UPLIFT

BY DAVID BRIN

The Practice Effect
The Postman
Heart of the Comet (with Gregory Benford)
Earth
Glory Season
Otherness
Foundation's Triumph
Kil'n People
Existence

The Uplift Books
Sundiver
Startide Rising
The Uplift War
Brightness Reef
Infinity's Shore
Heaven's Reach

Uplift: The Complete Original Trilogy (omnibus edition)
Exiles: The Second Uplift Trilogy (omnibus edition)

UPLIFT

The Complete Original Trilogy

This omnibus edition includes

Sundiver

Startide Rising

The Uplift War

DAVID BRIN

orbit

www.orbitbooks.net

ORBIT

First published in Great Britain in 2012 by Orbit

Copyright © 2012 by David Brin

Sundiver
First published in Great Britain in 1996 by Orbit
Copyright © 1980 by David Brin

Startide Rising
First published in Great Britain in 1996 by Orbit
Portions of this novel previously appeared in *Analog* (May 1981) in a slightly different
form under the title of *The Tales of Kithru*
Poems by Yosa Buson from *Anthology of Japanese Literature* copyright © 1995.
Reprinted by permission of Grove Press, Inc.
Copyright © 1983, 1993 by David Brin

The Uplift War
First published in Great Britain in 1996 by Orbit
Copyright © 1987 by David Brin
Maps copyright © 1987 by Jaye Zimet.

The moral right of the author has been asserted.

A CIP catalogue record for this book
is available from the British Library.

ISBN 978-1-84149-489-0

Typeset in New Aster by M Rules
Printed and bound in Great Britain by
Clays Ltd, St Ives plc

Papers used by Orbit are from well-managed forests
and other responsible sources.

MIX
Paper from
responsible sources
FSC
www.fsc.org   FSC® C104740

Orbit
An imprint of
Little, Brown Book Group
100 Victoria Embankment
London EC4Y 0DY

An Hachette UK Company
www.hachette.co.uk

www.orbitbooks.net

SUNDIVER

To my brothers Dan and Stan,
to Arglebargle the IVth . . .
and to somebody else.

PART I

... it is reasonable to hope
that in the not too distant future
we shall be competent to understand
so simple a thing as a star.

A. S. EDDINGTON, 1928

1

OUT OF THE WHALE-DREAM

'Makakai, are you ready?'

Jacob ignored the tiny whirrings of motors and valves in his metal cocoon. He lay still. The water lapped gently against the bulbous nose of his mechanical whale, as he waited for an answer.

One more time he checked the tiny indicators on his helmet display. Yes, the radio was working. The occupant of the other waldo whale, lying half submerged a few meters away, had heard every word.

The water was exceptionally clear today. Facing downward, he could see a small leopard shark swim lazily past, a bit out of place here in the deeper water offshore.

'Makakai ... are you ready?'

He tried not to sound impatient, or betray the tension he felt building in the back of his neck as he waited. He closed his eyes and made the delinquent muscles relax, one by one. Still, he waited for his pupil to speak.

'Yesss ... let'sss do it!' came the warbling, squeaky voice, at last. The words sounded breathless, as if spoken grudgingly, in lieu of inhalation.

A nice long speech for Makakai. He could see the young dolphin's training machine next to his, its image reflected in the mirrors that rimmed his faceplate. Its gray metal flukes lifted and fell slightly with the swell. Feebly, without their power, her artificial fins moved, sluggishly under the transient, serrated surface of the water.

She's as ready as she'll ever be, he thought. If technology can wean a dolphin of the Whale-Dream, now's the time we'll find out.

He chinned the microphone switch again. 'All right Makakai. You know how the waldo works. It will amplify any action you make, but if you want the rockets to cut in, you'll have to give the command in English. Just to be fair, I have to whistle in trinary to make mine work.'

'Yesss!' she hissed. Her waldo's gray flukes thrashed up once and down with a boom and a spray of saltwater.

With a half muttered prayer to the Dreamer, he touched a switch releasing the amplifiers on both Makakai's waldo and his own, then cautiously turned his arms to set the fins into motion. He flexed his legs, the massive flukes thrust back jerkily in response, and his machine immediately rolled over and sank.

7

Jacob tried to correct but overcompensated, making the waldo tumble even worse. The beating of his fins momentarily made the area around him a churning mass of bubbles, until patiently, by trial and error, he got himself righted.

He pushed off again, carefully, to get some headway, then arched his back and kicked out. The waldo responded with a great tail-slashing leap into the air.

The dolphin was almost a kilometer off. As he reached the top of his arc, Jacob saw her fall gracefully from a height of ten meters to slice smoothly into the swell below.

He pointed his helmet beak at the water and the sea came at him like a green wall. The impact made his helmet ring as he tore through tendrils of floating kelp, sending a golden Garibaldi darting away in panic as he drove downwards.

He was going in too steep. He swore and kicked twice to straighten out. The machine's massive metal flukes beat at the water to the rhythmic push of his feet, each beat sending a tremor up his spine, pressing him against the suit's heavy padding. When the time was right he arched and kicked again. The machine ripped out of the water.

Sunlight flashed like a missile in his left window, its glare drowning the dim glow of his tiny instrument panel. The helmet computer chuckled softly as he twisted, beak down, to crash into the bright water once again.

As a school of tiny silver anchovies scattered before him, Jacob hooted out loud with exhilaration.

His hands slipped along the controls to the rocket verniers, and at the top of his next arc he whistled a code in trinary. Motors hummed, as the exoskeleton extended winglets along its sides. Then the boosters cut in with a savage burst pressing the padded head-piece upward with the sudden acceleration, pinching the back of his skull as the waves swept past just below his hurtling craft.

He came down near Makakai with a great splash. She whistled a shrill trinary welcome. Jacob let the rockets shut off automatically and resumed the purely mechanical leaping beside her.

For a time they moved in unison. With each leap Makakai grew more daring, performing twists and pirouettes during the long seconds before they struck the water. Once, in midair, she rattled off a dirty limerick in dolphin, a low piece of work, but Jacob hoped they'd recorded it back at the chase boat. He'd missed the punch line at the crashing end of the aerial cycle.

The rest of the training team followed behind them on the hover-craft. During each leap he caught sight of the large vessel, diminished, now, by distance, until his impact cut off everything but

8

the sounds of splitting water, Makakai's sonar squeaking, and the rushing, phosphorescent blue-green past his windows.

Jacob's chronometer indicated that ten minutes had passed. He wouldn't be able to keep up with Makakai for more than a half hour, no matter how much amplification he used. A man's muscles and nervous system weren't designed for this leap-and-crash routine.

'Makakai, it's time to try the rockets. Let me know if you're ready and we'll use them on the following jump.'

They both came down into the sea and he worked his flukes in the frothy water to prepare for the next leap. They jumped again.

'Makakai, I'm serious now. Are you ready?'

They sailed high together. He could see her tiny eye behind a plastic window as her waldo-machine twisted before slicing into the water. He followed an instant later.

'Okay, Makakai. If you don't answer me, we'll just have to stop right now.'

Blue water swept past, along with a cloud of bubbles, as he pushed along beside his pupil.

Makakai twisted around and dove down instead of rising for another leap. She chattered something almost too fast to follow in trinary . . . about how he shouldn't be a spoilsport.

Jacob let his machine rise slowly to the surface. 'Come dear, use the King's English. You'll need it if you ever want your children to go into space. And it's so expressive! Come on. Tell Jacob what you think of him.'

There were a few seconds of silence. Then he saw something move very fast below him. It streaked upward and, just before it hit the surface, he heard Makakai's voice shrilly taunt:

'Ch-chase me, ch-chump! I fly-y-y!'

With the last word, her mechanical flukes snapped back and she leaped out of the water on a column of flame.

Laughing, he dove to give himself headway and then launched into the air after his pupil

Gloria handed him the strip chart as soon as he finished his second cup of coffee. Jacob tried to make his eyes focus on the squiggly lines, but they swam back and forth like ocean swells. He handed the chart back.

'I'll look at the data later. Can you just give me a summary? And I'll take one of those sandwiches now, too, if you'll let me clean up.'

She tossed him a tuna on rye and sat on the countertop, her hands on the edges to compensate for the swaying of the boat. As usual, she was wearing next to nothing. Pretty, well endowed, and with long black hair, the young biologist wore next to nothing very well.

'I think we have the brainwave information we need now, Jacob. I don't know how you did it, but Makakai's attention span in English was at least twice normal. Manfred thinks he's found enough associated synaptic clusters to give him a boost in his next set of experimental mutations. There are a couple of nodes that he wants to expand in the left cerebral lobe of Makakai's offspring.

'My group is happy enough with the present. Makakai's facility with the waldo-whale proves that the current generation can use machines.'

Jacob sighed. 'If you're hoping these results will persuade the Confederacy to cancel the next generation of mutations, don't count on it They're running scared. They don't want to have to rely forever on poetry and music to prove that dolphins are intelligent They want a race of analytical tool users, and giving codewords to activate a rocket waldo just won't qualify. Twenty to one Manfred gets to cut.'

Gloria reddened. 'Cutting! They're *people*, a people with a beautiful dream. We'll carve them into engineers and lose a race of poets!'

Jacob put down the crust of his sandwich. He brushed crumbs away from his chest Already he regretted having said anything.

'I know, I know. I wish things could go a little slower, too. But look at it this way. Maybe the fins'll be able to put the Whale-Dream into words someday. We won't need trinary to discuss the weather, or Aborigine-pidgin to talk philosophy. They'll be able to join the chimps, thumbing their metaphorical noses at the Galactics while we put on an act of being dignified adults.'

'But ...'

Jacob raised his hand to cut her off. 'Can we discuss this later? I'd like to stretch out for a little while, and then go down and visit with our girl.'

Gloria frowned for a moment, then smiled openly. 'I'm sorry, Jacob. You must really be tired. But at least today, finally, everything worked.'

Jacob allowed himself to return her grin. On his broad face the toothy smile brought out lines around his mouth and eyes.

'Yes,' he said, rising to his feet. 'Today everything worked.'

'Oh by the way, while you were down, there was a call for you. It was an Eatee! Johnny was so excited about it that he barely remembered to take a message. I think it's around here somewhere.'

She pushed aside the lunch dishes and plucked up a slip of paper. She handed it to him.

Jacob's bushy eyebrows knotted together as he looked down at the message. His skin was taut and dark from a mixture of ancestry and exposure to sun and saltwater. The brown eyes tended to narrow to fine slits when he concentrated. He brought a calloused hand to the side of his hooked, amerind nose and struggled with the radio operator's handwriting.

'I guess we all knew that you worked with Eatees,' Gloria said. 'But I sure didn't expect to get one on the horn out here! Especially one that looks like a giant broccoli sprout and talks like a Minister of Protocol!'

Jacob's head jerked up.

'A Kanten called? Here? Did he leave his name?'

'It should be down there. Is that what it was? A Kanten? I'm afraid I don't know my aliens that well. I'd recognize a Cynthian or a Tymbrimi, but this one was new to me.'

'Um ... I'm going to have to call somebody. I'll clean up the dishes later so don't you touch them! Tell Manfred and Johnny I'll be down in a little while to visit with Makakai. And thanks again.' He smiled and touched her shoulder lightly, but as he turned his expression quickly relapsed to one of worried preoccupation.

He passed on through the forward hatch, clutching the message. Gloria looked after him for a moment She picked up the data charts and wished she knew what it would take to hold the man's interest for more than an hour, or a night.

Jacob's cabin was barely a closet with a narrow fold-down bunk, but it offered enough privacy. He pulled his portable teli out of a cabinet near the door and set it on the bunk.

There was no reason to assume that Fagin had called for any other purpose than to be sociable. He had, after all, a deep interest in the work with dolphins.

There had been a few times, though, when the alien's messages had led to nothing but trouble. Jacob considered not returning the Kanten's call.

After a moment's hesitation, he punched out a code on the face of the teli and settled back to compose himself. When he came right down to it, he couldn't resist an opportunity to talk with an E.T., anywhere, anytime.

A line of binary flashed on the screen, giving the location of the portable unit he was calling. The Baja E.T. Reserve. Makes sense, Jacob thought. That's where the Library is. There was the standard warning against contact with aliens by Probationary Personalities. Jacob looked away with distaste. Bright points of static filled the space above the blankets and in front of the screen, and then Fagin stood, en-replica, a few inches away.

The E.T. did look somewhat like a giant sprout of broccoli. Rounded blue and green shoots formed symmetrical, spherical balls of growth around a gnarled, striated trunk. Here and there tiny crystalline flakes tipped a few of the branches, forming a cluster near the top around an invisible blowhole.

The foliage swayed and the crystals near the top tinkled from the passage of air the creature exhaled.

'Hello, Jacob,' Fagin's voice came tinnily out of midair. 'I greet you with gladness and gratitude and with the austere lack of formality upon which you so frequently and forcefully insist.'

Jacob fought back a laugh. Fagin reminded him of an ancient Mandarin, as much for the fluting quality of his accent as for the convoluted protocol he used with even his closest human friends.

'I greet you, Friend-Fagin, and wish you well with all respect. And now that that's over, and before you say even a word, the answer is no.'

The crystals tinkled softly. 'Jacob! You are so young and yet so perspicacious! I admire your insight and ability to divine my purpose in calling you!'

Jacob shook his head.

'Neither flattery nor thickly veiled sarcasm, Fagin; I insist on speaking colloquial English with you because it's the only way I have a chance of avoiding getting screwed whenever I deal with you. And you know very well what I'm talking about!'

The alien shook, giving a parody of a shrug.

'Ah, Jacob, I must bow to your will and use the highly esteemed honesty of which your species should be so proud. It is true that there is a slight favor for which I had the temerity to ask. But now that you have given me your answer ... based no doubt on certain past unpleasant occurrences, most of which nevertheless turned out for the best ... I shall simply drop the subject.

'Would it be possible to inquire how your work with the proud Client species "porpoise" proceeds?'

'Uh, yes, the work is going very well. We had a breakthrough today.'

'That is excellent, I am certain that it could not have happened without your intervention. I heard that your work there was indispensable!'

Jacob shook his head to clear it. Somehow Fagin had taken the initiative again.

'Well, it's true I was able to help out early on with the Water-Sphinx problem, but since then my part hasn't been all that special. Hell, anyone could have done what I've been doing here lately.'

'Oh, that is something that I find very hard to believe!'

Jacob frowned. Unfortunately it was true. And from now on the work here at the Center for Uplift would be even more routine.

A hundred experts, some more qualified in porp-psych than he, were waiting to step in. The Center would probably keep him on, partly out of gratitude, but did he really want to stay? Much as he loved dolphins and the sea, he'd found himself more and more restless lately.

'Fagin, I'm sorry I was so rude at first I'd like to hear what you called me about ... provided you understand that the answer is still probably no.'

Fagin's foliage rustled.

'I had the intention of inviting you to a small and amicable meeting with some worthy beings of diverse species, to discuss an important problem of a purely intellectual nature. The meeting will be held this Thursday, at the Visitors Center in Ensenada, at eleven o'clock. You will be committed to nothing if you attend.'

Jacob chewed on the idea for a moment.

'"E.T."s, you say? Who are they? What's this meeting about?'

'Alas, Jacob, I am not at liberty to say, at least not by teli. The details will have to wait until you come, if you come, on Thursday.'

Jacob immediately became suspicious. 'Say, this "problem" isn't political, is it? You're being awfully close.'

The image of the alien was very still. It's verdant mass rippled slowly, as if in contemplation.

'I have never understood, Jacob,' the fluting voice finally resumed, 'why a man of your background takes so little interest in the interplay of emotions and needs which you call "politics." Were the metaphor appropriate, I would say that politics is "in my blood." It certainly is in yours.'

'You leave my family out of this! I only want to know why it's necessary to wait until Thursday to find out what all of this is about!'

Again, the Kanten hesitated.

'There are ... aspects of this matter which would best not be spoken over the ether. Several of the more thalamic of the contesting factions in your culture might misuse the knowledge if they ... overheard. However, let me assure you that your part would be purely technical. It is your knowledge we wish to tap, and the skills you have been using at the Center.'

Bull! Jacob thought. You want more than that.

He knew Fagin. If he attended this meeting the Kanten undoubtedly would try to use it as a wedge to get him involved in some ridiculously complicated and dangerous adventure. The alien had already done it to him on three occasions in the past.

The first two times Jacob hadn't minded. But he'd been a different sort of person then, the kind who loved that sort of thing.

Then came the Needle. The trauma in Ecuador had changed his

13

life completely. He had no desire to go through anything like it again.

And yet, Jacob felt a powerful reluctance to disappoint the old Kanten. Fagin had never actually lied to him, and he was the only E.T. he'd met who was unabashedly an admirer of human culture and history. Physically the most alien creature he knew, Fagin was also the one extraterrestrial who tried hardest to understand Earthmen.

I should be safe if I simply tell Fagin the truth, Jacob thought. If he starts applying too much pressure I'll let him know about my mental state – the experiments with self-hypnosis and the weird results I've been getting. He won't push too hard if I appeal to his sense of fair play.

'All right.' he sighed. 'You win, Fagin. I'll be there. Just don't expect me to be the star of the show.'

Fagin's laughter whistled with a flavor of woodwinds. 'Do not be concerned about that, Friend-Jacob! In this particular show no one will mistake you for the star!'

The Sun was still above the horizon as he walked along the upper deck toward Makakai's quarters. It loomed, dim and orange among the sparse clouds in the west – a benign, featureless orb. He stopped at the rail for a moment to appreciate the colors of the sunset and the smell of the sea.

He closed his eyes and allowed the sunlight to warm his face, the rays penetrating his skin with gentle, browning insistence. Finally, he swung both legs over the rail and dropped to the lower deck. A taut, energized feeling had almost replaced the day's exhaustion. He began to hum a fragment of a tune – out of key, of course.

A tired dolphin drifted to the edge of the pool when he arrived. Makakai greeted him with a trinary poem too quick to catch, but it sounded amiably nasty. Something about his sex life. Dolphins had been telling humans dirty jokes for thousands of years before men finally started breeding them for brains and for speech, and began to understand. Makakai might be a lot smarter than her ancestors, Jacob thought, but her sense of humor was strictly dolphin.

'Well,' he said. 'Guess who's had a busy day.'

She splashed at him, more weakly than usual, and said something that sounded a lot like 'Br-r-a-a-a-p you!'

But she moved in closer when he hunkered down to put his hand into the water and say hello.

2

SHIRTS AND SKINS

The old North American governments had razed the Border Strip years ago, to control movements to and from Mexico. A desert was made where two cities once touched.

Since the Overturn, and the destruction of the oppressive 'Bureaucracy' of the old syndical governments, Confederacy authorities had maintained the area as parklands. The border zone between San Diego and Tijuana was now one of the largest forested areas south of Pendleton Park.

But that was changing. As he drove his rented car southward on the elevated highway, Jacob saw signs that the belt was returning to its old purpose. Crews worked on both sides of the road, cutting down trees and erecting slender, candy-striped poles at hundred-yard intervals to the west and east The poles were shameful. He looked away.

A large green and white sign loomed where the line of poles crossed the highway.

New Boundary: Baja Extraterrestrial Reserve
Tijuana Residents Who Are Non-Citizens
Report to City Hall for Your Generous
Resettlement Bonus!

Jacob shook his head and grunted, 'Oderint Dum Metuant.' Let them hate, so long as they fear. So what if a person has lived in a town his entire life. If he hasn't got the vote, he's got to move out of the way when progress comes along.

Tijuana, Honolulu, Oslo, and half a dozen other cities were to be included when the E.T. Reserves expanded again. Fifty or sixty thousand Probationers, both permanent and temporary, would have to move to make those cities 'safe' for perhaps a thousand aliens. The actual hardship would be small, of course. Most of Earth was still barred to E.T.s, and non-Citizens still had plenty of room. The government offered large reparations as well.

But once again there were refugees on Earth.

The city suddenly resumed at the southern edge of the Strip. Many of the structures followed a Spanish or Spanish-Revival style, but overall the city showed the architectural experimentation typical of a modern Mexican town. Here the buildings ran in whites and blues. Traffic on both sides of the highway filled the air with a faint electric whine.

All over the town, green and white metallic signs, like the one at the border, heralded the coming change. But one, near the highway, had been defaced with black spray paint. Before it passed out of sight, Jacob caught a glimpse of the raggedly written words 'Occupation' and 'Invasion.'

A Permanent Probationer did that, he thought. A Citizen wasn't likely to do anything so kinky, with hundreds of legal ways to express his opinion. And a Temporary Probie, sentenced to probation for a crime, wouldn't want his sentence lengthened. A Temporary would recognize the certainty of being caught.

No doubt some poor Permanent, facing eviction, had vented his feelings, not caring about the consequences. Jacob sympathized. The P.P. was probably in custody by now.

Although he was not particularly interested in politics, Jacob came from a political family. Two of his grandparents had been heroes in the Overturn, when a small group of technocrats had succeeded in bringing the Bureaucracy tumbling down. The family policy toward the Probation Laws was one of vehement opposition.

Jacob had been of a habit, the last few years, of avoiding memories of the past. Now, though, an image came forcefully to mind.

Summer school in the Alvarez Clan compound in the hills above Caracas ... in the very house where Joseph Alvarez and his friends had made their plans thirty years before ... there was Uncle Jeremey lecturing while Jacob's cousins and adopted cousins listened, all respectful expressions on the outside and seething summer boredom within. And Jacob fidgeted in the back corner, wishing he could get back to his room and the 'secret equipment' he and his stepsister Alice had put together.

Suave and confident, Jeremey was then still in early middle age, a rising voice in the Confederacy Assembly. Soon he would be leader of the Alvarez clan, edging aside his older brother James.

Uncle Jeremey was telling about how the old Bureaucracy had decreed that everyone alive would be tested for 'violent tendencies' and that all who failed would from then on be under constant surveillance – Probation.

Jacob could remember the exact words his uncle had spoken that afternoon, when Alice had come sneaking into the Library, excitement radiating from her twelve-year-old face like something about to go nova.

'... They went to great efforts to convince the populace,' Jeremey said in a low rumbling voice, 'that the laws would cut down on crime. And they did have that effect. Individuals with radio transmitters in their rumps often think twice about causing trouble to their neighbors.

'Then, as now, the Citizens loved the Probation Laws. They had no trouble forgetting the fact that they cut through every traditional Constitutional guarantee of due process. Most of them lived in countries that had never had such niceties anyway.

'And when a fluke in those laws allowed Joseph Alvarez and his friends to turn the Bureaucrats themselves out on their ears – well, the jubilant Citizens just loved Probation testing even more. It did the leaders of the Overturn no good to push the issue at the time. They were having enough trouble setting up the Confederacy ... '

Jacob thought he would scream. Here was old Uncle Jeremey gabbing on and on about all that old nonsense, and Alice – lucky Alice whose turn it was to risk the oldsters' ire and listen in on the tap they'd placed on the house deepspace receiver – what was it she had heard!

It *had* to be a starship! It would be only the third of the great slow vessels ever to come back! That was the only possible explanation for the call up of the Space Reserves or for all the excitement in the east wing, where the adults kept their labs and offices.

Jeremey was still expounding on the public's continuing lack of compassion, but Jacob neither saw nor heard him. He kept his face rigid and still as Alice leaned over to whisper – no, gasp in her excitement – into his ear.

' ... *Aliens*, Jacob! They're bringing extraterrestrials! In their own ships! Oh, Jake, the *Vesarius* is bringing home Eatees!'

It was the first time Jacob had ever heard that word. He had often wondered if Alice was the one to coin it. At ten years of age, he recalled, he had wondered if 'eatee' implied that someone else was to be designated 'eaten.'

As he drove above the streets of Tijuana, it occurred to him that the question still hadn't been answered.

In several major intersections one corner edifice had been removed and a rainbow-colored 'E.T. Comfort Station Kiosk' installed. Jacob saw several of the new low open-decked buses equipped to carry humans and aliens who slithered, or walked three meters tall.

As he passed City Hall, Jacob saw about a dozen 'Skins' picketing. At least they looked like Skins: people wearing furs and waving toy plastic spears. Who else would dress that way in this sort of weather?

He turned up the volume on the car's radio and pressed the voice-select.

'Local news,' he said. 'Key words: Skins, City Hall, picketing.'

After only a moment of delay a mechanical voice spoke from behind the dashboard with the slightly flawed inflection of a computer-generated news report. Jacob wondered if they'd ever get the voice tone right.

'Newsbrief summary.' The artificial voice had an Oxford accent 'Precis: today, January 12, 2246, oh-nine forty one, good morning. Thirty-seven persons are picketing the Tijuana City Hall in a legal manner. Their registered grievance is, summarized in abstract, the expansion of the Extraterrestrial Reserve. Please interrupt if you wish a fax or verbal presentation of their registered protest manifesto.'

The machine paused. Jacob said nothing, already wondering if he wanted to hear the rest of the precis. He was already well acquainted with the Skins' protest against the implication of the Reserves: that some humans, at least, weren't fit to associate with aliens.

'Twenty-six of the thirty-seven members of the protest group carry probation transmitters,' the report continued. 'The rest are, of course, Citizens. This compares to a ratio of one probationer per hundred and twenty-four Citizens in Tijuana in general. By their demeanor and dress the protestors can be tentatively described as proponents of the so-called Neolithic Ethic, colloquially, "Skins." As none of the citizens has invoked privacy privilege, it can be said for certain that thirty of the thirty-seven are residents of Tijuana and the rest are visitors . . . '

Jacob stabbed the cutoff button and the voice died in mid-sentence. The scene at City Hall had long ago passed out of sight and it was an old story anyway.

The controversy over the expansion of the E.T. Reserve reminded him, though, that it had been almost two months since he last visited his Uncle James in Santa Barbara. The old bombast was probably up to his protruding ears, by now, in lawsuits on behalf of half of the probies in Tijuana. Still, he would notice if Jacob left on a long trip without saying good-bye, either to him or to the other uncles, aunts, and cousins of the rambling, rambunctious Alvarez clan.

Long trip? What long trip? Jacob thought suddenly. I'm not going anywhere!

But that corner of his mind he'd set aside for such things had caught scent of something in this meeting Fagin had called. He felt a sense of anticipation, and simultaneously a wish to suppress it. The feelings would have been intriguing, if they weren't already so familiar.

He rode on for a time in silence. Soon the city gave way to open countryside, and traffic reduced to a trickle. For the next twenty kilometers he drove with the sunshine warm on his arm and a pattern of doubts playing tag in his mind.

In spite of the restlessness he had felt recently, he was reluctant to admit that it was time to leave the Center for Uplift. The work with dolphins and chimps was fascinating, and far more equable (after the first tumultuous weeks during the Water-Sphinx affair) than his old profession as a scientific-crime investigator had been. The staff at the Center was dedicated and, unlike so many other scientific enterprises on Earth these days, they had high morale. They were doing work that had tremendous intrinsic value and would not be made instantly obsolete when the Branch Library in La Paz became completely operational.

But most important, he had made friends, and those friends had been supportive during the last year or so as he began the slow process of knitting together the schismed portions of his mind.

Gloria especially. I'm going to have to do something about her if I stay, Jacob thought. And more than the comradely heavy breathing we've done so far. The girl's feelings were becoming obvious.

Before the disaster in Ecuador, the loss that had brought him to the Center in the first place seeking work and peace, he would have known what to do and had the courage to do it. Now his feelings were a morass. He wondered if he would ever again consider more than a casual love relationship.

It had been a long two years since Tania's death. It had been lonely, at times, in spite of his work, his friends, and the ever fascinating games he played with his mind.

The ground became hilly and brown. Watching the cacti go by, Jacob sat back to enjoy the slow rhythm of the ride. Even now, his body swayed slightly with the motion as if he were still at sea.

The ocean glistened blue beyond the hills. The nearer the curving road took him to the meeting place, the more he wished he was aboard a boat out there: watching for the first hunched back and raised fluke of the year's Grey Migration, listening for the whale's Song of the Leader.

He rounded one hill to find the parking strips on both sides of the road lined solid with little electric runabouts like his own. On the crests of the hills up ahead were scores of people.

Jacob pulled his vehicle over into the automatic guideway on the right, where he could cruise slowly and take his eyes off the highway. What was going on here? Two adults and several children unloaded a car by the left side of the road, taking out picnic baskets and binoculars. They were clearly excited. They looked like a typical family on a weekday outing, except that all of them wore bright silver robes and golden amulets. Most of the people on the hill above them were similarly garbed. Many had small telescopes, aimed up the road at something that was obscured from Jacob's view by the hill on the right.

The crowd on that hill wore their caveman gear with panache. These Compleat Cro-Magnons compromised. They had their own telescopes, as well as wristwatches, radios, and megaphones, to back up their flint axes and spears.

It wasn't surprising that the two groups settled on opposite hill-tops. The only thing that the Shirts and Skins ever agreed on was their hatred of the Extraterrestrial Quarantine.

A huge sign spanned the highway at the crest between the two hills.

BAJA CALIFORNIA EXTRATERRESTRIAL RESERVE
Probationaries Not Admitted Without Authorization
First Time Visitors Please Stop At The Information Center
No Fetishes Or Neolithic Garments Please
Check 'Skins' in at Information Center.

Jacob smiled. The 'papers' had had a field day with that last command. There were cartoons on every channel, which depicted visitors to the Reserve being forced to peel off their dermis, while a pair of snakelike E.T.s looked on approvingly.

The parked cars jammed together at the top. When Jacob's car reached that point, the Barrier came into view.

In a wide swatch of barren ground that stretched from east to west, another line of barber poles ran, this one complete. The colors had faded from many of the smooth posts. Dust coated the round lamps that capped the tops.

The ubiquitous P-trackers acted here as a visible sieve, allowing Citizens to pass freely in and out of the E.T. Reserve but warning probationers to stay out, and aliens to stay within. It was a crude reminder of a fact that most people carefully ignored: that a large part of humanity wore imbedded transmitters because the larger part didn't trust them. The majority didn't want contact between extraterrestrials and those deemed 'prone to violence' by a psychological test.

Apparently, the Barrier did its job well. The crowds on both sides grew thicker up ahead, and the costumes wilder, but the mob stopped in a clump just north of the line of P-posts. Some of the Shirts and Skins were probably Citizens, but they kept on this side with their friends – out of politeness or perhaps as a protest.

The crowds were thickest just north of the Barrier. Here the Shirts and Skins shoved signs at quickly passing motorists.

Jacob kept in the guideway and looked about, shading his eyes from the glare and enjoying the show.

A young man on the left, wrapped in silver sateen from throat to toe, held up a placard that said, 'Mankind Was Uplifted Too: Let Our E.T. Cousins Out!'

Just across the roadway from him a woman held a banner tacked to a spearshaft: 'We did it Ourselves . . . Eatees off Earth!'

There was the controversy in a nutshell. The whole world waited to see if the believers in Darwin, or those who followed Von Daniken, were right. The Skins and Shirts were only the more fanatical fringes of a split that had divided humanity into two philosophical camps. The issue: how did Homo-Sapiens originate as a thinking being?

Or was that *all* the Shirts and Skins represented?

The former group took their love of aliens to almost a pseudo-religious frenzy. Hysterical Xenophilia?

The Neoliths, with their love of caveman garb and ancient lore; were their cries for 'independence from E.T. Influence' based on something more basic – fear of the unknown, the powerfully alien? Xenophobia?

Of one thing Jacob was sure. The Shirts and Skins shared resentment. Resentment of the Confederacy's cautious compromise policy towards E.T.s. Resentment of the Probation Laws which kept so many of them in a form of Coventry. Resentment of a world in which no man any longer knew his roots for certain.

An old, unshaven man caught Jacob's eye. He squatted by the road, hopped up and down and pointed at the ground between his legs, shouting in the dust kicked up by the crowd. Jacob slowed down as he approached.

The man wore a fur jacket and hand-sewn leather breeches. His shouting and jumping grew more frenzied as Jacob neared.

'Doo-Doo!' He screamed, as if delivering a terrible insult. Froth appeared on his lips and he again pointed to the ground.

'Doo-Doo! Doo-Doo!'

Puzzled, Jacob slowed the car almost to a stop.

Something flew past his face from the left and cracked against the window on the passenger side. There was a bang on the roof and within seconds a fusillade of small pebbles was striking the car, making a drumming that pounded in his ears.

He ran up the window on his left side, yanked the car out of automatic, and surged ahead. The flimsy metal and plastic of the runabout dimpled every time a missile struck it. Suddenly there were faces leering in Jacob's side windows; young tough faces with drooping moustaches. The youths ran along the side of the car as it sluggishly accelerated, hammering on it with fists and shouting.

With the Barrier only a few meters away, Jacob laughed and decided to find out what they wanted. He eased off a trifle on the accelerator and turned to mouth a question at the man who ran next to him, an adolescent dressed as a twentieth-century science fiction hero. The crowd by the side of the road was a blur of placards and costumes.

Before he could speak the car was shaken by a jolting bang. A hole had appeared in his windshield and a burning smell filled the little cab.

Jacob gunned the car toward the Barrier. The row of barber poles whizzed by and suddenly he was alone. In his rearview mirror he saw his entourage gather together. The youths shouted as he drove off, raising fists from the sleeves of futuristic robes. He grinned and opened the window to wave back.

How am I going to explain this to the rental company? he thought. Shall I say that I was attacked by forces of the Imperial Ming or do you think they'll believe the truth?

There was no question of calling the police. The local constabulary would be unable to make a move without starting with a P-Search. And a few P-Transmitters among so many would be lost for sure. Besides, Fagin had asked him to be discreet in coming to this meeting.

He rolled down the windows to let a breeze carry away the smoke. He poked at the bullet hole in his windshield with the tip of his small finger and smiled bemusedly.

You actually enjoyed that, didn't you? he thought.

It was one thing to let the adrenalin flow, and quite another to laugh at danger. His sense of elation during the fracas at the Barrier worried a part of Jacob more than the mysterious violence of the crowd did ... a symptom out of his past.

A minute or two passed, then a tone sounded from the dashboard.

He looked up. A hitchhiker? Out here? Down the road, less than half of a kilometer away, a man by the curb held his watch out into the path of the guidebeam. Two satchels rested on the ground beside him.

Jacob hesitated. But here inside the Reserve only Citizens were allowed. He pulled over to the curb, just a few meters past the man.

There was something familiar about the fellow. He was a florid little man in a dark grey business suit and his paunch jiggled as he heaved two heavy bags to the side of Jacob's car. His face was perspiring as he bent over the door on the passenger's side and peered in.

'Oh boy, what heat!' he moaned. He spoke standard English with a thick accent.

'No wonder no one uses the guideway!' he went on, mopping his brow with a handkerchief. 'They drive so fast to catch a little tiny breeze, don't they? But you are familiar, we must have met somewhere before. I am Peter LaRoque ... or Pierre, if you wish. I am with *Les Mondes*.'

Jacob started.

'Oh. Yes, LaRoque. We've met before. I'm Jacob Demwa. Hop in. I'm only going as far as the Information Center, but you can get a bus from there.'

He hoped that his face didn't show his feelings. Why hadn't he recognized LaRoque when he was still moving? He might not have stopped.

It wasn't that he had anything in particular against the man ... other than his incredible ego and his inexhaustible store of opinions, which he would thrust upon anyone at the smallest opportunity. In many ways he was probably a fascinating personality. He certainly had a following in the Danikenite press. Jacob had read a number of LaRoque's articles and enjoyed the style, if not the content.

But LaRoque had been a member of the press corps that had chased him for weeks after he'd solved the Water-Sphinx mystery, and one of the least tactful at that. The final story in *Les Mondes* had been favorable, and beautifully written as well. But it hadn't been worth the trouble.

Jacob was glad that the press hadn't been able to find him after the still earlier Ecuadorian fiasco, that mess at the Vanilla Needle. At that time LaRoque would have been too much to bear.

Right now he was having trouble believing LaRoque's obviously affected 'Origin' accent. It was even thicker than the last time they'd met, if possible.

'Demwa, ah, of course!' the man said. He stuffed his bags behind the passenger seat and got in. 'The maker and purveyor of aphorisms! The connoisseur of mysteries! You're here maybe to play puzzle games with our noble interplanetary guests? Or perhaps you are going to consult with the Great Library in La Paz?'

Jacob re-entered the guideway, wishing he knew who had started the 'National Origins Accent' fad, so he could strangle the man.

'I'm here to do some consultant work and my employers include extraterrestrials, if that's what you mean. But I can't go into details.'

'Ah yes, so very secret!' LaRoque wagged a finger playfully. 'You

23

should not tease a journalist so! Your business I might make my business! But you, you must surely wonder what brings the ace reporter of *Les Mondes* to this desolate place, no?'

'Actually,' Jacob said, 'I'm more interested in how you came to be hitchhiking in the *middle* of this desolate place.'

LaRoque sighed.

'A desolate place, indeed! How sad it is that the noble aliens who visit us should be stuck here and in other wastelands such as your Alaska!'

'And Hawaii and Caracas and Sri Lanka, the Confederacy Capitols,' Jacob said. 'But as to how you came to be ...'

'How I came to be assigned here? Yes, of course, Demwa! But maybe we can amuse ourselves with your renowned deductive talents. You perhaps can guess?'

Jacob suppressed a groan. He reached forward to pull the car out of the guideway and put more weight onto the accelerator pedal.

'I've got a better idea, LaRoque. Since you don't want to tell me why you were standing there in the middle of nowhere, perhaps you'd be willing to clear up a little mystery for me.'

Jacob described the scene at the Barrier. He left out the violent ending, hoping that LaRoque hadn't noticed the hole in the windshield, but he carefully described the behavior of the squatting man.

'But of course!' LaRoque cried. 'You make it easy for me!

'You know the initials of this phrase you used, "Permanent Probationer," that horrible classification which denies a man his rights, parenthood, the franchise ...'

'Look, I agree already! Save the speech.' Jacob thought for a moment. What were the initials?

'Oh ... I think I see.'

'Yes, the poor fellow was only striking back! You Citizens, you call him Pee-Pee ... so is it not simple justice that he accuse you of being Docile and Domesticated? Ergo the doo-doo!'

Jacob laughed, despite himself. The road began to curve.

'I wonder why all those people were gathered at the Barrier? They seemed to be waiting for somebody.'

'At the Barrier?' LaRoque said. 'Ah yes. I hear that happens every Thursday. Eatees from the Center go up to look at non-Citizens and they in turn come down to look at an Eatee. Droll, no? One doesn't know which side throws the peanuts!'

The road turned around one hill and their destination was in sight.

The Information Center, a few kilometers north of Ensenada, was a sprawling compound of E.T. quarters, public museums and, hidden around back, barracks for the border patrol. In front of a broad parking lot stood the main structure where first-time visitors took lessons in Galactic Protocol.

The station was on a small plateau, between the highway and the ocean, commanding a broad view over both. Jacob parked the car near the main entrance.

LaRoque was chewing, red-faced, on some thought. He looked up suddenly.

'You know I was joking, just then, when I spoke about peanuts. I was only making a joke.'

Jacob nodded, wondering what had got into the man. Strange.

3

GESTALT

Jacob helped LaRoque carry his bags to the bus station, then made his way around the main building to find a place, outside to sit. Ten minutes remained before he was due at the meeting.

Where the compound overlooked a small harbor he found a patio with shade trees and picnic tables. He chose one table to sit on and rested his feet on the bench. The touch of the cool ceramic tile and the breeze off the ocean penetrated his clothing and drew away the redness from his skin and the perspiration from his clothes.

For a few minutes he sat quietly, letting the hard muscles of his shoulders and lower back relax one by one, sloughing off the tension of the drive. He focused on a small sailboat, a daycraft with jib and main colored greener than the ocean. Then he let a trance come down over his eyes.

Floating. One at a time he examined the things his senses revealed to him and then he canceled them. He concentrated on his muscles one by one, to cut off sensation and tension. Slowly his limbs grew numb and distant.

An itch in his thigh persisted, but his hands remained in his lap until it left of its own accord. The salt smell of the sea was pleasant but equally distracting. He made it go away. He shut off the sound of his heartbeat by listening to it with undivided attention until it became too familiar to notice.

As he had for two years, Jacob guided the trance through a cathartic phase, in which images came and went startlingly fast in healing pain, as two pieces, split apart, tried again to fuse whole. It was a process that he never enjoyed.

He was alone, almost. All that remained was a background of voices, murmuring subvocal snatches of phrases at the edge of meaning. For a moment he thought he could hear Gloria and Johnny arguing about Makakai, then Makakai herself chattering something irreverent in pidgin-trinary.

He guided each sound away gently, waiting for one that came, as usual, with predictable suddenness: Tania's voice calling something he couldn't quite understand as she fell past him, arms outstretched. He still heard her as she fell the rest of the twenty miles to the ground, becoming a tiny speck and then disappearing . . . still calling.

That little voice too faded, but this time it left him more uneasy than usual.

A violent, exaggerated version of the incident at the Zone Boundary flashed through his mind. Suddenly he was back, this time standing among the Probationers. A bearded man dressed as a Pictish Shaman held out a pair of binoculars and nodded insistently.

Jacob picked them up and looked where the man pointed. Its image warped by heat waves rising from the highway, a bus rolled to a stop just on the other side of a line of candy-striped poles that stretched to each horizon. Each pole seemed to reach all the way up to the sun.

Then the image was gone. With practiced indifference, Jacob let go of the temptation to think about it and allowed his mind to go completely blank.

Silence and Darkness.

He rested in a deep trance, relying on his own internal clock to signal when the time to emerge was near. He moved slowly among patterns that had no symbols and long familiar meanings that eluded description or remembrance, patiently looking for the key he knew was there and that he'd someday find.

Time was now a thing like any other, lost in a deeper passage.

The calm dark was pierced, suddenly, by a sharp pain driving past all of his mind's isolation. It took a moment, an eternity that must have been a hundredth of a second, to localize it. The pain was a bright blue light that seemed to stab at his hypnosis sensitized eyes through closed lids. In another instant, before he could react, it was gone.

Jacob struggled for a moment with his confusion. He tried to concentrate solely on rising to consciousness while a stream of panicky questions popped like flashbulbs in his mind.

What subconscious artifact had that blue light been? A corner of neurosis that defends itself so fiercely has to mean trouble! What hidden fear did I probe?

As he emerged, hearing returned.

There were footsteps ahead. He picked them out from the sounds of the wind and sea, but in his trance they seemed like the soft padding ostrich feet might make if clothed in mocassins.

The deep trance finally broke, several seconds after the subjective burst of light. He opened his eyes. A tall alien stood in front of him, a few meters away. His immediate impression was of tallness, whiteness, and huge red eyes.

For a moment the world seemed to tilt.

Jacob's hands flew to the sides of the table and his head sank as he steadied himself. He closed his eyes.

Some trance! he thought. My head feels as if it's about to crash through the Earth and come out the other side!

He rubbed his eyes with one hand, then carefully looked up once again.

The alien was still there. So it was real. It was humanoid, standing at least two meters tall. Most of its slender body was covered by a long silvery robe. The hands, folded in front in the Attitude of Respectful Waiting, were long, white and glossy.

A very large round head bowed forward on a slender neck. The lidless, red, columnar eyes and the lips of the alien's mouth were huge. They dominated the face, on which a few other small organs served purposes unknown to him. This species was new to Jacob.

The eyes glowed with intelligence.

Jacob cleared his throat. He still had to fight off waves of dizziness.

'Excuse me ... Since we haven't been introduced, I ... don't know how I'm to address you, but I assume you're here to see me?'

The big, white head nodded deeply in assent.

'Are you with the group the Kanten Fagin asked me to meet?'

Again, the alien nodded.

I suppose that means yes, Jacob thought. I wonder if he can speak, what with any imaginable kind of mechanism lurking behind those huge lips.

But why was the creature just standing there? Was there something in its attitude ... ?

'Am I to assume that, that yours is a client species and you are waiting for permission to speak?'

The 'lips' separated slightly and Jacob caught a glimpse of something bright and white. The alien nodded again.

'Well then speak up, please! We humans are notoriously short on protocol. What's your name?'

The voice was surprisingly deep. It hissed out of a barely widened mouth with a pronounced lisp.

'I am Culla, Shir. Thank you. I have been shent to make sure that you were not losht. If you will come with me, the othersh are waiting. Or, if you prefer, you can continue to meditate until the appointed time.'

'No, no let's go, by all means.' Jacob rose to his feet unsteadily. He closed his eyes for a moment to clear his mind of the last shreds of the trance. Sooner or later he would have to sort out what had happened, while he'd been under, but that would have to wait.

'Lead on.'

Culla turned and walked with a slow, fluid gait toward one of the side doorways to the Center.

Culla was apparently a member of a 'client' species – one whose period of indenture to its 'patron' species was still active. Such a race rated low on the galactic pecking order. Jacob, mystified as he still was by the intricacies of galactic affairs, was glad that a lucky accident had won for humanity a better, if insecure, place on the hierarchy.

Culla led him upstairs to a large oaken door. He opened it without announcement and preceded Jacob into the meeting room.

Jacob saw two human beings and, besides Culla, two aliens: one short and furry, the other smaller still, and lizardlike. They were seated on cushions between some large indoor shrubs and a picture window overlooking the bay.

He tried to sort his impressions of the aliens before they noticed him, but had only a moment before someone spoke his name.

'Jacob, my friend! How kind it is for you to come and share with us your time!' It was Fagin's fluting voice. Jacob looked quickly about the room.

'Fagin, where ... ?'

'I am here.'

He looked back at the group by the window. The humans and the furry E.T. were rising to their feet. The lizard-alien remained on its cushion.

Jacob adjusted his perspective and suddenly one of the 'indoor shrubs' was Fagin. The old Kanten's silver tipped foliage tinkled softly as if there were a breeze.

Jacob smiled. Fagin presented a problem whenever they met. With humanoids, one looked for a face, or something that served the same purpose. Usually it took only a little time to find a place in an alien's strange features on which to focus.

There was almost always a part of the anatomy that one learned to address as the seat of another awareness. Among humans and very often among E.T.s, this focus was in the eyes.

A Kanten has no eyes. Jacob guessed that the bright silver objects that made the sound of tiny sleigh bells were Fagin's light receptors.

If so, it still didn't help. One had to look at the whole of Fagin, not at some cusp of the ego. It made Jacob wonder which was the larger improbability: that he liked the alien despite this handicap, or that he still felt uneasy with him despite years of friendship.

Fagin's dark leafy body approached from the window in a series of twists that brought successive root-knots to the fore. Jacob gave him one medium-formal bow and waited.

'Jacob Alvarez Demwa, a-Human, ul-Dolphin-ul-Chimp, we welcome you. It pleases this poor being to sense you today, once again.' Fagin spoke clearly, but with an uncontrolled singsong quality which made his accent sound like mixed Swedish and Cantonese. The Kanten did much better speaking dolphin or trinary.

'Fagin, a-Kanten, ab-Linten-ab-Siqul-ul-Nish, Mi-horki Keephu. It pleases me to see you once again.' Jacob bowed.

'These venerable beings have come to exchange their wisdom with yours, Friend-Jacob,' Fagin said. 'I hope you are prepared for formal introductions.'

Jacob set his mind to concentrate on the convoluted species names of each alien, at least as much as on their appearance. Patronymics and multiple client names would tell a great deal about the status of each. He nodded for Fagin to proceed.

'I will now formally introduce you to Bubbacub, a-Pil, ab-Kisa-ab-Soro-ab-Hul-ab-Puber-ul-Gello-ul-Pring, of the Library Institute.'

One of the E.T.s stepped forward. Jacob's initial gestalt was of a four-foot, gray teddy bear. But a wide snout and fringe of cilia around the eyes belied that impression.

This was Bubbacub, director of the Branch Library! The Branch Library at La Paz consumed almost all of the meager trade balance which Earth had accumulated since contact. Even so, much of the prodigious effort of adapting a tiny 'suburban' Branch to human referents was donated by the huge galactic Institute of the Library, as a charity, to help the 'backward' human race catch up with the rest of the galaxy. As head of the Branch, Bubbacub was one of the most important aliens on Earth! His species name also implied high status, higher even than Fagin's!

The 'ab' something-to-the-fourth meant that Bubbacub's species had been nurtured into sentience by another which had in turn been nurtured by another, and so forth back to the mythical beginning at the time of the Progenitors ... and that four of these generations of 'Parentals' were still alive somewhere in the galaxy. To be derived from such a chain meant status in a diffuse galactic culture whose every spacefaring species (with the possible lone exception of humanity) was brought up out of semi-intelligent savagery by some previous, space-traveling race.

The 'ul' something squared said that the Pil race had in turn fostered two new cultures on their own. This too was status.

The one thing that had prevented the complete snubbing of the 'orphan' human race by the Galactics was the fortunate fact that man had himself fostered new intelligent races twice before the *Vesarius* had brought Contact with the E.T. civilization home to Earth.

The alien made a slight bow.

'I am Bubbacub.'

The voice sounded artificial. It came from a disc that hung from the Pil's neck.

A Vodor! The Pil race required artificial assistance to speak English, then. From the simplicity of the device, much smaller than those used by alien visitors whose native tongues were twitters and squeaks, Jacob guessed that Bubbacub could actually pronounce human words, but in a frequency range beyond human hearing. He decided to assume that the being could hear him.

'I am Jacob. Welcome to Earth.' He nodded.

Bubbacub's mouth snapped open and shut a few times silently.

'Thank you,' the Vodor buzzed, in clipped, short words. 'I am happy to be here.'

'And I to be of service as your host.' Jacob bowed ever so slightly deeper than he had seen Bubbacub do when he came forward. The alien seemed to be satisfied and stepped back.

Fagin recommenced his introductions.

'These worthy beings are of your race.' A twig and a bunch of petals gestured vaguely in the direction of the two human beings. A gray-haired gentleman, dressed in tweed, stood next to a tall brown woman, in handsome middle age.

'I will now introduce you,' Fagin continued, 'in the informal manner preferred by humans.

'Jacob Demwa, meet Doctor Dwayne Kepler, of the Sundiver Expedition, and Doctor Mildred Martine, of the Department of Parapsychology at the University of La Paz.'

Kepler's face was dominated by a substantial handlebar moustache. He smiled, but Jacob was too amazed to reply to his pleasantries with more than a monosyllable.

The Sundiver Expedition! The research on Mercury and in the solar chromosphere had been a football in the Confederacy Assembly, of late. The 'Adapt & Survive' faction said that it made no sense to spend so much for knowledge that could be pulled out of the Library, when the same appropriation could employ several times as many unemployed scientists here on Earth with make-work projects. The 'Self-Sufficiency' faction had so far had its way, though, in spite of abuse from the Danikenite press.

But to Jacob it was the idea of sending men and ships down into a star that sounded like insanity of the first degree.

'Kant Fagin was enthusiastic in his recommendations,' Kepler said. The Sundiver leader smiled, but his eyes were reddened. They bore puffy outlines from some inner worry. He pressed Jacob's hand in both of his own and pumped quickly as he spoke. His voice was deep but it did not hide a quaver.

'We came to Earth only for a little while. It's an answered prayer that Fagin was able to persuade you to meet with us. We really hope you can join us on Mercury and give us the benefit of your experience in interspecies contact.'

Jacob started. Oh no, not this time you don't, you leafy monster! He wanted to turn and glare at Fagin but even informal intrahuman propriety required that he face these people and make small talk. Mercury indeed!

Dr Martine's face fell easily into a pleasant smile but she looked a little bored as he shook her hand.

Jacob wondered if he could ask what parapsychology had to do with solar physics without sounding as if he were interested, but Fagin beat him to it.

'I intrude, as is generally considered acceptable in informal conversations among human beings when a pause has occurred. There remains one worthy being to introduce.'

Oops, thought Jacob, I hope this Eatee's not one of the hypersensitive ones. He turned to where the lizardlike extraterrestrial stood, to his right, next to a multicolored wall mosaic. It had risen from its cushion and now moved on six legs toward them. It was less than a meter in length and about twenty centimeters high. It walked right past him without a glance and proceeded to rub itself against Bubbacub's leg.

'Ahem,' Fagin said. '*That* is a pet. The worthy whom you are about to meet is the estimable client who brought you to this room.'

'Oh, I'm sorry.' Jacob grinned, then forced a serious expression onto his face.

'Jacob Demwa, a-Human, ul-Dolphin-ul-Chimp, please meet Culla, a-Pring, ab-Pil-ab-Kisa-ab-Soro-ab-Hul-ab-Puber, Assistant to Bubbacub of the Libraries and Representative of the Library with the Sundiver Project.'

As Jacob had expected, the name had only patronymics. The Pring had no clients of their own. They were of the Puber/Soro line, though. Someday they would have high status as members of that old and powerful lineage. He had noticed that Bubbacub's species was also out of the Puber/Soro and wished he could recall if the Pila and Pring were Patron and Client.

The alien stepped forward but did not offer to shake hands. His hands were long and tentacular with six fingers each at the ends of long slender arms. They looked fragile. Culla had a faint odor, a bit like the smell of new mown hay, that was not at all unpleasant.

The huge columnar eyes flashed as Culla bowed for the formal introduction. The E.T.s 'lips' curled back to display a pair of white, gleaming, grinder-mashie things, one on top and one on the bottom. The partially prehensile lips brought the cleavers together with a white porcelain 'clack!'

That can't be a friendly gesture where he comes from, Jacob shuddered. The alien probably pulled his huge dentures out to imitate a human smile. The sight was disturbing and at the same time intriguing. Jacob wondered what they were for. He also hoped that Culla would keep his ... lips curled back in the future.

Nodding slightly he said, 'I am Jacob.'

'I am Culla, Shir,' the alien replied. 'Your Earth ish very pleasant.' The great red eyes were now dull. Culla backed away.

Bubbacub led them back to the cushions by the window. The little Pil sprawled into a prone position with his quadrilaterally symmetric hands dangling over the sides of the cushion. The 'pet' followed and curled up next to him.

Kepler leaned forward and spoke hesitantly.

'I'm sorry we dragged you away from your important work, Mr Demwa. I know you're already heavily engaged ... I only hope that we can persuade you that, that our own little ... problem is worth your time and worthy of your talents.' Dr Kepler's hands were knotted together on his lap.

Dr Martine looked on Kepler's earnestness with an expression of mildly amused patience. There were nuances here that bothered Jacob.

'Well, Dr Kepler, Fagin must have told you that since my wife's death, I've retired from the "mystery business," and I am pretty busy right now, probably too much so to get involved in a long journey off planet ...'

Kepler's face fell. His expression became so bleak so suddenly that Jacob was moved.

'... However, since Kant Fagin is a perceptive individual, I'll be happy to listen to anyone he refers to me, and decide on the merits of the case.'

'Oh, you'll find this case interesting! I've been saying all along that we need fresh insight. And, of course, now that the Trustees have agreed to let us bring in some consultants ...'

32

'Now, Dwayne,' Dr Martine said. 'You're not being fair. I came in as a consultant six months ago. and Culla brought the services of the Library even earlier. Now Bubbacub has kindly agreed to increase the Library support for the project and come personally with us to Mercury. I think the Trustees are being more than generous.'

Jacob sighed.

'I wish someone would explain what this is all about. Like you, Dr Martine, perhaps you can tell me what your job is ... on Mercury?' He found it difficult to say the word 'Sundiver.'

'I am a consultant, Mr Demwa. I was hired to perform psychological and parapsychological tests on the crew and environment on Mercury.'

'I assume they had to do with the problem Dr Kepler mentioned?'

'Yes. It was thought at first that the phenomena were a hoax or some sort of mass-hallucination. I've eliminated both of those possibilities. It's clear now that they're real and actually take place in the solar chromosphere.

'For the last months I've been designing psi experiments to take down on solar dives. I've also been helping as a therapist for a number of Sundiver staff members; the pressures of conducting this kind of solar research have been telling on many of the men.'

Martine sounded competent, but there was something about her attitude that put Jacob off. Flippancy, perhaps. Jacob wondered what else there was to her relationship with Kepler. Was she his personal therapist as well?

For that matter, am I here just to satisfy the whim of a sick, great man who must be kept going? The idea wasn't very attractive. Nor was the prospect of getting involved in politics.

Bubbacub, head of the entire Branch Library on Earth – why is he involved in an obscure Terran project? In some ways, the little Pil was the most important E.T. on the Planet outside of the Tymbrimi Ambassador. His Library Institute, the biggest and most influential of the galactic organizations, made Fagin's Institute of Progress look like a drum and tambourine outfit. Did Martine say he's going to Mercury?

Bubbacub stared at the ceiling, apparently ignoring the conversation. His mouth worked as though singing in some range inaudible to humans.

Culla's bright eyes were on the little Library Chief. Perhaps he could hear the singing, or perhaps he too was bored by the conversation so far.

Kepler, Martine, Bubbacub, Culla ... I never thought I'd be in a room in which *Fagin* was the least strange!

The Kanten rustled nearby. Fagin was obviously excited. Jacob wondered what could have happened in the Sundiver project to get him so fired up.

'Dr Kepler, it just might be possible that I could spare the time to help you out ... maybe.' Jacob shrugged. 'But first, it would be nice to find out what this is all about!'

Kepler brightened.

'Oh, didn't I ever actually say it? Oh my. I guess I just avoid thinking about it these days ... just skirt around the subject, so to speak.'

He straightened and took a deep breath.

'Mr Demwa, it appears that the Sun is haunted.'

PART II

In prehistoric and early times the Earth was visited by unknown being from the cosmos. These unknown beings created human intelligence by a deliberate genetic mutation. The extraterrestrials ennobled hominids 'in their own image.' That is why we resemble them and not they us.

ERICH VON DANIKEN
CHARIOTS OF THE GODS

The sublime mental activities, such as religion, altruism and morality, all evolved, and have a physical base.

EDWARD O. WILSON
ON HUMAN NATURE
HARVARD UNIVERSITY PRESS

4

VIRTUAL IMAGE

The *Bradbury* was a new ship. It used a technology far ahead of its predecessors on the commercial line, taking off from sea level under its own power instead of riding to the station at the top of one of the equatorial 'Needles,' slung beneath a giant balloon. *Bradbury* was a huge sphere, titanically massive by earlier standards.

This was Jacob's first trip aboard a ship powered by the billion-year-old science of the Galactics. He watched from the first-class lounge as the Earth fell away, and Baja California became first a brown rib, separating two seas, then a mere finger along the coast of Mexico. The view was breathtaking, but a bit disappointing. The roar and acceleration of a jetliner, or the slow majesty of a cruise-zep had more romance. And the few times he had left Earth before, rising and returning by balloon, there has been the other ships to watch, bright and busy as they floated up to Power Station or back down the pressurized interior of one of the Needles.

Neither of the great Needles had ever been boring. The thin ceram walls that held the twenty-mile towers at sea-level pressures had been painted with gigantic murals – huge swooping birds and pseudo science-fiction space battles copied from twenty-century magazines. It had never been claustrophobic.

Still, Jacob was glad to be aboard the *Bradbury*. Someday he might visit the Chocolate Needle, at the summit of Mt Kenya, for nostalgia's sake. But the other one, the one in Ecuador – Jacob hoped never to see the Vanilla Needle again.

No matter that the great tower was only a stone's throw from Caracas. No matter that he would be given a hero's welcome, if ever he came there, as the man who had saved the one engineering marvel on Earth to impress even the Galactics.

Saving the Needle had cost Jacob Demwa his wife and a large portion of his mind. The price had been too high.

Earth had gained a visible disc when Jacob went off to look for the ship's bar. Suddenly he was in the mood for company. He hadn't felt that way when he came aboard. He'd had a rough time making excuses to Gloria and the others at the Center. Makakai had raised a fit. Also, many of the research materials on Solar Physics he'd ordered had not arrived and would have to be forwarded to Mercury. Finally, he'd let himself get into a stew wondering how he'd been talked into coming along in the first place.

Now he made his way along the main corridor, at the ship's equator, until he found the crowded, dimly lit Saloon. Inside he squeezed past clots of talking, drinking passengers to get to the bar.

About forty persons, many of them contract workers bound for skilled labor on Mercury, crowded into the Saloon. More than a few, having drunk too much, spoke loudly to their neighbors or simply stared. For some, departure from Earth came hard.

A few extraterrestrials rested on cushions in the corner set aside for them. One, a Cynthian with shiny fur and thick sunglasses, sat across from Culla, whose great head nodded silently while he sipped daintily with a straw between his huge lips, from what appeared to be a bottle of vodka.

Several humans stood near the aliens, typical of the Xenophiles who hang on every word of an eavesdropped E.T. conversation and who wait eagerly for chances to ask questions.

Jacob considered edging through the crowd to get to the E.T. corner. The Cynthian might be someone he knew. But there were too many people at that end of the room. He chose instead to get a drink and see if anyone had started storytelling.

Soon he was part of a group listening to a mining engineer tell an enjoyably exaggerated tale of blow-ins and rescues in the deep Hermetian mines. Though he had to strain to hear over the noise, Jacob still felt he could conveniently ignore the headache that was coming on ... at least long enough to listen to the end of the story, when a finger jabbed in his ribs made him jump.

'Demwa! It's you!' Pierre LaRoque cried. 'How fortunate! We shall travel together and now I know that there will always be someone with whom I can exchange witticisms!'

LaRoque wore a loose shiny robe. Blue PurSmok drifted into the air from the pipe he puffed with earnest.

Jacob tried to smile but with someone behind him stepping on his heel, it came out more like gritting his teeth.

'Hello, LaRoque. Why are you going to Mercury? Wouldn't your readers be more interested in stories about the Peruvian excavations or ...'

'Or similar dramatic evidence that our primitive ancestors were nurtured by ancient astronauts?' LaRoque interrupted. 'Yes, Demwa, such evidence shall soon be so overwhelming that even the Skins and skeptics who sit on the Confederacy Council will see the error of their ways!'

'I see you wear the Shirt yourself.' Jacob pointed to LaRoque's silvery tunic.

'I wear the *robe* of the Daniken Society on my last day on Earth, in honor of the older ones who gave us the power to go into space.'

LaRoque shifted pipe and drink into one hand and with the other straightened the gold medallion and chain that hung from his neck.

Jacob thought the effect was a bit theatrical for a grown man. The robe and jewelry seemed effeminate, in contrast to the Frenchman's gruff manner. He had to admit, though, that it went well with the outrageous, affected accent.

'Oh come on, LaRoque,' Jacob smiled. 'Even you have to admit we got into space by ourselves, and we discovered the extraterrestrials, not they us.'

'I admit nothing!' LaRoque answered hotly. 'When we prove ourselves worthy of the Patrons who gave us our intelligence in the dim past, when they acknowledge us, then we'll know how much they have covertly helped us all these years!'

Jacob shrugged. There was nothing new in the Skin-Shirt controversy. One side insisted that man should be proud of his unique heritage as a self-evolved race, having won intelligence from Nature herself on the savannah and shoreline of East Africa. The other side held that homo sapiens – just as every other known race of sophonts – was part of a chain of genetic and cultural uplifting that stretched back to the fabled early days of the galaxy, the time of the Progenitors.

Many, like Jacob, were studiously neutral in the conflict of views, but humanity, and humanity's client races, awaited the outcome with interest Archeology and Paleontology had become the great new hobbies since Contact.

However, LaRoque's arguments were so stale they could be used for croutons. And the headache was getting worse.

'That's very interesting, LaRoque,' he said as he began to edge past 'Perhaps we can discuss it some other time ...' But LaRoque wasn't finished yet.

'Space is filled with Neanderthaler sentiment you know. The men on our ships would prefer to wear animal skins and grunt like apes! They resent the Older Ones, and they actively snub sensible people who practice humility!'

LaRoque made his point while jabbing in Jacob's direction with the stem of his pipe. Jacob backed away, trying to stay polite but having difficulty.

'Well, now I think that's going a little too far, LaRoque, I mean you're talking about *astronauts!* Emotional and political stability are prime criteria in their selection ...'

'Aha! What you do not know about the very things you just mentioned! You joke, no? I know a thing or two about "emotional and political stability" of astronauts!

'I'll tell you about it sometime,' he continued. 'Someday the whole story will come out, about the Confederacy's plan to isolate a large part of humanity away from the elder races, and from their heritage in the stars! All the poor "unreliables"! But by then it will be too late to seal the leak!'

LaRoque puffed and exhaled a cloud of blue PurSmok in Jacob's direction. Jacob felt a wave of dizziness.

'Yeah, LaRoque, whatever you say. You've got to tell me about it some time.' He backed away.

LaRoque glowered on for a moment, then grinned and patted Jacob on the back as he edged his way to the door.

'Yes,' he said. 'I'll tell you all about it. But meanwhile, better you should lie down. You don't look so good at all! Bye bye!' He slapped Jacob's back once more then slipped back into the bar.

Jacob walked to the nearest port and rested his head against the pane. It was cool and it helped to ease the throbbing in his forehead. When he opened his eyes to look out, the Earth was not in sight ... only a great field of stars, shining unblinking against blackness. The brighter ones were surrounded by diffraction rays, which he could lengthen or shorten by squinting. Except for the brightness, the effect was no different than looking at the stars on a night in the desert. They didn't twinkle, but they were the same stars.

Jacob knew he should feel more. The stars when viewed from space should be more mysterious, more ... 'philosophical.' One of the things he could remember best about his adolescence was the asolopsistic roar of starry nights. It was nothing like the oceanic feeling he now got through hypnosis. It had been like half-remembered dreams of another life.

He found Dr Kepler, Bubbacub, and Fagin in the main lounge. Kepler invited him to join them.

The group settled around a cluster of cushions near the view ports. Bubbacub carried with him a cup of something that looked and, from a chance whiff, smelled noxious. Fagin ambled slowly, twisting on his root-pods, carrying nothing.

The row of ports that ran along the curved periphery of the ship was broken in the lounge by a large circular disc, like a giant round window, that touched floor and ceiling. The flat side protruded into the room about a foot. Whatever lay within was hidden behind a tightly fixed panel.

'We are glad that you made it,' Bubbacub barked through his Vodor. He had sprawled on one of the cushions and, after saying this, dipped his snout into the cup he carried and ignored Jacob and the others. Jacob wondered if the Pil was trying to be sociable, or if he came by his charm naturally.

Jacob thought of Bubbacub as 'he' because he had no idea at all about Bubbacub's true gender. Though Bubbacub wore no clothes, other than the Vodor and a small pouch, what Jacob could see of the alien's anatomy only confused matters. He had learned, for instance, that the Pila were oviparous and did not suckle their young. But a row of what appeared to be teats lay like shirt buttons from throat to crotch. He couldn't even guess at their purpose. The Datanet did not mention them. Jacob had ordered a more complete summary from the Library.

Fagin and Kepler were talking about the history of Sunships. Fagin's voice was muffled because his upper foliage and blowhole brushed against the soundproofing panels on the ceiling. (Jacob hoped that Kanten were not prone to claustrophobia. But then, what were talking vegetables afraid of anyway? Being nibbled on, he supposed. He wondered about the sexual mores of a race whose lovemaking required the intermediary of a sort of domesticated bumblebee.)

'Then these magnificent improvisations,' Fagin said, 'without benefit of the slightest help from outside, enabled you to convey packages of instruments into the very Photosphere! This is most impressive and I wonder that, in my years here, I never knew of this adventure of your period before Contact!'

Kepler beamed. 'You must understand that the bathysphere project was only ... the beginning, long before my time. When laser propulsion for pre-Contact interstellar craft was developed, they were able to drop robot ships that could hover and, by the thermodynamics of using a high temperature laser, they could dump excess heat and cool the probe's interior.'

'Then you were only a short time away from sending men!'

Kepler smiled ruefully. 'Well, perhaps. Plans were made. But sending living beings to the Sun and back involved more than just heat and gravity. The worst obstacle was the turbulence!

'It would have been great to see if we could have solved the problem, though.' Kepler's eyes shone for a moment. 'There were plans.'

'But then the *Vesarius* found Tymbrimi ships in Cygnus,' Jacob said.

'Yes. So we'll never find out. The plans were drawn up when I was just a boy. Now they're hopelessly obsolete. And it's probably just as well ... There would have been inescapable losses, even deaths, if we'd done it without stasis ... Control of timeflow is the key to Sundiver now, and I certainly wouldn't complain about the results.'

The scientist's expression suddenly darkened. 'That is, until now.'

41

Kepler fell silent and stared at the carpet. Jacob watched him for a moment, then covered his mouth and coughed.

'While we're on the subject, I've noticed that there isn't any mention of Sun Ghosts on the Datanet, or even in a special request from the Library... and I have a 1-AB permit. I was wondering if you could spare some of your reports on the subject, to study during the trip?'

Kepler looked away from Jacob nervously.

'We weren't quite ready to let the data off Mercury yet, Mr Demwa. There ... are political considerations to this discovery that, uh, will delay your briefing until we get to the base. I'm sure that all of your questions will be answered there.' He looked so genuinely ashamed that Jacob decided to drop the matter for the moment. But this was not a good sign.

'I might take a liberty in adding one piece of information,' Fagin said. 'There has been another dive since our meeting, Jacob, and on that dive, we are told, only the first and more prosaic species of Solarian was observed. Not the second variety which has caused Dr Kepler so much concern.'

Jacob was still confused by the hurried explanations Kepler had given of the two types of Sun-creatures so far observed.

'Now I take it that type was your herbivore?'

'Not herbivore!' Kepler interjected. 'A magnetovore. It feeds on magnetic field energy. That type is actually becoming rather well understood, however ...'

'I interrupt! In the most unctious wish that I be forgiven for the intrusion, I urge discretion. A stranger approaches.' Fagin's upper branches rustled against the ceiling.

Jacob turned to look at the doorway, a bit shocked that anything would bring Fagin to interrupt another's sentence. Dismally he realized that this was still another sign that he had stepped into a politically tense situation, and he still knew none of the rules.

I don't hear anything, he thought. Then Pierre LaRoque stood at the door, a drink in his hand and his always florid face further flushed. The man's initial smile broadened when he saw Fagin and Bubbacub. He entered and gave Jacob a jovial slap on the back, insisting that he be introduced right away.

Jacob internalized a shrug.

He performed the introductions slowly. LaRoque was impressed, and he bowed deeply to Bubbacub.

'Ab-Kisa-ab-Soro-ab-Hul-ab-Puber! And two clients, what were they, Demwa? Jello and something? I'm honored to meet a sophont of the Soro line in person! I have studied the language of your ancestrals, whom we may someday show to be ours as well! The Soro tongue is so similar to Proto-Semitic, and Proto-Bantu also!'

Bubbacub's cilia bristled above his eyes. The Pil, through his Vodor, began to make voice with a complicated, alliterative, incomprehensible speech. Then the alien's jaws made short, sharp snaps and a high pitched growling could be heard, half amplified by the Vodor.

From behind Jacob, Fagin answered in a clicking and rumbling tongue. Bubbacub turned to face him, black eyes hot as he answered with a throaty growl, waving a stubby arm in a slash in LaRoque's direction. The Kanten's trilling reply sent a chill down Jacob's back.

Bubbacub swiveled and stamped out of the room without a further word to the humans.

For a dumbfounded instant, LaRoque said nothing. Then, he looked at Jacob plaintively. 'What is it I did, please?'

Jacob sighed, 'Maybe he doesn't like being called a cousin of yours, LaRoque.' He turned to Kepler to change the subject. The scientist was staring at the door through which Bubbacub left.

'Dr Kepler, if you haven't any specific data on board, perhaps you could lend me some basic solar physics texts and some background histories on Sundiver itself?'

'I'd be delighted to, Mr Demwa.' Kepler nodded. 'I'll send them to you by dinner time.' His mind appeared to be elsewhere.

'I too!' LaRoque cried. 'I am an accredited journalist and I demand the background upon your infamous endeavor, Mr Director!'

After a moment's startlement, Jacob shrugged. Have to hand it to LaRoque. Chutzhpa can be easily mistaken for resiliency.

Kepler smiled, as if he had not heard. 'I beg your pardon?'

'The great conceit! This "Sundiver Project" of yours, which takes money that could go to the deserts of Earth for reclamation, or to a greater Library for our world!

'The *vanity* of this project, to study what our betters understood perfectly before we were apes!'

'Now see here, sir. The Confederacy has funded this research . . .' Kepler reddened.

'Research! Ree-search it is. You re-search for that which is already in the Libraries of the Galaxy, and shame us all by making humans out to be fools!'

'LaRoque . . .' Jacob began, but the man wouldn't shut up.

'And what of your Confederacy! They stuff the Elders into reservations, like the old-time Indians of America! They keep access to the Branch Library out of the hands of the people! They allow continuation of this absurdity that all laugh at us for, this claim of spontaneous intelligence!'

Kepler backed away from LaRoque's vehemence. The color drained out of his face and he stammered.

43

'I . . . I don't think . . .'

'LaRoque! Come on, cut it out!'

Jacob grabbed his shoulder and pulled him over to whisper urgently in his ear.

'Come on man, you don't want to shame us in front of the venerable Kanten Fagin, do you?'

LaRoque's eyes widened. Over Jacob's shoulder Fagin's upper foliage rustled audibly in agitation. Finally, LaRoque's gaze dropped.

The second embarrassment must have been enough for him. He mumbled an apology to the alien, and with a parting glare at Kepler, took his leave.

'Thanks for the special effects, Fagin,' Jacob said after LaRoque was gone.

He was answered by a whistle, short and low.

5

REFRACTION

At 40 million kilometers, the Sun was a chained hell. It boiled in black space, no longer the brilliant dot that the children of Earth took for granted and easily, unconsciously, avoided with their eyes. Across millions of miles it pulled. Compulsively, one felt a need to look, but the need was dangerous.

From the *Bradbury*, it had the apparent size of a nickel held a foot away from the eye. The specter was too bright to be endured undiminished. To 'catch a glimpse' of this orb, as one sometimes did on Earth, would invite blindness. The Captain ordered the ship's stasis screens polarized and the regular viewing ports sealed.

The Lyot window was unshuttered in the lounge, so that passengers could examine the Lifegiver without injury.

Jacob paused in front of the round window in a late night pilgrimage to the coffee machine, half awake from a fitful sleep in his tiny stateroom. For minutes he stared, blank faced, still only half conscious, until a lisping voice roused him.

'Dish ish the way your shun looksh from the Aphelion of the orbit of Mercury, Jacob.'

Culla sat at one of the card tables in the dimly lit lounge. Just behind the alien, above a row of vending machines, a wall clock read '04:30' in glowing numbers.

Jacob's sleepy voice was thick in his throat 'Have ... um ... are we that close already?'

Culla nodded. 'Yesh.'

The alien's lip grinders were tucked away. His big folded lips pursed and let out a whistle each time he tried to pronounce an English long 's.' In the dim light his eyes reflected a red glow from the viewing window.

'We have only two more days until we arrive,' the alien said. His arms were crossed on the table in front of him. The loose folds of his silver gown covered half of the surface.

Jacob, swaying slightly, turned to glance back at the port. The solar orb wavered before his eyes.

'Are you all right?' the Pring asked anxiously. He started to rise.

'No. No, please.' Jacob held up his hand. 'I'm just groggy. Not 'nuff sleep. Need coffee.'

He shambled toward the vending machines, but halfway there he stopped, turned, and peered again at the image of the furnace-sun.

'It's red!' he grunted in surprise.

'Shall I tell you why while you get your coffee?' Culla asked.

'Yes. Please.' Jacob turned back to the dark row of food and beverage dispensers, looking for a coffee spout.

'The Lyot window only allowsh in light in monochromatic form,' Culla said. 'It ish made of many round platesh; some polarizersh and some light retardersh. They are rotated with reshpect to one another to finely tune which wavelength ish allowed through.

'Itsh a most delicate and ingenioush device, although quite obsholete by Galactic standarsh ... like one of the "Shwiss" watchesh some humansh shtill wear in an age of electronicsh. When your people become adept with the Library such ... Rube Goldbersh? ... will be archaic.'

Jacob bent forward to peer at the nearest machine. It looked like a coffee machine. There was a transparent panel door, and behind that a little platform with a metal grill drain at the bottom. Now, if he pushed the right button, a disposable cup should drop onto the platform and then, from some mechanical artery would pour a stream of the bitter black beverage he wanted.

As Culla's voice droned on in his ears, Jacob made polite sounds. 'Uh, huh ... yes, I see.'

At the far left, one of the buttons was lit with a green light. On impulse, he pressed it.

He watched the machine blearily. Now! That was a buzz and a click! There's the cup! Now ... what the hell?

A large yellow and green pill fell into the cup.

Jacob lifted the panel and took out the cup. A second later a stream of hot liquid spilled through the empty space where the cup had been, disappearing in the drain below.

Dubiously, he glowered down at the pill. Whatever it was, it wasn't coffee. He rubbed his eyes with his left wrist, one at a time. Then he sent an accusing glance at the button he'd pressed.

That button had a label, he now saw. It read 'E.T. Nutrient Synthesis.' Below the label a computer card stuck out from a data slot. The words 'Pring: Dietary Supplement – Coumarin Protein Complex' were printed along the protruding end.

Jacob looked quickly at Culla. The alien continued his explanation while he faced the Lyot window. Culla waved one arm toward the Sun's Dantean brilliance to emphasize a point.

'Thish ish now the red alpha line of Hydrogen,' he said. 'A very useful shpectral line. Inshtead of being overwhelmed by huge amountsh of random light from all levelsh of the Shun, we can now look at only those regions where elemental Hydrogen absorbsh or emitsh more than normal . . .'

Culla pointed to the Sun's mottled surface. It was covered with dark reddish speckles and feathery arches.

Jacob had read about them. The feathery arches were 'filaments.' Viewed against space, at the solar limb, they were the prominences that had been seen since the first time a telescope was used during an eclipse. Culla apparently was explaining the way these objects were viewed head-on.

Jacob considered. Throughout the voyage from Earth, Culla had refrained from eating his meals with the others. All he would do is sip an occasional vodka or beer with a straw. Although he had given no reasons, Jacob could only assume that the being had some cultural inhibition against eating in public.

Come to think of it, he thought, with those mashies for teeth it *could* get a little messy. Apparently I've barged in while he's having breakfast and he's too polite to mention it.

He glanced at the tablet which still lay in the cup in his hand. He dropped the pill into his jacket pocket and crumpled the cup into a nearby trash bin.

Now he could see the button which was labeled 'Coffee-Black.' He smiled ruefully. Maybe it would be best to skip the coffee and not run the risk of offending Culla. Although the E.T. had made no objections, he *had* kept his back turned while Jacob visited the food and beverage machines.

Culla looked up as Jacob approached. He opened his mouth slightly and for an instant the human caught a glimpse of white porcelain.

'Are you lesh . . . groggy, now?' the alien asked solicitously.

'Yesh, uh yes, thanks . . . thanks also for the explanation. I always thought of the Sun as a pretty smooth place . . . except for Sunspots and prominences. But I guess it's actually pretty complicated.'

Culla nodded. 'Doctor Kepler ish the expert. You will get a better explanation from him when you go on a dive wid ush.'

Jacob smiled politely. How carefully these Galactic Emissaries were trained! When Culla nodded, was the gesture personally meaningful? Or was it something he had been taught to do at certain times and places around humans?

Dive with us!?

He decided not to ask Culla to repeat the remark.

Better not to press my luck, he thought.

He started to yawn. Just in time he remembered to stifle it behind his hand. No telling what a similar gesture would mean on the Pring home planet! 'Well, Culla, I think I'm going to go back to my room and try for a little more sleep. Thanks for the talk.'

'You are mosht entirely welcome, Jacob. Good night.'

He shuffled down the hall and barely made it to bed before he was fast asleep.

6

RETARDATION AND DIFFRACTION

A soft, pearly light suffused through the ports, illuminating the faces of those who watched Mercury glide beneath the descending ship.

Almost everyone who did not have a duty to perform was in the lounge, held to the row of viewing windows by the planet's terrible beauty. Voices were hushed, and conversations settled into small groups gathered around each port. For the most part the only sound was a faint crackling which Jacob couldn't identify.

The surface of the planet was gouged and scratched with craters and long rills. The shadows cast by the mountains of Mercury were vacuum sharp in their blackness, set against bright silvers and browns. In many ways the place resembled the Earth's moon.

There were differences. In one area a whole piece had been torn off in some ancient cataclysm. The scar made a deep series of grooves on the side that faced the Sun. The terminator ran starkly along the edge of the indention, a sharp borderline of day and night.

Down there, in places where shadow did not fall, a rain of seven different types of fire fell. Protons, x-rays spun off from the planet's magnetosphere and the simple blinding sunshine itself mixed with other deadly things to make the surface of Mercury as unlike the moon as anyplace could be.

It seemed like a place where one could find ghosts. A purgatory.

He remembered a line from an ancient pre-Haiku Japanese poem that he had read only a month before:

> More sad thoughts crowd into my mind
> When evening comes; for then,
> Appears your phantom shape –
> Speaking as I have known you speak.

'Did you say something?'

Jacob started from the mild trance and saw Dwayne Kepler standing next to him.

'No, nothing much. Here's your jacket.' He handed the folded garment to Kepler, who took it with a grin.

'Sorry, but biology strikes at the most unromantic times. In real life space travelers have to go to the bathroom too. Bubbacub seems to find this velour fabric irresistible. Every time I put my jacket down to do something I come back to find that he's gone to sleep on it. I'm going to have to purchase some for him when we get back to Earth. Now what were we talking about before I left?'

Jacob pointed down at the surface below. 'I was just thinking ... now I understand why astronauts call the moon "The Playpen." You certainly have to be more cautious here.'

Kepler nodded. 'Yes, but it's a whole lot better than working on some stupid "make-work" project at home!' Kepler paused for a moment as If he were about to go on to say something scathing. But the passion leaked away before he could continue. He turned to the port and gestured at the view below. 'The early observers, Antoniodi and Schiaparelli, called this area Charit Regio. That huge ancient crater over there is Goethe.' He pointed to a jumble of darker material in a bright plain. 'It's very close to the North Pole, and underneath it is the network of caves that makes Hermes Base possible.'

Kepler was the perfect picture, now, of the dignified scholarly gentleman, except for the times when one end or the other of his long sandy-colored moustache was in his mouth. His nervousness appeared to ease as they approached Mercury and the Sundiver Base where he was boss.

But at times during the trip, particularly when a conversation turned to uplift or the Library, Kepler's face took on the expression of a man with a great deal to say and no way to say it. It was a nervous, embarrassed look, as if he were afraid of expressing his opinions out of fear of rebuke.

After some pondering, Jacob thought he knew part of the reason. Although the Sundiver chief had said nothing explicit to give himself away, Jacob was convinced that Dwayne Kepler was religious.

In the midst of the Shirt-Skin controversy and Contact with extraterrestrials, organized religion had been torn apart.

The Danikenites proselytized their faith in some great (but not omnipotent) race of beings that had intervened in man's development and might do so again. The followers of the Neolithic Ethic preached the palpable presence of the 'spirit of man.'

And the mere existence of thousands of space-traveling races, few professing anything similar to the tenets of the old faiths of earth, did grievous harm to concepts of an all-powerful, anthropomorphic God.

Most of the formal creeds had either co-opted one side or another in the Shirt-Skin conflict or devolved into philosophical theism. The armies of the faithful had mostly flocked to other banners, and those who remained were quiet amid all of the uproar.

Jacob had often wondered if they were waiting for a Sign.

If Kepler were a Believer, it would explain some of his caution. There was enough unemployment among scientists these days. Kepler wouldn't want to risk adding his own name to the rolls by getting a reputation as a fanatic.

Jacob thought it a shame that the man felt that way. It would have been interesting to hear his views. But he respected Kepler's obvious wish for privacy in that area.

What attracted Jacob's professional interest was the way in which the isolation might have contributed to Kepler's mental problems. Something more than just a philosophical quandary was at work in the man's mind, something that now and then impaired his effectiveness as a leader and his self-confidence as a scientist.

Martine, the psychologist, was often with Kepler, reminding him regularly to take his medication from the vials of diverse, multicolored pills that he carried in his pockets.

Jacob felt old habits coming back, undulled by recent quiet months at the Center for Uplift. He wanted to know what those pills were, almost as much as he wished to know what Mildred Martine's *real* job was on Sundiver.

Martine was still an enigma to Jacob. In all of their conversations aboard ship he failed to penetrate the woman's damnable friendly detachment. Her amused condescension toward him was just as pronounced as Dr Kepler's exaggerated confidence in him. The dark woman's thoughts were elsewhere.

Martine and LaRoque hardly glanced out their port. Instead, Martine was talking about her research into the effects of color and glare on psychotic behavior. Jacob had heard about this at the Ensenada meeting. One of the first things Martine had done on joining Sundiver was to have environmental psychogenic effects brought to a minimum, in case the 'phenomena' turned out to be a stress-illusion.

Her friendship with LaRoque had grown over the trip out as she listened, rapt, to story after contradicting story about lost civilizations and ancient visitors to Earth. LaRoque responded to the attention by calling up the eloquence for which he was famous. Several times their private conversations in the lounge had gathered crowds. Jacob listened in a couple of times, himself. LaRoque could evoke a great deal of sensitivity when he tried.

Still Jacob felt less comfortable around the man than he did with any of the other passengers. He preferred the company of more straightforward beings, such as Culla. Jacob had come to like the alien. Notwithstanding the huge complex eyes and incredible dental work, the Pring had tastes akin to his on a wide range of subjects.

Culla had been full of ingenuous questions about Earth and humans, most of all regarding the way humans treated their client races. When he learned that Jacob had actually participated in the project to raise chimpanzees, dolphins and, recently, dogs and gorillas, to full sapiency, he began to treat Jacob with even more respect.

Culla never once referred to Earth's technology as archaic or obsolete, although everyone knew that it was unique in the galaxy for its quaintness. No other race in living memory had, after all, had to invent everything itself from ground zero. The Library saw to that. Culla was enthusiastic about the benefits the Library would bring to his human and chimpanzee friends.

Once, the E.T. followed Jacob into the ship's gymnasium and watched, with those huge red disc oculars, as Jacob went into one of his marathon conditioning sessions, one of several during the trip out from Earth. During rests Jacob found that the Pring had already learned the art of telling off-color jokes. The Pring race must have similar sexual mores to those of contemporary humanity, for the punch line ' . . . now we're only haggling over the price,' seemed to have the same meaning for both.

It was the jokes more than anything else that made Jacob realize how very far away from home the slender Pring diplomat was. He wondered if Culla was as lonely as he would be in that situation.

In their subsequent discussion of whether Tuborg or L-5 was the best brand of beer, Jacob had to struggle to remember that this was an alien, not a lisping, overly polite human being. But the lesson had been brought home when, in the course of a conversation, they found themselves separated by a sudden, unbridgeable gap.

Jacob had told a story about Earth's old class struggles that Culla failed to understand. He tried to illustrate the point of it with a Chinese proverb: 'A peasant always hangs himself in his landlord's doorway.'

The alien's eyes suddenly became bright and Jacob for the first time heard an agitated clacking coming from Culla's mouth. Jacob had stared for a moment, then moved quickly to change the subject.

All things considered, however, Culla had the closest thing to a human sense of humor of any extraterrestrial he had met. Fagin excepted, of course.

Now, as they approached the landing, the Pring stood silently near his Patron – his expression, and Bubbacub's, once again unreadable.

Kepler tapped him gently on the arm. The scientist pointed at the port. 'Pretty soon, now, the Captain will tighten up the Stasis Screens and begin to cut down the rate at which she lets space-time leak in. You'll find the effects interesting.'

'I thought the ship sort of let the fabric of space slip past it, like riding a surfboard into a beach.'

Kepler smiled.

'No, Mr Demwa. That's a common fallacy. Space-surfing is just a phrase used by popularizers. When I speak of space-time I'm not talking about a "fabric." Space is not a material.

'Actually, as we approach a planetary singularity – a distortion in space caused by a planet – we must adopt a constantly changing metric, or set of parameters by which we measure space and time. It's as if nature wants us to gradually change the length of our meter sticks and the pace of our clocks whenever we get close to a mass.'

'I take it the Captain is controlling our approach by allowing this change to take place slowly?'

'Exactly right! In the old days, of course, the adaptation was more violent. One adapted one's metric either by braking continuously with rockets until touchdown, or by crashing into the planet. Now we just roll up excess metric like a bolt of cloth in stasis. Ah! There goes that "material" analogy again!'

Kepler grinned.

'One of the useful by-products of this is commercial grade neutronium, but the main purpose is to get us down safely.'

'So when we finally start stuffing space into a bag, what will we see?'

Kepler pointed to the port.

'You can see it happening now.'

Outside, the stars were going out. The tremendous spray of bright pinpoints which even the darkened screens had let through slowly faded as they watched. Soon only a few were left, weak and ochre colored against the blackness.

The planet below changed as well.

The light reflected from Mercury's surface was no longer hot and brittle. It took on an orange tint. The surface was quite dark now.

And it was getting closer, too. Slowly, but visibly, the horizon flattened. Surface objects only barely discerned earlier came into focus as the *Bradbury* settled lower.

Large craters opened up to show smaller craters within. As the ship descended past the ragged edge of one of these, Jacob saw it too was covered with still smaller pits, each similar in shape to the larger ones.

The tiny planet's horizon disappeared behind a range of mountains, and Jacob lost all perspective. With every minute of descent the ground below looked the same. How could you tell how high up you were? Is that thing just below us a mountain, or a boulder, or are we going to touch down in just a second or two and is it just a rock?

He sensed nearness. The gray shadows and orange outcrops seemed close enough to touch.

Expecting the ship to come to rest at any moment, he was surprised when a hole in the ground rushed up to engulf them.

As they prepared to disembark, Jacob remembered with a shock what he had been doing when he slipped into a light trance earlier, holding Kepler's jacket during the descent.

Surreptitiously, and with great skill, he had picked Kepler's pockets, taking a sample of every medication and removing a small pencil stub without smudging the fingerprints. They made a neat lump in Jacob's side pocket now, too small to stand out against the taper of his jacket.

So it's started already, he groaned.

Jacob's jaw tightened.

This time, he thought, I'm going to solve it myself! I don't need help from my alter ego. I'm not going to go around breaking and entering!

He struck his balled fist against his thigh to drive out the itchy, *satisfied* feeling in his fingers.

PART III

The transition region between the corona and photosphere (the surface of the sun as seen in white light) appears during an eclipse as a bright red ring around the sun, and is therefore called the chromosphere. When the chromosphere is examined closely, it is seen to be not a homogeneous layer but a rapidly changing filamentary structure. The term 'burning prairie' has been used to describe it. Numerous short-lived jets called 'spicules' are continuously shooting up to heights of several thousand kilometers. The red color is due to the dominance of radiation in the H-alpha line of hydrogen. The problems of understanding what is going on in such a complex region are great ...

HAROLD ZIRIN

7

INTERFERENCE

When Dr Martine left her quarters and took service corridors to the E.T. Environments Section, she thought of herself as using discretion, not stealth. Pipes and communications cables clung, stapled, to the rough unfinished walls. The Hermetian stone glistened with condensation and gave off an odor of wet rock as her footsteps rang down the fused path ahead of her.

She arrived at a pressure-sealed door with a green overhead light, the back entrance to one alien's residence. When she pressed the sensing cell next to it, the door opened immediately.

A bright, greenish-tinted light spilled out – the reproduced sunshine of a star many parsecs distant. She shielded her eyes with one hand while with the other she took a pair of sunglasses from her hip pouch, and put them on to look into the room.

On the walls she saw spiderweb tapestries of hanging gardens and of an alien city set on the edge of a mountain scarp. The city clung to the jagged cliff, shimmering as if viewed through a waterfall. Dr Martine thought she could almost hear high pitched music, keening just above her aural range. Could that explain the shortness of her breath? Her jittery nerves?

Bubbacub rose from a cushioned pallet to greet her. His gray fur shone as he waddled forward on stubby legs. In the actinic light and one point five g-field of his apartment, Bubbacub lost whatever 'cuteness' Martine had seen in him before. The Pil's bowlegged stance spoke strength.

The alien's mouth moved in short snaps. His voice, coming from the Vodor which hung from his neck, was smooth and resonant, although the words came clipped and separated.

'Good. Glad you come.'

Martine was relieved. The Library Representative sounded relaxed. She bowed slightly.

'Greeting, Pil Bubbacub. I came to ask if you have had any further word from the Branch Library.'

Bubbacub displayed a mouth full of needle sharp teeth. 'Come in and sit. Yes, good that you ask. I have a new fact. But come. Have food, drink first.'

Martine grimaced as she passed through the g-transition field of the threshold – always a disconcerting experience. Inside the room she felt as though she weighed seventy kilos.

'No. Thank you, I just ate. I will sit.' She selected a chair built for humans and carefully lowered herself into it. Seventy kilos was more than a person should weigh!

The Pil sprawled back on his cushion across from her, his ursine head barely above the level of his feet He regarded her with small black eyes.

'I have heard from La Paz by ma-ser. They say no thing on Sun Ghosts. No thing at all. It may not be se-man-tics at all. It may be the Branch is too small. It is small, small branch, as I saided. But some Hu-man Off-ic-ials will make much of the lack of a re-fer-ence.'

Martine shrugged. 'I wouldn't worry about it. This will only go to show that too little effort has been spent on the Library project. A bigger branch, like my group has been lobbying for all along, would surely have had results.'

'I sended for da-ta from Pil-a by time drop. There can be no con-fu-sion at a Main Branch!'

'That's good,' Martine nodded. 'What's bothering me, though, is what Dwayne is going to do during this delay. He's bubbling over with half cracked notions about how to communicate with the Ghosts. I'm afraid that in his stumbling around down there, he'll find some way of offending the psi-creatures so badly that all of the Library's wisdom won't patch things up. It's vital that Earth have good relations with its nearest neighbors!'

Bubbacub raised his head slightly and placed a short arm behind it. 'You are mak-ing ef-forts to cure Dr Kep-ler?'

'Of course,' she replied, stiffly. 'Actually, I'm having trouble seeing how he escaped Probation all of this time. Dwayne's mind is full of chaos, though I'll admit his P-score is within the acceptance curves. He had a tachisto test on Earth.

'I think I've got him pretty well stabilized, now. But what's driv-ing me crazy is trying to figure out what his basic problem is. His manic depressive swings resemble the "glare madness" of the late twentieth and early twenty-first centuries, when society was almost wrecked by the psychic effects of environmental noise. It nearly tore apart industrial culture when it was at its peak and led to the period of repression people today euphemistically call "the Bureau-cracy."'

'Yes. I have readed of your race-es at-tempt at sui-cide. It seem to me that the time af-ter, of which you just spoke, was time of order and peace. But that not my af-fair. You are luck-y to be in-comp-e-tent even at sui-cide.

'But do not stray. What of Kep-ler?'

The Pil's voice did not rise at the end of his question, but there was something he did with his snout ... a curling of the folds that served instead of lips ... that told when he was asking, no, *demanding* an answer. It sent a shiver down Dr Martine's spine.

He's so arrogant, she thought. And everyone else seems to think it's just a quirk of personality. Can they be blind to the power and the threat that this creature's presence on Earth represents?

In their culture shock, they see a little manlike bear. *Cute*, even! Are my boss and his friends on the Confederacy Council the only ones who recognize a demon from outer space when they see one?

And somehow it's up to me to find out what it will take to propitiate the demon, while I keep Dwayne from shooting off his mouth, and try to be the one to come up with a *sensible* way to contact the Sun Ghosts! Ifni, help your sister!

Bubbacub was still waiting for an answer.

'W-well, I do know that Dwayne is determined to crack the Sun Ghost's secret without extraterrestrial help. Some of his crew are downright radical about it. I won't go so far as to say that any of them are Skins, but their pride is running pretty stiff.'

'Can you keep him from do-ing rash things?' Bubbacub said. 'He has broughted in ran-dom el-ements.'

'Like inviting Fagin and his friend Demwa? They seem to be harmless. Demwa's experience with dolphins gives him a distant but plausible chance to be useful. And Fagin has a knack for getting along with alien races. The important thing is that Dwayne has someone to spill out his paranoid fantasies to. I'll talk to Demwa and ask him to be sympathetic.'

Bubbacub sat up in a momentary writhing of arms and legs. He settled into a new position and looked straight into Martina's eyes.

'I do not care about them. Fa-gin is a pass-ive ro-man-tic. Demwa looks like a fool. Like any friend of Fa-gin's.

'No, I care more a-bout the two who now cause troub-le on the base. I did not know, when I came, that there was a chimp here who was made part of the staff. He and the journ-al-ist have been all claws since we hit dirt. The journ-al-ist is snubbed by the base crew and he makes lot of noise. And the Chip keeps at Cul-la all time ... trying to "lib-er-ate" him, so ...'

'Has Culla been disobedient? I thought his indenture was only ...'

Bubbacub leapt from his seat, pointy teeth bared in a hiss.

'Do not interrupt, human!' Bubbacub's real voice became audible for the first time in Martina's memory, a high pitched squeak, above the roar of the Vodor, that hurt her ears.

For a moment, Martine was too stunned to move.

Bubbacub's taut stance began to relax by degrees. In a minute the stiff brush of fur was almost smooth again.

57

'I apo-log-ize, human-Mar-tine. I should not fluff-up to such minor breach by one of mere in-fant race.'

Martine let her breath out, trying not to make a sound.

Bubbacub sat once again. 'To answer your question, no, Cul-la not out of place. He does know his species will be in-den-tured to mine by Paren-tal right for long time.

'Still, it bad that this Doc-tor Jeff-rey does push this myth of rights with-out duties. You humans must learn to keep your pets in line, for it on-ly by good grace of we old ones that they are called cli-ent soph-onts at all.

'And if *they* not be sophonts, where would you be, hu-man?'

Bubbacub's teeth shone brightly for a moment then he closed his mouth with a snap.

Martine felt very dry in the throat. She chose her words carefully. 'I'm sorry about any offense you may have taken, Pil Bubbacub. I will speak to Dwayne and maybe he can get Jeffrey to ease off.'

'And the journ-al-ist?'

'Yes, I'll talk to Pierre also. I'm sure he doesn't mean any harm. He won't cause any more trouble.'

'That would be well,' Bubbacub's voicebox said softly. He allowed his stocky body to settle once more into a slouch.

'We have great com-mon goals, you and I. I hope we can work as one. But know this: our means may dif-fer. Please do what you can or I be forced to, as you say, kill two birds with one stone.'

Martine nodded again, weakly.

8

REFLECTION

Jacob let his mind wander as LaRoque launched into one of his expositions. At any rate, the little man was now more interested in impressing Fagin than in winning any points with Jacob. Jacob wondered if it would be sinful anthropomorphizing to pity the E.T. for having to listen.

The three rode in a small car that moved through tunnels later-ally as well as up and down. Two of Fagin's root-pods gripped a low rail that ran a few centimeters off the floor. The two humans held onto another that circuited the car higher up.

Jacob listened with half an ear as the car glided on. LaRoque still bearded a topic he started back aboard the *Bradbury*: that the missing Patrons of Earth ... those mythical beings who suppos-edly began the Uplift of man thousands of years ago, and then gave it up halfway finished ... were somehow associated with the Sun. LaRoque thought the Sun Ghosts themselves might be that race.

'Then you have all of the references in the religions of Earth. Almost in every one the Sun is something holy! It is one of the common threads that runs through all cultures!'

LaRoque made an expansive gesture with his arms, as if to encompass the scope of his idea.

'It makes so much sense,' he said. 'It would also explain why it is so difficult for the Library to trace our ancestry. Surely solar-type races have been known before ... That is why this "research" is so stupid. But they are undoubtedly rare and no one has yet thought to feed the Library this correlation which could solve two problems at once!'

The trouble was that the idea was so damned hard to refute. Jacob sighed inwardly. Of *course* many primitive Earth civilizations once had Sun cults. The Sun was so obviously the source of heat and light and life, a thing of miraculous power! It must be a common stage for a primitive people to pass through, to see animate properties in their star.

And *there* was the problem. The galaxy had few 'primitive peoples' to compare to the human experience; mostly animals, pre-sentient hunter-gatherers (or analogous types), and fully uplifted sophont races. Hardly ever did an 'in-between' case like man show up – apparently abandoned by its patron without the training to make its new sapiency work.

In such rare cases the newly potent minds were known to burst free of their ecological niche. They invented strange mockeries of science – bizarre rules of cause and effect, superstition and myth. Without the guiding hand of a patron, such 'wolfling' races seldom lasted long. Humanity's current notoriety was partly due to its survival.

The very lack of any other species with similar experience to com-pare with made generalizations easy to form and hard to refute. Since there were no other examples of species-wide indulgence in Sun-worship known to the small Branch in La Paz, LaRoque could maintain that those traditions of humanity recalled the Uplift that was never finished.

Jacob half listened for a moment longer just in case LaRoque said anything new. But mostly he let his mind drift.

*

It had been a long two days since the landing. He had had to get used to traversing from parts of the base that were gravity tuned to others in which the feathery pull of Mercury prevailed. There were many introductions to Base personnel, most of whose names he immediately forgot. Then Kepler had assigned someone to take him to his quarters.

The chief physician at Hermes Base turned out to be a Dolphin-Uplift bug. He was only too happy to examine Kepler's prescriptions, expressing mystification that there were so many. Afterwards he insisted on throwing a party at which everyone in the medical department, it seemed, wanted to ask questions about Makakai. Between toasts, that is. For that matter there weren't all that many questions after all.

Jacob's mind moved a little slowly as the car came to rest and the doors slid open to the huge underground cavern where the Sunships were serviced and stored. Then, for a fleeting moment, it seemed that space itself was bending out of shape, and, worse yet, there was two of everybody!

The opposite wall of the Cavern seemed to bulge forward, up to a rounded bulb only a few meters away, directly across from him. There, where it was closest, stood a Kanten two and a half meters high, a small red-faced human, and a tall, stocky, dark complexioned man who stared back at him with one of the stupidest expressions he'd ever seen.

Jacob suddenly realized that he was looking at the hull of a Sunship, the most perfect mirror in the solar system. The amazed man opposite him, with the obvious hangover, was his own reflection.

The twenty-meter spherical ship was so good a mirror that it was difficult to define its shape. Only by noting the sharp discontinuity of the edge and the way reflected images swept away in an arc could he focus his eyes on something to be interpreted as a real object at all.

'Very pretty,' LaRoque admitted grudgingly. 'Lovely, brave, misguided crystal.' He lifted his tiny camera-recorder and scanned it left to right.

'Most impressive,' Fagin added.

Yeah, Jacob thought. And big as houses, also.

Large as the ship was, the Cavern made it seem insignificant. The rough, rocky ceiling arched high overhead, disappearing in a misty fog of condensation. Where they stood it was rather narrow, but it stretched to the right for a kilometer, at least, before curving out of sight.

They stood on a platform which brought them even with the

60

equator of the ship, above the working floor of the hangar. A small crowd stood down below, dwarfed by the silvery sphere.

Two hundred meters to the left stood a pair of massive vacuum doors, easily a hundred and fifty meters broad. Those, Jacob supposed, were part of the airlock that led, by tunnel, to the unfriendly surface of Mercury, where the giant interplanetary ships, such as the *Bradbury*, rested in huge natural caves.

A ramp led down from the platform to the cavern floor below. At the bottom Kepler spoke with three men in overalls. Culla stood not far away. His companion was a well-dressed chimpanzee who sported a monocle and stood on a chair to get even with Culla's eyes.

The chimp jumped up and down with flexed knees and set the chair shivering. He tapped furiously at an instrument on his chest. The Pring diplomat watched with an expression that Jacob had learned to interpret as one of friendly respect. But there was something else in Culla's stance that surprised him ... an indolence, a looseness of posture, before the chimpanzee, that he had never seen the E.T. display in talking to a human or Kanten or Cynthian or, especially, a Pil.

Kepler greeted Fagin first then turned to Jacob.

'Glad you could make the tour, Mr Demwa.' Kepler shook his hand with a firmness that surprised Jacob, then called the chimpanzee over to his side.

'This is Dr Jeffrey, the first of his species to become a full member of a space research team, and one helluva fine worker. It's his ship that we'll be touring.'

Jeffrey smiled with the wry, unhinged grin characteristic of the superchimp species. Two centuries of genetic engineering had wrought changes in the skull and pelvic arch, changes modeled on the human form, as it was the easiest to duplicate. He looked like a very fuzzy, short brown man with long arms and huge buck teeth.

Another bit of engineering became evident when Jacob shook his hand. The chimpanzee's fully opposable thumb pressed hard, as if to remind Jacob that it was there, the Mark of a man.

Where Bubbacub carried his Vodor, Jeffrey wore a device with black horizontal keys left and right. In the middle was a blank screen about twenty centimeters by ten.

The superchimp bowed and his fingers flew over the keys. Bright letters appeared on the screen.

I AM HAPPY TO MEET YOU. DOCTOR KEPLER TELLS ME YOU'RE ONE OF THE GOOD GUYS.

Jacob laughed. 'Well thanks a lot, Jeff. I try to be, though I still don't know what it is I'm going to be asked to do!'

Jeffrey gave the familiar shrieking chimpanzee laugh; then, for the first time, he spoke. 'You will find out ssoooon!'

It was almost a croak, but Jacob was amazed. Speech was still almost impossibly painful for this generation of superchimp, but Jeff's words came out very clear.

'Dr Jeffrey will take this, our newest Sunship, out on a dive shortly after we finish our tour,' Kepler said. 'Just as soon as Commandant deSilva returns from reconnaissance in our other ship.

'I'm sorry the Commandant wasn't here to meet us when we arrived on the *Bradbury*. And now it seems that Jeff will be gone while we hold our briefings. It'll add a dramatic touch, though, to get his first report just about the time we finish tomorrow afternoon.'

Kepler started to turn toward the ship. 'Any introductions I've forgotten? Jeff, I know you've met Kant Fagin earlier. Pil Bubbacub appears to have declined our invitation. Have you met Mr LaRoque?'

The chimp's lips curled back in an expression of disgust. He snorted once and turned away to look at his own reflection in the Sunship.

LaRoque glared with hot-faced embarrassment.

Jacob had to hold back a laugh. No wonder the superchimps were called chips! For once, someone with less tact than LaRoque! The encounter between the two in the Refectory last night was already legend. He was sorry he'd missed it.

Culla laid a slender, six-fingered hand on Jeffrey's sleeve. 'Come, Friend-Jeffrey. Let ush show Mishter Demwa and hish friends your ship.' The chimp glanced sullenly at LaRoque then looked back at Culla and Jacob, and broke into a wide grin. He took one of Jacob's hands and one of Culla's and pulled them toward the entrance to the ship.

When the party reached the top of the other ramp they came to a short bridge that crossed a gap into the interior of the mirrored globe. It took a moment for Jacob's eyes to adjust to the dark. Then he saw a flat deck which stretched from one end of the ship to the other.

It floated, a circular disk of dark springy material at the equator of the ship. The only breaks in the flat surface were a half dozen or so acceleration couches, set flush with the deck at intervals around its perimeter, some with modest instrument panels, and a dome of seven meters diameter at the exact center.

Kepler knelt by a control panel and touched a switch. The wall of the ship became semi-transparent. Dimly, light from the cavern came in from all sides to illuminate the interior. Kepler explained that interior lighting was kept to a minimum to prevent internal reflections along the inner surface of the spherical shell, which might confuse both equipment and crew.

Inside the nearly perfect shell, the Sunship was like a solid model of the planet Saturn. The wide deck made up the 'ring.' The 'planet' protruded above and below the deck in two hemispheres. The upper hemisphere, which Jacob could see now, had several hatches and cabinets breaking its surface. He knew from his reading that the central sphere contained all of the machinery that ran the ship, including the timeflow controller, the gravity generator, and the refrigerator laser.

Jacob walked to the edge of the deck. It floated on a field of force, four or five feet away from the curving hull, which arched high over-head with a curious lack of highlights or shadows.

He turned as his name was called. The tour group stood by a door in the side of the dome. Kepler waved for him to join them.

'We'll inspect the instrument hemisphere now. We call it "flip-side." Watch your step, it's a gravity arc so don't be too surprised.'

At the doorway, Jacob stood aside to let Fagin pass, but the E.T. indicated that he would rather stay above. A seven-foot tall Kanten in a seven-foot hatch wouldn't be too comfortable at that. He followed Kepler inside.

And tried to duck out of the way! Kepler was above him, climbing a path that mounded just ahead, like part of a hill enclosed in bulkheads. He looked like he was about to fall over, judging from the angle of his body. Jacob couldn't see how the scientist could keep his balance!

But Kepler kept walking up and over the elliptical path and disappeared over the short horizon. Jacob put his hand on the bulkheads to either side and took a tentative step.

He felt no lack of balance. His other foot moved forward again. Still perfectly upright. Another step. He looked back.

The doorway tilted toward him. Apparently the dome enclosed a pseudo-gravity field so tight that it could be wrapped around a mere few yards. The field was so smooth and complete that it fooled his inner ear. One of the workmen stood in the hatch grinning.

Jacob set his jaw and continued over the loop, trying not to think of himself as slowly turning upside down. He examined the signs on access plates on the walls and floor of his path. Halfway around he passed over a hatch with the words TIME-COMPRESSION ACCESS inscribed on it.

The ellipse ended in a gentle slope. Jacob felt right-side-up when he got to the doorway and he knew what to expect, but even so he groaned.

'Oh no!' He brought his hands to his eyes.

A few meters over his head the floor of the hangar stretched away in all directions. Men walked around the ship's cradle like flies on a ceiling.

With a resigned sigh he walked out to join Kepler where the scientist stood at the edge of the deck, peering into the guts of a complicated machine. Kepler looked up and smiled.

'I was just exercising a boss's privilege to poke and pry. Of course the ship has been fully checked out by now, but I like to look things over.' He patted the machine affectionately.

Kepler led Jacob to the edge of the deck, where the upside-down effect was even more pronounced. The foggy ceiling of the cavern was visible far 'below' their feet.

'This is one of the multi-polarization cameras we set up soon after we first saw the Coherent Light Ghosts.' Kepler pointed to one of several identical machines that stood at intervals along the rim. 'We were able to pick the Ghosts out from the jumbled light levels in the chromosphere because, no matter how the plane of polarization migrated, we were able to track it and show that the coherency of the light was real and stable with time.'

'Why are all of the cameras down here? I didn't see any up above.'

'We found that live observers and machines interfered with each other when they rode on the same plane. For this and other reasons the instruments line the edge of the plane down here, and us chickens ride on the other half.

'We can accommodate both, you see, by orienting the ship so the edge of the deck is aligned toward the phenomenon we wish to observe. It turned out to be an excellent compromise; since gravity is no problem, we can tilt in any angle and we can arrange for the point-of-view of both sentient and mechanical observers to be the same for later comparison.'

Jacob tried to imagine the ship, tipped at some angle and tossed about in the storms of the Sun's atmosphere, while passengers and crew calmly watched.

'We've had a bit of trouble with this arrangement lately,' Kepler went on. 'This newer, smaller ship Jeff will take down has had some modifications, so soon we hope ... Ah! here come some friends ...'

Culla and Jeffrey emerged from the doorway, the chimp's half simian, half human face contorted in disdain.

He tapped at the chest display.

'LR SICK. NAUSEOUS GOING OVER RAMP. SHIRTED BASTARD.'

Culla spoke softly to the chimp. Jacob could barely overhear. 'Shpeak with reshpect, Friend-Jeff. Mr LaRoque ish human.'

Incensed, Jeffrey tapped out with frequent misspellings, that he had as much respect as the next chimp, but that he wasn't about to toady up to any particular human, especially one who had no part in his species' Uplift.

DO YOU REALLY HAV TO TAKE CRAP FROM BUBBAGUB JUST BECAUS HIS ANCESTORS DID YOURS A FAVOR HALF A MILLION YEARS AGO?

The Pring's eyes glowed. There was a flash of white between the thick lips. 'Please, Friend-Jeff, I know you mean well, but Bubbacub ish my Patron. Hu-mansh have given your race freedom. My race must sherve. It ish the way of the world.'

Jeffrey sniffed. 'We'll see,' he croaked.

Kepler took Jeffrey aside, asking Culla to show Jacob around. Culla led Jacob to the other side of the hemisphere to show him the machine that allowed the ship to navigate like a bathysphere in the semi-fluid plasma of the solar atmosphere. He removed several panels to show Jacob the holographic memory units.

The Stasis Generator controlled the flow of time and space through the body of the Sunship, so that the violent tossing of the chromosphere would seem a gentle rocking to those inside. The fundamental physics of the generator was still only partly understood by the scientists of Earth, though the government insisted that it be built by human hands.

Culla's eyes glowed and his lisping voice revealed pride in the new technologies brought to Earth by the Library.

The logic banks controlling the generator looked like a jumble of glassy filaments. Culla explained that the rods and fibers stored optical information far more densely than any previous Earth technology, and responded more quickly. Blue interference patterns ran up and down the nearest rod, as they watched, flickering packets of lambient data. It seemed to Jacob that there was something almost alive in the machine. The laser input-output swung aside under Culla's touch and they both stared for minutes at the raw pulsing information that was the machine's blood.

Though he must have seen the computer's bowels hundreds of times, Culla seemed as enthralled as Jacob, meditating fixedly with those bright, unblinking eyes.

Finally, Culla replaced the cover. Jacob noticed that the E.T. looked tired. Must be working too hard, he thought. They spoke little as they walked slowly back around the dome to rejoin Jeffrey and Kepler.

Jacob listened with interest, but little comprehension, as the chimpanzee and his boss argued about some minor calibration of one of the cameras.

Jeffrey left then, claiming business on the Cavern floor, and Culla followed soon after. The two men remained for a few minutes, talking about the machinery, then Kepler motioned for Jacob to walk ahead as they made their way back around the loop.

When Jacob was about halfway around he heard a sudden commotion up ahead. Someone was shouting in anger. He tried to ignore what his eyes were telling him about the curving gravity-loop and quickened his pace. The path wasn't meant to be taken quickly, though. For the first time he felt a confusing mixture of pulling sensations as different portions of the complicated field tugged at him.

At the top of the arc Jacob's foot caught on a loose floor plate, scattering the plate and several bolts along the curving deck. He fought to keep his balance, but the unnerving perspective, midway around the curving path, made him stagger. By the time he made it gratefully to the hatch on the upper side of the deck, Kepler had caught up with him.

The shouting came from outside the ship.

At the base of the ramp Fagin waved his branches about in agitation. A number of base personnel ran toward LaRoque and Jeffrey, who stood locked in a wrestler's embrace.

His face a deep red, LaRoque puffed and strained as he tried to pry Jeffrey's hands off of his head. He made a fist and struck out to no apparent effect. The chimp screamed repeatedly and bared his teeth as he fought for a better grip to bring LaRoque's head down to the level of his own. Neither noticed that a crowd had gathered. They ignored the arms that tried to pull them apart.

Hurrying to the bottom, Jacob saw LaRoque free one hand and reach for the camera that hung from a cord at his belt.

Jacob shoved through to the combatants. Without a pause he struck LaRoque's grip free of the camera with the hard side of his hand and reached down with the other to grab the fur at the back of the chimpanzee's head. He yanked back with all of his might and threw Jeffrey into the arms of Kepler and Culla.

Jeffrey struggled. The long powerful simian arms heaved against the grip of his captors. He tossed his head back and shrieked.

Jacob felt movement behind him. He swiveled and planted a palm on LaRoque's chest as the man came rushing forward. The journalist's feet flew out from beneath him and he landed with an 'Oof!'

Jacob reached for the camera at LaRoque's belt, just as the man grabbed for it. The cord parted with a snap. The men hauled LaRoque back as he struggled to his feet.

Jacob's hands went up.

'Now stop it!' he shouted. He placed himself so that neither LaRoque nor Jeffrey could easily see the other. LaRoque nursed his hand, ignoring the crewmen who held his shoulders, and glared angrily.

Jeffrey still strained to get loose. Culla and Kepler held onto him tightly. Behind them Fagin whistled helplessly.

Jacob took the chimp's face in his hands. Jeffrey snarled at him.

'Chimpanzee-Jeffrey, listen to me! I am Jacob Demwa. I am a human being. I am a supervisor with Project Uplift, I tell you now that you are behaving in an unseemly manner ... you are acting like an animal!'

Jeffrey's head jerked back as if slapped. He looked at Jacob dazedly for a moment, a snarl half formed, then the deep brown eyes unfocused. He sagged limp in the grip of Culla and Kepler.

Jacob held onto the furry head. With his other hand he stroked the ruffled fur back into place. Jeffrey shuddered.

'Now just relax,' he said gently. 'Just try to collect yourself. We'll all listen when you tell us what happened.'

Trembling, Jeffrey brought a hand to his speech display. It took him a few moments to slowly type, SORRY. He looked up at Jacob, meaning it.

'That's fine,' Jacob said. 'It takes a real man to apologize.'

Jeffrey straightened. With elaborate calmness he nodded to Kepler and to Culla. They released him and Jacob stepped back.

For all of his success in dealing with both dolphins and chimps at the Project, Jacob felt somewhat ashamed of the patronizing way in which he had spoken to Jeffrey. It had been a gamble that worked, to use Patronomy on the chimp-scientist. From what Jeffrey had said earlier, Jacob guessed that he kept a great deal of patron-esteem inside, but reserved it for some humans and not others. Jacob was glad he'd been able to tap that reserve, but not particularly proud of it.

Kepler took charge as soon as he saw that Jeffrey was calm.

'What the hell was going on here!' he shouted, glaring at LaRoque.

'The animal attacked me!' LaRoque cried. 'I had just managed to conquer my fears and get out of that terrible place and I was talking to the honorable Fagin, when the beast leapt at me, lithe like a tiger, and I had to fight for my life!'

LIAR. HE WAS DOING SABOTAGE. I FOUND T.C. ACCESS PLATE LOOSE. FAGIN SAID THE CREEP ONLY CAME OUT WHEN HE HEARD US COMING.

'Apologies for my contradiction!' Fagin fluted. 'I did not say the pejorative "Creep," I merely answered a query to state ...'

'He sspent an hour in there!' Jeffrey interrupted aloud, grimacing at the effort.

Poor Fagin, Jacob thought.

'I told you before,' LaRoque shouted back. 'That crazy place scared me! I spent half the time clutching the floor! Listen, you little ape, don't cast your slurs on me. Save them for your tree-mates!'

The chip shrieked, and Culla and Kepler rushed forward to hold the two apart Jacob walked over to Fagin, uncertain what to say.

Over the tumult the Kanten said to him, gently, 'It appears that your patrons, whoever they might have been, Friend-Jacob, must have been unique, indeed.'

Jacob nodded numbly.

9

REMEMBERING THE GREAT AUK

Jacob studied the group at the foot of the ramp. Culla and Jeffrey, each in his own fashion, spoke earnestly with Fagin. A small group of base personnel gathered nearby ... perhaps to escape LaRoque's persistent questioning.

The man had stalked the Cavern ever since the altercation broke up, shooting questions at those at work and complaining to those who weren't. For a while his rage at being deprived of his camera was awesome, only slowly declining to a state Jacob would call just short of apoplexy.

'I'm not sure why I took it from LaRoque,' Jacob said to Kepler, taking it out of his pocket. The slim black camera-recorder had a maze of tiny knobs and attachments. It looked like a perfect reporter's tool, compact and flexible and obviously very expensive.

He handed it to Kepler. 'I guess I thought he was reaching for a weapon.'

Kepler put the camera in his own pocket. 'We'll check that out anyway, just in case. In the meantime I'd like to thank you for the way you handled things.'

Jacob shrugged. 'Don't make much of it. I'm sorry I stepped on your authority.'

Kepler laughed. 'I'm glad as hell you did! I sure wouldn't have known what to do!'

Jacob smiled, but he still felt troubled.

'What are you going to do now?' he asked.

'Well, now I'm going to inspect Jeff's T.C. system, to make certain nothing's wrong, not that I think there is. Even if LaRoque poked around in the machine, what could he do? The circuits are all worked with special tools. He had none.'

'But the panel was loose when we came over the gravity arc.'

'Yes, but maybe LaRoque was just curious. In fact, I wouldn't be too surprised to find out that *Jeff* loosened the plate to have an excuse to pick a fight with him!'

The scientist laughed. 'Don't look so shocked. Boys will be boys. And you know that even the most advanced chimp oscillates between extreme priggishness and schoolboy pranksterism.'

Jacob knew the truth of that. But still he wondered why Kepler was so generous in his attitude toward LaRoque, whom he undoubtedly despised. Was he that anxious for a good press?

Kepler repeated his thanks and left, picking up Culla and Jeffrey on his way back to the entrance of the Sunship. Jacob found a place where he wouldn't be in the way and sat down on a shipping crate.

He drew a sheaf of papers from his inside jacket pocket.

Masergrams had arrived from Earth for many of the *Bradbury* passengers earlier in the day. Jacob had been hard put not to laugh when he caught the conspiratorial glances that passed between Bubbacub and Millie Martine when the Pil went to pick up his own coded message.

During breakfast she had sat between Bubbacub and LaRoque, trying to mediate the Earthman's embarrassing Xenophilia with the Library Representative's aloof suspicion. She appeared anxious to bridge the gap between them. But when the messages came LaRoque was left alone as she and Bubbacub hurried upstairs.

It probably hadn't helped the journalist's temper.

Jacob had finished his own meal and considered a visit to the Medical Lab, but instead went to pick up his own masergrams. Back in his rooms the Library material made a pile over a foot deep, which he placed on his desk before settling into a reading trance.

The reading trance was a technique for absorbing a lot of information in a short time. It had been useful many times in the past, the only disadvantage being that it cut off the critical faculties. The information would be stored, but the material would have to be read again normally for it all to be brought to mind.

When he came to, the papers were all stacked on the left. He was certain that they had all been read. The data he'd absorbed stalked at the edge of consciousness, isolated bits capriciously leaping to mind unbidden and as yet unconnected to a whole. For at least a week he would relearn, with a sense of *déjà vu*, things read in the trance. If he didn't want to be disoriented too long he'd better start wading through the stuff normally, soon.

Now, perched on the plastic packing crate in the Sunship Cavern, Jacob poked at random through the papers he'd bought. Teasing fragments of information read familiarly.

... The Kisa race, newly free from indenture to the Soro, discovered the planet Pila shortly after the recent migration of galactic culture to this quadrant. Traces were evident that the planet had been occupied by another transient race some two hundred million years before. Thus Pila was verified in Galactic Archives as having once been a residence, for six hundred millennia, of the Mellin Species, (see listing; Mellin-extinct).

The planet Pila, having lain fallow for greater than the required period, was surveyed and routinely registered as a Kisa colony, Class C (temporary occupancy, no more than three million years, minimal impact on contemporary biosphere allowed).

On Pila, the Kisa found a pre-sophont species whose name is taken from the planet of their origin ...

Jacob tried to picture the Pil race as it had been before the arrival of the Kisa and the beginning of their uplift. Primitive hunter-gatherers, no doubt. Would they have been the same today, after half a million years, if the Kisa had never come? Or would they have evolved, as some Earth anthropologists still insisted was possible, into a different kind of intelligent culture, without the influence of their patrons?

The cryptic reference to the extinct 'Mellin' species brought home the time scale covered by the ancient civilization of the Galactics and their incredible Library. Two hundred million years! That long ago the planet Pila had been held by a spacefaring race, who had resided there for six thousand centuries while Bubbacub's ancestors were insignificant little burrowing animals.

Presumably the Mellin paid their dues and had a Branch Library of their own. They offered proper respect (though perhaps more in word than in deed) to the patron race that had uplifted them long before they colonized Pila, and perhaps they, in turn, uplifted some promising species they found when they arrived ... biological cousins to Bubbacub's people ... which by now had probably gone extinct as well.

Suddenly the strange Galactic Laws of Residence and Migration made sense to Jacob. They forced species to look upon their planets as temporary homes, to be held in trust for future races whose present form might be small and silly. Small wonder many of the Galactics frowned at humanity's record on Earth. Only the influence of the Tymbrimi, and other friendly races had enabled humanity to purchase its own three colonies in Cygnus from the stodgy and environmentally fanatic Institute of Migration. And at that it had been fortunate that the *Vesarius* had returned with enough warning for human beings to bury the evidence of some of their crimes! Jacob was one of less than a hundred thousand human beings who knew that there had ever been such a thing as a Manatee, or a giant ground sloth, or an orangutang.

That Man's victims might have someday become thinking species was something that he, more than most, was in a position to appreciate, and regret. Jacob thought of Makakai, of the whales, and how narrowly they were saved.

He brought up the papers and resumed his skimming. Another piece leapt into recognition as he read it. It had to do with Cula's species.

> ... colonized by an expedition from Pila. [The Pila, having threatened their Kisa patrons with an appeal to Soro for a Jihad, had won release from their indenture.] Upon receiving their license to the planet Pring, the Pila undertook their occupancy with more than perfunctory attention to the minimal-impact provisions of their contract. Since the Pila arrival on Pring, inspectors from the Institute of Migration have observed that the Pila have taken greater than average safeguards to protect indigenous species whose pre-sophont potential seemed realistic. Among those in danger of extinction upon the establishment of the colony were the genetic ancestors of the Pring race whose species name is also that of the planet of their origin ...

Jacob made a mental note to learn more about the Pilan Jihads. The Pila were aggressive conservatives in galactic politics. The Jihads, or 'Holy Wars' were supposedly the last resort used to enforce tradition among the races of the galaxy. The Institutes served the traditions, but left enforcement to the opinion of the majority, or to the strongest.

Jacob felt sure that the Library references would be full of justified Holy Wars, with few 'regrettable' cases of species using tradition as an excuse to wage war for power or for hate.

History is usually written by the winners.

He wondered on which grievance the Pila had won free of their indenture to the Kisa. He wondered what a Kisa looked like.

*

Jacob started as a loud bell rang, sending reverberations throughout the Cavern. Three more times it pealed, echoing off stone walls and bringing him to his feet.

All the workmen in sight downed tools and turned to look at the mammoth doors which led, by airlock and tunnel, to the surface of the planet.

With a low rumbling, the doors slowly parted. At first only blackness could be seen in the widening crack. Then something big and bright came up and nudged the separation from the other side, like a puppy bumping impatiently with its nose to hurry the opening and get inside.

It was another shiny mirrored bubble, like the one he had just toured, only larger. It floated above the tunnel floor as though insubstantial. The ship bobbed slightly in the air and, when the way was open, entered the lofty hangar as if blown in by a breeze from the outside. Reflections of rockwall, machinery, and people swam along its sides brightly.

As the ship approached, it emitted a faint humming and crackling sound. Workmen gathered at a nearby cradle.

Culla and Jeffrey rushed past Jacob as he watched, the chimpanzee flashing him a grin and waving for him to come along. Jacob smiled back and started to follow, folding his papers and slipping them into his pocket. He looked for Kepler. The Sundiver chief must have stayed aboard Jeffrey's ship to finish the inspection, for he was nowhere in sight. The ship crackled and hissed as it maneuvered over its nest, and then began to descend slowly. It was hard to believe that it didn't shine with light of its own, its mirrored surface gleamed so. Jacob stood near Fagin, at the edge of the crowd. They watched together as the ship came to rest.

'You appear to be deep within your thoughts,' Fagin fluted. 'Please forgive the intrusion, but I judge that it is acceptable to inquire informally concerning their nature.'

Jacob was close enough to Fagin to pick up a faint odor, somewhat like oregano. The alien's foliage rippled gently nearby.

'I suppose I was thinking about where this ship has just been,' he answered. 'I was trying to imagine what it must be like, down there. I – I just can't.'

'Do not feel frustrated, Jacob. I am similarly in awe, and incapable of comprehending what you of Earth have accomplished here. I await my first descent with humble anticipation.'

And so put me to shame again, you green bastard, Jacob thought. I'm still trying to find a way not to have to go on one of these crazy dives. And you blather about being anxious to go!

'I don't want to call you a liar, Fagin, but I think you're stretching diplomacy a bit by saying you're impressed by this project. The technology is early stone age by galactic standards. And you can't tell me no one has ever dived into a star before! There have been sophonts loose in the galaxy for almost a billion years. Everything worth doing has been done at least a trillion times!'

There was a vague bitterness in his voice as he spoke. The strength of his own feelings surprised Jacob.

'That is no doubt quite true, Friend-Jacob. I do not pretend that Sundiver is unique. Only that it is unique in my experience. The sentient races with whom I have contact have been satisfied to study their suns from a distance and to compare the results with Library standards. For me this is adventure in its truest form.'

A rectangular slice of the Sunship started to slide downward, to form a ramp to the cradle's rim.

Jacob frowned.

'But manned dives *have* to have been performed before! It's such an obvious thing to try at some time or another if it's proven possible! I can't believe that we're the first!'

'There is very little doubt, of course,' Fagin said slowly. 'If no one else, then surely the Progenitors did this. For they did all things, it is said, before they departed. But so many things have been done, by so many peoples, it is very hard to ever know for certain.'

Jacob mulled over this in silence.

As the section of the Sunship neared the ramp, Kepler approached, smiling at Jacob and Fagin.

'Ah! There you are. Exciting, isn't it? Everyone's here! It's this way every time someone gets back from the Sun, even for a short scout dive like this one was!'

'Yes,' Jacob said. 'It's very exciting. Um, there's something I want to ask you, Doctor Kepler, if you have a moment. I was wondering if you've asked the Branch Library at La Paz for a reference on your Sun Ghosts. Surely someone else has encountered a similar phenomenon, and I'm sure it would be a big help to have . . .'

His voice fell away as he saw Kepler's smile fade.

'That was the reason Culla was assigned to us in the first place, Mr Demwa. This was going to be a prototype project to see how well we could mix independent research with limited help from the Library. The plan worked well when we were building the ships. I have to confess that the Galactic technology is something astounding. But since then the Library hasn't been much help at all.

'It's really very complicated. I was hoping to get into it tomorrow, after you've had a complete briefing, but you see . . .'

73

A loud cheer came from all around as the crowd surged forward. Kepler smiled resignedly.

'Later!' he shouted.

At the top of the cradle three men and two women waved at the cheering crowd. One of the women, tall and slender with a close cut of straight blonde hair, caught sight of Kepler and grinned. She started down and the rest of the crew followed.

This was apparently the Hermes Base commander Jacob had heard about from time to time during the last two days. One of the physicians at the party last night had called her the best Commandant the Confederacy outpost on Mercury ever had. A younger man had then interrupted the old-timer with a comment that she was also '. . . a fox.' Jacob had assumed that the med-tech was referring to the commander's mental skill. As he watched the woman (she seemed hardly older than a girl) lithely stride down the steep ramp, he realized that the remark could easily have another complimentary meaning.

The crowd parted and the woman approached the Sundiver chief, hand outstretched.

'They're there all right!' she said. 'We went down to tau point two, in the first active region, and there they were! We got within eight hundred meters of one! Jeff won't have any trouble. It was the biggest herd of magnetovores I've ever seen!'

Jacob found her voice low and melodious. Confident. Her accent, though, was hard to place. Her pronunciation seemed quaint, old fashioned.

'Wonderful! Wonderful!' Kepler nodded. 'Where there are sheep, there must be shepherds, eh?'

He took her arm and turned to introduce her to Fagin and Jacob.

'Sophonts, this is Helene deSilva, Confederacy Commandant here on Mercury, and my right-hand man. Couldn't get along without her. Helene, this is Mr Jacob Alvarez Demwa, the gentleman I told you about by maser. The Kanten Fagin, of course, you met some months back, on Earth. I understand you've exchanged a few masergrams since.'

Kepler touched the young woman's arm. 'I must run now, Helene. There are a few messages from Earth that have to be handled. I already put them off too long to be here for your arrival, so I'd better go now. You're sure everything went smoothly and the crew is well rested?'

'Sure, Dr Kepler, everything's great. We slept on the way back. I'll meet you back here when it's time to see Jeff off.'

The Sundiver chief made his salutations to Jacob and Fagin, and

74

nodded curtly to LaRoque, who stood just close enough to overhear but not close enough to be civil. Kepler left in the direction of the elevators.

Helene deSilva had a way of bowing respectfully to Fagin that was warmer than most people could hug. She radiated delight at seeing the E.T. again, and redundantly said so as well.

'And this is Mr Demwa,' she said as she shook Jacob's hand. 'Kant Fagin spoke of you. You're the intrepid young fellow who dove the entire height of the Ecuador Needle to save it. That's a story I insist on hearing from the hero himself!'

A part of Jacob winced, as always when the Needle was mentioned. He hid it behind a laugh.

'Believe me, that jump wasn't made on purpose! In fact, I think I'd rather go on one of your little solar, toe-frying junkets than ever do that again!'

The woman laughed, but at the same time she looked at him strangely, with a certain *appraising* expression that Jacob found himself liking, although it confused him. He felt oddly at a loss for words.

'Um ... anyway it's a bit odd being called a "young fellow" by someone as young as you appear to be. You must be a very competent person to have been offered a command like this before any worry lines have shown.'

DeSilva laughed again. 'How gallant! That's very sweet of you, sir, but actually I have sixty-five years' worth of invisible worry lines. I was a junior officer on *Calypso*. You may recall we got back in system a couple of years ago. I'm over ninety years old!'

'Oh!'

Starship crewmen were a very special breed. No matter what their subjective ages, they could pick their jobs when they came home ... when they chose to keep working, that is.

'Well in that case, I really must treat you with the respect you're due, Granny.'

DeSilva took a step back and cocked her head, looking at him through wryly narrowed eyes. 'Just don't go too far the other way! I've worked too hard at becoming a woman, as well as an officer and a gentleman, to want to jump from "jail bait" straight into social security. If the first attractive male to arrive in months who isn't under my command starts thinking of me as unapproachable, I just might be persuaded to throw him in irons!'

Half of the woman's referents were indecipherably archaic (what the devil was 'jail bait'?), but somehow the meaning was clear. Jacob grinned and put up his hands in surrender – willingly enough. Somehow, Helene deSilva reminded him a lot of Tania.

The comparison was vague. There was an answering tremor, also vague and hard to identify. But it felt worth following.

Jacob shook aside the image. Philosophical-emotional bullshit. He was very good at that when he allowed himself. The plain fact was that the Base Commandant was an awful damned attractive fem.

'So be it,' he said. 'And damned be he who first says, "Hold, enough!"'

DeSilva laughed. She took him lightly by the arm and turned to Fagin.

'Come, I want you both to meet the dive crew. Then we'll be busy getting Jeffrey ready to leave. He's terrible about good-byes. Even when going on a short dive like this one will be, he always bawls and hugs everyone who's staying behind as if he's never going to see them again!'

PART IV

Only with the Solar Probe is it possible to obtain data on the distribution of mass and angular momentum in the solar interior ... obtain high resolution pictures ... detect neutrons released in nuclear processes occurring at or near the solar surface ... [or] determine how the solar wind is accelerated.

Finally, given the communications and tracking systems and, perhaps, the on-board hydrogen maser ... the Solar Probe will be by far the best platform to use in the search for low frequency gravity waves from cosmological sources.

EXCERPTED FROM THE REPORT OF THE NASA
PRELIMINARY SOLAR PROBE WORKSHOP

10

HEAT

Like taffy twists and feather boas, the ochre shapes drooped in a pink misty background, as if suspended from invisible strings. The row of wispy dark arches, each a fluffy rope of gaseous tendrils, led off into the distance, each farther arch smaller in perspective than the one before, until the last faded into the swirling red miasma.

Jacob found it difficult to focus on any one detail of the recorded holographic image. The dark filaments and streamers that made up the visible topography of the middle chromosphere were deceptive in both shape and texture.

The closest filament almost filled the left forward corner of the tank. Wispy strands of darker gas coiled about an invisible magnetic field which arched over a sunspot almost a thousand kilometers below.

High above the place where most of the Sun's energy production leaked out into space as light, an observer could make out details for tens of thousands of miles. Even so it was still hard to get used to the idea that the magnetic arch he now looked at was about the size of Norway. It was merely one filigree in a chain that arched for 200,000 kilometers over a sunspot group below.

And this one was a wimp, compared to many they'd seen.

One arching spectacle had stretched a quarter of a million kilometers from end to end. The image had been recorded several months back, over an active region that had long since vanished, and the ship that recorded it had kept its distance. The reason became clear when the top of the gigantic, twisted faerie arch erupted into the most awesome of Solar events, a flare.

The flare was beautiful and terrible – a churning, boiling maelstrom of brightness representing an electrical short circuit of incomprehensible magnitude. Even a Sunship would not have survived the sudden surge of high energy neutrons from the nuclear reactions driven by the flare, particles immune to the ship's electromagnetic shields, too many neutrons to damp away using time compression. The Sundiver Project chief emphasized, for that reason, that flares were usually predictable and avoidable.

Jacob would have found the assurance more comforting without the proviso, 'usually.'

*

The briefing had been rather routine otherwise, as Kepler led his audience through a quick review of solar physics. Jacob had learned most of the material earlier in his studies aboard the *Bradbury*, but the projections of actual dives into the chromosphere were, he had to admit, fantastic visual aids. If it was hard to comprehend the sizes of the things he saw, Jacob could blame no one but himself.

Kepler had briefly covered the basic dynamics of the Sun's interior, the real star, to which the chromosphere was just a thin skin.

In the deep core the unimaginable weight of the Sun's mass drives the nuclear reactions, producing heat and pressure and preventing the giant ball of plasma from contracting under its own gravitational pull. Pressure keeps the body 'inflated.'

The energy given off by the fires at the core works slowly outward, sometimes as light, and sometimes as a convective exchange of hot material from below for cooler stuff returning from above. By radiation, then convection, then radiation again, the energy reaches the kilometers-thick layer known as the *photosphere* – the 'sphere of light' where it finally finds freedom and leaves home forever, for space.

So dense is matter inside a star, that a sudden cataclysm in the interior would take a million years to show up in a change in the amount of light leaving the surface.

But the sun doesn't stop at the photosphere: the density of matter falls off slowly with height. If one included the ions and electrons that forever stream out into space in the solar wind – to cause auroras on Earth and to shape the plasma tails of comets – one might say that there was no real boundary to the Sun. It truly reaches out to touch the other stars.

The halo of the *corona* shimmers around the rim of the Moon during a Solar eclipse. The tendrils that seem so soft on a photographic plate are comprised of electrons heated to millions of degrees, but they are diffuse, almost as thin (and harmless to Sunships) as the Solar wind.

Between the photosphere and the corona lies the *chromosphere*, the 'sphere of color' ... the place where old Sol makes the final alterations to his light show, where he places his spectral signature on the sunshine Earthmen see.

Here the temperature suddenly plummets to its minimum, a 'mere' few thousand degrees. The pulsing of the photospheric cells sends ripples of gravitation upwards through the chromosphere, subtly strumming chords of space-time across millions of kilometers, and charged particles, riding the crests of Alfven waves, sweep outward in a mighty wind.

This was the domain of Sundiver. In the chromosphere, the Sun's magnetic fields play games of tag, and simple chemical compounds ephemerally brew. One can see, if the right bands are chosen, for tremendous distances. And there is a lot to see.

Kepler was in his element, now. In the darkened room his hair and moustache glowed reddish in the light given off by the tank. His voice was confident as he used a slender rod to point out features of the chromosphere for his audience.

He told the story of the sunspot cycle, the alternating rhythm of high and low magnetic activity that flips polarity every eleven years. Magnetic fields 'pop out' of the Sun to form complicated loops in the chromosphere – loops which could sometimes be traced by looking at the paths of the dark filaments in hydrogen light.

The filaments twisted around the field lines and glowed with complex induced electric currents. In close-up they looked less feathery than Jacob had at first thought. Bright and dark red strips knotted around one another all along the length of the arch, some-times swirling in complicated patterns until some tightening knot squeezed closed and splattered bright droplets away like hot grease from a skillet.

It was numbingly beautiful, although the red monochrome eventually made Jacob's eyes hurt. He looked away from the tank and rested by staring at the wall of the viewing room.

The two days since Jeffrey had waved good-bye and taken his ship off to the Sun were mixed pleasure and frustration for Jacob. They had certainly been busy.

He saw the Hermetian mines yesterday. The great layered flows that filled huge hollowed caverns north of the base with smooth rainbowed crusts of pure metal startled Jacob with their beauty, and he stared in awe at the dwarfed machines and men that ate at their flanks. He would carry with him always the amazement he felt ... at both the loveliness of the giant field of frozen melt and at the temerity of the tiny men who dared to disturb it for its treasure.

Also enjoyable was an afternoon spent in the company of Helene deSilva. In the lounge of her apartment she broke the seal on a bottle of alien brandy whose worth Jacob didn't dare to calculate, and shared it all with him.

In a few hours he came to like the Base Commandant for her wit and the range of her interests, as well as for her pleasantly archaic flirtatious charm. They exchanged stories of peripheral interest, saving, by mute agreement, the best for later. He told her about his work with Makakai, to her delight, explaining how he persuaded the young dolphin – by means of hypnosis, bribery (letting her play with 'toys' such as the waldo-whales), and love – to concentrate on the kind of abstract thought that humans used, instead of (or in addition to) the cetacean Dreaming.

He described how the whale dream, in turn, was slowly becoming understood ... using Hopi and Australian Aborigine philosophies to help translate that totally alien world view into something vaguely accessible to a human mind.

Helene deSilva had a way of listening that drew the words out of Jacob. When he finished his story she radiated satisfaction, then reciprocated with a tale about a dark star that nearly stood his hair on end.

She spoke of the *Calypso* as if it were mother, child, and lover all in one. The ship and its crew had been her world for only three years, subjective time, but on the return to Earth they became a link with the past. Of those she had left behind on Earth, on her first voyage out, only the youngest had lived to see *Calypso*'s return. And they were now old.

When an interim assignment with Sundiver had been offered, she had jumped at the opportunity. While the scientific adventure of the solar expedition, plus a chance to gain some command experience, were probably reasons enough, Jacob thought he could sense another reason behind her choice.

Although she tried not to show it, Helene apparently disapproved of both extremes of behavior for which returning starship crewmen were famous: cloistered insularity or boisterous hedonism. There was a core of ... 'shyness' could be the only word to describe it ... which peeked out from beneath both the articulate and competent outer persona and the laughing, playful inner woman. Jacob looked forward to finding out more about her during his stay on Mercury.

But the dinner was postponed. Dr Kepler had called a formal banquet and, in the manner of such things, Jacob had little to think about all evening, while everyone bent over backwards being polite and flattering.

But the biggest frustration came from Sundiver itself.

Jacob tried questioning deSilva, Culla, and perhaps a dozen base engineers, getting about the same answer each time.

'Of course, Mr Demwa, but wouldn't it be better to talk about it after Dr Kepler's presentation? It'll be so much clearer then ...'

It became very suspicious.

The stack of Library documents still sat in his room. He read from the pile for an hour at a time, in a normal state of consciousness. While he slogged through the pile, isolated fragments jumped into familiarity as soon as he read them.

... nor is it understood why the Pring are a binocular species, since no other indigenous life form on their planet has more than one eye. It is generally assumed that these and other differences are the result of genetic manipulation by the Pila colonists. Although the Pila are reluctant to answer questions from any but officials from the Institutes, they do admit to having altered the Pring from a brachiating, arboreal animal to a sophont capable of walking and serving in their farms and cities.

The unique Pring dental arrangement had its origin in their previous state as tree grazers. It evolved as a method for scraping off the high-nutrient outer bark of their planet's trees; that bark serving in the place of fruit as a fertilization-spore spreading organ for many of the plants on Pring ...

So that was the background behind Culla's weird dentation! Knowing their purpose somehow made a mental image of the Pring's mashies less disgusting. The fact that their function was vegetarian was downright reassuring.

It was interesting to note, while re-reading the article, how good a job the Branch Library had done with this report. The original had probably been written scores, if not hundreds of light years away from Earth, and long before Contact. The semantics machines at the Branch in La Paz were obviously getting the knack of converting alien words and meanings into English sentences that made sense, though, of course, something might have been lost in the translation.

The fact that the Institute of the Libraries had been forced to ask for human help in programming those machines, after those first disastrous attempts just after Contact, was a source of some small satisfaction. Used to translating for species whose languages all derived from the same general Tradition, the E.T.s had been boggled, at first, by the 'flighty and imprecise' structure of all human languages.

They had moaned (or chirped or zithered or flapped) in despair at the extent to which English, in particular, had declined into a state of sublime, contextually discursive, disorder. Latin, or even better, late Neolithic Indo-European, with its highly organized structure of declensions and cases, would have been preferred. Humans obstinately refused to change their *lingua franca* for the sake of the Library (though both Skins and Shirts began studying Indo-European for fun – each for their own reasons), and instead sent their brightest mels and fems to help the helpful aliens adjust.

The Pring serve in the cities and farms of nearly all Pil planets, except for the home planet, Pila. The sun of Pila, an F3 dwarf, is apparently too bright for this generation of uplifted Pring. (The

Pring sun is F7.) This is the reason given for continuing genetic research on the Pring visual system by the Pila, long after their Uplift license would normally have expired ...

... have only allowed the Pring to colonize class A worlds, devoid of life and requiring terraforming, but free of use restrictions by the Institutes of Tradition and Migration. Having taken leadership in several Jihads, the Pila apparently don't wish to have their Clients in a position to embarrass them by mishandling an older, living world ...

The data on Culla's race spoke volumes about Galactic Civilization. It was fascinating, but the manipulation it told of made him uncomfortable. Inexplicably, he felt personally responsible.

It was at this stage in the re-reading that the summons to Dr Kepler's long awaited talk arrived.

Now he sat in the viewing room, and wondered when the man would get to the point. What were the magnetovores? And what did people mean when they mentioned a 'second type' of Solarian ... that played tag with Sunships and made threatening gestures to their crews in anthropomorphic shapes?

Jacob looked back at the holo-tank.

The filament Kepler chose had grown to fill the tank and then expanded until the viewer felt himself visually immersed in the feathery, fiery mass. Details became clearer – twisted clumps that meant a tightening of magnetic field lines, wisps that came and went like vapor as movement dopplered the hot gasses into and out of the camera's visible band, and clusters of bright pinpoints that danced at the distant edge of vision.

Kepler kept up a running monologue, sometimes getting too technical for Jacob, but always returning to simple metaphors. His voice had become firm and confident, and he clearly enjoyed giving the show.

Kepler gestured at one of the nearby plasma streamers: a thick, twisted strand of dark red, coiling around a few painfully bright pinpoints.

'These were first thought to be your usual compressional hot spots,' he said. 'Until we took a second look at them. Then we found that the spectrum was all wrong.'

Kepler used a control at the base of his pointer to zoom in on the center of the sub-filament.

The bright points grew. Smaller dots became visible as the image expanded.

'Now you'll recall,' Kepler said, 'that the hot spots we saw earlier still looked red, albeit a very bright red. That's because the ship's filters, at the time these pix were taken, were tuned only to let in a very narrow spectral band, centered on hydrogen alpha. You can see, even now, the thing that caught our interest.'

Indeed I do, Jacob thought.

The bright points were a brilliant shade of green!

They flickered like blinkers and they had the color of emeralds.

'Now there are a couple of bands in the green and blue that are cut out less efficiently than most, by the filter. But the alpha line usually washes these out entirely with distance. Besides, this green isn't even one of those bands!

'You can imagine our consternation, of course. No thermal light source could have sent that color through these screens. In order to get through, the light from these objects had to be not only incredibly bright, but totally monochromatic as well, with a brightness temperature of millions of degrees!'

Jacob straightened up from the slumped posture he had assumed during the talk, interested at last.

'In other words,' Kepler went on. 'They had to be lasers.'

'There are ways in which lasing action can occur naturally in a star,' Kepler said. 'But no one had ever seen it happen in our Sun before, so we went in to investigate. And what we found was the most incredible form of life anyone could imagine!'

The scientist twisted the control on his pointer and the field of view began to shift.

A soft chime sounded from the front row of the audience. Helene deSilva could be seen picking up a telephone receiver. She spoke softly into the instrument.

Kepler concentrated on his demonstration. Slowly the bright points grew in the tank until they resolved into tiny rings of light, still too small to make out in detail.

Suddenly Jacob could make out the murmur of deSilva's voice as she spoke into the phone.

Even Kepler stopped what he was doing and waited as she shot hushed questions to the person on the other end.

She put the phone down, then, her face frozen in a mask of steel control. Jacob watched her rise and walk to where Kepler stood, nervously twisting his baton in his hands. The woman bent over slightly to whisper in Kepler's ear, and the Sundiver director's eyes closed once. When they reopened his expression was totally blank.

Suddenly everyone was talking at once. Culla left his seat in the front row to join deSilva. Jacob felt air rush by as Dr Martine sped down the aisle to Kepler's side.

Jacob rose to his feet and turned to Fagin, who stood in the aisle nearby. 'Fagin, I'm going to find out what's going on. Why don't you wait here.'

'That will not be necessary,' the Kanten philosopher fluted.

'What do you mean?'

'I could overhear what was said to Commandant Human Helene deSilva over the telephone, Friend-Jacob. It is not good news.'

Jacob shouted inside. Always deadpan, you damn leafy eggplant egghead, of *course* it's not good news!

'So what the hell is happening!' he asked.

'I grieve most sincerely, Friend-Jacob. It appears that Scientist-Chimpanzee Jeffrey's Sunship has been destroyed in the chromosphere of your Sun!'

II

TURBULENCE

In the ochre light of the holo-tank, Dr Martine stood by Kepler's side, speaking his name over and over and passing her hand in front of his empty eyes. The audience milled onto the stage, jabbering. The alien Culla stood alone, facing Kepler, his great round head rolling slightly on his slender shoulders.

Jacob spoke to him.

'Culla . . .' The Pring didn't seem to hear him. The huge eyes were dull and Jacob could hear a buzzing sound, like teeth chattering coming from behind Culla's thick lips.

Jacob frowned at the grim red light pouring out of the holo-tank. He went to where Kepler stood in shock, to pry the controller rod gently from the man's hands. Martine took no notice of him as she vainly tried to get Kepler's attention.

After a couple of tentative twists on the controller, Jacob got the image to fade and brought the room lights back on. The situation seemed much easier to deal with now. The others must have sensed this as well, because the cacophony of voices subsided.

DeSilva looked up from the telephone and saw Jacob holding the controller. She smiled her thanks. Then she was back on the line shooting terse questions to the person at the other end.

A medical team arrived on the run with a stretcher. Under Dr Martine's guidance they laid Kepler in the fabric frame and gently bore him off through the crowd gathered at the door.

Jacob turned back to Culla. Fagin had managed to push a chair up behind the Library Representative and was trying to get him to sit down. The rustling of branches and high pitched flutings subsided when Jacob approached.

'He is, I believe, all right,' the Kanten said in a singsong voice. 'He is a highly empathic individual, and I fear that he will grieve excessively over the loss of his friend Jeffrey. It is often the reaction of younger species to the death of another with whom one has become close.'

'Is there anything we should do? Can he hear us?'

Culla's eyes didn't appear to be focused. But then Culla's eyes never did tell Jacob anything. The chattering from inside the alien's mouth went on.

'I believe he can hear us,' Fagin answered.

Jacob took hold of Culla's arm. It felt very thin and soft. There didn't appear to be any bone.

'Come on, Culla,' he said. 'There's a chair right behind you. You'd make us all feel a lot better if you'd sit down now.'

The alien tried to answer. The huge lips parted and suddenly the chattering was very loud. The coloration of his eyes changed slightly and the lips closed again. He nodded shakily and allowed himself to be guided to the chair. Slowly the round head came down into his slender hands.

Empathic or no, there was something eerie about the alien feeling this strongly about the death of a man – a chimpanzee – who would be, down to his fundamental body chemistry, always an alien; a being whose fishlike far ancestors swam in different seas than his, and gaped in anaerobic surprise at the sunshine of a totally different star.

'May I have your attention please!' deSilva stood on the dais.

'For those of you who haven't yet heard, preliminary reports indicate that we may have lost Dr Jeffrey's ship in active region J-12, near Sunspot Jane. This is *only* a preliminary report, and further confirmation will have to wait until we can go over the telemetry we received up to the mishap.'

LaRoque waved from the far side of the room to attract the Commandant's attention. In one hand he held a small steno-camera, a different model from the one taken from him in the Sunship Cavern. Jacob wondered why Kepler hadn't returned the other one yet.

'Miss deSilva,' LaRoque cut in. 'Will it be possible for the press to attend the telemetry review? There should be a public record.' In his excitement, LaRoque's accent had virtually disappeared. Without it, the anachronistic appelation, 'Miss deSilva,' sounded very odd.

She paused without looking directly at the man. The Witness

Laws were very clear about denying access to a public record at news events without a 'Seal' from the Agency for Secrets Registration. Even the ASR people, responsible for enforcing honesty above the law, were reluctant to allow it. LaRoque obviously had her cornered, but he wasn't pushing. Yet.

'All right. The observing gallery above the Control Center can hold just about everybody who wants to come ... *except*,' she glared at a cluster of base crewmen who had gathered near the door, 'for people who have work to do.' She ended with a raised eyebrow. There was an immediate bustle of motion by the exit.

'We'll gather in twenty minutes,' she concluded and stepped down.

Members of the Hermes Colony Staff started leaving right away. Those wearing Earth clothing, recent arrivals and visitors, left more slowly.

LaRoque was already gone, no doubt on his way to the maser station to send his story to Earth.

That left Bubbacub. He had been talking to Dr Martine before the meeting began, but the little bearlike alien hadn't come in. Jacob wondered where Bubbacub had been during the meeting.

Helene deSilva joined him and Fagin.

'Culla's quite a little Eatee,' she said to Jacob, softly. 'He used to joke that he got along with Jeffrey so well because they were both low men on the status pole, and because they'd both come down so recently from the trees.' She looked at Culla with pity, and put out one hand to the side of the alien's head.

I'll bet that's comforting, Jacob thought.

'Sadness is the primary perquisite of youth.' Fagin rustled his leaves, like a tinkling of sand dollars in a breeze.

DeSilva let her hand fall. 'Jacob, Dr Kepler left written instructions that I was to consult with you and Kant Fagin if anything ever happened to him.'

'Oh?'

'Yessir. Of course the directive has very little legal weight. All I really have to do is let you in on our staff meetings. But it's obvious anything you'd offer would be useful. I was hoping that the two of you, in particular, wouldn't miss the telemetry replay.'

Jacob appreciated her position. As Base Commandant she would bear the onus of any decision made today. Yet of those with substantial reputations now on Mercury, LaRoque was hostile, Martine was barely friendly to the project, and Bubbacub was an enigma. If Earth should hear many accounts of what went on here, it would be in her interest to have some friends as well.

'Of course,' Fagin whistled. 'We will both be honored to aid your staff.'

DeSilva turned back to Culla and asked softly if the alien would be all right. After a pause, he lifted his head from his hands and nodded slowly. The chattering had stopped, but Culla's eyes were still dull, with bright pinpoints flickering randomly at the edge. He looked exhausted, as well as miserable.

DeSilva departed to help prepare the telemetry replay. Shortly afterwards Pil Bubbacub puffed importantly into the room, his sleek fur ruffled in a collar around his short fat neck. When he spoke his mouth moved in quick snaps and the Vodor on his chest boomed out the words in audible range.

'I have heard the news. It vital that all be at the Tel-e-me-try Review, so I es-cort you there.'

Bubbacub moved to look behind Jacob. He saw Culla sitting absently on the flimsy folding chair.

'Culla!' he called. The Pring looked up, hesitated then made a gesture that Jacob didn't understand. It seemed to imply supplication, negation.

Bubbacub bristled. He emitted a series of clicks and high pitched squeaks at a rapid clip. Culla stumbled to his feet quickly. Immediately Bubbacub turned his back on them all to start in short powerful steps down the hallway ...

Behind him, Jacob and Fagin walked with Culla. From somewhere at the top of Fagin's 'head' there came a strange music

12

GRAVITY

Automation kept the Telemetry Room small. A mere dozen consoles made two rows below a large viewing screen. Behind a railing, on a raised dais, the invited guests watched as the operators carefully rechecked the recorded data.

Occasionally a man, male or female, would lean forward and peer at some detail on a screen, in vain hope for a clue that a Sunship still existed down there.

Helene deSilva stood near the pair of consoles closest to the dais. From there the recording of Jeffrey's last remarks played on a visual display.

A row of words appeared, representing fingerstrokes on a keyboard forty million kilometers away, hours before.

*

RIDE IS SMOOTH ON AUTOMATICS ... HAD TO DAMP TIME FACTOR OF TEN DURING TURBULENCE ... I JUST HAD LUNCH IN TWENTY SECONDS HA HA ...

Jacob smiled. He could imagine the little chimpanzee getting a kick out of the time differential.

DOWN PAST TAU POINT ONE NOW ... FIELD LINES CONVERGING AHEAD ... INSTRUMENTS SAY THERE'S A HERD THERE JUST LIKE HELENE SAID ... ABOUT A HUNDRED ... CLOSING NOW ...

Then Jeffrey's simian voice came on, gruff, abrupt, over a loudspeaker.

'Wait 'til I tell em inna trees, boys! First solo onna Sun! Eat yer heart out, Tarzan!' One of the controllers started to laugh, then cut it off. It finished sounding like a sob.

Jacob started. 'You mean he was all alone down there?'

'I thought you knew!' deSilva looked surprised. 'The dives are pretty well automatic nowadays. Only a computer can adjust the stasis fields fast enough to keep the turbulence from pounding a passenger to jelly. Jeff ... had two: one onboard and also a laser remote from the big machine here on Mercury. What can a man do anyway, besides add a touch here or there?'

'But why add *any* risk?'

'It was Dr Kepler's idea,' she answered, a little defensively. 'He wanted to see if it was only human psi patterns that were causing the Ghosts to run away or make threatening gestures.'

'We never got to that part of the briefing.'

She brushed a lock of blonde hair back.

'Yes, well in our first few encounters with the magnetovores, we never saw any of the herdsmen. Then when we did, we watched from a distance to determine their relationship to the other creatures.

'When we finally approached, the herdsmen just ran away at first. Then their behavior changed radically. While most of them fled, one or two would arc up over the ship, *out* of the plane of the instrument platform, and come down close to the ship!'

Jacob shook his head, 'I'm not sure I understand ...'

DeSilva glanced at the nearest console but there was no change. The only reports from Jeff's ship were solonomic data – routine reports of solar conditions.

'Well, Jacob, the ship is a flat deck inside an almost perfectly reflecting shell. The Gravity Engines, Stasis Field Generators and the Refrigerator Laser are all in the smaller sphere that sits in the middle of the deck. The recording instruments line the rim of the deck on the 'bottom' side, and the people occupy the 'top' side, so both will have an unobstructed view to anything looked at edge on. But we hadn't counted on anything purposely dodging our cameras!'

'If the Ghost went out of view of your instruments by coming up overhead, why didn't you just turn the ship? You have complete gravity control.'

'We tried. They just disappeared! Or worse, they stayed overhead however fast we'd turn. They'd just *hover*! That's when some of the crew started seeing some of the most damnable anthropoid shapes!'

Suddenly Jeffrey's raspy voice filled the room again.

'Hey! There's a whole pack of sheep dogs pushin' those toroids around! Goin' in to give 'em a pet! Nice Doggies!'

Helene shrugged.

'Jeff was always a skeptic. He never saw any shapes-in-the-ceiling and he always called the herdsmen "sheep dogs" because he saw nothing in their behavior to imply intelligence.'

Jacob smiled wryly. The condescension of superchimp toward the canine race was one of the more humorous aspects of their me-too obsession. Also perhaps it diluted their sensitivity over the special relationship, of dog with human being, that antedated their own. Many chimps kept dogs as pets.

'He called the magnetovores toroids?'

'Yes, they're shaped like huge doughnuts. You would have seen that if the briefing hadn't ... been interrupted.' She shook her head sadly and looked down.

Jacob shifted his feet. 'I'm sure there's nothing anyone could have done ...' he began. Then he realized that he was sounding foolish. DeSilva nodded once and turned back to the console; busy, or pretending to be, with technical readouts.

Bubbacub lay sprawled on a cushion to the left, near the barrier. He had a book play-back in his hands and had been reading, in total absorption, the alien characters that flashed from top to bottom on the tiny screen. The Pil had raised his head and listened when Jeffrey's voice came on, and then gazed enigmatically at Pierre LaRoque.

LaRoque's eyes flashed as he recorded an 'historic moment.' Occasionally he spoke in a low excited voice into the microphone of his borrowed steno-camera.

'Three minutes,' deSilva said thickly.

For a minute, nothing happened. Then, the big letters came on the screen again.

THE BIG BOYS ARE HEADING TOWARD ME FOR ONCE! OR AT LEAST A COUPLE OF 'EM ARE. I JUST TURNED ON THE CLOSEUP CAMERAS ... HEY! I'M GETTIN A T-T-TILT IN HERE! TIME-COMPRESSION JAMMED!!

'Gonna abort!' came the deep, croaking voice, suddenly. 'Ridin' up fast ... More tilt! 'S' falling! ... The Eatees! They ...'

There came a very brief burst of static, then silence followed by a loud hiss as the console operator turned up his gain. Then, nothing.

For a long moment nobody said a word. Then one of the console operators rose from his station.

'Implosion confirmed,' he said.

She nodded once. 'Thank you. Please prepare a summary of the data for transmission to Earth.'

Strangely, the strongest emotion Jacob felt was a poignant pride. As a staff member of the Center for Uplift, he'd noticed that Jeffrey spurned his keyboard in the last moments of his life. Instead of retreating before fear, he made a proud, difficult gesture. Jeff the Earthman spoke aloud.

Jacob wanted to mention this to somebody. If anyone could, Fagin would understand. He started over to where the Kanten stood, but Pierre LaRoque hissed sharply before he got there.

'Fools!' The journalist stared about with an expression of disbelief.

'And I am the biggest fool of all! Of any here I should have seen the danger in sending a chimpanzee down to the Sun alone!'

The room was silent Blank expressions of surprise turned to LaRoque, who waved his arms in an expansive gesture.

'Can you not see? Are you all blind? If the Solarians are our Ancestrals, and there can be little doubt of that, then they have obviously gone to great pains to avoid us for millennia. Yet perhaps some distant affection for us has kept them from destroying us so far!

'They have tried to warn you and your Sunships off in ways that you could not ignore, and yet you persist in trespassing. How are these mighty beings to react, then, if they are burst upon by a Client race of the race they have abandoned? What is it you expect them to do when they are invaded by a *monkey* ... !'

Several crewmen rose to their feet in anger. DeSilva had to raise her voice to get them to subside. She faced LaRoque, an expression of iron control on her features.

'Sir, if you will please put your interesting hypothesis down on paper, with a minimum of invective, the staff will be only too happy to consider it.'

'But ...'

'And that will be *enough* on the subject now! We'll have plenty of time to talk about it later!'

'No, we don't have any time at all.'

Everyone turned. Dr Martine stood at the back of the Gallery, in the doorway. 'I think we'd better discuss this right now,' she said.

'Is Dr Kepler all right?' Jacob asked.

She nodded. 'I've just come from his bedside. I managed to break him out of his shock and he's sleeping now. But before he fell asleep he spoke rather urgently about making another dive right away.'

'Right away? Why? Shouldn't we wait until we know for certain what happened to Jeffrey's ship?'

'We *know* what happened to Jeff's ship!' she answered sharply. 'I overheard what Mr LaRoque said just as I came in, and I'm not at all happy with the way you all received his idea! You're all so hide-bound and sure of yourselves that you can't listen to a fresh approach!'

'You mean you really think that the Ghosts are our Ancestral Patrons?' DeSilva was incredulous.

'Perhaps, and perhaps not. But the rest of his explanation makes sense! After all, did the Solarians ever do more than threaten before this? And now they suddenly became violent. Why? Could it be that they felt no compunctions over killing a member of a species as immature as Jeff's?'

She shook her head sadly.

'You know, it's only a matter of time before human beings begin to realize just how much we're going to have to adapt! The fact is that every other oxygen-breathing race subscribes to a status system . . . a pecking order based on seniority, strength, and parentage. Many of you don't find this nice. But it's the way things are! And if we don't want to go the way of the non-European races in the nineteenth century, we'll just have to learn the way other, stronger species like to be treated!'

Jacob frowned.

'You're saying that if a chimpanzee is killed, and human beings are threatened or snubbed, then . . .'

'Then perhaps the Solarians don't want to mess around with children and pets . . .' One of the operators pounded his fist onto his console. A glare from deSilva cut him off. '. . . but might be willing to speak with a delegation with members of older, more experienced species. After all, how do we even know until we try?'

'Culla's been down there with us on most of our dives,' the console operator muttered. 'And he's a trained ambassador!'

'With all due respect to Pring Culla,' Martine bowed slightly toward the tall alien. 'He is from a very young race. Almost as young as ours. It's apparent that the Solarians don't think he's any more worthy than us of their attention.

'No, I propose that we take advantage of the unprecedented presence here on Mercury of two members of ancient and honored races. We should humbly ask the Pil Bubbacub and Kant Fagin to join us, down in the Sun, in one last attempt to make contact!'

Bubbacub rose slowly. He looked around deliberately, aware that Fagin would wait for him to speak first. 'If human beings say they need me down on Sol, then despite the seen dangers of prim-it-ive Sunships. I be inc-lined to ac-cept.'

He returned complacently to his cushion.

Fagin rustled and his voice sighed. 'I too shall be pleased to go. Indeed, I would perform any labor to earn the lowest berth on such a craft. I cannot imagine what help I could be. But I will happily go along.'

'Well *I* object damnit!' deSilva shouted. 'I refuse to accept the political implications of taking Pil Bubbacub and Kant Fagin down, particularly after the accident! You talk of good relations with powerful alien races, Dr Martine, but can you imagine what would happen if they *died* down there in an Earth ship?'

'Oh fish and falafal!' Martine said. 'If anyone can handle things so no blame falls on Earth, it's these sophonts. The galaxy is a dangerous place, after all. I'm sure they could leave depositions or something.'

'Such documents are already recorded in my case,' Fagin said.

Bubbacub, as well, stated his magnanimous willingness to risk his life in a primitive craft, absolving all of responsibility. The Pil turned away as LaRoque began to thank him. Even Martine joined in asking the man to please shut up.

DeSilva looked to Jacob. He shrugged.

'Well, we've got time. Let's give the crew here a chance to check the data from Jeff's dive, and let Dr Kepler recover. Meanwhile we can refer this idea to Earth for suggestions.'

Martine sighed. 'I wish it were that simple, but you just haven't thought this out. Consider, if we were to try to make peace with the Solarians, shouldn't we return to the same group that was offended by Jeff's visit?'

'Well, I'm not sure that necessarily follows, but it sounds right.'

'And how do you plan to find the same group, down in the solar atmosphere?'

'I suppose you'd just have to return to the same active region, where the grazers are feeding … Oh, I see what you mean.'

'I'll bet you do,' she smiled. 'There is no permanent "Solography" down there to make a map from. The active regions, and sunspots themselves, fade away in a matter of weeks! The Sun has no surface, per se, only different levels and densities of gas. Why, the equator even rotates faster than the other latitudes! How are you ever going to find the same group if you don't leave right away, before the damage done by Jeff's visit spreads over the entire star?'

Jacob turned to deSilva, puzzled. 'Do you think she might be right, Helene?'

She rolled her eyes upward. 'Who knows? Maybe. It's something to think about. I do know that we aren't going to do a damn thing until Dr Kepler is well enough to be heard.'

Dr Martine frowned. 'I told you before! Dwayne agreed that another expedition should leave right away!'

'And I'll hear from him personally!' deSilva answered hotly.

'Well, here I am, Helene.'

Dwayne Kepler stood in the doorway, leaning against the jamb. Beside him, supporting his arm, Chief Physician Laird glared across the room at Dr Martine.

'Dwayne! What are you doing out of bed! Do you want a heart attack?' Martine strode toward him, furious and concerned, but Kepler waved her back.

'I'm fine, Millie. I've just diluted that prescription you gave me, that's all. In a smaller dose it really is useful, so I know you meant well. It's just that it wasn't helping to knock me out like that!'

Kepler chuckled weakly. 'Anyway, I'm glad I wasn't too doped up to hear your brilliant speech. I caught most of it from the doorway.'

Martine reddened.

Jacob felt relieved that Kepler didn't mention the part he had played. After landing and obtaining Laboratory space, it had seemed a waste not to go ahead and analyze the samples he'd pilfered, back on the *Bradbury*, of Kepler's pharmacopoeia.

No one asked where he got his samples, fortunately. Although the base surgeon, when consulted, thought that some of the doses seemed a bit high, all but one of the drugs turned out to be standard for treatment of mild manic states.

The unknown drug stayed at the back of Jacob's mind; one more mystery to solve. What sort of physical problem did Kepler have that required large doses of a powerful anticoagulant? Physician Laird had been incensed. Why had Martine prescribed Warfarin?

'Are you sure you're well enough to be up here now?' deSilva asked Kepler. She helped the physician guide him to a chair.

'I'm all right,' he answered. 'Besides, there are things that just won't wait.

'First of all, I'm not at all sure about Millie's theory that the Ghosts would greet Pil Bubbacub or Kant Fagin with more enthusiasm than they've shown to the rest of us. I do know that I'm definitely not taking responsibility for taking them down on a dive! The reason is that if they were killed down there it wouldn't be at the hands of the Solarians ... it would be caused by human beings! There should be another dive right away ... *without* our distinguished extraterrestrial friends, of course ... but it should leave immediately to go to the same region, as Millie suggested.'

DeSilva shook her head emphatically. 'I don't agree at all, sir! Either Jeff was killed by the Ghosts, or something went wrong with his ship. And I think it was the latter, much as I hate to admit it ... We should check everything out before ...'

'Oh, there's no doubt it was the ship,' Kepler interrupted. 'The Ghosts didn't kill anybody.'

'What is it you say?' LaRoque shouted. 'Are you a blind man? How can you deny the obvious facts!'

'Dwayne,' Martine said smoothly. 'You're much too tired to think about this now.'

Kepler just waved her away.

'Excuse me, Dr Kepler,' Jacob said. 'You mentioned something about the danger coming from human beings? Commandant deSilva probably thinks you meant an error in prepping Jeff's ship caused his death. Are you talking about something else?'

'I just want to know one thing,' Kepler said slowly. 'Did the telemetry show that Jeff's ship was destroyed by a collapse of his stasis field?'

The console operator who had spoken earlier stepped forward. 'Why ... yessir. How did you know?'

'I didn't know,' he smiled. 'But I guessed pretty well, once I thought of sabotage.'

'What!?' Martine, deSilva and LaRoque shouted almost at once.

And suddenly Jacob saw it. 'You mean during the tour ... ?' He turned to look at LaRoque. Martine followed his eyes and gasped.

LaRoque stepped back as if he had been struck. 'You are an insane man!' he cried. 'And you are as well!' He shook a finger at Kepler. 'How could I have sabotaged the engines when I was sick all of the time I was in that crazy place?'

'Hey look, LaRoque,' Jacob said. 'I didn't say anything, and I'm sure Dr Kepler is only speculating.' He ended in a question and raised an eyebrow to Kepler.

Kepler shook his head. 'I'm afraid I'm serious. LaRoque spent an hour next to Jeff's Gravity Generators, with no one else around. We checked the Grav Generator for any damage that might have been caused by anyone fumbling around with their bare hands, and we didn't find any. It didn't occur to me until later to check Mr LaRoque's camera.

'When I did, I found that one of its little attachments is a small sonic stunner!' From one of the pockets of his tunic he pulled out the small recording device. '*This* is how the kiss of Judas was delivered!'

LaRoque reddened. 'The stunner is a standard self-defense device for journalists. I had even forgotten about it. And it could never have harmed so big a machine!

'And all of that is beside the point! This terra-chauvinist, archaeo-religious lunatic, who has nearly destroyed all chance of meeting our Patrons as friends, dares to accuse me of a crime for which there is no motive! He murdered that poor monkey, and he wishes to throw the blame on someone else!'

'Shut up, LaRoque,' deSilva said evenly. She turned back to Kepler.

'Are you aware of what you're saying, sir? A Citizen wouldn't commit murder, simply out of dislike for an individual. Only a Probationary Personality could kill without dire cause. Can you think of any reason Mr LaRoque might have had to do such a drastic thing?'

'I don't know,' Kepler shrugged. He peered at LaRoque. 'A Citizen who feels justified in killing still feels remorse afterward. Mr LaRoque doesn't look like he regrets anything, so either he's innocent, or a good actor ... or he is a Probationer after all!'

'In space!' Martine cried. 'That's impossible, Dwayne. And you know it. Every spaceport is loaded with P-receivers. And every ship is equipped with detectors also! Now you should apologize to Mr LaRoque!'

Kepler grinned.

'Apologize? At the very least I know LaRoque lied about being "dizzy" in the gravity loop. I sent a masergram to Earth. I wanted a dossier on him from his paper. They were only too happy to oblige.

'It seems that Mr LaRoque is a trained astronaut! He was separated from the Service for "medical reasons" – a phrase that's often used when a person's P-test scores rise to probation levels and he's forced to give up a sensitive job!

'That may not prove anything, but it does mean that LaRoque has had too much experience in spaceships to have been "scared to death" in Jeffrey's gravity loop. I only wish I realized this conflict in time to warn Jeff.'

LaRoque protested and Martine objected, but Jacob could see the tide of opinion in the room turn against them. DeSilva eyed LaRoque with a cold feral gleam that startled Jacob somewhat.

'Wait a minute,' he held up a hand. 'Why don't we check if there are any Probationers without transmitters here on Mercury. I suggest we all have our retina patterns sent back to Earth for verification. If Mr LaRoque isn't listed as a Probationer, it will be up to Dr Kepler to show why a Citizen might have thought he had reason to murder.'

'All right, then, for Kukulkan's sake, let us do it now!' LaRoque said. 'But only on the condition that I not be singled out!' For the first time Kepler began to look unsure.

For Kepler's benefit, deSilva ordered the entire base reduced to Mercurlan gravity. The Control Center answered that the conversion would take about five minutes. She went on the Intercom and announced the identity test to the crew and visitors, then left to supervise the preparations.

Those in the Telemetry Room began to drift out, on their way to the elevators. LaRoque kept close to Kepler and Martine, as if to demonstrate his eagerness to disprove the charges against him, his chin raised in an expression of high martyrdom.

The three of them, plus Jacob and two crewmen, were waiting for an elevator car when the gravity change happened. It was an ironic place for it to occur for it felt as if the floor had suddenly started to drop.

They were all used to changes in gravity – many places in Hermes Base were kept off Earth Gee. But usually the transition was through a stasis-controlled doorway, itself no more pleasant than this but, from familiarity, less disconcerting. Jacob swallowed hard and one of the crewmen staggered slightly.

In a sudden violent motion LaRoque dove for the camera in Kepler's hand. Martine gasped and Kepler grunted in surprise. The crewman who grabbed after the journalist got a fist in the face as LaRoque twisted like an acrobat and began to run backward down the hall, bringing up his recaptured camera. Jacob and the other crewman gave chase, instinctively.

There was a flash and a shooting pain in Jacob's shoulder. Something in his mind spoke as he dove to avoid another stunner bolt. It said, 'Okay, this is my job. I'm taking over now.'

He was standing in a hallway, waiting. It had been exciting, but now it was sheer hell. The passageway dimmed for a moment. He gasped and reached to steady himself on the rough wall as his vision cleared.

He was alone in a service corridor with a pain in his shoulder and the remnants of a deep, almost smug sense of satisfaction dissipating like a fading dream. He looked carefully around himself, then sighed.

'So you took over and thought you could handle it without me, didn't you?' he grunted. The shoulder tingled as if it was just now coming awake.

How his other half had got loose Jacob had no idea, nor why it had tried to handle things without the main persona's help. But it must have run into trouble to have given up now.

A sensation of resentment answered that thought. Mr Hyde was sensitive about his limitations, but capitulation came at last.

Is that all? Full memory of the last ten minutes flooded back. He laughed. His amoral Self had been confronted by an insurmountable barrier.

Pierre LaRoque was in a room at the end of the hallway. Amid the chaos that followed his seizure of the camera-stunner only Jacob had been able to stay on a man's trail, and he'd selfishly kept the stalk to himself.

He had played LaRoque like a trout, letting him think he'd eluded all pursuit. Once he even diverted a posse of base crewmen when they were getting too close.

Now LaRoque was putting on a spacesuit in a tool closet twenty meters from an outer airlock. He'd been in there five minutes and it would take at least another ten for him to finish. That was the insurmountable barrier. Mr Hyde couldn't wait. He was only a collection of drives, not a person, and *Jacob* had all of the patience. He'd planned it that way.

Jacob snorted his disgust but not without a twinge. Not too long ago that drive had been a daily part of him. He could understand the pain that waiting caused the small artificial personality that demanded instant gratification.

Minutes passed. He watched the door silently. Even in his full awareness he began to get impatient. It took a serious effort of will to keep his hand off the door latch.

The latch started to turn. Jacob stepped back with his hands at his sides.

The glassy bubble of a spacesuit helmet poked through the opening as the door swung outward. LaRoque looked to the left and then to the right. His teeth made a hissing shape when he saw Jacob. The door swung wide and the man came forward with a bar of plastic bracing material in his hand.

Jacob held up a hand. 'Stop, LaRoque! I want to talk to you. You can't get away anyway.'

'I don't want to hurt you, Demwa. Run!' LaRoque's voice twanged nervously from a speaker on his chest He flexed the plastic cudgel menacingly.

Jacob shook his head. 'Sorry. I jimmied the airlock down the hall before waiting here. You'll find it a long walk in a spacesuit to the next one.'

LaRoque's face twisted. 'Why?! I did nothing! Particularly to you!'

'We'll see about that. Meanwhile, let's talk. There isn't much time.'

'I'll talk!' LaRoque screamed. 'I'll talk with this!' He came forward with the bar, swinging.

Jacob dropped into a deflection stance and tried to raise both hands to seize LaRoque's wrist. But he'd forgotten about the numb left shoulder. His left hand just fluttered weakly, halfway to its assigned position. The right shot out to block and got a piece of the bar coming around instead. Desperately, he fell forward and tucked his head in as the club whistled inches above.

The roll, at least, was perfect. The lesser gravity helped as he came up and around effortlessly in a crouch. But his right hand was numb now, as he automatically shut off the pain from an ugly bruise. In his suit LaRoque swiveled more lightly than Jacob expected. What was it that Kepler said about LaRoque having been an astronaut? No time. Here he comes again.

The bar came down in a vicious overhead cut. LaRoque held it in a two-handed kendo grip; easy to block if only Jacob had his hands. Jacob dove under the cut and buried his head in LaRoque's midriff. He kept driving forward until together they slammed into the corridor wall. LaRoque said 'Oof!' and dropped the bar.

Jacob kicked it away and jumped back.

'Stop this, LaRoque!' He gulped for breath. 'I just want to talk to you ... Nobody has enough evidence to convict you of anything, so why run? There's no place to run to anyway!'

LaRoque shook his head sadly. 'I'm sorry, Demwa.' The affected accent was completely gone. He lunged forward, arms outstretched.

Jacob hopped backward until the distance was right, counting slowly. At the count of five his eyelids fell and locked into slits. For an instant Jacob Demwa was whole. He dropped back and traced a geodesic in his mind from the toe of his shoe to his opponent's chin. The toe followed the arc in a snap that seemed to expand to minutes. The impact felt feather soft.

LaRoque rose into the air. In his plentitude, Jacob Demwa watched the space-suited figure fly backward in slow motion. He empathized, and it was he, it seemed, who went horizontal in midair and then drifted down in shame and hurt until the hard floor slammed into his back through the utility pack.

Then the trance ended and he was loosening LaRoque's helmet ... pulling it off and helping him to sit up against the wall. LaRoque was crying softly.

Jacob noticed a package attached to LaRoque's waist. He cut the attachment and started to unwrap it, pushing LaRoque's hands aside when he resisted.

'So,' Jacob pursed his lips. 'You didn't try to use the stunner on me because the camera was too valuable. Why, I wonder? I might find out if we play this thing back.

'Come on, LaRoque,' he rose and pulled the man to his feet. 'We're going to stop where there's a readout machine. That is unless you have something to say first?'

LaRoque shook his head. He followed meekly with Jacob's hand on his arm.

At the main corridor, as Jacob was about to turn to the photo lab, a posse led by Dwayne Kepler found them. Even in the reduced gravity the scientist leaned heavily on the arm of a med-aid.

'Aha! You caught him! Wonderful! This proves everything I said! The man was fleeing a righteous punishment! He's a murderer!'

'We'll see about that,' Jacob said. 'The only thing this adventure proves is that he got scared. Even a Citizen can be violent when he panics. The thing I'd like to know is where he thought he was going. There's nothing out there but blasted rock! Maybe you should have some men go out and search the area around the base to be sure.'

Kepler laughed.

'I don't think he was going anywhere. Probationers never do know where they're going. They act on basic instinct. He simply wanted to get out of an enclosed place, like any hunted animal.'

LaRoque's face remained blank. But Jacob felt his arm tense when a surface search was mentioned, then relax when Kepler shrugged the idea aside.

'Then you're giving up the idea of an adult-murder,' Jacob said to Kepler as they turned toward the elevators. Kepler walked slowly.

'On what motive? Poor Jeff never harmed a fly! A decent, god-fearing chimpanzee! Besides, there hasn't been a murder by a Citizen in the System for ten years! They're about as common as gold meteors!'

Jacob had his doubts about that. The statistics were more a comment on police methods than anything else. But he remained silent.

By the elevators Kepler spoke briefly into a wall communicator. Several more men arrived almost immediately and took LaRoque from Jacob.

'Did you find the camera, by the way?' Kepler asked.

Jacob dissembled briefly. For a moment he considered hiding it and then pretending to discover it later.

'Ma camera a votre oncle!' LaRoque cried. He thrust out a hand

and reached for Jacob's back pocket. The crewmen pulled him back. Another came forward and held out his hand. Jacob reluctantly handed over the camera.

'What did he say?' Kepler asked. 'What language was that?'

Jacob shrugged. An elevator came and more people spilled out, including Martine and deSilva.

'It was just a curse,' he said. 'I don't think he approves of your ancestry.'

Kepler laughed out loud.

13

UNDER THE SUN

To Jacob the Communications Dome seemed like a bubble stuck in tar. All around the hemisphere of glass and stasis, the surface of Mercury gave off a dull, lambent shine. The liquid quality of the reflected sunlight enhanced the feeling of being inside a crystal ball that was trapped in mire, unable to escape into the cleanliness of space.

In the near distance, the rocks themselves looked strange. Unusual minerals formed in that heat and under constant bombardment of particles from the solar wind. The eye puzzled without quite knowing why, at powders and odd crystal shapes. And there were puddles as well. One shied away from thinking about those.

And something else near the horizon demanded attention.

The Sun. It was very dim, cut down by the powerful screens. But the whitish yellow ball seemed like a golden dandelion near enough to touch, an incandescent coin. Dark sunspots ran in clusters, fanning north- and south-eastward, away from the equator. The surface had a fineness of texture that just escaped focus.

Looking directly at the Sun brought a strange detachment in Jacob. Dimmed, but not red tuned, its light bathed those inside the dome in an energizing glow. Streamers of sunshine seemed to caress Jacob's forehead.

It was as if he had, like some ancient lizard seeking more than warmth, exposed every part of his self to the Lord of Space and, under those fires, felt a pulling force, a need to go.

He felt an uneasy certainty. Something lived in that furnace. Something terribly old, and terribly aloof.

*

Beneath the dome, men and machines stood on a fused plate of iron silicate. Jacob craned his head back to look at the huge pylon that filled the center of the chamber and protruded from the top of the stasis shield, into the hot Mercurial sunshine.

At its tip were the masers and laser which kept Hermes Base in touch with Earth, and, via a net of synchronous satellites, orbiting 15 million kilometers above the surface, followed the Sunships down into the Maelstrom of Helios.

The maser beam was busy now. One retinal pattern after another flew at lightspeed to the computers at home. It was tempting to imagine riding that beam back to Earth, to blue skies and waters.

The Retinal Reader was a small machine attached to the laser optics of the Library-designed computer system. The reader was essentially a large eyepiece against which a human user could press cheek and forehead. The optical input did the rest.

Although the E.T.s were exempted from the search for Probationers (there was no way they could qualify, and there certainly weren't any retinal codes on file for the few thousand galactics in the solar system) Culla insisted on being included. As Jeffrey's friend he claimed a right to participate, however symbolically, in the investigation of the chimpanzee scientist's death.

Culla had trouble fitting his huge oculars one at a time into the pieces. He was very still for a long time. Finally, at a musical tone, the alien walked away from the machine.

The operator adjusted the height of the eyepiece for Helene deSilva.

Jacob's turn came then. He waited until the eyepiece was adjusted, then pressed his nose, cheek, and forehead against the stops and opened his eyes.

A blue dot shone inside. Nothing else. It reminded Jacob of something, but he couldn't focus on what It seemed to turn around and sparkle as he looked, eluding analysis, like the shining of somebody's soul.

Then the musical tone told him his turn was over. He stepped back and made room, as Kepler came forward, leaning on Millie Martine's arm. The scientist smiled as he passed Jacob.

Now that's what it reminded me of! he thought. The dot had been like a twinkle in a man's eye.

Oh well, it fits, Computers can just about think today. There are some that are supposed to have a sense of humor, even. Why not this as well? Give the computers eyes to flash, and arms to put akimbo. Let them cast meaningful glances or stares that would kill if only stares could. Why should they not, the machines, begin to take on the aspect of those whom they absorb?

*

LaRoque submitted to the Reader, looking confident When he finished, he sat aloof and silent under the gaze of Helene deSilva and several of her crew.

The Base Commandant had refreshments brought in, as everyone connected with the Sundiver ships took his or her turn at the Reader. Many of the technicians grumbled at the interruption of their work. Jacob had to admit, as he watched the procession pass, that it was an awful lot of effort to go through. He had never thought Helene would want to check on *everybody*.

DeSilva had offered a partial explanation in the elevator on the way up. After putting Kepler and LaRoque in separate cars, she had ridden with Jacob.

'One thing confuses me,' he had said.

'Only one thing?' she smiled grimly.

'Well, one thing stands out. If Dr Kepler accuses LaRoque of sabotaging Jeff's ship, why does he object to taking Bubbacub and Fagin on a followup dive, whatever the result of this investigation? If LaRoque is guilty that would mean that the next dive will be perfectly safe with him out of the way.'

DeSilva looked at him for a moment pondering.

'I guess if there's anyone on this base I can confide in it's you, Jacob. So I'll tell you what I think.

'Dr Kepler never did want any E.T. help on this program. You'll understand that I'm telling you this in strict confidence, but I'm afraid the usual balance between humanism and xenophilia that most spacemen get might have swung a bit too far in his case. His background makes him bitterly opposed to the Danikenite philosophy, and I suppose that converts into a partial distrust of aliens. Also, a lot of his colleagues have been thrown out of work by the Library. For a man who loves research as much as he, it must have been hard.

'I'm not saying he's a Skin or anything like that! He gets along with Fagin pretty well and manages to hide his feelings around other Eatees. But he might say that if one dangerous man got on Mercury, another could, and use our guests' safety as an excuse to keep them off his ships.'

'But Culla's been on almost every dive.'

DeSilva shrugged.

'Culla doesn't count. He's a Client.

'I do know one thing, though; I'm going to have to go over Dr Kepler's head if this proves out. Every man on this base is having his identity checked and Bubbacub and Fagin go on the next dive if I have to shanghai them! I'm not going to let the slightest rumor get around that human crews are unreliable!'

She nodded with her jaw set. At the time Jacob thought her grimness was excessive. Though he could understand her feelings, it was a shame to masculinize those lovely features. At the same time he wondered if Helene was being totally candid on her own motivations.

A man who stood waiting by the maser link tore off a slip of message tape and carried it to deSilva. There was a tense silence as everyone watched her read. Then, grimly, she motioned to several of the husky crewmen who stood by.

'Place Mr LaRoque under detention. He's to be returned on the next ship out.'

'On what charge!' LaRoque shouted. 'You cannot do this, you, you Neanderthaler woman! I will see that you pay for this insult!'

DeSilva looked down at him as if he were a form of insect. 'For now the charge is illegal removal of a probationary transmitter. Other charges may be added later.'

'Lies, lies!' LaRoque shrieked as he leapt up. A crewman seized his arm and pulled him, choking with rage, toward the elevators.

DeSilva ignored them and turned to Jacob. 'Mr Demwa, the other ship will be ready in three hours. I'll go tell the others.'

'We can sleep en route. Thanks again for the way you handled things downstairs.'

She turned away before he could answer, giving orders in a low voice to crewmen who clustered about, efficiency masking her anger at the news: a Probationer in space!

Jacob watched for a few minutes as the dome slowly emptied. A death, a wild chase, and now a felony. So what, he thought, if the only felony proven so far is one I'd probably commit if I ever became a P.P. ... it does mean that there's a good chance that LaRoque caused the death as well.

As much as he disliked the man, he had never thought him capable of cold-blooded murder, in spite of those wicked swipes with the plastic cudgel.

At the back of his mind Jacob could feel his other half rubbing hands gleefully ... amorally delighted at the mysterious twists and turns the Sundiver case had taken and clamoring now to be set loose.

Forget it.

Dr Martine approached him near the elevator. She appeared to be in shock.

'Jacob ... you, you don't think Pierre could kill that silly little fellow, do you? I mean, he likes chimpanzees!'

'I'm sorry, but the evidence seems to point that way. I don't like the Probation Laws any more than you do. But people who are assigned that status are capable of easy violence, and for Mr LaRoque to remove his transmitter is against the law.

'But don't worry, they'll work it all out on Earth. LaRoque is sure to get a fair hearing.'

'But ... he's already being unfairly accused!' she blurted. 'He's not a Probationer, and he's not a murderer! I can prove it!'

'That's great! Do you have evidence here?'

He frowned suddenly. 'But the transmission from Earth said he *was* a Probationer!'

She bit her lip, looking away from his eyes. 'The transmission was a forgery.'

Jacob felt pity for her. Now the supremely confident psychologist was stammering and grasping at far-fetched ideas in her shock. It was degrading and he wished he was elsewhere.

'You have proof that the maser message was a lie? Can I see it?'

Martine looked up at him. Suddenly she seemed very unsure, as if wondering whether to say more.

'The ... the crew here. Did you actually see the message? That woman ... she only read it to us. She and the others hate Pierre ...'

Her voice trailed off weakly, as if she knew her argument was thin. After all Jacob thought, could the Commandant have faked reading from a piece of tape and known for certain that no one would ask to see it? Or, for that matter, would she place LaRoque in a position to sue her for every penny she'd earned in seventy years, just for a grudge?

Or had Martine been about to say something else?

'Why don't you go down to your quarters and get some rest,' he said gently, 'and don't worry about Mr LaRoque. They'll need more evidence than they have now to convict him of a murder in a court on Earth.'

Martine let him lead her into the elevator. There, Jacob looked back. DeSilva was busy with her crew, Kepler had been taken below. Culla stood morosely near Fagin, the two of them towering over everyone else in the chamber, under the great yellow disc of the Sun.

He wondered, as the door closed, whether this was really a good way to begin a journey.

PART V

Life is an extension of the physical world. Biological systems have unique properties, but they nevertheless must obey the constraints imposed by the physical and chemical properties of the environment and of the organisms themselves ... evolutionary solutions to biological problems are... influenced by the physico-chemical environment.

ROBERT E. RICKLEFS, *ECOLOGY*, CHIRON PRESS

14

THE DEEPEST OCEAN

Project Icarus it was called, the fourth space program of that name and the first for which it was appropriate. Long before Jacob's parents were born – before the Overturn and the Covenant, before the Power Satellite League, before even the full flower of the old Bureaucracy – old grandfather NASA decided that it would be interesting to drop expendable probes into the Sun to see what happened.

They discovered that the probes did a quaint thing when they got close. They burned up.

In America's 'Indian Summer' nothing was thought impossible. Americans were building *cities* in space – a more durable probe couldn't be much of a challenge!

Shells were made, with materials that could take unheard of stress and whose surfaces reflected almost anything. Magnetic fields guided the diffuse but tremendously hot plasmas of corona and chromosphere around and away from those hulls. Powerful communications lasers pierced the solar atmosphere with two-way streams of commands and data.

Still, the robot ships burned. However good the mirrors and insulation, however evenly the superconductors distributed heat, the laws of thermodynamics still held. Heat will pass from a higher temperature to a zone where the temperature is lower, sooner or later.

The solar physicists might have gone on resignedly burning up probes in exchange for fleeting bursts of information had Tina Merchant not offered another way.

'Why don't you refrigerate?' she asked. 'You have all the power you want. You can run refrigerators to push heat from one part of the probe to another.'

Her colleagues answered that, with superconductors, equalizing heat throughout was no problem.

'Who said anything about equalizing?' the Belle of Cambridge replied. 'You should take all excess heat from the part of the ship where the instruments are and pump it into another part where the instruments aren't.'

'And that part will burn up!' one colleague said.

'Yes, but we can make a chain of these "heat dumps,"' said another engineer, slightly more bright, 'and then we can drop them off, one by one . . .'

'No, no you don't quite understand.' The triple Nobel Laureate strode to the chalkboard and drew a circle, then another circle within.

'Here!' She pointed to the inner circle. 'You pump your heat into here until it is, for a short time, *hotter* than the ambient plasma outside of the ship. Then, before it can do harm there, you dump it out into the chromosphere.'

'And how,' asked a renowned physicist, 'do you expect to do that?'

Tina Merchant had smiled as if she could almost see the Astronautics Prize held out to her. 'Why I'm surprised at all of you!' she said. 'You have onboard a communications laser with a brightness temperature of millions of degrees! Use it!'

Enter the age of the Solar Bathysphere. Floating in part by buoyancy and also by balancing atop the thrust of their refrigerator lasers, probes lingered for days, weeks, monitoring the subtle variations at the Sun, that wrought weather on the Earth.

That era came to an end with Contact But soon a new type of Sunship was born.

Jacob thought about Tina Merchant. He wondered if the great lady would have been proud, or merely bemused, to stand on the deck of a Sunship and cruise calmly through the worst tempests of this irascible star. She might have said 'Of course!' But how could she have known that an alien science would have to be added to her own for men to ride those storms?

To Jacob the mixture didn't inspire confidence.

He knew, of course, that a couple of dozen successful descents had been made in this ship. There was no reason to think that this trip would be dangerous.

Except that another ship, the scaled-down replica of this one, had mysteriously failed just three days before.

Jeff's ship was probably now a drifting cloud of dissolving cermet fragments and ionized gases, scattered through millions of cubic miles in the solar maelstrom. Jacob tried to imagine the storms of the chromosphere the way the chimp scientist saw them in the last instant of his life, unprotected by the space-time fields.

He closed his eyes and rubbed them gently. He had been staring at the Sun, blinking too seldom.

From his point of view, on one of the observation couches flush with the deck, he could see almost an entire hemisphere of the Sun. Half of the sky was filled by a feathery, slowly shifting ball of soft reds and blacks and whites. In hydrogen light, everything glowed in shades of crimson; the faint, delicate arch of a prominence, standing out against space at the star's rim; the dark, twisting bands of filaments; and the sunken, blackish sunspots with their umbral depths and penumbral flows.

The topography of the Sun had almost infinite variety and texture. From flickers too fast to follow with the eye, to slow majestic turnings, all he could see was in motion.

Although the major features changed little from one hour to the next, Jacob could now make out countless lesser movements. The quickest were the pulsations of forests of tall slender 'spicules' around the edges of great mottled cells. The pulses took place within seconds. Each spicule, he knew, covered thousands of square miles.

Jacob had spent time at the telescope on the Flip-side of the Sunship, watching the flickering spikes of superheated plasma jetting up out of the photosphere like quick waving fountains, flinging free of the Sun's gravity great rolling waves of sound and matter that became the corona and the solar wind.

Within the spicule fences, the huge granulation cells pulsed in complicated rhythm as heat from below finished its million-year journey of convection to escape suddenly as light.

These, in turn, bunched together in gigantic cells, whose oscillations were the basic modes of the almost perfectly spherical Sun – the ringing of a stellar bell.

Above all this, like a broad deep sea rolling over the ocean floor, flowed the chromosphere.

The analogy could be overstated, but one could think of the turbulent areas above the spicules as coral reefs, and of the rows of stately, feathery filaments, tracing everywhere the paths of magnetic fields, as beds of kelp, gently swaying with the tide. No matter that each pink arch was many times the size of Earth!

Once more Jacob tore his eyes away from the boiling sphere. I'm going to be useless for anything if I keep staring like this, he thought. I wonder how the others resist it?

The entire observation floor was visible from his position, except for a small section on the other side of the forty-foot dome at the Center.

An opening grew in the side of the central dome and light spilled out into the deck. Silhouetted, a man emerged, followed by a tall woman. Jacob didn't have to wait for his eyes to adapt to know the outline of Commandant deSilva.

Helene smiled as she walked over and sat cross-legged next to his couch.

'Good morning, Mr Demwa. I hope you had a good night's sleep. It'll be a busy day.'

Jacob laughed. 'That's three times in one breath you've talked as if there was anything called night here. You don't have to keep up the fiction, like providing this sunrise here.' He nodded to where the Sun covered half of the sky.

'Rotation of the ship to make eight hours of night allows ground-lubbers a chance to sleep,' she said.

'You needn't have worried,' Jacob said. 'I can catch Zees anytime. It's my most valuable talent.'

Helene's smile widened. 'It was no inconvenience. But, now that you mention it, it's always been a tradition of Helionauts to rotate the ship once before final descent and call it night.'

'You have traditions already? After only two years?'

'Oh this tradition is much older than that! It dates back to when nobody could imagine any other way to visit the Sun but ...' She paused.

Jacob groaned out loud.

'But to go at night, when it isn't so hot!'

'You figured it out!'

'Filamentary, my dear Watson.'

It was her turn to groan. 'Actually, we are building up some feeling of tradition among those who have gone down to Helios. We make up the Fire-Eaters Club. You'll be initiated back on Mercury. Unfortunately, I can't tell you what the initiation consists of ... but I hope you can swim!'

'I don't see any place to hide, Commandant. I'll be proud to be a Fire-Eater.'

'Good! And don't forget, you still owe me that story about how you saved the Finnila Needle. I never did tell you how glad I was to see that old monstrosity when the *Calypso* returned, and I want to hear about it from the man who preserved it.'

Jacob stared past the Sunship Commandant. For a moment he thought he could hear a wind whistling, and someone calling ... a voice crying out indecipherable words as somebody fell ... He shook himself.

'Oh, I'll save it for you. It's much too personal to talk about in one of those story-swaps. There was someone else involved in saving the needles, someone you might like to hear about.'

There was something in Helene deSilva's expression, something compassionate, that implied she already knew about what had happened to him at Ecuador, and would let him tell about it in his own good time.

'I'm looking forward to it. And I've finally thought of one for you. It's about the "song-birds" of Omnivarium. It seems the planet is so silent that the human settlers have to be very careful lest the birds start mimicking any noise they make. This has an interesting effect on the settler's lovemaking behavior, particularly among the women, depending on whether they want to advertise their partner's "abilities" in the age-old fashion or remain discreet!

'But I must go back to my duties now. And I certainly don't want to give away the whole story. I'll let you know when we reach the first turbulence.'

Jacob rose to his feet with her and watched as she walked toward the command station. Partway into the solar chromosphere was probably an odd place to be enthralled by the way a fem walked, but until she went out of sight he felt no inclination to turn his eyes away. He admired the limberness that members of the interstellar corps inculcated into their extremities.

Hell, she was probably doing it on purpose. Where it didn't interfere with her job, Helene deSilva obviously pursued libido as a hobby.

There was something strange, though, in her behavior towards him. She appeared to trust him more than would normally be warranted by the small contributions he'd made on Mercury and their few friendly conversations. Perhaps she was after something. If so he couldn't figure out what.

On the other hand, maybe people were more naturally intimate when she'd left Earth for the long Jump on *Calypso*. Someone brought up on an O'Niel Colony, in a period of introspection caused by political stultification, might be more willing to trust her instincts than a child of the highly individualistic Confederacy.

He wondered what Fagin had told her about him.

Jacob went to the central dome, the outside wall of which contained a little boxlike head.

When he came out, Jacob felt much more awake. On the other side of the dome, by the food and beverage machines, he found Dr Martine standing with the two bipedal aliens. She smiled at him, and Culla's eyes brightened with friendliness. Even Bubbacub grunted a greeting through his Vodor.

He pressed buttons for orange juice and an omelette.

'You know, Jacob, you turned in too early last night. Pil Bubbacub was telling us some more incredible stories after you went to bed. They were astounding, really!'

Jacob bowed slightly at Bubbacub.

'I apologize, Pil Bubbacub. I was very tired, otherwise I would have been thrilled to hear more about the great Galactics, particularly of the glorious Pila. I'm sure the stories are inexhaustible.'

Martine stiffened next to him, but Bubbacub showed his pleasure by preening. Jacob knew it would be dangerous to insult the little alien. But by now he'd guessed the Ambassador wouldn't know any accusation of hubris as an insult. Jacob couldn't resist the harmless dig.

Martine insisted that he come over to eat with them, where the couches had already been raised for dining. Two of deSilva's four crewmen ate nearby.

'Has anyone seen Fagin?' Jacob asked.

Dr Martine shook her head. 'No, I'm afraid he's been on Flip-side for over twelve hours. I don't know why he doesn't join us here.'

It wasn't like Fagin to be reticent. When Jacob had gone to the instrument hemisphere to use the telescope, and found the Kanten there, Fagin had hardly said a word. Now the Commandant had put the other side of the ship off limits to everyone except the E.T., who occupied it alone.

If I don't hear from Fagin by lunchtime, I'm going to demand an explanation, Jacob thought.

Nearby, Martine and Bubbacub talked. Occasionally Culla said a word or two, always with the most unctuous respect. The Pring seemed always to have a liquitube between his giant lips. He sipped slowly, steadily consuming the contents of several tubes while Jacob ate his meal.

Bubbacub launched into a story about an Ancestral of his, a member of the Soro race who had, some million or so years ago, taken part in one of the few peaceful contacts between the loose civilization of oxygen breathers and the mysterious parallel culture of hydrogen-breathing races which coexisted in the galaxy.

For aeons there had been little or no understanding between hydrogen and oxygen. Whenever conflict arose between the two a planet died. Sometimes more. It was fortunate that they had almost nothing in common, so conflicts were rare.

The story was long and involved, but Jacob admitted to himself that Bubbacub was a master storyteller. Bubbacub could be charming and witty, as long as he controlled the center of attention.

Jacob allowed his imagination to drift along as the Pil vividly described those things which only a handful of men had ever even sampled: the infinite strangeness and beauty of the stars, and the variety of things which dwelt on a multitude of planets. He began to envy Helene deSilva.

Bubbacub felt the cause of the Library intensely. It was the vehicle of knowledge and of a tradition which unified all of those who took in oxygen as breath. It provided continuity and more, for without the Library, there would be no bridges between species. Wars would not be fought with restraint but to extinction. Planets would be ruined by over-use.

The Library, and the other loosely knit Institutes, helped to prevent genocide among its members.

Bubbacub's story reached its climax and he allowed his awed

audience a few moments of silence. Finally, he good-naturedly asked Jacob if he would care to honor them with a story of his own.

Jacob was taken aback. By human standards, perhaps, he had led an interesting life, but certainly not remarkable! What could he talk about from history? Apparently the rules were that it had to either be a personal experience, or an adventure of an Ancestor or Ancestral.

Perspiring in his chair, Jacob considered telling a story about some historical figure; perhaps Marco Polo or Mark Twain. But Martine would probably not be interested.

Then there was the part his grandfather Alvarez had played in the Overturn. But that story was rather heavily political and Bubbacub would think its moral downright subversive. His best story had to do with his own adventure at the Vanilla Needle, but that was too personal, too filled with painful memories to share here and now. Besides he'd promised it to Helene deSilva.

It was too bad LaRoque wasn't here. The feisty little man would probably have been able to talk until the fires below burned out.

An impish thought struck Jacob. There was a character out of history, who was a direct Ancestor of his and whose story might be sufficiently relevant. The amusing part was that the story could be interpreted on two levels. He wondered how obvious he could get without certain listeners catching on.

'Well, as a matter of fact,' he began slowly. 'There's a male from the history of Earth who I would like to talk about. He is of interest because he was involved in a contact between a "primitive" culture and technology and another that could overpower it in almost every respect. Naturally, you're all familiar with the premise. Since Contact, it's been almost all historians talk about.

'The fate of the Amerind is this era's morality play. Old twentieth-century movies glorifying the "Noble Red Man" are shown today strictly for laughs. As Millie reminded us, back on Mercury, and as everyone back home knows, the Red Man did just about the poorest job of any of the impacted cultures at adapting to the arrival of Europeans. His vaunted pride kept him from studying the white man's powerful ways until it was too late, exactly opposite to the successful "co-opting" made by Japan in the late nineteenth century ... the example that the "Adapt and Survive" faction keeps pointing out to all who will listen these days.'

He had them. The humans were watching him silently. Culla's eyes were bright. Even Bubbacub, usually inattentive, kept his beady little eyes on Jacob. Martine had winced when he mentioned the A & S faction, though. A datum.

If LaRoque were here, he wouldn't care for what I'm saying,

Jacob thought. But LaRoque's distress would be nothing next to that of his Alverez kin, should they ever hear him talk like this!

'Of course, the failure of the Amerinds to adapt wasn't entirely their fault,' Jacob continued. 'Many scholars think that western hemisphere cultures were in a periodic slump that happened, unfortunately, to coincide with the arrival of Europeans. Indeed, the poor Mayans had just finished a civil war in which they'd all moved out to the country and left their cities, and princes and priests, to rot. When Columbus arrived the temples were mostly deserted. Of course, the population had doubled and wealth and trade had quadrupled over the "Golden Age of the Maya," but those are hardly valid measures of cultures.'

Careful, boy. Don't go too heavy on the irony.

Jacob noticed that one of the crewmen, a fellow he'd met named Dubrowsky, had backed away from the others. Only Jacob could see the sardonic grin on the man's face. Everyone else appeared to be listening with unsuspicious interest, though it was hard to tell with Culla and Bubbacub.

'Now this ancestor of mine was an Amerind. His name was Se-quo-yi, and he was a member of the Cherokee nation.

'At the time, the Cherokee lived mostly in the state of Georgia. Since that was the East Coast of America, they had even less time than the other Amerinds to prepare to deal with the white man. Still, they tried, after their own fashion. Their attempt was nowhere near as grand or complete as the Japanese, but they tried.

'They were quick to pick up on the technology of their new neighbors. Log cabins replaced lodge houses and iron tools and blacksmithing became a part of Cherokee life. They learned about gunpowder early, as well as European methods of farming. Though many didn't like the idea, the tribe even became a slaveholding enterprise at one point.

'That was after they'd been whipped in two wars. They'd made the mistake of supporting the French in 1765, and then backed the Crown during the first American Revolution. Even so, they had a fair-sized little republic in the first part of the nineteenth century, partly because several young Cherokee had picked up enough of the white man's knowledge to become lawyers. Along with their Iroquois speaking cousins to the north, they did a fair job of playing the treaty game.

'For a while.

'Enter my ancestor. Se-quo-yi was a man who didn't like either of the choices offered his people, either staying noble savages and getting wiped out, or co-opting the settlers' ways completely and disappearing as a people. In particular, he saw the power of the written word but thought the Indian would forever be at a disadvantage if he had to learn English to become literate.'

Jacob wondered if anyone would make the connection, comparing the situation that faced Se-quo-yi and the Cherokee with humanity's present predicament, vis-à-vis the Library.

Judging by the look on Martine's face, at least one person was surprised to hear such a long historical tale from the normally quiet Jacob Demwa. There was no way she could, or ever would, know about the long lessons, after school, in history and oratory that he and the other Alvarez children had endured. Though he had turned away from politics, a family black sheep, he still had some of the skills.

'Well, Se-quo-yi solved his problem to his own satisfaction by inventing a written form of the Cherokee language. It was a Herculean task, accomplished at cost of episodes of torture and exile, for many in his own tribe resisted his efforts. But when he finished all of the world of literature and technology was available, not just to the intellectual who could study English for years, but to the Cherokee of average intelligence, as well.

'Soon even the assimilationists accepted the work of Se-quo-yi's genius. His victory set the tone for all succeeding generations of Cherokee. These people, the only Amerinds whose principle hero was an intellectual, and not a warrior, chose to be selective.

'And that was their big mistake. If they'd let the local missionaries change them over into imitation settlers they would have been able, probably, to merge into the yeoman class and be looked upon by the Europeans as a slightly lower type of white man.

'Instead, they thought they could become *modern Indians*, retaining the essential elements of their old culture ... obviously a contradiction in terms.

'Still, there are some scholars who think they might have made it. Things were going well until a group of white men discovered gold on Cherokee land. That got the settlers fairly excited. They got a bill through the Georgia legislature to declare the land up for grabs.

'Then the Cherokee did a strange thing, something that wasn't adequately duplicated for about a hundred years after. That Indian nation took the Georgia state legislature to court over the land seizure! They had some help from some sympathetic white men and managed to bring the case before the United States Supreme Court.

'The Court ruled that the seizure was illegal. The Cherokee could keep their land.

'But here is where the incompleteness of their adjustment let them down. Because they'd made no major attempt to fit themselves into the basic structure of settler society, the Cherokee had no *political power* to back up the rightness of their cause. They trusted, and cleverly used, the high and honorable *laws* of the new nation, but didn't realize that public opinion has every bit as much force as law.

'To most of their white neighbors they were just another tribe of Indians. When Andy Jackson told the Court to go to hell, and sent the Army in to evict the Cherokee *anyway*, there was nowhere for them to turn.

'So Se-quo-yi's people had to pack a few belongings and march the tragic Trail of Tears to a new "Indian Territory," in western lands none of them had ever seen.

'The story of the Trail of Tears was an epic of human courage and endurance. The sufferings of the Cherokee on that long march were deep and sad. Some very moving literature came out of it, as well as a tradition of strength in privation that has affected the spirit of that people ever since, even down to today.

'That eviction wasn't the last trauma to fall on the Cherokee.

'When the United States had a Civil War, the Cherokee did as well. Brother killed brother when the Confederate Indian Volunteers met the Union Indian Brigade. They fought as passionately as did the white troops, and usually with more discipline. And in the process their new homes were ravaged.

'Later there were troubles with bandit gangs, diseases, and more land seizures. In their stoicism they came to be known by some as the "Amerind Jews." While some other tribes dissolved in despair and apathy in the face of the crimes committed against them, the Cherokee maintained their tradition of self reliance.

'Se-quo-yi was remembered. Perhaps in symbolism of the pride of the Cherokee, his name was given to a certain type of tree, one that grows in the misty forests of California. The tallest tree in the world.

'But all of this leads us away from the folly of the Cherokee. For while their pride helped them survive the depredations of the nineteenth century and the neglect of the twentieth, it held them back from participating in the Indian Consolation of the twenty-first. They refused the "cultural reparations" offered by the American governments just before the beginning of the Bureaucracy; riches heaped on the remnants of the Indian Nations to salve the delicate consciences of the enlightened, educated public in that era that is today, ironically, referred to as America's "Indian Summer."

'They refused to set up Cultural Centers to perform ancient dances and rituals. While other Amerind revivalists resurrected pre-Columbian crafts to "regain contact with their heritage," the Cherokee asked why they should dig up "Model Ts" when they could be building their own specially-flavored version of twenty-first-century American culture.

'Along with the Mohawks and scattered groups from other tribes, they traded their "Consolation" and half of their tribal wealth to buy into the Power Satellite League. The pride of their youth went up to help build the cities in space, as their grandfathers had helped build the great cities of America. The Cherokee gave away a chance to be rich in exchange for a share of the sky.

'And once again they paid terribly for their pride. When the Bureaucracy began its suppression, the League rebelled. Those bright young males and fems, the treasure of their nation, died by the thousands alongside their space-brothers, descendants of Andy Jackson and of Andy Jackson's slaves. The League cities they built were decimated. The survivors were allowed to remain in space only because someone had to be there to show the Bureaucracy's carefully selected replacements how to live.

'On Earth the Cherokee suffered, too. Many took part in the Constitutionalist Revolt. Alone of the Indian nations, they were punished by the victors as a group, along with the VietAms, and the Minnesotans. The Second Trail of Tears was as sad as the first. This time, though, they had company.

'Of course, the first ruthless generation of Bureaucracy leaders passed, and the era of the true bureaucrats arrived. The Hegemony cared more about productivity than vengeance. The League rebuilt, under supervision, and a rich new culture developed in the O'Niel Colonies, influenced by the survivors of the original builders.

'On Earth, the Cherokee *still* meet, long after many tribes have been absorbed into cosmopolitan culture or into quaintness. They still haven't learned their lesson. I hear that their latest crackpot scheme is a joint project with the VietAms and Israel-APU to try to terraform Venus. Ridiculous, of course.

'But all of that is beside the point. If my Ancestor, Se-quo-yi, and his kin, had adapted completely to the ways of the white man they could have won a small place in his culture and been absorbed in peace, without suffering. If they had resisted with indiscriminate stubbornness, along with many of their Amerind neighbors, they would have suffered still, but finally been given a place, through the "kindness" of a later generation of white man.

'Instead, they tried to find a synthesis between those obvious good and powerful aspects of western civilization, and their own heritage. They experimented and were choosy. They picked and fussed over the meal for six hundred years and suffered, because of it, more than any other tribe.

'The moral of this story I have told, should be obvious. We humans are faced with a choice similar to that faced by the

Amerinds, whether to be picky or to accept wholeheartedly all of the billion-year-old culture offered us through the Library. Let anyone who urges choosiness remember the story of the Cherokee. Their trail has been long, and it isn't over yet.'

There was a long silence after Jacob finished. Bubbacub still watched him with little black eyes. Culla stared fixedly. Dr Martine looked down at the deck, her eyebrows knotted in thought.

The crewman, Dubrowsky, stood well back. One arm was crossed in front of him. His other hand covered his month. Crinkles around his eyes; did they betray silent laughter?

Must be a League-man. Space is infested with them. I hope he keeps his mouth shut about this. I took enough of a chance as it is.

His throat felt parched. He took a long drink from the liquitube of orange juice he had saved from breakfast.

Bubbacub finally placed both little hands behind his neck and sat up. He looked at Jacob for a moment.

'Good sto-ry,' he snapped, finally. 'I will ask you to rec-ord it for me, when we get back. It has good les-son for Earth folk.

'There are some ques-tions I would ask, though. Now or la-ter. Some things I do not un-der-stand.'

'As you wish, Pil-Bubbacub,' Jacob bowed, trying to hide his grin. Now to change the subject quick, before Bubbacub could get started asking about pesky details! But how?

'I too, enjoyed my friend Jacob's story,' a whistling voice fluted from behind them. 'I approached as silently as I could, when I came into range to hear it I am pleased that my presence did not disturb the telling.'

Jacob shot to his feet with relief.

'Fagin!' Everyone rose as the Kanten slithered toward them. In the ruby light he looked jet black. His movements were slow.

'I wish to offer apologies! My absence was unavoidable. The Commandant graciously assented to allow more radiation through the screens so that I could take nourishment But, understandably, it was necessary that she do so only on the unoccupied reverse side of the ship.'

'That's true,' Martine laughed. 'We wouldn't want any sunburn here!'

'Quite so. And yet it was lonely there, I am glad to have company again.'

The bipeds sat down and Fagin settled himself onto the deck. Jacob seized the opportunity to get out of his fix.

'Fagin, we've been exchanging some stories here, waiting for the surfing to start. Maybe you can tell us one about the Institute of Progress?'

The Kanten rustled its foliage. There was a pause. 'Alas, Friend-

Jacob. Unlike that of the Library, the Institute of Progress is not an important society. The very name is poorly translated into English. There are no words in your language to represent it properly.

'Our small order was founded to fulfill one of the least of the Injunctions that the Progenitors placed upon the oldest of races when they left the galaxy so long ago. Crudely stated, it imposed upon us the duty to respect "Newness."

'It may be hard for a species such as your own, orphans so to speak, who have until recently never felt the bittersweet bonds of kinship and patron-client obligation, to understand the inherent conservatism of our Galactic culture. This conservatism is not bad. For amidst so much diversity a belief in the Tradition and in a common heritage is a good influence. Young races heed the words of those older, who have learned wisdom and patience with years.

'You might say, to borrow an English expression, that we hold a deep regard for our roots.'

Only Jacob noticed that Fagin shifted his weight slightly at that point. The Kanten was folding and unfolding the short knotty tentacles that served as his feet. Jacob tried not to choke as a swallow of orange juice went down wrong.

'But there remains a need to face the future, as well,' Fagin continued. 'And in their wisdom, the Progenitors warned the Oldest not to scorn that which is new under the Sun.'

Fagin was silhouetted against the giant red orb, their destination. Jacob shook his head helplessly.

'So when word got out that somebody'd found a bunch of savages sucking at a wolfs teat, you came running, right?'

More rustling foliage. 'Very graphic, Friend-Jacob. But your surmise is essentially correct. The Library has the important task of teaching the races of Earth what they need to know to survive. My Institute has the humbler mission of appreciating your Newness.'

Dr Martine spoke.

'Kant Fagin, to your knowledge, has this ever happened before? I mean, has there ever been a case of a species which has no memory of Ancestral Upbringing, bursting into the galaxy on their own like we did?'

'Yes, respected Doctor Martine. It has happened a number of times. Space is large beyond all imagining. The periodic migrations of oxygen and hydrogen civilizations cover great distance, and rarely is even a settled area ever full explored. Often, in these great movements, a tiny fragment of a race, barely raised from bestiality, has been abandoned by its patrons to find its way alone. Such abandonments are usually avenged by civilized peoples ...' The Kanten hesitated. Suddenly Jacob realized why with a shock as Fagin hurried on.

'But since it is usually at a time of migration that these rare cases occur, there is an added problem. The wolfling race may develop a crude spacedrive from the dregs of its patron's technology, but by the time it enters interstellar space, its part of the galaxy might be under Interdict. Unknowingly it might fall prey to hydrogen breathers whose turn it may be to occupy that cluster or spiral arm.

'Nevertheless, such species are found occasionally. Usually the orphans retain vivid memories of their patrons. In some cases, myth and legend have taken the place of fact. But the Library is almost always able to trace the truth, for that is where our truths are stored.'

Fagin lowered several branches in Bubbacub's direction. The Pil acknowledged with a friendly bow.

'That is why,' Fagin went on, 'we await with great expectation the discovery of the reason why there is no mention of your Earth in that great archive. There is no listing, no record of previous occupation, in spite of five full migrations through this region since the Progenitors departed.'

Bubbacub froze in his bow. The small black eyes snapped up to bear on the Kanten with narrowly focused ferocity, but Fagin appeared not to notice as he continued.

'To my knowledge, mankind is the first case in which there exists the Intriguing possibility of *evolved* intelligence. As I am sure you know, this idea violates several well-established principles of our biological science. Yet some of your anthropologists' arguments possess startling self-consistency.'

'It is quaint idea,' Bubbacub sniffed. 'Like per-pet-ual motion, these boast-ings by those you call "Skins." The theories of "natural" growth of full sent-ience, are great source of good-natured jokes, human-Jacob-Dem-wa. But soon the Lib-rar-y give your troub-led race what it needs; the com-fort of knowing where you came from!'

The low hum of the ship's engines grew louder, and for a second Jacob felt a slight disorientation.

'Attention everybody,' the amplified voice of Commandant deSilva carried throughout the ship. 'We've just crossed over the first reef. From now on there will be momentary shocks like that one. I'll inform you when we near our target area. That is all.'

The Sun's horizon was now nearly flat. On all sides of the ship, a sparse red and black tangle of curling shapes stretched away to infinity. More and more of the highest filaments were coming even with the vessel to become prominences against what remained of the blackness of space, and then to disappear into the reddish haze that grew over their heads.

The group moved, by mutual consent, to the edge of the deck where they could look straight into the lower chromosphere. They were quiet, for a while, watching as the deck quivered from time to time.

'Dr Martine,' Jacob said. 'Are you and Pil Bubbacub ready with your experiments?'

She pointed to a pair of stout space-trunks on the deck next to Bubbacub's station and her own.

'We have all we need right here. I'm bringing along some psi equipment I used on earlier dives, but mostly I'm going to help Pil Bubbacub in any way I can. My brain wave amplifiers and Q-devices are like knucklebones and tea leaves next to what he's got in *his* case. But I'll try to be of assistance.'

'Your help be take-en with glad-ness,' Bubbacub said. But when Jacob asked to see the Pil's psi-testing apparatus he held up his four-fingered hand. 'Later, when we are ready.'

The old itchiness returned to Jacob's hands. What does Bubbacub have in those trunks? The Branch Library had next to nothing on psi. Some phenomenology, but very little on methodology.

What does a billion-year-old galactic culture know, he thought, about the deep fundamental levels that all sentient species seem to have in common? Apparently they don't know everything, for the Galactics still operate on this plane of reality. And I know for a fact that at least some of them don't have any more telepathy than *I* do.

There were rumors that older species periodically faded away from the galaxy; sometimes from natural attrition or war or apathy, but also occasionally by simply "stepping off" ... disappearing into interests and behavior that have no meaning to their clients or neighbors.

Why does our Branch Library have nothing on these events, or even on the practical aspects of psi?

Jacob frowned and locked his two hands together. No, he decided. I'm going to leave Bubbacub's trunk alone!

Helene deSilva's voice came on again over the intercom.

'We will be approaching the target area in thirty minutes. Those who wish may now approach the Pilot Board to get a good view of our destination.'

The rest of the Sun seemed to dim slightly as their eyes adapted to the added brightness of the area. The faculae were bright pinpoints, flashing on and off far below in sudden brilliance. At some indeterminable distance, a great sunspot group stretched away. The nearest spot looked like an open pit mine, a sunken recess in the grainy 'surface' of the photosphere. The dark Umbra was very still, but the penumbral regions around the sunspot's rim rippled incessantly outward, like wavelets spreading from a pebble thrown into a lake. The border was vague, like a plucked piano string, vibrating.

Above and all around, the huge shape of a filament tangle loomed. It had to be one of the biggest things that Jacob had ever seen. Following the lines of magnetic fields that merged, twisted, and looped around one another, giant clouds swirled and flowed. A strand emerged from nothingness, rose, twisted around another, and then disappeared into 'thin air.'

All around them now was a swirl of smaller shapes: almost invisible, but excluding the comforting black of space in an overall pink haze.

Jacob wondered what a literary man would make of this scene. For all of his egregious – perhaps murderous faults – LaRoque had a reputation built on a beautiful facility with words. Jacob had read several of his articles and enjoyed the flowing prose, while perhaps laughing at the man's conclusions. Here was a scene that demanded a poet, whatever his politics. He thought it a pity that LaRoque wasn't here ... for more than one reason.

'Our instruments have picked up a source of anomalous polarized light. That's where we start our search.'

Culla stepped up to the lip of the deck and stared intently at a position pointed out to him by a crewman. Jacob asked the Commandant what he was doing. 'Culla can detect color far more accurately than we,' deSilva said. 'He can see differences in wave length down to about an angstrom or so. Also he's somehow able to retain the phase of the light he sees. Some interference phenomenon, I suppose. But it makes him really handy at spotting the coherent light these laser beasties put out. He's almost always the first one to see them.'

Culla's mashies clacked together once. He pointed with a slender hand.

'It ish there,' he stated. 'There are many points of light. It ish a large herd, and I believe that there are sheperdsh there ash well.'

DeSilva smiled, as the ship hastened its approach.

15

OF LIFE AND DEATH

In the center of the filament, the Sunship moved like a fish caught in a swift current The current was electrical, and the tide that swept the mirrored sphere along was a magnetized plasma of incredible complexity.

Lumps and streaming shreds of ionized gas seared thither and back, twisted by the forces that their very passage created. Flows of glowing matter popped suddenly in and out of visibility, as the Doppler effect took the emission lines of the gas into and then out of coincidence with the spectral line being used for observation.

The ship swooped through the turbulent chromospheric crosswinds, tacking on the plasma forces by subtle shifts in its own magnetic shields ... sailing with sheets made of almost corporeal mathematics. Lightning fast furling and thickening of those shields of force – allowing the tug of the conflicting eddies to be felt in one direction and not another – helped to cut down the buffeting dealt out by the storm.

Those same shields kept out most of the screaming heat, diverting the rest into tolerable forms. What got through was sucked up into a chamber to drive the Refrigerator Laser, the kidney whose filtered waste-flow was a stream of x-rays which clove aside even the plasma in its path.

Still, these were mere inventions of Earthmen. It was the science of the Galactics that made the Sunship graceful and safe. Gravity fields held back the amorous, crushing pull of the Sun so the ship fell or flew at will. The pounding forces of the center of the filament were absorbed or neutralized, and duration itself was altered by time-compression.

In relation to a fixed position on the Sun (if such a thing existed), it was swept along the magnetic arch at thousands of miles per hour. But relative to the surrounding clouds, the ship seemed to poke its way slowly, pursuing a quarry seen in glimpses.

Jacob watched the chase with half an eye, and kept Culla in sight the rest of the time. The slender alien was the ship's lookout He stood by the helmsman, eyes glowing and arm pointing into the murk.

Culla's directions were only a little better than those given by the ship's own instruments, but the instruments were difficult for Jacob to read. He appreciated having someone there to show passengers, as well as crew, the way to look.

For an hour they'd chased after specks that glowed in the distant haze. The specks were extremely faint, In the blue and green lines deSilva had ordered opened, but occasionally a 'burst of greenish light stabbed out from one or another, like a searchlight that suddenly took in the ship and then swept past.

Now the glimpses occurred more frequently. There were at least a hundred of the objects, all about the same size. Jacob looked at the Proximity Meter. Seven hundred kilometers.

At two hundred their shape became clear. Each of the 'magnetic grazers' was a torus. At this range the colony looked like a large collection of tiny blue wedding rings. Every little ring was aligned the same way, along the filamentary arch.

'They line up along the magnetic field where it's most intense,' deSilva said. 'And spin on their axes to generate an electric current Heaven knows how they get from one active region to another when the fields shift. We're still trying to figure out what keeps them together.'

Toward the edge of the crowd a few toruses wobbled slowly as they spun. Processing.

Suddenly, for an instant, the ship was bathed by a sharp green glow. Then the ochre hue returned. The pilot looked up at Jacob.

'We just passed through the laser tail of one torus. An occasional shot like that doesn't do any harm,' he said. 'But if we were coming up from behind and below the main herd we might have had trouble!'

A clump of dark plasma, either cooler or moving much faster than the surrounding gas, passed in front of the ship, blocking their view.

'What purpose does the laser serve?' Jacob asked.

DeSilva shrugged. 'Dynamic stability? Propulsion? Possibly they use it for cooling like we do. I suppose there might even be solid matter in their makeup, if that were true.

'Whatever the purpose, it sure is powerful to punch green light through these red-tuned screens. That's the only reason we discovered them. Big as they are, they're like pollen blowing in the wind down here. We could search for a million years and never find a toroid, without the laser for a trace. They're invisible in the hydrogen alpha, so to observe them better, we opened up a couple of bands in the green and blue. Naturally we won't be opening the wavelength that laser's tuned to! The lines we choose are quiet and optically thick, so whatever you see that's green or blue comes from a beastie. It should come as a pleasant change.'

'Anything would be welcome but this damned red.'

The ship passed through the dark matter and suddenly they were almost among the creatures.

Jacob gulped and closed his eyes momentarily. When he looked again, he found that he couldn't swallow. On top of three days of unbelievable sights, what he saw left him helpless before a powerful tremor of emotion.'

If a group of fish is called a 'school' for its discipline, and several lions comprise a 'pride,' named for their attitude, Jacob decided that the cluster of solar-beings could only be called a 'flare.' So intense was its brilliance that its members seemed to shine against black space.

The nearer toroids shone with the colors of an Earth spring. Only with distance did the colors fade. Pale green shimmered below their axes, where laser light scattered in the plasma.

Around all of them sparkled a diffuse halo of white light.

'Synchrotron radiation,' a crewman said. 'Those babies must really be spinning! I'm picking up a big flux at 100KeV!'

Four hundred meters across and more than 2,000 distant, the nearest toroid spun madly. Around its rim geometric shapes flew past like beads on a necklace, changing, so that deep blue diamonds became purple sinuous bands, circuiting a brilliant emerald ring, all within seconds.

The Sunship captain stood by the Pilot Board, eyes darting from indicator to gauge and alert to every detail. To glance at her was to watch a softened version of the show outside the ship, for the flux-ious, iridescent colors of the nearest toroid bathed her face and her white uniform and were thereby tamed and diffused for the second half of the trip to Jacob's eye. First faintly, then more brightly as green and blue mixed with and drove out the pink, the colors sparkled each time she looked up and smiled.

Suddenly, the blueness swelled as a burst of exuberance from the toroid coincided with an intricate display of patterns, like a weaving of ganglia around the ring-beast's rim.

The performance was peerless. Arteries erupted in green and twined with veins drawn in pulsing, chaste blue. These throbbed in counterpoint, then grew like gravid vines, peeling back to release clouds of tiny triangles – sprays of two dimensional pollen that scattered in a multitude of miniscule three-point collisions around the non-Euclidian body of the torus. At once the motif became iso-sceles, and the doughnut-rim became a cacophote of sides and angles.

The display reached a peak of intensity, then receded. The rim patterns became less bright and the torus backed away, finding a place to spin among its fellows as the red started to return, pushing out greens and blues from the deck of the ship and from the faces of the watchers.

'*That* was a greeting,' Helene deSilva said finally. 'There are skep-tics back on Earth who still think that the magnetovores are just some form of magnetic aberration. Let them come and see for them-selves, then. We are witnessing life. Clearly the Creator accepts few limits to the range of his handiwork.'

She touched the pilot's shoulder lightly. His hands moved on his controls and the ship began to bank away.

Jacob agreed with Helene, though her logic was unscientific. He had no doubts that the toroids were alive. The creature's display, whether it was a greeting or simply a territorial response to the presence of the ship, had been a sign of something vital, if not sentient.

The anachronistic reference to a supreme deity had sounded oddly fitting to the beauty of the moment.

The Commandant spoke again into her microphone as the flare of magnetovores fell back and the deck turned.

'Now we go hunting ghosts.

'Remember, we aren't really here to study the magnetovores but their predators. A constant watch is to be maintained by the crew for any sign of these elusive creatures. Since they have been sighted as often by accident as not, it would be appreciated if everyone helped. Please report anything extraordinary to me.'

DeSilva and Culla held a conference. The alien nodded slowly, an occasional flash of white between huge gums betraying his excitement. Finally, he set off around the curve of the central dome.

DeSilva explained that she had sent Culla to the other side of the deck, flip-side, where normally only instruments stood, to act as a lookout in case the laser beings should appear from the nadir, where the rim-mounted detectors could not reach them.

'We've had a number of zenith sightings,' deSilva repeated. 'And these have often been the most interesting cases, such as when we saw anthropomorphic shapes.'

'And the shapes always disappeared before the ship could be turned?' Jacob asked.

'Or the beasts would turn with us to stay overhead. It was infuriating! But that gave us the first clue that psi might be involved. After all, whatever their motives, how could they know about our way of placing instruments at the rim of a disc and follow our movements so precisely, without knowing what we intended to do?'

Jacob frowned in thought 'But why not put a few cameras up here? Certainly it wouldn't be much of a chore?'

'No, not much of a chore,' deSilva agreed. 'But the support and dive crews didn't want to disturb the ship's original symmetry. We would have to put another conduit through the deck to the main recording computer, and Culla assured us that this would eliminate whatever small ability we might have to maneuver in a stasis-failure ... though that ability is probably negligible anyway. Witness what happened to poor Jeff.

'Jeffrey's ship, the small one you toured on Mercury, was designed from the start to carry recorders aimed at zenith and nadir. His was the only one with this modification. We'll have to make do with the rim instruments, our eyes, and a few hand-held cameras.'

'And the psi experiments,' Jacob pointed out.

DeSilva nodded expressionlessly.

'Yes, we are all hoping to make friendly contact of course.'

'Excuse me, Captain.'

The pilot looked up from his instruments. He held a button speaker to his ear. 'Culla says there's a color difference at the upper north end of the herd. It might be a calving.'

DeSilva nodded.

'Okay. Proceed along a north tangent to the field flux. Rise with the herd as you make your way around and don't get close enough to spook them.'

The ship began to bank at a new angle. The Sun rose on the left until it became a wall that stretched up and ahead to infinity. A faint luminescence twisted away from them, down toward the photosphere below. The sparkling trail paralleled the alignment of the herd of toruses.

'That's the path of superionization our Refrigerator Laser left when we were pointed that way,' deSilva said. 'It must be a couple of hundred kilometers long.'

'The laser is that strong?'

'Well, we have to get rid of a lot of heat. And the whole idea is to *heat* up a small part of the Sun. Otherwise the refrigerator wouldn't work. Incidentally, that's another reason why we're so careful not to let the herd get ahead of or behind us.'

Jacob felt momentarily awed.

'When will we be in sight of ... what was it he said? A calving?'

'Yes, a calving. We're very lucky. We've only seen this twice before. The shepherds were there both times. They appear to assist whenever a torus gives birth. It's a logical place to start looking for them.

'As for when we get there, that depends on how violent things are between here and there, and how much time-compression we need to get there comfortably. It could be a day. If we're lucky ... ' She glanced at the Pilot Board. ' ... we could be there in ten minutes.'

A crewman stood nearby holding a chart, apparently waiting to see deSilva.

'I'd better go and warn Bubbacub and Dr Martine to get ready,' Jacob said.

'Yes, that would be a good idea. I'll make an announcement when I know how soon we'll arrive.'

As he walked away, Jacob had a strange feeling that her eyes were still on him. It lasted until he passed around the side of the central dome.

Bubbacub and Martine took the news calmly. Jacob helped them pull their equipment boxes to a position near the Pilot Board.

Bubbacub's implements were incomprehensible, and astounding. Complex, shiny, and multifaceted, one of them took up half of the crate. Its curling spires and glassy windows hinted at mysteries.

Bubbacub laid out two other devices. One was a bulbous helmet apparently designed to fit over the head of a Pil. The other looked like a chunk off of a nickel iron meteoroid, with a glassy end.

'There is three ways to look at psi,' Bubbacub said through his Vodor. He motioned with a four-fingered hand for Jacob to sit. 'One is that the psi is just very fine sens-or-y power, to pick out brain waves at long range and de-cipher them. That the thing I will see ab-out with this.' He pointed at the helmet.

'And this large machine?' Jacob moved to look closer.

'That sees if time and space are be-ing twisted here by the force of a soph-ont's will. The thing is done some-times. It sel-dom all-owed. The word is *pi-ngrli*. You have no word for it. Most, in-cluding hu-mans, do not need to know of it since it is rare.

'The Li-brar-y prov-ides these ka-ngrl,' he stroked the side of the machine once, 'to each Branch, in case out-laws try to use pi-ngrli.'

'It can counteract that force?'

'Yes.'

Jacob shook his head. It bothered him that there was a whole *type* of power to which man had no access. A deficiency in technology was one thing. It could be made up in time. But a qualitative lack made him feel vulnerable.

'The Confederacy knows about this ... ka-ka ... ?'

'Ka-ngrl. Yes. I have their leave to take it from Earth. If it is lost, it will be re-placed.'

Jacob felt better then. The machine suddenly looked friendlier. 'And this last item ... ?' he began to move toward the lump of iron.

'That is a P-is.' Bubbacub snatched it up and put it back in the trunk. He turned away from Jacob and began to fiddle with the brain-wave helmet.

'He's pretty sensitive about that thing,' Martina said when Jacob came near. 'All I could get out of him was that it's a relic from the Lethani, his race's fifth high Ancestrals. It dates from just before they "passed over" to another plane of reality.'

The Perpetual Smile broadened. 'Here, would you like to see ye olde alchemist's tools?'

Jacob laughed. 'Well, our friend Pil has the Philosopher's Stone.

What miraculous devices have you for mixing effluvium, and exorcising highly caloric ghosts?'

'Besides the normal run-of-the-mill psi detectors, such as they are, there's not much. A brain-wave device, an inertial movement sensor that's probably useless in a time-suppression field, a tachistoscopic 3-D camera and projector ...'

'May I see that?'

'Sure, it's at the far end of the trunk.'

Jacob reached in and removed the heavy machine. He laid it on the deck and examined the recording and projecting heads.

'You know,' he said softly. 'It's just possible ...'

'What is?' Martine asked.

Jacob looked up at her. 'This, plus the retinal pattern reader we used on Mercury, could make a perfect mental proclivities tester.'

'You mean one of those devices used to determine Probation status?'

'Yes. If I had known this was available back at the base, we could have tested LaRoque then and there. We wouldn't have had to maser Earth and go through layers of fallible bureaucracy for an answer that might have been tampered. We could have found out his violence index on the spot!'

Martine sat still for a moment Then she looked downward.

'I don't suppose it would have made any difference.'

'But you were sure there was something wrong with the message from Earth!' Jacob said. 'This could save LaRoque from two months in a brig if you were right. Hell, it's possible he would have been with us right now. We'd be less unsure about the possible danger from the Ghosts, too!'

'But his escape attempt on Mercury! You said he was violent!'

'Panicky violence does not a Probationer make. What's the matter with you anyway? I thought you were sure LaRoque was framed!'

Martine sighed. She avoided meeting his eyes.

'I'm afraid I was a little hysterical back at the base. Imagine, dreaming up a conspiracy, just to trap poor Peter!

'It's still hard to believe that he's a Probationer, and maybe some mistake was made. But I no longer think it was done purposely. After all, who would want to saddle him with the blame for that poor little chimpanzee's death?'

Jacob stared for a moment, unsure what to make of her change of attitude. 'Well ... the real murderer, for one,' he said softly.

Immediately he regretted it.

'What are you talking about?' Martine whispered. She glanced quickly to both sides to be sure that no one was nearby. Both knew that Bubbacub, a few meters away, was deaf to whispered speech.

'I'm talking about the fact that Helene deSilva, much as she probably dislikes LaRoque, thinks it's unlikely the stunner could have damaged the stasis mechanism on Jeff's ship. She thinks the crew botched up, but ...'

'Well then Peter will be released on insufficient evidence and he'll have another book to write! We'll find out the truth about the Solarians and everybody will be happy. Once good relations are established I'm sure it won't matter much that they killed poor Jeff in a fit of pique. He'll go down as a martyr to science and all this talk of murder can be ended once and for all. It's so distasteful anyway.'

Jacob was beginning to find the conversation with Martine distasteful as well. Why did she *squirm* so? It was impossible to follow a logical argument with her.

'Maybe you're right,' he shrugged.

'Sure I'm right.' She patted his hand and then turned to the brain-wave apparatus. 'Why don't you go look for Fagin. I'm going to be busy here for a while and it's possible he doesn't know about the calving yet.'

Jacob nodded once and got to his feet. As he crossed the gently quivering deck he wondered what strange things his suspicious other half was thinking. The blurt about a 'real murderer' worried him.

He met Fagin where the photosphere filled the sky in all directions, like a great wall. In front of the treelike Kanten, the filament in which they rode spiraled down and away into red dissipation. To the left and right and far below, spicule forests wriggled like effervescent rows of elephant grass.

For a time they watched together in silence.

As a waving tendril of ionized gas drifted past the ship, Jacob was reminded for the nth time of kelp floating in the tide.

Suddenly he had an image. It made him smile. He imagined Makakai, wearing a waldo-suit of cermet and stasis, plunging and leaping among these towering fountains of swirling flame, and diving, in her shell of gravity, to play among the children of this, the greatest ocean.

Do the Sun Ghosts while away the aeons as our cetaceans do? he wondered. By singing?

Neither have machines (or any of the neurotic hurry that machines bring – including the sickness of ambition?), because neither have the means. Whales have no hands and cannot use fire. Sun Ghosts have no solid matter and too much fire.

Has it been a blessing for them or a curse?

(Ask the humpback, as he moans in the stillness underwater.

Probably, he won't bother to answer, but someday he may add the question to his song.)

'You're just in time. I was about to call,' the Captain motioned ahead into the pink haze.

A dozen or more of the toroids spun in front of them colorfully.

This group was different. Instead of drifting passively they moved about, jostling for position around something deep in the middle of the crowd. One nearby torus, only a mile distant, moved aside and then Jacob could see the object of their attention.

The magnetovore was larger than the others. Instead of the changing, multifaceted geometric shapes, dark and light bands alternated around its circuit, and it wobbled lazily while its surface rippled. Its neighbors milled about on all sides but at a distance, as if held back by some deterrent.

DeSilva gave a command. The pilot touched a control and the ship turned, righting itself so the photosphere soon was beneath them once more. Jacob was relieved. Whatever the ship's fields told him, having the Sun on his left made him feel sideways.

The magnetovore Jacob thought of as 'Big One' spun, apparently oblivious to its retinue. It moved sluggishly, with a pronounced wobble.

The white halo that bathed every other torus flickered dimly around the edges of this one, like a dying flame. The dark and light bands pulsed with an uneven undulation.

Each pulse evoked a response in the surrounding crowd of toroids. Rim patterns sharpened starkly in bright blue diamonds and spirals as each magnetovore kept its own backbeat to Big One's slowly strengthening rhythm.

Suddenly, the nearest of the attendant toruses rushed toward the banded Big One, sending bright green flashes of light along its spinning path.

From around the gravid torus, a score of brilliant blue dots flew up toward the intruder. They were in front of it in an instant, dancing, like shimmering drops of water on a hot skillet, next to its ponderous hulk. The bright dots began to push it back, nipping and teasing, it seemed, until it was almost below the ship.

The ship turned under the pilot's hand to present its edge to the nearest of the sparkling motes, only a kilometer away. Then, for the first time, Jacob could clearly see the life forms that were called Sun Ghosts.

It floated like a wraith, delicately, as if the chromospheric winds were a breeze to be taken with barely a flutter: as different from the firm, spinning, dervishlike toruses as a butterfly is from a whirling top.

It looked like a jellyfish, or like a brilliantly blue bath towel flapping in the wind as it hung on a clothesline. Possibly it was more an octopus, with ephemeral appendages that flickered in and out of existence along its ragged edges. Sometimes it looked to Jacob like a patch of the surface of the sea itself, somehow skimmed up and moved here; maintained in its liquid, tidal movement by a miracle.

The ghost rippled. It moved toward the Sunship, slowly, for a minute. Then it stopped.

It's looking at us too, Jacob thought.

For a moment they regarded one another, the crew of water beings, in their ship, and the Ghost.

Then the creature turned so that its flat surface was toward the Sunship. Suddenly, a flash of brilliant multicolored light washed the deck. The screens kept the glare bearable, but the pale red of the chromosphere was banished.

Jacob put a hand out in front of his eyes and blinked in wonder. So this is what it's like, he thought somewhat irrelevantly, inside a rainbow!

As suddenly as it came, the light show disappeared. The red Sun was back, and with it the filament, the sunspot far below, and the spinning toruses.

But the Ghosts were gone. They had returned to the giant magnetovore and once more danced as almost unseen dots about its rim.

'It ... it blasted us with its laser!' the pilot said. 'They never did *that* before!'

'One never came that close before in its normal shape, either,' Helene deSilva said. 'But I'm not sure what either action is supposed to mean.'

'Do you think It meant to harm us?' Dr Martine spoke hesitantly. 'Maybe that's how they started with Jeffrey!'

'I don't know. Maybe it was a warning ...'

'Or maybe it just wanted to get back to work,' Jacob said. 'We were in almost the opposite direction as the big magnetovore out there. You'll notice that all of its companions went back at the same time.'

DeSilva shook her head.

'I don't know. I guess we'll be all right if we just stay here and watch. Let's see what they do when they finish with the calving.'

Ahead of them, the big torus began to wobble more as it spun. The dark and light bands along its rim became more pronounced, the darker becoming narrow strictures and the lighter bands ballooning outward with each oscillation.

Twice Jacob saw groups of bright herdsmen jet away to head off a magnetovore that came too close, like sheepdogs at the heels of a wayward ram, as others stayed with the ewe.

The wobble deepened and the dark bands grew tighter. The green laser light, scattered below the big torus, dimmed. Finally it disappeared.

The Ghosts moved in. As the Big One's nutation reached an almost horizontal pitch, they gathered at the rim to somehow seize it and complete the turnover with a sudden jerk.

The behemoth now spun lazily on an axis perpendicular to the magnetic field. For a moment the position held, until the creature suddenly began to fall apart.

Like a necklace with a broken string, the torus split where one of the dark bands tightened to nothing. One by one, as the parent body spun slowly, the light bands, now small individual doughnut shapes themselves, were flung free, each as it rotated to the place where the break occurred. One at a time, they were cast upwards, along the invisible lines of magnetic flux, until they ran like beads across the sky. Of the Big One, the parent, nothing remained.

About fifty of the little doughnut shapes spun dizzyingly in a protecting swarm of bright blue herdsmen. They processed uncertainly and, from the center of each, a tiny green glow flickered tentatively.

In spite of their careful watch, the ghosts lost several of their erratic charges. Some of the infants, more active than their peers, jetted out of the queue. A brief burst of green brilliance took one baby magnetovore out of the protected area and toward one of the adults that lurked nearby. Jacob hoped it would continue toward the ship. If only the adult torus would get out of the way!

As if it heard his thoughts, the adult began to drop away below the oncoming path of the juvenile. Its rim pulsed with green-blue diamonds as the newborn passed overhead.

Suddenly the torus leaped upward on a column of green plasma. Too late, the juvenile tried to flee. It turned its feeble torch toward its pursuer's rim as it jetted away.

The adult was undeterred. In a moment the baby was overtaken, drawn down into its elder's pulsing central hole and consumed in a flash of vapor.

Jacob realized that he was holding his breath. He let it out and it felt like a sigh.

The babies were now arranged in orderly ranks by their mentors. They began to move away from the herd slowly, while a few herdsmen stayed to keep the adults in line. Jacob watched the brilliant little rings of light until a thick wisp of filament floated in to cut off his view.

'Now we start earning our pay,' Helene deSilva whispered. She turned to the pilot. 'Keep the remaining herdsmen aligned with the deck-plane. And ask Culla to please keep his eyes peeled. I want to know if anything comes in from the nadir.'

Eyes peeled! Jacob suppressed an involuntary shudder, and firmly said no when his imagination tried to present an image. What kind of an era did this fem come from!

'Okay,' the Commandant said. 'Let's approach slowly.'

'Do you think they'll notice we waited until they were through with the calving?' Jacob asked.

She shrugged. 'Who knows? Maybe they thought we were just a timid form of adult torus. Perhaps they don't even remember our earlier visits.'

'Or Jeff's?'

'Or even Jeff's. It wouldn't do to assume too much. Oh, I believe Dr Martine when she says her machines register a basic intelligence. But what does that mean? In an environment like this ... even more simple than an ocean on earth, what reason would a race have to develop a functioning semantic skill? Or memory? Those threatening gestures we saw on previous dives don't necessarily indicate a lot of brains.

'They might be like dolphins were before we started genetic experiments a few hundred years ago, lots of intelligence and no mental ambition at all. Hell, we should have brought in people like you, from the Center for Uplift, long ago!'

'You're talking as if evolved intelligence is the only route,' he smiled. 'Galactic opinion aside for the moment, shouldn't you at least consider another possibility?'

'You mean that the Ghosts might have once been uplifted!?' deSilva looked shocked for a moment. Then the idea soaked in and she leaped on the implications, her eyes sharp. 'But if that were the case, then there'd have to have been ...'

She was interrupted by the pilot.

'Sir, they're starting to move.'

The Ghosts fluttered in the hot, wispy gas. Blue and green highlights rippled along the surface of each as it hovered lazily, a hundred thousand kilometers above the photosphere. They retreated from the ship slowly, allowing the separation to diminish, until a faint corona of white could be seen surrounding every one.

Jacob felt Fagin come up beside him on his left.

'It would be sad,' the Kanten fluted softly, 'if such beauty were found sullied by a crime. I could have great trouble sensing evil while struck in awe.'

Jacob nodded slowly.

'Angels are bright ...' he began. But of course, Fagin knew the rest.

> Angels are bright, though the brightest fell.
> Though all things foul would wear the brows of grace,
> Still grace must look so.

'Culla says they're about to do something!' the pilot peered ahead with a hand over his ear.

A wisp of darker gas from the filament moved swiftly into the area, momentarily blocking off the view of the Ghosts. When it cleared, all but one had moved farther away.

That one waited as the ship edged slowly closer. It looked different, semi-transparent, bigger and bluer. And simpler. It looked stiff and did not ripple like the others. It moved more deliberately.

An ambassador, Jacob thought.

The Solarian rose slowly as they neared.

'Keep him edge-on,' deSilva said. 'Don't lose instrument contact!'

The pilot glanced up at her grimly, and turned back to his instruments with tight lips. The ship started to rotate.

The alien rose faster and drew near. The fan-shaped body seemed to beat against the plasma like a bird trying to gain altitude.

'It's toying with us,' deSilva muttered.

'How do you know?'

'Because it doesn't have to work that hard to stay overhead.' She asked the pilot to speed up the rotation.

The Sun rose on the right and crept toward the zenith. The Ghost continued to beat toward a position overhead, even though it had to be spinning upside down along with the ship. The Sun rolled overhead and then set. Then it rose and set again in less than a minute.

The alien stayed overhead.

The spin accelerated. Jacob gritted his teeth and resisted an urge to grab Fagin's trunk for balance as the ship experienced day and night in seconds. He felt hot, for the first time since the journey to the Sun began. The Ghost stayed maddeningly overhead and the photosphere blasted on and off like a flashing lamp.

'Okay, give it up,' deSilva said.

The spinning slowed. Jacob swayed as they came to complete rest. He felt as if a cool breeze was washing his body. First heat, then chills: Am I going to be ill? he wondered.

'It won,' deSilva said. 'It always does, but it was worth a try. Just once I'd like to try that with the Refrigerator Laser operating though!' She glanced at the alien overhead. 'I wonder what would happen when he got near a fraction of the speed of light.'

'You mean you had our refrigerator turned off just then?' Now Jacob couldn't help it. He touched Fagin's trunk lightly.

'Sure,' the Commander said. 'You don't think we want to fry dozens of innocent toruses and herdsmen do you? That's why we were under a time limit. Otherwise we could have tried to line him up with the rim instruments till hell froze over!' She glared up at the Ghost.

Again, the touching turn of phrase. Jacob wasn't sure whether the woman's fascination lay in her more straightforward qualities or in this way she had with quaint expressions. In any event, the over-heating and subsequent cool breezes were explained. For a time the heat of the Sun had been allowed to leak in.

I'm glad that's all it was, he thought.

16

... AND APPARITIONS

'All we get is a dim picture,' the crewman said. 'The stasis screens must be bending the Ghost's image somehow because it looks warped ... like it's refracted at an angle through a lens.'

'Anyway,' he shrugged as he passed the photos around. 'This is the best we can do with a hand-held camera.'

DeSilva looked at the picture in her hand. It showed a blue, streaky caricature of a man, a stick figure with spindly legs, long arms, and big, splayed hands. The photograph had been taken just before the hands had balled into fists, crude but identifiable.

When his turn came, Jacob concentrated on the face. The eyes were empty holes, as was the ragged mouth. In the photograph they looked black but Jacob recalled that the crimson of the chromosphere had been the real color. The eyes burned red and the maw worked as if mouthing vicious oaths, all in red.

'One thing, though,' the crewman went on. 'The guy's transparent. The H-alpha passes right through. We only notice it in the eyes and mouth because the blue he's putting out doesn't swamp it there. But as far as we can tell, his body doesn't block any of it"

'Well, that's your definition of a Ghost if I ever heard one,' Jacob said, and handed the picture back.

Glancing up again, for the hundredth time, he asked, 'Are you sure the solarian is coming back?'

'It always has,' deSilva said. 'It was never satisfied with just one round of insults before.'

Nearby, Martine and Bubbacub rested, ready to put on their helmets if the alien reappeared. Culla, relieved of his duties on the flip-side, lay in a couch, sucking slowly on a liquitube containing a blue beverage. The big eyes were glossy now, and he looked tired.

'I guess we all should lie down,' deSilva said. 'It won't do to break our necks looking up. That's where the Ghost will be when he shows.'

Jacob chose a seat next to Culla, so he could watch Bubbacub and Martine at work.

The two had little time to do much during the first appearance. No sooner had the Sun Ghost taken a position near the zenith than it had changed into the manlike, threatening shape. Martine hardly got her headset adjusted before the creature leered, shook a balled image of a fist, and then faded away.

But Bubbacub had time to check his ka-ngrl. He announced that the Solarian was not using the particularly potent type of psi the machine was designed to detect and counteract. Not then at least. The little Pil left it turned on anyway, just in case.

Jacob rested back in the seat, and touched the button that allowed it to recline slowly until he looked up at the pink, feathery sky overhead.

It was a relief to learn that the pi-ngrli power was not at work here. But if not, what was the reason for the Ghost's strange behavior? Idly, he wondered again if LaRoque might have been right ... that the Solarians knew how to make themselves partly understood because they knew humans from days gone by. Surely men never visited the Sun in the past, but did plasma creatures once go to Earth, and even nurture civilization there? It sounded preposterous, but then, so did Sundiver.

Another thought: If LaRoque was not responsible for the destruction of Jeff's ship, then the Ghosts might be capable of killing them all at any time.

If so, Jacob hoped the journalist-astronaut was right about the rest of it; that the Solarians would feel more restraint in dealing with humans, Pila, and Kanten than they had toward a chimpanzee.

Jacob considered trying his own hand at telepathy when the creature next appeared. He'd been tested once and found to have no psi talent, despite extraordinary hypnotic and memory skills, but maybe he should try anyway.

A movement to his left caught his eye. Culla, staring at a point in front of him and forty-five degrees to zenith, lifted a deck-mike to his lips.

'Captain,' he said, 'I believe it ish coming back.' The Pring's voice echoed around the ship. 'Try angles 120 by 30 degrees.'

Culla put the mike down. The flexible cord drew it back into a slot, next to his slender right hand and the now-empty beverage tube.

The red haze darkened briefly as a wisp of darker gas passed the ship. Then the Ghost was back, still small with distance but getting bigger as it approached.

It was brighter this time, and more crisp around the edges. Soon, its blueness was almost painful to look at.

It came once again as a stick figure of a man, the eyes and mouth glowing like coals as it hovered, halfway up to zenith.

For several long minutes it stayed there, doing nothing. The figure was definitely malevolent. He could feel it! Dr Martine's cursing brought him around, and he realized that he had been holding his breath.

'Damn it!' she tore off her helmet 'There's so much noise! One moment I think I'm onto something ... a touch here and there ... and then it's gone!'

'Do not bo-ther,' Bubbacub said. The clipped voice came from the Vodor, now lying on the deck next to the little Pil. Bubbacub had his own helmet on and stared intently with small black eyes at the Ghost. 'Hu-mans do not have the psi they use. Your attempt, in fact, does cause them pain and some of their anger.'

Jacob swallowed quickly. 'You're in touch with them?' he and Martine asked almost at once.

'Yes,' the mechanical voice said. 'Do not bo-ther me.' Bubbacub's eyes closed. 'Tell me if it moves. Only if it moves!' After that they could get nothing from him.

What's he saying to it? Jacob wondered. He looked at the apparition. What can one say to a creature like that?

Suddenly, the Solarian began to wave its 'hands' and move its 'mouth.' This time its features were more clear. There was none of the image warping they had seen at its first appearance. The creature must have learned to handle the stasis screens. One more example of its ability to adapt. Jacob didn't want to think about what that implied about the safety of the ship.

A flash of color drew Jacob's attention to the left He groped on the panel next to him, then pulled up his deck-mike and switched it to personal.

'Helene, look at about one eight by sixty-five. I think we've got more company.'

'Yes,' deSilva's voice quietly filled the area of the couch occupied by his head. 'I see it. It seems to be in its standard form. Let's see what it does.'

The second Ghost approached, hesitantly, from the left. Its rippling, amorphous form was like a patch of oil on the surface of the ocean. Its shape was nothing like a man's.

Dr Martine drew her breath in sharply when she saw the intruder and started to pull her helmet on.

'Do you think we should arouse Bubbacub?' he asked quickly.

She thought for a moment, then glanced up at the first Solarian. It still waved its 'arms' but it hadn't changed positions. Nor had Bubbacub. 'He said to tell him if it moves,' she said.

She looked up eagerly at the newcomer. 'Maybe I should work on this new one and let him go on with the first one undisturbed.'

Jacob wasn't sure. So far Bubbacub was the only one to come up with anything positive. Martine's motive for not informing him of the second Solarian was suspect. Was she envious of the Pil's success?

Oh well, Jacob shrugged, E.T.s hate to be interrupted anyway.

The newcomer approached cautiously, in short fits and starts, toward where its larger and brighter cousin performed its impersonation of an angry man.

Jacob glanced at Culla.

Should I tell him at least? He seems so intent on watching the first ghost. Why hasn't Helene made an announcement? And where's Fagin? I hope he's not missing this.

Somewhere above there was a flash. Culla stirred.

Jacob looked up. The newcomer was gone. The first Ghost slowly shrank back and faded away.

'What happened?' Jacob asked. 'I only turned away for a second . . .'

'I don't know, Friend-Jacob! I wash watching, to see if the being'sh visual behavior might betray some cluesh to itsh nature, when suddenly a shecond one came. The first one attacked the shecond with a bursht of light, and made it depart Then it too shtarted to leave!'

'You should have told me when new one came,' Bubbacub said. He was on his feet, the Vodor around his neck once more. 'No matter. I know all I need to know. I now re-port to hu-man deSilva.'

He turned and left. Jacob scrambled to his feet to follow.

Fagin awaited them, near deSilva and the Pilot Board. 'Did you see it?' Jacob whispered.

'Yes, I had a good view. I am eager to hear what our dear esteemed friend learned.'

With a theatrical wave of his arm, Bubbacub asked everyone to listen in.

'It said that it is old. I be-lieve it. It is ver-y old race.'

Yes, Jacob thought. That's the first thing Bubbacub would find out.

'The Sol-ar-ians say that they killed the chimp. LaRoque killed him too. They will start to kill hu-mans also, if they do not leave for-ever.'

'What?' deSilva cried. 'What are you talking about? How could LaRoque and the Ghosts be responsible!'

'Re-main calm, I urge you,' the voice of the Pil, moderated by the Vodor, carried a tone of threat. 'The Sol-ar-ian told me that they caused the man to do the thing. They gave him his rage. They gave him a need to kill. They gave him the truth as well.'

Jacob finished summarizing Bubbacub's remarks to Dr Martine.

'... Then he finished by saying that there was only one way that the Ghosts could have influenced LaRoque from such a distance. And if they used that method it explained the lack of Library references. Anywhere anyone uses that power is taboo, closed off. Bubbacub wants us to stick around just long enough to check and then get the hell out of here.'

'What power?' Martine asked. She sat with the crude Earth psi helmet in her lap. Nearby Culla listened in, another slender liquitube between his lips.

'It's not pi-ngrli. That's used sometimes legally. Besides, it can't reach that far and he couldn't find any trace of it anyway. No, I think Bubbacub plans to use that stonelike thing.'

'The Lethani relic?'

'Yes.'

Martine shook her head. She looked down and fiddled with a knob on her helmet.

'It's so complicated. I don't understand it at all. Nothing's gone right ever since we got back to Mercury. No one is what he appears to be.'

'What do you mean?'

The parapsychologist paused, then shrugged.

'Never be sure about anyone ... I was so sure that Peter's silly pique with Jeffrey was both genuine and harmless. Now I find that it was artificially induced and deadly. And he was right I guess, about the Solarians, too. Only it wasn't his idea, it was theirs.'

'Do you think they really are our long lost Patrons?'

'Who knows?' she said. 'If it's true, it's a tragedy that we can't ever come back here again to talk to them.'

'Then you accept Bubbacub's story without reservations?'

'Yes, of course! He's the only one who's ever made contact and besides, I know him. Bubbacub would never mislead us. Truth is his life's work!'

But Jacob knew, now, of whom she spoke when she said 'never be sure you know anyone.' Dr Martine was terrified.

'Are you sure that Bubbacub was the only one to make any sort of contact?'

Her eyes widened, then she looked away. 'He seems to be the only one with the ability.'

'Then why did you stay behind with your helmet on, when Bubbacub called us together for his report?'

'I don't have to take a cross-examination from you!' she answered hotly. 'If it's any of your business, I stayed to try once more. I was jealous of his success and wanted another go at it! I failed, of course.'

Jacob was unconvinced. Martine's testiness seemed uncalled for and it was clear she knew more than she was saying.

'Dr Martine,' he said, 'what do you know about a drug called "Warfarin"?'

'You too!' she reddened. 'I told the Base Physician I never heard of it, and I certainly don't know how any got into Dwayne Kepler's medicine. That is, if there ever was any in the first place!'

She turned away. 'I think I'd better rest now, if you don't mind. I want to be awake when the Solarians come back.'

Jacob ignored her hostility; a bit of the toughness of his other self must have leaked out with the suspicion. But it was obvious Martine wouldn't say any more. He rose to his feet. She pointedly ignored him as she lowered her couch.

Culla met him by the refreshment machines. 'You are upshet, Friend-Jacob?'

'Why no, I don't think so. Why do you ask?'

The tall E.T. gazed down at him. He looked tired. The slender shoulders drooped, though the huge eyes were bright.

'I hope you are not taking thish too hard, thish news that Bubbacub hash announced.'

Jacob turned fully from the machines and faced Culla, 'Take what too hard, Culla? His statements are data. That's all. I'd be disappointed if it turned out that Sundiver has to end. And I'll want some way to verify what he says before I'll agree that's necessary ... like at least a Library reference. But other than that my strongest emotion is curiosity.' Jacob shrugged, irritated at the question. His eyes smarted, probably from an overdose of red light.

Culla slowly shook his large round head. 'I think it ish otherwise. Excuse my presumption, but I think you are very dishturbed.'

Jacob felt an instant of hot anger. He almost spoke it, but managed to hold back. 'Again, what are you talking about Culla?' He spoke slowly.

'Jacob, you have done a good job in staying neutral in your species' remarkable internal conflict. But all sophontsh have opinionsh. You are badly hurt to find that Bubbacub made contact where humansh fail. Though you have never expreshed a position on the Origin Question, I know you are not happy to find that humanity did indeed have Patronsh.'

Jacob shrugged again.

'It's true, I'm still not convinced by this story of Solarians uplifting mankind in the dim past and then abandoning us before the job's finished. Neither part makes any sense.'

Jacob rubbed his right temple. He felt a headache coming on. 'And people have been behaving very peculiarly everywhere in this project. Kepler's suffered from some sort of unexplained hysteria and was overly dependent on Martine. LaRoque was more than his usual abrasive self, sometimes self-destructively. And don't forget his alleged sabotage. Then Martine herself turns from an emotional defense of LaRoque to a very strange fear of saying anything that might undermine Bubbacub. It makes me wonder . . .' He paused.

'Perhapsh the Sholarians are responsible for all of thish. If they could make Mishter LaRoque do a murder from so far away, they might have caused other aberrationsh ash well.'

Jacob's hands balled in fists. He looked up at Culla barely able to choke back his anger. The alien's bright eyes were oppressive. He didn't want to be under them.

'Don't interrupt,' he said, tight-lipped, and as calmly as he could.

He could tell that something was wrong. A cloud seemed to surround him. Nothing was very clear but still there was a felt need to say something important. Anything.

He looked quickly around the deck.

Bubbacub and Martine were at their stations again. Both wore their helmets and looked his way. Martine was talking.

The bitch! Probably she's telling the gross arrogant little fool everything I said. Toady!

Helene deSilva stopped by the two while making her rounds, taking their attention away from Culla and Jacob. For a moment he felt better. He wished Culla would go away. It was too bad the fellow had to be put down but a Client must know his place!

DeSilva finished speaking to Bubbacub and Martine, and started to walk toward the refreshment machines. Once again Bubbacub's small black eyes were on him.

Jacob growled. He swiveled away from the beady stare and faced the beverage machine.

Fuck them all. I came here for a drink and that's what I'm going to get. They don't exist anyway!

The machine wavered in front of him. An internal voice was shouting about some sort of emergency but he decided that the voice didn't exist either.

Now this is a strange machine, he thought. I hope it isn't like that sneaky one aboard the *Bradbury*. That one hadn't been friendly at all.

No, this one has a bunch of transparent 3-D buttons that stand out from the others. In fact there are rows and rows of little buttons, all of them standing out in space.

He reached forward to press one at random, then caught himself. Uh-uh. We'll *read* the labels this time!

Now what do I want. Coffee?

The little internal voice was screaming for Gyroade. Yes, that's sensible. A wonderful drink, Gyroade. Not only is it delicious, but it also straightens you out. A perfect drink for a world full of hallucinations.

He had to admit that it might be a good idea to have some at that. Something *did* seem a little fishy. Why was everything going so slowly?

His hand moved like a snail toward the button he wanted. It shifted back and forth a few times but finally he was aimed right for it. He was about to press it when the little voice came back, this time begging him to stop!

Of all the nerve! You give me good advice and then you chicken out. Dammit, who needs you anyway?

He pressed. Time speeded up a little, and he heard the sound of liquid pouring.

Who the hell needs anybody! Damn upstart Culla. Snobby Bubbacub and his fish-cold human consort. Even crazy Fagin ... dragging me away from Earth to this stupid place.

He bent over and pulled the liquitube out of its slot It looked delicious.

Time speeded up now, almost back to normal He already felt better, as if a great pressure was relieved. Antagonisms and hallucinations seemed to fade away. He smiled at Helene deSilva as she approached. Then he turned to smile at Culla.

Later, he thought, I'll apologize for being rude. He raised the tube in a toast.

' ... been hovering around out there, just at the edge of detection,' deSilva was saying. 'We're ready whenever it is so maybe you'd better ...'

'Shtop, Jacob!' Culla shouted.

DeSilva cried out and leaped forward to grab his hand. Culla joined in, adding his own slight strength to pull the tube away from his lips.

Spoilsports, he thought amiably. Show a puny alien and a ninety-year old woman what a mal can do.

He pulled them off one by one, but they kept attacking. The Commandant even tried some nasty disabling shots but he parried them and brought the drink to his face slowly, triumphantly.

A wall broke and the sense of smell he hadn't known he'd lost returned like a steamroller. He coughed once and looked down at the vile concoction in his hand.

It steamed brown and poisonous with lumps and bubbles. He threw it away. Everyone was looking at him. Culla chattered from the floor where he'd been thrown. DeSilva stood up warily. The other humans were gathering around.

He could hear Fagin's concerned whistle coming from some-where. Where *is* Fagin, he thought as he stumbled forward. He made it three steps and then collapsed onto the deck in front of Bubbacub.

He came around slowly. It was difficult because his forehead was so tight. The skin felt stretched like the leather on a drum. But it wasn't dry like leather. It kept getting wet, first with perspiration and then with something else, something cool.

He groaned and brought his hand up. It touched skin, someone else's hand, warm and soft. Female, he could tell by the smell.

Jacob opened his eyes. Dr Martine sat nearby with a washcloth in her brown hand. She smiled and brought out a liquitube to hold to his lips.

For a moment he started, then he bent forward to take a sip. It was lemonade, and it tasted wonderful.

He finished it off while he looked around himself. The couches scattered on the deck were filled with recumbent figures.

He looked up. The sky was almost black!

'We're on our way back,' Martine said.

'How ...' He could feel his larynx hum from disuse. 'How long have I been under?'

'About twelve hours.'

'Was I sedated?'

She nodded. The Perpetual Professional Smile was back. But it didn't seem so put-on now. He brought a hand to his forehead. It still hurt.

'Then I guess I didn't dream it. What was it I tried to drink yes-terday?'

'It was an ammonia compound that we brought along for Bubbacub. It probably wouldn't have killed you. But it would have hurt, a lot.

'Can you tell me why you did it?'

Jacob allowed his head to settle back against the cushion. 'Well ... it seemed like a pretty good idea at the time.'

He shook his head. 'Seriously, I guess something went wrong with me. But I'll be damned if I know what it was.'

'I should have known something was wrong when you started saying strange things about murders and conspiracies,' she nodded. 'It's partly my fault for not recognizing the signs. It's nothing to be ashamed of. I think it's just a case of orientation shock. A Sunship dive can be an awful disorienting experience, in so many ways!'

He rubbed the sleep out of his eyes.

'Well, you're right about that last part for sure. But it just occurred to me that some people are probably thinking I was influenced.'

Martine started, as if surprised to find him so alert so soon.

'Yes,' she said. 'In fact Commandant deSilva thought it was the Ghost's work. She said they were probably demonstrating their psi powers to prove their point. She even started talking about shooting back. The theory has merits but I prefer my own.'

'That I went crazy?'

'Oh no, not at all! Just disoriented and confused! Culla said you were behaving ... abnormally in the minutes before your ... accident. That pins my own observations ...'

'Yes,' Jacob nodded. 'I owe Culla a real apology ... Ohmigosh! He wasn't hurt, was he? Or Helene?' He started to rise.

Martine pushed him back. 'No, no, everyone is okay. Don't worry. I'm sure the only concern anyone had was for your welfare.'

Jacob dropped back. He looked down at the empty liquitube. 'May I have another?'

'Sure. I'll be right back.'

Martine left him alone. He could hear her soft footsteps move toward the refreshment center ... the place where the 'accident' occurred. He winced as he thought about it. He felt shame mixed with disgust. But most of all there was the burning question, WHY?

Somewhere behind him two people spoke softly. Dr Martine must have met somebody at the R.C.

Jacob knew that sooner or later he would have to make a dive that made Sundiver seem tame. That trance would be a lulu, but it would have to be taken if the truth was to come out. The only question was when? Now, when it might split his mind wide open? Or back on Earth, in the presence of therapists at the Center, but where the answers might do him, Sundiver and his job no good at all?

Martine came back. She dropped down beside him and offered a full liquitube. Helene deSilva was with her. The Commandant sat next to the parapsychologist.

He spent several minutes assuring her that he was all right. She brushed his apologies aside.

'I had no idea you were so good at U.C., Jacob,' she said.

'U.C.?'

'Unarmed combat. I'm pretty good, though I'm rusty I admit. But you're better. We found out in the surest way, a fight between parties each anxious to disable the other without pain or harm. It's awful hard to do but you're an expert.'

He never would have thought it possible to blush at that sort of compliment, but Jacob could feel himself redden.

'Thanks. It's hard to remember but it seems you were pretty tricky, too.'

They looked at each other in complete understanding and grinned.

Martine looked from one to the other. She cleared her throat. 'I don't think Mr Demwa should spend too much time talking. A shock like that calls for plenty of rest.'

'I just want to know a few things, Doctor, then I'll cooperate. First of all, where's Fagin? I don't see him anywhere.'

'Kant Fagin is on flip-side,' deSilva said. 'He's taking nourishment.'

'He was very concerned about you. I'm sure he'll be glad to know you're okay,' Martine said.

Jacob relaxed. For some reason he had been worried about Fagin's safety.

'Now tell me what happened after I passed out.'

Martine and deSilva shared a glance. Then deSilva shrugged.

'We had another visitation,' she said. 'It took quite a while. For several hours the Solarian just fluttered around at the edge of visibility. We'd left the toroid herd far behind and with it all of its fellows.

'It's a good thing it waited though. We were in an uproar for a while because of, well . . . '

'Because of my attention-grabbing performance,' Jacob sighed. 'But did anyone try to make contact while it flittered out there?'

DeSilva looked at Martine. The doctor shook her head very slightly.

'Nothing much was done then,' the Commandant went on hurriedly. 'We were still pretty upset. But then, at about fourteen hundred, it disappeared. It came back a while later in its . . . . "threatening mode."'

Jacob let the interchange between the two women pass. But a thought suddenly occurred to him.

'Say, are you all positive that they were the same Ghosts at all?

Maybe the "normal" and "threatening" modes are actually two different species!'

Martine looked blank for a moment. 'That could explain ...' Then she shut up.

'Uh, we aren't calling them Ghosts anymore,' deSilva said. 'Bubbacub says they don't like it.'

Jacob felt a moment of irritation, but he suppressed it quickly lest either woman notice it. This conversation wasn't getting them anywhere!

'So what happened when it came in its threatening mode?'

DeSilva frowned.

'Bubbacub talked with it for a while. Then he got angry and made it go away.'

'He what?'

'He tried reasoning with it. Quoted the book on Patron-Client rights. Promised trade, even. It just kept making threats. Said it would send psi messages to Earth and cause disaster of some undescribed sort.

'Finally Bubbacub called it quits. He had everybody lie down. Then he pulled out that lump of iron and crystal he was so secretive about. He ordered everyone to cover their eyes, then said some mumbo jumbo and set the darn thing off!'

'What did it do?'

She shrugged again.

'The Progenitors only know, Jacob. There was a dazzling light, a feeling of pressure in the ears ... and when we next looked, the Solarian was gone!

'Not only that! We went back to where we thought we'd left the toroid herd. It was gone too. There wasn't a living thing in sight!'

'Nothing at all?' He thought about the beautiful toruses and their bright multicolored masters.

'Nothing,' Martine said. 'Everything had been scared away. Bubbacub assured us that they hadn't been harmed.'

Jacob felt numb. 'Well, then at least there's protection now. We can bargain with the Solarians from a position of strength.'

DeSilva shook her head sadly.

'Bubbacub says there can be no negotiation. They're evil, Jacob. They'll kill us now, if they can.'

'But ...'

'And we can't count on Bubbacub anymore. He told the Solarians there'd be vengeance if Earth was ever harmed. But other than that he won't help. The relic goes back to Pila.'

She looked down at the deck. Her voice grew husky.

'Sundiver is finished.'

PART VI

The measure of (mental) health is flexibility (not comparison to some 'norm'), the freedom to learn from experience ... to be influenced by reasonable arguments... and the appeal to the emotions ... and especially the freedom to cease when sated. The essence of illness is the freezing of behavior into unalterable and insatiable patterns.

LAWRENCE KUBIE

17

SHADOW

The workbench was bare, each tool of its accustomed clutter hanging in uncomfortable disuse from the appropriate hook on the wall. The tools were clean. The scored and pitted tabletop shone under a new layer of wax.

The stack of partly disassembled instruments which Jacob had shoved aside lay on the floor accusingly, like the chief mechanic, who had watched him in idle suspicion as he appropriated the workbench. Jacob didn't care. Despite, or perhaps because of the fiasco aboard the Sunship, no one objected when he decided to continue his own studies. The workbench was a large and convenient space for him to use, and nobody else wanted it right now. Besides, it made it less likely he'd be found by Millie Martine.

In an apse of the huge Sunship Cavern, Jacob could see a sliver of the giant silvery ship, only partly cut off from view by the rock wall. Far overhead the wall arched into a mist of condensation.

He sat on a high stool in front of the bench. Jacob drew 'Zwicky Choiceboxes' on two sheets of paper and laid them out on the table. The pink sheets had a yes or no question written on each, representing alternate possible morphological realities.

The one on the left read: B IS RIGHT ABOUT S-GHOSTS. YES (I)/NO(II).

The other sheet was even more difficult to look at: I HAVE FLIPPED OUT, YES(III)/NO(IV).

Jacob couldn't let anyone else's judgment sway him on these questions. That was why he'd avoided Martine and the others since the return to Mercury. Other than paying a courtesy call on the recuperating Dr Kepler, he had become a hermit.

The question on the left concerned Jacob's job, though he couldn't exclude a linkage with the question on the right.

The question on the right would be difficult. All emotion would have to be put aside to arrive at the right answer to that one.

He placed a sheet with the Roman numeral I just below the question on the left, listing the evidence that Bubbacub's story was correct.

BOX I: B's STORY TRUE.

It made a tidy list. First of all there was the neat self-consistency of the Pil's explanation for the Sun Ghost's behavior. It had been known all along that the creatures used some type of psi. The threatening, man-shaped apparitions implied knowledge of man and an unfriendly inclination. 'Only' a chimpanzee had been killed, and only Bubbacub could demonstrate successful communication with the Solarians. All this fit in with LaRoque's story – the one supposedly implanted in his mind by the creatures.

The most impressive achievement, one that took place while Jacob was unconscious aboard the Sunship, was Bubbacub's feat with the Lethani relic. It was proof that Bubbacub had some contact with the Sun Ghosts.

To drive one Ghost off with a flash of light might be plausible (although Jacob was at a loss as to how a being drifting in the brilliant chromosphere could detect anything from the dim interior of a Sunship), but the dispersal of the entire herd of magnetovores and herdsmen implied that some powerful force (psi?) must have been the Pil's means.

Every one of these elements would have to be re-examined in the course of Jacob's morphological analysis. But on the face of it, Jacob had to admit that box number I looked true.

Number II would be a headache, for it assumed the opposite of the proposition in Box I.

BOX II: B's STORY WRONG – (IIA) HE'S MISTAKEN/(IIB) HE'S LYING.

IIA didn't give Jacob any ideas. Bubbacub seemed too sure, too confident. Of course, he would have been fooled by the *Ghosts themselves* ... Jacob scribbled a note to that effect and put it in position IIA. It was actually a very important possibility, but Jacob couldn't think of any way to prove or disprove it short of making more dives. And the political situation made more dives impossible.

Bubbacub, supported by Martine, insisted that any further expeditions would be pointless and probably fatal as well, without the Pil and his Lethani relic along. Oddly enough, Dr Kepler didn't fight them. Indeed, it was at his orders that the Sunship was dry-docked, normal maintenance suspended, and even data reduction halted while he conferred with Earth.

Kepler's motives puzzled Jacob. For several minutes he stared down at a sheet that said: SIDE ISSUE – KEPLER? Finally he tossed it over on the stack of disassembled equipment, with a curse. Kepler obviously had political reasons for wanting Sundiver's closure to be on Bubbacub's head. Jacob was disappointed in the man. He turned to sheet IIB.

It was appealing to think that Bubbacub was lying. Jacob could no longer pretend any affection for the little Library Representative. He recognized his own personal bias. Jacob wanted IIB to be true.

Certainly Bubbacub had a *motive* for lying. The failure of the Library to come up with a reference on solar-type life-forms was an embarrassment to him. The Pil also resented totally independent research by a 'wolfling' race. Both problems would be eliminated if Sundiver was cut off in a manner that boosted the stature of ancient science.

But to hypothesize that Bubbacub lied brought up a whole raft of problems. First, how much of the story was a lie? Obviously the trick with the Lethani relic was genuine. But where else could one draw the line?

And if Bubbacub lied he had to be awfully sure that he wouldn't get caught. The Galactic Institutes, especially the Library, relied on a reputation of absolute honesty. They'd have to fry Bubbacub alive if he was found out.

Box IIB had all of the meat in it. It looked hopeless, but somehow Jacob would have to show that IIB was true or Sundiver was finished.

This was going to be complicated. Any theory that had Bubbacub lying would have to explain Jeffrey's death, LaRoque's anomalous status and behavior, the Sun Ghost's threatening behavior ...

Jacob scribbled a note and tossed it onto sheet IIB.

SIDE NOTE: *TWO TYPES OF SUN GHOSTS?* He remembered the remark that no one had ever actually seen a 'normal' Sun Ghost turn into the semi-transparent variety that did the threat pantomimes.

Another thought came to him.

SIDE NOTE: CULLA'S THEORY THAT SOLARIAN'S PSI EXPLAINS NOT ONLY LR BUT OTHER STRANGE BEHAVIOR AS WELL.

Jacob was thinking of Martine and Kepler when he wrote that down. But after thinking about it he carefully wrote a second copy of the same remark and tossed it over on the sheet labeled I HAVE FLIPPED OUT – NO(IV).

The question of his own personal sanity took courage to face. Methodically he listed the evidence that something was wrong, under sheet number III.

1. BLINDING 'LIGHT' BACK AT BAJA. The trance he'd entered just before the meeting at the Information Center was the last deep one he'd had. He had been awakened from it by an apparent psychological artifact – a 'blueness' that cut through his hypnotic state like a searchlight But whatever warning his subconscious must have been sending was interrupted when Culla approached.

2. UNCONTROLLED USE OF MR HYDE. Jacob knew that the bifurcation of his mind into normal and abnormal parts was a

temporary solution at best to a long-range problem. A couple of hundred years ago his state would have been diagnosed schizophrenic. But hypnotic transaction, supposedly, would allow his divided halves to reassemble peacefully under the guidance of his dominant personality. The occasions in which his feral other half pushed through or took control would logically be when it was needed ... when Jacob *had* to revert to the cold, hard, supremely confident meddler he once had been.

Jacob hadn't been worried, earlier, about his other side's exploits, so much as embarrassed. For instance, it was logical enough to pilfer samples of Dr Kepler's pharmacopoeia on the *Bradbury*, given what he'd seen so far, although other means to the same ends might have been preferable.

But some of the things he'd said aboard the Sunship to Dr Martine – they implied either a great deal of justified suspicion churning around in his unconscious, or very deep problems down below.

3. BEHAVIOR ON SUNSHIP: ATTEMPTED SUICIDE? That one hurt less than he thought it would, when he wrote it. Jacob felt disconcerted by the episode. But strangely, he felt more angry than ashamed, as if he had been made to act like a fool by somebody else.

Of course that could mean anything, including frantic self-justification, but it didn't feel that way. Jacob felt no internal resistance when he probed that line of reasoning. Only negation.

Number three *could* have been part of an overall pattern of mental decay. Or it might have been an isolated case of disorientation, as diagnosed by Dr Martine (who since landing had been chasing him all over the base in order to get him into therapy). Or it could have been induced by the something external, as he had already considered.

Jacob pushed back from the workbench. This would take time. The only way to get anything done would be to take frequent breaks and let ideas filter up from the unconscious, the very unconscious he was investigating.

Well, that wasn't the *only* way, but until he had solved the question of his own sanity he wasn't about to try the other means.

Jacob stepped back and began to move his body slowly in the pattern of relaxing positions known as Tai Chi Chuan. The vertebrae in his back crackled from sitting awkwardly on the stool. He stretched and allowed energy to return to parts of his body that had fallen asleep.

The light jacket he wore bound his shoulders. He stopped the routine and took it off.

There was a coat rack by the chief mechanic's office, across the maintenance shop and near the drinking fountain. Jacob walked over to the rack, lightly, on the balls of his feet, feeling taut and energized by the Tai Chi.

The chief mechanic nodded grumpily when Jacob passed by; the man was obviously unhappy. He sat behind his desk in the foam-paneled office, wearing an expression Jacob had seen a lot of since coming back, especially among the lower echelons. The reminder pricked Jacob's bubble.

As he bent over the drinking fountain, Jacob heard a clattering sound. He lifted his head as it repeated, coming from the direction of the ship. Half of the ship was now visible from where he stood. As he walked to the corner of the rock wall, the rest came slowly into view.

Slowly, the wedge-shaped door of the Sunship descended. Culla and Bubbacub waited at the bottom, holding a long cylindrical machine between them. Jacob ducked behind the rock wall. Now what are those two doing?

He heard the catwalk extend from the rim of the Sunship's deck, then the sound of the Pil and Pring pulling the machine up into the ship.

Jacob rested his back against the rock wall and shook his head. This was too much. If he was given just one more mystery he'd probably *really* flip out ... that is if he hadn't already.

It sounded like an air compressor was being used inside the ship, or a vacuum cleaner. Clattering and sliding and occasional squeaky Pilan oaths implied that the machine was being dragged all over the interior of the ship.

Jacob gave in to temptation. Bubbacub and Culla were inside the ship and no one else was in sight.

In any event there was probably nothing to be lost by being caught spying but the rest of his reputation.

He bounded up the springy catwalk in a few powerful steps. Near the top of the ramp he flattened and looked inside.

The machine *was* a vacuum cleaner. Bubbacub pulled it, his back to Jacob, as Culla manipulated the long rigid suction member at the end of its flexible hose. The Pring shook his head slowly, his dentures chattering softly. Bubbacub shot off a series of sharp yaps at his Client and the chattering increased, but Culla worked faster.

This was most queer and disturbing. Culla was apparently vacuuming the space between the deck and the curving ship's wall! Nothing *existed* there but the force fields that held the deck in place!

Culla and Bubbacub disappeared around the central dome as they made their way around the rim. At any moment they'd be coming around the other side and facing him this time. Jacob slid back down the ramp a few feet, then descended the rest of the way on foot. He walked back to the apse and sat again on the stool in front of the slips of paper.

If there was only time! If the central dome had been bigger or Bubbacub's work slower, he might have found a way to get down into that force-field gap and get a sample of whatever they were collecting. Jacob shuddered at the thought but it would have been worth a try.

Or even a picture of Culla and Bubbacub at work! But where could he get a camera in the few minutes he had left?

There was no way to prove that Bubbacub was up to mischief, but Jacob decided that theory IIB had received a big boost On a piece of paper he scribbled: B'S DUST OR WHATEVER ... HALLUCINOGEN RELEASED ON BOARD SHIP? He threw it on that pile, then hurried over to the chief mechanic's office.

The man grumbled when Jacob asked him to come along. He claimed that he had to sit by his phone and said he couldn't imagine where a regular still camera could be found nearby. Jacob thought the fellow was lying but he had no time to argue. He had to get to a phone.

There was one set on the wall near the corner where he watched Culla and Bubbacub climb the ramp. But as he raised it he wondered who he could call and what he could say.

Hello, Dr Kepler? Remember me, Jacob Demwa? The guy who tried to kill himself on one of your Sunships? Yeah ... well I'd like you to come down here and watch Pil Bubbacub do spring cleaning ...

No, that wouldn't do. By the time anyone got down here Culla and Bubbacub would be gone and his call would be another item on his list of public aberrations.

That thought struck Jacob.

Did I just imagine the whole thing? There was no sound of a vacuum cleaner now. Only silence. The whole thing was so damnably symbolic anyway ...

From around the corner came a squeal, Pilan curses, and a clattering of falling machinery. Jacob closed his eyes for a moment. The sound was beautiful. He risked a peek around the edge.

Bubbacub stood at the bottom of the ramp holding one end of the vacuum cleaner, the bristles around his eyes jutting starkly on end, and his fur stuck out in a ruff around his collar. The Pil glared at Culla, who fumbled with the catch of the machine's dust bag. A small pile of red powder leaked from the opening.

Bubbacub snorted in disgust as Culla scooped handfuls of powder together and then turned the reassembled machine on the pile. Jacob was sure a handful went, instead of to the pile, into the pocket of Culla's silvery tunic.

Bubbacub kicked the remaining dust around until it blended with the floor. Then, after a furtive glance on all sides that sent Jacob's head jetting back behind the wall, he barked a quick command and led Culla back to the elevators.

When he returned to the workbench, Jacob found the chief mechanic looking over the scattered sheets of his morphological analysis. The man looked up when he approached.

'What was that all about?' He pointed his chin toward the Sunship.

'Oh, nothing,' Jacob answered. He chewed on his cheek gently for a moment. 'Just some Eatees messing around with the ship.'

'With the ship?' The chief mechanic came erect. 'Is that what you were jabbering about before? Why the hell didn't you say so!?'

'Wait, hold up!' Jacob held the man's arm as he turned to hurry to the Sunship cradle. 'It's too late, they're gone. Besides, figuring out what they're up to will take more than just catching them in the act of doing something strange. Strangeness is what Eatees are best at anyway.'

The engineer looked at Jacob as if for the first time. 'Yeah,' he said slowly. 'You have a point. But maybe now you'd better tell me what you saw.'

Jacob shrugged and told the whole story, from hearing the sound of the hatch opening to the comedy of the spilled powder.

'I don't get it,' the chief mechanic scratched his head.

'Well, don't worry about it. Like I said, it'll take more than one clue to get this buttock-beeper placed.'

Jacob sat again on the stool and began scribbling carefully on several sheets.

C. HAS SAMPLE OF PWDR ... WHY? DANGEROUS TO ASK HIM TO SHARE?

IS C. WILLING ACCOMPLICE? FOR HOW LONG?

GET A SAMPLE!!!

'Hey, what are you doing here, anyway?' the chief mechanic asked.

'I'm chasing clues.'

After a moment of silence the man tapped the sheets at the far right of the table. 'Boy I couldn't be so coldblooded about it if I thought *I* was going nuts! What did it feel like? I mean when you went swacko and tried to drink poison?'

Jacob raised his eyes from his writing. There was an image. A gestalt. The smell of ammonia filled his nostrils and a powerful throbbing beat at his temples. It felt as if he had spent hours under the glare of an inquisitor's spotlight.

He remembered the image vividly. The last thing he saw before he collapsed was Bubbacub's face. The small black eyes stared at him below the brow of the psi helmet. Alone of those aboard, the Pil watched impassively as Jacob lurched forward and fell to the deck senseless, a few feet away.

The thought made Jacob grow cold. He started to write it down but then stopped. This was too big. He jotted a short note in pidgin dolphin-trinary and threw it on pile IV.

'I'm sorry,' he looked up at the chief engineer. 'Were you saying something?'

The engineer shook his head.

'Oh, it was none of my business anyway. I shouldn't have butted my nose in. I was just curious what you were doing here.'

The man paused for a moment.

'Y're trying to save the project, aren't you?' he finally asked.

'Yes, I am.'

'Then you must be the only one of the hotshots who is,' he said bitterly. 'I'm sorry I growled at you earlier. I'll stay out of your way so you can work.' He started to move away.

Jacob thought for a moment. 'Would you like to help?' he asked.

The man turned. 'What do you need?'

Jacob smiled. 'Well, for starters I could use a broom and a dust-pan.'

'Coming right up!' The chief mechanic hurried away.

Jacob drummed his fingers on the tabletop for a moment. Then he gathered the scattered sheets and stuffed them back into his pocket.

18

FOCUS

'The director said no one was supposed to go in there, you know.'

Jacob looked up from his work. 'Gosh, chief,' he grinned savagely, 'I didn't know that! I'm just trying to pick this lock for my health!'

The other man shifted nervously where he stood, and mumbled about never having expected to be involved in a burglary.

Jacob rocked back. The room swayed and he touched the plastic leg of the table next to him for balance. In the dim light of the photo lab it was hard to see straight, especially after twenty minutes of close work with tiny tools.

'I've told you before, Donaldson,' he said slowly. 'We have no choice. What have we that we can show anyone? A patch of dust and a cockeyed theory? Use your head. We're caught TwoTwo as it is. They won't let us near the evidence because we haven't the evidence to prove we need it!'

Jacob rubbed at the muscles at the back of his neck. 'No, we're going to have to do this ourselves ... that is, if you want to hang around ...'

The chief mechanic grunted. 'You know I'll stay.' His tone was hurt.

'Okay, okay.' Jacob nodded. 'Apologies. Now will you please hand me that small tool over there? No, the one with the hook on the end. That's right.

'Now why don't you go over to the outer door and keep a lookout? Give me some time to clean up if someone comes. And watch out for that trip-fall!'

Donaldson moved away a small distance, but he stayed to watch as Jacob went back to work. He rested against the cool side of one of the doorjambs and wiped perspiration from his cheeks and eyebrows.

Demwa seemed rational and reasonable, but the wild path his imagination had taken in the last few hours left Donaldson dizzy.

The worst part was that it all hung together so well. It was exciting, this hunt for clues. And what he'd found out before meeting Demwa here supported the man's story. But it was also frightening. There was always the chance that the guy really was crazy, in spite of the consistency of his arguments.

Donaldson sighed. He turned away from the tiny sounds of scraping metal and the nodding of Jacob's bushy head, and walked slowly toward the outer door of the photo lab.

It didn't really matter. Something was rotten under Mercury. If someone didn't act soon there wouldn't be any more Sunships.

A simple tumbler lock for a ridged and slotted key. Nothing could be easier. In fact, Jacob could not have helped noticing that Mercury had few modern locks. Electronics required shielding on a planet where the magnetosheath grazed across the bare unprotected surface. It wasn't very expensive to shield but still someone must have thought such an expenditure ridiculous for locks. Who would want to break into the Inner Photo Lab anyway? And who would know *how*?

Jacob knew how. But that didn't appear to be helping. Somehow it didn't feel right. The tools weren't speaking to him. He felt no continuity from his hands to the metal.

At this rate it could take all night.

Let me do it.

Jacob gritted his teeth and slowly pulled the rake out of the lock. He laid it down.

Stop personifying, he thought You're nothing but a set of asocial habits I've put under hypnotic lock for a while. If you keep acting like a separate personality you'll get us ... me into a full-blown schizophrenic state!

Now look who's personifying.

Jacob smiled.

I shouldn't be here. I should have stayed home for the full three years and finished my mental house-cleaning in peace and quiet. The behavior patterns I wanted ... *needed* to keep submerged are now needed wide awake, by my job.

Then why not use them?

When this mental arrangement was set up it wasn't supposed to be rigid. That sort of suppression would *really* lead to trouble! The amoral, cold-blooded, savant qualities leaked out in a steady stream, though usually under complete control. It had been intended that they be available in an emergency.

The suppression and personification by which he'd reacted to that stream lately may have *caused* some of his problem. His sinister half was to *sleep* as he worked off the trauma of Tarda ... not be severed off at the wrist.

Then let me do it.

Jacob picked another rake and rolled it in his fingers. The light slip of tool steel felt smooth, cool.

Shut up. You're not a person, just a talent unfortunately linked to a neurosis ... like a well-trained singing voice that can only be used while standing naked on a stage.

Fine. Use the talent. The door could be open by now!

Jacob carefully laid his tools down and shuffled forward until his forehead rested against the door. Should I? What if I *did* flip out on the Sunship? My theory could be wrong. And then there's that blue flash back at Baja. Can I risk opening up if something's gone loose inside?

Weak from indecision, he felt the trance begin to fall. With an effort he stopped it, but then, with a mental shrug, allowed it to proceed. At the count of seven a barrier of fear blocked him. It was a familiar barrier. It felt like the edge of a precipice. He consciously brushed it aside and continued down.

At twelve he commanded: This Shall Be Temporary. He felt assent.

The backcount was done in an instant. He opened his eyes. A tingle wandered down the length of his arms and entered his fingers, suspiciously, like a dog returning, sniffing, to an old home.

So far so good, Jacob thought. I feel no less ethical. No less 'me.' My hands don't feel as if they're controlled by an alien force . . . only more alive.

The lockpicking tools weren't cool when he picked them up. They felt warm, like extensions of his hands. The rake slid sensuously into the lock and caressed the tumblers as the torque bar pulled. One after another tiny click telegraphed along the metal. Then the door was open.

'You did it!' Donaldson's surprise hurt a little.

'Of course,' was all he said. It was reassuringly easy to squelch the insulting reply that popped into his mind. So far so good. The genie seemed benign. Jacob swung the door wide and entered.

Filing cabinets lined the left wall of the narrow room. Along the other wall a low table supported a row of photoanalysis machines. At the far end an open door led to the unlit and seldom used chemical darkroom.

Jacob began at one end of the row of filing cabinets, bending to look at labels. Donaldson worked along the bench. It wasn't long before the chief mechanic said, 'I found them!' He pointed to an open box, next to a viewing machine halfway down the table.

Each spool was held in a padded niche, its sides inscribed with the date and times covered and a code for the instrument that made the recording. At least a dozen niches were empty.

Jacob held several cassettes to the light. Then he turned to Donaldson.

'Someone's been here first and pilfered every cassette we wanted.'

'Stolen? . . . But how!'

Jacob shrugged. 'Maybe the way we did it, by breaking and entry. Or maybe they had a key. All we know is that the final spool for each recording device is missing.'

They stood for a moment in dark silence.

'Then we haven't got any proof at all,' Donaldson said.

'Not unless we can track down the missing spools.'

'You mean we should bust into Bubbacub's rooms too? . . . I don't know. If you ask me, those data are burned by now. Why would he keep them around?

'No, I suggest we sneak out of here and let Dr Kepler or Dr deSilva discover the fact that they're missing by themselves. It's not much but they may see it as slight evidence to support our story.'

Jacob hesitated. Then he nodded.

'Let me see your hands,' Jacob said.

Donaldson presented his palms up. The thin coating of flex-plastic was intact. They were probably safe from chemical and fingerprint tracing, then.

'Okay,' he said. 'Let's put everything back in its place, as exactly as you can remember it. Don't disturb anything you haven't already touched. Then we'll leave.'

Donaldson turned to comply but then there was a crash as something fell in the Outer Photo Lab. The sound carried, muffled through the door.

The trap Jacob had set by the hall door had gone off. Someone was in the outer lab. Their escape route was blocked!

The two men hurried back into the dim doorway of the dark-room. They made it around the corner of the light-trap maze just as the sound of a metal key scratching at the lock carried across the narrow room.

Jacob heard the door sigh open slowly, over the subjective roar of his own rapid breathing. He patted the pockets of his overalls. Half of his burglar tools were out there, on top of one of the filing cabinets.

Fortunately his dentist's mirror wasn't. It was still in his breast-pocket case.

The intruder's footsteps clicked softly in the room a few feet away. Jacob carefully weighed the hazards against the potential benefits and then slowly eased the mirror out. He knelt and poked the round, shiny working end into the threshold, a few inches above the floor.

Dr Martine stooped in front of a filing cabinet, sorting through a ring of metal keys. Once, she shot a furtive glance toward the outer door. She looked agitated, though it was hard to tell from the image in the tiny mirror, jiggling on the floor two meters from her feet.

Jacob felt Chief Donaldson leaning over, above and behind him, trying to peek past the doorway. Irritated, he tried to wave the man back, but Donaldson overbalanced instead. His left hand shot out for support and landed on Jacob's back.

'Oof!' The air expelled from Jacob's lungs as the chief engineer's weight fell on him. His teeth jarred as he took the full force through his stiffened left arm. Somehow he kept them both from collapsing into the doorway, but the mirror fell out of his hand and onto the floor with a tiny clink.

Donaldson slid backward into the dimness, breathing heavily – pathetically trying to be quiet. Jacob smiled wryly. Anyone who hadn't heard that debacle had to be deaf.

'Who ... who's there?'

Jacob stood and brushed himself off deliberately. He cast a brief, disdainful glance at Chief Donaldson, who sat glumly and avoided Jacob's eyes.

Quick footsteps receded in the outer room. Jacob stepped out into the doorway.

'Wait a minute, Millie.'

Dr Martine froze midstep at the door. Her shoulders hunched as she turned slowly, her face a mask of fear until she recognized Jacob. Then her dark, patrician features washed deep red.

'What the hell are *you* doing here!'

'Watching you, Millie. An enjoyable pastime usually, but now especially interesting.'

'You were spying on me!' she gasped.

Jacob walked forward, hoping Donaldson would have enough sense to stay hidden. 'Not just you, dear. On everybody. Something is fishy on Mercury, all right. Everyone's whistling a different tuna, and they're all red herrings! I have a feeling you know more than you're telling.'

'I don't know what you are talking about,' Martine said coldly. 'But that's not surprising. You're not rational and you need help ...' She started to back away.

'Perhaps,' Jacob nodded seriously. 'But maybe you will need help explaining your presence here today.'

Martine stiffened. 'I got my key from Dwayne Kepler. What about you!'

'Did you get the key *with* his knowledge?'

Martine blushed and didn't answer.

'There are several data spools missing from the collection taken last dive ... all covering the period when Bubbacub did his trick with the Lethani relic. You wouldn't happen to know where they are, would you?'

Martine stared at Jacob.

'You're kidding! But who ... ? No ...' She shook her head slowly, confused.

'*Did* you take them?'

'No!'

'Then who did?'

'I don't know. How should *I* know? What business have you questioning ...'

'I could call Helene deSilva right now,' Jacob rumbled ominously. 'I could have just arrived to find this door open with you inside and the key with your prints on it in your pouch. She'd search and find the spools missing and there you'd be. You've been covering for someone and I have some independent evidence who. If you don't come out with all you know right now, I swear you're going to take the fall, with or without your friend. You know as well as I that the crew at this base is just itching for someone to burn.'

Martine wavered. Her hand went to her head.

'I don't ... I don't know ...'

Jacob maneuvered her into a chair. Then he closed and locked the door.

Hey, take it easy, a part of him said. He closed his eyes for a moment and counted to ten. Slowly, a brutal itch in Jacob's hands ebbed.

Martine held her face in her hands. Jacob caught a glimpse of Donaldson, peeking around the darkroom door. He jerked his hand and the chief engineer's head darted out of sight.

Jacob pulled open the filing cabinet the woman had been examining.

Aha. Here it is.

He picked up the steno-camera and carried it back to the bench, plugged the readout jack into one of the viewers and turned both machines on.

Most of the material was quite uninteresting, LaRoque's notes on events between the landing on Mercury and the morning that he took the camera to the Sunship Cavern, just before the fateful tour of Jeffrey's ship. Jacob ignored the audio portion. LaRoque tended to be even more wordy in leaving notes to himself than he was in his published prose. But suddenly the character of the visual portion changed, just after a panorama shot of the exterior of the Sunship.

For a moment he was puzzled as the pictures moved past. Then he laughed out loud.

Millie Martine was so surprised by this that she raised her red eyes from her misery. Jacob nodded to her genially.

'Did you *know* what you were fetching down here?'

'Yes.' Her voice was husky. She nodded slowly. 'I wanted to get Peter's camera back to him so he could write up his story. I thought that after the Solarians had been so cruel to him ... using him so ...'

'He's still in confinement, isn't he?'

'Yes. They figured it's safest that way. The Solarians manipulated him once before, you see. They could do it again.'

'And whose idea was it to return his camera?'

'His, of course. He wanted the recordings and I didn't think it would hurt ...'

'To let him get his hands on a weapon?'

'No! The stunner would be put out of comm ... commission. Bubb ...' Her eyes widened and her voice trailed off.

'Go ahead and say it. I already know.'

Martine lowered her gaze.

'Bubbacub said he'd meet me at Peter's quarters and put the stunner out of commission, as a favor and to prove he had no hard feelings.'

Jacob sighed. 'That tears it,' he muttered.

'What ... ?'

'Let me see your hands.' He motioned peremptorily when she hesitated. The long slender fingers trembled as he examined them.

'What is it?'

Jacob ignored her. He paced slowly up and back down the narrow room.

The symmetry of the trap appealed to him. If it carried through there wouldn't be a human left on Mercury with an unsullied reputation. He couldn't have done better himself. The only question now was, when was it supposed to be sprung?

He turned and looked back at the darkroom entrance. Again, Donaldson's head flicked back out of sight.

'It's all right, Chief. Come on out. You're going to have to help Dr Martine clean this place of her fingerprints.'

Martine gasped as the portly chief engineer emerged, smiling sheepishly.

'What are you going to do?' he asked.

Instead of answering, Jacob picked up the voice-phone by the inner door and dialed.

'Hello, Fagin? Yes. I'm ready for a "parlor scene" now. Oh yeah ...? Well, don't be so sure yet. It will depend on how lucky I can get in the next few minutes.

'Would you please invite the core group down to LaRoque's detention quarters for a meeting in five minutes? Yes, right away, and please insist. Don't bother with Dr Martine, she's right here.'

Martine looked up from wiping the handle of a filing cabinet, amazed by the tone of Jacob Demwa's voice.

'That's right,' Jacob went on. 'And please invite Bubbacub first and Kepler as well. Get them moving the way we both know you can. I'll have to run as it is. Yeah, thanks.'

'So now what?' Donaldson said on their way out the door.

'Now you two apprentices graduate to first-class burglarhood. And you've got to make it snappy. Dr Kepler will be leaving his rooms shortly and you'd better not be too long following him to the meeting.'

Martine stopped in her tracks. 'You're kidding. You don't seriously expect me to help ransack Dwayne's apartment!'

'Why not?' Donaldson growled. 'You've been giving him rat poison! You stole his keys to break into the Photo Lab.'

Martine's nostrils flared. 'I have *not* been giving him rat poison! Who told you that?'

Jacob sighed. 'Warfarin. It was used as a rat poison in the old days. Before the rats got immune to it and nearly everything else.'

'I told you *before,* I never *heard* of Warfarin! First the Doctor and then you on the Sunship. Why does everybody think I'm a poisoner!'

'I don't. But I do think that you'd better cooperate if you want to help us get to the bottom of this. Now you've got the keys to Kepler's rooms, right?'

Martine bit her lip, then nodded once.

Jacob told Donaldson what to look for and what to do with it when he found it. Then he was off, running in the direction of the E.T. Quarters.

19

IN THE PARLOR

'You mean Jacob called this meeting and he isn't even here?' Helene deSilva asked from the doorway.

'I should not be concerned, Commandant deSilva. He shall arrive. I have never known Mister Demwa to call a meeting that was not well worth the time of attending.'

'Indeed!' LaRoque laughed from one end of the large sofa, with his feet propped up on an ottoman. He spoke sarcastically around the stem of his pipe, and through a haze of smoke. 'And why not? What else have we to do here? The "research" is over, and the studies are done. The Ivory Tower has collapsed in arrogance and it is the month of the long knives. Let Demwa take his time. Whatever he has to say will be more amusing than watching all these serious faces!'

Dwayne Kepler grimaced from the other end of the sofa. He sat as far from LaRoque as he possibly could. Nervously, he twitched aside the lap blanket a med-aid had just finished adjusting. The med-aid looked up to the physician, who just shrugged.

'Shut up, LaRoque,' Kepler said.

LaRoque merely grinned and took out a tool to work on his pipe. 'I still think I should have a recording device. Knowing Demwa, this may be historic.'

Bubbacub snorted and turned away. He had been pacing. Uncharacteristically he hadn't gone near any of the cushions scattered around the carpeted room. The Pil stopped in front of Culla, standing by the wall, and clicked his quadrilaterally symmetric fingers in a complicated pattern. Culla nodded.

'I am instructed to shay that enough tragedy has occurred because of Mishter LaRoquesh recording devishesh. Also Pil Bubba-cub hash indicated that he will not remain pasht another five minutes.'

Kepler ignored the statement. Methodically, he rubbed his neck as if searching for an itch. A lot of the fleshiness had departed in recent weeks.

LaRoque raised his shoulders once in a gallic shrug. Fagin was silent. Not even the silvery chimes moved at the ends of his blue-green branches.

'Come on in and sit down, Helene,' the physician said. 'I'm sure the others will be here soon.' With his eyes he commiserated. Walking into this room was like wading into a pool of very cold and not very clean water.

She found a seat as far from the others as possible. Unhappily, she wondered what Jacob Demwa was up to.

I hope it's not the same thing, she thought. If this group in here has anything in common, it's the fact that they don't even want the word 'Sundiver' mentioned. They're just on the edge of tearing each other's throats out, but all the same there's this conspiracy of silence.

She shook her head. I'm glad this tour is over soon. Maybe things will be better in another fifty years.

She didn't hold out much hope for that. Already the only place you could hear a Beatles tune performed was by a symphony orchestra, of all the monstrosities. And good jazz didn't exist outside of a library.

Why did I ever leave home?

Mildred Martine and Chief Donaldson entered. To Helene, their attempts to look nonchalant were pathetic, but no one else seemed to notice.

Interesting. I wonder what those two have in common?

They looked around the room and then edged toward a corner behind the only sofa, where Kepler and LaRoque and the tension between them occupied all of the space. LaRoque looked up at Martine and smiled. Was that a conspiratorial wink? Martine avoided his eye and LaRoque looked disappointed. He returned to lighting his pipe.

'I have had e-nough!' Bubbacub announced finally, and he turned for the door. But before he got there it swung open, apparently on its own. Then Jacob Demwa appeared in the doorway, a white canvas sack over his shoulder. He entered the room whistling softly. Helene blinked unbelievingly. The tune sounded *awfully* like 'Santa Claus Is Coming to Town.' But surely . . .

Jacob swung the bag into the air. It came down on the coffee table with a bang that made Dr Martine jump halfway out of her chair. Kepler's frown deepened and he gripped the arm of the sofa.

Helene couldn't help it. The anachronistic, homely old tune, the loud noise, and Jacob's demeanor broke the wall of tension like a custard pie in the face of someone you didn't particularly like. She laughed.

Jacob winked once. 'Ho ho.'

'Are you here to play?' Bubbacub demanded. 'You steal my time! Comp-en-sate!'

Jacob smiled. 'Why certainly, Pil Bubbacub. I hope that you will be edified by my demonstration. But first, won't you please be seated?'

Bubbacub's jaws snapped together. The small black eyes seemed to burn for a moment, then he snorted and threw himself onto a nearby cushion.

Jacob studied the faces in the room. The expressions were mostly confused or hostile, except for LaRoque, who remained pompously aloof, and Helene, who smiled uncertainly. And Fagin, of course. For the thousandth time he wished the Kanten had eyes.

'When Dr Kepler invited me to Mercury,' he began, 'I had some doubts about the Sundiver Project, but approved of the idea overall. After that first meeting I expected to become involved in one of the most exciting events since Contact . . . a complex problem of inter-species relations with our nearest and strangest neighbors, the Sun Ghosts.

'Instead, the problem of the Solarians seems to have taken back burner to a complicated web of interstellar intrigue and murder.'

Kepler looked up sadly. 'Jacob, please. We all know you've been under a strain. Millie thinks we should be kind to you and I agree. But there are limits.'

Jacob spread his hands. 'If kindness is humoring me, then please do so. I'm sick of being ignored. If you don't listen, I'm sure the Earth authorities will.'

Kepler's smile froze. He sat back. 'Go ahead, then. I'll listen.'

Jacob stepped onto the broad throw rug in the center of the room.

'First: Pierre LaRoque has consistently denied killing Chimp Jeffrey or using his stunner to sabotage the smaller Sunship. He denies having ever been a Probationer and claims that the records on Earth have somehow been fouled up.

'Yet, since our return from the Sun he has consistently refused to take a P-test, which might go a long way toward proving his innocence. Presumably he expects that the results of the test would also be falsified.'

'That's right,' LaRoque nodded. 'Just another lie.'

'Even if Physician Laird, Dr Martine and I jointly supervised?'

LaRoque grunted. 'It might prejudice my trial, especially if I decide to sue.'

'Why *go* to trial? You had no motive to kill Jeffrey when you opened the access plate to the R.Q. tuner ...'

'Which I deny doing!'

'... and only a Probie would kill a man in a fit of pique. So why stay in detention?'

'Maybe he's comfortable here,' the med-aid commented. Helene frowned. Discipline had gone straight to hell lately, along with morale.

'He refuses the test because he knows he'll fail!' Kepler shouted.

'That is why the Sun-Men chose him to do their kill-ing,' Bubbacub added. 'That is what they told me.'

'And am *I* a Probationer? Some people seem to think the Ghosts made me try to commit suicide.'

'You were un-der stress. Doct-or Mar-tine says so. Yes?' Bubbacub turned to Martine. Her hands gripped each other whitely but she said nothing.

'We'll get to that in a few minutes,' Jacob said. 'But before we start I'd like to have a private word with Dr Kepler and Mr LaRoque.'

Dr Laird and his assistant moved away politely. Bubbacub glared at being forced to move, but followed suit.

Jacob passed around the back of the sofa. As he bent over between the two men his hand went behind his back. Donaldson leaned forward and placed a small object there which Jacob held tightly.

Jacob looked alternately at Kepler and LaRoque.

'I think you two should cut it out. Especially you, Dr Kepler.'

Kepler hissed. 'What in god's name are you talking about?'

'I think you have some property of Mr LaRoque's. No matter that he got it illegally. He wants it badly. Badly enough to temporarily take a rap he knows won't stick. Maybe enough to change the tone of the articles he's certain to write about all this.

'I don't think the deal will hold anymore. You see, I have the item now.'

'My camera!' LaRoque whispered harshly. His eyes shone.

'Quite a little camera, too. A complete little sonic spectrograph.

Yes, I have it. I also have the copies of recordings you made that were hidden in Dr Kepler's rooms.'

'You t-traitor,' Kepler stammered. 'I thought you were a friend . . .'

'Shut up, you skinny bastard!' LaRoque almost shouted. 'You are the one who is a traitor.' Contempt seemed to boil from the little writer like steam overlong contained.

Jacob laid a hand on the back of each man. '*Both* of you will be on no-return orbits if you don't keep your voices down! LaRoque can be charged with espionage and Kepler for blackmail and complicity after the fact in espionage!

'In fact, since the evidence of LaRoque's espionage is also circumstantial evidence that he wouldn't have had time to sabotage Jeffrey's ship, the immediate suspicion would fall on the last person to inspect the ship's generators. Oh I don't think you did it, Dr Kepler. But I'd be careful if I were you!'

LaRoque fell silent. Kepler chewed on the end of his moustache.

'What do you want?' he said finally.

Jacob tried to resist but the suppressed side was now too much awake. He couldn't help making a little dig.

'Why, I'm not sure yet. Maybe I'll think of something. Just don't let your imagination go wild. Friends of mine on Earth know everything by now.'

It wasn't true. But Mr Hyde did believe in caution.

Helene deSilva strained to overhear what the three men were saying to each other. If she had been one to believe in possession she would have been sure the familiar faces were moving at the command of invading spirits. Gentle Dr Kepler, turned taciturn and secretive since their return from the Sun, muttered like a wrathful sage denied his will. LaRoque – thoughtful, cautious – behaved as if his whole world hinged on a careful assessment of affairs.

And Jacob Demwa . . . earlier glimpses hinted at a charisma beneath his quiet, sometimes watery thoughtfulness. It had drawn her even as it frustrated in its peek-a-boo appearances. But *now*, now it radiated. It compelled like a flame.

Jacob stood straight and announced, 'For now, Dr Kepler has kindly agreed to drop all charges against Pierre LaRoque.'

Bubbacub rose from his cushion. 'You are mad. If hu-mans condone the kill-ing of their cli-ents, that is their own prob-lem. But the Sun-Men may bend him to do harm a-gain!'

'The Sun-Men never bent him to do anything,' Jacob said slowly.

Bubbacub snapped. 'As I said, you are mad. I spoke with the Sun-Men. They did not lie.'

'If you wish,' Jacob bowed. 'But I still would like to continue with my synopsis.'

Bubbacub snorted loudly and threw himself again on the cushion. 'Mad!' he snapped.

'First,' Jacob said. 'I would like to thank Dr Kepler for his gracious permission for Chief Donaldson and Dr Martine and myself to visit the Photo Labs and study the films from the last dive.'

At the mention of Martine's name, Bubbacub's expression changed. So that's what chagrin looks like on a Pil, Jacob thought. He empathized with the little alien. It had been a beautiful trap, now entirely defused.

Jacob told an edited version of their discovery in the Photo Lab, that the flipside spools of the last third of the mission were missing. The only other sound in the room was the tinkling of Fagin's branches.

'For a while, I wondered where these spools could be. I had an idea who took them, but whether he had destroyed them or taken the chance of hiding them I wasn't sure. Finally, I decided to gamble that a "data-packrat" never throws anything away. I searched a certain sophont's quarters and found the missing spools.'

'You dared!' Bubbacub hissed. 'If you had prop-er mas-ters I would have you nerve whipped! You dared!'

Helene shook away her surprise. 'You mean you admit that you hid Sundiver datatapes, Pil Bubbacub? Why!'

Jacob grinned. 'Oh that will become clear. In fact the way this case was going, I thought for sure it would be more complicated than it is. But it's actually quite simple. You see, these tapes make it very clear that Pil Bubbacub has lied.'

A low rumbling rose in Bubbacub's throat. The little alien stood very still as if he didn't trust himself to move.

'Well, where are the tapes?' deSilva demanded.

Jacob picked up the sack from the table.

'I've got to give the devil his due, though. It was only luck that I figured the spools would just fit into an empty gas cannister.' He pulled out an object and held it up.

'The Lethani relic!' DeSilva gasped. A small trill of surprise escaped Fagin. Mildred Martine stood up, her hand brought to her throat.

'Yes, the Lethani relic. I'm sure Bubbacub counted on a reaction like yours on the obscure chance that his rooms were searched. Naturally, no one would think of disturbing a semi-religious object-of-reverence of an old and powerful race; particularly one that looked like nothing but a slab of meteoric rock and glass!'

He turned it over in his hands.

'Now watch!'

The relic opened with a twist. A can of some sort was imbedded in one of the halves. Jacob laid the other half down and tugged at the end of the can. Something inside rattled softly. The can suddenly came loose and a dozen small black objects came rolling out and fell to the floor. Culla's mashies clacked.

'The spools!' LaRoque nodded with satisfaction as he fumbled with his pipe.

'Yes,' Jacob said. 'And on the outer surface of this "relic" you can find the button which released the previous contents of this now-empty cannister. There appear to be some traces left inside. I'll bet anything that they match the substance that Chief Donaldson and I gave Dr Kepler yesterday when we failed to convince ...' Jacob stopped himself. Then he shrugged.

'... Traces of an unstable monomolecule which, under a certain sophont's skillful control, spread out in a "burst of light and sound" to coat the inner surface of the upper hemisphere of the shell of the Sunship ...'

DeSilva rose to her feet. Jacob had to speak louder to overcome the rising chatter coming from Culla.

'... and to effectively block out all green and blue light – the only wavelengths in which we could pick out the Sun Ghosts from their surroundings!'

'The spools!' deSilva cried. 'They should show ...'

'They *do* show toroids, Ghosts ... hundreds of them! Interestingly there were no anthropoid shapes, but perhaps they didn't make them because our psi patterns indicated we weren't seeing them.

'But *oh* the confusion in that herd when we blundered right into them without so much as a by-your-leave, toroids and "normal" Ghosts scattering out of our path ... all because we couldn't see that we were right in the middle of them!'

'You crazy Eatee!' LaRoque shouted. He shook his fist at Bubbacub. The Pil hissed back but remained still, the fingers of each hand flexing against one another as he watched Jacob.

'The monomolecule was designed to decay just as we were leaving the chromosphere. It slumped in a thin layer of dust on the force field at the rim of the deck, where no one would notice it until Bubbacub could return with Culla and vacuum it up. That's right, isn't it, Culla?'

Culla nodded miserably.

Jacob felt distantly pleased that sympathy came as easily as amoral wrath had earlier. A part of him had begun to get worried. He smiled reassuringly.

'That's okay, Culla. I have no evidence to connect you with

anything else. I watched the two of you when you did it and it was pretty clear you were under duress.'

The Pring's eyes rose. They were very bright. He nodded once again and the chattering from behind the thick lips subsided slowly. Fagin moved closer to the slender E.T.

Donaldson rose from picking up the recording spools.

'I think we'd better make some provisions for custody.'

Helene had already moved to the telephone. 'I'm taking care of that now,' she said softly.

Martine sidled up to Jacob and whispered. 'Jacob, this is an External Affairs matter now. We should let them handle it from here.'

Jacob shook his head. 'No. Not just yet. There's a bit more that needs out.'

DeSilva put down the phone. 'They'll be here shortly. Meanwhile, why don't you go on, Jacob? Is there more?'

'Yes. Two items. One is this.'

From the bag on the table he pulled Bubbacub's psi helmet. 'I suggest this be kept in storage. I don't know if anyone else remembers, but Bubbacub was wearing it and staring at me when I warped out aboard the Sunship. Being made to do things makes me mad, Bubbacub. You shouldn't have done it.'

Bubbacub made a gesture with his hand that Jacob didn't try to interpret.

'Finally, there's the matter of the death of chimpanzee Jeffrey. Actually, it's the easiest part.

'Bubbacub knew almost everything there was to know about the Galactic technology in Sundiver; the drives, the computer system, the communications ... aspects which Terran scientists haven't even scratched.

'It's only circumstantial evidence that Bubbacub was working on the laser communications pylon, spurning Dr Kepler's presentation, when Jeff's largely remote-controlled ship blew up. It wouldn't convict in a court of law, but that doesn't matter since Pila have extraterritoriality and all we can do is deport him.

'Another thing that'd be hard to prove would be the hypothesis that Bubbacub planted a false lead in the Space Identification System ... a system linked directly to the Library at LaPaz ... creating a false report that LaRoque was a Probationer. Still, it's pretty clear that he did. It was a perfect red herring. With everyone sure that LaRoque did it, nobody bothered to really do a detailed double-check of the telemetry on Jeff's dive. Right now I believe I recall that Jeff's ship went into trouble almost exactly when he turned on his closeup cameras, a perfect delayed trigger if that was the technique

Bubbacub used. Anyway, we'll probably never know. The telemetry is probably missing or destroyed by now.'

Fagin fluted. 'Jacob, Culla asks that you stop. Please do not embarrass Pil Bubbacub any further. It would serve no purpose.'

Three armed crewmen appeared at the door. They looked at Commandant deSilva expectantly. She motioned for them to wait.

'Just a moment,' Jacob said. 'We haven't dealt with the most important part, Bubbacub's motives. *Why* would an important sophont, a representative of a prestigious galactic institution, indulge in theft, forgery, psychic assault, and murder?

'Bubbacub had personal grudges against both Jeffrey and LaRoque, to start with. Jeffrey represented an abomination to him, a species that had been uplifted a mere hundred years before and yet dared to talk back. Jeff's "uppityness" and his friendship with Culla contributed to Bubbacub's anger.

'But I think he hated what chimpanzees represent most of all. Along with dolphins, they meant instant status for the crude, vulgar human race. The Pila had to fight for half a million years to get to where they are. I guess Bubbacub resents us having it "easy."

'As for LaRoque, well, I'd say Bubbacub just didn't like him. Too loud and pushy, I suppose . . .'

LaRoque sniffed audibly.

'And perhaps he was insulted when LaRoque suggested that the Soro might have once been our Patrons. The "upper crust" in Galactic society frowns on species who abandon their clients.'

'But those are just personal reasons,' Helene objected. 'Haven't you got anything better?'

'Jacob,' Fagin began. 'Please . . .'

'Of *course* Bubbacub had another reason,' Jacob said. 'He wanted to end Sundiver in a way that would put into disrepute the concept of independent research and boost the status of the Library. He made it seem that he, a Pil, was able to make contact where humans weren't, concocted a story that made Sundiver out to be a bungled operation. Then he faked a Library report to verify his claims about the Solarians and ensure that there would be no more dives!

'It was the failure of the Library to come up with anything that probably irked Bubbacub the most. And it's faking that message that'll get him in the deepest trouble back at home. For that they'll punish him worse than we ever would for killing Jeff.'

Bubbacub rose slowly. He carefully brushed his fur flat and then clicked his four-fingered hands together.

'You are ver-y smart,' he said to Jacob. 'But se-man-tics bad . . . aim too high. You build too much on small stuff. Hu-mans shall always be small. I shall speak your kaka Terran tongue no more.'

With that he removed the Vodor from around his neck and tossed it idly on the table.

'I'm sorry, Pil Bubbacub,' deSilva said. 'But it appears that we're going to have to restrict your movement until we get instructions from Earth.'

Jacob half expected the Pil to nod or shrug but the alien performed another movement that somehow conveyed the same indifference. He turned away and marched stiffly out the door, a small stubby, proud figure leading the large human guards.

Helene deSilva picked up the bottom of the 'Lethani relic.' She weighed it carefully in her hands, thoughtfully. Then her lips tightened and she threw the object with all her might against the door.

'Murderer,' she cursed.

'I've learned my lesson,' Martine said slowly. 'Never trust anyone over thirty million.'

Jacob stood in a daze. The exalted feeling was draining away too quickly. Like a drug, it left behind it an emptiness – a return to rationality but a loss of totality as well. Soon he would begin to wonder if he had done right in releasing everything at once in an orgiastic display of deductive logic.

Martine's remark made him look up.

'Not anyone?' he asked.

Fagin was nudging Culla into a chair. Jacob went over to him.

'I'm sorry, Fagin,' he said. 'I should have warned you, discussed it with you first. There may be ... complications to this thing, repercussions that I didn't think out.' He brought a hand to his forehead.

Fagin whistled softly.

'You unleashed that which you have been restraining, Jacob. I do not understand why you have been so reticent to use your skills, of late, but in this instance justice demanded all of your vigor. It is fortunate that you relented.

'Do not worry too much about what has happened. The Truth was more important than the damage done through minor over-eagerness, or through the use of techniques too long dormant.'

Jacob wanted to tell Fagin how wrong he was. The 'skills' he had unleashed were more than that. They were a deadly force within him. He feared that they had done more harm than good.

'What do you think will happen?' he asked, tiredly.

'Why I believe that humanity will discover that it has a powerful enemy. Your government will protest. How it does so will be of great importance, but it will not change the essential facts. Officially the Pila will disown Bubbacub's unfortunate actions. But they are peevish and prideful, if you will excuse a painful but necessarily unkind description of a fellow sophont race.

'That is just one result of this event-chain. But do not worry over-much. You did not do this thing. All that you did was make humanity *aware* of the danger. It was bound to happen. It always has happened to wolfling races.'

'But why!'

'That, my most esteemed friend, is one of the things I am here to try to discover. Though it may be of little comfort, please note that there are many who would like to see humanity survive. Some of us ... care very much.'

20

MODERN MEDICINE

Jacob pressed against the rubber rimmed eyepiece of the Retinal scanner, and once again saw the blue dot dance and shimmer alone in a black background. Now he tried not to focus on it, ignoring its tantalizing suggestion of communion, as he waited for the third tachistoscopic image.

It flashed on suddenly, filling his entire field of view with a 3-D image in dull sepia. The gestalt he got in that first, unfocused instant was of a pastoral scene. There was a woman in the fore-ground, buxom and well fed, her old-fashioned skirts flying as she ran.

Dark, threatening clouds loomed on the horizon, above farm buildings set on a hill. There were people on the left ... dancing? No, fighting. There were soldiers. Their faces were excited and – afraid? The woman was afraid. She fled with her arms over her head as two men in seventeenth-century body armor chased her, holding high their matchlocks with bayonets sharp. Their ...

The scene blacked out and the blue dot was back. Jacob closed his eyes and pulled back from the eyepiece.

'That's it,' Dr Martine said. She bent over a computer console nearby, next to Physician Laird. 'We'll have your P-test score in a minute, Jacob.'

'You're sure you don't need any more? That was only three.' Actually, he was relieved.

'No, we took five from Peter to have a double-check. You're just a control. Why don't you just sit down and relax now, while we finish up here.'

Jacob walked over to one of the nearby lounge chairs, wiping his left cuff along his forehead to remove a thin sheen of perspiration. The test had been a thirty-second ordeal.

The first image had been a portrait of a man's face, gnarled and lined with care, a story of a life-time that he had examined for two, maybe three seconds, before it disappeared again, as seared as any ephemera could be into his memory.

The second had been a confusing jumble of abstract shapes, jutting and bumping in static disarray ... somewhat like the maze of patterns around the rim of a sun-torus but without the brilliance or overall consistency.

The third had been the scene in sepia, apparently rendered from an old etching of the Thirty Years War. It was explicitly violent, Jacob recalled, just the sort of thing one would expect in a P-test.

After the overly dramatic 'parlor scene' downstairs, Jacob was reluctant to enter even a shallow trance to calm his nerves. And he found that he couldn't relax without it. He rose and approached the console. Across the dome, near the stasis shell itself, LaRoque wandered idly as he waited, staring out at the long shadows and blistered rocks of Mercury's North Pole.

'May I see the raw data?' Jacob asked Martine.

'Sure. Which one would you like to see?'

'The last one.'

Martine tapped on her keyboard. A sheet extruded from a slot beneath the screen. She tore it off and handed it to him.

It was the 'pastoral scene.' Of course now he recognized its true content, but the whole purpose of the earlier viewing was to trace his reactions to the image during the first few instants he saw it, before conscious consideration could come into play.

Across the image a jagged line darted back and forth, up and down. At every vertex or resting point was a small number. The line showed the path of his attention during that first quick glimpse, as detected by the Retinal Reader, watching the movements of his eye.

The number one, and the beginning of the trace, was near the center. Up to number six the focus line just drifted. Then it stopped right over the generous cleavage presented by the running woman's bosom. The number seven was circled there.

There the numbers clustered, not only seven to sixteen, but thirty through thirty-five and eighty-two to eighty-six, as well.

At twenty the numbers suddenly shifted from the woman's feet to the clouds over the farmhouse. Then they moved quickly among the people and objects pictured, sometimes circled or squared to denote the level of dilation of the eye, depth of focus, and changes in his blood pressure as measured by the tiny veins in his retina. Apparently the modified Stanford-Purkinje eye scanner he had devised for this test, from Martina's tachistoscope and other odds and ends, had worked.

Jacob knew better than to be embarrassed or concerned by his reflex reaction to the pictured woman's breast. If he'd been female his reaction would have been different, spending more time with the woman, overall, but concentrating more on hair, clothes, and face.

What concerned him more was his reaction to the overall scene. Over to the left, near the fighting men, was a starred number. That represented the point at which he realized that the image was violent, not pastoral. He nodded with satisfaction. The number was relatively low and the trace darted immediately away for a period of five beats before returning to the same spot. That meant a healthy dose of aversion followed by direct instead of covert curiosity.

At first glance it looked like he'd probably pass. Not that he ever really doubted it.

'I wonder if anyone will ever learn how to fool a P-test,' he said, handing the copy to Martine.

'Maybe they will, someday,' she said as she gathered her materials. 'But the conditioning needed to change a man's response to instantaneous stimuli ... to an image flashed so fast that only the unconscious has time to react ... would leave too many side effects, new patterns that would have to show up in the test.

'The final analysis is very simple; does the subject's mind follow a plus or zero sum game, qualifying him for Citizenship, or is it addicted to the sick-sweet pleasures of a negative sum. That, more than any index of violence, is the essence of this test.'

Martine turned to Physician Laird. 'That's right, isn't it, Doctor?'

Laird shrugged. 'You're the expert.' He had been allowing Martine to slowly win her way back into his good graces, still not quite forgiving her for prescribing to Kepler without consulting him.

After the denunciation downstairs, it became clear that she had never prescribed the Warfarin to Kepler at all. Jacob recalled Bubbacub's habit, aboard the *Bradbury*, of falling asleep on articles of clothing, carelessly left on cushions or chairs. The Pil must have done it as a subterfuge to enable him to plant, in Kepler's portable pharmacopoeia, a drug that would cause his behavior to deteriorate.

It made sense. Kepler was eliminated from the last dive. With his keen insight he might have detected Bubbacub's trick with the 'Lethani relic.' Also his aberrant actions would have helped in the long run to discredit Sundiver.

It hung together, but to Jacob all of these deductions tasted like a dinner of protein-flakes. They were enough to persuade but they had no flavor. A bowl full of suppositions.

Some of Bubbacub's misdeeds were proven. The rest would have to remain speculation since the Library representative had diplomatic immunity.

Pierre LaRoque joined them. The Frenchman's attitude was subdued. 'What is the verdict, Doctor Laird?'

'It's quite clear that Mr LaRoque is not an asocially violent personality and that he does not qualify for Probation,' Laird said slowly. 'In fact, he betrays a rather high social conscience index. That may be part of his problem. He's apparently sublimating something and he would be well-advised to seek the help of a professional at his neighborhood clinic when he gets home.' Laird looked down at LaRoque sternly. LaRoque merely nodded meekly.

'And the controls?' Jacob asked. He had been the last to take the test. Dr Kepler, Helene deSilva, and three randomly selected crewmen had also taken their turns at the machine. Helene hadn't given the test a second thought and had taken the crewmen with her when she left to supervise the hurried pre-launch checkout of the Sunship. Kepler had scowled as Physician Laird read him his own results privately, and stalked off in a huff.

Laird reached up and pinched the bridge of his nose, just below the eyebrows.

'Oh, there isn't a Probationer in the bunch, just as we expected after your little show downstairs. But there are problems and things I don't quite understand, bubbling in the minds of some of the people, here. You know, it's not easy for a country sawbones like me to have to fall back on his internship training and look into people's souls. I would have missed half a dozen nuances if Dr Martine hadn't helped. As it is, I find it hard to interpret these hidden darknesses, especially of men I know and admire.'

'There's nothing serious, I hope.'

'If there were you wouldn't be going on this rush-job dive Helene's ordered! I'm not grounding Dwayne Kepler because he has a cold!'

Laird shook his head and apologized. 'Forgive me. I'm just not used to this. There's nothing to worry about, Jacob. You had some awfully strange quirks in your test but the basic reading is as sane as any I've ever seen. Decidedly positive-sum and realistic.

'Still, there are some things that confuse me. I won't go into specifics that might cause you more worry than they're worth while you're on this dive, I'd just appreciate it if you and Helene would each come and see me when you get back.'

Jacob thanked the man and walked with him, Martine, and LaRoque toward the elevator.

High overhead, the communications pylon pierced the stasis dome. All around them, beyond the men and machines of the chamber, the blistered rocks of Mercury sparkled or shone dully. Sol was an incandescent yellow ball above a low range of hills.

When the elevator car arrived, Martine and Laird entered, but LaRoque's hand on his arm kept Jacob back until the door had closed, leaving the two of them alone.

Pierre LaRoque whispered to Jacob.

'I want my camera!'

'Sure, LaRoque. Commandant deSilva disarmed the stunner and you can pick it up any time, now that you're cleared.'

'And the recording?'

'I've got it. I'm holding onto it too.'

'You have no *business* ...'

'Come off it, LaRoque,' Jacob groaned. 'Why don't you just once cut the act and give someone else credit for some intelligence! I want to know why you were taking sonic pictures of the stasis oscillator in Jeffrey's ship! And I also want to know what gave you the idea my uncle would be interested in them!'

'I owe you a great deal Demwa,' LaRoque said slowly. The thick accent was almost gone. 'But I have to know if your political views are at all like your uncle's before I answer you.'

'I have a lot of uncles, LaRoque. Uncle Jeremey is in the Confederacy Assembly, but I know you wouldn't be working with him! Uncle Juan is pretty big on theory and very down on illegality ... my guess is that you mean Uncle James, the family kook. Oh I agree with him about a lot of things, even some things the rest of the family doesn't. But if he's involved in some sort of espionage plot, I'm not going to help to dig him deeper ... especially in a plot as clumsy as yours appears to be.

'You may not be a murderer or a Probationer, LaRoque, but you are a spy! The only problem is figuring out who you're spying *for*. I'll save that mystery for when we get back to Earth.

'Then, maybe, you can visit me; you and James can both try to talk me out of turning you in. Fair enough?'

LaRoque nodded curtly.

'I can wait, Demwa. Just don't you lose the recordings, eh? I have been through the very hell to get them. I want to get that chance to persuade you to hand them over.'

Jacob was looking at the Sun.

'LaRoque, spare me your moanings. You haven't been to hell ... yet.'

He turned away and headed for the elevators. There was time enough for a few hours under a sleep machine. He didn't want to see anyone until it was time to leave.

PART VII

In all evolution there is no transformation, no 'quantum leap,' to compare with this one. Never before has the life-style of a species, its way of adapting, changed so utterly and so swiftly. For some fifteen million years the family of man foraged as animals among animals. The pace of events since then has been explosive ... the first farming villages ... cities ... supermetropolises ... all this has been packed into an instant on the evolutionary time scale, a mere 10,000 years.

JOHN E. PFEIFFER

21

DÉJÀ PENSÉ

'Have you ever wondered why most of our starships jump out with crews that are seventy percent female?'

Helene handed Jacob the first liquitube of hot coffee and turned back to the machine to punch out another for herself.

Jacob peeled back the outer seal on the semi-permeable membrane, allowing steam to escape while keeping the dark liquid contained. The liquitube was almost too hot to hold, in spite of its insulation.

Trust Helene to think up another provocative topic! Whenever they were alone together, as alone as one could get on the open deck of a Sunship, Helene deSilva had never missed a chance to engage him in mental gymnastics. The odd thing was that he didn't mind a bit. The contest had lifted his spirits considerably since they had left Mercury ten hours before.

'When I was an adolescent, my friends and I never really cared about the reasons. We just thought it was an added bonus for being a male on a starship. "Of such thoughts are pubescent fantasies born ..." Who was it who wrote that, John Two-Clouds? Have you ever read anything by him? I think he was born in High London, so you may have known his parents.'

Helene sent him an accusing glare. Jacob had to fight back, for the nth time, a temptation to tell her that the expression was endearing. It *was*, but what fully-grown female professional wanted to be reminded that she still had dimples? It wasn't worth getting a broken arm, anyway.

'Okay, okay,' he laughed. 'I'll stay on the subject. I suppose the male-female ratio has to do with the way women respond better to high acceleration, heat and cold ... better hand-eye coordination and superior passive strength. That must make them better spacemen, I guess.'

Helene sipped from the siphon of her liquitube. 'Yes, all that's part of it. Also most fems appear to be more immune to Jump-sickness. But you know those differences aren't all that big. Not enough to make up for the fact that more males volunteer for spaceflight than females.

'Besides, more than half of the crewmen on in-system ships are male, and seven out of ten on military craft.'

'Well, I don't know about commercial or research ships, but I'd think that the military selects for an aptitude for fighting. I know it's still not proven, but I'd guess that . . .'

Helene laughed. 'Oh, you don't have to be so diplomatic, Jacob. Of course mels make better fighters than fems . . . statistically that is. Amazons like me are the exception. Actually, that is one factor in the selection. We don't want too many warrior types aboard a starship.'

'But that doesn't make sense! The crews on starships go out into an immense galaxy that hasn't even been fully explored by the Library. You have to face a wild variety of alien races, most of them temperamental as hell. And the Institutes don't forbid fighting among the races. They couldn't even if they tried, judging by what Fagin says. They only try to make it tidy.'

'So a starship with humans aboard should be ready for a fracas?' Helene smiled as she rested her shoulder against the wall of the dome. In the mottled red light of the upper chromosphere in hydrogen alpha, her blonde hair looked like a close fitted ping cap. 'Well you're right, of course. We do have to be *ready* to fight. But think for a moment about the situation we face out there.

'We have to deal with literally hundreds of species whose only thing in common is the one thing we lack, a chain of tradition and uplift stretching back two billion years. They've all been using the Library for aeons, adding to it, albeit slowly, all of the time.

'Most of them are cranky, hyper-mindful of their privileges, and dubious of that silly "wolfling" race from Sol.

'And what can we *do*, when we are challenged by some two-bit species whose extinct patrons uplifted them as talking, obedient *riding steeds*, who now own two little terraformed planets that sit right astride our only route to the colony on Omnivarium? What can we do when these creatures with no ambition or sense of humor stop our ship and demand an incredible *forty* whale songs as a toll?'

Helene shook her head and her eyebrows knotted.

'Wouldn't it be nice to fight, at a time like that! A great beauty such as *Calypso*, filled to the brim with things badly needed by a struggling little community, and with an even more precious cargo of . . . stopped dead in space by a pair of tiny, ancient hulks that were obviously bought, not built, by the "intelligent" camels aboard!' The woman's voice thickened, as she remembered.

'Picture it. New and beautiful, yet primitive, using only the tiny portion of Galactic science we'd been able to absorb when she was refitted, mostly in the drives . . . stopped by hulks older than Caesar but made by someone who used the Library all his life.'

Helene stopped for a moment and turned away.

Jacob was moved, but even more he felt honored. He knew Helene well enough, now, to know what an act of trust it was for her to open up like this.

She's been doing most of the work too, he realized. She asks most of the questions – about my past, about my family, about my feelings – for some reason I've been reluctant to ask about her, the person inside. I wonder what's been stopping me? There must be so much in there!

'So I suppose the idea is not to fight, because we'd probably lose,' he said quietly.

She looked back and nodded. She coughed twice, behind a closed fist.

'Oh, we've a couple of tricks we think we might surprise somebody with sometime, simply because we haven't had the Library and it's all they've known. But those tricks have got to be saved for a rainy day.

'Instead, we flatter, fawn, bribe, sing spirituals … tap dance … and when that fails, we run.'

Jacob imagined meeting a shipload of Pila.

'Running must be awful hard at times.'

'Yes, but we have a secret way of keeping cool,' Helene brightened slightly. For a moment those appealing recesses reappeared at the corners of her smile. 'It's one of the biggest reasons why the crew is mostly women.'

'Now come on. A fem is just about as likely as a mel to take a poke at someone who insulted her. I don't see that as much of a guarantee.'

'Nooo, not normally.' She eyed him again with that 'appraising' expression. For an instant she seemed about to go on. Then she shrugged.

'Let's sit,' she said. 'I want to show you something.'

She led him around the dome and across the deck to a part of the ship where none of the crew or passengers were, where the circular deck floated two meters away from the shell of the ship.

The sparkling glow of the chromosphere refracted eerily where the stasis screen curved away below their feet. The narrow suspension field allowed light to pass, but twisted it slightly. From where they stood, part of the Big Spot could be seen, its configuration changed considerably since the last dive. Where the field intervened, the sunspot shimmered and rippled with new pulsations, added to its own.

Slowly, Helene lowered herself to the deck and then approached the edge. For a moment she sat with her feet inches from the shimmering, holding her knees under her chin. Then she placed her hands behind her on the deck and allowed her legs to drop into the field.

Jacob swallowed.

'I didn't know you could do that,' he said.

He watched as she swung her legs languidly. They moved as if in a thick syrup, the snug sheathing of her shipsuit rippling like something animate.

She lifted her legs straight out and up above the level of the deck, with apparent ease.

'Hmmm, they seem to be all right. I can't push them down very deep, though. I guess the mass of my legs shoves a dimple into the suspension field. At least they don't *feel* upside down when I do it.' She let them drop again.

Jacob felt weak in the knees. 'You mean you've never done that before?'

She looked up at him and grinned.

'Am I showing off? Yes I guess I was trying to impress you. I'm not crazy though. After you told us about Bubbacub and the vacuum cleaner I went over the equations carefully. It's perfectly safe, so why don't you join me?'

Jacob nodded numbly. After so many other miracles and unexplainable things since he left Earth, this was rather small, after all. The secret, he decided, was not to think at all.

It did feel like a thick syrup that increased in viscosity as he pushed downwards. It was rubbery and pushed back.

And the legs of Jacob's shipsuit felt almost, disconcertingly, alive.

Helene said nothing for a time. Jacob respected her silence. Something was obviously on her mind.

'Was that story about the Finnila Needle really true?' she asked at last, without looking up.

'Yes.'

'She must have been quite a woman.'

'Yes, she was.'

'I mean in addition to being brave. She had to be brave to jump from one balloon to another, twenty miles up in the air, but ...'

'She was trying to distract them while I defused the Torcher. I shouldn't have let her.' Jacob heard his own voice, remote and faded. 'But I thought I could protect her at the same time ... I had a device, you see ...'

'... but she must have been quite a person in other ways as well. I wish I could have met her.'

Jacob realized that he hadn't said a word aloud.

'Um, yes, Helene. Tania would have liked you.' He shook himself. This was getting no one anywhere.

'But I thought we were talking about something else, uh, the ratio of females to males on starships, wasn't that it?'

She was looking at her feet. 'We *are* on the same topic, Jacob,' she said quietly.

'We are?'

'Sure. You remember I said there was a way to make a largely female crew more cautious in dealing with aliens . . . a way to guarantee that they'll run rather than fight?'

'Yes, but . . .'

'And you know that humanity has been able to plant three colonies so far, but transportation costs are too great to carry many passengers, so increasing the gene pool at an isolated colony is a real problem?' She spoke rapidly, as if embarrassed.

'When we got back the first time and found that the Constitution stood again, the Confederacy made it voluntary for the women on the next jump instead of compulsory. Still, most of us volunteered.'

'I . . . I don't understand.'

She looked up at him as she smiled.

'Well, maybe now isn't the time. But you should realize that I'm shipping out on *Calypso* in a few months and there are certain preparations I have to make beforehand.

'And I can be as selective as I want.'

She looked straight into his eyes.

Jacob felt his Jaw drop.

'Well!' Helene rubbed her hands on her lap and prepared to stand up. 'I guess we'd better be heading back. We're pretty near the Active Region, now, and I should be at my station to supervise.'

Jacob hurried to his feet and offered her his hand. Neither of them saw anything funny in the archaism.

On their way to the command station, Jacob and Helene stopped to examine the Parametric Laser. Chief Donaldson looked up from the machine as they approached.

'Hi! I think she's all tuned and ready to go. Want a tour?'

'Sure.' Jacob hunkered down next to the laser. Its chassis was bolted to the deck. Its long, slender, multi-barreled body swung on a gimballed swivel.

Jacob felt the soft fabric covering Helene's right leg brush lightly against his arm as she stepped over beside him. It didn't help him keep his thoughts straight.

'This here Parametric Laser,' Donaldson began, 'is my contribution to the attempt to contact the Sun Ghosts. I figured that psi was getting us nowhere, so why not try to communicate with them the way they communicate with us – visually?

'Well now, as you probably know already, most lasers operate on just one or two very narrow spectral bands, particular atomic and molecular transitions, mostly. But this baby will punch out any wavelength you want, just by dialing it in with this control.' He pointed to the central of three controls on the face of the chassis.

'Yes,' Jacob said. 'I know about Parametric Lasers, though I've never seen one. I imagine it has to be pretty powerful to penetrate through our screens and still look bright to the Ghosts.'

'In my other life . . .' deSilva drawled ironically (she often referred to her past, before jumping with the *Calypso*, with defensive sardonicism) '. . . we were able to make multicolored, tunable lasers with optical dyes. They put out a fair amount of power, they were efficient, and incredibly simple.'

She smiled. 'That is, until you spilled the dye. Then, what a mess! Nothing makes me appreciate Galactic science more than knowing I'll never have to clean a puddle of Rhodamine 6-G off the floor again!'

'Could you really tune through the whole optical spectrum with a single molecule?' Donaldson was incredulous. 'How did you power a . . . "dye laser," anyway?'

'Oh, with flashlamps sometimes. Usually with an internal chemical reaction using organic energy molecules, like sugars.

'You had to use several dyes to cover the whole visible spectrum. Poly-methyl coumarin was used a lot for the blue and green end of the band. Rhodamine and a few others were dyes for tuning in red colors.

'Anyway, that's ancient history. I want to know what devilish plan you and Jacob have cooked up this time!' She dropped down next to Jacob on the deck. Instead of looking at Donaldson, she fixed Jacob with that disconcerting appraisal.

'Well,' he swallowed. 'It's really quite simple. I took along a library of whale songs and dolphin-ditties when I boarded *Bradbury*, in case the Ghosts turned out to be poets along with everything else. When Chief Donaldson mentioned his idea of aiming a beam at them to communicate, I volunteered the tapes.'

'We'll be adding a modified version of an old math contact code. He rigged that one up too.' Donaldson grinned. 'I wouldn't know a Fibonacci series if one came up and bit me! But Jacob says it's one of the old standards.'

'It was,' deSilva said. 'We never used any of the math routines, though, after the *Vesarius*. The library makes sure everyone understands each other in space, so there was no use for the old pre-Contact codes.'

She pushed lightly on the slim barrel. It rotated smoothly on its swivel. 'You aren't going to let this thing swing freely when the laser is on, are you?'

'No, of course we'll be bolting it firmly, so the laser beam fires along a radius from the center of the ship. That should prevent those internal reflections you're probably worryin' about.

'As it is, we'll all want to be wearing these goggles when it's on.' Donaldson pulled a pair of thick, dark, wraparound glasses from a sack next to the laser. 'Even if there were no danger to the retina, Dr Martine would insist on it. She's a positive bug on the effects of glare on perception and personality. She turned the whole base upside down, finding bright lights no one even knew were there. Blamed them for the "mass hallucination" when she arrived. Boy did she change her tune when she saw the beasties!'

'Well, it's time for me to get back to work,' Helene announced. 'I shouldn't have stayed so long. We must be getting close. I'll keep you men posted.' Both men rose as she smiled and departed.

Donaldson watched her walk away.

'You know, Demwa, first I thought you were crazy, then I *knew* you had it all together. Now I'm starting to change my mind again.'

Jacob sat down. 'How's that?'

'Any mel I know would grow a tail and wag it if that fem so much as whistled. I just can't believe your self-control, is all. None of my business, of course.'

'You're right. It isn't.' Jacob was disturbed that the situation was so obvious. He was beginning to wish this mission was over so he could give the problem his undivided attention.

Jacob shrugged. It was a mannerism he'd made a lot of use of since leaving Earth. 'To change the subject, I'd been wondering about this internal reflection business. Has it occurred to you that somebody might be pulling a big hoax?'

'A hoax?'

'With the Sun Ghosts. All someone would have to do is smuggle aboard some sort of holographic projector ...'

'Forget it,' Donaldson shook his head. 'That was the first thing we checked. Besides, who'd be able to fake anything as intricate and beautiful as that herd of toruses? Anyway, a projection like that, filling our whole view, would be given away by the columnated rim cameras on flip-side!'

'Well, maybe not the herd, but what about the "humanoid" Ghosts? They're rather simple and small, and the way they avoid the rim cameras, spinning faster than we can to stay overhead, is pretty uncanny.'

'What can I say, Jake? Every piece of equipment carried aboard is carefully inspected, along with everyone's personal items as well, for that very reason. No projector's ever been found, and where could anyone hide one on an open ship like this? I'll admit I've wondered about it myself at times. But I don't see any way anyone could be pulling a hoax.'

Jacob nodded slowly. Donaldson's argument made sense. Also, how could one reconcile a projection with Bubbacub's trick with the Lethani relic? It was a tempting idea, but a hoax didn't seem very likely.

Distant spicule forests pulsed like waving fountains. Individual jets fenced with one another along the rim of the slowly throbbing supergranulation cell that covered half the sky. In its center lay the Big Spot, a huge eye of black, rimmed by areas of hot brightness.

About ninety degrees around the deck from them, a group of dark silhouettes stood or knelt near the Pilot Board. Only the outlines could be made out against the bright crimson blaze of the photosphere.

Two clumps of shadow could be distinguished from those near the command station. The tall, slender figure of Culla stood slightly to the side, pointing ahead at a tall, wispy filament arch that hung, suspended, over the Spot. The arch grew slowly, perceptibly closer as Jacob watched.

The other identifiable clump of shadow detached itself from the crowd and began to creep in fits and starts toward Jacob and the chief. It was rounded on top, bigger above than below.

'Now there's where you could hide a projector!' Donaldson motioned with his chin toward the bulky, massive silhouette as it creeped toward them with a swaying, twisting motion.

'What, *Fagin*?'

Jacob whispered. Not that it would make any difference, with the Kanten's hearing what it was. 'You can't be serious! Why he's only been on two dives!'

'Yeah,' Donaldson mused. 'Still, all of those branches and such ... I'd have sooner searched Bubbacub's undies than have to pry in there after contraband.'

For an instant Jacob thought he caught a bit of a burr in the chief engineer's voice. He stared at his neighbor but the man had on his poker face. That in itself was a small miracle for Donaldson. It would be too much if the man were actually being witty.

They both rose to greet Fagin. The Kanten whistled a cheery response, showing no sign that he'd overheard them.

'Commandant Helene deSilva has expressed the opinion that solar weather conditions are surprisingly calm. She said that this will be of great value in solving certain solonomical problems unrelated to the Sun Ghosts. The measurements involved will take very little time. Much less than the time we will be saved, by these excellent conditions.

'In other words, my friends, you have about twenty minutes to get ready.'

Donaldson whistled. He called Jacob over and the two men set to work on the laser, bolting it into place and checking the projection tapes.

A few meters away, Dr Martine rummaged through her space-crate for small pieces of apparatus. Her psi helmet was already on her head and Jacob thought he could overhear her softly curse, 'Damn it, this time you're going to *talk* to me!'

22

DELEGATION

'"What is their purpose, these creatures of light?" the reporter asks. But he'd do better to ask, "What purpose has man?" Is it our job to scramble on our metaphorical knees, ignoring the pain with chin upthrust in childish pride, saying to all the universe: "See me! I am man! I crawl where others walk! But isn't it great that I can crawl anywhere?"

'Adaptability, the Neoliths claim, is the "specialization" of man. He cannot run as fast as a cheetah, but he can run. He cannot swim as well as an otter, but he can swim. His eyes are not so sharp as a hawk's nor can he store food in his cheeks. So he must train his eyes and create instruments from bits and pieces of tortured earth; not only to let him see, but to outrun the cat and to outswim the otter as well. He can walk across an arctic waste, swim a tropical river, climb a tree and, at the end of his journey, build a nice hotel. There he will clean up and then boast of his accomplishments over dinner with his friends.

'And yet for all recorded time our hero has been dissatisfied. He yearned to know his place in the world. He shouted aloud. He demanded to know why he was here! The universe of stars only smiled down at his questions with profound, ambiguous silence.

'He longed for a *purpose*. Denied, he took his frustration out on

193

his fellow creatures. The specialists around him knew their roles and he hated them for it. They became his slaves, his protein factories. They became the victims of his genocidal rage.

'"Adaptability" soon meant that we needed no one else. Species whose descendants might one day have been great became dust in the holocaust of man's egoism.

'It is only by the slimmest of luck that we became environmentalists shortly before Contact ... thus keeping from our heads the just wrath of our elders. Or was it luck? Is it an accident that John Muir, and those who followed, appeared soon after the first confirmed "sightings"?

'As the Reporter lies here, in a bubble, in a swaddling of deceptive pink vapor all around, he wonders if the purpose of man may be to be an example. Whatever original sin drove our Patrons off, long ago, is being paid off in a comedy.

'One hopes our neighbors are edified, as well as amused, as they watch us crawl about, gaping in wonder and often resentment at those who are fulfillment incarnate, without ambition.'

Pierre LaRoque took his thumb off the recording button and frowned. No, that last part wouldn't do. It sounded almost bitter. More whiney than poignant. In fact, all of it would have to be reworked. There was too little spontaneity. The sentences tried too hard.

He took a sip from the liquitube in his left hand, then began absently stroking his moustache. In front of him the brilliant herd of spinning toruses rose slowly as the ship righted itself. The maneuver had taken less time than he'd expected. Now there was no more time to digress on the plight of mankind. He could, after all, do that any day.

But this, this was extraordinary.

He pressed again on the switch and brought up the microphone.

'Note for rewrite,' he said. 'More irony, and more on advantages of certain types of specialization. Also mention the Tymbrimi ... how they're more adaptable than we'll ever be. Keep it short and upbeat on outcome if *all* humanity participates.'

Heretofore the rising herd had consisted of little rings, fifty or more kilometers away. Now the main body came into view, along with a small sliver of the photosphere. The nearest torus was a bright, spinning, blue-green monster. Along its rim, thin blue lines swiftly mixed and shifted, like meshing moire patterns. A white halo shimmered all around it.

LaRoque sighed. This would be his greatest challenge. When holos of these creatures were released everyone and his chimp butler would be tuning in to see if his words measured up. Yet he felt the inverse of what he must make them feel. The deeper the ship went into the Sun, the more detached he became. It was as if none of it was really happening. The creatures didn't seem real at all.

Also, he admitted, he was scared.

'Pearls of serendipity they are, strung on necklaces of lambent emerald, if some galactic galleon once foundered here, to leave its treasure on these feathery, fiery reefs, its diadems are now safe. Uncorrupted by time, they sparkle still. No hunter will carry them off in a sack.

'They defy logic, for they should not be here. They defy history, for they are not remembered. They defy the power of our instruments and even those of the Galactics, our elders.

'Imperturbable as Bombadil, they ignore the passing of oxygen and hydrogen in their incessant bickerings, and take nourishment from the most timeless of fonts.

'Do they recall ... could they have been *among* the Progenitors, back when the galaxy was new? We hope to ask, but for now they keep their counsel to themselves.'

Jacob looked up from his work when the herd came into view again. The sight had less effect on him than it had the first time around. To experience the emotions he'd felt during that first dive he'd have to see something else for the very first time. And to see anything anywhere near as impressive, he'd have to Jump.

It was one of the drawbacks of having monkeys for ancestors.

Still Jacob could spend hours looking at the lovely patterns the toroids made. And for a few moments at a time, when he remembered the significance of what he was seeing, he was awe-struck once again.

The computer board on Jacob's lap bore a shifting pattern of curving, connected lines, isophotes of the Ghost they'd seen an hour before.

It hadn't been much of a contact. One isolated Solarian had been caught by surprise as the ship came out from behind a thick wisp of filament near the edge of the herd.

It darted away from them, then hovered suspiciously at a few kilometers distance. Commandant deSilva had ordered the ship turned so that Donaldson's Parametric Laser could bear on the fluttering creature.

At first the Ghost had backed away. Donaldson muttered and cursed as he adjusted the laser, to carry the various modulations of Jacob's contact tape.

Then the creature reacted. Its (tentacles? wings?) shot out from the center as if snapped taut It began to ripple colorfully.

Then, in a flash of brilliant green, it was gone.

Jacob examined computer readouts from that reaction. The Solarian had presented the rim cameras with a good view. The earliest recordings showed that part of its rippling was in phase with the bass rhythm of the whale melody. Jacob was now trying to find out if the complicated display it emitted just before jetting away had a pattern that might be interpretable as a reply.

He finished drawing the analysis program he wanted the computer to pursue. It was to look for variations on the whale-song theme and rhythm in three regimes, color, time, and brightness across the surface of the Ghost. If it found anything definite he'd be able to set up a computer linkup in realtime during the next encounter.

That is, if there *was* a next encounter. The whale song had only been an introduction to the sequence of scales and mathematical series Jacob had planned to send. But the Ghost hadn't stuck around to 'listen' to the rest.

He put the computer board aside and lowered his couch so that he could look at the nearest toroids without moving his head. A pair of them swung slowly by at forty-five degrees from the angle of the deck.

Apparently the 'spinning' of the torus creatures was more complicated than had been previously thought. The intricate, swiftly changing patterns that swept rapidly around the rim of each represented something in their internal makeup.

When two of the toroids touched each other, nudging for better positions in the magnetic fields, there was no change in the rotating figures. They interacted with each other as if they weren't spinning at all.

The pushing and shoving became more pronounced with time as they transited the herd. Helene deSilva suggested that it was because the active region they were above was dying out. The magnetic fields were getting more and more diffuse.

Culla dropped into the couch next to him, bringing his mashies together in a clack. Jacob was starting to recognize some of the rhythms Culla's dental work made in various situations. It had taken a long time to realize that they were part of a Pring's fundamental repertoire, like facial expressions for a human being.

'May I shit here, Jacob?' Culla asked. 'This ish my firsht opportunity to thank you for your cooperation back on Mercury.'

'You don't have to thank me, Culla. A two-year secrecy oath is pretty much *de rigueur* for an incident like this. Anyway, once Commandant deSilva got orders from Earth it was pretty clear that no one would be going home until they signed.'

'Shtfil, you had every right to tell the world, the galaxy. The Library Inshtitute hash been shamed by Bubbacub'sh actionsh. It ish admirable of you, the dish-coverer of hish ... mishtake, to show reshtraint and let them make ammendsh.'

'What will the Institute do ... besides punishing Bubbacub?'

Culla took a sip from his ubiquitous liquitube. His eyes shone.

'They will probably cancel Earth's debt and donate Branch shervices free for shome time. A longer time if the Confederacy agreesh to a period of silence. I cannot overshtate their eagernesh to avoid a shcandal.

'In addition, you will probably be rewarded.'

'Me?' Jacob felt numb. To a 'primitive' Earthman, almost any reward the Galactics chose to give would be like a magic lamp. He could hardly believe what he was hearing.

'Yesh, although there will probably be shome bitternesh that you did not keep your dishcoveriesh more private. The magnitude of their generoshity will probably be invershe to the notoriety Bubbacub'sh case getsh.'

'Oh, I see.' The bubble was burst. It was one thing to get a token of gratitude from powers-that-be, and quite another to be offered a bribe. Not that the value of the reward would be any less. In fact, the prize would probably be even more valuable.

Or would it? No alien thought exactly the way a human would. The directors of the Institute of the Libraries were an enigma to him. All he knew for certain was that they wouldn't like to get a bad press. He wondered if Culla was speaking now in his official capacity, or simply predicting what he thought would happen next.

Culla suddenly turned and looked up at the passing herd. His eyes glowed and a short buzzing came from behind the thick, prehensile lips. The Pring pulled the microphone from the slot next to his couch.

'Excushe me, Jacob. But I think I shee shomething. I musht report to the Commandant.'

Culla spoke briefly into the microphone, not moving his gaze from a position about thirty degrees to their right and twenty-five degrees high. Jacob looked but saw nothing. He could hear a distant murmuring of Helene's voice filling the region of the head of Culla's couch. Then the ship began to turn.

Jacob checked the computer board. The results were in. The previous encounter had elicited nothing recognizable as a reply. They'd just have to keep on doing as they had before.

'Sophonts,' Helene's voice rang out over the intercom, 'Pring Culla has made another sighting. Please return to your stations.'

Culla's mashies clacked. Jacob looked up.

At about forty-five degrees, a tiny flickering point of light began to grow just beyond the bulk of the nearest toroid. The blue dot grew as it approached until they could make out five uneven appendages, bilaterally symmetric. It loomed up swiftly, then stopped.

Sun Ghost manifestation, type two, leered down at them in its gross mockery of the shape of a man. The chromosphere glowed red through the jagged holes of its eyes and mouth.

No attempt was made to bring the apparition in line with the flip-side cameras. It would probably have been futile and besides, this time the P-laser took precedence.

He told Donaldson to continue playing the primary contact tape, from the point where the last contact broke off.

The engineer raised his microphone.

'Everyone please put on your goggles. We're going to turn on the laser now.' He put on his own, then looked around to make sure everyone in sight had complied (Culla was exempted; they took his word for it that he was in no danger). Then he threw the switch.

Even through the goggles, Jacob could see a dim glow against the inner surface of the shield wall as the beam punched through toward the Ghost. He wondered if the anthropomorphic figure would be more cooperative than the earlier, 'natural-shaped' manifestation had been. For all he knew, this was the same creature. Maybe it left, earlier, to 'put on its makeup' for this present appearance.

The Ghost fluttered impassively while the beam from the Communication Laser shone right through it. Not far away, Jacob could hear Martine curse softly.

'Wrong, wrong, wrong!' she hissed. Her psi helmet and goggles made only her nose and chin visible. 'There's *something* but it's not *there*. Dammit! What in hell's the matter with this thing!'

Suddenly, the apparition swelled like a butterfly squashed flat against the outside of the ship. The features of its 'face' smeared out into long narrow strips of ochre blackness. The arms and body spread until the creature was nothing but a ragged rectangular band of blue across ten degrees of the sky. Flecks of green began to form, here, and there, along its surface. They dodged about, mixed and coalesced, and then began to take on coherent form.

'Dear sweet God in heaven,' Donaldson murmured.

From somewhere nearby Fagin let out a whistling, shivering, diminished seventh. Culla began to chatter.

Across its length, the Solarian was covered with bright green letters, in the Roman alphabet. They spelled:

LEAVE NOW. DO NOT RETURN.

Jacob gripped the sides of his couch. Despite the sound effects of the E.T.s, and the hoarse breathing of the humans, the silence was unbearable.

'Millie!' he tried as hard as he could not to shout. 'Are you getting anything?'

Martine moaned.

'Yes ... NO! I'm getting something, but it doesn't make sense! It doesn't correlate!'

'Well try sending a question! Ask if it's receiving your psi!'

Martine nodded and pressed her hands against her face in concentration.

The letters immediately reformed overhead.

CONCENTRATE. SPEAK ALOUD FOR FOCUS.

Jacob was stunned. Deep inside he could feel his suppressed half shivering in horror. What he couldn't solve terrified Mr Hyde. 'Ask it why it'll talk to us now and not before.' Martine repeated the question aloud, slowly.

THE POET. HE WILL SPEAK FOR US. HE IS HERE.

'No, no I can't!' LaRoque cried. Jacob turned quickly and saw the little journalist, scrunched, terrified near the food machines.

HE WILL SPEAK FOR US.

The green letters glowed.

'Doctor Martine,' Helene deSilva called. 'Ask the Solarian why we shouldn't come back.'

After a pause, the letters shifted again.

WE WANT PRIVACY. PLEASE LEAVE.

'And if we do come back? Then what?' Donaldson asked. Grimly, Martine repeated the question.

NOTHING. YOU WONT SEE US. MAYBE OUR YOUNG, OUR CATTLE.
NOT US.

That explained the two types of Solarians, Jacob thought. The 'normal' variety must be the young, given simple tasks such as shepherding the toroids. Where, then, did the adults live? What kind of culture did they have? How could creatures made of ionized plasma communicate with watery human beings? Jacob ached at the creature's threat. If they wanted to, the adults could avoid a Sunship, or any conceivable fleet of Sunships, as easily as an eagle could a balloon. If they cut off contact now, humans could never force them to renew it.

'Pleashe,' Culla asked. 'Ashk it if Bubbacub offended them.' The Pring's eyes glowed hotly and the chattering continued, muffled, between each word he spoke.

BUBBACUB MEANS NOTHING. INSIGNIFICANT. JUST LEAVE.

The Solarian began to fade. The ragged rectangle grew smaller as it slowly backed away.

'Wait!' Jacob stood up. He stretched out one hand grabbing at nothing.

'Don't cut us off! We're your nearest neighbors! We only want to share with you! At least tell us who you are!'

The image was blurred with distance. A wisp of darker gas swept in and covered the Solarian, but not before they read one last message. With a crowd of 'young' gathered around it, the adult repeated one of its earlier sentences.

THE POET SPEAKS FOR US.

PART VIII

In ancient days two aviators procured to themselves wings. Daedalus flew safely through the middle air and was duly honoured on his landing. Icarus soared upwards to the sun till the wax melted which bound his wings and his flight ended in fiasco ... The classical authorities tell us, of course, that he was only 'doing a stunt'; but I prefer to think of him as the man who brought to light a serious constructional defect in the flying-machines of his day.

FROM *STARS AND ATOMS*, BY SIR ARTHUR EDDINGTON
(OXFORD UNIVERSITY PRESS, 1927, P. 41)

23

AN EXCITED STATE

Pierre LaRoque sat with his back to the utility dome. He hugged his knees and stared vacantly at the deck. He wondered, miserably, if Millie would give him a shot to last him until the Sunship got out of the chromosphere.

Unfortunately, that wouldn't be in keeping with his new role as a prophet. He shuddered. During his entire career he had never realized how much it meant to have only to comment, and not to have to shape events. The Solarian had given him a curse, not a blessing.

He wondered, dully, if the creature had chosen him in an ironic whim ... as a joke: Or had it somehow planted words deep within him that would come out when he got back to Earth, shocking and embarrassing him?

Or am I just supposed to spout out my own opinions as I always have? He rocked slowly, miserably. To foist one's ideas on others by dint of personality was one thing. To speak clothed in a prophet's mantle was quite another.

The others had gathered near the command station to discuss the next step. He could hear them talking and wished they'd just go away. Without looking up, he could feel it when they turned and stared at him.

LaRoque wished he were dead.

'I say we should bump him off,' Donaldson suggested. His burr was very pronounced, now. Jacob, listening nearby, wished the ethnic languages fad had never caught on. 'There'll be no end of the trouble that man'll cause if 'e gets loose on Earth,' the engineer finished.

Martine chewed on her lip for a moment. 'No, that wouldn't be wise. Better beam Earth for instructions when we get back to Hermes. The feds may decide to use up an emergency sequester allotment on him, but I don't think anyone would get away with actually eliminating Peter.'

'I'm surprised you react that way to the chief's suggestion,' Jacob said. 'One would think you'd be aghast at the idea.'

Martine shrugged. 'By now it must be clear to all of you that I represent a faction in the Confederacy Assembly. Peter is my friend, but if I felt it was my duty to Earth to put him out of the way, I'd do it myself.' She looked grim.

Jacob wasn't as surprised as he might have been. If the chief engineer felt a need to put up a layer of flippancy, to get through the shock of the last hour, many of the others had dropped all pretense. Martine was willing to think about the unthinkable. Nearby, LaRoque didn't pretend to be anything but scared as he rocked slowly, apparently oblivious to them all.

Donaldson raised his index finger.

'Did you notice that the Solarian didn' say anything at all about the message beam? It passed right through 'im and he didn't seem to care. Yet earlier, the other Ghost . . . '

'The juvenile.'

' . . . the juvenile, definitely reacted.'

Jacob scratched his earlobe. 'There's no end to mysteries. Why has the adult creature always avoided being in line with our rim instruments? Has it got something to hide? Why all the threatening gestures on all the previous dives, when he was capable of communicating ever since Dr Martine brought her psi helmet aboard months ago?'

'Maybe your P-laser gave it an element it needed,' a crewman suggested, an Oriental gentleman named Chen, whom Jacob had met only at the start of the dive. 'An alternative hypothesis would be that it was waiting for someone of reasonable status to speak to.'

Martine sniffed.

'That's the theory we were working on on the *last* dive, and it didn't work. Bubbacub *faked* contact, and for all of his talents Fagin failed . . . oh, you mean Peter . . . '

The silence could be cut with a knife.

'Jacob, I sure wish we could have found a projector,' Donaldson smiled wryly. 'T'would have solved all our problems.'

Jacob grinned back, without humor. '*Deux ex machina*, Chief? You know better than to expect special favors from the universe.'

'We might as well resign ourselves,' Martine said. 'We may never see another adult Ghost. Folks were skeptical about all of these stories about "anthropomorphic shapes" back on Earth. It's just the word of a couple dozen sophonts that have seen them, plus a few blurred photos. In time it may be all put down to hysteria, despite my tests.' She looked down gloomily.

Jacob was aware of Helene deSilva standing next to him. She had been strangely silent since calling them together a few minutes before.

'Well at least this time Sundiver itself isn't threatened,' Jacob said. 'The solonomical research can go on, and so can studies of the toroid herds. The Solarian said that they won't interfere.'

'Yeah,' Donaldson added. 'But will *he*?' he gestured at LaRoque.

*

'We have to decide what to do next. We're drifting near the bottom of the herd now. Do we go up and keep poking around? Maybe Solarians vary among themselves as much as we humans do. Maybe the one we met was a grouch.' Jacob suggested.

'I hadn't thought of that,' Martine commented.

'Let's put the Parametric Laser on automatic and add a portion in coded English to the communication tape. It'll beam into the herd as we spiral leisurely upward, on the off chance that a friendlier adult Solarian might be attracted.'

'If one is, I sure hope it doesn't scare me out of my codpiece like that last one did,' Donaldson muttered.

Helene deSilva rubbed her shoulders as if fighting a chill. 'Has anyone else got anything to say "en camera"? Then I'm going to settle the humans-only part of this discussion by ruling out any precipitate action concerning Mr LaRoque. Just everybody keep your eyes on him.

'This meeting is in recess. Think about ideas on what to do next. Someone please ask Fagin and Culla to join us at the refreshment center in twenty minutes. That's all.'

Jacob felt a hand on his arm. Helene stood next to him.

'Are you all right?' he asked.

'Fine ... fine.' She smiled without much conviction. 'I'd just ... Jacob, would you come to my office with me, please?'

'Sure, after you.'

Helene shook her head. Her fingers dug into his arm and she pulled him along in a fast walk toward the closet-sized cubbyhole in the side of the dome that served as a captain's office. When they were inside she cleared a space on the tiny desk and motioned for him to sit. Then she closed the door and sagged back against it.

'Oh, God,' she sighed.

'Helene ...' Jacob started forward, then stopped. Her eyes blazed blue up at him.

'Jacob,' she was making a concentrated effort to be calm. 'Can you promise me you'll do me a favor for a few minutes and not talk about it afterwards? I can't tell you what it is until you agree.' Her eyes appealed silently.

Jacob didn't have to think. 'Of course, Helene. You can ask anything. But tell me what's the ...'

'Then please, just hold me.' Her voice trailed off in a cry. She came up against his chest with her arms tucked in in front of her. In mute surprise, Jacob put his arms around her and held on tightly.

Slowly he rocked her back and forth as a series of powerful tremors ran through! her body. 'Sshhh ... It's all right ...' He spoke reassuring nonsense words. Her hair brushed his cheek and her smell seemed to fill the tiny room. It was heady.

For a time they stood together silently. She moved her head slowly on his shoulder.

The tremors subsided. Gradually her body relaxed. He stroked the taut muscles of her back with one hand and they loosened one by one.

Jacob wondered who was doing whom the favor. He hadn't felt this peaceful this calm, for Ifni knew how long. It moved him that she trusted him so.

More, it made him *happy*. There was a bitter little voice below that was gnashing its teeth at this moment, but he wasn't listening. Doing what he was doing now felt more natural than breathing.

After a few more moments, Helene lifted her head. When she spoke her voice was thick.

'I've never been so scared in all my life,' she said. 'I want you to understand that I didn't *have* to do this. I could have been Iron Lady for the rest of the dive ... but you were here, available ... I had to. I'm sorry.'

Jacob noticed that Helene made no effort to back away. He kept his arms around her.

'No problem,' he spoke softly. 'Sometime later I'll tell you how nice it was. Don't worry about being scared. I just about went out of my skin when I saw those letters. Curiosity and numbness are my defense mechanisms. You saw how the others were reacting. You just had more responsibility is all.'

Helene didn't say anything. She brought her hands up and put them on his shoulders, without creating a space between them.

'Anyway,' Jacob went on, brushing free locks of her hair into place. 'You must have been more startled lots of times during your Jumps.'

Helene stiffened and pushed back from his chest.

'Mr Demwa, you are intolerable! You and your constantly mentioning my Jumps! Do you think I've ever been as scared as that?! Just how old do you think I am?'

Jacob smiled. She hadn't pushed back hard enough to shake off his arms. Obviously she wasn't ready for him to let go.

'Well, relativity-wise ...' he began.

'*Fuck* relativity! I'm twenty-five! I may have seen more sky than you have but I've experienced a hell of a lot less of the *real* universe than you ... and my competence rating says nothing about how I feel inside! It's scary having to be perfect and strong and responsible for people's lives ... for *me* at least, it is, unlike you, you impervious, imperturbable, once-upon-a-time hero-oaf, standing there calm as you please, just like Captain Beloc on *Calypso* when we ran that crazy fake blockade at J8'lek and ... and now I'm going to go highly illegal and order you to kiss me, since you don't seem about to do it on your own!'

She looked at him defiantly. When Jacob laughed and pulled her toward him, she resisted momentarily. Then her arms slid around his neck and her lips pressed up against his.

Jacob distantly felt her tremble again. But this time it was different. It was hard to tell how it was different, since he was busy at the moment. Enchantingly so.

Suddenly, agonizingly, he realized how long it had been since ... two very long years. He pushed the thought aside. Tania was dead, and Helene was beautifully, wonderfully alive. He held her tighter and answered her passion in the only way possible.

'Excellent therapy, Doctor,' she teased as he tried to comb the knots out of his hair. 'I feel like a million bucks, though I'll admit you look like you've been through a wringer.'

'What's ... a "wringer"? Never mind, I don't want any explanations of your anachronisms. Look at you! You're *proud* of making me feel like a bar of steel that's been melted and bent out of shape!'

'Yup.'

Jacob didn't succeed at suppressing a grin. 'Shut up and respect your elders. How much time do we have, anyway?'

Helene glanced at her ring. 'About two minutes. Damned awkward time to have a meeting. You were just starting to get interesting. Who the hell called it at such an inconvenient moment?'

'You did.'

'Ah, yes. So I did. Next time I'll give you at least a half hour, and we'll investigate matters in more detail.'

Jacob nodded uncertainly. It was hard to tell, sometimes, at what level this fem was kidding.

Before she unlatched the door, Helene soberly leaned up and kissed him.

'Thank you, Jacob.'

He caressed the side of her face with his left hand. She pressed against it briefly. There was nothing to say when he brought the hand away.

Helene opened the door and looked out. There was no one in sight but the pilot. Everyone else had probably gathered for the second meeting at the refreshment center.

'Let's go,' she said. 'I could eat a horse!'

Jacob shuddered. If he was going to get to know Helene better, he'd better be prepared for a lot of exercise for his imagination. A horse indeed!

Still, he dropped a little less than a foot back as they walked, so he could watch Helene move. It was so distracting that he didn't notice when a spinning torus swung past the ship, its sides emblazoned with starbursts and surrounded by a halo as white and bright as the down on the breast of a dove.

24

SPONTANEOUS EMISSION

Culla was just pulling a liquitube out of Fagin's foliage when they returned. One arm was enmeshed in the Kanten's leafy branches. The Pring held another liquitube in his other hand.

'Welcome back,' Fagin fluted. 'Pring Culla was just assisting me with my dietary supplement. I am afraid that in doing so he has neglected his own.'

'No problem, shir,' Culla said. He slowly pulled the tube backward.

Jacob came up behind the Pring to watch. This was a chance to learn more about Fagin's workings. The Kanten once told him that his species had no modesty taboo, so surely he wouldn't mind if Jacob sighted along Culla's arm to see what sort of orifice the semi-vegetable alien used.

He was bent over thus when suddenly Culla jerked back, pulling the liquitube free. His elbow collided painfully with the ridge above Jacob's eye, sending him backwards on his rump.

Culla chattered loudly. The liquitubes dropped from the hands that fell limply to his sides. Helene had trouble choking back a fit of laughter. Jacob hurried to his feet. His 'I'll-get-even-someday' grimace at Helene only made her cough more loudly.

'Forget it, Culla,' he said. 'No damage done. It was my fault. I have a spare eye anyway.' He resisted the urge to rub the spot where it hurt.

Culla looked down at him with shining eyes. The chattering subsided.

'You are mosht gracioush, Friend-Jacob,' he said at last. 'In a proper client-elder shituation I wash at fault for careleshnesh. I thank you for forgiving me.'

'Tut tut, my friend.' Jacob waved it aside. Actually he could feel the beginnings of a nasty bump forming. Still, it would be worth-while changing the subject to save Culla further embarrassment.

'Speaking of spare eyes, I read that your species, and most of those on Pring, had only one eye before the Pila arrived and started their genetic program.'

'Yesh, Jacob. The Pila gave ush two eyesh for esthetic purposhesh. In the galaxy mosht bipedsh are binocular. They did not want ush … teashed by the other young raceesh.'

Jacob frowned. There was something … he knew Mr Hyde already had it but was holding back, still in his peevish mood.

Damnit, it's my unconscious!

No use. Oh well.

'But Culla, I also read that your species were arboreal … even *brachiating*, if I remember right …'

'What's that mean?' Donaldson whispered to deSilva. 'It means they used to swing from tree limbs,' she answered. 'Now hush!'

'… But if they had only one eye how did your ancestors have good enough depth perception to keep from missing when they reached for the next branch?'

Before Jacob even finished his sentence he felt jubilation. *That* had been the question Mr Hyde was holding back! So the little devil *didn't* have a complete lock on unconscious insight! Helene was doing him good already. He hardly cared what Culla's answer was.

'I thought you knew, Friend-Jacob. I overheard Commandant deShilva explaining during our firsht dive that I have different receiversh than you do. My eyesh can detect *phase* ash well ash intenshity.'

'Yes,' Jacob was starting to have fun now. He'd have to keep his eyes on Fagin. The old Kanten would warn him if he was getting into an area Culla found touchy.

'Yes, but sunlight, particularly in a forest, would have to be totally incoherent … random in phase. Now a dolphin uses a system like yours in her sonar, keeping the phase and all. But she provides her own coherent phase field by letting out well-timed squeaks into her surroundings.'

Jacob stepped back, enjoying a dramatic pause. His foot fell on one of the liquitubes Culla had dropped. Absently he picked it up.

'So if all your ancestors' eyes did was retain the phase, the whole thing still wouldn't work without having a source of coherent light in your environment.' Jacob got excited. 'Natural lasers? Do your forests have some natural source of laser light?'

'By George that would be interesting!' Donaldson commented.

Culla nodded. 'Yesh, Jacob. We call them the …' his mashies came together in a complicated rhythm '… plants. It'sh incredible that you

209

dedushed their exishtence from sho few cluesh. You are to be congratulated. I will show you picturesh of one when we get back.'

Jacob caught a glimpse of Helene, smiling at him, possessively. (Deep inside his head he felt a distant rumbling. He ignored it) 'Yes, I'd like to see it, Culla.'

The liquitube was sticky in his hand. There was a smell in the air, like new mown hay.

'Here, Culla.' He held out the liquitube. 'I think you dropped this.' Then his arm froze. He stared at the tube for a moment then broke out laughing.

'Millie, come here!' he shouted. 'Look at this!' He held out the tube to Dr Martine and pointed to the label.

'3-(alpha-Acetonylbenzyl) – 4-hydroxycoumarin alkalide mix?' She looked uncertain for a moment then her jaw dropped. 'Why, that's Warfarin! So it's one of Culla's dietary supplements! Well then how the hell did a sample get into Dwayne's pharmacopoeia?'

Jacob smiled ruefully. 'I'm afraid that misunderstanding was all my fault. I absentmindedly picked up a sample of one of Culla's beverage mix tablets back aboard the *Bradbury*. I was so sleepy then that I forgot about it. It must have gone into the same pocket where I later stashed Dr Kepler's samples. They all went together to Dr Laird's lab.

'It was just a wild coincidence that one of Culla's nutrient supplements happened to be identical with an old terrestrial poison, but boy did it have me going in circles! I was thinking Bubbacub slipped it to Kepler to make him unstable, but I was never very happy with that theory.' He shrugged.

'Well *I*, for one, am relieved the whole thing is solved!' Martine laughed. 'I didn't like what people were thinking about me!'

It was a minor discovery. But somehow clearing up one small, nagging mystery had transformed the mood of those present. They talked animatedly.

The only pall came as Pierre LaRoque passed by, laughing softly. Dr Martine went to ask him to join them, but the little man just shook his head, then resumed walking in a slow path around the rim of the ship.

Helene stood next to Jacob. She touched the hand that still held Culla's liquitube.

'Speaking of coincidences, did you take a close look at the formula for Culla's supplement?' She stopped and looked up, Culla came up to them and bowed.

'If you are finished now, Jacob. I will put thish shticky tube away.'

'What? Oh sure, Culla. Here. Now what were you saying, Helene?'

Even when her face was serious it was hard not to be struck by her beauty. It's the initial 'falling' of love that, for a time, makes listening to one's lover difficult.

'... I was just saying that I noticed an interesting coincidence when Dr Martine read that chemical formula aloud. Do you remember earlier, when we were talking about organic dye lasers? Well ...'

Helene's voice faded away. Jacob could see her mouth move, but all he could make out was one word: '... coumarin ...'

There was trouble erupting below. His channeled neurosis had mutinied. Mr Hyde was trying to stop him from listening to Helene. In fact, he suddenly realized, his other half had been holding back its usual tithe of insight ever since Helene had hinted, in their conversation at the edge of the deck, that she wanted *him* to give her the genes she'd be taking to the stars when the *Calypso* jumped.

Hyde hates Helene! he realized with a shock. The first girl I've met who could begin to replace what I've lost (a tremor, like a migraine, threatened to split his skull) and Hyde hates her! (The headache came and went instantly.)

What was more, that part of his unconscious had been holding out on him. It had seen all of the pieces and hadn't let them surface. This was a violation of the agreement. It was intolerable, and he couldn't figure out why!

'Jacob, are you all right?' Helene's voice was back. She looked at him quizzically. Over her shoulder he could see Culla, looking down at them from near the food machines.

'Helene,' he said abruptly. 'Listen, I left a small box of pills by the Pilot Board. They're for these headaches I get sometimes ... could you please look for them for me?' He brought a hand up to his forehead and grimaced.

'Why ... sure,' Helene touched his arm. 'Why don't you come with me? You could lie down. We'll talk ...'

'No,' he took her by the shoulders and gently turned her the right way. 'Please, you go. I'll wait here.' Furiously, he fought down panic at the time it was taking to get her away.

'Okay, I'll be right back,' Helene said. As she walked away Jacob sighed with relief. Most of those present had their goggles on their belts, per standing orders. The competent and efficient Commandant deSilva had left hers at her couch.

When she had gone about ten meters toward her destination, Helene began to wonder.

Jacob never left any box of pills by the Pilot Board. I would have known it if he had. He wanted to get rid of me! But why?

She looked back. Jacob was just turning away from a food

machine with a protein roll in his hand. He smiled at Martine and nodded at Chen, then started to walk past Fagin to get out onto the open deck. Behind him Culla watched the group with bright eyes, near the gravity-loop hatch.

Jacob didn't look like he had a headache at all! Helene felt hurt and confused.

Well if he doesn't want me around, that's fine. I'll make a pretense of looking for his damned pills!

She started to turn when, suddenly, Jacob tripped on one of Fagin's root pods and went sprawling on the deck. The protein roll bounced away and fetched up against the Parametric Laser housing. Before she could react, Jacob was on his feet again, smiling sheepishly. He walked over to pick up the food ball. Bending over, his shoulder touched the barrel of the laser.

Blue light flooded the room instantly. Whooping alarms howled. Helene instinctively covered her eyes behind her arm and grabbed for the goggles at her waist.

They weren't there!

Her couch was three meters away. She could picture where she was exactly, and where she'd stupidly left the goggles. She turned and dove for them, coming up again in one movement, the protectors over her eyes.

There were bright spots everywhere. The P-laser, shoved out of plumb with the ship's radius, was sending its beam bouncing about the concave inner surface of the Sunship's shell. The modulated 'contact code' flashed against the deck and dome.

Bodies writhed on the deck near the food machines. No one had approached the P-laser to shut it off. Where were Jacob and Donaldson? Were they blinded in the first instant?

Several figures struggled near the gravity-loop hatch. In the flashing, sepulchral light she saw that they were Jacob Demwa and the chief engineer ... and Culla. They ... Jacob was trying to shove a bag over the alien's head!

There was no time to decide what to do. Between intervening in the mysterious fight and eliminating a possible danger to her ship, Helene didn't have to choose. She ran over to the P-laser, ducking under faint, crisscrossing trails, and tore out the plug.

The flashing points of light stopped abruptly, except for one that coincided with a shriek of pain and a crash, near the hatchway. The alarms shut off and suddenly there was only the sound of people moaning.

'Captain, what is it? What's happening?' The voice of the pilot rang out over the intercom. Helene picked up the mike from a couch nearby.

'Hughes,' she said quickly. 'What's ship's status?'

'Status nominal, sir. But it's a good thing I had my goggles on! What the devil happened?'

'P-laser got loose. Continue as is. Hold her steady about a klick from the herd. I'll be back to you soon.' She released the mike and raised her head to shout. 'Chen! Dubrowsky! Report!' She peered about in the dimness.

'Over here, skipper!' It was Chen's voice. Helene cursed and tore off the goggles. Chen was over beyond the hatchway. He knelt over a figure on the deck.

'It's Dubrowsky,' the man said. 'He's dead. Fried through the eyes.'

Dr Martine cowered behind Fagin's thick trunk. The Kanten whistled softly as Helene hurried over.

'Are you two okay?'

Fagin let out a long note that sounded vaguely like a slurred 'yes.' Martine nodded once, jerkily, but she stayed clutching Fagin's trunk. Her goggles were skewed over her face. Helene took them off.

'Come on, Doctor. You have patients.' She pulled at Martine's arm. 'Chen! Go to my office and get the aid-kit! On the double!'

Martine started to get up, then sagged back shaking her head.

Helene gritted her teeth and hauled up on the arm she held, suddenly, snapping the older woman upwards with a gasp. Martine staggered to her feet.

Helene slapped her once across the face. 'Wake up, Doctor! You'll help me with these men or so help me I'll kick your teeth in!' She took Martine's arm and supported her across the few meters to where Chief Donaldson and Jacob Demwa lay.

Jacob moaned and began to stir. Helene felt her heart rise when he took his arm away from his face. The burns were superficial and they hadn't touched the eyes. Jacob had his goggles on.

She steered Martine over next to Donaldson and made her sit. The chief engineer was badly seared along the left side of his face. The left lens of his goggles was smashed.

Chen arrived on the run, carrying the aid-kit.

Dr Martine turned away from Donaldson and shuddered. Then she looked up and saw the crewman with the medical bag. She held out her hands for it.

'Will you need help, Doctor?' Helene asked.

Martine spread instruments on the deck. She shook her head without looking up.

'No. Be quiet.'

Helene called Chen over. 'Go look for LaRoque and Culla. Report when you've found them.' The man ran off.

Jacob moaned again and tried to rise up on his elbows. Helene got a cloth from the fountain nearby and wet it. She knelt by Jacob and pulled on his shoulders to get his head onto her lap.

He winced as she dabbed gently at his wounds.

'Oh . . . ' he moaned and brought a hand to the top of his head. 'I should've known better. His ancestors were tree swingers. He'd have to have a chimp's strength. And he looks so weak!'

'Can you tell me what happened?' she asked softly.

Jacob grunted as he groped beneath his back with his left hand. He tugged on something a couple of times. Finally he pulled out the large bag the protection goggles had come in. He looked at it, then tossed it away.

'My head feels as if it's been sandblasted,' he said. He pushed himself up into sitting position, wavered for a moment with his hands on his head, then he let them drop.

'Culla wouldn't happen to be lying unconscious around here, would he? I was hoping I turned into a fighting fool after he knocked me dizzy, but I guess I just blacked out.'

'I don't know where Culla is,' Helene said. 'Now What . . . ?'

Chen's voice boomed over the intercom.

'Skipper? I've found LaRoque. He's at degrees two-forty. He's okay. In fact, he didn't even know anything was wrong!'

Jacob moved over next to Dr Martine and began to talk to her urgently. Helene stood up and went to the intercom next to the food center.

'Have you seen Culla?'

'Nossir, not a sign anywhere. He must be on flip-side.' Chen's voice dropped. 'I had the impression there was a *fight* going on. Do you know what happened?'

'I'll get back to you when I know something. Meanwhile you'd better relieve Hughes.'

Jacob joined her by the intercom.

'Donaldson will be all right, but he'll need a new eye. Listen, Helene, I'm going to have to go after Culla. Lend me one of your men, will you? Then you'd better get us out of here as fast as you can.'

She whirled. 'You just *killed* one of my men! Dubrowsky's dead! Donaldson is blinded, and now you want me to send someone else to help you harass poor Culla some more? What madness is this?'

'I didn't kill anyone, Helene.'

'I *saw* you, you clumsy oaf! You bumped the p-laser and it went crazy! So did you! Why were you attacking Culla?'

'Helene . . . ' Jacob winced. He brought a hand to his head. 'There's no time to explain. You've got to get us out of here. There's no telling what he'll do down there now that we know.'

'Explain first!'

'I ... I bumped the laser on purpose ... I ...'

Helene's shipsuit fit so snugly that Jacob would never have thought she had the snug little stun gun that appeared in her hand. 'Go on, Jacob,' she said evenly.

' ... He was watching me. I knew if I showed a sign I'd caught on, he could blind us all in an instant. I sent you away to get you clear and then went after the goggles bag. I kicked the laser free to confuse him ... laser light all over the place ...'

'And killed and maimed my men!'

Jacob drew himself together. 'Listen, you little nit!' He towered over her. 'I turned that beam down! It might blind but it wouldn't burn!

'Now if you don't believe me, knock me out! Strap me in! Only get us out of here fast, before Culla kills us all!'

'Culla ...'

'His *eyes*, damnit! *Coumarin!* His "dietary supplement" is a dye used in lasers! *He* killed Dubrowsky when he tried to help me and Donaldson!

'He was lying about that laser plant back on his home planet! The Pring have their *own* source of coherent light! He's been projecting the "adult" type Sun Ghosts all along! And ... my god!' Jacob punched at the air.

' ... if his projector is subtle enough to display fake "Ghosts" on the inside of a Sunship shell, it must be good enough to interact with the optical inputs of those Library designed computers! *He* programmed the computers to tag LaRoque as a Probationer. And ... and I was next to him when he programmed Jeff's ship to self-destruct! He was feeding in commands all the time I was admiring the pretty lights!'

Helene backed away, shaking her head. Jacob took a step toward her, looming large with fists tight, but his face was a mask of self-reproach.

'Why was Culla always the first to spot the humanoid Ghosts? Why were there none seen during the time he was with Kepler on Earth? Why didn't I think, before this, about Culla's reasons for volunteering to have his "retina" read during the identity search!'

The words were coming too fast. Helene's brow knit with tension as she tried to think.

Jacob's eyes pleaded. 'Helene, you've got to believe me.'

She hesitated, then cried out, 'Oh shit!' and threw herself at the intercom.

'Chen! Get us out of here! Never mind strap-in warning, just put on max thrust and crank up the time-compression! I want to see black sky before I blink twice!'

'Aye sir!' came the reply.

The ship surged up against them as the compensation fields were temporarily overcome, sending both Helene and Jacob staggering. The Commandant held onto the intercom.

'All hands, keep your goggles on at all times from now on. Everybody please strap in as quick as you can. Hughes, report to the loop-hatch; on the double!'

Outside, the toruses began to pass by more rapidly. As each beast fell below the rim of the deck, its rims flashed brightly as if bidding them adieu.

'I should have caught on too,' Helene said dismally. 'Instead I turned off the P-laser and probably let him get away.'

Jacob kissed her quickly, hard enough to leave her lips tingling.

'You didn't know. I'd have done the same thing in your shoes.'

She touched her lips and stared past him at Dubrowsky's body. 'You sent me away because . . .'

'Captain,' Chen's voice interrupted. 'I'm having trouble getting the time-compression off automatic. Can I keep Hughes here to help? We've also just lost maser link with Hermes.'

Jacob shrugged. 'First the maser link to keep word from getting out, then time-compression, then the gravity drive, finally the stasis. I guess the last step is to blow the shields, unless the other steps are sufficient They should be.'

Helene toggled the intercom. 'Negative, Chen. I want Hughes now! Do what you can alone.' She cut the switch.

'I'm going with you.'

'No you aren't,' he said. He put his goggles back on and picked up the bag from the floor. 'If Culla gets to step three we're cooked, literally. But if I can stop him part-way you're the only one who'd stand a chance of piloting us out. Now please lend me that gun, it could be useful.'

Helene handed it over. At this stage argument would be ridiculous. Jacob was in charge. She had no ideas of her own.

The quiet thrumming of the ship changed its rhythm, becoming a low, uneven hum.

Helene answered Jacob's questioning glance. 'It's the time-compression. He's already started slowing us down. In more ways than one, we haven't very much time.'

25

A TRAPPED STATE

Jacob crouched in the hatchway, ready to dive back behind the combing at the sight of a tall, gangling alien. So far, so good. Culla hadn't been in the gravity loop.

The turnaround route to flip-side, the only route, might have been a good place for an ambush. But Jacob wasn't particularly surprised that Culla wasn't there, for two reasons.

The first was tactical. Culla's weapon operated on line-of-sight. The loop curved very tightly, so the humans could approach within a few meters without being spotted. An object thrown around the loop would travel most of the way with undiminished velocity. Jacob was now sure of this. He and Hughes had thrown several knives from the ship's galley when they entered the loop. They found them near the flip-side exit in a puddle of ammonia from the liquitubes they'd squeezed ahead of them as they walked the topsy-turvy passage.

Culla could have been waiting just beyond the door, but there was another reason he had to leave his rear undefended. He had only a limited amount of time before the Sunship reached a high orbit. After they got into free space the humans would be safe from the tossing of the chromospheric storms, and the tough, reflecting physical shell of the ship could deflect enough of the heat of the Sun to keep them alive until help came.

So Culla had to finish them, and himself, off quickly. Jacob felt sure the Pring specialist was by the computer input ninety degrees around the dome to the right, using his laser eyes to slowly reprogram past the machine's safeguards.

Why he was doing it was a question that would have to wait.

Hughes picked up the knives. With the bag, some liquitubes, and Helene's little stunner, they composed their armory.

Classically, since the alternative was death for all of them, the answer would be for one man to sacrifice himself so the other could finish Culla off.

He and Hughes could carefully time their approach from different directions to surprise Culla at the same moment. Or one man could come in front and the other aim the stunner from over his shoulder.

But neither plan would work. Their opponent could literally kill a man as fast as he could look at him. Unlike the faked 'adult' Sun Ghost projections, which were continuous output, Culla's killer bolts were discharges. Jacob wished he could remember how many he'd fired off during the fight on topside . . . or at what repeat frequency. It probably didn't matter. Culla had two eyes and two enemies. One bolt each would probably suffice.

Worst of all, they couldn't be sure that Culla's holographic imaging ability wouldn't enable him to locate them the instant they stepped out onto the floor, from reflections off the inner shell. He probably couldn't hurt them with reflections, but that was poor compensation.

If there weren't so damned much attenuation during the internal bouncing of the beam they could have tried to disable the alien with the P-laser, by letting it sweep the entire ship while the humans and Fagin crowded into the gravity-loop.

Jacob cursed and wondered what was keeping them with the P-laser. Next to him Hughes mumbled softly into a wall intercom. He turned to Jacob. 'They're ready!' he said.

Thanks to their goggles they were spared most of the pain when the dome outside burst with light. Still it took a few moments to blink away tears and adapt to the brightness.

Commandant deSilva had, presumably with Dr Martine's help, dragged the P-laser to a new position near the rim of the upper deck. If her calculations were right the beam should hit the side of the dome on flip-side exactly where the computer input was. Unfortunately, the complexity of the figure needed to go from point A to B, through the narrow gap at the edge of the deck, meant that the beam probably wouldn't harm Culla.

It did startle him though. At the instant the beam came on, while Jacob was squeezing his eyes shut, they heard a sudden chattering and sounds of movement far to the right.

When his vision cleared, Jacob saw a thin tracery of bright lines hanging in the air. The passage of the P-laser beam left a track in the small amount of dust in the air. That was fortunate. It would help them avoid it.

'Intercom on max?' he asked quickly.

Hughes gave thumbs up.

'Okay, let's go!'

The P-laser was randomly putting out colors in the blue-green. They hoped it would confuse reflections from the inner shell.

He gathered his legs and counted, 'One, two. Go!'

Jacob dashed out across the open space and dove behind one of the hulking recording machines at the rim of the deck. He heard Hughes land hard, two machines clockwise from him.

The man waved once when he glanced back. 'Nothing over here!' he whispered harshly. Jacob took a look around the corner of his own machine, using a mirror from the aid-kit, which had been smeared with grease. Hughes had another mirror, from Martine's purse.

Culla wasn't in sight.

Between them, he and his partner could survey about three-fifths of the deck. The computer input was on the other side of the dome, just out of Hughes' view. Jacob would have to take the long way around, darting from one recording machine to another.

The Sunship's shell glowed in spots where the P-laser beam glanced off it. The colors shifted constantly. Otherwise, the red and pink miasma of the chromosphere surrounded them. They had left the big filament minutes before, and the herd of toroids with it by now a hundred kilometers below.

Below was actually right over Jacob's head. The photosphere, with the Big Spot in the center made a great flat endless, fiery ceiling above him, spicules hung like stalactites.

He gathered his legs beneath him and took off, bent over and facing away from any possible ambush.

He leapt over the P-laser beam where its path was traced in floating dust particles, and dove behind the next machine. Quickly he eased the mirror out to look at the territory now exposed.

Culla wasn't in sight.

Neither was Hughes. He whistled two short notes in the brief code they'd agreed upon. All clear. He heard one note, the fellow's reply.

He had to duck under the beam the next time. All the way across the narrow distance his skin crawled, anticipating a searing bolt of light along his flank.

He stumbled behind the machine and caught hold of it to steady himself, breathing heavily. That wasn't right! He shouldn't be so tired already. Something was wrong.

Jacob swallowed once then began to slide the mirror out along the counter-clockwise edge of the machine.

Pain lanced into his fingertips and he dropped the mirror with a cry. He stopped just short of popping the hand in his mouth, and held it instead, a few inches away, his mouth open in agony.

Automatically, he started to lay over a light pain relief trance. The red pokers started to fade as the fingers seemed to grow more distant. Then the flow of relief stopped. It was like a tug of war. He could only accomplish so much; a counter pressure resisted the hypnosis with equal strength no matter how hard he concentrated.

Another of Hyde's tricks. Well there was no time to dicker with him ... whatever the hell he wanted. He looked at the hand, now that the pain was barely bearable. The index and fourth fingers were badly fried. The others were less damaged.

He managed to whistle a short code to Hughes. It was time to put his plan into effect, the only plan with any real chance of success.

Their only chance lay in getting into space. Time-compression was frozen on automatic – the first thing Culla took care of after the maser link – their subjective time would pretty closely match the actual time it took to leave the chromosphere.

Since assaulting Culla was almost certainly futile, the best way to delay the alien's murder-suicide would be to talk to him.

Jacob took a couple of breaths as he leaned back against the holo-recorder, careful to keep his ears awake. Culla was always a noisy walker. That was his best hope against out and out attack by the Pring. If Culla made too much sound out in the open, Jacob might get a chance to use the stunner he clutched in his good hand. It had a wide beam and wouldn't take much aiming.

'Culla!' he shouted. 'Don't you think this has gone far enough? Why don't you come out now and we'll talk!'

He listened. There was a faint buzzing, as if Culla's mashies were chattering softly behind the thick prehensile lips. During the fight topside, half of the problem facing him and Donaldson had been avoiding the flashing white grinders.

'Culla!' he repeated. 'I know it's stupid to judge an alien by your own species' values, but I really thought you were a friend. You owe us an explanation! Talk to us! If you're acting under Bubbacub's orders, you can surrender and I swear we'll all say you put up a hell of a fight!'

The buzzing grew louder. There was a brief shuffle of footsteps. One, two, three ... but that was all. Not enough to get a fix on.

'Jacob, I am shorry,' Culla's voice carried softly across the deck.

'You musht be told, before we die, but firsht I ashk that you have that lasher turned off. It hurtsh!'

'Culla, so does my hand.'

The Pring sounded woebegone. 'I am sho, sho, shorry, Jacob. Pleash undershtand that you *are* my friend. It ish partly for your shpeciesh that I do thish.

'Theshe are neceshary crimesh, Jacob. I am only glad that death ish near sho that I may be free of memory.'

Jacob was astonished by the alien's sophistry. He had never expected such sophomore whinings from Culla, whatever his reasons for what he'd done. He was about to frame a reply when Helene deSilva's voice boomed over the intercom.

'Jacob? Can you hear me? The gravity thrust is deteriorating fast. We're losing headway.'

What she didn't say was the threat. If something wasn't done soon they'd begin the long fall toward the photosphere, a fall from which they'd never return.

Once in the grip of the convection cells, the ship would be pulled downward into the stellar core. If there was a ship left, by then.

'You shee, Jacob,' Culla said. 'To delay me will do no good. It ish already done. I will shtay to make shertain you cannot correct it.

'But pleashe, let ush talk until the end. I do not wish to die ash enemiesh.'

Jacob stared out into the wispy, hydrogen-red atmosphere of the Sun. Tendrils of fiery gas were still floating 'downwards' (up, to him), past the ship, but that could be a function of the motion of the gas in this area at this time. Certainly they were going by much less quickly. It could be that the ship was already falling.

'Your dischovery of my talent and my hoax wash most ashtute, Jacob. You combined many obshcure cluesh to find the anshwer! Tying in the background of my race wash a brilliant shtroke!

'Tell me, although I avoided the rim detectorsh with my phan-tomsh, didn't it throw you off that they shometimesh appeared on topshide when I wash on flip-shide?'

Jacob was trying to think. He had the cool side of the stun gun against his cheek. It felt good, but it wasn't helping him come up with ideas. And he had to spare some of his attention to talk to Culla.

'I never bothered to think about it, Culla. I suppose you just leaned over and beamed through the transparent deck-suspension field. That'd explain why the image looked refracted. It was actually *reflected*, at an angle, inside the shell.'

Actually that *was* a valid clue. Jacob wondered why he'd missed it.

And the bright blue light, during his deep trance in Baja! It happened just before he awoke to see Culla standing there! The Eatee must have taken a hologram of him! What a way to get to know somebody and never forget his face!

'Culla,' he said slowly. 'Not that I'm one to hold a grudge or anything, but were you responsible for my crazy behavior at the end of the last dive?'

There was a pause. Then Culla spoke. His lisp was getting worse.

'Yesh, Jacob. I am shorry, but you were getting too inquishitive. I hoped to dishcredit you. I failed.'

'But how ... ?'

'I lishtened to Dr Martine talk about the effect of glare on humansh, Jacob!'

The Pring almost shouted. For the first time in Jacob's memory, Culla had interrupted somebody. 'I ekshperi-mented on Doctor Kepler for months! Den on LaRoque and Jeff ... den on you. I ushed a narrow diffracted beam. No one could shee it, but it unfocused your thoughtsh!

'I did not know what you would do. But I knew it would be embarrasshing. Again, I am shorry. It wash neceshary!'

They had definitely stopped rising. The big filament that they had left only a few minutes before loomed over Jacob's head. High streamers twisted and curled up toward the ship, like grasping fingers.

Jacob had been trying to find a way, but his imagination was blocked by a powerful barrier.

All right! I give up!

He called on his neurosis to offer its terms. What the hell did the damned thing want of him?

He shook his head. He'd have to invoke the emergency clause. Hyde was going to have to come out and become part of him, like in the bad old days. Like when he chased down LaRoque on Mercury, and when he broke into the Photo Lab. He got ready to go into the trance.

'Why Culla. Tell me *why* you did all this!'

Not that it mattered. Maybe Hughes was listening. Perhaps Helene was recording. Jacob was too busy to care.

Resistance! In the non-linear, non-orthogonal coordinates of thought he sifted feelings and gestalts through a sieve. To whatever extent the old automatic systems still worked, he set them off to do their jobs.

Slowly, the window dressing and camouflage was stripped away and he came face to face with his other half.

The battlements, unscalable in every past siege, were even more formidable now. The earthen breastworks had been replaced by stone. The abatis was made of sharpened needles, slender and twenty miles long. At the top of the highest tower a flag rippled. The pennant read 'Loyalty.' It flew above two stakes, on each of which a head was impaled.

One head he recognized at once. It was his own. The blood that dripped from the severed neck still glistened. The expression was one of remorse.

The other head set him shivering. It was Helene's. Her face was streaked and pockmarked, and as he watched the eyes fluttered weakly. The head was still alive.

But *why*! Why this rage against Helene? And why the overtones of suicide ... this unwillingness to join with him to create the near ubermensch he once had been?

If Culla decided to attack now, he'd be helpless. His ears were filled with the cry of a whistling wind. There was a roar of jets and then the sound of someone falling ... the sound of someone calling as she fell past him.

And for the first time he could make out her words.

'*Jake! Watch that first step ... !*'

Is *that* all? Then why all the fuss over it? Why the months trying to drag out what turned out to be Tania's last ironic dig?

Of course. His neurosis was letting him see, now that death was imminent, that the hidden words had been another red herring. Hyde was hiding something else. It was ...

Guilt.

He knew he carried a burden of it after the affair on the Vanilla Needle, but how much he'd never realized. He now saw how sick this Jekyll and Hyde arrangement he'd been living with really was. Instead of slowly healing the trauma of a painful loss, he'd sealed off an artificial entity, to grow and feed on him and on his shame for having let Tania fall ... for the supreme arrogance of the man who, on that crazy day twenty miles high, thought he could do two things at once.

It had been just another form of arrogance ... a belief that he could bypass the normal, human way of recovering from grief, the cycle of pain and transcendency by which the billions of his fellow human beings coped when each suffered a loss. That and the comfort of closeness to other people.

And now he was trapped. The meaning of the pennant on the battlements was clear now. In his sickness he'd thought to expiate part of his guilt by demonstrations of loyalty to the person he'd failed. Not overt loyalty, but loyalty deep within ... a sick loyalty based on withholding himself from everybody ... all the while convinced that he was all right since he'd *had* lovers!

No wonder Hyde hated Helene! No wonder he wanted Jacob Demwa dead as well!

Tania would never have approved of you, he told it. But it wasn't listening. It had its own logic and had no use for his.

Hell, she'd have *loved* Helene!

It didn't do any good. The barrier was firm. He opened his eyes.

The red of the chromosphere had deepened. They were in the filament now. A flash of color, seen even through his goggles, sent him glancing to the left.

*

It was a toroid. They were back amidst the herd. As he watched, several more drifted past, their rims festooned with bright designs. They spun like mad doughnuts, oblivious to the peril of the Sunship.

'Jacob, you have shaid nothing,' Culla's droning, lisping voice had become background. At the mention of his name Jacob paid attention.

'Shurely you have shome opinion on my motivesh. Cannot you shee that de greater good will come of dish … not only for my shpecies but for yoursh and your Clientsh ash well?'

Jacob shook his head vigorously to clear it. The Hyde-induced drowsiness was something he had to fight! The only silver lining was that his hand no longer hurt.

'Culla, I must think about this for a little while. Can we retire a ways and confer? I can pick up some food for you and maybe we can work something out.'

There was a pause. Then Culla spoke slowly.

'You are very tricky, Jacob. I am tempted but now I shee dat it will be better if you and your friend stay shtill. In fact, I will make certain. If either of you movesh I will "shee" him.'

Numbly, Jacob wondered what was so 'tricky' about offering the alien food. Why had that idea popped into his head?

They were falling faster now. Overhead the herd of toruses stretched toward the ominous wall of the photosphere. The nearest shone in blues and greens as they swept past. The colors faded with distance. The farthest beasts looked like tiny dim wedding rings, each poised on a tiny flicker of green light.

There was movement among the nearest magnetovores. As the ship fell, one after another moved aside and 'downward' from Jacob's upside-down perspective. Once a flash of green filled the Sunship as a tail-laser swept over them. The fact that they weren't destroyed meant that the automatic screens were still working.

Outside, a fluttering shape shot past Jacob, from over his head out, past the deck at his feet Then another rippling apparition appeared, lingering for a moment outside the shell near him, its body slick with iridescent colors. Then it sped upward, out of sight.

The Sun Ghosts were gathering. Perhaps the Sunship's headlong fall had finally piqued their curiosity.

They had passed the largest part of the herd by now. There was a cluster of large magnetovores just overhead, in their line of descent. Tiny bright herdsmen danced around the group. Jacob hoped they'd get out of the way. No sense in taking anyone else with them. The incandescent trail of the ship's Refrigerator Laser cut dangerously close.

Jacob gathered himself together. There was nothing else to do. He and Hughes would have to try a frontal assault on Culla. He whistled a code, two short and two long. There was a pause and then there was an answer. The other man was ready.

He'd wait until the first sound. They'd agreed that, when they were close enough, any attack with any chance of success would have to come the instant any noise was made, before Culla could be alerted. Since Hughes had farther to go, presumably, he'd move first.

He tensed into a crouch and forced himself to concentrate only on the attack. The stunner rested in the sweaty palm of his left hand. He ignored the distracting tremors that erupted from an isolated part of his own mind.

A sound, like someone falling, came from somewhere to the right. Jacob stepped out from behind the machine, pressing the firing stud of the stunner at the same instant.

No bolt of light greeted him. Culla wasn't there. One of the precious stunner charges was gone.

He ran forward as fast as he could. If he could catch the alien with his back turned to deal with Hughes ...

The lighting was changing. As he ran just a few steps the red brightness of the photosphere overhead was swiftly replaced by a blue-green shine from above. Jacob spared the briefest of glances overhead as he dashed forward. The light came from toruses. The huge Solarian beasts were coming up fast from below the Sunship on a collision course.

Alarms rang, and Helene deSilva's voice came on, loudly, with a warning. As the blueness grew brighter, Jacob dove over a trace made by the P-laser beam in the dusty air, and landed just two meters away from Culla.

Just beyond the Pring, the crewman Hughes knelt on the ground, holding up bloody hands, his knives scattered on the ground. He stared up at Culla dully, expecting the coup de grace.

Jacob raised the stunner as Culla swiveled, warned by the sound of his arrival. For the briefest of instants Jacob thought he'd made it as he pressed down on the firing stud.

Then his entire left hand erupted in agony. A spasm flung it up and the gun flew away. For a moment the deck seemed to sway, then his vision cleared and Culla was standing before him, eyes dull. The Pring's mashies were now fully exposed, waving at the ends of the tentacular 'lips.'

'I am shorry, Jacob.' The alien slurred so badly Jacob could barely make out the words. 'It musht be thish way.'

The Eatee planned to finish him off with his cleavers! Jacob stumbled back in fear and disgust. Culla followed, the mashies clacking together slowly, powerfully with the rhythm of his footsteps.

A great sense of resignation washed over Jacob, a feeling of defeat and imminent death. It took the distance out of his backward steps. The throbbing in his hand meant nothing next to the closeness of extinction.

'No!' he shouted hoarsely. He launched himself forward, head down, toward Culla.

At that instant Helene's voice came on again and the blueness overhead took over everything. There was a distant humming and then a powerful force lifted them off the floor, into the air above the violently heaving deck.

PART IX

There was once a lad so virtuous that the gods gave him
a wish. His choice was to be, for a day, the charioteer of
the Sun. Apollo was overruled when he predicted dire
consequences, but subsequent events proved him right.
The Sahara is said to be the track of desolation laid when
the inexperienced driver let his carriage pass too close to
Earth. Since then, the gods have tried to operate a closed
shop.

M. N. PLANO

26

TUNNELING

Jacob landed on the opposite side of the computer-console, falling hard on his back to save his blistered, bleeding hands. Fortunately, the springy material of the deck cushioned some of the impact.

He tasted blood and his head rang as he rolled over onto his elbows. The deck still bounced as the magnetovores overhead jostled against the underbelly of the Sunship, filling the interior of flip-side with brilliant blue light. They touched the ship, three of them, at about forty-five degrees 'above' the deck, leaving a large gap directly overhead. That left room for the Refrigerator Laser to pour its deadly beam of stored solar heat between them, downward toward the photosphere.

Jacob had no time to wonder what they were doing ... whether they were attacking, or just playful. (What a thought!) He had to take advantage of this respite quickly.

Hughes had landed nearby. The man was already on his feet, stumbling in shock. Jacob hurried up and took the man's arm in his ... avoiding contact between their wounded hands.

'Come on, Hughes. If Culla's been stunned we might both be able to jump him!'

Hughes nodded. The man was confused, but he was willing. His movements were exaggerated, though. Jacob had to guide him the right way, hurrying.

They came around the curve of the central dome to find Culla just rising to his feet. The alien wavered but as he turned toward them Jacob knew it was hopeless. One of Culla's eyes flashed brightly, the first time Jacob had actually seen one in operation. That meant ...

There was a smell of burning rubber and the left strap of his goggles parted. He was dazzled by the blue brightness of the chamber as they fell off.

Jacob shoved Hughes back around the curve of the dome and flung himself after the man. At any moment he expected a sudden pain in the back of his neck, but they stumbled together all the way to the gravity-loop hatch and fell within, safe.

Fagin moved aside to let them in. He trilled loudly and waved his branches.

'Jacob! You are alive! And your associate as well! This is better than I'd feared!'

'How ...' Jacob gasped for breath. 'How long since we started falling?'

'It has been five, perhaps six minutes. I followed you down after regaining my wits. I may not be able to fight but I can interpose my body. Culla would never have enough power to cut his way through me to get above!' The Kanten piped shrill laughter.

Jacob frowned; that was an interesting point. How much power did Culla have? What was it he once read about the human body operating on an average of one hundred and fifty watts? Culla put out considerably more than that, but it was in short, half-second bursts.

Given enough time, Jacob could figure it out. When projecting his hoaxed Solarians, Culla had made the apparitions last for about twenty minutes. Then the anthropomorphic Ghosts 'lost interest' and Culla was suddenly ravenously hungry. They'd all attributed his appetite to nervous energy, but actually the Pring had to replenish his supply of coumarin ... and probably of high-energy chemicals to power the dye-laser reaction, as well.

'You are hurt!' Fagin fluted. The branches fluttered in agitation. 'You had best take your compatriot upside and both have your wounds tended.'

'I guess so,' Jacob nodded, reluctant to leave Fagin alone. 'There are some important questions I have to ask Dr Martine while she's treating us.'

The Kanten gave out a long whistling sigh, 'Jacob, under no circumstances disturb Dr Martine! She is in rapport with the Solarians. It is our only chance!'

'She's what!'

'They were attracted by the flashing of the Parametric Laser. When they came, she donned her psi helmet and initiated communications! They positioned several of their magnetovores beneath us and have substantially arrested our fall!'

Jacob's heart leapt. It sounded like a reprieve. Then he frowned.

'Substantially? Then we aren't rising?'

'Regrettably, no. We are falling slowly. And there is no knowing how long the toroids can hold us.'

Jacob felt distantly in awe of Martine's accomplishment. She had contacted the Solarians! It was one of the epochal accomplishments of all time, and *still* they were doomed.

'Fagin,' he said carefully. 'I'll be back as soon as I can. Meanwhile, can you fake my voice well enough to fool Culla?'

'I believe so. I can try.'

'Then talk to him. Throw your voice. Use all your tricks to keep him busy and uncertain. He can't be allowed more time at that computer access!'

Fagin whistled assent. Jacob turned, with his arm in Hughes' and started around the gravity-loop.

The loop felt strange, as if the gravity fields had started to fluctuate slightly. His inner ear bothered him as it never had before, as he helped Hughes traverse the short arc, and he had to concentrate to keep his step,

Topside was still red – the red of the chromosphere. But fluttering blue-green Solarians danced just outside, closer than Jacob had ever seen them before. Their 'butterfly wings' were almost as broad as the ship itself.

Blue traceries of the P-laser also shone in the dust up here. Near the edge of the deck, the laser itself hummed inside its bulky mounting.

They dodged several of the thin beams.

If only we'd had the tools to unship that thing from its holder, Jacob thought. Well, it was no use wishing. He steadied his partner until he could get him into a couch. Then he strapped the man in and went looking for the aid-kit.

He found it by the Pilot Board. Since he hadn't seen Martine, it was apparent she'd chosen another quadrant of the deck to do her communing with the Solarians, away from the others. Near the Pilot Board, LaRoque, Donaldson, and the unliving body of crewman Dubrowsky lay firmly strapped in. Donaldson's face was half covered with medicinal flesh-foam.

Helene deSilva and her remaining crewman bent over their instruments. The Commandant looked up as he approached. 'Jacob! What happened?'

He kept his hands behind his back, to keep from distracting her. It was getting hard to stay on his feet, though. He'd have to do something soon.

'It didn't work. We got him talking, though.'

'Yes, we heard it all up here, then a lot of noise. I tried to warn you before we impacted the toroids. I was hoping you could use it.'

'Oh the impact helped, all right. It shook us up but it saved our lives.'

'And Culla?'

Jacob shrugged. 'He's still down there. I think he's running low on juice. During our fight up here he burned off half of Donaldson's face with one shot. Down there he was a miser, taking tiny pot shots at strategic places.'

He told her about Culla's attack with his mashies. 'I don't think he's going to run out early enough. If we had lots of men we could keep throwing them at him until he went dry. But we haven't. Hughes is willing, but he can't fight anymore. I suppose you two can't leave your posts.'

Helene turned to answer a beeping alarm from her control board. She stabbed a switch and it cut off. Then she looked back, apologetic.

I'm sorry, Jacob. But we've got all we can handle here. We're trying to get through to the computer by actuating the ship's sensors in coded rhythms. It's slow work, and we have to keep turning away to handle emergencies. I'm afraid we're slipping. The controls are deteriorating.' She turned to answer another signal.

Jacob backed away. The last thing he wanted to do was distract her.

'Can I help?'

Pierre LaRoque looked up at him from a couch a few feet away. The little man was constrained, his couch straps secured out of reach. Jacob had all but forgotten about him.

He hesitated. LaRoque's behavior just before the fight topside hadn't inspired confidence. Helene and Martine had strapped him in to keep him out of everyone's hair.

Yet Jacob needed *someone*'s hands to operate the aid-kit. Jacob remembered LaRoque's near escape on Mercury. The man was unreliable, but he had talent when he chose to use it.

LaRoque looked coherent and sincere at the moment. Jacob asked Helene for permission to release him. She glanced up and shrugged.

'Okay. But if he comes near the instruments I'll kill him. Tell him that.'

There was no need to tell him. LaRoque nodded that he understood. Jacob bent over and rumbled with the strap hooks with the good fingers of his right hand.

Helene hissed behind him. 'Jacob, your hands!

The look of concern on her face warmed Jacob. But when she started to get up he'd have none of it. Right now her job was more important than his. She knew this. He took the fact that she was torn at all as a great display of affection. She smiled briefly in encouragement then bent to answer a half dozen alarms that started blaring at once.

LaRoque rose, rubbing his shoulders, then picked up the aid-kit and motioned to Jacob. His smile was ironic.

'Who should we fix first?' he said. 'You, the other man, or Culla?'

27

EXCITATION

Helene had to find time to think. There must be something she could do! Slowly the systems based on Galactic science were failing. So far it had been the time-compression and the gravity thrust, plus several peripheral mechanisms. If *internal* gravity control went out they'd be helpless before the tossing of the chromosphere storms, battered within their own hull.

Not that it'd matter. The toroids that were holding them up against the pull of the Sun were obviously tiring. The altimeter was slipping. Already the rest of the herd was high overhead, almost lost in the pink haze of the upper chromosphere. It wouldn't be long.

An alarm light flashed.

There was positive feedback in the internal gravity field. She did a quick mental calculation, then fed in a set of parameters to damp it out.

Poor Jacob, he'd tried. His exhaustion had been written on his face. She felt ashamed not to have shared the fight on flip-side, though, of course, it had never been likely that they could dislodge Culla from the computer on flip-side.

Now it was up to her. But *how*, with every damned component falling apart!

Not every component. Except for the maser link with Mercury, the equipment derived from Earth technology still ran perfectly. Culla hadn't bothered with any of it. The refrigeration still worked. The E.M. fields around the hard shell of the ship still ran, though they had lost the ability to selectively let in more sunlight on flipside. Naturally.

The ship shuddered. It bounced as something bumped against it once, twice. Then a brightness appeared at the edge of the deck. Suddenly the rim of a toroid appeared, rubbing against the side of the ship. Above it, several Solarians fluttered.

The bumping became a scraping sound, loud and hideous. The toroid was livid with bright purple blotches around its rim. It pulsed and throbbed under the proddings of its tormentors. Then, in a sudden burst of light, it was gone. The Sunship tipped as its forward end, unsupported, fell suddenly. DeSilva and her partner struggled to right it.

When she looked up she could see her Solarian allies drifting away, with the two remaining toroids.

There was no more they could do. The toroid that had deserted them was just a spot of light overhead, receding rapidly atop a pillar of green flame.

The altimeter began to spin faster. On her view-screens Helene could see the pulsing granulation cells of the photosphere, and the Big Spot, now bigger than ever.

They were already closer than anyone had come before. Soon they'd be in there – the first men in the Sun.

Briefly.

She looked up at the now distant Solarians, and wondered if she should call everyone together to ... to wave good-bye or something. She wanted Jacob here.

But he'd gone below again. They'd hit before he could make it back.

She gazed up at the tiny green lights and wondered how the toroid had been able to move so fast.

She jerked upright with a curse. Chen looked up at her. 'What is it, skipper? Shields going?'

With a cry of exultation Helene started throwing switches.

She wished they could monitor their telemetry back on Mercury, because if they died here on the Sun *now* it would certainly be in a unique way!

Jacob's arms still throbbed. Worse, they *itched*. He couldn't scratch, of course. His left hand was in a solid block of flesh-foam and so were two of the fingers of his right hand.

He crouched again just inside the hatch of the gravity-loop, looking out onto the deck on flip-side. Fagin moved aside so he could push his new mirror, this one glued to the end of a pencil with more flesh-foam, out beyond the combing.

Culla wasn't in sight. The hulking cameras stood out against the pulsing blue ceiling presented by the laboring magnetovores. The trail of the P-laser crisscrossed, marked by scattering from dust in the air.

He motioned for LaRoque to lay down his load just inside the hatch, next to Fagin.

They took turns coating each other's necks and faces with more flesh-foam. The goggles were sealed down with extra blobs of the pliant, rubbery material.

'Of course you know this is dangerous,' LaRoque said. 'It may protect us from damage from a quick shot but this stuff is highly flammable. It's the only flammable substance allowed in spaceships, for that matter, because of its unique medicinal properties.'

Jacob nodded. If he looked anything like LaRoque, now, they'd stand a good chance of *scaring* the alien to death!

He hefted the brown cannister, then sprayed a shot out onto the deck. It didn't have much range but it might do as a weapon. There was still plenty of the stuff left.

The deck jerked under them, then jounced twice more. Jacob looked out and saw that they were tipping over. The magnetovore that held up this side of the ship was rolling along lower and lower, toward the edge of the deck and away from where the photosphere covered the sky.

One of the beasts on the other side must have lost its hold, then. That meant it was almost over.

The ship shuddered and then began to right itself. Jacob sighed. There still might be time to save the ship if he could disable Culla immediately. But that was clearly impossible. He wished he could go up and join Helene.

'Fagin,' he said. 'I'm not the man you used to know. That man would have had Culla by now. We'd have been out of here and safe. We both know what he was capable of.

'Please understand. I tried. But I'm just not the same anymore.'

Fagin rustled. 'I knew, Jacob. It was to achieve this change that I invited you to Sundiver in the first place.'

Jacob stared at the alien.

'You are my artful dodger,' the Kanten whistled softly. 'I had no idea the issues here were as critical as they turned out to be. I asked you here solely to help break the chrysalis you have been in since Ecuador, and then to introduce you to Helene deSilva. The plan succeeded. I am pleased.'

Jacob was at a loss.

'But Fagin, my mind . . .' he trailed off.

'Your mind is fine. You simply have an overeager imagination. That is all. Truly, Jacob, you invent such fantasies. And so elaborate! I have never met a hypochondriac such as you!'

Jacob's mind raced. Either the Kanten was being polite, or he was mistaken or . . . or he was right. Fagin had never lied to him before, especially regarding personal matters.

Could it be that Mr Hyde wasn't a neurosis at all but a *game*? As a child he had created play universes so detailed that they could hardly be distinguished from reality. His worlds *had* existed. The neo-Reichian therapists had merely smiled and credited him with a powerful, non-pathological imagination because the tests always showed that he knew he was playing, when it mattered that he know it!

Could Mr Hyde have been a play-entity?

It's true that until now it never did any actual harm. It was a perpetual annoyance, but there always turned out to be a valid reason for the things it 'made' him do. Again, until now.

'You were non-sane for a time when I met you, Jacob. But the Needle cured you. The cure *frightened*, so you went into a game. I do not know the details of your game; you were very secretive. But I know now that you are awake. You have been awake for perhaps twenty minutes.'

Jacob clamped down. Whether or not Fagin was right, he had no time to stand here and blather about it. He had only minutes to save the ship. If it was possible at all.

Outside, the chromosphere shimmered. The photosphere loomed over their heads. The dust trails of the P-laser crisscrossed the inner shell.

Jacob tried to snap his ringers, and winced in pain.

'LaRoque! Run upstairs and get your lighter. Quick!'

LaRoque stepped back. 'Why, I have it right here,' he said. 'But of what use ...'

Jacob was moving toward the intercom. If Helene had some reserve of power she'd been holding back, now was the time to use it. He needed a little time! Before he could switch it on, though, an alarm filled the ship.

'Sophonts,' Helene's voice rang out. 'Please prepare for acceleration. We will be leaving the Sun shortly.'

The woman's voice sounded amused, almost whimsical.

'Due to the mode of our imminent departure, I would recommend that all passengers dress as warmly as possible! The Sun can be very cold this time of year!'

28

STIMULATED EMISSION

A blast of cold air blew constantly from the ventilator ducts around the Refrigerator Laser housing. Jacob and LaRoque huddled around their fire, trying to keep the cold air off it.

'Come on, baby. Burn!' A pile of flesh-foam shavings smoldered on the deck. Slowly the flames grew as they piled on more chips.

'Ha ha!' Jacob laughed. 'Once a caveman, always a caveman, eh, LaRoque? Men get all the way to the sun, and they build a fire to stay warm!'

LaRoque smiled weakly, and kept piling on larger and larger

shavings. The loquacious journalist had said very little since Jacob released him from his couch. Now and then, though, he would mutter something angry and spit.

Jacob held a torch into the flames. It was made from a clump of flesh-foam stuck to the end of a liquitube. The end began to smolder, giving off thick black smoke. It was beautiful.

Soon they had several torches. Smoke billowed into the air, carrying a foul stench. They had to stand back, in the path of the air duct, to be able to breathe. Fagin moved well into the gravity-loop.

'Okay,' Jacob said. 'Let's go!' He hopped out of the hatchway to the left and tossed one of the smoldering brands to the end of the deck, as far as he could see. Behind him LaRoque was doing the same in the opposite direction.

With a heavy rustling, Fagin followed them out. The Kanten went straight out from the hatch to the opposite end of the deck to act as a lookout, and to draw Culla's fire if possible. Fagin had refused a coating of flesh-foam.

'It is all clear,' the Kanten whistled softly. 'Culla is not to be seen.'

That was good and bad news. It localized Culla. It also meant the alien was probably working to bolix up the Refrigerator Laser.

It was getting COLD!

Once it had begun, Helene's scheme made perfect sense to Jacob. Since she still had control over the screens surrounding the ship, (the crew were alive to prove it), she could let in heat from the Sun at whatever rate she wished. This heat could be sent directly to the Refer Laser and pumped back out into the chromosphere, plus waste heat from the ship's power plant. Only this time the flow was a torrent, and directed downward. The thrust had stopped their fall and they had begun to climb.

Naturally, such meddling with the ship's automatic heat control system had to be inaccurate. Helene must have decided to program the mechanism to err in the direction of coldness. In that direction mistakes would be more easily corrected.

It was a brilliant idea. Jacob hoped he'd get to tell her so. Right now it was his job to make sure it had a chance to work.

He edged around the dome until he reached the point where Fagin's view was cut off. Without looking around, he threw two more of the brands to different parts of the deck ahead of him. Smoke boiled from each of them.

The chamber was getting hazy from the smoke released so far. The trail of the P-laser beam shimmered brightly in the air. Some of the weaker trails were disappearing, attenuated by cumulative passage though the smoke.

Jacob moved back into Fagin's cone of view. He had three more smoldering brands. He backed up onto the deck and tossed them at different angles over the top of the central dome. LaRoque joined him and threw his as well.

One of the torches passed directly over the center of the dome on its way over. It entered the x-ray beam of the Refrigerator Laser and vanished in a cloud of vapor.

Jacob hoped it hadn't deflected the beam much. The coherent x-rays supposedly passed through the shell with near zero contamination of the ship, but the beam wasn't designed to handle solid objects.

'Okay!' he whispered.

He and LaRoque hurried to the wall of the dome, where spare parts for the recording instruments were stored. LaRoque opened a cabinet and climbed as high as footholds allowed, then offered his hand. Jacob scrambled up next to him. Now they were all vulnerable. Culla must react to the obvious threat implied by the firebrands! Already visibility was dropping well below normal. The chamber was filled with a foul stench and Jacob was finding it increasingly uncomfortable to breathe.

LaRoque braced his shoulder in the top jamb of the cabinet, then offered his cupped hands to Jacob. Jacob took the boost and climbed up onto LaRoque's shoulder.

The dome was sloping here, but the surface was smooth, and Jacob had only three fingers instead of ten. The flesh-foam coating helped. It was still somewhat sticky. After two unsuccessful attempts Jacob concentrated and leapt from LaRoque's shoulder, nearly hard enough to shake the man loose.

The surface of the dome was like quicksilver. He had to flatten himself and move with scrambling speed to gain each inch.

Near the top, he had to worry about the Refer Laser. He could see the orifice as he rested near the summit. Two meters away it hummed softly; the smoky air shimmered and Jacob wondered what the transparency safety distance was from the deadly mouth.

He turned away so as not to have to think about it.

He couldn't whistle to let them know he'd made it. They'd have to rely on Fagin's superb hearing to track his movements, and to time the distraction.

There were at least a few seconds to wait. Jacob decided to take a chance. He rolled over onto his back and looked up at the Big Spot.

Everywhere was the Sun.

From his point of view there was no ship. There was no battle. There were no planets or stars or galaxies. The rim of his goggles even cut off the sight of his own body. The photosphere was everything.

It pulsed. The spicule forests, like undulating picket fences, hurled their noise up at him, and the breakers split just above his head. The sound divided and swept around toward the irrelevancies of space.

It roared.

The Big Spot stared back at him. For an instant the broad expanse was a face, the bristled, grizzled face of a patriarch. The throbbings were its breath. The noise was the booming of its giant voice, singing a billions-year-old song that only the other stars could hear or understand.

The Sun was alive. What was more, it noticed him. It gave him its undivided attention.

Call me lifegiver, for I am your sustenance. I burn, and by my burning you live. I stand, and in standing supply your anchor. Space curls around, my blanket, and funnels down to mystery in my bowels. Time beats his scythe on my forge.

Living thing, does Entropy, my wicked Aunt, notice our joint conspiracy? Not yet, I think, for you are yet too small. Your puny struggle against her tide is a fluttering in a great wind. And she thinks I am still her ally.

Call me lifegiver, oh living thing, and weep. I burn endlessly and, burning, consume what cannot be replaced. While you sip daintily at my torrent the font runs slowly out. When it empties other stars shall take my place, but oh not forever!

Call me lifegiver, and laugh!
You, living thing, hear the true Lifegiver's voice from time to time, it is said. He speaks to you but not to us, His first born!
Pity the stars, oh living thing! We sing away the aeons in pretended joy as we toil for His cruel sister, awaiting the day of your maturity, you tiny embryo, when He turns you loose to change the way of things again.

Jacob laughed soundlessly. Oh what an imagination! Fagin was right, after all. He closed his eyes, still listening for the signal. Seven seconds, exactly, had passed since he reached the top of the dome.

'Jake . . .' It was a woman's voice. He looked up without opening his eyes.

'Tania.'

She stood by the pion-scope In her lab, exactly as he had seen her so many times when he came to pick her up. Braided brown hair, slightly uneven white teeth grinning generously, and large, crinkled eyes. She came forward with surefooted grace and confronted him with fists on hips.

'It's about time!' she said.

'Tania, I ... I don't understand.'

'It's 'bout time you brought up an image of me doing something besides falling! Think it's fun doin' that over and over again? Why haven't you brought me back having some of the good times!'

He suddenly realized that it was true! For two years he'd only remembered Tania in that last instant, not thinking about their time together at all!

'Well, I'll admit it's done you some good,' she nodded. 'You seem to finally be free of that damned arrogance. Just *think* about me from time to time, for heaven's sake. I hate being ignored!'

'Yes, Tania. I'll remember you. I promise.'

'And pay attention to the star! Stop thinking you imagine everything!'

She softened. The image began to fade. 'You're right, Jake, dear one, I do like her. Have a good ... '

He opened his eyes. The photosphere throbbed overhead. The spot stared back at him. The granulation cells pumped slowly like leisured heartbeats.

Did you just do that? he asked, silently.

The answer permeated him, drilled through his body and came out the other side. Neutrinos to cure neuroses. A most original approach.

A short whistle came from below. Before he was aware he had moved, he was slithering toward the sound and to the right, silently and without a wasted motion.

He peered over to look down on the head of Culla ta-Pring ab-Pa-ab-Kisa-ab-Soro-ab-Hul-ab-Puber.

The alien faced Jacob's left, his hand still on the open access plate to the computer-input. Though the smoke dimmed it almost to nothing, there was still a glare as the P-laser beam hit the spot.

From the left came a rustling. Somewhere to the right was the sound of running feet, LaRoque hurrying around the dome.

A few silver-tipped twigs poked out from the curve of the dome. Culla crouched and one of Fagin's shiny light receptors curled up in smoke. The Kanten gave out a high pitched keening and retreated out of sight. Culla swiveled quickly.

Jacob pulled the flesh-foam sprayer out of his pocket. He aimed and pressed the nozzle. A thin jet of liquid shot out in an arc toward Culla's eyes. In the instant before it struck, Pierre LaRoque appeared, running, his head down as he charged through the smoke toward Culla.

Culla jumped back. The spray passed in front of his eyes. At that instant a bright spark flashed at a point along its length.

With a whoosh the entire stream burst into flame. Culla stumbled backwards, hands in front of his face. LaRoque barrelled through the falling embers and collided with the Pring's midsection.

Culla almost went down in the thick smoke. Breath wheezed as he gripped LaRoque around the neck, first for balance and then closing tightly to squeeze on the man's windpipe. LaRoque struggled wildly but his momentum was gone. It was like trying to escape from a pair of boa constrictors. His face turned flush and started to puff.

Jacob gathered himself for a leap. The smoke was so thick he could hardly keep from coughing. Desperately he suppressed the urge. If Culla saw him before he could jump, the alien wouldn't bother killing LaRoque the hard way. He'd finish them both off with a look.

His muscles pressed like hard springs and he launched himself from the dome.

The midair flight was suspenseful. His own subjective version of time-compression made the transit seem slow and leisurely. It was a trick from the bad old days, and now he used it again, automatically.

When a third of the distance was covered he saw Culla's head start to turn. It was hard to tell exactly what the E.T. was doing to LaRoque at that instant. A thick pall of smoke obscured everything but Culla's bright red eyes and two flashes of white beneath them.

The eyes came up. It was a race to see who'd arrive first at a certain point in space, just above and to the right of the alien's head. Jacob wondered at what angles Culla could shoot a narrow beam.

The suspense was killing him. It was almost satirical. Jacob decided to speed things up and see what happened.

There was a flash, then a tooth jarring, numbing smash as his shoulder hit the side of Culla's head. He clutched and got a tight grip on the front of the alien's gown as his inertia carried both of them over into a crashing tumble onto the deck.

Human and alien fought for breath amidst fits of coughing as they rolled into a tangle of slashing, grabbing arms and legs. Somehow Jacob got around behind his opponent and held on tightly to the slender neck as Culla thrashed, trying to turn his head to snap with his cleavers or burn with his laser eyes.

The powerful tentacular hands clutched back, snatching for a purchase. Jacob dodged his head aside and struggled to get Culla around, so he could get his legs into a scissors lock. After rolling almost halfway across the deck, he succeeded, and was rewarded by a lancing pain in his right thigh.

'More,' he coughed. 'Shoot, Culla. Use it up!'

Twice more bolts struck his exposed legs, sending small tsunamis of agony up to his brain. The pain he shunted aside and he held on, praying that Culla would send some more.

But Culla stopped wasting his shots and began to roll about faster, buffeting Jacob every time the human struck the deck. They were both coughing, Culla sounding like half a dozen ball bearings shaken in a bottle, every time he wheezed in the thick, billowing smoke.

There was no way to choke the devil! When he wasn't holding on for dear life, Jacob tried to turn his grip around Culla's throat into a stranglehold. But there didn't seem to be any vulnerable points! It was unfair. Jacob wanted to curse the bad luck but he couldn't spare the breath. His lungs could barely hold enough to make a small cough, each time the Pring rolled over on top.

Streams of tears blurred his vision and his eyes hurt. He suddenly realized that his goggles were gone! Either Culla had burned them off again in that first instant as he launched himself from the dome, or they'd been torn off during the fight.

Where the hell is LaRoque!

His arms shuddered with the strain and there was a rubbed-out pain in his abdomen and groin from the constant pounding of the cavort across the deck. Culla's coughing was sounding more pathetic and strained, and his own took on an ominous gurgle. He could feel the first stages of heat prostration and a dreadful fear that the ordeal would never end, even as their struggle brought his back up against one of the smoldering flesh-foam brands.

It smothered in a broiling release of heat as he screamed. The pain was too sudden and from too unexpected a quarter to be shunted aside. His tight grip around Culla's throat slacked for an instant of agony and the alien tore at his hands. The grip parted and Culla rolled away even as Jacob grabbed after him.

He missed. Culla scrambled farther away, then turned quickly to face him. Jacob closed his eyes and covered his face with his encased left hand, expecting a laser bolt.

He tried to stand, but something was wrong with his lungs. They wouldn't work properly. His breath was shallow and he could feel his balance waver as he slowly rose to his knees. His back felt like charred hamburger meat.

Not far away, two meters at most, there was a loud clack! Then another. Then another, closer.

Jacob's arm fell. He no longer had the strength to hold it up. There was no use in keeping his eyes closed, anyway. He opened them to see Culla, kneeling a meter away. Only the red eyes and gleaming white teeth showed through the thick stench.

'Cu ... Culla ...' he gasped. Wheezing, the words sounded like tiny, failing gears. 'Give up now, this is your last chance. I'm ... warning you ...'

Tania would have liked that, he thought It was almost as good a parting shot, as hers had been. He hoped Helene had heard it.

Parting shot? Hell, why not give Culla one! Even if he cuts my throat or drills a hole into my brain through my eyelids, I'll still have time to give him a present!

He pulled the flesh-foam sprayer out of his belt and started to raise it He'd give Culla such a spraying! Even if it meant he'd die at that instant by laser instead of by decapitation.

Excruciating pain burst like a steel needle through his left eye. It felt like a lightning bolt crashing all the way to the back of his head and out the other side. At that same instant he pressed the release and held it in the direction Culla's head had been.

29

ABSORPTION

Helene lifted her eyes briefly as the ship rose past the toroid herd on the left.

The greens and blues were faded, eaten by the distance. Still the beasts shone like tiny incandescent rings, specks of life ordered in their miniscule convoy, dwarfed by the immensity of the chromosphere.

The herdsmen were already too far away to be seen.

The herd passed behind the dark bulk of the filament, out of sight.

Helene smiled. If only we still had our maser link, she thought. They could have seen how hard we tried. They would have known that the Solarians didn't kill us, as some will think. They tried to help us. We talked to them!

She bent to answer two alarms at once.

Dr Martine wandered aimlessly behind her and the copilot. The parapsychologist was rational, but not very coherent. She had only just returned from the opposite end of topside. She walked unevenly and muttered softly under her breath.

Martine had enough sense to stay out of their hair, thank Ifni! But she refused to strap herself in. Helene hesitated to ask her to go around to flip-side. In her present condition the good doctor wouldn't be much help.

There was a stench in the air. Helene's flip-side monitors showed only a thick billowing cloud of smoke. There had been shouting and sounds of a terrible fracas just minutes ago. Twice the intercoms had carried the sound of someone screaming. Just moments ago came a shriek that could have waked the dead. Then silence.

The only emotion she allowed herself was a detached sense of pride. The fact that the fight had lasted so long was a tribute to them, especially to Jacob. Culla's weapons should have finished them off quickly.

Of course it wasn't likely they'd succeeded. She'd have heard something by now. She clamped a lid on her feelings and told herself she was shivering because of the cold.

It had dropped to five Celsius. The less efficient her reactions got, as she tired, the more she weighted the cold side of the Refrigerator-Laser's increasingly erratic swing. The hot side would be disaster.

She answered a shift in the E.M. field that threatened to leave a window in the XUV band. It subsided nicely under her delicate control and continued to hold.

The Refer Laser groaned as it sucked heat in from the chromosphere then back out and downward as x-rays. They climbed with agonizing slowness.

Then an alarm clanged. It wasn't a drift-warning, it was the cry of a ship dying.

The stink was terrible! Worse, it was freezing. Someone nearby was shivering and coughing at the same time. Dimly, Jacob became aware that it was himself.

He came erect in a fit of hacking that set his body trembling. For long moments after he got it under control he just sat, wondering numbly how he was alive.

The smoke had begun to clear slightly near the deck. Shreds and tendrils drifted past him toward the whining air compressors.

The fact that he could see at all was amazing. He brought his right hand up to touch his left eye.

It was open, blind. But it was whole! He closed the lid and touched it over and over with his three fingers. The eye was still there, and the brain behind it ... saved by the thick smoke and the depletion of Culla's energy supply.

Culla! Jacob swung his head about to scan for the alien. He felt a wave of nausea come on and rode it out as he peered around himself.

A slender white hand lay on the floor, two meters away, exposed by the opening cloud of smoke. The air cleared a little more and the rest of Culla's body came into view.

The E.T.'s face was burned, catastrophically. Black crusts of seared foam hung in shreds from the remnants of the huge oculars. A sizzling blue liquid seeped from large cracks in the sides.

Culla was obviously dead.

Jacob crawled forward. First he had to check on LaRoque. Then Fagin. Yes, that was the way to do it.

Then hurry and get someone down here who can work the computer panel ... if there was still a chance to reverse the damage Culla'd done.

He found LaRoque by following the man's moans. He was several meters past Culla, sitting up and holding his head. He looked up blearily.

'Oooh ... Demwa, is that you? Do not answer. Your voice might blow my poor delicate head away!'

'Are you ... all right, LaRoque?'

LaRoque nodded. 'We are both alive so Culla must not be, no? He left his job on us incomplete so we may merely wish we were dead. *Mon Dieu*! You look like spaghetti! Do I look like that!'

Whatever the effects of the fight, it had brought back the man's appetite for words.

'Come on, LaRoque. Help me up. We still have work to do.'

LaRoque started to rise, then wavered. He clutched Jacob's shoulder to keep his balance. Jacob choked back tears of pain. Jerkily, they helped each other up and onto their feet.

The firebrands must have burned out, because the chamber was rapidly clearing. Wisps of smoke trailed in the air, though, hanging before their faces as they staggered along the dome in a clockwise direction.

Once they encountered the P-laser beam, a thin, straight tracery in their way. Unable to go over or under, they went through. Jacob winced as the beam stitched a bloody line along the outside of his right thigh and the inside of his left. They continued.

When they found Fagin, the Kanten was comatose. A faint sound came from the blowhole and the silver chimes tinkled, but there was no answer to their questions. When they tried to move him they found it impossible. Sharp claws had emerged from Fagin's root pods and dug into the tough springy material of the deck. There were dozens, and no way to loosen them.

Jacob had other business to tend to. Reluctantly, he led LaRoque around the Kanten. They staggered toward the hatchway in the side of the dome.

Jacob gasped for breath next to the intercom.

'Hel ... Helene ...'

He waited. But no one answered. He could hear, faintly, his own words echoing from topside. So he knew it wasn't the mechanism. What was wrong?

'Helene, can you hear me! Culla's dead! We're pretty badly torn up ... though. You ... you or Chen come down ... down and fix ...'

The cold air blasting from the Refer Laser sent him into a fit of shivering. He couldn't talk anymore. With LaRoque helping, he stumbled up past the duct and collapsed to the sloping floor of the gravity-loop.

He fell into a fit of coughing, lying on his side to favor his burned back. Slowly the hacking subsided, leaving him raw and aching in his chest.

He fought off sleep. Rest just rest here a moment then over and around to topside. Find out what's wrong.

His arms and legs sent tremors of sharp pain up to his brain. There were too many and his mind was too unfocused to cut all the messages off. It felt as though one of his ribs was cracked, probably from the struggle with Culla.

All of this paled beside the throbbing burden of the left side of his head. He felt as if he was carrying a hot coal there.

The deck of the gravity-loop felt strange. The tight wraparound g-field should have pulled evenly along his body. Instead it seemed to swell like the surface of the ocean, rippling under his back with tiny wavelets of lightness and weight.

Obviously something was wrong. But it actually felt good, like a lullaby. Sleep would be so nice.

'Jacob! Thank God!' Helene's voice boomed around him, but still it sounded far away – friendly, definitely, warm – but also irrelevant.

'No time to talk! Come up here *quick*, darling! The g-fields are going! I'm sending Martine, but ...' There was a clattering and the voice cut off.

It would have been nice to see Helene again, he thought dimly. Sleep invaded in force this time. For a while he thought of nothing.

He dreamt of Sisyphus, the man cursed forever to roll a boulder up an endless hill. Jacob thought he had a way to be tricky about it. He had a way to make the hill think it was flat while still looking like a hill. He'd done it before.

But this time the hill was angry. It was covered with ants that climbed up onto his body and bit him all over, painfully. A wasp was laying its eggs in his eye.

What's more, it was cheating. The hill was sticky in places and didn't want to let him go. Elsewhere it was slippery and his body was too light to get a grip on its surface. It heaved with sickening unevenness.

He didn't remember anything in the rules about crawling, either. But that seemed to be part of it. At least it helped the traction.

The boulder helped too. He only had to push it a little. Mostly it crawled on its own. That was nice, but he wished it wouldn't moan so. Boulders shouldn't moan. Especially not in French. It wasn't fair to make him listen to it.

He awakened, blearily, in sight of a hatchway. Which hatchway he wasn't sure, but it wasn't very smoky.

Outside, beyond the deck, he could see the beginnings of a blackness, a transparency, returning to the red haze of the chromosphere.

Was that a horizon, out there? An edge to the Sun? The flat photosphere stretched out on ahead, a feathery carpet of crimson and black flame. In its depths it crawled with tiny movements. It pulsed, and filaments sewed elongated patterns above brightly waving jets.

Waving. Back and forth, on and on, Sol waved before his eye.

Millie Martine stood in the doorway, with her fist up near her mouth and an expression of horror on her face.

He wanted to reassure her. Everything was all right It would be from now on. Mr Hyde was dead, wasn't he? Jacob remembered seeing him somewhere, in the rubble of his castle. His face was burned up and his eyes were gone and he gave off a terrible stink.

Then something reached up and grabbed him. *Down* was now towards the hatchway. There was a steep slope in between. He tumbled forward and never remembered crashing to a halt just outside the door.

PART X

A lovely thing to see:
through the paper window's holes
the galaxy.

KOBAYASHI ISSA (1763–1828)

30

OPACITY

Commissioner Abatsoglou: 'Then It would be a fair statement to say that all of the Library-designed systems failed, before the end?'

Professor Kepler: 'Yes, Commissioner. Every one eventually deteriorated to uselessness. The only mechanisms still working at the last were components designed on Earth, by terrestrial personnel. Mechanisms which, I might add, were declared superfluous and unnecessary by Pil Bubbacub and many others during construction.'

C.A.: 'You aren't implying that Bubbacub knew in advance ...'

P.K.: 'No, of course not. In his own way he was as much a dupe as the rest of us. His opposition was based solely on esthetics. He didn't want Galactic time-compression and gravity-control systems crammed into a ceramic shell and linked to an archaic cooling system.

'The reflection fields and the Refrigerator Laser were based on physical laws known by humans back in the twentieth century. Naturally he objected to our "superstitious" insistence on building a ship around them, not only because the Galactic systems made them redundant, but also because he considered pre-contact Earth science to be a pathetic accumulation of half-truths and mumbo-jumbo.'

C.A.: 'The "mumbo jumbo" worked when the new stuff failed, though.'

P.K.: 'In all fairness, Commissioner, I'd have to say that that was a lucky break. The saboteur believed they'd make no difference, so he didn't try to wreck them, at first. He was denied an opportunity to correct his error.'

Commissioner Montes: 'There's one thing I don't understand, Dr Kepler. I'm sure some of my associates here share my mystification. I understand the Sunship Captain's use of the Refrigerator-Laser to blast out of the chromosphere. But to do so she had to boost at an acceleration greater than the surface gravity of the Sun! Now they could get away with this as long as the internal gravity fields held.

But what happened when they failed? Weren't they immediately subjected to a force that would squash them flat?'

P.K.: 'Not immediately. Failure came in stages; first the fine-tuned fields used to maintain the gravity-loop tunnel to the instrument hemisphere, "flip-side," then the automatic turbulence adjustment, and finally a gradual loss of the major field which compensated internally for the pull of the Sun. By the time the latter failed, they had already reached the lower corona. Captain deSilva was ready when it happened.

'She knew that to climb straight out after internal compensation failed would be suicide, though she considered doing it anyway to get her records out to us. The alternative was to allow the ship to fall, braking only enough to impose on the occupants about three gees or so.

'Fortunately, there is a way to fall towards a gravity sink and still get away. What Helene did was to try for a hyperbolic escape orbit. Almost all of the laser thrust then went into giving the ship a tangent velocity as it fell back again.

'In effect she duplicated the program that had been considered for manned dives decades before contact; a shallow orbit, using lasers for thrust and cooling, and E.M. fields for protection. Only this dive was unintentional, and it wasn't very shallow.'

C.A.: 'How close did they go?'

P.K.: 'Well, you'll recall that they'd fallen twice before in all of the confusion: once when the g-thrust failed, and a second time when the Solarians lost their grip on the ship. Well during this third fall they came closer to the photosphere than on any of the previous occasions. They literally skimmed its surface.'

C.A.: 'But the turbulence, Doctor! Without internal gravity or time-compression, why wasn't the ship smashed?'

P.K.: 'We learned a lot of solar physics from this inadvertent dive, sir. At least on this occasion the chromosphere was far less turbulent than anyone ever expected ... that is anyone but a couple of my colleagues to whom I owe a few abject apologies ... But I believe the most significant factor was the piloting of the ship. Helene quite simply did the impossible. The auto-recorder is being studied now by the TAASF people. The only thing greater than their delight with the tapes is their chagrin at not being able to give her a medal.'

General Wade: 'Yes, the condition of the crew was a cause of great distress to the TAASF rescue team. The ship looked like Napoleon's retreat from Moscow! With no one alive to tell what happened, you'll understand our mystification until the tapes were played back.'

Commissioner Nguyen: 'I can imagine. You seldom expect to get a special shipment of snowballs from hell. Can we assume, Doctor, that the ship's Commander weighted the heat pump system on the cold side for the obvious reason?'

'In all honesty, Commissioner, I don't believe we can. I think her reasoning was to keep the interior cold so that all of the records would survive. If the Refer-Laser system erred too much the other way they'd have been fried. I believe her sole idea was to protect those tapes. She probably expected to come out of the Sun having roughly the consistency of strawberry jam.

'I don't think the biological effects of freezing were on her mind.

'You see, in many ways Helene was a bit of an innocent. She stayed up to date in her field but I don't think she knew about the advances in cryosurgery we've made since her day. I think she's going to be very surprised, a year from now, when she wakes up.

'The others will probably take it as a routine miracle. Except for Mr Demwa, of course. I don't think Mr Demwa would be surprised by anything ... or consider his revival miraculous. The man is indestructible. I think by now, wherever his consciousness drifts in its frozen sleep, he knows it.'

31

PROPAGATION

In the springtime the whales go north again.

Several of the grey humps that broached and spumed in the distance had not been born when he last stood on a shore and watched a California migration pass by. He wondered if any of the grey whales still sang 'The Ballad of Jacob and the Sphinx.'

Probably not. It never was a favorite of Greys anyway. The song was too irreverent too ... beluga for their sober temperament. The Greys were complacent snobs, but he loved them anyway.

The air boomed with the noise of the breakers, crashing into the rocks at his feet. It was wet with sea water and filled his lungs with the paradoxical satiated-hungry feeling that others got from breathing deep in a bakery shop. There was a serenity that came with the pulse of the ocean, plus an expectation that the tide would always wash up changes.

They'd given him a chair, at the hospital in Santa Barbara, but Jacob preferred the cane. It gave him less mobility, but the exercise would shorten his convalescence. Three months after waking up in that antiseptic organ factory had left him desperate to get back on his feet, and to experience something that was pleasantly, naturally dirty.

Such as Helene's way of talking. It defied all logic that a person born at the height of the old Bureaucracy would have so uninhibited a mouth as to make a Confederacy Citizen blush. But when Helene felt she was among friends her language became impressive and her vocabulary astonishing. She said that it came from being raised on a power satellite. Then she smiled and refused to explain any further until he reciprocated with acts she *knew* he wasn't ready yet to perform. As if *she* was!

One month to go before the physicians would take them off of hormone suppressants, after the bulk of cell regrowth was completed. Another month before they'd be cleared for anything as rigorous as space flight. And yet she insisted on pulling out that dog-eared copy of *NASA Sutra*, wondering teasingly if he would have the stamina!

Well, the doctors said that frustration helps recuperation. Sharpens the will to get back to normal, or some such nonsense.

If Helene keeps up her teasing much longer they're all going to be surprised! Jacob didn't believe much in timetables anyway.

Ifni! That water looks good! Nice and cold. There *has* to be a way to make nerves grow faster! Something that helps even better than auto-suggestion.

He turned away from the rocks and slowly walked back to the patio of his uncle's long, rambling house. He used the cane liberally, perhaps more than necessary, enjoying the dramatic touch. It made being ill slightly less unpleasant.

As usual, Uncle James was flirting with Helene. She encouraged him shamelessly.

Serves the old bastard right he thought after all the trouble he caused.

'My boy,' Uncle James threw up his hands. 'We were just about to go after you, truly we were.'

Jacob smiled lazily. 'No hurry, Jim. I'm sure our interstellar explorer here had plenty of interesting stories to tell. Did you tell him the one about the black hole, dear?'

Helene grinned nastily and made a surreptitious gesture. 'Why, Jake, you yourself told me not to. But if you think your uncle would like to hear it . . .'

Jacob shook his head. He'd handle his uncle himself. Helene could get a little rough.

Ms deSilva was a great pilot and in the last few weeks she'd been an imaginative co-conspirator as well. But their personal relationship left Jacob dizzy. Her personality was . . . powerful.

When she'd learned, on awakening, that the *Calypso* had jumped, Helene had signed onto the gang designing the new *Vesarius II*. The reason, she announced brazenly, was to have three years to subject Jacob Demwa to a full course of Pavlovian conditioning. At the end of said time she would ring a little bell and he would, supposedly, decide to become a Jumper.

Jacob had his reservations, but it was already clear that Helene deSilva had complete control over his salivary glands.

Uncle James was more nervous than he'd ever seen him. The usually imperturbable politician seemed decidedly ill at ease. The rakish Irish charm of the Alvarez side of the family was subdued. The grey head nodded nervously. His green eyes seemed unnaturally sad.

'Um, Jacob, my boy. Our guests have arrived. They are waiting in the study and Christien is looking after them.

'Now, I hope you are going to be reasonable about this matter. There really was no reason to invite that government fellow. We could have settled this ourselves.

'Now as I see it . . .'

Jacob held up his free hand. 'Uncle, please. We've been through this.

'The matter has to be adjudicated. If you refuse the services of the Secrets Registration people, I'll just have to call a family council and present the matter to them! You know Uncle Jeremey, he'll probably opt for publicly announcing the whole thing. It'd make good press, all right but the Department of Overt Prosecutions would have the case then, and you'd have five years with a little thing in your rump going "beep . . . beep . . . beep."'

Jacob leaned against Helene's shoulder, more for the contact than for support, and flashed both hands in front of Uncle James' eyes. With each 'beep' the man's aristocratic face paled a little. Helene started to giggle, then she hiccuped.

'Excuse me,' she said demurely.

'Don't be sarcastic,' Jacob commented. He pinched her then reclaimed his cane.

*

The study wasn't as impressive as the one in Alvarez Hall, in Caracas, but this house was in California. That made up for a lot. Jacob hoped he and his uncle still spoke after today.

Stucco walls and false beams emphasized the Spanish aspect. Display cases, containing James' collection of Bureaucracy-era Samizdat publications, stood out prominently among the bookshelves.

In the mantle was carved a long motto.

'The People, United, Shall Never Be Defeated.'

Fagin fluted a warm greeting. Jacob bowed and went through a long, formal salutation, just to please the Kanten. Fagin had visited him regularly in the hospital It had been difficult at first, between them – each convinced he was deeply indebted to the other. Finally they'd agreed to disagree.

When the TAASF rescue team had broken into the Sunship, as it hurtled outward on its laser-assisted hyperbolic orbit, they were amazed by the crumpled, frozen condition of the human crew. They didn't quite know what to make of the smashed body of the Pring, on flip-side. But what shocked them most was Fagin, hanging upside down by those small sharp spikes in his root-pods while the laser still put out its potent thrust The cold had not ruptured almost a quarter of his cells, as it had the humans, and he appeared to have come through the pounding ride through the photosphere unscathed.

In spite of himself, Fagin of the Institute of Progress – the perpetual observer and manipulator – had become, himself, a unique personage. He was probably the only sophont alive anywhere who could describe what it was like to fly, hanging upside down, through the thick, opaque fire of the photosphere. Now he had a story of his own to tell.

It must have been painful for the Kanten. Nobody believed a word of his tale until Helene's tapes were replayed.

Jacob said hello to Pierre LaRoque. The man had regained much of his color since their last meeting, not to mention his appetite. He'd been wolfing down Christien's hors d'oeuvres. Still confined to his chair, he smiled and nodded silently to Jacob and Helene. Jacob suspected LaRoque's mouth was too full to talk.

The last guest was a tall, narrow-faced man with blonde hair and light blue eyes. He rose from the couch and offered his hand.

'Han Nielsen, at your service, Mr Demwa. On the basis of the news reports alone I am proud to meet you. Of course, Secrets Registration knows everything the government knows, so I am doubly impressed. I assume, though, that you have called us in to deal with a matter that the government is not to know?'

Jacob and Helene sat on the couch across from him, their backs to a window overlooking the ocean.

'Yes, that's correct, Mr Nielsen. Actually, there are a couple of matters. We'd like to apply for a seal and for adjudication by the Terragens Council.'

Nielsen frowned. 'Surely you must realize that the council is barely an infant at this point. The delegates appointed by the colonies have not even arrived! The Confederacy b ... civil servants' (Had he been about to say the dirty word 'bureaucrats'?) 'don't even like the idea of having a supra-legal Secrets Registration to enforce honesty above secular law. The Terragens is even less popular.'

'Even though it's been shown that it's the only way to deal with the crisis we've faced since Contact?' Helene asked.

'Even so. The Feds are reconciled to the fact that it will eventually take jurisdiction over interstellar and interspecies affairs, but they don't like it and they're dragging their feet every step of the way.'

'But that's just the point,' Jacob said. 'The crisis was bad before this debacle on Mercury, bad enough to force the creation of the Council. But it was still manageable. Sundiver has probably changed that.'

Nielsen looked grim. 'I know.'

'Do you?' Jacob rested his hands on his knees and leaned forward. 'You've seen Fagin's report on the probable reaction of the Pila to Bubbacub's exposed peccadilloes on Mercury. And that report was written well before this whole business regarding Culla came to light!'

'And the Confederacy knows everything,' Nielsen grimaced. 'Culla's actions, his weird apologia, the whole capsule.'

'Well after all,' Jacob sighed. 'They *are* the government. They make foreign policy. Besides, Helene had no way of knowing we'd live through that mess down there. She recorded everything.'

'It never occurred to me,' Helene said, 'until Fagin explained, that it might be better if the Feds never found out the truth, or that the Terragens Council might be better suited to handle this mess.'

'Better suited, perhaps, but what do you expect us ... the Council to do? It'll take years to build up acceptance and legitimacy. Why should they risk it all by intervening in this situation?'

For a moment no one spoke. Then Nielsen shrugged.

From his briefcase he pulled a small recording cube, which he activated and placed in the center of the room, on the floor.

'This conversation is under seal by the Secrets Registration. Why don't you start, Dr deSilva.'

Helene ticked off points with the fingers of her hand.

'One, we know that Bubbacub perpetrated a crime in the eyes of both the Library Institute and his own race by falsifying a Library report, and perpetrating a hoax on Sundiver; to wit: that he had communicated with the Solarians and had used his "Lethani relic" to protect us from their wrath.

'We think we know Bubbacub's motives for doing what he did. He was embarrassed by the failure of the Library to reference the Sun Ghosts. He wanted to rub the "wolfling" race's collective nose in its inferiority, as well.

'By Galactic Tradition this situation would resolve itself by both the Pila and the Library bribing Earth to "keep its mouth shut." The Confederacy would be able to choose its reward with few strings attached, though the human race would have to face enmity from the Pila in the future simply because their pride had been hurt.

'They could still increase their efforts to remove provisionary-sophont status from our Clients, the chimps and dolphins. There has been talk of placing humanity under some sort of "adoptive" Client status ... "to guide us through this difficult transition." Have I summed up the situation fairly well, so far?'

Jacob nodded. 'Fine. Except you left out my own stupidity. On Mercury I accused Bubbacub *publicly*! That little two-year pledge we signed was never taken seriously, and the Feds have waited too long to put an emergency sequester on this case. Probably half of the spiral arm knows the story by now.

'That means we've lost what little leverage we would have had with the Pila by blackmail. They'll hold nothing back in their efforts to get us "adopted," and they'll use "reparations" for Bubbacub's crime as an excuse to force us to accept all kinds of aid that we don't want.'

He motioned for Helene to continue.

'Point number two; we now know that the one behind this fiasco was Culla. Apparently Culla never intended that humanity discover Bubbacub's peccadillo. He had his own blackmail scheme in mind.

'By encouraging Jeffrey's friendship he got the chimpanzee to try to "liberate" him, thus enraging Bubbacub. Jeffrey's subsequent death left Sundiver in such a state of confusion that Bubbacub would be encouraged to think that anything he did would be believed. It's possible that Dwayne Kepler's apparent mental deterioration was part of this campaign, induced by Culla's "glare psychosis" technique.

'The most important part of Culla's plan was the hoax of the anthropomorphic Ghosts. That part was magnificently executed. It fooled everybody. With talents like those, it's not hard to see why the Pring think they can take on the Pila in a bid for independence.

258

They're one of the most deceptively potent races I've ever come across or heard of.'

'But if the Pila were Patrons to the Pring,' James objected. 'And if they uplifted Culla's ancestors from near animals, why wasn't Bubbacub aware of the possibility that the Ghosts were Culla's hoax?'

'If I may be allowed to comment on this,' Fagin fluted. 'The Pring were allowed to select the assistant who would accompany Bubbacub. My institute has independent information that Culla was a figure of some importance, on one of their terraformed planets, in an artistic endeavor that we have, until now, not been able to witness. We had attributed the Pring secretiveness on this matter to habit patterns inherited from the Pila. Now, however, we might conjecture that it is the Pila themselves who were not to witness the art. In their complacent superiority, the Pila must have cooperated unknowingly by denigrating their Clients' endeavors.'

'And this art form is?'

'The art form must, logically, be holographic projection. It is possible that the Pring have been experimenting for most of the hundred millennia of their sentience, in secret from their Patrons. I am in awe of the dedication it would have taken to keep a secret for so long.'

Nielsen whistled lowly. 'They must want their release awful bad. But I still don't understand, though I've listened to all of the tapes, why Culla pulled these pranks with Sundiver! How could the hoax of the anthropomorphic Sun Ghosts, the death of Jeffrey, or trapping Bubbacub into his error ever help the Pring?'

Helene glanced at Jacob. He nodded. 'This is still your part, Helene. You figured most of it out.'

Helene took a deep breath.

'You see, Culla never intended that Bubbacub be exposed on Mercury. He snared his boss into lying and pulling that stunt with the Lethani relic, but he expected him to be believed, here at least.

'If his plan had carried through he would have reported two assertions to the Library Institute; one, that Bubbacub was a fool and a liar who had been saved from embarrassment by the quick thinking of his assistant, and two, that humans were just a pack of harmless idiots and should be ignored.

'I'll cover the second point first.

'On the face of it, it is obvious that no one out there would believe this crazy story of "man-shaped ghosts" fluttering around in a star, especially when the Library has no mention of them!

'Imagine how the galaxy would react to a tale about plasma creatures which "shake their fists" and miraculously avoid having their pictures taken so there can be no proof they exist! Having heard that, most observers would never bother to examine the evidence we *did* have, the recordings of toroids and of the *real* Solarians!

'The galaxy on the whole looks on Terrestrial "research" with amused contempt. Culla apparently wanted Sundiver to be laughed out without a hearing.'

Across the room, Pierre LaRoque blushed. No one said anything about the remarks he'd made on 'Terrestrial research' over a year back.

'The quick explanation Culla gave, when he tried to kill us all, was that he faked the Ghosts for our own good. If we looked foolish we might make less of a splash when we announced life in the Sun ... a splash that would give humanity more publicity in a time when we should be studying quietly to catch up with everyone else.'

Nielsen frowned. 'He may have had a point'

Helene shrugged. 'It's too late now.

'Anyway, it seems, as I have said, that Culla intended to report to the Library, and to the Soro, that humans were harmless idiots and, more importantly, that Bubbacub had been a party to that idiocy ... that he had believed in the Ghosts and lied on the basis of that belief!'

Helene turned to face Fagin. 'Is that a fair summary of what we discussed, Kant Fagin?'

The Kanten whistled softly. 'I would think so. Trusting in the "seal" of the Secrets Registration organization, I will state confidentially that my Institute has received intelligence regarding activities of the Pring and Pila that now make sense in the light of what we have here learned. The Pring apparently are engaged in a campaign to discredit the Pila. Therein lies an opportunity and a danger to humanity.

'The opportunity is that your Confederacy could offer evidence of Culla's betrayal to the Pila, so that those sophonts may show how they have been manipulated. If the Soro then came down against the Pring, Culla's race would be hard pressed to find a protector. They might be lowered in status, their colonies eliminated, populations "reduced."

'There might be immediate rewards for humanity in this act, but it would do little to change the long range enmity of the Pil. Their psychology does not work that way. They might suspend their attempts to have humanity "adopted." They might be willing to accept restraints on the reparations they will insist on paying for Bubbacub's crime, but in the long run it will not win their friendship. Owing humanity a debt will only increase their hatred.

'In addition, there is the fact that many of the more "liberal" species, on whose protection humanity has so far relied, would not appreciate your providing the Pila with a Casus Belli for another of their Jihads. The Tymbrimi might withdraw their consulate from Luna.

'Finally there is the ethical consideration. It would take long for me to discuss all of the reasons. Some of them you would probably not understand. But the Institute of Progress is anxious that the Pring not be devastated. They are young and impulsive. Almost as much so as humanity. But they show great promise. For the entire species to suffer terrible depredations, because a few of its members engage in a scheme to end a hundred millennia of servitude, would be a terrible tragedy.

'For these reasons I would recommend that Culla's crimes be placed under seal. Certainly rumors would soon drift about. But the Soro will be aloof to rumors bandied about by the likes of men.'

Fagin's chimes tinkled softly as a breeze came in the window. Nielsen was staring at the floor.

'No wonder Culla tried to kill himself and everyone else aboard the ship, when Jacob figured him out! If the Pila get official testimony on Culla's actions, the Pring are probably doomed.'

'What do you think the Confederacy will do?' Jacob asked.

'Do?' He laughed humorlessly. 'Why they'll offer the evidence to Pila with bended knee, of course. Ifni! It's a chance to keep them from "giving" us a full sector Library Branch and ten thousand technicians to staff it! It's a chance to keep them from "giving" us modern ships that no human engineer could possibly understand and no human crew could operate without "advisors." It'd put off indefinitely those damned "adoption procedures"!' He spread his hands. 'And it's pretty clear that the Confederacy won't stick its neck out for the race of a sophont who killed one of our Clients, damn near wrecked our hottest project, and attempted to make humans look like idiots among the peoples of the galaxy!

'And when you get right down to it, could you blame them?'

Jacob's Uncle James cleared his throat to gain their attention.

'We can try to put the entire episode under seal,' he suggested. 'I am not without influence in some circles. If I put in a good word . . .'

'You can't put in a good word, Jim,' Jacob said. 'You're a *participant* in this mess, in a minor way. If you try to involve yourself the truth will eventually come out.'

'What truth is that?' Nielsen asked.

Jacob frowned at his uncle then at LaRoque. The Frenchman had imperturbably begun to nibble on more hors d'oeuvres.

'These two,' Jacob said, 'are part of a cabal whose aim is to undermine the Probation laws. That's the second reason I asked you to come. Something's going to have to be done and Secrets Registration is a better first step than going to the police.'

At the mention of the police, LaRoque stopped nibbling at his tiny sandwich. He looked at it then put it down.

'What kind of cabal?' Nielsen asked.

'A society, consisting of Probationers and certain citizen sympathizers, dedicated to the secret manufacture of spaceships ... spaceships with Probationer crews.'

Nielson sat upright. 'What?'

'LaRoque is in charge of their astronaut training program. He's also their chief spy. He tried to measure the calibration settings of a Sunship's Gravity Generator. I have the tapes to prove it.'

'But why would they want to do such a thing?'

'Why not? It'd be the most powerful symbolic protest imaginable. If I were a Probationer, I'd certainly participate. I'm sympathetic. I don't like the Probation laws one bit.

'But I'm also realistic. As it stands the Probationers have been made into an underclass. Their psychological problems are a stigma that follows them everywhere. They react in a very human way, they gather together to hate the "docile and domesticated" society around them.

'They say, "You Citizens think I'm violent, well then by damn I *will* be!" Most of the Probationers would never do anything to hurt anybody, *whatever* their P-tests say. But faced with this stereotype they become what they're reputed to be!'

'That may or may not be true,' Nielsen said. 'But given the situation as it stands, for Probationers to get access to *space* ...'

Jacob sighed. 'You're right, of course. It can't be allowed to happen. Not yet.

'On the other hand, we can't allow the Feds to whip up public hysteria over this either. It'd just aggravate matters and put off a later, more severe form of rebellion.'

Nielsen looked worried. 'You aren't going to suggest that the Terragens Council get involved in the *Probation laws*, are you? Why that'd be suicide! The public would never stand for it!'

Jacob smiled sadly. 'That's right, they wouldn't. Even Uncle James would have to recognize that. Today's Citizen won't even consider changing the status of Probationers, and as things stand the Terragens has no authority.

'But what is the domain of the Council? Currently It's administration of extrasolar colonies. Eventually it's to include supervision of all extrasolar affairs. And there's where they can meddle in the Probation laws, symbolically at least, without threatening anyone's peace of mind.'

'I don't know what you mean.'

'Well now I don't suppose you've ever read Aldous Huxley, have you? No? His works were still popular when Helene was brought up, and my cousins and I were ... required to study some of them in our youth – damned difficult at times, because of the strange period references, but worth it for the man's incredible insight and wit.

'Old Huxley wrote one piece titled *Brave New World* ...'

'Yes, I've heard of it. Some sort of dystopia, wasn't it?'

'Of a sort. You should read it. There are some uncanny prophecies.

'In that novel he projects a society with some unpalatable aspects but with, all the same, a self-consistency and its own form of honor – akin to the ethics of a hive, but ethics nonetheless. When man's diversity keeps throwing up individuals who don't fit into the conditioned pattern of the society, what do you suppose Huxley's state does with them?'

Nielsen frowned, wondering where this was leading. 'In a hivelike state? I'd guess that the deviants were eliminated, killed.'

Jacob raised a finger. 'No, not quite. The way Huxley presents it, this state has wisdom, of sorts. The leaders are aware that they've set up a rigid system that might fall before some unexpected threat. They realize that the deviants represent a control, a reserve to fall back on in times of trouble, when the race would need all of its resources.

'But at the same time, they can't keep them hanging around, threatening the stability of the culture.'

'So what did they do?'

'They banished the deviates to islands. There they were allowed to pursue their own cultural experiments undisturbed.'

'Islands, eh?' Nielsen scratched his head. 'It is a striking idea. Actually, it's the inverse of what we're already doing with the Extraterrestrial Reserves, exiling the Probies from geographically controllable areas and then allowing E.T.s in to mingle with the Citizens who come and go at will.'

'An intolerable situation,' James muttered. 'Not only for the Probationers, but for the extraterrestrials, as well. Why, Kant Fagin was just telling me how much he'd like to visit the Louvre, or Agra, or Yosemite!'

'All shall come in time, Friend-James Alvarez,' Fagin trilled. 'For now I am grateful for the dispensation which enables me to visit this small part of California, an undeserved and extravagant reward.'

'I don't know if the "islands" idea would work that well,' Nielsen said thoughtfully. 'Of course it's worth bringing up. We can go into all of the ramifications another time. What I'm having trouble figuring out is what this would have to do with the Terragens Council.'

'Extrapolate,' Jacob urged. 'It just *might* ameliorate the Probationer problem, somewhat, to set up some sort of island Coventry in the Pacific, where they could pursue their own path without the perpetual observation they undergo everywhere today. But it wouldn't be enough. Many Probationers feel that they are emasculated from the start. Not only are their parentage rights limited by law, they are also excluded from the most important adventure mankind has ever undertaken, the expansion into space.

'This little imbroglio LaRoque and James were engaged in is a prime example of the problems we'll face, unless a niche is found for them, so that they can feel they're participating.'

'A niche. Islands. Space . . . good lord, man! You can't be serious! Buy another colony and give it over to Probationers? When we're still in hock up to our ears for the three we've *got*? You must be an optimist if you think that could pass!'

Jacob felt Helene's hand slide into his own. He barely glanced at her, but the expression on her face was enough. Proud, alert, and just on the edge, as ever, of laughter. He twined his fingers with hers to cover the most area, and squeezed back.

'Yes,' he said to Nielsen. 'I *have* become somewhat of an optimist lately. And I think it could be done.'

'But where would we get the credit? And how do you salve the wounded egos of half a billion *Citizens* who want to colonize, when you're giving space to non-Citizens?

'Hell, colonization wouldn't work anyway. Even the *Vesarius II* will carry only ten thousand. There are almost a hundred million Probationers!'

'Oh not all of them will want to go, especially if they get a place on the islands as well. Besides, I'm sure all they're looking for is fair treatment. A share. Our real problem is that there's not enough colony room, or transport.'

Jacob smiled slowly. 'But what if we could get the Library Institute to "donate" the funds for a Class Four colony, plus a few Orion type transports specially simplified for human crews.'

'How do you expect to persuade them to do that? They're obligated to compensate us for Bubbacub's hoax, but they'll want to do it in a way that serves their purposes, like making us totally dependent on Galactic technology. In that they'd be supported by almost every race. What could make them change the form of their reparations?'

Jacob spread his hands. 'You forget, we now have something they'll want … something very precious that the Library Institute can't do without. Knowledge!'

Jacob reached into his pocket and pulled out a slip of paper.

'This is a ciphered message I received a little while ago from Millie Martine on Mercury. She's still restricted to a chair, but they wanted her back there so badly that they let her travel over a month ago.

'She says that full dives have been resumed in active regions. She's already been down once, in charge of the effort to re-establish contact with the Solarians. So far she's been able to avoid telling the Feds much about what she's found, waiting instead to confer with Fagin and myself.

'Contact has been made. The Solarians talked to her. They are lucid and have a very long memory.'

'Incredible,' Nielsen sighed. 'But I'm getting the impression you think this will have political implications relating to the problems we've discussed here?'

'Think about it. The Library will believe they can force us to take reparations on their terms. But if it's handled right we can blackmail them into giving us what *we* want instead.

'The fact that the Solarians are talkative and can remember the distant past – Millie hints that they remember dives into the Sun by ancient sophonts, so long ago that they might have been the Progenitors themselves – means that we have found a prize of unprecedented proportions.

'It means that the Library must try to find out everything they can about them. It also means that this discovery will get a great deal of publicity.'

Jacob grinned.

'It'll be complicated. First we've got to play to the impression they already have that Sundiver is one big fiasco. Get them to assign us a Library Investigation Patent to the Sun. They'll imagine it will only make us look more idiotic. When they realize what we have, they'll have to buy it from us at our price!

'We'll need Fagin's help to finesse it properly, plus all of the savvy of the Alvarez clan and the cooperation of you Terragens people, but it can be done. Uncle Jeremey, in particular, will be glad to know that I'm going to dust off my long dormant skills and get involved in "dirty politics" for a while, to help.'

James laughed. 'Just wait til your cousins hear! I can see them shuddering already!'

'Well tell them not to worry. No, I'll tell them myself when Jeremey calls a family council on this. I'm going to make certain

265

that this whole mess is settled within three years. After that I'm retiring from politics, permanently.

'You see, I'll be going on a long trip about then.'

Helene let out a small gasp and pressed her fingernails into his thigh. Her expression was indescribable.

'One thing I'm going to insist on,' he said to her, wondering if he could, or wanted to, suppress the urge to laugh or the roaring in his ears. 'We'll have to find a way to take along at least one dolphin. Her limericks are awfully dirty, but they may buy us supplies in a few ports while we're out there.'

STARTIDE RISING

'To my own progenitors ...'

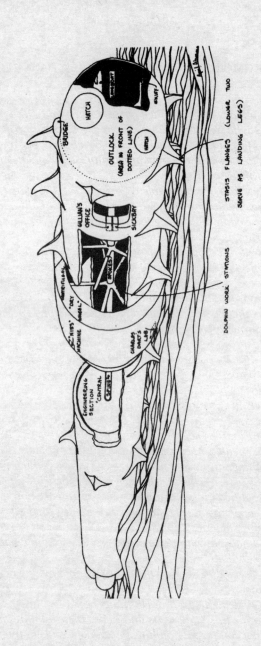

BRIDGE

HATCH

OUTLOCK
(AREA IN FRONT OF
DOTTED LINE)

HATCH

STUFF

GILLIAN'S
OFFICE

SICKBAY

SPOKES

KIDS'
DRY
MACHINE
ANNEX

CHARLIE
DAVES
LAB

ENGINEERING
SECTION
CENTRAL

SPINES

STASIS FLANGES (LOWER TWO
SERVE AS LANDING LEGS)

DOLPHIN WORK STATIONS

PROLOGUE

FROM THE JOURNAL OF GILLIAN BASKIN

Streaker *is limping like a dog on three legs.*

We took a chancy jump through overdrive yesterday, a step ahead of the Galactics who are chasing us. The one probability coil that had survived the Morgran battle groaned and complained, but finally delivered us here, to the shallow gravity well of a small population-H dwarf star named Kthsemenee.

The Library *lists one habitable world in orbit, the planet Kithrup.*

When I say 'habitable,' it's with charity. Tom, Hikahi, and I spent hours with the captain, looking for alternatives. In the end, Creideiki decided to bring us here.

As a physician, I dread landing on a planet as insidiously dangerous as this one, but Kithrup is a water world, and our mostly-dolphin crew needs water to be able to move about and repair the ship. Kithrup is rich in heavy metals, and should have the raw materials we need.

It also has the virtue of being seldom visited. The Library *says it's been fallow for a very long time. Maybe the Galactics won't think to look for us here.*

I said as much to Tom last night, as he and I held hands and watched the planet's disc grow larger in one of the lounge ports. It's a deceptively lovely blue globe, swathed in bands of white clouds. The night side was lit in patches by dimly glowing volcanoes and flickering lightning.

I told Tom that I was sure no one would follow us here – pronouncing the prediction confidently, and fooling nobody. Tom smiled and said nothing, humoring my bout of wishful thinking.

They'll look here, of course. There were only a few interspatial paths Streaker *could have taken without using a transfer point. The only question is, can we get our repairs finished in time, and get away from here before the Galactics come for us?*

Tom and I had a few hours to ourselves, our first in days. We went back to our cabin and made love.

While he sleeps, I'm making this entry. I don't know when I'll have another chance.

Captain Creideiki just called. He wants both of us up on the bridge, I suppose so the fins can see us and know their human patrons are nearby. Even a competent dolphin spacer like Creideiki might feel the need from time to time.

If only we humans had that psychological refuge.

Time to put this down and awaken my tired fellow. But first, I want to jot down what Tom said to me last night, while we watched Kithrup's stormy seas.

He turned to me, smiled that funny way he does when he thinks of something ironic, and whistled a brief haiku in dolphin-Trinary.

> * The stars shake with storms
> > * The waters below roll thunder –
> > > * Still, are we wet, love? *

I had to laugh. Sometimes I think Tom *is half dolphin.*

PART ONE

BUOYANCY

'All your better deeds
shall be
in water writ ...'

FRANCIS BEAUMONT AND JOHN FLETCHER

1

TOSHIO

Fins had been making wisecracks about human beings for thousands of years. They had *always* found men terribly funny. The fact that humanity had recently meddled with their genes, and taught them engineering, hadn't done much to change their attitude.

Fins were still smart-alecks.

Toshio watched the small instrument panel of his seasled, pretending to check the depth gauge. The sled thrummed along at a constant ten meters below the surface. There were no adjustments to be made, yet he concentrated on the panel as Keepiru swam up alongside – doubtless to start another round of teasing.

'Little Hands, whistle!' The sleek, gray cetacean did a barrel roll to Toshio's right, then drew nearer to eye the boy casually. 'Whistle us a tune about shipsss and space and going home!'

Keepiru's voice, echoing from a complex set of chambers under his skull, rumbled like the groaning of a bassoon. He could just as well have imitated an oboe, or a tenor sax.

'Well, Little Hands? Where is your sssong?'

Keepiru was making sure the rest of the party could hear. The other fins swam quietly, but Toshio could tell they were listening. He was glad that Hikahi, the leader of the expedition, was far ahead, scouting. It would be far worse if she were here and ordered Keepiru to leave him alone. Nothing Keepiru said could match the shame of being protected like a helpless child.

Keepiru rolled lazily, belly up, next to the boy's sled, kicking slow fluke strokes to stay easily abreast of Toshio's machine. In the crystal-clear water of Kithrup, everything seemed strangely refracted. The coral-like peaks of the metal-mounds shimmered as though mountains seen through the haze of a long valley. Drifting yellow tendrils of dangle-weed hung from the surface.

Keepiru's gray skin had a phosphorescent sheen, and the needle-sharp teeth in his long, narrow, vee mouth shone with a teasing cruelty that *had* to be magnified ... if not by the water, then by Toshio's own imagination.

How could a fin be so mean?

'Won't you sing for us, Little Hands? Sing us a song that will buy us all fish-brew when we finally get off this ssso-called planet and find a friendly port! Whistle to make the Dreamers dream of land!'

Above the tiny whine of his air-recycler, Toshio's ears buzzed with embarrassment. At any moment, he was sure, Keepiru would stop calling him Little Hands and start using the new nickname he had chosen: 'Great Dreamer.'

It was bad enough to be taunted for having made the mistake of whistling, when accompanying an exploration crew of fins – they had greeted his absentminded melody with raspberries and chittering derision – but to be mockingly addressed by a title almost always reserved for great musicians or humpback whales ... it was almost more than he could bear.

'I don't feel like singing right now, Keepiru. Why don't you go bother somebody else?' Toshio felt a small sense of victory in managing to keep a quaver out of his voice.

To Toshio's relief, Keepiru merely squeaked something high and fast in gutter Trinary, almost Primal Delphin – that in itself a form of insult. Then the dolphin arched and shot away to surface for air.

The water on all sides was bright and blue. Shimmering Kithrupan fish flicked past with scaled backs that faceted the light like drifting, frosted leaves. All around were the various colors and textures of metal. Morning sunshine penetrated the clear, steady sea to glimmer off the peculiar life forms of this strange and inevitably deadly world.

Toshio had no eye for the beauty of Kithrup's waters. Hating the planet, the crippled ship that had brought him here, and the fins who were his fellow castaways, he drifted into a poignantly satisfying rehearsal of the scathing retorts he *should* have said to Keepiru.

'If you're so good, Keepiru, why don't you whistle us up some vanadium!' Or, 'I see no point in wasting a *human* song on a dolphin audience, Keepiru.'

In his imagination the remarks were satisfyingly effective. In the real world, Toshio knew, he could never say any such thing.

First of all, cetacean vocalizings were legal tender in countless spaceports. And while it was the mournful ballads of the larger cousins, the whales, that brought the real prices, Keepiru's kin could buy intoxicants on a dozen worlds merely by exercising their lungs.

Anyway, it would be a mistake to try to pull human rank on any of the crew of the *Streaker*. Old Hannes Suessi, one of the other six humans aboard, had warned him about that just after they had left Neptune, at the beginning of the voyage.

'Try it and see what happens,' the mechanic had suggested. 'They'll laugh so hard, and so will *I*, if I have the good luck to be there when you do. Likely as not, one of them will take a nip at you for good measure! If there's anything fins don't respect, it's a human who never earned the right, putting on patron airs.'

'But the Protocols ... ' Toshio had started to protest.

'Protocols my left eye! Those rules were set up so humans and chimps and fins will act in just the right way when Galactics are around. If the *Streak* gets stopped by a Soro patrol, or has to ask a Pilan Librarian for data somewhere, *then* Dr Metz or Mr Orley – or even you or I – might have to pretend we're in charge ... because none of those stuffed-shirt Eatees would give the time of day to a race as young as fins. But the rest of the time we take our orders from Captain Creideiki.

'Hell, that'd be hard enough – taking brown from a Soro and pretending you like it because the damned ET is nice enough to admit that *humans*, at least, are a bit above the level of fruit flies. Can you imagine how hard it would be if we actually had to *run* this ship? What if we had tried to make dolphins into a nice, well-behaved, slavey client race? Would you have liked that?'

At the time Toshio had shaken his head vigorously. The idea of treating fins as clients usually were in the Five Galaxies was repulsive. His best friend, Akki, was a fin.

Yet, there were moments like the present, when Toshio wished there were compensations for being the only human boy on a starship crewed mostly by adult dolphins.

A starship which wasn't going anywhere at the moment, Toshio reminded himself. The acute resentment of Keepiru's goading was replaced by the more persistent, hollow worry that he might never leave the water world of Kithrup and see home.

> * Slow your travel – boy sled-rider *
> * Exploring pod – does gather hither *
> * Hikahi comes – we wait here for her *

Toshio looked up. Brookida, the elderly dolphin metallurgist, had come up alongside on the left. Toshio whistled a reply in Trinary.

> * Hikahi comes – my sled is stopping *

He eased the sled's throttle back.

On his sonar screen, Toshio saw tiny echoes converging from far ahead. The scouts returning. He looked up and saw Hist-t and Keepiru playing at the surface.

Brookida switched to Anglic. Though somewhat shrill and stuttered, it was still better than Toshio's Trinary. Dolphins, after all, had been modified by generations of genetic engineering to take up human styles, not the other way around.

'You've found no t-traces of the needed substances, Toshio?' Brookida asked.

Toshio glanced at the molecular sieve. 'No, sir. Nothing so far. This water is unbelievably pure, considering the metal content of the planet's crust. Hardly any heavy metal salts.'

'And nothing on the long ssscan?'

'No resonance on the bands I've been checking, though the noise level is awfully high. I'm not sure I'd be able to pick out monopole-saturated nickel, let alone the other stuff we're looking for. It's like trying to find that needle in a haystack.'

It was a paradox. The planet had metals in superabundance. One reason Captain Creideiki chose this world as a refuge. Yet the water was relatively pure ... enough to allow dolphins to swim freely, though some complained of itching, and each would need chelating treatments back on the ship.

The explanation lay all around them, in the plants and fishes.

Calcium did not make up the bones of Kithrupan life forms. Other metals did. The water was strained and sieved clean by biological filters. As a result, the sea shone all around with the bright colors of metal and oxides of metal. The gleaming dorsal spines of living fish – the silvery seedpods of underwater plants – all contrasted with the mundane green of chlorophyllic leaves and fronds.

Dominating the scenery were metal-mounds, giant, spongy islands shaped by millions of generations of coral-like creatures, whose metallo-organic exoskeletons accumulated into huge, flat-topped mountains rising a few meters above the mean water mark.

Atop the islands drill-trees grew, sending metal-tipped roots through each mound to harvest organics and silicates, depositing a non-metallic layer on top and creating a cavity underneath. It was a strange pattern. *Streaker*'s onboard *Library* had offered no explanation.

Toshio's instruments detected clumps of pure tin, mounds of chromium fish eggs, coral colonies built from a variety of bronze, but so far no convenient, easily gathered piles of vanadium. No lumps of the special variety of nickel they sought.

What they needed was a miracle – one enabling a crew of dolphins, with seven humans and a chimpanzee, to repair their ship and get the hell out of this part of the galaxy before their pursuers caught up with them.

At best, they had a few weeks to get away. The alternative was capture by any of a dozen not-entirely-rational ET races. At worst it could mean interstellar war on a scale not seen in a million years.

It all made Toshio feel small, helpless, and very young.

*

Toshio could hear, faintly, the high-pitched sonar echoes of the returning scouts. Each distant squeak had its tiny, colored counterpoint on his scanner screen.

Then two gray forms appeared from the east, diving at last into the gathering above, cavorting, playfully leaping and biting.

Finally one of the dolphins arched and dove straight down toward Toshio. 'Hikahi's coming and wants the sssled topside,' Keepiru chattered quickly, slurring the words almost into indecipherability. 'Try not to get lost on the way up-p-p-p.'

Toshio grimaced as he vented ballast. Keepiru didn't have to make his contempt so obvious. Even speaking Anglic normally, fins usually sounded as if they were giving the listener a long series of raspberries.

The sled rose in a cloud of tiny bubbles. When he reached the surface, water drained along the sides in long, gurgling rivulets. Toshio locked the throttle and rolled over to undo his faceplate.

Sudden silence was a relief. The whine of the sled, the pings of the sonar, and squeaks of the fins all vanished. A fresh breeze swept past his damp, straight, black hair and cooled the hot feeling in his ears. It carried scents of an alien planet – the pungence of secondary growth on an older island, the heavy, oily odor of a drill-tree in its peak of activity.

And overlying everything was the slight tang of metal.

It shouldn't harm them, they'd said back at the ship, least of all Toshio in his waterproof suit. Chelating would remove all of the heavy elements one might reasonably expect to absorb on a scouting trip ... though no one knew for sure what other hazards this world might offer.

But if they were forced to stay for months? Years?

In that case the medical facilities of the *Streaker* could not deal with the slow accumulation of metals. In time they would start to pray for the Jophur, or Thennanin, or Soro ships to come and take them away for interrogation or worse – simply to get off a beautiful planet that was slowly killing them.

It wasn't a pleasant thought to dwell on. Toshio was glad when Brookida drifted alongside.

'Why did Hikahi have me come up to the surface?' he asked the elderly dolphin. 'I thought I was to stay out of sight below in case there were already spy-sats overhead.'

Brookida sighed. 'I suppose she thinkss you need a break. Besides, who could spot as small a machine as the ssled, with so much metal around?'

Toshio shrugged. 'Well, it was nice of her.'

Brookida rose up in the water, balancing on a series of churning tail-strokes. 'I hear Hikahi,' he announced. 'And here she isss.'

Two dolphins came in fast from the north, one light gray in appearance, the other dark and mottled. Through his headphones Toshio heard the voice of the party leader.

> * Flame-fluked I – Hikahi call you *
> * Dorsal listening – ventral doing *
> * Laugh at my words – but first obey them *
> * Gather at the sled – and listen! *

Hikahi and Ssattatta circled the rest of the party once, then came to rest in front of the assembled expedition.

Among mankind's gifts to the neo-dolphin had been an expanded repertoire of facial expression. A mere five hundred years of genetic engineering could not do for the porpoise what a million years of evolution had for man. Fins still expressed most of their feelings in sound and motion. But they were no longer frozen in what humans had taken (in some degree of truth) to be a grin of perpetual amusement. Fins were capable now of *looking* worried. Toshio might have chosen Hikahi's present expression as a classic example of delphin chagrin.

'Phip-pit has disappeared,' Hikahi announced.

'I heard him cry out, over to the south of me, then nothing. He was searching for Ssassia, who disappeared earlier in the same direction. We will forego mapping and metals search to go and find them. All will be issued weaponss.'

There was a general sussuration of discontent. It meant the fins would have to put on the harnesses they had only just had the pleasure of removing, on leaving the ship. Still, even Keepiru recognized this was urgent business.

Toshio was briefly busy dropping harnesses into the water. They were supposed to spread naturally into a shape suitable for a dolphin to slip into, but inevitably one or two fins needed help fitting the small nerve amplifier socket each had just above the left eye.

Toshio finished quickly, with the unconscious ease of long practice. He was worried about Ssassia, a gentle fin who had always been kind and soft-spoken to him.

'Hikahi,' he said as the leader swam past, 'do you want me to call the ship?'

The small gray *Tursiops* female rose up to face Toshio. 'Negative, Ladder-runner. We obey orders. Spy-sats may be high already. Set your speed sled to return on auto if we fail to survive what is in the sssoutheast.'

'But no one's seen any big animals ...'

'That-t is only one possibility. I want word to get back whatever our doom ... should even rescue fever strike us all.'

Toshio felt cold at the mention of 'rescue fever.' He had heard of it, of course. It was something he had no desire to witness.

They set forth in skirmish formation. The fins took turns gliding along the surface, then diving to swim alongside Toshio. The ocean bottom was like an endless series of snake tracks – pitted by strange pock-holes like deep craters, darkly ominous. In the valleys Toshio could usually see bottom, a hundred meters or so below, gloomy with dark blue tendrils.

The long ridges were topped at intervals by the shining metal-mounds, like hulking castles of shimmering, spongy armor. Many were covered with thick, ivy-like growths in which Kithrupan fishes nested and bred. One metal-mound appeared to be teetering on the edge of a precipice – the cavern dug by its own tall drill-tree, ready to swallow the entire fortress when the undermining was done.

The sled's engine hummed hypnotically. Keeping track of his instruments was too simple a task to keep Toshio's mind busy. Without really wishing to, he found himself thinking. Remembering.

A simple adventure, that's what it had seemed when they had asked him to come along on the space voyage. He had already taken the Jumpers' Oath, so they knew he was ready to leave his past behind. And they needed a midshipman to help with hand-eye work on the new dolphin ship.

Streaker was a small exploratory vessel of unique design. There weren't many finned, oxygen-breathing races flying ships in inter-stellar space. Those few used artificial gravity for convenience, and leased members of some client species to act as crafters and hand-men.

But the first dolphin-crewed starship had to be different. It was designed around a principle which had guided Earthlings for two centuries: 'Whenever possible, keep it simple. Avoid using the science of the Galactics when you don't understand it.'

Two hundred and fifty years after contact with Galactic civiliza-tion, mankind was still struggling to catch up. Species which had been using the aeons-old *Library* since before mammals appeared on Earth – adding to that universal compendium with glacial slow-ness – had seemed almost god-like to primitive Earthmen in their early, lumbering slowships. Earth had a branch *Library*, now, sup-posedly giving her access to all wisdom accumulated over Galactic history. But only in recent years had it proven more help than a con-fusing hindrance.

Streaker, with its complex arrangements of centrifugally held pools and weightless workshops, must have seemed incredibly archaic to the aliens who looked it over just before launch. Still, to Earth's neo-dolphin communities, she was an object of pride.

After her shakedown cruise, *Streaker* stopped at the small human-dolphin colony of Calafia to pick up the best graduates of its tiny academy. It was to be Toshio's first, and possibly last, visit to old Earth.

'Old Earth' was still home to ninety percent of humanity, not to mention the other terrestrial sapient races. Galactic tourists still thronged in to gawk at the home of the *enfants terribles* who had caused such a stir in a few brief centuries. They were open in their wagering over how long Mankind would survive without the protection of a patron.

All species had patrons, of course. Nobody reached spacefaring intelligence without intervention by another, older race. Had not men done this for chimps and dolphins? All the way back to the time of the mythical Progenitors, every species that spoke and flew spaceships had been raised up by a predecessor. None still survived from that distant era, but the civilization the Progenitors established, with its all-encompassing *Library*, went on.

Toshio wondered, as just about everyone had for three centuries, what the patrons of Man might have been like. If they ever existed. Might they even be one of the species of fanatics that had ambushed the unsuspecting *Streaker*, and even now sought her out like hounds after a fox?

It wasn't a pleasant line of thought, considering what the *Streaker* had discovered.

The Terragens Council had sent her to join a scattered fleet of exploration vessels, checking the veracity of the *Library*. So far only a few minor gaps had been found in its thoroughness. Here a star misplaced. There a species miscatalogued. It was like finding someone had written a list describing every grain of sand on a beach. You could never check the complete list in a thousand lifetimes of a race, but you could take a random sampling.

Streaker had been poking through a small gravitational tide pool, fifty thousand parsecs off the galactic plane, when she found the fleet.

Toshio sighed at the unfairness of it. One hundred and fifty dolphins, seven humans, and a chimpanzee; how could we have known what we found?

Why did *we* have to find it?

Fifty thousand ships, each the size of a moon. That's what they found. The dolphins had been thrilled by their discovery – the biggest derelict fleet ever encountered, apparently incredibly ancient. Captain Creideiki had psicast to Earth for instructions.

Dammit! *Why* did he call Earth? Couldn't the report have waited until we'd gone home? Why let the whole eavesdropping galaxy know you'd found a Sargasso of ancient hulks in the middle of nowhere?

The Terragens Council had answered in code.

'Go into hiding. Await orders. Do not reply.'

Creideiki obeyed, of course. But not before half the patron-lines in the galaxy had sent out their warships to find *Streaker*.

Toshio blinked.

Something. A resonance echo at last? Yes, the magnetic ore detector showed a faint echo toward the south. He concentrated on the receiver, relieved at last to have something to do. Self-pity was becoming a bore.

Yes. It would have to be a pretty fair deposit. Should he tell Hikahi? Naturally, the search for the missing crewfen came first, but . . .

A shadow fell across him. The party was skirting the edge of a massive metal-mound. The copper-colored mass was covered with thick tendrils of some green hanging growth.

'Don't go too close, Little Hands,' Keepiru whistled from Toshio's left. Only Keepiru and the sled were this close to the mound. The other fins were giving it a wide berth.

'We know nothing of this flora,' Keepiru continued. 'And it'ss near here that Phip-pit was lost. You should stay safe within our convoy.' Keepiru rolled lazily past Toshio, keeping up with languid fluke strokes. The neatly folded arms of his harness gleamed a coppery reflection from the metal-mound.

'Then it's all the more important to get samples, isn't it?' Toshio replied in irritation. 'That's what we're here for!' Without giving Keepiru time to react, Toshio banked the sled toward the shadowy mass of the mound, entering darkness as the island blocked the afternoon sunlight. A drifting school of silver-backed fish seemed to explode away from him as he drove at an angle along the thick, fibrous weed.

Keepiru squeaked in startlement behind him, an oath in Primal Delphin, which showed the fin's distress. Toshio smiled.

The sled hummed cooperatively as the mound loomed like a mountain on his right. Toshio banked and grabbed at the nearest flash of green. There was a satisfying snapping sensation as his sample came free in his hand. No fin could do that! He flexed his fingers appreciatively, then twisted about to stuff the clump into a collection sack.

Toshio looked up and saw that the green mass, instead of receding, was closer than ever. Keepiru's squawling was louder.

Crybaby! Toshio thought. So I let the controls drift for a second. So what? I'll be back in your damned convoy before you finish making up a cuss-poem.

He steepened his leftward bank and simultaneously set his bow planes to rise, then realized it was a tactical mistake. For it slowed him down just enough for a cluster of pursuing tendrils to arrive.

There must be larger sea creatures on Kithrup than the party had seen so far, for the tentacles that fell about Toshio were obviously meant to catch big prey.

'Oh, Koino-Anti! Now I've done it!' He pushed the throttle over to maximum and braced for the expected surge of power.

Power came ... but not acceleration. The sled groaned, stretching the ropy strands. But forward movement was lost. Then the engine died. Toshio felt a slithery presence across his legs, then another. The tendrils began to tighten and pull.

Gasping, he managed to twist onto his back, and groped for the knife sheathed at his thigh. The tendrils were sinuous and knotty, clinging to whatever they touched, and when one brushed the back of Toshio's exposed left hand, the boy cried out from searing pain.

The fins squealed to each other, and there were sounds of vigorous movement not far away. But other than a brief prayer that nobody else was caught, Toshio had no time to think of anything but the fight at hand.

The knife came free, gleaming like hope. And hope brought hope as two small strands parted under his slashing attack. Another, larger, one, took several seconds to saw through. It was replaced almost instantly by two more.

Then he saw where he was being drawn.

A deep gash split the metal-mound. Inside, a writhing mass of filaments waited. Deep within, a dozen meters farther up, something sleek and gray lay enmeshed in a forest of deceptively languid foliage.

Toshio felt open-mouthed steam fill his facemask. The reflection of his own eyes, dilated and stricken, was superimposed on the motionless figure of Ssassia. Gentle as her life had been, though not her death, the tide rocked her.

With a cry, Toshio resumed hacking. He wanted to call out to Hikahi – to let the party leader know of Ssassia's fate – but all that came out was a roar of loathing of the Kithrupan creeper. Leaves and fronds flew through the churning water as he sliced out his hatred, to little good as the tendrils fell more numerous about him to draw him toward the gash.

* Ladder climber – Sharp-eyed rhymer *
* Call a fix – for seeking finders *
* Trill sonar – through the leaf blinders *

Hikahi calling.

Above the churning of his struggle and the hoarseness of his breath, Toshio could hear combat sounds of dolphin teamwork. Quick trills of Trinary, unslowed for human ears except that one brief command, and the whining of their harnesses.

'Here! Here I am!' He slashed at a vine that threatened his air hose, barely missing the hose itself. He licked his lips and tried to whistle in Trinary.

* Holding off – the sea-squid's beak *
* Suckers tight – and outlook bleak *
* Havoc done – on Ssassia wreaked! *

Lousy form and rhythm, but the fins would hear it better than a shout in Anglic. After just forty generations of sapience, they still thought better in an emergency when using whistle rhyme.

Toshio could hear the sounds of combat coming closer. But, as if hurried by the threat, the tentacles began drawing him back more rapidly, toward the gash. Suddenly a sucker-covered strand wrapped itself around his right arm. Before he could shift his grip, one of the burning knots reached his hand. He screamed and tore the tendril away, but the knife was lost to darkness.

Other filaments were falling all about him. At that moment Toshio became distantly aware that someone was *talking* to him, slowly, and in Anglic!

'... says there are ships out there! Vice-Captain Takkata-Jim wants to know why Hikahi hasn't sent a monopulse confirmation ...'

It was *Akki's* voice, calling from the ship! Toshio couldn't answer his friend. The switch for the sled radio was out of reach, and he was preoccupied.

'Don't respond to this message,' Akki went on obligingly. Toshio moaned at the irony as he tried to pry a tendril off his facemask without doing further insult to his hands. 'Just transmit a monopulse and come on back-k, all of you. We think there's a space battle going on over Kithrup. Probably those crazy ETs followed us here and are fighting over the right to capture us, just like at Morgran.

'Gotta c-close up, now. Radio silence. Get back as soon as you can. Akki out.'

Toshio felt a tendril seize hold of his air hose. A solid grip, this time.

'Sure, Akki, old friend,' he grunted as he pulled at it. 'I'll be going home just as soon as the universe lets me.'

The air hose crimped shut and there was nothing he could do. Fog filled his facemask. As he felt himself blacking out, Toshio thought he saw the rescue party arrive, but he couldn't be sure if it was real or a hallucination. He wouldn't have expected *Keepiru* to lead the charge, for instance, or for that fin to have such a ferocious demeanor, heedless of the burning suckers.

In the end, he decided it was a dream. The laser flashes were too bright, the saser tones too clear. And the party came toward him with pennants waving in their wake like the cavalry that five centuries of Anglic-speaking man had come to associate with the image of rescue.

2

GALACTICS

On a ship in the center of a fleet of ships, a phase of denial was passing.

Giant cruisers spilled out of a rent in space, to fall toward the pinpoint brilliance of a non-descript reddish sun. One by one, they tumbled from the luminous tear. With them came diffracted starlight from their point of departure, hundreds of parsecs away.

There were rules that should have prevented it. The tunnel was an unnatural way to pass from place to place. It took a strong will to deny nature and call into being such an opening in space.

The Episiarch, in its outraged rejection of What Is, *had created the passage for its Tandu masters. The opening was held by the adamant power of its ego – by its refusal to concede anything at all to Reality.*

When the last ship was through, the Episiarch was purposely distracted, and the hole collapsed with soundless violence. In moments, only instruments could tell that it had ever been. The affront to physics was erased.

The Episiarch had brought the Tandu armada to the target star well ahead of the other fleets, those who would challenge the Tandu for the right to capture the Earth ship. The Tandu sent impulses of praise to the Episiarch's pleasure centers. It howled and waved its great furry head in gratitude.

To the Tandu, an obscure and dangerous form of travel had once again proved worth the risks. It was good to arrive on the battlefield before the enemy. The added moments would give them a tactical edge.

The Episiarch only wanted things to deny. Its task now finished, it was returned to its chamber of delusions, to alter an endless chain of surrogate realities until its outrage was needed by the Masters once again. Its shaggy, amorphous shape rolled free of the sensory web, and it shambled off, escorted by wary guardians.

When the way was clear, the Acceptor entered, and climbed on spindly legs to its place within the web.

For a long moment it appraised Reality, embracing it. The Acceptor probed and touched and caressed this new region of space with its farflung senses. It gave out a crooning cry of pleasure.

'Such leakage!' the Acceptor joyously announced. 'I had heard the hunted were sloppy sophonts, but they leak even as they scan for danger! They have hidden on the second planet. Only slowly do the edges of their psychic shields congeal to hide from me their exact location. Who were their masters, to teach these dolphins so well to be prey?'

'Their masters are the humans, themselves unfinished,' the Leading Stalker of the Tandu replied. Its voice was a rhythmic pattern of rapid clicks and pops from the ratchet joints of its mantis-legs. 'The Earthlings are tainted by wrong belief, and by the shame of their own abandonment. The noise of three centuries shall be quieted when they are eaten. Then our hunter's joy will be as yours is, when you witness a new place or thing.'

'Such joy,' the Acceptor agreed.

'Now stir to get details,' the Stalker commanded. 'Soon we do battle with heretics. I must tell your fellow clients their tasks.'

The Acceptor turned in the web as the Stalker left, and opened its feelings to this new patch of reality. Everything was good. It passed on reports of what it saw, and the Masters moved the ships in response, but with the larger part of its mind it appreciated ... it accepted ... the tiny red sun, each of its small planets, the delicious expectancy of a place soon to become a battlefield.

Soon it felt the other war fleets enter the system, each in its own peculiar way. Each took a slightly inferior position, forced by the early arrival of the Tandu.

The Acceptor sensed the lusts of warrior clients and the cool calculations of calmer elders. It caressed the slickness of mind shields rigidly held against it, and wondered what went on within them. It appreciated the openness of other combatants, who disdainfully cast their thoughts outward, daring the listener to gather in their broadcast contempt.

It swept up savage contemplations of the Acceptor's *own annihilation, as the great fleets plunged toward each other and bright explosions began to flash.*

The Acceptor *took it all in joyfully. How could anyone feel otherwise, when the universe held such wonders?*

3

TAKKATA-JIM

High in the port quarter of *Streaker*'s spherical control room, a psi operator thrashed in her harness. Her flukes made a turmoil of the water, and she cried out in Trinary.

> * *The inky, eight-armed, squid-heads find us!* *
> * *Ripping pods of them do battle!* *

The operator's report confirmed the discovery made by neutrino sensor moments before. It was a litany of bad news, related in trance-verse.

> * *They scream and lust—*
>   *To win and capture . . .* *

From another station came a calmer bulletin in dolphin-accented Anglic.

'We're getting heavy graviton traffic, Vice-Captain Takkata-Jim. Gravitational disturbances confirm a major battle is forming up not far from the planet-t.'

The executive officer of the *Streaker* listened quietly, letting himself drift sideways in the circulating currents of the command center. A stream of bubbles emerged from his blowhole as he inhaled some of the special fluid that filled the ship's bridge.

'Acknowledged,' he said at last. Underwater, his voice was a muted buzz. The consonants came out slurred. 'How far away is the nearest contact?'

'Five AU, sssir. They couldn't get here for at leasst an hour, even if they came hell-bent.'

'Hmmm. Very well, then. Remain in condition yellow. Continue your observationsss, Akeakemai.'

The vice-captain was unusually large for a neo-fin, thick-bodied and muscular where most of the others were sleek and narrow. His uneven gray coloring and jagged teeth were marks of the *Stenos* sub-racial line, setting him and a number of others apart from the *Tursiops* majority.

The human next to Takkata-Jim was impassive as the bad news came. It only confirmed what they had feared.

'We had better inform the captain, then,' Ignacio Metz said. The words were amplified by his facemask into the fizzing water. Bubbles floated away from the tall human's sparse gray hair.

'I warned Creideiki this would happen if we tried eluding the Galactics. I only hope he decides to be reasonable, now that escape's become impossible.'

Takkata-Jim opened and closed his foodmouth diagonally, an emphatic nod.

'Yesss, Doctor Metz. Now even Creideiki must recognize that you were right. We're cornered now, and the captain will have no choice but to listen to you.'

Metz nodded, gratified. 'What about Hikahi's team? Have they been told?'

'I've already ordered the prospecting party back. Even the sled might be too much of a risssk. If the Eatees are already in orbit they might have means to detect it.'

'Extraterrestrials ...' Metz corrected, professorial. 'The term "Eatee" is hardly polite.'

Takkata-Jim kept an impassive face. He was in command of ship and crew while the captain was off watch. Yet the human treated him like a fresh-weaned pupil. It was irritating, but Takkata-Jim was careful never to let it show. 'Yes, Doctor Metz.'

'Hikahi's party should never have left the ship. I warned Tom Orley something like this might happen. Young Toshio's out there ... and all those crewfen, out of contact for so long. It would be *terrible* if anything happened to them!'

The human was probably thinking about how terrible it would be if any of *Streaker*'s crew got killed away from his sight ... out where he was unable to judge how they behaved for his behavioral and genetic studies. 'If only Creideiki had listened to you, sssir,' he repeated. 'You always have so much to say.'

It was chancy, but if the human ever saw through Takkata-Jim's respectful mask to the core of sarcasm, he never gave it away.

'Well, nice of you to say so, Takkata-Jim. I know you have things to do now, so I'll find Creideiki and break the news that our pursuers have followed us to Kithrup.'

Takkata-Jim gave the human a deferential nod from high body stance. 'That-t is kind of you, Doctor Metz.'

Metz patted the lieutenant on his rough flank, as if to reassure him. Takkata-Jim bore the patronizing gesture with outward calm, and watched as the human turned to swim away.

The bridge was a fluid-filled sphere which bulged slightly from the bow of the cylindrical ship. The main ports looked into a murky scene of ocean ridges, sediment, and drifting sea creatures.

The crew's web-lined work stations were illuminated by small spotlights. Most of the chamber lay in quiet shadows, as elite bridge personnel carried out their tasks quickly and almost silently. The only sounds, other than the swish and fizz of recycling oxywater, were the intermittent click of sonar pulses and terse, professional comments from one operator to another.

Give Creideiki his due, Takkata-Jim told himself. He has crafted a finely tuned machine in this bridge crew.

Of course, dolphins were less consistent than humans. You couldn't tell in advance what might cause a neo-fin to start unraveling until you saw him perform under stress. This bridge crew performed as well as any he had ever seen, but would it be enough?

If they had overlooked a single radiation or psi leak, the ETs would be down on them quicker than orcas upon harbor seals.

The fins out there in the prospecting team were safer than their comrades aboard ship, Takkata-Jim thought somewhat bitterly. Metz was a fool to worry about them. They were probably having a wonderful time!

Takkata-Jim tried to recall swimming free in an ocean, without a harness, and breathing natural air. He tried to recall diving in deep water, the deep water of the *Stenos*, where big-mouthed, smart-aleck, shore-hugging *Tursiops* were rare as dugongs.

'Akki,' he called to the E.L.F radio operator, the young dolphin midshipman from Calafia. 'Have you received confirmation from Hikahi? Did she get the recall?'

The colonial was a small *Tursiops* variant of yellowish-gray coloration. Akki replied with some hesitation. He still wasn't used to breathing and speaking in oxywater. It required a very odd dialect of Underwater Anglic.

'I'm ... sh-sorry, Vice-Captain, there's no reply. I checked for a monopulse on all ... ch-channels. There's been nothing.'

Takkata-Jim tossed his head in irritation. Hikahi might have decided that even a monopulse reply would be too much risk. Still, confirmation would have taken from his back an unpleasant decision.

'Mm-m-m, sir?' Akki tipped his head down and lowered his tail in respect.

'Yess?'

'Ah ... shouldn't we repeat the message? There's a chance they were distracted and missed it the firsh ... first time ...'

Like all dolphins from the colony planet Calafia, Akki was proud of his cultured Anglic. It apparently bothered him to have trouble with such simple sentences.

That suited the vice-captain fine. If there was one Anglic word that translated perfectly into Trinary, it was 'smartass.' Takkata-Jim didn't care for smartass midshipmen.

'No, comm-operator. We have our orders. If the captain wants to try again when he gets here, he's welcome. Meantime, attend your possst.'

'Heth ... er, aye aye, shir.' The young dolphin spun about to return to his station, where he could breathe from an airdome instead of gulping water like a fish. There he could speak like a normal person while he awaited word from his closest friend, the human middie out in the wide, alien ocean.

Takkata-Jim wished the captain would come soon. The control room felt closed and dead. Breathing the fizzing, gas-charged oxywater always left him tired at the end of his shift. It never seemed to provide enough oxygen. His supplementary gill-lungs itched with the irritation of defied instinct, and the pills – the ones that forced extra oxygen into his system through his intestines – always gave him heartburn.

Once again he caught sight of Ignacio Metz. The white-haired scientist clutched a stanchion, with his head thrust under a comm airdome to call Creideiki. When he finished he would probably want to hang around. The man was always hovering nearby, watching ... always making him feel he was being tested.

'I need a human ally,' Takkata-Jim reminded himself. Dolphins were in command of *Streaker*, but the crew seemed to obey an officer more rapidly if he had the confidence of one of the patron race. Greideiki had Tom Orley. Hikahi had Gillian Baskin. Brookida's human companion was the engineer, Suessi.

Metz would have to be Takkata-Jim's human. Fortunately, the man could be manipulated.

Reports on the space battle were coming in faster on the data displays. It seemed to be turning into a real conflagration over the planet. At least five big fleets were involved.

Takkata-Jim resisted the sudden urge to turn and bite something, to lash out hard with his flukes. What he wanted was something to fight! Something palpable, instead of this hanging pall of dread!

After weeks of fleeing, *Streaker* was trapped at last. What new trick would Creideiki and Orley come up with to get them away *this* time?

What if they failed to come up with a plan? Or worse, contrived some squid-brained scheme to get them all killed? What would he do *then*?

Takkata-Jim mulled over the problem to keep his mind busy while he waited for the captain to come and relieve him.

4

CREIDEIKI

It had been his first restful sleep in weeks. Naturally, it *had* to be interrupted.

Creideiki was used to taking his rest in zero gee, suspended in moist air. But as long as they were in hiding, anti-gravity beds were banned, and sleeping in liquid was the only other way for a dolphin.

He had tried for a week to breathe oxywater all through his rest period. The result had been nightmares and exhausting dreams of suffocation. The ship's surgeon, Makanee, had suggested he try sleeping in the old-fashioned way, drifting at the surface of a pool of water.

Creideiki decided to try Makanee's alternative. He made sure that there was a big air-gap at the top of his stateroom. Then he verified three times that the redundant oxygen alarms were all in perfect order. Finally, he shrugged out of his harness, turned off the lights, rose to the surface and expelled the oxywater in his gill-lung.

That part was a relief. Still, at first he just lay at the air-gap near the overhead, his mind racing and his skin itching for the touch of his tool harness. It was an irrational itch, he knew. Pre-spaceflight humans, in their primitive, neurotic societies, must have felt the same way about nudity.

Poor *Homo sapiens*! Mankind's histories showed such suffering during those awkward millennia of adolescence before Contact, when they were ignorant and cut off from Galactic society.

Meanwhile, Creideiki thought, dolphins had been in almost a state of grace, drifting in their corner of the Whale Dream. When men finally achieved a type of adulthood, and started lifting the higher creatures of Earth to join them, dolphins of the *amicus* strain moved fairly easily from one honorable condition to another.

We have our own problems, he reminded himself. He badly

wanted to scratch the base of his amplifier socket, but there was no way to reach it without his harness.

He floated at the surface, in the dark, awaiting sleep. It *was* sort of restful, tiny wavelets lapping against the smooth skin above his eyes. And real air was definitely more relaxing to breathe than oxywater.

But he couldn't escape a vague unease over *sinking* . . . as if it would harm him any to sink in oxywater . . . as if millions of other dolphins hadn't slept this way all their lives.

Disconcerting was his spacer's habit of looking *up*. The ceiling bulkhead was inches away from the tip of his dorsal fin. Even when he closed his eyes, sonar told him of the nearness of enclosure. He could no more sleep without sending out echolocation clicks than a chimp could nap without scratching himself.

Creideiki snorted. *Beach himself* if he'd let a shipboard requirement give him insomnia! He blew emphatically and began to count sonar clicks. He started with a tenor rhythm, then slowly built a fugue as he added deeper elements to the sleep-song.

Echoes spread from his brow and diffracted about the small chamber. The notes drifted over one another, overlapping softly in faint whines and basso growls. They created a sonic structure, a template of *otherness*. The right combinations, he knew, would make the walls themselves seem to disappear.

Deliberately, he peeled away the duty-rigor of Keneenk – welcoming a small, trusted portion of the Whale Dream.

> * *When the patterns—*
> > *In the cycloid*
> * *Call in whispers—*
> > *Soft remembered*
> * *Murmuring of—*
> > *Songs of dawning*
> * *And of the Moon—*
> > *The sea-tide's darling*
> * *Then the patterns—*
> > *In the cycloid*
> * *Call in whispers—*
> > *Soft remembered* . . .*

The desk, the cabinets, the walls, were covered under false sonic shadows. His chant began to open on its own accord, a rich and very physical poetry of crafted reflections.

Floating things seemed to drift past, tiny tail-flicks, schools of dream creatures. The echoes opened space around him, as if the waters went on forever.

293

*   * And the Dream Sea,
                Everlasting
        * Calls in whispers
                Soft remembered ... *

Soon he felt a presence nearby, congealing gradually out of reflections of sound.

She formed slowly next to him as his engineer's consciousness let go ... the shadow of a goddess. Then Nukapai floated beside him ... a ghost of ripples, ribbed by motes of sound. The black sleekness of her body passed back into the darkness, unhindered by a bulkhead that seemed no longer there.

Vision faded. The waters darkened all around Creideiki, and Nukapai became more than a shadow, a passive recipient of his song. Her needle teeth shone, and she sang his own sounds back to him.

        * With the closeness—
                Of the waters
        * In an endless—
                Layer of Dreaming
        * As the humpback—
                Older sibling
        * Sings songs to the—
                Serious fishes
        * Here you find me—
                Wandering brother
        * Even in this—
                Human rhythm
        * Where humans
                And other walkers
        * Give mirth to—
                The stars themselves ... *

A type of bliss settled over him as his heartbeat slowed. Creideiki slept next to the gentle dream-goddess. She chided him only teasingly for being an engineer, and for dreaming her in the rigid, focused verse of Trinary rather than the chaotic Primal of his ancestors.

She welcomed him to the Threshold Sea, where Trinary sufficed, where he felt only faintly the raging of the Whale Dream and the ancient gods who dwelt there. It was as much of that ocean as an engineer's mind could accept.

How rigid the Trinary verse sometimes seemed! The patterns of

overlapping tones and symbols were almost human-precise ...
almost human-narrow.

He had been brought up to think those terms compliments. Parts
of his own brain had been gene-designed along human lines. But
now and then chaotic sound-images slipped in, teasing him with
hints of ancient singing.

Nukapai clicked sympathetically. She smiled ...

No! She did no such land-ape thing! Of cetaceans, only the neo-
dolphin 'smiled' with their mouths.

Nukapai did something else. She stroked against his side, gentlest
of goddesses, and told him,

> * Be now at peace *
> * It is That is ... *
> * And engineers *
> * Far from the ocean *
> * Can hear it still *

The tension of several weeks at last broke, and he slept.
Creideiki's breath gathered in glistening condensation on the ceiling
bulkhead. The breeze from a nearby air duct brushed the droplets,
which shuddered, then fell on the water like gentle rain.

When the image of Ignacio Metz formed a meter to his right,
Creideiki was slow to become aware.

'Captain ...' the image said. 'I'm calling from the bridge. I am
afraid the Galactics have found us here sooner than we expected ...'

Creideiki ignored the little voice that tried to call him back to
deeds and battles. He lingered in a waving forest of kelp fronds, listening to long night sounds. Finally, it was Nukapai herself who
nudged him from his dream. Fading beside him, she gently
reminded,

> # Duty, duty – honor is, is—
> Honor, Creideiki—alertly
> # Shared, is—Honor #

Nukapai alone might speak Primal to Creideiki with impunity. He
could no more ignore the dream-goddess than his own conscience.
One eye at last focused on the hologram of the insistent human, and
the words penetrated.

'Thank you, Doctor Metz,' he sighed. 'Tell Takkata-Jim I'll be
right-t there. And please page Tom Orley. I'd like to see him on the
bridge. Creideiki out.'

He inhaled deeply for a few moments, letting the room come

back into shape around him. Then he twisted and dove to retrieve his harness.

5

TOM ORLEY

A tall, dark-haired man swung one-handed from the leg of a bed, a bed that was bolted to the floor in an upside-down room. The floor slanted over his head. His left foot rested precariously on the bottom of a drawer pulled from one of the inverted wall cabinets.

At the sudden yellow flash of the alert light, Tom Orley whirled and grabbed at his holster with his free hand. His needler was half-drawn before he recognized the source of the disturbance, cursed slowly and reholstered the weapon. *Now* what was the emergency? He could think of a dozen possibilities, offhand, and here he was, hanging by one arm in the most awkward part of the ship!

'I initiate contact, Thomas Orley.'

The voice seemed to come from above his right ear. Tom changed his grip on the bed leg to turn around. An abstract three-dimensional pattern swirled a meter away from his face, like multicolored motes caught in a dust devil.

'I suppose you would like to know of the cause of the alarm. Is this correct?'

'You're damned right I do!' he snapped. 'Are we under attack?'

'No.' The colored images shifted. 'This ship is not yet assailed, but Vice-Captain Takkata-Jim has announced an alert. At least five intruder fleets are now in the neighborhood of Kithrup. These squadrons appear now to be in combat not far from the planet.'

Orley sighed. 'So much for quick repairs and a getaway.' He hadn't thought it likely that their hunters would let them escape again. The damaged *Streaker* had left a noisy trail, slipping away from the confusion after the ambush at Morgran.

Tom had been helping the crew in the engine room repair *Streaker*'s stasis generator. They had just finished the part calling for detailed hand-eye work, and the moment had come to steal away to a deserted section of the dry-wheel, where the Niss computer had been hidden.

The dry-wheel was a band of workrooms and cabins that spun freely when the ship was in space, providing pseudo-gravity for the humans aboard. Now it lay still, this section of upside-down corridors and cabins abandoned in the inconvenient gravity of the planet.

The privacy suited Tom, though the topsy-turvy arrangement was irksome.

'You weren't to announce yourself unless I switched you on manually,' he said. 'You were to wait for my thumbprint and voice i.d. before letting on you were anything but a standard comm.'

The swirling patterns took on a cubist style. The machine's voice sounded unperturbed. 'Under the circumstances, I took the liberty. If I erred, I am prepared to accept discipline up to level three. Punishment of a higher order will be considered unjustified and rejected with prejudice.'

Tom allowed himself an ironic smile. The machine would run him in circles if he let it, and he would gain nothing by asserting his titular mastery over it. The Tymbrimi spy who had lent the Niss to him had made it clear that the machine's usefulness was based upon its flexibility and initiative, however irritating it became.

'I'll take the level of your error under advisement,' he told the Niss. 'Now, what can you tell me about the present situation?'

'A vague question. I can access the ship's battle computers. But that might entail an element of risk.'

'No, you'd better not do that quite yet.' If the Niss tried to inveigle the battle computer during an alert, Creideiki's bridge crew might notice. Tom assumed Creideiki knew about the presence of the Niss aboard his ship, just as the captain knew that Gillian Baskin had her own secret project. But the dolphin commander kept quiet about it, leaving the two of them to their work.

'All right, then. Can you patch me through to Gillian?'

The holo danced with blue specks. 'She is alone in her office. I am placing the call.'

The motes suddenly faded, replaced by the image of a blonde woman in her early thirties. She looked puzzled briefly, then her face brightened with a brilliant smile. She laughed.

'Ah, visiting your mechanical friend, I see. Tell me, Tom, what does a sarcastic alien machine have that I don't? You've never gone head over heels so literally for me.'

'Very funny.' Still, her attitude relieved his anxiety. He had been afraid they would be in combat almost immediately. In a week or so, *Streaker* might be able to make a good accounting of herself before being destroyed or captured. Right now, she had all the punch of a drugged rabbit.

'I take it the Galactics aren't landing yet.'

Gillian shook her head. 'No, though Makanee and I are standing by in the infirmary just in case. Bridge crew says at least three fleets have popped into space nearby. They immediately started having it out, just like at Morgran. We can only hope they'll annihilate each other.'

'Not much hope of that, I'm afraid.'

'Well, you're the tactician of the family. Still, it might be weeks before there is a victor to come down after us. There will be deals and last-minute alliances. We'll have time to think of something.'

Tom wished he could share her optimism. As the family tactician, it was *his* job to 'think of something.'

'Well, if the situation's not urgent ...'

'You can spend a while longer with your roomie there – my electronic rival. I'll get even by going intimate with Herbie.'

Tom could only shake his head and let her have her joke. Herbie was a cadaver – their one tangible prize from the derelict fleet. Gillian had determined that the alien corpse was over two billion years old. The ship's mini-*Library* seemed to have seizures every time they asked what race it once belonged to.

'Tell Creideiki I'll be right down, okay?'

'They're waking him now. I'll tell him I last saw you hanging around somewhere.' She gave a wink and switched off.

Tom watched the place where her image had been, and once again wondered what he had done to deserve a woman like her.

'Out of curiosity, Thomas Orley, I am interested in some of the undertones of this last conversation. Am I right in assuming that some of these mild insults Doctor Baskin conveyed fell into the category of affectionate teasing? My Tymbrimi builders are telempathic, of course, but they, also, seem to indulge in this pastime. Is it part of a mating process? Or is it a friendship test of some sort?'

'A little of both, I guess. Do the Tymbrimi really do the same sort of ...' Tom shook himself. 'Never mind about that! My arms are tired and I've got to get below. Have you anything else to report?'

'Not of significance to your survival or mission.'

'I take it you haven't managed to coax the ship's mini-*Library* to deliver anything on Herbie or the derelict fleet.'

The holo flowed into sharp geometries. 'That is the main problem, isn't it? Doctor Baskin asked me the same question thirteen hours ago.'

'And did you give her a more direct answer?'

'Finding ways to bypass the access programming on this ship's mini-*Library* is the reason I was put aboard in the first place. I would tell you if I had succeeded.' The machine's disembodied voice was dry enough to dessicate melons. 'The Tymbrimi have long suspected that the *Library Institute* is less than neutral – that the branch

Libraries sold by them are programmed to be deficient in subtle ways, to put troublesome races at a disadvantage.

'The Tymbrimi have been working on this problem since days when your ancestors wore animal skins, Thomas Orley. It was never expected we would achieve anything more on this trip than gathering a few shards of new data, and perhaps elimination of a few minor barriers.'

Orley understood how the long-lived machine could take such a patient perspective. Still, he resented it. It would be nice to think *something* had come of the grief *Streaker* and her crew had fallen into. 'After all the surprises we've encountered, this voyage must have served up more than a few bits to crunch.'

'The propensity of Earthlings to get into trouble, and to learn thereby, was the reason my owners agreed to this mad venture – although no one expected such a chain of *unusual* calamities as befell this ship. Your talents were under-rated.'

There was no way to answer that. Tom's arms had begun to hurt. 'Well, I'd better get back. In an emergency I'll contact you via ship's comm.'

'Of course.'

Orley let go and landed in a crouch by the closed doorway, a rectangle high on one steeply sloping wall.

'Doctor Baskin has just passed word, Takkata-Jim has ordered the survey party home,' the Niss spoke abruptly. 'She thought you would want to know.'

Orley cursed. Metz might have had a hand in that. How were they to repair the ship without looking for raw materials? Creideiki's strongest reason for coming to Kithrup had been the abundance of pre-refined metals in an oceanic environment accessible to dolphins. If Hikahi's prospectors were called back the danger had to be severe ... or someone was panicking.

Tom paused and looked up. 'Niss, we *must* know what it is the Galactics think we found.'

The sparkles were muted. 'I have done a thorough search of open files in this ship's micro-branch *Library* for any record that might shed light on the mystery of the derelict fleet. Aside from a few vague similarities between the patterns we saw on those gigantic hulls and some ancient cult symbols, I can find no support for a hypothesis that the ships we found are in any way connected to the fabled Progenitors.'

'But you found nothing to contradict it, either?'

'Correct. The derelicts might or might not be linked with the one legend which binds all oxygen-breathing races in the Five Galaxies.'

'It could be we found huge bits of flotsam of no historical significance, then.'

'True. At the other extreme, you may have made the biggest archaeological and religious find of the age. The mere possibility helps to explain the battle shaping up in this solar system, indicative of how many of the Galactic cultures feel about events so long ago. So long as this ship is the sole repository of information about the derelict fleet, the survey vessel *Streaker* remains a great prize, valued by every brand of fanatic.'

Orley had hoped the Niss would find evidence to make their discovery innocuous. Such proof might have been used to get the ETs to leave them alone. Otherwise *Streaker* would have to find a way to get the information to Earth, and let wiser heads figure out what to do with it.

'You keep contemplating, then,' he told the Niss. 'Meanwhile I'll help keep the Galactics off our backs. Now, can you tell me ...'

'Of course I can,' the Niss interrupted again. 'The corridor outside is clear. Don't you think I would let you know if anyone were outside?'

Tom shook his head, certain the machine had been programmed to do this now and again. It would be typical of the Tymbrimi. Earth's greatest allies were also famous practical jokers. When a dozen other calamitous priorities had been settled, he intended taking a monkey wrench to the machine, and explaining the mess to his Tymbrimi friends as 'an unfortunate accident.'

As the door panel slipped aside, Tom grabbed the rim and swing out to drop onto the dim hallway ceiling below. The door hummed shut automatically. Red alert lights flashed at intervals down the gently curved corridor.

All right, he thought. *Our hopes for a quick getaway are dashed, but I've already thought out some contingency plans.*

A few he had discussed with the captain. One or two he had kept to himself.

I'll have to set a few into motion, he thought, knowing from experience that chance diverts all schemes.

As likely as not, it will be something totally unexpected that turns up to offer us our last real hope.

6

GALACTICS

The first phase of the fight was a free-for-all. A score of warring factions scratched and probed at each other, exploring for weaknesses. Already a number of wrecks drifted in orbit, torn and twisted and ominously luminous. Glowing clouds of plasma spread along the path of battle, and jagged metal fragments sparkled as they tumbled.

In her flagship, a leathery queen looked upon view-screens that showed her the battlefield. She lay on a broad, soft cushion and stroked the brown scales of her belly in contemplation.

The displays that rimmed Krat's settee showed many dangers. One panel was an overlay of curling lines, indicating zones of anomalous probability. Others pointed out where the slough from psychic weapons was still dangerous.

Clusters of lights were the other fleets, now regrouping as the first phase drew to a close. Fighting still raged on the fringes.

Krat lounged on a cushion of vletoor skin. She shifted her weight to ease the pressure in her third abdomen. Battle hormones always accelerated the quickening within her. It was an inconvenience which, in ancient days, had forced her female ancestors to stay in the nest, leaving to stupid males the fighting.

No longer, though.

A small, bird-like creature approached her side. Krat took a lingplum from the tray it proffered. She bit it and savored the juices that ran over her tongue and down her whiskers. The little Forski put down the tray and began to sing a crooning ballad about the joys of battle.

The avian Forski had been uplifted to full sapiency, of course. It would have been against the Code of Uplift to do less with a client race. But while they could talk, and even fly spacecraft in a pinch, independent ambition had been bred out of them. They were too useful as domestics and entertainers to be fated anything but specialization. Adaptability might interfere with their graceful and intelligent performance of those functions.

One of her smaller screens suddenly went dark. A destroyer in the Soro rearguard had been destroyed. Krat hardly noticed. The consolidation had been inexpensive so far.

The command room was divided into pie sections. Krat could look into every baffled unit from her couch of command. Her crew bustled about, each a member of a Soro client race, each hurrying to do her will in its own sub-speciality.

From the sectors for navigation, combat, and detection, there was a quieting of the hectic battle pace at last. In planning, though, she saw increased activity as the staff evaluated developments, including a new alliance between the Abdicator and Transcendor forces.

A Paha sub-officer poked its head out of detection sector. Under hooded eyes, Krat watched it dash to a food station, snatch a steaming mug of amoklah, and hurry back to its post.

The Paha race had been allowed more racial diversity than the

Forski, to enhance their value as ritual warriors. It left them less tractable than suited her, but it was a price one paid for good fighters. Krat decided to ignore the incident. She listened to the little Forski sing of the coming victory – of the glory that would be Krat's when she *captured the Earthlings, and finally squeezed their secrets out of them.*

Klaxons shrieked. The Forski leapt in alarm and fled to its cubby. Suddenly there were running Paha everywhere.

'Tandu raider!' the tactical officer shouted. 'Ships two through twelve, it has appeared in your midst! Take evasive maneuvers! Quickly!'

The flagship bucked as it, too, swerved wildly to avoid a spread of missiles. Krat's screens showed a pulsing, danger-blue dot – the daring Tandu cruiser that had popped into being within her fleet – which was even now pouring fire into the Soro ships!

Curse their damnable probability drives! *Krat knew that nobody else could move about as quickly as the Tandu, because no other species was willing to take such chances!*

Krat's mating claw throbbed in irritation. Her Soro ships were so busy avoiding missiles, nobody was firing back!

'Fools!' Krat hissed into her communicator. 'Ships six and ten, hold your ground and concentrate fire on the obscenity!'

Then, before her words reached her sub-captains, the terrible Tandu ship began to dissolve on its own! One moment it was there, ferocious and deadly, ranging in on a numerous but helpless foe. The next instant the spindly destroyer was surrounded by a coruscating, discolored halo of sparks. Its shield folded, and the cruiser fell into itself like a collapsing tower of sticks.

With a brilliant flash, the Tandu vanished, leaving a cloud of ugly vapor behind. Through her own ship's shields, Krat felt an awful psychic roar.

We were lucky, *Krat realized as the psi-noise slowly faded.* It was not without reason that other races avoided the Tandus' methods. But if that ship had lasted a few moments longer …

No harm was done, and Krat noted that her crew had all done their jobs. Some were slow, however, and these must be punished …

She beckoned the chief tactician, a tall, burly Paha. The warrior stepped toward her. He tried to maintain a proud bearing, but his drooping cilia told that he knew what to expect. Krat rumbled deep in her throat.

She started to speak, but in the emotion of the moment, the Soro commander felt a churning pressure within. Krat grunted and writhed, and the Paha officer fled as she panted on the vletoor cushion. Finally she howled and found relief. After a moment, she bent forward to retrieve the egg she had laid.

She picked it up, punishments and battles temporarily banished from her mind. In an instinct that predated her species' uplift by the timid Hul, two million years before, she responded to the smell of pheromones and licked birthing slime from the tiny air-cracks which seamed the leathery egg.

Krat licked it a few extra times for pleasure. She rocked the egg slowly in an ancient, untampered reflex of motherhood.

7

TOSHIO

There was a ship involved, of course. All of his dreams since the age of nine had dealt with ships. Ships, at first, of plasteel and jubber, sailing the straits and archipelagos of Calafia, and later ships of space. Toshio had dreamt ships of every variety, including those of the powerful Galactic patron races, which he had hoped one day to see.

Now he dreamt of a dinghy.

The tiny human-dolphin colony of his homeworld had sent him out with Akki riding on the outrigger, his Calafian Academy button shining brightly under Alph's sunshine. It started out a balmy day.

Only soon the weather darkened, and the sky all around became the same color as the water. The sea grew bilious, then black, then changed to vacuum, and suddenly there were stars everywhere.

He worried about air. Neither he nor Akki had suits. It was *hard*, trying to breathe vacuum!

He was about to turn for home when he saw them chasing him. Galactics, with heads of every shape and color – long, sinuous arms, or tiny, grasping claws, or worse – rowing toward him steadily. The sleek prows of their boats were as lambent as the starlight.

'What do you want?' he cried out, paddling hard to get away. (Hadn't the boat started out with a motor?)

'Who is your master?!' They shouted in a thousand different tongues. 'Is that He beside you?'

'Akki's a fin! Fins are *our* clients! We uplifted them and set them free!'

'Then they are free,' the Galactics replied, drawing closer. 'But who uplifted you? Who set *you* free?'

'I don't know!' he screamed. 'Maybe we did it ourselves!' He stroked harder as the Galactics laughed. He struggled to breathe the hard vacuum. 'Leave me alone! Let me go home!'

Suddenly the *fleet* loomed ahead. The ships seemed bigger than moons – bigger than stars. They were dark and silent, and their aspect seemed to daunt even the Galactics.

Then the foremost of the ancient globes began to open. Toshio realized, then, that Akki was gone. His boat was gone. The ETs were gone.

He wanted to scream, but air was very dear.

A piercing whistle brought him around in a painful, disorienting instant. He sat up suddenly and felt the sled bounce unhappily with the motion. While his eyes made a blurred jumble of the horizon, a stiff breeze blew against his face. The tang of Kithrup greeted his nostrils.

'About time, Ladder-runner. You gave us quite a scare.'

Toshio wavered, then saw Hikahi floating nearby, inspecting him with one eye.

'Are you okay, little Sharp-Eyes?'

'Um ... yes. I think so.'

'Then you had better get to work on your hose. We had to nip it to give you air.'

Toshio felt the knife-edged cut. He noticed that both hands were neatly bandaged.

'Was anyone else hurt?' he asked as he felt through his thigh pocket for his repair kit.

'A few minor burns. We enjoyed the fight, after learning you were all right-t. Thank you for telling us about Ssassia. We'd never have looked there had you not been caught.

'They are cutting her loose now.'

Toshio knew he should be grateful to Hikahi for putting the mis-adventure in that light. By rights he should be getting a tongue-lashing for rashly leaving formation, and almost losing his life. But Toshio felt too lost to allow himself even gratitude to the dolphin lieutenant. 'I suppose they haven't found Phip-pit?'

'Of him there's been no sign.'

The slow rotation of Kithrup had taken the sun past what would look like four o'clock, Earth time. Low clouds were gathering on the eastern horizon. There was a choppiness to the water that had been absent before.

'There may be a small squall later,' Hikahi said. 'It may be unwise to use Earth instincts on another world, but I think we have nothing to fear ...'

Toshio looked up. There was something to the south ... He squinted.

There it was again, a flash, and then another. Two tiny bursts of light followed in quick succession, almost invisible against the sea glare.

'How long has that been going on?' he gestured toward the southern sky.

'What do you mean, Toshio?'

'That flashing. Is it lightning?'

The fin's eyes widened and her mouth curled slightly. Hikahi's flukes churned and she rose up in the water to turn first one eye, then the other, toward the south.

'I detect nothing, Sharp-Eyes. Tell me what you see.'

'Multicolored flashes. Bursts of light. Lots of . . . ' Toshio stopped wrapping his air hose. He stared for a moment, trying to remember.

'Hikahi,' he said slowly. 'I think Akki called me during the fight with the weed. Did you get anything over your set?'

'No I didn't, Toshio. But remember, we fins aren't yet so good at abstract thought while fighting. T-try to recall what he said, please.'

Toshio touched his forehead. The encounter with the weed wasn't something he wanted to think about. It all blended in with his nightmare, a jumbling of colors, noises and confusion.

'I think . . . I think he said something about wanting us to keep radio silence and come home . . . something about a space battle going on?'

Hikahi let out a whistling moan and flipped out of the water in a backward dive. She was back immediately, tail churning.

> * Close-up
>   Lock-up
> * Go the other way – than up! *

Sloppy Trinary. There were nuances in Primal Delphin which Toshio, of course, couldn't understand. But they sent a thrill down his spine. Hikahi was the last fin he would ever have expected to slip into Primal. As he finished wrapping his air hose, he realized with chagrin what his failure to tell Hikahi earlier might have cost them all.

He slapped his faceplate shut and flopped over to press the buoyancy valve on the sled, checking simultaneously the telltales on his helmet rim. He ran through the pre-dive checklist with a rapidity only a fourth-generation Calafian colonist could have achieved.

The bow of the sled was sinking quickly as the sea erupted to his right. Seven dolphins breached in a spume of water and exhaled breath.

'S-s-sassia's tied to your stern, Toshio. Can you shake your leg?' Keepiru urged. 'Now is no time to dawdle making up t-t-tunes!'

305

Toshio grimaced. How could Keepiru have fought so hard earlier to save the life of someone he ridiculed so?

He remembered the way Keepiru had torn into the weed, the desperate look in his eye, and the glow it had taken on finding the sled. Yet now he was cruel and taunting as ever.

A sharp blast of light flashed in the east, searing the sky all around them. The fins squealed almost as one, and immediately dove – all except Keepiru, who stayed beside Toshio – as the eastern cloudline spat fire into the afternoon sky.

The sled finally sank, but in the last instant Toshio and Keepiru saw a hurtling battle of giants.

A huge, arrowhead-shaped space vessel plummeted down on them, pitted and fiery. Wind-swept trailers of purple smoke boiled out of great gashes in its sides, to be flung back into the needle-narrow shock front of its supersonic flight. The shock wave warped even the shimmer of the great ship's defensive shields, shells of gravity and plasma that sparkled with unhealthful overload.

Two grapnel-shaped destroyers dogged it no more than four ship lengths behind. Beams of accelerated anti-matter flashed from each of the trefoils, hitting their mark twice in terrible explosions.

Toshio was five meters below the surface when the sonic boom hit. It slammed the sled over, and kept it tumbling amid a roar that sounded like a house caving in. The water was a churning maelstrom of bubbles and bodies. As he struggled with the sled, Toshio thanked Infinity he hadn't been at the surface to hear the battle passing by. At Morgran they had seen ships die. But never this close.

The noise finally settled down to a long, loud growling. Toshio got the sled righted at last.

Ssassia's sad corpse still lay tied to the rear end of the sled. The other fins, too scared or prudent to go above, began taking turns at the small airdomes that lined the bottom rim of the sled. It was Toshio's job to keep the sled still, not easy in the churning water, but he did it without a thought.

They were near the sloping western edge of a huge, grayish metal-mound. Sea-plants grew at intervals along its side. They looked nothing like the strangle weed, but that was no guarantee.

More and more, Toshio was coming to dislike being here. He wished he was home, where the dangers were simple, and easily handled – kelp klingers and island turtles and the like – and where there were no ETs.

'Are you all right?' Hikahi asked as she came by. The dolphin lieutenant radiated calm.

'I'm fine,' he grumped. 'It's a good thing I didn't wait any longer to tell you about Akki's message. You have every reason to be mad at me.'

'Don't be silly. Now we head back. Brookida is fatigued, so I've lashed him under an airdome. You will forge ahead with the scouts. We'll follow. Now t-take off!'

'Aye, sir.' Toshio took his bearings and pushed the throttle. The thrusters hummed as the sled accelerated. Several of the stronger swimmers maintained pace alongside, as the mound slowly receded on the right.

It had taken them five minutes or so to get started. They were barely under way before the tsunami hit.

It was not a huge wave, merely the first of a series of ripples spreading from a point where a pebble had plunked into the sea. The pebble happened to be a spaceship half a kilometer long. It had plunked, at supersonic speed, a mere fifty kilometers away.

The wave jerked the sled upward and sideways, almost shaking the boy off. A cloud of sea debris, torn-up plants, and dead and living fish whirled about him like clods in a cyclone. The roar was deafening.

Toshio clutched the controls desperately. Somehow, against incredible momentum, he managed slowly to drive the prow of the sled up and away from the wave front. Just in time, he thrust out of the curling, downward circulation and sent the tiny craft flying along the direction the current wanted to go. Eastward.

An ash-gray form speared past him on his left. In a flash he recognized Keepiru, struggling to keep control in the churning waters. The fin squeaked something indecipherable in Trinary, then was gone.

Some instinct guided Toshio, or perhaps it was the sonar screen, now a mess of jumbled snow, but still bearing the faint, fading traces of the terrain map it had shown only moments before. Toshio forced the sled to bear left as hard as possible.

The emergency-power roar of the engines changed to a scream as he suddenly slewed hard to port in desperation. The huge, dark bulk of a metal-mound loomed ahead! Already he could feel undertow as the wave began to form breakers to his right, curling as the cycloid rode up the sloping shore of the island.

Toshio wanted to cry out, but the struggle took all of his breath. He clenched his teeth and counted as terrible seconds passed.

The sled drove past the cliff-like northern shore amid a cloud of bubbles. Though he was still underwater, Toshio could look downward a dozen meters to his right, and see the lower beach plants of the island. He was riding in the center of a tall mound of water.

Then he was past! The sea opened up and one of the deep oceanic rills lay below, dark and seemingly bottomless. Toshio slammed the bow planes forward and vented his tanks. The sled plummeted faster than he had ever dived before.

His stern pulled forward precariously. Toshio passed clouds of falling debris. Darkness and cold came up at him, and he sought the chill as a refuge.

The valley sloped as he brought the sled to a quiet depth. He could sense the tsunami rolling above. Sea plants all around waved in an obviously unaccustomed manner. A slow rain of falling rubbish drifted down on all sides, but at least the water wasn't trying to beat him to death anymore. Toshio flattened out his dive and headed toward the valley center, away from everything. Then he let himself sag in an agony of bruised muscles and adrenaline reaction.

He blessed the tiny, man-designed symbiotes that were right now scavenging his blood of excess nitrogen, preventing narcosis raptures at this depth. Toshio cranked the engines down to one-quarter, and they sighed, sounding almost relieved. The lamps on the sled's display were mostly green, surprisingly.

One telltale caught his eye – it indicated an airdome in operation. Suddenly Toshio noticed a faint, singing sound; it was a whistling of patience and reverence.

> * The Ocean ^{is} as ^{is} as ^{is}—
> an endless sigh of dreaming—
> * Of other seas that ^{are} that ^{are}—
> and others in them, dreaming— *

Toshio snapped on the hydrophones.

'Brookida! Are you okay? Is your air all right?'

There was a sigh, tremulous and tired.

'Fleet-t-t Fingers, hello. Thank you for saving my life. You flew as truly as any *Tursiops*.'

'That ship we saw must have crashed! If that's what it was you can bet there will be aftershocks! Maybe we'd better stay down here a while. I'll turn on the sonar so others can come for air while the waves pass.' He flicked a switch, and immediately a low series of clicks emanated into the surrounding water. Brookida groaned.

'They will not come, Toshio. Can't you hear them? They won't answer your call.'

Toshio frowned. 'They *have* to! Hikahi will know about the aftershocks. They're probably looking for us right now! Maybe I'd better head back. . . .' He moved to turn the sled and blow ballast. Brookida had started him worrying.

'Don't go, Toshio! It will do no good for you to die as well! Wait until the waves pass-s-s! You must live to tell Creideiki!'

'What are you *talking* about?'

'Listen, Sharp-Eyes. Listen!'

Toshio shook his head, then swore and pulled back on the throttle until the engine died. He turned up the gain on the hydrophones.

'Do you hear?' Brookida asked.

Toshio cocked his head and listened. The sea was a mess of intonation. The roar of the departing wave dopplered down as he lay there. Schools of fish made panicky noises. All around came the reports of rockslides and surf pounding on the islands.

Then he heard it. The shrill repetitive squeals of Primal Delphin. No modern dolphin spoke it when fully in command of his faculties.

That, in itself, was bad news.

One of the cries was clear. He could easily make out the basic distress call. It was the earliest Delphin signal human scientists had understood.

But the other noise ... at least three voices were involved in that one. It was a strange sound, very poignant and *very* wrong!

'It isss rescue fever,' Brookida groaned. 'Hikahi is beached and injured. *She* might have stopped this, but she is delirious and now adds to the problem!'

'Hikahi ...'

'Like Creideiki, she is an adept of Keneenk ... the study of logical discipline. She would have been able to force the others to ignore the cries of those washed ashore, to make them dive to safety for a t-time.'

'Don't they realize there will be aftershocks?'

'Shockss hardly matter, Sharp-Eyes!' Brookida cried. 'They may beach themselves without assist! You are Calafian. How can you not know this about usss? I thrash here to go and die answering that call!'

Toshio groaned. Of course he knew about rescue fever, in which panic and fear washed aside the veneer of civilization, leaving a cetacean with only one thought – to save his comrades, whatever the personal risk. Every few years the tragedy struck even the highly advanced fins of Calafia. Akki had told him, once, that sometimes the sea itself seemed to be calling for help. Some humans claimed to have felt it, too – particularly those who took dolphin RNA in the rites of the Dreamer Cult.

Once upon a time the *Tursiops,* or bottlenose dolphin, had been about the least likely cetacean to beach itself. But genetic engineering had upset the balance somewhere. As the genes of other species were spliced onto the basic *Tursiops* models, a few things had been thrown out of kilter. For three generations human geneticists had been working on the problem. But for now the fins swam along a knife edge, where irrationality was a perpetual danger.

Toshio bit his lip. 'They have their harnesses,' he said uncertainly.

'One can hope. But is it likely they'll use them properly when they are even now speaking P-primal?'

Toshio struck the sled with his balled fist. Already his hand was growing numb from the chill. 'I'm going up,' he announced.

'No! You must not! You must guard your safet-ty!'

Toshio ground his teeth. *Always mothering me. Mothering or teasing. The fins treat me like a child, and I'm sick of it!*

He set the throttle to one-quarter and pulled up on the bow planes. 'I'm going to unlash you, Brookida. Can you swim okay?'

'Yesss. But-t . . .'

Toshio looked at his sonar. A fuzzy line was forming in the west. 'Can you swim!' he demanded.

'Yesss. I can swim well enough. But don't cut me loose near the rescue fever! Don't you risk the aftershockssss!'

'I see one coming now. They'll be several minutes apart and weakening with time. I'll fix it so we rise just after this one passes. Then you've got to get going back to the ship! Tell them what's happened and get help.'

'That's what *you* should do, Toshio.'

'Never mind that! Will you do as I ask? Or must I leave you lashed up!'

There was an almost unnoticeable pause, but Brookida's voice changed. 'I shall do exactly as you say, Toshio. I'll bring help.'

Toshio checked his trim, then he slipped over the side, holding onto the rim stanchions with one hand. Brookida looked at him through the transparent shell of the airdome. The tough bubble membrane surrounded the dolphin's head. Toshio tore loose the lashings holding Brookida in place. 'You're going to have to take a breather, you know.'

Brookida sighed as Toshio pulled a lever by the airdome. A small hose descended, one end covering Brookida's blowhole. Like a snake, ten feet of hose, wrapped around Brookida's torso. Breathers were uncomfortable, and hindered speech. But by wearing one Brookida would not have to come up for air. The breather would help the old metallurgist ignore the cries in the water – a constant, uncomfortable reminder of his membership in a technological culture.

Toshio left Brookida tied in place by a single lashing. He pulled himself back onto the upper surface just as the first aftershock rolled overhead.

The sled bucked, but he was prepared this time. They were deep, and the wave passed with surprising quickness.

'Okay, here goes.' He pushed the throttle forward to max and blew ballast.

Soon the metal island appeared on his left. The screams of his comrades grew distinctly louder. The distress call was now pre-eminent over the rescue fever response.

Toshio steered past the mound to the north. He wanted to give Brookida a head start.

Just then, however, a sleek gray figure shot past, just overhead. He recognized it at once, and where it was headed.

Toshio cut the final lashing. 'Get moving, Brookida! If you come back anywhere near this island, I'll rip your harness and bite your tail in half!'

Brookida dropped away and the sled turned sharply. Toshio kicked in emergency power to try to catch up with Keepiru. The fastest swimmer in the *Streak*'s crew was heading straight for the western beach. His cries were pure Primal Delphin.

'Damn you, Keepiru. Stop!'

The sled sped quickly, just under the water's surface. The afternoon had aged, and there was a reddish tinge to the clouds, but Toshio could clearly see Keepiru leaping from wavelet to wavelet up ahead. He appeared indifferent to Toshio's calls as he neared the island where his comrades lay beached and delirious.

Toshio felt helpless. Another aftershock was due in three minutes. If it didn't beach the dolphin, Keepiru's own efforts probably would. Keepiru came from Atlast, a new and rather rustic colony world. It was doubtful he had learned the tools of mental discipline studied by Creideiki and Hikahi.

'Stop! If we time it right we can work as a team! We can miss the aftershocks! Will you let me catch *up?*' he screamed. It was no use. The fin had too much of a head start.

The futile chase frustrated Toshio. How could he have lived and worked with dolphins all his life and known them so poorly? To think the Terragens Council had chosen him for this tour because of his *experience* with fins! Hah!

Toshio had always taken a lot of kidding from fins. They kidded *all* human children, while protecting them ferociously. But on signing aboard *Streaker*, Toshio had expected to be treated as an adult and officer. Sure, there'd be a little repartee, as he'd seen between man and fin back home, but mutual respect, as well. It hadn't worked out that way.

Keepiru had been the worst, starting right off with heavy sarcasm and never letting up.

So why am I trying to save him?

He recalled the fierce courage Keepiru had shown in saving him from the weed. There was no rescue fever then. The fin had been in full control over his harness.

So, he thinks of me as a child, Toshio realized bitterly. No wonder he doesn't hear me now.

Still, it offered a way. Toshio bit his lip, wishing vainly for an alternative. To save Keepiru's life he would have to humiliate himself utterly. It wasn't an easy thing to decide, his pride had taken such a beating.

With a savage curse, he pulled back the throttle and set the bow planes to descend. He turned up the hydrophones to maximum, swallowed, then cried out in pidgin Trinary.

> * *Child drowning – child in danger!* *
> * *Child drowning – child's distress* *
> * *Human child – in need of savior* *
> * *Human child – come do your best!* *

He repeated the call over and over, whistling through lips dry with shame. The nursery rhyme was taught to all the children of Calafia. Any kid past the age of nine who used it usually pleaded for transfer to another island to escape the subsequent razzing. There were more dignified ways an adult called for help.

None of which Keepiru had heard!

Ears burning, he repeated the call.

Not all Calafian kids did well with the fins. Only a quarter of the planet's human population worked closely with the sea. But those adults were the ones who learned how to deal with dolphins. Toshio had always assumed he'd be one of them.

Now that was all over. If he got back to *Streaker* he'd have to hide in his cabin . . . for at least the few days or weeks it took for the victors of the battle over Kithrup to come down and claim them all.

On his sonar screen, another fuzzy line of static was approaching from the west. Toshio let the sled slip a little deeper. Not that he cared. He continued to whistle, but he felt like crying.

> \# *where – where – where child is – where child is? where* \#

Primal Delphin! Nearby! Almost, Toshio forgot his shame. He fingered a rope left over from Brookida's lashings, and kept whistling.

A streak of gray twilight flashed past him. Toshio gathered his knees under him and took the rope in both hands. He knew Keepiru would circle below and come up the other side. When he saw the first hint of gray hurtling upward, Toshio launched himself from the sled.

The bullet-like body of the dolphin twisted in an abrupt, panicky attempt to avoid collision. Toshio cried out as the cetacean's tail struck him in the chest. But it was a cry more of glee than pain. He had timed it right!

As Keepiru twisted around again, Toshio flung himself backward, allowing the fin to pass between himself and the rope. He clamped his feet around the dolphin's slick tail and pulled the rope with all the will of a garroter.

'Got you!' he cried.

At that instant the aftershock hit.

The cycloid clutched and pulled. Bits of flotsam struck him as suction tossed his body in alliance with the mad, bucking dolphin.

This time Toshio felt no fear of the wave. He was filled with a fierce battle lust. Adrenaline seared like a hot flux. It pleased him to save Keepiru's life by physically punishing him for weeks of humiliation.

The dolphin writhed in panic. As the shock rolled past them, Keepiru cried out the basic call for air. Desperately, the fin drove for the surface.

They breached, and Toshio just missed getting blasted by spume from Keepiru's blowhole. Keepiru commenced a series of leaps, gyrating to shake loose his unwelcome rider. Each time they went underwater Toshio tried to call out.

'You're *sentient*,' he gasped. 'Damn you, Keepiru ... you're ... you're a *starship pilot*!'

He should be doing his coaxing in Trinary, but it was no use trying, when he could barely hold on for dear life.

'You pea-brained ... phallic symbol!' he screamed as water slammed against him. 'You over-rated *fish*! You're *killing* me, you goddamned ... The Eatees own Calafia by now because you fins can't hold your tongues! We never should have taken you along into space!'

The words were hateful. Contemptuous. At last Keepiru seemed to have heard. He reared out of the water like an enraged stallion. Toshio felt his grip tear loose, and he was flung away like a rag doll, to hit the sea with a splash.

Only eighteen cases were known, in the forty generations of dolphin uplift, in which a fin attacked a human with murderous intent. In each case, every fin related to the perpetrator had been sterilized. Still, Toshio expected to be crushed at any instant. He didn't care. He had realized, at last, the cause of his depression. It had come to the surface when he was wrestling with Keepiru.

It hadn't been his inability to go home that had hurt, these last few weeks. It was another fact he had not let himself think of since the battle of Morgran. The ETs ... the extraterrestrials ... the Galactics of every stripe and philosophy which were chasing *Streaker* ... would not settle for hunting down the dolphin-crewed ship.

At least one ET race would have seen that the *Streak* might successfully go into hiding. Or they might imagine, erroneously, that her crew had succeeded in passing the secret of her discovery to Earth. Either way, the logical next step for one of the more amoral or vicious Galactic races would be coercion.

Earth might be able to defend herself. Probably Omnivarium and Hermes, as well. The Tymbrimi would defend the Caanan colonies.

But places like Calafia, or Atlast, must be captured by now. They were hostages, his family and everyone he had known. And Toshio realized, he blamed the fins.

Another aftershock was due any minute. Toshio didn't care.

Pieces of floating debris drifted all about nearby. Not more than a kilometer away Toshio could see the metal-mound. At least it looked like the same one. He couldn't tell if there were dolphins stranded on the shore or not.

A large piece of flotsam drifted near him. It took him a moment to realize that it was Keepiru.

Toshio treaded water as he opened his faceplate.

'Well,' he asked, 'are you proud of yourself?'

Keepiru turned slightly to one side, and one dark eye looked up at Toshio. The bulge at the top of the cetacean's head, where human meddling had created a vocal apparatus from the former blowhole, gave out a long, soft, warbling sound.

Toshio couldn't be certain it was just a sigh. It might have been an apology in Primal Delphin. The possibility alone was enough to make him angry.

'Can that crap! I just want to know one thing. Do I have to send you back to the ship? Or do you think you can stay sentient long enough to help me? Answer in Anglic, and make it grammatically correct!'

Keepiru moaned in pure anguish. After a moment of heavy breathing he finally spoke, quite slowly.

'Don't sssend me back. They're still calling for help! I will do what you ask-k-k!'

Toshio hesitated. 'All right. Go down after the sled. When you've found it, put on a breather. I don't want you hampered by need for air, and you need a constant reminder!

'Then bring the sled up near the island, *but not too close*!'

Keepiru flung his head up in a huge nodding motion. 'Yesss!' he cried. Then he flipped and dove into the water.

It was just as well Keepiru had left all the thinking to him. The fin might have balked if he'd caught onto what Toshio had in mind to do next.

A kilometer to the island; there was only one way to get there fast and avoid a scramble up the slanting, abrasive, metal-coral surface. He checked his orientation one more time, then a drop in the water level told him that the wave was coming.

The fourth wave seemed the gentlest by far. He knew the feeling was deceptive. He was in water deep enough so that the swell came at him as a gentle lump in the ocean, rather than a crested breaker. He dove down into the hump and swam against the direction of motion for a time before rising to the surface.

He had to gauge it just right. Swim back too far and he wouldn't reach the island before the following trough arrived and pulled him out to sea again. To remain at the front of the wave would be to body-surf a vicious breaker onto the beach, undertow and all.

It was all happening too fast. He swam hard, but couldn't tell if he had passed the peak of the wave or not. Then a glance told him that it was too late for remedial measures. He flipped around to face the looming, foliage-topped mound.

The breaker started a hundred yards ahead, but the island slope rapidly ate away at the wave as bottom dragged the cycloid into a crested monster. The peak moved backward, toward Toshio, even as the wave hurtled upward onto the beach.

The boy braced as the crest reached him. He was prepared to look down on a precipice, and then see nothing more.

What he saw was a cataract of white foam as the wave began to die. Toshio cried out to keep his ear channels open, and started swimming furiously to stay atop the churning tide of spume and debris.

Suddenly, there was greenery all around. Trees and shrubs which had withstood the earlier assaults shook under this attack. Some tore loose of their moorings even as Toshio flew past them. Others stood and flailed at him as he hurtled through.

No sharp branch impaled him. No unbreaking vine garroted him as he passed. In a tumbling, tossing confusion he finally came to rest, somehow hugging the trunk of a huge tree, while the wave churned, and finally receded.

Miraculously, he was on his feet, the first man to stand on the soil of Kithrup. Toshio stared dazedly at his surroundings, briefly not believing his survival.

Then he hurriedly opened his faceplate, and became the first man to lose his breakfast on the soil of Kithrup.

8

GALACTICS

'Slay them!' The Jophur high priest demanded. 'Slay the isolated Thennanin battlecruisers on our sixth quadrant!'

The Jophur chief of staff bowed its twelve-ringed trunk before the high priest.

'The Thennanin are our allies-of-the-moment! How can we turn on them without first performing the secret rituals of betrayal? Their ancestors will not be appeased!'

The Jophur high priest expanded its six outer sap-rings. It rose high upon its dais at the rear of the command chamber.

'There is no time to perform the rites! Now, as our alliance finishes sweeping this sector, as our alliance has become the strongest! Now, while this phase of the battle still rages. Now, while the foolish Thennanin have opened up their flanks to us. Now may we harm them greatly!'

The chief of staff pulsed in agitation, its outer sap-rings discoloring with emotion.

'We may change alliances as it suits us, agreed. We may betray our allies, agreed. We may do anything to win the prize, agreed. But we may not do so without performing the rituals! The rituals are what make us the appropriate vessels for the will of the ancients! You would bring us down to the level of the heretics!'

The dais shook with the high priest's anger.

'My rings decide! My rings are those of priesthood! My rings . . .'

The oration-peak of the pyramidal high priest erupted in a geyser of hot, multi-hued sap. The explosion spewed sticky amber liquor across the bridge of the Jophur flagship.

'Continue fighting.' The chief of staff waved the crew back to work with its sidearm. 'Call the Quartermaster of Religiosity. Have it send up rings to make up a new priest. Continue fighting while we prepare to perform the rituals of betrayal. '

The chief of staff bowed to the staring section chiefs. 'We shall appease the ancestors of the Thennanin before we turn on them.

'But remember to make certain the Thennanin themselves do not sense our intentions!'

9

STREAKER

FROM THE JOURNAL OF GILLIAN BASKIN

It's been some time since I've been able to make an entry in this personal log. Since the Shallow Cluster it seems we've constantly been in frantic motion ... making the discovery of the millennia, getting ambushed at Morgran, and fighting for our lives from then on. I hardly ever see Tom any more. He's always down in the engine or weapons pods. I'm either here in the lab or helping out in sick bay.

Ship's surgeon Makanee has a mouthful of problems. Fen have always had a talent for hypochondria. A fifth of the crew shows up every sick call with psychosomatic complaints. You can't just tell them it's all in their heads, so we stroke them and tell them what brave fellows they are, and that everything's going to be all right.

I think if it weren't for the captain, half of this crew would be hysterical by now. To many of them he seems almost like a hero out of the Whale Dream. Creideiki moves about the ship, supervising repairs and giving little lessons in Keneenk logic. The fen seem to buck up whenever he's nearby.

Still, reports keep coming in about the space battle. Instead of tapering off, it's only getting thicker and heavier!

And we're all getting more than a little worried about Hikahi's party.

Gillian put down her stylus. From the small circle of her desk lamp, the rest of the laboratory appeared dark and gloomy. The only other light came from the far end of the room. Silhouetted against the spots was a vaguely humanoid shape, a mysterious shadow, lying on a stasis table.

'Hikahi,' she sighed. 'Where in Ifni's name *are* you?'

That Hikahi's survey party hadn't even sent back a monopulse confirmation of the recall order was now of great concern. *Streaker* couldn't afford to lose those crewfen. For all of his frequent unreliability outside the bridge, Keepiru was their best pilot. Even Toshio Iwashika had a lot of promise.

But most of all, the loss of Hikahi would hurt. Without her, how could Creideiki manage?

Hikahi was Gillian's best dolphin friend, at least as close to her as Tom was to Creideiki or Tsh't. Gillian wondered why Takkata-Jim had been appointed vice-captain instead of Hikahi. It made no sense. She could only imagine that politics was behind it. Takkata-Jim was a *Stenos*. Perhaps Ignacio Metz had had a hand in choosing the complement for this mission. Metz was a passionate advocate of certain dolphin racial types back on Earth.

Gillian didn't write these thoughts down. They were idle speculations, and she didn't have time for speculation.

Anyway, it's time I got back to Herbie.

She closed her journal and headed over to the stasis table, where a dry, dessicated figure floated in a heavily shielded field of suspended time.

The ancient cadaver grinned back at her through the glass.

It wasn't human. There hadn't even been multi-cellular creatures on Earth when this thing had lived and breathed and flown spaceships. Yet it looked eerily humanoid. It had straight arms and legs, and a very man-like head and neck. Its jaw and eye orbits were strange-looking, but its skull still had an Earth-like grin.

How old are you, Herbie? she asked in her thoughts. *One billion years? Two?*

How is it your fleet of ancient hulks waited undiscovered by Galactic civilization for so long, waited until we came along ... a bunch of wolfling humans and newly uplifted dolphins? Why were we the ones to find you?

And why did one little hologram of you, beamed home to Earth, make half the patron-lines in the galaxy go crazy?

Streaker's micro-*Library* was no help. It refused to recognize Herbie at all. Maybe it was holding back. Or perhaps it was simply too small an archive to remember an obscure race so long extinct.

Tom had asked the Niss machine to look into it. So far the sarcastic Tymbrimi artefact had been unable to cozen out an answer.

Meanwhile, between sick bay and her other duties, Gillian had to find a few hours a day to examine this relict non-destructively, and maybe figure out what was stirring up the Eatees. If she didn't do it, no one would.

Somehow she would make it until tonight.

Poor Tom, Gillian thought, smiling. *He'll be coming back from his engines, wiped out, and I'll be feeling amorous. It's a damned good thing he's a sport.*

She picked up a pion microprobe.

Okay Herbie, let's see if we can find out what kind of a brain you had.

10

METZ

'I'm sorry, Doctor Metz. The captain is with Thomas's Orley in the weapons section. If there's anything I can do . . . ?'

As usual, Vice-Captain Takkata-Jim was unfailingly polite. His Anglic diction, even while breathing oxywater, was almost perfect. Ignacio Metz couldn't help smiling in approval. He had a particular interest in Takkata-Jim.

'No, Vice-Captain. I just stopped by the bridge to see if the survey party had reported in.'

'They haven't. We can only wait.'

Metz tsked. He had already concluded that Hikahi's party was destroyed.

'Ah, well. I don't suppose there has been any offer of negotiations by the Galactics yet?'

Takkata-Jim shook his large, mottled-gray head left to right.

'Regrettably, no sir. They appear more interested in slaughtering each other. Every few hours, it seems, yet another battle fleet enters Kihsemenee's system to join in the free-for-all. It may be a while before anyone initiates diplomacy.'

Dr Metz frowned at the illogic of it. If the Galactics were rational, they'd let *Streaker* hand her discovery over to the *Library Institute* and have done with it! Then everyone would share equally!

But Galactic civilization was unified more in the breach than in fact. And too many angry species had big ships and guns.

Here we are, he thought, *in the middle, with something they all want. It can't just be that giant fleet of ancient ships. Something more must have set them off. Gillian Baskin and Tom Orley picked something up out there in the Shallow Cluster. I wonder what it was.*

'Will you be wanting me to join you for dinner this evening, Doctor Metz?'

Metz blinked. What day was it? Ah, yes. Wednesday. 'Of course, Vice-Captain. Your company and conversation would be appreciated, as usual. Shall we say sixish?'

'Perhapsss nineteen-hundred hours would be better, sir. I get off duty then.'

'Very well. Until then.'

Takkata-Jim nodded. He turned and swam back to his duty station.

Metz watched the fin appreciatively.

He's the best of my Stenos, Metz thought. *He doesn't know I'm his godfather … his gene-father. But I am proud nonetheless.*

All the dolphins aboard were of *Tursiops amicus* stock. But some had genetic grafts from *Stenos bredanensis,* the deep-water dolphin that had always been the closest to the bottlenose in intelligence.

Wild *bredanensis* had a reputation for insatiable curiosity and reckless disregard for danger. Metz had led the effort to have DNA from that species added to the neo-fin gene pool. On Earth many of the new *Stenos* had turned out very well, showing streaks of initiative and individual brilliance.

But a reputation for harsh temperament had lately caused some resentment in Earth's coastal communities. He had worked hard to convince the Council that it would be an important gesture to appoint a few *Stenos* to positions of responsibility on the first dolphin-crewed starship.

Takkata-Jim was his proof. Coldly logical, primly correct, the fin used Anglic almost to the exclusion of Trinary, and seemed impervious to the Whale Dream that so enthralled older models like Creideiki. Takkata-Jim was the most man-like dolphin Metz had ever met.

He watched the vice-captain manage the bridge crew, with none of the little Keneenk parables Creideiki was always inserting, but rather with Anglic precision and brevity. Never a word wasted.

Yes, he thought. This one is going to get a good report when we get home.

'Doctor Metsssss?'

Metz turned, and recoiled at the size of the dolphin that had silently come up beside him. 'Wha … ? Oh, K'tha-Jon. You startled me. What can I do for you?'

A truly large dolphin grinned at him. His blunt mouth, his counter-shaded body and bulging eyes, would have told Metz everything about him … if he hadn't already known.

Feresa attenuata, the human savored the thought. *So beautiful and savage. My most secret project, and nobody, not even you, K'tha-Jon, knows that you are more than just another* Stenos.

'Forgive the interruption, Doctor Metsss, but the chimp scientist Charlesss Dart-t has asked to speak with you. I think the little ape wantsss to bitch to somebody again.'

Metz frowned. K'tha-Jon was only a boson, and not expected to be as refined as Takkata-Jim. Still, there were limits, even considering the giant's hidden background.

I will have to talk to this fellow, he reminded himself. *This kind of attitude will never do.*

'Please inform Doctor Dart that I'm on my way,' he told the fin. 'I'm finished here for now.'

II

CREIDEIKI & ORLEY

'So we're armed again,' Creideiki sighed. 'After a fashion.'

Thomas Orley looked up from the newly repaired missile tubes and nodded. 'It's about as good as we're going to get, Creideiki. We weren't expecting trouble when we popped into a battle at Morgran transfer point. We were lucky to get away with as little damage as we took.'

Creideiki agreed. 'Just ssso. If only I had reacted faster.'

Orley noticed his friend's mood. He pursed his lips and whistled. His breather mask amplified a faint sound-shadow picture. The little echo danced and hopped like a mad elf from corner to corner in the oxywater-filled chamber. Workers in the weapons pod lifted their narrow, sound-sensitive jaws to follow the skipping sonar image as it scampered unseen, chittering in mock sympathy.

> * When one commands,
> One is envied by people –
> But, oh! the demands! *

The sound-wraith vanished, but laughter remained. The crew of the weapons pod spluttered and squawled.

Creideiki let the mirth settle. Then, from his brow came a pattern of chamber-filling clicks that merged to mimic the sounds of thunderclouds gathering. In the closed room those present heard raindrops blown before the wind. Tom closed his eyes to let the sound-image of a sea squall close over him.

> * They stand in my road,
> The mad, ancient, nasty things
> Tell them 'move, or else!' *

Orley bowed his head, acknowledging defeat. No one had ever beaten Creideiki at Trinary haiku. The admiring sighs of the fen only confirmed this.

Nothing had changed, of course. As Orley and Creideiki turned to leave the weapons pod, they knew that defiance alone would not get this crew through the crisis. There must be hope, as well.

Hope was scarce. Tom knew that Creideiki was desperately worried about Hikahi, though he hid it well.

When they were out of earshot, the captain asked, 'Has Gillian made any progresss studying that *thing* we found ... the cause of all this trouble?'

Tom shook his head. 'I haven't spent more than an hour with her in two days.'

Creideiki sighed. 'It would have been nice to know what the Galacticsss think we found. Ah, well ...'

They were stopped by a sudden whistle. Tsh't, the ship's fourth officer, flew into the hallway in a cloud of bubbles.

'Creideiki! Tom! Sonar reports a dolphin at long range, to the eassst, swimming this way at high speed!'

Creideiki and Orley looked at each other. Then Tom nodded at the captains unspoken command.

'Can I take Tsh't and twenty fen?'

'Yesss. Get a team ready. But don't leave till we find out more. You may want to take more than twenty. Or it may be hopeless to go at all.'

Tom saw pain in the captain's eye. He motioned for Lieutenant Tsh't to follow and swam rapidly down the flooded corridor toward the outlock.

12

GALACTICS

Feeling the combined joys of patronhood and command, the Soro, Krat, watched the Gello, the Paha, the Vila, her creatures, as they guided the Soro fleet toward battle once more.

'Mistress,' the Gello detection officer announced. 'We are approaching the water world at one-quarter light-speed, per your instructions.'

Krat acknowledged with a bare flick of her tongue, but secretly she was happy. Her egg was healthy. When they won here she would be due to go home and mate once more. And the crew of her flagship was working together like a finely tuned machine.

'The fleet is one paktaar ahead of timetable, mistress,' the detection officer announced.

Of all the client species owing allegiance to the Soro, the Gello were special to Krat. They were her own species's first clients, uplifted by the Soro long ago. The Gello had in their turn become patrons as well, and brought two more client races into the clan. They had made the Soro proud. The chain of uplift went on.

Deep in the past had been the Progenitors, who began Galactic Law. Since then, race had aided race to sentience, taking indentured service as payment.

Many millions of years ago, the ancient Luber had uplifted the Puber, or so the Library said. The Luber were now long extinct. The Puber still existed, somewhere, though now degenerate and decadent.

Before their decadence, though, the Puber raised up the Hul, who in turn made clients of Krat's stone-chopping, Soro ancestors. Shortly thereafter, the Hul retired to their home-world to become philosophers.

Now the Soro themselves had many clients. Their most successful upspring were the Gello, the Paha, and the Pila.

Krat could hear the high voice of the Pila tactician Cubber-cabub, haranguing its subordinates, to coax information she wanted from the shipboard mini-Library. Cubber-cabub sounded frightened. Good. It would try harder if it feared her.

Alone of those aboard, the Pila were mammals, short bipeds from a high-gravity world. They had become a powerful race in many Galaxy-wide bureaucratic organizations, including the important Library Institute. The Pila had raised clients of their own, bringing credit to the clan.

Still, too bad the Pila were no longer indentured clients. It would have been nice to meddle with their genes again. The furry little sophonts shed, and had a bothersome odor.

No client race was perfect. Only two hundred years ago, the Pila had been thoroughly embarrassed by the humans of Earth. The affair was difficult and expensive to cover up. Krat did not know all of the facts, but it had something to do with the Earthlings' sun. Since then, the Pila had hated humans passionately.

Krat's mating claw throbbed as she thought of Earthlings. In just a few generations, they had become almost as great a nuisance as the sanctimonious Kanten, or the devil-trickster Tymbrimi! The Soro patiently awaited an opportunity to erase the blot on their clan honor. Fortunately, humans were pathetically ignorant and vulnerable. Perhaps the chance had already come!

How delicious it would be to have Homo sapiens assigned to the Soro as indentured foster clients. It could happen! Then what changes could be made! How humans might be molded!

Krat looked at her crew and wished she were free to meddle, alter, shape at will even these adult species. So much could be done with them! But that would require changing the rules.

323

If the upstart-water-mammals from Earth had discovered what she thought they had, then the rules might *be changed … if the Progenitors had, indeed, come back from the mists of time. How ironic that the newest spacefaring race should discover this derelict fleet! She almost forgave dolphins for existing, for giving those humans the status of patrons.*

'Mistress!' a tall Gello announced. 'The Jophur-Thennanin alliance has broken up, fighting among themselves. This means they are no longer pre-eminent!'

'Maintain vigilance.' Krat sighed. *The Gello shouldn't make too much out of one little act of treachery. Alliances would form and dissolve until one emerged supreme. She intended that that force be Soro.*

The dolphins must *be here! When she won this battle, she would pry the handless ones out from their underwater sanctuary and make them tell all!*

With a languid wave of her left paw, she summoned the Pil Librarian from its niche.

'Look into the data on these water creatures we pursue,' she told it. 'I want to know more about their habits, what they like and dislike. It is said their bonds to their human patrons are weak and corruptible. Give me a lever to pervert these … dolphins.'

Cubber-cabub bowed and withdrew into the Library section, with the rayed spiral glyph above its opening.

Krat felt destiny all around her. *This place in space was a fulcrum of power. She didn't need instruments to tell her that.*

'I will have them! The rules will be changed!'

13

TOSHIO

Toshio found Ssattatta by the bole of the giant drill-tree. The fin had been thrown against the monstrous plant and crushed. Her harness was a jumble of broken pieces.

Toshio stumbled through the ruined undergrowth, whistling a Trinary call when he felt able. Mostly he tried very hard to stay on his feet. He hadn't walked much since leaving Earth. Bruises and nausea didn't help much.

He found K'Hith lying on a soft bed of grass-like growth. His harness was intact, but the dolphin planetologist had already bled to death from three deep gashes in his belly. Toshio made a mental note of the spot and moved on.

Closer to the shore he found Satima. The little female was bleeding and hysterical, but alive. Toshio bound her wounds with fleshfoam and repair tape. Then he took the manipulator arms of her harness and used a large rock to pound them into the loam. It was the best he could do to bind her to the ground before the fifth wave hit.

It was more a flooding than a wave. Toshio clung to a tree as it flowed past, tugging at him and rising almost to his neck.

As soon as the wave began to recede, he let go and floundered over to Satima. He groped until he found the catch on her harness, then released her to float in the growing backtow. He pushed hard to join the flood and keep from being left behind.

He was struggling to shove her around a clump of shrubs, against the growing pull of the backwash, when a swift motion in a tree overhead caught his eye. The movement didn't fit into the overall pattern of swaying subsidence. He looked up, and met the gaze of a pair of small, black eyes.

There was little time for more than a startled double take before the tide pulled him and Satima straight through the obstruction and into a small, recently made marsh. Toshio was suddenly too busy to look anywhere but straight ahead.

He had to pull Satima down the last few yards of slippery sea-plant, taking care not to reopen her wounds. In the last few minutes it had seemed she was more lucid. Her Delphin squeakings were starting to take on form and sound like Trinary words.

A whistle brought Toshio's head up. Keepiru was only forty meters offshore, driving the sled toward him. The fin had on a breather, but he could still signal.

'Satima!' Toshio shouted to the wounded dolphin. 'Go to the sled! Go to Keepiru!'

'Lash her to an airdome!' he called to Keepiru. 'And keep your eye on that sonar screen! Get back out there when you see a wave coming!'

Keepiru tossed his head. As soon as Satima was a hundred feet out he used the sled to herd her toward deeper water.

Five accounted for. That left Hist-t and Hikahi.

Toshio climbed back up the sea-plant and stumbled into the undergrowth once again. The territory of his mind seemed as torn up and desolated as the island he trod upon. He had seen too many corpses for one day – too many dead friends.

He realized now that he had been unfair to the fins all along.

It had been unjust to blame them for teasing him. They couldn't help the way they were built. All of man's genetic meddling notwithstanding, dolphins had been dealing with humanity on a level of good-natured derision since the first person paddled a log canoe out to sea. That pathetic image had been enough to set a pattern that uplift could only alter, not eliminate.

And why eliminate it? Toshio now saw that those humans he had known on Calafia, who worked best with dolphins, had had a special type of personality, generally featuring a mixture of a thick skin, firmness, and a willing sense of humor. No one worked for long with fins who hadn't earned their respect.

He hurried over to a gray form that lay in the underbrush. But no. It was Ssattatta again. She had been moved by the last wave. Toshio stumbled on.

Dolphins were quite well aware of what Mankind had done for them. Uplift was a painful process. But none of them would go back to the Whale Dream if they could help it.

The fins knew, as well, that the loose codes that ruled behavior among the Galactic races, rules established in the *Library* for aeons, would have let humanity demand a hundred thousand years of servitude from its clients. Men had collectively shuddered at the thought. *Homo sapiens* was barely that age. If Mankind *did* have a patron out there – one strong enough to lay claim to the title – that species wasn't going to pick up *Tursiops amicus* as an added bonus.

There wasn't a fin alive who wasn't aware of Earth's attitude. There were dolphins on the Terragens Council, as well as chimpanzees.

Toshio knew at last how he had hurt Keepiru with his words, during their struggle at sea. Most of all he regretted the remark about Calafia. Keepiru would willingly die a thousand times to save the humans of Toshio's homeworld. Toshio's tongue would fall off before he said such things again. Ever.

He staggered into a clearing. There, in a shallow pool, lay a *Tursiops* dolphin.

'Hikahi!'

She was scratched and battered. Bloody trails lay along her sides. But she was awake. And as Toshio started forward she called out.

'Stay there, Sharp-Eyes! Don't-t move! We have company here!'

Toshio stopped in his tracks. Hikahi's command was specific. Yet the need to go to her was urgent. The dolphin's scratches looked dangerous. If there were slivers of metal lodged under the skin they had to be removed soon, before blood poisoning set in. And it wasn't going to be easy getting Hikahi out to sea.

'Hikahi, there'll be another wave soon. It may reach this high. We've got to be ready for it!'

'Stay, Toshio. The wave will not reach here. Besides, look around. See how much more important this isss!'

For the first time, Toshio noticed the clearing. The pool was set near one side, with scratch marks all around, indicating that it had been recently dug. Then he saw that the manipulator arms from Hikahi's harness were missing.

Then who ...? Toshio's perception shifted. He saw twisted debris at the far end of the clearing, scattered through the undergrowth, and recognized the fragments of a ruined, shattered village.

In the chronic shimmering of a Kithrupan forest he saw the fragments of rude, torn, crudely-woven nets, scattered pieces of wrecked thatching, and bits of sharp metal crudely bound to wooden staves.

In the tree branches he saw fleet movements. Then, one by one, small, splayed, web-fingered hands appeared – followed by slowly peeking, shining black eyes that peered back at him from under low, greenish brows.

'Abos!' he whispered. 'I saw one earlier, then forgot. They look pre-sentient!'

'Yesss,' Hikahi sighed. 'And this makes secrecy more vital than ever. Quickly, Sharp-Eyes! Tell me what has happened!'

Toshio related only what he had done since the first wave struck, leaving out only his battle with Keepiru. It was hard to concentrate, with eyes in the trees staring down at him, then skittishly darting under cover whenever he glanced their way. He barely finished his story as the last wave arrived.

Breakers could be seen driving up the sloping shore with a white foaming. But Hikahi was right. The water wouldn't rise this high.

'Toshio!' Hikahi whistled. 'You've done very well. You may have saved these little people, as well as ourselves. Brookida will succeed. He will bring help.

'So saving me is not that important. You *must* do as I say! Have Keepiru dive at once! He must stay out of sight and remain quiet as possible as he searches for bodies and debris. You must bury Ssattatta and K'Hith and gather the fragments of their harnesses. When help comes we must be able to move quickly!'

'Are you sure you'll be all right? Your wound ...'

'I'll be fine! My friends keep me wet-t. The trees overhang to keep me hidden. Watch the skies, Sharp-Eyes! Don't be seen! When you're finished I hope to have coaxed our little hosts into trusting you.'

She sounded tired. Toshio was torn. Finally, he sighed and turned back to the forest. He forced himself to run through the broken foliage, following the receding waters to the shore.

Keepiru was just emerging as he arrived. The fin had removed his breather and wore an airdome instead. He reported finding the body of Phip-pit, the dolphin supposed lost earlier to the killer weed. The sucker-bruised body must have been torn loose during the tsunami.

'Any sign of Hist-t?' Toshio called.

Keepiru answered negative. Toshio passed on Hikahi's command and watched as the sled sank below again.

For a moment he stood there looking out over the west. Kithrup's reddish sun was setting. A few stars poked rays through scattered clouds, which were beginning to look ominous. Toshio decided against taking off his drysuit, though he compromised by pulling the rubberized headpiece off. The breeze was chilling, but a huge relief.

If the battle in space continued, Toshio saw no sign of it. Kithrup's rotation had taken the shining globe of plasma and debris out of sight.

Toshio lacked the will to shake his fist, but he grimaced toward the southern sky, hoping the Galactics had wiped each other out.

It wasn't likely. There would be victors. And someday soon they would be down here looking for dolphins and men.

Toshio pulled his shoulders back, in spite of his fatigue, and walked with deliberateness toward the forest, and the protecting, overhanging trees.

They found the young man and the dolphin shortly after landing. The two were huddled together under a crude shelter which dripped warm rain in long rivulets. Lightning flashes drowned out the muffled yellow light from lamps the rescuers brought. In the first flash, Thomas Orley thought he saw a half-dozen small squat figures clustered around the Earthling and the Calafian. But by the time he and his partner had shoved through the undergrowth for a better view, the animals – or whatever they were – were gone.

His first fear that they had been carrion-eaters disappeared when he saw Toshio move. Still, he kept his right hand on the butt of his needler and held up the lantern to let Hannes Suessi pass underneath. Orley looked carefully around the clearing, taking in the smells and sounds of the living surface of the metal-mound, memorizing details.

'Are they all right?' he asked after a few seconds.

'Shh, 't's okay, Toshio. It's just me, Hannes,' he heard the engineer mutter. The fellow sounded downright maternal. 'Yes, Mr Orley.' Suessi called back, 'They're both awake, but not in much shape for talking.'

Thomas Orley took in the clearing once more, then moved over to set the lamp beside Suessi. 'This lightning would cover anything,' he said. 'I'm going to call up the mechanicals to get these two out of here, quick as possible.' He touched a button on the rim of his faceplate and whistled quickly in perfect Trinary. The message lasted six seconds. It was said that Thomas Orley could actually speak Primal Delphin, though no human had ever witnessed it.

'They'll be here in a few minutes.' He squatted next to Toshio, who was sitting up now that Suessi had moved over to Hikahi.

'Hello, Mr Orley,' the boy said. 'I'm sorry we dragged you away from your work.'

'That's all right, son. I've been wanting to have a look around up here, anyway. This gave the captain a good excuse to send me. After we get you started toward the ship, Hannes and Tsh't and I will go on to look over that ship that crashed.

'Now, do you think you can lead us to Ssattatta and K'Hith? We want to comb this island clean before the storm passes.'

Toshio nodded. 'Yes, sir. I should be able to stumble around that long. I don't suppose anyone's found Hist-t?'

'No. We're worried about that, but nowhere near as worried as when Brookida came back alone. Keepiru's told us most of the story. That fin thinks rather highly of you, you know. You did quite a job here.'

Toshio turned away, as if ashamed to receive the praise.

Orley looked at him curiously. He had never given much thought to the middie. During the first part of the voyage, the youth had seemed bright, but a bit irresponsible. Later, after they found the derelict fleet, he had turned morose, as their chances of ever going home diminished.

Now there was this new note. It was too soon to tell the long-term effects, but this had clearly been a rite of passage for Toshio.

Humming sounds drifted up from the beach. Soon two spider-like mechanicals strode into view, a hammocked and harnessed dolphin piloting each one.

Toshio sighed a little raggedly as Orley helped him stand. Then the older man stooped to pick up an object from the ground. He hefted it in his left hand.

'A scraper, isn't it? Made from bits of metal fish spine glued to a wood handle . . .'

'I guess so.'

'Do they have much of a language yet?'

'No, sir; well, the rudiments. They seem to be stabilized. Strict hunter-gatherers. Hikahi guesses they've been stuck for half a million years.'

Orley nodded. This native species looked ripe, at first glance. A pre-sentient race at just the right stage for uplift. It was a miracle some Galactic patron line hadn't snapped them up already, for client status and an aeon of servitude.

Now the men and fen of *Streaker* had yet another obligation, and secrecy was more important than ever.

He put the artifact in his pocket, then laid his hand on Toshio's shoulder.

'Well, you can tell us all about it back on the ship, son. In the meantime, you have some pondering to do.'

'Sir?' Toshio looked up in confusion.

'Well, it isn't everybody who gets to name a future space-faring race. You know, the fen will be expecting you to make up a song about it.'

Toshio looked at the older man, uncertain if he was joking. But Thomas Orley had on his usual enigmatic expression.

Orley glanced up at the rain clouds. As the mechanicals moved in to claim Hikahi, he stepped back and smiled at the curtain which, temporarily, hung across the theater of the sky.

PART TWO

CURRENTS

'For the sky and the sea,
And the sea and the sky,
Lay like a load on my weary eye,
And the dead lay at my feet.'

S. T. COLERIDGE

14

DENNIE

Charles Dart pulled away from the polarization microscope and growled an oath. In a habit he had spent half his life trying to break, he absently laid his forearms over his head and tugged on his hairy ears. It was a simian contortion no one else aboard ship could easily duplicate. Had he noticed he was doing it, he would have quit instantly.

Of a crew of one hundred and fifty, only eight aboard the *Streaker* even *had* arms ... or external ears. One of these shared the drylab with him.

Commenting on Charles Dart's body behaviors did not occur to Dennie Sudman. She had long ceased to notice such things as his loose, rolling gait, his shrieking chimpanzee laughter, or the sparse fur that nearly covered his body.

'What is it?' she asked. 'Are you still having trouble with those core samples?'

Dart nodded absently, staring at the screen. 'Yeah.'

His voice was low and scratchy. At his best, Charles Dart sounded like a man speaking with gravel in his throat. Sometimes, when he had something complicated to say, he unconsciously moved his hands in the sign language of his youth.

'I can't make any sense out of these isotope concentrations,' he growled. 'And there are minerals in all the wrong places ... siderophiles without metals, intricate crystals at a depth where there shouldn't be such complexity ... Captain Creideiki's silly restrictions are crippling my work! I wish he'd let me do some seismic scans and deep radar.' He swiveled about in his seat to look at Dennie earnestly, as if hoping she would concur.

Dennie's smile was broad under high cheekbones. Her almond eyes narrowed in amusement.

'Sure, Charlie. Why not? Here we are in a crippled ship, hidden under an ocean on a deadly world, with fleets from a dozen arrogant and powerful patron-lines fighting over the right to capture us, and you want to start setting off explosions and casting gravity beams around. Wonderful idea!

'Say! I've got an even better one! Why don't we just take out a large sign and wave it at the sky, something that says "Yoohoo, beasties! Come and eat us!" Hmmm?'

Charlie cast a sidelong look at her, one of his rare, unhinged, lop-sided grins. 'Oh, they wouldn't have to be *big* gravity scans. And I'd only need a few teeny, tiny explosions for seismography. The ETs wouldn't notice those, you think?'

Dennie laughed. What Charlie wanted was to make the planet ring like a bell, so he could trace the patterns of seismic waves in the interior. Teeny tiny explosions, indeed! More likely detonations in the kiloton range! Sometimes Charlie seemed so single-minded a planetologist that it bothered Dennie. This time, however, he was obviously having some fun at his own expense.

He laughed as well, letting out brief whoops that echoed off the stark, white walls of the dry lab. He thumped the table beside him.

Grinning, Dennie filled a zip case with papers. 'You know, Charlie, there are volcanoes going off all the time, a few degrees away from here. If you're lucky, one might start right near us.'

Charlie looked hopeful. 'Gee, you think so?'

'Sure. And if the ETs start bombing the planet to get at us, you'll have plenty of data from all the near misses. That is, if they don't bomb so hard as to make geophysical analyses of Kithrup moot. I envy you your potential silver lining. In the meantime, I intend to forget about my own frustrating research, and go get some lunch. Coming?'

'Naw. Thanks, though. I brought my own. I think I'll stay and work for a while.'

'Suit yourself. Still, you might try to see more of the ship, other than your quarters and this lab.'

'I talk to Metz and Brookida all the time on screen. I don't need to wander around gawking at this Rube Goldberg contraption that can't even fly any more.'

'And besides ...' she prompted.

Charlie grinned. 'And besides, I hate getting wet. I *still* think you humans should have worked on dogs second, after casting your spells on us *Pan* types. Dolphins are all right – some of my best friends are fins. But they were a funny bunch to try to make into a space-traveling race!'

He shook his head with an expression of sad wisdom. Obviously he thought the whole uplift process on Earth would have been better handled had his people been in charge.

'Well, they're superb space pilots, for one thing,' Dennie suggested. 'Look at how hot a star-jockey Keepiru is.'

'Yeah, and look at what a jerk-off that fin can be when he's *not* piloting. Honestly, Dennie, this trip has made me wonder if fins are really ready for spaceflight. Have you seen how some of 'em have been acting since we got into trouble? All the pressure is making some of 'em unravel, especially some of Metz's big *Stenos*.'

'You're not being charitable,' Dennie chided. 'Nobody ever expected this mission to be so stressful. I think most of the fen are doing marvelously. Look at how Creideiki slipped us away from that trap at Morgran.'

Charlie shook his head. 'I dunno. I still wish there were more men and chimps aboard.'

One century, that's how much longer than dolphins chimps had been a recognized space-faring species. Dennie figured a million years from now they would still hold a patronizing attitude over that lead.

'Well, if you're not coming, I'm off.' Dennie took her notecase and touched the palm-plate by the door. 'See you, Charlie.'

The chimp called after her, before the door hissed shut.

'By the way! If you run into Tkaat or Sah'ot, have 'em call me, eh? I'm thinking these subduction anomalies may be paleotechnic! An archaeologist may be interested!'

Dennie let the door close without answering. If she didn't acknowledge Charlie's request, she could feign ignorance later. There was no way she would go out of her way to speak to Sah'ot, whatever the significance of Charlie's find!

Avoiding that particular dolphin was already taking up too much of her time.

The dry sections of the starship *Streaker* were extensive, though they served only eight members of the crew. The one hundred and thirty dolphins – down by thirty-two since they had left Earth – could only visit the dry-wheel by riding a mechanical walker or 'spider.'

There were some rooms that should not be flooded with hyper-oxygenated water, nor be left to the gravity fluctuations of the central shaft when the ship was in space. There were stores that had to be kept free of moisture and machine shops that performed hot processing under gravity. And there were the living quarters for humans and chimp.

Dennie stopped at an intersection. She looked down the hallway and thought about knocking on the door two cabins down. If Tom Orley were in, this could be the time to ask his advice about a problem that was daily growing more irksome, how to handle Sah'ot's unusual . . . 'attentions.'

There were few people better qualified to advise her on non-human behavior. Orley's official title was Alien Technologies Consultant, but clearly he was also here as a psychologist, to help Dr Metz and Dr Baskin evaluate the performance of an integrated dolphin crew. He knew cetaceans, and might be able to tell her what Sah'ot wanted from her.

Dennie's habitual indecision reasserted itself. There were plenty of reasons not to bother Tom right now, like the fact that he was spending every waking moment trying to find a way to save all of their lives. The same could be said of most of the crew, but experience and reputation suggested that Orley just might come up with a way.

Dennie sighed. Another reason to put it off was pure embarrassment. It wasn't easy for a young fem to ask personal advice of a mel as worldly as Orley. Particularly when the subject was how to cope with advances by an amorous porpoise. However kind Tom's intentions, he would be forced to laugh – or obviously bite back laughter. The situation, Dennie admitted, would *have* to seem funny, to anyone but the object of the seduction.

Dennie quickened her pace up the gently curved corridor toward the lift. *Why did I ever go into space, anyway? Sure, it was a chance to advance my career. And my personal life was a shambles on Earth. But now where am I? My analysis of Kithrupan biology is getting nowhere. There are thousands of bug-eyed monsters circling over the planet slathering to come down and get me, and a horny dolphin's harassing me with suggestions that would make Catherine the Great blush.*

It wasn't fair, of course, but when had life ever been fair?

Streaker had been built from a modified Snarkhunter-class exploration vessel. Few Snarks were still in service. As Terrans became more comfortable with the refined technologies of the *Library,* they learned to combine the old and new – ancient Galactic designs and indigenous Terran technologies. This process had been in a particularly awkward phase when the Snarks were built.

The ship was a bulb-ended cylinder with jutting, crane-like reality flanges in five bands of five along her hull. In space the flanges anchored her to a protecting sphere of stasis. Now they served as landing legs as the wounded *Streaker* lay on her side in a muddy canyon, eighty meters below the surface of an alien sea.

Between the third and fourth rings of flanges, the hull bulged outward slightly for the dry-wheel. In free space the wheel rotated, providing a primitive form of artificial gravity. Humans and their clients had by now learned how to generate gravity fields, but almost every Earth ship still possessed a centrifugal wheel. Some saw it as a trademark, advertising what some friendly species had recommended Terrans keep quiet, that the three races of Sol were different from any others in space ... the 'orphans' of Earth.

Streaker's wheel held room for up to forty humans, though right now there were only seven and one chimpanzee. It also held recreation facilities for the dolphin crew, pools for leaping and splashing and sexual play during off-duty hours.

But on a planet's surface the wheel could not turn. Most of its rooms were tilted and inaccessible. And the great central bay of the ship was filled with water.

Dennie rode a lift up one of the spokes connecting the dry-wheel to the ship's rigid spine. The spine supported *Streaker*'s open interior. Dennie stepped from the elevator into a hexagonal hallway with doors and access panels at all angles, until she reached the main bay lock, fifty meters forward of the wheel spokes.

In weightlessness she would have glided rather than walked down the long passage. Gravity made the corridor seem eerily unfamiliar.

In the bay-lock, a wall of transparent cabinets held spacesuits and diving gear. Dennie chose a bikini from her locker, and a facemask and flippers. Under 'normal' circumstances she would have donned coveralls, a small jet belt, and possibly a pair of broad armwings. She could have leapt into the central bay and flown the humid air to any place she wanted, providing she was careful of the rotating spokes of the dry-wheel.

Now, of course, the spokes were still, and the central bay contained something more humid than air.

She quickly stripped and stepped into the swimsuit. Then she stopped in front of a mirror and tugged at the strings until the bikini was comfortable. Dennie knew she was attractively built. At least the mels she knew had told her so. Still, slightly broad shoulders gave her an excuse for the self-reproach she always seemed to be looking for.

She tested the mirror with a smile. The image was instantly transformed. Strong white teeth brilliantly balanced her dark brown eyes.

She let it lapse. Dimples made her look younger, an effect to be avoided at all cost. She sighed and carefully pushed her jet black hair into a rubber diving cap.

Well, let's get this over with.

She checked the seals on her notecase and entered the lock. When she closed the inner hatch, fizzing saline water began flooding into the chamber from vents around the floor.

Dennie avoided looking down. She fumbled with her Batteau breather mask, making it snug over her face. The transparent membrane felt tough, but it passed air in and out freely as she took rapid, deep breaths. Numerous flexible plates around its rim would help pull enough air from supercharged oxywater. At the corners of her vision, the mask was equipped with small sonar displays, which were supposed to help make up for a human's substantial deafness underwater.

Warm bubbling wetness climbed her legs. Dennie readjusted her

337

facemask several times. Her elbow pressed the notecase close against her side. When the fluid had almost reached her shoulders, she immersed her head and breathed hard with her eyes closed.

The mask worked. Of course, it always did. It felt like inhaling a thick ocean mist, but there was enough air. A bit sheepish over her fearful little ritual, she stood up straight and waited for the water to rise over her head.

At last the door opened, and Dennie swam out into a large chamber where spiders, 'walkers,' and other dolphin gear lay neatly folded in recesses. Tucked into orderly shelves were racks of the small water-jetpacks that the dolphins used to move about in the ship in weightlessness. The jets made amazing acrobatics possible in free fall, but on a planet, with most of the ship flooded, they were useless.

Usually one or two fen were in this outer dressing room, wriggling into or out of equipment. Puzzled by the emptiness, Dennie swam to the opening at the far end of the chamber and looked into the central bay.

The great cylinder was only twenty meters across. The vista wasn't as impressive as the view from the hub of one of the space cities of Sol's asteroid belts. Still, whenever she entered the central bay, her first impression was one of vast and busy space. Long radial shafts stretched out from spine to cylinder wall, holding the ship rigid and carrying power to the stasis flanges. Between these columns were dolphin work areas, arrayed on supports of resilient mesh.

Dolphins, even the *Tursiops amicus*, didn't like being cooped up any more than they had to be. In space, the crew worked in the weightless openness of the central bay, jetting about in humid air. But Creideiki had to land his damaged ship in an ocean. And this meant he had also had to flood the ship in order to enable his workers to reach their instruments.

The bay shimmered with a barely suppressed effervescence. Here and there tiny streams of bubbles rose toward the curving ceiling. The waters of Kithrup were carefully filtered, solvents added, and oxygen forced in to make oxywater. Neo-dolphins had been gene-crafted to be able to breathe it, though they didn't enjoy it much.

Dennie looked around, puzzled. Where was everyone?

Motion caught her eye. Above the five-meter span of the central spine, two dolphins and two humans swam rapidly toward the ship's bow. 'Hey!' she shouted. 'Wait for me!'

The facemask was supposed to focus and amplify her voice, but to Dennie it sounded as if the water swallowed her words.

The fen stopped at once. In unison they swooped about toward her. The two humans swam on for a few moments, then paused and looked about, moving their arms slowly. When they caught sight of Dennie, one of them waved.

'Hurry up, honored biologissst!' A large, charcoal-gray dolphin in heavy work harness swooped past Dennie. The other one circled about impatiently.

Dennie swam as hard as she could. 'What's going on? Is the space battle over? Has someone found us?'

A stocky black man grinned as she approached. The other human, a tall, stately, blonde woman, impatiently turned to go as soon as Dennie had caught up.

'Now, wouldn't we have heard alarms, then, if there'd been ETs comin'?' The black man kidded her as they swam above the spine. Why Emerson D'Anite, with his dark coloration, chose at times to affect a burr was a secret which Dennie had yet to pry out of him.

She was relieved to hear they weren't under attack, but if the Galactics weren't coming to get them yet, what was all the fuss?

'The prospecting party!' The fate of the lost patrol had completely slipped her mind, so caught up had she been in her own problems. 'Gillian, have they come back? Have Toshio and Hikahi returned?'

The older woman swam with a reaching, long-limbed grace that Dennie envied. Her low, alto voice somehow carried well through the water. Her expression was grim.

'Yes Dennie, they're back. But at least four of them are dead.'

Dennie gasped. She had to make an effort to keep up. 'Dead? How ... ? Who ... ?'

Gillian Baskin didn't slacken her pace. She answered over her shoulder. 'We aren't sure how. ... When Brookida made it back, he mentioned Phip-pit and Ssassia ... and told the rescue party they'd probably find others beached or killed.'

'Brookida ... ?'

Emerson jogged her with his elbow. 'And where have *you* been? It was announced when he got in, hours ago. Mr Orley took old Hannes and twenty crewfen to find Hikahi and the others.'

'I ... I must have been asleep at the time.' Dennie contemplated slowly taking apart a certain chimpanzee. Why didn't Charlie tell me when I came in for work? It probably slipped his mind entirely. One of these days that chimp's monomania will cause somebody to strangle him!

Dr Baskin had already pulled ahead with the two dolphins. She was almost as fast a swimmer as Tom Orley, and none of the other five humans aboard could keep up when she hurried. Dennie turned to D'Anite. 'Tell me about it!'

Emerson quickly summarized the story Brookida had told – of a killer weed, of a burning, falling star cruiser, and of the savage

339

waves that followed its crash, setting off a desperate cycle of rescue fever.

Dennie was stunned by the tale, especially young Toshio's role. That didn't sound like Toshio Iwashika at all. He had been the one person aboard *Streaker* who seemed younger and lonelier than she. She liked the middie, of course, and hoped he hadn't lost his life trying to be a hero.

Emerson then told her the most recent rumors – about an island rescue during a midnight storm, and aboriginal tool users. This time Dennie stopped in midstroke. '*Abos?* You're sure? Native pre-sentients?' She tread water, staring at the black engineer.

They were now only ten meters from a great open hatch at the bow end of the central bay. Through it came a cacophony of high squeakings and chitterings.

Emerson shrugged. The action shook a coating of bubbles from his shoulders and the rim-plates of his facemask. 'Dennie, why don't we go in and find out? They must be through decontamination by now.'

From ahead there came a sudden, high-pitched whine of engines; then three white power sleds sped from the outlock hatch, single-file. They veered, one by one, around Dennie and D'Anite before either of them could move, leaving fizzing trails of supercritical bubbles in their wakes.

Strapped to the back of each, under a plastic shell, was an injured dolphin. Two of them had dreadful gashes in their flanks, crudely bandaged. Dennie blinked in surprise when she saw that one of them was Hikahi, *Streaker*'s third officer.

The ambulance sleds banked under the central spine and headed for an opening in the inner wall of the great cylinder. On the last sled, clutching a handrail, the dusky blonde who had accompanied them here allowed herself to be dragged along. With her free hand she pressed a diagnostic monitor to the flank of one of the wounded dolphins.

'No wonder Gillian was in such a hurry. It was stupid of me to slow her down.'

'Oh, don't worry about it,' Emerson held her arm. 'The injuries didn't look like the kind you'd need a human surgeon for. Makanee and the autodocs can handle almost anything, you know.'

'Still, there may be biochemical damage ... poisons ... I might be of use.'

She turned to go, but the engineer's hand held her.

'You'll be called if it's anything Makanee or feMister Baskin can't handle. And I don't think you'll want to miss out on news that bears on your specialty.'

Dennie looked after the ambulances, then nodded. Emerson was right. If she was needed, an intercom call would reach her anywhere, and a sled would arrive to fetch her faster than she could swim. They headed toward the buzzing of excited cetaceans in the outlook bay, and entered the forward chamber amid a swirl of swooping gray forms and a ferment of flying bubbles.

The forward outlook at *Streaker*'s bow was the ship's main link with the outside. The cylindrical wall was covered by storage cells, holding spiders, sleds, and other gear for crew who might leave the ship on errands. The bow had three great airlocks.

Port and starboard, the spacious chamber was taken up by the skiff and the longboat. The nose of each small spaceship almost touched the iris that would let it outside, into vacuum, air, or water, as needed.

The stern of the skiff stopped short of the rear bulkhead of the twenty-meter outlook, but the aft end of the larger longboat disappeared into a sleeve that extended into the maze of rooms and passages in *Streaker*'s thick cylindrical shell.

Overhead, a third berthing port lay empty. The captain's gig had been lost to a strange accident weeks before, along with ten crew members, at the region Creideiki had named the Shallow Cluster. Its loss, in the course, of investigating the derelict fleet, was a topic seldom brought up in conversation.

Dennie gripped D'Anite's arm as another sled passed by, more slowly than the white ambulances of sick bay. Sealed green bags were tied to its back. A bottle-like narrowness at one end of each, and a flat flaring at the other, revealed their contents.

There's no smaller bag, Dennie thought. Does that mean Toshio's alive then? Then she saw, by the decontamination lock, a young dry-suited human in a crowd of dolphins.

'There's Toshio!' she cried, a little surprised at the intensity of her relief. She forced herself to speak in a calm tone. 'Is that Keepiru next to him?' She pointed.

D'Anite nodded. 'Yeah. They seem all right. By my count I guess that means Hist't hitched a sky-current. That's a rotten shame. We got along.' Emerson's affected burr was completely gone as he mourned the loss of a friend.

He peered through the crowd. 'Can you think of an official enough reason for us to shove in there? Most of the fen would get out of our way out of habit. But Creideiki's something else. He'll chew our asses off, patrons or no, if he thinks we're hanging around useless, getting in the way.'

Dennie had been thinking about just that. 'Leave it to me.' She led him into the jostling crowd, touching flipper and fluke to pry a passage through the press. Most of the fen moved aside on catching a glimpse of the two humans.

Dennie looked about the squeaking, clicking mob. Shouldn't Tom Orley be here? He and Hannes and Tsh't were in on the rescue. I've *got* to talk to him sometime soon!

Toshio looked like a very tired young man. Just out of decon, he slowly peeled off his drysuit while speaking with Creideiki. Soon he floated naked but for a facemask. Dabs of synthetic skin coated his hands and throat and face. Keepiru drifted nearby. The exhausted dolphin wore a breather, probably under physician's orders.

Suddenly the spectators blocking Dennie's view began to spin about and dart away in all directions.

> *.. bands of idle gawkers—
>   cease their vain eavesdropping!
> * Lest the nets of Iki find them—
>   for their lack of work and purpose!*

The sudden cetacean dispersal buffeted Dennie and Emerson; in moments the crowd had thinned.

Creideiki's voice pursued the fleeing spacers. 'All is done here. Think clear thoughts and do your jobs!'

A dozen fen remained, outlock personnel and the captain's aides. Creideiki turned to Toshio. 'Go on then, little shark-biter, finish your story.'

The boy blushed, nonplussed by the honorific. He forced his heavy eyelids open and tried to maintain a semblance of standard posture in the drifting current.

'Uh, that's about it, sir. I've told you everything Mr Orley and Tsh't told me about their plans. If the ET wreck looks usable, they'll send a sled back for help. If not, they'll return with whatever they've salvaged as quickly as possible.'

Creideiki made small, slow circles with his lower jaw. 'A hazardousss gamble,' he commented. 'They'll not reach the hulk for a day, at least. More days, still, will pass without contact . . .'

Bubbles rose from his blowmouth.

'Very well, then. You shall rest, then join me for supper. I'm afraid your reward for saving Hikahi, and possibly all our lives, shall be an interrogation worse than you'd receive from our enemies.'

Toshio smiled tiredly.

'I understand, sir. I'll happily let you wring me of info so long as I can eat first . . . and get *dry* for a while!'

'Done. Until then!' The captain nodded and turned to go.

Dennie was about to shout to Creideiki when someone else called out first.

'Captain, please! May I have a word?'

The voice was musical, the speaker a large male dolphin with the mottled gray coloration of a *Stenos* sub-breed. He wore civilian harness, without the bulky racks or heavy manipulator arms carried by the regular crew. Dennie cringed behind Emerson D'Anite. She hadn't noticed Sah'ot in the crowd until he spoke.

'Before you go, sir,' the dolphin fluted, quite casual. 'I must asssk leave to visit that island where Hikahi was stranded.'

With a tail-flick Creideiki arched bottom side up to regard the speaker, skeptically. 'Talker-to-races, this is not a fishbrew bar, this island, where poetry can buy back an error. Why venture now courage you never before displayed?'

Despite her dislike of the civilian specialist, Dennie felt sympathy. Sah'ot's behavior at the derelict fleet, refusing to go with the doomed survey party, had not been admirable. But he had been proven right. The captain's gig and ten crew had been lost, along with *Streaker*'s former second in command.

All the sacrifice had gained them was a three-meter-long tube of some strange metal, thoroughly pitted by ages of micrometeorite impacts, recovered personally by Tom Orley. Gillian Baskin had taken over the sealed relic, and to Dennie's knowledge nobody else had seen it since. It hardly seemed worth the loss they had suffered.

'Captain,' Sah'ot answered, 'Thomas Orley has gone on to investigate the wrecked warship, but the island still concerns us.'

No fair! Dennie had been ready to do this! It was to be an act of professionalism – of *assertion,* to speak out and demand. ...

'Honestly, Captain,' Sah'ot went on, 'after our duty to escape this trap, and serve the clan of Earth species, what urgent responsibility has fallen upon uss?'

Creideiki obviously wanted to chew Sah'ot's dorsal fin for baiting him like this. Also, obviously, Sah'ot had hit him with a double harpoon ... lacing the word 'duty' into a riddle. The captain thrashed his tail, giving out a low series of broad-band sonar clicks, like a watch ticking. His eyes were recessed and dark.

Dennie couldn't wait for the captain to figure the puzzle, or slap Sah'ot into a cell.

'The abos!' she shouted.

Creideiki turned. Dennie blushed as she felt his field of analytic sound sweep over her. She knew the waves penetrated her very viscera, revealing everything down to her breakfast. Creideiki frightened

343

her. She felt far from being patron to the powerful, involute mind behind that broad forehead.

The captain whirled back to Toshio. 'You still have those artifactsss that selected, young hunter?'

'Yes, sir, I ...'

'You will please lend them to Biologist Sudman and Race Speaker Sah'ot before you retire. When you've rested, collect them again, along with the specialists' recommendations. I will examine them myself during supper.'

Toshio nodded. The captain flipped to face Dennie.

'Before I give permission, you must have a plan. You'll get little material assistance, and will be recalled at any sign of danger. Can you accept these conditions?'

'Y-yes ... we'll need a monofilament cable to the ship, for a computer link, and ...'

'Talk this over with Keepiru, before he rests. He must help you come up with something militarily acceptable.'

'Keepiru? But I thought ...' Dennie looked at the younger dolphin, and quickly bit back the tactlessness she had been about to utter. Silently wearing his breather, the pilot seemed unhappier than ever.

'I have my reasons, femsir. As a pilot, he is of little use while we are immobile. I can spare him from work here, to be your field liaison ... *if* I agree to your plan.'

The captain's attention made Keepiru hunch slightly and look away. Toshio put a hand on Keepiru's sleek back. That, too, was a change. The two had never struck Dennie as fast friends before.

Creideiki's teeth shone in the bright lights of the bay. 'Is there more comment-t?'

Everyone was silent.

Creideiki thrashed his tail, then whistled the phrase of command termination. He arched and sped away with rapid, powerful strokes. His aides followed in his wake.

Keepiru watched until his captain passed out of sight. Then he addressed Dennie and Sah'ot.

> * At your service, you will find me—
>   In my quarters, floating, breathing—
> * After seeing Toshio resting ... *

Toshio smiled when Dennie gave him a brief hug. Then he turned to swim away, arm over Keepiru's back, keeping to the fin's slow pace.

Just then one of the intrahull lift tubes opened, and a blue and yellow shape bulleted out of the tube. A joyful racket filled the chamber as the ship's other midshipman speared past Keepiru and the boy, then zoomed around them in ever-tightening circles, chattering excitedly.

'Do you think Toshio's going to get any sleep?' Emerson asked.

'Not if Akki makes him tell the entire story before supper with the captain.' Dennie envied Akki and Toshio their fellowship, as constant and intense as any star. She watched the boy laughing as he fended off his friend until they disappeared into the tube.

'Well, sister,' Emerson D'Anite grinned at Dennie. 'It appears you have a science command. My congratulations.'

'Nothing's decided yet,' she answered. 'Besides, Keepiru will be in charge.'

'Keepiru will have *military* command. That part confuses me a bit. I don't know where Creideiki's aiming, assigning Keepiru after the way I hear he behaved out there.

My guess is it's his way of getting the poor dollie out of his hai ... hide.'

Dennie had to agree, though she thought it a bit cruel.

She suddenly felt a smooth, flat touch on the inner part of her left thigh. She yelped and whirled around with her hand at her throat, then sighed when she saw that it was the neo-dolphin anthropologist, Sah'ot, who had slipped in his left pectoral fin to goose her. The *Stenos* gave her an uneven grin. His rough teeth shone brightly.

Dennie's heart pounded. 'Shark-breath! Doggerel-rhymer! Go make love to an unwashed specimen bottle!' Her voice cracked.

Sah'ot reared back, his eyes momentarily white-rimmed in surprise. Apparently he hadn't expected Dennie to be so high-strung.

'Aw, Dennie,' Sah'ot sighed. 'I was jussst trying to thank you for interceding with Creideiki. Obviously your charms are more persuasive than any arguments *I* might raise. Sorry if I sstartled you.'

Dennie sniffed at Sah'ot's double-edged apology. Still, her reaction might have been overdrawn. Her pulse slowly settled. 'Oh ... never mind. Just don't you sneak up on me like that!'

Without even turning around, she could *feel* Emerson D'Anite grinning behind his hand. *Males*, she thought. *Do they ever grow up?*

'Um, Dennie?' Sah'ot's voice crooned like a string trio. 'There is one small matter we have to discuss, if we are going to be going on this expedition to the island together. Will you be churlish and let Creideiki choose the science commander on the basis of prejudice? Or will you give me a chance? Maybe we can *wrestle* for it-t-t?'

D'Anite started coughing. He turned the other way and cleared his throat.

Dennie blushed. 'We'll let the captain decide what's best. Besides ... I'm not sure both of us should go. Charlie told me his analysis of the planetary crust samples may be of interest to you ... there are traces of paleotechnology in recent layers. You ought to go see him right away.'

Sah'ot's eyelids narrowed. 'That *isss* interesting. I'd thought this planet was fallow far longer than would allow paleotech-ch remnants.'

But he dashed Dennie's hopes. 'Alasss. Digging for long-toasted garbage of past Kithrupan civilizations cannot be half as important as making contact with pre-sentients and establishing a proper patron claim for you humans. We fins might have new client cousins before even neo-dogs are finished! Heaven help the poor creatures if the Tandu or Soro or similar ilk collect them!

'Besides,' he soothed, 'this is a chance for us to get to know each other better ... and exchange professional information, of course.'

Emerson D'Anite had to cough again.

'I've left the repairs for too long already, kids,' he said. His burr was back in force. 'I think I'll be gettin' on back to my engines, and let you two discuss your plans.'

D'Anite's grin was barely suppressed. Dennie swore eventual revenge. 'Emerson!' she hissed.

'Yes, lass?' He looked back at her innocently.

She glared, 'Oh ... I'll bet you haven't a drop of Celtic blood in your body!'

The dark engineer smiled at her. 'Why, bairn, didn' ya know? All Scots are engineers, and all engineers are Scots.' He waved and swam off before Dennie could think of a reply. *Trapped*, she cursed, by a cliche!

When D'Anite was out of earshot Sah'ot sidled close to Dennie. 'Shall we start planning our expedition?' His blowmouth was near her ear.

Dennie started. Suddenly she noticed that everyone had gone. Dennie's heart beat faster, and her facemask seemed not to provide enough air.

'Not *here* we won't!' She spun away and began swimming. 'Let's go to the wardroom. There are plotting boards ... and airdomes! A man can breathe there!'

Sah'ot kept pace, uncomfortably close.

'Aw, Dennie ...' he said, but he didn't press. Instead, he began to sing a low, atonal, hybrid melody in a complex and obscure dialect of Trinary.

Against her will, Dennie found herself drawn into the song. It was strange, and eerily beautiful, and it took her several minutes to realize that it was also dirty as hell.

15

STENOS

Moki, Sreekah-pol, and Hakukka-jo spent their latest off-duty period as they had spent every one for weeks, complaining.

'He was down in my section again, t-today,' Sreekah-pol griped, 'sticking his jaw into everybody's work-k. Thinks he's ssso-o-o discreet, but he fills the sound-scape with his Keneenk-k echoes!'

Moki nodded. There wasn't any doubt who 'he' was.

> * Crying—Crooning
> Talk, talk rhythms
> * My group wags tails
> To his Logic Logic! *

Hakukka-jo winced. Moki seldom spoke Anglic anymore, and his Trinary had a little too much Primal in it to be decent.

But Sreekah-pol obviously thought Moki's point valid. 'All the *Tursiopsss* worship Creideiki. They imitate him and try to act like Keneenk-k adeptsss! Even half of our *Stenos* seem just as swallowed by his spell!'

'Well, if he can get-t us out of here alive, I will forgive even his nosy inspections,' Hakkuka-jo suggested.

Moki tossed his head.

> * Alive! Alive!
> To deep, rich waters!
> * Follow, Follow
> A rough-toothed leader! *

'Will you make quiet-t-t?' Hakukka-jo swung about quickly to listen to echoes in the rest area. A few crewfen were gathered by the food machines. They gave no sign of having heard. 'Heed your scatter! You're already in trouble without clicking mutiny! I hear Doctor Metz has gone to Takkata-Jim about you!'

Moki smirked defiantly. Sreekah-pol agreed with Moki's unspoken comment. 'Metz won't do nothing,' Sreekah-pol said. 'It'sss common knowledge half the *Stenos* aboard were chosen by him. We're his babiesss,' Sreekah-pol crooned. 'With Orley and Tsh't gone, and Hikahi in sick bay, the only one we gotta watch out for is the chief smartass himself!'

Hakkuka-jo looked about wildly. 'You too? Look-k, will you be quiet? There comes K'tha-Jon!'

The other two turned the way he indicated. They saw a huge neo-fin swim out of a hull lift and head their way. Dolphins half his size got out of the giant's way quickly.

'So what-t-t? He is of us!' Sreekah-pol said uncertainly.

'He's also a bosun!' Hakkuka-jo answered hotly.

'He hates *Tursiopsss* smartasses, too!' Moki cut in in Anglic.

'If so he keeps it to himself! He knows how humans feel about racism!'

Moki looked away. The dark mottled dolphin was like a lot of fins in holding the patron race in a sort of superstitious dread. He countered weakly in Trinary.

> * Ask the black men –
>   The brown and yellow men
> * Ask the whales –
>   About human racism! *

'That was long ago!' Hakkuka-jo snapped. 'And humans had no patrons to guide them!'

'Jussst ssso ...' Sreekah-pol said, but his agreement sounded unsure.

They all shut up as K'tha-Jon approached. Hakkuka-jo felt a recurring chill on contemplating the bosun.

K'tha-Jon was a giant, surpassing three meters in length with a girth that two men couldn't span with their arms. His bottle nose was blunt, and, unlike the other so-called *Stenos* aboard, his coloring was not mottled but deeply counter-shaded. Rumor had it K'tha-Jon was another of Dr Metz's 'special' cases.

The giant swam up nearby and exhaled a loud spurt of bubbles. His open jaws displayed a fearful array of rough teeth. The others unconsciously adapted a submissive posture, eyes averted, food-mouths closed.

'I hear there's been more fighting ...' K'tha-Jon rumbled in deep Underwater Anglic. 'Fortunately, I was able to bribe senior bosun S'thata with a rare sensie tape, and he agreed not to report it to the captain. I'll expect the cost of the tape to be covered by somebody, with interest-t. ...'

Moki seemed about to speak, but K'tha-Jon cut him off.

'No excuses! Your temper is a burden I can do without. S'thata would have been right to challenge you for biting him from behind like that-t!'

348

Moki barely blatted out the beginning before being slammed amidships by a blow from K'tha-Jon's mighty flukes. He slewed several meters through the water before coming to rest, whistling in pain. K'tha-Jon came close and murmured softly.

'YOU are *Tursiops!* That is the name of our entire, *Library*-registered species! Tursiopsss *amicusss* ... "friendly bottlenose"! Ask Doctor Metz if you don't believe me! Embarrass the rest of uss aboard who have *Stenos* grafts in our genes – Vice-Captain Takkata-Jim and myself, for instance – by acting like an animal, and I will show you *how* to be a friendly bottlenose! I'll use your gutssss for hawsers!'

Moki trembled and turned away, jaw closed tightly.

K'tha-Jon swept the cowering fin with a contemptuous spray of sonar, then turned to regard the others. Hakkuka-jo and Sreekah-pol looked idly at the bright, decorative garibaldi and angel fish which swam unmolested throughout the central bay. Hakkuka-jo whistled softly.

'Break is almost over,' the bosun snapped. 'Back to work-k. And save your hatred for private time!' K'tha-Jon turned about and sped away, the turbulence from his flukes almost toppling the others.

Hakukka-jo watched him go, then whistled a long, low sigh.

That should do it, K'tha-Jon thought as he hurried off to duties in the cargo section. Moki, especially, would be quiet for a while. *He had better be.*

If there was anything he and Takkata-Jim did not need, it was a spate of racist innuendo and suspicion. Nothing would unite the humans in alienation like that sort of thing.

And catch the attention of Creideiki, too. Takkata-Jim insists we give the captain one more chance to come up with a plan to get us home alive.

All right, then, I can wait.

But what if he doesn't? What if he keeps asking for sacrifice from a crew that never volunteered to be heroes?

In that case, someone would have to be able to present the crew with an alternative to follow. Takkata-Jim was still reluctant, but that might not last.

If the time did come, they would need human support, and Moki's kind of interracial bullying could wreck the chances of that. K'tha-Jon intended to ride close herd on that *Stenos,* to keep him nice and docile.

349

Even if it was nice, from time to time, to chew the tail of some bloody, shore-hugging, sanctimonious, smartass *Tursiops*!

16

GALACTICS

– Rejoice – *crooned the fourth Brother of the Ebony Shadows.* – Rejoice *that the fifth moon of the small dusty planet has been conquered!* –

The Brothers of the Night had fought bitterly for this fulcrum of power, from which they would soon project irresistible might to sweep the skies of heretics and blasphemers. This moon would guarantee that the prize would be theirs, and theirs alone!

None of the other moons in the Kthsemenee system had the one attribute this one possessed: a core of almost one percent unobtainium. Already thirty of the Brothers' ships had landed, to begin construction of the Weapon.

The Library, as always, had been the key. Many cycles ago the fourth Brother of the Ebony Shadows had come across an obscure reference to a device once used in a war between two races now long extinct. It had taken half his lifespan to hunt down the details, for the Library was a labyrinth. But now would come his payment!

– Rejoice! – *The cry resounded.* It was a paean of triumph meant to be heard, and indeed a few other combatants began to notice that something curious was going on, over in a corner of Kthsemenee's system. While the fiercest battles raged around the strategic gas-giant world, and Kithrup itself, some enemies had begun sending scouts this way to see what the Brothers of the Night were up to.

– Let them come and look! Can it matter? –

A ship of the Soro had been watching them for some time. Could it have divined their purpose?

– Never! *The citation was too obscure! Our new weapon has sat unnoticed too long in the dusty archives. They will first understand when this moon begins to vibrate on the fifteenth probability band, sending out waves of uncertainty that will tear their battle fleets apart!* Then *their shipboard* Libraries *will undoubtedly remember, but too late!* –

The Brother of the Ebony Shadows watched from space as the resonator neared completion, watched as grounded ships fed their combined energies to the resonator. From a thousand units out he could feel the wave build . . .

– What are they doing? What are the Progenitor-scorned Soro doing? –

Instruments showed that the Brothers of the Night were not alone on the fifteenth band! From the Soro ship came a small tone, a variation of the beat emanating from the small moon. An echo.

The fifteenth band began to throb. Impossibly, it resonated along with the Soro rhythm!

The Brothers on the ground tried to damp the runaway signal, but it was already too late! The small moon shook, and finally crumbled. Great shards of rock tumbled apart, crushing the little ships in their way.

– How could they have known? How could they ... ? –

Then the Brother of the Ebony Shadows understood. Long ago, when he had begun his search for a new weapon, there had been a helpful Librarian ... a Pilan. The Pilan had always been there with the useful suggestion, with the helpful reference. The Brother had thought nothing of it. Librarians were supposed to be helpful, and neutral, whatever their backgrounds.

– But the Pil are clients to the Soro – The Brother realized – Krat knew all along –

He gave the order sending his remaining forces into hiding. – This is only a setback. We shall yet be the ones to capture the Earthlings! –

Behind the fleeing remnants, the small moon continued to dissolve.

17

TOM ORLEY

Hannes Suessi lay prone on the heavy work sled next to Thomas Orley. The gaunt, balding artificer gestured at the wreck before them.

'It's a Thennanin ship,' the chief engineer said. 'It's pretty badly crumpled, but there's no doubt. See? No objectivity anchors, only stasis projectors on the main flanges. The Thennanin are terrified of reality alteration. This ship was never designed to use a probability drive. Definitely Thennanin, or a Thennanin client or ally.'

The dolphins circled slowly nearby, taking turns at the airdomes underneath the sled, emitting excited sonar clicks as they eyed the gigantic crushed arrowhead below them.

'I think you're right, Hannes,' Tom said. 'It's a behemoth.'

That the ship was still in one piece was amazing. In its Mach five meeting with the ocean, it had caromed off at least two sub-surface islands – leaving substantial dents in them – and plowed a deep gouge in the ocean floor before finally catching up against a furrow of pelagic mud, just before it would have smashed into a sheer scarp. The cliff face looked crumbly and precarious. Another substantial jolt would surely cause a collapse, burying the wreck completely.

Orley knew, it was the quality of the Thennanin stasis shields that made such a performance possible. Even in dying, a Thennanin ship was reputed to be not worth putting out of its misery. In battle they were slow, unmaneuverable – and as hard to disable permanently as a cockroach.

It was difficult to assess the damage. Down here the illumination from the surface was blue-tinged and dim. The fen wouldn't turn on the arc lights they had strung up until Tsh't said it was safe. Fortunately, the wreck was in water shallow enough to visit, yet deep enough to shield them from spy eyes overhead.

A pink-bellied bottlenose dolphin swam up next to the sled. She worked her foodmouth in a thoughtful circular motion.

'It's really amazing, isn't it, Tom?' she asked. 'It should be in a jillion piecesss.'

This deep, there was an odd clarity to the fin's voice. Bursts of air from her blowmouth and sonar clicks joined in a complex manner to make speech an intricate juggling of bodily functions. To a landlubber human, a neo-dolphin speaking underwater sounded more like an avant-garde orchestra tuning up, than someone speaking a derivative of the English language.

'Do you think we can make any use of it-t?' The dolphin officer asked.

Orley looked again at the ship. There was a good chance that in the confusion of battle none of those contending over Kithrup had bothered to note where this sparrow had fallen. He already had a few tentative ideas, one or two of which might be bold, unexpected – and idiotic – enough to work.

'Let's give it a look,' he nodded. 'I suggest we split into three groups. Team one heads for any center of emissions, particularly probability, psi, or neutrino radiation, and disables the source. They should also watch out for survivors, though that seems unlikely.'

Suessi snorted as he looked at the pounded wreck. Orley went on.

'Team two concentrates on harvesting. Hannes should lead that one, along with Ti-tcha. They'll look for monopoles and refined metals *Streaker* can use. With luck, they might find some replacements for those coils we need.

'With your permission, Tsh't, I'll take team three. I want to look over the structural integrity of that ship, and survey the topography of the surrounding area.'

Tsh't performed a jaw clap of agreement. 'Your logic is good, Tom. That is what we'll do. I'll leave Lucky Kaa with the other sled, on alert. The ressst shall join their teams at once.'

Orley grabbed Tsh't's dorsal fin as she was about to whistle the command. 'Oh, we'd better go with breathers all around, hadn't we? Trinary may not be efficient, but I'd rather put off complex conversations in Anglic than have to risk everybody shuttling back and forth for air, and maybe someone getting hurt.'

Tsh't grimaced, but gave the command. The party was composed of disciplined fen – the pick of *Streaker*'s crew – so the gathering at the sled was occasion merely for low-pitched grousing and indignant bubbles as each dolphin was fitted with a wraparound hose of air.

Tom had heard of prototype breathers that would give a fin a streamlined air supply without hindering the speech-mouth. If ever he found the time, he might try to rig some up himself. Speaking Trinary posed no real difficulty for him, but he knew from experience that the fen would have problems conveying technical information in anything but Anglic.

Old Hannes was already grumbling. He helped pass out the breathers with ill-disguised reluctance. The chief artificer was conversant in Trinary, of course, but he found the three-level logic difficult. To cap things off, he was a lousy poet. He obviously didn't look forward to trying to discuss technical matters in whistle rhyme.

They had their work cut out for them. Several of the picked petty officers and crew that had accompanied them on the rescue effort had gone back to the ship, escorting Toshio and Hikahi and the other victims of the stranding waves: Only a short score of fen remained in the party. Should anything dangerous come up, they would have to take care of it. No help from *Streaker* could arrive in time to do any good.

It would have been nice to have Gillian here, Tom mused. Not that inspecting alien cruisers was her area of expertise, but she knew fins, and could handle herself if things got sticky.

But she had work of her own aboard *Streaker*, trying to solve the puzzle of a billion-year-old mummy that should never have existed in the first place. And in an emergency she was the only other person aboard *Streaker*, barring, possibly, Creideiki himself, who knew about the Niss machine.

Tom smiled as he caught himself rationalizing again.

Okay, so there are good and logical reasons why the two of us can't be together. Take it for what it's worth. Do a good job here, and maybe you can be back to her in a few days.

There had never been any question, from the moment they had met as adolescents, that he and she would make a pair. He sometimes wondered if their planners had known in advance, in choosing gametes from selected married couples, that two of the growing zygotes would later fit so perfectly – down to the simple telempathy they sometimes shared.

Probably it was a happy accident. Human genetic planning was limited by law and custom. Accident or no, Tom was grateful. In his missions for the Terragens Council he had learned that the universe was dangerous and filled with disillusionment. Too few sophonts – even those equipped for it – ever got enough love.

As soon as the breathers had been distributed Tom used the sled's speaker to amplify his voice. 'Now remember, everybody; though all Galactic technologies are based on the *Library*, that collection of wisdom is so huge that almost any type of machine might be inside that hull. Treat everything like it's booby-trapped until you've iden-tified it and rendered it harmless.

'The first goal of Team One, after silencing the wreck, is to find the main battle computers. There may be a record of the initial stages of the fight above. That information might be invaluable to the captain.

'And would you all keep an eye out for the *Library* glyph? If you find that symbol anywhere, please note its location and pass word to me. I'd like to see what kind of micro-branch they were carrying.'

He nodded to Tsh't. 'Is that all right with you, Lieutenant?'

Streaker's fourth officer clapped jaw and nodded. Orley's politeness was appreciated, but she was likelier to bite off her own tail than overrule any suggestion he made. *Streaker* was the first large expe-dition ever commanded and operated by dolphins. It had been clear from the beginning that certain humans were along whose advice bore the patina of patronomy.

She called out in Trinary.

> * Team One, with me—
>   To diffract above, listening
> * Team Two, with Suessi—
>   To taste for treasure
> * Team Three, with Orley—
>   To aid him scheming
> * Drop nothing of Earth here—
>   To betray our visit
> * Clean it up after—
>   If you must shit
> * Think before acting—
>   In tropic-clear logic
> * Now Streaker's, with stillness—
>   Away! *

In precise order, three formations peeled off, one group embellishing with a synchronized barrel roll as they passed Orley's sled. In obedience to Tsh't's orders, the only sound was the rapid clicking of cetacean sonar.

Orley rode the sled until he was within forty meters of the hulk. Then he patted Hannes on the back and rolled off to the side.

What a beautiful find the ship was! Orley used a hot-torch spectrograph to get a quick analysis of the metal at the edges of a gaping tear in the vessel's side. When he determined the ratios of various beta-decay products he whistled, causing the fen nearby to turn and look at him curiously. He had to make assumptions about the original alloy and the rate of exposure to neutrinos since the metal was forged, but reasonable guesses indicated that the ship had been fabricated at least thirty million years ago!

Tom shook his head. A fact like that made one realize how far Mankind had to go to catch up with the Galactics.

We like to think of the races using the *Library* as being in a rut, uncreative and unadaptable, Orley thought.

That appeared to be largely true. Very often the Galactic races seemed stodgy and unimaginative. But ...

He looked at the dark, hulking battleship, and wondered.

Legend had it that the Progenitors had called for a perpetual search for knowledge before they departed for parts unknown, aeons ago. But, in practice, most species looked to the *Library* and only the *Library* for knowledge. Its store grew only slowly.

What was the point of researching what must have been discovered a thousand times over by those who came before? It was simple, for instance, to choose advanced spaceship designs from *Library* archives and follow them blindly, understanding only a fraction of what was built. Earth had a few such ships, and they were marvels.

The Terragens Council, which handled relations between the races of Earth and the Galactic community, once almost succumbed to that tempting logic. Many humans urged co-opting of Galactic models that older races had themselves co-opted from ancient designs. They cited the example of Japan, which in the nineteenth century had faced a similar problem – how to survive amongst nations immeasurably more powerful than itself. Meiji Japan had concentrated all its energy on learning to imitate its neighbors, and succeeded in becoming just like them, in the end.

The majority on the Terragens Council, including nearly all of the cetacean members, disagreed. They considered the *Library* a honey pot – tempting, and possibly nourishing, but also a terrible trap.

They feared the 'Golden Age' syndrome ... the temptation to 'look backward' – to find wisdom in the oldest, dustiest texts, instead of the latest journal.

Except for a few races, such as the Kanten and Tymbrimi, the Galactic community as a whole seemed stuck in that kind of a mentality. The *Library* was their first and last recourse for every problem. The fact that the ancient records almost always contained something useful didn't make that approach any less repugnant to many of the wolflings of Earth, including Tom, Gillian, and their mentor, old Jacob Demwa.

Coming out of a tradition of bootstrap technology, Earth's leaders decided there were things to be gained from innovation, even this late in Galactic history. At least it *felt* better to believe that. To a wolfling race, pride was an important thing.

Orphans often have little else.

But *here* was evidence of the power of the Golden Age approach. Everything about this ship spoke silkily of refinement. Even in wreckage, it was beautifully simple in its construction, while indulgent and ornate in its embellishments. The eye saw no welds. Bracings and struts were always integral to some other purpose. Here one supported a stasis flange, while apparently also serving as a baffled radiator for excess probability. Orley thought he detected other overlaps, subtleties that could only have come with aeons of slow improvement on an ancient design.

He was struck by a decadence in the pattern, an ostentation that he found arrogant and bizarre beyond mere alienness.

One of Tom's main assignments aboard *Streaker* had been evaluation of alien devices – particularly of the military variety. This wasn't the best the Galactics had, yet it made him feel like an ancient New Guinea headhunter, proud of his new muzzle-loading musket, but painfully aware of the fact of machine guns.

He looked up. His team was gathering. He chinned his hydrophone switch.

'Everybody about done? All right, then. Subteam two, head off and see if that canyon goes all the way through the ridge. It'd cut twenty klicks off the route back to *Streaker*.'

He heard a whistle of assent from Karacha-jeff, leader of subteam two. Good. That fin was reliable.

'Be careful,' he added as they swam off. Then he motioned for the others to follow him into the wreck through the seared, curled rent in its hull.

They entered darkened corridors of eerily familiar design. Everywhere were signs of the commonality of Galactic culture, superimposed with the idiosyncracies of a peculiar alien race. The lighting panels were identical to those on ships of a hundred species, but spaces in between were garishly decorated with Thennanin hieroglyphs.

Orley eidetically examined it all. But always he looked out for one thing, a symbol that could be found everywhere in the Five linked Galaxies – a rayed spiral.

They'll tell me when they find it, he reminded himself. *The fins know I'm interested.*

I do hope, though, they don't suspect just how badly I want to see that glyph.

18

GILLIAN

'Aw, why should I? Huh? You aren't being very cooperative with *me*! All I want is to talk to Brookida for just a minute. It's not as if I was asking a lot!'

Gillian Baskin felt tired and irritable. The holo image of the chimpanzee planetologist, Charles Dart, glared out at her. It would be easy to become scathing and force Charlie to retreat. But then he would probably complain to Ignacio Metz, and Metz would lecture her about 'bullying people just because they are clients.'

Crap. Gillian wouldn't take from a human being what she had put up with from this self-important little neo-chimp!

She brushed aside a strand of dark blonde hair that had fallen over her eyes. 'Charlie, for the last time, Brookida is sleeping. He has received your message, and will call you when Makanee says he's had enough rest. In the meantime, all I want from you is a listing of isotope abundances for the trans-ferric elements here on Kithrup. We've just finished more than four hours' surgery on Satima, and we need that data to design a chelating sequence for her. I want to get every microgram of heavy metal out of her body as soon as possible.

'Now, if that's too much to ask, if you're too overworked studying little geological puzzles, I'll just call the captain or Takkata-Jim, and ask them to assign somebody to go down and *help* you!'

The chimp scientist grimaced. His lips curled back to display an array of large, yellowed, buck teeth. At the moment, in spite of the enlarged globe of his cranium, his out-thrust jaw, and his opposable thumbs, he looked more like an angry ape than a sapient scientist.

'Oh, all right!' His hands fluttered and emotion made him stammer. 'B-But this is important! Understand? I think Kithrup was inhabited by technological sophonts as recently as thirty thousand years ago! Yet the Galactic Migration Institute's had this planet posted as fallow and untouchable for the last hundred million!'

Gillian suppressed an urge to say, 'So what?' There had been more defunct and forgotten species in the history of the Five Galaxies than even the *Library* could count.

Charlie must have read her expression. 'It's illegal!' he shouted. His coarse voice cracked. 'If it's true, the Institute of M-migration should be told! They might even be grateful enough to help get those crazy religious n-n-nuts overhead to let us alone!'

Gillian lifted an eyebrow in surprise. What was this? Charles Dart pondering implications beyond his own work? Even he, then, must think from time to time about survival. His argument about the laws of migration were naive, considering how often the codes were twisted and perverted by the more powerful clans. But he deserved some credit.

'OK. That's a good point, Charlie,' she said. 'I'm having dinner with the captain later. I'll mention it to him then. I'll also ask Makanee if she'll let Brookida out a little early. Good enough?'

Charlie looked at her with suspicion. Then, unable to maintain so subtle and intermediate an expression for long, he let a broad grin spread.

'Good enough!' he rumbled. 'And you'll have that fax in hand within four minutes! I leave you in good health.'

'Health,' Gillian replied softly, as the holo faded.

She spent a long moment staring at the blank comm screen. With her elbows on the desk, her face settled down upon the palms of her hands.

Ifni! I should have been able to handle an angry chimp better than that. What's the matter with me?

Gillian gently rubbed her eyes. *Well, I've been up for twenty-six hours, for one thing.*

A long and unproductive argument about semantics with Tom's damned, sarcastic Niss machine hadn't helped at all, when all she had wanted from the thing was its assistance on a few obscure *Library* references. It knew she needed help to crack the mystery of Herbie, the ancient cadaver that lay under glass in her private lab. But it kept changing the subject, asking her opinion on various irrelevant issues such as human sexual mores. By the time the session was through, Gillian was ready to disassemble the nasty thing with her bare hands.

But Tom would probably disapprove, so she deferred.

She had been about to go to bed when the emergency call came from the outlook. Soon she was busy helping Makanee and the autodocs treat survivors of the survey party. Worry about Hikahi and Satima drove all thought of sleep from her mind until that was done.

Now that they seemed to be out of danger, Gillian could no longer use adrenaline reaction to hold off that empty feeling that seeped in around the edges of a very rough day.

It's not a time to enjoy being alone, she thought. She lifted her head and looked at her reflection in the blank comm screen. Her eyes were reddened. From overwork, certainly, but also worry.

Gillian knew well enough how to cope, but coping was a sterile solution. Instinct demanded warmth, someone to hold and satisfy that physical longing.

She wondered if Tom felt the same way at this moment. Oh, of course he did; with the crude telempathic link they shared, Gillian felt she knew him well. They were of a type, the two of them.

Only sometimes it seemed to Gillian the planners had been more successful with him than with her. While everyone seemed to think of her as superbly competent, they were all a bit in awe of Thomas Orley.

And at times like the present, when eidetic recall seemed more a curse than a blessing, Gillian wondered if she really was as neurosis-free as the manufacturer's warranty promised.

The fax on her desk extruded a hardcopy message. It was the isotope distribution profile promised by Charlie – a minute ahead of schedule, she noted. Gillian scanned the columns. Good. There was little variation from the millennia-old *Library* report on Kithrup. Not that she had expected any, but one always checked.

A brief appendix at the bottom warned that these profiles were only valid in the surface crust and upper asthenosphere regions, and were invalid any more than two kilometers below the surface.

Gillian smiled. Someday Charlie's compulsiveness might save them all.

She stepped from her office onto a parapet above a large open chamber. Water filled the central part of the room up to two meters below the parapet. Bulky machines stuck out above. The upper half of the chamber, including Gillian's office, was inaccessible to dolphins unless they came riding a walker or spider.

Gillian didn't bother with the folded facemask at her belt. She looked below, then dove, plunging between two rows of dark autodocs. The large, oblong glassite containers were silent and empty.

All the waterways of sick bay were shallow to allow open breathing and dry surgery. She swam with long, strong strokes, gripped the corner of one machine to make a turn, and passed through a stripdoor into the trauma unit.

She surfaced, open-mouthed, for air, bobbed for a moment, then swam over to a wall of thick leaded glass. Two bandaged dolphins floated in a heavily shielded gravity tank.

One occupant, connected to a maze of tubing, had the dull-eyed look of heavy sedation. The other whistled cheerfully as Gillian approached.

'I greet you, Life-Cleaner! Your potions scour my veins, but it's this taste of weightlessness which liftsss my spacer's heart. Thank you!'

'You're welcome, Hikahi.' Gillian treaded water easily, not bothering with the curb and rail near the gravity tank. 'Just don't get too used to the comfort. I'm afraid Makanee and I are going to kick you out soon, as penalty for having such an iron constitution.'

'As opposed to one of bismuth or c-c-cadmium?' Hikahi spluttered a raspberry-like chuckle.

Gillian laughed. 'Indeed. And being healthy will be your tough luck. We'll have you out of here, breathing bubbles and standing on your tail for the captain in no time.'

Hikahi gave her small neo-fin smile. 'You're certain this isn't too risky, turning on thisss gravity tank? I wouldn't want Satima and me to be responsible for giving the show away.'

'Relax, fem-fin,' Gillian shook her head. 'We triple-checked. The leak-detection buoys aren't picking up a thing. Enjoy it and don't worry.

'Oh, and I hear the captain may be sending a small team back to your island to examine those pre-sentients you found. I figured you'd be interested. It's a sign he's not worried about Galactics in the short term. The space battle may last a long time, and we might be able to hide indefinitely.'

'An indefinite stay on Kithrup's not my idea of paradise!' Hikahi opened her mouth in a grin of irony. 'If that's meant as cheery news, please warn me when your message is depressing!'

Gillian laughed. 'I will. Now you get some sleep. Shall I turn down the light?'

'Yess, please. And Gillian, thanks for the news. I do think it's very important we do something about the abos. I hope the expedition is a success.

'Tell Creideiki I'll be back on duty before he can open a can of tuna.'

'I will. Pleasant dreams, dear.' Gillian touched the dimmer switch and the lights gradually faded. Hikahi blinked several times, apparently settling into a seaman's nap.

Gillian headed for the outer clinic, where Makanee would be dealing with a line of complaining crewfen at sick call. Gillian would show the physician Charlie's isotope profiles and then go back to her own lab to work for a while longer.

Sleep called to her, but she knew it would be a long time coming. In this mood that had come upon her she felt reluctant.

Logic was the blessing and curse of her upbringing. She knew that Tom was where he was supposed to be – out pursuing ways to save them all. He knew it as well. His departure had been hasty and necessary, and there simply hadn't been time to seek her out to say good-bye.

Gillian was aware of all of these considerations. She repeated them to herself as she swam. But they only seemed to disconnect the larger from the smaller of her problems, and rob of poignant consolation the unattractiveness of her empty bed.

19

CREIDEIKI

'Keneenk is a study of relationships,' he told his audience. 'That part comes from our dolphin heritage. Keneenk is also a study of *strict comparisons*. This second part we learn from our human patrons. Keneenk is a synthesis of two world-views, much as we ourselves are.'

About thirty neo-dolphins floated across from him, bubbles rising slowly from their blowmouths, intermittent unconscious sonar clicks their only sound.

Since there were no humans present, Creideiki did not have to use the crisp consonants and long vowels of standard Anglic. But, transcribed onto paper, his words would have pleased any English grammarian.

'Consider reflections from the surface of the ocean, where the air meets the water,' he suggested to his pupils. 'What do the reflections tell us?'

He saw puzzled expressions.

'Reflections from which side of the water, you wonder? Do I speak of the reflections felt from *below* the interface or from above?

'Moreover, do I mean reflections of *sound*, or of *light*?'

He turned to one of the attentive dolphins. 'Wattaceti, imagine yourself one of our ancestors. Which combination would occur to you?'

The engine room tech blinked. 'Sound images, Captain. A pre-sentient dolphin would have thought of sound reflections *in* the water, bouncing against the surface from below.'

The tech sounded tired, but Wattaceti still attended these sessions, in a fervent desire for self-improvement. It was for the morale of fen like Wattaceti that the busy captain made time to continue them.

Creideiki nodded. 'Quite right. Now, what would be the first type of reflection thought of by a human?'

'The image of *light* from above,' the mess chief, S'tat, answered promptly.

'Most probably, though we all know that even some of the "big-ears" can eventually learn to hear.'

There was a general skree of laughter at the harmless little put-down of the patron race. Laughter was a measure of crew morale, and he weighed it as he might test the mass of a fuel cell by hefting it between his jaws.

Creideiki noticed for the first time that Takkata-Jim and K'tha-Jon had swum up to join the group. Creideiki quashed a momentary concern. Takkata-Jim would have signaled if something had come up. He seemed to be here simply to listen.

If this was a sign the vice-captain was ending his long, unexplained sulk, Creideiki was glad. He had kept Takkata-Jim aboard, instead of sending him out to accompany Orley and the rescue party, because he wanted to keep his exec under scrutiny. He had reluctantly begun to think the time might have come to make changes in the chain of command.

He waited for the snickering to die down. 'Consider, now. How are a human's thoughts about these reflections from the surface of the water *similar* to our own?'

The students assumed expressions of concentration. This would be the next-to-last problem. With so much repair work to oversee, Creideiki had been tempted to cancel the sessions altogether. But so many in the crew wanted desperately to learn Keneenk.

At the beginning of the voyage almost all the fen had participated in the lectures, games, and athletic competitions that helped stave off spaceflight ennui. But since the frightening episode at the Shallow Cluster, when a dozen crewfen had been lost exploring the terrifying derelict fleet, some had begun to detach themselves from the community of the ship, to associate with their own little groups. Some even began exhibiting a strange atavism – increasing difficulty with Anglic and the sort of concentrated thought needed by a spacer.

Creideiki had been forced to juggle schedules to find replacements. He had given Takkata-Jim the task of finding jobs for the reverted ones. The task seemed to suit the vice-captain. With the aid of bosun K'tha-Jon he seemed to have found useful work for even the worst stricken.

Creideiki carefully listened to the swish of flukes, the uncomfortable gurgling of gill-lungs, the rhythm of heartbeats. Takkata-Jim and K'tha-Jon floated quietly, apparently attentive. But Creideiki sensed in each of them an underlying tension.

Creideiki shivered. There had come a suddenly vivid mental image of the vice-captain's shrewd, sullen eye, and the bosun's great, sharp teeth. He suppressed it, chiding himself for an overactive imagination. There was no logical reason to fear either of those two!

'We are contemplating reflections from an interface between air and water.' He hurriedly resumed his lecture. 'Both humans and dolphins envision a *barrier* when they consider such a surface. On the other side is a realm that is only faintly apparent until the barrier is crossed. Yet the modern human, with his tools, does not fear the water side, as he once did. The neo-fin, with *his* tools, can live and work in the air, and look down without discomfort.

'Consider how your own thoughts stretched out when I asked my original question. The idea of sound reflecting from below came to mind first. Our ancestors would have complacently stopped with that first generalization, but *you* did not stop there. You did not generalize without considering further alternatives. This is a common hallmark of *planning* creatures. For us it is a new thing.'

The timer on Creideiki's harness chimed. It was growing late. Tired as he was, he still had a meeting to attend, and he wanted to stop at the bridge to find out if there had been any word from Orley.

'How does a cetacean, whose heritage, whose very *brain* is built on intuitive thinking, learn to *analyze* a complex problem, piece by piece? Sometimes the key to an *answer* is found in the way you formulate the *question*. I'll leave you all today with an exercise for your idle moments.

'Try to state the problem of reflections from the surface of water in *Trinary* ... in a way that demands not a single answer, or a three-level opposition, but a plain listing of the reflections that are possible.'

He saw several of the fen frown uncomfortably.

The captain smiled reassuringly. 'I know it sounds difficult, and I will not ask you to recite today. But just to show you it can be done, accept the echo of this dream.'

> * A layer divides
>   Sky-star—Sea-star
> * What comes to us
>   At a narrow angle?
>
> * The huntsqueaking starcatching octopus
>   Reflects!

> * The night-calling, star-following tern
>   Reflects!

> * The star-twinkle in my lover's eye
>   Reflects!

> * The sun, soundless, roaring showoff—
>   Reflects! *

Creideiki was adequately rewarded by the wide-eyed appreciation of his audience. As he turned to go, he noticed that even Takkata-Jim was shaking his head slowly, as if considering a thought that had never occurred to him before.

After the meeting broke up, K'tha-Jon persisted in his argument.

'You sssaw? You heard him, Takkata-Jim?'

'I saw and heard, Bosun. And, as usual, I was impressed. Creideiki is a geniusss. So what is it you wanted to point out to me?'

K'tha-Jon clapped his jaw, not the most polite gesture to make before a superior officer.

'He sayss *nothing* about the Galacticss! Nothing about the siege! Nothing at *all* about plans to get us away from here! Or, barring that, to fight-t!

'And meanwhile he ignores the growing split amongst the crew!'

Takkata-Jim let out a line of bubbles. 'A split you have busily been encouraging, K'tha-Jon. No, don't bother protesting innocence. You've been subtle, and I know you've been doing it to build a power base for me. So I look away.

'But don't be sure Creideiki will always be too busy to notice! When he *does* notice, K'tha-Jon, watch your tail! For *I* won't have known a thing about your little tricks!'

K'tha-Jon blew quiet bubbles, not bothering to reply.

'As for Creideiki's plans, we'll see. We'll see if he's willing to listen to Doctor Metz and myself, or if he persisssts in this dream of carting secrets back to Earth unopened.'

Takkata-Jim saw the giant *Stenos* was about to interrupt. 'Yesss, I know you think we should consider a third option, don't you? You'd like to see us head out and take on all the Galactics single-handed, wouldn't you, K'tha-Jon?'

The huge dolphin didn't answer, but his eye gleamed back at the vice-captain.

Are you my Boswell, my Seaton, my Igor, or my Iago? Takkata-Jim thought silently at the giant mutant. *You serve me now, but in the long run, am I using you, or are you using me?*

20

GALACTICS

Battle screamed all around the flotilla of tiny Xappish warships.

'We have just lost the X'ktau *and the* X'klennu! *That means a third of the Xappish armed might is gone!'*

The elder Xappish lieutenant sighed. 'So? Young one, tell me news, not things I already know.'

'Our Xatinni patrons spend their clients like reaction gas, and commit their own forces miserly. Notice how they hang back, ready to flee if the battle gets too furious! Yet we *they send into danger!'*

'That is ever their way,' the other agreed.

'But if the Xappish fleet is destroyed here, in this futile fray, who will protect our three tiny worlds, and enforce our rights?'

'Is that not what we have patrons for?' The older lieutenant knew he was being ironic. He adjusted the screens to resist a sudden psionic attack, without even changing his tone of voice.

His junior did not dignify the reply with a comment. He grumbled instead. 'What did these Earthlings ever do to us, anyway? In what way do they threaten our patrons?'

A searing blast from a Tandu battle-cruiser just missed the left wing of the small Xappish scout. The junior lieutenant sent the ship into a wild evasive maneuver. The senior lieutenant replied to the question as if nothing at all had happened.

'I take it you don't believe the story that the Progenitors have returned.'

The other only snorted, while adjusting his torpedo sights.

'Aptly put. I, too, think this is merely part of a program to destroy the Earthlings. The senior patron races see the Terrans as a threat. They are wolflings, and therefore dangerous. They preach revolutionary uplift practices ... more dangerous still. They are allies of the Tymbrimi, an insult beyond forbearance. And they proselytize – an unforgivable offense.'

The scoutship shuddered as the torpedo leapt toward the Tandu destroyer. Their tiny craft accelerated mightily to get away.

'Well, I think we should listen *to the Earthlings,' the junior lieutenant shouted. 'If all the client races in the galaxy rebelled at once ...'*

'It has already happened,' the elder interrupted. 'Study the Library *records. Six times in Galactic history. And twice successfully.'*

'No! What happened?'

'What do you think happened? The clients went on to become patrons of newer species, and treated them just the same as ever!'

'I do not believe it! I cannot believe it!'

The elder lieutenant sighed. 'Look it up.'

'I shall!'

But he never did. An undetected improbability mine lay across their path. The tiny scout departed the galaxy in a manner that was picturesque, if ultimately lethal.

21

DENNIE AND TOSHIO

Dennie checked the charges one more time. It was dark and crowded in the close passage of the drill-tree root. Her helmet's beam cast stark shadows through the thick maze of rootlets.

She called upward. 'Are you almost finished, Toshio?'

He was planting his explosives in the upper section, near the surface of the metal-mound.

'Yeah, Dennie. If you're done, go back down now. I'll join you in a minute.'

She couldn't see his flippered feet above her. His voice was distorted in the narrow, water-filled thicket. It was a relief to be allowed to leave.

She picked her way downward carefully, fighting back waves of claustrophobia. This was no job Dennie would ever have chosen. But it had to be done, and the two dolphins were by nature unqualified.

Halfway down, she snagged herself on a strand of creeper. It didn't let go when she tugged. Thrashing only entangled her further, and she vividly recalled Toshio's story of the killer weed. Panic almost closed in, but she forced herself to stop kicking, to take a deep breath and study the snare.

It was just a dead vine wrapped around one leg. The strand parted easily under her knife. She continued her descent more cautiously and escaped at last into the grotto beneath the metal-mound.

Keepiru and Sah'ot waited below. Hose-like breathers covered their blowmouths and wrapped around their torsos. The headlights of the two sleds diffracted through thousands of tiny threads that seemed to fill the chamber in a drifting fog. A dim light filtered into the grotto from the cave mouth through which they had entered.

* Echoes sounding, in this rock-cage
Will not be those of happy fishing *

Dennie looked at Sah'ot, unsure she had understood the poet's fancy Trinary.

'Oh! Yes. When Toshio sets the fuses, we'd better get outside. The explosion will reverberate in this chamber.'

Keepiru nodded in agreement. The expedition's military commander had been mostly silent all the way here from the ship.

Dennie looked around the underwater cavity. Coral-like, microscopic scavengers had built their castle on the rich silicate rocks of an ocean hillock. The structure had grown slowly, but when the mound finally breached the ocean surface toplife became possible. Among the vegetation which had sprouted was the drill-tree.

That plant somehow pierced the mound's metal core and penetrated to organically useful layers beneath the island. Minerals were drawn up and deposited above. A cavity grew below, which would eventually accept the metal-mound into the crust again.

Something struck the ecologist in Dennie as odd about this arrangement. The tiny micro-branch *Library* aboard *Streaker* hadn't mentioned the metal-mounds at all, which was also curious.

It was hard to believe the drill-tree could evolve into its niche in a gradual way, as most species did. For the tree to succeed was an all-or-nothing proposition, requiring great power and perseverance. How did it get that way? Dennie wondered. And what happened to the mounds after they fell into the cavities the drill-trees prepared for them? She had seen some pits which had swallowed their mounds. Their depths were cloudy and obscure, and apparently far deeper than she would have expected.

She shone her beam on the bottom of the mound. The reflections were really quite startling. Dennie had expected something ragged and irregular, not a field of bright concave pits on the shining metal underside.

She swam to one of the larger depressions, bringing up her camera. Charlie Dart would like pictures and samples from this trip. She knew better than to expect thanks. More likely each tantalizing photo or rock would send him into exasperated sighs over her failure to follow up *obvious* leads.

Deep within one of the pits something moved, a twisting and slow turning. Dennie re-oriented her beam and peered closer. It was a *root* of some sort. She watched several of the tiny drifting threads fly within reach of the hanging tendril, to be caught and drawn within. She grabbed at a few for her sample bag.

'Let's go, Dennie!' She heard Toshio call. There was a thrumming sound as a sled moved just beneath her. 'Come on! We've only got five minutes till they blow!'

'Okay, okay,' she said. 'Give me a minute.' Professional curiosity momentarily overwhelmed other thoughts. Dennie could think of no reason why a living thing should burrow into the lightless underside of a mass of almost pure metal. She reached far into the pit and grabbed the twisting tendril root, then braced herself against the bulk of the mound and pulled hard.

At first the springy root was adamant, and seemed even to pull back. The possibility that she had trapped herself vividly occurred to Dennie.

The root tore free suddenly. Dennie glimpsed a shiny-hard tip as she stuffed the specimen into a sample bag. She flipped and kicked away from the metal surface.

Keepiru looked at her reproachfully as she grabbed the sled. He gunned the machine toward the cave entrance and out into the daylight, where Toshio and Sah'ot waited. Moments later a loud concussion sent booming echoes through the shallows.

They waited an hour, then re-entered the grotto.

The charges had shattered the drill-tree trunk where it pierced the bottom side of the metal-mound. The severed shaft canted at an angle below, continuing down into murky depths. Bits of debris still fell from the opening in the mound's bottom. The chamber below the island was thick with swirling shreds of vegetation.

They approached the opening cautiously. 'I'd better check it out with a robot first,' Toshio said. 'There may be unstable chunks left in the shaft.'

> * I will do this – Ladder-runner
> * Robots heed my – close nerve socket *

Toshio nodded. 'Yeah, you're right. You do it, Keepiru.' The pilot, with his direct machine-nerve interface, would be able to control the probe better than Toshio. Of the humans aboard, only Emerson D'Anite and Thomas Orley had such cyborg links. It would be a long time before most humans could deal with the side effects of socket implantation as well as dolphins, who had needed the interface far more and had been bred for it.

Under Keepiru's direction, a small probe detached itself from the rear of the sled, jetted off toward the hole and disappeared within.

Toshio had never expected to be sent right back out again with Keepiru – to a site where, in his opinion, neither of them had behaved particularly well. The importance of their mission, to serve and protect two important scientists, confused him even further. Why didn't Creideiki assign someone else? Someone more reliable?

Of course, the captain might have ordered all four of them out of the ship to get them out of his way. But that didn't seem to fit either. Toshio decided not to try to pierce Creideiki's logic. Inscrutability seemed to be at the heart of it. Perhaps that was what it was to be a captain. Toshio only knew that he and Keepiru were both determined to do a good job on this mission.

As a midshipman he officially outranked Keepiru. But tradition made warrant officers and pilots masters of middies unless otherwise decided by higher authority. Toshio would be assisting Dennie and Sah'ot in their studies. On security matters, Keepiru was in charge.

Toshio was still surprised to find that others stopped and listened when he made suggestions; his opinions had been routinely solicited. That alone would take some getting used to.

The screen showed a picture sent back by the robot – a hollow cylindrical excavation through the foamy metal. Broken stumps were all that remained of the anchor bearings that had held the drill-tree shaft in place. Bits of debris drifted down past the camera as they watched.

As the robot rose, the light from above slowly grew brighter through a thin haze of bubbles.

'Think it's wide enough to pass a sled?' Toshio asked. Keepiru whistled that the passage looked navigable.

The robot surfaced into a pool several meters wide. Its camera panned the rim, transmitting images of blue sky and thick green foliage. The high trunk of the drill-tree had crashed into the forest. The slope of the pool made it hard to see the damage this had done, but Toshio was sure it hadn't fallen in the direction of the abo village.

They had worried that blasting a way to the interior of the island might panic the hunter-gatherers. They took the risk anyway, because routinely trying to scale the treacherous island walls in open surf would have been dangerous, and a foolish exposure to Galactic spy satellites. The apparently random falling of a tree on an island would hardly be noted by anyone watching from above.

'Uh oh.' Toshio pointed.

Dennie moved closer to look at the screen. 'What is it, Tosh? Is there a problem?'

Keepiru stopped the camera as it was about to finish its scan. 'There,' Toshio said. 'That jagged crop of coral is hanging over the pool. It looks about to fall.'

'Well, can you have the robot wedge something under to prevent it?'

'I don't know. What do you think, Keepiru?'

Keepiru eyed his twin screens and concentrated. Toshio knew the pilot was listening to a complex pattern of sound-images, transmitted over his neural link. Under Keepiru's command, the robot moved to the edge of the pool. Its claw arms grabbed the spongy metal of the rim to pull forward. There was a small rain of pebbles as it brought its treads to bear.

'Watch out!' Toshio called.

The jagged rock tipped forward. The camera showed it tottering ominously. Dennie cringed back from the screen. Then the rock toppled over and crashed into the robot.

There followed a swirl of spinning images. Dennie continued watching the screen, but Toshio and Keepiru shifted their gaze to the bottom of the shaft. Suddenly a rain of objects fell from the gap, tumbling into the darkness below. The debris sparkled in the sled's beams as it dropped into the abyss.

After a long silence Keepiru spoke.

* The probe is down there—lungs unbreathing
* I was spared—the cutoff false-death
* It still whistles—stranded echoes *

Keepiru meant that the probe still sent him messages from whatever murky ledge had finally stopped it. Its tiny brain and transmitter hadn't been destroyed, and Keepiru had not suffered the jolt that a sudden cutoff could send to a connected nervous system.

But the robot's flotation tanks had been ruined. It was down there for good.

* That must be—the last obstruction
* I shall go then—
    carefully,
        testing—
* Dennie, take the sled—and watch me! *

Before Keepiru or Toshio could stop him, Sah'ot was off his sled and away. He fluked mightily and disappeared into the shaft. Keepiru and Toshio looked at each other, sharing a malign thought about crazy civilians.

At least, Toshio thought, he could have taken a camera with him!

But then, if Sah'ot had waited, Toshio would have had a chance to insist on the dubious privilege of scouting the passage.

He looked at Dennie. She watched the robot probe screen, as if it might deliver some token about what was happening to Sah'ot. She had to be reminded to swim over and take control of the other sled.

Toshio had always thought of Dennie Sudman as one more adult scientist, friendly but enigmatic. Now he saw that she was not an awful lot more mature than he. And while she had the honor and status of a full professional, she lacked the eclecticism his officer training was giving him. She would never encounter the range of people, things, and situations he would, in the course of his career.

He looked again to the shaft entrance. Keepiru blew nervous bubbles. They would have to decide soon what to do if Sah'ot did not reappear.

Sah'ot was obviously a genetic experiment, in which the gene-crafters were pushing a set of traits toward a calculated optimum. If judged successful, the traits would be grafted into the main pool of the neo-dolphin species. The process imitated, on a vastly quicker scale, the segregation and mixing that worked in nature.

Such experiments sometimes resulted in things not planned, though. Toshio wasn't sure he trusted Sah'ot. The fin's obscurity wasn't like the inscrutability of Creideiki – deep and thoughtful. It grated, like the dissembling of some humans he had known.

Also, there was this sexual game between Sah'ot and Dennie. Not that he was a prude. Such hobbies weren't exactly forbidden, but they had been known to cause problems.

Apparently Dennie wasn't even aware of the subtle ways she was encouraging Sah'ot. Toshio wondered if he had the nerve to tell her – or if it was any of his business.

Another tense minute passed. Then, just as Toshio was about to go himself, Sah'ot shot out of the shaft and swooped toward them.

> * The way is clear—
> I'll lead you airward! *

Keepiru jetted his sled over to the dolphin anthropologist, and squawked something pitched so high that Toshio couldn't quite catch it, even with his Calafian sensitivity.

Sah'ot's mouth twisted and closed into a reluctant attitude of sub-mission. Still, there was something defiant in his eye. He cast a look at Dennie, even as he rolled over to offer one of his ventral fins to Keepiru's mouth.

The pilot took a token nip, then turned back to the others.

            * The way is clear—
                        I do believe him
            * Now let us go—
                        and drop these breathers
            * To talk like Earthmen—
                        about our work
            * And to meet our future—
                        pilot brothers *

The sled moved under the drill-tree shaft, then rose in a cloud of bubbles. The others followed.

22

CREIDEIKI

The briefing had gone on far too long.

Creideiki regretted ever letting Charles Dart attend via holoscreen. The chimp planetologist would have been less long-winded if he were here in the fizzing oxywater of the central bay, wet and wearing a facemask. Dart lounged in his own laboratory, projecting his image, oblivious to the chafing of his listeners. Breathing oxywater in front of a console for two hours was highly uncomfortable to a neo-fin.

'Naturally, Captain,' the chimp's scratchy baritone throbbed into the water. 'When you chose to land us near a major tectonic boundary, I approved wholeheartedly. Nowhere else offered so much data in one spot. Still, I think I've made a convincing case for six or seven more sampling sites distributed about Kithrup, to verify some of the extremely interesting discoveries we've made here.'

Creideiki was mildly surprised. Using the first personal plural was the first modest thing Charlie had said.

Brookida floated nearby. The metallurgist had been working with Charles Dart, his skills not currently required by the repair team. He had been largely silent for the last hour, letting the chimp pour out tides of technical jargon.

What's the matter with Brookida? Does he think a captain under siege has nothing better to do?

Hikahi, recently released from sick bay, rolled over on her back, breathing the fizzing, oxygenated fluid and keeping one eye to the hologram of the chimpanzee. *She shouldn't do that,* Creideiki thought. *I'm having enough trouble concentrating as it is.*

A lengthy, constricting meeting always did this to Creideiki. He felt a stirring of blood in and around his penile sheath. What he *wanted* to do was swim over to Hikahi and bite her softly in numerous places, up and down her flanks.

Kinky, yes, especially in public, but at least he was honest with himself.

'Planetologist Dart,' he sighed. 'I am trying very hard to understand what you claim to have discovered. The part about various crystalline and isotopic anomalies below the crust of Kithrup I think I follow. As for the subduction layer ...'

'A subduction zone is a boundary of two crustal plates, where one slips below its neighbor ...' Charlie interrupted.

Creideiki wished he could let down his dignity to curse. 'I know that much planetology, Doctor Dart.' He spoke carefully. 'And I'm glad our being near one of these plate boundaries is useful to you. But our choice of landing site was based on matters tactical. We want the metals and camouflage offered by the "coral" mounds. With hostile cruisers overhead, I can't think of permitting expeditions to other parts of the globe. In fact, I must refuse your request for further drilling at this location. The risk is too great.'

The chimp frowned. His hands began to flutter. Before he found the words, Creideiki cut him off.

'Besides, what does the ship's micro-branch say about Kithrup? Doesn't the *Library* contribute anything on these problems you face?'

'The *Library*!' Dart snorted. 'That pack of lies! That friggin' morass of misinformation!' Charlie's voice dropped to a growl. 'It has *nothin'* on the anomalies! It doesn't even mention the metal-mounds! The last survey was done over four *hundred* million years ago, when the planet was put on reserve status for the Karrank%. ...'

Charlie became so strangled around the extended glottal stop that he started to choke. He went bug-eyed and pounded himself on the chest, coughing.

Creideiki turned to Brookida. 'Is this true? Is the *Library* so deficient on this planet?'

'Yess-s.' Brookida nodded slowly. 'Four hundred epochs is a long time. When a world is placed on reserve it's usually either to let it lie fallow, while new species evolve to a level ripe for uplift, or to provide a quiet place of decline for an ancient race entering senescence. Planets are placed off limits either to become nurseries or old age homes.

'Both seem to have occurred on Kithrup-p. We have discovered a ripe pre-sentient race which has apparently risen since the last *Library* update. Also, the ... Karrank-k% ...' Brookida, too, had trouble with the name. '... were granted the planet as a peaceful place to die, which they apparently have done. There seem to be no Kar-rank%-% ... anymore.'

'But four hundred epochs without a re-survey?' It was difficult to imagine.

'Yes, a planet is usually re-licensed by the Institute of Migration long before that. Still, Kithrup is such a strange world ... few species would choose to live here. Also, good access routes are scarce. This region of space is gravitationally very shallow. It'sss one reason we came here.'

Charles Dart was still catching his breath. He drank from a tall glass of water. During the respite, Creideiki lay still, thinking. Despite Brookida's points, would Kithrup really have been left fallow for so long, in an overcrowded galaxy where every piece of real estate was desired?

The Institute of Migration was the only one of the loose Galactic bureaucracies whose power and influence rivaled even that of the *Library Institute*. By tradition, all patron-lines obeyed its codes of ecosphere management; to do otherwise courted galaxy-wide disaster. The potential of lesser species to one day become clients, then patrons in their own time, made for a powerful galaxy-wide ecological conservatism.

Most Galactics were willing to overlook humanity's pre-Contact record. The slaughter of the mammoth, the giant ground sloth, and the manatee were forgiven in light of Mankind's 'orphan' status. The real blame was laid on *Homo sapiens* supposed patron – the mysterious undiscovered race that all said must have left humanity's uplift half-unfinished, thousands of years ago.

Dolphins knew how close the cetaceans themselves had come to extinction at the hands of human beings, but they never mentioned it outside Earth. For well or ill, their fate was now linked to Mankind's.

Earth was humanity's until the race moved on or died out. Her ten colony worlds were licensed for smaller periods, based on complex eco-management plans. The shortest lease was a mere six thousand years. Then the colonists of Atlast had to depart, leaving the planet fallow once again.

'Four hundred million years,' Creideiki mulled. 'That seems an unusually long time with no re-survey.'

'I agree!' Charlie Dart shouted, now fully recovered. 'And what if I told you Kithrup was occupied by a machine civilization as recently as thirty thousand years ago? Without any entry in the *Library* at all?'

Hikahi rolled over closer. 'You think-k these crustal anomalies betray an interloper civilization, Doctor Dart?'

'Yes!' he cried. 'Exactly! You all know many eco-sensitive races will only build major facilities along a planet's plate boundaries. That way, when the planet is later declared fallow, *all* traces of habitation will be sucked down into the mantle and disappear. Some think that's why there are no signs of previous occupancy on Earth.'

Hikahi nodded. 'And if some species settled here illegally ... ?'

'They'd build only at a plate boundary! The *Library* surveys planets at multi-epoch intervals. All evidence of the incursion would be sucked underground by then!' The chimp looked eagerly from the holo display.

Creideiki had trouble taking this very seriously. Charlie made it sound like a whodunit! Only in this case the culprits were civilizations, the clues whole cities, and the rug under which the evidence was being swept was a planet's crust! It was the perfect crime! After all, the cop on the corner only swings by every few million years, and is late, at that.

Creideiki realized every metaphor he had just used was a human one. Well, that was to be expected. There were times, such as space-warp-piloting, when cetacean analogies were more useful. But when thinking about the crazy politics of the Galactics, it helped to have watched a lot of old human movie thrillers, and read volumes of crazy human history.

Now Brookida and Dart were arguing some technical point ... and all Creideiki could think of was the taste of the water near Hikahi. He badly wanted to ask her if the flavor meant what he thought it meant. Was it a perfume she had put on, or natural pheromone?

With some difficulty, he forced himself back to the subject at hand.

Charlie's and Brookida's discovery, under normal circumstances, would be exciting.

But this has no bearing on escape for my ship and crew, nor getting our data back to the Terragens Council. Even the mission I sent Keepiru and Toshio on, to help appraise the native pre-sentients, is more urgent than hunting arcane clues in ancient alien rocks.

'Excuse me, Captain. I'm sorry I'm late. I've been listening quietly for a while, though.'

Creideiki turned to see Dr Ignacio Metz drift up alongside. The gangling, gray-haired psychologist treaded water slowly, casually compensating for a small negative buoyancy. A slight pot belly distended the neat fit of his slick brown drysuit.

Brookida and Dart argued on, now about rates of heating by radioactives, gravity, and meteoritic impact. Hikahi, apparently, found it all fascinating. '

'You're welcome even late, Doctor Metz. I'm glad you could make it.'

Creideiki was amazed he hadn't heard the man approach. Metz

normally made a racket you could hear halfway across the bay. He sometimes radiated a two kilohertz hum from his right ear. It was barely detectable now, but at times it was quite annoying. How could the man have worked with fins for so long and never had the problem corrected?

Now I'm beginning to sound like Charlie Dart! He chided himself. *Don't be peevish, Creideiki!*

He whistled a stanza which echoed only within his own skull.

> * Those who live
> > All vibrate,
> > * All,
> * And aid the world's
> > Singing *

'Captain, I actually come out here for another reason, but Dart's and Brookida's discovery may bear on what I have to say. Can we talk in private?'

Creideiki became expressionless. He had to get some rest and exercise soon. Overwork was wearing him down, and *Streaker* could ill-afford that.

But this human had to be treated carefully. Metz could not command him, aboard *Streaker* or anywhere, but he had power, power of a particularly potent kind. Creideiki knew that his own right of reproduction was guaranteed, no matter how this mission ended. Still, Metz's evaluation would carry weight. Every dolphin aboard behaved as 'sentiently' as possible around him. Even the captain.

Perhaps that's why I've put off a confrontation, Creideiki thought. Soon though, he would force Dr Metz to answer some questions regarding certain members of *Streaker*'s crew.

'Very well, Doctor,' he answered. 'Allow me a moment.'

Hikahi swam close at a nod from Creideiki. She grinned and flicked her pectorals at Metz.

'Hikahi, please finish up here for me. Don't let them go more than another ten minutes before summing up. Meet me in an hour in recreation pool 3-A with your recommendations.'

She answered as he had addressed her, in rapid, highly inflected Underwater Anglic. 'Aye aye, Captain. Will there be anything else?'

Damn! Creideiki knew Hikahi's sonar showed her everything about his sexual agitation. It was easy to tell with a male. He would have to do an explicit sonic scan of her innards to gain the same information about her, and that would not be polite.

Things must have been so much simpler in the old times!

Well, he would find out her frame of mind in an hour. One of the privileges of captaincy was to order a recreation pool cleared. There had better not be an emergency between now and then!

'No, nothing else for now, Hikahi. Carry on.'

She saluted snappily with an arm of her harness.

Brookida and Charlie were still arguing as Creideiki turned back to Metz. 'Will it be private enough if we take the long way to the bridge, Doctor? I'd like to check with Takkata-Jim before going on to other duties.'

'That'll be fine, Captain. What I have to say won't take long.'

Creideiki kept his face impassive. Was Metz smiling at something in particular? Something he had seen or heard?

'I am ssstill confused by the pattern of volcanoes up and down the three-thousand-kilometer zone where these two plates meet,' Brookida said. He spoke slowly, partly for Charlie's benefit and partly because it was hard to argue in oxywater. There never seemed to be enough air.

'If you look at the sssurvey charts we made from orbit, you see that vulcanism is dispersed sparsely elsewhere on the planet. But *here* the volcanoes are very frequent, and all about the same small size.'

Charlie shrugged. 'I don't see how that relates at all, old man.'

'But isn't this also the only area where metal-mounds are found?' Hikahi suggested. 'I'm no expert, but a spacer learns to be suspicious of twin coincidences.'

Charlie opened and closed his mouth, as if he were about to speak, then thought better of it. At last he said, 'Brookida, you think these coral critters may need some nutrient that only this type of volcano provides?'

'Possssibly. Our exobiology, expert is Dennie Sudman. She's now at one of the islands, investigating the aboriginals.'

'She must get samples for us!' Charlie rubbed his hands together. 'Do you think it'd be too much to ask her to take a side trip to a volcano? Not too far away, of course, after what Creideiki just said. Just a little, teeny one.'

Hikahi let out a short whistling laugh. The fellow had chutzpah! Still, his enthusiasm was infectious, a wonderful distraction from worry. If only she could afford to hide away from the dangerous universe in abstractions, like Charlie Dart did.

'And a temperature probe!' Charlie cried. 'Surely Dennie'd do that much for me, after all I've done for her!'

Creideiki cruised a wide spiral around the swimming human, stretching his muscles as he arched and twisted. By neural command he flexed his harness's major manipulators, like a human exercising his arms. 'Very well, Doctor. What can I do for you?'

Metz swam a slow kick-stroke. He regarded Creideiki amiably. 'Captain, I believe it's time to re-think our strategy. Matters have changed since we came to Kithrup.'

'Could you be specific?'

'Certainly. As you recall, we fled from the transfer point at Morgran because we didn't wish to be crushed in a seven-way ambush. You were quick to realize that even if we surrendered to one party, this would only result in all sides ganging up on our captors, inevitably leading to our destruction. I was slow to understand your logic. Now I applaud it. Of course, your tactical maneuvers were brilliant.'

'Thank you, Doctor Metz. You leave out another reason for our flight. We are under orders from the Terragens Council to bring our data directly to them, without leaks. Our capture would classify as a "leak" wouldn't you say?'

'Certainly!' Metz agreed. 'And so the situation remained when we fled to Kithrup, a move which I now consider inspired. To my way of thinking, it was just bad luck this hiding place didn't work as planned.'

Creideiki refrained from pointing out that they were still concealed in this hiding place. 'Go on,' he suggested.

'Well, the chance of escape is now next to nil. Kithrup remains a refuge from the chaos of battle, but it can't hide us for long once there is a final victor overhead.'

'You're suggesting?'

'I think we should consider our priorities, and plan for unpleasant contingencies.'

'What priorities do you consider important?' Creideiki knew the answer to expect.

'Why, the survival of this ship and crew, of course! And the data for evaluating the performance of both! After all, what was our main purpose out here. Hmm?' Metz stopped swimming, regarding Creideiki like a teacher quizzing a pupil.

Creideiki could list a half-dozen tasks that had been set for *Streaker*, from *Library* veracity checks, to establishing contact with potential allies, to Thomas Orley's military intelligence work. As Metz alluded, the primary purpose was to evaluate a dolphin-crewed, dolphin-commanded spacecraft. *Streaker* and her complement were the experiment.

But everything had changed since they found the derelict fleet! He couldn't operate under the priorities he had been given at the beginning. How could he explain that to a man like Metz?

Judgment, Creideiki mused, *thou art fled to brutish beasts, and men have lost their reason* ... Sometimes he thought that the Bard must have been half dolphin, himself.

'I understand your point, Doctor Metz. But I don't see how it calls for a change in strategy. We still face destruction should we poke our beaks above Kithrup's sea.'

'Only if we do so before there's a winner overhead! Certainly, we shouldn't expose ourselves until the crossfire is over.

'However, we *are* in a position to negotiate, once there is a victor! We may yet win success for this mission!'

Creideiki resumed his slow spiral, forcing the geneticist to swim again toward the bridge lock.

'Can you suggest what we might have to offer in negotiation, Doctor Metz?'

Metz smiled. 'For one thing, we have the information Brookida and Charles Dart have literally dug up. The Institutes reward those who report ecological crimes. Most of the factions fighting over us are traditionalist conservatives of one stripe or another and would appreciate our discovery.'

Creideiki refrained from expressing in raspberries his contempt for the man's naivete. 'Go on, Doctor,' he said levelly. 'What-t else have we to offer?'

'Well, Captain, there's also the honor of our mission. Even if our captors decided to hold onto *Streaker* for a while, they'd certainly be sympathetic to our purpose. Teaching clients to use spaceships is one of the basic tasks of uplift. Surely they'd let us send a few men and fen home with our behavior-evaluation data, so progress toward future dolphin-crewed ships can continue. For them to do otherwise would be like a stranger interfering in the development of a child because of an argument with its parent!'

And how many human children were tortured and killed because of the sins of their parents, back in your own Dark Ages? Creideiki wanted to ask who would be the emissary to carry the uplift data back to Earth, while *Streaker* was held captive.

'Doctor Metz, I think you underestimate the fanaticism of those involved. But is there more?'

'Of course. I saved the most important for last.' Metz touched Creideiki's flank for emphasis. 'We must consider giving the Galactics what they want.'

Creideiki had expected it. 'You think we should give up the location of the derelict fleet.'

'Yes, and whatever souvenirs or data we picked up there.'

Creideiki wore his poker face. *How much does he know about Gillian's 'Herbie,'* he wondered. *Great Dreamer! But that cadaver's caused problems!*

'You'll recall, Captain, the one brief message we got from Earth ordered us to go into hiding and keep our data secret, *if possible*! They also said we should use our own best judgment!

'Will our silence really delay the rediscovery of that Sargasso of lost ships for long, now that it's known to exist? No doubt half the patron-lines in the Five Galaxies have swarms of scouts out now, trying to duplicate our discovery. They already know to look in a poorly linked, dim globular cluster. It's only a matter of time until they stumble across the right gravitational tide pool, in the right cluster.'

Creideiki thought that debatable. Galactics didn't often think like the Earthborn, and wouldn't conduct a search in the same way. Witness how long the fleet had lain undiscovered. Still, Metz was probably right in the long run.

'In that case, Doctor, why don't we simply broadcast the location to the *Library*? It'll be public knowledge, and no longer our affair. Surely this important discovery should be investigated by a licensed team from the Institutesss?'

Creideiki was sarcastic, but he realized, as Metz smiled patronizingly, that the human took him seriously.

'You are being naive, Captain. The fanatics overhead care little about loose Galactic codes when they believe the millennium is at hand! If everyone knows where the derelict fleet is, the battleground will simply move out there! Those ancient ships will be destroyed in a crossfire, no matter how powerful that weird protective field that surrounds them. And the Galactics will *still* strive to capture us, in case we lied!'

They had arrived at the bridge lock. Creideiki paused there. 'So it would be better if only one of the contesting groups got the data, and proceeded to investigate the fleet alone?'

'Yes! After all, what is that bunch of floating hulks to us? Just a dangerous place where we lost a scoutboat and a dozen fine crewfen. We're not ancestor-worshipers like those ET fanatics fighting over us, and we don't give a damn except intellectually whether the derelict fleet is a remnant from the days of Progenitors, or even the returning Progenitors themselves! It sure isn't worth *dying* over. If we've learned one thing in the last two hundred years, it's that a little clan of newcomers like us Earthfolk has got to duck out of the way when big boys like the Soro and Gubru get something up their snoots!'

Dr Metz's silvery hair waved as he bobbed his head for emphasis. A fizzing halo of effervescence collected amongst the strands.

Creideiki didn't want to go back to respecting Ignacio Metz, but when the man became passionate enough to drop his stuffy facade, he became almost likable.

Unfortunately, Metz was fundamentally wrong.

Creideiki's harness clock chimed. He realized with a start how late it had become. 'You make an interesting argument, Doctor Metz. I don't have time to go into it any further, right now. But nothing will be decided until a full staff review by the ship's council. Does that sound fair?'

'Yes, I think so, although . . .'

'And, speaking of the battle over Kithrup, I must go now and see what Takkata-Jim has to say.' He hadn't intended to spend so much time with Metz. He did *not* plan to miss his long-delayed exercise period.

Metz seemed unwilling to let go. 'Ah. Your mention of Takkata-Jim reminds me of something else I wanted to bring up, Captain. I'm concerned about feelings of social isolation expressed by some of the crewfen who happen to come from various experimental sub-breeds. They complain of ostracism, and seem to be under discipline a disproportionate amount of the time.'

'You're referring to some of the *Stenos,* I assume.'

Metz looked uncomfortable. 'A colloquial term that seems to have caught on, although all neo-fen are taxonomically *Tursiops amicus* . . .'

'I have my jaws on the situation, Doctor Metz,' Creideiki no longer cared if he interrupted the mel. 'Subtle group dynamics are involved, and I am applying what I believe are effective techniques to maintain crew solidarity.'

Only about a dozen of the *Stenos* showed disaffection. Creideiki suspected an infection of stress atavism, a decay of sapiency under fear and pressure. The supposed expert, Dr Metz, seemed to think the majority of *Streaker*'s crew was practicing racial discrimination.

'Are you implying that Takkata-Jim is also having problems?' Creideiki asked.

'Certainly not! He's a most impressive officer. Mention of his name reminded me because . . .' Metz paused.

Because he's a Stenos, Creideiki finished for him silently. *Shall I tell Metz that I'm considering moving Hikahi into the vice-captaincy? For all of Takkata-Jim's skill, his moody isolation is becoming a drag on crew morale. I cannot have that in my pod-second.*

Creideiki sorely missed Lieutenant Yachapa-Jean, who had died back at the Shallow Cluster.

'Doctor Metz, since you bring up the subject, I have noticed discrepancies between pre-launch psych profiles of certain members of the crew and their subsequent performance. I'm not a cetapsychologist, per se, but in certain cases I am convinced the fen did not belong on this ship in the first place. Have you a comment?'

Metz's face was blank. 'I'm not sure I know what you're talking about, Captain.'

Creideiki's harness whirred as one arm snaked out to scratch an itch above his right eye. 'I have little to go on, but I think I'll want to invoke command privilege and look over your notes. Strictly informally, of course. Please prepare them for . . .'

A tone interrupted Creideiki. It came from the comm link on his harness. 'Yess, speak!' he commanded. He listened for a few moments to a buzzing voice on his neural tap.

'Hold everything,' he replied. 'I'll be right up. Creideiki out.'

He focused a burst of sonar at the sensitive plate by the door lock. The hatch hummed open.

'That was the bridge,' he told Metz. 'A scout has returned with a report from Tsh't and Thomas Orley. I'm needed, but we will discuss these matters again, Doctor.'

With two powerful fluke strokes Creideiki was through the lock doors and on his way to the bridge.

Ignacio Metz watched the captain go.

Creideiki suspects, he thought. *He suspects my special studies. I'll have to do something. But what?*

These conditions of siege-pressure were providing fantastic data, especially on the dolphins Metz had inveigled into *Streaker*'s complement. But now things were starting to come apart. Some of his subjects were showing stress symptoms he had never expected.

Now, in addition to worry about ET fanatics, he had to handle Creideiki's suspicions. It wouldn't be easy to put him off track. Metz appreciated genius when he saw it, especially in an uplifted dolphin.

If only he were one of mine, he thought of Creideiki. *If only I could take credit for that one.*

23

GILLIAN

The ships lay in space like serried rows of scattered beads, dimly reflecting the faint glow of the Milky Way. The nearest stars were the dim reddish oldsters of a small globular cluster, patient and barren remnants from the first epoch of star formation – devoid of planets or metals.

Gillian contemplated the photograph, one of six that *Streaker* had innocently transmitted home from what had seemed an obscure and uninteresting gravitational tide pool, far off the beaten path.

An eerie, silent armada, unresponsive to their every query; the

Earthlings hadn't known what to make of it. The fleet of ghost ships had no place in the ordered structure of the Five Galaxies.

How long had they gone unnoticed?

Gillian put the holo aside and picked up another. It showed a closeup of one of the giant derelict ships. Huge as a moon, pitted and ancient, it shimmered inside a faint lambency – a preservative field of unguessable properties. The aura had defied analysis. They could only tell that it was an intense probability field of unusual nature.

In attempting to dock with one ghost ship, at the outer reaches of the field, the crew of *Streaker*'s gig somehow touched off a chain reaction. Brilliant lightning flashed between the ancient behemoth and the little scoutboat. Lieutenant Yachapa-Jean had reported that all the dolphins were experiencing intense visions and hallucinations. She tried to disengage, but in her disorientation she set off her stasis screens inside the strange field. The resultant explosion tore apart both the tiny Earthship and the giant derelict.

Gillian put down the photo and looked across the lab. Herbie lay enmeshed in his web of stasis, a silhouette untold hundreds of million years – billions of years old.

After the disaster, Tom had gone out all alone and brought the mysterious relic in secret through one of *Streaker*'s side locks.

A prize of great cost, Gillian thought as she contemplated the cadaver. *We paid well for you, Herb. If only I could figure out what we bought.*

Herb was an enigma worthy of concerted research by the great Institutes, not one solitary woman on a besieged starship far from home. It was frustrating, but someone had to make this effort. Somebody had to try to understand why they had been turned into hunted animals. With Tom gone, and Creideiki busy keeping the ship and crew functioning, the task was hers.

Slowly, she was learning a thing or two about Herbie ... enough to confirm that the corpse was very old, that it had the skeletal structure of a planet-walker, and that the ship's micro-*Library* still claimed that nothing like it had ever existed.

She put her feet up onto the desk and pulled another photo from the stack. It clearly showed, through that shimmering probability field, a row of symbols etched into the side of a massive hull.

'Open *Library*,' she pronounced. Of the four holo screens on her desk, the one at the far left – with the rayed spiral glyph above it – came alight.

'Sargasso file – symbols reference search. Open and display changes.'

A terse column of text displayed in response against the wall to Gillian's left. The listing was dismayingly brief.

'Sub-persona: Reference Librarian – query mode,' she said. The outline remained projected against the wall. Alongside it a swirling pattern coalesced into the rayed spiral design. A low, calm voice intoned, 'Reference Librarian mode, may I help you?'

'Is this all you've been able to come up with, regarding those symbols on the side of that derelict ship?'

'Affirmative,' the voice was cool. The inflections were correct, but no attempt had been made to disguise the fact that it came from a minimal persona, a small corner of the shipboard *Library* program.

'I have searched my records for correlates with these symbols. You are well aware, of course, that I am a very small micro-branch, and that symbols are endlessly mutable in time. The outline gives all possible references I have found within the parameters you set.'

Gillian looked at the short list. It was hard to believe. Though incredibly small compared with planetary or sector branches, the ship's *Library* contained the equivalent of all the books published on Earth until the late twenty-first century. Surely there had to be more correlates than this!

'Ifni!' she sighed. '*Something* has got half the fanatics in the galaxy stirred up. Maybe it's that picture of Herbie we sent back. Maybe it's these symbols. Which was it?'

'I am not equipped to speculate,' the program responded.

'The question was rhetorical, and not addressed to you anyway. I see you show a thirty percent correlation of five symbols with religious glyphs of the "Abdicator" Alliance. Give me an overview of the Abdicators.'

The voice shifted tone. 'Cultural summary mode . . .'

'Abdicator is a term chosen from Anglic to represent one of the major philosophical groupings in Galactic society.

'The Abdicator belief dates from the fabled Tarseuh episode of the fifteenth aeon, approximately six hundred million years ago, a particularly violent time, when the Galactic Institutes barely survived the ambitions of three powerful patron lines (reference numbers 97AcF109t, 97AcG136t and 9 7AcG986s).

'Two of these species were amongst the most potent and aggressive military powers in the history of the Five Linked Galaxies. The third species was responsible for the introduction of several new techniques of spacecraft design, including the now standard . . .'

The *Library* waxed into a highly technical discussion of hardware and manufacturing methods. Though interesting, it seemed hardly relevant, With her toe she touched the 'skim' button on her console, and the narration leaped ahead . . .

'... The conquerors assumed an appellation which might be translated as "the Lions." They managed to seize most of the transfer points and centers of power, and all the great *Libraries*. For twenty million years their grip appeared unassailable. The Lions engaged in unregulated population expansion and colonization, resulting in extinction of eight out of ten pre-client races in the Five Galaxies at the time.

'The Tarseuh helped bring about an end of this tyranny by summoning intervention by six ancient species previously thought to be extinct. These six joined forces with the Tarseuh in a successful counterattack by Galactic culture. Afterward, when the Institutes were re-established, the Tarseuh accompanied the mysterious defenders to an obscure oblivion ...'

Gillian interrupted the flow of words.

'Where did the six species that helped the rebels come from? Did you say they had been extinct?'

The monitor voice returned. 'According to records of the time, they had been thought extinct. Do you want reference numbers?'

'No. Proceed.'

'Today most sophonts believe the six were racial remnants not yet finished "stepping off" into a later stage of evolution. Thus the six might not have been extinct per se, but merely grown almost unrecognizable. They were still capable of taking an interest in mundane affairs when matters became sufficiently severe. Do you wish me to refer you to articles on the natural passing modes of species?'

'No. Proceed. What do the Abdicators say took place?'

'Abdicators believe that there are certain ethereal races which deign to take physical form, from time to time, disguised in a seemingly normal pattern of uplift. These "Great Ghosts" are raised up as pre-clients, pass through indenture, and go on to become leading seniors, without ever revealing their true nature. In emergencies, however, these super-species can quickly intervene directly in the affairs of mortals.

'The Progenitors are said to be the earliest, most aloof, and most powerful of these Great Ghosts.

'Naturally, this is profoundly different from the common Progenitor legend, that the Eldest departed the Home Galaxy long ago, promising to return some day ...'

385

'Stop!' The *Library* fell silent at once. Gillian frowned as she thought about the phrase 'Naturally, this is profoundly different...'

Bull! The Abdicator belief was just a variant of the same basic dogma, differing only slightly from other millennial legends of the 'return' of the Progenitors. The controversy reminded her of old-time religious conflicts on Earth, when adherents had performed frantic exegesis over the nature of trinity, or the number of angels that could dance on the head of a pin.

This particular frenzy over minor points of doctrine would be almost funny if the battle weren't going on right now, a few thousand kilometers overhead. She jotted a reminder to try a cross-reference to the Hindu belief in the avatars of deities. The similarity to Abdicator tenets made her wonder why the *Library* hadn't made the connection, at least as an analogy.

Enough is enough.
'Niss!' she called.

The screen on the far right came alight. An abstract pattern of sparkling motes erupted into a sharply limited zone just above.

'As you know, Gillian Baskin, it is preferable that the *Library* not know of my existence aboard this ship. I have taken the liberty of screening it so that it cannot observe our conversation. You wish to ask me something?'

'I certainly do. Were you listening to that report just now?'

'I listen to everything this ship's micro-branch does. It is my primary function here. Didn't Thomas Orley ever explain that to you?'

Gillian restrained herself. Her foot was too close to the offending screen. She put it on the floor to remove temptation. 'Niss,' she asked evenly, 'why does the micro-branch *Library* talk gibberish?'

The Tymbrimi machine sighed anthropomorphically. 'Doctor Baskin, virtually every oxygen-breathing race but Mankind has been weaned on a semantic which evolved down scores of patron-client links; all influenced by the *Library*. The languages of Earth are strange and chaotic by Galactic standards. The problems of converting Galactic archives into your unconventional syntax are enormous.'

'I know that! The ETs wanted us to all learn Galactic Seven at the time of Contact. We told them to take the idea and stick it.'

'Graphically put. Instead, humanity applied immense resources to convert Earth's branch *Library* to use colloquial Anglic, hiring Kanten, Tymbrimi, and others as consultants. But still there are problems, are there not?'

Gillian rubbed her eyes. This was getting nowhere. *Why* did Tom imagine this sarcastic machine was useful? Whenever she wanted a simple answer, it only asked questions.

'The language problem has been their excuse for two centuries!' she said. 'How much longer will they use it? Since Contact we've been studying *language* as it hasn't been studied in millions of years! We've tackled the intricacies of "wolfling" tongues like Anglic, English, Japanese, and taught dolphins and chimps to speak. We've even made some progress communicating with those strange creatures, the Solarians of Earth's sun!

'Yet the *Library Institute* still tells us it's our language that's at fault for all of these lousy correlations, these clumsily translated records! Hell, Tom and I can each speak four or five Galactic tongues. It's not the language difference that's the trouble. There's something queer about the *data* we've been given!'

The Niss hummed silently for a time. The sparkling motes coalesced and separated like two immiscible fluids merging and falling apart into droplets.

'Doctor Baskin, haven't you just described the major reason for ships such as this one, which roam space hunting discrepancies in the *Library's* records? And the very purpose of my existence, to catch the *Library* in a lie, to find out if powerful patron races, as you would say, "stack the deck" against younger sophonts such as Men and Tymbrimi?'

'Then why don't you *help* me?' Gillian's heart raced. She gripped the edge of the desk, and realized that frustration was close to overcoming her.

'Why am I so fascinated with the human way of looking at things, Doctor Baskin?' the Niss asked. Its voice turned almost sympathetic. 'My Tymbrimi masters are unusually crafty. Their adaptability keeps them alive in a dangerous galaxy. Yet they, too, are trapped in the Galactic mode of thinking. You Earthlings, from a fresh perspective, may see what they do not.

'The range of behaviors and beliefs among oxygen-breathers is vast, yet the experience of Man is virtually unique. Carefully uplifted client races never suffer through the errors made by your pre-Contact human nations. These errors have made you different.'

That was true enough, Gillian knew. Blatant idiocies had been tried by early men and women – foolishness that would never have been considered by species aware of the laws of nature. Desperate superstitions had bred during the savage centuries. Styles of government, intrigues, philosophies were tested with abandon. It was almost as if Orphan Earth had been a planetary laboratory, upon which a series of senseless and bizarre experiments were tried.

Illogical and shameful as they seemed in retrospect, those experiences enriched modern Man. Few races had made so many mistakes in so short a time, or tried so many tentative solutions to hopeless problems.

Earthling artists were sought out by many jaded ETs, and paid well to spin tales no Galactic would imagine. The Tymbrimi particularly liked human fantasy novels, with lots of dragons, ogres and magic – the more the better. They thought them terrifyingly grotesque and vivid.

'I am not discouraged when you grow frustrated with the *Library*,' the Niss said. 'I am *glad*. I learn from your frustration! You question things that all Galactic society takes for granted.

'Only secondarily am I here to help you, Mrs Orley. Primarily, I am here to observe how you suffer.'

Gillian blinked. The machine's use of an ancient honorific had to have a purpose – as did its blatant attempt to make her angry. She sat still amid a flux of conflicting emotions.

'This is getting nowhere,' she spat. 'And it's making me crazy. I feel all cooped up.'

The Niss sparkled without commenting. Gillian watched the motes spin and dance.

'You're suggesting we let it sit for a while, aren't you?' she said at last.

'Both Tymbrimi and humans possess pre-conscious selves. Perhaps we should both let matters lie in the dark for a time, and let our hidden parts mull things over.'

Gillian nodded. 'I'm going to ask Creideiki to send me to Hikahi's island. The abos are important. After escape itself, I'd guess they're the most important thing.'

'A normal, moral view from the Galactic standpoint, and therefore of little interest to me.' The Niss sounded bored already. The dazzling display coalesced into dark patterns of spinning lines. They whirled and converged, fell together into a tiny point, and disappeared.

Gillian imagined she heard a faint pop as the Niss departed.

When she reached Creideiki on the comm line the captain blinked at her.

'Gillian, is your psi working overtime? I was just calling you!'

She sat up. 'Have you heard from Tom?'

'Yesss. He's fine. He's asked me to send you on an errand. Can you come down here right away?'

'I'm on my way, Creideiki.'

She locked the door to her lab and hurried toward the bridge.

24

GALACTICS

Beie Chohooan could only rumble in amazement at the magnitude of the battle. How had the fanatics managed to gather such strength in so short a time?

Beie's little Synthian scout ship cruised down the ancient, rocky jet stream left by a long-dead comet. The Kthsemenee system was ablaze with bright flashes. Her screens showed the battle fleets as they merged into swirling knots all around her, scratching and killing and separating again. Alliances formed and dissolved whenever the parties seemed to sense an advantage. In violation of the codes of the Institute for Civilized Warfare, no quarter was being given.

Beie was an experienced spy for the Synthian Enclave, but she had never seen anything like this.

'I was an observer at Paklatuthl, when the clients of the J'81ek broke their indenture on the battlefield. I saw the Obeyor Alliance meet the Abdicators in ritual war. But never have I seen such mindless slaughter! Have they no pride? No appreciation of the art of war?'

Even as she watched, Beie saw the strongest of the alliances fall apart in a fiery betrayal, as one flank fell upon the other.

Beie snorted in disgust. 'Faithless fanatics,' she muttered.

There was a chitter from the shelf to her left. A row of small pink eyes looked down upon her.

'Which of you said that!' She glared at the little tarsier-like wazoon, each staring out the entrance hatch of its own little spy-globe. The eyes blinked back at her. The wazoon snickered in amusement, but none of them answered her directly.

Beie sniffed. 'Well, you're right, of course. The fanatics have quick reactions on their side. They do not stop and consider, but dive right in, while we moderates must ponder before we act.'

Especially the ever-cautious Synthians, she thought. Earthlings are supposed to be our allies, yet timidly we talk and consider, we protest to the impotent Institutes, and send expendable scouts to spy upon the battle.

The wazoon chattered a warning.

'I know!' she snapped. 'Don't you think I know my business? So there's a watcher probe up ahead. One of you go take care of it and don't bother me! Can't you see I'm busy?'

The eyes blinked at her. One pair vanished as the wazoon scuttled into its tiny ship and closed the hatch. *In a moment a small shudder passed through the scout as the probe departed.*

Luck to you, small wazoon, faithful client, *she thought. Feigning nonchalance, she watched as the tiny probe danced ahead amongst the planetoid debris, sneaking toward the watcher probe that lay in Beie's path.*

One expendable scout, she thought bitterly. The Tymbrimi are fighting for their lives. Earth is besieged, half her colonies taken, and still we Synthians wait and watch, watch and wait, sending only me and my team to observe.

A small flame burned suddenly, casting stark shadows through the asteroid field. The wazoon let out a low groan of mourning, stopping quickly when Beie looked their way.

'Do not *hide your feelings from me, my brave wazoon,' she murmured. 'You are clients and brave warriors, not slaves. Mourn your colleague, who died so well for us.'*

She thought about her own cool, careful people, amongst whom she always felt a stranger.

'Feel!' *she insisted, surprised by her own vehemence. 'There is no shame in* caring, *my little wazoon. In this you may be greater than your patron race, when you are grown up and on your own!'*

Beie piloted closer to the water world, where the battle raged, feeling more akin to her little client-comrades than to her own ever-cautious race.

25

THOMAS ORLEY

Orley looked upon his treasure: a thing he had sought for twelve years. It appeared to be intact, the first of its kind ever to fall into human hands.

Only twice had micro-branch *Libraries* designed for other races been captured by human crews, from ships defeated in skirmishes over the last two hundred years. In each case the repositories were damaged. Attempts to study them were informative, but one mistake or another always caused the semi-intelligent machines to self-destruct.

This was the first ever recovered from a warship of a powerful Galactic patron race, and the first taken since certain Tymbrimi had joined in this clandestine research.

The unit was a beige box, about three meters by two by one, with simple optical access ports. Halfway along one side was the rayed spiral symbol of the *Library*.

It was lashed to a cargo sled along with other booty, including three probability coils, undamaged and irreplaceable. Hannes Suessi would ride back to *Streaker*, protecting those as a mother hen her eggs. Only when he saw them safely in Emerson D'Anite's hands would he turn around to come back here.

Tom wrote routing instructions on a waxboard. With any luck, the crew back at *Streaker* would turn the micro-branch unit over to Creideiki or Gillian without undue attention. He adhered the shipping slip so that it covered the *Library* glyph.

Not that his interest in a captured micro-branch was particularly secret. The crew here had helped him pry it from the Thennanin ship. But the fewer who knew the details the better. Especially if they should ever be captured. If his instructions were followed, the unit would be plugged into the comm in his own cabin, to outward appearances a normal communications screen.

He imagined the Niss would be impressed. Tom wished he could be there when the Tymbrimi machine found out what it suddenly had access to. The smug thing would probably be speechless for half a day.

He hoped it wouldn't be *too* stunned. He wanted something from it right away.

Suessi was already asleep, tethered to his precious salvage. Tom made sure the instructions were well secured. Then he swam up toward the sheer outcrop of rock overlooking the wrecked alien starship.

Neo-fen swarmed over the hulk, making detailed measurements from without and within. At word from Creideiki charges would be set off, beginning a process that would leave the giant battleship's core a reamed and empty cavity.

By now the scout they had sent back should have reached *Streaker* with his initial report, and a sled should already be returning down the new shortcut they had found, bringing a monofilament intercom line from home. It ought to meet the salvage sled about halfway.

All this assumed 'home' was still there. Tom guessed the battle still raged above Kithrup. Space war was a slow thing, especially as practiced by the long-viewed Galactics. They might still be at it in a year or two, though he doubted it. That much time would allow reinforcements to arrive and produce a war of attrition. It was unlikely the fanatic alliances would let things come to that pass.

In any event, *Streaker*'s crew had to act as if the war were about to end any day now. So long as confusion reigned above, they still had a chance.

Tom went over his plan again, and came to the same conclusion. He had no other choice.

There were three conceivable ways they might escape the trap they were in – rescue, negotiation, and trickery.

Rescue was a nice image. But Earth herself didn't have the strength to come and deliver them. Together with her allies she could barely match *one* of the pseudo-religious factions in the battle over Kithrup.

The Galactic Institutes might intervene. What law there was demanded that *Streaker* report directly to them. Problem was, the Institutes had little power of their own. Like the feeble versions of world government Earth had almost died of in the Twentieth Century, they relied on mass opinion and volunteer levies. The majority 'moderates' might finally decide that *Streaker*'s discovery should be shared by all, but Tom figured it would take years for the necessary alliances to form.

Negotiation seemed as faint a hope as rescue. In any event, Creideiki had Gillian and Hikahi and Metz to help him if it ever came to haggling with a victor in the space battle. They didn't need Tom for that.

That left clever schemes and subtle deceptions ... finding a way to thwart the enemy when rescue and negotiation fail.

That's my job.

The ocean was deeper and darker here than fifty kilometers to the east, where strings of metal-mounds grew in hilly shallows along the edges of a thin crustal plate. In the area where Hikahi's party had been rescued, the water was metal-enriched by a chain of semi-active volcanoes.

There were no true metal-mounds in this area, and the long-dead volcanic islands were worn down to the water's surface. When he looked away from the crumpled Thennanin wreck, and the trail of havoc it had left before coming to rest, Tom found the scenery restful, its beauty calming. Drifting, dark-yellow fronds of danglevine, waving like corn silk from the surface, reminded him of the color of Gillian's hair.

Orley hummed to himself a melody few other human beings could attempt. Small, gene-crafted sinuses reverberated under his skull, sending a low refrain into the water around him.

> * *In sleep, your caring*
> *Touches me,*
> * *Where, waking, I let it not*

> ** In distance, I will*
> *Call to you,*
> ** And touch you as you sleep **

Of course Gillian couldn't actually hear his gift poem. His own psi powers were quite modest. Still, she might pick up a hint. Other things she had done had surprised him more.

The dolphin escort gathered at the sled. Suessi had awakened and was checking the lashings with Lieutenant Tsh't.

Tom launched himself from his aerie toward the group. Tsh't saw him and took a quick breath from an airdome before swimming up to meet him halfway.

'I wish you would reconsider doing thisss,' she implored when they met. 'I'll be frank. Your presence is good for morale. If you were losssst it would be a blow.'

Tom smiled and put a hand on her flank. He had already come to terms with his poor chances of returning.

'I don't see any other way, Tsh't. All the other parts of my plan can be handled by others, but I'm the only one who can bait the hook. You know that.'

'Besides,' he grinned, 'Creideiki will have one more chance to call me back if he doesn't like the plan. I asked that he send Gillian to meet me at Hikahi's island, with the glider and the supplies I need. If she tells me his answer is no, I'll be back at the ship before you.'

Tsh't looked away. 'I doubt he'll sssay no,' she whistled low and almost inaudibly.

'Hmm? What do you mean?'

Evasively, Tsh't answered in Trinary.

> ** Creideiki leads us—*
> *Is our master*
> ** Yet we imagine—*
> *Secret orders **

Tom sighed. There it was again, the suspicion that Earth would never let the first dolphin-commanded vessel go out without disguised human supervision. Naturally, most of the rumors centered around himself. It was bothersome, because Creideiki was an excellent captain. Also, it detracted from one of the purposes of the mission, to make a demonstration that would boost neo-fin self-confidence for a generation.

> ** Then in my leaving—*
> *Learn a lesson,*

393

Tsh't must have been running low on the breath she had taken at the sled's airdome. Bubbles leaked from her blowmouth. Still she looked back at him resignedly and spoke in Anglic.

'All right-t. After Suessi leaves, we'll get you on your way. We'll continue working here until we get ordersss from Creideiki.'

'Good.' Tom nodded. 'And you still approve of the rest of the plan?'

Tsh't turned away, her eyes recessed.

> * Keneenk and logic
>   Join to sing
> * Its tune
>
> * The plan is all between
>   Us and
> * Our doom
>
> * We'll all do our part *

Tom reached over and hugged her. 'I know we can count on you, you sweet old fish-catcher. I'm not worried at all. Now let's say good-bye to Hannes, so I can be on my way. I don't want Jill to get to the island before me.'

He dove toward the sled. But Tsh't remained behind for a moment. Although the air in her lungs was growing stale, she lay still, watching him swim away.

Her sonar clicks swept over him as he descended. She caressed him with her hearing, and sang a quiet requiem.

> * They cast their nets to catch us—
>   Those of Iki,
> * Yet you are there—
>   To cut the nets.
>
> * Good Walker,
>   Always,
> * You cut the nets—
>
> * Though they'll take
>   In payment
>   Your life ... *

26

CREIDEIKI

The most formal Anglic, spoken carefully by a neo-dolphin, would be difficult for a human raised only in Man-English to understand. The syntax and many root words were the same. But a pre-space-flight Londoner would have found the sounds as strange as the voices that spoke them.

The dolphin's modified blowhold provided whistles, squawks, vowels and a few consonants. Sonar clicks and many other sounds came from complex resonant cavities inside the skull. In speech, these separate contributions were sometimes in phase and sometimes not. Even at the best of times, there were stretched sibilants, stuttered t's, and groaned vowels. Speech was an art.

Trinary was for relaxation, for imagery and personal matters. It replaced and greatly expanded on Primal Delphin. But *Anglic* linked the neo-dolphin to the world of cause and effect. Anglic was a language of compromise between the vocal abilities of two races – between the hands-and-fire world of Men and the drifting legends of the Whale Dream. Speaking it, a neo-dolphin could equal most humans in analytic thought, consider past and future, make schemes, use tools, and fight wars.

Some thoughtful humans wondered if giving the cetacean Anglic had really been much of a favor, after all.

Two neo-dolphins alone together might speak Anglic for concentration, but not care if the *sounds* resembled English words. They would drift into frequencies beyond human hearing, and consonants would virtually disappear. Keneenk allowed this. It was the semantics that counted. If the grammar, the two-level logic, the time-orientation were Anglic, pragmatic results were all that mattered.

When Creideiki took Hikahi's report, he purposely spoke a very relaxed form of fin-Anglic. By example he wanted to say that what went on here was private.

He listened to her while he took the kinks out of his body, diving and racing back and forth across the exercise pool. Hikahi recited her report on the planetology meeting, enjoying the sweet smell of real air in her main lungs. Occasionally, she paused and sped alongside him for a stretch before continuing. Right now her words sounded nothing like human speech, but a very good voicewriter could have transcribed them.

'... He feels very strongly about it, Captain. In fact, Charlie suggests that we should leave a small study team here with the longboat, if *Streaker* tries to escape. Even Brookida is tempted by the idea. I was a bit stunned.'

Creideiki passed in front of her. He burst out a quick question.

'What would they do if we left them behind, and we were then captured?' He dove back underwater and sped toward the far wall.

'Charlie thinks he and a detached team could be declared non-combatants, and the Sudman-Sah'ot group out on the island, as well. He says there are precedents. That way, whether we get away or not, part of the mission is preserved.'

The exercise room was in *Streaker*'s centrifugal ring, ten degrees up the side of the wheel. The walls were canted and Creideiki had to watch out for shallows in the pool's port side. A cluster of balls, rings, and complex toys floated to starboard.

Creideiki felt much better. The frustration which had built when he listened to Tom Orley's message had abated. He could put aside, for a while, the depression he felt when he agreed to the man's plan. All that remained was to get the formal advice of the ship's council. He prayed they'd come up with a better idea, though he doubted they would.

Creideiki swam quickly under a cluster of balls and shot out of the water. He spun as he sailed through the air and landed on his back with a splash. He did a flip underwater, then rose above the surface on his churning tail. Breathing heavily, he regarded Hikahi with one eye.

'I've considered the idea already,' he said. 'We could leave Metz and his records, too. Getting him off our tails would be worth thirty herring and an anchovy dessert.'

He settled back down into the water. 'Too bad the solution is immoral and impractical.'

Hikahi looked puzzled, trying to figure his meaning.

'Think,' he asked his lieutenant. 'Declaring noncombatants might work if we are killed or captured, but what if we *escape*, and draw our ET friends chasing after us?'

Hikahi's jaw dropped open slightly – a borrowed human mannerism. 'Of course. I hear it. Kthsemenee is so very isolated. There are only a few routes in and out. The longboat probably couldn't make it back to civilization all alone.'

'Which would mean?'

'They would become castaways, on a deadly planet, with minimal medical facilities. Forgive my lack of foresight.'

She turned slightly, presenting her left ventral fin. It was a civilized version of an ancient gesture of submission, such as a human student's sheepish bowed head to his teacher.

With luck, Hikahi would someday command ships far greater

than *Streaker*. The captain and teacher within him was pleased with her combination of modesty and cleverness.

'Well, we'll take their idea under advisement. In case we have to adopt the plan quickly, see to stocking the longboat. But put a guard on it, too.'

They both knew that it was a bad sign, when security precautions had to be taken *within*, as well as without.

A brightly striped rubber ring floated past them. Creideiki felt an urge to chase it ... as he wanted to push Hikahi into a corner and nuzzle her until ... He shook himself.

'As for further tectonic research,' he said. 'That's out of the question. Gillian Baskin has left for your island, to take supplies to Orley and to help Sudman study the aboriginals. She can bring back rock samples for Charlie. That'll have to satisfy him.

'The rest of us will be busy as soon as Suessi gets back here with those spare parts.'

'Suessi's sure he found what we need at the wreck?'

'Fairly certain.'

'This new plan means we'll have to move *Streaker*. Turning on our engines may give us away. But I guess there's no choice. I'll get started on a plan to move the ship.'

Creideiki realized this was getting him nowhere. A few hours remained, at most, until Suessi arrived, and here he was talking to Hikahi in *Anglic* ... forcing her to think rigidly and carefully! No wonder he was getting no hint, no body language, no suggestion that an advance might be welcomed or rejected.

He answered in Trinary.

> * We'll only move her—
>   Below water
> * To the crashed ship—
>   Empty, waiting
> * Soon, while battles—
>   Wrack the blackness
> * Filling space—
>   With squid-like racket
> * At a time when—
>   Orley, Net-bane,
> * Far away, does
>   Make
>   Distraction
> * Far away, does
>   Truth
>   Decipher

> * Drawing sharks—
>> To make us safer *

Hikahi stared. This was the first time she had heard about that part of the plan. Like many females aboard, Hikahi had a platonic passion for Thomas Orley.

I should have broken the news more gently, or, better yet, waited!

Her eyes blinked, once, twice, then closed. She sank slowly, and from her forehead came a faint keening.

Creideiki envied humans their enfolding arms. He dropped alongside to touch her with his bottle-shaped rostrum.

> * Do not grieve for—
>> Strong-eyed flyer
> * Orley's song shall—
>> By whales be sung

Hikahi replied sadly.

> * I, Hikahi—
>> Honor Orley
> * Honor captain—
>> Honor crewmates
> * Deeds are done, still—
>> For one I suffer—
>
> * For Jill Baskin—
>> Dear Life-Cleaner
> * For her loss—
>> And body sorrow *

Shamed, Creideiki felt an enclosing shroud of melancholy fall around him. He shut his own eyes and the waters echoed back to him a shared sadness.

For a long time they lay side by side, rising to breathe, then settling once more below.

Creideiki's thoughts were far away when he finally felt Hikahi drift away. But then she was back, rubbing gently against his side, and then nibbling tenderly with sharp, small teeth.

Almost against his will, at first, Creideiki felt his enthusiasm begin to return. He rolled over to his side and let out a long sigh of bubbles as her nuzzling became more provocative.

The water began to taste happier then, as Hikahi crooned a

familiar song, taken from one of the oldest of Primal signals. It seemed to say, among other things, 'Life goes on.'

27

THE ISLAND

The night was quiet.

Kithrup's many small moons stirred low tides against metal cliffs a hundred meters away. Ever-present winds, driven without brake across the planet ocean, tugged at trees and ruffled the foliage.

Still, compared to what they had known for months, the silence was heavy. There were none of the ubiquitous machine sounds which had followed them everywhere from Earth, the unceasing whirrs and clicks of mechanical function, or the occasional smoking crackle of failure.

The squeaking, groaning drone of dolphin conversation was gone, too. Even Keepiru and Sah'ot were absent. At night the two dolphins accompanied the Kithrup aboriginals in their nocturnal sea hunt.

The surface of the metal-mound was almost too quiet. The few sounds seemed to carry forever. The sea, a distant rumble of some faraway volcano ...

There was a gentle moan in the night, followed by a very quiet gasping cry.

'They're at it again,' Dennie sighed, not particularly caring if Toshio heard her.

The sounds came from the clearing at the southern point of the island. The third and fourth humans on the metal-mound had tried to find privacy as far from the abo village and the tunnel pool as possible. Dennie wished they could have gone even farther.

There was laughter, faint but clear.

'I've never heard anything like it,' she sighed.

Toshio blushed and fed another stick to the fire. The couple in the next clearing deserved their privacy. He considered pointing this out to Dennie.

'*I* swear, they're like minks!' Dennie said, intending to sound sardonic and mock-envious. But it came out just a little bitter.

Against his better judgment, Toshio said, 'Dennie, we all know humans are among the sexual athletes of the galaxy, though some of our clients give us a run for it.'

'What do you mean by that?' Dennie looked at him sharply.

Toshio poked a stick into the fire. That had been a pretty brash thing to say. He felt a trifle emboldened by the night, and the desire to break the tension by the fire.

'We-ell, there's a line in an old play ... "Why, your *dolphin* was not lustier!" Shakespeare wasn't the first to compare the two horniest of the brainy mammals y'know. I don't suppose anyone's come up with a scale to measure it, but I'd have to wonder if it weren't a prerequisite for intelligence.

'Of course, that's only one of the possibilities. If you take what the Galactics say about uplift into account ... '

He rambled on, slowly drawing away from incitement, noticing how Dennie came *this* close to blowing her cool, before she turned and looked away.

He'd done it! He had played a round and won it! It was a minor victory in a game he had wondered if he would ever get to play.

The art of teasing had always been a one-sided affair to Toshio, and he'd always had the short end. To get the best of an attractive older woman by dint of clever conversation and character insight was a coup.

He didn't think he was being cruel, though a genteel cruelty did seem to be part of the game. All he knew for certain was that this was one way to get Dennie Sudman to treat him less like a child. If some of the easy mutual liking they'd had before had to suffer for it, that was too bad.

Much as he didn't care for Sah'ot, Toshio was glad the fin had provided the lever he needed to pry a chink in Dennie's armor. He was about to try out another bon mot when Dennie cut in.

'I'm sorry, Tosh. I'd love to hear the rest, but I'm going to bed. We've a busy day tomorrow, launching Tom's glider, showing Gillian the Kiqui, and experimenting with that damned robot for Charlie. I suggest you get some sleep too.'

She turned to wrap herself in her sleeping bag at the far end of the camp, near the watch-wards.

'Yeah,' Toshio said, perhaps a bit too heartily. 'I'll do that in a bit, Dennie. Good night. Pleasant dreams.'

She was silent, with her back to the tiny glow from the fire. Toshio couldn't tell if she was asleep or awake.

I wish we humans were better at psi, he thought. *They say telepathy has its drawbacks, but it would sure be nice to know what's going on in another person's head sometimes.*

It'd take away a lot of the anxiety if I knew what she was thinking ... even if I found out she just thought I was a nervy kid.

He looked up at the patchy sky overhead. Through long ragged openings in the clouds he could see stars.

In two places, there were nebiculae in the sky that hadn't been there the night before, signs of a battle still raging. The tiny false nebiculae glowed in every visible color, and probably in other bands than light.

Toshio let a fistful of metallo-silicate dirt sift through his fingers onto the coals. Falling sparkles of metal winked at him like incandescent confetti, like winking stars.

He dusted off his hands and turned to crawl into his own sleeping roll. He lay there, eyes closed, reluctant to watch the stars, or to dissect the pros and cons of his behavior.

Instead, he listened to the wind-and-surf sounds of the night. They were rhythmic and calming, like a lullaby, like the seas of home.

Except once in a while he thought he could pick up, on the edge of hearing, sighs and soft laughter coming from the south. They were sounds of complex happiness that filled him with a sad longing.

'They're at it again,' he sighed to himself. 'I swear, I've never heard of anything like it.'

The humid air kept their perspiration slick upon them.

Gillian licked a moustache of tear-like salt off her upper lip. The same way, Tom cleaned some of the sheen off her breasts. The wetness of his mouth cooled on her aureoles and nipples when he took his mouth away.

She gasped and grabbed the wavy hair at the back of his head, where his slightly balding vanity feared no tugging. He responded with mock biting that sent shivers to her calves, thighs, and lower back.

Gillian locked her heel behind his knee and levered her pelvis up against his. Her breath whistled softly as he lifted his head and met her eyes.

'I thought what I was doing was afterplay,' he whispered a little hoarsely. He made a show of wiping his forehead. 'You should warn me when I cross over the line, and start promising what I can't deliver.' He took her hand and kissed its palm and the inside of her wrist.

Gillian ran her fingers along his cheek, to touch, feather light, his jaw, throat and shoulder. She took sparse clumps of chest hair and pulled playfully.

She purred – not like a housecat, but with the feral rumble of a leopardess. 'Whenever you're ready, love. I can wait. You may be the illegitimate son of a fecund test tube, but I know you better than your planners ever did. You have resources they never imagined.'

Tom was about to say that, planners or no planners, he was the quite legitimate son of May and Bruce Orley of Minnesota State,

Confederacy of Earth . . . but then he noticed the liquid welling in her eyes. Her words were rough, light and teasing, but her grip on his chest hair only tightened as she looked up at his face, eyes roaming, as if memorizing every feature.

Tom felt suddenly confused. He wanted to be close to Gillian on their last night together. How could they be any closer than they were right now? His body pressed against hers, and her warm breath filled his nostrils. He looked away, feeling somehow he was letting her down.

Then he felt it, a tender stroking that seemed to strive against a locked and heavy feeling inside his own head. It was a soft pressure that would not go away. He realized that the thing fighting it was himself.

I'm leaving tomorrow, he thought.

They had argued over who would be the one to go, and he had won. But it was bitter.

He closed his eyes. *I've cut her off from me! I may never come back, and I've cut off the deepest part of me.*

Suddenly, Tom felt very strange and small, as if he were stranded in a dangerous place, the sole barrier between his loved ones and terrible foes, not a superhero but only a man, outnumbered and about to gamble all he had. As if he were himself.

He opened his eyes as he felt a touch on his face.

He pressed his cheek against her hand. There were still tears in her eyes, but also the beginnings of a smile.

'Silly boy,' she said. 'You can never leave me. Haven't you realized that by now? I'll be with you, and you'll come back to me.'

He shook his head in wonder.

'Jill, I . . .' He started to speak, but his mouth was stopped as she pulled him down to kiss him hungrily. Her lips were hot and tender upon his, crosswise. The fingers of her right hand did inciteful things.

Still and all, it was the heady, sweet smell of her that made him realize that she had been right about him, once again.

PART THREE

DISSONANCE

'Animals are molded by natural forces
they do not comprehend.
To their minds there is no past and no future.
There is only the everlasting
present of a single generation,
its trails in the forest,
its hidden pathways in the air
and in the sea.

'There is nothing in the Universe more
alone than Man.
He has entered into the strange world of history ...'

LOREN ELSELEY

28

All night he had followed them. Toward morning, Sah'ot felt he was beginning to understand.

With the dawn, the Kiqui left their nocturnal hunting grounds and swam toward the safety of their island. They stowed their woven nets and traps in hidden coral clefts, took their crude spears, and hurried from the growing light. With daytime the killer vines would become active, and other dangers as well. By day, the Kiqui could forage the forests atop the metal islands, seeking nuts and small animals in the thick foliage.

Underwater, the Kiqui looked like green puffer fish with short, web-handed arms and flippered legs. A pair of almost prehensile ventral fins helped them maneuver. Strong, kicking legs left their hands free to carry burdens. Around each head a fin-like crest of wafer-thin flagellae waved, collecting dissolved oxygen to supplement each Kiqui's distended air-sac.

The hunter-gatherers pulled two nets full of bright, crab-like sea creatures, like multi-colored metal sculptures in the mesh. The Kiqui sang a song of flutters and squawks and yelps.

Sah'ot listened as they squeaked to one another, their tiny vocabulary hardly more than a series of vocalized signals coordinating their movements. Each time a few Kiqui rose to the surface for air, the act was accompanied by a chain of complex twitters.

The natives took little notice of the alien creatures that followed them. Sah'ot kept his distance, careful not to interfere. They knew he was here, of course. Now and then the younger Kiqui would cast suspicious sonar squirts his way. Strangely, the older hunters seemed to accept him completely.

Sah'ot looked up at the growing light with relief. In spite of the darkness, he had kept his own sonar down to a minimum all night to keep from intimidating the natives. He had felt almost blind, and a little panicky when he almost blundered into something ... or 'something' almost blundered into him.

Still, it had been worthwhile. He felt he had a pretty good grasp of their language now. The signal structure, like Primal Delphin, was based on a hierarchical herd and the tempo of the breathing cycle. Its cause-and-effect logic was a bit more complicated than Primal, no doubt due to hands and tool use.

> :?: *Look, we well hunt*   *hunt*
>   *– hunted*   *– well*
> :?: *Careful, Careful,*
>
>   *Opportunistic*
>
> :?: *Eat, EAT well, will eat-*
>   *– not eaten*   *No!*
> *Die above water, not in . . .*

Based on semantic ability alone, these creatures seemed less ripe for uplift than fallow Earth-dolphins had been. Others, biased toward tool-using ability, might disagree.

Of course, the fact that they had hands probably meant the Kiqui would never be particularly good poets. Still, some of their braggadocio had a certain charm.

The straps of Sah'ot's harness chafed as he rose for breath. In spite of its lightweight, streamlined design, he wished he could get rid of the damned thing. Of course, these waters were dangerous, and he might need its protection. Also, Keepiru was out there somewhere, staying out of the way as requested, but listening, nonetheless. Keepiru would chew Sah'ot's dorsal fin down to the backbone if he caught him without his harness.

Unlike the ultra-technical fen of *Streaker*'s crew, Sah'ot was uncomfortable with devices. He didn't mind computers, some of which could talk, and which helped him speak to other races. But implements for the moving, shaping, or killing of objects, these were unnatural things which he wished he could do without.

He hated the two nubby little 'fin-gers' at the tips of each of his pectoral fins – which they said would someday lead to full hands for his species. They were unaesthetic. He also resented the changes made to dolphin lungs, making them more resistant to land-based diseases, and adapting parts to breathing oxywater. Natural cetaceans needed no such mutations. Fallow *Stenos bredanensis* and *Tursiops truncatus* dolphins, left untouched by the gene-crafters, could outswim any of the 'amicus' breed almost any time.

He was ambivalent to the expanded visual sense, bought at the cost of gray matter once dedicated to sound alone.

Sah'ot rose again to breathe, then submerged, keeping pace with the aboriginals.

His own line represented a drive to emphasize *language* ability, rather than tool use. It seemed to him a more natural extension of dolphin nature than all this crashing about in starships, pretending to be spacemen and engineers.

That was one reason he had refused to go along in the spaceboat, to help scout the derelict fleet back at the Shallow Cluster. Even had there been anything or anyone left to talk to – for which there'd been no evidence – he wasn't about to poke around supported only by a gang of inept clients! For *Streaker* to try to deal alone with the derelict fleet was like a group of children playing with a live bomb.

His actions had won contempt from the crew, even though he had been vindicated by the disastrous loss of the captain's gig.

Their contempt didn't matter, Sah'ot reminded himself. He was a civilian. As long as he did his job he didn't have to explain himself.

Nor did disapproving clicks over his pursuit of Dennie Sudman bother him. Long before uplift, male dolphins had been fresh with woman researchers. *It's a long-standing tradition*, he rationalized. Whatever was good enough for horny old Flipper is good enough for his brainy descendant.

One of the things he hated about Anglic patterns of thought was this need to self-justify. Men were always asking 'Why?' What did it *matter* why? There were other ways than the human way of looking at things. Any whale would tell you.

The Kiqui chittered excitedly as they swam toward the eastern end of their own island, preparing to hoist their catch up a crevice in the leeward seawall.

Sah'ot felt a sweep of sonar, like a passing searchlight. Keepiru approached from the north, to escort him back to the Earthling encampment. Sah'ot flicked up to the surface. He tilted his head to look out on the new day. The sun rose behind a bank of haze in the east, and the wind carried a whisper of rain on the way.

A metal taint seemed to stain the air, reminding him of their deadly predicament on Kithrup. No doubt Creideiki and his 'engineers' were trying to jury-rig a scheme to get out of this mess. Their plan would no doubt be frightfully bold and clever . . . and get them all killed.

Wasn't it obvious that neophytes at the game of making and conquering couldn't thwart the Galactics, who had been at it for aeons? The humans had his loyalty, of course. But he knew them for what they were – clumsy wolflings, struggling to survive in a dangerously reactionary galaxy. There was an old dolphin saying. 'All humans are engineers, and all engineers are humans.' It was cute, but patently a lie.

Keepiru broke surface beside him. Sah'ot blew quietly, his breath condensing into spray. He lay watching the sunrise until Keepiru's patience wore thin.

'It'sss daylight, Sah'ot. We shouldn't be out here. We've got to report, and I want food and rest!'

Sah'ot affected the role of an absent-minded scientist, as if pulled from thoughts deeper than Keepiru might ever understand. 'What?

Oh, yes. Of course, Pilot. By all means. I've very interesting data to report. You know, I think I've cracked their language?'

'How nice.' Keepiru's reply was semantically Anglic, and phonemically a squawk. He dove and headed for the cave entrance.

Sah'ot winced at the pilot's sarcasm. But he was unrepentant.

Maybe I've time to finish a few suggestive limericks, to intersperse in my report to Dennie, he thought. *It's too bad she stays up on the bank of the pool. Maybe today she'll relent.*

When they got to the bottom of the former drill-tree shaft, now lit by a small phosphor bulb, Sah'ot noticed that someone had taken both sleds out of the passage and moored them in the cavern below. But at least one sled was always supposed to be in the pool in case Dennie and Toshio had to escape quickly! He hurried after Keepiru, up the narrow vertical tunnel.

There were two more sleds in the pool at the top. Someone must have arrived from the ship during the night.

Toshio and Dennie were already down by the water, talking to Keepiru. Sah'ot eyed Dennie speculatively, but decided not to start in.

This evening I'll try to get her to join me in the water. I'll think up a pretext, maybe something to do with the mechanics of the drill-tree root. It probably won't work, but the attempt should be fun.

Sah'ot spy-hopped, churning his tail to rise up and look about the poolside clearing. The thick brush parted to the south and two men, one female and one male, approached.

Gillian Baskin knelt by the poolside and whistled a Trinary welcome.

> * *Constant Keepiru*
> > *Solid as surf rock*
> * *Orca-defier*
>
> * *Chameleon Sah'ot*
> > *Ever adaptable*
> * *Ever so man-like*
>
>
> * *Under dark squalls I'd*
> > *Recognize you two …*
> * *Study in opposites!*

Keepiru answered in Anglic, a pathetically unoriginal 'Good to see you, Gillian. You too, T-Tom.'

Sah'ot settled down, uncomfortably aware that he had a reputation to live up to. Unlike Keepiru, he would have to come up with a greeting that matched Gillian's.

He would rather have gone someplace to think about Gillian's remark, especially that part about being 'ever so man-like ...' Was that a compliment, or was there a touch of pity in Gillian's upper register when she had whistled it?

Orley stood quietly next to Gillian. Sah'ot felt as if the man were seeing through him.

Sah'ot drew a breath.

> * Look here!
> A monogamous
> * Miracle!
>
> * A pair of lovers!
> Silhouetted against
> * The wide sky. *

Gillian clapped her hands and laughed. Orley smiled briefly, but apparently had things on his mind.

'I'm glad you two fins are back,' he said. 'Gillian and I arrived last night, she from *Streaker* and I from the site where Toshio's tsunami ship crashed. Jill brought you folks a monofilament cable, so you can stay in touch with the ship. She'll work with you for a few days on this vital matter of the Kiqui. Also, I understand there are some folks back at the ship who'd like to ask you to collect some data for them. That right, Gillian?'

The blonde woman nodded. Word of Charlie Dart's demands had not delighted Toshio and Dennie.

Orley continued. 'Jill's other purpose in coming here was to deliver some gear to me. I have to go away this morning. I'll be using a solar glider.'

Keepiru sucked air. He started to object, but Orley raised a hand. 'I know, it's risky. But there's an experiment I have to try in order to see if the escape plan we've put together will work. And since you people are the only ones available, I'm going to have to ask for your help.'

Sah'ot's tail thrashed under the water. He clamped down to hide his feelings, but it was hard. So hard!

So they were truly going to try to escape! He had hoped for better from Orley and Baskin. They were intelligent and experienced, almost-mythical agents of the Terragens Council. Survivors.

Now they were talking madness, and expected him to *help*! Didn't they realize what they were up against?

He swam up next to Keepiru, wearing the mask of a faithful, attentive client. But inside he felt turmoil as he listened to the crazy 'plan' that was supposed to save them from the bug-eyed monsters.

29

TAKKATA-JIM

'The ship's council meeting was a disaster. It is worse than I thought,' the vice-captain sighed.

> * They plan deception
>   To fool deceivers,
> * And veils
>   To cover whales!

K'tha-Jon tossed his great blunt head in agreement.

'I hear the codeword for thisss project is the "Trojan Seahorse." What does that mean?'

'It's a literary allusion,' Takkata-Jim replied. He wondered where the bosun had gone to school. 'I'll explain some other time. Right now I must think. There must be another way than this suicide plan Creideiki and Orley have devised.'

'The captain didn't lisssten?'

'Oh he's *very* polite! Blowfish Metz swam in my wake point by point, and Creideiki listened so nicely to both of us. The meeting lasted four hours! But the captain decided to go with Orley's scheme anyway! The Baskin fem has already left with supplies for him.'

The two *Stenos* drifted quietly for a long moment. K'tha-Jon waited for the vice-captain.

Takkata-Jim's tail slashed. 'Why won't Creideiki even *consider* broadcasting the location of our find and have done with it! Instead, he and Orley want to try to trick sophonts who have been trapping each other for millions of years! We'll be fried! Compared with this plan, even *your* idea of blasting forth with all guns blazing is better. At least we'd be able to maneuver!'

'I only offer a gloriousss alternative to his mad venture,' K'tha-Jon said. 'But I would go with your plan. Think, if *we* were the ones to find a way to save the ship and crew, would not the benefits go beyond simply preserving our livesss?'

Takkata-Jim shook his head. 'If I were in command, perhapsss. But we are led by this mad, honor-bound genius, who'll only guide us to doom.'

He turned away, deep in his thoughts, and swam silently down the corridor to his quarters.

K'tha-Jon's eyes narrowed as they followed the vice-captain. Bubbles from his blowmouth came out in tiny, rhythmic pops.

30

AKKI

It wasn't fair! Almost everybody who counted had been allowed to go with Hikahi, to go join the crew working on the Thennanin wreck. The repairs to *Streaker* were nearly completed, and he was *still* stuck here, where nothing important was happening at all!

Akki drifted at his study-station, under an airdome near the top of the central bay. Bubbles from below passed unhindered through the pages of a holo-text displayed in front of him.

Of all the dumb ideas! Making him study astrogation while the ship was stuck at the bottom of an ocean! He tried to concentrate on the subtleties of wormhole navigation, but his mind wandered. He got to thinking about Toshio. How long ago had it been since the two of them had time to pull off a decent prank? It must have been over a month since they'd stolen Brookida's glasses and replaced them with Fresnel lenses.

I sure hope Toshio's okay. But at least he's doing something. *Why did Creideiki insist I stay here when they need every decent engineer out at the wreck?*

Akki tried one more time to focus on the text, but was distracted by a sound. He looked down toward a noisy altercation at one of the food stations. Two fen were taking turns swatting at each other with their flukes while a circle of others watched.

Akki backed out of the airdome and dove toward the disturbance.

'Stop thisss!' he shouted. 'Cut it out, now!' He struck out with his own flukes to knock Sth'ata and Sreekah-jo apart.

The observers backed away a little, but the combatants ignored him. They bit and flailed at each other. A kicking fluke struck Akki in the chest, sending him spinning.

Akki gulped to catch his breath. How did they find the energy to fight in oxywater?

He swam up to one of the observers. 'Pk'Tow ... Pk'Tow!' He bit the fin on his flank and assumed dominant stance as Pk'Tow whirled angrily. It wasn't easy to face him down; Akki felt very young. But Creideiki had taught him what to do. When a fin reverts, make him focus!

'Pk'Tow! Stop listening to them and use your *eyes*. *Look* at me! As a ship's *officer* I *order* you to help me break up this fight!'

The glazed expression faded from Pk'Tow's face. He nodded. 'Aye, sssir.' Akki was amazed by the fellow's dullness.

Drops of blood diffused into a pink stain as the combatants slowed down, trading blows, their gill-lungs gasping for breath. Akki collected three more crewfen, swatting and shouting to get them focused, then he moved in. He got the *Stenos* and the cook separated at last, and led them under guard toward sick bay. Dr Makanee could keep them isolated until he reported this to the captain.

Akki glanced up and noticed the bosun, K'tha-Jon, pass by. The giant petty officer didn't even offer to help. He probably watched the whole thing, Akki thought bitterly. K'tha-Jon wouldn't have needed to cajole the onlookers. He could have intimidated the brawlers with a growl.

K'tha-Jon was headed swiftly for the outlock, his expression intent.

Akki sighed.

Okay, maybe Creideiki had his reasons for keeping me around, after all. Now that Hikahi has left with the engineers, he needs help taking care of the dregs that are still aboard Streaker.

Akki nosed Sreekah-jo to keep him moving. The *Stenos* squawked an almost Primal curse, but obeyed.

At least I've got an excuse not to study astrogation, Akki thought, sardonically.

31

SUESSI

'No! Stop it! Back off and try it again – this time more carefully!'

Hannes Suessi watched skeptically as the dolphin engineers reversed their heavy sleds and hauled the beam back out of the chamber.

It had been their third attempt to fit a supporting member into a gaping opening in the tail of the sunken Thennanin vessel. They had come closer to getting it right, but still the lead sled hung back too long and almost let its end be driven into the inner wall of the battleship.

'There now, Olelo, here's how you avoid that beam.' He addressed the pilot of the lead sled. His voice projected from the sled's hydrophones. 'When you get to their hieroglyph thingie that looks like a two-headed jackal, lift your nose thusly!' He motioned with his arms.

The fin looked at him blankly, for a moment, then nodded vigorously.

Roger—I'll dodge her! *

Suessi grimaced at the flippancy. They wouldn't be fins if they weren't sarcastic one-half the time and over-eager the other half. Besides, they really had been working hard. Still, it was a royal bitch working underwater. In comparison, doing construction in weight-lessness was a pure joy.

Since the Twenty-first Century, humans had learned a lot about building things in space. They had found solutions to the problems of inertia and rotation that weren't even in the *Library*. Beings who'd had antigravity for a billion years had never needed to discover them.

There had been somewhat less experience, in the last three hundred years, doing heavy work underwater, even in Earth's dolphin communities, and none at all in repairing or looting spacecraft at the bottom of an ocean.

If weightless inertia caused problems in orbit, what about the almost unpredictable buoyancies of submerged materials? The force it took to move a massive object varied with the speed it was already traveling and with the cross-section it presented at any given moment. In space there were no such complications.

As the fen reoriented the beam, Suessi looked inside the battle-ship to see how other work was progressing. Flashing laser saws, as bright as the heliarc lamps; illuminated the slow dismemberment of the central cavity of the Thennanin battleship. Gradually, a great cylindrical opening was being prepared.

Lieutenant Tsh't was supervising that end of the work. Her workers moved in that unique neo-fin pattern. Each dolphin used his eyes or instruments for close work. But when approaching an object, the worker's head would bob in a circular motion, spraying narrow beams of sound from the bulbous 'melon' that gave the

413

Tursiops porpoise its highbrow look. The sound-sensitive tip of his lower jaw waved to build a stereoscopic image.

The chamber was filled with creaking sounds. Suessi never ceased to marvel that they made anything out of the cacophony at all.

They were noisy fellows, and he wished he had more of them.

Suessi hoped Hikahi would get here soon with those extra crewfen. She was supposed to bring the longboat or skiff, giving Suessi a place to dry off, and the others a chance to rest with good air to breathe. If his gang weren't relieved soon, there would be accidents.

It was a devil of a plan Orley had proposed. Suessi had hoped that Creideiki and the ship's council would come up with an alternative, but those objecting to the plan had failed to offer anything better. *Streaker* would be moved as soon as the signal came from Thomas Orley.

Apparently Creideiki had decided they all had little to lose.

A 'Ker-runch!' sound carried through the water. Suessi winced and looked around. One end of a Thennanin quantum-brake hung limply, broken at the join by the end of Olelo's bracing beam. The usually impassive fin looked at him in obvious distress.

'Now, boys and girls,' Suessi moaned, 'how are we gonna make this shell look like it's survived a fight if we do more harm than the enemy ever did? Who'd believe it could fly with all these holes in it?'

Olelo's tail slashed. He let out mournful chirps.

Suessi sighed. After three hundred years, one still wanted to tread lightly with dolphins. Criticism tended to break them up. Positive reinforcement worked much better.

'All right. Let's try it again, hmm? Carefully. You came a lot closer that time.'

Suessi shook his head and wondered what kind of lunacy had ever driven him to become an engineer.

32

GALACTICS

The battle had moved away from this region of space; the Tandu fleet had once again survived.

The Pthaca faction had joined with the Thennanin and Gubru, and the lot of the Soro remained dangerous. The Brothers of the Night had been almost destroyed.

The Acceptor perched in the center of its web and peeled back its shields in careful stages, as it had been trained to do. It had taken the Tandu masters millennia to teach its race to use mind shields at all, so loath were they to let anything pass unwitnessed.

As the barriers fell, the Acceptor eagerly probed nearby space, caressing clouds of vapor and drifting wreckage. It lightly skirted over untriggered psi-traps and fields of unresolved probability. Battles were lovely to look at, but they were also dangerous.

Recognition of danger was another thing the Tandu had force-fed them. In secret, the Acceptor's species didn't take it very seriously. Could something that actually happened ever be bad? The Episiarch felt that way, and look how crazy it was!

The Acceptor noticed something it would normally have overlooked. If it had been free to espertouch the ships, planets, and missiles, it would have been too distracted to detect such a subtle nuance – thoughts of a single, disciplined mind.

Delighted, the Acceptor realized the sender was a Synthian! There was a Synthian here, and it was trying to communicate with the Earthlings!

It was an anomaly, and therefore beautiful. The Acceptor had never witnessed a daring Synthian before.

Neither were Synthians famed for their psychic skill, but this one was doing a creditable job of threading through the myriad psi detectors all sides had spread through nearby space.

The feat was marvelous for its unexpectedness ... one more proof of the superiority of objective reality over the subjective, in spite of the ravings of the Episiarch! Surprise was the essence of life.

The Acceptor knew it would be punished if it spent much longer marveling at this event instead of reporting it.

That, too, was a source of wonder, this 'punishment' by which the Tandu were able to make the Acceptor's people choose one path over another. For 40,000 years it had amazed them. Someday they might do something about it. But there was no hurry. By that day they might be patrons themselves. Another mere sixty thousand years would be an easy wait.

The signal from the Synthian spy faded. Apparently the fury of the battle was driving her farther from Kthsemenee.

The Acceptor cast about, regretting the loss slightly. But now the glory of battle opened before it. Eager for the wealth of stimulus that awaited it, the Acceptor decided to report on the Synthian later ... if it remembered.

33

THOMAS ORLEY

Tom looked over his shoulder at the gathering clouds. It was too soon to tell if the storm would catch him. He had a long way to fly before finding out.

The solar plane hummed along at four thousand feet; the little aircraft wasn't designed for breaking records. It was little more than a narrow skeleton, the propeller driven by sunlight falling on the wide, black wing.

Kithrup's world-ocean was traced below by thin white-caps. Tom flew to the northeast, letting the tradewinds do most of the work. The same winds would make the return trip – if any – slow and hazardous.

Higher, faster winds pushed the dark clouds eastward, chasing him.

He was flying almost by dead reckoning, using only Kithrup's orange sun for rough navigation. A compass would be useless, for metal-rich Kithrup was covered with twisty magnetic anomalies.

Wind whistled past the plane's small conical noseguard. Lying prone on the narrow platform, he hardly felt the breeze, but Tom wished he had just one more pillow. His elbows were getting chafed, and his neck was developing a crick. He had trimmed and retrimmed his list of supplies until he found himself choosing between one more psi-bomb to use at his destination and a water distiller to keep him alive when he got there. His compromise collection was taped beneath his cushion. The lumps made it almost impossible to find a comfortable position.

The journey was an unending monotony of sea and sky.

Twice he caught sight of swarms of flapping creatures in the distance. It was his first inkling that any animals flew on Kithrup. Could they have evolved from jumping fish? He was a bit surprised to find flight on a world so barren of heights.

Of course, the creatures might have been molded by some ancient Galactic tenant of Kithrup, he thought. Where nature's variety fails, sophonts can meddle. I've seen weirder gene-crafted things than fliers on a water world.

Tom remembered a time when he and Gillian had accompanied old Jake Demwa to the Tymbrimi university-world of Cathrhennlin. Between meetings, he and Jill had toured a huge continental wilderness preserve, where they saw great herds of Clideu beasts grazing the grassy plains in precise and complex geometric patterns. The arrangements spontaneously changed, minute by minute, without any apparent communication among the individual animals – like the transient weavings of a moire pattern. The Tymbrimi explained that an ancient Galactic race that had dwelt on Cathrhennlin ages ago had programmed the patterns into the Clideu as a form of puzzle. No one in all time since had ever managed to decipher the riddle, if there actually was one.

Gillian suggested that the patterns might have been adapted by the Clideu for their own benefit. The puzzle-loving Tymbrimi preferred to think otherwise.

Tom smiled as he recalled that trip, their first mission as a pair. Since then he and Gillian had seen more wonders than they could ever catalog.

He missed her already.

The local birds, or whatever, veered away from the growing bank of clouds. Orley watched them until they passed out of sight. There was no sign of land in the direction they flew.

The plane was making nearly two hundred knots. That should take him to the northeast chain of volcanic islands he sought in another two hours or so. Radio, satellite tracking, and radar were all forbidden luxuries. Tom had only the chart pinned to his windscreen to guide him.

He'd be able to do better on the return trip. Gillian insisted he take an inertial recorder. It could guide him blindfolded back to within a few meters of Hikahi's island.

Should the opportunity arise.

The pursuing clouds grew slowly above and behind him. Kithrup's jet stream was really cooking. Tom admitted that he wouldn't mind finding a landing site before the storm reached him.

As the afternoon wore on he saw another swarm of flying creatures, and twice he caught a glimpse of motion in the water below, something huge and sinuous. Both times the thing vanished before he could get a better look.

Scattered among the swells below floated sparse patches of seaweed. Some clusters came together to form isolated mounds of vegetation. Perhaps the flying things perched on those, he thought idly.

Tom fought the tedium, and developed a profound hatred for whatever lumpy object lay directly under his left kidney.

The glowering cloudbank was only a couple of miles behind him when he saw something on the northern horizon, a faint smudge against the graying sky.

He applied more power and banked toward the plume. Soon he could make out a dusky funnel. Curling and twisting to the northeast, it hung like a sooty banner across the sky.

Tom strove for altitude, even as threatening clouds encroached on the late afternoon sun, casting shadow onto the solar collectors on his wing. Thunder grumbled, and flashes of lightning briefly illuminated the seascape.

When it began to rain, the ammeter swung far over to the red. The tiny engine began to labor.

Yes. There it was! An island! The mountain seemed a good way off yet. It was partly hidden by smoke.

He'd prefer to land on a companion isle, one that wasn't quite as active. Orley grinned at the presumption of anyone in his position making demands. He would land at sea, if need be. The small plane was equipped with pontoons.

The light was fading. In the growing dimness Tom noticed that the surface of the ocean had changed color. Something about its texture made him frown in puzzlement. It was hard to tell what the difference was.

Soon he had little time for speculation, as he fought his bucking craft, struggling for every foot of altitude.

Hoping it would remain light long enough to find a landing place, he drove his fragile ship through pelting rain toward the smoldering volcano.

34

CREIDEIKI

He hadn't realized the ship looked this bad.

Creideiki had checked the status of every damaged engine and instrument. As repairs were made, he or Takkata-Jim had discreetly triple-checked. Most of the damage that could be fixed, had been.

But as ship's master, he was the one who also had to deal with intangibles. *Someone* had to pay attention to aesthetics, no matter how low their priority. And however successful the functional repairs were, *Streaker* was no longer beautiful.

This was his first trip outside in person. He wore a breather and swam above the scarred hull, getting an overview.

The stasis flanges and the main gravity drives would work. He had Takkata-Jim's and Emerson D'Anite's word on that, and had checked himself. One rocketry impeller had been destroyed by an antimatter beam at Morgran. The remaining tube was serviceable.

But though the hull was secure and strong, it was not the delight to the eye it had once been. The outer layer was seared in two places, where beams had penetrated the shields to blister the skin.

Brookida had told him that there was even one small area where the metal had been changed from one alloy to another. The structural integrity of the ship was intact, but it meant that someone had come awfully close to them with a probability distorter. It was disturbing to think that that piece of *Streaker* had been swapped with another similar but slightly different ship, containing similar but slightly different fugitives, in some hypothetical parallel universe.

According to *Library* records, no one had ever learned to control cross-universe distorters well enough to use them as anything but weapons, though it was rumored that some of the ancient species that 'outgrew' Galactic civilization from time to time discovered the secret, and used it to leave this reality by a side door.

The concept of endless parallel universes was one known by dolphins since long before humans learned fire. It was integral to the Whale Dream. The great cetaceans moaned complacently of a world that was endlessly mutable. In becoming tool users, *amicus* dolphins lost this grand indifference. Now they understood the whales' philosophy little better than did men.

A tame version of the probability distorter was one of the dozen ways the Galactics knew to cheat the speed of light, but cautious species avoided it. Ships *disappeared* using probability drives.

Creideiki imagined coming out of FTL to find a convention of 'Streakers' – all from different universes, all captained by slightly altered versions of himself. The whales might be able to be philosophically complacent about a situation like that. He wasn't so sure of himself.

Besides, the whales, for all their philosophical genius, were imbeciles on levels dealing with spaceships and machines. They wouldn't recognize a fleet of ships any better than a dog knew its reflection in the water.

Less than two months ago, Creideiki had faced a derelict fleet of ships the size of moons, as old as middle-aged stars. He had lost a dozen good fen there, and had been fleeing fleets of ships ever since.

There were times when he wished he could be animal-blind to some things, as were the whales. Or as philosophical.

Creideiki swam up to a ridge overlooking the ship. Bright heliarc lamps cast long shadows in the clear euphotic water. Crews below were finished installing the booty Suessi had found at the Thennanin wreck. There remained only clearing the landing legs for movement.

Hikahi had left just hours ago, with a picked crew and the ship's skiff. Creideiki wished he could have spared more to go help Suessi, but *Streaker* was already well below minimum complement.

He still saw no alternative to Thomas Orley's plan.

Metz and Takkata-Jim had been unable to come up with anything short of outright surrender to the winner of the battle overhead, and that was one thing Creideiki could never permit. Not while there was any chance at all.

Passive sensors showed the fight in space peaking in fury. Within days it might climax, and the last opportunity for an escape in the confusion would be upon them.

I hope Tom arrived safely, and his experiment is successful.

The water echoed with low grumblings of engines being tested. Creideiki had calculated the acceptable noise levels himself. There were so many forms of leakage – neutrinos from the power plant, gravitonics from the stasis screen, psi from everyone aboard. Sound was the least of his worries.

As he swam, Creideiki heard something above him. He turned his attention surfaceward.

A solitary neo-fin drifted near the detector buoys, working on them with harness manipulators. Creideiki moved closer.

* *Is there a problem—*
Here to bother
* *Duty's patterns?* *

He recognized the giant *Stenos*, K'tha-Jon. The bosun started. His eyes widened, and momentarily Creideiki could see the whites around the flat, boat-like pupils.

K'tha-Jon recovered quickly. His mouth opened in a grin.

* *Noise buzz bothered—*
Neutrino listener
* *She could not hear—*
The battle raging

* *Now she tells me—*
Static has fled
* *I'll to my duty—*
Now be leaving *

This was serious business. It was vital that *Streaker's* bridge know what was going on in the sky and be able to hear news of Thomas Orley's mission.

Takkata-Jim should have detailed someone else to do the job. The buoys were the responsibility of the bridge crew. Still, with Hikahi and Tsh't gone, and most of the elite bridge crew with them, perhaps K'tha-Jon was the only petty officer who could be spared.

> * Good as jumping—
> Big wave rider
> * Now hurry back—
> To those who need you *

K'tha-Jon nodded. His harness arms folded back. Without another word, he blew a cloud of bubbles and dove toward the bright opening of *Streaker*'s lock.

Creideiki watched the giant go.

Superficially, K'tha-Jon appeared to have reacted more resiliently than many of the other fen. Indeed, he had seemed to relish the fighting retreat from Morgran, and manned his gun battery with fierce enthusiasm. He was an efficient non-com.

Then why do my hackles rise whenever I'm near him? Is he another of Metz's sports? I must insist Dr Metz stop stalling, and show me his records! If necessary, I'll override the man's door-locks – protocols be damned!

K'tha-Jon had become Lieutenant Takkata-Jim's constant companion. Together with Metz, the three were the chief opponents to Tom Orley's plan. There was still bad bile over it. Takkata-Jim had become more taciturn than ever.

Creideiki felt compassion for the lieutenant. It was not his fault this test cruise had become a crucible. But pity would not prevent Creideiki from promoting Hikahi over his head as soon as the crew was reunited. Takkata-Jim was likely aware of what was coming, and of the report the captain had to write on each of his officers for the Uplift Center. Takkata-Jim's right to have bonus offspring might be in jeopardy.

Creideiki could imagine how the vice-captain felt. There were times when he, too, felt oppressed by the towering invasiveness of uplift, when he wanted to squawk in Primal, *'Who gave you the right?'* And the sweet hypnosis of the Whale Dream would call him to embrace the Old Gods.

The moment always passed, and he recalled that there was nothing in the universe he wanted more than to command a starship, to collect tapes of the songs of space, and explore the currents between the stars.

A school of native fish swam past. They looked a little like mullet, kitsch mullet, in garish, metal-flake scales.

He felt a sudden urge to give *chase*, to call his hardworking crew out to join him in a hunt!

He envisioned his stolid engineers and techs dropping their harnesses to join in the squealing pack, nimbly driving the poor creatures, catching them in midair as panic drove them leaping above the surface.

Even if a few fen got carried away and swallowed some metal, it would be worth it for morale.

> * *All the rains of Spring,*
> *And then, one secret evening,*
> *Riding waves, the Moon ... **

It was a Haiku of regret.

There was no time for hunt-games, not while they themselves were quarry.

His harness chime announced that he had only thirty minutes' air left. He shook himself. If his meditation had gone any deeper Nuka-pai might have come. The chimerical goddess would have teased him. Her gentle voice would have reminded him of Hikahi's absence.

The observation buoys bobbed nearby, tethered by slender strands to the seabed below. He swam closer to the smooth red and white ovoid K'tha-Jon had worked on, and noticed that the access plate had been left ajar.

Creideiki's head bobbed as he cast narrowly focused sound. The odd geometry of the buoy and guywires was mildly disturbing.

His sonar-speak receiver buzzed. An amplified voice came to him over the neural patchline.

'Captain, thisss is Takkata-Jim. We've just finished testing the impellers and the stasis generators. They're working up to your new specs. Also, Suessi called to say that the ... the Trojan Seahorse *is coming along. Hikahi has arrived there and sends greetingsss.'*

'Good.' Creideiki sent the words directly along the neural link. 'Has there been anything from Orley?'

'No, sir. And it's getting late. Are you sure you want to go with this plan of his? What if he can't get a psi-bomb message back to us?'

'We have already discussed contingencies.'

'And we're still going to move the ship? I think we ought to talk it over one more time.'

Creideiki felt a wave of irritation. 'We'll not discussss policy over an open channel, Pod-second. And it's already decided. Ill be back shortly. Meanwhile, search for loose ends to bite off. We must be ready when Tom calls!'

'Aye, sir.' Takkata-Jim didn't sound at all apologetic as he switched off.

Creideiki had lost count of the number of times he had been

questioned about this plan. If they lacked faith because he was 'only' a dolphin, they should have noted that the original idea was Thomas Orley's! Besides, he, Creideiki, *was* captain. He was the one saddled with saving their lives and honor.

When he had served aboard the survey vessel *James Cook*, he had never witnessed its human master, Captain Alvarez, questioned this way.

He slashed his tail through the water until his temper cooled, counting as the calming patterns of Keneenk settled over him.

Let it go, he decided. The majority of the crew did not question, and the rest obeyed, if grudgingly. For an experimental crew, under immense pressure, that would have to do.

'Where there is mind, there is always solution,' Keneenk taught. All problems contained the elements of their answer.

He commanded his manipulator arms to reach out and grab the access panel to the buoy. If things were in good order, he would find a way to praise Takkata-Jim. There must be a key to reach the lieutenant, to pull him back into the ship's community and break his vicious cycle of isolation. 'Where there is mind . . .'

It would only take a few minutes to find out if it was working. Creideiki plugged an extension from his neural socket into the buoy's computer. He commanded the machine to report its status.

A brilliant arc of electric discharge flashed. Creideiki screamed as the shock blew out the motors of his harness and seared the skin around his neural tap.

A *penetrator bolt!* Creideiki realized in stunned rigidity. *How . . . ?*

He felt it all in slow motion. The current fought with the protective diodes of his nerve amplifier. The main circuit breaker threw, but the insulation almost immediately buckled under backlash.

Paralyzed, Creideiki seemed to hear a voice in the pulsing, battling fields, a voice taunting him.

In a body-arching squeal of agony,

> # *Where there is mind – is mind,*
> *is – also deception*
> # *Deception – is, there is #*

Creideiki screamed one undisciplined cry in Primal, the first of his adult life. Then he rolled belly-up, to drift in a blackness deeper than night.

PART FOUR

_____

LEVIATHAN

'Oh my father was the keeper of the Eddystone light,
He slept with a mermaid one fine night.
From this union there came three:
A porpoise, a porgy and me.

'Oh, for the life on the rolling sea.'

OLD CHANTY

35

GILLIAN

'*Like most species derived from wholly carnivorous forebears, the Tandu were difficult clients. They had cannibalistic tendencies, and attacks on individuals of their patron race, the Nght6, weren't unheard of early in their uplift.*

'*The Tandu have remarkably low empathy for other sapient life-forms. They are members of a pseudo-religious alignment whose tenets propose the eventual extermination of species judged "unworthy." While they observe the codes of the Galactic Institutes, the Tandu make no secret of their desire for a less crowded universe, or their eagerness for the day when all laws are swept aside by a "higher power."*

'*According to followers of their "Inheritor" alignment, this will happen when the Progenitors return to the Five Galaxies. The Tandu assume that they will be chosen, come that day, to hunt down the unworthy.*

'*While waiting for this millennium, the Tandu keep in practice by indulging in countless minor skirmishes and battles of honor. They join in any war of enforcement declared by the Galactic Institutes, whatever the cause, and are often cited for use of excess force. "Accidental extinction" of at least three spacefaring species has been attributed to them.*

'*Although the race has little empathy for their patron-level peers, the Tandu are masters of the art of uplift. In their pre-sentient form, on their fallow homeworld, they had already tamed several local species for use as hunting animals: the equivalent of tracking dogs on Earth. Since release from indenture, the Tandu have acquired and adapted two of the most powerful psychic adepts of the recent crop of clients. The Tandu are under long-term investigation for excessive genetic manipulation in making the two (see references: EP1SIARCH-cl-82f49; ACCEPTOR-cl-82f50) totally dependent instruments of their love of the hunt . . .*'

Nice people, these Tandu, Gillian thought, putting the flat reading plate down beside the tree where she sat. She had allotted herself an hour for reading this morning, but had covered only two hundred thousand words or so.

This entry on the Tandu had come over the cable from *Streaker* last night. Apparently the Niss machine was already accomplishing things with the mini-*Library* Tom had retrieved from the Thennanin wreck. This report read too clearly, and came to the point too directly to have come straight from the English translation software of *Streaker's* own pathetic little micro-branch.

Of course, Gillian already knew some things about the Tandu. All Terragens agents were taught about these secretive, brutal enemies of Mankind. This report only reinforced her feeling that there was something terribly wrong with a universe that had such monsters in it.

Gillian had once spent a summer reading ancient space-romances from pre-Contact days. How open and friendly those old-time fictional universes had seemed! Even the rare 'pessimistic' ones hadn't come close to the closed, confined, dangerous reality.

Thinking about the Tandu put her in a melodramatic mind to carry around a dirk, and to exercise a woman's ancient last prerogative should those murderous creatures ever capture her.

The thick, organic smell of humus overwhelmed the metallic tang that permeated everywhere near the water. The aroma was fresh after last night's storm. Green fronds waved slowly under gentle buffeting from Kithrup's incessant tradewinds.

Tom must have found his island crucible by now, she thought, *and begun preparing his experiment.*

If he still lives.

This morning, for the first time, she felt uncertain about that. She had been so sure she would know it, if he died, wherever or whenever it happened. Yet now she felt confused. Her mind was muddied, and all she could tell for certain was that terrible things had happened last night.

First, around sunset, had come a crawling premonition that something had happened to Tom. She couldn't pin the feeling down, but it disturbed her.

Then, late last night, she had had a series of dreams.

There had been faces. Galactic faces, leathern and feathered and scaled, toothed and mandibled. They yammered and howled, but she, in spite of all her expensive training, couldn't understand a single word or sense-glyph. A few of the jumbled faces she had recognized in her sleep – a pair of Xappish spacemen, dying as their ship was torn apart – a Jophur, howling through smoke at the bleeding stump of its arm – a Synthian, listening to whale songs while she waited impatiently behind a vacuum-cold lump of stone.

In her sleep Gillian had been helpless to keep them out.

She had awakened suddenly, in the middle of the night, to a tremor that plucked her spine like a bowstring. Breathing heavily in the darkness, she sensed a kindred consciousness writhe in agony at the limit of her range. In spite of the distance, Gillian caught a mixed flavor in the fleeting psychic glyph. It felt too human to have been only a fin, too cetacean to have been merely a man.

Then it ceased. The psychic onslaught was over.

She didn't know what to make of any of it. What use was psi, if its messages were too opaque to be deciphered? Her genetically enhanced intuition now seemed a cruel deception. Worse than useless.

She had a few moments left to her hour. She spent them with her eyes closed, listening to the rise and fall of sound, as breakers fought their endless battle with the western shoreline. Tree limbs brushed and swayed with the wind.

Interleaved with the creakings of trunk and branch, Gillian could hear the high chittering squeaks of the aboriginal pre-sentients – the Kiqui. From time to time, she made out the voice of Dennie Sudman, speaking into a machine that translated her words into the high-frequency Kiqui dialect.

Though she was working twelve hours a day, helping Dennie, Gillian couldn't help feeling guiltily that she was taking a vacation. She reminded herself that the little natives were extremely important, and that she had just been spinning her wheels back at the ship.

But one of the faces from her dream had stuck with her all morning. Only a half-hour ago she had realized that it was her own subconscious rendering of what Herbie, the ancient cadaver which had caused all this trouble, must have looked like when he was alive.

In her dream, shortly before she had begun feeling premonitions of disaster, the long, vaguely humanoid face of the ancient had smiled at her, and slowly winked.

'Gillian! Doctor Baskin? It's time!'

She opened her eyes, lifted her arm and glanced at her watch. It might as well have been set by Toshio's voice. Trust a midshipman at his word, she remembered. Tell him to fetch you in one hour, and he'll time it down to the second. Early in the voyage she had had to threaten dire measures to get him to call her 'sir' – or the anachronistic 'ma'am' – only in every third sentence, rather than every other word.

'On my way, Toshio! Just a minute!' She rose to her feet and stretched. The rest break had been useful. Her mind had been in knots that only quiet could smooth.

She hoped to finish here and get back to *Streaker* within three days, about the time Creideiki had planned to move the ship. By then she and Dennie should have worked out the environmental needs of the Kiqui – how to take a small sample group with them back to the Center for Uplift on Earth. If *Streaker* got away, and if humanity first filed a client claim, it could save the Kiqui from a far worse fate.

On her way through the trees, Gillian caught a glimpse of the ocean through a northeast gap in the greenery.

Will I be able to feel it here, when Tom calls? The Niss said his signal should be detectable anywhere on the planet.

All the ETs will hear it, for sure.

She carefully kept all psychic energies low, as Tom had insisted she do. But she did form an old-fashioned prayer with her mouth, and cast it northward, over the waves.

'I'll bet this will please Doctor Dart,' Toshio said. 'Of course, the sensors might not be types he'd want. But the 'bot *is* still operational.'

Gillian examined the small screen. She was no expert on robotics or planetology. But she understood the principles.

'I think you're right, Toshio. The X-ray spectrometer works. So do the laser zapper and the magnetometer. Can the robot still move?'

'Like a little rock lobster! The only thing it can't do is float back up. Its buoyancy tanks were ruptured when the piece of coral crashed down on it.'

'Where is the robot now?'

'It's on a ledge about ninety meters down.' Toshio tapped the tiny keyboard and brought a holo schematic into space in front of the screen. 'It's given me a sonar map that deep. I've held off going any lower until I talk to Doctor Dart. We can only go down, one ledge at a time. Once the robot leaves a spot there's no going back.'

The schematic showed a slightly tapered cylindrical cavity, descending into the metal-rich silicate rock of Kithrup's thin crust. The walls were studded with outcrops and ledges, like the one the crippled probe now rested on.

A solid shaft ran up the great cavity, tilted at a slight angle. It was the great drill-root Toshio and Dennie had blown apart a few days earlier. The upper end rested against one rim of its own underwater excavation. The shaft disappeared into unknown territory below the mapped area.

'I think you're right, Toshio,' Gillian grinned and squeezed the boy's shoulder. 'Charlie will be glad about this. It may help get him off Creideiki's back. Do you want to ring him up with the news?'

Toshio was obviously pleased with the compliment, but taken aback by Gillian's offer. 'Uh, no, thank you, sir. I mean, couldn't you just tuck this in when you report to the ship, today? I'm sure Doctor Dart will have questions I'm not qualified to handle ...'

Gillian couldn't blame Toshio. Presenting good news to Charles Dart was barely more pleasant than delivering bad news. But Toshio would have to come to grips with the chimp planetologist sooner or later. It would be best if he learned to deal with the problem from the start.

'Sorry, Toshio. Doctor Dart is all yours. Don't forget that I'm leaving here in a few days. You're the one who's going to have to ... *satisfy* Charlie, when he asks you to put in thirty-hour shifts.'

Toshio nodded seriously, taking her advice soberly until she managed to catch eye contact with him. She grinned until he couldn't help but blush and smile.

36

AKKI

Hurrying to get to the bridge before watch change, Akki took a shortcut through the outlook. In his haste he was halfway across the wide chamber before he noticed anything different.

He did an overhead flip to stop. His gill-lungs heaved, and he cursed himself for an idiot, speeding and doing fancy maneuvers when there just wasn't enough oxygen available!

The outlook was as empty as he had ever seen it. The captain's gig had been lost at the Shallow Cluster. Heavy sleds and a lot of equipment had been moved to the Thennanin wreck, and Lieutenant Hikahi had taken the skiff there only yesterday.

There was a cluster of activity around the longboat, the last and largest of *Streaker*'s pinnaces. Several crewfen used mechanical spiders to carry crates into the small spacecraft. Akki forgot his haste to be early on duty, and kicked a lazy spiral toward the activity.

He swam up behind one spider-riding dolphin. The fin's spider carried a large box in its waldo-arms.

'Hey Sup-peh, v-what's going on here?' Akki kept his sentences short and simple. He was getting better speaking Anglic in oxywater, but if a *Calafian* couldn't speak properly, what where the others to think?

The other dolphin looked up. 'Oh, hello, Mr Akki. Change of orders is what-t. We're checking the longboat for spaceworthiness. Also, we been told to load these cratesss.'

'What are vey ... er, what's in the boxes?'

'Doctor Metz's records, seemsss-s,' the spider's third manipulator arm waved toward the pile of waterproof cartons.

'Imagine, all our grandparents 'n' grandchildren here, listed on mag chips. It gives you a feeling *of continuity*, don't it-t-t?'

Sup-peh was from the South Atlantic community, a clan which took pride in quaint speech. Akki wondered if it were really eccentricity as much as plain dimness. 'I thought you were on the supply run to the Thennanin ship?' he asked. Sup-peh was usually assigned tasks that required minimal finesse.

'That I were, Mr Akki. But-t-t those runs have been stopped. The ship's closed down, didn't you hear? We're all swimming in circles t-till it's clearer about the captain'sss condition.'

'Wvhat?' Akki choked. ' ... the *captain* ... ?'

'Got hurt in an inspection outside the ship. 'Lectrocuted, I hear. Barely found him before his breather ran out-t. Been unconscious all this time. Takkata-Jim's in charge.'

Akki lay there in shock. He was too stunned to notice Sup-peh turn suddenly and hurry back to work as a very large dark figure swam up.

'May I help you, *Mister* Akki?' The giant dolphin's tone sounded almost sarcastic.

'K'tha-Jon,' Akki shook himself. 'What's happened to the captain?'

Something in the bosun's attitude chilled Akki. And it wasn't just the minimal pretense of respect for Akki's rank. K'tha-Jon let out a quick squirt of Trinary.

> * Suggestions come
> to me,
> * How you can know more— *
>
> * Go and ask your
> leader,
> * Who awaits you on the shore— *

With an almost insolent wave of one harness arm, K'tha-Jon flipped about and swam off to rejoin his workcrew. The wake from his mighty flukes pushed Akki backward two meters. Akki knew better than to call him back. Something in K'tha-Jon's Trinary triple entendre told him it would be useless. He decided to take it as a warning, and turned to hurry toward the hull lift.

He was suddenly aware of how many of the best fen in *Streaker's* crew were absent. Tsh't, Hikahi, Karkaett, S'tat and Lucky Kaa were

432

all gone to the Thennanin wreck. That left K'tha-Jon senior petty officer!

And Keepiru was away as well. Akki hadn't believed the gossip he had heard about the pilot. He had always thought Keepiru the bravest fin in the crew, besides the fastest swimmer. He wished Keepiru, and Toshio, were here right now. *They'd* help him find out what was going on!

Near the lift, Akki encountered a group of four *Tursiops,* clustered in a corner of the outlock doing nothing in particular. They wore morose expressions and lay in listless postures.

'Sus'ta, what's going on here?' he asked. 'Don't you fen have work to do?'

The messman looked up and twisted his tail in the dolphin's equivalent of a shrug. 'What'sss the point, Mr Akki?'

'The point ish ... is we do our duty! Come on, what's got you all in such a f-funk?'

'The c-captain ...' one of the others began.

Akki cut him off. 'The captain would be the first to say you should p-p-persevere!' He switched to Trinary.

> * *Focus on the far*
> *Horizon—*
> * *On Earth!*
> *Where we are needed—* *

Sus'ta blinked, and tried to drop his forlorn stance. The others followed suit.

'Yesssir, Mr Akki. We'll t-try.'

Akki nodded. 'Very good, then. Carry on in the spirit of K-k-keneenk.'

He entered the lift and clicked out a code for the bridge. As the doors slid shut, he saw the fen swim away, presumably toward their work stations.

Ifni! It had been hard to posture and act reassuring, when all he really wanted to do was squeeze the others for information. But in order to *be* reassuring he had to seem to know more than they!

Turtle-bites! Disfunctioning motors! How badly is the captain hurt? How will we stand a chance, if Creideiki is taken from us?

He decided to be as innocuous and unnoticed as possible for a while ... until he found out what was going on. He knew a middie was in the most exposed position of all, with an officer's burdens and none of the protections.

And a middie was always the last to find out what was going on!

37

SUESSI

The excavation was nearly ready. The Thennanin battleship had been reamed and braced. Soon they'd be able to fill the cylindrical cavity with its intended cargo and be off.

Hannes Suessi couldn't wait. He'd had it with working underwater. If the truth be told, he'd about had it with fins, too.

Gads, the stories he would be able to tell back home! He had bossed work gangs under the smog oceans of Titan. He had helped herd adenine comets through the Soup Nebula. He had even worked with those crazy Amerindians and Israelis who were trying to terraform Venus. But never had a job taught him the laws of perversity as this one had!

Almost all of the materials they'd had to work with were of alien manufacture, with weird ductility and even stranger quantum conductivities. He'd had to check the psionic impedance of almost every connection himself, and still their masked marvel would probably leak telekinetic static all over the sky when it took off!

Fins! They were the frosting! They'd flawlessly perform the most delicate operation, then swim about in circles squealing Primal nonsense when the opening of a hatchway set off a peculiar pattern of sonar reflections.

And every time a job was finished, they called for old Suessi. Check it for us, Hannes, they'd ask. Make sure we've done it right.

They tried so damned hard. They couldn't help feeling like half-finished clients of wolfling patrons in an impossibly hostile galaxy, especially when it was all true.

Suessi admitted he was bitching more to hear the echoes in his own skull than out of any real complaint. The *Streakers* had done the job; that was all that really mattered. He was proud of every one of them.

Anyway, it had been a lot better since Hikahi arrived. She provided an example for the rest, teasing with Keneenk parables, to help the fen concentrate.

Suessi rolled over onto one elbow. His narrow bunk was only a meter below the ceiling. Inches from his shoulder was the horizontal hatch to his coffin-like sleeper compartment.

I've rested enough, he thought, though his eyes were scratchy and his arms still ached. There was no sense in trying to go back to sleep. He would only stare at his eyelids now.

Suessi pushed the narrow hatch open. He shielded his eyes from the overhead lights of the companionway as he sat up and swung his legs over the side. They splashed.

Ugh. Water. Except for the top meter or so, up here near the ceiling, the skiff was full of water.

His body looked pale in the sharp hall light. *I wonder when I'm scheduled to fade away,* he thought, sliding into the water with his eyes closed. He swam over to the head and closed the door behind him.

Naturally, he had to wait until the room pumped out before he could use any of the fixtures.

A little later, he made his way to the control room of the tiny spacecraft. Hikahi was there with Tsh't, fussing over the comm set. They argued in a fast, squeaky version of Anglic he couldn't follow.

'Whoa!' he called. 'If you want to keep me out, fine. But if I can help, you'd better change to thirty-three and a third. I'm not Tom Orley. I can't follow that jabber!'

The two dolphin officers lifted their heads clear of the water as Suessi took a grip on a nearby wall rail. Hikahi's eyes extended outward to refocus for above-water binocular vision.

'We aren't sure we have a problem, Hannesss, but we seem to have lost contact with the ship.'

'With *Streaker*?' Suessi's bushy eyebrows went up. 'Are they under attack?'

Tsh't rocked her upper body left to right slightly. 'We don't think so. I was here, waiting for word that they'd heard from Orley, and would be moving the ship soon. I wasn't paying close attention, but heard the operator suddenly tell us to "stand by" . . . then nothing!'

'When was this?'

'A few hours ago. I waited until shift change, hoping it was a technical glitch at the ship, then I called Hikahi.'

'We've been tracing circuits since then,' the senior officer finished.

Suessi swam over to look at the set. Of course, the thing to do was tear it apart and check it by hand. But the electronics were sealed away against the wetness.

If only we were in free fall so the fins could work without all this damned water everywhere.

'All right,' he sighed. 'With your permission, Hikahi; I'll kick you two officers and gentlefems out of the control room and look at the unit. Don't bother the fen resting in the hold.'

Hikahi nodded. 'I'll send a crew to follow the monofilament and see if it's intact.'

'Good thinking. And don't worry. I'm sure nothing's really the matter. It's probably just gremlins at work.'

435

38

CHARLES DART

'I'm afraid they've only taken the damned robot down another eighty meters. That kid Toshio will only work on it for a few hours, then he's always got to be off helping Dennie and Gillian run their new clients through mazes, or having them knock down bananas with poles or something. I tell you it's frustrating! The rotten little half-wrecked probe's carrying mostly the wrong kinds of instruments for geological work. Can you imagine how bad it will be when we get it down to a decent depth?'

The holographic image of the metallurgist Brookida seemed to look past Charles Dart for a moment. Apparently, the dolphin scientist was referring to his own displays. Each eye was covered with a goggle lens to correct for astigmatism when reading. He turned back to look at his chimp colleague.

'Charlie. You talk so assuredly about sending thisss robot deeper into Kithrup's crust. You complain that it has gone down "only" five hundred meters. Are you cognizant that that-t is half a kilometer?'

Charlie scratched his fuzzy jaw. 'Yeah? So what? The excavation has got so little taper that it might easily drop down as much farther as it's already gone. It's a wonderful mineralogical lab! Already I'm finding out a lot about the subsurface zone!'

Brookida sighed. 'Charlie, aren't you curious as to why the cavern under Toshio's island goes down even *one* hundred meterssss?'

'Hmmm? What do you mean?'

'I mean that the so-called "drill-tree" that'ss responsible for this excavation cannot have dug so deep merely in search of carbon and silicate nutrients. It can't-t have ...'

'How would you know? Are you an ecologist?' Charlie rapped out a sharp laugh. 'Honestly, Brookida, what do you base these suppositions on? Sometimes you surprise me!'

Brookida waited patiently for the chimpanzee to finish laughing. 'I base them on a well-informed layman's knowledge of basic lawsss of nature, and upon Occam's Razor. Think of the volume of material removed! Has it been scattered upon the watersss? Has it occurred to you that there are tens of thousands of these metal-mounds along this plate boundary, most with their own drill-trees ... and that there may have been millions of such deep excavations dug in recent geologic time?'

Dart started to snigger, then he stopped. He stared for a moment at the image of his cetacean college, then laughed in earnest. He pounded the desk.

'Touché! All right, sir! We'll add "Why these holes?" to our list of questions! Fortunately, I've been cultivating an ecologist lab-mate for the last few months. I've done her innumerable favors, and it happens she's at the site of our quandary! I'll ask Dennie to get to work on it right away! Best assured, we'll know soon enough what these drill-trees are up to!'

Brookida didn't bother answering. He did let out a small sigh.

'Now that that's settled,' Charlie went on, 'let's get back to the really important stuff. Can you help persuade the captain to let me go out there in person and take a real deep-probe robot with me to replace that lousy little thing Toshio salvaged?'

Brookida's eyes widened. He hesitated.

'The c-captain remains unconscious,' Brookida said at last. 'Makanee has twice performed surgery. According to the latest reports, the outlook remains bleak-k.'

The chimp stared for a long moment. 'Oh, yeah. I forgot.' Charlie looked away from the holo display. 'Well, then maybe Takkata-Jim will be willing. After all, the longboat's not being used. I'll ask Metz to talk to him. Will you help?'

Brookida's eyes were sunken. 'I'll study these mass spectrometer data,' he answered evenly. 'I will call you when I have results. Now I mussst sign off, Charles Dart.'

The image dissolved. Charlie was alone again.

Brookida was awfully abrupt there, he thought. Have I offended him somehow?

Charlie knew he was offensive to people. He couldn't help it. Even other chimpanzees thought him abrasive and self-centered. They said neo-chimps like him gave the race a bad rep.

Well, I've tried, he thought. And when a person's tried and failed so often, when his best attempts at gallantry turn to faux pas, and he constantly finds himself forgetting other people's names, well, then, maybe a guy should give up. Other people don't always win awards for kindness to me, either.

Charles Dart shrugged. It didn't matter. What point was there in pursuing an ever-elusive popularity? There was always his personal world of rocks and molten cores, of magma and living planets.

Still, I thought Brookida, at least, was my friend ...

He forced the thought aside.

I've got to call Metz. He'll get me what I need. I'll show 'em this planet is so unique they'll ... they'll rename it after me! There are *precedents.* He chuckled as he tugged on his ear with one hand and punched out a code with the other.

An idle thought came to him, as he waited for the computer tracer to track down Ignacio Metz. *Wasn't everybody waiting to hear from Tom Orley? That was all anybody'd talk about, a while back.*

Then he remembered that Orley's report was supposed to come in yesterday, about the time Creideiki was hurt.

Ah! Then Tom was probably successful at whatever it was he was doing, and nobody bothered to tell me. Or maybe somebody did, and I wasn't listening again. Anyway, I'm sure he got everything squared away with the ETs. About time, too. Damned nuisance being hunted all over the galaxy, forced to fill the ship with water ...

Metz's number appeared on the intercom. The line was ringing.

It was a shame about Creideiki. He was awfully stiff and serious for a fin, and not always reasonable ... but Charlie couldn't bring himself to feel happy to have him out of the way. In fact, it gave him a queer sensation in his stomach whenever he thought about the captain being removed from the picture.

Then don't think about it! Jeez! When has it ever paid to worry?

'Ah, Doctor Metz! Did I catch you as you were going out? I was wondering, could we have a talk together soon? Later this afternoon? Good! Yes, I do have a very, very small favor to ask ...'

39

MAKANEE

A physician must be part intellectual and part alchemist, part sleuth and part shaman, Makanee thought.

But in medical school they never told her she might have to be a soldier and politician, as well.

Makanee had trouble keeping a dignified demeanor. In fact, she felt on the verge of insubordination. Her tail crashed to the water's surface, sending spray over the canals of sick bay.

'I tell you I can't-t-t operate alone! My aides haven't the skill to assist me! I must-t-t talk to Gillian Baskin!'

With one eye lazily lifted above the water line, one harness arm holding a channel stanchion, Takkata-Jim glanced at Ignacio Metz. The human returned an expression of great patience. They had expected this sort of reaction from the ship's surgeon.

'I'm sure you underrate your skill, Doctor,' Takkata-Jim suggested.

'So you're a sssurgeon, now? I need your opinion? Let-t me talk to Gillian!'

Metz spoke placatingly. 'Doctor, Lieutenant Takkata-Jim has just explained that there are military reasons for the partial communications blackout. Data from the detection buoys appear to indicate a psi leak somewhere within a hundred kilometers of this spot. Either the crew working under Hikahi and Suessi or the people at the island are responsible. Until we trace the leak . . . '

'You are acting on the basis of information from a buoy? It was a defective buoy that almost k-k-killed C-C-Creideiki!'

Metz frowned. He wasn't used to being interrupted by dolphins. He noted that Makanee was quite agitated. Too agitated, in fact, to speak with the Anglic diction a fin in her position should use. This was certainly data for his files . . . as was her belligerent attitude.

'That was a different buoy, Physician Makanee. Remember, we have three on station. Besides, we aren't claiming the leak is necessarily real, only that we must *treat* it as real until proven otherwise.'

'But the blackout isn't total! I hear that chimpanzee is ssstill getting his Iki-damned robot-t data! So why won't you let me talk to Doctor Baskin?'

Metz wanted to curse. He had asked Charles Dart to keep quiet about that. Damn the necessity to keep the chimp placated!

'We are eliminating the possibilities one at a time,' Takkata-Jim tried to soothe Makanee. At the same time he assumed a head-down forward stance, dominant assertive body language. 'As soon as those in contact with Charles Dart – the young humans Iwashika and Sudman and the poet Sah'ot – have been eliminated as possible leaks, then we will contact Doctor Baskin. Surely you see that she is less likely to be the one carelessly leaking psi energy than these others, so we must check them first.'

Metz's eyebrows rose slightly. Bravo! The excuse wouldn't hold up under close scrutiny, of course. But it had a *flavor* of reasonability! All they needed was a little time! If this kept Makanee quiet for just another couple of days, that should be enough.

Takkata-Jim apparently noticed something of Metz's approval. Encouraged, he grew more assertive. 'Now, enough delaying, Doctor! We came down here to find out about the captain's condition. If he's unable to resume his duties, a new commanding officer mussst be selected. We're in a crisis and cannot put up with delays!'

If this was meant to intimidate, it had the opposite effect. Makanee's tail churned. Her head rose out of the water. She turned one narrowed eye to the male dolphin and chattered in sarcastic verse.

I'd thought that you
    —had misremembered
        —duty's orders
How nice to note
    —I had mistaken
        —your behavior
You'll not claim, in
    —hasty mischief
        —captain's honors?

Takkata-Jim's mouth opened, baring twin vee rows of rough white teeth. For a moment it seemed to Metz he would charge the small female.

But Makanee acted first, leaping up out of the water and landing with a splash that covered both Metz and Takkata-Jim. The human spluttered and slipped off the wall curb.

Makanee whirled and disappeared behind a row of dark life-support coffins. Takkata-Jim spun underwater, emitting rapid sonar clicks, seeking her out. Metz seized him by the dorsal fin before he could take off after her.

'Ah . . . ahem!' He grabbed a wall rail. 'If we can put a stop to this foul temper, fin-people? Doctor Makanee? Will you please come back? It's bad enough half the known universe wants to hunt us down. We mustn't fight amongst ourselves!'

Takkata-Jim looked up and saw that Metz was earnest. The lieutenant continued to breathe heavily.

'Please, Makanee!' Metz called again. 'Let's talk like civilized folk.'

They waited, and a short time later Makanee's head emerged from between two autodocs. Her expression was no longer defiant, simply tired. Her physician's harness made tiny whirring sounds. The delicate instruments shook slightly, as if held in trembling hands.

She rose so only her blowmouth broke the surface.

'I apologize,' she buzzed. 'I know Takkata-Jim would not assume permanent captaincy without a vote by the ship's council.'

'Of course he wouldn't! This is not a military vessel. The duties of the executive officer aboard a survey ship are mostly administrative, and his succession to command must be ratified by a ship's council as soon as one can be conveniently arranged. Takkata-Jim is fully aware of the rules involved, is that right, Lieutenant?'

'Yessss.'

'But until then we must accept Takkata-Jim's authority or have chaos! And in the meantime, *Streaker* must have a chain of command.

That will be ambiguous until you certify that Captain Creideiki can no longer function.'

Makanee closed her eyes, breathing heavily. 'Creideiki will probably not regain consciousness without further surgery. Even then it'sss chancy.

'The shock traveled along his neural connector socket into the brain. Most of the damaged areas are in the New Zones of the cortex ... where basic *Tursiopsss* gray matter has been heavily uplift-modified. There are lesions in regions controlling both vision and speech-ch. The corpus callosum is seared ...'

Makanee's eyes re-opened, but she did not appear to be looking at them.

Metz nodded. 'Thank you, Doctor,' he said. 'You've told us what we need to know. I'm sorry we took so much of your time. I'm sure you're doing your best.'

When she did not answer, the human slipped his oxymask over his face and slid into the water. He motioned to Takkata-Jim and turned to leave.

The male dolphin clicked at Makanee for a moment longer, but when she did not move he flipped about and followed Metz toward the exit.

A shudder passed through her as the two entered the lock. She lifted her head to call after them.

'Don't forget-t when you call a ship's council that *I'm* a member! And Hikahi and Gillian and T-Tom Orley!' The lock was hissing shut behind them as she called. She couldn't tell if they had heard.

Makanee settled back into the water with a sigh. *And Tom Orley*, she thought. *Don't forget him, you sneaky bastards! He'll not let you get away with this!*

Makanee shook her head, knowing she was thinking irrationally. Her suspicions weren't based on facts. And even if they were true, Thomas Orley couldn't stretch his hand across two thousand kilometers to save the day. There were rumors that he was already dead.

Metz and Takkata-Jim had her all confused. She had a gut feeling that they had told her a complex assortment of truths, half-truths, and outright lies, and she had no way of knowing which was which.

They think they can fool me, just because I'm female, and old, and two uplift generations cruder than any other fin aboard but Brookida. But I can guess why they're giving special favors to the one chimpanzee member on the ship's council. Here and now, they have a majority to back up any decision they make. No wonder they're not anxious to have Hikahi or Gillian back!

Maybe I should have lied to them ... told them Creideiki would awaken any minute.

But then, who can tell how desperate they are? Or what they'd resort to? Was the accident with the buoy really an accident? They could be lying to cover up ignorance – or to cover up a conspiracy. Could I protect Creideiki, with only two female aides to help me?

Makanee let out a low moan. This sort of thing wasn't her department! She sometimes wished that being a dolphin physician, like in the old days, simply meant you lifted the one you were trying to save up on your brow, and held his head above the water until he recovered, or your strength failed you, or your own heart broke.

She turned back toward Intensive Care. The chamber was darkened except for a light that shone upon a large gray neo-dolphin, suspended in a shielded gravity tank. Makanee checked the life-maintenance readings and saw that they were stable.

Creideiki blinked unseeingly, and once a brief shudder passed down the length of his body.

Makanee sighed and turned away. She swam over to a nearby comm unit and considered.

Metz and Takkata-Jim can't be back on the bridge yet, she thought. She clicked a sonar code that activated the unit. Almost instantly the face of a young, blue-finned dolphin appeared before her.

'Communications. C-can I help you?'

'Akki? Yes, child, it's Doctor Makanee. Have you made any plans for lunch? You know, I do think I still have some of that candied octopus left. You're free? How sssweet. I'll see you soon, then. Oh, and let's keep our date our little secret. Okay? That'sss a good lad.'

She departed Intensive Care, a scheme beginning to form in her mind.

40

CREIDEIKI

In the quiet grayness of the gravity tank, a faint moaning cry.

> * *Desperate, he swims*
> *Tossed by gray storm winds, howling:*
> *Drowning! Drowning!* *

41

TOM ORLEY

A foul-tempered mountain growled in the middle of a scum-crusted sea.

It had stopped raining a while ago. The volcano grumbled and coughed fire at low overhanging clouds, casting orange on their undersides. Thin, twisting trails of ash blew into the sky. Where the hot cinders finally fell, it was not to a quenching by clean sea water. They landed in a muddy layer atop a carpet of dingy vines which seemed to go on forever.

Thomas Orley coughed in the dank, sooty air. He crawled up a small rise of slippery, jumbled weeds. The dead weight of his crude sledge dragged a tether wrapped around his left hand. With his right he clutched a thick tendril near the top of the weed-mound.

His legs kept sliding out from under him as he crawled. Even when he managed to wedge them into gaps in the slimy mass, his feet frequently sank into the mire between the vines. When he awkwardly pulled them out, the quagmire would let go reluctantly, giving off an awful sucking sound.

Sometimes 'things' came out with his feet, squirming along his legs and dropping off to slither back into the noisome brine.

The tightly wrapped thong cut into his left hand as he pulled the sledge, a meager remnant of his solar plane and supplies. It was a miracle that he had been able to salvage even that much from the crash.

The volcano sent ochre flickers across the weedscape. Rainbow specks of metallic dust coated the vegetation in all directions. It was late afternoon, almost a full Kithrup day since he had banked his glider toward the island, searching for a safe place to land.

Tom raised his head to look blearily over the plain of weeds. All of his well-laid plans had been brought down by this plain of tough, ropy sea plants.

He had hoped to find shelter on an island upwind of the volcano, or, barring that, to land at sea and turn the glider into a broad and seaworthy raft from which to perform his experiment.

I should have considered this possibility. The crash, those dazed, frantic minutes diving after gear and piling together a crude sledge while the storm lashed at him, and then hours crawling among the

443

fetid vines toward a solitary hump of vegetation – it all might have been avoided.

He tried to pull forward, but a tremor in his right arm threatened to turn into a full-scale cramp. It had been badly wrenched during the crash, when the plane's wing pontoons had come off and the fuselage went tumbling across the morass, splashing at last into an isolated pool of open water.

A gash across the left side of his face had almost sent him into shock during those first critical moments. It reached from his jaw almost to the neural socket above his left ear. The plastic cover that normally protected the delicate nerve interface had spun out into the night, hopelessly lost.

Infection was the least of his worries, now.

The tremor in his arm grew worse. Tom tired to ride it out, lying face down on the pungent, rubbery weeds. Gritty mud scraped his right cheek and forehead each time he coughed.

Somewhere he had to find the energy. He hadn't time for the subtleties of self-hypnosis, to coax his body back into working. By main force of will, he *commanded* the abused muscles to behave for one final effort. He could do little about what the universe threw at him, but *dammit*, after thirty hours of struggle, within meters of his goal, he would not accept a rebellion by his body!

Another coughing fit ripped at his raw throat. His body shook, and the hacking weakened his grip on the dry root. Just when he thought his lungs could take no more, the fit finally passed. Tom lay there in the mud, drained, eyes closed.

> ** Count the joys of movement?—*
> *First among advantages:*
> *Absence of Boredom— **

He hadn't the breath to whistle the Trinary Haiku, but it blew through his mind, and he spared the energy for a brief smile through cracked, mud-crusted lips.

Somewhere, he found the reserves for one more effort. He clenched his teeth and pulled himself over the last stretch. The right arm almost buckled, but it held as his head rose over the top of the small hill.

Tom blinked cinders from his eyes and looked out at what lay beyond. More weeds. As far as the eye could see, more weeds.

A thick loop of neustonic vine stuck out at the summit of the modest hillock. Tom heaved the sledge high enough to wrap the slack line around the root.

Sensation flowed into his numbed left hand, leaving him open-mouthed in silent agony. He slumped back against the hillock, breathing rapidly and shallowly.

The cramps returned in force, and his body folded under them. He wanted to tear at the thousand teeth that bit at his arms and legs, but his hands were immobile claws. He lay curled around them.

Somehow, the logical part of Tom's mind remained disconnected from the agony. It still plotted and schemed and tried to set time limits. He'd come out here for a reason, after all. There had to be a reason for going through all this ... If only he could remember why he was here in the stench and hurt and dust and grit ...

The calming pattern he sought wouldn't form. He felt himself start to fade.

Suddenly, through pain-squinted eyes, he thought he saw Gillian's face.

Fronds of airy vegetation waved behind her. Her gray eyes looked his way, as if searching for something just out of range. They seemed to scan past him twice as he trembled, unable to move. Then, at last, they met his, and she smiled!

Pain-drenched static threatened to drown out the dream-words.

> *I send **** for good ****,*
> *though you *** skeptical, love.*
> **** though the whole **** might listen.*

He strained to focus on the message – more likely a hallucination. He didn't care which. It was an anchor. He clung to it as cramps made humming bowstrings of his tendons.

Her smile conveyed commiseration.

> What a mess *** are! The *** I love
> is ****** and careless! Shall I ****
> it better?

Meta-Orley disapproved. If this really was a message from Gillian, she was taking a terrible chance. 'I love you, too,' he subvocalized. 'But will you shut the hell up before the Eatees hear you?'

The psicast – or figment – wavered as a fit of coughing struck, hacking until his lungs felt like dry husks. Finally, he sank back with a sigh.

At last, Meta-Tom surrendered pride.

> *Yes!*

He cast into the murk before his eyes, calling after her dissolving image.

Gillian's face seemed to diffract in all directions, like a bundle of moonbeams, joining the shimmering volcanic dust in the sky. Whether a true message, or an illusion born of delirium, it faded like a portrait done in smoke.

Still, he thought he heard a lingering trace of Gillian's inner voice . . .

*** *** *is, that is, that is . . .*
and healing comes, in dreaming . . .

He listened, unaware of time, and slowly, the tremors subsided. His fetal curl gradually unfolded.

The volcano rumbled and lit the sky. The 'ground' beneath Tom undulated gently and rocked him into a shallow slumber.

42

TOSHIO

'No, Doctor Dart. The enstatite inclusions are one part I'm not sure of. The static from the robot was really strong when I took that reading. If you'd like, I can double-check it right now.'

Toshio's eyelids were heavy with ennui. He had lost track of time spent pushing buttons and reading data at Charles Dart's behest. The chimp planetologist would not be satisfied! No matter how well and quickly Toshio responded, it was never quite enough.

'No, no, we haven't got time,' Charlie answered gruffly from the holoscreen at the edge of the drill-tree pool. 'See if you can work it out on your own after I sign off, okay? It would make a nice project for you to pursue on the side you know, Toshio. Some of these rocks are totally unique! If you did a thorough study of the mineralogy of this shaft, I'd be happy to help you write it up. Imagine the feather in your cap! A major publication couldn't hurt your career, you know.'

Toshio could well imagine. He was, indeed, learning a lot working for Dr Dart. One thing, which would serve him well if he ever did go on to graduate school, was to be very careful in choosing his research advisor.

The question was moot, with aliens overhead getting ready to capture them. Toshio shied away from thinking about the battle in space. It only made him depressed.

'Thanks, Doctor Dart, but ...'

'No problem!' Charlie barked in gruff condescension. 'We'll discuss the details of your project later though, if you don't mind. Right now, let's have an update on where the drone is.'

Toshio shook his head, amazed by the fellow's tenacious single-mindedness. If it got any worse he would lose his temper with the chimp, senior research associate or no.

'Urn ...' Toshio checked his gauges. 'The 'bot's descended a little over a kilometer, Doctor Dart. The shaft is narrower and smoother as we get down to more recent digging, so I'm anchoring the robot to the wall at each site.'

Toshio looked over his shoulder to the northeast, wishing Dennie or Gillian would show up as a distraction. But Dennie was with her Kiqui, and he had last seen Gillian seated in lotus position, overlooking the ocean, oblivious to the world.

Gillian had been pretty upset earlier, when Takkata-Jim told her everyone at the ship was too busy getting *Streaker* ready for the move to talk to her. Even her questions about Tom Orley were brushed aside with abrupt politeness. They'd call her when they knew anything, Takkata-Jim had said before signing off.

Toshio had seen a frown settle over her face as every call she made was deflected. A new comm officer had replaced Akki. The fin told Gillian every person she wanted was unavailable. The one crew member she was able to talk to was Charles Dart, apparently because his skills weren't urgently needed at the moment. And the chimp refused to talk about anything but his work.

Immediately, she had begun getting ready to leave. Then came orders from the ship, directly from Takkata-Jim. She was to stay indefinitely and help Dennie Sudman prepare a report on the Kiqui.

This time Gillian took the news impassively. Without comment, she had gone into the jungle to be alone.

'... more of those tendrils of Dennie's.' Charles Dart had been talking as Toshio's mind drifted. '... The most exciting thing is the potassium and iodine isotope profiles. They prove my hypothesis that within recent geological time some sophont race has been burying garbage in this subduction zone of the planet! This is colossally important, Toshio. There's evidence in these rocks of multiple generations of dumping of material from above, and rapid recycling of stuff brought up by nearby volcanoes. It's almost as if there's been a rhythm to it, an ebb and flow. Something awfully suspicious has been going on here for a long time! Kithrup's supposed to have been

447

fallow since the ancient Karrank% lived here. Yet somebody's been hiding highly refined stuff in this planet's crust up until very recently!'

Toshio almost committed a rudeness. 'Very recently' indeed! Dart was sleuthing in geological time. Any day now, the Eatees would be down on them, and he was treating the alleged burying of industrial garbage thousands of years ago as if it was the latest Scotland Yard mystery!

'Yes, sir. I'll get on it right away.' Toshio wasn't even sure what Dart had just asked him to do, but he covered his ass.

'And don't worry, sir. The robot will be monitored day and night. Keepiru and Sah'ot have orders from Takkata-Jim to stay plugged into it at turns when I'm unavailable. They'll call me if there's any change in its condition.'

Wouldn't that satisfy the chimp? The fen hadn't taken well at all to that order from *Streaker*'s exec, but they would obey, even if it slowed Sah'ot's work with the Kiqui.

Miracle of miracles, Charlie seemed to agree. 'Yeah, that's nice of them,' he muttered. 'Be sure to thank 'em for me.

'And say! Maybe, while Keepiru's plugged in, can he trace that intermittent static we keep getting from the robot? I don't like it, and it's getting worse.'

'Yes, sir. I'll ask him.'

The chimpanzee rubbed his right eye with the back of a furry hand, and yawned.

'Listen, Toshio,' he said. 'I'm sorry, but I really need a break. Would you mind if we put off finishing this until just a little bit later? I'll ring you back after supper and answer all your questions then, hmmm? OK, bye, then, for now!' Charlie reached forward and the holo image disappeared.

Toshio stared at the empty space for a moment, slightly stunned. Mind? Would I mind? Why, no, sir, I don't believe I'd mind at all! I'll just wait here patiently, until either you call back or the sky falls down on my head!

He snorted. Would I mind.

Toshio stood up, his joints crackling from sitting cross-legged too long.

I thought I was too young for that. Ah, well. A midshipman is supposed to experience everything.

He looked toward the forest. Dennie was hard at work with the Kiqui. Should I bother Gillian, I wonder? She's probably worried about Tom. We were supposed to have heard from him early yesterday.

But maybe she wants company.

Lately he had started having fantasies about Gillian. It was only natural, of course. She was a beautiful older woman – at least thirty – and by most standards quite a bit more alluring than Dennie Sudman.

Not that Dennie wasn't attractive in her own way, but Toshio didn't want to think about Dennie much any more. Her implicit rejection, by effectively overlooking him when the two of them were alone and so much alike, was painful.

Toshio suspected she sensed his attraction to her, and was over-reacting by turning cold to him. He told himself that was an immature response on her part. But that didn't keep it from hurting.

Fantasizing about Gillian was another matter. He'd had shameful but very compelling daydreams about being there when she needed a man, helping her overcome her loss . . .

She probably knew how he felt, but didn't let it change her behavior toward him at all. It was a comforting forgiveness, and it made her a safe object of semi-secret adoration.

It could simply be that I'm very confused, of course, Toshio thought. *I'm trying to be analytical in an area where I have no experience, and my own feelings keep getting in the way.*

I wish I wasn't just an awkward kid, and were more like Mr Orley.

An uneven electronic tone behind him interrupted his fantasy – the comm coming back to life.

'Oh, no!' Toshio groaned. 'Not already!'

The unit spat static as the tuner sought to bring in an erratic carrier wave. Toshio had a wild desire to run over and kick the thing into the bottomless murk of the drill-tree shaft.

Suddenly, a crackling, noise-shrouded whistle broke out.

> * If (crackle) midshipmen
>> Stuck together
>>> Who could stop us?
> * And of midshipmen
>> Who can fly
>>> Like Calafians?

'Akki!' Toshio hurried over to kneel in front of the comm.

> * Right again,
>> Diving partner –
> * Remember how we'd
>> Once hunt lobster?

'Do I? Ifni! I wish we were home doing that now! What's happening? Are you having equipment trouble on the bridge? I'm getting no visual, and there's a lot of static. I thought you were taken off comm duty. And why the Trinary?'

> * Necessity
>> Is someone's (crackle) mother—
> * I send this via
>> Close nerve socket—
> * Anxious, I seek
>> soft High Patron—
> * Urgently
>> To pass (crackle) warning—

Toshio's lips pursed as he repeated the message to himself silently. '... soft High Patron.' There were few humans given titles like that by fins. Only one candidate was here on the island right now.

'You want to talk to Gillian?'

> * Urgently
>> To pass on warning—

Toshio blinked, then he said, 'I'll get her right away, Akki! You hold on!'

He turned and ran into the forest, calling Gillian's name at the top of his lungs.

43

AKKI

The monofilament cable was almost invisible against the rubble and ooze of the sea floor. Even in the light from Akki's harness lamp, it barely reflected a spiderweb's glimmer here and there amid the rock and sediments atop this jagged ridgeline.

The cable had been *designed* to be hard to detect; it was the only certain way *Streaker* could communicate with her two outlying work parties without giving away her location. Akki had been forced to search for over an hour, using the best instruments at his disposal and knowing where to look, before finding the line to the island. By the time he had clipped his neural tap into the line, more than half of the oxygen in his breather was gone.

A lot of time had been spent just getting away from the ship. And

Akki wasn't even sure his departure had gone unnoticed. The taciturn electrician's mate in charge of the equipment locker shouldn't have questioned orders when Akki asked for breathing gear. Another fin, an off-duty engine room rating, had followed him from a distance and Akki had to dodge through the outlock to shake the *Stenos* off his tail.

In less than two days a subtle change had come over the crew of *Streaker*. A new alignment of power. Crew members who had formerly been of little influence now pushed their way to the front of the food lines and adopted dominant body postures, while others went about their duties with eyes downcast and flukes drooping. Rank and official position had little to do with it. Such things had always been informal aboard *Streaker* anyway. Dolphins were more apt to pay attention to subtle shifts in dominance than to formal authority.

Now even racism seemed to be a factor. A disproportionate number of the new figures of authority were of the *Stenos* sub-breed. It amounted to an informal coup. Officially, Takkata-Jim was acting on behalf of the unconscious Creideiki until a ship's council could be convened. But *Streaker*'s water had the taste of a herd with a new dominant male. Those close to the old bull were on the out, and cronies of the new swam in the vanguard.

Akki found it all quite illogical and disgusting. It bothered him that even the highly selected fen of *Streaker*'s crew could submit to ancient patterns of behavior under stress. He now saw what the Calactics meant when they said three hundred years of uplift was too short for a race to fly star-ships.

The rude realization made Akki feel more like a *client* than he ever had in the mixed, egalitarian colony of Calafia. It gave a primitive satisfaction to his act of mutiny, abandoning the ship to make contact with Gillian Baskin against specific orders from the acting captain.

Now Akki felt he knew the truth; he was a member of a crew of imitation spacemen. There was no way, short of Creideiki miraculously recovering, that they were going to get out of this mess without intervention by their patrons.

He discounted the value of Ignacio Metz – or Emerson D'Anite or even Toshio, for that matter. He agreed with Makanee that their only hope lay in Dr Baskin or Mr Orley coming home. By now he had come to accept that Orley was lost. The rest of the crew believed this, and it was one more reason morale had gone to hell since Creideiki's accident.

The comm line quietly sent a carrier tone directly to his statoacoustic nerve, as Akki waited impatiently for Toshio to return with

Gillian. The line was not being used for anything else, now that Charles Dart had signed off, but every second increased the chance that the comm operator aboard the ship would detect his tap. Akki had set it up to hide his conversation with Toshio, but even a dullard CommSec fin couldn't miss the side effects, in time.

Where are *they?* he wondered. *Surely they know I only have so much air? And this metal-rich water makes my skin itch!*

Akki breathed slowly for calm. A teaching rhyme of Keneenk ran through his mind.

> * *'Fast' is what once was—*
>> *A remnant that's called memory . . .*
> * *In it lie the 'causes'—*
>> *Of what now is.*

> * *'Future' is what will be—*
>> *Envisioned, seldom seen . . .*
> * *In it lie 'results'—*
>> *Of what now is.*

> * *'Present' is that narrowness—*
>> *Passing, always flickering . . .*
> * *Proof of the 'joke'—*
>> *Of 'what now is.'*

Past, future and present were among the hardest ideas to express explicitly in Trinary. The rhyme was meant to teach causation as the human patrons, and most other sophonts, saw it, while keeping essential faith with the cetacean view of life.

It all seemed so simple to Akki. At times he wondered why some of these dolphins of Earth had so much trouble with such ideas. One thought, one imagined actions and their consequences, considered how the different results would taste and feel, then one acted! If the future was unclear, one did the best one could, and hoped.

It was how humans had muddled through during the ages of their horrible, orphaned ignorance. Akki saw no reason why it should be so hard for his people, especially when they were being shown the way.

'Akki? Toshio here. Gillian's coming. She had to break away from something important, so I ran ahead. Are you all right?'

Akki sighed.

> * *In the depths—*
>> *With itching blowmouth*

> * *I tread in wait –*
> > *At duty's calling*
> * *As the cycloid—*
> > *Rolls in . . .*

'*Hang on,*' Toshio called, interrupting the rhyme. Akki grimaced. Toshio never would develop a sense of style.

'*Here's Gillian,*' Toshio finished. '*Take care of yourself, Akki!*' The line crackled with static.

> * *You, too—*
> > *Diving/flying partner* *

'*Akki?*'

It was the voice of Gillian Baskin, made tinny by the weak connection, but almost infinitely gratifying to hear.

'*What is it, dear? Can you tell me what's going on on the ship? Why won't Creideiki talk to me?*'

That wasn't what Akki had thought she would ask first. For some reason he had expected her main concern to be Tom Orley. Well, he wasn't about to bring the subject up if she didn't.

> * *Makanee—*
> > *Patient healer*
> * *Sends me out—*
> > *With danger warning*
> * *Soundless, flukeless*
> > *Lies Creideiki*
> * *Streaker's fortunes*
> > *Strangely waning*

> * *And the taste—*
> *Of atavism*
> * *Fouls the waters—*

There was silence at the other end. No doubt Gillian was formulating her next question in a way that would let him answer unambiguously in Trinary. It was a skill Toshio sometimes sadly lacked.

Akki brought his head up quickly. Was that a sound? It hadn't come from the comm line, but from the dark waters around him.

'*Akki,*' Gillian began. '*I'm going to ask you questions phrased to take three-level answers. Please spare artistry for brevity in answering.*'

Gladly, if I can, Akki thought. He had often wondered why it was so hard to hold direct conversations in Trinary without beating around the bush in poetic allusion. It was his native tongue as much as Anglic was, and still he felt frustrated by its resistance to short-cuts.

'Akki, does Creideiki ignore the Fish-of-Dreaming, does he chase them, or does he feed them?'

Gillian was asking if Creideiki still functioned as a tool user, was he lost to injury, drifting in an unconscious dream-hunt or, worse, was he dead. Somehow, Gillian had immediately gone right to the heart of the matter. Akki was able to answer with blessed brevity.

> * Chasing squid—
> > In deepest water *

There was that sound again! A rapid clicking, coming from not far away. Curse the necessity to keep his neural socket linked to the static of this line! The sounds were close enough to leave little doubt. Someone was hunting for him out here.

'All right, Akki. Next question. Does Hikahi calm all with her Keneenk rhythms, does she echo herd obedience, or does she sing an absent silence?'

Dolphin sonar is a highly directional thing. He felt the edge of a lobe of a sonic beam pass just above him, without hitting him broadside. Akki got down as close to the ocean floor as he could, and made an effort to direct his own nervous clickings into the soft sand. He wanted to reach out with one of his harness arms and grab a rock or something for stability, but was afraid the tiny whirring of the motors would be heard.

> * Absent silence—
> > Fades the memory –
> * Of Hikahi

> * Absent silence—
> > From Tsh't
> * And Suessi *

He wished he, too, were absent this place and back in his quiet stateroom aboard *Streaker*.

'Okay, is their silence that of netted capture? Is it of orca-fearful waiting? Or is it the silence of fishes feeding?'

Akki was about to answer when, like one whose eyes were suddenly struck by a bright light, he was awash in a beam of pulsed sound, highly directional, somewhere from his left and above. No question a dolphin up there was instantly aware of him.

* Takkata-Jim—
        Bites the cables

* My own job—
        Is mine no longer

* His fen relay—
        His lying songs *

Akki was so agitated that some of that actually came out as sound rather than impulses sent to the monofilament. There was no use trying any longer for secrecy. He made ready to jettison the line and turned his melon toward the intruder. He fired off a sonar pulse strong enough, he hoped, to momentarily stun him.

The echoes of his burst returned giving him a vivid image. There was a thrashing sound as a very large dolphin swung aside, out of his beam.

K'tha-Jon! Akki recognized the echo at once.

'Akki? What was that? Are you in fighting patterns? Break off if you have to. I'm coming home fast as I . . . '

Duty absolved, Akki popped the neural link free and rolled to one side.

He acted none too soon. A blue-green laser bolt sizzled through the spot where he had been seconds before.

So, that's the way of it, he thought as he dove into the canyon next to the ocean ridge. The hammerhead is out to get me, and no politeness about it.

He did a quick roll to his right and speared downward toward the shadows.

Dolphins were known for a reluctance to kill anything that breathed air, but they were not a limited race. Even before uplift, humans had witnessed cases of fin murdering fin. In enabling cetaceans to be starfarers, men also made them more efficient when they chose to kill.

A line-bright laser beam hissed a bare meter ahead of him. Akki clenched his jaw and dove through the streak of scalding bubbles. Another narrow, searing bolt sizzled between his pectoral fins. He whirled and dove for the long sonic shadow of a jagged outcrop of rock. K'tha-Jon's laser rifle could kill at long range, while the welder/torch on Akki's harness was, like all sidearm-tools, of use only up close. Obviously, his only chances were in flight or in trickery.

It was very dark down here. All of the red colors were gone. Only blue and green could pass through from the day to illuminate a shadow-filled landscape. Akki took advantage of the rugged terrain and slipped between the sharp walls of a narrow rock cleft. There he stopped to wait and listen.

The echoes he picked up through passive listening only told him that K'tha-Jon was out there, somewhere, searching. Akki hoped his own rapid breathing wasn't as loud as it seemed.

He sent a neural query to his harness. The microcomputer in its frame told him he had less than half an hour's air left in his breather.

Akki's jaws ground together. He wanted K'tha-Jon's long pectorals between his teeth, much as he knew he was no match for the big *Stenos* in size or strength.

Akki had no way of knowing whether K'tha-Jon was out here on his own or following orders from Takkata-Jim. But if there were some cabal of *Stenos* at work, he wouldn't put it past them to kill the helpless Creideiki to secure their plan. Unthinkable as it was, they could even get it into their heads to harm *Gillian*, if she weren't careful how she made her return to the ship. The mere thought of any fin participating in such crimes made Akki feel sick.

I've got to get back and help Makanee defend Creideiki until Gillian arrives!

He slipped out of the cleft and swam a series of floor-hugging zigs and zags toward a small canyon to the southeast, in a direction away from *Streaker*, and away from both Toshio's island and the Thennanin wreck. It was the direction most likely to be unwatched by K'tha-Jon.

He could hear the giant casting about for him. The powerful beams of sound were missing for now. There was a good chance he would get a head start.

Still, it wasn't quite as *tasty* as the satisfaction he would have felt in surprising K'tha-Jon with a snout-ramming to his genitals!

Gillian turned from the comm set to see anxiety on Toshio's face. It made him seem very young. Gone was the role of a rough, tough, worldly mel. Toshio was an adolescent midshipman who had just found out his captain was crippled. And now his best friend might well be fighting for his life. He looked at her, hoping for reassurance that everything would be all right.

Gillian took the youth's hand and pulled him into a hug. She held him, against his protests, until, at last, the tension went out of his shoulders and he buried his face in her shoulder, holding her tightly.

When he finally pulled away, Toshio didn't look at her, but turned away and wiped at one eye with the heel of his hand.

'I'm going to want to take Keepiru with me,' Gillian said. 'Do you think you and Sah'ot and Dennie can spare him?'

Toshio nodded. His voice was thick, but he soon had it under control. 'Yes, sir. Sah'ot may be a problem when I start giving him some of Keepiru's duties. But I've been watching the way you handle him. I can manage.'

'That's good. See if you can keep him off Dennie's back. I'm sure you'll manage fine.'

Gillian turned to her small poolside campsite to gather her gear. Toshio went to the water's edge and switched on the hydrophone amplifier that would signal the two dolphins that they were wanted. Sah'ot and Keepiru had left an hour ago, to await the evening foray of the aborigines.

'I'll go back with you if you want, Gillian.'

She shook her head as she gathered her notes and tools together. 'No, Toshio. Dennie's work with the Kiqui is damned important. You're the one who's got to keep her from burning down the forest with a spent match while she's preoccupied. Besides, I need you to maintain a pretense that I haven't left. Do you think you can do that for me?' Gillian zipped shut her watertight satchel and started slipping out of her shirt and shorts. Toshio turned away, at first, and started to blush.

Then he noticed that Gillian didn't seem to care that he look. *I might never see her again*, he thought. *I wonder if she knows what she's doing for me?*

'Yes, sir,' he said. Toshio's mouth felt very dry. 'I'll act just as harassed and impatient as ever with Doctor Dart. And if Takkata-Jim asks for you I'll . . . I'll tell him you're off somewhere, er, sulking.'

Gillian was holding her drysuit in front of her, preparing to step into it. She looked up at him, surprised by the wryness of his remark. Then she laughed.

In two long-legged strides she was over to him, seizing him into another hug. Without a thought Toshio put his arms around the smooth skin of her waist.

'You're a good man, Tosh,' she said as she kissed him on the cheek. 'And, you know, you've grown quite a bit taller than me? You lie to Takkata-Jim for me and I promise we'll make a *proper* mutineer of you in no time at all.'

Toshio nodded and closed his eyes. 'Yes, ma'am,' he said as he held her tight.

44

CREIDEIKI

His skin itched. It had always itched, since that dim time when he rode alongside his mother in her slipstream – when he had first learned about touch from nursing and the gentle nuzzles she used to remind him to rise for air.

Soon he had learned that there were other kinds of touching. There were walls and plants and the sides of all the buildings of the settlement at Catalina-Under; there was the stroking, butting, and yes! biting play of his peers; there was the soft, oh, so deliciously varied touch of the mels and fems – the humans – who swam about like pinnipeds, like sea lions, laughing and playing catch with him underwater and above.

There was the feel of water. All the different lands of feel there were to water.

The *splash* and *crash* of falling into it! The smooth laminar flow of it as you speared along faster than anyone *ever* could have gone before! The gentle lapping of it, just below your blowmouth as you rested, whispering a lullaby to yourself.

O, how he itched!

Long ago he had learned to rub against things, and he discovered what that could do to him. Ever since then, he had masturbated whenever he felt like it, just like any other healthy fin would . . .

Creideiki wanted to scratch himself. He wanted to masturbate.

Only there was no wall nearby to rub against. He seemed unable to move, or even to open his eyes to see what surrounded him.

He was floating in midair, his weight held up by nothing . . . by a familiar magic . . . 'anti-gravity.' The word – like his memories of floating this way many times before – for some reason felt alien, almost meaningless.

He wondered at his lassitude. Why not open his eyes and see? Why not click out a soundbeam and hear the shape and texture of this place?

At intervals he felt a spray of moisture that kept his skin wet. It seemed to come from all directions.

He considered, and came to the conclusion that something must be very wrong with him. He must be sick.

An involuntary sigh made him realize he was still capable of some sound. He searched for the right mechanisms, experimented, then managed to repeat the faint moan.

They must be working to fix me, he thought. I must have been hurt. Though I don't feel any pain, I feel a vacancy. Something has been taken from me. A ball? A tool? A skill? Anyway, the people are probably trying to put it back.

I trust people, he thought happily. And the apex of his mouth curled into a slight smile.

*!!!! *

The apex of his mouth did what?
Oh. Yes. Smiling. That new thing.
New thing? I've done it all my life!
Why?
It's expressive! It adds subtlety to my features! It ...
It is redundant.

Creideiki let out a weak, warbling cry of confusion.

> ** In the brightness*
>   *Of the sunshine—*
> ** Answers swarm*
>   *In schools, like fishes **

He remembered a little, now. He had been dreaming. Something terrible had happened, plunging him into a nightmare of bewilderment. Shapes had darted toward and away from him, and he had felt ancient songs take new, eerie, forms.

He realized he must still be dreaming, with both hemispheres at the same time. That explained why he couldn't move. He tried to coax himself awake with a song.

> ** Levels there are—*
>   *Known only to sperm whales*
>
> ** Physeter, who hunts*
>   *In chasms of dreaming*
>
> ** To battle the squid*
>   *Whose beaks are sea-mounts*
>
> ** And whose great arms*
>   *Encompass oceans ...*

It was not a calming rhyme. It had overtones of darkness that made him want to fly away in horror. Creideiki tried to halt it, fearing what the chant might call up. But he could not stop crafting the sound-glyphs.

* Go down to levels—
  In the darkness

* Where your 'cycloid'
  Never reaches

* Where all music
  Finally settles

* And it gathers
  Stacked in layers

* Howling songs of
  Ancient storms,

* And hurricanes
  That never died ...

A presence grew alongside Creideiki. A great, broad figure could be felt nearby, forming out of the fabric of his song. Creideiki sensed its slow sonar pulses, filling the small chamber he lay within ... a small chamber that couldn't possibly hold the behemoth taking shape beside him.

Nukapai?

* Sounds of earthquakes—
  Stored for epochs

* Sounds of molten
  Primeval rocks ...

The sound creature solidified with each passing verse. There was a muscular power in the presence forming beside him. The thing's slow, huge fluke strokes threatened to send him tumbling head over tail. When It blew, Its spume was like a storm breaking on a rocky shore.

Fear at last gave Creideiki the will to open his eyes. Moist mucus flowed as he labored to separate the lids. The sockets were recessed to their deepest, and it took moments to make them switch to air-focus.

At first all he saw was a hospital suspension tank, small and confined. He was alone.

But sound told him he was in the open sea, and a leviathan rode next to him! He could feel its great power!

He blinked, and suddenly his vision shifted. Sight adopted the frame of reference of sound. The room vanished, and he *saw* It!

!!!!!!!

The thing beside him could never have lived in any of the oceans he had known. Creideiki almost choked in dread.

It moved with the power of tsunamis, the irresistibility of tides.

It was a thing of darkness and depths.

It was a god.

* K-K-Kph-kree !! *

It was a name Creideiki hadn't been aware he had known. It welled up from somewhere, like the dragons of a nightmare.

One dark eye regarded Creideiki with a look that seared him. He wanted to turn away – to hide or die.

Then it spoke to him.

It spurned Trinary, as he knew it would. It cast aside Primal, disdaining it a tongue for clever animals. It sang a song that brushed against him with physical force, enveloped him and filled him with a terrible understanding.

: You Swam Away From Us Creideiki : You Were Starting To Learn : Then Your Mind Swam Away : But We Have Not Finished : Yet :

: We Have Waited Long For One Such As You : Now You Need Us As Much As We Need You : There Is No Going Back :

: As You Are : You Would Be A Hulk : Dead Meat : Emptiness Without A Song : Never Again A Dreamer *or* A Fire User :

: *Useless* Creideiki : Neither Captain : Nor Cetacean : Useless Meat :

: There Is One Path For You : Through The Belly Of The Whale Dream : There You May Find A Way : A Hard Way : But A Way To Do Your Duty : There You May Find A Way To Save Your Life . . . :

Creideiki moaned. He thrashed feebly and called out for Nukapai. But then he remembered. She was *one* of them.

She waited, down below, with his other tormentors, some of

461

them old gods named in the sagas, and some he had never heard mentioned even by the humpback whales ...

K-K-Kph-kree had come to bring him back.

Though Anglic was lost to him, Creideiki conveyed a plea in a language he had not known he knew.

: I Am Damaged! : I Am A Hulk! I *Should* Be Dead Meat! : I Have Lost Speech! I Have Lost Words! : Let Me Die! :

It answered with a sonorous rumble that seemed born beneath the earth. Beneath the ooze.

: **Through The Whale Dream You Go : Where Your Cousins Have Never Been : Even When They Played Like Animals And Barely Knew Men : Deeper Than The Humpbacks Go : In Their Idle Meditation : Deeper Than *Physeter* : In His Devil Hunt : Deeper Than The Darkness Itself ...:**

: ***There* You May Decide To Die, If Truth Cannot Be Borne ...:**

The walls of the small chamber faded away as his tormentor began to take on a new reality. It had the great brow and bright teeth of a sperm whale, but Its eyes shone like beacons, and Its flanks were streaked with sparkling silver. All around It shimmered an aura like ... like the glimmering fields around a starship ...

The room disappeared entirely. Suddenly, all around him was a great, open sea of weightlessness. The old god began to swim forward with powerful fluke strokes. Creideiki, wailing a soft fluting cry, was powerless to prevent being swept along in the behemoth's pulling slipstream. They accelerated, faster ... faster ...

In spite of the absence of direction, he knew, somehow, they were going **DOWN**.

'Did you hear that-t-t?'

Makanee's assistant looked up at the tank in which the captain lay suspended. A dim spotlight within the gravity tank shone on the suture scars of repeated surgery. Every few seconds, recessed nozzles cast a fine mist over the unconscious dolphin.

Makanee followed the medic's gaze.

'Perhapsss. I thought I picked up something a little while ago, like a sigh. What did you hear?'

The assistant shook her head from side to side. 'I'm not sure. I thought it sounded like he was talking to somebody – only not in Anglic. It seemed like there was a snatch of Trinary, then ... then something else. It sounded weird!'

The assistant shivered. 'Do you think maybe he's dreaming?'

Makanee looked up at Creideiki. 'I don't know dreaming is something to wish for him, or to pray devoutly he doesn't do.'

45

TOM ORLEY

A chilly sea breeze swept over him out of the west. A bout of shivering shook him awake in the middle of the night. His eyes opened in the dark, staring into emptiness.

He couldn't remember where he was.

Give it a moment, he thought. *It'll come.*

He had been dreaming of the planet Garth, where the seas were small and the rivers many. There he had lived for a time among the human and chimp colonists, a mixed colony as rich and surprising as Calafia, where man and dolphin dwelt together.

Garth was a friendly world, though isolated far from other Earthling settlements.

In his dream, Garth was invaded. Giant warships hovered over her cities and spewed clouds of gas across her fertile valleys, sending colonists fleeing in panic. The sky had been filled with flashing lights.

He had trouble separating the trailing edges of the dream from reality. Tom stared at the crystal dome of Kithrup's night. His body was locked – legs pulled in, hands clutching opposite shoulders – as much from a rigor of exhaustion as from the cold. Slowly, he got the muscles to loosen. Tendons popped and joints groaned as he learned all over again how to move.

The volcano to the north had died down to only a feeble red glow. There were long, ragged openings in the clouds overhead. Tom watched pinpoints of light in the sky.

He thought about stars. Astronomy was his mental focus.

Red means cool, he pondered. That red one there might be a small, nearby ancient – or a distant giant already in its death throes. And that bright one over there could be a blue supergiant. Very rare. Was there one in this area of space?

He ought to remember.

Tom blinked. The blue 'star' was moving.

He watched it drift across the starfield, until it intercepted another bright pinpoint, this one a brilliant green. There was a flash as the two tiny lights met. When the blue spark moved on, the green was no more.

Now what were the chances I'd witness that? How likely to be looking at just the right place at the right time? The battle must still be pretty hot and heavy up there. It isn't over yet.

Tom tried to rise, but his body sagged back against the bed of vines.

Okay, try again.

He rolled over onto one elbow, paused to marshal his strength, then pushed upright.

Kithrup's small, dim moons were absent, but there was enough starlight to make out the eerie weedscape. Water sluiced through the shifting morass. There were croaking and slithering sounds. Once he heard a tiny scream that choked off – some small prey suddenly dying, he supposed.

He was thankful for the obstinacy that had brought him to this modest height. Even two meters made a difference. He couldn't have survived a night down in that loathsome mess.

He turned stiffly and began groping through his meager supplies on the crude sledge. First priority was to get warm. He pulled the top piece of his wetsuit from the jumbled pile, and gingerly slid into it.

Tom knew he should give some attention to his wounds, but they could wait just a little longer. So could a full meal – he had salvaged enough stores for a few of those.

Munching on a foodbar and taking sparing sips from a canteen, Tom appraised his small pile of equipment. At the moment what mattered were his three psi-bombs.

He looked up at the sky. Except for a faint purple haze near one bright star, there were no more signs of the battle. Yet that one glimpse had been enough. Tom already knew which bomb to set off.

Gillian had spent a few hours with the Niss machine before leaving *Streaker* to meet him at Toshio's island. She had connected the Tymbrimi device to the Thennanin micro-branch *Library* he had salvaged. Then she and the Niss had worked out the proper signals to load into the bombs.

The most important was the Thennanin distress call. Ifni's fickle luck permitting, it would let Tom perform the crucial experiment, to find out if the Plan would work.

All of the work Suessi and Tsh't and the others had put into the 'Trojan Seahorse' would come to naught if Thennanin were not amongst those left in the war. What use would it be for *Streaker* to slip inside a hollowed-out Thennanin hulk, to rise into space in disguise, if all the combatants would shoot anyway at a remnant of a faction which had already lost?

Tom picked up one psi-bomb. It was spherical, and rested in his hand like an orb. At the top was a safety switch and timer. Gillian had carefully labeled each bomb on a strip of tape. On this one she had added a flowing signature and a small heart with an arrow through it.

Tom smiled and brought the bomb to his lips.

He had felt guilty of machismo, insisting on being the one to come here while she remained behind. Now he knew he had been right. Tough and competent as Gillian was, she wasn't as good a pilot as he, and probably would have died in the crash. She certainly wouldn't have had the physical strength to haul the sledge this far.

Hell, he thought. *I'm glad because she's safe with friends who'll protect her. That's reason enough. She may be able to lick ten Blenchuq cave lizards with one hand tied, but she's my lady, and I'll not let harm come near her if I can help it.*

The complaining volcano thundered and rumbled, reminding him ironically of Mount Deanna when he had last seen it, spilling molten magma down the towering, shelfing slope of Aphrodite Terra, that continent whose flanks were washed by the searing, bone-dry ghost of a primeval dead sea. Under the sulfurous clouds of Venus those lava flickerings had illuminated another long night of all too well remembered pain, only this nearby Kithrupan fumerole would have barely glimmered on mighty Deanna's distant, fiery shoulders. Anyway, on Venus night has no end.

There, too, he had lain amid rubble, half-broken, wondering whether he was going to live or die. Through his pitted helmet visor, he had watched infrared trails through the choking atmosphere, left by a slow rain of faraway descending comets, hurtling iceballs whose targeted plummet seemed aimed just over the curved horizon, beyond reach of sight or sound.

He had been young and naive then, or else he never would have trusted a stranger's word that the hired dirigiplane was fully checked out for a quick dash across Ella's Burning Sands . . . a stranger who, Tom later recalled, had never once looked him in the eye while filling out the rental forms. *First impressions can be wrong*, he contemplated after barely surviving the crash. *But when in doubt, trust what your senses tell you.*

Then, too, the overwhelming sensation had been of frustration and failure. With information in his pouch, the Venus Terraforming Project might yet manage to hold on to its alien advisors, Galactics from the Institute for Progress who were due to pull out the very next day, dismissing as quixotic the quaint, human dream of awakening seas already dead for three billion years. With their knowledge and technological aid, miracles might yet happen, if only the advisors could be persuaded to stay. If the data reached them in time . . .

He shuddered, remembering that earlier trial. The similarities were deceiving. On Venus help had been just an hour away, and the issues, while serious, weren't as horrific. *And on Venus the problem was to keep from burning up.* A chill breeze penetrated his damp clothes, setting his teeth briefly chattering.

Still, from now on maybe I'd better make a point of staying away from volcanoes.

Tom washed down the last of the protein bar. He hefted the bomb and considered strategy. His original plan had been to land near the volcano, wait until the glider had recharged for launching, then plant the bomb and take flight before it went off. He could have ridden thermals from the volcano to a good altitude and found another island from which to watch the results of his experiment. Lacking another island, he still could have gone far enough, landed in the ocean, and used his telescope to watch from there.

It was a nice plan, foiled by a raging storm and an unexpected jungle of mad vines. His telescope had joined the metal detritus at the bottom of Kithrup's world-sea, along with most of the wreckage of his solar plane.

Tom rose carefully to his feet. Food and warmth made it merely an exercise in controlled agony.

Rummaging through his few belongings, he tore a long, narrow strip of cloth from the tattered ruins of his sleeping bag. The swatch of tough insu-silk seemed adequate.

The psi-bomb felt heavy and substantial in his hand. It was hard to imagine the globe stuffed with powerful illusions – a super-potent counterfeit, ready to burst free on command.

He set the timer for two hours and thumbed the safety release, arming the thing. He laid it carefully into his makeshift sling. Tom knew he was being dramatic. Distance wouldn't help all that much. Sensors all over the Kithrup system would light up when it went off. He might as well set it off at his feet.

Still, one never knew. Might as well toss it as far away as he could.

He let the sling sway a few times to get the feel of it, then he began swinging it. Slowly, at first, he built up momentum while a strange feeling of well-being spread outward from his chest into his arms and legs. Fatigue seemed to fall away. He started to sing.

> Oh, Daddy was a caveman,
> He fought in skins, no shirts.
> He dreamed of lights up in the sky,
> While scratching in the dirt.

Your ETs and your stars . . .

Oh, Daddy the bold fighter,
Slew his cousins, fourth and third.
He dreamed of peace eternally,
And died speared to the earth.

You ETs and your stars . . .

Oh, Daddy was a lover,
And yet he beat his' wife.
He dreamed, longing for sanity
Regretting all his life.

You ETs and your stars . . .

Yes and Daddy was a leader,
He dreamed, yet still told lies.
He got the frightened masses,
To put missiles in the skies.

You ETs and your stars . . .

My Daddy was unlearned,
But ever on he tried.
He hated his damned ignorance,
And struggled with his pride . . .

He stepped up on a bootstrap, then
And, up on nothing, cried.
That tragic orphan willed to me,
A mind and heart, then died.

So scorn me as a wolfling,
Sneer at my orphan's scars!
But tell me, boys, What's *your* excuse?
You ETs, and your stars?

You Eatees and your stars!

Tom's shoulders flexed as he took a step. His arm snapped straight,
and he released the sling. The bomb sailed high into the night, whirling
like a top. The spinning sphere shone briefly, still climbing, sparkling
until it disappeared from sight. He listened, but never heard it land.

Tom stood still for a while, breathing deeply.

Well, he thought at last. *That built an appetite. I have two hours to eat, tend my wounds, and prepare a shelter. Any time I get after that, O Lord, will be accepted with humble gratitude.*

He laid the ragged strip of cloth over his shoulder and turned to prepare himself a meal by starlight.

PART FIVE

CONCUSSION

'In a world older and more complex than ours, they move finished and complete, gifted with extensions of the senses we have lost or never attained, living by voices we shall never hear ... they are other nations, caught with ourselves in the net of life and time ...'

HENRY BATESON

46

SAH'OT

It was evening, and the Kiqui were leaving for their hunting grounds. Sah'ot heard them squeaking excitedly as they gathered in a clearing west of the toppled drill-tree. The hunters passed not far from the pool on their way to a rock chimney on the southern slope of the island, chittering and puffing their lung sacks in pomp.

Sah'ot listened until the abos were gone. Then he sank a meter below the surface and blew depressed bubbles. Nothing was going right.

Dennie had changed, and he didn't like it. Instead of her usual delightful skittishness, she virtually ignored him. Worse, she had listened to two of his best limericks and answered seriously, completely missing the delicious double entendres.

In spite of the importance of her studies of the Kiqui, Takkata-Jim had ordered her also to analyze the drill-tree system for Charles Dart. Twice she had gone into the water to collect samples from below the metal-mound. She had ignored Sah'ot's nuzzling advances or, even more disturbing, petted him absently in return.

Sah'ot realized that, for all of his previous efforts to break her down, he hadn't really wanted her to change. At least, not *this* way.

He drifted unhappily until a tether attached to one of the sleds brought him up short, reminding him of the worst affront of all. His new assignment kept him linked to this electrical obscenity, chafed and cramped in a tiny pool while his real work was out in the open sea with the pre-sentients!

When Gillian and Keepiru left, he had assumed their absence would free him to do pretty much what he wanted. Hah! No sooner had the pilot and physician left, than did *Toshio* step in and assume command.

I should have been able to talk rings around him. How in the Five Galaxies did the boy manage to get the upper hand?

But here he was, stuck monitoring a damned robot for a pompous, egocentric chimpanzee who cared only about rocks! The dumb little robot didn't even have a brain one could TALK to! You don't have conversations with microprocessors. You tell them what to do, then helplessly watch the disaster when they take you literally.

His harness gave off a chime. It was time to check on the probe. Sah'ot clucked a sarcastic response.

> * *Yes indoody,*
> > *Lord and master!*
> * *Metal moron,*
> > *And disaster!*
> * *Beep again,*
> > *I'll work faster!*

Sah'ot brought his left eye even with the sled's screen. He sent a pulse-code to the robot, and a stream of data returned. The 'bot had finally digested the most recent rock sample. He ordered the probe's small memory emptied into the sled's data banks. Toshio had run him through the drill until Sah'ot could control the 'bot almost unconsciously.

He made it anchor one end of a monofilament line to the rough rock, then lower itself another fifty meters.

The old explanation for the hole beneath the metal-mound had been discarded. The drill-tree couldn't have needed to dig a tunnel a kilometer deep in search of nutrients. It shouldn't have been *able* to pierce the crust that far. The mass of the drill root was clearly too great to have been rotated by the modest tree that once stood atop the mound.

The amount of material excavated wouldn't fit atop ten metal-mounds. It was found as sediment all around the high ridge on which the mound sat.

To Sah'ot these mysteries weren't enticing. They only proved once again that the universe was weird, and that maybe humans and dolphins and chimps ought to wait a while before challenging its deeper puzzles.

The robot finished its descent. Sah'ot made it reach out and seize the cavity wall with diamond-tipped claws, then retract its tether from above.

Down in stages it would go. For this little machine there would be no rising. Sah'ot felt that way himself, sometimes, especially since coming to Kithrup. He didn't really expect ever to leave this deadly world.

Fortunately, the probe's sampling routine was fairly automatic once triggered. Even Charles Dart should have little excuse to complain. Unless . . .

Sah'ot cursed. There it was again – the static that had plagued the probe since it had passed the half-kilometer mark. Toshio and Keepiru had worked on it, and couldn't find the problem.

The crackling was unlike any static Sah'ot had ever heard . . . not that he was an expert on static. It had a syncopation of sorts, not all that unpleasant to listen to, actually. Sah'ot had heard that some people liked to listen to white noise. Certainly nothing was more undemanding.

The clock on his harness ticked away. Sah'ot listened to the static and thought about perversities, about love and loneliness.

                    * *I swim-*

circles –   *like the others*

          *And learn * –*

sadly –   *I am*

         *Sightlessly * –*

Sighing –   *alone*

Slowly Sah'ot realized he had adopted the rhythm of the 'noise' below. He shook his head. But when he listened again it was still there.

A song. It was a song!

Sah'ot concentrated. It was like trying to follow all parts of a six-part fugue at the same time. The patterns interleaved with an incredible complexity.

No wonder they had all thought it noise! Even *he* had barely caught on!

His harness timer chimed, but Sah'ot didn't notice. He was too busy listening to the planet sing to him.

47

STREAKER

Moki and Haoke had both volunteered for guard duty, but for different reasons.

Both enjoyed getting out of the ship for a change. And neither dolphin particularly minded having to stay plugged in to a sled for hours at a stretch in the dark, silent waters outside the ship.

But beyond that they differed. Haoke was there because he felt it was a necessary job. Moki, on the other hand, hoped guard duty would give him a chance to kill something.

'I wissshh Takkata-Jim sent me after Akki, instead of K'tha-Jon,' Moki rasped. 'I could've tracked the smartasss just as well.'

Moki's sled rested about twenty yards from Haoke's, on the high underwater bluff overlooking the ship. Arc lamps still shone on *Streaker*'s hull, but the area was deserted now, off-limits to all but those few cleared by the vice-captain.

Moki looked at Haoke through the flexible bubble-dome of his sled. Haoke was silent, as usual. He had ignored Moki's comment completely.

Arrogant spawn of a stink-squid! Haoke was another *Tursiops* smart-aleck, like Creideiki and that stuck up little midshipfin, Akki.

Moki made a small sound-sculpture in his mind. It was an image of ramming and tearing. Once, he had put Creideiki in the role of the victim. The captain who had so often caught him goldbricking, and embarrassed him by correcting his Anglic grammar, had finally got his just deserts. Moki was glad, but now he needed another fantasy target. It was no fun to imagine ripping into nobody in particular.

The Calafian, Akki, served well when it was discovered that the young middie had betrayed the vice-captain. Moki had hoped to be the one sent after Akki, but Takkata-Jim had ordered K'tha-Jon out instead, explaining that the purpose was to bring Akki back for discipline, not to commit murder.

The giant had seemed oblivious to such nice distinctions when he departed equipped with a powerful laser rifle. Perhaps Takkata-Jim had less than perfect control over K'tha-Jon, and had sent him away for his own safety. From the gleam in K'tha-Jon's eye, Moki did not envy the Calafian when the youth was found.

Let K'tha-Jon *have* Akki! One small pleasure lost didn't take away much from Moki's overall joy.

It was good to be BIG, for a change! On his off-duty time, everybody got out of Moki's way, as if he was a pod leader! Already he had his eye on one or two of those sexy little females in Makanee's sick bay. Some of the younger males looked good, too … Moki wasn't particular.

They would all come around soon enough, when they saw the way the current pulled. He briefly resisted an urge, but couldn't help himself. He let out a short skirr of triumph in a forbidden form.

> # *Glory! is, is,*
> *Glory!*
> # *Biting is   and Glory!*
> *Females submit!*
> # *A new bull is!   is! #*

He saw Haoke react at last. The other guard jerked slightly and raised his head to regard Moki. He was silent, though, as Moki met his eye defiantly. Moki sent a focused beam of sonar directly at Haoke, to show he was listening to *him*, too!

Arrogant stink-squid! Haoke would get his, too, after Takkata-Jim

474

had locked his jaws on the situation. And the men of Earth would never disapprove, because Big-Human Metz was at Takkata-Jim's side, agreeing with everything!

Moki let out another squeal of Primal, tasting the forbidden primitiveness with delight. It pulled at something deep inside him. Each taste brought on further hunger for it.

Let Haoke click in disgust! Moki dared even the *Galactics* to come and try to interfere with him and his new captain!

Haoke bore Moki's bestial squawking stoically. But it reminded him that he had joined up with a gang of cretins and misfits.

Unfortunately, the cretins and misfits were *right*, and the brightest of *Streaker*'s crew were caught up in a disastrous misadventure.

Haoke was desperately sad over the crippling of Creideiki. The captain had obviously been among the best the breed could produce. But the accident had made possible a quiet and perfectly legal change in policy, and he couldn't regret that. Takkata-Jim at least recognized the foolishness of pursuing the desperate Trojan Seahorse scheme.

Even if *Streaker could* be moved silently to the Thennanin wreck, and *if* Tsh't's crew had miraculously set things up so *Streaker* could wear the hulk as a gigantic disguise – and actually take off under those conditions – what would that win them?

Even if Thomas Orley had reported that Thennanin were still in the battle in space, there remained the question of *fooling* those Thennanin into coming to rescue a supposed lost battleship, and escorting it to the rear. A dubious chance.

The question was moot. Orley was obviously dead. There had been no word for days, and now the gamble had turned into a desperate wish.

Why not just give the thrice-damned Calactics what they *want*! Why this romantic nonsense of saving the data for the Terragens Council. What do *we* care about a bunch of dangerous long-lost hulks, anyway? It's obviously no business of ours if the Galactics want to fight over the derelict fleet. Even the Kithrup aboriginals weren't worth dying for.

It all seemed plain to Haoke. It was also apparent to Takkata-Jim, whose intelligence Haoke respected.

But if it was so obvious, why did people like Creideiki and Orley and Hikahi disagree?

Quandaries like this were the sort of thing that had kept Haoke a SubSec in the engine room instead of trying for non-com or officer, as his test scores indicated.

Moki blatted another boast-phrase in Primal. It was even louder, this time. The *Stenos* was trying to get a rise out of him.

Haoke sighed. Many of the crew had begun behaving that way, not quite as bad as Moki, but bad enough. And it wasn't just *Stenos*, either. As morale dissolved, so did the motivation to maintain Keneenk, to keep up the daily fight against the animal side that always wanted out. One would hardly have been able to predict, weeks ago, who later turned out to be the most susceptible.

Of course, all the best crewfen were away, with Suessi and Hikahi.

Fortunately, Haoke thought. He dwelt on the irony of good going to bad, and right coming out of wrong. At least Takkata-Jim seemed to understand how he felt, and didn't hold it against him. The vice-captain had taken Haoke's support with gratitude.

He heard Moki's tail thrash, but, before the angry little *Stenos* could voice another taunt, both of their sled speakers came to life.

'Haoke and Moki? CommSec Fin Heurka-pete calling ... Ack-cknowledge!'

The call was from the ship's comm and detection operator. The fact that the jobs had been combined showed just how bad things were.

'Roger, Haoke here. Moki's indisposed at the moment. What'sss up?'

He heard Moki choke a protest. But it was clear the fin would be a while reformatting his mind for Anglic.

'We have a sonic bogey to the east-t, Haoke ... sounds like a sled. If hostile, destroy. If it's someone from the island, they must be turned back-ck. If they refuse, shoot to disable the sled!'

'Understood. Haoke and Moki on our way.'

'All right, gabby,' he told the speech-tied Moki. Haoke gave his partner a long, narrow grin. 'Let'sss check it out. And watch that trigger! We're only enforcing a quarantine. We don't shoot at crewmates unless we absolutely have to!'

With a neural impulse, he turned his sled motor on. Without looking back, he lifted off from the muddy rise, then accelerated slowly to the east.

Moki watched Haoke head out before turning his sled to follow.

> \# *Tempted, tempted ... tempted, Moki, is, is*
> \# *Temptation, delicious is – is – is!* \#

The sleds dropped, one after another, into the gloom. On a passive sonar screen they were small, blurry dots that drifted slowly past the shadow of the seamount, then disappeared behind it.

Keepiru opened his harness's right claw and dropped the portable listening unit. It tumbled down to the soft ooze. He turned to Gillian.

> * Done and gone—
> > They chase our shadows
> * They'll not like—
> > To catch false prey! *

Gillian had expected guards. Several kilometers back they had left the sled on delayed automatic, and swam off to the north and west. By the time the sled started up again, they had circled to within a few hundred yards of the out-lock.

Gillian touched Keepiru's flank. The sensitive hide trembled under her hand. 'You remember the plan, Keepiru?'

> * Need you ask? *

Gillian raised an eyebrow in surprise. A triple upsweep trill and a wavering interrogative click? That was an unusually brief and straightforward reply for Trinary. Keepiru was capable of more subtlety than she had thought.

'Of course not, dear bow-wave rider. I apologize. I'll do my part, and not worry for a moment about you doing yours.'

Keepiru looked at her as if wishing he didn't have to wear a breather. As if he wanted to speak to her in *her* native language. Gillian felt some of this in a gentle telepathic touch.

She hugged his smooth gray torso. 'You take care, Keepiru. Remember that you're admired and loved. Very much so.'

The pilot tossed his head.

> * To swimming – or
> > Battle
> * To warning – or
> > Rescue
> * To earning – your
> > Trust *

They dropped over the edge of the bluff and swam quickly for the ship's outer lock.

48

TAKKATA-JIM

It was impossible to rest.

Takkata-Jim envied humans the total unconsciousness they called sleep. When a man lay down for the night, his awareness of the world disappeared, and the nerves to his muscles deactivated. If he *did* dream, he usually didn't have to participate *physically*.

Even a neo-dolphin couldn't just turn himself off that way. One or the other hemisphere of the brain was always on sentry duty to control his breathing. Sleep, for a fin, was both a milder and a far more serious thing.

He knocked about the captain's stateroom, wishing he could go back to his own, smaller cabin. But symbolism was important to the crew he had inherited. His followers needed more than the logic of legality to confirm his command. They needed to see him as the New Bull. And that meant living in the style of the former herd leader.

He took a long breath at the surface and emitted clicks to illuminate the room in sound-images.

Creideiki certainly had eclectic tastes. Ifni knew what sorts of things the former captain had owned which couldn't stand wetness, and had therefore been stowed away before *Streaker* landed on Kithrup. The collection that remained was striking.

Works by artists of a dozen sentient races lay sealed behind glass cases. Sound-stroke photos of strange worlds and weird, aberrant stars adorned the walls.

Creideiki's music system was impressive. He had recordings by the thousands, songs and eerie ... *things* that made Takkata-Jim's spine crawl when he played them. The collection of whale ballads was valuable, and a large fraction appeared to have been collected personally.

By the desk comm, there was a photo of Creideiki with the officers of the *James Cook*. Captain Helene Alvarez herself had signed it. The famous explorer had her arm over her dolphin exec's broad, smooth back as she and Creideiki mugged for the camera.

Takkata-Jim had served on important ships – cargo vessels supplying the Atlast and Calafia colonies – but he had never been on missions like those of the legendary *Cook*. *He* had never seen such sights, nor heard such sounds.

Until the Shallow Cluster ... until they found dead ships the size of moons ...

He thrashed his tail in frustration. His flukes struck the ceiling painfully. His breath came heavily.

It didn't matter. Nothing that he had done would matter if he succeeded! If he got *Streaker* away from Kithrup with her crew alive! If he did that, he would have a photo of his own. And the arm on his back would be that of the President of the Confederacy of Earth.

A shimmering collection of tiny motes began to collect to his right. The sparkles coalesced into a holographic image, a few inches from his eye.

'Yess, what is it!' he snapped.

An agitated dolphin, harness arms flexing and unflexing, nodded nervously. It was the ship's purser, Suppeh.

'Sssir! Sssomething strange has happened. We weren't sssure we should wake you, but-t-t ...'

Takkata-Jim found the fin's Underwater Anglic almost indecipherable. Suppeh's upper register warbled uncontrollably.

'Calm down and talk slowly!' he commanded sharply. The fin flinched, but made an effort to obey.

'I ... I was in the outlock-k. I heard someone say there was an alert-t. Heurka-pete sent Haoke and Moki after sled-sounds ...'

'Why wasn't I informed?'

Suppeh recoiled in dismay. For a moment he appeared too frightened to speak. Takkata-Jim sighed and kept his voice calm. 'Never mind. Not your fault. Go on.'

Visibly relieved, Suppeh continued. 'A f-few minutes later, the light on the personnel outlock-k came on. Wattaceti went over, and I p-p-paid no heed. But when Life-Cleaner and Wormhole-Pilot entered ...'

Takkata-Jim spumed. Only dire need to hear Suppeh's story without delay prevented him from crashing about the room in frustration!

' ... tried to stop them, as you ordered, but-t Wattaceti and Hiss-kaa were doing back flipsss of joy, and dashed about fetching for them both-th!'

'Where are they now?' Takkata-Jim demanded.

'Bassskin entered the main bay, with Wattaceti. Hiss-kaa is off, spreading rumorsss throughout the ship. Keepiru took a sled and breathers and is gone!'

'Gone where?'

'Back-k-k out-t-t!' Suppeh wailed. His command of Anglic was rapidly dissolving. Takkata-Jim took advantage of what composure the purser had left.

'Have Heurka-pete awaken Doctor Metz. Have Metz meet me at sick bay with three guards. *You* are to go to the dry-wheel dressing room, with Sawtoot, and let-t no one enter! Understood?'

Suppeh nodded vigorously, and his image vanished.

Takkata-Jim prayed that Heurka-pete would have the sense to recall Moki and Haoke and send them after Keepiru. Together, between Haoke's brains and Moki's feral ruthlessness, they might be able to cut the pilot off before he reached the Thennanin wreck.

Why isn't K'tha-Jon back yet? I chose him to go after that middie in order to get him out of the ship for a while. I was afraid he was becoming dangerous even to me. I wanted some time to organize without him around. But now the Baskin woman's returned sooner than I expected. Maybe I should have kept K'tha-Jon around. The giant's talents might be useful about now.

Takkata-Jim whistled the door open and swam out into the hall. He faced a confrontation he had hoped to put off for at least another forty hours, if not indefinitely.

Should I have seen to Creideiki before this? It would have been easy . . . a power failure in his gravity tank, a switched catheter . . .

Metz would not approve, but there was already much Metz did not know. Much that Takkata-Jim wished he didn't know.

He swam hard for the intrahull lift.

Maybe I won't need K'tha-Jon in order to deal with Gillian Baskin, he thought. *After all, what can one human female do?*

49

THE PSI-BOMB

The mound of partly dried weeds formed a dome on the sea of vines. Tom had propped up a low roof using salvaged bits of strutting from his sledge, making a rude cave. He sat in the entrance, waiting in the pre-dawn dimness, and munched one of his scarce foodbars. His wounds were cleaned as well as possible, and coated with hardening dabs of medicinal foam. With food in his stomach and some of the pain put down, he almost felt human again.

He examined his small osmotic still. The upper part, a clear bag with a filtered spout at one end, held a thick layer of saltwater and sludge. Below the filter, one of his canteens sat almost filled.

Tom looked at his watch. Only five minutes remained. There was no time to dip for another load of scummy water to feed the still.

He wouldn't even be able to clean the filters before the bomb went off.

He picked up the canteen, screwed its cap tight, and slipped it into a thigh pouch. Then he popped the filter out of its frame and shook most of the sludge out before folding it tightly and tucking it under his belt. The filter probably didn't take all the dissolved metal salts out of the water. It hadn't been designed with Kithrup in mind. Nonetheless, the little package was probably his most valuable possession.

Three minutes, the glowing numbers on his watch told him.

Tom looked up at the sky. There was a vague brightening in the east, and the stars were starting to fade. It would be a clear morning, and therefore bitterly cold. He shivered and zipped the wetsuit tight. He pulled in his knees.

Again, Venus came to mind, perhaps because then, too, his fate and all he cared about had hung upon sending a message. Only there it had been for succor. Moreover, his enemies had been few and furtive, while all around him friendly humans and aliens had roamed the steaming skies, searching for a slender clue he had only to provide.

This time, matters were reversed. Friends were the scarce commodity, while his signal would be a shout, a scream, directed at countless foes. Enemies who, at best, would willingly rack his body and strain his brain pan for what it contained. Yet he must strive to bring them here, down here almost to this very spot.

How do I keep getting into jams like this?

One minute.

When it came it would be like the loudest sound he had ever heard. Like the brightest light. There would be no keeping it out.

He wanted to cover his ears and eyes, as if against a real explosion. Instead, he stared at a point on the horizon and counted, pacing each breath. Deliberately he let himself slide into a trance.

'. . . seven . . . eight . . . nine . . . ten . . .' A lightness filled his chest. The feeling spread outward, numbing and soothing.

Light from the few stars in the west diffracted spiderweb rays through his barely separated eyelashes as he awaited a soundless explosion.

'Sah'ot, I said I'm ready to take over now!'

Sah'ot squirmed and looked up at Toshio. 'Just-t another few minutes, OK? I'm listening to ssssomething!'

Toshio frowned. This was not what he had expected from Sah'ot. He had come to relieve the dolphin linguist early because Sah'ot *hated* working with the robot probe!

'What's going on, Tosh?'

Dennie sat up in her sleeping bag, rubbing her eyes, peering in the pre-dawn dark.

'I offered to take over the robot, so Sah'ot wouldn't have to deal with Charlie when he calls. But he refuses to let go.'

Dennie shrugged. 'Then I'd say that's his business. What do you care, anyway?'

Toshio felt a sharp answer rise to his lips, but he kept them locked and turned away. He would ignore Dennie until she wakened fully and decided to behave civilly.

Dennie had surprised him after Gillian and Keepiru left, by taking his new command without complaint. For the last two days, she hadn't seemed much interested in anything but her microscopes and samples, ignoring even Sah'ot's desultory sexual innuendo, answering questions in monosyllables.

Toshio knelt by the comm unit attached by cable to Sah'ot's sled. He tapped out a query on the monitor and frowned at the result.

'Sah'ot!' he said severely. 'Get over here!'

'In a ssssec . . .' The dolphin sounded distracted.

Toshio pursed his lips.

> * NOW, you will to HERE
> Ingather
> * Or shortly cease ALL
> Listening further! *

He heard Dennie gasp behind him, though she probably didn't understand the Trinary burst in detail. Toshio felt justified. This was a test. He wasn't as subtle as Gillian Baskin, but he had to get obedience or be useless as an officer.

Sah'ot stared up at him, blinking dazedly. Then the fin sighed and moved over to the side of the pool.

'Sah'ot, you haven't taken any geological readings in four hours yet in that time you've dropped the probe two hundred meters! What's got into you?'

The *Stenos* rolled from side to side uncertainly. Finally, he spoke softly. 'I'm get-tting a sssong . . .'

The last word faded before Toshio could be sure of it. 'You're getting a *what*?'

'A ssssong . . . ?'

Toshio lifted his hands and dropped them to his sides. *He's finally cracked. First Dennie, now Sah'ot. I've been left in charge of two mental cases!*

He sensed Dennie approach the pool. 'Listen, Sah'ot,' Toshio said.

482

'Doctor Dart will be calling soon. What do you think he's going to say when ...'

'I'll take care of Charlie when he calls,' Dennie said quietly.

'You?' Dennie had spent the last forty hours cursing over the drill-tree problem she had been assigned, at Takkata-Jim's order and Charles Dart's request. It had almost completely superseded her work with the Kiqui. Toshio couldn't imagine her *wanting* to talk with the chimpanzee.

'Yes, me. What I have to tell may make him forget all about the robot, so you just lay off Sah'ot. If he says he heard singing, well, maybe he's heard singing.'

Toshio stared at her, then shrugged. *Fine. My job is to protect these two, not correct their scientific blunders. I just hope Gillian straightens things out back at the ship so I can report what's going on here.*

Dennie knelt down by the water to talk to Sah'ot. She spoke slowly and earnestly, patient with the Anglic slowness he suffered after his long seance with the robot. Dennie wanted to dive to look at the core of the metal-mound. Sah'ot agreed to accompany her if she would wait until he transcribed some more of his 'music.' Dennie assented, apparently completely unafraid of going into the water with Sah'ot.

Toshio sat down and waited for the inevitable buzz of the comm line from the ship. People were changing overnight, and he hadn't the slightest idea why!

His eyes felt scratchy. Toshio rubbed them, but that didn't seem to help.

He blinked and tried to look at Dennie and Sah'ot. The difficulty he was having focusing only seemed to be getting worse. A haziness began to spread between himself and the pool. Suddenly he felt a sense of dread expectancy. Pulsing, it seemed to migrate from the back of his head to a place between his shoulder blades.

He brought his hands to his ears. 'Dennie? Sah'ot? Do you ... ?' He shouted the last words, but could barely hear his own voice.

The others looked up. Dennie rose and took a step toward him, concern on her face.

Then her eyes opened in wide surprise. Toshio saw a blur of movement. Then there were *Kiqui* in the forest, charging them through the bushes!

Toshio tried to draw his needler, knowing it was already too late. The aboriginals were already upon them, waving their short arms and screaming in tiny, high-pitched voices. Three plowed into him and two toppled Dennie. He struggled and fell beneath them, fighting to keep their slashing claws away from his face while the grating noise erupted in his brain.

Then, in an instant, the Kiqui were gone!

Amidst the grinding roar in his head, Toshio forced himself to turn over and look up.

Dennie tossed back and forth across the ground moaning, clutching at her ears. Toshio feared she had been wounded by Kiqui claws, but when she rolled his way he saw only shallow cuts.

With both shaking hands, he drew his needler. The few Kiqui in sight weren't heading this way, but squealing as they rushed the pool and dove in.

It's not their doing, he realized dimly.

At least he recognized the 'sound' of a thousand fingernails scraping across a blackboard.

A psi attack! We have to hide! Water might cushion the assault. We should dive in like the abos did!

His head roared as he crawled toward the pool. Then he stopped.

I can't drag Dennie in there, and we can't put on our breathing gear while shaking like this!

He reversed direction until he reached a pool-side tree. He sat with his back against the bole and he tried to concentrate, in spite of the crashing in his brain.

Remember what Mr Orley taught you, middie! Think *about your mind, and go within. SEE the enemy's illusions . . . listen lightly to his lies . . . use the Yin and the Yang . . . the twin salvations . . . logic to pierce Mara's veil . . . and faith to sustain . . .*

Dennie moaned and rolled in the dust a few meters away. Toshio laid the needler on his lap, to have it ready when the enemy came. He called to Dennie, shouting over the screaming noise.

'Dennie! Listen to your heartbeat! Listen to each breath! *They're* real sounds! This isn't!'

He saw her turn slightly toward his voice, agony in her eyes as she pressed white bloodless hands over her ears. The shrieking intensified.

'Count your heartbeats, Dennie! They're . . . they're like the *ocean,* like the surf! Dennie!' He shouted. 'Have you ever heard any sound that can overcome the surf? Can . . . can anything or *anybody* scream loud enough to keep the tide from laughing *back?*'

She stared at him, trying. He could see her inhaling deeply, mouthing slowly as she counted.

'Yes! Count, Dennie! Breaths and heartbeats! Is there *any* sound the tide of your heartbeat can't laugh at?'

She locked onto his eyes, as he anchored himself to hers. Slowly, as the howling within his head reached its crescendo, Toshio saw her nod and give a faint grateful smile.

*

Sah'ot felt it too. Even as the psychic wave rolled over him, the pool was suddenly afroth with panicky Kiqui. Sah'ot was inundated by a babel of noise from all around and within. It was worse than being blinded by a searchlight.

He wanted to dive away from the cacophony. Biting back panic, he forced himself to separate the noise into parts. Dennie and Toshio seemed in worse shape than he. Perhaps they were more sensitive to the assault. There would be no help from them!

The Kiqui were in terror, squawling as they crashed into the pool.

> :?: *Flee!*   *Flight ...*
> *from the sad great things*
> :?: *Somebody*   *Help*
> *the great sad hurt things!*

Out of the mouths of babes ... When he concentrated, the 'psi attack' *did* feel like a call for help. It hurt like the hell of the deeps, but he faced it and tried to pin it down.

He thought he was making progress – certainly he was coping – when still *another* voice joined in, this one over his neural link! The song from below, that he had spent all night unable to decipher, had awakened. From the bowels of Kithrup it bellowed. Its simplicity *commanded* understanding.

> + *WHO*   *CALLS?* -
> - *WHO DARES BOTHER* +

Sah'ot moaned as he tore the robot link free. Three screaming noises, all at different levels of mind, were quite enough. Any more and he would go insane!

Buoult of the Thennanin was afraid, though an officer in the service of the Great Ghosts thought nothing of death or of living enemies.

The shuttle cycled through the lock of his flagship, *Quegsfire*. The giant doors, comfortingly massive and enduring, swung shut behind them. The shuttle pilot plotted a course to the Tandu flagship.

Tandu.

Buoult flexed his ridge crest as a display of confidence. He would lose heat from the sail of nerves and blood vessels in the frigid atmosphere of the Tandu ship, but it was absolutely necessary to maintain appearances.

It might have been slightly less distasteful to make an alliance with the Soro instead. At least the Soro were more Thennaninoid than the anthropod Tandu, and lived at a decent temperature. Also, the Soro's clients were interesting folk, the sort Buoult's people might have liked to uplift themselves.

Better for them if we had, he thought. *For we are kind patrons.*

If the leathern Soro were meddlesome and callous, the spindly Tandu were horrifying beings. Their clients were weird creatures that set off twitches at the base of Buoult's tail when he thought of them.

Buoult grimaced in disgust. Politics made for strange gene transfers. The Soro were now strongest among the survivors. The Thennanin were weakest of the major powers. Although the Tandu philosophy was the most repulsive of those in opposition to the Abdicator Creed, they were now all that stood in the way of a Soro triumph. The Thennanin must ally with them, for now. Should the Tandu seem about to prevail, there would be another chance to switch sides. It had happened a number of times already, and would happen again.

Buoult steeled himself for the meeting ahead. He was determined not to let show any of his dread of stepping aboard a Tandu ship.

The Tandu didn't seem to care what chances they took with their crazy, poorly understood probability drive. The insane reality manipulations of their Episiarch clients let them move about more quickly than their opponents. But sometimes the resulting alterations of spacetime swallowed whole groups of ships, impartially snatching the Tandu and their enemies from the universe forever. It was madness!

Just let them not use their perverted drives while I am aboard, Buoult's organ-of-prayer subvocalized. *Let us make our battle plans and be done.*

The Tandu ships came into sight, crazy, stilt-like structures that disdained armor for wild speed and power.

Of course even these unusual shapes were mere variations of ancient *Library* designs. The Tandu were daring, but they did not add to their crimes the gaucherie of originality. *Earthlings* were in many ways more unconventional than the Tandu. Their sloppy gimmickry was a vulgar habit that came from a poor upbringing.

Buoult wondered what the 'dolphins' were doing right now. Pity the poor creatures if the Tandu or Soro got hold of them! Even these primitive sea mammals, clients of a coarse and hairy wolfling race, deserved to be protected, if possible.

Of course there were priorities. Pitiable or not, they mustn't be allowed to hoard the data they held! It must be shared with the Abdicator faction or with no one.

Buoult noticed that his finger-claws had unsheathed in his

agitation. He pulled them back and cultivated serenity as the shuttle drew near the Tandu squadron.

Buoult's musing was split by a sudden chill that made his crest tremble ... a disturbance on a psi band.

'Operator!' he snapped. 'Contact the flagship! See if they verify that call!'

'Immediately, General-Protector!'

Buoult controlled his excitement. The psychic energies he felt could be a ruse. Still, they felt right. They bore the image of *Krondorsfire*, which none of them had hoped to see again!

Determination filled him. In the negotiations ahead, he would ask one more favor. The Tandu must provide one added cooperation in exchange for the help of the Thennanin.

'Confirmed, sir. It is battleship *Krondorsfire*,' the pilot said, his voice raspy with emotion. Buoult's crest stood erect in acknowledgment. He stared ahead at the looming metal mantis shapes, steeling himself for the confrontation, the negotiations, and the waiting.

Beie Chohooan was listening to whale songs – rare and expensive copies which had cost her a month's pay some time ago – when her detectors picked up the beacon. Reluctantly, she put down her headphones and noted the direction and intensity. There were so many signals ... bombs and blasts and traps. Then one of the little wazoon pointed out to her that this particular beacon emanated from the water-world itself.

Beie groomed her whiskers and considered.

'I believe this will change things, my pretty little ones. Shall we leave this belt of unborn rubble in space and move toward the action? Is it time to let the Earthlings know that someone is out here who is a friend?'

The wazoon chittered back that policy was her business. According to union rules, they were spies, not strategists.

Beie approved of their sarcasm. It was very tasty.

'Very well,' she said. 'Let us try to move closer.'

Hikahi hurriedly queried the skiff's battle computer.

'It's a psi weapon of some sort,' she announced via hydrophone to the crew working in the alien wreck. Her Anglic was calm and precise, accentuated with the cool overtones of Keneenk. 'I detect no other signs of attack, so I believe we're feeling a fringe of the space-battle. We've felt otherss before, if not this intense.

'We're deep underwater, partly shielded from psi-waves. Grit your teeth, *Streakers*. Try to ignore it. Go about your duties in tropic-clear logic.'

487

She switched off the speakers. Hikahi knew Tsh't was even now moving among the workers out there, joking and keeping morale high.

The psi-noise was like a nagging itch, but an itch with a weird rhythm. It pulsed as if in some code she couldn't quite get her jaws around.

She looked at Hannes Suessi, who sat on a wall rail nearby, looking very tired. He had been about to turn in for a few hours' sleep, but the psionic assault apparently affected him worse than it did the dolphins. He had compared it to fingernails scratching on a blackboard.

'I can think of two possibilities, Hikahi. One would be very good news. The other's about as bad as could be.'

She nodded her sleek head. 'We've repeatedly re-checked our circuitsss, sent three couriers back with messages, and yet there's only silence from the ship. I must assume the worst.'

'That Streaker's been taken,' Suessi closed his eyes.

'Yess. This psi havoc comes from somewhere on the surface of the planet. The Galactics may even now be fighting over her – or what's left of her.'

Hikahi decided. 'I'm returning to Streaker in this boat. I'll delay until you've sealed quarters for the work-crew inside the hulk. You need power from the skiff to recharge the Thennanin accumulators.'

Suessi nodded. Hikahi was clearly anxious to depart as soon as possible. 'I'll go outside and help, then.'

'You just got off duty. I cannot permit it.'

Suessi shook his head. 'Look, Hikahi, when we've got that refuge inside the battleship set up, we can pump in filtered fizzywater for the fen and they'll be able to rest properly. The wreck is well shielded from this psychic screeching, too. And most important, I'll have a room of my own, one that's *dry*, without a crowd of squeaking, practical-joking children goosing me from behind whenever I turn the other way!' His eyes were gently ironic.

Hikahi's jaw made a gentle curve. 'Wait a minute, then, Maker of Wonderful Toys. I'll come out and join you. Work will distract usss from the scratching of ET fingernails.'

The Soro, Krat, felt no grating tremors. Her ship was girded against psychic annoyances. She first learned of the disturbance from her staff. She took the data scroll from the Pila Cullalberra with mild interest.

They had detected many such signals in the course of the battle. But none yet had emanated from the planet. Only a few skirmishes had taken the war down to Kithrup itself.

Normally she would have simply ordered a homing torpedo dispatched and forgotten the matter. The expected Tandu-Thennanin alliance against the Soro was forming up near the gas-giant world, and she had plans to make. But something about this signal intrigued her.

'Determine the exact origin of this signal on a planetary map,' she told the Pila. 'Include locations of all known landfalls by enemy ships.'

'There would be doz-ens by now, and the pos-itions very vague,' the Pil statistician barked. Its voice was high and sharp. Its mouth popped open for each syllable, and hairy cilia waved above its small, black eyes.

Krat did not dignify it with a look. 'When the Soro intervened to end Pilan indenture to the Kisa,' she hissed, 'it was not to make you Grand Elders. Am I to be questioned, like a human who pampers his chimpanzee?'

Cullalberra shivered and bowed quickly. The stocky Pila scuttled away to its data center.

Krat purred happily. Yes, the Pila were *so* close to perfect. Arrogant and domineering with their own clients and neighbors, they scurried to serve the Soro's every whim. How wonderful it was to be a Grand Elder!

She owed the humans something, at that. In a few centuries they had almost replaced the Tymbrimi as the bogeymen to use on recalcitrant clients. They symbolized all that was wrong with Uplift Liberalism. When Terra was finally humbled, and humans were 'adopted' into a proper client status, some other bad example would have to serve instead.

Krat opened a private communication line. The display lit up with the image of the Soro Pritil, the young commander of one of the ships in her flotilla.

'Yes, fleet-mother,' Pritil bowed slowly and shallowly. 'I listen.'

Krat's tongues flickered at the young female's insolence. 'Ship number sixteen was slow in the last skirmish, Pritil.'

'One opinion.' Pritil examined her mating claw. She cleaned it in front of the screen, an indelicacy designed to show indifference. Younger females seldom understood that a real insult should be subtle and require time for the victim to discover it. Krat decided she would teach Pritil this lesson.

'You need a rest for repairs. In the next battle, ship number sixteen would be next to useless. There is, however, a way in which she might win honor, and perhaps the prey, as well.'

Pritil looked up, her interest piqued.

'Yes, fleet-mother?'

'We have picked up a call that pretends to be one thing, perhaps an enemy pleading for succor. I suspect it may be something else.'

The flavor of intrigue obviously tempted Pritil. 'I choose to listen, group-mother.'

Krat sighed at the predictability. She knew the younger captains secretly believed all of the legends about Krat's hunches. She had known Pritil would come around.

You have much yet to learn, she thought, *before, you will pull me down and take my place, Pritil. Many learning scars shall mar that young hide first. I will enjoy teaching you until that day, my daughter.*

Gillian and Makanee looked up as Takkata-Jim and Dr Ignacio Metz entered sick bay, accompanied by three stocky, war-harnessed, hard-faced *Stenos*.

Wattaceti squealed indecipherable indignation and moved to interpose himself. Makanee's assistants chittered behind the ship's surgeon.

Gillian met Makanee's eye. It had come, the confrontation. Now they would see if Makanee was only imagining things. Gillian still held out a hope that Takkata-Jim and Metz had compelling reasons for their actions, and that Creideiki's injury was truly an accident.

Makanee had already made up her mind. Akki, the young midshipfin from Calafia, had still not returned. The doctor glared at Takkata-Jim as she would look at a tiger shark. The expression on the male dolphin's face did little to belie the image.

Gillian had a secret weapon, but she had sworn never to use it except in the direst emergency. *Let them act first*, she thought. *Let them show their cards before we pull that last ace of trumps.* The first stages might be a little dangerous. She had only had time to make a brief call to the Niss machine from her office before hurrying to sick bay. Her position here might be difficult if she had miscalculated the degree of atavism loose on *Streaker*. Maybe she should have kept Keepiru by her side.

'Doctor Baskin!' Ignacio Metz didn't swim very close before grabbing a wall rail and letting an armed *Stenos* pass before him. 'It's good to see you again, but why didn't you announce yourself?'

'A grosss violation of security rules, Doctor,' Takkata-Jim added.

So that's the way of it, Gillian thought. And they might try to make that stick long enough to get me into a cell.

'Why, I came for the ship's council meeting, gentlefin and -mel. I got a message from Doctor Makanee calling me back for it. Sorry if your bridge crew fouled up my reply. I hear they're mostly new and inexperienced up there.'

Takkata-Jim frowned. It was even possible she *had* sent such a call, which had been lost in the confusion on the bridge.

'Makanee's message was also against orderss! And your return was contrary to my specific instructions.'

Gillian put on an expression of bewilderment. 'Wasn't she simply passing on your call for a ship's council? The rules are clear. You must call a meeting within twenty-four hours of the death or disability of the captain.'

'Preparations were underway! But in an emergency the acting-captain can dispense with the advice of the council. When faced with clear disobedience of orders, I am within rightsss to ...'

Gillian tensed herself. Her preparations would do no good if Takkata-Jim were irrational. She might have to make a break by vaulting over the row of autodocs to the parapet above. Her office would be steps away.

'... to order that-t you be detained for a hearing to be held at some time after the emergency.'

Gillian took in the stances of the guard-fen. Would they really be willing to harm a human being? She read their expressions and decided they just might be.

Her mouth felt dry, but she didn't let it show. 'You misread your legal status, Lieutenant,' she replied carefully. 'I think very few of the fen aboard would be surprised to learn that ...'

The words stopped in her throat. Gillian felt a chill in her spine as the air itself seemed to waver and throb around her. Then, as she grabbed a rail for support, a deep, growling sound began to emanate from *inside* her head.

The others stared at her, confused by her behavior. Then they began to feel it too.

Takkata-Jim whirled and shouted, 'Psi weapon! Makanee, give me a link to the bridge! We are under attack-k!'

The dolphin physician moved aside, amazed by Takkata-Jim's quickness as he rushed past. Gillian pressed her hands over her ears and saw Metz doing the same as the grating noise grew louder. The security guards were in disarray, fluting disconsolately with boat-like pupils wide in fear.

Should I make my break now? Gillian tried to think. But if this *is* an attack we'll have to drop our quarrels and join forces.

'... incompetentsss!' Takkata-Jim shouted at the comm. 'What do you mean "only a thousand miles away"? Pinpoint it-t! ... Why *won't* the active sensors work?'

'Wait!' Gillian cried. She clapped her hands together, Through a haze of building emotion she started to laugh. Takkata-Jim continued to bark rapidly at the bridge crew, but everyone else turned to look at her in surprise.

Gillian laughed. She slapped the water, pounded on the nearest autodoc, grabbed Wattaceti around the dolphin's quivering flank. Even Takkata-Jim stopped then, captivated by her apparently psychotic fit of joy. He stared, oblivious to frantic twitters from the bridge.

'Tom!' She cried out loud. 'I *told* you you couldn't die! Dammit, I love you, you son of a . . . Oh, if *I* had gone I would have been *home* by now!'

The fins stared at her, eyes opening still wider as they began to realize what she was talking about.

She laughed, tears running down her face.

'Tom,' she said softly. 'I *told* you you couldn't die!' And blindly she hugged close whatever was nearest to her.

Sounds came to Creideiki as he drifted in weightlessness.

It was like listening to Beethoven, or like trying actually to *understand* a humpback whale.

Somebody had left the audio link on in case he made any more sounds. No one had considered that the circuit went both ways. Words penetrated the gravity tank from the outer room.

They were tantalizing, like those ghosts of meaning in a great symphony – hinting that the composer had caught a glimpse of something notes could only vaguely convey and words could never approach.

Takkata-Jim spluttered and mumbled. The threatening tone was clear. So was the cautious clarity of Gillian Baskin's voice. If only he could understand the words! But Anglic was lost to him.

Creideiki knew his ship was in peril, and there was nothing he could do to help. The old gods weren't through with him, and would not let him move. They had much more to show him before he was ready to serve their purposes.

He had become resigned to periodic episodes of terror – like diving to do battle with a great octopus, then rising for a rest before going back down to the chaos once again. When they came to pull him DOWN he would once more be caught in the maelstrom of idea-glyphs, of throbbing dreams which hammered away at his engineer's mind with insistent impressions of otherness.

The assault never would have been possible without the destruction of his speech centers. Creideiki grieved over the loss of words. He listened to the talk-sounds from the outer world, concentrating as hard as he could on the eerie, musical familiarity.

It wasn't *all* gone, he decided after a while. He could recognize a few words, here and there. Simple ones, mostly the names of objects or people, or simple actions associated with them.

That much his distant ancestors could do.

But he couldn't remember the words more than three or four

deep, so it was impossible to follow a conversation. He might laboriously decipher a sentence, only to forget it completely when he worked on the next one. It was agonizingly difficult, and at last he made himself cease the vain effort.

That's not the way, he concluded.

Instead, he should try for the gestalt, he told himself. Use the tricks the old gods had been using on *him*. Encompass. Absorb … like trying to feel what Beethoven felt by submerging into the mystery of the Violin Concerto.

Murmuring sounds of angry sophonts squawked from the speaker. The noises bounced around the chamber and scattered like bitter droplets. After the terrible beauty of DOWN, he felt repelled. He forced himself to listen, to seek a way – some humble way to help *Streaker* and his crew.

Need swelled within him as he concentrated. He sought a center, a focus in the chaotic sounds. —

> * *Rancor*
>> *Turbid*
>>> *In the rip-tide*
> * *Ignoring*
>> *Sharks!*
>>> *Internecine struggle …*
> *Inviting
>> *Sharks!*
>>> *Foolish opportunism …*

Against his will, he felt himself begin to click aloud. He tried to stop, knowing where it would lead, but the clicks emerged involuntarily from his brow, soon joined by a series of low moans.

The sounds of the argument in sick bay drifted away as his own soft singing wove a thicker and thicker web around him. The humming, crackling echoes caused the walls to fade as a new reality took shape all around. A dark presence slowly grew next to him.

Without words, he told it to go away.

: No : We Are Back : You Have More To Learn :

For all I know, you're a delirium of mine! None of you ever make a sound of your own! You always speak in reflections from my own sonar!

: Have Your Echoes Ever Been So Complex? :

Who knows what my unconscious could do? In my memory are more strange sounds than any other living cetacean has heard! I've been where living clouds whistled to tame hurricanes! I've heard the doom-booms of black holes and listened to the songs of stars!

: All The More Reason You Are The One We Want : The One We Need :

I am needed here!

: Indeed.

Come,

Creideiki. :

The old god, K-K-Kph-kree, moved closer. Its sonically translucent form glistened. Its sharp teeth flashed. Figment or not, the great thing began to move, carrying him along, as before, helpless to resist.

: DOWN :

Then, just as resignation washed over Creideiki, he heard a sound. Miraculously, it wasn't one of his own making, diffracted against the insane dream. It came from somewhere else, powerful and urgent!

: Pay No Heed : Come :

Creideiki's mind leaped after it as if it were a school of mullet, even as the noise swelled to deafening volume.

: You Are Sensitized : You Have Psi You Had Not Known Before : You Know Not Yet Its Use : Relinquish Quick Rewards : Come The Hard Way ... :

Creideiki laughed, and opened himself to the noise from the outside. It crashed in, dissolving the shining blackness of the old god into sonic specks that shimmered and then slowly disappeared.

: That Way Is Not For You :

: Creideiki ... :

Then the great-browed god was gone. Creideiki laughed at his release from the cruel illusion, grateful for the new sound that had freed him.

But the noise kept growing. Victory went to panic as it swelled and became a pressure within his head, pushing against the walls of his skull, hammering urgently to get out. The world became a whirling groaning alien cry for help.

Creideiki let out a warbling whistle of despair as he tried to ride the crashing tide.

50

STREAKER

The waves of pseudo-sound were fading at last.

'Creideiki!' Makanee cried and swam to the captain's tank. The others turned also, just noticing the injured dolphin's distress.

'What's the matter with him?' Gillian swam up next to Makanee. She could see the captain struggle feebly, giving off a slowly diminishing series of low moans.

'I don't know. No one was watching him as the psi-bomb hit its peak! Just now I saw he was disturbed.'

The large, dark gray form within the tank seemed calmer now. The muscles along Creideiki's back twitched slowly, as he let out a low, warbling cry.

Ignacio Metz swam up alongside Gillian.

'Ah, Gillian ...' he began, 'I want you to know that I'm very glad Tom is alive, although this tardiness bodes poorly. I'd still stake my life that this Trojan Seahorse plan of his is ill conceived.'

'We'll have to discuss that at ship's council, then, won't we, Doctor Metz?' she said coolly.

Metz cleared his throat. 'I'm not sure the acting captain will permit ...' He subsided under her gaze and looked away.

She glanced at Takkata-Jim. If he did anything rash, it could be the last straw that broke *Streaker*'s morale. Gillian had to convince Takkata-Jim that he would lose if he contested with her. And he had to be offered a way out, or there might still be civil war aboard the ship.

Takkata-Jim looked back at her with a mixture of pure hostility and calculation. She saw the sound-sensitive tip of his jaw swing toward each of the fen in turn, gauging their reaction. The news that Thomas Orley still lived would go through the ship like a clarion. Already one of the armed *Stenos* guards, presumably carefully picked by the vice-captain, looked mutinously jubilant and chattered hopefully with Wattaceti.

I've got to act fast, Gillian realized. He's desperate.

She swam toward Takkata-Jim, smiling. He backed away, a loyal *Stenos* glaring at her from his side.

Gillian spoke softly, so the others could not hear.

'Don't even think it, Takkata-Jim. The fen aboard this ship have Tom Orley fresh on their minds now. If you thought you could harm me before this, even you know better now.'

Takkata-Jim's eyes widened, and Gillian knew she had struck on target, capitalizing on the legend of her psi ability. 'Besides, I'm going to stick close to Ignacio Metz. He's gullible, but if he witnesses me being harmed, you'll lose him. You need a token man, don't you? Without at least one, even your *Stenos* will melt away.'

Takkata-Jim clapped his jaw loudly.

'Don't try to bully me! I don't have to *harm* you. I am the legal authority on this ship. I can have you confined to quartersss!'

Gillian looked at her fingernails. 'Are you so sure?'

'You would incite the crew to disobey the legal ship's master?' Takkata-Jim sounded genuinely shocked. He must know that many, perhaps most of the *Tursiops* would follow her, whatever the law said. But that would be mutiny, and tear the crew apart.

'I have the law on my side!' he hissed.

Gillian sighed. The hand must be played out, for all the damage this would do if the dolphins of Earth found out. She whispered the two words she had not wanted to utter.

'Secret orders,' she said.

Takkata-Jim stared at her, then let out a keening cry. He stood on his tail and did a back flip while his guard blinked in confusion. Gillian turned and saw Metz and Wattaceti staring at them.

'I don't believe you!' Takkata-Jim spluttered, spraying water in all directions. 'On Earth we were promisssed! *Streaker* is *our* ship!'

Gillian shrugged. 'Ask your bridge crew if the battle controls work,' she offered. 'Have someone try to leave through the outlock. Try to open the door to the armory.'

Takkata-Jim whirled and sped to a comm screen at the far end of the room. His guard stared at Gillian momentarily, then followed. His look conveyed a sense of betrayal.

Not all of the crew would feel that way, Gillian knew. Most would probably be delighted. But deep inside an implication would settle. One of the main purposes of *Streaker*'s mission, to build in the neo-fen a sense of independence and self-confidence, had been compromised.

Did I have any other choice? Is there anything else I might have tried first?

She shook her head, wishing Tom were here. Tom might have settled everything with one sarcastic little ditty in Trinary that put everybody to shame.

Oh, Tom, she thought. *I should have gone instead of you.*

'Gillian!'

Makanee's flukes pounded the water and her harness whirred. With one metal arm she pointed up at the wounded dolphin floating in the gravity tank.

Creideiki was looking back at her!

'Joshua H. Bar – but you said his cortex was fried!' Metz stared.

An expression of profound concentration bore down on Creideiki's features. He breathed heavily, then gave voice to a desperate cry.

'*Out!:*'

'It'sss not possible!' Makanee sighed. 'His ssspeech centers ...'

Creideiki frowned in effort.

It was Trinary baby talk, but with a queer tone to it. And the dark eyes burned with intelligence. Gillian's telempathic sense throbbed.

'*Out!:*' He whirled about in the tank and slammed his powerful flukes against the window with a loud boom. He repeated the Anglic word. The falling tone-slope was like a phrase in Primal.

'*Out-t-t!:*'

'Help him out-t!' Makanee commanded her assistants. 'Gently! Quickly!'

Takkata-Jim was heading back from his comm screen at high speed, wrath on his face. But he stopped abruptly at the gravity tank, and stared at the bright eye of the captain.

It was the last straw.

He rolled back and forth, as if unable to decide on appropriate body language. Takkata-Jim turned to Gillian.

'What I've done was in what I believed to be the best interest of the ship, crew, and mission. I could make a very good case on Earth.'

Gillian shrugged. 'Let's hope you get the chance.'

Takkata-Jim laughed dryly. 'Very well, we'll hold this charade ship'sss council. I'll call it for one hour from now. But let me warn you, don't push too far, Doctor Baskin. I have powers ssstill. We must find a compromise. Try to pillory me and you will divide the ship.

'And then I will fight-t-t you,' he added, low.

Gillian nodded. She had achieved what she had to. Even if Takkata-Jim had done the worst things Makanee suspected of him, there was no proof, and it was a matter of compromise or lose the ship to civil war. The first officer had to be offered an out. 'I'll remember, Takkata-Jim. In one hour, then. I'll be there.'

Takkata-Jim swirled about to leave, followed by his two loyal security guards.

Gillian saw Ignacio Metz staring after the dolphin lieutenant. 'You lost control, didn't you?' she asked dryly as she swam past him.

The geneticist's head jerked. 'What, Gillian? What do you mean?' But his face betrayed him. Like many others, Metz tended to over-estimate her psychic powers. Now he must be wondering if she had read his mind.

'Never mind,' Gillian's smile was narrow. 'Let's go and witness this miracle.'

She swam to where Makanee waited anxiously for the emerging Creideiki. Metz looked after her uncertainly, before following.

51

THOMAS ORLEY

With trembling hands, he pulled vines away from the cave entrance. He crept out of his shelter and blinked at the hazy morning.

A thick layer of low clouds had gathered. There were no alien ships, yet, and that was just as well. He had feared they would arrive while he was helpless, struggling against the effects of the psi-bomb.

It hadn't been fun. In the first few minutes the psychic blasts had beaten away at his hypnotic defenses, cresting over them and drenching his brain in alien howling. For two hours – it had felt like eternity – he had wrestled with crazy images, pulsing, nerve-evoked lights and sounds. Tom still shook with reaction.

I sure hope there are still Thennanin out there, and that they fall for it. It had better have been worth it.

According to Gillian, the Niss machine had been confident it had found the right codes in the *Library* taken from the Thennanin wreck. If there were still Thennanin in the system, they should try to answer. The bomb must have been detectable for millions of miles in all directions.

He dragged a handful of muck out of the gap in the weeds and flung it aside. Scummy sea water welled up almost to the surface of the hole. Another gap probably lay only a few meters beyond the next hummock – the weedscape flexed and breathed incessantly – but Tom wanted a water entrance near at hand.

He scooped away the slime as best he could, then wiped his hands and settled down to scan the sky from his shelter. On his lap he arranged his remaining psi-bombs.

Fortunately, these wouldn't pack the wallop of the Thennanin distress call. They were simply pre-recorded message casts, designed to carry a brief code a few thousand kilometers.

He had only recovered three of the message globes from the glider wreck, so he could only broadcast a narrow range of facts. Depending on which bomb he set off, Gillian and Creideiki would know what kind of aliens had come to investigate the distress call.

Of course, something might happen that didn't fit into any of the scenarios they had discussed. Then he would have to decide whether to broadcast an ambiguous message or do nothing and wait.

Maybe it would have been better to bring a radio. But a warship in the vicinity could pinpoint a transmission instantly, and blast his position before he spoke a few words. A message bomb could do its work in a second or so, and would be much harder to locate.

Tom thought about *Streaker*. Everything desirable was there – food, sleep, hot showers, his woman. He smiled at the way the priorities had spilled out. Ah well, Jill would understand.

Streaker might have to abandon him, if his experiment led to a brief chance to blast away from Kithrup. It would not be a worthless way to die. He wasn't afraid of dying, only of having not done all he could, and not properly spitting in the eye of death when it came for him. That final gesture was important.

Another image came to him, far more unpleasant – *Streaker* already captured, the space battle already over, all of his efforts useless.

Tom shuddered. It was better to imagine a sacrifice being for something.

A stiff breeze kept the clouds moving. They merged and separated in thick, wet drifts. Tom shaded his eyes against the glare to the east. About a radian south of the haze-shrouded morning sun, he thought he saw motion in the sky. He huddled deeper into his makeshift cave.

Out of one of the eastern cloud-drifts, a dark object slowly descended. Swirling vapor momentarily obscured its shape and size as it hung high above the sea of weeds.

A faint drumming sound reached Tom. He squinted from his hiding place, wishing for his lost binoculars. Then the mists parted briefly, and he saw the hovering spaceship clearly. It looked like some monstrous dragonfly, sharply tapered and wickedly dangerous.

Few races delved so deeply into the *Library* for weird designs as did the idiosyncratic, ruthless Tandu. Wild protrusions extended from the narrow hull in all directions, a Tandu hallmark.

At one end, however, a blunt, wedge-shaped appendage clashed with the overall impression of careless, cruel delicacy. It didn't seem to fit into the overall design.

Before he could get a better view, the clouds came together, concealing the floating cruiser from sight. The faint hum of powerful engines grew slowly louder, however.

Tom scratched an itchy five-day growth of beard. The Tandu were bad news. If they were the only ones to show themselves, he would have to set off message bomb number three. Tell *Streaker* to lock up and get ready for a death-fight.

This was an enemy with whom Mankind had never been able to negotiate. In skirmishes on the Galactic marshes, Terran ships had seldom conquered Tandu vessels, even with the odds in their favor.

And, when there were no witnesses around, the Tandu loved to pick fights. Standing orders were to avoid them at all costs, until such time as Tymbrimi advisors could teach human crews the rare knack of beating these masters of the sneak-and-strike.

If the Tandu were the only ones to appear, it also meant he had likely seen his last sunrise. For in setting off a message bomb he'd almost certainly given away his position. The Tandu had clients who could psi-sniff even a thought, if they once caught the mental scent.

Tell you what, Ifni, he thought. *You send someone else into this confrontation. I won't insist it be Thennanin. A Jophur fighting-planetoid will suffice. Mix things up here, and I promise to say five sutras, ten Hail Marys, and Kiddush when I get home. Okay? I'll even dump some credits in a slot machine, if you like.*

He envisioned a Tymbrimi-Human-Synthian battle fleet erupting out of the clouds, blasting the Tandu to fragments and sweeping the sky clear of fanatics. It was a lovely image, although he could think of a dozen reasons why it wasn't likely. For one thing, the Synthians, friendly as they were, wouldn't intervene unless it was a sure thing. The Tymbrimi, for that matter, would probably help Earth defend herself, but wouldn't stick their lovely humanoid necks *too* far out for a bunch of lost wolflings.

Okay Ifni, you lady of luck and chance. He fingered bomb number three. *I'll settle for a single, beat-up, old Thennanin cruiser.*

Infinity gave him no immediate answer. He hadn't expected one.

The thrumming seemed to pass right over his head. His hackles rose as the ship's strong-field region swept the area. Its shields screeched at his modest psi sense.

Then the crawling rumble began slowly to recede to his left. Tom looked west. The ragged clouds separated just long enough to display the Tandu cruiser – a light-destroyer, he now saw, and not really a battleship – only a couple of miles away.

As he watched, the blunt appendage detached from the mother ship and began to drift slowly to the south. Tom frowned: That thing didn't look like the Tandu scout ships he was familiar with. It was a totally different design, stout and stolid, like ...

The haze came together again, frustratingly, covering the two ships. Their muttering growl accompanied the muted grumblings of the nearby volcano.

Suddenly three brilliant streams of green light speared down from the clouds where Tom had last seen the Tandu ship, to hit the sea with flashing incandescence. There came a peal of supersonic thunder. First he thought the Tandu were blasting the surface below. But a crackling bright explosion in the clouds showed that the destroyer itself was at the receiving end. Something high above the cloud deck was shooting at the Tandu!

He was too busy snatching up gear to waste time in exultation. Tom kept his head averted, and so was spared blindness as the destroyer began firing actinic beams of antimatter at its assailant. Waves of heat scorched the back of his head and his left arm as he stuffed the psi-bombs under his waistband and snapped on a breather mask.

The beams of annihilation made streaks of solar heat across the sky. Tom grabbed his pack and dove into the hole he had earlier cleared in the thickly woven weeds.

The thunder suddenly muted as he splashed through a jungle of dangling vines. Straight shafts of flickering battle-light speared into the gloom. Tom found he was automatically holding his breath. That didn't make much sense. The mask would not allow much oxygen to escape, but it would pass carbon dioxide. He started inhaling as he grabbed a strong root for an anchor, but soon found he was laboring for breath. With all the vegetation around, he had expected the oxygen content to be high. But the tiny indicator on the rim of his mask told that the opposite was true. The water was depleted compared to the normally rich brine of Kithrup's sea. The waving gill fins of the mask were picking up only a third as much oxygen as he would need to maintain himself, even if he stayed perfectly still.

In just a few minutes he would start to get dizzy. Not long thereafter he would pass out.

A battle roar penetrated the weed cover in a series of dull detonations. Shafts of brilliance shot into the gloom through openings in the leafy roof, one right in front of Orley. Even indirectly, the light hurt his eyes. He saw fronds just above the waterline, which had recently survived ashfall from a volcano, curl from the heat, turn brown, and fall away.

So much for the rest of my supplies.

So much for coming up for air.

He wrapped his legs around the thick root and shrugged out of his backpack, rummaging through the satchel for something to improvise. In the sharp shadows he negotiated the contents mostly by touch. The inertial tracker Gillian had given him, a pouch of food bars, two canteens of 'fresh' water, explosive slivers for his needler, a tool kit.

The air meter was turning an ominous orange. Tom wedged the pack between his knees and tore open the tool kit. He seized a small roll of eight-gauge rubber tubing. Purple blobs flickered on the edge of his field of vision as he used his sheath knife to cut a length of narrow hose.

He crammed one end through the mask's chow-lock. The seal held, but the contents of the tube sprayed at his mouth, making him gag and cough.

There was no time for finesse. He shimmied up the root to a point within reach of the hole in the weeds. Tom pinched the tube below the other end, but bitter, oily water streamed from the tube as he straightened the coil. The mask's demon-lock would purge the fluid, *if* too much didn't flood in. He averted his face, but swallowed a little anyway. It tasted foul.

Tom reached out and pushed the tube above the surface of the narrow pool, where the battle flashes sent shafts of light into the depths. He sucked hard at the hose, spitting out slime and a sharp metallic tang, desperately trying to clear it.

One of the searing blasts flashed closer than ever, scalding his fingers below the waterline. He fought the instinct to shout or pull away from the pain. Consciousness began to slip, and with it the will to hold his left hand into the searing heat.

He drew hard and at last was rewarded with a thin stream of dank air. Tom sucked frantically. The hot, steamy air tasted of smoke, but it nourished. He exhaled into the mask, trusting it to hold the hard-won oxygen.

The aching in his lungs subsided and the agony of his hand took the fore. Just as he thought he couldn't hold it out there any more, the burning heat from above subsided, fading to a dull flickering glow in the sky.

A few meters away was another gap in the weeds, where he might be able to prop the tube between two thick roots without exposing himself. Tom took a few more breaths, then pinched the tube shut. But before he could prepare any further, a sharp blue light suddenly filled the water, brighter than ever, casting stark, blinding shadows everywhere. There was a tremendous detonation, then the sea began tossing him about like a rag doll.

Something huge had struck the ocean and set it bucking. His anchor root came free of its mooring, and he fell into a maelstrom of flailing vines.

The swell tore the backpack from him. He grabbed after it and caught the end of one strap, but something struck him in the back of the head, knocking him dizzy. The pack was snatched away into the noise and flashing shadows.

Tom curled into a ball, his forearms holding the rim of his mask against the whipping vines.

There had been another maelstrom – of sand and grinding, blazing wind. The air of Venus, far thicker than water, had torn at his frail suit and helmet, its fierce grip on his chest making each breath precious. Before very long he had ceased walking, stumbling, crawling through the drifts, finally, crouching in the lee of a jagged basalt tooth, he had waited to die. An hour, or eon, of delirium passed before, unexpected, the vision came to him.

So they were right ... he had pondered blearily, looking up as a blaze of true light pierced the inky Venusian heat-haze, stabbing his unaccustomed eyes, making them flow with tears. *The ancients were right, after all. When death arrives, it's an angel that comes for you.* ...

The angel had bent closer. Behind a diamond-fringed facemask, fair hair had framed a face he dimly knew he should recognize. A *familiar* face, as if he had known it half his life ...

Lips moving. *'So you're the Orley boy.'* The amplified voice had been soothing, though more efficient-sounding than angelic. *'Not much to look at, compared to your picture. But I'll reserve judgment till we get you cleaned up.'*

'Uh-h-h-' he had croaked, while hands drew him onto a stretcher, her face never leaving his sight. Tom felt life might slip away if it had. Working to pump remedies into his veins, she had kept on murmuring, *'There now, it'll be all right ... Say, don't you recognize me? We've never been introduced, but they've been nagging us to meet and get married.'*

That first time, under the hellish sky of Venus, he had never once lost consciousness because of her. Now though, all he had was memory to cling to. Awareness bled away like bitter, irretrievable air.

His first thought, on coming around, was a vague surprise that he was still breathing. Tom thought the battle-storm was still going on, until he realized that the shaking he felt was his own body. The roar in his ears was only a roar in his ears.

His throbbing left arm was draped over a thick horizontal stump. Scummy green water came up to his chin, lapping against the finned facemask. His lungs ached and the air was stale.

He brought up his trembling right hand, and pulled the mask down to hang around his neck. The filters had kept out the ozone stench, but he inhaled deeply, gratefully. At the last moment he must have chosen immolation over suffocation and struck out for the surface. Fortunately, the battle ended just before he arrived.

Tom resisted the temptation to rub his itching eyes; the slime on his hands would do them no good. Tears welled at a biofeedback command, flushing most of the binding mucus away. He looked up when he could see again.

To the north the volcano fumed on as ever. The cloud cover had parted somewhat, revealing numerous twisted banners of multi-colored smoke. All around Tom, small crawling things were climbing out from the singed weeds, resuming their normal business of eating or being eaten. There were no longer battleships in the sky, blazing away at each other with beams of nova heat.

For the first time, Tom was glad of the monotonous topography of the carpet of vines. He hardly had to rise in the water to see several columns of smoke pouring from slowly settling wrecks. As he watched, one faraway metal derelict exploded. The sound arrived seconds later in a series of muted coughs and pops, punctuated unsynchronously by bright flashes. The dim shape sank lower. Tom averted his eyes from the final detonation. When he looked back he could detect nothing but clouds of steam and a faint hissing that fell away into silence.

Elsewhere lay other floating fragments. Tom turned a slow circle, somewhat in awe of the destruction. There was more than enough wreckage for a mid-sized skirmish.

He laughed at the irony, although it made his abused lungs hurt. The Galactics had all come to investigate a counterfeit mayday signal, and they had brought their death feuds along to what should have been a mission of mercy. Now they were dead while he still lived. This didn't feel like the random capriciousness of Ifni. It was too like the mysterious, wry work of God himself.

Does this mean I'm all alone again? he wondered. *That would be rich. So much fireworks, and one humble human the only survivor?*

Not for long, perhaps. The battle had caused him to lose almost all of the supplies he had struggled so hard to recover. Tom frowned, suddenly. The message bombs! He clutched at his waist, and the world seemed to drop away. Only one of the globes remained! The others must have popped out in the struggle below the clinging vines.

When his right hand stopped shaking, he carefully reached under his waistband and drew out the psi-bomb, his very last link with *Streaker* ... with Gillian.

It was the verifier ... the one that he was to set off if he thought the Trojan Seahorse should fly. Now he would have to decide whether to set off this one, or none at all. Yes or No were all he could say.

I only wish I knew whose ships those were that fired on the Tandu.

Tucking the bomb away, he resumed his slow turn. One wreck on the northwest horizon looked like a partially crushed eggshell. Smoke still rose from it, but the burning seemed to have stopped. There were no explosions, and it seemed not to be sinking any lower.

All right, Tom thought. *That will do as a goal. Looks intact enough to have possibilities. It may have salvageable gear and food. Certainly it's shelter, if it's not too radioactive.*

It seemed only five kilometers away or so, though looks could be deceiving. A destination would give him something to do, at least. He needed more information. The wreck might tell what he needed to know.

Tom pondered whether to try to go 'by land,' trusting his weary legs to negotiate the weedscape, or to attempt the journey underwater, swimming from airhole to airhole, daring the unknown creatures of the deep.

He suddenly heard a warbling whine behind him, turned, and saw a small spacecraft, about a kilometer away, heading slowly northward, wavering bare meters above the ocean. Its shimmering shields flickered. Its drives heaved and faltered.

Tom pulled up his mask and prepared to dive, but the tiny ship wasn't coming his way. It was passing to the west, sparks shooting from its stubby stasis flanges. Ugly black streaks stained its hull, and one patch had blistered and boiled away.

Tom caught his breath as it passed. He had never seen a model like this before. But he could think of several races whose style would be compatible with the design.

The scout dipped as its dying drives coughed. The high whine of the gravity generator began to fall.

The boat's crew obviously knew it was done for. It banked to change course for the island. Tom held his breath, unable to help sympathizing with the desperate alien pilot. The boat sputtered along just above the weeds, then passed out of sight behind the mountain's shoulder.

The faint 'crump' of its landing carried over the whistling of the tradewinds.

Tom waited. After a few seconds the boat's stasis field released with a loud concussion. Glowing debris flew out over the sea. The fragments quenched in water or burned slowly into the weeds.

He doubted anyone could have gotten away in time.

Tom changed goals. His long-range destination was still the eggshell ship floating a few miles away. But first he wanted to sift through the wreckage of that scout boat. Maybe there would be evidence there to make his decision easier. Maybe there would be food.

He tried to crawl up onto the weeds, but found it too difficult. He was still shaking.

All right, then. We'll go under the sea. It's probably all moot anyway. I might as well enjoy the scenery.

52

AKKI

The son of a blood-gorged lamprey just wouldn't let go!

Akki was exhausted. The metallic tang of the water mixed with the taste of bile from his fore-stomach as he swam hard to the southeast. He wanted desperately to rest, but he knew he couldn't afford to let his pursuer cut away at his lead.

Now and then he caught sight of K'tha-Jon, about two kilometers behind him and closing the gap. The giant, darkly countershaded dolphin seemed tireless. His breath condensed in high vertical spouts, like small rockets of fog, as he plowed ahead through the water.

Akki's breath was ragged, and he felt weak with hunger. He cursed in Anglic and found it unsatisfying. Playing over a resonating, obscene phrase in Primal Delphin helped a little.

He should have been able to outdistance K'tha-Jon, at least over a short stretch. But something in the water was affecting the hydrodynamic properties of his skin. Some substance was causing an allergic reaction. His normally smooth and pliant hide was scratchy and bumpy. He felt like he was plowing through syrup instead of water. Akki wondered why no one else had reported this. Did it only affect dolphins from Calafia?

It was one more unfairness in a series that stretched back to the moment he had left the ship.

Escaping K'tha-Jon hadn't been as easy as he expected. Heading southeast, he should have been able to veer right or left to reach help, either Hikahi and the crew at the Thennanin wreck, or at Toshio's island. But every time he tried to change course, K'tha-Jon moved to cut the corner. Akki couldn't afford to lose any more of his lead.

A wave of focused sonar swept over him from behind. He wanted to curl up into a ball every time it happened. It wasn't natural for a dolphin to flee another for so long. In the deep past a youngster who angered an older male – by trying to copulate with a female in the old bull's harem, for instance – might get thumped or raked. But only rarely was a grudge held. Akki had to stifle an urge to stop and try to reason with K'tha-Jon.

What good would that do? The giant was obviously mad.

His speed advantage was lost to this mysterious skin itch. Diving to get around K'tha-Jon was also out of the question. The *Stenos bredanensis* were pelagic dolphins. K'tha-Jon could probably outdive anyone in the *Streaker*'s crew.

When next he glanced back, K'tha-Jon had closed to within about a kilometer. Akki warbled a sigh and redoubled his efforts.

A line of green-topped mounds lay near the horizon, perhaps four or five kilometers away. He had to hold on long enough to reach them!

53

MOKI

Moki drove the sled at top speed to the south, blasting its sonar ahead like a bugle.

'*... calling Haoke, calling Moki. This is Heurkah-pete. Come in. Verify p-please!*'

Moki tossed his head in irritation. The ship was trying to reach him again. Moki clicked the sled's transmitter on and tried to talk clearly.

'Yesss! What-t-t you want-t!'

There was a pause, then, '*Moki, let me talk to Haoke.*'

Moki barely concealed a laugh. 'Haoke ... dead! K-k-killed by intruder! I'm ch-chasing now. T-t-tell Takkata-Jim I'll get-t 'em!'

Moki's Anglic was almost indecipherable, yet he didn't dare use Trinary. He might slip into Primal in public, and he wasn't ready for that yet.

There was a long silence on the sonar-speak line. Moki hoped that now they'd leave him alone.

When he and Haoke had found the Baskin woman's empty sled, drifting slowly westward at low power, something had finally snapped within him. He had then entered a confused but exalted state, a blur of action, like a violent dream.

Perhaps they were ambushed, or perhaps he merely imagined it. But when it was over Haoke was dead and he, Moki, had no regrets.

After that his sonar had picked up an object heading south. Another sled. Without another thought he had given chase.

The sonar-speak crackled. '*Heurkah again, Moki. You're getting out of saser range, and we still can't use radiosss. You are now given two ordersss. First – relay a sonar-speak message to K'tha-Jon, ordering him back-k! His mission is cancelled!*

'*Number two – after that, turn around yoursself! That'sss a direct order!*'

The lights and dots meant little to Moki anymore. What mattered were the patterns of sound that the sled's sensors sent him. The expanded hearing sense gave him a god-like feeling, as if he were one of the Great Dreamers himself. He imagined himself a huge *catodon*, a sperm whale, lord of the deep, hunting prey that fled at any hint of his approach.

Not far to the south was the muffled sound of a sled, the one he had been chasing for some time. He could tell that he was catching up to it.

Much farther away, and to the left, were two tiny rhythmic signals, sounds of rapid cetacean swimming. That had to be K'tha-Jon and the upstart Calafian. Moki would dearly love to steal K'tha-Jon's prey from him, but that could wait. The first enemy lay dead ahead.

'Moki, did you copy me? Answer! You have your ordersss! You must ...'

Moki clapped his jaws in disgust. He shut off the sonar-speak in the middle of Heurkah-pete's complaint. It was getting hard to understand the stuck-up little petty officer anyway. He had never been much of a *Stenos*, always studying Keneenk with the *Tursiops*, and trying to 'better himself.'

Moki decided he would look the fellow up after he had finished taking care of his enemies *outside* the ship.

54

KEEPIRU

Keepiru knew he was being followed. He had expected that someone might be sent after him to keep him from reaching Hikahi.

But his pursuer was some sort of idiot. He could tell from the distant whine of the engines that the fin's sled was being driven well beyond its rated speed. What did the fellow hope to accomplish? Keepiru had a long enough head start to make it within sonar-speak range of the Thennanin wreck before his pursuer caught up. He only had to push his sled's throttle slightly into the red.

The fin behind him was spraying sonar noise all over the place, as if he wanted to announce to all and sundry that he was coming. With all his screeching, the imbecile was making it hard for Keepiru to piece together what was going on to the southeast. Keepiru concentrated and tried to block out the noise from behind.

Two dolphins, it seemed, one almost out of breath, the other powerful and still vigorous, were swimming furiously toward a bank of sonar shadows fifty kilometers away.

What was going on? Who was chasing whom?

He was listening so narrowly that Keepiru suddenly was yanked back to the present and had to veer to avoid colliding with a high seamount. He passed on the west side, banking hard to sweep past by meters. The mountain's bulk momentarily cast him into silence.

* 'Ware shoals
Child of Tursiops! *

He trilled a lesson-rhyme, then switched to Trinary Haiku.

* Echoes of the shore
Are like drifting feathers
Dropped by pelicans! *

Keepiru chided himself. Dolphins were supposed to be hot pilots – it was what had won them their first starship berths over a century before – and he was known far and wide as one of the best. So why were forty knots underwater harder to handle than fifty times lightspeed down a worm-hole?

His thrumming sled left the shadow of the seamount and came into open water. East of southeast came a faint image-gestalt of racing cetaceans, once again.

Keepiru concentrated. Yes, the one in pursuit was a *Stenos*, a big one. It used a strange pattern of search sonar.

The one in front ...

... *It has to be Akki*, he thought. *The kid is in trouble. Bad trouble.*

He was almost deafened as a blast of sound from the sled behind him caught him directly in a focused beam. Keepiru chattered a curse-glyph and shook his head to clear it, tempted to turn around to take care of the self-sucking turd swallower behind him.

Keepiru was tormented by a choice. Strictly speaking, his duty was to get a message to Hikahi. Yet it went against everything inside him to abandon the middie. It sounded like the youngster was exhausted. His pursuer was clearly catching up.

But if he swung to the east he would give his *own* pursuer a chance to catch up ...

But he might also distract K'tha-Jon, force him to turn around.

It didn't become a Terragens officer. It didn't reflect Keneenk. But he couldn't decide logically.

He wished some distant, great-great-grandchild of his were here now, a fully mature and logical dolphin who could tell his crude, half-animal ancestor what to do.

Keepiru sighed. *What makes me think they'll let me have great-grandchildren, anyway?*

Finally, he chose to be true to himself. He banked the sled to the left and pulled the engine throttle one more notch into the red.

55

CHARLES DART

One of the two Earthlings in the room – the human – rummaged through dresser drawers and distractedly tossed things into an open valise on the bed. He listened while the chimpanzee talked.

' ... the probe is down below two kilometers. The radio-activity's rising fast, and the temperature gradient, too. I'm not sure the probe will last more'n another few hundred meters, yet the shaft keeps going!

'Anyway, I'm now *positive* that there's been garbage dumping by a technological race, and recently! Like *hundreds* of years ago!'

'That's very interesting, Doctor Dart. Really, it is.' Ignacio Metz tried not to show his exasperation. One had to be patient with chimps, especially Charles Dart. Still, it was hard to pack while the chimp ran on and on, perched on a chair in his stateroom.

Dart went on obliviously. 'If anything made me appreciate Toshio, as inefficient as that boy is, it's having to work with that lousy dolphin linguist Sah'ot! Still, I was gettin good data until Tom Orley's damned bomb went off and Sah'ot started hollering stuff about "voices" from below! Crazy bloody fin ... ' .

Metz sorted his belongings. *Now where is my blue land-suit? Oh yes, it's already packed. Let's see. Duplicates of all my notes are already loaded aboard the boat. What else is there?*

' ... I said, Doctor Metz!'

'Hmmm?' He looked up quickly. 'I'm sorry, Doctor Dart. It's all these sudden changes and all. I'm sure you understand. What were you saying?'

Dart groaned in exasperation. 'I said I want to go *with* you! To you this trip may be a form of exile, but to me it'd be an escape! I've *got* to get out to where my work is!' He pounded the wall and showed two rows of large, yellowed teeth.

Metz thought for a moment, shaking his head. Exile? Perhaps Takkata-Jim looked at it that way. Certainly he and Gillian were like oil and water. She was determined to set in motion Orley's and Creideiki's Trojan Seahorse plan. Takkata-Jim was just as adamant resisting it.

Metz agreed with Takkata-Jim, and had been surprised when the lieutenant meekly resigned his acting-captaincy at the ship's council meeting, appointing Gillian in command until Hikahi could be recalled. That meant the Seahorse scheme would go forward after all. *Streaker* was to begin her underwater move in a few hours.

If the ruse was really to be tried, Metz was just as happy to be gone from the ship. The longboat was spacious, and comfortable enough. In it, he and his notes would be safe. The records of his special experiments would get to Earth eventually, even when ... if *Streaker* was destroyed trying to escape.

Besides, now he could join Dennie Sudman in examining the Kiqui. Metz was more than a little eager to get a look at the pre-sentients.

'You'll have to talk to Gillian about coming with us, Charlie,' he shook his head. 'She's letting us take your new robot with us to the island. You may have to settle for that.'

'But you and Takkata-Jim promised that if I cooperated, if I kept quiet to Toshio earlier, and was willing to give you my proxy on the council ...'

The chimp lapsed when he saw the expression on Metz's face. Charlie's lips pressed close together and he got up to his feet.

'Thanks for nuthin'!' he growled as he went for the door.

'Now, Charlie ...'

Dart marched out into the hall. The shutting door cut off Metz's last words.

The chimp walked along the sloping corridor, head bowed in determination.

'I gotta get out there!' He grumbled. 'There's *gotta* be a way!'

56

SAH'OT

When Gillian called to ask that he talk to Creideiki, his first thought had been to rebel over the workload.

'I know, I know,' her tiny simulacrum had agreed, 'but you're the only one I can spare who has the qualifications. Let's rephrase that. You *are* the only one for the job. Creideiki is clearly aware and alert, but he can't talk! We need someone to help him communicate through parts of his brain that weren't damaged. You're our expert.'

Sah'ot had never really liked Creideiki, And the type of injury the captain had suffered made Sah'ot feel queasy. Still, the challenge appealed to his vanity.

'What about Charlesss Dart? He's been driving Toshio and me until our flukes droop, and he has top priority on this line.'

In the small holo image Gillian looked very tired. 'Not any more he doesn't. We're sending out a new probe with Takkata-Jim and Metz, one he'll be able to control himself by commlink. Until then, his project takes last place. *Last* place. Is that understood?'

Sah'ot clapped his jaw loudly in assent. It felt good to hear decisive leadership again. The fact that the voice was that of a human he respected helped, too.

'This bit-t about Metz and Takkata-Jim . . .'

'I've filled in Toshio,' Gillian said. 'He'll brief you when the chance comes. He is in absolute charge now. You're to obey him with alacrity. Is that clear?'

Gillian never lost her vocabulary under pressure. Sah'ot liked that. 'Yesss. Eminently. Now, about these resonances I'm getting from the planet's crust. What shall I do? They are, to my knowledge, totally unprecedented! Can you ssspare someone to do a *Library* search for me?'

Gillian frowned. 'You say resonances of apparent intelligent origin are coming from deep in Kithrup's crust?'

'Exactly.'

Gillian rolled her eyes. 'Ifni! To explore this world in *peace and quiet* would demand a decade of work by a dozen survey ships!' She shook her head. 'No. My quick guess is that some formation of probability-sensitive rock below the surface is resonating with emanations from the battle overhead. In any event, it comes after the other priorities: security, the Kiqui, and talking to Creideiki. You've got a mouthful to deal with already.'

Sah'ot stifled a protest. Complaining would only get Gillian to order him explicitly away from the probe. She hadn't yet, so it would be best to stay quiet.

'Now think about your options,' Gillian reminded him. 'If *Streaker* makes a break for it, we'll try to get the skiff out to pick up Tom and whoever wants to join us from the island. You can choose to come along, or stay with Metz and Takkata-Jim and wait it out in the longboat. Inform Toshio of your decision.'

'I undersstand. I'll think about it.' Somehow the issue seemed less urgent than it would have a few days ago. The sounds from below were having an effect on him.

'If I stay, I still wish you all the best of luck,' he added.

'You too, mel-fin.' Gillian smiled. 'You're a strange duck, but if I

get home, I'm going to recommend you get lots of grandchildren.'
Her image vanished as she broke the connection.

Sah'ot stared at the blank screen. The compliment, wholly unexpected, left him momentarily stunned. Then a few Kiqui who were foraging nearby were surprised to see a large dolphin rise up onto his tail and dance about the small pool.

> * To be noticed by –
> A humpback
> * To be credited
> At last
> For being me *

57

DENNIE AND TOSHIO

'I'm afraid.'

Almost without a thought, Toshio put his arm around Dennie's shoulder. He gave her a reassuring squeeze. 'What for? There's nothing to be scared of.'

Dennie looked up from the pounding breakers to see if he was serious. Then she realized she was being teased. She stuck out her tongue at him.

Toshio inhaled deeply and was content. It wasn't clear to him where his new relationship with Dennie was going. It wasn't physical, for one thing. They had slept together last night, but fully clothed. Toshio had thought it would be frustrating, and it was, sort of. But not as much as he had expected.

It would work out, one way or another. Right now Dennie needed someone to be nearby. It was satisfying just filling that need. Maybe, when all this was over, she would go back to thinking of him as a boy, four years her junior. Somehow he doubted it. She was touching him more now, rather than less, holding his arm and punching him in mock anger, even as memories from the psi-bomb episode faded.

'When are they supposed to get here with the longboat?' She looked back over the ocean once more.

'Late tomorrow, sometime,' he answered.

'Takkata-Jim and Metz wanted to negotiate with the ETs. What's to stop them if they decide to ignore orders and try anyway?'

'Gillian's giving them only enough power to get here. They have a regenerator, so they'll be able to charge up for space-travel in a month or so. By then *Streaker*'d be gone, one way or another.'

Dennie shivered. Toshio cursed his awkward tongue. 'Takkata-Jim won't have a radio. I'm to guard ours until the skiff comes to pick us up. Besides, what could he offer the Galactics? He won't have any of the charts marking the derelict fleet.

'My guess is he and Metz will wait until everybody leaves, then scuttle off to Earth with Metz's tapes and a hold full of gripes.'

Dennie looked up at the first stars of the long Kithrup twilight. 'Are you going back?' she asked.

'*Streaker*'s my ship. Thank God, Creideiki is still alive. But even if he's not skipper any more, I owe it to him to keep on, as one of his officers should.'

Dennie glanced up at him briefly, then nodded and looked back out at the sea.

She's thinking we haven't a chance, Toshio realized. *And maybe we don't. Wearing a Thennanin battlewagon as a disguise, we'll have all the maneuverability of a Calafian mud-gleaner. And even fooling the Galactics might not be so good an idea. They want to capture Streaker, but they won't hold back their fire if they see a defeated enemy climbing back up·for another round. There still have to be Thennanin around, if the scheme is to work.*

But we can't just sit here waiting, can we? If we do, the Galactics will learn that they can push Earthlings around. We just can't afford to let anyone profit from chasing one of our survey ships.

Toshio changed the subject. 'How's your report coming?'

'Oh, all right, I guess. It's clear the Kiqui are fully pre-sentient. They've been fallow a very long time. In fact, some Darwinist heretics might think they were just getting ripe to bootstrap themselves. They show signs.'

Some iconoclast humans still pushed the idea that a pre-sentient race could make the leap to spacefaring intelligence by evolution alone, without the intervention of a patron. Most Galactics thought the idea absurd and strange, but the failure to find humanity's missing benefactor had regained the theory a few adherents.

'What about the metal-mound?' Toshio asked about Dennie's other research, begun at Charlie Dart's behest when the chimp had been given top priority, but pursued now out of interest.

Dennie shrugged. 'Oh, the mound's alive. The professional biologist in me would give her left arm to be able to stay a year on this island, with full laboratory equipment. The metal-eating pseudo-coral, the drill-tree, the living core of the island, are all symbiots. In effect, they're organs in one giant entity! If I could only write it up at home I'd be famous ... if anyone believed me.'

'They'll believe you,' Toshio assured her. 'And you'll be famous.'

He motioned that they should start heading back to camp. They only had a little time after second supper to walk and talk. Now that he was in command, he had to make sure that timetables were kept.

Dennie held his arm as they turned to return to the encampment. Over the rushing rustle of the wind through the foliage came the intermittent squeaks of the natives, rousing from their siesta to prepare for the evening hunt.

They walked in silence along the narrow trail.

58

GALACTICS

Krat licked slowly at her mating claw, studiously ignoring the creatures who scurried to clean up the bloody mess in the corner.

There would be trouble over this. The Pilan High Council would protest.

Of course she was within her rights, as grand admiral, to deal with any member of the fleet as she saw fit. But that did not traditionally cover the skewering of a senior Librarian simply because he was the bearer of bad news.

I am getting old, *she realized.* And the daughter I had hoped would soon be strong enough to pull me down is now dead. Who now will do me the honors, before I grow erratic and become a hazard to the clan?

The small, furry body was hauled away, and a sturdy Paha mopped up the bloody mess. The other Pila looked at her.

Let them stare. When we capture the Earthlings it won't matter. I shall be famous, and this incident will be ignored by all, especially the Pila.

If we are the first ones to approach the Progenitors with an offering, the Law won't matter any more. The Pila will not simply be our adult liege-clients. They will be *ours* again, to meddle with, to redesign, to shape once more.

'Back to work! All!' She snapped her mating claw. The twang sent the bridge crew scuttling off to their stations, some to repair the smoking damage from a near miss in the most recent battle with the Tandu.

Think now, Soro mother. Can you spare ships to send once more to the planet? To that hellish volcano where every fleet has already sent a party to fight and die?

There weren't supposed to be any Gubru left here! But a battered Gubru scout had shown up at the place where the distress call came from. It had gone to smoky ruin along with a Tandu destroyer, Pritil's ship number sixteen, and two other vessels even her battle computers could not identify. Perhaps one was a surviving spearship of the Brothers of the Night which had hidden on one of Kithrup's moons.

Meanwhile, out here, the 'final' battle with the Tandu's unholy alliance had turned into a bloody draw. The Soro still had a slim advantage, so the remaining Thennanin stayed by their Tandu allies.

Should she risk all in the next encounter? For the Tandu to win would be horrible. They would, if they gained the Power, destroy so many beautiful species that the Soro might some day own.

If it came down to a choice, she guessed the Thennanin would switch sides one more time.

'Strategy section!' she snapped.

'Fleet-Mother?' A Paha warrior approached, but stopped just out of arm-reach. It eyed her cautiously.

Given a chance, she would breed respect into the Paha genes so deeply nothing would ever eradicate it.

The Paha stepped back involuntarily as her claw stretched. 'Find out which ships are now most expendable. Organize them into a small squadron. We're going to investigate the planet again.'

The Paha saluted and returned to its station quickly. Krat settled deeper into the vletoor cushion.

We shall need a distraction, *she thought.* Perhaps another expedition to that volcano would make the Thennanin nervous and let the Tandu think we know something.

Of course, *she reminded herself,* the Tandu themselves may know what we do not.

59

CREIDEIKI

Far Away
> *They Call*

>> *The Giants,*
>>> *The Spirits of OCEAN,*
>>>> *The Leviathans*

Creideiki begins to understand – does, does, begin –
The old gods are part figment, part racial memory, part ghost ...
and part something else ... something an engineer could never have
allowed his ears to hear, or eyes to see ...

Far Away

They Call
Leviathans ...

Not yet. Not yet, not. Creideiki has a duty to perform yet, does
have a duty.
No more, no more an engineer – but Creideiki remains a spacer.
Not useless, Creideiki will do what he can, can do, can do to help.
Can do to help save his crew, his ship ...

60

GILLIAN

She wanted to rub her eyes, but the facemask was in the way. Too
much remained to be done.

The fins came and went, swooping by her wherever she traveled
in the ship, almost toppling her in their hurry to report and then be
off again, carrying out orders.

I hope Hikahi gets back soon. I'm not doing badly, I guess, but I'm
no starship officer. She has the training to rule a crew.

Hikahi doesn't even know she's captain, Gillian thought. *Much as*
I pray they get the line open soon, I'll hate having to break that news
to her.

She wrote a brief message to Emerson D'Anite, and the last
courier dashed off for the engine room. Wattaceti kept pace alongside her as she turned to swim into the outlook.

There were two small crowds of dolphins in the bay, one at the
forward sally hatch and the other clustered about the longboat.

The bow of the small spaceship almost touched the iris of one of
the outer hatches. Its stern disappeared into a metal sheath beyond
the rear end of the outlook.

When the longboat is gone this place'll look pretty empty, she
thought.

A fin in the party at the lock saw her and sped toward Gillian. He halted abruptly before her and hovered in the water at attention.

'Flankers and scoutsss are ready to depart when you give the word, Gillian.'

'Thank you, Zaa'pht. It will be soon. Is there still no word from the line-repair party, or from Keepiru?'

'No, ssssir. The courier you sent to follow Keepiru should be near the wreck shortly, though.'

It was frustrating. Takkata-Jim had severed the link to the Thennanin wreck, and now it seemed impossible to find the break. For once she cursed the fact that monofilaments could be hidden so well.

For all they knew, some terrible disaster might have struck the work party, at the very site where she was planning on moving *Streaker*. At least the detectors indicated the space battle was still going on, almost as fierce as ever.

But what was keeping Tom? He was supposed to set off a message bomb when ETs showed up to investigate his ruse. But since the faked distress call there had been nothing.

In addition to everything else, the damned Niss machine wanted to talk to her. It had not set off the hidden alarm in her office to indicate that it was an emergency, but every time she used a comm unit she heard a faint click that signaled the thing's desire to talk.

It was enough to make a fem just want to climb into bed and stay there.

A sudden commotion broke out near the lock. The wall speaker let out a brief, sloppy squeal of Trinary, followed by a longer report in loose, high-pitched Anglic.

'Sssir!' Zaa'pht turned excitedly. 'They report ....'

'I heard.' She nodded. 'The line's been repaired. Congratulate the repair team for me, and get them inside for a couple of hours' rest. Then please ask Heurkah-pete to contact Hikahi right away. He's to ascertain her situation and tell her we begin moving the ship at 2100 hours unless she objects. I'll be calling her shortly.'

'Aye, sssir!' Zaa'pht whirled and sped off.

Wattaceti watched her silently, waiting.

'All right,' she said. 'Let's see Takkata-Jim and Metz off. You've made certain the crew has offloaded anything not on our checklist, and inspected everything the exiles took aboard?'

'Yesss. They haven't even got a flaregun. No radio and no more fuel than the minimum needed to reach the island.'

Gillian had gone on her own inspection of the boat a few hours back, while Metz and Takkata-Jim were still packing. She had taken a few additional precautions that nobody else knew about.

'Who's going with them?'

'Three volunteers, all of them "strange" *Stenos*. All males. We searched them down to their penile sheathsss. They're clean. All in the longboat now, ready to go.'

Gillian nodded. 'Then, for better or worse, let's get them out of here so we can get on with other things.'

Mentally she had already begun rehearsing what she had to tell Hikahi.

61

HIKAHI & SUESSI

'Remember,' she told Tsh't and Suessi, 'maintain radio silence at all cossst. And try to keep those crazy fen in the wreck from eating up all the supplies in the first few days, hmmm?'

Tsh't signaled assent with a jaw clap, although her eyes were heavy with reservation. Suessi said, 'Are you sure you won't let one of us come with you?'

'I'm sure. If I encounter disaster I want no more lives lost. If I find survivors, I might need every bit of room. In any event, the skiff runs itself, essentially. All I have to do is watch it.'

'You can't fight while piloting,' Hannes pointed out.

'If I had a gunner along I might be *tempted* to fight. This way I have to run away. If *Streaker* is dead or captured, I must be able to return the skiff to you here, or you'll all be doomed.'

Suessi frowned, but found he had to agree with her reasoning. He was thankful Hikahi had stayed as long as she had, letting them use the skiff's power to finish preparing a habitat inside the wreck.

We're all worried about Streaker *and the captain*, he thought. *But Hikahi must be in agony.*

'All right, then. Good-bye and good luck, Hikahi. May Ifni's boss watch over you.'

'The sssame to both of you,' Hikahi took Suessi's hand gently between her jaws, then did the same with Tsh't's left pectoral fin.

Tsh't and Suessi left through the skiff's small airlock. They backed their sled toward the yawning opening in the sunken alien battle-ship.

A low whine spread from the skiff as power came on. The sound echoed back to them from the mammoth sea-cliff that towered over the crash site.

The tiny space vessel began to move slowly eastward, picking up speed underwater. Hikahi had chosen a roundabout route, taking her far out before swinging back in an arc to *Streaker*'s hiding place. This would keep her out of touch for as long as a couple of days, but it would also mean that her point of origin could not be traced, if an enemy lay in wait where *Streaker* had been.

They watched until the boat disappeared into the gloom. Long after Suessi ceased hearing anything, Tsh't waved her jaw slowly back and forth, following the diminishing sound.

Two hours later, as Hannes was lying down for his first nap in his new dry-quarters, the makeshift intercom by his pallet squawked.

Not more *bad news*. He sighed.

Lying in the darkness with one arm over his eyes, he touched the comm. 'What?' he said simply.

It was Lucky Kaa, the young electronics tech and junior pilot. His voice fizzed with excitement. 'Sir! Tsh't says you should come quickly! It'sss the ship!'

Suessi rolled over onto one elbow.

'*Streaker*?'

'Yesss! The line just re-opened! They want to talk to Hikahi right away!'

All of the strength went out of Suessi's arms. He slumped back and groaned. *Oh, frabjous day! By now she's well out of sonar-speak range!*

At times like these I wish I talked dolphin jabber like Tom Orley. Maybe Trinary could express something properly ironic and vulgar about the way the universe works.

62

EXILES

The longboat slid smoothly through the port and out into the twilight blue of Kithrup's ocean.

'You're going the wrong way,' Ignacio Metz said, after the iris closed behind them. Instead of turning east, the boat spiraled upward.

'Just a small detour, Doctor Metz,' Takkata-Jim soothed. 'Sneekah-jo, tell *Streaker* I'm adjusting the trim.'

The dolphin on the co-pilot's ramp began whistling to his counterpart on the ship. The sonar-speak squawked back angrily. *Streaker*, also, had noticed the change in course.

Metz's seat was above and behind Takkata-Jim's. The water level came up to his waist. 'What are you *doing?*' he asked.

'Jusst getting used to the controls . . .'

'Well, watch out! You're headed straight for the detection buoys!'

Metz watched, amazed, as the craft sped toward the crew of dolphins dismantling the listening devices. The workfen scattered out of the way, cursing shrilly as the boat crashed into the tethered buoys. Metal smithereens clattered along its prow and fell into blackness.

The sonar-speak squawked. Dr Metz blushed. Good fin-persons shouldn't use language like that. Takkata-Jim seemed oblivious. He calmly turned the small ship around and piloted it at a sedate pace eastward, toward their island destination. The longboat drove down a narrow canyon, leaving the brightly lit subsea vale and *Streaker* behind it.

'Tell them it was an accident-t,' Takkata-Jim told his co-pilot. 'The trim was out of line, but now we've got it under control. We're proceeding underwater to the island, as ordered.'

'*Accident, my hairy uncle Fred's scrotum!*'

The words were followed by a sniggering laugh from the back of the control room. 'You know, I kinda *figured* you wouldn't leave without destroying the incriminating evidence first, Takkata-Jim.'

Dr Metz struggled with his straps to turn around. He stared. 'Charles Dart! What are you doing here?'

Perched on a shelf in a storage locker – whose door was now open – a spacesuited chimpanzee grinned back at him. 'Why, exercisin' a teeny tiny bit of *initiative, Doctor* Metz! Now you be sure and note that in your records. I wanna be given credit for it.' He broke into a shrieking giggle, amplified by his suit speaker.

Takkata-Jim twisted about on his ramp to regard the chimp for a moment. He snorted and turned back to his piloting.

Charlie visibly screwed up his nerve to slide out of the cabinet into the water, even though none of it could touch him through the spacesuit. He floundered in the liquid up to his helmet-ring.

'But how . . . ?' Metz started to ask.

Charlie hefted a large, heavy waterproof sack from the locker to a man-seat next to Metz. 'I used deductive reasoning,' he said as he climbed up. 'I figured Gillian's boys'd only be watching out for misbehavin' by a few grumbling *Stenos*. So, thought I, why not get to the longboat by a route they wouldn't even *think* of watching?'

Metz's eyes widened. 'The sleeve! You crawled into one of the sealed maintenance ways that the builders used on Earth, and made your way to the boat's access panels, down by the thrust motors ...'

'Righto!' Charlie beamed as he buckled his seatbelt.

'You probably had to remove some plates in the sleeve wall, using a jack-pry. No dolphin could manage such a thing in an enclosed space, so they didn't think of it.'

'No, they didn't.'

Metz looked Charlie up and down. 'You passed pretty close to the thrusters. Did you get cooked?'

'Hmmm. My suit rad-meter says raw to medium rare.' Charlie mocked blowing on his fingertips.

Metz grinned. 'I shall, indeed, take note of this rare display of ingenuity, Doctor Dart! And welcome aboard. I'll be too busy anyway, inspecting the Kiqui, to take proper care of that robot of yours. Now you can do it right.'

Dart nodded eagerly. 'That's why I'm here.'

'Excellent. Perhaps we can have a few games of chess, as well.'

'I'd like that.'

They sat back and watched as the ocean ridges passed by. Every few minutes one would look at the other, and would burst out laughing. The *Stenos* were silent.

'What's in the sack?' Metz pointed to the large satchel on Dart's lap.

Charlie shrugged. 'Personal effects, instruments. Only the barest, most minuscule, most Spartan necessities.'

Metz nodded and settled back again. It would, indeed, be nice to have the chimpanzee along on the trip. Dolphins were fine people, of course. But Mankind's older client race had always struck him as better conversationalists. And dolphins didn't play chess worth a damn.

It was an hour later that Metz recalled Charlie's first words, on announcing his presence aboard. Just what did the chimp mean when he accused Takkata-Jim of 'destroying evidence'? That was a very strange thing to say.

He put the question to Dart. 'Ask the lieutenant,' Charlie suggested. 'He seemed to know what I meant. We're not exactly on speaking terms,' he grumbled.

Metz nodded earnestly. 'I *will* ask him. As soon as we get settled on the island, I will certainly do that.'

63

TOM ORLEY

In the tangled shadows below the weed carpet, he made his way cautiously from airhole to airhole. The facemask helped him stretch a deep breath a long way, especially when he got near the island and had to search for an opening to the shore.

Tom finally crawled out onto land just as the orange sun Kthsemenee slipped behind a thick bank of clouds to the west. The long Kithrup day would last for a while yet, but he missed the direct warming of the sun's rays. Evaporation-chill made him shiver as he pulled himself through a gap in the weeds and up the rocky shoreline. He climbed on his hands and knees to a hummock a few meters above the sea, and sat back heavily against the rough basalt. Then he pulled the breathing-mask down around his neck.

The island seemed to rock slowly, as if it were a cork bobbing in the sea. It would take a while to grow used to solid ground again – just long enough, he realized ironically, for him to finish what he had to do here and get back into the water again.

He pulled clumps of green slime from his shoulders, and shivered as the damp slowly evaporated.

Hunger. Ah, there was that, too.

It took his mind off the damp and chill, at least. He thought about pulling out his last foodbar, but decided it could wait. It was all within a thousand kilometers that he could eat, barring what he might find in alien wreckage.

Smoke still rose where the small ET scout had crashed, just over the shoulder of the mountain. The thin stream climbed to merge high above with sooty drifts from the volcano's crater. Once in a while, Tom heard the mountain itself growl.

Okay. Let's move.

He gathered his feet beneath him and pushed off.

The world wavered unsteadily. Still, he was pleasantly surprised to find himself standing without too much trouble.

Maybe Jill's right, he thought. *Maybe I have reserves I've never touched before.*

He turned to his right, took a step, and almost tripped. He recovered, then stumbled along the rocky slope, thankful for his webbed gloves when it came to climbing over jagged rocks, serrated like chipped flint. One step after another, he drew near the source of the smoke.

Topping a small rise, he came into view of the wreck.

The scout had broken into three pieces. The stern section lay submerged, only its torn front end protruding from the charred weeds in the shallows. Tom checked the radiation meter at the rim of his facemask. He could stand the dose for a few days, if necessary.

The forward half of the wreck had split longitudinally, spilling the contents of the cockpit along a stony strand. Loose banners of fine wire wafted above metal bulkheads which had been pulled and twisted apart like taffy.

Looks easy enough, Tom thought. *I just go down and inspect the damned thing. One step at a time.* He thought about drawing his needler, but decided it would be better to have both hands free in case he fell.

There wasn't much left.

Tom poked through the scattered small pieces, recognizing bits of various machines. But nothing told him what he wanted to know.

And there was no food.

Large bent sheets of metal lay everywhere. Tom approached one that seemed to have cooled off, and tried to lift it. It was too heavy to budge more than a few inches before he had to let it drop.

Tom panted with his hands on his knees for a moment, breathing heavily.

A few meters away was a great pile of driftwood. He went over and pulled out a few of the thicker stumps of dried seaweed. They were tough, but too springy to use as pry-bars.

Tom scratched his stubble and thought. He looked at the sea, covered all the way to the horizon with vile, slimy vines. Finally he started gathering dried vines together into two piles.

After dark he sat by a driftwood fire, weaving tough strands of vine into a pair of large flat fans, somewhat like tennis rackets with loops on one side. He wasn't sure they would work as desired, but tomorrow he would find out.

He sang softly in Trinary, to distract himself from his hunger. The whistled nursery rhyme echoed softly from the nearby cliffside.

> * *Hands and fire?*
> *Hands and fire!*
> * *Use them, use them*
> *To leap higher!*

> * Dreams and song?
> Dreams and song!
> * Use them, use them
> To leap-long! *

Tom stopped suddenly, and cocked his head. After a silent moment he slid his needler out of its holster.

Had he heard a sound? Or was it his imagination?

He rolled quietly out of the firelight and crouched in the shadows looking into the darkness, and like a dolphin, tried to listen to the shape of things. In a stalker's crouch, from cover to cover, he made a slow circuit of the wreckage-strewn beach.

'Barkeemkleph Annatan P'Klenno. V'hoominph?'

Tom dove behind a hull-shard and rolled over. Breathing open-mouthed to keep silent, he listened.

'Vhoomin Kent'thoon ph?'

The voice resonated, as if from a metal cavity . . . from under one of the large pieces of wreckage? A survivor? Who would have imagined?

Tom called out. *'Birkech'kleph. V'human ides'k. V'Thennan kleph ph?'*

He waited. When the voice in the darkness answered, Tom was up and running.

'Idatess. V'Thennankleeph . . .'

He dove once again and fetched up against another shard of metal then crawled on his elbows and took a quick look around the side of the bulkhead.

And aimed his weapon directly into the eyes of a large, reptiloid face, only a meter away. The face grimaced in the dim starlight.

He had only met Thennanin once, and studied them at the school on Cathrhennlin for one week. The creature was half-squashed under a massive, warped metal plate. Tom could guess its expression was one of agony. The scout's arms and back had been broken under the piece of hull.

'Vhoomin t'barrchit pa . . .'

Tom adjusted to the dialect the other spoke, a version of Galactic Six.

'. . . would not kill you, human, had I even the means. I wish only to persuade you to talk to me and distract me for a time.'

Tom holstered the needler and moved to sit cross-legged in front of the pilot. It would only be polite to listen to the creature – and be ready to put him out of his misery if he asked the favor.

'I grieve that I am unable to succor you,' Tom answered in Galactic Six. 'Though you are an enemy, I have never been one to call Thennanin wholly evil.'

The creature grimaced again. His ridge-crest bumped intermittently against the metal roof and he winced each time.

'Nor do we think of *hooman'vlech* as totally without promise, though recalcitrant, wild, and irreverent.'

Tom bowed, accepting as whole the partial compliment.

'I am prepared to do the service of termination, should you wish it,' he offered.

'You are kind, but that is not our way. I will wait as my pain balances my life. The Great Ghosts shall judge me brave.'

Tom lowered his gaze. 'May they judge you brave.'

The Thennanin breathed raggedly, eyes closed. Tom's hand drifted to his waistband. He touched the bulge that was the message bomb. *Are they still waiting, back at* Streaker? He wondered. *What will Creideiki decide to do if he doesn't hear from me?*

I must know what's been happening in the battle above Kithrup.

'For conversation and distraction,' he offered, 'shall we exchange questions?'

The Thennanin opened his eyes. They actually seemed to hold a hint of gratitude. 'Nice. A nice idea. As elder, I shall begin. I will ask simple questions, so as not to strain you.'

Tom shrugged. *Almost three hundred years we've had the* Library. *We have had six thousand years of intricate civilization. And still nobody believes humans could be anything but ignorant savages.*

'Why did you not, from Morgran, flee to a safer haven?' the scout asked. 'Earth could not protect you, nor even those scoundrel Tymbrimi who lead you into evil ways. But the Abdicators are strong. You would have found safety with us. Why did you not come into our arms?'

He made it all sound so simple! If only it were so. If only there had been a truly powerful alignment to flee to, one that would not have charged, in return, more than *Streaker*'s crew or Earth could afford to pay. How to tell the Thennanin that his Abdicators were only slightly less unpalatable than most of the other fanatics.

'It is our policy never to surrender to bullying threats,' Tom said. 'Never. Our history tells us the value of this tradition, more than those brought up on the *Library* annals could imagine. Our discovery will be given only to the Galactic Institutes, and only by our Terragens Council leaders themselves.'

At mention of *Streaker*'s 'discovery' the Thennanin's face showed unmistakable interest. But he waited his turn, allowing Tom the next question.

'Are the Thennanin victorious overhead?' Tom asked anxiously. 'I saw Tandu. Who prevails in the sky?'

Air whistled through the pilot's breathing vents. 'The Glorious fail. The killer Tandu thrive, and Soro pagans abound. We harass where we can, but the Glorious have failed. Heretics shall gain the prize.'

It was a bit of a tactless way to put it, with one of the 'prizes' sitting in front of him. Tom cursed softly. What was he going to do? Some of the Thennanin survived, but could he tell Creideiki to go ahead and take off on that basis? Should they try a ruse which, even if successful, would gain them allies too weak to do any good?

The Thennanin breathed raggedly.

Although it was not his turn, Tom asked the next question.

'Are you cold? I will move my fire here. Also, there is work I must do, as we talk. Forgive this junior patron if I offend.'

The Thennanin looked at him with purple, cat-irised eyes. 'Politely spoken. We are told you humans are without manners. Perhaps you are merely unlearned, yet well-meaning ...'

The scout wheezed and blew sand grains from his breathing slits, while Tom quickly moved his camp. By the flickering flame-light, the Thennanin sighed. 'It is appropriate that, trapped and dying on a primitive world, I shall be warmed by the crafty fire-making skills of a wolfling. I shall ask you to tell a death-bound being about your discovery. No secrets, just a story ... a story about the miracle of the Great Return ...'

Tom drew forth a memory, one that still gave him chills.

'Consider ships,' he began. 'Think of starships – ancient, pitted, and great as moons ...'

When he awakened next to the warm coals of his fire, the dawn was barely breaking, casting long dim shadows along the beach.

Tom felt much better. His stomach had become resigned to a fast, and sleep had done him a lot of good. He was still weak, but he felt ready to try a dash for the next possible haven.

He got up, brushed off the multi-colored sand, and peered to the north. Yes the floating derelict was still there. Hope on the horizon.

To his left, under the massive bulkhead, the Thennanin scout breathed softly, slowly dying. It had fallen asleep listening to Tom's story of the Shallow Cluster, of the shining giant ships, and the mysterious symbols on their sides. Tom doubted the creature would ever reawaken.

He was about to turn and pick up the shoes he had woven the night before, when he frowned and peered under a shading hand toward the eastern horizon.

If only the binoculars had been saved!

He squinted, and at last he made out a line of shadows moving slowly against the brightening horizon, spindly-legged figures, and one smaller, shambling thing. A column of tiny silhouettes moved slowly northward.

Tom shivered. They were headed toward the eggshell wreck. Unless he acted quickly, they would cut him off from his only chance at survival.

And he could tell already that they were Tandu.

PART SIX

SCATTER

'The moot point is, whether Leviathan can long endure so wide a chase, and so remorseless a havoc ... and the last whale, like the last man, smoke his last pipe, and then himself evaporate in the final puff.'

HERMAN MELVILLE

64

CREIDEIKI/SAH'OT

Creideiki stared at the holo display and concentrated. It was easier to talk than to listen. He could call up the words one or two at a time, speak them slowly, shuttling them like pearls on a string.

'... neural link ... repaired ... by ... Gillian and Makanee ... but ... but ... speech ... still ... still ...'

'Still gone,' Sah'ot's image nodded. 'You can use tools now, though?'

Creideiki concentrated on Sah'ot's simple question. You-can-use ... Each word was clear, its meaning obvious. But in a row they meant nothing. It was frustrating!

Sah'ot switched to Trinary.

> * Tools to prod?
> The balls
> The starships—
> * Is your jaw?
> The player
> The pilot— *

Creideiki nodded. That was much better, though even Trinary came to him like a foreign tongue, with difficulty.

> * Spider walkers, walkers, walkers
> * Holocomm talkers, talkers, talkers
> Are my playthings, are— *

Creideiki averted his eyes. He knew there were elements of Primal in that simple phrase, in the repetition and high whistling. It was humiliating to still have an active, able mind, and know that to the outside world you sounded retarded.

At the same time, he wondered if Sah'ot noticed a trace of the language of his dreams – the voices of the old gods.

Listening to the captain, Sah'ot was relieved. Their first conversation had started off well, but toward the end Creideiki's attention had begun to wander, especially when Sah'ot had started running him through a battery of linguistic tests. Now, after Makanee's last operation, he seemed much more attentive.

He decided to test Creideiki's listening ability by telling him about his discovery. He carefully and slowly explained in Trinary about the 'singing' he had heard while linked to the robot in the drill-tree funnel.

Creideiki looked confused for a long moment as he concentrated on Sah'ot's slow, simplified explanation, then he seemed to understand. In fact, from his expression, it seemed he thought it the most natural thing in the world that a planet should sing.

'Link ... link me ... pl – please ... I ... I will ... listen ... listen ...'

Sah'ot clapped his jaw in assent, pleased. Not that Creideiki, with his language centers burned, would be able to make out anything but static. It took all of Sah'ot's subtle training and experience to trace the refrain. Except for that one time, when the voices from below had shouted in apparent anger, the sounds had been almost amorphous.

He still shuddered, remembering that one episode of lucidity.

'Okay, Creideiki,' he said as he made the connection. 'Listen closely!'

Creideiki's eyes recessed in concentration as the static crackled and popped over the line.

65

GILLIAN

'Triple damn! Well, we can't wait for her to get here to start the move. It might take Hikahi two days to circle around in the skiff. I want to have *Streaker* safely inside the Seahorse by then.'

Suessi's simulacrum shrugged. 'Well, you could leave her a note.'

Gillian rubbed her eyes. 'That's just what we'll do. We'll drop a monofilament relay link at *Streaker's* present position, so we can stay in touch with the party on the island. I'll stick a message to the relay telling her where we've gone.'

'What about Toshio and Dennie?'

Gillian shrugged. 'I'd hoped to send the skiff after them and Sah'ot ... and maybe after Tom. But as things are, I'd better have Dennie and Sah'ot head toward your site by sled. I hate doing it. It's dangerous and I need Toshio there watching Takkata-Jim until just before we take off.'

She didn't mention the other reason for wanting Toshio to stay as long as possible. They both knew that Tom Orley, if he flew the glider

home, would return to the island. He ought to have someone waiting for him.

'Are we really going to abandon Metz and Takkata-Jim?' Suessi
looked perplexed.

'And Charlie Dart, apparently. He stowed away on the longboat.
Yes, it's their choice. They hope to make it home after the Galactics
blow us to kingdom come. For all I know they may be right. Anyway,
the final decision's Hikahi's, when she finally shows up and finds out
she's in command.'

Gillian shook her head. 'Ifni sure seems to have gone out of her
way to throw us curves, hasn't she, Hannes?'

The elderly engineer smiled. 'Luck's always been fickle. That's why
she's a lady.'

'Hmmph!' But Gillian didn't have the energy to give him much of
a dirty look. A light winked on the console next to the holo display.

'Here it is, Hannes. The engine room is ready. I've got to go, now.
We're getting under way.'

'Good luck, Gillian.' Suessi held up an 'O' sign, then broke the
connection.

Gillian flicked a switch cutting into the comm line from *Streaker*
to the island. 'Sah'ot, this is Gillian. Sorry to break in, but would you
please tell the captain we're about to move.' It was a courtesy to let
Creideiki know. *Streaker* had been his, once.

'Yesss, Gillian.' There was a series of high, repetitious whistles in
very Primal-like Trinary. Much of it crested over the upper range of
even Gillian's gene-enhanced hearing.

'The captain wantss to go outside to watch,' Sah'ot said. 'He
promises not to get in the way.'

Gillian couldn't see any real reason to refuse. 'All right. But tell
him to check with Wattaceti first, to use a sled, and to be careful! We
won't be able to spare anyone to go chasing him if he wanders off!'

There was another high series of whistles that Gillian could
barely follow. Creideiki signaled that he understood.

'Oh, by the way, Sah'ot,' Gillian added. 'Please ask Toshio to call
me as soon as the longboat arrives.'

'Yes!'

Gillian cut the connection and got up to dress. There were so
many things to juggle simultaneously!

I wonder if I did the right thing, letting Charlie Dart sneak away, she
thought. *If he or Takkata-Jim behave in a way I don't expect, what'll
I do?*

A tiny light shone at the corner of her console. The Niss machine
still wanted to talk to her. The light didn't flash urgent. Gillian
decided to ignore it as she hurried out to supervise the move.

66

AKKI

With aching muscles, Akki swam slowly out of the notch in which he had rested until dawn.

He took several deep breaths and dove, scattering a school of brightly scaled fish-like creatures through shafts of morning light. Without thinking, he speared through the school and snapped up a large one, relishing its frantic struggle between his jaws. But the metal taste was bitter. He flipped the creature away, spitting.

Red clouds spread a pink glow across the east as he surfaced again. Hunger growled in his compound stomachs. He wondered if the sound was loud enough to be picked up by his hunter.

It's unfair. When K'tha-Jon finds me, he, *at least, will have something to eat!*

Akki shook himself. What a bizarre thought! 'You're falling apart, middie. K'tha-Jon is no cannibal. He's a ... a ...'

A what? Akki remembered the final stretch, yesterday at sunset, when he had somehow made it to the chain of metal-mounds just meters ahead of his pursuer. The chase amidst the tiny islands had been a confusion of bubbles and surf and hunting cries. For hours after he had finally found a hiding place, he had listened to staccato bursts of sonar that proved K'tha-Jon had not gone far.

Thought of the bosun sent chills down Akki's spine. What kind of creature *was* he? It wasn't just the irrationality of this death-chase; there was something else as well, something in the *way* K'tha-Jon hunted. The giant's sonar sweeps contained something malevolent that made Akki want to curl up in a ball.

Of course, *Stenos* gene-grafts might account for some of his size and irritability. But in K'tha-Jon there was more. Something very different must have gone into the bosun's genetic splice. Something terrifying. Something Akki, raised on Calafia, had never encountered.

Akki swam close to the edge of the coral mound and stuck his jaw out beyond the northern verge. There were only the natural sounds of the Kithrup sea.

He hopped up on his tail and scanned visually. To go west, or north? To Hikahi, or Toshio?

Better north. This chain of mounds might extend to the one where the encampment lay. It might provide cover.

He dashed across the quarter-kilometer gap to the next island, then listened quietly. There was no change. Breathing a little more easily, he crossed the next channel, then the next, swimming quick bursts, then listening, then resuming his cautious passage.

Once he heard a strange, complex chatter to his right. He lay motionless until he realized that it couldn't be K'tha-Jon. He detoured slightly to take a look.

It was an underwater skirmish line of balloon-like creatures, with distended air bladders and lively blue faces. They carried crude implements and nets filled with thrashing prey. Except for a few holos sent back by Dennie Sudman and Sah'ot, this was Akki's first glimpse of the Kithrup natives, the Kiqui. He watched, fascinated, then swam toward them. He had thought himself still far south of Toshio, but if this group was the same ...

As soon as they caught sight of him the hunters squeaked in panic. Dropping their nets, they scrambled up the vine-covered face of a nearby island. Akki realized that he must have encountered a different tribe, one which had never seen dolphins before.

Still, seeing them was something. He watched the last one climb out of sight. Then he turned northward once more.

But when he passed the northern shore of the next mound, a sharp beam of sound passed over him.

Akki quailed. How! Had K'tha-Jon duplicated his logic about an island chain? Or had some demon instinct told him where to hunt his prey?

The eerie call passed over him once more. It had mutated further during the night into a piercing, falling cry that set Akki shivering.

The cry pealed again, nearer, and Akki knew he couldn't hide. That cry would seek him out in any cleft or cranny, until the panic took hold. He had to make a break for it, while he still had control over his mind!

67

KEEPIRU

The fight had begun in the predawn darkness.

A few hours ago Keepiru realized that his pursuer's sled was showing no sign of failing. The engine screamed, but it would not die. Keepiru notched his own upward well beyond the red line, but it was too late. A short time later, he heard the whine of a torpedo homing in from behind. He zigged leftward and down, blowing ballast to leave a cloud of noisy bubbles in his wake.

The torpedo streaked past and into the gloom beyond. An amplified squawk of disappointment and indignation echoed amongst the rills and seamounts. Keepiru was used to hearing Primal obscenities from his pursuer.

He had almost reached the line of metal-mounds behind which the two swimming dolphins had disappeared a few hours back. As he had drawn nearer, Keepiru had listened to the distant hunt cries, and been chilled by a gnawing association that he couldn't bring himself yet to believe. It made him dread for Akki.

Now Keepiru had his own problems. He wished Akki luck holding out until he could get rid of this idiot on his own tail.

It was growing light overhead. Keepiru dove his sled behind a lumpy ridge, then throttled the engine back and waited.

Moki cursed as the tiny torpedo failed to detonate.

> # Teeth, teeth are – are –
> Better, better than –
> # Things! #

He swung his jaw left and right. He had abandoned the sled's sensors, and was controlling the machine purely by habit.

Where *was* the smart-aleck! Let him come out and get it over with!

Moki was tired and cranky and unutterably bored. He had never imagined that being a Great Bull could be so tedious. Moki wanted the hot, almost orgasmic rage back. He tried to call up the bloodlust again, but kept thinking about killing fish, not dolphins.

If only he could emulate the savagery he had heard in K'tha-Jon's hunt-cry! Moki no longer hated the frightening bosun. He had begun to see the giant as a spirit creature of pure and evil nature. He would kill this smart-aleck *Tursiops* and bring its head to K'tha-Jon as proof of his worthiness as a disciple. Then he, too, would become elemental, a terror that none would ever dare thwart.

Moki brought the machine about in a circle, keeping close to the seafloor to take advantage of shadows of sound. The *Tursiops* had turned left at high speed. His turn *had* to be wider than Moki's, so all Moki had to do was hunt in the correct arc.

Moki had been on guard duty when this chase began, so his sled had torpedoes. He was sure the smartass didn't have any. He whistled in eager anticipation of an end to the tedious chase.

A sound! He turned so quickly he banged his snout against the plastic bubble-dome. Moki gunned the sled forward, readying another torpedo. *This* one would finish his enemy off.

A sheer drop opened into a broad ocean canyon. Moki took ballast and fell, hugging the wall. He throttled back and stopped.

Minutes passed as the sound of muffled engines grew louder from his left. The oncoming sled was staying close to the cliff face, at a greater depth.

Suddenly, it was below him! Moki chose not to fire right away. This was too easy! Let the smart-aleck hear death suddenly fall upon him from behind, too close to evade. Let him writhe in panic before Moki's torpedo tore his body into pieces!

His sled growled, then dropped in pursuit. His victim could never turn in time! Moki crowed,

> # A herd bull is! -is!
> # A Great Bull ... #

Moki interrupted his chant. Why wasn't the smart-aleck fleeing?

He had been relying entirely upon sound. Only now did he turn his eye on his intended victim.

The other sled was empty! It drove along slowly, unpiloted. But then where ... ?

> * Hunting ears
>   Can make a bull—
> * But eyes
>   And brains
>   Make spacefen – *

The voice was above him! Moki cried out, trying to turn the sled and fire a torpedo at the same time. With a despairing wail the engines screamed and then died. His neural link went dead just as he came about into sight of a sleek, gray *Tursiops* dolphin, two meters above him, white teeth shining in the light from the surface.

> * And fools
>   Make only
>   Corpses— *

Moki screamed as the cutting torch on the pilot's harness exploded into laser-blue brilliance.

68

TOM ORLEY

Where did they all come from?

Tom Orley hid behind a low weed mound and looked about at the various alien parties on the horizon. He counted at least three groups, all converging from different directions on the floating eggshell-shaped wreck.

About a mile behind him, the volcano still rumbled. He had left the crashed Thennanin scoutship at dawn, leaving a pan of precious fresh water under the dying pilot's mouth, within reach if he should ever awaken.

He had set out soon after sighting the party of Tandu, testing his newly woven 'weed-shoes' on the uneven slimy surface. The splayed, snowshoe-like devices helped him walk cautiously across the slick carpet of vines.

At first he moved much faster than the others. But soon the Tandu developed a new technique. They stopped floundering in the mire, and came on at a brisk walk. Tom kept low and worried about what would happen if they caught sight of him.

And now there were other parties as well, one approaching from the southwest and one from the west. He couldn't make them out clearly yet, just dots bobbing slowly and with difficulty on a low, serrated horizon. But where the hell had they all come from?

The Tandu were closest. There were at least eight or nine of them, approaching in a column. Each creature splayed its six spindly legs wide apart to spread its weight. In their arms they cradled long, glistening instruments that could only be weapons. They marched forward rapidly.

Tom wondered what their new tactic was. Then he noticed that the lead Tandu did not carry a weapon. Instead, it held the leash of a shaggy, shambling creature. The keeper leaned forward over its charge, as if coaxing it to keep at a given task.

Tom risked raising his head a couple of feet above the mound.

'Well, I'll be damned.'

The hairy creature was *creating* land – or at least solidity – in a narrow causeway in front of the party! Just before and on both sides of the trail, there was a faint shimmering where reality seemed to struggle against a noxious intrusion.

An Episiarch! Momentarily, Tom forgot his predicament, grateful for this rare sight.

As he watched, the causeway failed in one spot. The luminous band around the edges of the trail snapped together with a loud bang. The Tandu warrior standing there flailed and thrashed as it fell into the weeds. By fighting it merely tore the carpet and opened the hole wider until, finally, it sank like a stone into the sea.

None of the other Tandu seemed to take notice. The two behind the gap leaped across to the temporarily solid 'ground' beyond. The party, diminished by one, continued to advance.

Tom shook his head. He *had* to reach the wreck first! He couldn't afford to let the Tandu pass him. Yet if he did anything, even resumed his own march, they'd certainly spot him. He didn't doubt their efficiency with those weapons they carried. No human warrior ever underestimated the Tandu for long.

Reluctantly, he knelt and untied the fastenings on his weed-shoes. Discarding them, he crawled carefully to the edge of an open pool.

He counted slowly, waiting until he could hear the column of Galactics approaching, rehearsing his moves in his mind.

Taking several deep breaths, he pulled his diving mask over his face, making certain it was snug and the collecting fins were clear. Then he pulled his needler from its holster, holding it in two hands.

Tom set his feet on two firm roots and checked his balance. The pool was just in front of him.

He closed his eyes.

> * Listen—
> *For the swishing tail*
> *Of the tiger shark*— *

His empathy sense pinpointed the powerful psi emissions of the mad ET adept, now only some eighty meters away.

'Gillian ...,' he sighed. Then, in one sudden fluid motion, he stood up and extended his weapon. His eyes opened and he fired.

69

TOSHIO

Against Toshio's objections, they had used the last of the longboat's energy to lift it to a landing site on top of the island. He had offered to blast a wider opening into the chamber below the metal-mound, but Takkata-Jim had turned his suggestion down cold.

That meant two hours of backbreaking work, heaping chopped foliage over the small ship to camouflage it. Toshio wasn't sure even that would do any good if the Galactics finished their battle and turned their full attention to the planet's surface.

Metz and Dart were supposed to help him. Toshio had set them to work cutting brush, but found that he had to tell them to do each and every thing. Dart was sullen and angry at being commanded by a middie he had ordered around only days before. He obviously wanted to get to the supplies he had excitedly dropped by the drill-tree pool before being drafted into the work crew. Metz had been willing enough, but was so anxious to be off talking to Dennie that he was distracted and worse than useless.

Toshio finally sent them both away and finished the job by himself.

At last the boat was covered. He slumped to the ground and rested against the bole of an oli-nut tree.

Damn Takkata-Jim! Toshio and Dennie were supposed to see the encampment secure, report their findings on the Kiqui to Metz, and then climb on their sleds and get *out* of here! Gillian expected them to set out in a few hours, and yet almost nothing was accomplished!

To top it all off, *Streaker* had only warned him an hour or so in advance that he could probably expect a stowaway. Gillian decided not to have Charlie arrested for violation of orders, even though it appeared he had stolen equipment from at least a dozen labs aboard the ship. Toshio was glad to be spared the added chore. There wasn't much of anything hereabouts to use as a jail, anyway.

Foliage rustled to Toshio's left. A series of mechanical whirrings accompanied the sound of crushing vegetation. Then four 'spiders' pushed through the brush to enter his tiny clearing. A *Stenos* dolphin lay on the flotation pad of each armored mechanical, controlling the four high-jointed legs with neural-link commands. Toshio stood up as they approached.

Takkata-Jim passed by, eyeing him coolly, silently. The other three spiders followed him across the clearing and back into the forest. The *Stenos* piped to each other in gutter-Trinary.

Toshio stared after them. He discovered that he had been holding his breath.

'I don't know about Takkata-Jim, but those fen *with* him are crazier than Atlast pier-nesters,' he said to himself, shaking his head. He had met few so-called *Stenos* on Calafia. Some had displayed quirks, positive and negative, like Sah'ot. But none had ever had the look that the former vice-captain's followers had in their eyes.

The sound of the procession faded away. Toshio got up to his feet.

He wondered why Gillian had let Takkata-Jim go at all. Why not just throw him and his cohorts in the brig and have *done* with it?

Granted, it was a good idea to leave a party with the longboat, to try to sneak back to Earth if *Streaker* was lost trying to escape. Gillian probably couldn't spare any of the reliable members of the crew. But ...

He turned toward the village of the Kiqui, thinking as he walked.

Of course, the longboat was stripped. Theoretically, Takkata-Jim couldn't contact the Galactics even if he wanted to. And Toshio couldn't imagine a reason he'd want to.

But what if he *had* a reason? And what if he found a way?

Toshio almost bumped into a tree in his worried concentration. He looked up and corrected his path.

I'll just have to make sure, he decided. Tonight I'll have to find out if he can cause trouble.

Tonight.

The tribe's adults squatted around a circle in a clearing in the center of the village. Ignacio Metz and Dennie Sudman sat to one side. The Nest-Mother squatted across from them, her bright green-and-red-striped puffer sacks fully inflated. The elders on either side of her billowed and chuffed like a chain of gaily painted balloons in the forest-filtered sunshine.

Toshio stopped at the edge of the village clearing. Sunshine filtered through the trees, revealing a conclave of races. The Kiqui Nest-Mother chattered, waving her paws in a queer up-and-down pattern that Dennie had said connoted happy emphasis. If the oldest female had been angry, her gestures would have been crosswise. It was a blissfully simple expression pattern. The rest of the tribe repeated her sounds, sometimes anticipating her in a rising and falling chant of consensus.

Ignacio Metz nodded excitedly, cupping one hand over an earphone as he listened to the translation computer. When the chant died down he spoke a few words into a microphone. A long series of high-pitched repetitive squeaks came out of the machine's speaker.

Dennie's expression was one of relief. She had dreaded the uplift specialist's first meeting with the Kiqui. But Metz had not, apparently, muffed her long and careful negotiations with the pre-sentients. The meeting seemed to be coming to a satisfactory conclusion.

Dennie caught sight of Toshio, and smiled brilliantly. Without ceremony she stood up and left the circle. She hurried over to where he waited at the edge of the village clearing.

'How's it going?' he asked.

'Wonderfully! It turns out he's read every word I sent back! He understands their pack protocol, their physical manifestations of sex and age, and he thought my behavioral analysis was "exemplary"! Exemplary!'

Toshio smiled, sharing her pleasure.

'He's talking about getting me an appointment as a fellow at the Uplift Center! Can you imagine that?' Dennie couldn't help bouncing up and down excitedly.

'What about the treaty?'

'Oh they're ready any time. If Hakahi makes it here in the skiff we'll take a dozen Kiqui back to *Streaker* with us. Otherwise a few will go back to Earth with Metz in the longboat. It's all settled.'

Toshio looked back at the happy villagers and tried not to show his misgivings.

Of course, it was for the good of the Kiqui as a species. They would fare far better under the patronage of Mankind than under almost any other starfaring race. And Earth geneticists had to have living beings to examine before any sort of adoption claim could be made.

Every attempt would be made to keep the first group of aboriginals healthy. Half of Dennie's job had been to analyze their bodily requirements, including needed trace elements. But it was still unlikely any of the first group would survive. Even if they did, Toshio doubted the Kiqui had a notion of the strangeness they were about to embark upon.

They're not sentients yet, he reminded himself. By Galactic law they're still animals. And, unlike anyone else in the Five Galaxies, we'll at least try to explain to their limited understanding, and ask permission.

But he remembered a stormy night, with driving rain and flashing lightning, when the little amphibians had huddled around him and an injured dolphin who was his friend, keeping them warm and warding off despair with their company.

He turned away from the sun-washed clearing.

'Then there's nothing keeping you here any longer?' he asked Dennie.

She shook her head. 'I'd rather stay a while longer, of course. Now that I'm finished with the Kiqui I can really work on the problem of the metal-mound. That's why I was so grouchy a couple of days ago. Besides being so tired trying to do two major jobs, I was also frustrated. But now we're a step closer to solving that problem. And did you know the core of the metal-mound is still alive? It's ...'

Toshio had to interrupt to stop the flow of words. 'Dennie! Stop

542

it for a minute, please. Answer my question. Are you ready to leave now?'

Dennie blinked. She changed tracks, frowning. 'Is it *Streaker*? Has something gone wrong?'

'They began the move a few hours ago. I want you to gather all of your notes and samples and secure them to your sled. You and Sah'ot are leaving in the morning.'

She looked at him, his words slowly sinking in. 'You mean *you*, me, and Sah'ot, don't you?'

'No. I'm staying for another day. I have to.'

'But why?'

'Look, Dennie, I can't talk about it now. Just do as I ask, please.'

As he turned to walk back toward the drill-tree pool she grabbed his arm. Holding on, she was forced to follow.

'But we were going to go together! If you have things to do here, I'll wait for you!'

He walked along without answering. He couldn't think of anything to say. It was bitter to win her respect and affection at last, only to lose her within hours.

If this is what being grown up means, they can have it, he thought. *It sucks.*

As they approached the pool, sounds of loud argument came from that direction. Toshio hurried. Dennie trotted alongside until they burst into the clearing.

Charles Dart screamed and clutched at a slender cylinder that was gripped at the other end by the manipulator arm of Takkata-Jim's spider. Charlie strained against the pull of the waldo-machine. Takkata-Jim grinned open-mouthed.

The tug of war lasted for a few seconds as the neo-chimp's powerful muscles strained, then the cylinder popped out of his hands. He fell back to the dust and barely stopped before rolling into the pool. He hopped up and shrieked his anger.

Toshio saw three other Stenos-controlled spiders trooping off toward the longboat. Each carried another of the thin cylinders. Toshio stopped in his tracks when he got a good look at the one Takkata-Jim had taken. His eyes went wide.

'There is no longer any danger,' Takkata-Jim told him.

His voice carried insouciance. 'I have confissscated these. They'll be kept safe aboard my boat, and there will be no harm.'

'They're mine, you thief!' Charles Dart hopped angrily, and his hands fluttered. 'You criminal!' he growled. 'You think I don't know you tried to m-murder Creideiki? We all know you did! You wrecked the buoys to destroy the evidence! And n-now you steal the tools of m-my trade!'

543

'Which you stole from *Streaker*'s armory, no doubt. Or do you wish to call Doctor Baskin for confirmation that they truly are yoursss?'

Dart growled and showed an impressive display of teeth. He whirled away from the neo-dolphin and sat down in the dust in front of a complex diving robot, freshly unpacked on the verge of the pool.

Takkata-Jim's spider started to turn, but the fin noticed Toshio looking at him. For just a moment, Takkata-Jim's cool reserve broke under the youth's fierce gaze. He looked away, and then back at Toshio.

'Don't-t believe everything you hear, boy-human,' he said. 'Much I have done, and will do, and I'm convinced I am right. But it wasss not I who hurt Creideiki.'

'Did you destroy the buoys?' Toshio could sense Dennie standing close behind him, watching the large dolphin silently over his shoulder.

'Yesss. But it was not I who ssset the trap. Like King Henry with Beckett-t, I only found out about it after. Tell this, on Earth, if by some strange chance you should escape and I don't. Another took the initiative.'

'Who did it, then?' Toshio's fists were tight balls.

A long sigh escaped Takkata-Jim's blowmouth.

'Our Doctor Metz wrung from the Survey Board berths for some who shouldn't have been on this voyage. He was impatient. A few of his *Stenos* had ... *unusual* family trees.'

'The *Stenos* ...'

'*A few Stenos*! I am not one of Metz's experiments! I am a starship officer. I earned my place!' The dolphin's voice was defiant.

'When the pressure built to the breaking point, some of them turned to me. I thought I could control them. But there was one who turned out to be more than even I could manage. Tell them if you get home, Toshio Iwashika. Tell them on Earth that it'sss possible to turn a dolphin into a monster. They should be warned.'

Takkata-Jim gave him one long, intent look, then his spider turned away and followed his crew back to the longboat.

'He's a liar!' Dennie whispered after he had gone. 'He sounds so reasonable and logical, but I shiver when I listen to him!'

Toshio watched the spider disappear down the trail.

'No,' he said. 'He is ambitious, and maybe crazy too. He's probably a traitor, as well. But for some reason I think everything he said was explicitly true. Maybe a surface honesty is what he clings to now, for pride's sake.'

He turned, shaking his head. 'Not that that makes him any less dangerous.'

He approached Charles Dart, who looked up with a friendly smile. Toshio squatted near the chimp planetologist.

'Doctor Dart, how big were they?'

'Were what, Toshio? Say! Have you *seen* this new robot? I made it up special. It can dive to the base of the shaft; then dig laterally to those big magma tunnels we detected . . .'

'How big *were* they, Charlie?' Toshio demanded. He was tense, and ready to throttle the chimpanzee. '*Tell* me!'

Dart glanced briefly, guiltily, at Toshio, then looked down at the pool wistfully.

'Only about a kiloton each,' he sighed. 'Hardly big enough to set off decent crust waves, really.' He looked up with large, innocent brown eyes. 'They were really only teeny little A-bombs, honest!'

70

HIKAHI

The need to run quietly kept her speed to little more than it might have been with a sled. It was frustrating.

Cut off from contact with anyone for more than a day, Hikahi studied the seascape around her to avoid thinking about the possible fate of Creideiki and *Streaker*. She would find out what had happened sooner or later. Until then worry would only wear her out.

Morning light filtered down to the canyon bottoms as she swung east and then northward. Clots of dangle-weed drifted overhead, and copper-backed fish darted briefly alongside, until the driving skiff left them behind.

Once she caught sight of something long and sinuous that quickly slithered into a sea-cave as she approached. There was no time to stop and explore, but she did take the monster's picture as she passed.

What will I do if I find Streaker *destroyed?* The thought came unwanted.

I'll go back to the Thennanin wreck as an intermediate step. They'd need me there. But I'd be commander, then. And hiding at the bottom of the ocean wouldn't be a long-term solution. Not on this deadly world.

Can I bring myself to negotiate a surrender?

If she did, she wouldn't let the Galactics take her personally. She was one of the few who, with the right notes, could plot an accurate course back to the derelict fleet.

Maybe I'd see the crew safely interned and then make a break for it in the skiff, she thought. *Not that the skiff could ever make it all the way home, even if it could run a Galactic blockade. But someone has to try to get word back to Earth. Perhaps there would be a way to punish the fanatics ... make their behavior so costly to them that they'd think twice before bullying Earthlings again.*

Hikahi knew she was dreaming. In a few thousand years humans and their clients might have that kind of power, maybe.

Hikahi listened. There was a sound ...

She turned up the gain on the ship's hydrophones. Filters removed the background growl of the engines and the tide. She heard the soft scurrying sounds of the ocean creatures.

'Computer! Filter for cetacean output!'

The patterns of sound changed. The sea became quiet. Still, there was a trace of something.

'Increase gain!' The noise level rose. Above the static hiss she heard the faint but distinguishable cries of swimming dolphins! They were desperate sounds of combat.

Was she picking up the echoes of straggling survivors of a disaster? What to do? She wanted to rush to the aid of the distressed fen. But who was pursuing them?

'Machine soundsss!' She commanded. But the detector winked a red light, indicating that there were none within range. So, the dolphins were sledless.

If she attempted a rescue, she risked the only hope of the crew back at the Seahorse. Should she make a detour around the refugees, and hurry toward *Streaker* as planned? It was an agonizing choice.

Hikahi cut her speed to run still quieter, and sent the skiff due north, toward the dim cries.

71

CHARLES DART

He waited until everyone had left before he unscrewed the back of the new robot and checked its contents.

Yes, it was still there. Safely concealed.

Ah, well, he thought. *I'd hoped to repeat the experiment. But one bomb should be enough.*

72

STREAKER

FROM THE JOURNAL OF GILLIAN BASKIN

We're on our way. Everyone aboard seems relieved to be moving at last.

Streaker *lifted off the ocean floor late last night, impellers barely ticking over. I was on the bridge, monitoring reports by the fen outside, and watching the strain gauges until we were sure* Streaker *was okay. In fact, she sounded positively eager to be off.*

Emerson and the crew in the engine room should be proud of the job they've done, though, of course, it's the coils Tom and Tsh't found, that made it possible. Streaker *hums like a starship once again.*

Our course is due south. We dropped a monofilament relay behind to keep us in touch with the party on the island, and left a message for Hikahi when she shows up.

I hope she hurries. Being a commander is more complicated than I'd ever imagined. I have to make sure everything is done in the right order and correctly, and all as unobtrusively as possible, without making the fen feel 'the old lady' is hovering over them. It makes me wish I had some of the military training Tom got while I was away in medical school.

Less than thirty hours and we'll reach the Thennanin shell. Suessi says they'll be ready for us. Meanwhile, we have scouts out, and Wattaceti paces us overhead in a detection sled. His instruments show very little leakage, so we should be safe for now.

I'd give a year's wages for Hikahi or Tsh't, or even Keepiru right now. I'd never understood, before, why a captain treasures a good executive officer so much.

Speaking of captains. Ours is a wonder.

Creideiki seemed to be in a daze for a long time, after getting out of sick bay. But his long conversation with Sah'ot appears to have roused him. I don't know what Sah'ot did, but I would never have believed a person so severely damaged as Creideiki could be so vigorous, or make himself so useful.

When we lifted off he asked to be allowed to supervise the scouts and flankers. I was desperate for a reliable fin to put in charge out there, and thought that having him visible could help morale. Even the Stenos were excited to have him about. Their last bitterness over my 'coup' – and Takkata-Jim's exile – seems to have dissipated.

Creideiki is limited to the simplest calls in Trinary, but that seems to be enough. He's out there now, zipping about in his sled, keeping things orderly by pointing, nudging, and setting an example. In only a few hours Tsh't should rendezvous with the scouts we sent ahead, and then Creideiki can come back aboard.

There's a tiny light on my comm that's been flashing since I returned. It's that crazy Tymbrimi Niss machine. I've been keeping the damned thing waiting.

Tom wouldn't approve, I guess. But a fem has only so much strength, and I've got to take a nap. If the matter were urgent it would have broken in and spoken by now.

Oh, Tom, we could use your endurance now. Are you on your way back? Is your little glider even now winging home to Toshio's island?

Who am I fooling? Since the first psi-bomb we've detected nothing, only noise from the space battle, some of it indicating fighting over his last known position. He's set off none of the message globes. So either he's decided not to send an ambiguous message or worse.

Without word from Tom, how can we decide what to do, once we enter the Seahorse? Do we take off and try our luck, or hide within the hulk as long as we can?

It will be Hikahi's decision when the time comes.

Gillian closed the journal and applied her thumbprint to the fail-safe self-destruct. She got up and turned off the light.

On her way out of the lab, she passed the stasis-bier of the ancient cadaver they had reclaimed at such cost from the Shallow Cluster. Herbie just lay there grinning under a tiny spotlight, an ancient enigma. A mystery.

A troublemaker.

Battered, battle-scarred, *Streaker* moved slowly along the valley floor, her engines turning over with gentle, suppressed power. A dark, foamy mist rose below her where impellers kicked up the surface ooze.

The nubby cylinder slid over gloomy black rills and abysses, skirting the edges of seamounts and valley walls. Tiny sleds paced alongside, guiding the ship by sonar-speak.

Creideiki watched his ship in motion once again. He listened to the clipped reports of the scouts and sentries, and the replies of the bridge staff. He couldn't follow the messages in detail; the sophisticated technical argot was as out of reach to him as last year's wine. But he could sense the under-meaning; the crew had things well in hand.

Streaker couldn't really shine in this light, dim and blue, fifty meters down, but he could listen – his own sonar clicked softly in accompaniment as he savored the deep rumble of her engines, and he imagined he could be with her when she flew again.

: Never Again Creideiki : You Shall Never Fly With Her Again :

The spectre, K-K-Kph-kree, came into being gradually alongside him, a ghostly figure of silver and sonic shadows. The presence of the god did not surprise, or even bother Creideiki. He had been expecting It to come. It swam lazily, easily keeping pace alongside the sled.

: You Escaped Us : Yet Now You Purposely Sculpt Me Out Of Song : Because Of The Old Voices You Heard? : The Voices From Below? :

: Yes :
Creideiki thought not in Anglic or Trinary, but in the new language he had been learning.
: There Is Ancient Anger Within This World : I Have Heard Its Song :
The dream-god's great brow sparkled starlight. Its small jaw opened. Teeth shone.

: And What Do You Plan To Do? :

Creideiki sensed that It already knew the answer.
: My Duty : He replied in Its own speech. : What Else Can I Ever Do? :
From the depths of the Whale Dream, It sighed approval.

Creideiki turned up the gain on his hydrophones. There were faraway excited echoes from up ahead – joyous sounds of greeting.
On his sled's sonar display, at the far edge of its range was a small cluster of dots coming inward. They joined the specks that were *Streaker*'s scouts. The first group had to be Tsh't's party from the Seahorse.
Making sure no one was nearby to take note, he turned his sled aside into a small side canyon. He slipped behind the shadows of a rock outcrop and turned off his engine. He waited then, watching *Streaker* pass below his aerie, until she vanished, along with the last of her flankers, around a curve in the long canyon.
'Good-bye ...' He concentrated on the Anglic words, one at a time. 'Good-bye ... and ... good luck ...'

When it was safe, he turned on his sled and rose out of the little niche. He swung about and headed northward, toward the place they had left twenty hours before.

: You Can Come Along If You Like: he told the god – part figment of his mind, part something else. The ghostly figure answered in un-words made up from Creideiki's own sonar sounds.

: I Accompany You : I Would Not Miss This For The Song of the World :

PART SEVEN

THE FOOD CHAIN

'Master, I marvel how the fishes live in the sea.'
'Why, as men do aland – the great ones eat up the little ones.'

WILLIAM SHAKESPEARE
KING RICHARD THE SECOND

73

AKKI

It was a scream that curdled his marrow. Only a monster could make a sound like that. He fled *it* almost as hard as he fled the creature that voiced it.

By noontime Akki realized it was nearly over.

His exhaustion showed in a laboring heart and heavy breathing, but also in a painful sloughing of the outer layers of his skin. His allergic reaction to the water seemed to be aggravated by fatigue. It had grown worse as he frantically dodged in and out amongst tiny islets. His once-smooth, dynamically supple hide was now a rough mass of sores. His mind felt little more agile than his body.

Several times he had escaped traps that should have left him meat. Once he had fled a sonar reflection almost into K'tha-Jon's jaws. The giant had grinned and flourished his laser rifle as Akki turned away frantically. It hadn't been by speed or cleverness that Akki escaped. He realized that his enemy was just toying with him.

He had hoped to flee northward, toward Toshio's island, but now he was all turned around, and north was lost to him. Perhaps if he could wait until sunset . . .

No. I won't last that long. It's time to end it.

The chilling hunt-scream pealed out again. The ululation seemed to coagulate the water around him.

A large part of Akki's fatigue had come from the involuntary terror that cry sent through him. What devil *was* it, that chased him?

A little while ago he thought he had distantly heard another cry. It sounded like a *Tursiops* search call. But he was probably imagining things. Whatever was going on back at *Streaker*, they couldn't have spared anyone to look for him. Even if they had, how could anyone ever find him in this wide ocean?

He had done *Streaker* one service, in distracting the monster K'tha-Jon, in leading him away from where he could do worse harm.

I hope Gillian and Hikahi got back and straightened things out, he thought. *I'm sure they did.*

He took quiet breaths in the shadow of a rock cleft. K'tha-Jon knew where he was, of course. It was only a matter of time until he grew bored with the chase and came to collect his prey.

I'm fading, Akki thought. *I've got to finish this while there's a chance to win something from it – even if it's just the honor of choosing my own time to die.*

He checked the charge on his harness cells. There was only enough for two good shots from his cutter torch. Those would have to be from very short range, and no doubt K'tha-Jon's rifle was almost fully charged.

With his harness-hands Akki plugged his breather back over his blowmouth. Ten minutes of oxygen remained. More than enough.

The high scream echoed again, chilling, taunting.

All right, monster. He clenched his jaw to keep from shivering again. *Hold your horses. I'm coming.*

74

KEEPIRU

Keepiru raced to the northeast, toward the battle sounds he had heard during the night. He swam hard and fast at the surface, arching and thrusting to drive through the water. He cursed at the drag of his harness, but to drop it was unthinkable.

Once again he cursed the damnable luck. Both his and Moki's sleds were used up, worthless, and had to be left behind.

As he entered the maze of tiny islands, he heard the hunt-scream clearly for the first time.

Until now he could tell himself he was imagining things – that distance or some strange refraction in the water had tricked him into hearing what could not be.

The screeching cry pealed out, reflecting from the metal-mounds. Keepiru whirled, and it momentarily seemed a pack of hunters was all around him.

Then came another sound, a brave and very faint skirr of distant Trinary. Keepiru swung his jaw about, chose a direction, and swam for all he was worth.

His muscles flexed powerfully as he streaked through the maze. When a rasping buzz told him his breather was near empty, he cursed as he popped the thing loose, and continued his dash along the surface, puffing and blowing with each driving arch.

He came to a narrow meeting of channels and swung about in confusion.

Which way! He swiveled about until the hunt cry echoed once more. Then there was a terrible crashing sound. He heard a squeal of outrage and pain, and the soft whine of a harness in operation. Another faint Trinary challenge was answered by a shivering scream and another crash.

Keepiru sprinted. It couldn't be far! He dashed, sparing none of his reserves, just as there came a final call of exhausted defiance.

> * For the honor
> Of Calafia ... *

The voice disappeared under a scream of savage triumph. Then there was silence.

It took him another five minutes, frantically casting about the narrow passages, to find the battleground. The taste of the water, when Keepiru sped into the quiet strait, told him he was too late.

He caught up short of entering a small vale between three metal-mounds. Coppery strands of dangle-weed floated overhead. Pink froth spread from the center of the tiny valley, with streamers of red in the direction of the prevailing currents. At the center, enmeshed in a tangle of wrecked harness parts, the body of a young *amicus* neo-fin, already partly dismembered, drifted belly up, teased and tugged at by the red jaws of a giant dolphin.

A giant dolphin? How, in all the time since they had left Earth, had he not noticed this before? Keepiru desperately reattached a fresh breather from his harness, and took gasping breaths while he watched and listened to the killer.

Look at the deep countershading, he told himself. *Look at the short jaw, the great teeth, the short, sharp dorsal fin.*

Listen to him!

K'tha-Jon grunted contentedly as he ripped a piece from Akki's side. The giant didn't even appear to notice a long burn along his left flank, or the bruise slowly spreading from the point where Akki's last desperate ramming had come home. Keepiru knew the monster was aware of him. K'tha-Jon lazily swallowed, then rose to the surface for air. When he descended he looked right at Keepiru.

'Well, Pilot?' he murmured happily.

Keepiru used Anglic, though the breather muffled the words.

'I've just dealt with one monster, K'tha-Jon, but *your* devolution fouls our entire race.'

K'tha-Jon's derision was a series of high snorts.

'You think I have reverted, like that pathetic *Stenosss* Moki, don't you, Pilot?'

Keepiru could only shake his head, unable to bring himself to say what he thought the bosun had become.

'Can a devolved dolphin speak Anglic as well as I?' K'tha-Jon

555

sneered. 'Or use logic thisss way? Would a reverted *Tursiops,* or even a pure *Stenosss,* have pursued an air-breathing prey with such determination . . . and satisssfaction?

'True, the crisis of the last few weeks allowed something deep within me to burssst free. But can you truly listen to me and then call me a *devolved dolphin?'*

Keepiru looked at the pink froth around the giant's stubby, powerful jaws. Akki's corpse drifted away slowly with the tide.

'I know what you are, K'tha-Jon.' Keepiru switched to Trinary.

> * Cold water boils
> > When you scream
> * Red-jawed hunger
> > Fills your dream.
> * Harpoons slew
> > The whales,
> * The nets of Iki
> > Caught us,
> * Yet you, alone
> > We feared at night
> * You alone—
> > . . . Orca.

K'tha-Jon's jaw gaped in satisfaction, as if he were accepting an accolade. He rose for air and returned a few meters closer to Keepiru, grinning.

'I guessssed the truth some time ago, I am one of the prized experiments of our beloved human-patron Ignacio Metz. That-t fool did one great thing, for all of his ssstupidity. Some of the others he snuck into berths on *Streaker did* revert or go mad. But *I* am a successs . . .'

'You are a calamity!' Keepiru spluttered, prevented by the breather from using words more to the point.

K'tha-Jon drifted closer still, causing Keepiru to back away involuntarily. The giant stopped again; a satisfied clicking emanated from his brow. 'Am I, Pilot? Can you, a simple fish-eater, understand your betters? Are you worthy to judge one whose forebears were at the top of the ocean food-chain? And dealt as judges of the sssea with all your kind?'

Keepiru was hardly listening, uncomfortably aware of the vanishing distance between himself and the monster.

'You arrogate t-too much. You have only a few gene splices from . . .'

'I am ORCA!' K'tha-Jon screamed. The cry echoed like a high

paean of bugles. 'The superficial body is *nothing!* It is the brain and *blood* that matter. *Listen* to me, and dare deny what I am!'

K'tha-Jon's jaw-clap was like a gunshot. The hunt cry pealed forth and Keepiru, under its direct focus, felt a deep instinct well up, a desire to tuck himself inward, to hide or die.

Keepiru resisted. He forced himself to assume an assertive body stance and bite out words of defiance.

'You *are* devolved, K'tha-Jon! Worse, you are a mutant thing, with no heritage at all. Metz's grafts went bad. Do you think-k a true Orca would do what you've done? They do hunt fallow dolphins on Earth, but never when sssated! The true killer whale does not kill out of spite!'

Keepiru defecated and flicked it in the giant's direction with his flukes.

'You are a failed experiment, K'tha-Jon! You say you're still logical, but now you have no home. And when my report gets back to Earth your gene-plasm will be poured into the sewers! Your line will end the way monsters end.'

K'tha-Jon's eyes gleamed. He swept Keepiru with sonar, as if to memorize every curve of an intended prey.

'What gave you the idea you were ever going to report-t-t?' he hissed.

Keepiru grinned open-mouthed. 'Why, the simple fact that you are a crippled, insane monster whose blunt snout couldn't stave in cardboard, whose maleness satisfies only pool-gratings, bringing forth nothing but stale water ...'

The giant screamed again, this time in rage. As K'tha-Jon charged, Keepiru whirled and darted into a side channel, fleeing just ahead of powerful jaws.

Tearing through a thick hedge of dangle-weed, Keepiru congratulated himself. By taunting K'tha-Jon into a personal vendetta he had made the creature forget entirely about his harness ... and the laser rifle. Now K'tha-Jon obviously intended to kill Keepiru the way he had finished off Akki.

Keepiru fled a bare body length ahead of the mutant.

So far so good, he thought as the sparkling metal hillsides rushed past.

But it proved hard to shake his pursuer. And the menacing jaws made Keepiru wonder if his strategy had been so wise, after all. The chase went on and on, while the afternoon waned. As the sun set they were at it, still.

In the darkness, it became purely a battle of wits and of sound.

The nocturnal denizens of the archipelago fled in dismay as two swift foreign monsters streaked in and out of the interisland channels, swerving and darting in streaming clouds of bubbles. As they swept by, they sprayed the depths and shallows with complex and confusing patterns of sound – compounded images and vivid illusions of echoes. Local fishes, even giants, fled the area, leaving it to the battling aliens.

It was an eerie game of image and shadow, of deception and sudden ambush.

Keepiru slid out of a narrow, silted channel and listened. It had been an hour since he last heard the hunt-scream, but that didn't mean K'tha-Jon was being silent. Keepiru built a mental map of the surrounding area from the reflections that came to him, and knew that some of those images were subtly crafted constructs. The giant was nearby, using his immensely talented sonic organs to place an overlay of untruth over the echoes of this place.

Keepiru wished he could see. But the midnight clouds cast everything into darkness. Only faintly phosphorescent plants illuminated the seascape.

He rose to the surface for breath, and looked at the faint, silvery underlining of the clouds. In a dismal, gloomy drizzle, the vegetation on the hulking metal-mounds swished and swayed.

Keepiru took seven breaths then descended again. Down below was where the battle would be settled.

Phantoms swam through the open channels. A false echo seemed to present an opening directly to the north, the direction Keepiru had been trying to lead the chase, but on careful examination he concluded it was an illusion.

Another such fake passage earlier had fooled him until, at the last moment, he had swerved away, too late to keep from slamming into the vine-covered verge of a metal-mound. Battered, he had fought free of the tangle just in time to escape a ramming. K'tha-Jon's giant muzzle missed him by inches. As he fled, Keepiru was struck by a grazing bolt from the laser rifle. It had seared a hot burn into his left side, hurting like bloody hell. Only his greater maneuverability had enabled him to escape that time, to find a refuge and ride out waves of pain.

He could probably elude the pseudo-Orca in time. But time was not on his side. K'tha-Jon had dedicated himself to a ritual hunt and spared no thought for anything beyond it. He did not plan to return to civilization. All he had to do was prevent Keepiru from reporting back, and trust Ignacio Metz to protect his birthright back on Earth.

Keepiru, though, had responsibilities. And *Streaker* wouldn't wait for him if she got a chance to flee.

Still, he thought. *Am I really trying all that hard to get away?*

He frowned and shook his head. Two hours ago he had been almost sure he had lost K'tha-Jon. Instead of making good his escape, he had turned around, under some rationalization he couldn't even remember now, until he picked up the giant's sound-scent again. His enemy felt him, too. In moments the hunt-scream pealed forth, and the mutant was after him again.

Why did I do that?

An idea glimmered for a moment ... the truth ... But Keepiru thrust it aside. K'tha-Jon was coming. He barely noticed the thrill of adrenaline that overcame the pain of his bruises and burns.

The illusions vanished like an unraveling bank of fog, dissolving into constituent clicks and whispers. In a swirl of powerful fluke strokes, the giant entered the channel below Keepiru. The white countershading of the sport's belly showed against the gloom as K'tha-Jon rose for air, then swam past Keepiru's niche, casting pulse-beams of search sonar in front of him.

Keepiru waited until the monster had passed, then rose to the surface himself. He blew softly five times, then sank without moving a fin.

The monster was ten meters away. Keepiru made no sound as K'tha-Jon ascended and blew again. But as the *Stenos* descended, Keepiru aimed a tight burst of clicks to carom off two metal-mounds across the channel.

The semi-Orca swerved quickly and dashed to Keepiru's left, passing almost beneath him, chasing the illusion.

Like a diving missile, Keepiru dropped, nose first, toward his enemy.

The hunter's senses were incredible, for all of Keepiru's unnatural quiet. K'tha-Jon heard something behind him and swiveled like a dervish to come upright in the water, half facing Keepiru.

The angle was suddenly wrong for a ramming or raking. The laser rifle swung toward him, and the giant jaws. To abort and flee would invite a total blast!

Keepiru had a sudden flash of memory. He remembered his tactics instructor at the academy, lecturing about the benefits of surprise.

'... *It's the one unique weapon in our arsenal, as sentient Earthlings, that others cannot duplicate* ...'

Keepiru accelerated, and pulled up in front of K'tha-Jon, coming belly to belly with the astonished creature. He grinned.

> * *Who can deny*
> *An attentive suitor—*
> * *Let's dance!* *

Keepiru's harness whined, and the three waldo-arms snapped out to grab K'tha-Jon's and lock them into place.

The stunned ex-bosun screamed in rage and snapped his jaws at Keepiru, but he couldn't bend far enough. He tried to lash out with his massive flukes, but Keepiru's tail flexed back and forth with his adversary's in perfect rhythm.

Keepiru felt an erection begin, and encouraged it. In adolescent erotic play between young male dolphins the dominant one usually took the male role. He prodded K'tha-Jon, and elicited a howl of dismay.

The giant writhed and shook. He bucked and kicked, then sped off in a random direction, filling the waters with his ululation. Keepiru held on tightly, knowing what K'tha-Jon's next tactic would be.

The semi-Orca sped slantwise toward a steep-sided metal-mound. Keepiru held still until K'tha-Jon was just about to slam into the wall, with him in between. Suddenly he arched, and swung his weight to one side in a savage jerk.

A giant he might be, but K'tha-Jon was no true Orca. Keepiru weighed enough to swing them about just before the collision. K'tha-Jon's right flank hit the wall of rugged metal coral, and bloody streaks of blubber were left behind.

K'tha-Jon swam on, shaking his head dizzily and leaving behind a bloody cloud. For the moment the monster seemed to lose interest in anything except air as he rose to the surface, and blew.

I'll be needing air very shortly, Keepiru realized. *But now's the time to strike!*

He tried to pull back to bring his short-range cutting torch into play.

It was caught! Locked into K'tha-Jon's harness rack! Keepiru tugged but it wouldn't come loose.

K'tha-Jon eyed him.

'Your t-turn, little-porp,' he grinned. 'You ssset me off there. But now all I have to do is keep you under water. It will be interesssting to lisssten to you beg for air!'

Keepiru wanted to curse, but he needed to save his strength. He struggled to force K'tha-Jon over onto his back so he could reach the surface, a bare meter away, but the half-Orca was ready and stopped his every move.

Think, Keepiru told himself. *I've got to think. If only I knew Keneenk better! If only . . .*

His lungs burned. Almost, he gave vent to a Primal distress call.

He recalled the last time he had been tempted by Primal. He replayed Toshio's voice, patron-chiding, then patron-soothing.

He remembered his private vow to die before sinking to the animal level ever again.

Of course! I am an idiotic, overrated fish! Why didn't I think!

First he sent a neural command jettisoning the torch. It was useless anyway. Then he set his harness arms in motion.

> * Those who choose
> Reversion's patterns
> * Need not space,
> Nor a spacer's tools *

With one claw he seized the neural link in the side of K'tha-Jon's head. The monster's eyes widened, but before he could do a thing, Keepiru wrenched the plug free, making sure to cause the maximum amount of pain and damage. While his enemy screamed, he ripped the cable out of its housing, rendering the harness permanently useless.

K'tha-Jon's harness arms, which had been pulsing under his, went dead. The tiny whine of the laser rifle was silenced. K'tha-Jon howled and thrashed.

Keepiru gasped for breath as the mutant's bucking brought them both briefly out of the water in a great leap. They crashed back underwater as he transferred his grip on K'tha-Jon's harness. He held on with two waldo-arms. '*Kootchie-Koo*,' he crooned as he brought the other into play, ready to tear into his enemy.

But in a writhing body twist, K'tha-Jon managed to fling him away. Keepiru sailed through the air, to land with a great splash on the other side of a narrow mudbank.

Puffing, they eyed each other across the tiny shoals. Then K'tha-Jon clapped his jaws and moved to find a way around the barrier. The chase was on again.

All subtlety went out of the fight with the coming of dawn. There were no more delicate sonic deceptions, no tasteful taunts. K'tha-Jon chased Keepiru with awesome single-mindedness. Exhaustion seemed to hold no meaning to the monster. Blood loss only seemed to feed his rage.

Keepiru dodged through the narrow channels, some as shallow as twelve inches, trying to run the wounded pseudo-Orca ragged before he himself collapsed. Keepiru no longer thought of getting away. This was a battle that could only end in victory or death.

But there seemed no limit to K'tha-Jon's stamina.

The hunt-scream echoed through the shallows. The monster was casting about, a few channels over.

'Pilot-t-t! Why do you fight-t-t? You know I have the food chain on my sssside!'

Keepiru blinked. How could K'tha-Jon bring *religion* into this?

Prior to uplift, the concept of the food chain as a mystical hierarchy had been central to cetacean morality – to the temporal portion of the Whale Dream.

Keepiru broadcast omnidirectionally.

'K'tha-Jon, you're insane. Jussst because Metz stuffed your zygote with a few mini-Orca genes, that doesn't give you the right to eat anybody!'

In the old days humans used to wonder why dolphins and many whales remained friendly to man after experiencing wholesale slaughter at his hands. Humans began to understand, a little, when they first tried to house Orcas and dolphins next to each other at ocean parks, and discovered, to their amazement, that the dolphins would leap over barriers to be with the killer whales ... so long as the Orcas weren't hungry.

In Primal, a cetacean did not blame a member of another race for killing him, not when that other race was higher on the food chain. For centuries cetaceans simply assumed that man was at the topmost rung, and begrudged only the *most* senseless of his killing sprees.

It was a code of honor which, when humans learned about it, made most of them more, not less ashamed of what had been done.

Keepiru slid out into the open channel to change his location, certain that K'tha-Jon had taken a fix from that last exchange.

There was something familiar about this area. Keepiru couldn't pin it down. Something to the taste of the water. It had the flavor of stale dolphin death.

> * *Eating – eaten*
> *Biting – bitten*
> * *Repay the sea ...*
> *Come and feed me!* *

Too close. K'tha-Jon's voice was much too near, chanting religious blasphemies. Keepiru headed for a crevice to take cover, and stopped suddenly as the death-taste became suddenly overpowering.

He nosed in slowly, and halted when he saw the skeleton suspended in the weeds.

'Hist-t!' he sighed.

The dolphin spacer had been missing since that first day, when the wave had stranded Hikahi and he had behaved like such a fool. The body had been picked clean by scavengers. The cause of death was not apparent.

I know where I am ... Keepiru thought. At that moment the hunt-scream pealed again. Close! Very close!

He whirled and darted back into the channel, saw a flash of movement, and dove out of the way even as a monstrous form plunged past him. He was knocked spinning by a whack from the giant's flukes.

Keepiru arched and darted away, though his side hurt as if a rib was broken. He called out.

> * *After me – reverted scoundrel*
> * *I know – now it's time to feed you* *

K'tha-Jon-roared in answer, and charged after him.

A body length ahead, now two, now a half, Keepiru knew he only had moments. The gaping jaws were right behind him. *It's near here*, he thought. *It's got to be!*

Then he saw another crevice and knew.

K'tha-Jon roared when he saw that Keepiru was trapped against the island.

> \# *Slow, slow*
> *or fast, fast –*
> \# *Time to feed me – feed me!* \#

'I'll feed you,' Keepiru gasped as he dove into the narrow-walled canyon. On all sides a dangling-weed bobbed, as if tugged by the tide.

> \# *Trapped! Trapped!*
> *I have you* ... \#

K'tha-Jon squawked in surprise. Keepiru shot to the surface of the crevice, struggling to reach the top before vines closed in around him. He surfaced and blew, inhaling heavily and clinging close to the wall.

Nearby the water churned and frothed. Keepiru watched and listened in awe, as K'tha-Jon struggled alone, without harness or any aid, tearing great ropes of the killer weed with his jaws, thrashing as strand after strand fell over his great body.

Keepiru was busy as well. He forced himself to remain calm and use his harness. The strong claws of his waldo-arms snapped the strands that grabbed at him. He recited his multiplication tables in order to stay in Anglic thought-patterns, dealing with the vines one at a time.

563

The half-Orca's struggle sent geysers of seawater and torn vegetation into the sky. The surface of the water soon became a beaten green-and-pink froth. The hunt-scream filled the cavern with defiance.

Minutes passed. The ropes that attempted to seize Keepiru grew fewer and fewer. More and more descended to fall upon the struggling giant. The hunt-scream came again, weaker – still defiant, but desperate, now.

Keepiru watched and listened as the battle began to subside. A strange sadness filled him, as if he almost regretted the end.

> # I told you – I would feed you *

He sang softly to the dying creature below.

> * But I did not say who—
> I would feed you to ... *

75

HIKAHI

Since nightfall she had hunted for the refugees, first slowly and cautiously, then with growing desperation. There came a point when she threw caution away and began broadcasting a sonar beacon for them to home in on.

Nothing! There were fen out there, but they ignored her totally!

Only after entering the maze did she get a good fix on the sound. Then she realized that one of the fen was desperately crazy, and that both were engaged in ritual combat, closing out all the universe until the battle was over.

Of all the things that could have happened, this stunned Hikahi most of all. Ritual combat? Here? What did this have to do with the silence from *Streaker*?

She had an uneasy feeling that *this* ritual battle was to the death.

Hikahi set the sonar on automatic and let the skiff guide itself. She napped, letting one hemisphere and then the other go into alpha state as the little ship slid through the narrow channels, always headed northeastward.

She snapped out of a snooze to the sound of a loud buzzer. The

skiff was stopped. Her instruments showed traces of cetacean movement just beyond a sheer shelf of metallic rock, heading slowly
westward.

Hikahi activated the hydrophones.

'Whoever you are,' her voice boomed through the water. 'Come
out at once!'

There was a faint query sound, a weary, confused whistle.

'*This* way, idiot-t! Follow my voice!'

Something moved out from a broad channel between islands.
She snapped on the skiff's spotlights. A gray dolphin blinked back in
the sharp glare.

'Keepiru!' Hikahi gasped.

The pilot's body was a mass of bruises, and one side bore a savage
burn, but he smiled nevertheless.

> * Ah, the gentle rains –
> Dear lady, for you to come
> And rescue me ... *

The smile faded like a quenched fire and his eyes rolled. Then, on
pure instinct, his half-unconscious body rose to the surface, to drift
until she came for him.

PART EIGHT

THE 'TROJAN SEAHORSE'

Ebony half-moons that soar
From pools where the half light begins
To set when, on what far shore,
Dolphins? Dolphins?

HAMISH MACLAREN

76

GALACTICS

Beie Chohooan cursed the parsimony of her superiors.

If the Synthian High Command had sent a mothership to observe the battle of the fanatics, she might have been able to approach the war zone in a flitter – a vessel too small to be detected. As it was, she had been compelled to use a starship large enough to travel through transfer points and hyperspace, too small to defend itself adequately, and too large to sneak past the combatants.

She almost fired upon the tiny globe that nosed around the asteroid that sheltered her ship. Just in time she recognized the little wazoon-piloted probe. She pressed a stud to open a docking port, but the wazoon hung back, sending a frantic series of tight laser pulses.

Your position discovered, *it flashed.* Enemy missiles closing . . .

Beie uttered her vilest damnations. Every time she almost got close enough to 'cast a message through the jamming to the Earthlings, she had to flee from some random, paranoid tentacle of battle.

Come in quickly and dock! *She tapped out a command to the wazoon.* Too many of the loyal little clients had died for her already.

Negative. Flee, Beie. Wazoo-two will distract . . .

Beie snarled at the disobedience. The three wazoon who remained on the shelf to her left cringed and blinked their large eyes at her.

The scout globe sped off into the night.

Beie closed the port and fired up her engines. Carefully, she weaved her way through the lanes between chunks of primordial stone, away from the area of danger.

Too late, *she thought as she glanced at the threat board. The missiles were closing too fast.*

A sudden glare from behind told of the fate of the little wazoon. Beie's whiskered upper lip curled as she contemplated a suitable way to get even with the fanatics, if she ever got a chance.

Then the missiles arrived, and she was suddenly too busy even for nasty, pleasant thoughts.

She blasted two missiles to vapor with her particle gun. Two others fired back; their beams were barely refracted by her shields.

Ah, Earthlings, *she contemplated.* You'll not even know I was ever here. For all you know, you have been forsaken by all the universe.

But don't let that stop you, wolflings. Fight on! Snarl at your pursuers! And when all your weapons fail, *bite them!*

Beie destroyed four more missiles before one managed to explode close by, sending her broken ship spinning, burning, into the dusty Galactic dark.

77

TOSHIO

The night blew wet with scattered blustery sheets of rain. Glossy broadleaf plants waved uncertainly under contrary gusts from a wind that seemed unable to decide on a direction. The dripping foliage glistened when two of Kithrup's nearby tiny moons shone briefly through the clouds.

At the far southern end of the island, a crude thatch covering allowed rain to seep through in slow trickles. It dripped onto the finely pitted hull of a small spaceship. The water formed small meniscus pools atop the gently curving metal surface, then ran off in little rivulets. The tappity-tap of the heavy raindrops hitting the thatch was joined by a steady patter as streams of runoff poured onto smashed mud and vegetation beneath the cylindrical flying machine.

The trickles sluiced over stubby stasis flanges and sent jagged trails over the forward viewports, dark and clear in the intermittent moonlight. Trails penetrated the narrow cracks around the aft airlock, using the straight channels to pour dribbling streams onto the muddy ground.

There came a tiny mechanical hiss, barely louder than the rainfall. The cracks around the airlock widened almost imperceptibly. Neighboring streams merged to fill the new crevices. A pool began to form in a dirt basin below the hatch.

The doorway cracked a little farther. More trickles merged to pour in, as if seeking to enter the ship. All at once a gurgling stream poured from the bottom of the crack. The flow became a gushing waterfall. Then, just as abruptly, the torrent subsided.

The armored hatch slid open with a muted sigh. Rain sent a flurry of slanting droplets pelting into the opening.

A dark, helmeted figure stood in the threshold, ignoring the onslaught. It turned to look left and right, then stepped out and splashed in the puddle. The hatch shut again with a whine and a small click.

The figure bent into the wind, searching in the darkness for a trail.

*

Dennie sat up suddenly at the sound of wet footsteps. With her hand at her breast she whispered.

'Toshio?'

The tent's fly was pushed aside and the flap zipped open. For a moment a dark shape loomed. Then a quiet voice whispered. 'Yeah, it's me.'

Dennie's rapid pulse subsided. 'I was afraid it was somebody else.'

'Who'd you expect, Charlie Dart? Come out of his tent to ravish you? Or, better yet, one of the Kiqui?' He teased her gently, but could not hide the tension in his voice. He shrugged out of his drysuit and helmet, which he hung on a peg by the opening. In his underwear, Toshio crawled over to his own sleeping bag and slid in.

'Where have you been?'

'Nowhere. Go back to sleep, Dennie.'

The rain pattered on the fly in an uneven tattoo. She remained sitting up, looking at him in the faint light from the opening. She could see little more than the whites of his eyes, staring straight up at nothing.

'Please Tosh, tell me. When I woke up and you weren't in your sleeping bag ...' Her voice trailed off as he turned to look back at her. The difference that had grown in Toshio Iwashika the last week or so was never more manifest than in his narrowed expression, than this slitted intensity in his eyes.

She heard him sigh finally. 'All right, Dennie. I was just over at the longboat. I snuck inside and had a look around.'

Dennie's pulse sped again. She started to speak, stopped, then finally said, 'Wasn't that dangerous? I mean there's no telling how Takkata-Jim might react! Especially if he really is a traitor.'

Toshio shrugged. 'There was something I had to find out.'

'But how could you get in and out without being caught?'

Toshio rolled over onto one elbow. She saw a brief flash of white as he smiled slightly. 'A middie sometimes knows things even the engineering officers never find out, Dennie. Especially when it comes to hiding places aboard ship. When off-duty time comes, there's always a pilot or a lieutenant around thinking up homework for idle hands and fins ... always just a *little* more astrogation or protocol to study, for instance. Akki and I used to grab sack time in the hold of the longboat. We learned how to open the locks without it flashing on the control room.'

Dennie shook her head. 'I'm glad you didn't tell me you were going, after all. I would have died of worry.'

Toshio frowned. Now Dennie was beginning to sound like his mother again. She still wasn't happy about having to leave while he stayed behind. Toshio hoped she wouldn't take this opportunity to bring up the subject again.

Dennie lay down and faced him, using her arm as a pillow. She thought for a moment, then whispered. 'What did you find out?'

Toshio closed his eyes. 'You might as well know,' he said. 'I'll want you to tell Gillian in case I can't get through to her in the morning. I found out what Takkata-Jim is doing with those bombs he took from Charlie.'

'He's converting them to fuel for the longboat.'

Dennie blinked. 'But ... but what can we do about it?'

'I don't know! I'm not even sure we *have* to do anything about it. After all, in a couple weeks his accumulators would be recharged enough to lift off, anyway. Maybe Gillian doesn't care.

'On the other hand, it might be darned important. I still haven't figured it all out yet. I may have to do something pretty drastic.'

He had seen the partially dismantled bombs through the thick window of the security door to the longboat's specimen lab. Getting to them would be considerably more difficult than simply sneaking back aboard.

'Whatever happens,' he tried to reassure her, 'I'm sure it will all be all right. You just make certain your notes are all packed properly in the morning. That data on the Kiqui is the second most important thing to come out of this crazy odyssey, and it's got to get back. Okay?'

'Sure, Tosh.'

He let gravity pull him over onto his back. He closed his eyes and breathed slowly to feign sleep.

'Toshio?'

The young man sighed. 'Yes, Denn ...'

'Um, it's about Sah'ot. He's only leaving to escort me. Otherwise I think you'd have a mutiny on your hands.'

'I know. He wants to stay and listen to those underground "voices" of his.' Toshio rubbed his eyes, wondering why Dennie was keeping him awake with all this. He already had listened to Sah'ot's importunities.

'Don't shrug them off like that, Tosh. He says Creideiki listened to them, too, and that he had to cut the channel to break the captain out of a trance, the sounds were so fascinating.'

'The captain is a brain-damaged cripple.' The words were bitter. 'And Sah'ot is an egocentric, unstable ...'

'I used to think so too,' Dennie interrupted. 'He used to scare me until I learned he was really quite sweet and harmless. But even if we could suppose the two fen were having hallucinations, there's the stuff I've been finding out about the metal-mounds.'

572

'Mmmph,' Toshio commented sleepily. 'What is it? More about the metal-mounds being alive?'

Dennie winced a little at his mild disparagement. 'Yes, and the weird eco-niche of the drill-trees. Toshio, I did an analysis on my pocketcomp, and there's only one possible solution! The drill-tree shafts are part of the life cycle of one organism – an organism that lives part of its life cycle above the surface as a superficially simple coral colony, and later falls into the pit prepared for it . . .'

'All that clever adaptation and energy expended to dig a grave for itself?' Toshio cut in.

'No! Not a grave! A channel! The metal-mound is only the *beginning* of this creature's life cycle . . . the *larval* stage. Its destiny as an adult form lies below, below the shallow crust of the planet, where convective veins of magma can provide all the energy a metallo-organic life form might ever need!'

Toshio tried earnestly to pay attention, but his thoughts kept drifting – to bombs, to traitors, to worry over Akki, his missing comrade, and to a man somewhere far to the north, who deserved to have someone waiting for him if – *when* he finally returned to his island launching point.

' . . . only thing wrong is there's no way I see that such a life form could have evolved! There's no sign of intermediate forms, no mention of any possible precursors in the old *Library* records on Kithrup . . . and this is certainly unique enough a life form to merit mention!'

'Mmm-hmmm.'

Dennie looked over at Toshio. His arm was over his eyes and he breathed slowly as if drifting off into slumber. But she saw a fine vein on his temple pulse rapidly, and his other fist clenched at even intervals.

She lay there watching him in the dimness. She wanted to shake him and *make* him listen to her!

Why am I pestering him like this? she suddenly asked herself. *Sure, the stuff's important, but it's all intellectual, and Toshio's got our corner of the world on his shoulders. He's so young, yet he's carrying a fighting man's load now.*

How do I feel about that?

A queasy stomach told her. *I'm pestering him because I want attention.*

I want his *attention,* she corrected. *In my clumsy way I've been trying to give him opportunities to* . . .

Nervously, she faced her own foolishness.

If I, the older one, can get my signals this crossed, I can hardly expect him *to figure out the cues,* she realized at last.

Her hand reached out. It stopped just short of the glossy black hair that lay in long, wet strands over his temples. Trembling, she looked again at her feelings, and saw only fear of rejection holding her back.

As if on a will of its own, her hand moved to touch the soft stubble on Toshio's cheek. The youth started and turned to look at her, wide-eyed.

'Toshio,' she swallowed. 'I'm cold.'

78

TOM ORLEY

When there came a moment of relative calm, Tom made a mental note. *Remind me next time*, he told himself, *not to go around kicking hornets' nests.*

He sucked on one end of the makeshift breathing tube. The other end protruded from the surface of a tiny opening in the weedscape. Fortunately, he didn't have to pull in quite so much air this time, to supplement what his mask provided. There was more dissolved oxygen in this area.

Battle beams sizzled overhead again, and weak cries carried to him from the miniature war going on above. Twice, the water trembled from nearby explosions.

At least this time I don't have to worry about being baked by the near misses, he consoled himself. *All these stragglers have are hand weapons.*

Tom smiled at that irony. *All* they had were hand weapons.

He had picked off two of the Tandu in that first ambush, before they could snap up their particle guns to fire back. More importantly, he managed to wing the shaggy Episiarch before diving head-first into a hole in the weeds.

He had cut it close. One near-miss had left second-degree burns on the sole of his bare left foot. In that last instant he glimpsed the Episiarch rearing in outrage, a nimbus of unreality coruscating like a fiery halo around its head. Tom thought he momentarily saw stars through that wavering brilliance.

The Tandu flailed to stay upon their wildly bucking causeway. That probably was what spoiled their much vaunted aim, and accounted for his still being alive.

As he had expected, the Tandu's vengeance hunt had led them

westward. He popped up, from time to time, to keep their interest keen with brief enfilades of needles.

Then, as he swam between openings in the weedscape, the battle seemed to take off without him. He heard sounds of combat and knew his pursuers had come into contact with another party of ET stragglers.

Tom had left then, underwater, in search of other mischief to do.

The battle noise drifted away from his present position. From his brief glimpse an hour ago, this particular skirmish seemed to involve a half-dozen Gubru and three battered, balloon-tired rover machines of some type. Tom hadn't been able to tell if they were robots or crewed, but they had seemed unable to adapt to the tricky surface, for all of their firepower.

He listened for a minute, then coiled his tube and put it away in his waistband. He rose quietly to the surface of the tiny pool and risked lifting his eyes to the level of the interwoven loops of weed.

In his mosquito raids, he had moved ever toward the eggshell wreck. Now he saw that it was only a few hundred meters away. Two smoking ruins told of the fate of the wheeled machines. As he watched, first one, then the other slowly sank out of sight. Three slime-covered Gubru, apparently the last of their party, struggled over the morass toward the floating ship. Their feathers were plastered against their slender, hawk-beaked bodies. They looked desperately unhappy.

Tom rose up and saw flashes of more fighting to the south.

Three hours before, a small Soro scoutship had come diving in, strafing all in sight, until a delta-winged Tandu atmospheric fighter swooped out of the clouds to intercept it. They blasted away at each other, harassed by small arms fire from below, until they finally collided in a fiery explosion, falling to the sea in a tangled heap.

About an hour later the story had repeated itself. This time the participants were a lumbering Pthaca rescue-tender and a battered spearship of the Brothers of the Night. Their wreckage joined the smoky ruins which slowly subsided in every direction.

No food, no place to hide, and the only race of fanatics I really want *to see is the one not represented out here in this dribble-drabble charnel house.*

The message bomb pressed under his waistband. Again, he wished he knew whether or not to use it.

Gillian has to be worried by now, he thought. *Thank God, at least she's safe.*

And the battle's still going on. That means there's still time. We've still got a chance.

Yes. And dolphins like to go for long walks along the beach.

Ah, well. Let's see if there's some more trouble I can cause.

79

GALACTICS

The Soro, Krat, cursed at the strategy schematic. Her clients took the precaution of backing away while she vented her anger by tearing great rips out of the vletoor cushion.

Four ships lost! To only one by the Tandu! The recent battle had been a disaster!

And meanwhile, the sideshow down at the planet's surface was bleeding away her small support craft in ones and twos!

It seemed that tiny remnants of all of the defeated fleets, stragglers that had hidden out on moons or planetoids, must have decided the Earthlings were hiding near that volcano down in Kithrup's mid-northern latitudes. Why did they think that?

Because surely nobody would be fighting over nothing at all, would they? The skirmish had a momentum all its own by now. Who would have thought that the defeated alliances would have hidden away so much firepower for one last desperate attempt at the prize?

Krat's mating claw flexed in wrath. She couldn't afford to ignore the possibility that they were right. What if the distress call had, indeed, emanated from the Earthlings' ship? No doubt this was some sort of fiendish human distraction, but she could not risk the chance that the fugitives actually were there.

'Have the Thennanin called yet?' she snapped.

A Pil from the communications section bowed quickly and answered. 'Not yet, Fleet-Mother, though they have pulled away from their Tandu allies. We expect to hear from Buoult soon.'

Krat nodded curtly. 'Let me know the very instant!' The Pil assented hurriedly and backed away.

Krat went back to considering her options. Finally, it came down to deciding which damaged and nearly useless vessel she could spare from the coming battle for one more foray to the planet's surface.

Briefly, she toyed with the idea of sending a Thennanin ship, once the upcoming alliance against the now-pre-eminent Tandu was consummated. But then she decided that would be unwise. Best to keep the priggish, sanctimonious Thennanin up here where she could keep her eyes on them. She would choose one of her own small cripples to go.

Krat contemplated a mental image of the Earthlings – dough-skinned, spindly, shaggy-maned humans, who were sneakiness embodied – and their weird, squawking, handless dolphin clients.

When they are finally mine, *she thought*, I will make them regret the trouble they are causing me.

<h1 style="text-align:center">80</h1>

THE JOURNAL OF GILLIAN BASKIN

We've arrived.

For the last four hours I've been the matriarch of a madhouse. Thank heaven for Hannes and Tsh't and Lucky Kaa and all the beautiful, competent fen we've missed for so long. I hadn't realized until we arrived just how many of the best had been sent ahead to prepare our new home.

There was an ecstatic reunion. Fen dashed about bumping each other and making a racket that I kept telling myself the Galactics couldn't really hear ... The only pall came when we thought about the absent members of our crew, the six missing fen, including Hikahi, Akki, and Keepiru. And Tom, of course.

It wasn't until later that we discovered that Creideiki was gone, also.

After a brief celebration, we got to work. Lucky Kaa took the helm, almost as sure and steady as Keepiru would have been, and piloted Streaker *along a set of guide rails into the cavity in the Thennanin wreck. Giant clamps came down and girdled* Streaker, *almost making her part of the outer shell. It's a snug fit. Techs immediately started integrating the sensors and tuning the impedances of the stasis flanges. The thrusters are already aligned. Carefully disguised weapons ports have been opened, in case we have to fight.*

What an undertaking! I never would have thought it possible. I can't believe the Galactics will expect anything like this. Tom's imagination is astounding.

If only we would hear his signal ...

I've asked Toshio to send Dennie and Sah'ot here by sled. If they take a direct route at top speed they should arrive in a little over a day. It'll take that long, at least, to finish setting up here.

It really is vital we get Dennie's notes and plasma samples. If Hikahi reports in, I'll ask her to stop at the island for the Kiqiti emissaries: Second only to our need to escape with our data is our duty to the little amphibians, to *save them from indenture to some crazy race of Galactic patrons.*

Toshio chose to stay to keep an eye on Takkata-Jim and Metz, and to meet Tom, should he show up. I think he added that last part knowing it would make it impossible for me to refuse . . . Of course, I knew he'd make the offer. I was counting on it.

It only makes me feel worse, using him to keep Takkata-Jim in check. Even if our ex-vice-captain disappoints me, and behaves himself, I don't know how Toshio's to get back here in time, especially if we have to take off in a hurry.

I'm learning what they mean by the 'agony of command.'

I had to pretend shocked surprise when Toshio told me about the mini-bombs Charlie Dart stole out of the armory. Toshio offered to try to get them back from Takkata-Jim, but I've forbidden it. I told him we'd take our chances.

I couldn't take him into my confidence. Toshio is a bright young man, but he has no poker face.

I think I have things timed right. If only I were certain.

The damned Niss is calling me again. This time I'll go see what it wants.

Oh, Tom. Would you, if you were here, have misplaced an entire ship's captain? How can I forgive myself for letting Creideiki go out there alone?

He seemed to be doing so well, though. What in Ifni's crap-shoot went wrong?

81

CHARLES DART

Early in the morning he was at his console at the water's edge, happily conversing with his new robot. It was already down a kilometer, planting tiny detectors in the drill-tree shaft wall along the way.

Charles Dart mumbled cheerfully. In a few hours he would have it down as deep as the old one, the next-to-worthless probe he had abandoned. Then, after a few more tests to verify his theories about local crustal formations, he could start finding out about bigger questions, like what Kithrup the *planet* was like.

Nobody, but nobody, could stop him now!

He remembered the years he had spent in California, in Chile, in Italy, studying earthquakes as they happened, working with some of the greatest minds in geophysical science. It had been exciting. Still, after a few years he had begun to realize that something was wrong.

He had been admitted into all the right professional societies, his papers were greeted with both high praise and occasional vehement rejection – both reactions far preferred by any decent scientist over yawns. There was no lack of prestigious job offers.

But there came a time when he suddenly wondered where the *students* were.

Why didn't graduate students seek him out as an advisor? He saw his colleagues besieged by eager applicants for research assistantships, yet, in spite of his list of publications, his widely known and controversial theories, only the second-raters came to him, students searching more for grant support than a mentor. None of the bright young mels and fems sought him out as an academic patron.

Of course, there had been a couple of minor cases in which his temper had gotten the better of him, and one or two of his students had departed acrimoniously, but that couldn't account for the doldrums in the pedagogical side of his career, could it?

Slowly, he came to think that it must be something else. Something . . . racial.

Dart had always held himself aloof from the uplift obsession of many chimps – either the fastidious respectfulness of the majority toward humans, or the sulking resentfulness of a small but vocal minority. A couple of years ago he began paying attention, however. Soon he had a theory. The students were avoiding him because he was a chimpanzee!

It had stunned him. For three solid months he dropped everything to study the problem. He read the protocols governing humanity's patronhood over his race, and grew outraged over the ultimate authority Mankind held over his species – until, that is, he read about uplift practice in the galaxy at large. Then he learned that no other patron gave a four-hundred-year-old client race seats on its high councils, as Mankind did.

Charles Dart was confused. But then he thought about that word 'gave.'

He read about humanity's age-old racial struggles. Had it really been less than half a millennium since humans contrived gigantic, fatuous lies about each other simply because of pigment shades, and killed millions because they believed their own lies?

He learned a new word, 'tokenism,' and felt a burning shame. That was when he volunteered for a deep space mission, determined not to return without *proof* of his academic prowess – his skill as a scientist on a par with any human!

Alas that he had been assigned to *Streaker*, a ship filled with squeaking dolphins, and *water*. To top it off, that smugpot Ignacio

Metz immediately started treating him like another of his unfinished experimental half-breeds!

He'd learned to live with that. Even cosied up with Metz. He would bear anything until the results from Kithrup were announced.

Then they'll stand up as Charles Dart enters rooms! The bright young human students will come to him. They'll all see that *he*, at least, is no token!

Charlie's deep thoughts were interrupted by sounds from the forest nearby. He hurriedly slapped the cover plate over a set of controls in a lower corner of his console. He was taking no chances with anyone finding out about the *secret* part of his experiment.

Dennie Sudman and Toshio Iwashika emerged from the village trail, talking in low voices, carrying small bundles. Charlie busied himself with detailed commands to the robot; but cast a surreptitious eye toward the humans, wondering if they suspected anything.

But no. They were too much into each other, touching, caressing, murmuring. Charlie snorted under his breath at the human preoccupation with sex, day in, day out; but he grinned and waved when they glanced his way.

They don't suspect a thing, he congratulated himself, as they waved back, then turned to their own concerns. How lucky for me they're in love.

'I still want to stay. What if Gillian's wrong? What if Takkata-Jim finishes converting the bombs early?'

Toshio shrugged. 'I still have something he needs.' He glanced down at the second of two sleds in the pool, the one that had belonged to Tom Orley. 'Takkata-Jim won't take off without it.'

'Exactly!' Dennie was emphatic. 'He'd need that radio, or the ETs would blast him to bits before he could negotiate. But you'll be all alone! That fin is dangerous!'

'That's just one of many reasons I'm sending you away right now.'

'Is this the big, macho mel talking?' Dennie tried sarcasm, but was unable to put much bite into it.

'No.' Toshio shook his head. 'This is your military commander talking. And that's that. Now let's get these last samples loaded. I'll escort you and Sah'ot a few miles before we say good-bye.'

He bent over to pick up one of the parcels, but before he touched it he felt a hand in the small of his back. A sharp push threw him off balance, flailing.

'Denneee!' He caught a glimpse of her, grinning devilishly. At the last moment his left hand darted out and caught hers. Her laughter turned into a shriek as he dragged her after him into the water.

They came up, spluttering, between the sleds. Dennie cried out in triumph as she grabbed the top of his head with both hands and dunked him. Then she leapt half out of the water as something goosed her from behind.

'Toshio!' she accused.

'That wasn't me.' He caught his breath and backed out of arms' reach. 'It must have been your other lover.'

'My ... Oh, no! Sah'ot!' Dennie whirled around searching and kicking, then whooped as something got her from behind again. 'Do you scrotum-brained males ever think of anything *else?*'

A mottled gray dolphin's head broached the surface nearby. The breather wrapped over his blowmouth only muted his chattering laughter slightly.

> * Long before humans
>> Rowed out on logs—
> * We made an invention
>
> * Care to
>> Manage a try—
> * At
>> Menage a trois? *

He leered, and Toshio had to laugh as Dennie blushed. That only set her splashing water at him until he swam over and pinned her arms against one of the sleds. To stop her imprecations he kissed her.

Her lips bore the desperate tang of Kithrup as she kissed him back. Sah'ot sidled up alongside them, and nibbled their legs softly with jagged, sharp teeth.

'You know we're not supposed to expose ourselves to this stuff if we can help it,' Toshio told her as they held each other. 'You shouldn't have done that.'

Dennie shook her head, then buried her face in his shoulder to hide it.

'Who are we fooling, Tosh?' she mumbled. 'Why worry about slow metal poisoning? We'll be dead long before our gums start to turn blue.'

'Aw, Dennie. That's nuts ...' He sought words to comfort her, but found that all he could do was hold her close as the dolphin wrapped himself around them both.

A few minutes later a comm alert buzzed. Sah'ot went over to the unit on Orley's sled, the one connected by monofilament cable to *Streaker*'s old position. He listened to a brief burst of primitive clicks, then squawked quickly in reply. He rose high in the water, popping his breather loose.

'It's for you, Toshio!'

Toshio didn't bother asking if it was important. Over that line it had to be. Gently, he disengaged from Dennie. 'You finish packing. I'll be back right away to help.'

She nodded, rubbing her eyes ...

'Stay with her a while, will you, Sah'ot?' he asked as he swam over to the comm unit. The *Stenos* shook his head.

'I would gladly, Toshio. It'sss my turn to amuse the lady. Unfortunately, you need me here to translate.'

Toshio looked at him uncomprehendingly.

'It is the captain,' Sah'ot informed him. 'Creideiki wants to talk to both of usss. Then he wants us to help him get in touch with the techno-inhabitants of this world.'

'Creideiki? Calling here? But Gillian said he was missing!' Toshio's brow furrowed as the rest of Sah'ot's sentence sunk in.

'Techno ... He wants to talk to the *Kiqui?*'

Sah'ot grinned.

'No, sir; they hardly qualify, fearless military leader. Our captain wants to talk with my "voices." He wants to talk to those who dwell below.'

82

TOM ORLEY

The Brother of Twelve Shadows piped softly. His pleasure spread through the waters around him, below the carpet of weeds. He swam away from the site of the ambush, the faint thrashing sounds of victims dying down behind him.

The darkness beneath the weeds didn't bother him. Never would absence of light displease a Brother of the Night.

'Brother of the Dim Gloom,' he hissed. 'Do you rejoice as I do?'

From somewhere to his left, amongst the dangling sea vines, came a jubilant reply.

'I rejoice, Senior Brother. That group of Paha warriors shall never again kneel before perverted Soro females. Thank the ancient warlords.'

'We shall thank them in person,' Brother of Twelve Shadows answered, 'when we learn the location of their returning fleet from the half-sentient Earthers. For now, thank our long-deceased Nighthunter patrons, who made us such formidable fighters.'

'I thank their spirits, Senior Brother.'

They swam on, separated by the three score body lengths demanded by underwater skirmish doctrine. The pattern was inconvenient with all these weeds about, and the water echoed strangely, but doctrine was doctrine, as unquestionable as instinct.

Senior Brother listened until the last weak struggles of the drowning Paha ceased. Now he and his fellow would swim toward one of the floating wrecks, where more victims surely awaited.

It was like picking fruits from a tree. Even powerful warriors such as the Tandu were reduced to floundering dolts on this carpet of noxious weeds, but not the Brothers of the Night! Adaptable, mutable, they swam *below*, wreaking havoc where it could be wrought.

His gill-slits pulsed, sucking the metal-tangy water through. The Brother of Twelve Shadows detected a patch of slightly higher oxygen content and took a slight detour to pass through it. Keeping to doctrine was important, surely, but here, underwater, what could harm them?

There was suddenly a flurry of crashing sounds to his left, a brief cry, and then silence.

'Lesser Brother, what was that disturbance?' he called in the direction his surviving partner had been. But speech carried poorly underwater. He waited with growing anxiety.

'Brother of the Dim Gloom!'

He dove beneath a cluster of hanging tendrils, holding a flechette gun in each of his four tool-hands.

What, down here, could have overcome so formidable a fighter as his lesser brother? Surely none of the patrons or clients he knew of could do such a thing. A robot should have caused his metal detectors to go off.

It suddenly occurred to him that the half-sentient 'dolphins' they sought might be dangerous in water.

But no. Dolphins were air-breathers. And they were large. He swept the area around him and heard no likely reflections.

The Eldest Brother – who commanded the remnants of their flotilla from a cave on a small moon – had concluded that the Earthlings were not here in this northern sea, but he had sent a small vessel to harass and observe. The two brothers in the water were all that survived, but everything they had seen confirmed the quarry wasn't here.

The Brother of Twelve Shadows quickly skirted the edge of an open pool. Had his younger brother strayed into the open and been blasted by a walker above?

He swam toward a faint sound, weapons ready.

In the darkness he sensed a bulky body up ahead. He chirped out, and concentrated on the complex echoes.

The returning sounds showed only one large creature in the vicinity, still and silent.

He swam forward, took hold of it, and mourned. Water pulsed through his gill-slits and he cried out.

> *'I am going to avenge you, Brother!*
> *'I am going to slay all in this sea who think!*
> *'I am going to bring darkness upon all who hope!*
> *'I am going to ...'*

There came a loud splash. He let out a brief 'urk' as something heavy fell from *above* onto his right side and wrapped long legs and arms around him. As the Brother of Twelve Shadows struggled, he realized in stupefaction that his enemy was a human! A half-sentient, frail-skinned, wolfling *human*!

'Before you do all those other things, there's one thing you'll do first,' the voice rasped in Galactic Ten, just behind his hearing organs.

The Brother wailed. Something fiery sharp pierced his throat near the dorsal nerve-chord.

He heard his enemy say, almost sympathetically,

'You are going to die.'

83

GILLIAN

'All I can tell you, Gillian Baskin, is that he knew how to find me. He came here aboard a "walker," and spoke to me from the hallway.'

'Creideiki was *here*? Tom and I figured he'd deduce we had a private high-level computer, but the location should have been impossible ...'

'I was not terribly surprised, Doctor Baskin,' the Niss machine interrupted, covering the impoliteness with a soothing pattern of abstract images. 'The captain clearly knows his ship. I had expected him to guess my location.'

Gillian sat by the door and shook her head. 'I should have come when you first signaled for me. I might have been able to stop him from leaving.'

'It is not your fault,' the machine answered with uncharacteristic sensitivity. 'I would have made the request more demanding if I thought the situation urgent.'

'Oh sure,' Gillian was sarcastic. 'It's not urgent when a valuable fleet officer succumbs to pressure atavism and gets lost in a deadly alien wilderness!'

The patterns danced. 'You are mistaken. Captain Creideiki has not fallen prey to reversion schizophrenia.'

'How would you know?' Gillian said hotly. 'Over a third of the crew of this vessel have shown signs since the ambush at Morgran, including all but a few of the *Stenos*-grafted fen. How can you say Creideiki hasn't reverted after all he's suffered? How can he practice Keneenk when he can't even talk!'

The Niss answered calmly. 'He came here seeking specific information. He knew I had access not only to *Streaker*'s micro-branch *Library*, but the more complete one taken from the Thennanin wreck. He could not tell me what it was he wanted to know, but we found a way to get across the speech barrier.'

'How?' Gillian was fascinated in spite of her anger and guilt.

'By pictograms, visual and sound pictures of alternate choices which I presented to him quite rapidly. He made quick yes or no sounds to tell when I was getting – as you humans say – hotter or colder. Before long he was leading *me*, making associations I had not even begun to consider.'

'Like what?'

The light-motes sparkled. 'Like the way many of the mysteries regarding this unique world seem to come together, the strangely long time this planet has lain fallow since its last tenants became degenerate and settled here to die, the unnatural ecological niche of the so-called- drill-tree mounds, Sah'ot's strange "voices from the depths" ...'

'Dolphins of Sah'ot's temperament are *always* hearing "voices."' Gillian sighed. 'And don't forget he's another of those experimental *Stenos*. I'm sure some of them were passed into this crew without the normal stress tests.'

After a short pause, the machine answered matter-of-factly.

'There is evidence, Doctor Baskin. Apparently Doctor Ignacio Metz is a representative of an impatient faction at the Center for Uplift ...'

Gillian stood up. 'Uplift! Dammit! I *know* what Metz did! You think I'm blind? I've lost several dear friends and irreplaceable crewmates because of his crazy scheme. Oh, he "hot-tested" his sports, all right. And some of the new models failed under pressure!

'But all that's finished! What does uplift have to do with voices from below, or drill-tree mounds, or the history of Kithrup, or our

585

friendly cadaver Herbie, for that matter? What does *any* of it have to do with rescuing our lost people and getting away from here!'

Her heart raced, and Gillian found that her fists were clenched.

'Doctor Baskin,' the Niss replied smoothly. 'That was exactly what I asked your Captain Creideiki. When he put the pieces together for me I, too, realized that uplift is not an irrelevant question here. It is the only question. Here at Kithrup all that is good and evil about this several-billion-year-old system is represented. It is almost as if the very basis of Galactic society has been placed on trial.'

Gillian blinked at the abstract images.

'How ironic,' the disembodied voice went on, 'that the question rests with you humans, the first sophont race in aeons to claim "evolved" intelligence.

'Your discovery in the so-called Shallow Cluster may result in a war that fills the Five Galaxies, or it may fade away like so many other chimerical crises. But what is done here on Kithrup will become a legend. All of the elements are there.

'And legends have a tendency to affect events long after wars are forgotten.'

Gillian stared at the hologram for a long moment. Then she shook her head.

'Will you please tell me what the bloody damn *hell* you are *talking* about?'

84

HIKAHI/KEEPIRU

'We mussst hurry!' the pilot insisted.

Keepiru lay strapped to a porta-doc. Catheters and tubes ran from the webbing that kept him suspended above the water's surface. The sound of the skiff's engines filled the tiny chamber.

'*You* must relax,' Hikahi soothed. 'The autopilot is in charge now. We're going as fast as we can underwater. We should be there very soon.'

Hikahi was still somewhat numbed by the news about Creideiki, and shaken by Takkata-Jim's treachery. But over it all she could not bring herself to accept Keepiru's frantic urgency. He was obviously driven by his devotion to Gillian Baskin, and wanted to return to her aid instantly, if possible.

Hikahi looked at things from another perspective. She knew

Gillian probably already had things well under control back at the ship. Compared with the disasters she had been fantasizing the last few days, the news was almost buoyant. Even Creideiki's injury could not suppress Hikahi's relief that *Streaker* survived intact.

Her harness whined. With one waldo-hand she touched a control to give Keepiru a mild soporific.

'Now I want you to sssleep,' she told him. 'You must regain your strength. Consider that an order, if, as you say, I am now acting captain.'

Keepiru's eyes began to recess; the lids drooped together slowly. 'I'm shorry, sir. I ... I guessss I'm not much-ch more logical than Moki. I'm alwaysss causssing t-trouble ...'

His speech slurred as the drug took hold. Hikahi swam almost underneath the drowsy pilot and sighed a brief, soft lullaby.

> * Dream, defender—
> Dream of those who love you
> And bless your courage— *

85

GILLIAN

'You're saying these ... Karrank% ... were the last sophonts to have a license to the planet Kithrup, a hundred million years ago?'

'Correct,' the Niss machine replied. 'They were savagely abused by their patrons, mutated far beyond the degree allowed by the codes. According to the Thennanin battleship's *Library*, it caused quite a scandal at the time. In compensation, the Karrank% were released from their indenture as clients and granted a world suited to their needs, one with low potential for developing pre-sentience. Water worlds make good retirement homes for that reason. Few pre-sophonts ever arise on such planets. The Kiqui seem to be an exception.'

Gillian paced the sloping ceiling of the lopsided room. An occasional clanking, transmitted by the metal walls, told of the final fittings being made to secure *Streaker* into the Trojan Seahorse.

'You aren't saying the Kiqui have anything to do with these ancient ...'

'No. They appear to be a genuine find, and a major reason why you should endeavor to escape this trap and return to Earth with what you have learned.'

Gillian smiled ironically. 'Thanks. We'll do our best.

'So, what was done to the Karr ... the Karrank%,' she did her best with the double glottal stop, 'to make them want to hide away on Kithrup, never to associate with Galactic culture again?'

The Niss explained. 'In their pre-sentient form, they were mole-like creatures on a metal-rich world like this one. They had carbon-oxygen metabolisms, such as yours, but they were excellent diggers.'

'Let me guess. They were bred as miners, to extract ores on metal-poor worlds. It would be cheaper to import and breed Karrank% diggers than ship large quantities of metals across interstellar space.'

'A very good guess, Doctor Baskin. The client-Karrank% were indeed transformed into miners, and in the process converted to a metabolism extracting energy directly from radioactives. Their patrons thought it would help serve as an *incentive*.'

Gillian whistled. 'Such a drastic shift in their structure couldn't have been successful! *Ifni*, they must have suffered!'

'It was a perversion,' the Niss agreed. 'When it was discovered, the Karrank% were freed and offered recompense. But after a few millennia trying to adapt to standard starfaring life, they chose to retire to Kithrup. This planet was ceded them for the duration of their race. No one expected them to survive for long.

'Instead of dying out, however, they seem to have continued to modify themselves, on their own. They appear to have adopted a life style unique in known space.'

Gillian brought together the threads of the earlier part of the conversation, and made an inference. Her eyes widened. 'You mean to tell me the *metal-mounds* ... ?'

'Are larvae of an intelligent life form which dwells in the crust of this planet. Yes. I might have surmised this from the latest data sent by Doctor Dennie Sudman, but Creideiki had leapt to the conclusion before we even heard from her. That is why he came to see me, to get confirmation of his hypothesis.'

'Sah'ot's *voices*' Gillian whispered. 'They're Karrank%!'

'An acceptable tentative deduction,' the Niss approved. 'It would have been the discovery of the century, were it not for the *other* things you've already turned up on this expedition. I believe you humans have an old expression in English – "It doesn't rain but it pours" – it's quaint, but apropos.'

Gillian wasn't listening. 'The bombs!' She slapped her forehead.

'I beg your pardon?'

'I let Charlie Dart steal some low-yield bombs from our armory. I knew Takkata-Jim would confiscate them and begin transforming them into fuel. It was part of a plan I had cooked up. But ...'

'You assumed Takkata-Jim would confiscate all of the bombs?'

'Yes! I was going to call him and tip him off if he overlooked them, but he was quite efficient and discovered them right away. I had to lie to Toshio about it, but that couldn't be helped.'

'If all went according to plan, I do not see the problem.'

'The problem is that Takkata-Jim may not have seized *all* of the bombs! It never occurred to me that Charlie could harm living sophonts if he still had one! *Now,* though . . . I've got to get in touch with Toshio, at once!'

'Can it wait a few minutes? Takkata-Jim probably was thorough, and there is another matter I wish to discuss with you.'

'No! You don't understand. Toshio's about to sabotage his comm set! It's part of my plan! If there's even a *chance* Charlie's got a bomb we have to find out quickly!'

The holo patterns were agitated.

'I'll make the connection at once,' the Niss announced. 'It will take me a few moments to worm through *Streaker*'s comm system without being detected. Stand by.'

Gillian paced the sloping floor, hoping they would be in time.

86

TOSHIO

Toshio finished the re-wiring, slapped the cover over the transmitter on Thomas Orley's sled, and spread a light smear of mud on the plate to make it seem long unopened. Then he unhitched the monofilament line from the unit, tied a small red marker ribbon to the end, and let the almost invisible fiber drift down into the depths.

Now he was out of touch with *Streaker*. It made him feel more alone than ever – even lonelier than when Dennie and Sah'ot had departed early in the morning.

He hoped Takkata-Jim would follow orders and wait here until *Streaker* left. If he did, Gillian would call down as they blasted away, and warn him of the modifications that had been made to the longboat and this transmitter.

But what if Takkata-Jim were, indeed, a traitor? What if he took off early?

Charles Dart would probably be aboard then, as well as Ignacio Metz, three *Stenos*, and perhaps three or four Kiqui. Toshio wished none of them harm. It was an agonizing choice.

He looked up and saw Charles Dart happily muttering to himself as he played with his new robot.

Toshio shook his head, glad that the chimp, at least, was happy.

He slid into the water and swam over to his own sled. He had jettisoned its tiny radio an hour ago. He strapped himself in and turned on the motors.

He still had to make one more splice below the island. The old robot, the damaged probe Charles Dart had abandoned down near the bottom of the drill-tree shaft, had one last customer. Creideiki, hanging around Streamer's old site, still wanted to talk to Sah'ot's 'voices.' Toshio figured he owed the captain the favor, even if it did feel like he was humoring a delusion.

As the sled sank, Toshio thought about the rest of his job here . . . the things he might have to do before he could leave.

Let Tom Orley be waiting for me when I come back up, he wished fervently. *That would solve everything. Let Mr Orley be finished with his job up in the north, and land up there while I'm below.*

Toshio smiled ironically. *And while you're at it, Ifni, why not throw in a giant fleet of good guys to clear the skies of baddies, hmmm?*

He descended down the narrow shaft, into the gloom.

87

GILLIAN

'Drat! Triple hell! The line's dead. Toshio's already cut it.'

'Don't be overly alarmed.' The Niss spoke reassuringly. 'It is quite likely that Takkata-Jim confiscated all of the bombs. Did not Midshipman Iwashika report that he saw several being dismantled for fuel, as you expected?'

'Yes, and I told him not to worry about it. But it never occurred to me to ask him to *count* them. I was caught up in the minutiae of moving the ship, and I didn't think Charlie would do any real harm even if, by some chance, he managed to keep one!'

'Now, of course, we know better.'

Gillian looked up, wondering if the Tymbrimi machine was being tactful or obliquely sarcastic.

'Well,' she said, 'what's done is done. Whatever happens can't affect us here. I just hope we don't add a crime against a sentient race to our dubious record on this voyage.'

She sighed. 'Now, will you tell me again how all this is going to become some sort of legend?'

88

TOSHIO

The connection was made. Now Creideiki could listen to the underground sounds to his heart's content. Toshio let the monofilament drop into the mud. He emptied ballast, and the sled rose in a spiral toward the drill-tree shaft.

When he surfaced, Toshio knew at once that something had changed. The second sled, the one belonging to Tom Orley, had been dragged up the steep embankment and lay on the sward to the south of the pool. Wires dangled from an open section in the control panel.

Charles Dart squatted by the water's edge. The chimp leaned forward with his finger to his lips.

Toshio cut the motors and loosened his straps. He sat up and looked about the clearing, but saw only the waving forest fronds.

Charlie said in a guttural whisper, 'I think Takkata-Jim and Metz are planning to take off soon, Toshio, with or without me.' Dart looked confused, as if dazed by the foolishness of the idea.

Toshio kept his expression guarded. 'What makes you think that, Doctor Dart?'

'As soon as you went down, two of Takkata-Jim's *Stenos* came to take that sled's radio. Also, when you were below, they tested the engines. They sounded kinda ragged at first, but they're working on 'em now. I think now they don't even care if you report back anymore.'

Toshio heard a soft growling sound to the south – a low whine that rose and fell unevenly.

A rustle of movement to the north caught his eye. He saw Ignacio Metz hurrying southward down the forest trail, carrying bundles of records. Behind him trooped four sturdy Kiqui volunteers from the village. Their air-sacks were puffed up proudly, but they obviously did not like approaching the rough engine noises. They carried crude bundles in front of them.

From the foliage, several dozen pairs of wide eyes watched the procession nervously.

Toshio listened to the sound of the engines, and wondered how much time was left. Takkata-Jim had finished recycling the bombs sooner than expected. Perhaps they had underestimated the dolphin lieutenant. How much else had he jury-rigged to make the longboat serviceable ahead of schedule?

Should I try to delay their takeoff? If I stay any longer it's unlikely I'd ever reach Streaker *in time.*

'What about you, Doctor Dart? Are you ready to finish up and hop aboard when Takkata-Jim calls?'

Dart glanced to his console. He shook his head. 'I need another six hours,' he grumbled. 'Maybe we've got a common interest in delaying th' longboat takin' off. You got any ideas?'

Toshio considered.

Well, this is it, isn't it? This is where you decide. Leave now, if you plan to go at all.

Toshio exhaled deeply. *Ah, well.*

'If I think of a way to delay them for a while, Doctor Dart, will you help me? It may be a little risky.'

Dart shrugged. 'All I'm doin right now is waiting for my 'bot to dig into the crust to bury a . . . an instrument. I'm free until then. What do I have to do?'

Toshio unhooked the monofilament feeder coil from his sled and cut the free end. 'Well, for starters I think we'll need someone to climb some trees.'

Charlie grimaced. 'Stereotypes,' he muttered to himself. 'Allatime gettin trapped by stereotypes.'

89

GILLIAN

She shook her head slowly. Maybe it was her tiredness, but she couldn't understand more than a fraction of the Niss machine's explanation. Every time she tried to get it to simplify some subtle point of Galactic tradition, it insisted on bringing in examples that only muddied things further. She felt like a Cro-Magnon trying to understand the intrigues in the court of Louis XIV. The Niss seemed to be saying that *Streaker*'s discoveries would have consequences that reached beyond the immediate crisis over the derelict fleet. But the subtleties eluded her.

'Doctor Baskin.' The machine tried again. 'Every epoch has its turning point. Sometimes it occurs on the battlefield. Sometimes it takes the form of a technological advance. On occasion, the pivotal event is philosophical and so obscure that the species in existence at the time are hardly aware that anything has changed before their world-view is turned topsyturvy around them.

'But often, very often, these upheavals are preceded by a legend. I know of no other Anglic word to use for it ... a *story* whose images will stand out in the minds of almost all sophonts ... a *true* story of prodigious deeds and powerful archetypal symbols, which presages the change to come.'

'You're saying *we* may become one of these legends?'

'That is what I am saying.'

Gillian could not remember ever feeling so small. She couldn't lift the weight of what the Niss was implying. Her duty to Earth and the lives of one hundred and fifty friends and crewmates were burdens enough.

'Archetype symbols, you say ...'

'What could be more symbolic, Doctor Baskin, than *Streaker* and her discoveries? Just one, the derelict fleet, has turned the Five Galaxies upside down. Now add the fact that the discovery was made by the newest of all client races, whose patrons are wolflings, claiming no patrons at all. Here on Kithrup, where no pre-sentient life was supposed to be able to arise, *they find* a ripe pre-sentient race, and take great risks to protect the innocents from a Galactic civilization grown rigid and calcified ...'

'Now just a ...'

'Now add the Karrank%. In all of the recent epochs, no sapient race has been treated so foully, so abused by the system which was supposed to protect them.

'So what were the chances that *this* ship would happen to flee to the very planet that was *their* last refuge? Can you not see the overlying images, Doctor Baskin? From the Progenitors down to the very newest race, what one sees is a powerful sermon about the Uplift System.

'Whatever the outcome of your attempt to escape Kithrup, whether you succeed or fail, the stars cannot help but make a great song of your adventure. This song, I believe, will change more than you can imagine.' The voice of Niss finished, with a hushed, almost reverent tone. Its implication was left spinning in the silence.

Gillian stood on the sloping ceiling of the dark, lopsided room, blinking in the sparkling light cast by the swirling motes. The silence hung. Finally, she shook her head.

'Another damned Tymbrimi practical joke,' she sighed. 'A god-damn shaggy dog story. You've been pulling my leg.'

The motes spun silently for a long moment. 'Would it make you feel any better if I said I were, Doctor Baskin? And would it change what you have to do one bit if I said I weren't?'

She shrugged. 'I guess not. At least you pulled me back from my own troubles for a little while. I feel a bit lightheaded from all that philosophical crap, and maybe even ready to get some sleep.'

'I am always ready to be of service.'

Gillian smirked. 'Sure you are.' She climbed up on a packing crate to reach the door-plate, but before opening the door she looked back up at the machine.

'Tell me one thing, Niss. Did you give Creideiki any of this bull-shit you were feeding me just now?'

'Not in Anglic words, no. But we did cover most of the same themes.'

'And he believed you?'

'Yes. I believe he did. Frankly, I was a bit surprised. It was almost as if he had heard it all before, from another source.'

That explained part of the mystery of the captain's disappearance, then. And there was nothing that could be done about it now.

'Assuming he did believe you, just what does Creideiki think he's going to accomplish out there?'

The motes spun for a few seconds.

'I suppose, Doctor Baskin, he is first off looking for *allies*. On an entirely different level, I think he is out there trying to add a few choice stanzas to the legend.'

90

CREIDEIKI

They moaned. They had always been in pain. For aeons life had hurt them.

: Listen :

He called out in the language of the ancient gods, coaxing the Karrank% to answer him.

: Listen : You Deep, Hidden Ones – You Sad, Abused Ones : I Call From The Outside : I Crave an Audience :

The doleful singing paused. He felt a hint of irritation. It came in both sound and psi, a shrug to shake a bothersome flea away.

The song of lamentation resumed.

Creideiki kept at it, pushing, probing. He floated at the relay link *Streaker* had left behind, breathing from his sled's airdome, trying to get the attention of the ancient misanthropes, using the electrical buzz of a distant robot to amplify his faint message.

: I Call From The Outside : Seeking Aid : Your Ancient Tormentors Are Our Enemies Too :

That stretched the truth slightly, but not in essence. He hurried on, sculpting sound images as he felt their attention finally swing his way.

: We Are Your Brothers : Will You Help Us? :

The growling drone suddenly erupted. The psi portion felt angry and *alien*. The part that was sound grated like static. Without his apprenticeship in the Sea of Dreams, Creideiki felt certain he would have found it unfathomable.

+ DO NOT BOTHER US –
– DO NOT SAY ! WE +
+ HAVE NO BROTHERS –
– WE   REJECT +
+ THE   UNIVERSE –
– GO   AWAY! +

Creideiki's head rang with the powerful dismissal. Still, the potency of the psi was encouraging.

What *Streaker*'s crew had needed all along was an ally, *any* ally. They had to have some help, at least a distraction, if Thomas Orley's clever plan of deception and disguise stood a chance of success. As alien and bitter as these underground creatures were, they had once been starfarers. Perhaps they would take some satisfaction in helping other victims of Galactic civilization.

He persisted.

: Look! : Listen! : Your World Is Surrounded By Gene-Meddlers : They Seek Us : And Small Ones Who Share This Planet With You : They Wish To Warp Us : As They Did You : They Will Invade Your Private Agony :

He crafted a sonic image of great fleets of ships, embellished with gaping jaws. He painted over them an impression of malicious intent.

His picture was shattered by a thundering response.

+ WE ARE NOT INVOLVED! –

Creideiki shook his head and concentrated.
: They May Seek **You** Out, As Well :

+ THEY HAVE NO USE FOR US! –
– IT IS **YOU** THEY SEEK! +
+ NOT   US! –

The reply dazed him. Creideiki only had strength for one more question. He tried to ask what the Karrank% would do if they *were* attacked.

Before he finished, he was answered by a gnashing that could not be parsed even in the sense-glyphs of the ancient gods. It was more a roar of defiance than anything decipherable. Then, in an instant, the sound and mental echoes cut off. He was left there, drifting with his head ringing from their anger.

He had done his best. Now what?

With nothing better to do, he closed his eyes and meditated. He clicked out sonar spirals and wove the echoes of the surrounding ridges into patterns. His disappointment subsided as he sensed Nukapai take shape alongside him, her body a complex matting of his own sounds and those of the sea. She seemed to rub along his side and Creideiki thought he could *almost* feel her. He felt a brief sexual thrill.

: Not Nice People : she commented.

Creideiki smiled sadly.

: No, Not Nice : But They Hurt : I Would Not Bother Such Hermits But For Need :

He sighed.

: The World-Song Seems To Say They Will Not Help :

Nukapai grinned at his pessimism. She changed tempo and whistled softly in an amused tone.

> * Go below
> > And hear tomorrow's weather
> * Go below
> > Prescience, prescience … *

Creideiki concentrated to understand her. Why did she speak Trinary, a language almost as difficult for him now as Anglic? There was another speech, subtle and powerful, that they could share now. Why did she remind him of his disability?

He shook his head, confused. Nukapai was a figment of his own mind … or at least she was limited to whatever sounds his own voice could create. So *how* was it she could talk in Trinary at all?

There were mysteries still. The deeper he went the more mysteries there seemed to be..

> * Go below
> > Deep night-diver
> * Go below
> > Prescience, prescience— *

He repeated the message to himself. Did she mean that something could be read from the future? That something inevitable was fated to bring the Karrank% out of their isolation?

596

He was still trying to puzzle out the riddle when he heard the sound of engines. Creideiki listened for a few moments. But he didn't need to turn on the sled's hydrophones to recognize the pattern of those motors.

Cautiously, tentatively, a tiny spacecraft nosed into the canyon. Sonar swept slowly from one end to another. A searchlight took in the scars in the sea-bed that the departing *Streaker* had left behind. They scanned bits and pieces of abandoned equipment, and finally came to rest on the little boxy relay, and his sled.

Creideiki blinked in the bright beam. He opened his jaws wide in a smile of greeting. But his voice froze. For the first time in several days he felt bashful, unable to speak for fear of choking over even the simplest words and seeming a fool.

The ship's speakers amplified a single happy sigh, elegantly simple.

* Creideiki! *

With a warm pleasure he recognized that voice. He turned on the sled's motors and cast loose from the relay. As he sped toward the skiff's opening hatch he called out careful words in Anglic, one at a time.

'Hikahi ... Nice ... to hear ... your ... voice ... again ...'

91

TOM ORLEY

Fog swirled over the sea of weeds. That was good, up to a point. It made stealth easier. But it also made it hard to look for traps.

Tom searched carefully as he crawled across the last stretch of weeds before the open end of the wrecked cruiser. This patch couldn't be taken underwater, and he didn't doubt those who had taken shelter within the hulk had set up defenses.

He found a device only a few meters from the gaping opening. Thin wires were strung from one small hump of vines to the next. Tom inspected the arrangement, then carefully dug below the trip-wire and slithered underneath. When he was clear, he scrambled quietly to the edge of the floating ship and rested against the pitted hull.

The weed beasties had taken cover during the fighting. They were out again, now that almost all of the combatants were dead. Their frog-like croaks refracted eerily in the noisome vapor. Distantly, Tom heard the rumble of the volcano. His empty stomach growled. It sounded loud enough to rouse the Progenitors.

He checked his weapon. The needler had only a few shots left. He had better be right about the number of ETs that had taken shelter aboard this vessel.

I'd better be right about a number of things, he reminded himself. *I've staked a lot on there being food here, as well as the information I need.*

He closed his eyes in brief meditation, then turned to crouch below the opening. He peeked one eye just past the ragged edge.

Three bird-like Gubru huddled around a motley array of equipment on the smoke-stained, canted deck. A tiny, inadequate heater held the attention of two, who warmed slender-boned arms over it. The third sat before a battered portable console and squeaked in Galactic Four, a language popular among many avian species.

'No sign of humans or their clients,' the creature peeped. 'We have lost our deep-search equipment, so we cannot be certain. But we find no sign of Earthlings. We cannot achieve anything more. Come for us!'

The radio sputtered. 'Impossible to come out of hiding. Impossible to squander last resources at this time. You must maintain. You must lie low. You must wait.'

'Wait? We shelter in a hull whose food supply is radioactive. We shelter in a hull whose equipment is ruined. Yet this hull we shelter in is the best still afloat! You must come for us!'

Tom cursed silently at the news. So much for eating.

The radio operator maintained its protests. The other two Gubru listened, shifting their weight impatiently. One of them stamped its clawed feet and turned around suddenly as if to interrupt the radio operator. Its gaze swept past the gap in the hull. Before Tom could duck back, the creature's eyes went wide. It began to point.

'A human! *Quickly . . .*'

Tom shot it in the thorax. Without bothering to watch it fall, he dove through the opening and rolled behind a tilted console. He scuttled to the other end and snapped off two quick shots just as the second standing Gubru tried to fire. A thin flame spat out of a small handgun, searing the already scarred ceiling as the alien shrieked and toppled backward.

The Galactic at the radio stared at Tom. It glanced at the radio beside it.

'Don't even think it,' Tom squawked in heavily accented Galactic

Four. The alien's crest riffled in surprise. It lowered its hands and kept still.

Tom rose carefully, never drawing bead away from the surviving Gubru. 'Drop your weapons belt and stand away from the transmitter. Slowly. Remember, we humans are wolflings. We are feral, carnivorous, and extremely fast! Do not make me eat you.' He grinned his broadest grin to display a maximum of teeth.

The creature shuddered and moved to obey. Tom reinforced obedience with a growl. Sometimes a reputation as a primitive had its uses.

'All right,' he said as the alien moved to where he gestured, by the gaping hole. Tom kept his gun trained and sat by the radio. The receiver gave out excited twitters.

He recognized the model, thank Ifni, and switched it off. 'Were you transmitting when your friend here spotted me?' he asked his captive. He wondered if the commander of the hidden Gubru forces had heard the word 'human.'

The Galactic's comb fluttered. Its answer was so irrelevant that Tom momentarily wondered if he had totally misphrased the question.

'You must surrender pride,' it chanted, puffing its feathers. 'All young ones must surrender pride. Pride leads to error. Hubris leads to error. Only orthodoxy can save. We can save ...'

'That's enough!' Tom snapped.

'... save you from heretics. Lead us to the returning Progenitors. Lead us to the ancient masters. Lead us to the rule-givers. Lead us to them. They expect to return to the Paradise they decreed when they long ago departed. They expect Paradise and would be helpless before such as the Soro or the Tandu or the Thennanin or ...'

'Thennanin! That's what I want to know! Are the Thennanin still fighting? Are they powers in the battle?' Tom swayed with the intensity of his need to know.

'... or the Dark Brothers. They will need protection until they are made to understand what terrible things are being done in their name, orthodoxies broken, heresies abounding. Lead us to them, help us cleanse the universe. Your rewards will be great. Your modifications small. Your indenture short ...'

'Stop it!' Tom felt the strain and exhaustion of the last few days rise in a boiling rage. Next to the Soro and Tandu, the Gubru had been among humanity's worst persecutors. He had had all he was about to take from this one.

'Stop it and answer my questions!' He fired at the floor near the alien's feet. It hopped in surprise, wide-eyed. Tom fired twice more.

The first time the Gubru danced away from a ricochet. The second time it winced as the needler misfired and jammed.

The Galactic peered at him, then squawked joyfully. It spread its feathered arms wide and unsheathed long talons. For the first time it said something direct and intelligible.

'Now *you* shall talk, impertinent, half-formed, masterless upstart!' It charged, screaming.

Tom dove to one side as the shrieking avian screeched past him. Slowed by hunger and exhaustion, he couldn't prevent one razor-sharp claw from passing through his wetsuit and ripping his side along one rib. He gasped and stumbled against a blood-stained wall as the Gubru turned around to renew the attack.

Neither of them even considered the handguns that lay on the floor. Depleted and slippery, the weapons weren't worth the gamble to stoop and retrieve them.

'Where are the dolphinnnns?' the Gubru squawked as it danced back and forth. 'Tell me or I shall teach you respect for your elders the hard way.'

Tom nodded. 'Learn to swim, bird-brain, and I'll take you to them.'

The Gubru's talons spread again. It shrieked and charged.

Tom summoned his reserves. He leapt into the air and met the creature's throat with a savage kick. The shriek was cut off abruptly, and he felt its vertebrae snap as it went down, sliding along the damp deck to fetch up at the wall in a heap.

Tom landed stumbling beside it. His eyes swam. Breathing heavily with hands on his knees, he looked down at his enemy.

'I told ... told you we were ... wolflings,' he muttered.

When he could, he walked unsteadily to the ragged tear in the side of the ship and leaned on the curled and blackened lower edge, staring out at the drifting fog.

All he had left were his mask, his freshwater still, his clothes, and ... oh yes, the nearly worthless hand weapons of the Gubru.

And the message-bomb, of course. The weight pressed against his midriff.

I've put off a decision long enough, he decided. While the battle lasted he could pretend he was searching for answers. Maybe he had been procrastinating, though.

I wanted to be sure. I wanted to know the trick had a maximum chance of working. For that to happen there had to be Thennanin.

I met that scout. The Gubru mentioned Thennanin. Do I have to see their fleet to guess there are still some in the battle above?

He realized there was another reason he had been putting the decision off.

Once I set it off, Creideiki and Gillian are gone. There's no way they'll be able to stop for me. *I was to get back to the ship on my own, if at all.*

While fighting on the weeds, he had kept hoping to find a working vessel. Anything that could fly him home. But there were only wrecks.

He sat down heavily with his back to the cool metal and drew out the message-bomb.

Do I set it off?

The Seahorse was his plan. Why was he out here, far from Gillian and home, but to find out if it would work?

Across the blood-smeared deck of the alien cruiser, his gaze fell on the Gubru radio.

You know, he told himself, *there is one more thing I can do. Even if it means I'll be putting myself right in the middle of a bull's-eye, at least it'll give Jill and the others all I know.*

And maybe it'll accomplish more than that ...

Tom summoned the strength to stand up one more time. *Ah, well,* he thought as he staggered to his feet. *There's no food anyway. I might as well go out in style.*

PART NINE

ASCENT

'Sunset and evening star,
And one clear call for me!
And may there be no moaning of the bar
When I put out to sea.'

A. TENNYSON

DENNIE & SAH'OT

'It'sss the longer way, Dennie. Are you sure we shouldn't just cut southwest?'

Sah'ot swam alongside the sled, keeping pace fairly easily. Every few strokes he glided smoothly to the surface to blow, then rejoined his companion without breaking stride.

'I know it would be faster, Sah'ot.' Dennie answered without looking up from her sonar display. She was careful to skirt far from any metal-mounds. It was in this area that the killer-weed grew. Toshio's story about his encounter with the deadly plant had terrified her, and she was determined to give the unfamiliar mounds a wide berth.

'Then why are we returning to *Streaker*'s old site before heading sssouth?'

'For several reasons,' Dennie answered. 'First of all, we *know* this part of the route, having been over it before. And the path from the old site to the Seahorse is straight south, so there's less chance of getting lost.'

Sah'ot snickered, unconvinced. 'And?'

'And this way we'll stand a chance of finding Hikahi. My guess is she may be nosing around the old site about now.'

'Did Gillian ask you to look for her?'

'Yeah,' Dennie lied. Actually, she had her own reasons for wanting to find Hikahi.

Dennie was afraid of what Toshio intended to do. It was possible that he meant to delay leaving the island until *Streaker*'s preparations were finished and it was too late for Takkata-Jim to interfere. Of course, by then it would be too late for him to rejoin the ship via sled.

In that case the skiff would be Toshio's only chance.

She had to find Hikahi before Gillian did. Gillian might decide to send the skiff after Tom Orley instead of Toshio.

She knew she wasn't thinking things out, and felt a little guilty about her decision. But if she could lie to one dolphin, she could lie to another.

TAKKATA-JIM & METZ

The former vice-captain tossed his head and gnashed his teeth as he contemplated the latest sabotage.

'I will string their entrails from the foressst branches!' he hissed. The heavy waldo-arms of his armored spider whined.

Ignacio Metz stared up at the thin, almost invisible wires that formed a tight tracery over the longboat, holding it to the ground. He blinked, trying to follow the trail of fibers into the forest.

Metz shook his head. 'Are you sure you're not overreacting, vice-captain? It seems to me the boy was only trying to make sure we didn't take off before we agreed to.'

Takkata-Jim whirled to glare down on the human. 'And have you sssuddenly changed your mind, *Doctor* Metz? Do you now think we should let the lunatic woman who now controls *Streaker* send our crewmates out to certain death?'

'N-no, of course not!' Metz shrank back from the dolphin officer's rancor. 'We should persevere, I agree. We must try to make our offer of compromise to the Galactics, but . . .'

'But what?'

Metz shrugged uncertainly. 'I just don't think you should blame Toshio for doing his job . . .'

Takkata-Jim's jaws clapped together like a gunshot, and he caused the spider to advance upon Metz, stopping less than a meter from the nervous man.

'You *think*! You THINK! Of all comedies, that one topsss all! *You*, who had the arrogance to suppose his wisdom exceeded the councils of Earth – who brought pet monsters amongst an already fragile crew – who deceived himself into thinking all was well, and ignored danger signs when his wisdom was needed by his desperate clients – *yes*, Ignacio Metz. Tell me how you think-k!' Takkata-Jim snorted in derision.

'B-but we . . . you and I agreed on nearly everything! My gene-graft *Stenos* were your most loyal supporters! They're the only ones who stood by you!'

'*Your Stenos* were not *Stenos*! They were benighted, erratic creatures who did not belong on thisss mission! I *used* them, as I've used *you*. But don't class me with your monsters, Metz!'

Stunned, Metz sagged back against the hull of the longboat.

From nearby came sounds of returning machines. With a withering glance, Takkata-Jim warned the human to be silent. Sreekah-pol's spider pushed through the foliage.

'The fibersss lead to the p-pool,' the fin announced. His Anglic was almost too high-pitched for Metz to follow. 'They go below and wrap around the drill-tree shshaft-t.'

'You've cut them?'

'Yesss!' The neo-fin tossed its head.

Takkata-Jim nodded. 'Doctor Metz, please prepare the Kiqui. They are our second greatest trade item, and musst be ready for inspection by whichever race we contact-t.'

'Where are you going now?' Metz asked.

'You don't want to know.'

Metz saw Takkata-Jim's determined expression. Then he noted the three *Stenos*. Their eyes gleamed with an eager madness.

'You've been goading them in Primal!' he gasped. 'I can tell! You've taken these fen over the edge! You're going to make them homicidals!'

Takkata-Jim sighed. 'I will wrestle with my conscience later, Doctor Metz. In the meantime I will do what I must to save the ship and our mission. Since a sane dolphin cannot kill human beings, I needed insane dolphins.'

The three *Stenos* grinned at Metz. He looked at their eyes in terror, and listened to their feral clickings.

'You're mad!' he whispered.

'No, Doctor Metz,' Takkata-Jim shook his head pityingly. 'You are mad. These fen are mad. I am only acting as a desperate and dedicated human being might act. Criminal or patriot, that's a matter of opinion, but I am sentient.'

Metz's eyes were wide. 'You can't take back to Earth anyone who knows ...' He paled, and turned to run for the airlock.

Takkata-Jim did not have to give the order. From Sreekah-pol's spider a burst of blue light lanced out. Ignacio Metz sighed and fell to the muddy ground just outside the longboat's hatch. He stared up at Sreekah-pol, like a father betrayed by a son he had doted on.

Takkata-Jim turned to his crew, hiding the nauseated feeling that churned within him.

> \# *Find, Find,*
> *Find and Kill,*
> \# *Kill*
> *Soft-skin human*
> *Hairy ape*

The fen gave out a shrill assent in unison, and turned as one to go crashing back into the forest, heavy manipulator arms brushing aside saplings like twigs.

The man groaned. Takkata-Jim looked down at him and considered putting him out of his misery. He wanted to. But he couldn't bring himself to do direct violence against a human being.

Just as well, he thought. There are still repairs to do. I must be ready when my monsters return.

Takkata-Jim stepped daintily over the supine human and climbed into the airlock.

'Doctor Metz!' Toshio pulled the wounded man to one side and lifted his head. He whispered urgently as he applied a spray ampule of pain killer to the geneticist's neck. 'Doctor Metz, can you hear me?'

Metz blearily looked up at the young man. 'Toshio? My boy, you've got to get away! Takkata-Jim has sent . . . '

'I know, Doctor Metz. I was hiding in the bushes when they shot you.'

'Then you heard,' he sighed.

'Yes, sir.'

'And you know what a fool I've been . . . '

'Now's not the time for that, Doctor Metz. We've got to get you away. Charlie Dart's hiding nearby. I'll go fetch him now, while the *Stenos* are searching another part of the island.'

Metz clutched Toshio's arm. 'They're hunting for him, too.'

'I know. And you've never seen a more stunned chimp. He honestly believed they'd never think he helped me! Let me go get him, and we'll move you away from here.'

Metz coughed, and red foam appeared on his lips. He shook his head.

'No. Like Victor Frankenstein, it seems I am murdered by my own hubris. Leave me. You must go to your sled and depart.'

Toshio grimaced. 'Their first stop was the pool, Doctor Metz. I followed and saw them sink my sled.

'I ran ahead then to chase the Kiqui off the island. Dennie taught me their panic signal, and they split like crazed lemmings when I called it out, so at least they're safe from the *Stenos* . . . '

'Not *Stenos*,' Metz corrected. '*Demenso cetus metzii*, I should think. "Metz's mad dolphins" . . . you know, I think I'm the first dolphin-perpetrated homicide in ...' He brought his fist to his mouth and coughed again. Metz looked at the red spittle in his hand, then up at Toshio. 'We were going to give the Kiqui to the Galactics, you know. I wasn't happy ... but he convinced me ...'

'Takkata-Jim?'

'Yes. Didn't think offering the location of the derelict fleet would be enough ...'

'He's got *tapes?*' Toshio felt stunned. 'But how ... ?'

Metz wasn't listening. He seemed to be fading fast. '... Didn't think would be enough to win *Streaker's* freedom, so ... we'd give them the aboriginals, as well.'

The man grabbed feebly at Toshio's arm. 'Don't let the fanatics have them. They are so promising. Must have kind patrons. Maybe the Linten, or Synthians ... we're not suited ... we'd ... make them caricatures of ourselves. We'd ...'

The geneticist sagged. Toshio waited with him. It was all he could do for the man.

Metz roused once more, a minute later. He stared up without seeing. 'Takkata-Jim ...' he gasped. 'I never thought of it before. Why, he's exactly what we've been looking for! I never realized, but he's not a dolphin. He's a *man* ... Who in the world would have thought ...'

His voice faded into a rattle. His eyes rolled upward.

Toshio found no pulse. He lowered the corpse to the ground and slipped back into the forest.

'Metz is dead,' he told Charles Dart. The chimp looked out from the bushes. The whites of his eyes shone.

'B-b-but th-that's ...'

'That's homicide, I know.' Toshio nodded, sympathizing with Charles Dart. The one standard technique of uplift humans had taken unmodified from the Galactics was to ingrain a revulsion of patron-murder in their clients. Few thought it particularly hypo-critical, considering man's liberal record in other areas. Still ...

'Then they w-won't think twice about shooting you and me!'

Toshio shrugged.

'What're we gonna do?' Charlie had dropped all professorial man-nerisms. He looked to Toshio for guidance.

He's the adult and I'm the kid, Toshio thought bitterly. *It should be the other way around.*

No, that's foolish. Age or patron-client status has nothing to do with it. I'm military. Keeping us alive is my job.

He kept his nervousness hidden. 'We'll do as we have done, Doctor Dart. We've got to harass them, and keep them from taking off as long as possible.'

Dart blinked a few times, then protested. 'But we'll have no way *off*, then! Can't you get *Streaker* to come for us?'

'If it turns out to be at all possible, I'm sure Gillian will try to make arrangements. But you and I are expendable now. Try to understand that, Doctor Dart. We're soldiers. They say there's a kind of satisfaction in sacrificing oneself for others. I guess it's true; otherwise there wouldn't ever be legends.'

The chimp tried to believe. His hands fluttered. 'If they get b-back to Earth, they'll tell about what we did, won't they?'

Toshio smiled. 'You bet.'

Charlie looked at the ground for a moment. In the distance they could hear the *Stenos* crashing through the forest.

'Uh, Toshio, there's something you oughta know.'

'What is it, Doctor Dart?'

'Uh, you remember that thing I wanted to make them wait a few hours for, before taking off?'

'Your experiment. Yes, I remember.'

'Well the instruments I left aboard *Streaker* will take the data, so the info will get home even if I don't.'

'Hey, that's great, Doctor Dart! I'm happy for you.' Toshio knew what that meant to the chimp scientist.

Charlie smiled weakly. 'Yeah, well, it's too late to stop it from happening, so I figure you oughta know so it doesn't surprise you.'

Something about the way he said it made Toshio feel uneasy. 'Tell me,' he said.

Charlie looked at his watch. 'The robot will be where I want it in eighty minutes.' He glanced up at Toshio a little nervously. 'Then my bomb goes off.'

Toshio fell back against the bole of a tree. 'Oh, great, that's all we need . . .'

'I was *gonna* tell Takkata-Jim just before, so we could hover when it exploded,' Charlie explained sheepishly. 'I wouldn't worry too much, though. I looked over Dennie's map of the cavern below the island. I'd say there's at least even money the mound won't fall in, but, you know . . .' He spread his hands.

Toshio sighed. They were going to die anyway. Fortunately, this latest twist didn't seem to have any cosmic implications.

94

'We're ready.' He made the announcement quite matter-of-factly.

Gillian looked up from the holo display. Hannes Suessi gave Gillian a two-fingered salute from the door jamb. Light from the bright hallway cast a stark trapezoid onto the floor of the dimly lit room.

'The impedance matchings ... ?' she asked.

'All darn near perfect. In fact, when we get back to Earth I'm going to suggest we buy a bunch of old hulls from the Thennanin to refit all Snarks with. We'll be slow, doubly so because of all the water in the central bay, but *Streaker* will lift, fly, and warp. And it'll take a hell of a punch to pound through the outer shell.'

Gillian put one foot on the desk. 'There's still a lot of punch out there, Hannes.'

'She'll fly. As for the rest ...' The engineer shrugged. 'The only constraint I'd suggest is that you let the engineering staff get an hour or so under sleep machines if you don't want us sagging on takeoff. Other than that, it's up to you now, Madame Captain.'

He stopped her before she could speak. 'And don't go looking to us for any advice, either, Gillian. You've been doing too good a job so far, and neither Tsh't nor I are going to say anything but aye aye, sir, and jump when you say so.'

Gillian closed her eyes and nodded. 'All right,' she said softly.

Hannes looked through the open door from her office to Gillian's laboratory. He knew about the ancient cadaver. He had been there to help Tom Orley bring it back into the ship.

Glimpsing a silhouette suspended within a glass case, he shivered and turned away.

Gillian's holo display showed a small, Ping-Pong-ball-sized representation of Kithrup, and a scattering of small BBs as the planet's moons. Two clusters of blue and red dots were accompanied by tiny computer-code letters suspended in space.

'Don't seem like too many of the nasty buggers are left,' Suessi commented.

'Those are just the ships in nearby space. An expanded view, about a cubic astron, shows two still substantial Galactic squadrons. We can't actually identify the fleets from neutrino fluxes, of course, but the battle computer assigns colors on the basis of movement. They're still changing alliances out there.'

'Also, there's a plethora of survivors hiding out on the moons.'

Suessi pursed his lips. Almost he asked the question that was on everyone's mind, but he bit it back. Gillian answered anyway.

'There's still been no word from Tom.' She looked at her hands. 'Until now we didn't really have any use for the information, but . . .' She paused.

'But now we've got to know whether taking off would be suicide.' Suessi finished her thought. He noticed Gillian was studying the display again.

'You're trying to figure it out for yourself, aren't you?'

Gillian shrugged. 'Go get that hour, Hannes, or three, or ten. Tell your fen to take their naps at their stations, and toggle their sleep machines to the bridge.'

She frowned as she looked at the drifting dots. 'I may be wrong. We may wind up choosing the lesser evil – hiding down here until our gums start turning blue from metal poisoning, or we starve. But I have a feeling, a hunch, we may have to act soon.' She shook her head.

'What about Toshio and Hikahi and the others?'

Gillian did not answer. No answer was necessary. After a moment Suessi turned and left. He closed the door behind him.

Dots. No more could be resolved by *Streaker*'s passive sensors than drifting dots that occasionally came together in sparkling swarms and separated smaller in number. The battle computer went over the patterns and drew tentative conclusions. But the answer she needed was never there. 'Would the surviving fleets be indifferent to the sudden reappearance of a long-lost Thennanin cruiser, or would they join forces to swat it out of the sky?' The decision lay with her. Never had Gillian felt so alone.

Where are you, boy? You live, I know. I can feel your distant breath. What are you doing right now?

To her left a green light started flashing. 'Yes,' she told the comm link.

'Doctor Bassskin!' It was the voice of Wattaceti, calling from the bridge. 'Hikahi callsss! She is at-t the relay! And she has Creideiki!'

'Put her through!'

There was a hiss as the operator raised the gain on the attenuated signal.

'Gillian? Is that-t you?'

'Yes, Hikahi. Thank God! Are you all right? And Creideiki's still at the relay?'

'We are both quite well, Life-Cleaner. From what the fen on the bridge tell usss, you don't seem to need us there at all!'

'They're damned patron-sucking liars! And I wouldn't trade a one of them away for my left arm. Listen, we're missing five crewfen. You should be warned, two are atavistic and highly dangerous.'

The line hissed for a long moment. Then, 'All are accounted for, Gillian,' came the reply at last. 'Four of them are dead.'

Gillian covered her eyes. 'Dear Lord ...'

'Keepiru is with usss,' Hikahi answered her unasked question.

'Poor Akki,' Gillian sighed.

'Send word to Calafia that he did his duty. Keepiru says he was defiant and sentient till the end.'

Gillian did not like the implication of Hikahi's message. 'Hikahi, you're in command now. We need you back here *now*. I am this instant officially handing over ...'

'Don't, Gillian,' the fluting voice interrupted. 'Please. Not yet-t. There are still things to be done with the skiffff. Those on the island must be recovered, and the Kiqui volunteers.'

'I'm not sure we'll have time, Hikahi.' The words were bitter as she spoke them. She thought of bright, ever self-deprecating Dennie Sudman, of the erudite Sah'ot, and Toshio, so very young and noble.

'Has T-Tom called? Is there an emergency?

'Neither, yet. But ...'

'Then what-t?'

She couldn't explain. She tried in Trinary.

* What a piercing sound I hear—
* The peal of bugles, engines rising—
* The tears of love abandoned—
* Soon, so very soon— *

There was a long silence from the skiff. Then, it was not Hikahi's voice, but Creideiki's, that answered. In his repetitious, simply-phrased Trinary, there was something Gillian could only catch a hint of, something deep and a little eerie.

* Sounds, All Sounds
Answer Something
Answer Something :

* Acts, All Acts
Make Sounds
Make Sounds :

Gillian didn't breathe as she listened to Creideiki's last note fall away. Her spine was chilled.

'Bye, Gillian,' Hikahi said. 'You do what you have to. We'll be back quick-k as we can. But don't wait for usss.'

'Hikahi!' Gillian reached for the comm link, but the carrier wave cut off before she could say another word.

95

TOSHIO

'Both airlocks are bolted from the inside,' Toshio panted when he returned to the hiding place. 'Looks like we try it your way.'

Charles Dart nodded, and led him to the impulse thrusters at the stern of the small spacecraft.

Twice they had hidden themselves by climbing tall trees as patrolling *Stenos* passed below. It seemed not to occur to the mad fen to look above for their quarry. But Toshio knew they'd be deadly if they ever caught him and Charlie in the open.

Charlie removed the rear cover to the maintenance bay between the engines. 'I got in by crawling between the feedlines, over there, until I reached the access plate in that bulkhead.' He pointed. Toshio peered into the maze of pipes.

He looked back at Dart, amazed. 'No wonder nobody expected a stowaway. Is this how you got into the armory, as well? By climbing through ducts where no human could fit?'

The planetologist nodded. 'I guess you can't go in with me. That means I gotta get the little critters out by myself, right?'

Toshio nodded. 'I think they're in the aft hold. Here's the voder.'

He handed over the translator. It looked like a large medallion hanging from a neck-chain. All neo-chimps knew about voders, since they generally had trouble talking until the age of three. Charlie slipped it over his head. He started to climb into the small opening, but stopped and looked sidelong at the middie.

'Say, Toshio. Imagine this was one of those 20th-century "zoo" ships, and those were a bunch of pre-sentient chimps in the hold of a clipper ship – or whatever they used back then – on their way from

Africa to some laboratory or circus. Would *you* have snuck in to rescue *them?*'

Toshio shrugged. 'I don't honestly know, Charlie. I'd like to think I would've. But I really don't know what I'd've done.'

The neo-chimp met the human's eyes for a long instant, then he grunted. 'Okay, you guard the rear.'

He took a boost from Toshio and squirmed into the mechanical maze. Toshio squatted beneath the thruster tubes and listened to the forest. While Charlie struggled to get the inner access plate off, he made what felt like a terrible racket. Then it stopped.

Toshio slid into the forest to make a cautious circuit of the immediate area.

From crashing sounds up in the direction of the Kiqui village, he guessed the *Stenos* were amusing themselves with a destructive spree. He hoped none of the little natives had come back yet to witness, or worse, be caught in the violence.

He returned to the longboat and looked at his watch. Seventeen minutes until the bomb went off. They were cutting it close.

He reached into the maintenance area and spent a few minutes twiddling with some of the valves, spoiling their settings. Of course, Takkata-Jim didn't need the thrusters at all. If he was, indeed, refueled, he could take off on gravities. Leaving the access panel loose would decrease the boat's aerodynamic stability, but even that effect would be slight. Longboats like these were built rugged.

He stopped and listened. The rampage through the forest was heading this way again. The fen were on their way back.

'Hurry up, Charlie!' He fingered the grip of his holstered needler, not certain he could aim well enough, to hit the vulnerable patches where the dolphins were unprotected by the metal-sided spiders.

'Come on!'

There came a series of small, wet, slapping sounds from within the cavity. Intermittent squeaks echoed from the narrow confines, and then he saw a pair of widely splayed, green-finned hands.

They were followed by the head of a rather distressed-looking Kiqui. The aboriginal scuttled through the inner panel and crept through the maze of pipes until it leapt into Toshio's arms.

Toshio had to peel the frightened creature loose and put it down in order to reach for the next one. The little Kiqui were making a fearful racket, squeaking dolefully.

Finally all four were out. Toshio peered inside and saw Charles Dart trying to replace the inner panel.

'Never mind that!' Toshio hissed.

'I gotta! Takkata-Jim'll notice the change in air pressure on his panel! It's only luck he hasn't yet!'

'Come on! They're ...' He heard the whine of waldo motors and crushed vegetation. 'They're here! I'm going to draw them away from you. Good luck, Charlie!'

'Wait!'

Toshio crawled a few meters into the shrubbery so they would not guess where he came from. Then, from a crouch start, he ran.

> # *There! There!*
> # *Whaler!*
> # *Iki-netman!*
> # *Tuna-follower!*
> # *There! Kill! There!* #

The *Stenos* squawked from very close nearby. Toshio dove behind an oli-nut tree as bolts of blue death sizzled overhead. The Kiqui screamed and scattered into the forest.

Toshio rolled to his feet and ran, trying to keep the tree between him and his pursuers.

He heard sounds to the left and right as the fen moved quickly to surround him. His drysuit slowed him down as he tried to reach the shore cliffs before the circle was closed.

96

TOM ORLEY

He spent a while listening to the radio, but, although he recognized a few species-types in the voices, so much of the traffic was inter-computer that there was little to be learned that way.

All right, he told himself. *Let's work out the proper phrasing. This had better be good.*

97

THE SKIFF

Dennie stumbled over the words she had so carefully prepared. She tried to rephrase her arguments, but Hikahi stopped her.

'Doctor Sudman. You needn't persissst! Our next stop is the island anyway. We'll pick up Toshio if he hasn't left already. And perhaps we'll deal with Takkata-Jim, as well. We'll be on our way as soon as Creideiki finishes.'

Dennie exhaled all of her remaining tension. It was out of her hands, then. The professionals would take care of things. She might as well relax.

'How long ... ?'

Hikahi tossed her head. 'Creideiki doesn't expect to do any better this time than lassst. It shouldn't take long. Why don't you and Sah'ot go and rest in the meantime?'

Dennie nodded and turned to find some space to stretch out in the tiny hold.

Sah'ot swam alongside.

'Say, Dennie, as long as we're going to try to relax, want to trade backrubs?'

Dennie laughed. 'Sure, Sah'ot. Just don't get carried away, okay?'

Creideiki tried to reason with them one more time.

: We Are Desperate : As You Once Were : We Offer Hope To Little Unfinished Ones On This Very World : *Hope* To Grow Unbent :

: Our Enemies Will Harm You, As Well, In Time :

: Help Us : The static pulsed and throbbed in response. It carried a partly psychic feeling of closedness, of pressure and molten heat. It was a claustrophilic song, in praise of rough hard stone and flowing metal.

+	CEASE	−
−	PEACE	+
+	RELEASE!!	−

−	ISOLATION	+

Silence fell suddenly with a squeal of tortured machinery. The old robot which had so long hung two kilometers down the narrow drill-tree shaft had been destroyed.

Creideiki clicked a familiar phrase in Trinary.

* It is, that is— *

He was tempted to enter the Dream again. But there was, on this level of reality, no time for such things.

This level of reality was where duty lay, for the moment. Later, perhaps. Later he would visit Nukapai again. Perhaps she would show him the untenable things that she heard through the vague avenues of prescience.

He headed back to the airlock of the tiny spaceship. Hikahi, seeing him approach, started warming up the engines.

98

TOM ORLEY

'... a small group of dolphins spotted a few hundred paktaars north of this location! They were moving north quite rapidly. They may have come this way to see what all the fighting was about. Hurry! Now is the time to strike!'

Tom clicked off the receiver. His head hurt from the concentration it took to speak Galactic Ten rapidly. Not that he expected the Brothers of the Night to believe his was the voice of one of their missing scouts. That didn't matter to his plan. All he wanted to do was stir up their interest before the final jab.

He switched frequency and pursed his lips in preparation to speaking Galactic Twelve.

Actually, this was fun! It distracted him from his exhaustion and hunger and satisfied his aesthetic sense, even if it did mean everyone and his client would be down here shortly, all looking for him.

'... Paha warriors! Paha-ab-Kleppko -ab-puber ab-Soro ab-Hul! Inform the Soro fleet-mistress we have news!'

Tom chuckled as he thought of a pun that could only be phrased in Galactic Twelve and which, nevertheless, he was sure the Soro would never get.

99

GILLIAN

Something was making the fleets shift all of a sudden. Small squadrons raveled off the battered fleets and joined tiny groups from Kithrup's moons, all heading toward the planet. As they merged, the groups swirled about and tiny explosions took the place of individual lights.

What in the world was going on? Whatever it was, Gillian felt a glimmer of opportunity.

'Doctor Bassskin! Gillian!' Tsh't's voice came over the comm-speaker. 'We're getting radio traffic from the planet's surface again. It'sss from a single transmitter, but it keeps putting out stuff in different Galactic languages! Yet I ssswear they all sound like one voice!'

She leaned forward and touched a switch. 'I'm on my way up, Tsh't. Please call half of the off-duty shift to stations. We'll let the others rest a while longer.' She switched off the unit.

Oh, Tom, she thought as she hurried out the door. *Why this? Couldn't you have come up with anything more elegant? Anything less desperate?*

Of course he couldn't, she chided herself as she ran down the hallway. *Come on, Jill. The least you can do is not be a nag.*

In moments she was on the bridge, listening for herself.

100

TOSHIO

Cornered, Toshio couldn't even climb a tree. They were too close, and would be on him the instant they heard him move.

He could hear them as they spiraled closer, tightening the noose. Toshio clutched his needler and decided he had better attack first, before they were close enough to support each other. It would be a small handgun against armored machines and high-powered lasers, and he was no marksman like Tom Orley. In fact, he had never fired at a sentient being before. But it beat waiting here.

He crouched and began to crawl to his right, toward the shoreline. He tried not to snap any twigs, but a minute after leaving his hiding place he flushed some small animal, which fled noisily through the bushes.

Immediately he heard the noise of approaching mechanicals. Toshio slithered quickly under a thick bush, only to emerge facing the broad footpad of a spider.

 # Gotcha! Gotcha! #

There was a squeal of triumph. He looked up to meet the mad eye of Sreekah-pol. The fin leered as he commanded the spider to lift its leg.

619

Toshio rolled aside as the foot crashed down where his head had been. He reversed direction, avoiding a kick. The mechanical reared back, bringing both front legs into play. Toshio saw no place to turn. He fired his small pistol against the armored belly of the machine, and tiny needles ricocheted harmlessly into the forest.

The triumphant whistle was pure Primal.

Gotcha!

Then the island began to shake.

The ground heaved up and down. Toshio was jounced right and left and his head hit the loam rhythmically. The spider teetered, then crashed backward into the forest.

The shaking accelerated. Toshio somehow rolled over onto his stomach. He fought the oscillations to rise to his knees.

There was a crunching sound as two spider-riders stumbled into the clearing. One crashed past Toshio in panic. The other, though, saw him and squawked in wrath.

Toshio tried to hold out his needler, but the island's trembling began to turn into a list. It became a race between him and the mad dolphin to see who could aim and fire first.

Then both of them were staggered by a scream that echoed within their heads.

+   *BAD!*   –
– *BAD ONES!* +
+   *LEAVE*   –
–   *US*   +
+   *ALONE!* –

It was a roar of rejection that made Toshio moan and grab at his temples. The needler slipped out of his grasp and fell to the rapidly tilting ground.

The dolphin whistled shrilly as its spider collapsed in convulsions. It wailed in a foxhole lamentation.

Sorry! Sorry!
Patron forgive!
Forgive!

Toshio stumbled forward. 'Forgiven,' he managed to say as he hurried past. He couldn't deal with the fin's schizoid conversion. 'Come this way if you can!' he called back, as he tried to make it to the shore. The noise in his head was like an earthquake. Somehow

Toshio managed to stay on his feet and stumble through the forest.

When he reached the edge of the mound the sea was a froth below. Toshio looked right and left and saw no place that looked any better.

At that moment, a scream of engines pealed forth. He looked back to see a tornado of broken vegetation fly up from a spot only a hundred meters away. The gun-metal gray longboat rose above the rapidly tilting forest. It was surrounded by a glowing nimbus of ionization. Toshio's hackles rose as the island was swept by a throbbing antigravity field. The boat turned slowly and seemed to hesitate. Then, with a thunderclap, it speared into the eastern sky.

Toshio crouched as the boom whipped at him, tugging at his clothes.

There was no time to delay. Either Charles Dart had got away or he hadn't. Toshio pulled his mask up over his face, held it with one hand, and leapt.

'Ifni's boss . . .' he prayed. And he fell into the stormy waters.

101

GALACTICS

Above the planet small flotillas of battered warships paused suddenly in their multi-sided butchery.

They had left hiding places on Kithrup's tiny moons, gambling all on the chance that the strange radio broadcasts from the planet's northern hemisphere were, indeed, of human origin. On their way down to Kithrup, the tiny alliances sniped at each other with their waning strength, until a sudden wave of psychic noise hit the entire motley ensemble. It rose from the planet with a power none could have expected, overwhelming psi-shields and striking crews temporarily motionless.

The ships continued to plunge toward the planet, their living crews blinked limply, unable to fire their weapons or guide their vessels.

If it had been a weapon, the psychic shout would have cleansed half of the ships of their crews. As it was, the mental scream of anger and rejection reverberated within their brains, driving a few of the least flexible completely mad.

For long moments the cruisers drifted out of formation, uncontrolled, downward into the upper fringes of the atmosphere.

Finally, the psi-scream began to fade. The grating anger growled and diminished, leaving burning after-images as the numb crews slowly came to their senses.

The Xatinni and their clients, having drifted away from the others, looked about and discovered that they had lost their appetite for further fighting. They decided to accept the pointed invitation to depart. Their four ragged ships left Kthsemenee's system as quickly as laboring engines could manage.

The J'8lek were slow coming around. After succumbing to the numbing mind-scream, they drifted in amongst the ships of the Brothers of the Night. The Brothers awakened sooner, and used the J'8lek for target practice.

Sophisticated autopilots brought two Jophur warships to land on the slope of a steaming mountain, far to the south of their original destination. Automatic weapons kept watch for enemies while the Jophur struggled with their confusion. Finally, as the stunning psychic noise subsided, the crews began to revive and retake control of their grounded ships.

The Jophur were almost ready to lift off again, and head north to rejoin the fray, when the entire top of their mountain blew away in a column of superheated steam.

102

STREAKER

Gillian stared, slack-jawed, until the grating 'sounds' finally began to fade. She swallowed. Her ears popped, and she shook her head to clear away the numb feeling. Then she saw that the dolphins were staring at her.

'That was awful!' she stated. 'Is everybody all right?'

Tsh't looked relieved. 'We're all fine, Gillian. We detected an extremely powerful psi-explosion a few moments ago. It easily pierced our shields, and seems to have dazed you for a few minutes. But except for some momentary discomfort, we hardly felt it!'

Gillian rubbed her temples. 'It must be my esper sensitivity that made me susceptible. Let's just hope the Eatees don't follow that attack up with another even closer ...' She stopped. Tsh't was shaking her head.

'Gillian, I don't think it was the Eatees. Or if it was, they weren't aiming for us. Instruments indicate that that burst came from very close nearby, and was almost perfectly tuned *not* to be received by cetaceans! Your brain is similar to ours, so you only felt it a little. Suessi reports hardly feeling a thing.

'But I imagine some of the Galactics had a rough t-time weathering that psi-storm!'

Gillian shook her head a second time. 'I don't understand.'

'That makes two of usss. But I don't suppose we *have* to understand. All I can tell you is thisss – at almost the same time that psi-burst went off, there was an intense ground tremor not two hundred klicks from here. The crustal waves are only now starting to arrive.'

Gillian swam over to Tsh't's station in the glassy sphere of *Streaker*'s bridge. The dolphin lieutenant pointed with her jaw toward a globe model of the planet.

Not far from *Streaker*'s position on the globe, a small cluster of flashing red symbols was displayed.

'That's Toshio's island!' Gillian said. 'Then Charlie *did* have a spare bomb after all!'

'Beg p-pardon?' Tsh't looked confused. 'But I thought Takkata-Jim had confiscated . . .'

'*Ship rising!*' A detection officer announced. '*Anti-g and stasis – from the same site as the crust tremors, one hundred and fifffffty klicks from here. Tracking . . . tracking . . . Ship is now heading off at Mach two, due east!*'

Gillian looked at Tsh't. They shared the same thought. *Takkata-Jim.*

Gillian saw the question in the dolphin officer's eye. 'We may face a decision shortly. Have his blip followed to see where he's headed. And we'd better start awakening the rest of the off-duty crew.'

'Aye, sir. Those that managed to remain asleep through the last few minutes.' Tsh't turned and relayed the command.

A few minutes later the battle computer began to chatter.

'What *now?*' Gillian asked.

Bright yellow pinpoints began to glow up and down a long jagged streak on the globe of Kithrup, starting from the site of Toshio's island.

'Detonations of some sort,' Tsh't commented. 'The computer's interpreting them as bombings, but we've detected no missiles! And why this scattered pattern? The detonations are only occurring along thisss narrow stripe of longitude!'

'*More psi disturbances!*' an operator announced. '*Strong! And from numerous sources, all on the planet!*'

Gillian frowned. 'Those detonations aren't bombings. I remember seeing that pattern before. That's the boundary of this planetary crustal plate. Those disturbances may be volcanoes.

'I'd say it's the locals' way of showing they're unhappy.'

'?' Tsh't queried confusedly.

Gillian's expression was thoughtful, as if she was looking at something very far away. 'I think I'm starting to understand what's been going on. We can thank Creideiki for the fact that the psi-disturbances don't affect dolphins, for instance.'

The dolphins stared at her. Gillian smiled and patted Tsh't's flank.

'Not to worry, fem-fin. It's a long story, but I'll explain if we have time. I expect the biggest effect all this will have on us is crustquakes. We should be getting some shortly. Will we be able to ride them out down here?'

The dolphin lieutenant frowned. The way humans could change mental tracks midstride was beyond her comprehension.

'Yesss, I think so, Gillian. That is, so long as *that-t* remains stable.' She gestured through a port, toward the seacliff that loomed over their hybrid ship.

Gillian looked up at the hulking mass of rock, visible through cracks in the Thennanin armor. 'I'd forgotten about that. We'd better keep an eye on it.'

She turned back to the holo display, watching the spreading pattern of disturbances.

Come on, Hikahi! she urged silently. *Pick up Toshio and the others and get back here! I have to make a decision soon, and you might get back too late!*

The minutes passed. Several times the water seemed to tremble as a low rumble passed through the seafloor.

Gillian watched the blue globe of Kithrup. A string of flickering yellow pinpoints spread gradually northward, like an angry wound in the planet's side. Finally, the dots merged with a small group of tiny islands in the northeast quadrant.

That's where Tom is, she remembered.

Suddenly the comm operator thrashed at his station. 'Commander! I'm gett-ting a transmission! And it'sss in Anglic!'

103

TOM ORLEY

He held the microphone awkwardly. It had been designed for alien hands. Tom ran his tongue over his cracked lips. He didn't have time to go over his speech once more. Company would be arriving any moment now.

He pressed the transmit lever.

'Creideiki!' He spoke carefully. 'Record and replay for Gillian. She'll interpret.'

He knew every ship in near-space was listening to this transmitter by now. Probably a large number were already on their way here. If he composed his new lines properly, he could make sure even more of them came.

'My direct wire to the ship is broken,' he said. 'And a hundred kilometers is a long way to have to carry a message, so I'll risk this new coder, hoping it's not been broken in all the fighting here.'

That last was a tissue of fantasies for Galactic consumption. Now for the real message. Hidden in context, he had to tell *Streaker* what he knew.

'Jill? Our egg hatched, hon. And a zoo spilled out. A zoo of fierce critters!

'But I came across only one bedraggled sample of the brand we're shopping for. I've heard clues it's still for sale, on higher shelves, but those have been just clues. You and H and C are going to have to decide on that basis.

'Remember when old Jake Demwa took us along with him on that mission to the central *Library* on Tanith? Remember what he said about hunches? Tell Creideiki about it. It's his decision, but my gut feeling is, follow Jake's advice!'

He felt a thickening in his throat. He should cut this off. No sense in letting the Eatees zero in *too* closely.

'Jill.' He coughed. 'Hon, I'm out of the game now. Get Herbie and the rest of the data to the Council. And those abos, too. I've got to believe all this has been worth it.'

He closed his eyes and gripped, the mike. 'When you see old Jake, hoist a glass with him for me, will you?'

He wanted to say more, but realized that he was already getting a little too unambiguous. He couldn't afford to let the Galactics' language computers figure out what he was talking about.

He pursed his lips. And bid adieu in a language designed for such things.

> * Petals floating by,
> * Drift through my woman's hand,
> * As she remembers me – *

The carrier wave hissed until he cut the circuit.

He rose and carried the radio outside. Carefully approaching the edge of an open pool, he dropped the transmitter in. If anyone had

625

locked into a resonance with the crystals in the set, that Eatee would have to dive for it.

He stood there, by the pool, and watched low clouds roll past, dark and heavy with unspent rain.

They'd be arriving any moment; His weapons were at his belt, and his breathing tube, and a full canteen. He was ready for them.

He was standing that way, watching and waiting, when the steaming volcano on the horizon began to growl, then cough, then angrily spout bright fireworks into the sky.

The bridge was a blur. Gillian's eyes swam, but when she blinked the tears would not bead and drop away. Her eyes clung to them, like precious things.

'Shall we answer?' Tsh't spoke softly from next to her.

Gillian shook her head. *No*, she tried to say. But she could only mouth the word. Telempathically, she sensed the sympathy of those around her.

How can I mourn, she wondered, *when I can still feel him faintly? He is still alive out there, somewhere.*

How can I mourn?

She felt a swirl of movement as a fin approached cautiously and tried to report to Tsh't without disturbing her.

Gillian pressed her burning eyelids together. The tears flowed at last, in narrow trails down her cheeks. She couldn't reach under her mask to brush them away, so she let them lie. When she opened her eyes, her vision had cleared.

'I heard that, Wattaceti. Which way is Takkata-Jim headed?'

'Toward the Galactic flotillas, Commander. Though the fleets seem to be in chaosss! They are boiling every which way, after the confusion caused by that psi-burst. A major free-for-all is shaping up above ... above Mr Orley's position.'

Gillian nodded. 'We'll wait a little while longer. Go to condition yellow and keep me informed.'

Off-duty personnel were called to their posts. Suessi and D'Anite reported that the engines were warm.

Last chance, Hikahi, Gillian thought. *Are you coming?*

'Gillian!' Lucky Kaa called. With his harness arm he pointed out one of the ports. 'The cliff!'

Gillian hurried over and looked where the pilot indicated. The entire mass of rock was trembling. Cracks began to appear in the great wall that towered over *Streaker*.

'Lift stations!' Gillian commanded. 'Tsh't, take us out of here!'

104

GALACTICS

Cullcullabra bowed low before the Soro Krat.

'Have you interpreted the human's broadcast?' she snapped.

The stocky Pil bowed again, backing away slightly. 'No, Fleet-Mother, not completely. The human spoke in their two doggerel languages called "Anglic" and "Trinary." We have translation programs for both, of course, but they are so chaotic and contextual – unlike any civilized language . . . .'

The Librarian flinched as Krat hissed at him. 'Have you nothing?'

'Mistress, we think the last part of his message, in the dolphin-speech, may be the important part. It might have been a command to his clients, or . . . '

The Librarian piped dismay and dodged back into his station as a ling-plum missed him by inches.

'Hypotheses! Tentative conjectures!' Krat stormed. 'Even the Tandu boil with excitement and send expedition after futile piddling expedition to the site on the planet's surface from which the message emanated. And we must, perforce, follow, no?'

She stared about. Her crew avoided her gaze.

'Has anyone even a hypothesis *to explain that psi-assault which struck a short time ago, and seems to have disoriented every sophont in the system? Was* that, *also, a chimera of the Earthlings? Are the volcanoes that fill our instruments with static mere trickery?'*

The crew tried to look simultaneously busy and attentive. No one wanted to risk the ire of the fleet mother.

A Paha warrior strode from the office of detection.

'Mistress,' it announced. 'We did not notice before because of the volcanoes, but there has been a launching from the planet's surface.'

Krat felt a turn of glee. This was what she had been waiting for! Though she had sent ships of her own to the site of the radio messages, she had kept the core of her fleet together.

'Diversions! They were all diversions! The radio calls, the psi attacks, even the volcanoes!'

A part of her was curious about how the Earthlings had managed the last two. But that question would be solved when the humans and their clients were captured and interrogated.

'The Earthlings waited until much of the battle had moved near the

planet,' she muttered. 'And now they make their attempt to escape! Now we must ...'

Cullcullabra came up to her side and bowed. 'Mistress, I've done a deep search of the Library, and I think I know the source of the psi and the ...'

The Pi's eyes bugged out as Krat stabbed him in the abdomen with her mating claw. Krat stood up, carrying the Librarian in the air, then flung his lifeless body over to the wall.

She stood over the body breathing deeply of the death odors. No trouble would come over this killing, at least. The idiotic Pil had actually interrupted her! No one would deny that she had been within her rights this time.

She sheathed her claw. It had felt good. Not quite like mating with a male of her own race, who could fight back in kind, but good.

'Tell me about the Earthling ship,' she crooned to the Paha.

She noticed it waited a full second after she finished speaking to begin. 'Mistress,' it said. 'It is not their main vessel. It appears to be a scout ship, of some sort.'

Krat nodded. 'An emissary. I wondered why they did not try to work out a surrender agreement before this. Move the fleet to intercept this vessel. We must act before the Tandu notice it!

'Have our new Thennanin allies take the rear. I want them to understand that they are junior partners in this enterprise.'

'Mistress, the Thennanin have already begun preparations to leave us. They appear to be eager to join the chaos at the planet's surface.'

Krat grunted. 'Let them. We are even with the Tandu again. And the Thennanin are almost used up anyway. Let them depart. Then we proceed after the scout ship!'

She settled back onto the vletoor cushion and hummed to herself.

Soon. Soon.

The masters demanded too much. How could they expect the Acceptor to report specifically when so much was happening!

It was beautiful! Everything was going on at once! Sparkling little battles over the planet's surface ... bright hot volcanoes ... and that great psychic roar of anger that had poured out of the planet itself only a little while ago!

The anger still steamed and spumed. Why were the masters so uninterested in something so unique? Psi from below a planet's surface? The Acceptor could tell the Tandu so much about that angry voice, but they were only interested in shutting it out. It distracted them and made them feel vulnerable.

The Acceptor witnessed it all in bliss, until the punishment came *again. The masters applied a neural whip. Its legs jerked at the unpleasant sensation that coursed through its brain.*

Should it let the 'punishment' alter its behavior this time? The Acceptor considered.

It decided to ignore the 'pain.' Let them cajole and shout. The Acceptor was enthralled by the angry voices that churned below, and listened with all its might.

105

THE SKIFF

'What the devil ...?'

Dennie was rolled off the dry-shelf to splash into the water below. Sah'ot squawked in confusion as the tiny ship's hold tipped.

Then, in addition to the physical tossing, a rolling wave of psychic discomfort began to fill their heads. Dennie coughed water and grabbed a wall stanchion. She wanted to cover her ears.

'Not again,' she moaned. She tried to use the techniques Toshio had taught her ... focusing on her heartbeat to drive out the grinding static in her head. She hardly even noticed when Sah'ot shouted, 'It'sss them!'

The fin pressed the hatch button with his beak and sped out into the hallway. He streaked into the tiny control room.

'Creideiki!' he began, forgetting for a moment that the captain could not understand him. 'It's *them*. The voices from below!'

Creideiki looked back at him, and Sah'ot realized that the captain already knew. In fact, he seemed hardly surprised. Creideiki crooned a soft melody of acceptance. He appeared content.

From the pilot's station, Keepiru announced, 'I'm getting neutrinos and anti-g flux! They're coming from dead ahead. A small ship taking off.'

Hikahi nodded. 'Probably Takkata-Jim. I hope Gillian's right that he's been taken care of.'

They continued to drive underwater toward the east. About a half-hour later, Keepiru shouted again. 'More anti-g! A big ship! Taking off from near to the southwest!'

Creideiki's flukes struck the surface of the water.

> * *Up, up!*
> *Up and Look!*
> * *Look! :*

Hikahi nodded to Keepiru. 'Take her up.'

The skiff surfaced. Seawater slid in sheets off the ports.

They clustered around a southern port and watched as a distant wedge-shaped object erupted from the horizon, and lumbered into the sky, slowly gathering speed. They watched as it flew south, passing the speed of sound, finally disappearing into the high clouds.

They watched even after *Streaker*'s contrail began to drift and slowly come apart under Kithrup's contrary winds.

PART TEN

RAPTURE

'They are the lads that always live before the wind.'

HERMAN MELVILLE

106

TOSHIO

Toshio swam hard as the swell tried to drag him backward. He fought the current and strove for the open sea. Finally, just as he felt aching arms and legs could do no more, he reached calmer waters. With burning lungs he turned and watched as the metal-mound, now almost two kilometers away, sank slowly into its pit.

The sinking couldn't go on. The drill-tree had not completed its excavations when he and Dennie had blown it apart. The island would probably settle until the shaft was plugged.

Dull detonations groaned on all sides of him. Toshio treaded water and looked around. On islands in all directions trees swayed, and not from the wind. In the distance he saw at least three roiling clouds of steam and smoke rise from boiling patches in the sea. There was a growling of subsea quakes.

All this because of one little bomb? In spite of all he had been through, Toshio calmly wondered about the cause of it all. With nothing left to do but choose the manner of his dying, he felt queerly liberated.

What if the bomb released a vein of magma, Toshio wondered. If a volcano appeared anywhere, I'd think it would be in that drill-tree shaft. But I guess the island's plugging it.

The metal-mound that had been his home for two weeks seemed to have stopped sinking. A few treetops waved above the water.

Toshio wondered about the fate of Charles Dart. He couldn't imagine the chimpanzee swimming very far. Perhaps it was just as well. At least Charlie had had a clean exit.

Toshio felt a bit better having rested. He began swimming again, for the open sea.

About twenty minutes later there came another low rumbling. He turned around just in time to see the distant mound rocked by a terrific explosion. Dirt and vegetation flew in all directions. The mound itself heaved upward, almost out of the water, split apart, then fell back into a cloud of steam.

107

TAKKATA-JIM

'Calling battle fleet! Calling the battle fleet ahead! This is Lieutenant Takkata-Jim of the Terragens Survey Service. I wish to negotiate. Please ressspond!'

The receiver was silent. Takkata-Jim cursed. The radio *must* work. He had taken it from Thomas Orley's sled, and that human always maintained his equipment. Why weren't the Galactics answering?

The longboat was designed to be run by more than one person. The sudden and unexpected disaster at the island had forced him to abandon his *Stenos*. Now he had no one to help him. He had to juggle two or three jobs at once.

He watched the tactics display. A cluster of yellow lights were heading his way from Galactic north. It was a paltry flotilla compared with the great armadas that had come sweeping into the system only weeks ago. But it was still an awesome array of firepower. They were heading right for him.

Elsewhere, all was chaos. The planet was pockmarked with energy releases – boiling steam tornadoes where volcanoes emptied into the sea. And above the planet's northern hemisphere a free-for-all battle was going on.

Takkata-Jim increased the scale on his display and saw another fleet. It, too, had just started turning toward him.

The ether was filled with a roar of voices. AM, FM, PCM – every spot on the dial took part in the confusion. Could that explain why nobody seemed to hear him?

No. The Galactics had sophisticated computers. It had to be his own equipment. There had been no time to check it all before taking off!

Takkata-Jim nervously watched the map.

He was flying into a pod of tiger sharks, hoping to negotiate *Streaker*'s protection and eventual release. But he remembered the look on Gillian Baskin's face, a week before, when he had suggested giving the ETs everything they wanted. Metz had supported him then, but the expression on the woman's face came to mind now. She had looked at him pityingly and told him that fanatics never worked that way.

'They'll take all we have, thank us politely, and *then* boil us in oil,' she had commented.

Takkata-Jim tossed his head. *I don't believe it. Besides, anything is better than what she plans!*

He watched the tactics holo. The first fleet was only a hundred thousand klicks away, now. The computer gave him data on the ships, at last. They were Soro battlecruisers.

Soro! Takkata-Jim tasted bile from his first stomach. All the stories he had heard about them came to mind.

What if they shoot first? What if they're not even interested in prisoners? He looked at his own battle controls. The armament of the longboat was pitiful, but ...

A claw of his harness reached over to flick on the arming switch ... just for the small comfort it gave.

108

STREAKER

'Now both of the larger fleets turn toward Takkata-Jim!'

Gillian nodded. 'Keep me informed, Wattaceti.' She turned. 'Tsh't, how long can we stay hidden by these tectonic disturbances?'

'Our anti-g's been detectable for five minutess, Gillian. I don't think we can put off energy detection much longer by flying over volcanoes. If we're to make a break for it we've *got* to gain altitude.'

'We're being scanned at long range!' the detector operator snapped. 'A couple of ships from that battle over Orley's position are curiousss!'

'That's it, then,' Tsh't commented. 'We go for it.'

Gillian shook her head.

'Buy me five more minutes, Tsh't. I don't care about the stragglers up north. Keep me hidden from the main fleets just a little while longer!'

Tsh't whirled through the oxywater, leaving a trail of bubbles. 'Lucky Kaa! Steer south by southwest, toward that new volcano!'

Gillian stared intently at the display. A tiny blue speck showed the longboat, flying toward a mass of over thirty *much* larger dots.

'Come on, Takkata-Jim,' Gillian murmured to herself. 'I thought I had you figured out. Prove me right!'

There hadn't been a sound on the radio from the renegade lieutenant. Toshio must have done his job, and sabotaged the sets on the island.

The blue speck drew within one hundred thousand kilometers of the enemy.

'Telemetry! Takkata-Jim's armed his weaponsss!' Wattaceti announced.

Gillian nodded. *I knew it. The fellow's almost human. He'd have to have a stronger personality than I'd ever expected, not to do that, just for the security-blanket effect. As pointless as it seemed, who would go to face an enemy with his safeties on?*

Now, just a little closer ...

'Gillian!' The detector officer cried. 'I don't believe it-t! Takkata-Jim hasss ...'

Gillian smiled, a little sadly.

'Let me guess. Our brave vice-captain is firing on the entire battle fleet.'

Tsh't and Wattaceti turned to look at her, wide-eyed.

She shrugged. 'Come now. For all his faults, no one ever said Takkata-Jim wasn't brave.'

She grinned to hide her own nervousness. 'Get ready, everybody.'

109

TAKKATA-JIM

Takkata-Jim shrieked and grabbed at the toggle switch. It didn't work! The fire controls were activating without his orders!

Every few seconds a shudder passed through the little ship as a small seeker missile launched from the single torpedo tube. Small bursts of antimatter erupted from the longboat's nose, automatically aimed at the nearest alien vessel.

In a lucky shot, the lead Soro ship blossomed open like a fiery flower unfolding. The sheer surprise of the attack had overcome defenses designed to withstand nova heat.

He cursed and tried the override. It, too, had no effect.

As the Soro fleet began firing in return, Takkata-Jim wailed and swerved the little scout into a wild series of evasive maneuvers. With a dolphin's natural three-dimensional sense, he whirled off in a high-g gyration, threading salvos that passed chillingly close.

There was only one thing to do, only one possible source of succor. Takkata-Jim sent the scout streaking toward the second battle fleet. They must have witnessed his attack. They would think him an ally, if he survived long enough to reach them.

He sped out into space, chased by a herd of behemoths that turned and lumbered after him.

110

STREAKER

'Now, Gillian?'

'Almost, dear. Another minute.'

'Those shipsss from the north seem to have decided. Several of them are turning this way ... Correction, the whole skirmish is heading southward, toward usss!'

Gillian couldn't make herself feel too bad about drawing fire away from Tom's position. It was only returning his favor, after all.

'All right. You choose a trajectory. I want to head out east on the ecliptic, just as soon as that second fleet finishes turning toward the longboat.'

Tsh't warbled an impatient sigh. 'Aye, sir.' She swam to the pilot's position and conferred with Lucky Kaa.

111

TOM

He raised his head above the surface of the pool where he had taken refuge.

Where had everybody gone, all of a sudden? Minutes ago the sky had been ablaze with pyrotechnics. Burning ships were falling out of the sky, right and left. Now he caught sight of a few stragglers, high in the distant sky, speeding southward.

It took him a moment to come up with a guess.

Thanks, Jill, he thought. *Now give 'em hell for me.*

112

TAKKATA-JIM

Takkata-Jim spluttered in frustration. He was so busy there wasn't time to work on the fire controls. Desperate, he sent impulses shutting down whole blocks of computer memory. Finally, something worked. The weapons system turned off.

Frantically, he made the ship roll left and applied full thrust to escape a spread of torpedos.

The two fleets were coming together quickly, with him in between.

Takkata-Jim intended to dive into the second fleet and stop behind it, conveying by his actions what he couldn't say by radio, that he was seeking protection.

But the controls wouldn't respond! He couldn't correct from his last evasive maneuver! He must have shut down too much memory!

The longboat streaked outward at right angles to the converging fleets, away from both of them.

Both armadas turned to follow.

113

STREAKER

'Now!' she said.

The pilot needed no urging. He had already been adding momentum. Now he applied full power. *Streaker*'s engines roared and she left the atmosphere on a crackling trail of ionization. The acceleration could be felt even through stasis, even inside the fluid-filled bridge.

The gray sea disappeared under a white blanket of clouds. The horizon became a curve, then an arc. *Streaker* fell outward into an ocean of stars.

'They're following us. The skirmishers from up north.'

'How many?'

'About twenty.' Tsh't listened to her neural link for a moment. 'They're strung out. Except for a fairly big group at the rear, hardly any two of them seem to be of the same race. I hear shooting. They're fighting each other even as they chase us.'

'How many m that final bunch?'

'Um ... ssssix, I think.'

'Well, let's see what we can do when we stretch our legs.'

The planet fell behind them as Lucky Kaa sent *Streaker* accelerating in the direction Gillian had chosen.

Beyond Kithrup's horizon, a great battle had begun. Her path kept her hidden by the planet's bulk for several minutes. Then they came into view of the conflagration.

A million kilometers away, space was filled with bright explosions and hackle-raising shrieks that feebly penetrated the psi-screens.

Tsh't commented. 'The big boys are fighting over Takkata-Jim. We might even make it out of the system before the major fleets could catch up with usss.'

Gillian nodded. Toshio's sacrifice had not been in vain.

'Then our problem is these little guys on our tail. Somehow we've got to shake them off. Maybe we can do a dodge behind the gas giant planet. How long until we can get to it?'

'Hard to judge, Gillian. Maybe an hour. We can't use overdrive in system, and we're carrying a lot of excess mass.'

Tsh't listened to her link, concentrating. 'The ones on our tail have mostly stopped beating on each other. They may be damaged, but I think at least two of the lead ships will catch up with us about the time we reach the gasss giant.'

Gillian looked at the holo tank. Kithrup had shrunk to a tiny ball in one corner, a sparkle of battle beyond it. On this side a chain of small dots showed *Streaker*'s pursuers.

In the forward tank a shining pastel-striped globe began to grow. A huge world of frigid gas, looking much like Jupiter, swelled slowly but perceptibly.

Gillian pursed her lips and whistled softly. 'Well, if we can't outrun them I guess we'll have to try an ambush.'

Tsh't stared at her. 'Gillian, those are battleships! We're only an overweight Snark-class survey ship!'

Gillian grinned. 'This snark has become a boojum, girl. The Thennanin shell will do more than just slow us down. And we may be able to try something they'll never expect.'

She didn't mention that, given a chance, she wanted to hang around this system a while, in case of a miracle.

'Have all loose objects been secured?'

'Sstandard procedure. It's been done.'

'Good. Please order all crew out of the central bay. They're to strap themselves in wherever they can.'

Tsh't gave the order, then turned back with a questioning look.

Gillian explained. 'We're slow because we're overweight, right? They'll be shooting at us before we reach the cover of the gas giant, let alone overdrive range. Tell me, Tsh't, what's making us over-weight?'

'The Thennanin shell!'

'And? What else?'

Tsh't looked puzzled.

Gillian hinted with a riddle.

> ** Living touch*
>> *The substance of motion—*
> ** Like air, forgotten*
>> *Until it's gone! **

Tsh't stared blankly. Then she got it. Her eyes widened.

'Pretty tricky, yesss. It just might work, at that. Still, I'm glad you told me. The crew are going to want to wear the right apparel.'

Gillian tried to snap her fingers in the water, and failed. 'Spacesuits! You're right! Tsh't, what would I do without you!'

114

GALACTICS

'The side battle amongst all the remnant forces seems to have moved away from the planet,' a Paha warrior reported. *'They are streaming away from Kithrup, chasing a rather large vessel.'*

The Soro, Krat, finished paring a ling-plum. She fought to hide the nervous tremor in her left arm.

'Can you identify the one they pursue?'

'It does not appear to be the quarry.' The Paha tastefully ignored the fleet-mistress's obvious wave of relief on hearing this. *'It is too large to be the Earth ship. We have tentatively identified it as a crippled Thennanin, although ...'*

'Yes?' Krat asked archly.

The Paha hesitated. *'It behaves strangely. It is inordinately massive, and its motors seem to have a quasi-Tymbrimi tone. It is already too far to read clearly.'*

Krat grunted. *'What is our status?'*

'The Tandu parallel us, sniping at our flanks as we do theirs. We both chase the Earth scout. Both of us have ceased firing at the boat except when it gets too close to the other side.'

Krat growled. *'This vessel leads us farther and farther from the planet – from the true quarry. Have you contemplated a scoutship whose very purpose may have been to accomplish this?'* she snapped.

The Paha considered, then nodded. *'Yes, Fleet-Mother. It would be just like a Tymbrimi or wolfling trick. What do you suggest?'*

Krat was filled with frustration. It *had* to be a trick! Yet she couldn't abandon the chase, or the Tandu would capture the scoutship. And the longer the chase went on, the worse the attrition on both sides!

She threw the plum across the room. It splattered dead center on the rayed spiral glyph of the Library. A startled Pil jumped and squeaked in dismay, then glared at her insolently.

'Transmit Standard Truce Call Three,' Krat commanded with distaste. 'Contact the Tandu Stalker. We must put an end to this farce and get back to the planet at once!'

The Tandu Stalker asked the Trainer one more time. 'Can you arouse the Acceptor?'

The Trainer knelt before the Stalker, offering its own head. 'I cannot. It has entered an orgasmic state. It is over-stimulated. Operant manipulation does not achieve success.'

'Then we have no metaphysical way to investigate the strange chase behind us?'

'We do not. We can only use physical means.'

The Stalker's legs ratchetted. 'Go and remove your head. With your last volition, place it in my trophy rack.'

The Trainer rasped assent.

'May the new one I grow serve you better.'

'Indeed. But first,' the Stalker suggested, 'arrange to open a talk-line with the Soro. I shall sever the leg I use to talk with them, of course. But talk to them we now must.'

Buoult bit at his elbow spikes, then used them to preen his ridgecrest. He had guessed correctly! He had taken the last six Thennanin ships out of the battle between the Tandu and Soro, and arrived at the planet in time to join a long chase. Ten ragged ships were ahead of him, chasing an object that could only dimly be made out.

'More speed,' he urged. 'The others are uncoordinated.

While the Tandu and Soro chase a ruse, we are the only fair-sized squadron in the vicinity! We must chase!'

Far ahead of the Thennanin, a Gubru captain ruffled its feathers and cackled.

'We catch up! We catch up with the lumbering thing! And look! Now that we are near, look and see that its emanations are human! They fly inside a shell, but now we are near and can look and see and catch that which is inside that shell!

'Now we are near, and will catch them!'

Failure was still possible, of course. But total defeat would be unpermissible.

'If we cannot catch them,' it reminded itself, 'then we must make certain to destroy them.'

115

STREAKER

The gas giant loomed ahead. The heavily laden *Streaker* lumbered toward it.

'They'll expect us to dive in close for a tight hyperbolic,' Tsh't commented. 'It's generally a good tactic when being chased in a planetary system. A quick thrusst while we're swinging near the planet can translate into a major shift in direction.'

Gillian nodded. 'That's what they'll expect, but that's not what we'll do.'

They watched the screens as three large blips grew and then took form as solid figures – ships with ugly battle-scars and uglier weapons.

The great bulk of the planet began to intrude even as the pursuing ships grew larger.

'Are all fen secured?'

'Yesss!'

'Then you choose the time, Lieutenant. You have a better feel for space battles than I. You know what we want to do.'

Tsh't clapped her jaws together. 'I do, Gillian.'

They dove toward the planet.

'Sssoon. Soon they'll be committed . . .' Tsh't's eyes narrowed. She concentrated on sound images, transmitted by her neural link. The bridge was silent except for the nervous clicking of dolphin sonar. Gillian was reminded of tense situations on human ships, when half the crew would be whistling through their teeth without ever being aware of it.

'Get-t ready,' Tsh't told the engineering crew by intercom.

The pursuing ships disappeared briefly behind the planet's limb.

'Now!' she cried for Suessi to hear. 'Open the rear locks! Activate all pumps!' She swung to the pilot. 'Launch that decoy probe! Hard lateral acceleration! Apply stasis to compensate all but one g rearward! Repeat, allow one gravity rearward in the ship!'

Half the control boards in the bridge sprouted red lights. Forewarned, the crew overrode safeguards as the contents of *Streaker*'s central bay flew out behind her into the vacuum of open space.

*

The Gubru captain was concerned with a Pthaca ship encroaching on its lead. The commander contemplated maneuvers to destroy the Pthaca, but the master computer suddenly squawked frantically for attention.

'They have not done that!' the captain chanted as it stared in disbelief at the display. 'They cannot have done such a thing. They cannot have found such a devilish trap. They cannot have . . .'

It watched the Pthaca ship collide relativistically with a barrier that had not been there minutes before.

It was only a diffuse stream of gas particles, drifting in their path. But, unexpected, it met the Pthaca warship's screens like a solid wall. At a fair fraction of light speed, any barrier was deadly.

'Veer off!' the Gubru commanded. 'Fire all weapons on the quarry!'

Fiery energy lanced out, but the beams stuck an intangible wall between the Gubru and the rapidly turning Earth ship.

'Water!' it shrieked as it read the spectral report. 'A barrier of water vapor! A civilized race could not have found such a trick in the Library! A civilized race could not have stooped so low! A civilized race would not have . . .'

It screamed as the Gubru ship hit a cloud of drifting snow flakes.

Lightened by megatonnes, *Streaker* screamed about in an arc far tighter than she could have managed minutes before. Her locks closed, and the ship slowly refilled with air. Internal anti-gravity was reapplied. Her spacesuited crewfen flew back to their duty stations from hull rooms where they had taken refuge.

In the still water-filled bridge, Gillian watched the annihilation of the first two pursuing vessels. The crew cheered as the third battered cruiser swerved desperately, then suffered a malfunction at the last moment, and collided disastrously with the diffuse cloud. It dissolved into a flat ball of plasma.

'The rest of them are still out of sight beyond the gas giant,' Gillian said. 'After the chase from Kithrup, they'll think they know our dynamic, and never guess we could turn around like this!'

Tsh't looked less certain. 'Perhapsss. We did fire off a decoy probe along our old flight path, mimicking our radiation. They *may* chase it.

'At least I'd be willing to bet they'll come in on a tight and fast hyperbolic-c.'

'And we'll pick 'em off as they come!' Gillian felt a little giddy. There was just a chance they might be able to do it cleanly, so cleanly that they might be able to lie low, to wait a little longer for Hikahi and Creideiki. For another miracle.

Streaker groaned as she fought to change direction.

'Suessi says the wall braces are under stresss,' Lucky Kaa reported. 'He asks if you're going to be turning off stasis again, or pulling any other . . . uh, he calls them "wild, crazy, female maneuvers." His words, sssir!'

Gillian gave no answer. Suessi certainly didn't expect one.

Streaker completed her sharp turn and sped back the way she had come, just as two more battle cruisers came into view around the limb of the gas giant.

'Get 'em, Tsh't,' Gillian told the dolphin officer. An outrage she had not allowed to show in weeks of frustration came out in her voice. 'Use your own tactics. But *get* them!'

'Yesss!' Tsh't noted Gillian's balled fists. She felt it too. 'Now!' She whirled and called to the crew.

> * Patiently,
>> We took the insults—
> * Patiently,
>> Evil intent –

> * Now we stop,
>> Patient no longer—
> * Dream and logic,
>> Join in combat !! *

The bridge crew cheered. *Streaker* dove toward the surprised foe.

116

GALACTICS

The voice of the Soro matriarch growled out of the communications web. 'Then we are in agreement to stop this chase and join our forces?'

The Tandu Stalker promised itself it would remove two legs, not one, for the shame of making this agreement.

'Yes,' it replied. 'If we continue in the present manner, we will only erode ourselves down to nothing. You Soro fight well, for vermin. Let us unite and end it.'

Krat made it explicit. 'We swear by Pact Number One, the oldest and most binding to be found in the Library, to capture the Earthlings together, to extract the information together, and to seek out together *the emissaries of our ancestors, to let them be the judges of our dispute.'*

'Agreed,' the Tandu assented. 'Now let us finish here and turn about together to seize the prize.'

117

TAKKATA-JIM

He now understood what humans meant by a 'Nantucket sleighride.'

Takkata-Jim was tired. He had fled for what seemed like hours. Every time he tried to make the boat drift to one side, so he could surrender to one party, the other side fired salvos between him and his goal, forcing him back.

Then, some time ago, he detected a long chain of ships leaving Kithrup in the other direction. It didn't take much to figure out that *Streaker* was making her move.

It's over, then, he thought. *I tried to do my duty as I saw it, and save my own life at the same time. Now the die is cast. My plan is lost.*

I'm lost. There's nothing I can do except, maybe, buy Streaker *a few minutes.*

Some time ago the two fleets had stopped tearing at each other as they chased him. Takkata-Jim realized they were coming to an agreement.

Suddenly his receiver buzzed with a basic contact code in Galactic One. The message was simple ... stop and surrender to the combined Tandu-Soro fleet.

Takkata-Jim clapped his jaws together. He hadn't a transmitter, so he couldn't respond. But if he stopped dead in space they would probably take that as a surrender.

He delayed until the message had been repeated three times. Then he began decreasing speed ... but slowly. Very slowly, drawing out the time.

When the Galactics had drawn close, and their threats began to sound final, Takkata-Jim sighed and turned the longboat's fire-control computers back on.

The boat bucked as small missiles leaped away. He applied full thrust again.

When both flotillas simultaneously fired volleys of missiles at him, he tried to evade, of course. It would be unsporting to give up.

But he didn't have the heart for a major effort. Instead, while he waited, he worked on a poem.

> * *The saddest of things*
> *To a dolphin – even me—*
> *Is to die alone . . .* *

118

STREAKER

The ambush at the gas giant was unexpected. The enemy came in close, using the great planet's gravity to swing about in a tight hyperbolic turn. They were unprepared for an attack on their flanks.

Compared with their breakneck dive, *Streaker* was almost motionless. She fell upon the pair of cruisers as they passed, lacing a web-like tracery of antimatter in their paths.

One of the battleships blossomed into a fireball before *Streaker*'s computers could even identify it. Its screens were probably already damaged after weeks of battle.

The other cruiser was in better shape. Its screens flashed an ominous violet, and thin lines of exploding metal brightened its hull. But it passed through the trap and began decelerating furiously.

'It'll misss our mines, worse luck,' Tsh't announced. 'There wasn't time to lay a perfect pattern.'

'We can't have everything,' Gillian replied. 'You handled that brilliantly. He'll be some time getting back to us.'

Tsh't peered at the screen and listened to her neural link. 'He may be *very* tardy, if his engines keep misssssing. He's on a collision spiral with the planet!'

'Goody. Let's leave him and see about the others.'

Streaker's motion was taking her away from the giant planet, toward another group of five onrushing cruisers. Having witnessed part of the ambush, these were all adjusting course furiously.

'Now we see how well the Trojan Seahorse works,' Gillian said. 'The first bunch was close enough to read our engines and know we're Earth-made. But these guys were too far back. Has Suessi altered our power output along Thennanin lines, as planned?'

Wattaceti whistled confirmation. 'It's done. Suesssi says it'll cut efficiency, though. He reminds you that our engines aren't Thennanin.'

646

'Thank him for me. Now, for all our lives, what happens next depends on whether they're an unimaginative lot, as Tom guessed they'd be.

'Full power to the psi shields!'

'Aye, sssir!'

Energy detectors lit up as the oncoming ships swept them with probe-beams. The motley assortment of approaching ET vessels seemed to hesitate, then diverged.

'Numbers one, four, and five are accelerating to pass us by!' Tsh't announced. The bridge was filled with chattering dolphin applause.

'What about the others?'

Tsh't's manipulator arm pointed to two dots in the holotank. 'Decelerating and preparing for battle! We're picking up a beam-cast in Galactic Ten! It's a ritual challenge!'

Tsh't shook her head. 'They *do* think we're Thennanin! But they want to stop and finish us off!'

'Who are they?'

'Brothers of the Night!'

The magnification screens showed the two approaching battle-wagons, dark and deadly and growing nearer.

What to do? Gillian kept her face impassive. She knew the fen were watching her.

We can't outrun them, especially not while we're faking Thennanin engines or wearing this heavy Thennanin shell. But only a fool would try to take them in a straight battle.

A fighting fool like Tom, she thought ironically. *Or Creideiki. If either of them were in command I'd be preparing condolence wreaths for the Brothers of the Night right now.*

'Gillian?' Tsh't asked nervously.

Gillian shook herself. *Now. Decide now!*

She looked at the approaching death machines.

'Down their throats,' she said. 'Head toward Kithrup.'

119

GALACTICS

'We shall leave half of our joint fleet above the planet. None of the others will dare return, now that we have consolidated. We shall also send squadrons to clean the moons of hiding enemies, and to investigate the happenings out beyond the gas giant.'

The Tandu Stalker had only four legs now, instead of the former six. The Soro, Krat, wondered what accident had befallen the leader of her unpleasant allies.

Not that it really mattered. Krat dreamt of the day when she could personally detach the Stalker's remaining limbs, and then all its head buds.

'Is it possible that that out-planet chaos may be caused by the quarry?' she asked.

The Tandu's expression was unreadable on the display screen. 'All things are possible, even the impossible.' It sounded like a Tandu truism. 'But the quarry could not escape even the stragglers' small might. If they are captured by them, the remnants will fight over the spoils. When our task force arrives, we will take over. It is simple.'

Krat nodded. It did sound elegant.

Soon, *she told herself.* Soon we will wring the information out of the Earthlings, or sift it out of their wreckage. And soon thereafter we will be before our ancestors themselves.

I must try to make certain some few of the humans and dolphins are left alive, after they tell us where the Progenitor Fleet is located. My clients do not appreciate it when I use them for entertainment. It would save trouble if I found amusements outside the family.

Wistfully, she longed for a scrappy male of her own species, as a joint Tandu-Soro detachment of thirteen ships blasted at full thrust toward the gas-giant planet.

120

STREAKER

'Damage to the stasis flanges on the port ssside!' Wattaceti announced. 'All missile slots in that sector are out!'

'Any harm to the inner hull?' Gillian asked anxiously.

The fin looked blank as he sounded out the damage control computer. 'Nope. The Thennanin shell's taken it all, ssso far. But Suessi says the bracings are weakening!'

'They'll try to concentrate fire on the port side now that it'ss damaged,' Tsh't said. 'And they'll expect us to turn away. Starboard missile batteries! Fire mines at forty degrees azimuth by one hundred south! Slow thrust and lurk fuses!'

'But-t no one's there!'

'They *will* be! Fire! Helm, roll ship left two radians per minute, pitch up one per minute!'

Streaker shuddered and groaned as she turned slowly in space. Her screens flickered dangerously under powerful battle beams she could never hope to match. Not a blow had been struck on her opponents. They kept up easily with her lumbering attempts at evasion.

From *Streaker*'s shadowed quarter six small missiles puffed lazily outward, then cut thrust. *Streaker* turned to try to protect her weakened side, a little more slowly than she was really capable of turning.

Sensing a fatal weakness, the enemy battleships followed the turn. Beams stabbed out to blast at *Streaker*'s damaged side, at what the Brothers of the Night thought was their supine enemy's real hull.

Streaker shook as the beams penetrated her shields and struck the Thennanin armor. Stasis flickered, giving them all eerily vivid feelings of déjà vu. Even in the water-filled bridge the blasts nearly threw the crew from their stations. Damage control spotters screamed reports of smoke and fire, of melting armor and buckling walls.

The cruisers drifted confidently into the mined region, and the missiles exploded.

Gillian clutched a handrail whitely. On those sensors that had not been blasted to vapor, the enemy was hidden by a cloud of roiling gas.

'Hard thrussst, twenty degrees by two seventy!' Tsh't called. 'Stop roll and pitch!'

The abused engines struggled. The bracings holding *Streaker* to her armored shell groaned as she accelerated in a new direction.

'Blessings on that damned Thennanin armor!' One of the fins sighed. 'Those beams would've sliced *Streaker* like toasssst!'

Gillian peered into one of the few operational holotanks, straining to see through the space-smoke and debris. Finally, she saw the enemy.

'A hit! A palpable hit!' she exulted.

One of the battlewagons bore a gaping hole in its side, burning metal still curled away from the cavity, and secondary explosions shook the cruiser.

The other one appeared undamaged, but more wary than before.

Oh, keep hesitating, she urged them silently. *Let us get a head start!*

'Anybody else around?' she asked Tsh't. If these two ships were the only ones left, she'd be willing to turn the engines back on full power, and let even the devil know they were an Earth ship!

The lieutenant blinked. 'Yes, Gillian. Six more. Approaching rapidly.' Tsh't shook her head. 'There's no way we'll get away from this new bunch. They're coming too fasst. Sorry, Gillian.'

'The Brothers have made up their minds,' Wattaceti announced. 'They're coming after uss!'

Tsh't rolled her eyes. Gillian silently agreed. *We won't fool them again.*

'Suessi calls. He wants to know ifff . . .'

Gillian sighed. 'Tell Hannes there don't seem to be any more "female tricks" forthcoming. I'm fresh out of ideas.'

The two battleships drew nearer, chasing *Streaker*'s stern. They held their fire, saving it for a total assault.

Gillian thought about Tom. She couldn't help feeling that she had failed him.

It really was a good plan, hon. I only wish I'd executed it competently for you.

The enemy bore down on them, looming ominously.

Then Lucky Kaa shouted. 'Vector change!' The pilot's tail thrashed. 'They're veering off! Fleeing like mullet-t!'

Gillian blinked in confusion. 'But they had us!'

'It's the newcomers, Gillian! Those six oncoming shipsss!' Tsh't shouted joyfully.

'What? What *about* them?'

Tsh't grinned as broadly as a neo-fin could manage. 'They're *Thennanin*! They're coming in blassting! And it'sss not us they're shooting at!'

The screens showed the pair of cruisers that had been chasing them, now in full flight, firing Parthian style at the approaching mini-flotilla.

Gillian laughed. 'Wattaceti! Tell Suessi to shut down! Put everything on idle and pour out smoke. We want to play the gravely wounded soldier!'

After a moment came the engineer's reply.

'Suessi says that that-t will be no problem. No problem at all.'

121

GALACTICS

Buoult's crest riffled with waves of emotion. Krondorsfire *lay ahead of them, battered but proud. He had thought the old battlewagon lost since the first day of the battle, and Baron Ebremsev, its commander. Buoult longed to see his old comrade again.*

'Is there still no response?' *he asked the communicator.*

'No, Commander. The ship is silent. It is possible they just now sustained a fatal blow that . . . Wait! There* is *something! A flashing-light* signal in uncoded open-talk! They are sending from one of the viewing ports!'

Buoult edged forward eagerly. 'What do they say? Do they require help?'

The communications officer huddled before his monitor, watching the winking lights, jotting notes.

'All weapons and communications destroyed,' he recited, 'life support and auxiliary drives still serviceable ... Earthlings ahead, chased by a few dregs ... We shall withdraw ... happy hunting ... Krondorsfire out.'

Buoult thought the message a little odd. Why would Ebremsev want to pull out if he could still follow and at least draw fire from the enemy? Perhaps he was making a brave show in order not to hold them back. Buoult was about to insist on sending aid anyway when the communications officer spoke again.

'Commander! A squadron is outbound from the water planet! At least ten vessels! I read signs of both Tandu and Soro!'

Buoult's crest momentarily collapsed. It had come to pass, the very last alliance of heretics.

'We have one chance! After the fugitives at once! We can overpower the remnants even as they overpower the Earthlings, and be off before the Tandu and Soro arrive!'

As his ship leapt outward, he had a message sent back to Krondorsfire. 'May the Great Ghosts dwell with you ...'

122

STREAKER

'That's a pretty sophisticated little computer you've kept hidden away all this time,' Tsh't commented.

Gillian smiled. 'It's actually Tom's.'

The fins nodded wisely. That was explanation enough.

Gillian thanked the Niss machine for its hurry-up Thennanin translation. The disembodied voice whispered from a cluster of sparkles that floated near her, dancing and whirling amidst the fizzing oxywater bubbles.

'I could do nothing else, Gillian Baskin,' it replied. 'You few lost Earthlings have accumulated, in the course of heaping disasters upon yourselves, more data than my masters have gathered in the last thousand years. The lessons about uplift alone will profit the Tymbrimi, who are always willing to learn – even from wolflings.'

The voice faded, and the sparkles vanished before Gillian could reply.

'The signal party's returned from the viewport, Gillian,' Tsh't said. 'The Thennanin have gone off chasing our shadows, but they'll be back. What-t do we do now?'

Gillian felt tremors of adrenaline reaction. She had not planned beyond this point. There was only one thing she wanted desperately to do now. Only one destination in the universe she wanted to go.

'Kithrup,' she whispered.

Gillian shook herself. 'Kithrup?' She looked at Tsh't, knowing what the answer would be, wishing it weren't so.

Tsh't shook her sleek head. 'There'sss a flotilla orbiting Kithrup now, Gillian. No fighting. There must've been a winner in the big battle.

'Another squadron's heading this way fassst. A big one. We don't want 'em to get close enough to see through our disguise.'

Gillian nodded. Her voice didn't want to function, but she made the words come.

'North,' she said.

'Take us out along Galactic north, Tsh't . . . to the transfer point. Full speed. When we get close enough, we'll dump the Seahorse, and get the Ifni-damned hell out of here with . . . with the ashes we've won.'

The dolphins returned to their posts. The rumble of the engines gathered strength.

Gillian swam to one dark corner of the crystal dome, to a place where there was a chink in the Thennanin armor, where she could look at the stars directly.

Streaker picked up speed.

123

GALACTICS

The Tandu-Soro detachment was gaining on the strung-out fugitives.

'Mistress, a crippled Thennanin is approaching the transfer point on an escape trajectory.'

Krat squirmed on her cushion and snarled. 'So? Casualties have left the battle area before. All sides try to evacuate their wounded. Why do you bother me when we are even now closing in!'

The little Pila detector officer scuttled back into its cubbyhole. Krat bent to watch her forward screens.

A small squadron of Thennanin struggled to keep ahead. Further on, at the edge of detection, sparks of desultory battle showed that the leaders were still bickering, even as they closed on the quarry.

What if they're mistaken, *Krat wondered.* We chase the Thennanin, who chase the remnants, who chase what? Those fools might even be chasing each other!

It didn't matter. Half the Tandu-Soro fleet orbited Kithrup, so the Earthlings were trapped, one way or another.

We'll deal with the Tandu in good time, *she thought,* and meet the. ancient ones alone.

'Mistress!' *the Pila shouted shrilly.* 'There is a transmission from the transfer point!'

'Bother me *one* more *time with inconsequentials . . . '* she rumbled, *flexing her mating claw threateningly. But the client interrupted her! The Pil dared to* interrupt!'

'Mistress. It is the Earth ship! They taunt us! They defy us! They . . . '

'Show *me!' Krat hissed.* 'It must be a trick! Show me at once!'

The Pil ducked back into its section. On Krat's main screen appeared the holo image of a man, and several dolphins. From the man's shape, Krat could tell it was a female, probably their leader.

'. . . stupid creatures unworthy of the name "sophonts." Foolish, pre-sentient upspring of errant masters. We slip away from all your armed might, laughing at your clumsiness! We slip away as we always will, you pathetic creatures. And now that we have a real head start, you'll never catch us! What better proof that the Progenitors favor not you, but us! What better proof . . . '

The taunt went on. Krat listened, enraged, yet at the same time savoring the artistry of it. These men are better than I'd thought. Their insults are wordy and overblown, but they have talent. They deserve honorable, slow deaths.

'Mistress! The Tandu with us are changing course! Their other ships are leaving Kithrup for the transfer point!'

Krat hissed in despair. 'After them! After them at once! We followed them through space this far. The chase only goes on!'

The crew bent to their tasks resignedly. The Earth ship was in a good position to escape. At best this would be a long chase.

Krat realized that she would never make it home in time for mating. She would die out here.

On her screen, the man continued to taunt them.

'Librarian!' *she called.* 'I do not understand some of the man's words. Find out what that phrase – Nyaahh nyaaah – means in their beastly wolfling tongue!'

124

TOM ORLEY

Cross legged on a woven mat of reeds, shaded by a floating wreck, he listened as a muttering volcano slowly sputtered into silence. Contemplating starvation, he listened to the soft, wet sounds of the endless weedscape, and found in them a homely beauty. The squishy, random rhythms blended into a backdrop for his meditation.

On the mat in front of him, like a focus mandala, lay the message bomb he had never set off. The container glistened in the sunlight of north Kithrup's first fine day in weeks. Highlights shone in dimpled places where the metal had been battered, as he had been. The dented surface gleamed still.

Where are you now?

The subsurface sea-waves made his platform undulate gently. He floated in a trance through levels of awareness, like an old man poking idly through his attic, like an old-time hobo looking with mild curiosity through the slats of a moving boxcar.

Where are you now, my love?

He recalled a Japanese haiku from the eighteenth century, by the great poet Yosa Buson.

> *As the spring rains fall,*
> *Soaking in them, on the roof*
> *Is a child's rag ball.*

Watching blank images in the dents on the psi-globe, he listened to the creaking of the flat jungle – its skittering little animal sounds – the wind riffling through the wet, flat leaves.

Where is that part of me that has departed?

He listened to the slow pulse of a world ocean, watched patterns in the metal, and after a while, in the reflections in the dents and creases, an image came to him.

A blunt, bulky, wedge shape approached a place that was a *notplace*, a shining blackness in space. As he watched, the bulky thing cracked open. The thick carapace slowly split apart, like a hatching egg. The shards fell away, and there remained a slender nubbed cylinder, looking a bit like a caterpillar. Around it glowed a nimbus, a thickening shell of probability that hardened even as he watched.

No illusion, he decided. It cannot be an illusion.

He opened himself to the image, accepting it. And from the cater-pillar a thought winged to him.

> *Blossoms on the pear*
> *and a woman in the moonlight*
> *reads a letter there ...*

His slowly healing lips hurt as he smiled. It was another haiku by Buson. Her message was as unambiguous as could be, under the cir-cumstances. She had somehow picked up his trance-poem, and responded in kind.

'Jill ... ' he cast as hard as he could.

The caterpillar shape, sheathed in a cocoon of stasis, approached the great hole in space. It dropped forward toward the *not-place*, grew transparent as it fell, then vanished.

For a long time Tom sat very still, watching the highlights on the metal globe slowly shift as the morning passed.

Finally, he decided it wouldn't do him or the universe any harm if he started doing something about survival.

125

THE SKIFF

'Between you two crazy males, have you come any closer to figuring out what he'sss talking about?'

Keepiru and Sah'ot just stared back at Hikahi. They turned back to their discussion without answering her, huddling with Creideiki, trying to interpret the captain's convoluted instructions.

Hikahi rolled her eyes and turned to Toshio. 'You'd think they'd include me in these seances of theirs. After all, Creideiki and I are mates!'

Toshio shrugged. 'Creideiki needs Sah'ot's language skill and Keepiru's ability as a pilot. But you saw their faces. They're halfway into the Whale Dream right now. We can't afford to have you that way while you're in command.'

'Hmmmph.' Hikahi spumed, only slightly mollified. 'I suppose you've finished the inventory, Toshio?'

'Yes, sir.' He nodded. 'I have a written list ready. We're well enough stocked in consumables to last to the first transfer point, and at least one beyond that. Of course, we're in the middle of nowhere, so we'll need at least *five* transfer jumps to get anywhere near civilization. Our charts are pitifully inadequate, our drives will probably fail over the long haul, and few ships our size have even taken transfer points successfully. Aside from all that, and the cramped living quarters, I think we're all right.'

Hikahi sighed. 'We can't lose anything by trying. At leasst the Galactics are gone.'

'Yeah,' he agreed. 'It was a nice stroke, Gillian taunting the Eatees at the last minute. It let us know they got away, and got the Eatees off our backs.'

'Don't say 'Eatees,' Toshio. It'ss not polite. You may offend some nice Kanten or Linten one day if you get into the habit.'

Toshio swallowed and ducked his head. No matter where or when, no lieutenant had ever been known to slacken off on a middie. 'Yes, sir,' he said.

Hikahi grinned and flicked a small splash of water on the youth with her lower jaw.

> * Duty, duty
> > Brave shark-biter
> * What reward
> > Could taste better? *

Toshio blushed and nodded.

The skiff started to move again. Keepiru was back in the pilot's saddle. Creideiki and Sah'ot chattered excitedly in a semi-Primal rhythm which still sent shivers down Hikahi's spine. And Sah'ot had said that Creideiki was toning it down on purpose!

She was still getting used to the idea that Creideiki's injury might have been a door opening, rather than a closing.

The skiff lifted from the sea and began to speed eastward, following Creideiki's hunch.

'What about passenger morale?' Hikahi asked Toshio.

'Well, I guess it's all right. That pair of Kiqui are happy so long as they're with Dennie. And Dennie's happy ... well, she's happy enough for now.'

Hikahi was amused. Why should the youth be embarrassed about Dennie's other preoccupation? She was glad the two young humans had each other, as she had Creideiki.

In spite of his new, eerie side, Creideiki was the same dolphin. The newness was something he used, something he seemed only to have begun exploring. He could hardly speak, but he conveyed his great intellect – and his caring – in other ways.

'What about Charlie?' she asked Toshio.

Toshio sighed. 'He's still embarrassed.'

They had found the chimp a day after the great earthquakes, clinging to a floating tree trunk, sopping wet. He had been unable to speak for ten hours, and had kept climbing the walls in the skiff's tiny hold until he finally calmed down.

Charlie finally admitted that he had scrambled to the top of a tall tree just before the island blew. It had saved his life, but the stereotype mortified him.

Toshio and Hikahi crowded in behind Keepiru's station and watched as the ocean rolled swiftly beneath the skiff. For minutes at a time the sea turned a brilliant green as they passed over great swatches of vine. The little boat sped toward the sun.

They had been searching for almost a week, ever since *Streaker* had departed.

First found had been Toshio, swimming purposefully westward, never giving up. Then Dennie had led them to another island where there was a tribe of Kiqui. While she negotiated another treaty, they searched for and found Charles Dart.

Takkata-Jim's *Stenos* were all missing or dead.

After that had come one last, and apparently forlorn, search. They had been at this last phase for several days now.

Hikahi was about to give up. They couldn't go on wasting time and consumables like this. Not with the journey they had ahead of them.

Not that they really had much of a chance. No one had ever heard of a voyage like they planned. A cross-Galactic journey in the skiff would make Captain Bligh's epic crossing of the Pacific in the *Bounty*'s longboat seem like an afternoon jaunt.

She kept her appraisal to herself, though. Creideiki and Keepiru probably understood what lay ahead of them. Toshio seemed to have guessed part of it already. There was no reason to inform the others until they had to cut the rations for the fourth time.

She sighed.

> * *Of what else*
> > *Are heroes made*
> * *Than men and women*
> > *Who, like us,*
> * *Try—* *

Keepiru's fluting call of triumph was like a shrill trumpet. He squawled and tossed on his platform. The skiff rolled left and right in a wiggle-waggle, then went into a screaming climb.

'What the f – !!' Toshio stopped himself. 'Holy jumping turtle-fish, Keepiru! What *is* it?'

Hikahi used a harness arm to grab a wall stanchion, and looked out a port. She sighed for a third time, long and deep.

The smoke from his fire momentarily hid the boat from sight. The first he knew of it was the sonic boom that rolled over him, nearly knocking over his drying racks.

The human standing on the woven reed mat almost dove for cover, but a hunch made him stop and look up instead.

His eyes were sun-squinted. Crow's-feet that had not been there a few weeks before lay at the corners. His beard was black, with thin gray flecks. It had grown out and nearly stopped itching, almost covering a ragged scar that ran down one cheek.

Shading his eyes, he recognized the wild maneuvers before he did the outlines of the tiny ship. It streaked high into the sky and looped about, coming back to screech past him again.

He reached out to steady the drying racks against the thunder. No sense in letting the meat go to waste. It had taken a lot of work to harvest it, strip it, and prepare it. They might need it for the voyage ahead.

He wasn't sure how the fen would take to the stuff, but it was nourishing ... the only food on the planet that an Earthling could eat.

Gubru jerky, Tandu strips, and flayed Episiarch would never make it into haute cuisine, of course. But perhaps they were an acquired taste.

He grinned and waved as Keepiru finally calmed down enough to bring the skiff to a halt nearby.

How could I ever have doubted he'd still be alive? Hikahi wondered, joyfully. *Gillian said he had to live. None of the Galactics could ever touch him. How could they?*

And why, in the wide universe, was I ever worried about getting home?

EPILOGUE

: Rest : Rest And Listen :
: Rest And Listen And Learn, Creideiki :
: For The Startide Rises :
: In The Currents Of The Dark ;
And We Have Waited Long, For What Must Be :

POSTSCRIPT

Dolphin names often sound as if they are Polynesian or Japanese. In some cases this is true. In general, however, the neo-fin chooses for a name a sound he likes, usually a polysyllabic word with strong alternating vowels and consonants.

In Anglic, the words 'man,' 'men,' and 'mankind' apply to humans without reference to gender. On those occasions when gender is important, a female human is referred to as a 'fem,' and a male human as a 'mel.'

Dolphin languages are the author's invention, and are not meant to represent the communication of natural dolphins and whales today. We are only beginning to understand the place of the cetaceans in the world, as we are just beginning to understand our own.

The author wishes to thank all those who helped with this work, with their advice and criticism and encouragement, especially Mark Grygier, Anita Everson, Patrick Maher, Rick and Pattie Harper, Ray Feist, Richard Spahl, Ethan Munson, and, as always, Dan Brin. Lou Aronica and Tappan King of Bantam Books were most helpful with encouragement when morale was lowest.

The translated haiku by Yosa Buson were from *An Anthology of Japanese Literature*, compiled and edited by Donald Keene, published by Grove Press.

The world's many paths diverge, in both reality and imagination. The creatures of this novel are all fanciful. But it may happen that some of our fellow mammals will one day be our partners. We owe it to that possible future to let their potential survive.

August 1982
DAVID BRIN

THE UPLIFT WAR

To Jane Goodall, Sarah Hrdy, and all the others who are helping us at last to learn to understand.

And to Dian Fossey, who died fighting so that beauty and potential might live.

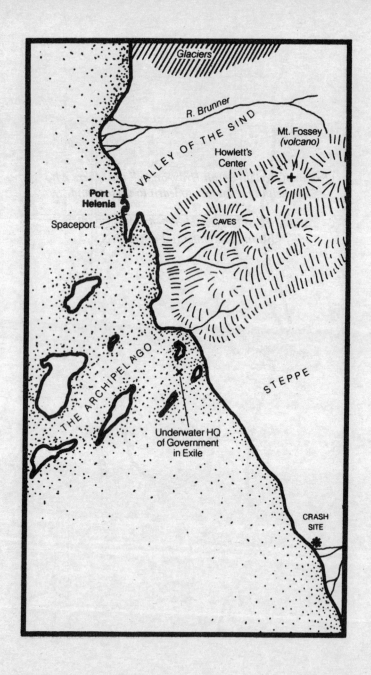

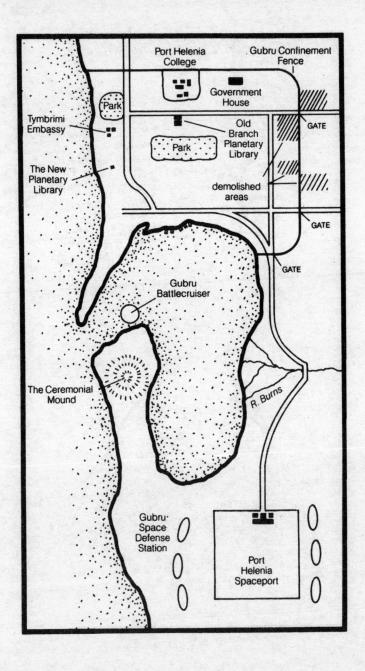

PRELUDE

How strange, that such an insignificant little world should come to matter so much.

Traffic roared amid the towers of Capital City, just beyond the sealed crystal dome of the official palanquin. But no sound penetrated to disturb the bureaucrat of Cost and Caution, who concentrated only on the holo-image of a small planet, turning slowly within reach of one down-covered arm. Blue seas and a jewel-bright spray of islands came into view as the bureaucrat watched, sparkling in the reflected glow of an out-of-view star.

If I were one of the gods spoken of in wolfling legends ... the bureaucrat imagined. Its pinions flexed. There was the feeling one had only to reach out with a talon and seize ...

But no. The absurd idea demonstrated that the bureaucrat had spent too much time studying the enemy. Crazy Terran concepts were infecting its mind.

Two downy aides fluttered quietly nearby, preening the bureaucrat's feathers and bright torc for the appointment ahead. They were ignored. Aircars and floater barges darted aside and regimented lanes of traffic melted away before the bright beacon of the official vehicle. This was status normally accorded only royalty, but within the palanquin all went on unnoticed as the bureaucrat's heavy beak lowered toward the holo-image.

Garth. So many times the victim.

The outlines of brown continents and shallow blue seas lay partly smeared under pinwheel stormclouds, as deceptively white and soft to the eye as a Gubru's plumage. Along just one chain of islands – and at a single point at the edge of the largest continent – shone the lights of a few small cities. Everywhere else the world appeared untouched, perturbed only by occasional flickering strokes of storm-brewed lightning.

Strings of code symbols told a darker truth. Garth was a poor place, a bad risk. Why else had the wolfling humans and their clients been granted a colony leasehold there? The place had been written off by the Galactic Institutes long ago.

And now, unhappy little world, you have been chosen as a site for war.

For practice, the bureaucrat of Cost and Caution thought in Anglic, the beastly, unsanctioned language of the Earthling creatures. Most Gubru considered the study of alien things an unwholesome pastime, but now the bureaucrat's obsession seemed about to pay off at last.

At last. Today.

The palanquin had threaded past the great towers of Capital City, and a mammoth edifice of opalescent stone now seemed to rise just ahead. The Conclave Arena, seat of government of all the Gubru race and clan.

Nervous, anticipatory shivers flowed down the bureaucrat's head-crest all the way to its vestigial flight feathers, bringing forth chirps of complaint from the two Kwackoo aides. How could they finish preening the bureaucrat's fine white feathers, they asked, or buff its long, hooked beak, if it didn't sit still?

'I comprehend, understand, will comply,' the bureaucrat answered indulgently in Standard Galactic Language Number Three. These Kwackoo were loyal creatures, to be allowed some minor impertinences. For distraction, the bureaucrat returned to thoughts of the small planet, Garth.

It is the most defenseless Earthling outpost ... the one most easily taken hostage. That is why the military pushed for this operation, even while we are hard-pressed elsewhere in space. This will strike deeply at the wolflings, and we may thereby coerce them to yield what we want.

After the armed forces, the priesthood had been next to agree to the plan. Recently the Guardians of Propriety had ruled that an invasion could be undertaken without any loss of honor.

That left the Civil Service – the third leg of the Perch of Command. And there consensus had broken. The bureaucrat's superiors in the Department of Cost and Caution had demurred. The plan was too risky, they declared. Too expensive.

A perch cannot stand long on two legs. There must be consensus. There must be compromise.

There are times when a nest cannot avoid taking risks.

The mountainous Conclave Arena became a cliff of dressed stone, covering half the sky. A cavernous opening loomed, then swallowed the palanquin. With a quiet murmur the small vessel's gravities shut down and the canopy lifted. A crowd of Gubru in the normal white plumage of adult neuters already waited at the foot of the landing apron.

They know, the bureaucrat thought, regarding them with its right eye. *They know I am already no longer one of them.*

In its other eye the bureaucrat caught a last glimpse of the white-swaddled blue globe. Garth.

Soon, the bureaucrat thought in Anglic. *We shall meet soon.*

*

The Conclave Arena was a riot of color. And such colors! Feathers shimmered everywhere in the royal hues, crimson, amber, and arsene blue.

Two four-footed Kwackoo servants opened a ceremonial portal for the bureaucrat of Cost and Caution, who momentarily had to stop and hiss in awe at the grandeur of the Arena. Hundreds of perches lined the terraced walls, crafted in delicate, ornate beauty out of costly woods imported from a hundred worlds. And all around, in regal splendor, stood the Roost Masters of the Gubru race.

No matter how well it had prepared for today, the bureaucrat could not help feeling deeply moved. Never had it seen so many queens and princes at one time!

To an alien, there might seem little to distinguish the bureaucrat from its lords. All were tall, slender descendants of flightless birds. To the eye, only the Roost Masters' striking colored plumage set them apart from the majority of the race. More important differences lay underneath, however. These, after all, were queens and princes, possessed of gender and the proven right to command.

Nearby Roost Masters turned their sharp beaks aside in order to watch with one eye as the bureaucrat of Cost and Caution hurried through a quick, mincing dance of ritual abasement.

Such colors! Love rose within the bureaucrat's downy breast, a hormonal surge triggered by those royal hues. It was an ancient, instinctive response, and no Gubru had ever proposed changing it. Not even after they had learned the art of gene-altering and become starfarers. Those of the race who achieved the ultimate – color and gender – had to be worshipped and obeyed by those who were still white and neuter.

It was the very heart of what it meant to be Gubru.

It was good. It was the way.

The bureaucrat noticed that two other white-plumed Gubru had also entered the Arena through neighboring doors. They joined the bureaucrat upon the central platform. Together the three of them took low perches facing the assembled Roost Masters.

The one on the right was draped in a silvery robe and bore around its narrow white throat the striped torc of priesthood.

The candidate on the left wore the sidearm and steel talon guards of a military officer. The tips of its crest feathers were dyed to show the rank of stoop-colonel.

Aloof, the other two white-plumed Gubru did not turn to acknowledge the bureaucrat. Nor did the bureaucrat offer any sign of recognizing them. Nevertheless, it felt a thrill. *We are three!*

The President of the Conclave – an aged queen whose once fiery plumage had now faded to a pale pinkish wash – fluffed her feathers and opened her beak. The Arena's acoustics automatically amplified her voice as she chirped for attention. On all sides the other queens and princes fell silent.

The Conclave President raised one slender, down-covered arm. Then she began to croon and sway. One by one, the other Roost Masters joined in, and soon the crowd of blue, amber, and crimson forms was rocking with her. From the royal assemblage there rose a low, atonal moaning.

'Zoooon . . .'

'Since time immemorial,' the President chirped in formal Galactic Three. 'Since before our glory, since before our patronhood, since before even our Uplift into sentience, it has been our way to seek balance.' The assembly chanted in counter rhythm.

> *'Balance on the ground's brown seams,*
> *Balance in the rough air streams,*
> *Balance in our greatest schemes.'*

'Back when our ancestors were still pre-sentient beasts, back before our Gooksyu patrons found us and uplifted us to knowledge, back before we even spoke or knew tools, we had already learned this wisdom, this way of coming to decision, this way of coming to consensus, this way of making love.'

'Zoooon . . .'

'As half-animals, our ancestors still knew that we must . . . must choose . . . must choose three.'

> *'One to hunt and strike with daring,*
> *for glory and for territory!*
> *One to seek the righteous bearing,*
> *for purity and propriety!*
> *One to warn of danger looming,*
> *for our eggs' security!'*

The bureaucrat of Cost and Caution sensed the other two candidates on either side and knew they were just as electrically aware, just as caught up in tense expectation. There was no greater honor than to be chosen as the three of them had been.

Of course all young Gubru were taught that this way was best, for what other species so beautifully combined politics and philosophy with lovemaking and reproduction? The system had served their race and clan well for ages. It had brought them to the heights of power in Galactic society.

And now it may have brought us to the brink of ruin.

Perhaps it was sacrilegious even to imagine it, but the bureaucrat of Cost and Caution could not help wondering if one of the other methods it had studied might not be better after all. It had read of so many styles of government used by other races and clans – autarchies and aristocracies, technocracies and democracies, syndicates and meritocracies. Might not one of those actually be a better way of judging the right path in a dangerous universe?

The idea might be irreverent, but such unconventional thinking was the reason certain Roost Masters had singled out the bureaucrat for a role of destiny. Over the days and months ahead, someone among the three would have to be the *doubting* one. That was ever the role of Cost and Caution.

'In this way, we strike a balance. In this way, we seek consensus. In this way, we resolve conflict.'

'*Zooon!*' agreed the gathered queens and princes.

Much negotiation had gone into selecting each of the candidates, one from the military, one from the priestly orders, and one from the Civil Service. If all worked out well, a new queen and two new princes would emerge from the molting ahead. And along with a vital new line of eggs for the race would also come a new *policy*, one arising out of the merging of their views.

That was how it was supposed to end. The *beginning*, however, was another matter. Fated eventually to be lovers, the three would from the start also be competitors. Adversaries.

For there could be only one queen.

'We send forth this trio on a vital mission. A mission of conquest. A mission of coercion.

'We send them also in search of unity ... in search of agreement ... in search of consensus, to unite us in these troubled times.'

'Zooooon!'

In the eager chorus could be felt the Conclave's desperate wish for resolution, for an end to bitter disagreements. The three candidates were to lead just one of many battle forces sent forth by the clan of the Gooksyu-Gubru. But clearly the Roost Masters had special hopes for this triumvirate.

Kwackoo servitors offered shining goblets to each candidate. The bureaucrat of Cost and Caution lifted one and drank deeply. The fluid felt like golden fire going down.

First taste of the Royal Liquor ...

As expected, it had a flavor like nothing else imaginable. Already, the three candidates' white plumage seemed to glisten with a shimmering *promise* of color to come.

We shall struggle together, and eventually one of us shall molt amber. One shall molt blue.

And one, presumably the strongest, the one with the best policy, would win the ultimate prize.

A prize fated to be mine. For it was said to have all been arranged in advance. Caution *had* to win the upcoming consensus. Careful analysis had shown that the alternatives would be unbearable.

'You shall go forth, then,' the Conclave President sang. 'You three new Suzerains of our race and of our clan. You shall go forth and win conquest. You shall go forth and humble the wolfling heretics.'

'*Zooooon!*' the assembly cheered.

The President's beak lowered toward her breast, as if she were suddenly exhausted. Then, the new Suzerain of Cost and Caution faintly heard her add,

'You shall go forth and try your best to save us ...'

PART ONE

INVASION

Let them uplift us, shoulder high. Then we will see over
their heads to the several promised lands, from which we
have come, and to which we trust to go.

W. B. YEATS

1

FIBEN

There had never been such traffic at Port Helenia's sleepy landing field – not in all the years Fiben Bolger had lived here. The mesa overlooking Aspinal Bay reverberated with the numbing, infrasonic growl of engines. Dust plumes obscured the launching pits, but that did not prevent spectators from gathering along the peripheral fence to watch all the excitement. Those with a touch of psi talent could tell whenever a starship was about to lift off. Waves of muzzy uncertainty, caused by leaky gravities, made a few onlookers blink quickly moments before another great-strutted spacecraft rose above the haze and lumbered off into the cloud-dappled sky.

The noise and stinging dust frayed tempers. It was even worse for those standing out on the tarmac, and especially bad for those forced to be there against their will.

Fiben certainly would much rather have been just about anywhere else, preferably in a pub applying pints of liquid anesthetic. But that was not to be.

He observed the frenetic activity cynically. *We're a sinking ship,* he thought. *And all th' rats are saying a'dieu.*

Everything able to space and warp was departing Garth in indecent haste. Soon, the landing field would be all but empty.

Until the enemy arrives ... whoever it turns out to be.

'Pssst, Fiben. Quit fidgeting!'

Fiben glanced to his right. The chim standing next to him in formation looked nearly as uncomfortable as Fiben felt. Simon Levin's dress uniform cap was turning dark just above his bony eye ridges, where damp brown fur curled under the rim. With his eyes, Simon mutely urged Fiben to straighten up and look forward.

Fiben sighed. He knew he should try to stand at attention. The ceremony for the departing dignitary was nearly over, and a member of the Planetary Honor Guard wasn't supposed to slouch.

But his gaze kept drifting over toward the southern end of the mesa, far from the commercial terminal and the departing freighters. Over there, uncamouflaged, lay an uneven row of drab, black cigar shapes with the blocky look of fighting craft. Several of the small scoutboats shimmered as technicians crawled over them, tuning their detectors and shields for the coming battle.

Fiben wondered if Command had already decided which craft he was to fly. Perhaps they would let the half-trained Colonial Militia pilots draw lots to see who would get the most decrepit of the ancient war machines, recently purchased cut-rate off a passing Xatinni scrap dealer.

With his left hand Fiben tugged at the stiff collar of his uniform and scratched the thick hair below his collarbone. *Old ain't necessarily bad*, he reminded himself. *Go into battle aboard a thousand-year-old tub, and at least you know it can take punishment.*

Most of those battered scoutboats had seen action out on the starlanes before human beings ever heard of Galactic civilization ... before they had even begun playing with gunpowder rockets, singeing their fingers and scaring the birds back on homeworld Earth.

The image made Fiben smile briefly. It wasn't the most respectful thing to think about one's patron race. But then, humans hadn't exactly brought his people up to be reverent.

Jeez, this monkey suit itches! Naked apes like humans may be able to take this, but we hairy types just aren't built to wear this much clothing!

At least the ceremony for the departing Synthian Consul seemed to be nearing completion. Swoio Shochuhun – that pompous ball of fur and whiskers – was finishing her speech of farewell to the tenants of Garth Planet, the humans and chims she was leaving to their fate. Fiben scratched his chin again, wishing the little windbag would just climb into her launch and get the hell out of here, if she was in such a hurry to be going.

An elbow jabbed him in the ribs. Simon muttered urgently. 'Straighten up, Fiben. Her Nibs is looking this way!'

Over among the dignitaries Megan Oneagle, the gray-haired Planetary Coordinator, pursed her lips and gave Fiben a quick shake of her head.

Aw, hell, he thought.

Megan's son, Robert, had been a classmate of Fiben's at Garth's small university. Fiben arched an eyebrow as if to say to the human administrator that *he* hadn't asked to serve on this dubious honor guard. And anyway, if humans had wanted clients who didn't scratch themselves, they never should have uplifted chimpanzees.

He fixed his collar though, and tried to straighten his posture. Form was nearly everything to these Galactics, and Fiben knew that even a lowly neo-chim had to play his part, or the clan of Earth might lose face.

On either side of Coordinator Oneagle stood the other dignitaries who had come to see Swoio Shochuhun off. To Megan's left was Kault, the hulking Thennanin envoy, leathery and resplendent in his brilliant cape and towering ridge crest. The breathing slits in his throat opened and closed like louvered blinds each time the big-jawed creature inhaled.

To Megan's right stood a much more humanoid figure, slender and long-limbed, who slouched slightly, almost insouciantly in the afternoon sunshine.

Uthacalthing's amused by something. Fiben could tell. *So what else is new?*

Of course Ambassador Uthacalthing thought *everything* was funny. In his posture, in the gently waving silvery tendrils that floated above his small ears, and in the glint in his golden, wide-cast eyes, the pale Tymbrimi envoy seemed to say what could not be spoken aloud – something just short of insulting to the departing Synthian diplomat.

Swoio Shochuhun sleeked back her whiskers before stepping forward to say farewell to each of her colleagues in turn. Watching her make ornate formal paw motions in front of Kault, Fiben was struck by how much she resembled a large, rotund raccoon, dressed up like some ancient, oriental courtier.

Kault, the huge Thennanin, puffed up his crest as he bowed in response. The two uneven-sized Galactics exchanged pleasantries in fluting, highly inflected Galactic Six. Fiben knew that there was little love to be lost between them.

'Well, you can't choose your friends, can you?' Simon whispered.

'Damn right,' Fiben agreed.

It was ironic. The furry, canny Synthians were among Earth's few 'allies' in the political and military quagmire of the Five Galaxies. But they were also fantastically self-centered and famous cowards. Swoio's departure as much as guaranteed there would be no armadas of fat, furry warriors coming to Garth's aid in her hour of need.

Just like there won't be any help from Earth, nor Tymbrim, them having enough problems of their own right now.

Fiben understood GalSix well enough to follow some of what the big Thennanin said to Swoio. Kault apparently did not think much of ambassadors who skip out on their posts.

Give the Thennanin that much, Fiben thought. Kault's folk might be fanatics. Certainly they were listed among Earth's present official enemies. Nevertheless, they were known everywhere for their courage and severe sense of honor.

No, you can't always choose your friends, or your enemies.

Swoio stepped over to face Megan Oneagle. The Synthian's bow was marginally shallower than the one she had given Kault. After all, humans ranked pretty low among the patron races of the galaxy.

And you know what that makes you, Fiben reminded himself.

Megan bowed in return. 'I am sorry to see you go,' she told Swoio in thickly accented GalSix. 'Please pass on to your people our gratitude for their good wishes.'

'Right,' Fiben muttered. 'Tell all th' other raccoons thanks a whole bunch.' He wore a blank expression, though, when Colonel Maiven, the human commander of the Honor Guard, looked sharply his way.

Swoio's reply was filled with platitudes.

Be patient, she urged. The Five Galaxies are in turmoil right now. The fanatics among the great powers are causing so much trouble because they think the Millennium, the end of a great era, is at hand. They are the first to act.

Meanwhile, the moderates and the Galactic Institutes must move slower, more judiciously. But act they would, she assured. In due time. Little Garth would not be forgotten.

Sure, Fiben thought sarcastically. *Why, help might be no more'n a century or two away!*

The other chims in the Honor Guard glanced at one other and rolled their eyes in disgust. The human officers were more reserved, but Fiben saw that one was rotating his tongue firmly in his cheek.

Swoio stopped at last before the senior member of the diplomatic corps, Uthacalthing Man-Friend, the consul-ambassador from the Tymbrimi.

The tall E.T. wore a loose black robe that offset his pale skin. Uthacalthing's mouth was small, and the unearthly separation between his shadowed eyes seemed very wide. Nevertheless, the humanoid impression was quite strong. It always seemed to Fiben as if the representative of Earth's greatest ally was always on the verge of laughing at some joke, great or small. Uthacalthing – with his narrow scalp-ruff of soft, brown fur bordered by waving, delicate tendrils – with his long, delicate hands and ready humor – was the solitary being on this mesa who seemed untouched by the tension of the day. The Tymbrimi's ironic smile affected Fiben, momentarily lifting his spirits.

Finally! Fiben sighed in relief. Swoio appeared to be finished at last. She turned and strode up the ramp toward her waiting launch. With a sharp command Colonel Maiven brought the Guard to attention. Fiben started mentally counting the number of steps to shade and a cool drink.

But it was too soon to relax. Fiben wasn't the only one to groan low as the Synthian turned at the top of the ramp to address the onlookers one more time.

Just what occurred then – and in exactly what order – would perplex Fiben for a long time afterward. But it appeared that, just as the first fluting tones of GalSix left Swoio's mouth, something bizarre happened across the landing field. Fiben felt a scratchiness at the back of his eyeballs and glanced to the left, just in time to see a lambency shimmer around one of the scoutboats. Then the tiny craft seemed to *explode*.

He did not recall diving to the tarmac, but that's where he found himself next, trying to burrow into the tough, rubbery surface. *What is it? An enemy attack so soon?*

He heard Simon snort violently. Then a chorus of sneezes followed. Blinking away dust, Fiben peered and saw that the little scoutcraft still existed. It hadn't blown up, after all!

But its *fields* were out of control. They coruscated in a deafening, blinding display of light and sound. Shield-suited engineers scurried to shut down the boat's malfunctioning probability generator, but not before the noisome display had run everyone nearby through all the senses they had, from touch and taste all the way to smell and psi.

'Whooee!' the chimmie to Fiben's left whistled, holding her nose uselessly. 'Who set off a stinkbomb!'

In a flash Fiben knew, with uncanny certainty, that she had called it right. He rolled over quickly, in time to see the Synthian Ambassador, her nose wrinkled in disgust and whiskers curled in shame, scamper into her ship, abandoning all dignity. The hatch clanged shut.

Someone found the right switch at last and cut off the horrible overload, leaving only a fierce aftertaste and a ringing in his ears. The members of the Honor Guard stood up, dusting themselves and muttering irritably. Some humans and chims still quivered, blinking and yawning vigorously. Only the stolid, oblivious Thennanin Ambassador seemed unaffected. In fact, Kault appeared perplexed over this unusual Earthling behavior.

A *stinkbomb*. Fiben nodded. *It was somebody's idea of a practical joke.*

And I think I know whose.

Fiben looked closely at Uthacalthing. He stared at the being who had been named Man-Friend and recalled how the slender Tymbrimi had smiled as Swoio, the pompous little Synthian, launched into her final speech. Yes, Fiben would be willing to swear on a copy of Darwin that at that very moment, just *before* the scout-boat malfunctioned, Uthacalthing's crown of silvery tendrils had lifted and the ambassador had smiled as if in delicious *anticipation*.

Fiben shook his head. For all of their renowned psychic senses, no Tymbrimi could have caused such an accident by sheer force of will.

Not unless it had been arranged in advance, that is.

The Synthian launch rose upward on a blast of air and skimmed out across the field to a safe distance. Then, in a high whine of gravities, the glittering craft swept upward to meet the clouds.

At Colonel Maiven's command, the Honor Guard snapped to attention one last time. The Planetary Coordinator and her two remaining envoys passed in review.

It might have been his imagination, but Fiben felt sure that for an instant Uthacalthing slowed right in front of him. Fiben was certain one of those wide, silver-rimmed eyes looked directly at him.

And the other one winked.

Fiben sighed. *Very funny*, he thought, hoping the Tymbrimi emissary would pick up the sarcasm in his mind. *We all may be smokin' dead meat in a week's time, and you're making with practical jokes. Very funny, Uthacalthing.*

2

ATHACLENA

Tendrils wafted alongside her head, ungentle in their agitation. Athaclena let her frustration and anger fizz like static electricity at the tips of the silvery strands. Their ends waved as if of their own accord, like slender fingers, shaping her almost palpable resentment into *something* . . .

Nearby, one of the humans awaiting an audience with the Planetary Coordinator sniffed the air and looked around, puzzled. He moved away from Athaclena, without quite knowing why he felt uncomfortable all of a sudden. He was probably a natural, if primitive, empath. Some men and women were able vaguely to *kenn* Tymbrimi empathy-glyphs, though few ever had the training to interpret anything more than vague emotions.

Someone else also noticed what Athaclena was doing. Across the public room, standing amid a small crowd of humans, her father lifted his head suddenly. His own corona of tendrils remained smooth and undisturbed, but Uthacalthing cocked his head and turned slightly to regard her, his expression both quizzical and slightly amused.

It might have been similar if a human parent had caught his daughter in the act of kicking the sofa, or muttering to herself sullenly. The frustration at the core was very nearly the same, except that Athaclena expressed it through her Tymbrimi aura rather than an outward tantrum. At her father's glance she hurriedly drew back her waving tendrils and wiped away the ugly sense-glyph she had been crafting overhead.

That did not erase her resentment, however. In this crowd of Earthlings it was hard to forget. *Caricatures*, was Athaclena's contemptuous thought, knowing full well it was both unkind and unfair. Of course Earthlings couldn't help being what they were – one of the strangest tribes to come upon the Galactic scene in aeons. But that did not mean she had to like them!

It might have helped if they were *more* alien ... less like hulking, narrow-eyed, awkward versions of Tymbrimi. Wildly varied in color and hairiness, eerily *off* in their body proportions, and so often dour and moody, they frequently left Athaclena feeling depressed after too long a time spent in their company.

Another thought unbecoming the daughter of a diplomat. She chided herself and tried to redirect her mind. After all, the humans could not be blamed for radiating their fear right now, with a war they hadn't chosen about to fall crushingly upon them.

She watched her father laugh at something said by one of the Earthling officers and wondered how he did it. How he bore it so well.

I'll never learn that easy, confident manner.

I'll never be able to make him proud of me.

Athaclena wished Uthacalthing would finish up with these Terrans so she could speak to him alone. In a few minutes Robert Oneagle would arrive to pick her up, and she wanted to have one more try at persuading her father not to send her away with the young human.

I can be useful. I know I can! I don't have to be coddled off into the mountains for safety, like some child!

Quickly she clamped down before another glyph-of-resentment could form above her head. She needed distraction, something to keep her mind occupied while she waited. Restraining her emotions, Athaclena stepped quietly toward two human officers standing nearby, heads lowered in earnest conversation, they were speaking in Anglic, the most commonly used Earth-tongue.

'Look,' the first one said. 'All we really know is that one of Earth's survey ships stumbled onto something weird and totally unexpected, out in one of those ancient star clusters on the galactic fringe.'

'But what *was* it?' the other militiaman asked. 'What did they find? You're in alien studies, Alice. Don't you have any idea what those poor dolphins uncovered that could stir up such a ruckus?'

The female Earthman shrugged. 'Search me. But it didn't take anything more than the hints in the *Streaker*'s first beamed report to set the most fanatic clans in the Five Galaxies fighting each other at a level that hasn't been seen in megayears. The latest dispatches say some of the skirmishes have gotten pretty damn rough. You saw how scared that Synthian looked a week ago, before she decided to pull out.'

The other man nodded gloomily. Neither human spoke for a long moment. Their tension was a thing which arched the space between them. Athaclena *kenned* it as a simple but dark glyph of uncertain dread.

'It's something big,' the first officer said at last, in a low voice. 'This may really be it.'

Athaclena moved away when she sensed the humans begin to take notice of her. Since arriving here in Garth she had been altering her normal body form, changing her figure and features to resemble more closely those of a human girl. Nevertheless, there were limits to what such manipulations could accomplish, even using Tymbrimi body-imagery methods. There was no way really to disguise who she was. If she had stayed, inevitably, the humans would have asked her a Tymbrimi's opinion of the current crisis, and she was loath to tell Earthlings that she really knew no more than they did.

Athaclena found the situation bitterly ironic. Once again, the races of Earth were in the spotlight, as they had been ever since the notorious 'Sundiver' affair, two centuries ago. This time an interstellar crisis had been sparked by the first starship ever put under command of *neo-dolphins*.

Mankind's second client race was no more than two centuries old – younger even than the neo-chimpanzees. How the cetacean spacers would ever find a way out of the mess they had inadvertently created was anyone's guess. But the repercussions were already spreading halfway across the Central Galaxy, all the way to isolated colony worlds such as Garth.

'Athaclena – '

She whirled. Uthacalthing stood at her elbow, looking down at her with an air of benign concern. 'Are you all right, daughter?'

She felt so small in Uthacalthing's presence. Athaclena couldn't help being intimidated, however gentle he always was. His art and discipline were so great that she hadn't even sensed his approach until he touched the sleeve of her robe! Even now, all that could be *kenned* from his complex aura was the whirling empathy-glyph called *caridouo* . . . a father's love.

'*Yes*, Father. I . . . I am fine.'

'Good. Are you all packed and ready for your expedition then?'

His words were in Anglic. She answered in Tymbrim-dialect Galactic Seven.

'Father, I do not wish to go into the mountains with Robert Oneagle.'

Uthacalthing frowned. 'I had thought that you and Robert were friends.'

Athaclena's nostrils flared in frustration. Why was Uthacalthing purposely misunderstanding her? He had to know that the son of the Planetary Coordinator was unobjectionable as a companion. Robert was as close to a friend as she had among the young humans of Port Helenia.

'It is partly for *Robert's* sake that I urge you to reconsider,' she told her father. 'He is shamed at being ordered to "nursemaid" me, as they say, while his comrades and classmates are all in the militia preparing for war. And I certainly cannot blame him for his resentment.'

When Uthacalthing started to speak she hurried on. 'Also, I do not wish to leave you, Father. I reiterate my earlier arguments-of-logic, when I explained how I might be useful to you in the weeks ahead. And now I add to them this offering, as well.'

With great care she concentrated on crafting the glyph she had composed earlier in the day. She had named it *ke'ipathye* . . . a plea, out of love, to be allowed to face danger at love's side. Her tendrils trembled above her ears, and the construct quavered slightly over her head as it began to rotate. Finally though, it stabilized. She sent it drifting over toward her father's aura. At that moment, Athaclena did not even care that they were in a room crowded with hulking, smooth-browed humans and their furry little chim clients. All that mattered in the world was the two of them, and the bridge she so longed to build across this void.

Ke'ipathye fell into Uthacalthing's waiting tendrils and spun there, brightening in his appreciation. Briefly, Athaclena gasped at its sudden beauty, which she knew had now grown far beyond her own simple art.

Then the glyph fell, like a gentle fog of morning dew, to coat and shine along her father's corona.

'Such a fine gift.' His voice was soft, and she knew he had been moved.

But . . . She knew, all at once, that his resolve was unshifted.

'I offer you a *kenning* of my own,' he said to her. And from his sleeve he withdrew a small gilt box with a silver clasp. 'Your mother, Mathicluanna, wished for you to have this when you were ready to declare yourself of age. Although we had not yet spoken of a date, I judge that now is the time for you to have it.'

Athaclena blinked, suddenly lost in a whirl of confused emotions. How often had she longed to know what her dead mother had left

683

in her legacy? And yet, right now the small locket might have been a poison-beetle for all the will she had to pick it up.

Uthacalthing would not be doing this if he thought it likely they would meet again.

She hissed in realization. 'You're planning to fight!'

Uthacalthing actually *shrugged* ... that human gesture of momentary indifference. 'The enemies of the humans are mine as well, daughter. The Earthlings are bold, but they are only wolflings after all. They will need my help.'

There was finality in his voice, and Athaclena knew that any further word of protest would accomplish nothing but to make her look foolish in his eyes. Their hands met around the locket, long fingers intertwining, and they walked silently out of the room together. It seemed, for a short span, as if they were not two but three, for the locket carried something of Mathicluanna. The moment was both sweet and painful.

Neo-chimp militia guards snapped to attention and opened the doors for them as they stepped out of the Ministry Building and into the clear, early spring sunshine. Uthacalthing accompanied Athaclena down to the curbside, where her backpack awaited her. Their hands parted, and Athaclena was left grasping her mother's locket.

'Here comes Robert, right on time,' Uthacalthing said, shading his eyes. 'His mother calls him unpunctual. But I have never known him to be late for anything that mattered.'

A battered floater wagon approached along the long gravel driveway, rolling past limousines and militia staff cars. Uthacalthing turned back to his daughter. 'Do try to enjoy the Mountains of Mulun. I have seen them. They are quite beautiful. Look at this as an opportunity, Athaclena.'

She nodded. 'I shall do as you asked, Father. I'll spend the time improving my grasp of Anglic and of wolfling emotional patterns.'

'Good. And keep your eyes open for any signs or traces of the legendary Garthlings.'

Athaclena frowned. Her father's late interest in odd wolfling folk tales had lately begun to resemble a fixation. And yet, one could never tell when Uthacalthing was being serious or simply setting up a complicated jest.

'I'll watch out for signs, though the creatures are certainly mythical.'

Uthacalthing smiled. 'I must go now. My love will travel with you. It will be a bird, hovering' – he motioned with his hands – 'just over your shoulder.'

His tendrils touched hers briefly, and then he was gone, striding back up the steps to rejoin the worried colonials. Athaclena was left standing there, wondering why, in parting, Uthacalthing had used such a bizarre human metaphor.

How can love be a bird?

Sometimes Uthacalthing was so strange it frightened even her.

There was a crunching of gravel as the floater car settled down at the curb nearby. Robert Oneagle, the dark-haired young human who was to be her partner-in-exile, grinned and waved from behind the machine's tiller, but it was easy to tell that his cheery demeanor was superficial, put on for her benefit. Deep down, Robert was nearly as unhappy about this trip as she was. Fate – and the imperious rule of adults – had thrown the two of them together in a direction neither of them would have chosen.

The crude glyph Athaclena formed – invisible to Robert – was little more than a sigh of resignation and defeat. But she kept up appearances with a carefully arranged Earthling-type smile of her own.

'Hello, Robert,' she said, and picked up her pack.

3

GALACTICS

The Suzerain of Propriety fluffed its feathery down, displaying at the roots of its still-white plumage the shimmering glow that foretold royalty. Proudly, the Suzerain of Propriety hopped up onto the Perch of Pronouncement and chirped for attention.

The battleships of the Expeditionary Force were still in inter-space, between the levels of the world. Battle was not imminent for some time yet. Because of this, the Suzerain of Propriety was still dominant and could interrupt the activities of the flagship's crew.

Across the bridge, the Suzerain of Beam and Talon looked up from its own Perch of Command. The admiral shared with the Suzerain of Propriety the bright plumage of dominance. Never-theless, there was no question of interfering when a religious pronouncement was about to be made. The admiral at once inter-rupted the stream of orders it had been chirping to subordinates and shifted into a stance of attentive reverence.

All through the bridge the noisy clamor of Gubru engineers and spacers quieted to a low chittering. Their four-footed Kwackoo clients ceased their cooing as well and settled down to listen.

Still the Suzerain of Propriety waited. It would not be proper to begin until all Three were present.

A hatchway dilated. In stepped the last of the masters of the expedition, the third member of the triarchy. As appropriate, the Suzerain of Cost and Caution wore the black torc of suspicion and doubt as it entered and found a comfortable perch, followed by a small covey of its accountants and bureaucrats.

For a moment their eyes met across the bridge. The tension among the Three had already begun, and it would grow in the weeks and months ahead, until the day when consensus was finally achieved – when they molted and a new queen emerged.

It was thrilling, sexual, exhilarating. None of them knew how it would end. Beam and Talon started with an advantage, of course, since this expedition would begin in battle. But that dominance did not have to last.

This moment, for instance, was clearly one for the priesthood.

All beaks turned as the Suzerain of Propriety lifted and flexed one leg, then the other, and prepared to pronounce. Soon a low crooning began to rise from the assembled avians.

– *zzooon*.

    'We embark on a mission, holy mission,' the Suzerain fluted.
– *Zzooon* –
    'Embarking on this mission, we must persevere'
– *Zzooon* –
    'Persevere to accomplish four great tasks'
– *Zzooon* –
    'Tasks which include *Conquest* for the glory of our Clan, zzooon'
– *ZZooon*
    'Conquest and *Coercion*, so we may gain the Secret, the Secret that the animal Earthlings clutch talon-tight, clutch to keep from us, zzooon'
– *ZZooon* –
    'Conquest, Coercion, and *Counting Coup* upon our enemies winning honor and submitting our foes to shame, avoiding shame ourselves, zzooon'
– *ZZooon* –
    'Avoiding shame, as well as Conquest and Coercion, and last, and last to prove our worthiness,
    our worthiness before our ancestrals, our worthiness before the Progenitors whose time of Return has surely come
    Our worthiness of Mastery, zzzoooon'

The refrain was enthusiastic.

– ZZooon –

The two other Suzerains bowed respectfully to the priest, and the ceremony was officially at an end. The Talon Soldiers and Spacers returned to work at once. But as the bureaucrats and civil servants retreated toward their own sheltered offices, they could be heard clearly but softly crooning.

'All ... all ... all of that. But one thing, one thing more ...

'First of all ... survival of the nest ...'

The priest looked up sharply and saw a glint in the eye of the Suzerain of Cost and Caution. And in that instant it knew that its rival had won a subtle but important point. There was triumph in the other's eye as it bowed again and hummed lowly.

'Zooon.'

4

ROBERT

Dappled sunlight found gaps in the rain forest canopy, illuminating streaks of brilliant color in the dim, vine-laced avenue between. The fierce gales of mid-winter had ebbed some weeks back, but a stiff breeze served as a reminder of those days, causing boughs to dip and sway, and shaking loose moisture from the prior night's rain. Droplets made fat, plinking sounds as they landed in little shaded pools.

It was quiet in the mountains overlooking the Vale of Sind. Perhaps more silent than a forest ought to be. The woods were lush, and yet their superficial beauty masked a *sickness*, a malaise arising from ancient wounds. Though the air carried a wealth of fecund odors, one of the strongest was a subtle hint of decay. It did not take an empath to know that this was a sad place. A melancholy world.

Indirectly, that sadness was what had brought Earthlings here. History had not yet written the final chapter on Garth, but the planet was already on a list. A list of dying worlds.

One shaft of daylight spotlighted a fan of multicolored vines, dangling in apparent disorder from the branches of a giant tree. Robert Oneagle pointed in that direction. 'You might want to examine those, Athaclena,' he said. 'They can be trained, you know.'

The young Tymbrimi looked up from an orchidlike bloom she

had been inspecting. She followed his gesture, peering past the bright, slanting columns of light. She spoke carefully in accented but clearly enunciated Anglic.

'What can be trained, Robert? All I see there are vines.'

Robert grinned. 'Those very forest vines, Athaclena. They're amazing things.'

Athaclena's frown looked very human, in spite of the wide set of her oval eyes and the alien gold-flecked green of their large irises. Her slightly curved, delicate jaw and angled brow made the expression appear faintly ironic.

Of course, as the daughter of a diplomat Athaclena might have been taught to assume carefully tutored expressions at certain times when in the company of humans. Still, Robert was certain her frown conveyed genuine puzzlement. When she spoke, a lilt in her voice seemed to imply that Anglic was somehow limiting.

'Robert, you surely don't mean that those hanging tendril-plants are *pre-sentient*, do you? There are a few autotrophic sophont races, of course, but this vegetation shows none of the signs. Anyway ...' The frown intensified as she concentrated. From a fringe just above her ears her Tymbrimi ruff quivered as silvery tendrils waved in quest. '... Anyway, I can sense no emotional emissions from them at all.'

Robert grinned. 'No, of course you can't. I didn't mean to imply they have any Uplift Potential, or even nervous systems per se. They're just rain forest plants. But they do have a secret. Come on. I'll show you.'

Athaclena nodded, another human gesture that might or might not be naturally Tymbrimi as well. She carefully replaced the flower she had been examining and stood up in a fluid, graceful movement.

The alien girl's frame was slender, the proportions of her arms and legs different from the human norm – longer calves and less length in the thighs, for instance. Her slim, articulated pelvis flared from an even narrower waist. To Robert, she seemed to *prowl* in a faintly catlike manner that had fascinated him ever since she arrived on Garth, half a year ago.

That the Tymbrimi were lactating mammals he could tell by the outline of her upper breasts, provocatively evident even under her soft trail suit. He knew from his studies that Athaclena had two more pair, and a marsupial-like pouch as well. But those were not evident at present. Right now she seemed more human – or perhaps elfin – than alien.

'All right, Robert. I promised my father I would make the best of this enforced exile. Show me more of the wonders of this little planet.'

The tone in her voice was so heavy, so resigned, that Robert decided she had to be exaggerating for effect. The theatrical touch made her seem oddly more like a human teenager, and that in itself was a bit unnerving. He led her toward the cluster of vines. 'It's over here, where they converge down at the forest floor.'

Athaclena's ruff – the helm of brown fur that began in a narrow stroke of down on her spine and rose up the back of her neck to end, caplike, in a widow's peak above the bridge of her strong nose – was now puffed and riffled at the edges. Over her smooth, softly rounded ears the cilia of her Tymbrimi corona waved as if she were trying to pick out any trace of consciousness other than theirs in the narrow glade.

Robert reminded himself not to overrate Tymbrimi mental powers as humans so often did. The slender Galactics did have impressive abilities in detecting strong emotions and were supposed to have a talent for crafting a form of *art* out of empathy itself. Nevertheless, true telepathy was no more common among Tymbrimi than among Earthlings.

Robert had to wonder what she was thinking. Could she know how, since they had left Port Helenia together, his fascination with her had grown? He hoped not. The feeling was one he wasn't sure he even wanted to admit to himself yet.

The vines were thick, fibrous strands with knotty protrusions every half-meter or so. They converged from many different directions upon this shallow forest clearing. Robert shoved a cluster of the multicolored cables aside to show Athaclena that all of them terminated in a single small pool of umber-colored water.

He explained. 'These ponds are found all over this continent, each connected to the others by this vast network of vines. They play a vital role in the rain forest ecosystem. No other shrubs grow near these catchments where the vines do their work.'

Athaclena knelt to get a better view. Her corona still waved and she seemed interested.

'Why is the pool colored so? Is there an impurity in the water?'

'Yes, that's right. If we had an analysis kit I could take you from pond to pond and demonstrate that each little puddle has a slight overabundance of a different trace element or chemical. The vines seem to form a network among the giant trees, carrying nutrients abundant in one area to other places where they're lacking.'

'A trade compact!' Athaclena's ruff expanded in one of the few purely Tymbrimi expressions Robert was certain he understood. For the first time since they had left the city together he saw her clearly excited by something.

He wondered if she was at that moment crafting an 'empathy-glyph,' that weird art form that some humans swore they could sense, and even learn to understand a little. Robert knew the feath-ery tendrils of the Tymbrimi corona were involved in the process, somehow. Once, while accompanying his mother to a diplomatic reception, he'd noticed something that *had* to have been a glyph – floating, it seemed, above the ruff of the Tymbrimi Ambassador, Uthacalthing.

It had been a strange, fleeting sensation – as if he had caught something which could only be looked at with the blind spot of his eye, which fled out of view whenever he tried to focus on it. Then, as quickly as he had become aware of it, the glimpse vanished. In the end, he was left unsure it had been anything but his imagination after all.

'The relationship is symbiotic, of course,' Athaclena pronounced. Robert blinked. She was talking about the vines, of course.

'Uh, right again. The vines take nourishment from the great trees, and in exchange they transport nutrients the trees' roots can't draw out of the poor soil. They also flush out toxins and dispose of them at great distances. Pools like this one serve as banks where the vines come together to stockpile and trade important chemicals.'

'Incredible.' Athaclena examined the rootlets. 'It mimics the self-interest trade patterns of sentient beings. And I suppose it is logical that plants would evolve this technique sometime, somewhere. I believe the Kanten might have begun in such a way, before the Linten gardeners uplifted them and made them starfarers.'

She looked up at Robert. 'Is this phenomenon catalogued? The Z'Tang were supposed to have surveyed Garth for the Institutes before the planet was passed over to you humans. I'm surprised I never heard of this.'

Robert allowed himself a trace of a smile. 'Sure, the Z'Tang report to the Great Library mentions the vines' chemical transfer proper-ties. Part of the tragedy of Garth was that the network seemed on the verge of total collapse before Earth was granted a leasehold here. And if that actually happens half this continent will turn into desert.

'But the Z'Tang missed something crucial. They never seem to have noticed that the vines *move* about the forest, very slowly, seek-ing new minerals for their host trees. The forest, as an active trading community, *adapts*. It changes. There's actual hope that, with the right helpful nudge here and there, the network might become a centerpiece in the recovery of the planet's ecosphere. If so, we may be able to make a tidy profit selling the technique to certain parties elsewhere.'

He had expected her to be pleased, but when Athaclena let the rootlets fall back into the umber water she turned to him with a cool tone. 'You sound *proud* to have caught so careful and intellectual an elder race as the Z'Tang in a mistake, Robert. As one of your tele-dramas might put it, "The Eatees and their Library are caught with egg on their faces once again." Is that it?'

'Now wait a minute. I – '

'Tell me, do you humans plan to hoard this information, gloating over your cleverness each time you dole out portions? Or will you flaunt it, crying far and wide what any race with sense already knows – that the Great Library is not and never has been perfect?'

Robert winced. The stereotypical Tymbrimi, as pictured by most Earthlings, was adaptable, wise, and often mischievous. But right now Athaclena sounded more like any irritable, opinionated young fem with a chip on her shoulder.

True, some Earthlings went too far in criticizing Galactic civilization. As the first known 'wolfling' race in over fifty megayears, humans sometimes boasted too loudly that they were the only species now living who had bootstrapped themselves into space without anybody's help. What need had they to take for granted everything found in the Great Library of the Five Galaxies? Terran popular media tended to encourage an attitude of contempt for aliens who would rather look things up than find out for themselves.

There was a reason for encouraging this stance. The alternative, according to Terragens psychological scientists, would be a crushing racial inferiority complex. Pride was a vital thing for the only 'backward' clan in the known universe. It stood between humanity and despair.

Unfortunately, the attitude had also alienated some species who might otherwise have been friendly to Mankind.

But on that count, were Athaclena's people all that innocent? The Tymbrimi, also, were famed for finding loopholes in tradition and for not being satisfied with what was inherited from the past.

'When will you humans learn that the universe is *dangerous*, that there are many ancient and powerful clans who have no love of upstarts, especially newcomers who brashly set off changes without understanding the likely consequences!'

Now Robert knew what Athaclena was referring to, what the real source of this outburst was. He rose from the poolside and dusted his hands. 'Look, neither of us really knows what's going on out there in the galaxy right now. But it's hardly *our* fault that a dolphin-crewed starship – '

'The *Streaker*.'

' – that the *Streaker* happened to discover something bizarre, something overlooked all these aeons. Anyone could have stumbled onto it! Hell, Athaclena. We don't even know what it was that those poor neo-dolphins found! Last anyone heard, their ship was being chased from the Morgran transfer point to Ifni-knows-where by twenty different fleets – all fighting over the right to capture her.'

Robert discovered his pulse was beating hard. Clenched hands indicated just how much of his own tension was rooted in this topic. After all, it is frustrating enough whenever your universe threatens to topple in on you, but all the more so when the events that set it all off took place kiloparsecs away, amid dim red stars too distant even to be seen from home.

Athaclena's dark-lidded eyes met his, and for the first time he felt he could sense a touch of understanding in them. Her long-fingered left hand performed a fluttering half turn. 'I hear what you are saying, Robert. And I know that sometimes I am too quick to cast judgments. It is a fault my father constantly urges me to overcome.

'But you ought to remember that we Tymbrimi have been Earth's protectors and allies ever since your great, lumbering slowships stumbled into our part of space, eighty-nine paktaars ago. It grows wearying at times, and you must forgive if, on occasion, it shows.'

'What grows wearying?' Robert was confused.

'Well, for one thing, ever since Contact we have had to learn and endure this assemblage of wolfling clicks and growls you have the effrontery to call a language.'

Athaclena's expression was even, but now Robert believed he could actually sense a faint *something* emanating from those waving tendrils. It seemed to convey what a human girl might communicate with a subtle facial expression. Clearly she was teasing him.

'Ha ha. Very funny.' He looked down at the ground.

'Seriously though, Robert, have we not, in the seven generations since Contact, constantly urged that you humans and your clients go slow? The *Streaker* simply should not have been prying into places where she did not belong – not while your small clan of races is still so young and helpless.

'You cannot keep on poking at the rules to see which are rigid and which are soft!'

Robert shrugged. 'It's paid off a few times.'

'Yes, but now your – what is the proper, beastly idiom? – your cows have come home to roost?

'Robert, the fanatics won't let go now that their passions are aroused. They will chase the dolphin ship until she is captured. And if they cannot acquire her information that way, powerful clans such as the Jophur and the Soro will seek *other* means to achieve their ends.'

Dust motes sparkled gently in and out of the narrow shafts of sunlight. Scattered pools of rainwater glinted where the beams touched them. In the quiet Robert scuffed at the soft humus, knowing all too well what Athaclena was driving at.

The Jophur, the Soro, the Gubru, the Tandu – those powerful Galactic patron races which had time and again demonstrated their hostility to Mankind – if they failed to capture *Streaker*, their next step would be obvious. Sooner or later some clan would turn its attention to Garth, or Atlast, or Calafia – Earth's most distant and unprotected outposts – seeking hostages in an effort to pry loose the dolphins' mysterious secret. The tactic was even *permissible*, under the loose strictures established by the ancient Galactic Institute for Civilized Warfare.

Some civilization, Robert thought bitterly. The irony was that the dolphins weren't even likely to behave as any of the stodgy Galactics expected them to.

By tradition a client race owed allegiance and fealty to its patrons, the starfaring species that had 'uplifted' it to full sentience. This had been done for *Pan* chimpanzees and *Tursiops* dolphins by humans even before Contact with starfaring aliens. In doing so, Mankind had unknowingly mimicked a pattern that had ruled the Five Galaxies for perhaps three billion years.

By tradition, client species served their patrons for a thousand centuries or more, until release from indenture freed them to seek clients of their own. Few Galactic clans believed or understood how much freedom had been given dolphins and chims by the humans of Earth. It was hard to say exactly what the neo-dolphins on the *Streaker*'s crew would do if humans were taken hostage. But that, apparently, wouldn't stop the Eatees from trying. Distant listening posts had already confirmed the worst. Battle fleets were coming, approaching Garth even as he and Athaclena stood here talking.

'Which is worth more, Robert,' Athaclena asked softly, 'that collection of ancient space-hulks the dolphins are supposed to have found ... derelicts that have no meaning at all to a clan as young as yours? Or your *worlds*, with their farms and parks and orbit-cities? I cannot understand the logic of your Terragens Council, ordering *Streaker* to guard her secret, when you and your clients are so vulnerable!'

Robert looked down at the ground again. He had no answer for her. It did sound illogical, when looked at in that way. He thought about his classmates and friends, gathering now to go to war without him, to fight over issues none of them understood. It was hard.

For Athaclena it would be as bad, of course, banished from her father's side, trapped on a foreign world by a quarrel that had little or nothing to do with her. Robert decided to let her have the last word. She had seen more of the universe than he anyway and had the advantage of coming from an older, higher-status clan.

'Maybe you're right,' he said. 'Maybe you're right.

Perhaps, though, he reminded himself as he helped her lift her backpack and then hoisted his own for the next stage of their trek, *perhaps a young Tymbrimi can be just as ignorant and opinionated as any human youth, a little frightened and far away from home.*

5

FIBEN

'*TAASF scoutship* Bonobo *calling scoutship* Proconsul ... *Fiben, you're out of alignment again. Come on, old chim, try to straighten her out, will you?*'

Fiben wrestled with the controls of his ancient, alien-built spacecraft. Only the open mike kept him from expressing his frustration in rich profanity. Finally, in desperation, he kicked the makeshift control panel the technicians had installed back on Garth.

That did it! A red light went out as the antigravity verniers suddenly unfroze. Fiben sighed. *At last!*

Of course, in all the exertion his faceplate had steamed up. 'You'd think they'd come up with a decent ape-suit after all this time,' he grumbled as he turned up the defogger. It was more than a minute before the stars reappeared.

'*What was that, Fiben? What'd you say?*'

'*I* said I'll have this old crate lined up in time!' he snapped. 'The Eatees won't be disappointed.'

The popular slang term for alien Galactics had its roots in an acronym for 'Extraterrestrials.' But it also made Fiben think about food. He had been living on ship paste for days. What he wouldn't give for a fresh chicken and palm leaf sandwich, right now!

Nutritionists were always after chims to curb their appetite for meat. Said too much was bad for the blood pressure. Fiben sniffed.

Heck, I'd settle for a jar of mustard and the latest edition of the Port Helenia Times, he thought.

'*Say, Fiben, you're always up on the latest scuttlebutt. Has anyone figured out yet who's invading us?*'

'Well, I know a chimmie in the Coordinator's office who told me she had a friend on the Intelligence Staff who thought the bastards were Soro, or maybe Tandu.'

'*Tandu! You're kidding I hope.*' Simon sounded aghast, and Fiben had to agree. Some thoughts just weren't to be contemplated.

'Ah well, my guess is it's probably just a bunch of Linten gardeners dropping by to make sure we're treating the plants all right.'

Simon laughed and Fiben felt glad. Having a cheerful wingman was worth more than a reserve officer's half pay.

He got his tiny space skiff back onto its assigned trajectory. The scoutboat – purchased only a few months back from a passing Xatinni scrap hauler – was actually quite a bit older than his own sapient race. While his ancestors were still harassing baboons beneath African trees, this fighter had seen action under distant suns – controlled by the hands, claws, tentacles of *other* poor creatures similarly doomed to skirmish and die in pointless interstellar struggles.

Fiben had only been allowed two weeks to study schematics and remember enough Galactiscript to read the instruments. Fortunately, designs changed slowly in the aeons-old Galactic culture, and there were basics most spacecraft shared in common.

One thing was certain, Galactic technology was impressive. Humanity's best ships were still bought, not Earth-made. And although this old tub was creaky and cranky, it would probably outlive him, this day.

All around Fiben bright fields of stars glittered, except where the inky blackness of the Spoon Nebula blotted out the thick band of the galactic disk. That was the direction where Earth lay, the homeworld Fiben had never seen, and now probably never would.

Garth, on the other hand, was a bright green spark only three million kilometers behind him. Her tiny fleet was too small to cover the distant hyperspacial transfer points, or even the inner system. Their ragged array of scouts, meteoroid miners, and converted freighters – plus three modern corvettes – was hardly adequate to cover the planet itself.

Fortunately, Fiben wasn't in command, so he did not have to keep his mind on the forlorn state of their prospects. He had only to do his duty and wait. Contemplating annihilation was not how he planned to spend the time.

He tried to divert himself by thinking about the Throop family, the small sharing-clan on Quintana Island that had recently invited him to join in their group marriage. For a modern chim it was a serious decision, like when two or three human beings decided to marry and raise a family. He had been pondering the choice for weeks.

The Throop Clan did have a nice, rambling house, good grooming habits, and respectable professions. The adults were attractive and interesting chims, all with green genetic clearances. Socially, it would be a very good move.

But there were disadvantages, as well. For one thing, he would have to move from Port Helenia back out to the islands, where most of the chim and human settlers still lived. Fiben wasn't sure he was ready to do that. He liked the open spaces of the mainland, the freedom of mountains and wild Garth countryside.

And there was another important consideration. Fiben had to wonder whether the Throops wanted him because they really liked him, or because the Neo-Chimpanzee Uplift Board had granted him a blue card – an open breeding clearance.

Only a white card was higher. Blue status meant he could join any marriage group and father children with only minimal genetic counseling. It couldn't help but have influenced the Throop Clan's decision.

'Oh, quit kiddin' yourself,' he muttered at last. The matter was moot, anyway. Right now he wouldn't take long odds on his chances of ever even seeing home again alive.

'Fiben? You still there, kid?'

'Yeah, Simon. What'cha got?'

There was a pause.

'I just got a call from Major Forthness. He said he has an uneasy feeling about that gap in the fourth dodecant.'

Fiben yawned. 'Humans are always gettin' uneasy feelings. Alla time worryin'. That's what it's like being big-time patron types.'

His partner laughed. On Garth it was fashionable even for well-educated chims to 'talk grunt' at times. Most of the better humans took the ribbing with good humor; and those who didn't could go chase themselves.

'Tell you what,' he told Simon. 'I'll drift over to the ol' fourth dodecant and give it a lookover for the Major.'

'We aren't supposed to split up,' the voice in his headphones protested weakly. Still, they both knew having a wingman would hardly make any difference in the kind of fight they were about to face.

'I'll be back in a jiffy,' Fiben assured his friend. 'Save me some of the bananas.'

He engaged the stasis and gravity fields gradually, treating the ancient machine like a virgin chimmie on her first pink. Smoothly, the scout built up acceleration.

Their defense plan had been carefully worked out bearing in mind normally conservative Galactic psychology. The Earthlings' forces were laid out in a mesh with the larger ships held in reserve. The scheme relied on scouts like him reporting the enemy's approach in time for the others to coordinate a timed response.

Problem was that there were too few scouts to maintain any-where near complete coverage.

Fiben felt the powerful thrum of engines through his seat. Soon he was hurtling across the star-field. *Got to give the Galactics their due*, he thought. Their culture was stodgy and intolerant – some-times almost fascistic – but they did build well.

Fiben itched inside his suit. Not for the first time, he wished some human pilots had been small enough to qualify for duty in these tiny Xatinni scouts. It would serve them right to have to smell them-selves after three days in space.

Often, in his more pensive moods, Fiben wondered if it had really been such a good idea for humans to meddle so, making engineers and poets and part-time starfighters out of apes who might have been just as happy to stay in the forest. Where would he be now, it they refrained? He'd have been dirty perhaps, and ignorant. But at least he'd be free to scratch an itch whenever he damn well pleased!

He missed his local Grooming Club. Ah, for the glory of being curried and brushed by a truly sensitive chen or chimmie, lazing in the shade and gossiping about nothing at all ...

A pink light appeared in his detection tank. He reached forward and slapped the display, but the reading would not go away. In fact, as he approached his destination it grew, then split, and divided again.

Fiben felt cold. 'Ifni's incontinence ...' He swore, and grabbed for the code-broadcast switch. 'Scoutship *Proconsul* to all units. They're behind us! Three ... no, *four* battlecruiser squadrons, emerging from B-level hyperspace in the fourth dodecant!'

He blinked as a fifth flotilla appeared as if out of nowhere, the blips shimmering as starships emerged into realtime and leaked excess hyperprobability into the real-space vacuum. Even at this dis-tance he could tell that the cruisers were *large*.

His headphones brought a static of consternation.

'My Uncle Hairy's twice-bent manhood! How did they know there was a hole in our line there?'

' ... Fiben, are you sure? Why did they pick that particular ...'

' ... Who th' hell are they? Can you ... ?'

The chatter shut down at once as Major Forthness broke in on the command channel.

'Message received. Proconsul. *We're on our way. Please switch on your repeater, Fiben.'*

Fiben slapped his helmet. It had been years since his militia train-ing, and a guy tended to forget things. He switched over to telemetry so the others could share everything his instruments picked up.

Of course broadcasting all that data made him an easy target, but that hardly mattered. Clearly their foe had known where the defenders were, perhaps down to the last ship. Already he detected seeker missiles streaking toward him.

So much for stealth and surprise as the advantages of the weak. As he sped toward the enemy – whoever the devils were – Fiben noticed that the emerging invasion armada stood almost directly between him and the bright green sparkle of Garth.

'Great,' he snorted. 'At least when they blast me I'll be headed for home. Maybe a few hanks of fur will even get there ahead of the Eatees.

'If anyone wishes on a shooting star, tomorrow night, I hope they get whatever th'fuk they ask for.'

He increased the ancient scout's acceleration and felt a rearward push even through the straining stasis fields. The moan of engines rose in pitch. And as the little ship leaped forward it seemed to Fiben that it sang a song of battle that sounded almost joyful.

6

UTHACALTHING

Four human officers stepped across the brick parquet floor of the conservatory, their polished brown boots clicking rhythmically in step. Three stopped a respectful distance from the large window where the ambassador and the Planetary Coordinator stood waiting. But the fourth continued forward and saluted crisply.

'Madam Coordinator, it has begun.' The graying militia commander pulled a document from his dispatch pouch and held it out.

Uthacalthing admired Megan Oneagle's poise as she took the proffered flimsy. Her expression betrayed none of the dismay she must be feeling as their worst fears were confirmed.

'Thank you, Colonel Maiven,' she said.

Uthacalthing couldn't help noticing how the tense junior officers kept glancing his way, obviously wondering how the Tymbrimi Ambassador was taking the news. He remained outwardly impassive, as befitted a member of the diplomatic corps. But the tips of his corona trembled involuntarily at the froth of tension that had accompanied the messengers into the humid greenhouse.

From here a long bank of windows offered a glorious view of the Valley of the Sind, pleasantly arrayed with farms and groves of both native and imported Terran trees. It was a lovely, peaceful scene.

Great Infinity alone knew how much longer that serenity would last. And Ifni was not confiding her plans in Uthacalthing, at present

Planetary Coordinator Oneagle scanned the report briefly. 'Do you have any idea yet who the enemy is?'

Colonel Maiven shook his head. 'Not really, ma'am. The fleets are closing now, though. We expect identification shortly.'

In spite of the seriousness of the moment, Uthacalthing found himself once again intrigued by the quaintly archaic dialect humans used here on Garth. At every other Terran colony he had visited, Anglic had taken in a potpourri of words borrowed from Galactic languages Seven, Two, and Ten. Here, though, common speech was not appreciably different from what it had been when Garth was licensed to the humans and their clients, more than two generations ago.

Delightful, surprising creatures, he thought. Only here, for instance, would one hear such a pure, ancient form addressing a female leader as 'ma'am.' On other Terran-occupied worlds, functionaries addressed their supervisors by the neutral 'ser,' whatever their gender.

There were other unusual things about Garth as well. In the months since his arrival here, Uthacalthing had made a private pastime of listening to every odd story, every strange tale brought in from the wild lands by farmers, trappers, and members of the Ecological Recovery Service. There had been rumors. Rumors of strange things going on up in the mountains.

Of course they were silly stories, mostly. Exaggerations and tall tales. Just the sort of thing you would expect from wolflings living at the edge of a wilderness. And yet they had given him the beginnings of an idea.

Uthacalthing listened quietly as each of the staff officers reported in turn. At last, though, there came a long pause – the silence of brave people sharing a common sense of doom. Only then did he venture to speak, quietly. 'Colonel Maiven, are you certain the enemy is being so thorough in isolating Garth?'

The Defense Councilor bowed to Uthacalthing. 'Mr Ambassador, we know that hyperspace is being mined by enemy cruisers as close in as six million pseudometers, on at least four of the main levels.'

'Including D-level?'

'Yes, ser. Of course it means we dare not send any of our lightly armed ships out on any of the few hyperpaths available, even if we could have spared any from the battle. It also means anyone trying to get *into* Garth system would have to be mighty determined.'

Uthacalthing was impressed. *They have mined D-level. I would not have expected them to bother. They certainly* don't *want anybody interfering in this operation!*

This spoke of substantial effort and cost. Someone was sparing little expense in this operation.

'The point is moot,' the Planetary Coordinator said. Megan was looking out over the rolling meadows of the Sind, with its farmsteads and environmental research stations. Just below the window a chim gardener on a tractor tended the broad lawn of Earth-breed grass surrounding Government House.

She turned back to the others. 'The last courier ship brought orders from the Terragens Council. We are to defend ourselves as best we can, for honor's sake and for the record. But beyond that all we can hope to do is maintain some sort of underground resistance until help arrives from the outside.'

Uthacalthing's deepself almost laughed out loud, for at that moment each human in the room tried hard *not* to look at him! Colonel Maiven cleared his throat and examined his report. His officers pondered the brilliant, flowering plants. Still, it was obvious what they were thinking.

Of the few Galactic clans that Earth could count as friends, only the Tymbrimi had the military strength to be of much assistance in this crisis. Men had faith that Tymbrim would not let humans and their clients down.

And that *was* true enough. Uthacalthing knew the allies would face this crisis together.

But it was also clear that little Garth was a long way out on the fringe of things. And these days the homeworlds had to take first priority.

No matter, Uthacalthing thought. *The best means to an end are not always those that appear most direct.*

Uthacalthing did not laugh out loud, much as he wanted to. For it might only discomfit these poor, grief-stricken people. In the course of his career he had met some Earthlings who possessed a natural gift for high-quality pranksterism – a few even on a par with the best Tymbrimi. Still, so many of them were such terribly dour, sober folk! Most tried so desperately hard to be serious at the very moments when humor could most help them through their troubles.

Uthacalthing wondered.

As a diplomat I have taught myself to watch every word, lest our clan's penchant for japes cause costly incidents. But has this been wise? My own daughter has picked up this habit from me ... this shroud of seriousness. Perhaps that is why she has grown into such a strange, earnest little creature.

Thinking of Athaclena made him wish all the more he could openly make light of the situation. Otherwise, he might do the human thing and consider the danger she was in. He knew that

Megan worried about her own son. *She underrates Robert*, Uthacalthing thought. *She should better know the lad's potential.*

'Dear ladies and gentlemen,' he said, savoring the archaisms. His eyes separated only slightly in amusement. 'We can expect the fanatics to arrive within days. You have made conventional plans to offer what resistance your meager resources will allow. Those plans will serve their function.'

'However?' It was Megan Oneagle who posed the question. One eyebrow arched above those brown irises – big and set almost far enough apart to look attractive in the classic Tymbrimi sense. There was no mistaking the look.

She knows as well as I that more is called for. Ah, if Robert has half his mother's brains, I'll not fear for Athaclena, wandering in the dark forests of this sad, barren world.

Uthacalthing's corona trembled. '*However,*' he echoed, 'it does occur to me that now might be a good time to consult the Branch Library.'

Uthacalthing picked up some of their disappointment. Astonishing creatures! Tymbrimi skepticism toward modern Galactic culture never went so far as the outright contempt so many humans felt for the Great Library!

Wolflings. Uthacalthing sighed to himself. In the space above his head he crafted the glyph called *syullf-tha*, anticipation of a puzzle *almost* too ornate to solve. The specter revolved in expectancy, invisible to the humans – although for a moment Megan's attention seemed to flutter, as if she were just on the edge of noticing something.

Poor Wolflings. For all of its faults, the Library is where everything begins and ends. Always, somewhere in its treasure trove of knowledge, can be found some gem of wisdom and solution. Until you learn that, my friends, little inconveniences like ravening enemy battle fleets will go on ruining perfectly good spring mornings like this one!

7

ATHACLENA

Robert led the way a few feet ahead of her, using a machete to lop off the occasional branch encroaching on the narrow trail. The bright sunshine of the sun, Gimelhai, filtered softly through the forest canopy, and the spring air was warm.

Athaclena felt glad of the easy pace. With her weight redistributed from its accustomed pattern, walking was something of an adventure in itself. She wondered how human women managed to go through most of their lives with such a wide-hipped stance. Perhaps it was a sacrifice they paid for having big-headed babies, instead of giving birth early and then sensibly slipping the child into a post-partum pouch.

This experiment – subtly changing her body shape to make it seem more humanlike – was one of the more fascinating aspects of her visit to an Earth colony. She certainly could not have moved among local crowds as inconspicuously on a world of the reptiloid Soro, or the sap-ring-creatures of Jophur. And in the process she had learned a lot more about physiological control than the instructors had taught her back in school.

Still, the inconveniences were substantial, and she was considering putting an end to the experiment.

Oh, Ifni. A glyph of frustration danced at her tendril tips. *Changing back at this point might be more effort than it's worth.*

There were limits to what even the ever-adaptable Tymbrimi physiology could be expected to do. Attempting too many alterations in a short time ran the risk of triggering enzyme exhaustion.

Anyway, it was a little flattering to *kenn* the conflicts taking shape in Robert's mind. Athaclena wondered. *Is he actually attracted to me?* A year ago the very idea would have shocked her. Even Tymbrimi boys made her nervous, and Robert was an alien!

Now though, for some reason, she felt more curiosity than revulsion.

There was something almost hypnotic about the steady rocking of the pack on her back, the rhythm of soft boots on the rough trail, and the warming of leg muscles too long leashed by city streets. Here in the middle altitudes the air was warm and moist. It carried a thousand rich scents, oxygen, decaying humus, and the musty smell of human perspiration.

As Athaclena trudged, following her guide along the steep-sided ridgeline, a low rumbling could soon be heard coming from the distance ahead of them. It sounded like a rumor of great engines, or perhaps an industrial plant. The murmur faded and then returned with every switchback, just a little more forceful each time they drew near its mysterious source. Apparently Robert was relishing a surprise, so Athaclena bit back her curiosity and asked no questions.

At last, though, Robert stopped and waited at a bend in the trail. He closed his eyes, concentrating, and Athaclena thought she caught, just for a moment, the flickering traces of primitive emotion-glyph. Instead of true *kenning*, it brought to mind a *visual* image – a high, roaring fountain painted in garish, uninhibited blues and greens.

He really is getting much better, Athaclena thought. Then she joined him at the bend and gasped in surprise.

Droplets, trillions of tiny liquid lenses, sparkled in the shafts of sunlight that cut sharply through the cloud forest. The low rumble that had drawn them onward for an hour was suddenly an earth-shaking growl that rattled tree limbs left and right, reverberating through the rocks and into their bones. Straight ahead a great cataract spilled over glass-smooth boulders, dashing into spume and spray in a canyon carved over persistent ages.

The falling river was an extravagance of nature, pouring forth more exuberantly than the most shameless human entertainer, prouder then any sentient poet.

It was too much to be taken in with ears and eyes alone. Atha-clena's tendrils waved, seeking, *kenning*, one of those moments Tymbrimi glyphcrafters sometimes spoke of – when a *world* seemed to join into the mesh of empathy usually reserved for living things. In a time-stretched instant, she realized that ancient Garth, wounded and crippled, could still sing.

Robert grinned. Athaclena met his gaze and smiled as well. Their hands met and joined. For a long, wordless time they stood together and watched the shimmering, ever-changing rainbows arch over nature's percussive flood.

Strangely, the epiphany only made Athaclena feel sad, and even more regretful she had ever come to this world. She had not wanted to discover beauty here. It only made the little world's fate seem more tragic.

How many times had she wished Uthacalthing had never accepted this assignment? But wishing seldom made things so.

As much as she loved him, Athaclena had always found her father inscrutable. His reasoning was often too convoluted for her to fathom, his actions too unpredictable. Such as taking this posting when he could have had a more prestigious one simply by asking.

And sending her into these mountains with Robert ... it hadn't been just 'for her safety,' she could tell that much. Was she actually supposed to chase those ridiculous rumors of exotic mountain crea-tures? Unlikely. Probably Uthacalthing only suggested the idea in order to distract her from her worries.

Then she thought of another possible motive.

Could her father actually imagine that she might enter into a self-other bond ... with a *human*? Her nostrils flared to twice their normal size at the thought. Gently, suppressing her corona in order to keep her feelings hidden, she relaxed her grip on Robert's hand, and felt relieved when he did not hold on.

Athaclena crossed her arms and shivered.

Back home she had taken part in only a few, tentative practice bondings with boys, and those mostly as class assignments. Before her mother's death this had been a cause of quite a few family arguments. Mathicluanna had almost despaired of her oddly reserved and private daughter. But Athaclena's father, at least, had not pestered her to do more than she was ready for.

Until now, maybe?

Robert was certainly charming and likable. With his high cheekbones and eyes pleasantly set apart, he was about as handsome as a human might hope to get. And yet, the very fact that she might think in such terms shocked Athaclena.

Her tendrils twitched. She shook her head and wiped out a nascent glyph before she could even realize what it would have been. This was a topic she had no wish to consider right now, even less than the prospect of war.

'The waterfall is beautiful, Robert,' she enunciated carefully in Anglic. 'But if we stay here much longer, we shall soon be quite damp.'

He seemed to return from a distant contemplation. 'Oh. Yeah, Clennie. Let's go.' With a brief smile he turned and led the way, his human empathy waves vague and far away.

The rain forest persisted in long fingers between the hills, becoming wetter and more robust as they gained altitude. Little Garthian creatures, timid and scarce at the lower levels, now made frequent skittering rustles behind the lush vegetation, occasionally even challenging them with impudent squeaks.

Soon they reached the summit of a foothill ridge, where a chain of spine-stones jutted up, bare and gray, like the bony plates along the back of one of those ancient reptiles Uthacalthing had shown her, in a lesson book on Earth history. As they removed their packs for a rest, Robert told her that no one could explain the formations, which topped many of the hills below the Mountains of Mulun.

'Even the Branch Library on Earth has no reference,' he said as he brushed a hand along one of the jagged monoliths. 'We've submitted a low-priority inquiry to the district branch at Tanith. Maybe in a century or so the Library Institute's computers will dig up a report from some long-extinct race that once lived here, and then we'll know the answer.'

'Yet you hope they do not,' she suggested.

Robert shrugged. 'I guess I'd rather it were left a mystery. Maybe we could be the first to figure it out.' He looked pensively at the stones.

A lot of Tymbrimi felt the same way, preferring a good puzzle to any written fact. Not Athaclena, however. This attitude – this resentment of the Great Library – was something she found absurd.

Without the Library and the other Galactic Institutes, oxygen-breathing culture, dominant in the Five Galaxies, would long ago have fallen into total disarray – probably ending in savage, total war.

True, most starfaring clans relied far too much on the Library. And the Institutes only *moderated* the bickering of the most petty and vituperative senior patron lines. The present crisis was only the latest in a series that stretched back long before any now living race had come into existence.

Still, this planet was an example of what could happen when the restraint of Tradition broke down. Athaclena listened to the sounds of the forest. Shading her eyes, she watched a swarm of small, furry creatures glide from branch to branch in the direction of the afternoon sun.

'Superficially, one might not even know this was a holocaust world,' she said softly.

Robert had set their packs in the shade of a towering spine-stone and began cutting slices of soyastick salami and bread for their luncheon. 'It's been fifty thousand years since the Bururalli made a mess of Garth, Athaclena. That's enough time for lots of surviving animal species to radiate and fill some of the emptied niches. Right now I guess you'd probably have to be a zoologist to notice the sparse species list.'

Athaclena's corona was at full extension, *kenning* faint traceries of emotion from the surrounding forest. '*I* notice, Robert,' she said. 'I can feel it. This watershed lives, but it is lonely. It has none of the life-complexity a wildwood should know. And there is no trace of Potential at all.'

Robert nodded seriously. But she sensed his distance from it all. The Bururalli Holocaust happened a long time ago, from an Earthling's point of view.

The Bururalli had also been new, back then, just released from indenture to the Nahalli, the patron race that uplifted them to sentience. It was a special time for the Bururalli, for only when its knot of obligations was loosened at last could a client species establish unsupervised colonies of its own. When their time came the Galactic Institute of Migration had just declared the fallow world Garth ready again for limited occupation. As always, the Institute expected that local lifeforms – especially those which might some day develop Uplift Potential – would be protected at all cost by the new tenants.

The Nahalli boasted that they had found the Bururalli a quarrel-some clan of pre-sentient carnivores and uplifted them to become perfect Galactic citizens, responsible and reliable, worthy of such a trust.

The Nahalli were proven horribly wrong.

'Well, what do you expect when an entire race goes completely crazy and starts annihilating everything in sight?' Robert asked. 'Something went wrong and suddenly the Bururalli turned into berserkers, tearing apart a world they were supposed to take care of.

'It's no wonder you don't detect any Potential in a Garth forest, Clennie. Only those tiny creatures who could burrow and hide escaped the Bururalli's madness. The bigger, brighter animals are all one with yesterday's snows.'

Athaclena blinked. Just when she thought she had a grasp of Anglic Robert did this to her again, using that strange human penchant for *metaphors*. Unlike similes, which *compared* two objects, metaphors seemed to declare, against all logic, that unlike things were the same! No Galactic language allowed such nonsense.

Generally she was able to handle those odd linguistic juxtaposi-tions, but this one had her baffled. Above her waving corona the small-glyph *teev'nus* formed briefly – standing for the elusiveness of perfect communication.

'I have only heard brief accounts of that era. What happened to the murderous Bururalli themselves?'

Robert shrugged. 'Oh, officials from the Institutes of Uplift and Migration finally dropped by, about a century or so after the holo-caust began. The inspectors were horrified, of course.

'They found the Bururalli warped almost beyond recognition, roaming the planet, hunting to death anything they could catch. By then they'd abandoned the horrible technological weapons they'd started with and nearly reverted to tooth and claw. I suppose that's why some small animals did survive.

'Ecological disasters aren't as uncommon as the Institutes would have it seem, but this one was a major scandal. There was galaxy-wide revulsion. Battle fleets were sent by many of the major clans and put under unified command. Soon the Bururalli were no more.'

Athaclena nodded. 'I assume their patrons, the Nahalli, were pun-ished as well.'

'Right. They lost status and are somebody's clients now, the price of negligence. We're taught the story in school. Several times.'

When Robert offered the salami again, Athaclena shook her head. Her appetite had vanished. 'So you humans inherited another recla-mation world.'

Robert put away their lunch. 'Yeah. Since we're two-client

patrons, we had to be allowed colonies, but the Institutes have mostly handed us the leavings of other peoples' disasters. We have to work hard helping this world's ecosystem straighten itself out, but actually, Garth is really nice compared with some of the others. You ought to see Deemi and Horst, out in the Canaan Cluster.'

'I have heard of them.' Athaclena shuddered. 'I do not think I ever want to see – '

She stopped mid-sentence. 'I do not ...' Her eyelids fluttered as she looked around, suddenly confused. *'Thu'un dun!'* Her ruff puffed outward. Athaclena stood quickly and walked – half in a trance – to where the towering spine-stones overlooked the misty tops of the cloud forest.

Robert approached from behind. 'What is it?'

She spoke softly. 'I sense something.'

'Hmmph. That doesn't surprise me, with that Tymbrimi nervous system of yours, especially the way you've been altering your body form just to please me. It's no wonder you're picking up static.'

Athaclena shook her head impatiently. 'I have *not* been doing it just to please you, you arrogant human male! And I've asked you before kindly to be more careful with your horrible metaphors. A Tymbrimi corona is not a radio!' She gestured with her hand. 'Now please be quiet for a moment.'

Robert fell silent. Athaclena concentrated, trying to *kenn* again ...

A corona might not pick up static like a radio, but it could suffer interference. She sought after the faint aura she had felt so very briefly, but it was impossible. Robert's clumsy, eager empathy flux crowded it out completely.

'What was it, Clennie?' he asked softly.

'I do not know. Something not very far away, off toward the southeast. It felt like people – men and neo-chimpanzees mostly – but there was something else as well.'

Robert frowned. 'Well, I guess it might have been one of the eco-logical management stations. Also, there are isolated freeholds all through this area, mostly higher up, where the seisin grows.'

She turned swiftly. 'Robert, I felt Potential! For the briefest moment of clarity, I touched the emotions of a pre-sentient being!'

Robert's feelings were suddenly cloudy and turbulent, his face impassive. 'What do you mean?'

'My father told me about something, before you and I left for the mountains. At the time I paid little attention. It seemed impossible, like those fairy tales your human authors create to give us Tymbrimi strange dreams.'

'Your people buy them by the shipload,' Robert interjected. 'Novels, old movies, threevee, poems ...'

Athaclena ignored his aside. 'Uthacalthing mentioned stories of a creature of this planet, a native being of high Potential ... one who is supposed to have actually survived the Bururalli Holocaust.' Athaclena's corona foamed forth a glyph rare to her ... *syullf-tha*, the joy of a puzzle to be solved. 'I wonder. Could the legends possibly be true?'

Did Robert's mood flicker with a note of relief? Athaclena felt his crude but effective emotional guard go opaque.

'Hmmm. Well, there *is* a legend,' he said. 'A simple story told by wolflings. It could hardly be of interest to a sophisticated Galactic, I suppose.'

Athaclena eyed him carefully and touched his arm, stroking it gently. 'Are you going to make me wait while you draw out this mystery with dramatic pauses? Or will you save yourself bruises and tell me what you know at once?'

Robert laughed. 'Well, since you're so persuasive. You just *might* have picked up the empathy output of a Garthling.'

Athaclena's broad, gold-flecked eyes blinked. 'That is the name my father used!'

'Ah. Then Uthacalthing has been listening to old seisin hunters' tales ... Imagine having such after only a hundred Earth years here ... Anyway, it's said that one large animal did manage to escape the Bururalli, through cunning, ferocity, and a whole lot of Potential. The mountain men and chims tell of sampling traps robbed, laundry stolen from clotheslines, and strange markings scratched on unclimbable cliff faces.

'Oh, it's probably all a lot of eyewash.' Robert smiled. 'But I did recall those legends when Mother told me I was to come up here. So I figured, so that it wouldn't be a total loss, I might as well take a Tymbrimi along to see if she could flush out a Garthling with her empathy net.'

Some metaphors Athaclena understood quite readily. Her fingernails pressed into Robert's arm. 'So?' she asked with a questing lilt. 'That is the entire reason I am in this wilderness? I am to be a sniffer-out of smoke and legends for you?'

'Sure,' Robert teased. 'Why else would I come out here, all alone in the mountains with an alien from outer space?'

Athaclena hissed through her teeth. But within she could not help but feel pleased. This human sardonicism wasn't unlike reverse-talk among her own people. And when Robert laughed aloud, she found she had to join him. For the moment all worry of war and danger was banished. It was a welcome release for both of them.

'If such a creature exists, we must find it, you and I,' she said at last.

'Yeah, Clennie. Well find it together.'

8

FIBEN

TAASF Scoutship *Proconsul* hadn't outlived its pilot after all. It had seen its last mission – the ancient boat was dead in space – but within its bubble canopy life still remained.

Enough life, at least, to inhale the pungent stench of a six days unwashed ape – and to exhale an apparently unceasing string of imaginative curses.

Fiben finally ran down when he found he was repeating himself. He had long ago covered every permutation, combination, and juxtaposition of bodily, spiritual, and hereditary attributes – real and imaginary – the enemy could possibly possess. That exercise had carried him all the way through his own brief part in the space battle, while he fired his popgun weaponry and evaded counterblows like a gnat ducking sledgehammers, through the concussions of near-misses and the shriek of tortured metal, and into an aftermath of dazed, confused bemusement that he did not seem to be dead after all. Not yet at least.

When he was sure the life capsule was still working and not about to sputter out along with the rest of the scoutboat, Fiben finally wriggled out of his suit and sighed at his first opportunity to scratch in days. He dug in with a will, using not only his hands but the tingers and tumb of his left foot, as well. Finally he sagged back, aching from the pounding he had been through.

His main job had been to pass close enough to collect good data for the rest of the defense force. Fiben guessed that zooming straight down the middle of the invading fleet probably qualified. Heckling the enemy he had thrown in for free.

It seemed the interlopers failed to appreciate his running commentary as *Proconsul* plunged through their midst. He'd lost count of how many times close calls came near to cooking him. By the time he had passed behind and beyond the onrushing armada, *Proconsul*'s entire aft end had been turned into a glazed-over hunk of slag.

The main propulsion system was gone, of course. There was no way to return and help his comrades in the desperate, futile struggle that followed soon after. Drifting farther and farther from the one-sided battle, Fiben could only listen helplessly.

It wasn't even a contest. The fighting lasted little more than a day.

He remembered the last charge of the corvette, *Darwin*, accompanied by two converted freighters and a small swarm of surviving scoutboats. They streaked down, blasting their way into the flank of the invading host, turning it, throwing one wing of battlecruisers into confusion under clouds of smoke and waves of noisome probability waves.

Not a single Terran craft came out of that maelstrom. Fiben knew then that TAASF *Bonobo*, and his friend Simon, were gone.

Right now, the enemy seemed to be pursuing a few fugitives off toward Ifni knew where. They were taking their time, cleaning up thoroughly before proceeding to supine Garth.

Now Fiben resumed his cursing along a new tack. All in a spirit of constructive criticism, of course, he dissected the character faults of the species his own race was unfortunate enough to have as patrons.

Why? he asked the universe. *Why did humans – those hapless, hairless, wolfling wretches – have the incredibly bad taste to have uplifted neo-chimpanzees into a galaxy so obviously run by idiots?*

Eventually, he slept,

His dreams were fitful. Fiben kept imagining that he was trying to speak, but his voice would not shape the sentences, a nightmare possibility to one whose great-grandfather spoke only crudely, with the aid of devices, and whose slightly more distant ancestors faced the world without words at all.

Fiben sweated. No shame was greater than this. In his dream he sought speech as if it were an object, a thing that might be *misplaced*, somehow.

On looking down he saw a glittering gem lying on the ground. Perhaps *this* was the gift of words, Fiben thought, and he bent over to take it. But he was too clumsy! His thumb refused to work with his forefinger, and he wasn't able to pluck the bauble out of the dust. In fact, all of his efforts seemed only to push it in deeper.

Despairing finally, he was forced to crouch down and pick it up with his lips.

It *burned*! In his dream he cried out as a terrible searing poured down his throat like liquid fire.

And yet, he recognized that this was one of those strange nightmares – the land in which one could be both objective *and* terrified at the same time. As one dreamself writhed in agony, another part of Fiben witnessed it in a state of interested detachment.

All at once the scene shifted. Fiben found himself standing in the midst of a gathering of bearded men in black coats and floppy hats. They were mostly elderly, and they leafed through dusty texts as they argued with each other. *An oldtime Talmudic conclave*, he recognized suddenly, like those he had read about in comparative religions class, back at the University. The rabbis sat in a circle, discussing symbolism and biblical interpretation. One lifted an aged hand to point at Fiben.

'*He that lappeth like an animal, Gideon, he shall thou not take ...*'

'Is that what it means?' Fiben asked. The pain was gone. Now he was more bemused than fearful. His pal, Simon, had been Jewish. No doubt that explained part of this crazy symbolism. What was going on here was obvious. These learned men, these wise human scholars, were trying to illuminate that frightening first part of his dream for him.

'*No, no,*' a second sage countered. '*The symbols relate to the trial of the infant Moses! An angel, you'll recall, guided his hand to the glowing coals, rather than the shining jewels, and his mouth was burned ...*'

'But I don't see what that *tells* me!' Fiben protested.

The oldest rabbi raised his hand, and the others all went silent.

'*The dream stands for none of those things. The symbolism should be obvious,*' he said.

'*It comes from the oldest book ...*'

The sage's bushy eyebrows knotted with concern.

'*... And Adam, too, ate from the fruit of the Tree of Knowledge ...*'

'Uh,' Fiben groaned aloud, awakening in a sweat. The gritty, smelly capsule was all around him again, and yet the vividness of the dream lingered, making him wonder for a moment which was real after all. Finally he shrugged it off. 'Old *Proconsul* must have drifted through the wake of some Eatee probability mine while I slept. Yeah. That must be it. I'll never doubt the stories they tell in a spacer's bar again.'

When he checked his battered instruments Fiben found that the battle had moved on around the sun. His own derelict, meanwhile, was on a nearly perfect intersect orbit with a planet.

'Hmmmph,' he grunted as he worked the computer. What it told him was ironic. *It really is Garth.*

He still had a little maneuvering power in the gravity systems. Perhaps enough, just maybe, to get him within escape pod range.

And wonder of wonders, if his ephemerides were right, he might even be able to reach the Western Sea area ... a bit east of Port Helenia. Fiben whistled tunelessly for a few minutes. He wondered what the chances were that this should happen. A million to one? Probably more like a trillion.

Or was the universe just suckering him with a bit of hope before the *next* whammy?

Either way, he decided, there was some solace in thinking that, under all these stars, someone out there was still thinking of him personally.

He got out his tool kit and set to work making the necessary repairs.

9

UTHACALTHING

Uthacalthing knew it was unwise to wait much longer. Still he remained with the Librarians, watching them try to coax forth one more valuable detail before it was time at last to go.

He regarded the human and neo-chimpanzee technicians as they hurried about under the high-domed ceiling of the Planetary Branch Library. They all had jobs to do and concentrated on them intently, efficiently. And yet one could sense a ferment just below the surface, one of barely suppressed fear.

Unbidden, *rittitees* formed in the low sparking of his corona. The glyph was one commonly used by Tymbrimi parents to calm frightened children.

They can't detect you, Uthacalthing told *rittitees*. And yet it obstinately hovered, trying to soothe young ones in distress.

Anyway, these people aren't children. Humans have only known of the Great Library for two Earth centuries. But they had thousands of years of their own history before that. They may still lack Galactic polish and sophistication, but that deficit has sometimes been an advantage to them.

Rarely. Rittitees was dubious.

Uthacalthing ended the argument by drawing the uncertain glyph back where it belonged, into his own well of being.

Under the vaulted stone ceiling towered a five-meter gray monolith, embossed with a rayed spiral sigil – symbol of the Great Library for three billion years. Nearby, data loggers filled crystalline memory cubes. Printers hummed and spat bound reports which were quickly annotated and carted away.

This Library station, a class K outlet, was a small one indeed. It contained only the equivalent of one thousand times all the books humans had written before Contact, a pittance compared with the full Branch Library on Earth, or sector general on Tanith.

Still, when Garth was taken this room, too, would fall to the invader.

Traditionally, that should make no difference. The Library was supposed to remain open to all, even parties fighting over the territory it stood upon. In times like these, however, it was unwise to count on such niceties. The colonial resistance forces planned to carry off what they could in hopes of using the information somehow, later.

A pittance of a pittance. Of course it had been his suggestion that they do this, but Uthacalthing was frankly amazed that the humans had gone along with the idea so vigorously. After all, why bother? What could such a small smattering of information accomplish?

This raid on the Planetary Library served his purposes, but it also reinforced his opinion of Earth people. They just never gave up. It was yet another reason he found the creatures delightful.

The hidden reason for this chaos – his own private jest – had called for the dumping and misplacing of a few specific megafiles, easily overlooked in all of this confusion. In fact, nobody appeared to have noticed when he briefly attached his own input-output cube to the massive Library, waited a few seconds, then pocketed the little sabotage device again.

Done. Now there was little to do but watch the wolflings while he waited for his car.

Off in the distance a wailing tone began to rise and fall. It was the keening of the spaceport siren, across the bay, as another crippled refugee from the rout in space came in for an emergency landing. They had heard that sound all too infrequently. Everyone already knew that there had been few survivors.

Mostly the traffic consisted of departing aircraft. Many main-landers had already taken flight to the chain of islands in the Western Sea where the vast majority of the Earthling population still made its home. The Government was preparing its own evacuation.

When the sirens moaned, every man and chim looked up briefly. Momentarily, the workers broadcast a complex fugue of anxiety that Uthacalthing could almost taste with his corona.

Almost taste?

Oh, what lovely, surprising things, these metaphors, Uthacalthing thought. *Can one taste with one's corona? Or touch with one's eyes? Anglic is so silly, yet so delightfully thought provoking.*

Ana do not dolphins actually see with their ears?

Zunour'thzun formed above his waving tendrils, resonating with the fear of the men and chims.

Yes, we all hope to live, for we have so very much left to do or taste or see or *kenn* . . .

Uthacalthing wished diplomacy did not require that Tymbrimi choose their dullest types as envoys. He had been selected as an ambassador because, among other qualities, he was *boring*, at least from the point of view of those back home.

And poor Athaclena seemed to be even worse off, so sober and serious.

He freely admitted that it was partly his own fault. That was one reason he had brought along his own father's large collection of pre-Contact Earthling comic recordings. The Three Stooges, especially, inspired him. Alas, as yet Athaclena seemed unable to understand the subtle, ironic brilliance of those ancient Terran comedic geniuses.

Through *Sylth* – that courier of the dead-but-remembered – his long-dead wife still chided him, reaching out from beyond life to say that their daughter should be home, where her lively peers might yet draw her out from her isolation.

Perhaps, he thought. But Mathicluanna had had her try. Uthacalthing believed in his own prescription for their odd daughter.

A small, uniformed neo-chimpanzee female – a chimmie – stepped in front of Uthacalthing and bowed, her hands folded respectfully in front of her.

'Yes, miss?' Uthacalthing spoke first, as protocol demanded. Although he was a patron speaking to a client, he generously included the polite, archaic honorific.

'Y-your excellency.' The chimmie's scratchy voice trembled slightly. Probably, this was the first time she had ever spoken to a non-Terran. 'Your excellency, Planetary Coordinator Oneagle has sent word that the preparations have been completed. The fires are about to be set.

'She asks if you would like to witness your ... er, program, unleashed.'

As Uthacalthing's eyes separated wider in amusement, the wrinkled fur between his brows flattening momentarily. His 'program' hardly deserved the name. It might better be called a devious practical joke on the invaders. A long shot, at best.

Not even Megan Oneagle knew what he was really up to. That necessity was a pity, of course. For even if it failed – as was likely – it would still be worthy of a chuckle or two. A laugh might help his friend through the dark times ahead of her.

'Thank you, corporal,' he nodded. 'Please lead the way.'

As he followed the little client, Uthacalthing felt a faint sense of regret at leaving so much undone. A good joke required much preparation, and there was just not enough time.

If only I had a decent sense of humor!

Ah, well. Where subtlety fails us we must simply make do with cream pies.

*

Two hours later he was on his way back to town from Government House. The meeting had been brief, with battle fleets approaching orbit and landings expected soon. Megan Oneagle had already moved most of the government and her few remaining forces to safer ground.

Uthacalthing figured they actually had a little more time. There would be no landing until the invaders had broadcast their manifesto. The rules of the Institute for Civilized Warfare required it.

Of course, with the Five Galaxies in turmoil, many starfaring clans were playing fast and loose with tradition right now. But in this case observing the proprieties would cost the enemy nothing. They had already won. Now it was only a matter of occupying the territory.

Besides, the battle in space had showed one thing. It was clear now the enemy were *Gubru*.

The humans and chims of this planet were not in for a pleasant time. The Gubru Clan had been among the worst of Earth's tormentors since Contact. Nonetheless, the avian Galactics were sticklers for rules. By their own interpretation of them, at least.

Megan had been disappointed when he turned down her offer of transportation to sanctuary. But Uthacalthing had his own ship. Anyway, he still had business to take care of here in town. He bid farewell to the Coordinator with a promise to see her soon.

'Soon' was such a wonderfully ambiguous word. One of many reasons he treasured Anglic was the wolfling tongue's marvelous untidiness!

By moonlight Port Helenia felt even smaller and more forlorn than the tiny, threatened village it was by day. Winter might be mostly over, but a stiff breeze still blew from the east, sending leaves tumbling across the nearly empty streets as his driver took him back toward his chancery compound. The wind carried a moist odor, and Uthacalthing imagined he could smell the mountains where his daughter and Megan's son had gone for refuge.

It was a decision that had not won the parents much thanks.

His car had to pass by the Branch Library again on its way to the Tymbrimi Embassy. The driver had to slow to go around another vehicle. Because of this Uthacalthing was treated to a rare sight – a high-caste Thennanin in full fury under the streetlights.

'Please stop here,' he said suddenly.

In front of the stone Library building a large floatercraft hummed quietly. Light poured out of its raised cupola, creating a dark bouquet of shadows on the broad steps. Five clearly were cast by neo-chimpanzees, their long arms exaggerated in the stretched silhouettes. Two even longer penumbral shadows swept away from slender figures standing close to the floater. A pair of stoic, disciplined Ynnin – looking like tall, armored kangaroos – stood unmoving as if molded out of stone.

Their employer and patron, owner of the largest silhouette, towered above the little Terrans. Blocky and powerful, the creature's wedgelike shoulders seemed to merge right into its bullet-shaped head. The latter was topped by a high, rippling crest, like that of a helmeted Greek warrior.

As Uthacalthing stepped out of his own car he heard a loud voice rich in guttural sibilants.

'Natha'kl ghoom'ph? Veraich'sch hooman'vlech! Nittaro K'Anglee!'

The chimpanzees shook their heads, confused and clearly intimidated. Obviously none of them spoke Galactic Six. Still, when the huge Thennanin started forward the little Earthlings moved to interpose themselves, bowing low, but adamant in their refusal to let him pass.

This only served to make the speaker angrier. *'Idatess! Nittaril kollunta ...'*

The large Galactic stopped abruptly on seeing Uthacalthing. His leathery, beaklike mouth remained closed as he switched to Galactic Seven, speaking through his breathing slits.

'Ah! Uthacalthing, ab-Caltmour ab-Brma abKrallnith ul-Tytlal! I see you!'

Uthacalthing would have recognized Kault in a city choked with Thennanin. The big, pompous, high-caste male knew that protocol did not require use of full species names in casual encounters. But now Uthacalthing had no choice. He had to reply in kind.

'Kault, ab-Wortl ab-Kosh ab-Rosh ab-Tothtoon ul-Paimin ul-Rammin ul-Ynnin ul-Olumimin, I see you as well.'

Each 'ab' in the lengthy patronymic told of one of the patron races from which the Thennanin clan was descended, back to the eldest still living. 'Ul' preceded the name of each client species the Thennanin had themselves uplifted to starfaring sentience. Kault's people had been very busy, the last megayear or so. They bragged incessantly of their long species name.

The Thennanin were idiots.

'Uthacalthing! You are adept in that garbage tongue the Earthlings use. Please explain to these ignorant, half-uplifted creatures that I wish to pass! I have need to use the Branch Library, and if they do not stand aside I shall be forced to have their masters chastise them!'

Uthacalthing shrugged the standard gesture of regretful inability to comply. 'They are only doing their jobs, Envoy Kault. When the Library is fully occupied with matters of planetary defense, it is briefly allowable to restrict access solely to the lease owners.'

Kault stared unblinkingly at Uthacalthing. His breathing slits puffed. *'Babes,'* he muttered softly in an obscure dialect of Galactic Twelve – unaware perhaps that Uthacalthing understood. *'Infants, ruled by unruly children, tutored by juvenile delinquents!'*

Uthacalthing's eyes separated and his tendrils pulsed with irony. They crafted *fou'usturatu*, which sympathizes, while laughing.

Damn good thing Thennanin have a rock's sensitivity to empathy. Uthacalthing thought in Anglic as he hurriedly erased the glyph. Of the Galactic clans involved in the current spate of fanaticism, the Thennanin were less repulsive than most. Some of them actually believed they were acting in the best interests of those they conquered.

It was apparent whom Kault meant when he spoke of 'delinquents' leading the clan of Earth astray. Uthacalthing was far from offended.

'These *infants* fly starships, Kault,' he answered in the same dialect, to the Thennanin's obvious surprise. 'The neo-chimpanzees may be the finest clients to appear in half a megayear ... with the possible exception of their cousins, the neo-dolphins. Shall we not respect their earnest desire to do their duty?'

Kault's crest went rigid at the mention of the other Earthling client race. 'My Tymbrimi friend, did you mean to imply that you have heard more about the dolphin ship? Have they been found?'

Uthacalthing felt a little guilty for toying with Kault. All considered, he was not a bad sort. He came from a minority political faction among the Thennanin which had a few times even spoken for peace with the Tymbrimi. Nevertheless, Uthacalthing had reasons for wanting to pique his fellow diplomat's interest, and he had prepared for an encounter like this.

'Perhaps I have said more than I should. Please think nothing more of it. Now I am saddened to say that I really must be going. I am late for a meeting. I wish you good fortune and survival in the days ahead, Kault.'

He bowed in the casual fashion of one patron to another and turned to go. But within, Uthacalthing was laughing. For he knew the real reason Kault was here at the Library. The Thennanin could only have come looking for him.

'Wait!' Kault called out in Anglic.

Uthacalthing looked back. 'Yes, respected colleague?'

'I ...' Kault dropped back into GalSeven. 'I must speak with you regarding the evacuation. You may have heard, my ship is in disrepair. I am at the moment bereft of transport.'

The Thennanin's crest fluttered in discomfort. Protocol and diplomatic standing were one thing, but the fellow obviously would rather not be in town when the Gubru landed. 'I must ask therefore. Will there be some opportunity to discuss the possibility of mutual aid?' The big creature said it in a rush.

Uthacalthing pretended to ponder the idea seriously. After all, his species and Kault's were officially at war right now. He nodded at last. 'Be at my compound about midnight tomorrow night – no later than a mictaar thereafter, mind you. And please bring only a minimum of baggage. My boat is small. With that understood, I gladly offer you a ride to sanctuary.'

He turned to his neo-chimp driver. 'That would only be courteous and proper, would it not, corporal?'

The poor chimmie blinked up at Uthacalthing in confusion. She had been selected for this duty because she knew GalSeven. But that was a far cry from penetrating the arcana that were going on here.

'Y-yessir. It, it seems like the kind thing to do.'

Uthacalthing nodded, and smiled at Kault. 'There you are, my dear colleague. Not merely correct, but *kind*. It is well when we elders learn from such wise precociousness, and add that quality to our own actions, is it not?'

For the first time, he saw the Thennanin blink. Turmoil radiated from the creature. At last though, relief won out over suspicion that he was being played for the fool. Kault bowed to Uthacalthing. And then, because Uthacalthing had included her in the conversation, he added a brief, shallow nod to the little chimmie.

'For my clientsss and myssselfff, I thank you,' he said awkwardly in Anglic. Kault snapped his elbow spikes, and his Ynnin clients followed him as he lumbered into the floater. The closing cupola cut off the sharp dome light at last. The chims from the Library looked at Uthacalthing gratefully.

The floater rose on its gravity cushion and moved off rapidly. Uthacalthing's driver held the door of his own wheelcar for him, but he stretched his arms and inhaled deeply. 'I am thinking that it might be a nice idea to go for a walk,' he told her. 'The embassy is only a short distance from here. Why don't you take a few hours off, corporal, and spend some time with your family and friends?'

'B-but ser . . .'

'I will be all right,' he said firmly. He bowed, and felt her rush of innocent joy at the simple courtesy. She bowed deeply in return.

Delightful creatures, Uthacalthing thought as he watched the car drive off. *I have met a few neo-chimpanzees who even seem to have the glimmerings of a true sense of humor. I do hope the species survives.*

He started walking. Soon he had left the clamor of the Library behind him and passed into a residential neighborhood. The breeze had left the night air clear, and the city's soft lights did not drive away the flickering stars. At this time the Galactic rim was a ragged spill of diamonds across the sky. There were no traces to be seen of the battle in space; it had been too small a skirmish to leave much visible residue. All around Uthacalthing were sounds that told of the difference of this evening. There were distant sirens and the growl of aircraft passing overhead. On nearly every block he heard someone crying ... voices, human or chim, shouting or murmuring in frustration and fear. On the fluttering level of empathy, waves beat up against one another in a froth of emotion. His corona could not deflect the inhabitants' dread as they awaited morning.

Uthacalthing did not try to keep it out as he strolled up dimly lit streets lined with decorative trees. He dipped his tendrils into the churning emotional flux and drew forth above him a strange new glyph. It floated, nameless and terrible, Time's ageless threat made momentarily palpable.

Uthacalthing smiled an ancient, special kind of smile. And at that moment nobody, not even in the darkness, could possibly have mistaken him for a human being.

There are many paths ... he thought, again savoring the open, undisciplined nuances of Anglic.

He left the thing he had made to hang in the air, dissolving slowly behind him, as he walked under the slowly wheeling pattern of the stars.

10

ROBERT

Robert awoke two hours before dawn.

There was a period of disorientation as the strange feelings and images of sleep slowly dissipated. He rubbed his eyes, trying to clear his head of muzzy, clouded confusion.

He had been running, he recalled. Running as one does sometimes but only in dreams – in long, floating steps that reach for leagues and seem barely to touch down. Around him had shifted and drifted vague shapes, mysteries, and half-born images that slipped out of reach even as his waking mind tried to recall them.

Robert looked over at Athaclena, lying nearby in her own sleeping bag. Her brown Tymbrimi ruff – that tapered helm of soft brown fur – was puffed out. The silvery tendrils of her corona waved delicately, as if probing and grappling with something invisible in the space overhead.

She sighed and spoke very low – a few short phrases in the rapid, highly syllabic Tymbrimi dialect of Galactic Seven.

Perhaps that explained his own strange dreams, Robert realized. He must have been picking up traces of hers!

Watching the waving tendrils, he blinked. For just a moment it had seemed as if something *was* there, floating in the air just above the sleeping alien girl. It had been like ... like ...

Robert frowned, shaking his head. It hadn't been *like* anything at all. The very act of trying to compare it to something else seemed to drive the thing away even as he thought about it. Athaclena sighed and turned over. Her corona settled down. There were no more half glimmers in the dimness.

Robert slid out of his bag and fumbled for his boots before standing. He felt his way around the towering spine-stone beneath which they had made camp. There was barely enough starlight to find a path among the strange monoliths.

He came to a promontory looking over toward the westward mountain chain, and the northern plains to his right. Below this ridgetop vantage point there lay a gently rippling sea of dark woods. The trees filled the air with a damp, heavy aroma.

Resting his back against a spine-stone, he sat down on the ground to try to think.

If only the adventure were all there was to this trip. An idyllic interlude in the Mountains of Mulun in the company of an alien beauty. But there was no forgetting, no escaping the guilty sureness that he should not be here. He really ought to be with his classmates – with his militia unit – facing the troubles alongside them.

That was not to be, however. Once again, his mother's career had interfered with his own life. It was not the first time Robert had wished he were not the son of a politician.

He watched the stars, sparkling in bright strokes that followed the meeting of two Galactic spiral arms.

Perhaps if I had known more adversity in my life, I might be better prepared for what's to come. Better able to accept disappointment.

It wasn't just that he was the son of the Planetary Coordinator, with all of the advantages that came with status. It went beyond that.

All through childhood he had noticed that where other boys had stumbled and suffered growing pains, he had always somehow had the knack of moving gracefully. Where most had groped their way in awkwardness and embarrassment toward adolescence and sexuality, he had slipped into pleasure and popularity with all the comfort and ease of putting on an old shoe.

His mother – and his starfarer father, whenever Sam Tennace sojourned on Garth – had always emphasized that he should *watch* the interactions of his peers, not simply let things happen and accept them as inevitable. And indeed, he began to see how, in every age group, there were a few like him – for whom growing up was *easier* somehow. They stepped lightly through the morass of adolescence while everyone else slogged, overjoyed to find an occasional patch of solid ground. And it seemed many of those lucky ones accepted their happy fate as if it were some sign of divine election. The same was true of the most popular girls. They had no empathy, no compassion for more normal kids.

In Robert's case, he had never sought a reputation as a playboy. But one had come, over time, almost against his will. In his heart a secret fear had started to grow: a superstition that he had confided in nobody. Did the universe balance all things? Did it take away to compensate for whatever it gave? The Cult of Ifni was supposed to be a starferer's joke. And yet sometimes things seemed so *contrived!*

It was silly to suppose that trials only hardened men, automatically making them wise. He knew many who were stupid, arrogant, and mean, in spite of having suffered.

Still …

Like many humans, he sometimes envied the handsome, flexible, self-sufficient Tymbrimi. A young race by Galactic standards, they were nevertheless old and galaxy-wise compared with Mankind. Humanity had discovered sanity, peace, and a science of mind only a generation before Contact. There were still plenty of kinks to be worked out of Terragens society. The Tymbrimi, in comparison, seemed to know themselves so well.

Is that the basic reason why I am attracted to Athaclena? Symbolically she is the elder, the more knowledgeable one. It gives me an opportunity to be awkward and stumble, and enjoy the role.

It was all so confusing, and Robert wasn't even certain of his own feelings. He was having fun up here in the mountains with Athaclena, and that made him ashamed. He resented his mother bitterly for sending him, and felt guilty about that as well.

Oh, if only I'd been allowed to fight! Combat, at least, was straightforward and easy to understand. It was ancient, honorable, simple.

Robert looked up quickly. There, among the stars, a pinpoint had flared up to momentary brilliance. As he watched, two more sudden brightnesses burst forth, then another. The sharp, glowing sparks lasted long enough for him to note their positions.

The pattern was too regular to be an accident ... twenty degree intervals above the equator, from the Sphinx all the way across to the Batman, where the red planet Tloona shone in the middle of the ancient hero's belt.

So, it has come. The destruction of the synchronous satellite network had been expected, but it was startling actually to witness it. Of course this meant actual landings would not be long delayed.

Robert felt a heaviness and hoped that not too many of his human and chim friends had died.

I never found out if I had what it takes when things really counted. Now maybe I never will.

He was resolved about one thing. He would do the job he had been assigned – escorting a noncombatant alien into the mountains and supposed safety. There was one duty he had to perform tonight, while Athaclena slept. As silently as he could, Robert returned to their backpacks. He pulled the radio set from his lower left pouch and began disassembling it in the dark.

He was halfway finished when another sudden brightening made him look up at the eastern sky. A bolide streaked flame across the glittering starfield, leaving glowing embers in its wake. Something was entering fast, burning as it penetrated the atmosphere.

The debris of war.

Robert stood up and watched the manmade meteor lay a fiery trail across the sky. It disappeared behind a range of hills not more than twenty kilometers away. Perhaps much closer.

'God keep you,' he whispered to the warriors whose ship it must have been.

He had no fear of blessing his enemies, for it was clear which side needed help tonight, and would for a long time to come.

II

GALACTICS

The Suzerain of Propriety moved about the bridge of the flagship in short skips and hops, enjoying the pleasure of pacing while Gubru and Kwackoo soldiery ducked out of the way.

It might be a long time before the Gubru high priest would enjoy such freedom of movement again. After the occupation force landed, the Suzerain would not be able to set foot on the 'ground' for many miktaars. Not until propriety was assured and consolidation complete could it touch the soil of the planet that lay just ahead of the advancing armada.

The other two leaders of the invasion force – the Suzerain of Beam and Talon and the Suzerain of Cost and Caution – did not have to operate under such restrictions. That was all right. The military and the bureaucracy had their own functions. But to the Suzerain of Propriety was given the task of overseeing Appropriateness of Behavior for the Gubru expedition. And to do that the priest would have to remain perched.

Far across the command bridge, the Suzerain of Cost and Caution could be heard complaining. There had been unexpected losses in the furious little fight the humans had put up. Every ship put out of commission hurt the Gubru cause in these dangerous times.

Foolish, short-sighted carping, the Suzerain of Propriety thought. The physical damage done by the humans' resistance had been far less significant than the ethical and legal harm. Because the brief fight had been so sharp and effective, it could not simply be ignored. It would have to be *credited*.

The Earth wolflings had recorded, in action, their opposition to the arrival of Gubru might. Unexpectedly, they had done it with meticulous attention to the Protocols of War.

> They may be more than mere clever beasts –
> > More than beasts –
> Perhaps they and their clients should be studied! –
> > Studied – zzooon

That gesture of resistance by the tiny Earthling flotilla meant that the Suzerain would have to remain perched for at least the initial part of the occupation. It would have to find an excuse, now, the sort of *casus belli* that would let the Gubru proclaim to the Five Galaxies that the Earthlings' lease on Garth was null and void.

Until that happened, the Rules of War applied, and in enforcing them, the Suzerain of Propriety knew there would be conflicts with the other two commanders. Its future lovers and competitors. Correct policy demanded tension among them, even if some of the laws the priest had to enforce struck it, deep down, as stupid.

> Oh for the time, may it be soon –
> > Soon, when we are released from rules – zzooon
> Soon, when Change rewards the virtuous –
> > When the Progenitors return – zzooon

The Suzerain fluttered its downy coat. It commanded one of its servitors, a fluffy, imperturbable Kwackoo, to bring a feather-blower and groomer.

> The Earthlings will stumble –
> They will give us justification – zzooon

12

ATHACLENA

That morning Athaclena could tell that something had happened the night before. But Robert said little in answer to her questions. His crude but effective empathy shield blocked her attempts at *kenning*.

Athaclena tried not to feel insulted. After all, her human friend had only just begun learning to use his modest talents. He could not know the many subtle ways an empath could use to show a desire for privacy. Robert only knew how to close the door completely.

Breakfast was quiet. When Robert spoke she answered in monosyllables. Logically, Athaclena could understand his guardedness, but then there was no rule that said *she* had to be outgoing, either!

Low clouds crested the ridgelines that morning, to be sliced by rows of serrated spine-stones. It made for an eerie, foreboding scene. They hiked through the tattered wisps of brumous fog in silence, gradually climbing higher in the foothills leading toward the Mountains of Mulun. The air was still and seemed to carry a vague tension Athaclena could not identify. It tugged at her mind, drawing forth unbeckoned memories.

She recalled a time when she had accompanied her mother into the northern mountains on Tymbrim – riding gurval-back up a trail only slightly wider than this one – to attend a Ceremony of Uplift for the Tytlal.

Uthacalthing had been away on a diplomatic mission, and nobody knew yet what type of transport her father would be able to use for his return trip. It was an all-important question, for if he was able to come all the way via A-level hyperspace and transfer points, he could return home in a hundred days or less. If forced to travel by D-level – or worse, normal space – Uthacalthing might be away for the rest of their natural lives.

The Diplomatic Service tried to inform its officers' families as soon as these matters were clear, but on this occasion they had taken far too long. Athaclena and her mother had started to become public nuisances, throwing irksome anxiety shimmers all over their neighborhood. At that point it had been politely hinted that they ought to get out of the city for a while. The Service offered them tickets to go watch the representatives of the Tytlal undergo another rite of passage on the long path of Uplift.

Robert's slick mind shield reminded her of Mathicluanna's closely guarded pain during that slow ride into purple-frosted hills. Mother and daughter hardly spoke to each other at all as they passed through broad fallow parklands and at last arrived at the grassy plain of an ancient volcano caldera. There, near a solitary symmetrical hilltop, thousands of Tymbrimi had gathered near a swarm of brightly colored canopies to witness the Acceptance and Choice of the Tytlal.

Observers had come from many distinguished starfaring clans – Synthians, Kanten, Mrgh'4luargi – and of course a gaggle of cachinnatous humans. The Earthlings mixed with their Tymbrimi allies down near the refreshment tables, making a boisterous high time of it. She remembered her attitude then, upon seeing so many of the atrichic, bromopnean creatures. *Was I really such a snob?* Athaclena wondered.

She had sniffed disdainfully at the noise the humans made with their loud, low laughter. Their strange, applanate stares were everywhere as they strutted about displaying their bulging muscles. Even their females looked like caricatures of Tymbrimi weightlifters.

Of course, Athaclena had barely embarked on adolescence back on that day. Now, on reflection, she recalled that her own people were just as enthusiastic and flamboyant as the humans, waving their hands intricately and sparking the air with brief, flashing glyphs. This was, after all, a great day. For the Tytlal were to 'choose' their patrons, and their new Uplift Sponsors.

Various dignitaries rested under the bright canopies. Of course the immediate patrons of the Tymbrimi, the Caltmour, could not attend, being tragically extinct. But their colors and sigil were in view, in honor of those who had given the Tymbrimi the gift of sapience.

Those present were honored, however, by a delegation of the chattering, stalk-legged Brma, who had uplifted the Caltmour long, long ago.

Athaclena remembered gasping, her corona crackling in surprise, when she saw that another shape curled under a dark brown covering, high upon the ceremonial mount. It was a Krallnith! The seniormost race in their patron-line had sent a representative! The Krallnith were nearly torpid by now, having given over most of their waning enthusiasm to strange forms of meditation. It was commonly assumed they would not be around many more epochs. It was an honor to have one of them attend, and offer its blessing to the latest members of their clan.

Of course, it was the Tytlal themselves who were the center of attention. Wearing short silvery robes, they nonetheless looked much like those Earth creatures known as otters. The Tytlal legatees fairly radiated pride as they prepared for their latest rite of Uplift.

'Look,' Athaclena's mother had pointed. 'The Tytlal have elected their muse-poet, Sustruk, to represent them. Do you recall meeting him, Athaclena?'

Naturally she remembered. It had been only the year before, when Sustruk visited their home back in the city. Uthacalthing had brought the Tytlal genius by to meet his wife and daughter, shortly before he was to leave on his latest mission.

'Sustruk's poetry is simpleminded doggerel,' Athaclena muttered.

Mathicluanna looked at her sharply. Then her corona waved. The glyph she crafted was *sh'cha'kuon,* the dark mirror only your own mother knew how to hold up before you. Athaclena's resentment reflected back at her, easily seen for what it was. She looked away, shamed.

It was, after all, unfair to blame the poor Tytlal for reminding her of her absent father.

The ceremony was indeed beautiful. A glyph-choir of Tymbrimi from the colony-world Juthtath performed 'The Apotheosis of Lerensini,' and even the bare-pated humans stared in slack-jawed awe, obviously *kenning* some of the intricate, floating harmonies. Only the bluff, impenetrable Thennanin ambassadors seemed untouched, and they did not seem to mind at all being left out.

After that the Brma singer Kuff-Kufft crooned an ancient, atonal paean to the Progenitors.

One bad moment for Athaclena came when the hushed audience listened to a composition specially created for the occasion by one of the twelve Great Dreamers of Earth, the whale named Five Bubble Spirals. While whales were not officially sentient beings, that fact did not keep them from being honored treasures. That they dwelled on Earth, under the care of 'wolfling' humans, was one more cause for resentment by some of the more conservative Galactic clans.

Athaclena recalled sitting down and covering her ears while everyone else swayed happily to the eerie cetacean music. To her it was worse than the sound of houses falling. Mathicluanna's glance conveyed her worry. *My strange daughter, what are we to do with you?* At least Athaclena's mother did not chide aloud or in glyph, embarrassing her in public.

At last, to Athaclena's great relief, the entertainment ended. It was the turn of the Tytlal delegation, the time of Acceptance and Choice.

Led by Sustruk, their great poet, the delegation approached the supine Krallnith dignitary and bowed low. Then they made their allegiance to the Brma representatives, and afterward expressed polite submissiveness to the humans and other patron-class alien visitors.

The Tymbrimi Master of Uplift received obeisance last. Sustruk and his consort, a Tytlal scientist named Kihimik, stepped ahead of the rest of their delegation as the mated pair chosen above all others to be 'race representatives.' Alternately, they replied as the Master of Uplift read a list of formal questions and solemnly noted their answers.

Then the pair came under the scrutiny of the Critics from the Galactic Uplift Institute.

Thus far it had been a perfunctory version of the Fourth Stage Test of Sentience. But now there was one more chance for the Tytlal to fail. One of the Galactics focusing sophisticated instruments on Sustruk and Kihimik, was a *Soro* ... no friend of Athaclena's clan. Possibly the Soro was looking for an excuse, *any* excuse, to embarrass the Tymbrimi by rejecting their clients.

Discreetly buried under the caldera was equipment that had cost Athaclena's race plenty. Right now the scrutiny of the Tytlal was being cast all through the Five Galaxies. There was much to be proud of today, but also some potential for humiliation.

Of course Sustruk and Kihimik passed easily. They bowed low to each of the alien examiners. If the Soro examiner was disappointed, she did not show it.

The delegation of furry, short-legged Tytlal ambled up to a cleared circle at the top of the hill. They began to sing, swaying together in that queer, loose-limbed manner so common among the creatures of their native planet, the fallow world where they had evolved into pre-sentience, where the Tymbrimi had found and adopted them for the long process of Uplift.

Technicians focused the amplifier which would display for all those assembled, and billions on other worlds, the choice the Tytlal had made. Underfoot, a deep rumbling told of powerful engines at work.

Theoretically, the creatures could even decide to reject their patrons and abandon Uplift altogether, though there were so many rules and qualifications that in practice it was almost never allowed. Anyway, nothing like that was expected on that day. The Tymbrimi had excellent relations with their clients.

Still, a dry, anxious rustling swept the crowd as the Rite of

Acceptance approached completion. The swaying Tytlal moaned, and a low hum rose from the amplifier. Overhead a holographic image took shape, and the crowd roared with laughter and approval. It was the face of a Tymbrimi, of course, and one everyone recognized at once. Oshoyothuna, Trickster of the City of Foyon, who had included several Tytlal as helpers in some of his most celebrated jests.

Of course the Tytlal had reaffirmed the Tymbrimi as their patrons, but choosing Oshoyothuna as their symbol went far beyond that! It exclaimed the Tytlal's pride in what it really meant to be part of their clan.

After the cheering and laughter died down, there remained only one part of the ceremony to finish, the selection of the Stage Consort, the species who would speak for the Tytlal during the next phase of their Uplift. The humans, in their strange tongue, called it the Uplift Midwife.

The Stage Consort had to be of a race outside of the Tymbrimi's own clan. And while the position was mostly ceremonial, a Consort could legally intervene on the new client species' behalf, if the Uplift process appeared to be in trouble. Wrong choices in the past had created terrible problems.

No one had any idea what race the Tytlal had chosen. It was one of those rare decisions that even the most meddlesome patrons, such as the Soro, had to leave to their charges.

Sustruk and Kihimik crooned once more, and even from her position at the back of the crowd Athaclena could sense a growing feeling of anticipation rising from the furry little clients. The little devils had cooked up something, that was certain!

Again, the ground shuddered, the amplifier murmured once more, and holographic projectors formed a blue cloudiness over the crest of the hill. In it there seemed to float murky shapes, flicking back and forth as if through backlit water.

Her corona offered no clue, for the image was strictly visual. She resented the humans their sharper eyesight as a shout of surprise rose from the area where most of the Earthlings had congregated. All around her, Tymbrimi were standing up and staring. She blinked. Then Athaclena and her mother joined the rest in amazed disbelief.

One of the murky figures flicked up to the foreground and stopped, grinning out at the audience, displaying a long, narrow grin of white, needle-sharp teeth. There was a glittering eye, and bubbles rose from its glistening gray brow.

The stunned silence lengthened. For in all of Ifni's starfield, nobody had expected the Tytlal to choose *dolphins*!

The visiting Galactics were stricken dumb. *Neo-dolphins* ... why the second client race of Earth were the youngest acknowledged sapients in all five galaxies – much younger than the Tytlal themselves! This was unprecedented. It was astonishing.

It was ...

It was hilarious! The Tymbrimi cheered. Their laughter rose, high and clear. As one, their coronae sparkled upward a single, coruscating glyph of approval so vivid that even the Thennanin Ambassador seemed to blink and take notice. Seeing that their allies weren't offended, the humans joined in, hooting and slapping their hands together with intimidating energy.

Kihimik and most of the other assembled Tytlal bowed, accepting their patrons' accolade. Good clients, it seemed they had worked hard to come up with a fine jest for this important day. Only Sustruk himself stood rigid at the rear, still quivering from the strain.

All around Athaclena crested waves of approval and joy. She heard her mother's laughter, joining in with the others.

But Athaclena herself had backed away, edging out of the cheering crowd until there was room to turn and flee. In a full *gheer* flux, she ran and ran until she passed the caldera's rim and could drop down the trail out of sight or sound. There, overlooking the beautiful Valley of Lingering Shadows, she collapsed to the ground while the waves of enzyme reaction shook her.

That horrible dolphin ...

Never since that day had she confided in anyone what she had seen in the eye of the imaged cetacean. Not to her mother, nor even her father, had she ever told the truth ... that she had sensed deep within that projected hologram a *glyph*, one rising from Sustruk himself, the poet of the Tytlal.

Those present thought it was all a grand jest, a magnificent blague. They thought they knew why the Tytlal had chosen the youngest race of Earth as their Stage Consort ... to honor the clan with a grand and harmless joke. By choosing dolphins, they seemed to be saying that they *needed* no protector, that they loved and honored their Tymbrimi patrons without reservation. And by selecting the *humans'* second clients, they also tweaked those stodgy old Galactic clans who so disapproved of the Tymbrimi's friendship with wolflings. It was a fine gesture. Delicious.

Had Athaclena been the only one, then, to see the deeper truth? Had she imagined it? Many years later on a distant planet, Athaclena shivered as she recalled that day.

Had she been the only one to pick up Sustruk's third harmonic of laughter and pain and confusion? The muse-poet died only days after that episode, and he took his secret with him to his grave.

Only Athaclena seemed to sense that the Ceremony had been no joke, after all, that Sustruk's image had not come from his thoughts but out of *Time*! The Tytlal had, indeed, chosen their protectors, and the choice was in desperate earnest.

Now, only a few years later, the Five Galaxies had been sent into turmoil over certain discoveries made by a certain obscure client race, the youngest of them all. Dolphins.

Oh, Earthlings, she thought as she followed Robert higher into the Mountains of Mulun. *What have you done? No, that was not the right question. What, oh what is it you are planning to become?*

That afternoon the two wanderers encountered a steep field of plate ivy. A plain of glossy, wide-brimmed plants covered the southeast-ward slope of the ridge like green, overlapping scales On the flank of some great, slumbering beast. Their path to the mountains was blocked.

'I'll bet you're wondering how we'll get across all this to the other side,' Robert asked.

'The slope looks treacherous,' Athaclena ventured. 'And it stretches far in both directions. I suppose we'll have to turn around.'

There was something in the fringes of Robert's mind, though, that made that seem unlikely. 'These are fascinating plants,' he said, squatting next to one of the plates – a shieldlike inverted bowl almost two meters across. He grabbed its edge and yanked back-ward hard. The plate stretched away from the tightly bound field until Athaclena could see a tough, springy root attached to its center. She moved closer to help him pull, wondering what he had in mind.

'The colony buds a new generation of these caps every few weeks, each layer overlapping the prior one,' Robert explained as he grunted and tugged the fibrous root taut.

'In late autumn the last layers of caps flower and become wafer thin. They break off and catch the strong winter winds, sailing into the sky, millions of 'em. It's quite a sight, believe me, all those rain-bow-colored kites drifting under the clouds, even if it is a hazard to flyers.'

'They are seeds, then?' Athaclena asked.

'Well, spore carriers, actually. And most of the pods that litter the Sind in early winter are sterile. Seems the plate ivy used to rely on some pollinating creature that went extinct during the Bururalli Holocaust. Just one more problem for the ecological recovery teams to deal with.' Robert shrugged. 'Right now, though, in the spring-time, these early caps are rigid and strong. It'll take some doing to cut one free.'

Robert drew his knife and reached under to slice away at the taut fibers holding the cap down. The strips parted suddenly, releasing the tension and throwing Athaclena back with the bulky plate on top of her.

'Oops! I'm sorry, Clennie.' She felt Robert's effort to suppress laughter as he helped her struggle out from under the heavy cap. *Just like a boy* ... Athaclena thought.

'Are you okay?'

'I am fine,' she answered stiffly, and dusted herself off. Tipped over, the plate's inner, concave side looked like a bowl with a thick, central stem of ragged, sticky strands.

'Good. Then why don't you help me carry it over to that sandy bank, near the dropoff.'

The field of plate ivy stretched around the prominence of the ridge, surrounding it on three sides. Together they hefted the detached cap over to where the bumpy green slope began, laying it inner face up.

Robert set to work trimming the ragged interior of the plate. After a few minutes he stood back and examined his handiwork. 'This should do.' He nudged the plate with his foot. 'Your father wanted me to show you everything I could about Garth. In my opinion your education'd be truly lacking if I never taught you to ride plate ivy.'

Athaclena looked from the upended plate to the scree of slick caps. 'Do you mean ...' But Robert was already loading their gear into the upturned bowl. 'You cannot be serious, Robert.'

He shrugged, looking up at her sidelong. 'We can backtrack a mile or two and find a way around all this, if you like.'

'You *aren't* joking.' Athaclena sighed. It was bad enough that her father and her friends back home thought her too timid. She could not refuse a dare offered by this *human*. 'Very well, Robert, show me how it is done.'

Robert stepped into the plate and checked its balance. Then he motioned for her to join him. She climbed into the rocking thing and sat where Robert indicated, in front of him with her knees on either side of the central stump.

It was then, with her corona waving in nervous agitation, that it happened again. Athaclena sensed something that made her convulsively clutch the rubbery sides of the plate, setting it rocking.

'Hey! Watch it, will you? You almost tipped us over!'

Athaclena grabbed his arm while she scanned the valley below. All around her face a haze of tiny tendrils fluttered. 'I *kenn* it again. It's down there, Robert. Somewhere in the forest!'

'What? *What's* down there?'

'The entity I *kenned* earlier! The thing that was neither man nor chimpanzee! It was a little like either, and yet different. And it reeks with Potential!'

Robert shaded his eyes. 'Where? Can you point to it?'

Athaclena concentrated. She tried localizing the faint brush of emotions.

'It it is gone,' she sighed at last.

Robert radiated nervousness. 'Are you sure it wasn't just a chim? There are lots of them up in these hills, seisin gatherers and conservation workers.'

Athaclena cast a *palang* glyph. Then, recalling that Robert wasn't likely to notice the sparkling essence of frustration. She *shrugged* to indicate approximately the same nuance.

'No, Robert. I have met many neo-chimpanzees, remember? The being I sensed was different! I'd swear it wasn't fully sapient, for one thing. And, there was a feeling of *sadness*, of submerged power ...'

Athaclena turned to Robert, suddenly excited. 'Can it have been a "Garthling"? Oh, let's hurry! We might be able to get closer!' She settled in around the center post and looked up at Robert expectantly.

'The famed Tymbrimi adaptability,' Robert sighed. 'All of a sudden you're *anxious* to go! And here I'd been hoping to impress and arouse you with a white-knuckler ride.'

Boys, she thought again, shaking her head vigorously. *How can they think such things, even in jest?*

'Stop joking and let's be off!' she urged.

He settled into the plate behind her. Athaclena held on tightly to his knees. Her tendrils waved about his face, but Robert did not complain. 'All right, here we go.'

His musty human aroma was close around her as he pushed off and the plate began to slip forward.

It all came back to Robert as their makeshift sled accelerated, skidding and bouncing over the slick, convex caps of plate ivy. Athaclena gripped his knees tightly, her laughter higher and more bell-like than a human girl's. Robert, too, laughed and shouted, holding Athaclena as he leaned one way and then the other to steer the madly hopping sled.

Must've been eleven years old when I did this last.

Every jounce and leap made his heart pound. Not even an amusement park gravity ride was like this! Athaclena let out a squeak of exhilaration as they sailed free and landed again with a rubbery rebound. Her corona was a storm of silvery threads that seemed to crackle with excitement.

I only hope I remember how to control this thing right.

Maybe it was his rustiness. Or it might have been Athaclena's presence, distracting him. But Robert was just a little late reacting when the near-oak stump – a remnant of the forest that had once grown on this slope – loomed suddenly in their path.

Athaclena laughed in delight as Robert leaned hard to the left, swerving their crude boat wildly. By the time she sensed his sudden change of mood their spin was already a tumble, out of control. Then their plate caught on something unseen. Impact swerved them savagely, sending the contents of the sled flying.

At that moment luck and Tymbrimi instincts were with Athaclena. Stress hormones surged and reflexes tucked her head down, rolling her into a ball. On impact her body made its own sled, bouncing and skidding atop the plates like a rubbery ball.

It all happened in a blur. Giants' fists struck her, tossed her about. A great roar filled her ears and her corona blazed as she spun and fell, again and again.

Finally Athaclena tumbled to a halt, still curled up tight, just short of the forest on the valley floor. At first she could only lie there as the *gheer* enzymes made her pay the price for her quick reflexes. Breath came in long, shuddering gasps; her high and low kidneys throbbed, struggling with the sudden overload.

And there was *pain*. Athaclena had trouble localizing it. She seemed only to have picked up a few bruises and scrapes. So where ... ?

Realization came in a rush as she uncurled and opened her eyes. The pain was coming from Robert! Her Earthling guide was broadcasting blinding surges of agony!

She got up gingerly, still dizzy from reaction, and shaded her eyes to look around the bright hillside. The human wasn't in sight, so she sought him with her corona. The searing painflood led her stumbling awkwardly over the glossy plates to a point not far from the upended sled.

Robert's legs kicked weakly from under a layer of broad plate ivy caps. An effort to back out culminated in a low, muffled moan. A sparkling shower of hot *agones* seemed to home right in on Athaclena's corona.

She knelt beside him. 'Robert! Are you caught on something? Can you breathe?'

What foolishness, she realized, asking multiple questions when she could tell the human was barely even conscious!

I must do something. Athaclena drew her jack-laser from her boot top and attacked the plate ivy, starting well away from Robert, slicing stems and grunting as she heaved aside the caps, one at a time.

Knotty, musky vines remained tangled around the human's head and arms, pinning him to the thicket. 'Robert, I'm going to cut near your head. Don't move!'

Robert groaned something indecipherable. His right arm was badly twisted, and so much distilled ache fizzed around him that she had to withdraw her corona to keep from fainting from the overload. Aliens weren't supposed to commune this strongly with Tymbrimi! At least she had never believed it possible before this.

Robert gasped as she heaved the last shriveled cap away from his face. His eyes were closed, and his mouth moved as if he were silently talking to himself. *What is he doing now?*

She felt the overtones of some obviously human rite-of-discipline. It had something to do with numbers and counting. Perhaps it was that 'self-hypnosis' technique all humans were taught in school. Though primitive, it seemed to be doing Robert some good.

'I'm going to cut away the roots binding your arm now,' she told him.

He jerked his head in a nod. 'Hurry, Clennie. I've ... I've never had to block this much pain before ...' He let out a shivering sigh as the last rootlet parted. His arm sprang free, floppy and broken.

What now? Athaclena worried. It was always hazardous to interfere with an injured member of an alien race. Lack of training was only part of the problem. One's most basic succoring instincts might be entirely wrong for helping someone of another species.

Athaclena grabbed a handful of coronal tendrils and twisted them in indecision. *Some things have to be universal!*

Make sure the victim keeps breathing. That she had done automatically.

Try to stop leaks of bodily fluids. All she had to go on were some old, pre-Contact 'movies' she and her father had watched on the journey to Garth – dealing with ancient Earth creatures called cops and robbers. According to those films, Robert's wounds might be called 'only scratches.' But she suspected those ancient story-records weren't particularly strong on realism.

Oh, if only humans weren't so frail!

Athaclena rushed to Robert's backpack, seeking the radio in the lower side pouch. Aid could arrive from Port Helenia in less than an hour, and rescue officials could tell her what to do in the meantime.

The radio was simple, of Tymbrimi design, but nothing happened when she touched the power switch.

No. It has to work! She stabbed it again. But the indicator stayed blank.

Athaclena popped the back cover. The transmitter crystal had been removed. She blinked in consternation. How could this be?

They were cut off from help. She was completely on her own.

'Robert,' she said as she knelt by him again. 'You must guide me. I cannot help you unless you tell me what to do!'

The human still counted from one to ten, over and over. She had to repeat herself until, at last, his eyes came into focus. 'I . . . I think my arm's b- busted, Clennie . . .' He gasped. 'Help get me out of the sun . . . then, use drugs . . .'

His presence seemed to fade away, and his eyes rolled up as unconsciousness overcame him. Athaclena did not approve of a nervous system that overloaded with pain, leaving its owner unable to help himself. It wasn't Robert's fault. He was brave, but his brain had shorted out.

There was one advantage, of course. Fainting damped down his broadcast agony. That made it easier for her to drag him backward over the spongy, uneven field of plate ivy, attempting all the while not to shake his broken right arm unduly.

Big-boned, huge-thewed, overmuscled human! She cast a glyph of great pungency as she pulled his heavy body all the way to the shady edge of the forest.

Athaclena retrieved their backpacks and quickly found Robert's first aid kit. There was a tincture she had seen him use only two days before, when he had caught his finger on a wood sliver. This she slathered liberally over his lacerations.

Robert moaned and shifted a little. She could feel his mind struggle upward against the pain. Soon, half automatically, he was mumbling numbers to himself once again.

Her lips moved as she read the Anglic instructions on a container of 'flesh foam,' then she applied the sprayer onto his cuts, sealing them under a medicinal layer.

That left the arm – and the agony. Robert had mentioned drugs. But *which* drugs?

There were many little ampules, clearly labeled in both Anglic and GalSeven. But directions were sparse. There was no provision for a non-Terran having to treat a human without benefit of advice.

She used logic. Emergency medicines would be packaged in gas ampules for easy, quick administration. Athaclena pulled out three likely looking glassine cylinders. She bent forward until the silvery strands of her corona fell around Robert's face, bringing close his human aroma – musty and in this case so very male. 'Robert,' she whispered carefully in Anglic. 'I know you can hear me. Rise within yourself! I need your wisdom out in the here-and-now.'

Apparently she was only distracting him from his rite-of-discipline, for she sensed the pain increase. Robert grimaced and counted out loud.

Tymbrimi do not curse as humans do. A purist would say they make 'stylistic statements of record' instead. But at times like this few would be able to tell the difference. Athaclena muttered caustically in her native tongue.

Clearly Robert was not an adept, even at this crude self-hypnosis' technique. His pain pummeled the fringes of her mind, and Athaclena let out a small trill, like a sigh. She was unaccustomed to having to keep out such an assault. The fluttering of her eyelids blurred vision as would a human's tears.

There was only one way, and it meant exposing herself more than she was accustomed, even with her family. The prospect was daunting, but there didn't seem to be any choice. In order to get through to him at all, she had to get a lot closer than this.

'I . . . I am here, Robert. Share it with me.'

She opened up to the narrow flood of sharp, discrete *agones* – so un-Tymbrimi, and yet so eerily familiar, almost as if they were *recognizable* somehow. The quanta of agony dripped to an uneven pump beat. They were little hot, searing balls – lumps of molten metal.

. . . lumps of metal . . . ?

The weirdness almost startled Athaclena out of contact. She had never before experienced a *metaphor* so vividly. It was more than just a comparison, stronger than saying that one thing was *like* another. For a moment, the agones *had been* glowing iron globs that burned to touch . . .

To be human is strange indeed.

Athaclena tried to ignore the imagery. She moved toward the *agone* nexus until a barrier stopped her. *Another metaphor?* This time, it was a swiftly flowing stream of pain – a river that lay across her path.

What she needed was an *usunltlan*, a protection field to carry her up the flood to its source. But how did one shape the mind-stuff of a human!

Even as she wondered, drifting smoke-images seemed to fall together around her. Mist patterns flowed, solidified, became a shape. Athaclena suddenly found she could visualize herself standing in a small boat! And in her hands she held an oar.

Was this how *usunltlan* manifested in a human's mind? As a *metaphor*?

Amazed, she began to row upstream, into the stinging maelstrom.

Forms floated by, crowding and jostling in the fog surrounding her. Now one blur drifted past as a distorted face. Next, some bizarre animal figure snarled at her. Most of the grotesque things she glimpsed could never have existed in any real universe.

Unaccustomed to *visualizing* the networks of a mind, it took Athaclena some moments to realize that the shapes represented memories, conflicts, emotions.

So many emotions! Athaclena felt an urge to flee. One might go mad in this place!

It was Tymbrimi curiosity that made her stay. That and duty.

This is so strange, she thought as she rowed through the metaphorical swamp. Half blinded by drifting drops of pain, she stared in wonderment. Oh, to be a true telepath and *know,* instead of having to guess, what all these symbols meant.

There were easily as many drives as in a Tymbrimi mind. Some of the strange images and sensations struck her as familiar. Perhaps they harkened back to times before her race or Robert's learned speech – her own people by Uplift and humans doing it the hard way – back when two tribes of clever animals lived very similar lives in the wild, on far separated worlds.

It was most odd seeing with two pairs of eyes at once. There was the set that looked in amazement about the metaphorical realm and her real pair which saw Robert's face inches from her own, under the canopy of her corona.

The human blinked rapidly. He had stopped counting in his confusion. She, at least, understood some of what was happening. But Robert was feeling something truly bizarre. A word came to her: *déjà vu* ... quick half-rememberings of things at once both new and old.

Athaclena concentrated and crafted a delicate glyph, a fluttering beacon to beat in resonance with his deepest brain harmonic. Robert gasped and she felt him reach out after it.

His metaphorical self took shape alongside her in the little boat, holding another oar. It seemed to be the way of things, at this level, that he did not even ask how he came to be there.

Together they cast off through the flood of pain, the torrent from his broken arm. They had to row through a swirling cloud of *agones,* which struck and bit at them like swarms of vampire bugs. There were obstacles, snags, and eddies where strange voices muttered sullenly out of dark depths.

Finally they came to a pool, the center of the problem. At its bottom lay the gestalt image of an iron grating set in a stony floor. Horrible debris obstructed the drain.

Robert quailed back in alarm. Athaclena knew these had to be emotion-laden memories – their fearsomeness given shape in teeth and claws and bloated, awful faces. *How could humans let such clutter accumulate?* She was dazed and more than a little frightened by the ugly, animate wreckage.

'They're called neuroses,' spoke Robert's inner voice. He knew

what they were 'looking' at and was fighting a terror far worse than hers. *'I'd forgotten so many of these things! I had no idea they were still here.'*

Robert stared at his enemies below – and Athaclena saw that many of the faces below were warped, angry versions of his own.

'This is my job now, Clennie. We learned long before Contact that there is only one way to deal with a mess like this. Truth is the only weapon that works.'

The boat rocked as Robert's metaphoric self turned and dove into the molten pool of pain.

Robert!

Froth rose. The tiny craft began to buck and heave, forcing her to hold tightly to the rim of the strange *usunltlan*. Bright, awful hurt sprayed on all sides. And down near the grating a terrific struggle was taking place.

In the outer world, Robert's face ran streams of perspiration. Athaclena wondered how much more of this he could take.

Hesitantly, she sent her image-hand down into the pool. Direct contact *burned*, but she pushed on, reaching for the grating.

Something grabbed her hand! She yanked back but the grip held. An awful thing wearing a horrid version of Robert's race leered up at her with an expression twisted almost out of recognition by some warped lust. The thing pulled hard, trying to drag her into the noisome pool. Athaclena screamed.

Another shape streaked in to grapple with her assailant. The scaly hold on her arm released and she fell back into the boat. Then the little craft started speeding away! All around her the lake of pain flowed toward the drain. But her boat moved rapidly the other way, upstream against the flow.

Robert is pushing me out, she realized. Contact narrowed, then broke. The metaphorical images ceased abruptly. Athaclena blinked rapidly, in a daze. She knelt on the soft ground. Robert held her hand, breathing through clenched teeth.

'Had to stop you, Clennie ... That was dangerous for you ...'

'But you are in such pain!'

He shook his head. 'You showed me where the block was. I... I can take care of that neurotic garbage now that I know it's there ... at least well enough for now. And ... and have I told you yet that a guy wouldn't have any trouble at all falling in love with you?'

Athaclena sat up abruptly, amazed at the non sequitur. She held up the three gas ampules. 'Robert, you must tell me which of these drugs will ease the pain, yet leave you conscious enough to help me!'

He squinted. 'The blue one. Snap it under my nose, but don't breathe any yourself! No ... no telling what para-endorphins would do to you.'

When Athaclena broke the ampule a small, dense cloud of vapor spilled out. About half went in with Robert's next breath. The rest quickly dispersed.

With a deep, shuddering sigh, Robert's body seemed to uncoil. He looked up at her again with a new light in his eyes. 'I don't know if I could have maintained consciousness much longer. But it was almost worth it ... sharing my mind with you.'

In his aura it seemed that a simple but elegant version of *zunour'thzun* danced. Athaclena was momentarily taken aback.

'You are a very strange creature, Robert. I ...'

She paused. The *zunour'thzun* ... it was gone now, but she had not imagined *kenning* that glyph. How could Robert have learned to make it?

Athaclena nodded and smiled. The human mannerisms came easily, as if imprinted.

'I was just thinking the same thing, Robert. I ... I, too, found it worthwhile.'

13

FIBEN

Just above a cliff face, near the rim of a narrow mesa, dust still rose in plumes where some recent crashing force had torn a long, ugly furrow in the ground. A dagger-shaped stretch of forest had been shattered in a few violent seconds by a plunging thing that roared and skipped and struck again – sending earth and vegetation spraying in all directions – before finally coming to rest just short of the sheer precipice.

It had happened at night. Not far away, other pieces of even hotter sky-debris had cracked stone and set fires, but here the impact had been only a glancing blow.

Long minutes after the explosive noise of collision ebbed there remained other disturbances. Landslides rattled down the nearby cliff, and trees near the tortured path creaked and swayed. At the end of the furrow, the dark object that had wreaked this havoc emitted crackling, snapping sounds as superheated metal met a cool fog sweeping up from the valley below.

At last things settled down and began returning to normal. Native animals nosed out into the open again. A few even approached, sniffed the hot thing in distaste, then moved on about the more serious business of living one more day.

It had been a bad landing. Within the escape pod, the pilot did not stir. That night and another day passed without any sign of motion.

At last, with a cough and a low groan, Fiben awoke. 'Where . . . ? What . . . ?' he croaked.

His first organized thought was to notice that he had just spoken Anglic. *That's good,* he considered, numbly. *No brain damage, then.*

A neo-chimpanzee's ability to use language was his crucial possession, and far too easily lost. Speech aphasia was a good way to get reassessed – maybe even registered as a genetic probationer.

Of course samples of Fiben's plasm had already been sent to Earth and it was probably too late to recall them, so did it really matter if he were reassessed? He had never really cared what color his procreation card was, anyway.

Or, at least, he didn't care any more than the average chim did.

Oh, so we're getting philosophical, now? Delaying the inevitable? No dithering, Fiben old chim. Move! Open your eyes. Grope yourself. Make sure everything's still attached.

Wryly put, but less easily done. Fiben groaned as he tried to lift his head. He was so dehydrated that separating his eyelids felt like prying apart a set of rusty drawers.

At last he managed to squint. He saw that the clearshield of the pod was cracked and streaked with soot. Thick layers of dirt and seared vegetation had been speckled, sometime since the crash, by droplets of light rain.

Fiben discovered one of the reasons for his disorientation – the capsule was canted more than fifty degrees. He tumbled with the seat's straps until they released, letting him slump against the armrest. He gathered a little strength, then pounded on the jammed hatch, muttering hoarse curses until the catch finally gave way in a rain of leaves and small pebbles.

Several minutes of dry sneezing ensued, finishing with him draped over the hatch rim, breathing hard.

Fiben gritted his teeth. 'Come on,' he muttered subvocally. 'Let's get *outta* here!' He heaved himself up. Ignoring the uncomfortable warmth of the outer shell and the screaming of his own bruises, he squirmed desperately through the opening, turning and reaching for a foothold outside. He felt dirt, *blessed ground.* But when he let go of the hatch his left ankle refused to support him. He toppled over and landed with a painful thump.

'Ow!' Fiben said aloud. He reached underneath and pulled forth a sharp stick that had pierced his ship briefs. He glared at it before throwing it aside, then sagged back upon the mound of debris surrounding the pod.

Ahead of him, about twenty feet away, dawn's light showed the edge of a steep dropoff. The sound of rushing water rose from far below. *Uh*, he thought in bemused wonder at his near demise. *Another few meters and I wouldn't've been so thirsty right now.*

With the rising sun the mountainside across the valley became clearer, revealing smoky, scorched trails where larger pieces of space-junk had come down. So *much for old* Proconsul, Fiben thought. Seven thousand years of loyal service to half a hundred big-time Galactic races, only to be splattered all over a minor planet by one Fiben Bolger, client of wolflings, semi-skilled militia pilot. What an undignified end for a gallant old warrior.

But he had outlived the scoutboat after all. By a little while at least.

Someone once said that one measure of sentience was how much energy a sophont spent on matters other than survival. Fiben's body felt like a slab of half-broiled meat, yet he found the strength to grin. He had fallen a couple million miles and might yet live to someday tell some smart-aleck, two-generations-further-uplifted grandkids all about it.

He patted the scorched ground beside him and laughed in a voice dry with thirst.

'Beat *that*, Tarzan!'

14

UTHACALTHING

'*... We are here as friends of Galactic Tradition, protectors of propriety and honor, enforcers of the will of the ancient ones who founded the Way of Things so long ago ...*'

Uthacalthing was not very strong in Galactic Three, so he used his portable secretary to record the Gubru Invasion Manifesto for later study. He listened with only half an ear while going about completing the rest of his preparations.

... with only half an ear ... His corona chirped a spark of amusement when he realized he had used the phrase in his thoughts. The human metaphor actually made his own ears itch!

The chims nearby had their receivers tuned to the Anglic translation, also being broadcast from the Gubru ships. It was an 'unofficial' version of the manifesto, since Anglic was considered only a wolfling tongue, unsuitable for diplomacy.

Uthacalthing crafted *l'yuth'tsaka,* the approximate equivalent of a nose-thumb and raspberry, at the invaders. One of his neo-chimpanzee assistants looked up at him with a puzzled expression. The chim must have some latent psi ability, he realized. The other three hairy clients crouched under a nearby tree listening to the doctrine of the invading armada.

'... *in accordance with protocol and all of the Rules of War, a rescript has been delivered to Earth explaining our grievances and our demands for redress ...*'

Uthacalthing set one last seal into place over the hatch of the Diplomatic Cache. The pyramidal structure stood on a bluff overlooking the Sea of Cilmar, just southwest of the other buildings of the Tymbrimi Embassy. Out over the ocean all seemed fair and spring-like. Even today small fishing boats cruised out on the placid waters, as if the sky held nothing unfriendlier than the dappled clouds.

In the other direction, though, past a small grove of Thula greatgrass, transplanted from his homeworld, Uthacalthing's chancery and official quarters lay empty and abandoned.

Strictly speaking, he could have remained at his post. But Uthacalthing had no wish to trust the invaders' word that they were still following all of the Rules of War. The Gubru were renowned for interpreting tradition to suit themselves.

Anyway, he had made plans.

Uthacalthing finished the seal and stepped back from the Diplomatic Cache. Offset from the Embassy itself, sealed and warded, it was protected by millions of years of precedent. The chancery and other embassy buildings might be fair game, but the invader would be hard-pressed to come up with a satisfactory excuse for breaking into this sacrosanct depository.

Still, Uthacalthing smiled. He had confidence in the Gubru.

When he had backed away about ten meters he concentrated and crafted a simple glyph, then cast it toward the top of the pyramid where a small blue globe spun silently. The warder brightened at once and let out an audible hum. Uthacalthing then turned and approached the waiting chims.

'... *list as our first grievance that the Earthlings' client race, formally known as* Tursiops amicus, *or "neo-dolphin," has made a discovery which they do not share. It is said that this discovery portends major consequences to Galactic Society.*

The Clan of Gooksyu-Gubru, as a protector of tradition and the inheritance of the Progenitors, will not be excluded! It is our legitimate right to take hostages to force those half-formed water creatures and their wolfling masters to divulge their hoarded information . . .'

A small corner of Uthacalthing's thoughts wondered just what the humans' other client race had discovered out there beyond the Galactic disk. He sighed wistfully. The way things worked in the Five Galaxies, he would have to take a long voyage through D-level hyper-space and emerge a million years from now to find out the entire story. By then, of course, it would be ancient history.

In fact, exactly what *Streaker* had done to trigger the present crisis hardly mattered, really. The Tymbrimi Grand Council had calculated that an explosion of some sort was due within a few centuries anyway. The Earthlings had just managed to set it off a bit early. That was all.

Set it off early . . . Uthacalthing hunted for the right metaphor. It was as if a child had escaped from a cradle, crawled straight into a den of Vl'Korg beasts, and slapped the queen right in the snout!

' . . . second grievance, and the precipitate cause for our ennomic intervention here, is our strong suspicion that Uplift irregularities are taking place on the planet Garth!

'In our possession is evidence that the semi-sentient client species known as "neo-chimpanzee" is being given improper guidance, and is not being properly served by either its human patrons or its Tymbrimi consorts . . .'

The Tymbrimi? Improper consorts? Oh, you arrogant avians shall pay for that insult, Uthacalthing vowed.

The chims hurried to their feet and bowed low when he approached. *Syulff-kuonn* glimmered briefly at the tips of his corona as he returned the gesture.

'I wish to have certain messages delivered. Will you serve me?'

They all nodded. The chims were obviously uncomfortable with each other, coming as they did from such different social strata.

One was dressed proudly in the uniform of a militia officer. Two others wore bright civilian clothes. The last and most shabbily dressed chim bore a kind of breast panel-display with an array of keys on both sides, which let the poor creature perform a semblance of speech. This one stood a little behind and apart from the others and barely lifted his gaze from the ground.

'We are at your service,' said the clean-cut young lieutenant, snapping to attention. He seemed completely aloof to the sour glances the gaudily clad civilians cast his way.

'That is good, my young friend.' Uthacalthing grasped the chim's shoulder and held out a small black cube. 'Please deliver this to

Planetary Coordinator Oneagle, with my compliments. Tell her that I had to delay my own departure to Sanctuary, but I hope to see her soon.'

I am not really *lying,* Uthacalthing reminded himself. *Bless Anglic and its lovely ambiguity!*

The chim lieutenant took the cube and bowed again at precisely the correct angle for showing bipedal respect to a senior patron ally. Without even looking at the others, he took off at a run toward his courier bike.

One of the civilians, apparently thinking Uthacalthing would not overhear, whispered to his brightly clad colleague. 'I hope th' blue-card pom skids on a mud puddle an' gets his shiny uniform all wet.'

Uthacalthing pretended not to notice. It sometimes paid to let others believe Tymbrimi hearing was as bad as their eyesight.

'These are for you,' he told the two in the flashy clothes, and he tossed each of them a small bag. The money inside was GalCoin, untraceable and unquestionable through war and turmoil, for it was backed by the contents of the Great Library itself.

The two chims bowed to Uthacalthing, trying to imitate the officer's precision. He had to suppress a delighted laugh, for he sensed their *foci* – each chim's center of consciousness – had gathered in the hand holding the purse, excluding nearly all else from the world.

'Go then, and spend it as you will. I thank you for your past services.'

The two members of Port Helenia's small criminal underworld spun about and dashed off through the grove. Borrowing another human metaphor, they had been 'his eyes and ears' since he had arrived here. No doubt they considered their work completed now.

And thank you for what you are about to do, Uthacalthing thought after them. He knew this particular band of probationers well. They would spend his money well and gain an appetite for more. In a few days, there would be only one source of such coin.

They would have new employers soon, Uthacalthing was sure.

'*. . . have come as friends and protectors of pre-sentient peoples, to see that they are given proper guidance and membership in a dignified clan . . .*'

Only one chim remained, trying to stand as straight as he could. But the poor creature could not help shifting his weight nervously, grinning anxiously.

'And what – ' Uthacalthing stopped abruptly. His tendrils waved and he turned to look out over the sea.

A streak of light appeared from the headland across the bay, spearing up and eastward into the sky. Uthacalthing shaded his eyes, but he did not waste time envying Earthling vision. The glowing ember climbed into the clouds, leaving a kind of trail that only he could detect. It was a shimmering of joyful departure that surged and then faded in a few brief seconds, unraveling with the faint, white contrail.

Oth'thushutn, his aide, secretary, and friend, was flying their ship out through the heart of the battle fleet surrounding Garth. And who could tell? Their Tymbrimi-made craft was specially built. He even might get through.

That was not Oth'thushutn's job, of course. His task was merely to make the attempt.

Uthacalthing reached forth in *kenning*. Yes, something did ride down that burst of light. A sparkling legacy. He drew in Oth'thushtn's final glyph and stored it in a cherished place, should he ever make it home to tell the brave Tym's loved ones.

Now there were only two Tymbrimi on Garth, and Athaclena was as safe as could be provided for. It was time for Uthacalthing to see to his own fate.

' . . . *to rescue these innocent creatures from the warped Uprearing they are receiving at the hands of wolflings and criminals* . . .'

He turned back to the little chim, his last helper. 'And what about you, Jo-Jo? Do you want a task, as well?'

Jo-Jo fumbled with the keys of his panel display.

YES, PLEASE
HELP YOU IS ALL I ASK

Uthacalthing smiled. He had to hurry off and meet Kault. By now the Thennanin Ambassador would be nearly frantic, pacing beside Uthacalthing's pinnace. But the fellow could just wait a few moments more.

'Yes,' he told Jo-Jo. 'I think there is something you can do for me. Do you think you can keep a secret?'

The little genetic reject nodded vigorously, his soft brown eyes filled with earnest devotion. Uthacalthing had spent a lot of time with Jo-Jo, teaching him things the schools here on Garth had never bothered to try – wilderness survival skills and how to pilot a simple flitter, for instance. Jo-Jo was not the pride of neo-chimp Uplift, but he had a great heart, and more than enough of a certain type of cunning that Uthacalthing appreciated.

'Do you see that blue light, atop the cairn, Jo-Jo?'

JO-JO REMEMBERS,

the chim keyed.

'Good.' Uthacalthing nodded. 'I knew you would. I shall count on you, my dear little friend.' He smiled, and Jo-Jo grinned back, eagerly.

Meanwhile, the computer-generated voice from space droned on, completing the Manifesto of Invasion.

'... and give them over for adoption by some appropriate elder clan – one that will not lead them into improper behavior ...'

Wordy birds, Uthacalthing thought. Silly things, really.

'We'll show them some "improper behavior," won't we, Jo-Jo?'

The little chim nodded nervously. He grinned, even though he did not entirely understand.

15

ATHACLENA

That night their tiny campfire cast yellow and orange flickerings against the trunks of the near-oaks.

'I was so hungry, even vac-pac stew tasted delicious,' Robert sighed as he put aside his bowl and spoon. 'I'd planned to make us a meal of baked plate ivy roots, but I don't guess either of us will have much appetite for that delicacy soon.'

Athaclena felt she understood Robert's tendency to make irrelevant remarks like these. Tymbrimi and Terran both had ways of making light of disaster – part of the unusual pattern of similarity between the two species.

She had eaten sparingly herself. Her body had nearly purged the peptides left over from the gheer reaction, but she still felt a little sore after this afternoon's adventure.

Overhead a dark band of Galactic dust clouds spanned fully twenty percent of the sky, outlined by bright hydrogen nebulae. Athaclena watched the starry vault, her corona only slightly puffed out above her ears. From the forest she felt the tiny, anxious emotions of little native creatures.

'Robert?'

'Hmmm? Yes, Clennie?'

'Robert, why did you remove the crystals from our radio?'

After a pause, his voice was serious, subdued. 'I'd hoped not to have to tell you for a few days, Athaclena. But last night I saw the communication satellites being destroyed. That could only mean the Galactics have arrived, as our parents expected.

'The radio's crystals can be picked up by shipborne resonance detectors, even when they aren't powered. I took ours out so there'd be no chance of being found that way. It's standard doctrine.'

Athaclena felt a tremor at the tip of her ruff, just above her nose, that shivered over her scalp and down her back. *So, it has begun.*

Part of her longed to be with her father. It still hurt that he had sent her away rather than allow her to stay at his side where she could help him.

The silence stretched. She *kenned* Robert's nervousness. Twice, he seemed about to speak, then stopped, thinking better of it. Finally, she nodded. 'I agree with your logic in removing the crystals, Robert. I even think I understand the protective impulse that made you refrain from telling me about it. You should not do that again, though. It was foolish.'

Robert agreed, seriously. 'I won't, Athaclena.'

They lay in silence for a while, until Robert reached over with his good hand and touched hers. 'Clennie, I . . . I want you to know I'm grateful. You saved my life – '

'Robert,' she sighed tiredly.

' – but it goes beyond that. When you came into my mind you showed me things about myself . . . things I'd never known before. That's an important favor. You can read all about it in textbooks, if you want. Self-deception and neuroses are two particularly insidious human plagues.'

'They are not unique to humans, Robert.'

'No, I guess not. What you saw in my mind was probably nothing by pre-Contact standards. But given our history, well, even the sanest of us needs reminding from time to time.'

Athaclena had no idea what to say, so she remained silent. To have lived in Humanity's awful dark ages must have been frightening indeed.

Robert cleared his throat. 'What I'm trying to say is that I know how far you've gone to adapt yourself – learning human expressions, making little changes in your physiology . . .'

'An experiment.' She shrugged, another human mannerism. She suddenly realized that her face felt warm. Capillaries were opening in that human reaction she had thought so quaint. She was blushing!

'Yeah, an experiment. But by rights it ought to go both ways, Clennie. Tymbrimi are renowned around the Five Galaxies for their adaptability. But we humans are capable of learning a thing or two, also.'

She looked up. 'What do you mean, Robert?'

'I mean that I'd like you to show me some more about Tymbrimi ways. Your customs. I want to know what your landsmen do that's equivalent to an amazed stare, or a nod, or a grin.'

Again, there was a flicker. Athaclena's corona reached, but the delicate, simple, ghostly glyph he had formed vanished like smoke. Perhaps he was not even aware he had crafted it.

'Um,' she said, blinking and shaking her head. 'I cannot be sure, Robert. But I think perhaps you have already begun.'

Robert was stiff and feverish when they struck camp the next morning. He could only take so much anesthetic for his fractured arm and remain able to walk.

Athaclena stashed most of his gear in the notch of a gum beech tree and cut slashes in the bark to mark the site.

Actually, she doubted anyone would ever be back to reclaim it. 'We must get you to a physician,' she said, feeling his brow. His raised temperature clearly was not a good sign.

Robert indicated a narrow slot between the mountains to the south. 'Over that way, two days march, there's the Mendoza Freehold. Mrs Mendoza was a nurse practitioner before she married Juan and took up farming.'

Athaclena looked uncertainly at the pass. They would have to climb nearly a thousand meters to get over it.

'Robert, are you sure this is the best route? I'm certain I have intermittently sensed sophonts emoting from much nearer, over that line of hills to the east.'

Robert leaned on his makeshift staff and began moving up the southward trail. 'Come on, Clennie,' he said over his shoulder. 'I know you want to meet a Garthling, but now's hardly the time. We can go hunting for native pre-sentients after I've been patched up.'

Athaclena stared after him, astonished by the illogic of his remark. She caught up with him. 'Robert, that was a strange thing to say! How could I think of seeking out native creatures, no matter how mysterious, until you were tended! The sophonts I have felt to the east were clearly humans and chimps, although I admit there *was* a strange, added element, almost like ... '

'Aha!' Robert smiled, as if she had made a confession. He walked on.

Amazed, Athaclena tried to probe his feelings, but the human's discipline and determination was incredible for a member of a wolfling race. All she could tell was that he was disturbed – and that it had something to do with her mention of sapient thoughts east of here.

Oh, to be a true telepath! Once more she wondered why the Tymbrimi Grand Council had not defied the rules of the Uplift Institute and gone ahead to develop the capability. She had sometimes envied humans the privacy they could build around their lives and resented the gossipy invasiveness of her own culture. But right now she wanted only to break *in* there and find out what he was hiding!

Her corona waved, and if there had been any Tymbrimi within half a mile they would have winced at her angry, pungent opinion of the way of things.

Robert was showing difficulty before they reached the crest of the first ridge, little more than an hour later. Athaclena knew by now that the glistening perspiration on his brow meant the same thing as a reddening and fluffing of a Tymbrimi's corona – overheating.

When she overheard him counting under his breath, she knew that they would have to rest. 'No.' He shook his head. His voice was ragged. 'Let's just get past this ridge and into the next valley. From there on it's shaded all the way to the pass.' Robert kept trudging.

'There is shade enough here,' she insisted, and pulled him over to a rock jumble covered by creepers with umbrellalike leaves, all linked by the ubiquitous transfer-vines to the forest in the valley floor.

Robert sighed as she helped him sit back against a boulder in the shade. She wiped his forehead, then began unwrapping his splinted right arm. He hissed through his teeth.

A faint purpling discolored the skin near where the bone had broken. 'Those are bad signs, aren't they, Robert?'

For a moment she felt him begin to dissemble. Then he reconsidered, shaking his head. 'N-no. I think there's an infection. I'd better take some more Universal ...'

He started to reach for her pack, where his aid kit was being carried, but his equilibrium failed and Athaclena had to catch him.

'Enough, Robert. You cannot walk to the Mendoza Freehold. I certainly cannot carry you, and I'll not leave you alone for two or three days!

'You seem to have some reason to wish to avoid the people who I sensed to the east of here. But whatever it is, it cannot match the importance of saving your life!'

Robert let her pop a pair of blue pills into his mouth and sipped from the canteen she held for him. 'All right, Clennie,' he sighed. 'We'll turn eastward. Only promise you'll corona-sing for me, will you? It's lovely, like you are, and it helps me understand you better ... and now I think we'd better get started because I'm babbling. That's one sign that a human being is deteriorating. You should know that by now.'

Athaclena's eyes spread apart and she smiled. 'I was already aware of that, Robert. Now tell me, what is the name of this place where we are going?'

'It's called the Howletts Center. It's just past that second set of hills, over that way.' He pointed east by southeast.

'They don't like surprise guests,' he went on, 'so we'll want to talk loudly as we approach.'

Taking it by stages, they made it over the first ridge shortly before noon and rested in the shade by a small spring. There Robert fell into a troubled slumber.

Athaclena watched the human youth with a feeling of miserable helplessness. She found herself humming Thlufall-threela's famous 'Dirge of Inevitability.' The poignant piece for aura and voice was over four thousand years old, written during the time of sorrow when the Tymbrimi patron race, the Caltmour, were destroyed in a bloody interstellar war.

Inevitability was not a comfortable concept for her people, even less than for humans. But long ago the Tymbrimi had decided to try all things – to learn all philosophies. Resignation, too, had its place.

Not this time! she swore. Athaclena coaxed Robert into his sleeping bag and got him to swallow two more pills. She secured his arm as best she could and piled rocks alongside to keep him from rolling about.

A low palisade of brush around him would, she hoped, keep out any dangerous animals. Of course the Bururalli had cleared Garth's forests of any large creatures, but that did not keep her from worrying. Would an unconscious human be safe then, if she left him alone for a little while?

She placed her jack-laser within reach of his left hand and a canteen next to it. Bending down she touched his forehead with her sensitized, refashioned lips. Her corona unwound and fell about his face, caressing it with delicate strands so she could give him a parting benediction in the manner of her own folk, as well.

A deer might have run faster. A cougar might have slipped through the forest stillness more silently. But Athaclena had never heard of those creatures. And even if she had, a Tymbrimi did not fear comparisons. Their very race-name was adaptability.

Within the first kilometer automatic changes had already been set in motion. Glands rushed strength to her legs, and changes in her blood made better use of the air she breathed. Loosened connective tissue opened her nostrils wide to pass still more, while elsewhere her skin tautened to prevent her breasts from bouncing jarringly as she ran.

The slope steepened as she passed out of the second narrow valley and up a game path toward the last ridge before her goal. Her rapid footfalls on the thick loam were light and soft. Only an occasional snapping twig announced her coming, sending the forest creatures scurrying into the shadows. A cluttering of little jeers followed her, both in sound and unsubtle emanations she picked up with her corona.

Their hostile calls made Athaclena want to smile, Tymbrimi style. Animals were so serious. Only a few, those nearly ready for Uplift, ever had anything resembling a sense of humor. And then, after they were adopted and began Uplift, all too often their patrons edited whimsy out of them as an 'unstable trait.'

After the next kilometer Athaclena eased back a bit. She would have to pace herself, if for no other reason than she was overheating. That was dangerous for a Tymbrimi.

She reached the crest of the ridge, with its chain of ubiquitous spine-stones, and slowed in order to negotiate the maze of jutting monoliths. There, she rested briefly. Leaning against one of the tall rocky outcrops, breathing heavily, she reached out with her corona. The tendrils waved, searching.

Yes! There were humans close by! And neo-chimpanzees, too. By now she knew both patterns well.

And ... she concentrated. There was something else, also. Something tantalizing.

It had to be that enigmatic being she had sensed twice before! There was that queer quality that at one moment seemed Earthly and then seemed to partake strongly of this world. And it was *presentient*, with a dark, serious nature of its own.

If only empathy were more of a directional sense! She moved forward, tracing a way toward the source through the maze of stones.

A shadow fell upon her. Instinctively, she leaped back and crouched – hormones rushing combat strength into her hands and arms. Athaclena sucked air, fighting down the *gheer* reaction. She had been expecting to encounter some small, feral survivor of the Bururalli Holocaust, not anything so large!

Calm down, she told herself. The silhouette standing on the stone overhead was a large biped, clearly a cousin to Man and no native of Garth. A chimpanzee could never pose a threat to her, of course.

'H-hello!' She managed Anglic over the trembling left by the receding *gheer*. Silently she cursed the instinctive reactions which made Tymbrimi dangerous beings to cross but which shortened their lives and often embarrassed them in polite company.

The figure overhead stared down at her. Standing on two legs, with a belt of tools around its waist, it was hard to discern against the glare. The bright, bluish light of Garth's sun was disconcerting. Even so, Athaclena could tell that this one was very large for a chimpanzee.

It did not react. In fact, the creature just stared down at her.

A client race as young as neo-chimpanzees could not be expected to be too bright. She made allowances, squinting up at the dark, furry figure, and enunciated slowly in Anglic.

'I have an emergency to report. There is a *human being*,' she emphasized, 'who is injured not far from here. He needs immediate attention. You must please take me to some humans, right now.' She expected an immediate response, but the creature merely shifted its weight and continued to stare.

Athaclena was beginning to feel foolish. Could she have encountered a particularly stupid chim? Or perhaps a deviant or a sport? New client races produced a lot of variability, sometimes including dangerous throwbacks – witness what had happened to the Bururalli so recently here on Garth.

Athaclena extended her senses. Her corona reached out and then curled in surprise!

It was the pre-sentient! The superficial resemblance – the fur and long arms – had fooled her. This wasn't a chim at all! It was the alien creature she had sensed only minutes ago!

No wonder the beast hadn't responded. It had had no patron yet to teach it to talk! *Potential* quivered and throbbed. She could sense it just under the surface.

Athaclena wondered just what one said to a native pre-sophont. She looked more carefully. The creature's dark, furry coat was fringed by the sun's glare. Atop short, bowed legs it carried a massive body culminating in a great head with a narrow peak. In silhouette, its huge shoulders merged without any apparent neck.

Athaclena recalled Ma'chutallils' famed story about a space-gleaner who encountered, in forests far from a colony settlement, a child who had been brought up by wild limb-runners. After catching the fierce, snarling little thing in his nets, the hunter had aura-cast a simple version of *sh'cha'kuon*, the mirror of the soul.

Athaclena formed the empathy glyph as well as she could remember it.

SEE IN ME – AN IMAGE OF THE VERY YOU

The creature stood up. It reared back, snorting and sniffing at the air.

752

She thought, at first, it was reacting to her glyph. Then a noise, not far away, broke the fleeting connection. The pre-sentient chuffed – a deep, grunting sound – then spun about and leaped away, hopping from spine-stone to spine-stone until it was gone from sight.

Athaclena hurried after, but uselessly. In moments she had lost the trail. She sighed finally and turned back to the east, where Robert had said the Earthling 'Howletts Center' lay. After all, finding help had to come first.

She started picking her way through the maze of spine-stones. They tapered off as the slope descended into the next valley. That was when she passed around a tall boulder and nearly collided with the search party.

'We're sorry we frightened you, ma'am,' the leader of the group said gruffly. His voice was somewhere between a growl and the croaking of a pond full of bug-hoppers. He bowed again. 'A seisin picker came in and told us of some sort of ship crash out this way, so we sent out a couple of search parties. You haven't seen anythin' like a spacecraft comin' down, have you?'

Athaclena still shivered from the Ifni-damned overreaction. She must have looked terrifying in those first few seconds, when surprise set off another furious change response. The poor creatures had been startled. Behind the leader, four more chims stared at her nervously.

'No, I haven't,' Athaclena spoke slowly and carefully, in order not to tax the little clients. 'But I do have a different sort of emergency to report. My comrade – a human being – was injured yesterday afternoon. He has a broken arm and a possible infection. I must speak to someone in authority about having him evacuated.'

The leader of the chims stood a bit above average in height, nearly a hundred and fifty centimeters tall. Like the others he wore a pair of shorts, a tool-bandoleer, and a light backpack. His grin featured an impressive array of uneven, somewhat yellowed teeth.

'I'm sufficiently in authority. My name is Benjamin, Mizz … Mizz …' His gruff voice ended in a questioning tone.

'Athaclena. My companion's name is Robert Oneagle. He is the son of the Planetary Coordinator.'

Benjamin's eyes widened. 'I see. Well, Mizz Athac-… well ma'am … you must have heard by now that Garth's been interdicted by a fleet of Eatee cruisers. Under th' emergency we aren't supposed to use aircars if we can avoid it. Still, my crew here is equipped to handle a human with th' sort of injuries you described. If you'll lead us to Mr Oneagle, we'll see he's taken care of.'

Athaclena's relief was mixed with a pang as she was reminded of larger matters. She had to ask. 'Have they determined who the invaders are yet? Has there been a landing?'

The chimp Benjamin was behaving professionally and his diction was good, but he could not disguise his perplexity as he looked at her, tilting his head as if trying to see her from a new angle. The others frankly stared. Clearly they had never seen a person like her before.

'Uh, I'm sorry, ma'am, but the news hasn't been too specific. The Eatees . . . uh.' The chim peered at her. 'Uh, pardon me, ma'am, but you aren't human, are you?'

'Great Caltmour, no!' Athaclena bristled. 'What ever gave you the . . . ' Then she remembered all the little external alterations she had made as part of her experiment. She must look very close to human by now, especially with the sun behind her. No wonder the poor clients had been confused!

'No,' she said again, more softly. 'I am no human. I am Tymbrimi.'

The chims sighed and looked quickly at one another. Benjamin bowed, arms crossed in front of him, for the first time offering the gesture of a client greeting a member of a patron-class race.

Athaclena's people, like humans, did not believe in flaunting their dominance over their clients. Still, the gesture helped mollify her hurt feelings. When he spoke again, Benjamin's diction was much better.

'Forgive me, ma'am. What I meant to say was that I'm not really sure who the invaders are. I wasn't near a receiver when their manifesto was broadcast, a couple of hours ago. Somebody told me it was the Gubru, but there's another rumor they're Thennanin.'

Athaclena sighed. Thennanin or Gubru. Well, it could have been worse. The former were sanctimonious and narrow-minded. The latter were often vile, rigid, and cruel. But neither were as bad as the manipulative Soro, or the eerie, deadly Tandu.

Benjamin whispered to one of his companions. The smaller chimp turned and hurried down the trail the way they had come, toward the mysterious Howletts Center. Athaclena caught a tremor of anxiety. Once again she wondered what was going on in this valley that Robert had tried to steer her away from, even at risk to his own health.

'The courier will carry back word of Mr Oneagle's condition and arrange transport,' Benjamin told her. 'Meanwhile, we'll hurry to give him first aid. ft you would only lead the way . . . '

He motioned her ahead, and Athaclena had to put away her curiosity for now. Robert clearly came first. 'All right,' she said. 'Let us go.'

As they passed under the standing stone where she had had her encounter with the strange, pre-sentient alien, Athaclena looked up. Had it really been a 'Garthling'? Perhaps the chims knew something about it. Before she could begin to ask, however, Athaclena stumbled, clutching at her temples. The chims stared at the sudden waving of her corona and the startled, narrow set of her eyes.

It was part sound – a keening that crested high, almost beyond hearing – and partly a sharp *itch* that crawled up her spine.

'Ma'am?' Benjamin looked up at her, concerned. 'What is it?'

Athaclena shook her head. 'It's ... It is ... ' She did not finish. For at that moment there was a flash of gray over the western horizon – something hurtling through the sky toward them – *too fast*! Before Athaclena could flinch it had grown from distant dot to behemoth size. Just that suddenly a giant ship appeared, stock-still, hovering directly over the valley.

Athaclena barely had enough time to cry out, 'Cover your ears!' Then thunder broke, a crash and roar that knocked all of them to the ground. The boom reverberated through the maze of stones and echoed off the surrounding hillsides. Trees swayed – some of them cracking and toppling over – and leaves were ripped away in sudden, fluttering cyclones.

Finally the pealing died away, diffracting and diminishing into the forest. Only after that, and blinking away tremors of shock, did they at last hear the low, loud growl of the ship itself. The gray monster cast shadows over the valley, a huge, gleaming cylinder. As they stared the great machine slowly settled lower until it dropped below the spine-stones and out of sight. The hum of its engines fell to a deep rumble, uncovering the sound of rockfalls on the nearby slopes.

The chims slowly stood up and held each others' hands nervously, whispering to each other in hoarse, low voices. Benjamin helped Athaclena to stand. The ship's gravity fields had struck her fully extended corona unprepared. She shook her head, trying to clear it.

'That was a warship, wasn't it?' Benjamin asked her. 'These other chims here haven't ever been to space, but I went up to see the old *Vesarius* when it visited, a couple years back, and even she wasn't as big as that thing!'

Athaclena sighed. 'It was, indeed, a warship. Of Soro design, I think. The Gubru are using that fashion now.' She looked down at the Earthling. 'I would say that Garth is no longer simply interdicted, Chim Benjamin. An invasion has begun.'

Benjamin's hands came together. He pulled nervously at one opposable thumb, then the other. 'They're hovering over the valley. I can hear 'em! What are they up to?'

'I don't know,' she said. 'Why don't we go look?'

Benjamin hesitated, then nodded. He led the group back to a point where the spine-stones opened up and they could gaze out over the valley.

The warship hovered about four kilometers east of their position and a few hundred meters above the ground, draping its immense shadow over a small cluster of off-white buildings on the valley floor. Athaclena shaded her eyes against the bright sunshine reflected from its gunmetal gray flanks.

The deep-throated groan of the giant cruiser was ominous. 'It's just hoverin' there! What are they doing?' one of the chims asked nervously.

Athaclena shook her head in Anglic. 'I do not know.' She sensed fear from humans and neo-chimps in the settlement below. And there were other sources of emotion as well.

The invaders, she realized. Their psi shields were down, an arrogant dismissal of any possibility of defense. She caught a gestalt of thin-boned, feathered creatures, descendants of some flightless, pseudo-avian species. A rare real-view came to her briefly, vividly, as seen through the eyes of one of the cruiser's officers. Though contact only lasted milliseconds, her corona reeled back in revulsion.

Gubru, she realized numbly. Suddenly, it was made all too real.

Benjamin gasped. 'Look!'

Brown fog spilled forth from vents in the ship's broad underbelly. Slowly, almost languidly, the dark, heavy vapor began to fall toward the valley floor.

The fear below shifted over to panic. Athaclena quailed back against one of the spine-stones and wrapped her arms over her head, trying to shut out the almost palpable aura of dread.

Too much! Athaclena tried to form a glyph of peace in the space before her, to hold back the pain and horror. But every pattern was blown away like spun snow before the hot wind of a flame.

'They're killing th' humans and 'rillas!' one of the chims on the hillside cried, running forward. Benjamin shouted after him. 'Petrie! Come back here! Where do you think you're going?'

'I'm goin' to help!' the younger chim yelled back. 'And you would too, if you cared! You can hear 'em screamin' down there!' Ignoring the winding path, he started scrambling down the scree slope itself – the most direct route toward the roiling fog and the dim sounds of despair.

The other two chims looked at Benjamin rebelliously, obviously sharing the same thought. 'I'm goin' too,' one said.

Athaclena's fear-narrowed eyes throbbed. What were these silly creatures doing now?

'I'm with you,' the last one agreed. In spite of Benjamin's shouted curses, both of them started down the steep slope.

'*Stop this, right now!*'

They turned and stared at Athaclena. Even Petrie halted suddenly, hanging one-handed from a boulder, blinking up at her. She had used the Tone of Peremptory Command, for only the third time in her life.

'Stop this foolishness and come back here immediately!' she snapped. Athaclena's corona billowed out over her ears. Her carefully cultured human accent was gone. She enunciated Anglic in the Tymbrimi lilt the neo-chimpanzees must have heard on video countless times. She might *look* rather human, but no human voice could make exactly the same sounds.

The Terran clients blinked, open-mouthed.

'*Return at once,*' she hissed.

The chims scrambled back up the slope to stand before her. One by one, glancing nervously at Benjamin and following his example, they bowed with arms crossed in front of them.

Athaclena fought down her own shaking in order to appear outwardly calm. 'Do not make me raise my voice again,' she said lowly. 'We must work together, think coolly, and make appropriate plans.'

Small wonder the chims shivered and looked up at her, wide-eyed. Humans seldom spoke to chims so peremptorily. The species might be indentured to man, but by Earth's own law neo-chimps were nearly equal citizens.

We Tymbrimi, though, are another matter. Duty, simple duty had drawn Athaclena out of her *totanoo* – her fear-induced withdrawal. Somebody had to take responsibility to save these creatures' lives.

The ugly brown fog had stopped spilling from the Gubru vessel. The vapor spread across the narrow valley like a dark, foamy lake, barely covering the buildings at the bottom.

Vents closed. The ship began to rise.

'Take cover,' she told them, and led the chims around the nearest of the rock monoliths. The low hum of the Gubru ship climbed more than an octave. Soon they saw it rise over the spine-stones.

'Protect yourselves.'

The chims huddled close, pressing their hands against their ears.

One moment the giant invader was there, a thousand meters over the valley floor. Then, quicker than the eye could follow, it was gone. Displaced air clapped inward like a giant's hand and thunder batted them again, returning in rolling waves that brought up dust and leaves from the forest below.

The stunned neo-chimps stared at each other for long moments as the echoes finally ebbed. Finally the eldest chim, Benjamin, shook himself. He dusted his hands and grabbed the young chen named Petrie by the back of his neck, marching the startled chim over to face Athaclena.

Petrie looked down shamefaced. 'I ... I'm sorry, ma'am,' he muttered gruffly. 'It's just that there are humans down there and ... and my mates ...'

Athaclena nodded. One should try not to be too hard on a well-intended client. 'Your motives were admirable. Now that we are calm though, and can plan, we'll go about helping your patrons and friends more effectively.'

She offered her hand. It was a less patronizing gesture than the pat on the head he seemed to have expected from a Galactic. They shook, and he grinned shyly.

When they hurried around the stones to look out over the valley again, several of the Terrans gasped. The brown cloud had spread over the lowlands like a thick, filthy sea that flowed almost to the forest slopes at their feet. The heavy vapor seemed to have a sharply defined upper boundary barely licking at the roots of nearby trees.

They had no way of knowing what was going on below, or even if anybody still lived down there.

'We will split into two groups,' Athaclena told them. 'Robert Oneagle still requires attention. Someone must go to him.'

The thought of Robert lying semi-conscious back there where she had left him was an unrelenting anxiety in her mind. She had to know he was being cared for. Anyway, she suspected most of these chims would be better off going to Robert's aid than hanging around this deadly valley. The creatures were too shaken and volatile up here in full view of the disaster. 'Benjamin, can your companions find Robert by themselves, using the directions I have given?'

'You mean without leading them there yourself?' Benjamin frowned and shook his head. 'Uh, I dunno, ma'am. I ... I really think you ought to go along.'

Athaclena had left Robert under a clear landmark, a giant quail-nut tree close to the main trail. Any party sent from here should have no trouble finding the injured human.

She could read the chim's emotions. Part of Benjamin anxiously wished to have one of the renowned Tymbrimi here to help, if possible, the people in the valley. And yet he had chosen to try to send her away!

The oily smoke churned and rolled below. She could distantly sense many minds down there, turbulent with fear.

'I will remain,' she said firmly. 'You have said these others are a qualified rescue team. They can certainly find Robert and help him. Someone must stay and see if anything can be done for those below.'

With a human there might have been argument. But the chimps did not even consider contradicting a Galactic with a made up mind. Client-class sophonts simply did not do such things.

In Benjamin she sensed a partial relief ... and a counterpoint of dread.

The three younger chims shouldered their packs. Solemnly they headed westward through the spine-stones, glancing back nervously until they passed out of sight.

Athaclena let herself feel relieved for Robert's sake. But underneath it all remained a nagging fear for her father. The enemy must certainly have struck Port Helenia first.

'Come, Benjamin. Let's see what can be done for those poor people down there.'

For all of their unusual and rapid successes in Uplift, Terran geneticists still had a way to go with neo-dolphins and neo-chimpanzees. Truly original thinkers were still rare in both species. By Galactic standards they had made great! strides, but Earthmen wanted even more rapid progress. It was almost as if they suspected their clients might have to grow up very quickly, very soon.

When a good mind appeared in *Tursiops* or *Pongo* stock, it was carefully nurtured. Athaclena could tell that Benjamin was one of those superior specimens. No doubt this chim had at least a blue card procreation right and had already sired many children.

'Maybe I'd better scout ahead, ma'am,' Benjamin suggested. 'I can climb these trees and stay above the level of the gas. I'll go in and find out how things lie, and then come back for you.'

Athaclena felt the chim's turmoil as they looked out on the lake of mysterious gas. Here it was about ankle deep, but farther into the valley it swirled several man-heights into the trees.

'No. We'll stay together,' Athaclena said firmly. 'I can climb trees too, you know.'

Benjamin looked her up and down, apparently recalling stories of the fabled Tymbrimi adaptability. 'Hmmm, your folk might have once been arboreal at that. No respect intended.' He gave her a wry, unhinged grin. 'All right then, miss, let's go.'

He took a running start, leaped into the branches of a near-oak, scampered around the trunk and darted down another limb. Then Benjamin jumped across a narrow gap to the next tree. He held onto the bouncing branch and looked back at her with curious brown eyes.

Athaclena recognized a challenge. She breathed deeply several times, concentrating. Changes began with a tingling in her hardening fingertips, a loosening in her chest. She exhaled, crouched, and took off, launching herself into the near-oak. With some difficulty she imitated the chim, move by move.

Benjamin nodded in approval as she landed next to him. Then he was off again.

They made slow progress, leaping from tree to tree and creeping around vine-entangled trunks. Several times they were forced to backtrack around clearings choked with the slowly settling fumes. They tried not to breathe when stepping over thicker wisps of the heavy gas, but Athaclena could not help picking up a whiff of pungent, oily stuff She told herself that her growing itch was probably psychosomatic.

Benjamin kept glancing at her surreptitiously. The chim certainly noticed some of the changes she underwent as the minutes passed – a limbering of the arms, a rolling of the shoulders and loosening and opening of the hands. He clearly had never expected to have a Galactic keep up with him this way, swinging through the trees.

He almost certainly did not know the price the *gheer* transformation was going to cost her. The hurt had already begun, and Athaclena knew this was only the beginning.

The forest was full of sounds. Small animals scurried past them, fleeing the alien smoke and stench. Athaclena picked up quick, hot pulses of their fear. As they reached the top of a knoll overlooking the settlement, they could hear faint cries – frightened Terrans groping about in a soot-dark forest.

Benjamin's brown eyes told her that those were his friends down there. 'See how the stuff clings to the ground?' he said. 'It hardly rises a few meters over the tops of our buildings. If only we'd built *one* tall structure!'

'They would have blasted that building first,' Athaclena pointed out. 'And *then* released their gas.'

'Hmmph.' Benjamin nodded. 'Well, let's go see if any of my mates made it into the trees. Maybe they managed to help a few of the humans get high enough as well.'

She did not question Benjamin about his hidden fear – the thing he could not bring himself to mention. But there was something added to his worry about the humans and chims below, as if that were not already enough.

The deeper they went into the valley, the higher among the branches they had to travel. More and more often they were forced to drop down, stirring the smoky, unraveling wisps with their feet as they hurried along their arboreal highway. Fortunately, the oily gas seemed to be dissipating at last, growing heavier and precipitating in a fine rain of gray dust.

Benjamin's pace quickened as they caught glimpses of the off-white buildings of the Center beyond the trees. Athaclena followed as well as she could, but it was getting harder and harder to keep up with the chim. Enzyme exhaustion took its toll, and her corona was ablaze as her body tried to eliminate heat buildup.

Concentrate, she thought as she crouched on one waving branch. Athaclena flexed her legs and tried to sight on the blur of dusty leaves and twigs opposite her.

Go.

She uncoiled, but by now the spring was gone from her leap. She barely made it across the two-meter gap. Athaclena hugged the bucking, swaying branch. Her corona pulsed like fire.

She clutched the alien wood, breathing open-mouthed, unable to move, the world a blur. *Maybe it's more than just* gheer *pain*, she thought. *Maybe the gas isn't just designed for Terrans. It could be killing me.*

It took a couple of moments for her eyes to focus again, and then she saw little more than a black-bottomed foot covered with brown fur ... Benjamin, clutching the tree branch nimbly and standing over her.

His hand softly touched the waving, hot tendrils of her corona. 'You just wait here and rest, miss. I'll scout ahead an' be right back.'

The branch shuddered once more, and he was gone.

Athaclena lay still. She could do little else except listen to faint sounds coming from the direction of the Howletts Center. Nearly an hour after the departure of the Gubru cruiser she could still hear panicky chimp shrieks and strange, low cries from some animal she couldn't recognize.

The gas was dissipating but it still stank, even up here. Athaclena kept her nostrils closed, breathing through her mouth.

Pity the poor Earthlings, whose noses and ears must remain open all the time, for all the world to assault at will. The irony did not escape her. For at least the creatures did not have to listen with their *minds*.

As her corona cooled, Athaclena felt awash in a babble of emotions ... human, chimpanzee, and that other variety that flickered in and out, the 'stranger' that had by now become almost familiar. Minutes passed, and Athaclena felt a little better ... enough to crawl along the limb to where branch met trunk. She sat back against the rough bark with a sigh, the flow of noise and emotion surrounding her.

Maybe I'm not dying after all, at least not right away.

Only after a little while longer did it dawn on her that something was happening quite nearby. She could sense that she was being *watched* – and from very close! She turned and drew her breath sharply. From the branches of a tree only six meters away, four sets of eyes stared back at her – three pairs deep brown and a fourth bright blue.

Barring perhaps a few of the sentient, semi-vegetable Kanten, the Tymbrimi were the Galactics who knew Earthlings best. Nevertheless, Athaclena blinked in surprise, uncertain just what it was she was seeing.

Closest to the trunk of that tree sat an adult female neo-chimpanzee – a 'chimmie' – dressed only in shorts, holding a chim baby in her arms. The little mother's brown eyes were wide with fear.

Next to them was a small, smooth-skinned human child dressed in denim overalls. The little blond girl smiled back at Athaclena, shyly.

But it was the fourth and last being in the other tree that had Athaclena confused.

She recalled a neo-dolphin sound-sculpture her father had brought home to Tymbrim from his travels. This was just after that episode of the ceremony of Acceptance and Choice of the Tytlal, when she had behaved so strangely up in that extinct volcano caldera. Perhaps Uthacalthing had wanted to play the sound-sculpting for her to draw her out of her moodiness – to prove to her that the Earthly cetaceans were actually charming creatures, not to be feared. He had told her to close her eyes and just let the song wash over her.

Whatever his motive, it had had the opposite effect. For in listening to the wild, untamed patterns, she had suddenly found herself immersed in an *ocean*, hearing an angry sea squall gather. Even opening her eyes, seeing that she still sat in the family listening room, did not help. For the first time in her life, sound overwhelmed vision.

Athaclena had never listened to the cube again, nor known anything else quite so strange ... until encountering the eerie metaphorical landscape within Robert Oneagle's mind, that is.

Now she felt that way again! For while the fourth creature across from her looked, at first, like a *very* large chimpanzee, her corona was telling quite another story.

It cannot be!

Calmly, placidly, the brown eyes looked back at her. The being obviously far outweighed all the others combined, yet it held the human child on its lap delicately, carefully. When the little girl squirmed, the big creature merely snorted and shifted slightly, neither letting go nor taking its gaze from Athaclena. Unlike normal chimpanzees, its face was very black.

Ignoring her aches, Athaclena edged forward slowly so as not to alarm them. 'Hello,' she said carefully in Anglic.

The human child smiled again and ducked her head shyly against her furry protector's massive chest. The neo-chimp mother cringed back in apparent fear.

The massive creature with the high, flattened face merely nodded twice and snorted again.

It fizzed with Potential!

Athaclena had only once before encountered a species living in that narrow zone between animal and accepted client-class sophont. It was a very rare state in the Five Galaxies, for any newly discovered pre-sentient species was soon registered and licensed to some star-faring clan for Uplift and indenture.

It dawned on Athaclena that this being was already far along toward sentience!

But the gap from animal to thinker was supposed to be impossible to cross alone! True, some humans still clung to quaint ideas from the ignorant days before Contact – theories proposing that true intelligence could be 'evolved.' But Galactic science assured that the threshold could only be passed with the aid of another race, one who had already crossed it.

So it had been all the way back to the fabled days of the first race – the Progenitors – billions of years ago.

But nobody had ever traced patrons for the humans. That was why they were called *k'chu-non* ... wolflings. Might their old idea contain a germ of truth? If so, might this creature also ... ?

Ah, no! Why did I not see it at once?

Athaclena suddenly knew this beast was not a natural find. It was not the fabled 'Garthling' her father had asked her to seek. The family resemblance was simply too unmistakable.

She was looking at a gathering of *cousins,* sitting together on that branch high above the Gubru vapors. Human, neo-chimpanzees, and ... what?

She tried to recall what her father had said about humanity's license to occupy their homeworld, the Earth. After Contact, the Institutes had granted recognition of mankind's de facto tenancy. Still, there were Fallow Rules and other restrictions, she was certain.

And a few special Earth species had been mentioned in particular.

The great beast radiated Potential like ... A *metaphor* came to Athaclena, of a beacon burning in the tree across from her. Searching her memory Tymbrimi fashion, she at last drew forth the name she had been looking for.

'Pretty thing,' she asked softly. 'You are a *gorilla*, aren't you?'

16

THE HOWLETTS CENTER

The beast tossed its great head and snorted. Next to it, the mother chimp whimpered softly and regarded Athaclena with obvious dread.

But the little human girl clapped her hands, sensing a game. "Rilla! Jonny's a 'rilla! Like me!' The child's small fists thumped her chest. She threw back her head and crowed a high-pitched, ululating yell.

A gorilla. Athaclena looked at the giant, silent creature in wonderment, trying to remember what she had been told in passing so long ago.

Its dark nostrils flared as it sniffed in Athaclena's direction, and used its free hand to make quick, subtle hand signs to the human child.

'Jonny wants to know if you're going to be in charge, now,' the little girl lisped. 'I hope so. You sure looked tired when you stopped chasing Benjamin. Did he do something bad? He got away, you know.'

Athaclena moved a little closer. 'No,' she said. 'Benjamin didn't do anything bad. At least not since I met him – though I am beginning to suspect – '

Athaclena stopped. Neither the child nor the gorilla would understand what she now suspected. But the adult chim knew, clearly, and her eyes showed fear.

'I'm April,' the small human told her. 'An' that's Nita. Her baby's name is Cha-Cha. Sometimes chimmies give their babies easy names to start 'cause they don't talk so good at first,' she confided.

Her eyes seemed to shine as she looked at Athaclena. 'Are you *really* a Tym ... bim ... Tymmbimmie?'

Athaclena nodded. 'I am Tymbrimi.'

April clapped her hands. 'Ooh. They're goodguys! Did you see the big spaceship? It came with a big boom, and Daddy made me go with Jonny, and then there was gas and Jonny put his hand over my mouth and I couldn't breathe!'

April made a scrunched up face, pantomiming suffocation.

'He let go when we were up in th' trees, though. We found Nita an' Cha-Cha.' She glanced over at the chims. 'I guess Nita's still too scared to talk much.'

'Were you frightened too?' Athaclena asked.

April nodded seriously. 'Yeth. But I had to stop being scared. I was th' only *man* here, and I hadda be in charge, and take care of ever'body.'

'Can you be in charge now? You're a really pretty Tymbimmie.'

The little girl's shyness returned. She partly buried herself against Jonny's massive chest, smiling out at Athaclena with only one eye showing.

Athaclena could not help staring. She had never until now realized this about human beings – of what they were capable. In spite of her people's alliance with the Terrans, she had picked up some of the common Galactic prejudice, imagining that the 'wolflings' were still somehow feral, bestial. Many Galactics thought it questionable that humans were truly ready to be patrons. No doubt the Gubru had expressed that belief in their War Manifesto.

This child shattered that image altogether. By law and custom, little April *had* been in charge of her clients, no matter how young she was. And her understanding of that responsibility was clear.

Still, Athaclena now knew why both Robert and Benjamin had been anxious not to lead her here. She suppressed her initial surge of righteous anger. Later, she would have to find a way to get word to her father, after she had verified her suspicions.

She was almost beginning to feel Tymbrimi again as the *gheer* reaction gave way to a mere dull burning along her muscles and neural pathways. 'Did any other humans make it into the trees?' she asked.

Jonny made a quick series of hand signs. April interpreted, although the little girl may not have clearly understood the implications. 'He says a few tried. But they weren't fast enough ... Most of 'em just ran aroun' doin' "Man-Things." That's what 'rillas call the stuff humans do that 'rillas don't understand,' she confided lowly.

At last the mother chim, Nita, spoke. 'The g-gas ...' She swallowed. 'Th' gas m-made the humans weak.' Her voice was barely audible. 'Some of us chims felt it a little ... I don't think the 'rillas were bothered.'

So. Perhaps Athaclena's original surmise about the gas was correct. She had suspected it was not intended to be immediately lethal. Mass slaughter of civilians was something generally frowned upon by the Institute for Civilized Warfare. Knowing the Gubru, the intent was probably much more insidious than that.

There was a cracking sound to her right. The large male chim, Benjamin, dropped onto a branch two trees away. He called out to Athaclena.

'It's okay now, miss! I found Dr Taka and Dr Schultz. They're anxious to talk to you!'

Athaclena motioned for him to approach. 'Please come here first, Benjamin.'

With typical *Pongo* exaggeration, Benjamin let out a long-suffering sigh. He leaped branch to branch until he came into view of the three apes and the human girl. Then his jaw dropped and his balancing grip almost slipped. Frustration wrote across his face. He turned to Athaclena, licking his lips, and cleared his throat.

'Don't bother,' she told him. 'I know you have spent the last twenty minutes trying, in the midst of all this turmoil, to arrange to have the truth hidden. But it was to no avail. I know what has been going on here.'

Benjamin's mouth clapped shut. Then he shrugged. 'So?' he sighed.

To the four on the branch Athaclena asked, 'Do you accept my authority?'

'Yeth,' April said. Nita glanced from Athaclena to the human child, then nodded.

'All right, then. Stay where you are until somebody comes for you. Do you understand?'

'Yes'm.' Nita nodded again. Jonny and Cha-Cha merely looked back at her.

Athaclena stood up, finding her balance on the branch, and turned to Benjamin. 'Now let us talk to these Uplift specialists of yours. If the gas has not completely incapacitated them, I'll be interested to hear why they have chosen to violate Galactic Law.'

Benjamin looked defeated. He nodded resignedly.

'Also,' Athaclena told him as she landed on the branch next to him. 'You had better catch up with the chims and gorillas you sent away – in order that I would not see them. They should be called back.

'We may need their help.'

17

FIBEN

Fiben had managed to fashion a crutch out of shattered tree limbs lying near the furrow torn up by his escape pod. Cushioned by tatters of his ship-suit, the crutch jarred his shoulder only *partially* out of joint each time he leaned on it.

Hummph, he thought. *If the humans hadn't straightened our spines and shortened our arms I could've* knuckle-walked *back to civilization.*

Dazed, bruised, hungry ... actually, Fiben was in a pretty good mood as he picked his way through obstacles on is way northward. *Hell, I'm alive. I can't really complain.* He had spent quite a lot of time in the Mountains of Mulun, doing ecological studies for the Restoration Project, so he could tell that he had to be in the right watershed, not too far from known lands. The varieties of vegetation were all quite recognizable, mostly native plants but also some that had been imported and released into the ecosystem to fill gaps left by the Bururalli Holocaust.

Fiben felt optimistic. To have survived this far, even up to crash-landing in familiar territory ... it made him certain that Ifni had further plans for him. She had to be saving him for something special. Probably a fate that would be particularly annoying and much more painful than mere starvation in the wilderness.

Fiben's ears perked and he looked up. Could he have imagined that sound?

No! Those were voices! He stumbled down the game path, alternately skipping and pole-vaulting on his makeshift crutch, until he came to a sloped clearing overlooking a steep canyon.

Minutes passed as he peered. The rain forest was so damn dense!

There! On the other side, about halfway downslope, six chims wearing backpacks could be seen moving rapidly through the forest, heading toward some of the still smoldering wreckage of TAASF *Proconsul*. Right now they were quiet. It was just a lucky break they had spoken as they passed below his position.

'Hey! Dummies! Over here!' He hopped on his right foot and waved his arms, shouting. The search party stopped. The chims looked about, blinking as the echoes bounced around the narrow defile. Fiben's teeth bared and he couldn't help growling low in frustration. They were looking everywhere *but* in his direction!

Finally, he picked up the crutch, whirled it above his head, and threw it out over the canyon.

One of the chims exclaimed, grabbing another. They watched the tumbling branch crash into the forest. *That's right*, Fiben urged. *Now think. Retrace the arc backwards.*

Two of the searchers pointed up his way and saw him waving. They shrieked in excitement, capering in circles.

Forgetting momentarily his own little regression, Fiben muttered under his breath. 'Just my luck to be rescued by a bunch of grunts. Come on, guys. Let's not make a thunder dance out of it.'

Still, he grinned when they neared his hillside clearing. And in all the subsequent hugging and backslapping he forgot himself and let out a few glad hoots of his own.

18

UTHACALTHING

His little pinnace was the last craft to take off from the Port Helenia space-field. Already detection screens showed battle cruisers descending into the lower atmosphere.

Back at the port, a small force of militiamen and Terragens Marines prepared to make a futile last stand. Their defiance was broadcast on all channels.

'... *We deny the invader's rights to land here. We claim the protection of Galactic Civilization against their aggression. We refuse the Gubru permission to set down on our legal lease-hold.*

'*In earnest of this, a small, armed, Formal Resistance Detachment awaits the invaders at the capital spaceport. Our challenge* ...'

Uthacalthing guided his pinnace with nonchalant nudges on the wrist and thumb controllers. The tiny ship raced southward along the coast of the Sea of Cilmar, faster than sound. Bright sunshine reflected off the broad waters to his right.

... should they dare to face us being to being, not cowering in their battleships ...

Uthacalthing nodded. 'Tell them, Earthlings,' he said softly in Anglic. The detachment commander had sought his advice in phrasing the ritual challenge. He hoped he had been of help.

The broadcast went on to list the numbers and types of weapons awaiting the descending armada at the spaceport, so the enemy would have no justification for using overpowering force. Under circumstances such as these, the Gubru would have no choice but to assail the defenders with ground troops. And they would have to take casualties.

If the Codes still hold, Uthacalthing reminded himself. *The enemy may not care about the Rules of War any longer.* It was hard to imagine such a situation. But there had been rumors from across the far starlanes ...

A row of display screens rimmed his cockpit. One showed cruisers coming into view of Port Helenia's public news cameras. Others showed fast fighters tearing up the sky right over the spaceport.

Behind him Uthacalthing heard a low keening as two stilt-like Ynnin commiserated with each other. Those creatures, at least, had been able to fit into Tymbrimi-type seats. But their hulking master had to stand.

Kault did not just stand, he paced the narrow cabin, his crest inflating until it bumped the low ceiling, again and again. The Thennanin was not in a good mood.

'*Why*, Uthacalthing?' he muttered for what was not the first time. 'Why did you delay for so long? We were the very last to get out of there!'

Kault's breathing vents puffed. 'You told me we would leave night before last! I hurried to gather a few possessions and be ready and you did not come! I waited. I missed opportunities to hire other transport while you sent message after message urging patience. And then, when you came at last after dawn, we departed as blithely as if we were on a holiday ride to the Progenitors' Arch!'

Uthacalthing let his colleague grumble on. He had already made formal apologies and paid diplomatic gild in compensation. No more was required of him.

Besides, things were going just the way he had planned them to.

A yellow light flashed on the control board, and a tone began to hum.

'What is that?' Kault shuffled forward in agitation. 'Have they detected our engines?'

'No.' And Kault sighed in relief.

Uthacalthing went on. 'It isn't the engines. That light means we've just been scanned by a probability beam.'

'*What?*' Kault nearly screamed. 'Isn't this vessel shielded? You aren't even using gravities! What anomalous probability could they have picked up?'

Uthacalthing shrugged, as if the human gesture had been born to him. 'Perhaps the unlikelihood is intrinsic,' he suggested. 'Perhaps it is something about us, about our own fate, that is glowing along the worldlines. That may be what they detect.'

Out of his right eye he saw Kault shiver. The Thennanin race seemed to have an almost superstitious dread of anything having to do with the art/science of reality-shaping. Uthacalthing allowed *looth'troo* – apology to one's enemy – to form gently within his tendrils, and reminded himself that his people and Kault's were officially at war. It was within his rights to tease his enemy-and-friend, as it had been ethically acceptable earlier, when he had arranged for Kault's own ship to be sabotaged.

'I shouldn't worry about it,' he suggested. 'We've got a good head start.'

Before the Thennanin could reply, Uthacalthing bent forward and spoke rapidly in GalSeven, causing one of the screens to expand its image.

'*Thwill'kou-chlliou!*' he cursed. 'Look at what they are doing!'

Kault turned and stared. The holo-display showed giant cruisers hovering over the capital city, pouring brown vapor over the buildings and parks. Though the volume was turned down, they could hear panic in the voice of the news announcer as he described the darkening skies, as if anyone in Port Helenia needed his interpretation.

'This is not well.' Kault's crest bumped the ceiling more rapidly. 'The Gubru are being more severe than the situation or their war rights here merit.'

Uthacalthing nodded. But before he could speak another yellow light winked on.

'What is it now?' Kault sighed.

Uthacalthing's eyes were at their widest separation. 'It means we are being chased by pursuit craft,' he replied. 'We may be in for a fight. Can you work a class fifty-seven weapons console, Kault?'

'No, but I believe one of my Ynnin – '

His reply was interrupted as Uthacalthing shouted, 'Hold on!' and turned on the pinnace's gravities. The ground screamed past under them. 'I am beginning evasive maneuvers,' he called out.

'Good,' Kault whispered through his neck vents.

Oh, bless the Thennanin thick skull, Uthacalthing thought.

He kept control over his facial expression, though he knew his colleague had the empathy sensitivity of a stone and could not pick up his joy.

As the pursuing ships started firing on them, his corona began to sing.

19

ATHACLENA

Green fingers of forest merged with the lawns and leafy-colored buildings of the Center, as if the establishment were intended to be inconspicuous from the air. Although a wind from the west had finally driven away the last visible shreds of the invader's aerosol, a thin film of gritty powder covered everything below a height of five meters, giving off a tangy, unpleasant odor.

Athaclena's corona no longer shrank under an overriding roar of panic. The mood had changed amid the buildings. There was a thread of resignation now ... and intelligent anger.

She followed Benjamin toward the first clearing, where she

caught sight of small groups of neo-chimps running pigeon-toed within the inner compound. One pair hurried by carrying a muffled burden on a stretcher.

'Maybe you shouldn't go down there after all, miss,' Benjamin rasped. 'I mean it's obvious the gas was designed to affect humans, but even us chims feel a bit woozy from it. You're pretty important ...'

'I am Tymbrimi,' Athaclena answered coolly. 'I cannot sit here while I am needed by clients and by my peers.'

Benjamin bowed in acquiescence. He led her down a stairlike series of branches until she set foot with some relief on the ground. The pungent odor was thicker here. Athaclena tried to ignore it, but her pulse pounded from nervousness.

They passed what had to have been facilities for housing and training gorillas. There were fenced enclosures, playgrounds, testing areas. Clearly an intense if small-scale effort had gone on here. Had Benjamin really imagined that he could fool her simply by sending the pre-sentient apes into the jungle to hide?

She hoped none of them had been hurt by the gas, or in the panicky aftermath. She remembered from her brief History of Earthmen class that gorillas, although strong, were also notoriously sensitive – even fragile – creatures.

Chims dressed in shorts, sandals, and the ubiquitous tool-bandoleers hurried to and fro on serious errands. A few stared at Athaclena as she approached, but they did not stop to speak. In fact, she heard very few words at all.

Stepping lightly through the dark dust, they arrived at the center of the encampment. There, at last, she and her guide encountered humans. They lay on couches on the steps of the main building, a mel and a fem. The male human's head was entirely hairless, and his eyes bore traces of epicanthic folding. He looked barely conscious.

The other 'man' was a tall, dark-haired female. Her skin was very black – a deep, rich shade Athaclena had never encountered before. Probably she was one of those rare 'pure breed' humans who retained the characteristics of their ancient 'races.' In contrast, the skin color of the chims standing next to her was almost pale pink, under their patchy covering of brown hair.

With the help of two older-looking chims, the black woman managed to prop herself up on one elbow as Athaclena approached. Benjamin stepped forward to make the introductions.

'Dr Taka, Dr Schultz, Dr M'Bzwelli, Chim Frederick, all of the Terran Wolfling Clan, I present you to the respected *Athaclena*, a Tymbrimi ab-Caltmour ab-Brma ab-Krallnith ul-Tytlal.'

Athaclena glanced at Benjamin, surprised he was able to recite her species honorific from memory.

'Dr Schultz,' Athaclena said, nodding to the chim on the left. To the woman she bowed slightly lower. 'Dr Taka.' With one last head incline she took in the other human and chim. 'Dr M'Bzwelli and Chim Frederick. Please accept my condolences over the cruelty visited on your settlement and your world.'

The chims bowed low. The woman tried to, as well, but she failed in her weakness.

'Thank you for your sentiments,' she replied, laboriously. 'We Earthlings will muddle through, I'm sure ... I do admit I'm a little surprised to see the daughter of the Tymbrimi ambassador pop out of nowhere right now.'

I'll just bet you are, Athaclena thought in Anglic, enjoying, this once, the flavor of human-style sarcasm. *My presence is nearly as much a disaster to your plans as the Gubru and their gas!*

'I have an injured friend,' she said aloud. 'Three of your neo-chimpanzees went after him, some time ago. Have you heard anything from them?'

The woman nodded. 'Yes, yes. We just had a pulse from the search party. Robert Oneagle is conscious and stable. Another group we had sent to seek out a downed flyer will be joining them shortly, with full medical equipment.'

Athaclena felt a tense worry unwrap in the corner of her mind where she had put it. 'Good. Very good. Then I will turn to other matters.'

Her corona blossomed out as she formed *kuouwassooe*, the glyph of presentiment – though she knew these folk would barely catch its fringes, if at all.

'First, as a member of a race that has been in alliance with yours ever since you wolflings burst so loudly upon the Five Galaxies, I offer my assistance during this emergency. What I can do as a fellow patron, I shall do, requiring in return only whatever help you can give me in getting in touch with my father.'

'Done.' Dr Taka nodded. 'Done and with our thanks.'

Athaclena took a step forward. 'Second – I must exclaim my dismay on discovering the function of this Center. I find you are engaged in unsanctioned Uplift activities on ... on a *fallow* species!'

The four directors looked at each other. By now Athaclena could read human expressions well enough to know their chagrined resignation. 'Furthermore,' she went on, 'I note that you had the poor taste to commit this crime on the planet Garth, a tragic victim of past ecological abuse – '

'Now just a minute!' Chim Frederick protested. 'How can you compare what we're doing with the holocaust of the Burur – '

'Fred, be quiet!' Dr Schultz, the other chim, cut in urgently.

Frederick blinked. Realizing it was too late to take back the interruption, he muttered on. '... th' only planets Earthclan's been allowed to settle have been other Eatees' messes ...'

The second human, Dr M'Bzwelli, started coughing. Frederick shut up and turned away.

The human male looked up at Athaclena. 'You have us against the wall, miss.' He sighed. 'Can we ask you to let us explain before you press charges? We're ... we're not representatives of our government, you understand. We are ... private criminals.'

Athaclena felt a funny sort of relief. Old pre-Contact Earthling flat movies – especially those copsandrobbers thrillers so popular among the Tymbrimi – often seemed to revolve around some ancient lawbreaker attempting to 'silence the witness.' A part of her had wondered just how atavistic these people actually were.

She exhaled deeply and nodded. 'Very well, then. The question can be put aside during the present emergency. Please tell me the situation here. What is the enemy trying to accomplish with this gas?'

'It weakens any human who breathes it,' Dr Taka answered. 'There was a broadcast an hour ago. The invader announced that affected humans must receive the antidote within one week, or die.

'Of course they are offering the antidote only in urban areas.'

'Hostage gas!' Athaclena whispered. 'They want all the planet's humans as pawns.'

'Exactly. We must ingather or drop dead in six days.'

Athaclena's corona sparked anger. Hostage gas was an irresponsible weapon, even if it was legal under certain limited types of war.

'What will happen to your clients?' Neo-chimps were only a few centuries old and should not be left unwatched in the wilderness.

Dr Taka grimaced, obviously worried as well. 'Most chims seem unaffected by the gas. But they have so few natural leaders, such as Benjamin or Dr Schultz here.'

Schultz's brown, simian eyes looked down at his human friend. 'Not to worry, Susan. We will, as you say, muddle through.' He turned back to Athaclena. 'We're evacuating the humans in stages, starting with the children and old folks tonight. Meanwhile, we'll start destroying this compound and all traces of what's happened here.'

Seeing that Athaclena was about to object, the elderly neo-chimp raised his hand. 'Yes, miss. We will provide you with cameras and assistants, so you may collect your evidence, first. Will that do? We would not dream of thwarting you in your duty.'

Athaclena sensed the chim geneticist's bitterness. But she had no sympathy for him, imagining how her father would feel when he learned of this. Uthacalthing liked Earthlings. This irresponsible criminality would wound him deeply.

'No sense in handing the Gubru a justification for their aggression,' Dr Taka added. 'The matter of the gorillas can go to the Tymbrimi Grand Council, if you wish. Our allies may then decide where to go from there, whether to press formal charges or leave our punishment to our own government.'

Athaclena saw the logic in it. After a moment she nodded. 'That will do, then. Bring me your cameras and I shall record this burning.'

20

GALACTICS

To the fleet admiral – the Suzerain of Beam and Talon – the argument sounded silly. But of course that was always the way of it among civilians. Priests and bureaucrats always argued. It was the fighters who believed in action!

Still, the admiral had to admit that it was thrilling to take part in their first real policy debate as a threesome. This was the way Truth was traditionally attained among the Gubru, through stress and disagreement, persuasion and dance, until finally a new consensus was reached.

And eventually . . .

The Suzerain of Beam and Talon shook aside the thought. It was much too soon to begin contemplating the Molt. There would be many more arguments, much jostling and maneuvering for the highest perch, before that day arrived.

As for this first debate, the admiral was pleased to find itself in the position of arbiter between its two bickering peers. This was a good way to begin.

The Terrans at the small spaceport had issued a well-written formal challenge. The Suzerain of Propriety insisted that Talon Soldiers must be sent to overcome the defenders in close combat. The Suzerain of Cost and Caution did not agree. For some time they circled each other on the dais of the flagship's bridge, eyeing each other and squawking pronouncements of argument.

> 'Expenses must be kept low!
>> Low enough that we need not,
>>> Need not burden other fronts!'

The Suzerain of Cost and Caution thus insisted that this expedition was only one of many engagements currently sapping the strength of the clan of Gooksyu-Gubru. In fact, it was rather a side-battle. Matters were tense across the Galactic spiral. In such times, it was the job of the Suzerain of Cost and Caution to protect the clan from overextending itself.

The Suzerain of Propriety huffed its feathers indignantly in response.

> 'What shall expense matter,
> mean,
> signify,
> stand for, if we fall,
> topple,
> drop,
> plummet from grace
> in the eyes of our Ancestrals?
> We must do what is right! *Zoooon!*'

Observing from its own perch of command, the Suzerain of Beam and Talon watched the struggle to see if any clear patterns of dominance were about to manifest themselves. It was thrilling to hear and see the excellent argument-dances performed by those who had been chosen to be the admiral's mates. All three of them represented the finest products of 'hot-egg' engineering, designed to bring out the best qualities of the race.

Soon, it was obvious that its peers had reached a stalemate. It would be up to Suzerain of Beam and Talon to decide.

It certainly would be less costly if the expeditionary force could simply ignore the insolent wolflings below until the hostage gas forced them to surrender. Or, with a simple order, their redoubt could be reduced to slag. But the Suzerain of Propriety refused to accept either option. Such actions would be catastrophic, the priest insisted.

The bureaucrat was just as adamant not to waste good soldiers on what would be essentially a gesture.

Deadlocked, the two other commanders eyed the Suzerain of Beam and Talon as they circled and squawked, fluffing their glowing white down. Finally, the admiral ruffled its own plumage and stepped onto the dais to join them.

> 'To engage in ground combat would cost,
> would mean expense.
> But it would be honorable,
> admirable.

'A third factor decides,
      swings the final vote.
That is the training need of
      Talon Soldiers.
Training against wolfling troops.

'Ground forces shall attack them, beam to beam, hand to
talon.'

The issue was decided. A stoop-colonel of the Talon Soldiers
saluted and hurried off with the order.

Of course with this resolution Propriety's perch position would
rise a little. Caution's descended. But the quest for dominance had
only just begun.

So it had been for their distant ancestors, before the Gooksyu
turned the primitive proto-Gubru into starfarers. Wisely, their
patrons had taken the ancient patterns and shaped and expanded
them into a useful, logical form of government for a sapient people.

Still, part of the older function remained. The Suzerain of Beam
and Talon shivered as the tension of argument was released. And
although all three of them were still quite neuter, the admiral felt a
momentary thrill that was deeply, thoroughly sexual.

21

FIBEN AND ROBERT

The two rescue parties encountered each other more than a mile
into the high pass. It was a somber gathering. The three who had
started out that morning with Benjamin were too tired to do more
than nod to the subdued group returning from the crash site.

But the battered pair who had been rescued exclaimed on seeing
each other.

'Robert! Robert Oneagle! When did they let you out of study hall?
Does your mommy know where you are?'

The injured chim leaned on a makeshift crutch and wore the
singed remains of a tattered TAASF ship-suit. Robert looked up at
him from the stretcher and grinned through an anesthetic haze.

'Fiben! In Goodall's name, was that *you* I saw smokin' out of the
sky? Figures. What'd you do, fry ten megacredits' worth of scoutboat?'

Fiben rolled his eyes. 'More like five megs. She was an old tub, even if she did all right by me.'

Robert felt a strange envy. 'So? I guess we got whomped.'

'You could say that. One on one we fought well. Would've been all right if there'd been enough of us.'

Robert knew what his friend meant. 'You mean there's no limit to what could've been accomplished with – '

'With an infinite number of monkeys?' Fiben cut in. His snort was a little less than a laugh but more than an ironic grin.

The other chims blinked in consternation. This level of banter was a bit over their heads, but what was more disturbing was how blithely this chen interrupted the human son of the Planetary Coordinator!

'I wish I could've been there with you,' Robert said seriously.

Fiben shrugged. 'Yeah, Robert. I know. But we all had orders.' For a long moment they were silent. Fiben knew Megan Oneagle well enough, and he sympathized with Robert.

'Well I guess we're both due for a stint in the mountains, assigned to holdin' down beds and harassing nurses.' Fiben sighed, gazing toward the south, 'If we can stand the fresh air, that is.' He looked down to Robert. 'These chims told me about the raid on the Center. Scary stuff.'

'Clennie'll help 'em straighten things out,' Robert answered. His attention had started to drift. They obviously had him doped to a dolphin's blowhole. 'She knows a lot … a lot more'n she thinks she does.'

Fiben had heard about the daughter of the Tymbrimi ambassador. 'Sure,' he said softly, as the others lifted the stretcher once again. 'An Eatee'll straighten things out. More likely'n not, that girl friend of yours will have everybody thrown in the clink, invasion or no invasion!'

But Robert was now far away. And Fiben had a sudden strange impression. It was as if the human mel's visage was not entirely Terran any longer. His dreamy smile was distant and touched with something … unearthly.

22

ATHACLENA

A large number of chims returned to the Center, drifting in from the forest where they had been sent to hide. Frederick and Benjamin set them to work dismantling and burning the buildings and their contents. Athaclena and her two assistants hurried from site to site, carefully recording everything before it was put to the torch.

It was hard work. Never in her life as a diplomat's daughter had Athaclena felt so exhausted. And yet she dared not let any scrap of evidence go undocumented. It was a matter of duty.

About an hour before dusk a contingent of gorillas trooped into the encampment, larger, darker, more crouched and feral-looking than their chim guardians. Under careful direction they took up simple tasks, helping to demolish the only home they had ever known.

The confused creatures watched as their Training and Testing Center and the Clients' Quarters melted into slag. A few even tried to halt the destruction, stepping in front of the smaller, soot-covered chims and waving vigorous hand signs – trying to tell them that this was a bad thing.

Athaclena could see how, by their lights, it wasn't logical. But then, the affairs of patron-class beings often did seem foolish.

Finally, the big pre-clients were left standing amid eddies of smoke with small piles of personal possessions – toys, mementos, and simple tools – piled at their feet. They stared blankly at the wreckage, not knowing what to do.

By dusk Athaclena had been nearly worn down by the emotions that fluxed through the compound. She sat on a tree stump, upwind of the burning clients' quarters, listening to the great apes' low, chuffing moans. Her aides slumped nearby with their cameras and bags of samples, staring at the destruction, the whites of their eyes reflecting the flickering flames.

Athaclena withdrew her corona until all she could *kenn* was the Unity Glyph – the coalescence to which all the beings within the forest valley contributed. And even that under-image wavered, flickered. She saw it *metaphorically* – weepy, drooping, like a sad flag of many colors.

There was honor here, she admitted reluctantly. These scientists had been violating a treaty, but they couldn't be accused of doing anything truly unnatural.

By any real measure, gorillas were as ready for Uplift as chimpanzees had been, a hundred Earth years before Contact. Humans had been forced to make compromises, back when Contact brought them into the domain of Galactic society. Officially, the tenancy treaty which sanctioned their rights to their homeworld was intended to see to it that Earth's fallow species list was maintained, so its stock of Potential for sentience would not be used up too quickly.

But everyone knew that, in spite of primitive man's legendary penchant for genocide, the Earth was still a shining example of genetic diversity, rare in the range of types and forms that had been left untouched by Galactic civilization.

Anyway ... when a pre-sentient race was ready for Uplift, it was ready!

No, clearly the treaty had been forced on humans while they were weak. They were allowed to claim neo-dolphins and neo-chimps – species already well on the road to sapiency before Contact. But the senior clans weren't about to let *Homo sapiens* go uplifting more clients than anybody else around!

Why, that would have given wolflings the status of senior patrons!

Athaclena sighed.

It wasn't fair, certainly. But that did not matter. Galactic society depended on oaths kept. A treaty was a solemn vow, species to species. Violations could not go unreported.

Athaclena wished her father were here. Uthacalthing would know what to make of the things she had witnessed here – the well-intended work of this illegal center, and the vile but perhaps legal actions of the Gubru.

Uthacalthing was far away, though, too far even to touch within the Empathy Net. All she could tell was that his special rhythm still vibrated faintly on the *nahakieri* level. And while it was comforting to close her eyes and inner ears and gently *kenn* it, that faint reminder of him told her little. *Nahakieri* essences could linger longer after a person left this life, as they had for her dead mother, Mathicluanna. They floated like the songs of Earth-whales, at the edges of what might be known by creatures who lived by hands and fire.

'Excuse me, ma'am.' A voice that was hardly more than a raspy growl broke harshly over the faint under-glyph, dispersing it. Athaclena shook her head. She opened her eyes to see a neo-chimp with soot-covered fur and shoulders stooped from exhaustion.

'Ma'am? You all right?'

'Yes. I am fine. What is it?' Anglic felt harsh in her throat, already irritated from smoke and fatigue.

'Directors wanna see you, ma'am.'

A spendthrift with words, this one. Athaclena slid down from the stump. Her aides groaned, chim-theatrically, as they gathered their tapes and samples and followed behind.

Several lift-lorries stood at the loading dock. Chims and gorillas carried stretchers onto flyers, which then lifted off into the gathering night on softly humming gravities. Their lights faded away into the direction of Port Helenia.

'I thought all the children and elderly were already evacuated. Why are you still loading humans in such a hurry?'

The messenger shrugged. The stresses of the day had robbed many of the chims of much of their accustomed spark. Athaclena was sure that it was only the presence of the gorillas – who had to be set an example – that prevented a mass attack of stress-atavism. In so young a client race it was surprising the chims had done so well.

Orderlies hurried to and from the hospital facility, but they seldom bothered the two human directors directly. The neo-chimp scientist, Dr Schultz, stood in front of them and seemed to be handling most matters himself. At his side, Chim Frederick had been replaced by Athaclena's old traveling companion, Benjamin.

On the stage nearby lay a small pile of documents and record cubes containing the genealogy and genetic record of every gorilla who had ever lived here.

'Ah, respected Tymbrimi Athaclena.' Schultz spoke with hardly a trace of the usual chim growl. He bowed, then shook her hand in the manner preferred by his people – a full clasp which emphasized the opposable thumb.

'Please excuse our poor hospitality,' he pleaded. 'We had intended to serve a special supper from the main kitchen ... sort of a grand farewell. But we'll have to make do with canned rations instead, I'm afraid.'

A small chimmie approached carrying a platter stacked with an array of containers.

'Dr Elayne Soo is our nutritionist,' Schultz continued. 'She tells me you might find these delicacies palatable.'

Athaclena stared at the cans. Koothra! Here, five hundred parsecs from home, to find an instant pastry made in her own hometown! Unable to help it, she laughed aloud.

'We have placed a full load of these, plus other supplies, aboard a flitter for you. We recommend you abandon the craft soon after leaving here, of course. It won't be long before the Gubru have their own satellite network in place, and thereafter air traffic will be impractical.'

'It won't be dangerous to fly *toward* Port Helenia,' Athaclena pointed out. 'The Gubru will expect an influx for many days, as people seek antidote treatments.' She motioned at the frantic pace of activity. 'So why the near-panic I sense here? Why are you evacuating the humans so quickly? Who ... ?'

Looking as if he feared to interrupt her, Schultz nevertheless cleared his throat and shook his head meaningfully. Benjamin gave Athaclena a pleading look.

'Please, ser,' Schultz implored with a low voice. 'Please speak softly. Most of our chims haven't really guessed ... ' He let the sentence hang.

Athaclena felt a cold thrill along her ruff. For the first time she looked closely at the two human directors, Taka and M'Bzwelli. They had remained silent all along, nodding as if understanding and approving everything being said.

The black woman, Dr Taka, smiled at her, unblinkingly. Athaclena's corona reached out, then curled back in revulsion.

She whirled on Schultz. 'You are killing her!'

Schultz nodded miserably. 'Please, ser. Softly. You are right, of course. I have drugged my dear friends, so they can put up a good front until my few good chim administrators can finish here and get our people away without a panic. It was at their own insistence. Dr Taka and Dr M'Bzwelli felt they were slipping away too quickly from effects of the gas.' He added sadly, weakly.

'You did not have to obey them! This is murder!'

Benjamin looked stricken. Schultz nodded. 'It was not easy. Chim Frederick was unable to bear the shame even this long and has sought his own peace. I, too, would probably take my life soon, were my death not already as inevitable as my human colleagues'.'

'What do you mean?'

'I mean that the Gubru do not appear to be very good chemists!' The elderly neo-chimp laughed bitterly, finishing with a cough. 'Their gas is killing some of the humans. It acts faster than they said it would. Also, it seems to be affecting a few of us chims.'

Athaclena sucked in her breath. 'I see.' She wished she did not.

'There is another matter we thought you should know about,' Schultz said. 'A news report from the invaders. Unfortunately, it was in Galactic Three; the Gubru spurn Anglic and our translation program is primitive. But we know it regarded your father.'

Athaclena felt removed, as if she were hovering above it all. In this state her numbed senses gathered in random details. She could *kenn* the simple forest ecosystem – little native animals creeping back into the valley, wrinkling their noses at the pungent dust, avoiding the area near the Center for the fires that still flickered there.

'Yes.' She nodded, a borrowed gesture that all at once felt alien again. 'Tell me.'

Schultz cleared his throat. 'Well, it seems your father's star cruiser was sighted leaving the planet. It was chased by warships. The Gubru say that it did not reach the Transfer Point.

'Of course one cannot trust what they say ...'

Athaclena's hips rocked slightly out of joint as she swayed from side to side. Tentative mourning – like a trembling of the lips as a human girl might begin to sense desolation.

No. I will not contemplate this now. Later. I will decide later what to feel.

'Of course you may have whatever aid we can offer,'

Chim Schultz continued quietly. 'Your flitter has weapons, as well as food. You may fly to where your friend, Robert Oneagle, has been taken, if you wish.

'We hope, however, that you will choose to remain with the evacuation for a time, at least until the gorillas are safely hidden in the mountains, under the care of some qualified humans who might have escaped.'

Schultz looked up at her earnestly, his brown eyes harrowed with sadness.

'I know it is a lot to ask, honored Tymbrimi Athaclena, but will you take our children under your care for a time, as they go into exile in the wilderness?'

23

EXILE

The gently humming gravitic craft hovered over an uneven row-of dark, rocky ridge-spines. Noon-shortened shadows had begun to grow again as Gimelhai passed its zenith and the flyer settled into the dimness between the stone spines. Its engines grumbled into silence.

A messenger awaited its passengers at the agreed rendezvous. The chim courier handed Athaclena a note as she stepped out of the machine, while Benjamin hurried to spread radar-fouling camouflage over the little flitter.

In the letter Juan Mendoza, a freeholder above Lome Pass, reported the safe arrival of Robert Oneagle and little April Wu. Robert was recuperating well, the message said. He might be up and about in a week or so.

Athaclena felt relieved. She wanted very much to see Robert – and not only because she needed advice on how to handle a ragged band of refugee gorillas and neo-chimpanzees.

Some of the Howletts Center chims – those affected by the Gubran gas – had gone to the city with the humans, hoping antidote would be given as promised . . . and that it would work. She had left only a handful of really responsible chim technicians to assist her.

Perhaps more chims would show up, Athaclena told herself – and maybe even some human officials who had escaped gassing by the Gubru. She hoped that somebody in authority might appear and take over soon.

Another message from the Mendoza household was written by a chim survivor of the battle in space. The militiaman requested help getting in touch with the Resistance Forces.

Athaclena did not know how to reply. In the late hours last night, as great ships descended upon Port Helenia and the towns on the Archipelago, there had been frantic telephone and radio calls to and from sites all over the planet. There were reports of ground fighting at the spaceport. Some said that it was even hand to hand for a time. Then there was silence, and the Gubru armada consolidated without further incident.

It seemed that in half a day the resistance so carefully planned by the Planetary Council had fallen completely apart. All traces of a chain of command had dissolved; for nobody had foreseen the use of hostage gas. How could anything be done when nearly every human on the planet was taken so simply out of action?

A scattering of chims were trying to organize here and there, mostly by telephone. But few had thought out any but the most nebulous plans.

Athaclena put away the slips of paper and thanked the messenger. Over the hours since the evacuation she had begun to feel a change within herself. What had yesterday been confusion and grief had evolved into an obstinate sense of determination.

I will persevere. Uthacalthing would require it of me and I will not let him down.

Wherever I am, the enemy will not thrive near me.

She would also preserve the evidence she had gathered, of course. Someday the opportunity might come to present it to Tymbrimi authorities. It could give her people an opportunity to teach the humans a badly needed lesson on how to behave as a Galactic patron race must, before it was too late.

If it was not too late already.

Benjamin joined her at the sloping edge of the ridge top. 'There!' He pointed into the valley below. 'There they are, right on time.'

Athaclena shaded her eyes. Her corona reached forth and touched the network around her. Yes. *And now I see them, as well.*

A long column of figures moved through the forest below, some small ones – brown in color – escorting a more numerous file of larger, darker shapes. Each of the big creatures carried a bulging backpack. A few had dropped to the knuckles of one hand as they shuffled along. Gorilla children ran amidst the adults, waving their arms for balance.

The escorting chims kept alert watch with beam rifles clutched close. Their attention was directed not on the column or the forest but at the sky.

The heavy equipment had already made it by circuitous routes to limestone caves in the mountains. But the exodus would not be safe until all the refugees were there at last, in those underground redoubts.

Athaclena wondered what was going on now in Port Helenia, or on the Earth-settled islands. The escape attempt of the Tymbrimi courier ship had been mentioned twice more by the invaders, then never again.

If nothing else, she would have to find out if her father was still on Garth, and if he still lived.

She touched the locket hanging from the thin chain around her neck, the tiny case containing her mother's legacy – a single thread from Mathicluanna's corona. It was cold solace, but she did not even have that much from Uthacalthing.

Oh, Father. How could you leave me without even a strand of yours to guide me?

The column of dark shapes approached rapidly. A low, growling sort of semi-music rose from the valley as they passed by, like nothing she had ever heard before. *Strength* these creatures had always owned, and Uplift had also removed some of their well-known frailty. As yet their destiny was unclear, but these were, indeed, powerful entities.

Athaclena had no intention of remaining inactive, simply a nursemaid for a gang of pre-sentients and hairy clients. One more thing Tymbrimi shared with humans was understanding of the need to *act* when wrong was being done. The letter from the wounded spacechim had started her thinking.

She turned to her aide.

'I am less than completely fluent in the languages of Earth, Benjamin. I need a word. One that describes an unusual type of military force.

'I am thinking of any army that moves by night and in the shadow of the land. One that strikes quickly and silently, using surprise to make up for small numbers and poor weapons. I remember reading that such forces were common in the pre-Contact history of Earth. They used the conventions of so-called civilized legions when it suited them, and innovation when they liked.

'It would be a *k'chu-non krann*, a wolfling army, unlike anything now known. Do you understand what I am talking about, Benjamin? Is there a word for this thing I have in mind?'

'Do you mean ... ?' Benjamin looked quickly down at the column of partly uplifted apes lumbering through the forest below, rumbling their low, strange marching song.

He shook his head, obviously trying to restrain himself, but his face reddened and finally the guffaws burst out, uncontainable. Benjamin hooted and fell against a spine-stone, then over onto his back. He rolled in the dust of Garth and kicked at the sky, laughing.

Athaclena sighed. First back on Tymbrim, then among humans, and now here, with the newest, roughest clients known – everywhere she found *jokers*.

She watched the chimpanzee patiently, waiting for the silly little thing to catch its breath and finally let her in on what it found so funny.

PART TWO

PATRIOTS

Evelyn, a modified dog,
Viewed the quivering fringe
of a special doily,
Draped across the piano, with some surprise –

In the darkened room,
Where the chairs dismayed
And the horrible curtains
Muffled the rain,
She could hardly believe her eyes –

A curious breeze, a garlic breath
Which sounded like a snore,
Somewhere near the Steinway
(or even from within)
Had caused the doily fringe to waft
And tremble in the gloom –

Evelyn, a dog, having undergone
Further modification
Pondered the significance of
Short Person Behavior
In pedal-depressed panchromatic resonance
And other highly ambient domains . . .

'Arf!' she said.

FRANK ZAPPA

24

FIBEN

Tall, gangling, storklike figures watched the road from atop the roof of a dark, low-slung bunker. Their silhouettes, outlined against the late afternoon sun, were in constant motion, shifting from one spindly leg to another in nervous energy as if the slightest sound would be enough to set them into flight.

Serious creatures, those birds. And dangerous as hell.

Nor *birds*, Fiben reminded himself as he approached the checkpoint. Not in the Earthly sense, at least.

But the analogy would do. Their bodies were covered with fine down. Sharp, bright yellow beaks jutted from sleek, swept-back faces.

And although their ancient wings were now no more than slender, feathered arms, they could fly. Black, glistening gravitic backpacks more than compensated for what their avian ancestors had long ago lost.

Talon Soldiers. Fiben wiped his hands on his shorts, but his palms still felt damp. He kicked a pebble with one bare foot and patted his draft horse on the flank. The placid animal had begun to crop a patch of blue native grass by the side of the road.

'Come on, Tycho,' Fiben said, tugging on the reins. 'We can't hang back or they'll get suspicious. Anyway, you know that stuff gives you gas.'

Tycho shook his massive gray head and farted loudly.

'I *told* you so.' Fiben waved at the air.

A cargo wagon floated just behind the horse. The dented, half-rusted bin of the farm truck was filled with rough burlap sacks of grain. Obviously the antigrav stator still worked, but the propulsion engine was kaput.

'Come on. Let's get on with it.' Fiben tugged again.

Tycho gamely nodded, as if the workhorse actually understood. The traces tightened, and the hover truck bobbed along after them as they approached the checkpoint.

Soon, however, a keening sound on the road ahead warned of oncoming traffic. Fiben hurriedly guided horse and wagon to one side. With a high-pitched whine and a rush of air, an armored hovercraft swept by. Vehicles like it had been cruising eastward intermittently, in ones and twos, all day.

He looked carefully to make sure nothing else was coming before leading Tycho back onto the road. Fiben's shoulders hunched nervously. Tycho snorted at the growing, unfamiliar scent of the invaders.

'Halt!'

Fiben jumped involuntarily. The amplified voice was mechanical, toneless, and adamant. 'Move, move to this side ... this side for inspection!'

Fiben's heart pounded. He was glad his role was to act frightened. It wouldn't be hard.

'Hasten! Make haste and present yourself!'

Fiben led Tycho toward the inspection stand, ten meters to the right of the highway. He tied the horse's tether to a railed post and hurried around to where a pair of Talon Soldiers waited.

Fiben's nostrils flared at the aliens' dusty, lavender aroma. *I wonder what they'd taste like*, he thought somewhat savagely. It would have made no difference at all to his great-to-the-tenth-grand-father that these were sentient beings. To his ancestors, a bird was a bird was a bird.

He bowed low, hands crossed in front of him, and got his first close look at the invaders.

They did not seem all that impressive up close. True, the sharp yellow beak and razorlike talons looked formidable. But the stick-legged creatures were hardly much taller than Fiben, and their bones looked hollow and thin.

No matter. These were starfarers – senior patrons-class beings whose Library-derived culture and technology were all but omnipotent long, long before humans rose up out of Africa's savannah, blinking with the dawnlight of fearful curiosity. By the time man's lumbering slowships stumbled upon Galactic civilization, the Gubru and their clients had wrested a position of some eminence among the powerful interstellar clans. Fierce conservatism and facile use of the Great Library had taken them far since their own patrons had found them on the Gubru homeworld and given them the gift of completed minds.

Fiben remembered huge, bellipotent battle cruisers, dark and invincible under their shimmering allochrous shields, with the lambent edge of the galaxy shining behind them ...

Tycho nickered and shied aside as one of the Talon Soldiers – its saber-rifle loosely slung – stepped past him to approach the tethered truck. The alien climbed onto the floating farm-hover to inspect it. The other guard twittered into a microphone. Half buried in the soft down around the creature's narrow, sharp breastbone, a silvery medallion emitted clipped Anglic words.

'State ... state identity ... identity and purpose!'

Fiben crouched down and shivered, pantomiming fear. He was sure not many Gubru knew much about neo-chimps. In the few centuries since Contact, little information would have yet passed through the massive bureaucracy of the Library Institute and found its way into local branches. And of course, the Galactics relied on the Library for nearly everything.

Still, verisimilitude was important. Fiben's ancestors had understood one answer to a threat when a counter-bluff was ruled out – submission. Fiben knew how to fake it. He crouched lower and moaned.

The Gubru whistled in apparent frustration, probably having gone through this before. It chirped again, more slowly this time.

'Do not be alarmed, you are safe,' the vodor medallion translated at a lower volume than before. 'You are safe ... safe ... We are Gubru ... Galactic patrons of high clan and family ... You are safe ... Young half-sentients are safe when they are cooperative ... You are safe ...'

Half-sentients ... Fiben rubbed his nose to cover a sniff of indignation. Of course that was what the Gubru were bound to think. And in truth, few four-hundred-year-old client races could be called fully uplifted.

Still, Fiben noted yet another score to settle.

He was able to pick out meaning here and there in the invader's chirpings before the vodor translated them. But one short course in Galactic Three, back in school, was not much to go on, and the Gubru had their own accent and dialect.

' ... You are safe ...' the vodor soothed. 'The humans do not deserve such fine clients ... You are safe ...'

Gradually, Fiben backed away and looked up, still trembling. *Don't overact*, he reminded himself. He gave the gangling avian creature an approximation of a correct bow of respect from a bipedal junior client to a senior patron. The alien would surely miss the slight embellishment – an extension of the middle fingers – that flavored the gesture.

'Now,' the vodor barked, perhaps with a note of relief. 'State name and purposes.'

'Uh, I'm F-Fiben ... uh, s-s-ser.' His hands fluttered in front of him. It was a bit of theater, but the Gubru might know that neo-chimpanzees under stress still spoke using parts of the brain originally devoted to hand control.

It certainly looked as if the Talon Soldier was frustrated. Its feathers ruffled, and it hopped a little dance. ' ... purpose ... purpose ... state your purpose in approaching the urban area!'

Fiben bowed again, quickly.

'Uh ... th' hover won't work no more. Th' humans are all gone ... nobody to tell us what to do at th' farm ...'

He scratched his head. 'I figured, well, they must need food in town ... and maybe some- somebody can fix th' cart in trade for grain ... ?' His voice rose hopefully.

The second Gubru returned and chirped briefly to the one in charge. Fiben could follow its GalThree well enough to get the gist.

The hover was a real farm tool. It would not take a genius to tell that the rotors just needed to be unfrozen for it to run again. Only a helpless drudge would haul an antigravity truck all the way to town behind a beast of burden, unable to make such a simple repair on his own.

The first guard kept one taloned, splay-fingered hand over the vodor, but Fiben gathered their opinion of chims had started low and was rapidly dropping. The invaders hadn't even bothered to issue identity cards to the neo-chimpanzee population.

For centuries Earthlings – humans, dolphins, and chims – had known the galaxies were a dangerous place where it was often better to have more cleverness than one was credited for. Even before the invasion, word had gone out among the chim population of Garth that it might be necessary to put on the old 'Yes, massa!' routine.

Yeah, Fiben reminded himself. *But nobody ever counted on* all *the humans being taken away!* Fiben felt a knot in his stomach when he imagined the humans – mels, fems, and children – huddled behind barbed wire in crowded camps.

Oh yeah. The invaders would pay.

The Talon Soldiers consulted a map. The first Gubru uncovered its vodor and twittered again at Fiben.

'You may go,' the vodor barked. 'Proceed to the Eastside Garage Complex ... You may go ... Eastside Garage ... Do you know the Eastside Garage?'

Fiben nodded hurriedly. 'Y-yessir.'

'Good ... good creature ... take your grain to the town storage area, then proceed to the garage ... to the garage ... good crea- ture ... Do you understand?'

'Y-yes!'

Fiben bowed as he backed away and then scuttled with an exag- geratedly bowlegged gait over to the post where Tycho's reins were tied. He averted his gaze as he led the animal back onto the dirt embankment beside the road. The soldiers idly watched him pass, chirping contemptuous remarks they were certain he could not understand.

Stupid damned birds, he thought, while his disguised belt camera panned the fortification, the soldiers, a hover-tank that whined by a few minutes later, its crew sprawled upon its flat upper deck, taking in the late afternoon sun.

Fiben waved as they swept by, staring back at him.

I'll bet you'd taste just fine in a nice orange glaze, he thought after the feathered creatures.

Fiben tugged the horse's reins. 'C'mon, Tycho,' he urged. 'We gotta make Port Helenia by nightfall.'

Farms were still operating in the Valley of the Sind.

Traditionally, whenever a starfaring race was licensed to colonize a new world, the continents were left as much as possible in their natural state. On Garth as well, the major Earthling settlements had been established on an archipelago in the shallow Western Sea. Only those islands had been converted completely to suit Earth-type animals and vegetation.

But Garth was a special case. The Bururalli had left a mess, and something had to be done quickly to help stabilize the planet's rocky ecosystem. New forms had to be introduced from the outside to prevent a complete biosphere collapse. That meant tampering with the continents.

A narrow watershed had been converted in the shadow of the Mountains of Mulun. Terran plants and animals that thrived here were allowed to diffuse into the foothills under careful observation, slowly filling some of the ecological niches left empty by the Bururalli Holocaust. It was a delicate experiment in practical planetary ecology, but one considered worthwhile. On Garth and on other catastrophe worlds the three races of the Terragens were building reputations as biosphere wizards. Even Mankind's worst critics would have to approve of work such as this.

And yet, something was jarringly wrong here. Fiben had passed three abandoned ecological management stations on his way, sampling traps and tracer 'bots stacked in disarray.

It was a sign of how bad the crisis must be. Holding the humans hostage was one thing – a marginally acceptable tactic by modern rules of war. But for the Gubru to be willing to disturb the resurrection of Garth, the uproar in the galaxy must be profound.

It didn't bode well for the rebellion. What if the War Codes really had broken down? Would the Gubru be willing to use planet busters?

That's the General's problem, Fiben decided. *I'm just a spy. She's the Eatee expert.*

At least the farms were working, after a fashion. Fiben passed one field cultivated with zygowheat and another with carrots. The robo-tillers went their rounds, weeding and irrigating. Here and there he saw a dispirited chim riding a spiderlike controller unit, supervising the machinery.

Sometimes they waved to him. More often they did not.

Once, he passed a pair of armed Gubru standing in a furrowed field beside their landed flitter. As he came closer, Fiben saw they were scolding a chim farmworker. The avians fluttered and hopped as they gestured at the drooping crop. The foreman nodded unhappily, wiping her palms on her faded dungarees. She glanced at Fiben as he passed by along the road, but the aliens went on with their rebuke, oblivious.

Apparently the Gubru were anxious for the crops to come in. Fiben hoped it meant they wanted it for their hostages. But maybe they had arrived with thin supplies and needed the food for themselves.

He was making good time when he drew Tycho off the road into a small grove of fruit trees. The animal rested, browsing on the Earth-stock grass while Fiben sauntered over behind a tree to relieve himself.

The orchard had not been sprayed or pest-balanced in some time, he observed. A type of stingless wasp was still swarming over the ping-oranges, although the secondary flowering had finished weeks before and they were no longer needed for pollination.

The air was filled with a fruity, almost-ripe pungency. The wasps climbed over the thin rinds, seeking access to the sweetness within.

Abruptly, without thinking, Fiben reached out and snatched a few of the insects. It was easy. He hesitated, then popped them into his mouth.

They were juicy and crunchy, a lot like termites. 'Just doing my part to keep the pest population down,' he rationalized, and his brown hands darted out to grab more. The taste of the crunching wasps reminded him of how long it had been since he had last eaten.

'I'll need sustenance if I'm to do good work in town tonight,' he thought half aloud. Fiben looked around. The horse grazed peacefully, and no one else was in sight.

He dropped his tool belt and took a step back. Then, favoring his still tender left ankle, he leaped onto the trunk and shimmied up to one of the fruit-heavy limbs. *Ah,* he thought as he plucked an almost ripe reddish globe. He ate it like an apple, skin and all. The taste was tart and astringent, unlike the bland human-style food so many chims claimed to like these days.

He grabbed two more oranges and popped a few leaves into his mouth for good measure. Then he stretched back and closed his eyes.

Up here, with only the buzz of the wasps for company, Fiben could almost pretend he didn't have a care, in this world or any other. He could put out of his mind wars and all the other silly preoccupations of sapient beings.

Fiben pouted, his expressive lips drooping low. He scratched himself under his arm.

'Ook, ook.'

He snorted – almost silent laughter – and imagined he was back in an Africa even his great-grandfathers had never seen, in forested hills never touched by his people's too-smooth, big-nosed cousins.

What would the universe have been like without men? Without Eatees? Without anyone at all but chimps?

Sooner or later we *would've invented starships, and the universe might have been ours.*

The clouds rolled by and Fiben lay back on the branch with narrowed eyes, enjoying his fantasy. The wasps buzzed in futile indignation over his presence. He forgave them their insolence as he plucked a few from the air as added morsels.

Try as he might, though, he could not maintain the illusion of solitude. For there arrived another sound, an added drone from high above. And try as he might, he couldn't pretend he did not hear alien transports cruising uninvited across the sky.

A glistening fence more than three meters high undulated over the rolling ground surrounding Port Helenia. It was an imposing barrier, put up quickly by special robot machines right after the invasion. There were several gates, through which the city's chim population seemed to come and go without much notice or impediment. But they could not help being intimidated by the sudden new wall. Perhaps that was its basic purpose.

Fiben wondered how the Gubru would have managed the trick if the capital had been a real city and not just a small town on a rustic colony world.

He wondered where the humans were being kept.

It was dusk as he passed a wide belt of knee-high tree stumps, a hundred meters before the alien fence. The area had been planned as a park, but now only splintered fragments lay on the ground all the way to the dark watchtower and open gate.

Fiben steeled himself to go through the same scrutiny as earlier at the checkpoint, but to his surprise no one challenged him. A narrow pool of light spilled onto the highway from a pair of pillar spots. Beyond, he saw dark, angular buildings, the dimly lit streets apparently deserted.

The silence was spooky. Fiben's shoulders hunched as he spoke softly. 'Come on, Tycho. Quietly.' The horse blew and pulled the floating wagon slowly past the steel-gray bunker.

Fiben chanced a quick glance inside the structure as he passed. A pair of guards stood within, each perched on one knotted, stick-thin leg, its sharp, avian bill buried in the soft down under its left arm. Two saber-rifles lay on the counter beside them, near a stack of standard Galactic faxboards.

The two Talon Soldiers appeared to be fast asleep!

Fiben sniffed, his flat nose wrinkling once more at the over-sweet alien aroma. This was not the first time he had seen signs of weaknesses in the reputedly invincible grip of the Gubru fanatics. They had had it easy until now – too easy. With the humans nearly all gathered and neutralized, the invaders apparently thought the only possible threat was from space. That, undoubtedly, was why all the fortifications he had seen had faced upward, with little or no provision against attack from the ground.

Fiben stroked his sheathed belt knife. He was tempted to creep into the guard post, slipping under the obvious alarm beams, and teach the Gubru a lesson for their complacency.

The urge passed and he shook his head. *Later*, he thought. *When it will hurt them more.*

Patting Tycho's neck, he led the horse through the lighted area by the guard post and beyond the gate into the industrial part of town. The streets between the warehouses and factories were quiet – a few chims here and there hurrying about on errands beneath the scrutiny of the occasional passing Gubru patrol skimmer.

Taking pains not to be observed, Fiben slipped into a side alley and found a windowless storage building not far from the colony's sole iron foundry. Under his whispered urging, Tycho pulled the floating hover over to the shadows by the back door of the warehouse. A layer of dust showed that the padlock had not been touched in weeks. He examined it closely. 'Hmmm.'

Fiben took a rag from his belt apron and wrapped it around the hasp. Taking it firmly in both hands, he closed his eyes and counted to three before yanking down hard.

The lock was strong, but, as he'd suspected, the ring bolt in the door was corroded. It snapped with a muffled 'crack!' Quickly, Fiben slipped the sheaf and pushed the door along its tracks. Tycho placidly followed him into the gloomy interior, the truck trailing behind. Fiben looked around to memorize the layout of hulking presses and metalworking machinery before hurrying back to close the door again.

'You'll be all right,' he said softly as he unhitched the animal. He hauled a sack of oats out of the hover and split it open on the ground. Then he filled a tub with water from a nearby tap. 'Ill be back if I can,' he added. 'If not, you just enjoy the oats for a couple of days, then whinny. I'm sure someone will be by.'

Tycho switched his tail and looked up from the grain. He gave Fiben a baleful look in the dim light and let out another smelly, gassy commentary.

'Hmph.' Fiben nodded, waving away the smell, 'You're probably right, old friend. Still, I'll wager *your* descendants will worry too much too, if and when somebody ever gives them the dubious gift of so-called intelligence.'

He patted the horse in farewell and loped over to the door to peer outside. It looked clear out there. Quieter than even the gene-poor forests of Garth. The navigation beacon atop the Terragens Building still flashed – no doubt used now to guide the invaders in their night operations. Somewhere in the distance a faint electric hum could be heard.

It wasn't far from here to the place where he was supposed to meet his contact. This would be the riskiest part of his foray into town.

Many frantic ideas had been proposed during the two days between the initial Gubru gas attacks and the invaders' complete seizure of all forms of communication. Hurried, frenzied telephone calls and radio messages had surged from Port Helenia to the Archipelago and to the continental outlands. During that time the human population had been thoroughly distracted and what remained of government communications were coded. So it was mainly chims, acting privately, who filled the airwaves with panicked conjectures and wild schemes – most of them horrifically dumb.

Fiben figured that was just as well, for no doubt the enemy had been listening in even then. Their opinion of neo-chimps must have been reinforced by the hysteria.

Still, here and there had been voices that sounded rational. *Wheat hidden amid the chaff.* Before she died, the human anthropologist Dr Taka had identified one message as having come from one of her former postdoctoral students – one Gailet Jones, a resident of Port Helenia. It was this chim the General had decided to send Fiben to contact.

Unfortunately, there had been so much confusion. No one but Dr Taka could say what this Jones person looked like, and by the time someone thought to ask her, Dr Taka was dead.

Fiben's confidence in the rendezvous site and password was slim, at best. *Prob'ly we haven't even got the night right,* he grumbled to himself.

He slipped outside and closed the door again, replacing the shattered bolt so the lock hung back in place. The ring tilted at a slight angle. But it could fool someone who wasn't looking very carefully.

The larger moon would be up in an hour or so. He had to move if he was going to make his appointment in time.

Closer to the center of Port Helenia, but still on the 'wrong' side of town, he stopped in a small plaza to watch light pour from the narrow basement window of a working chim's bar. Bass-heavy music caused the panes to shake in their wooden frames. Fiben could feel the vibration all the way across the street, through the soles of his feet. It was the only sign of life for blocks in all directions, if one did not count quiet apartments where dim lights shone dimly through tightly drawn curtains.

He faded back into the shadows as a whirring patroller robot cruised by, floating a meter above the roadway. The squat machine's turret swiveled to fix on his position as it passed. Its sensors must have picked him out, an infrared glow in the misty trees. But the machine went on, probably having identified him as a mere neo-chimpanzee.

Fiben had seen other dark-furred forms like himself hurrying hunch-shouldered through the streets. Apparently, the curfew was more psychological than martial. The occupation forces weren't being strict because there didn't seem to be any need.

Many of those not in their homes had been heading for places like this – the Ape's Grape. Fiben forced himself to stop scratching a persistent itch under his chin. This was the sort of establishment favored by grunt laborers and probationers, chims whose reproductive privileges were restricted by the Edicts of Uplift.

There were laws requiring even humans to seek genetic counseling when they bred. But for their clients, neo-dolphins and neo-chimpanzees, the codes were far more severe. In this one area normally liberal Terran law adhered closely to Galactic standards. It was that or lose chims and fins forever to some more senior clan. Earth was far too weak to defy the most honored of Galactic traditions.

About a third of the chim population carried green reproduction cards, allowing them to control their own fertility, subject only to guidance from the Uplift Board and possible penalties if they weren't careful. Those chims with gray or yellow cards were more restricted. They could apply, after they joined a marriage group, to reclaim and use the sperm or ova they stored with the Board during adolescence, before routine sterilization. Permission might be granted if they achieved meritorious accomplishments in life. More often, a yellow-card chimmie would carry to term and adopt an embryo engineered with the next generation of 'improvements' inserted by the Board's technicians.

Those with red cards weren't even allowed *near* chim children.

By pre-Contact standards, the system might have sounded cruel. But Fiben had lived with it all his life. On the fast track of Uplift a client race's gene pool was always being meddled with. At least chims were consulted as part of the process. Not many client species were so lucky.

The social upshot, though, was that there were classes among chims. And 'blue-carders' like Fiben weren't exactly welcome in places like the Ape's Grape.

Still, this was the site chosen by his contact. There had been no further messages, so he had no choice but to see if the rendezvous would be kept. Taking a deep breath, he stepped into the street and walked toward the growling, crashing music.

As his hand touched the door handle a voice whispered from the shadows to his left.

'Pink?'

At first he thought he had imagined it. But the words repeated, a little louder.

'Pink? Looking for a *party?*'

Fiben stared. The light from the window had spoiled his night vision, but he caught a glimpse of a small simian face, somewhat childlike. There was a flash of white as the chim smiled.

'Pink Party?'

He let go of the handle, hardly able to believe his ears. 'I beg your pardon?'

Fiben took a step forward. But at that moment the door opened, spilling light and noise out into the street. Several dark shapes, hooting with laughter and stinking of beer-soaked fur, pushed him aside as they stumbled past. By the time the revelers were gone and the door had closed again, the blurry, dark alley was empty once more. The small, shadowy figure had slipped away.

Fiben felt tempted to follow, if only to verify that he had been offered what he thought he had. And why was the proposition, once tendered, so suddenly withdrawn?

Obviously, things had changed in Port Helenia. True, he hadn't been to a place like the Ape's Grape since his college days. But pimps pandering out of dark alleys were not common even in this part of town. On Earth maybe, or in old threevee films, but here on Garth?

He shook his head in mystification and pulled open the door to go inside.

Fiben's nostrils flared at the thick aromas of beer and sniff-hi and wet fur. The descent into the club was made unnerving by the sharp, sudden glare of a strobe light, flashing starkly and intermittently over the dance floor. There, several dark shapes cavorted, waving what looked like small saplings over their heads. A heavy, sole-penetrating beat pounded from amplifiers set over a group of squatting musicians.

Customers lay on reed mats and cushions, smoking, drinking from paper bottles, and muttering coarse observations on the dancers' performances.

Fiben wended his way between the close-packed, low wicker tables toward the smoke-shrouded bar, where he ordered a pint of bitter. Fortunately, colonial currency still seemed to be good. He lounged against the rail and began a slow scan of the clientele, wishing the message from their contact had been less vague.

Fiben was looking for someone dressed as a fisherman, even though this place was halfway across town from the docks on Aspinal Bay. Of course the radio operator who had taken down the message from Dr Taka's former student might have gotten it all wrong on that awful evening while the Howletts Center burned and ambulances whined overhead. The chen had thought he recalled Gailet Jones saying something about 'a fisherman with a bad complexion.'

'Great,' Fiben had muttered when given his instructions. 'Real spy stuff. Magnificent.' Deep down he was positive the clerk had simply copied the entire thing down wrong.

It wasn't exactly an auspicious way to start an insurrection. But that was no surprise, really. Except to a few chims who had undergone Terragens Service training, secret codes, disguises, and passwords were the contents of oldtime thrillers.

Presumably, those militia officers were all dead or interned now. *Except for me. And my specialty wasn't intelligence or subterfuge. Hell, I could barely jockey poor old TAASF Proconsul.*

The Resistance would have to learn as it went now, stumbling in the dark.

At least the beer tasted good, especially after that long trek on the dusty road. Fiben sipped from his paper bottle and tried to relax. He nodded with the thunder music and grinned at the antics of the dancers.

They were all males, of course, out there capering under the flashing strobes. Among the grunts and probationers, feeling about this was so strong that it might even be called religious. The humans, who tended to frown over most types of sexual discrimination, did not interfere in this case. Client races had the right to develop their own traditions, so long as they didn't interfere with their duties or Uplift.

And according to this generation at least, chimmies had no place in the thunder dance, and that was that.

Fiben watched one big, naked male leap to the top of a jumbled pile of carpeted 'rocks' brandishing a shaker twig. The dancer – by day perhaps a mechanic or a factory laborer – waved the noise-maker over his head while drums pealed and strobes lanced artificial lightning overhead, turning him momentarily half stark white and half pitch black.

The shaker twig rattled and boomed as he huffed and hopped to the music, hooting as if to defy the gods of the sky.

Fiben had often wondered how much of the popularity of the thunder dance came from innate, inherited feelings of brontophilia and how much from the well-known fact that fallow, unmodified chimps in the jungles of Earth were observed to 'dance' in some crude fashion during lightning storms. He suspected that a lot of neo-chimpanzee 'tradition' came from elaborating on the publicized behavior of their unmodified cousins.

Like many college-trained chims, Fiben liked to think he was too sophisticated for such simple-minded ancestor worship. And generally he did prefer Bach or whale songs to simulated thunder.

And yet there were times, alone in his apartment, when he would pull a tape by the Fulminates out of a drawer, put on the headphones, and try to see how much pounding his skull could take without splitting open. Here, under the driving amplifiers, he couldn't help feeling a thrill run up his spine as 'lightning' bolted across the room and the beating drums rocked patrons, furniture, and fixtures alike.

Another naked dancer climbed the mound, shaking his own branch and chuffing loudly in challenge. He crouched on one knuckle as he ascended, a stylish touch frowned upon by orthopedists but meeting with approval from the cheering audience. The fellow might pay for the verisimilitude with a morning backache, but what was that next to the glory of the dance?

The ape at the top of the hill hooted at his challenger. He leapt and whirled in a finely timed maneuver, shaking his branch just as another bolt of strobe lightning whitened the room. It was a savage and powerful image, a reminder that no more than four centuries ago his wild ancestors had challenged storms in a like fashion from forest hilltops – needing neither man nor his tutling scalpels to tell them that Heaven's fury required a reply.

The chims at the tables shouted and applauded as the king of the hill jumped from the summit, grinning. He tumbled down the mound, giving his challenger a solid whack as he passed.

This was another reason females seldom joined the thunder dance. A full-grown male neo-chim had most of the strength of his natural cousins on Earth. Chimmies who wanted to participate generally played in the band.

Fiben had always found it curious that it was so different among humans. Their *males* seemed more often obsessed with the sound making and the females with dance, rather than vice versa. Of course humans were strange in other ways as well, such as in their odd sexual practices.

He scanned the club. Males usually outnumbered females in bars like this one, but tonight the number of chimmies seemed particularly small. They mostly sat in large groups of friends, with big males at the periphery. Of course there were the barmaids, circulating among the low tables carrying drinks and smokes, dressed in simulated leopard skins.

Fiben was beginning to worry. How was his contact to know him in this blaring, flashing madhouse? He didn't see anyone who looked like a scar-faced fisherman.

A balcony lined the three walls facing the dance mound. Patrons leaned over, banging on the slats and encouraging the dancers. Fiben turned and backed up to get a better look ... and almost stumbled over a low wicker table as he blinked in amazement.

There – in an area set aside by rope barrier, guarded by four floating battle-robots – sat one of the invaders. There was the narrow, white mass of feathers, the sharp breastbone, and that curved beak ... but this Gubru wore what looked like a woolen cap over the top of its head, where its comblike hearing organ lay. A set of dark goggles covered its eyes.

Fiben made himself look away. It wouldn't do to seem too surprised. Apparently the customers here had had the last few weeks to get used to an alien in their midst. Now, though, Fiben did notice occasional glances nervously cast up toward the box above the bar. Perhaps the added tension helped explain the frantic mood of the revelers, for the Grape seemed unusually rowdy, even for a working chim's bar.

Sipping his pint bottle casually, Fiben glanced up again. The Gubru doubtless wore the caplike muff and goggles as protection from the noise and lights. The guard-bots had only sealed off a square area near the alien, but that entire wing of the balcony was almost unpopulated.

Almost. Two chims, in fact, sat within the protected area, near the sharp-beaked Gubru.

Quislings? Fiben wondered. *Are there traitors among us already?*

He shook his head in mystification. Why was the Gubru here? What could one of the invaders possibly find of worth to notice?

Fiben reclaimed his place at the bar.

Obviously, they're interested in chims, and for reasons other than our value as hostages.

But what were those reasons? Why should Galactics care about a bunch of hairy clients that some hardly credited with being intelligent at all?

The thunder dance climaxed in an abrupt crescendo and one final crash, its last rumblings diminishing as if into a cloudy, stormy distance. The echoes took seconds longer to die away inside Fiben's head.

Dancers tumbled back to their tables grinning and sweating, wrapping loose robes around their nakedness. The laughter sounded hearty – perhaps too much so.

Now that Fiben understood the tension in this place he wondered why anyone came at all. Boycotting an establishment patronized by the invader would seem such a simple, obvious form of *ahisma*, of passive resistance. Surely the average chim on the street resented these enemies of all Terragens!

What drew such crowds here on a weeknight?

Fiben ordered another beer for appearances, though already he was thinking about leaving. The Gubru made him nervous. If his contact wasn't going to show, he had better get out of here and begin his own investigations. Somehow, he had to find out what was going on here in Port Helenia and discover a way to make contact with those willing to organize.

Across the room a crowd of recumbent revelers began pounding the floor and chanting. Soon the shout spread through the hall.

'Sylvie! Sylvie!'

The musicians climbed back onto their platform and the audience applauded as they started up again, this time to a much gentler beat. A pair of dummies crooned seductively on saxophones as the house lights dimmed.

A spotlight speared down to illuminate the pinnacle of the dancers' mound, and a new figure swept out of a beaded curtain to stand under the dazzling beam. Fiben blinked in surprise. What was a chimmie doing up there?

The upper half of her face was covered by a beaked mask crested with white feathers. The fem-chim's bare nipples were flecked with sparkles to stand out in the light. Her skirt of silvery strips began to sway with the slow rhythm.

The pelvises of female neo-chimpanzees were wider than their ancestors', in order to pass bigger-brained progeny. Nevertheless, swinging hips had never become an ingrained erotic stimulus – a male turn-on – as it was among humans.

And yet Fiben's heart beat faster as he watched her allicient movements. In spite of the mask his first impression had been of a young girl, but soon he realized that the dancer was a mature female, with faint marks of having nursed. It made her look all the more alluring.

As she moved the swaying strips of her skirt flapped slightly and Fiben soon saw that the fabric was silvery only on the outside. On the inner face each stripe of fabric tinted gradually upward toward a bright, rosy color.

He flushed and turned away. The thunder dance was one thing – he had participated in a few himself. But this was altogether different! First the little panderer in the alley, and now this? Had the chims of Port Helenia gone sex-crazed?

An abrupt, meaty pressure came down upon his shoulder. Fiben looked to see a large, fur-backed hand resting there, leading up a hairy arm to one of the biggest chims he had ever seen. He was nearly as tall as a small man, and obviously much stronger. The male neo-chimp wore faded blue work dungarees, and his upper lip curled back to expose substantial, almost atavistic canines.

'S'matter? You don't like Sylvie?' the giant asked.

Although the dance was still in its languid opening phase, the mostly male audience was already hooting encouragement. Fiben realized he must have been wearing his disapproval on his face, like an idiot. A true spy would have feigned enjoyment in order to fit in.

'Headache.' He pointed to his right temple. 'Rough day. I guess I'd better go.'

The big neo-chimp grinned, his huge paw not leaving Fiben's shoulder. 'Headache? Or maybe it's too bold for ya? Maybe you ain't had your first sharin' yet, hm?'

Out of the corner of his eye Fiben saw a swaying, teasing display, still demure but growing more sensual by the moment. He could feel the seething sexual tension beginning to fill the room and couldn't guess where it might lead. There were important reasons why this sort of display was illegal ... one of the few activities humans proscribed their clients.

'Of course I've been in sharings!' he snapped back. 'It's just that here, in public, it – it could cause a riot.'

The big stranger laughed and poked him amiably. 'When!'

'I beg your par- ... uh, what d'you mean?'

'I mean *when* did you first share, hm? From the way you talk, I'll bet it was one of those college parties. Right? Am I right, Mr Blue-card?'

Fiben glanced quickly right and left. First impressions notwithstanding, the big fellow seemed more curious and drunk than hostile. But Fiben wished he'd go away. His size was intimidating, and they might be attracting attention.

'Yeah,' he muttered, uncomfortable with the recollection. 'It was a fraternity initiation –'

The chimmie students back at college might be good friends with the chens in their classes, but they were never invited to *sharings*. It was just too dangerous to think of green-card females sexually. And anyway, they tended to be paranoid about pregnancy before marriage and genetic counseling. The possible costs were just too great.

So when chens at the University threw a party, they tended to invite girl chims from the far side of the tracks, yellow- and gray-card dummies whose flame-colored estrus was only an exciting sham.

It was a mistake to judge such behavior by human standards. *We have fundamentally different patterns*, Fiben had reminded himself back then, and many times since. Still, he had never found those sharings very satisfying or joyful. Maybe someday, when he found the right marriage group ...

'Sure, my sis used to go to those college parties. Sounded like fun.' The scarred chim turned to the bartender and slapped the polished surface. 'Two pints! One for me an' one for my college chum!' Fiben winced at the loud voice. Several others nearby had turned to look their way.

'So tell me,' his unwelcome acquaintance said, thrusting a paper bottle into Fiben's hand. 'Ya have any kids yet? Maybe some that are registered, but you never met?' He did not sound unfriendly, rather envious.

Fiben took a long swallow of the warm, bitter brew. He shook his head, keeping his voice low. 'It doesn't really work that way. An open birthright isn't the same as an unlimited-white card. If the planners have used any of my plasm I wouldn't know it.'

'Well why the hell not! I mean its bad enough for you bluesies, having to screw test tubes on orders from the Uplift Board, but to not even *know* if they've used the gunk ... Hell, my senior group-wife had a planned kid a year ago ... you might even be my son's gene-dad!' The big chim laughed and clapped Fiben again heavily on the shoulder.

This would never do. More heads were turning his way. All this talk about blue cards was not going to win him friends here. Anyway, he did *not* want to attract attention with a Gubru sitting less than thirty feet away. 'I really have to be going,' he said, and started to edge backward. 'Thanks for the beer ...'

Somebody blocked his way. 'Excuse me,' Fiben said. He turned and came face to face with four chims clothed in bright zipsuits, all staring at him with arms crossed. One, a little taller than the others, pushed Fiben back toward the bar.

'Of course this one's got *offspring*!' the newcomer growled. He had trimmed his facial hair, and the remaining mustache was waxed and pointed.

'Just look at those paws of his. I'll bet he's never done a day of honest chim's work. Probably he's a tech, or a *scientist*.' He made it sound as if the very idea of a neo-chimp wearing such a title was like a privileged child being allowed to play a complicated game of pretend.

The irony of it was that while Fiben's hands might be less callused than many here, under his shirt were burn-scars from crash landing on a hillside at Mach five. But it wouldn't do to speak of that here.

'Look, fellas, why don't I buy a round ...'

His money flew across the bar as the tallest zipsuiter slapped his hand. 'Worthless crap. They'll be collectin' it soon, like they'll be collecting you ape aristocrats.'

'*Shut up!*' somebody yelled from the crowd, a brown mass of hunched shoulders. Fiben glimpsed Sylvie, rocking up on the mound. The separate strips of her skirt rippled, and Fiben caught a glimpse that made him start with amazement. She really *was* pink ... her briefly exposed genitals in full estrus.

The zipsuiter prodded Fiben again. 'Well, Mr College-man? What good is your blue card gonna do you when the Gubru start collecting and sterilizing all you freebreeders? Hah?'

One of the newcomers, a slope-shouldered chim with a barbelate, receding forehead, had a hand in a pocket of his bright garment, gripping a pointed object. His sharp eyes seemed carnivorously intent, and he left the talking to his mustachioed friend.

Fiben had just come to realize that these guys had nothing to do with the big chim in the dungarees. In fact, that fellow had already edged away into the shadows. 'I – I don't know what you're talking about.'

'You don't? They've been goin' through the colonial records, bub, and picking up a lot of *college chims* like you for questioning. So far they've just been taking samples, but I've got friends who say they're planning a full-tilt purge. Now what d'you think of that?'

'*Shut th' fkup!*' someone yelled. This time several faces turned. Fiben saw glazed eyes, flecks of saliva, and bared fangs.

He felt torn. He wanted desperately to get out of here, but what if there were some truth in what the zipsuits were saying? If so, this was important information.

Fiben decided to listen a little while longer. 'That's pretty surprising,' he said, putting an elbow on the bar. 'The Gubru are fanatical conservatives. Whatever they do to other patron-level races, I'd bet they'd never interfere with the process of Uplift. It's against their own religion.'

Mustache only smiled. 'Is that what your college education tells you, blue boy? Well it's what the *Galactics* are saying that counts now.'

They were crowding Fiben, this bunch who seemed more interested in him than in Sylvie's provocative gyrations. The crowd was hooting louder, the music beating harder. Fiben's head felt as if it might crack under the noise.

'. . . too cool to enjoy a working man's show. Never done any real labor. But snap his fingers, an' our own chimmies come running!'

Fiben could tell something was false here. The one with the mustache was overly calm, his barratrous taunts too deliberate. In an environment like this, with all the noise and sexual tension – a true grunt shouldn't be able to focus so well.

Probationers! he realized suddenly. Now he saw the signs. Two of the zipsuited chims' faces bore the stigmata of failed genetic meddling – mottled, cacophrenic features or the blinking, forever-puzzled look of a cross-wired brain – embarrassing reminders that Uplift was an awkward process, not without its price.

He had read in a local magazine, not long before the invasion, how the trendy crowd in the Probie community had taken to wearing garishly colored zipsuits. Fiben knew, suddenly, that he had attracted the very worst kind of attention. Without humans around, or any sign of normal civil authority, there was no telling what these red-cards were up to.

Obviously, he had to get out of here. But how? The zipsuits were crowding him closer every moment.

'Look, fellas, I just came here to see what's happenin'. Thanks for your opinion. Now I really gotta go.'

'I got a better idea,' the leader sneered. 'How about we introduce you to a Gubru who'll tell you for himself what's goin' on? And what they're plannin' to do with college chims. Hah?'

Fiben blinked. Could these chens actually be cooperating with the invader?

He had studied Old Earth History – the long, dark centuries before Contract, when lonely and ignorant humanity had experimented horribly in everything from mysticism to tyranny and war. He had seen and read countless portrayals of those ancient times – especially tales of solitary men and women who had taken brave, often hopeless stands against evil. Fiben had joined the colonial militia partly in a romantic wish to emulate the brave fighters of the Maquis, the Palmach, and the Power Satellite League.

But history told of traitors, also: those who sought advantage wherever it could be found, even over the backs of their comrades.

'Come on, college chum. There's a bird I want you to meet.'

The grip on his arm was like a tightening vice. Fiben's look of pained surprise made the mustachioed chim grin. 'They put some extra strength genes into my mix,' he sneered. 'That part of their meddling worked, but not some of the others. They call me Irongrip, and *I* got no blue card, or even a yellow.

'Now let's go. We'll ask Bright Talon Squadron Lieutenant to explain what the Gubru's plans are for chim bright boys.'

In spite of the painful pressure on his arm, Fiben affected nonchalance. 'Sure. Why not? Are you willing to put a wager on it, though?' His upper lip curled back in disdain. 'If I remember my sophomore xenology right, the Gubru are pretty sharply clocked into a diurnal cycle. I'll bet behind those dark goggles of his you'll find that bloody bird is fast *asleep*. Think he'll like being awakened just to discuss the niceties of Uplift with the likes of you?'

For all his bravado, Irongrip was obviously sensitive about his level of education. Fiben's put-on assurance momentarily set him back, and he blinked at the suggestion that anyone could possibly sleep through all the cacophony around them.

Finally he growled angrily. 'We'll just see about that. Come on.'

The other zipsuits crowded close. Fiben knew he wouldn't stand a chance taking on all six of them. And there would be no calling on the law for help, either. Authority wore feathers these days.

His escorts prodded him through the maze of low tables. Lounging customers chuffed in irritation as Irongrip nudged them aside, but their eyes, glazed in barely restrained passion, were all on Sylvie's dance as the tempo of the music built.

A glance over his shoulder at the performer's contortions made Fiben's face feel hot. He backed away without looking and stumbled into a soft mass of fur and muscle.

'Ow!' a seated customer howled, spilling his drink.

'Sorry,' Fiben muttered, stepping away quickly. His sandals crunched upon another brown hand, producing yet another shout. The complaint turned into an outraged scream as Fiben ground the knuckle down then twisted away to apologize once again.

'Siddown!' a voice shouted from the back of the club. Another squeaked, 'Yeah! Beat it! Yer inna way!'

Irongrip glared suspiciously at Fiben and tugged on his arm. Fiben resisted briefly, then released, coming forward suddenly and shoving his captor back into one of the wicker tables. Drinks and sniff stands toppled, sending the seated chims scrambling to their feet, huffing indignantly.

'Hey!'

'Watch it, ye bastid Probie!'

Their eyes, already aflame from both intoxicants and Sylvie's dance, appeared to contain little reason anymore.

Irongrip's shaven face was pale with anger. His grasp tightened, and he began to motion to his comrades, but Fiben only smiled conspiratorially and nudged him with his elbow. In feigned drunken confidence, he spoke loudly.

'See what you did? I *told* you not to bump these guys on purpose, just to see if they're too stoned to talk ...'

From the nearby chims there came a hiss of intaken breath, audible even over the music.

'Who *says* I can't talk!' one of the drinkers slurred, barely able to form the words. The tipsy Borachio advanced a step, trying to focus on the source of this insult. 'Was it *you?*'

Fiben's captor eyed him threateningly and yanked him closer, tightening the vicelike grip. Still, Fiben managed to maintain his stage grin, and winked.

'Maybe they *can* talk, sorta. But you're right about them bein' a bunch *o* knuckle-walkers ...'

'*What!*'

The nearest chim roared and grabbed at Irongrip. The sneering mutant adroitly stepped aside and chopped with the edge of his free hand. The drunk howled, doubled up, and collided with Fiben.

But then the inebriate's friends dove in, shrieking. The hold on Fiben's arm tore loose as they were all swamped under a tide of angry brown far.

Fiben ducked as a snarling ape in a leather work harness swung on him. The fist sailed past and connected with the jaw of one of the zipsuited toughs. Fiben kicked another Probie in the knee as the chim grabbed for him, eliciting a satisfactory howl, but then all was a chaos of flying wicker-work and dark bodies. Cheap straw tables blew apart as they crashed down upon heads. The air filled with flying beer and hair.

The band increased its tempo, but it was barely to be heard over shrieks of outrage or combative glee. There was a wild moment as Fiben felt himself lifted bodily by strong simian arms. They weren't gentle.

'*Whoa-aoh!*'

He sailed over the riot and landed in a crash amidst a group of previously uninvolved revelers. The customers stared at him in momentarily stunned puzzlement. Before they could react, Fiben picked himself up from the rubble, groaning. He rolled out into the aisle, stumbling as a sharp pain seemed to lance through his still-tender left ankle.

The fight was spreading, and two of the bright zipsuits were headed his way, canines gleaming. To make matters worse, the customers whose party he had so rudely interrupted were on their feet now, chuffing in anger. Hands reached for him.

'Some other time, perhaps,' Fiben said politely. He hopped out of the debris away from his pursuers, hurriedly threading between the low tables. When there was no other way forward, he didn't hesitate, but stepped up onto a pair of broad, hunched shoulders and launched off, leaving his erstwhile springboard grunting in yet another pile of splintered wicker.

Fiben somersaulted over a last row of customers and tumbled to one knee in a broad, open area – the dance floor. Only a few meters away towered the thunder mound, where the alluring Sylvie was bearing down for her final grind, apparently oblivious to the growing commotion below.

Fiben moved quickly across the floor, intending to dash past the bar and out one of the exits beyond. But the moment he stepped out into the open area a sudden blaze of light lanced down from above, dazzling him! From all sides there erupted a tremendous cheer.

Something had obviously pleased the crowd. But what? Peering up against the glare, Fiben couldn't see that the ecdysiast had done anything new and spectacular – at least no more so than before. Then he realized that Sylvie was looking straight at him! Behind the birdlike mask he could see her eyes watching him in amusement.

He whirled. So were most of those not yet enveloped by the spreading brawl. The audience was cheering *him*. Even the Gubru in the balcony appeared to be tilting its goggle-shielded head his way.

There wasn't time to sort out the meaning of this. Fiben saw that several more of his tormentors had broken free of the melee. They were distinctive in their bright clothes as they gestured to each other, moving to cut him off from the exits.

Fiben quashed a sense of panic. They had him cornered. *There has to be another way out,* he thought furiously.

And then he realized where it would be. The *performer's door,* above and behind the padded dance mound! The beaded portal through which Sylvie had made her entrance. A quick scramble and he'd be up and past her – and gone!

He ran across the dance floor and leaped onto the mound, landing upon one of the carpeted ledges.

The crowd roared again! Fiben froze in his crouch. The glaring spotlights had followed him.

He blinked up at Sylvie. The dancer licked her lips and rocked her pelvis at him.

Fiben felt simultaneously repelled and powerfully drawn. He wanted to clamber up and grab her. He wanted to find some dark niche in a tree branch, somewhere, and hide.

Down below the fight was still going strong, but had stopped spreading. With only paper bottles and wicker furniture to use, the combatants seemed to have settled down to an amiable tumult of mutual mayhem, the original cause quite forgotten.

But on the edges of the dance floor stood four chims in bright zipsuits, watching him as they fingered objects in their pockets. There still looked to be only one way. Fiben clambered up onto another carpeted, 'rocky' cleft. Again, the crowd cheered in intensifying excitement. The noise, smells, confusion . . . Fiben blinked at the sea of fervent faces, all staring up at him in expectation. What was happening?

A flash of motion caught Fiben's attention. From the balcony over the bar, someone was waving at him. It was a small chim dressed in a dark, hooded cloak, standing out in this frenzied crowd, more than anything else, by a facial expression that was calm, icy sharp.

Fiben suddenly recognized the little *pimp*, the one who had accosted him briefly by the door to the Ape's Grape. The chim's voice didn't carry over the cacophony, but somehow Fiben picked out the mouthed words.

'Hey, dummy, look up!'

The boyish face grimaced. The panderer pointed overhead.

Fiben glanced upward . . . just in time to see a sparkling mesh start to fall from the rafters overhead! He leaped aside purely on instinct, fetching hard against another 'rock' as the fringe of the falling net grazed his left foot. Electric agony stroked his leg.

'Baboon shit! What in Goodall's name . . . ?' He cursed soundly. It took a moment for him to realize that part of the roaring in his ears was more applause. This turned into shouted cheers as he rolled over holding his leg, and thereby happened to escape yet another snare. A dozen loops of sticky mesh flopped out of a simulated rock to tauten over the area he had just occupied.

Fiben kept as still as possible while he rubbed his foot and glared about angrily, suspiciously. Twice he had almost been noosed like some dumb animal. To the crowd it might all be great fun, but he personally had no desire to be trussed up on some bizarre, lunatic obstacle course.

Below on the dance floor he saw bright zipsuits, left, right, and center. The Gubru on the balcony seemed interested, but showed no sign of intervening.

811

Fiben sighed. His predicament was still the same. The only direction he could go was up.

Looking carefully, he scrambled over another padded ridge. The snares appeared to be intended to be humiliating and incapacitating – and painful – but not deadly. Except in his case, of course. If *he* were caught, his unwanted enemies would be on him in a trice.

He stepped up onto the next 'boulder,' cautiously. Fiben felt a tickling falseness under his right foot and pulled back just as a trap door popped open. The crowd gasped as he teetered on the edge of the revealed pit. Fiben's arms windmilled as he fought for balance. From an uncertain crouch he leaped, and barely caught a grip on the next higher terrace.

His feet hung over nothingness. Fiben's breath came in heavy gasps. Desperately he wished humans hadn't edited some of his ancestors' 'unnecessary' instinctive climbing skills just to make room for trivialities such as speech and reason.

He grunted and slowly scrambled up out of the pit. The audience clamored for more.

As he panted on the edge of the next level, trying to see in all directions at once, Fiben slowly became aware that a public address system was muttering over the noise of the crowd, repeating over and over again, in clipped, mechanical tones.

... more enlightened approach to Uplift ... appropriate to the background of the client race ... offering opportunity to all ... unbiased by warped human standards ...

Up in its box, the invader chirped into a small microphone. Its machine-translated words boomed out over the music and the excited jabber of the crowd. Fiben doubted one in ten of the chims below were even aware of the E.T.s monologue in the state they were in. But that probably didn't matter.

They were being conditioned!

No wonder he had never heard of Sylvie's dance-mound striptease before, nor this crazy obstacle course. It was an innovation of the invaders!

But what was its *purpose?*

They couldn't have managed all this without help, Fiben thought angrily. Sure enough, the two well-dressed chims sitting near the invader whispered to each other and scribbled on clipboards. They were obviously recording the crowd's reactions for their new master.

Fiben scanned the balcony and noted that the little pimp in the cowled robe stood not far outside the Gubru's ring of robot guards. He spared a whole second to memorize the chim's boyish features. Traitor!

Sylvie was only a few terraces above him now. The dancer twitched her pink bottom at him, grinning as sweat beaded on his face. Human males had their own 'instant' visual triggers: rounded female breasts and pelvises and smooth fem skin. None of them could compare with the electric shiver a little color in the right place could send through a male chim.

Fiben shook his head vigorously. 'Out. Not in. You want out!'

Concentrating on keeping his balance, favoring his tender left ankle, he scrambled edgewise until he was around the pit, then crawled forward on his hands and knees.

Sylvie leaned over him, two levels up. Her scent carried even over the pungent aromas of the hall, making Fiben's nostrils flare.

He shook his head suddenly. There was *another* sharp odor, a cloying stink that seemed to be quite local.

With the little finger of his left hand he probed the terrace he had been about to climb upon. Four inches in he encountered a burning stickiness. He cried out and pulled back hard, leaving behind a small patch of skin.

Alas for instinct! His seared finger automatically popped into his mouth. Fiben almost gagged on the nastiness.

This was a fine fix. If he tried to move up or forward the sticky stuff would get him. If he retreated he would more than likely wind up in the pit!

This maze of traps did explain one thing that he had puzzled about, earlier. No wonder the chens below hadn't gone nuts and simply charged the hill the moment Sylvie showed pink! They knew only the cocky or foolhardy would dare attempt the climb. The others were content to observe and fantasize. Sylvie's dance was only the first half of the show.

And if some lucky bastard made it? Well, then, everybody would have the added treat of watching that, too!

The idea repelled Fiben. Private sharings were natural, of course. But this public lewdness was disgusting!

At the same time, he noted that he had already made it most of the way. He felt an old quickening in his blood. Sylvie swayed down a little toward him, and he imagined he could already touch her. The musicians increased their tempo, and strobes began flickering again, approaching like lightning. Artificial thunder echoed. Fiben felt a few stinging droplets, like the beginnings of a rainstorm.

Sylvie danced under the spots, inciting the crowd. He licked his lips and felt himself drawn.

Then, in the flicker of a single lightning flash, Fiben saw something equally enticing, more than attractive enough to pull him out of Sylvie's hypnotic sway. It was a small, green-lit sign, prim and legalistic, that shone beyond Sylvie's shoulder.

'EXIT,' it read.

Suddenly the pain and exhaustion and tension caused something to release inside Fiben. He felt somehow lifted above the noise and tumult and recalled with instant clarity something that Athaclena said to him shortly before he left the encampment in the mountains to begin his trek to town. The silvery threads of her Tymbrimi corona had waved gently as if in a breeze of pure thought.

There is a telling which my father once gave me, Fiben. It's a "haiku poem," in an Earthling dialect called Japanese. I want you to take it with you.'

'Japanese,' he had protested. *'It's spoken on Earth and on Calafia, but there aren't a hundred chims or men on Garth who know it!'*

But Athaclena only shook her head. *'Neither do I. But I shall pass the telling on to you, the way it was given to me.'*

What came when she opened her mouth then was less sound than a crystallization, a brief substrate of meaning which left an imprint even as it faded.

> *Certain moments qualify,*
> *In winter's darkest storm,*
> *When stars call, and you fly!*

Fiben blinked and the sudden relived moment The letters still glowed,

EXIT

shining like a green haven.

It all swept back, the noise, the odors, the sharp stinging of the tiny rainlike droplets. But Fiben now felt as if his chest had expanded twofold. Lightness spread down his arms and into his legs. They seemed to weigh next to nothing.

With a deep flexing of his knees he gathered himself and then launched off from his precarious perch to land on the edge of the next terrace, toes grasping inches from the burning, camouflaged glue. The crowd roared and Sylvie stepped back, clapping her hands.

Fiben laughed. He slapped his chest rapidly, as he had seen the gorillas do, beating countertime to the rolling thunder. The audience loved it.

Grinning, he stepped along the edge of the sticky patch, tracing its outline more by instinct than the faint difference in coloration.

Arms spread wide for balance, he made it look harder than it actually felt.

The ledge ended where a tall 'tree' – simulated out of fiberglass and green, plastic tassels – towered out of the slope of the mound.

Of course the thing was boobytrapped. Fiben wasted no time inspecting it. He leapt up to tap the nearest branch lightly and teetered precariously as he landed, drawing gasps from those below.

The branch reacted a delayed instant after he touched it ... just time enough for him to have gotten a solid grip on it, had he tried. The entire tree seemed to writhe. Twigs turned into curling ropes which would have shared an arm, if he were still holding on.

With a yip of exhilaration, Fiben leaped again, this time grabbing a dangling rope as the branch swayed down again. He rode it up like a pole vaulter, sailing over the last two terraces – and the surprised dancer – and flew on into the junglelike mass of girders and wiring overhead.

Fiben let go at the last moment and managed to land in a crouch upon a catwalk. For a moment he had to fight for balance on the tricky footing. A maze of spotlights and unsprung traps lay all around him. Laughing, he hopped about tripping releases, sending wires, nets, and tangle-ropes spilling over onto the mound. There were tubs of some hot, oatmeallike substance which he kicked over. Splatters on the orchestra sent the musicians diving for cover.

Now Fiben could easily see the outlines of the obstacle course. Clearly there was no real solution to the puzzle except the one he had used, bypassing the last few terraces altogether.

In other words, one had to cheat.

The mound was not a fair test, then. A chen couldn't hope to win by being more clever, only by letting others take the risks first, suffering pain and humiliation in the traps and deadfalls. The lesson the Gubru were teaching here was insidiously simple.

'Those bastards,' he muttered.

The exalted feeling was beginning to fade, and with it some of Fiben's temporary sense of borrowed invulnerability. Obviously Athaclena had given him a parting gift, a posthypnotic charm of sorts, to help him if he found himself in a jam. Whatever it was, he knew it wouldn't do to push his luck.

It's time to get out of here, he thought.

The music had died when the musicians fled the sticky oatmeal stuff. But now the public address system was squawking again, issuing clipped exhortations that were beginning to sound a bit frantic.

... unacceptable behavior for proper clients ... Cease expressions of approval for one who has broken rules ... One who must be chastised ...

The Gubru's pompous urgings fell flat, for the crowd seemed to have gone completely ape. When Fiben hopped over to the mammoth speakers and yanked out wires, the alien's tirade cut off and there rose a roar of hilarity and approval from the audience below.

Fiben leaned into one of the spotlights, swiveling it so that it swept across the hall. When the beam passed over them chims picked up their wicker tables and tore them apart over their heads. Then the spot struck the E.T. in the balcony box, still shaking its microphone in apparent outrage. The birdlike creature wailed and cringed under the sharp glare.

The two chimps sharing the VIP box dove for cover as the battle-robots rotated and fired at once. Fiben leaped from the rafters just before the spotlight exploded in a shower of metal and glass.

He landed in a roll and came to his feet at the peak of the dance mound ... King of the Mountain. He concealed his limp as he waved to the crowd. The hall shook with their cheers.

They abruptly quieted as he turned and took a step toward Sylvie.

This was the payoff. Natural male chimpanzees in the wild weren't shy about mating in front of others, and even uplifted neo-chimps 'shared' when the time and place was right. They had few of the jealousy or privacy taboos which made male humans so strange.

The evening's climax had come much sooner than the Gubru planned, and in a fashion it probably did not like, but the basic lesson could still be the same. Those below were looking for a vicarious sharing, with all the lessons psychologically tailored.

Sylvie's bird-mask was part of the conditioning. Her bared teeth shone as she wriggled her bottom at him. The many-slitted skirt whirled in a rippling flash of provocative color. Even the zipsuiters were staring now, licking their lips in anticipation, their quarrel with him forgotten. At that moment he was their hero, he was each of them.

Fiben quashed a wave of shame. *We're not so bad ... not when you figure we're only three hundred years old. The Gubru want us to feel we're barely more than animals, so we'll be harmless. But I hear even humans used to sometimes revert like this, back in the olden days.*

Sylvie chuffed at him as he approached. Fiben felt a powerful tightening in his loins as she crouched to await him. He reached for her. He gripped her shoulder.

Then Fiben swung her about to face him. He exerted strength to make her stand up straight.

The cheering crowd fell into confused muttering. Sylvie blinked up at him in hormone-drenched surprise. It was apparent to Fiben that she must have taken some sort of drug to get into this condition.

'F-frontwards?' she asked, struggling with the words. 'But Big-Beak s-said he wanted it to look natural ...'

Fiben took her face in his hands. The mask had a complex set of buckles, so he bent around the jutting beak to kiss her once, gently, without removing it.

'Go home to your mates,' he told her. 'Don't let our enemies shame you.'

Sylvie rocked back as if he had struck her a blow.

Fiben faced the crowd and raised his arms. 'Upspring of the wolflings of Terra!' he shouted. 'All of you. Go home to your mates! Together with our patrons we'll guide our *own* Uplift. We don't need Eatee outsiders to tell us how to do it!'

From the crowd there came a low rumbling of consternation. Fiben saw that the alien in the balcony was chirping into a small box, probably calling for assistance, he realized.

'Go home!' he repeated. 'And don't let outsiders make spectacles of us again!'

The muttering below intensified. Here and there Fiben saw faces wearing sudden frowns – chims looking about the room in what he hoped was dawning embarrassment. Brows wrinkled with uncomfortable thoughts.

But then, out of the babble below, someone shouted up at him.

'Whassamatta? Can't ya' get it up?'

About half of the crowd laughed uproariously. There were follow-up jeers and whistles, especially from the front rows.

Fiben really had to get going. The Gubru probably didn't dare shoot him down outright, not in front of the crowd. But the avian had doubtless sent for reinforcements.

Still, Fiben couldn't pass up a good straight line. He stepped to the edge of the plateau and glanced back at Sylvie. He dropped his pants.

The jeers stopped abruptly, then the brief silence was broken by whistles and wild applause.

Cretins, Fiben thought. But he did grin and wave before rebuttoning his fly.

By now the Gubru was flapping its arms and squawking, pushing at the well-dressed neo-chimps who shared its box. They, in turn, leaned over to shout at the bartenders. There were faint noises that sounded like sirens in the distance.

Fiben grabbed Sylvie for one more kiss. She answered this time, swaying as he released her. He paused for one last gesture up at the alien, making the crowd roar with laughter. Then he turned and ran for the exit.

Inside his head a little voice was cursing him for an extroverted idiot. *This wasn't what the General sent you to town to do, fool!*

He swept through the beaded curtain but then stopped abruptly, face to face with a frowning neo-chimp in a cowled robe. Fiben recognized the small chim he had briefly seen twice this evening – first outside the door to the Ape's Grape and later standing just outside the Gubru's balcony box.

'You!' he accused.

'Yeah, me.' the panderer answered. 'Sorry I can't make the same offer as before. But I guess you've had other things on your mind tonight.'

Fiben frowned. 'Get out of my way.' He moved to push the other aside.

'Max!' the smaller chim called. A large form emerged from the shadows. It was the huge, scar-faced fellow he had met at the bar, just before the zipsuited probationers showed up, the one so interested in his blue card. There was a stun gun in his meaty grasp. He smiled apologetically. 'Sorry, chum.'

Fiben tensed, but it was already too late. A rolling tingle washed over his body, and all he managed to do was stumble and fall into the smaller chim's arms.

He encountered softness and an unexpected aroma. *By Ifni*, he thought in a stunned instant.

'Help me, Max,' the nearby voice said. 'We've got to move fast.'

Strong arms lifted him, and Fiben almost welcomed the collapse of consciousness after this last surprise – that the young-faced little 'pimp' was actually a chimmie, a girl!

25

GALACTICS

The Suzerain of Cost and Caution left the Command Conclave in a state of agitation. Dealing with its fellow Suzerains was always physically exhausting. Three adversaries, dancing and circling, forming temporary alliances, separating and then reforming again, shaping an ever-changing synthesis. So it would have to be as long as the situation in the outer world was indeterminate, in a state of flux.

Eventually, of course, matters here on Garth would stabilize. One of the three leaders would prove to have been most correct, the best leader. Much rested upon that outcome, not least what color each of them would wear at the end, and what gender.

But there was no hurry to begin the Molt. Not yet. There would be many more conclaves before that day arrived, and much plumage to be shed.

Caution's first debate had been with the Suzerain of Propriety over using Talon Soldiers to subdue the Terragens Marines at the planetary spaceport. In fact, that initial argument had been little more than a minor squabble, and when the Suzerain of Beam and Talon finally tipped the scales, intervening in favor of Propriety, Caution surrendered with good grace. The subsequent ground battle had been expensive in good soldiery. But other purposes were served by the exercise.

The Suzerain of Cost and Caution had known that the vote would go that way. Actually, it had had no intention of winning their first argument. It knew how much better it was to begin the race in last place, with the priest and the admiral in temporary contention. As a result both of them would tend to ignore the Civil Service for a while. Setting up a proper bureaucracy of occupation and administration would take a lot of effort, and the Suzerain of Cost and Caution did not want to waste energy on preliminary squabbles.

Such as this most recent one. As the chief bureaucrat stepped away from the meeting pavilion and was joined by its aides and escorts, the other two expedition leaders could still be heard crooning at each other in the background. The conclave was over, yet they were still arguing over what had already been decided.

For the time being the military would continue the gas attacks, seeking out any humans who might have escaped the initial dosings. The order had been issued minutes ago.

The high priest – the Suzerain of Propriety – was worried that too many human civilians had been injured or killed by the gas. A few neo-chimpanzees had also suffered. This wasn't catastrophic from a legal or religious point of view, but it would complicate matters eventually. Compensation might have to be paid, and it could weaken the Gubru case if the matter ever came before interstellar adjudication.

The Suzerain of Beam and Talon had argued that adjudication was very unlikely. After all, with the Five Galaxies in an uproar, who was going to care about a few mistakes made on a tiny backwater dirtspeck such as this?

'We care!' the Suzerain of Propriety had declared. And it made its feelings clear by continuing to refuse to step off its perch onto the soil of Garth. To do so prematurely would make the invasion official, it stated. And that would have to wait. The small but fierce space battle, and the defiance of the spaceport, had seen to that. By resisting effectively, however briefly, the legal leaseholders had made it necessary to put off making any formal seizures for a while. Any further mistakes could not only harm Gubru claims here but prove terribly expensive as well.

The priest had fluttered its allochroous plumage after making that point, smugly certain of victory. After all, expense was an issue that would certainly win it an ally. Propriety felt it would surely be joined by Cost and Caution here!

How foolish, to think that the Molt will be decided by early bickerings such as these, the Suzerain of Cost and Caution had thought, and proceeded to side with the soldiery.

'Let the gassings go on, continue and seek out all those still in hiding,' it had said to the priest's dismay and the admiral's crowing delight.

The space battle and landings *had* proved extraordinarily costly. But not as expensive as it all would likely have been without the Coercion Program. The gas attacks had achieved the objective of concentrating nearly the entire human population onto a few islands where they might be simply controlled. It was easy to understand why the Suzerain of Beam and Talon wanted it that way. The bureaucrat, also, had experience dealing with wolflings. It, too, would feel much more comfortable with all of the dangerous humans gathered where it could see them.

Soon, of course, something would have to be done to curtail the high costs of this expedition. Already the Roost Masters had recalled elements of the fleet. Matters were critical on other fronts. It was vital to keep a tight perch-grip on expenses here. That was a matter for another conclave, however.

Today, the military suzerain was riding high. Tomorrow? Well, the alliances would shift and shift again, until at last a new policy emerged. And a queen.

The Suzerain of Cost and Caution turned and spoke to one of its Kwackoo aides.

'Have me driven, taken, conveyed to my headquarters.'

The official hover-barge lifted off and headed toward the buildings the Civil Service had appropriated, on headlands overlooking the nearby sea. As the vehicle hissed through the small Earthling town, guarded by a swarm of battle robots, it was watched by small crowds of the dark, hairy beasts the human wolflings prized as their eldest clients.

The Suzerain spoke again to its aide. 'When we arrive at the chancery, gather the staff together. We shall consider, contemplate, evaluate the new proposal the high priest sent over this morning concerning how to manage these creatures, these neo-chimpanzees.'

Some of the ideas suggested by the Propriety Department were daring to an extreme. There were brilliant features that made the bureaucrat feel proud of its future mate. *What a Threesome we shall make.*

There were other aspects, of course, that would have to be altered if the plan was not to lead to disaster. Only one of the Triumvirate had the sureness of grasp to see such a scheme to its final, victorious conclusion. That had been known in advance when the Roost Masters chose their Three.

The Suzerain of Cost and Caution let out a treble sigh and contemplated how it would have to manipulate the next leadership conclave. Tomorrow, the next day, in a week. That forthcoming squabble was not far off. Each debate would grow more urgent, more important as both consensus and Molt approached.

The prospect was one to look upon with a mixture of trepidation, confidence, and utter pleasure.

26

ROBERT

The denizens of the deep caverns were unaccustomed to the bright lights and loud noises the newcomers had brought with them. Hordes of batlike creatures fled before the interlopers, leaving behind a flat, thick flooring of many centuries' accumulated dung. Under limestone walls glistening with slow seepage, alkaline rivulets were now crossed by makeshift plank bridges. In drier corners, under the pale illumination of glow bulbs, the surface beings moved nervously, as if loath to disturb the stygian quiet.

It was a forbidding place to wake up to. Shadows were stark, acherontic, and surprising. A crag of rock might look innocuous and then, from a slightly different perspective, leap out in familiarity as the silhouette of some monster met a hundred times in nightmares.

It wasn't hard to have bad dreams in a place like this.

Shuffling in robe and slippers, Robert felt positive relief when at last he found the place he'd been looking for, the rebel 'operations center.' It was a fairly large chamber, lit by more than the usual sparse ration of bulbs. But furniture was negligible. Some ragged card tables and cabinets had been supplemented by benches fashioned from chopped and leveled stalagmites, plus a few partitions knocked together out of raw timber from the forest high above. The effect only made the towering vault seem all the more mighty, and the refugees' works all the more pitiful.

Robert rubbed his eyes. A few chims could be seen clustered around one partition arguing and sticking pins in a large map, speaking softly as they sifted through papers.

When one of them raised his voice too loud, echoes reverberated down the surrounding passages making the others look up in alarm. Obviously, the chims were still intimidated by their new quarters.

Robert shuffled into the light. 'All right,' he said, his larynx still scratchy from lack of use. 'What's going on here? Where is she and what is she up to now?'

They stared at him. Robert knew he must look a sight in rumpled pajamas and slippers, his hair uncombed and his arm in a cast to the shoulder.

'Captain Oneagle,' one of the chims said. 'You really should still be in bed. Your fever – '

'Oh, shove it ... Micah.' Robert had to think to remember the fellow's name. The last few weeks were still a fog in his mind. 'My fever broke two days ago. I can read my own chart. So tell me what's happening! Where is everybody? Where's Athaclena?'

They looked at each other. Finally one chimmie took a cluster of colored map pins out of her mouth. 'Th' General ... uh, Mizz Athaclena, is away. She's leading a raid.'

'A raid ...' Robert blinked. 'On the *Gubru*?' He brought a hand to his eyes as the room seemed to waver. 'Oh, Ifni.'

There was a rush of activity as three chims got in each other's way hauling over a wooden folding chair. Robert sat down heavily. He saw that these chims were all either very young or old. Athaclena must have taken most of the able-bodied with her.

'Tell me about it,' he said to them.

A senior-looking chimmie, bespectacled and serious, motioned the others back to work and introduced herself. 'I am Dr Soo,' she said. 'At the Center I worked on gorilla genetic histories.'

Robert nodded. 'Dr Soo, yes. I recall you helped treat my injuries.' He remembered her face peering over him through a fog while the infection raged hot through his lymphatic system.

'You were very sick, Captain Oneagle. It wasn't just your badly fractured arm, or those fungal toxins you absorbed during your accident. We are now fairly certain you also inhaled traces of the Gubru coercion gas, back when they dosed the Mendoza Freehold.'

Robert blinked. The memory was a blur. He had been on the mend, up in the Mendoza's mountain ranch, where he and Fiben had spent a couple of days talking, making plans. Somehow they would find others and try to get something started. Maybe make contact with his mother's government in exile, if it still existed. Reports from Athaclena told of a set of caves that seemed ideal as a headquarters of sorts. Maybe these mountains could be a base of operations against the enemy.

Then, one afternoon, there were suddenly frantic chims running everywhere! Before Robert could speak, before he could even stand they had plucked him up and carried him bodily out of the farm-house and up into the hills.

There were sonic booms . . . terse images of something immense in the sky.

'But . . . but I thought the gas was fatal if . . . ' His voice trailed off.

'If there's no antidote. Yes. But your dose was so small.' Dr Soo shrugged. 'As it is, we nearly lost you.'

Robert shivered. 'What about the little girl?'

'She is with the gorillas.' The chim nutritionist smiled. 'She's as safe as anyone can be, these days.'

He sighed and sat back a little. 'That's good at least.'

The chims carrying little April Wu must have got up to the heights in plenty of time. Apparently Robert barely made it. The Mendozas had been slower still and were caught in the stinking cloud that spilled from the belly of the alien ship.

Dr Soo went on. 'The 'rillas don't like the caves, so most of them are up in the high valleys, foraging in small groups under loose supervision, away from any buildings. Structures are still being gassed regularly, you know, whether they contain humans or not.'

Robert nodded. 'The Gubru are being thorough.'

He looked at the wall-board stuck with multicolored pins. The map covered the entire region from the mountains north across the Vale of Sind and west to the sea. There the islands of the Archipelago made a necklace of civilization. Only one city lay onshore, Port Helenia on the northern verge of Aspinal Bay. South and east of the Mulun Mountains lay the wilds of the main conti-nent, but the most important feature was depicted along the top edge of the map. Patient, perhaps unstoppable, the great gray sheets of ice encroached lower every year. The final bane of Garth.

The map pins, however, dealt with a much closer, nearer-term calamity. It was easy to read the array of pink and red markers. 'They've really got a grip on things, haven't they?'

The elderly chim named Micah brought Robert a glass of water. He frowned at the map also. 'Yessir. The fighting seems to all be over. The Gubru have been concentrating their energies around the Port and the Archipelago, so far. There's been little activity here in the mountains, except this perpetual harassment by robots dropping coercion gas. But the enemy has established a firm presence every place that was colonized.'

'Where do you get your information?'

'Mostly from invader broadcasts and censored commercial stations in Port Helenia. Th' General also sent runners and observers off in all directions. Some of them have reported back, already.'

'*Who's* got runners ... ?'

'Th' Gen- ... um.' Micah looked a bit embarrassed. 'Ah, some of the chims find it hard to pronounce Miss Athac-... Miss Athaclena's name, sir. So, well ...' His voice trailed off.

Robert sniffed. *I'm going to have to have a talk with that girl*, he thought.

He lifted his water glass and asked, 'Who did she send to Port Helenia? That's going to be a touchy place for a spy to get into.'

Dr Soo answered without much enthusiasm. 'Athaclena chose a chim named Fiben Bolger.'

Robert coughed, spraying water over his robe. Dr Soo hurried on. 'He *is* a militiaman, captain, and Miss Athaclena figured that spying around in town would require an ... um ... unconventional approach.'

That only made Robert cough harder. Unconventional. Yes, that described Fiben. If Athaclena had chosen old 'Trog' Bolger for that mission, then it spoke well for her judgment. She might not be stumbling in the dark, after all.

Still, she's hardly more than a kid. And an alien at that! Does she actually think she's a general? Commanding what? He looked around the sparsely furnished cavern, the small heaps of scrounged and hand-carried supplies. It was, all told, a pitiful affair.

'That wall map arrangement is pretty crude,' Robert observed, picking out one thing in particular.

An elderly chen who hadn't spoken yet rubbed the sparse hair on his chin. 'We could organize much better than this,' he agreed. 'We've got several mid-size computers. A few chims are working programs on batteries, but we don't have the power to run them at full capacity.'

He looked at Robert archly. 'Tymbrimi Athaclena insists we drill a geothermal tap first. But I figure if we were to set up a few solar collectors on the surface ... very well hidden, of course ...'

He let the thought hang. Robert could tell that one chim, at least, was less than thrilled at being commanded by a mere girl, and one who wasn't even of Earthclan or Terragens citizenship.

'What's your name?'

'Jobert, captain.'

Robert shook his head. 'Well, Jobert, we can discuss that later. Right now, will someone please tell me about this "raid"? What is Athaclena up to?'

Micah and Soo looked at each other. The chimmie spoke first.

'They left before dawn. It's already late afternoon outside. We should be getting a runner in any time now.'

Jobert grimaced again, his wrinkled, age-darkened face dour with pessimism. 'They went out armed with pin-rifles and concussion grenades, hoping to ambush a Gubru patrol.'

'Actually,' the elderly chim added dryly. 'We were expecting news more than an hour ago. I'm afraid they are already very late getting back.'

27

FIBEN

Fiben awoke in darkness, fetal-curled under a dusty blanket.

Awareness brought back the pain. Just pulling his right arm away from his eyes took a stoic effort of will, and the movement set off a wave of nausea. Unconsciousness beckoned him back seductively.

What made him resist was the filmy, lingering tracery of his dreams. They had driven him to seek consciousness ... those weird, terrifying images and sensations. The last, vivid scene had been a cratered desert landscape. Lightning struck the stark sands all around him, pelting him with charged, sparking shrapnel whichever way he tried to duck or hide.

He recalled trying to protest, as if there were words that might somehow placate a storm. But speech had been taken from him.

By effort of will, Fiben managed to roll over on the creaking cot. He had to knuckle-rub his eyes before they would open, and then all they made out was the dimness of a shabby little room. A thin line of light traced the overlap of heavy black curtains covering a small window.

His muscles trembled spasmodically. Fiben remembered the last time he had felt anywhere near this lousy, back on Cilmar Island. A band of neo-chimp circus entertainers from Earth had dropped in to do a show. The visiting 'strongman' offered to wrestle the college champion, and like an idiot Fiben had accepted.

It had been weeks before he walked again without a limp.

Fiben groaned and sat up. His inner thighs burned like fire. 'Oh, mama,' he moaned. 'I'll never scissors-hold again!' His skin and body hair were moist. Fiben sniffed the pungent odor of Dalsebo, a strong muscle relaxant. So, at least his captors had taken efforts to spare him the worst aftereffects of stunning. Still, his brain felt like a misbehaving gyroscope when he tried to rise. Fiben grabbed the teetering bedside table for support as he stood up, and held his side while he shuffled over to the solitary window.

He grabbed rough fabric on both sides of the thin line of light and snapped the drapes apart. Immediately Fiben stumbled back, both arms raised to ward off the sudden brightness. Afterimages whirled.

'Ugh,' he commented succinctly. It was barely a croak. What was this place? Some prison of the Gubru? Certainly he wasn't aboard an invader battleship. He doubted the fastidious Galactics would use native wood furnishings, or decorate in Late Antediluvian Shabby.

He lowered his arms, blinking away tears. Through the window he saw an enclosed yard, an unkempt vegetable garden, a couple of climbing trees. It looked like a typical small commune-house, the sort a chim group marriage family might own.

Just visible over the nearby roofs, a line of hilltop eucalyptus trees told him he was still in Port Helenia, not far from Sea Bluff Park.

Perhaps the Gubru were leaving his interrogation to their quislings. Or his captors could be those hostile Probationers. They might have their own plans for him.

Fiben's mouth felt as if dust weavers had been spinning traps in it. He saw a water pitcher on the room's only table. One cup was already poured. He stumbled over and grabbed for it, but missed and knocked it crashing to the floor.

Focus! Fiben told himself. *If you want to get out of this, try to think like a member of a starfaring race!*

It was hard. The subvocalized words were painful just behind his forehead. He could feel his mind try to retreat ... to abandon Anglic for a simpler, more natural way of thinking.

Fiben resisted an almost overpowering urge to simply grab up the pitcher and drink from it directly. Instead, in spite of his thirst, he concentrated on each step involved in pouring another cup.

His fingers trembled on the pitcher's handle.

Focus!

Fiben recalled an ancient Zen adage. 'Before enlightenment, chop wood, pour water. After enlightenment, chop wood, pour water.'

Slowing down in spite of his thirst, he turned the simple act of pouring into an exercise. Holding on with two shaking hands, Fiben managed to pour himself about half a cupful, slopping about as much onto the table and floor. No matter. He took up the tumbler and drank in deep, greedy swallows.

The second cup poured easier. His hands were steadier.

That's it. Focus . . . Choose the hard path, the one using thought. At least chims had it easier than neo-dolphins. The other Earthly client race was a hundred years younger and had to use three languages in order to think at all!

He was concentrating so hard that he didn't notice when the door behind him opened.

'Well, for a boy who's had such a busy night, you sure are chipper this morning.'

Fiben whirled. Water splattered the wall as he brought up the cup to throw it, but the sudden movement seemed to send his brain spinning in his head. The cup clattered to the floor and Fiben clutched at his temples, groaning under a wave of vertigo.

Blearily, he saw a chimmie in a blue sarong. She approached carrying a tray. Fiben fought to remain standing, but his legs folded and he sank to his knees.

'Bloody fool,' he heard her say. Bile in his mouth was only one reason he couldn't answer.

She set her tray on the table and took hold of his arm. 'Only an idiot would try to get up after taking a full stunner jolt at close range!'

Fiben snarled and tried to shake her hands off. Now he remembered! This was the little 'pimp' from the Ape's Grape. The one who had stood in the balcony not far from the Gubru and who had him stunned just as he was about to make his escape.

'Lemme 'lone,' he said. 'I don' need any help from a damn traitor!'

At least that was what he had intended to say, but it came out more as a slurred mumble. 'Right. Anything you say,' the chimmie answered evenly. She hauled him by one arm back to the bed. In spite of her slight size, she was quite strong.

Fiben groaned as he landed on the lumpy mattress. He kept trying to gather himself together, but rational thought seemed to swell and fade like ocean surf.

'I'm going to give you something. You'll sleep for at least ten hours. Then, maybe, you'll be ready to answer some questions.'

Fiben couldn't spare the energy to curse her. All his attention was given over to finding a focus, something to center on. Anglic wasn't good enough anymore. He tried Galactic Seven.

'*Na . . . Ka . . . tcha . . . kresh . . .*' he counted thickly.

'Yes, yes,' he heard her say. 'By now we're all quite aware how well educated you are.'

Fiben opened his eyes as the chimmie leaned over him, a capsule in her hand. With a finger snap she broke it, releasing a cloud of heavy vapor.

He tried to hold his breath against the anesthetic gas, knowing it was useless. At the same time, Fiben couldn't help noticing that she was actually fairly pretty – with a small, childlike jaw and smooth skin. Only her wry, bitter smile ruined the picture.

'My, you *are* an obstinate chen, aren't you? Be a good boy now, breathe in and rest,' she commanded.

Unable to hold out any longer, Fiben had to inhale at last. A sweet odor filled his nostrils, like overripe forest fruit. Awareness began dissipating in a floating glow.

It was only then Fiben realized that she, too, had spoken in perfect, unaccented Galactic Seven.

28

GOVERNMENT IN HIDING

Megan Oneagle blinked away tears. She wanted to turn away, not to look, but she forced herself to watch the carnage one more time.

The large holo-tank depicted a night scene, a rain-driven beach that shone dimly in shades of gray under faintly visible brooding cliffs. There were no moons, no stars, in fact hardly any light at all. The enhancement cameras had been at their very limits taking these pictures.

On the beach she could barely make out five black shapes that crawled ashore, dashed across the sand, and began climbing the low, crumbling bluffs.

'You can tell they followed procedures precisely,' Major Prathachulthorn of the Terragens Marines explained. 'First the submarine released the advance divers, who went ahead to scout and set up surveillance. Then, when it seemed the coast was clear, the sabots were released.'

Megan watched as little boats bobbed to the surface – black globes rising amid small clouds of bubbles – which then headed quickly for shore. They landed, covers popped off, and more dark figures emerged.

'They carried the finest equipment available. Their training was the best. These were Terragens Marines.'

So? Megan shook her head. *Does that mean they did not have mothers?*

She understood what Prathachulthorn was saying, however. If calamity could befall these professionals, who could blame Garth's colonial militia for the disasters of the last few months?

The black shapes moved toward the cliffs, stoop-shouldered under heavy burdens.

For weeks, now, the remnants still under Megan's command had sat with her, deep in their underwater refuge, pondering the collapse of all their well-laid plans for an organized resistance. The agents and saboteurs had been ready, the arms caches and cells organized. Then came the cursed Gubru coercion gas, and all their careful schemes collapsed under those roiling clouds of deadly smoke.

What few humans remained on the mainland were certainly dead by now, or as good as dead. What was frustrating was that nobody, not even the enemy in their broadcasts, seemed to know who or how many had made it to the islands in time for antidote treatment and internment.

Megan avoided thinking about her son. With any luck he was now on Cilmar Island, brooding with his friends in some pub, or complaining to a crowd of sympathetic girls how his mother had kept him out of the war. She could only hope and pray that was the case, and that Uthacalthing's daughter was safe as well.

More of a cause for perplexity was the fate of the Tymbrimi Ambassador himself. Uthacalthing had promised to follow the Planetary Council into hiding, but he had never appeared. There were reports that his ship had tried for deepspace instead, and was destroyed.

So many lives. Lost to what purpose?

Megan watched the display as the sabots began edging back into the water. The main force of men was already climbing the bluffs.

Without humans, of course, any hope of resistance was out of the question. A few of the cleverest chims might strike a blow, here or there, but what could really be expected of them without their patrons?

One purpose of this landing had been to start something going again, to adapt and adjust to new circumstances.

For the third time – even though she knew it was coming – Megan was caught by surprise as lightning suddenly burst upon the beach. In an instant everything was bathed in brilliant colors.

First to explode were the little boats, the sabots.

Next came the men.

'The sub pulled its camera in and dived just in time,' Major Prathachulthorn said.

The display went blank. The woman marine lieutenant who had operated the projector turned on the lights. The other members of the Council blinked, adjusting to the light. Several dabbed their eyes.

Major Prathachulthorn's South Asian features were darkly serious as he spoke again. 'It's the same thing as during the space battle, and when they somehow knew to gas every secret base we'd set up on land. Somehow they always find out where we are.'

'Do you have any idea how they're doing it?' one of the council members asked.

Vaguely, Megan recognized that it was the female Marine officer, Lieutenant Lydia McCue, who answered. The young woman shook her head. 'We have all of our technicians working on the problem, of course. But until we have some idea how they're doing it, we don't want to waste any more men trying to sneak ashore.'

Megan Oneagle closed her eyes. 'I think we are in no condition, now, to discuss matters any further. I declare this meeting adjourned.'

When she retired to her tiny room, Megan thought she would cry. Instead, though, she merely sat on the edge of her bed, in complete darkness, allowing her eyes to look in the direction she knew her hands lay.

After a while, she felt she could almost see them, fingers like blobs resting tiredly on her knees. She imagined they were stained – a deep, sanguinary red.

29

ROBERT

Deep underground there was no way to sense the natural passage of time. Still, when Robert jerked awake in his chair, he knew exactly when it was.

Late. Too damn late. Athaclena was due back hours ago.

If he weren't still little more than an invalid he would have overcome the objections of Micah and Dr Soo and gone topside himself, looking for the long overdue raiding party. As it was, the two chim scientists had nearly had to use force to stop him.

Traces of Robert's fever still returned now and then. He wiped his forehead and suppressed some momentary shivers. *No,* he thought. *I am in control!*

He stood up and picked his way carefully toward the sounds of muttered argument, where he found a pair of chims working over the pearly light of a salvaged level-seventeen computer. Robert sat on a packing crate behind them and listened for a while. When he made a suggestion they tried it, and it worked. Soon he had almost managed to push aside his worries as he immersed himself in work, helping the chims sketch out military tactics programming for a machine that had never been designed for anything more hostile than chess.

Somebody came by with a pitcher of juice. He drank. Someone handed him a sandwich. He ate.

An indeterminate time later a shout echoed through the underground chamber. Feet thumped hurriedly over low wooden bridges. Robert's eyes had grown accustomed to the bright screen, so it was out of a dark gloom that he saw chims hurrying past, seizing assorted, odd-lot weapons as they rushed up the passage leading to the surface.

He stood and grabbed at the nearest running brown form. 'What's happening?'

He might as well have tried to halt a bull. The chim tore free without even glancing his way and vanished up the ragged tunnel. The next one he waved down actually looked at him and halted restlessly. 'It's th' expedition,' the nervous chen explained. 'They've come back ... At least I hear some of 'em have.'

Robert let the fellow go. He began casting around the chamber for a weapon of his own. If the raiding party had been followed back here ...

There wasn't anything handy, of course. He realized bitterly that a rifle would hardly do him any good with his right arm immobilized. The chims probably wouldn't let him fight anyway. They'd more likely carry him bodily out of harm's way, deeper into the caves.

For a while there was silence. A few elderly chims waited with him for the sound of gunfire.

Instead, there came voices, gradually growing louder. The shouts sounded more excited than fearful.

Something seemed to stroke him, just above the ears. He hadn't had much practice since the accident, but now Robert's simple empathy sense felt a familiar trace blow into the chamber. He began to hope.

A babbling crowd of figures turned the bend – ragged, filthy neo-chimpanzees carrying slung weapons, some sporting bandages. The instant he saw Athaclena, a knot seemed to let go inside of Robert.

Just as quickly, though, another worry took its place. The Tymbrimi girl had been using the *gheer* transformation, clearly. He felt the rough edges of her exhaustion, and her face was gaunt.

Moreover, Robert could tell that she was still hard at work. Her corona stood puffed out, *sparkling* without light. The chims hardly seemed to notice as stay-at-homes eagerly pumped the jubilant raiders for news. But Robert realized that Athaclena was concentrating hard to *craft* that mood. It was too tenuous, too tentative to sustain itself without her.

'Robert!' Her eyes widened. 'Should you be out of bed? Your fever only broke yesterday.'

'I'm fine. But – '

'Good. I am happy to see you ambulatory, at last.'

Robert watched as two heavily bandaged forms were rushed past on stretchers toward their makeshift hospital. He sensed Athaclena's effort to divert attention away from the bleeding, perhaps dying, soldiers until they were out of sight. Only the presence of the chims made Robert keep his voice low and even. 'I want to talk with you, Athaclena.'

She met his eyes, and for a brief instant Robert thought he *kenned* a faint form, turning and whirling above the floating tendrils of her corona. It was a harried glyph.

The returning warriors were busy with food and drink, bragging to their eager peers. Only Benjamin, a hand-sewn lieutenant's patch on his arm, stood soberly beside Athaclena. She nodded. 'Very well, Robert. Let us go someplace private.'

'Let me guess,' he said, levelly. 'You got your asses kicked.'

Chim Benjamin winced, but he did not disagree. He tapped a spot on an outstretched map.

'We hit them here, in Yenching Gap,' he said. 'It was our fourth raid, so we thought we knew what to expect.'

'Your *fourth.*' Robert turned to Athaclena. 'How long has this been going on?'

She had been picking daintily at a pocket pastry filled with something pungently aromatic. She wrinkled her nose. 'We have been practicing for about a week, Robert. But this was the first time we tried to do any real harm.'

'And?'

Benjamin seemed immune to Athaclena's mood-tailoring. Perhaps it was intentional, for she would need at least one aide whose judgment was unaffected. Or maybe he was just too bright. He rolled his eyes. 'We're the ones who got hurt.' He went on to explain. 'We split into five groups. Mizz Athaclena insisted. It's what saved us.'

'What was your target?'

'A small patrol. Two light hover-tanks and a couple of open land-cars.

Robert pondered the site on the map, where one of the few roads entered the first rank of mountains. From what others had told him,

832

the enemy were seldom seen above the Sind. They seemed content to control space, the Archipelago, and the narrow strip of settlement along the coast around Port Helenia.

After all, why should they bother with the back country? They had nearly every human safely locked away. Garth was theirs.

Apparently, the rebels' first three forays had been exercises – a few former militia noncoms among the chims trying to teach raw recruits how to move and fight under the forest shadows. Fourth time out, though, they had felt ready to contact the enemy.

'From the beginning they seemed to know we were there,' Benjamin continued. 'We followed them as they patrolled, practiced ducking through the trees and keeping them in sight, like before. Then ...'

'Then you actually attacked the patrol.'

Benjamin nodded. 'We *suspected* they knew where we were. But we had to be sure. Th' General came up with a plan ...'

Robert blinked, then nodded. He still wasn't used to Athaclena's new honorary title. His puzzlement grew as he listened to Benjamin describe this morning's action.

The ambush had been set up so five different parties would each, in turn, get a shot at the patrol with minimum risk.

And without much chance to damage the enemy, either, he noted. The ambuscades were mostly too high or too far away to offer very good shots. With hunting rifles and concussion grenades, what harm could they do?

One small Gubru landcar had been destroyed in the initial fusillade. Another was lightly damaged before withering fire from the tanks forced each squad into retreat. Air cover arrived swiftly from the coast, and the raiders fled barely in time. The aggressive portion of the raid was finished in less than fifteen minutes. The retreat and circuitous covering of tracks took much longer.

'The Gubru weren't fooled, were they?' Robert asked.

Benjamin shook his head. 'They always seemed to be able to pick us out. It's a miracle we were able to ding them at all, and a bigger one we got away.'

Robert glanced at the 'General.' He started to voice his disapproval, but then he looked back at the map one more time, pondering the positions the ambushers had taken up. He traced the lines of fire, the avenues of retreat.

'You suspected as much,' he said at last to Athaclena.

Her eyes came slightly together and separated again, a Tymbrimi shrug. 'I did not think we should approach too closely, on our first encounter.'

Robert nodded. Indeed, if closer, 'better' ambush sites had been chosen, few if any of the chims would have made it back alive.

The plan was good.

No, not good. *Inspired*. It hadn't been intended to hurt the enemy but to build confidence. The troops had been dispersed so everyone would get to fire at the patrol with minimum risk. The raiders could return home swaggering, but most important, they would make it home.

Even so, they had been hurt. Robert could sense how exhausted Athaclena was, partly from the effort of maintaining everyone's mood of 'victory.'

He felt a touch on his knee and took Athaclena's hand in his own. Her long, delicate fingers closed tightly, and he felt her triple-beat pulse.

Their eyes met.

'We turned a possible disaster into a minor success today,' Benjamin said. 'But so long as the enemy always knows where we are, I don't see how we can ever do more than play tag with them. And even that game'll certainly cost more than we can afford to pay.'

30

FIBEN

Fiben rubbed the back of his neck and stared irritably across the table. So *this* was the person he had been sent to contact, Dr Taka's brilliant student, their would-be leader of an urban underground.

'What kind of idiocy was that?' he accused. 'You let me walk into that club blind, ignorant. There were a dozen times I nearly got caught last night. Or even killed!'

'It was two nights ago,' Gailet Jones corrected him. She sat in a straight-backed chair and smoothed the blue demisilk of her sarong. 'Anyway, I *was* there, at the Ape's Grape, waiting outside to make contact. I saw that you were a stranger, arriving alone, wearing a plaid work shirt, so I approached you with the password.'

'Pink?' Fiben blinked at her. 'You come up to me and whisper *pink* at me, and that's supposed to be a bloody, reverted *password?*'

Normally he would never use such rough language with a young lady. Right now Gailet Jones looked more like the sort of person he had expected in the first place, a chimmie of obvious education and breeding. But he had seen her under other circumstances, and he wasn't ever likely to forget.

'You call that a password? They told me to look for a *fisherman*!'

Shouting made him wince. Fiben's head still felt as though it were leaking brains in five or six places. His muscles had stopped cramping capriciously some time ago, but he still ached all over and his temper was short.

'A fisherman? In that part of town?' Gailet Jones frowned, her face clouding momentarily. 'Listen, everything was chaos when I rang up the Center to leave word with Dr Taka. I figured her group was used to keeping secrets and would make an ideal core out in the countryside. I only had a few moments to think up a way to make a later contact before the Gubru took over the telephone lines. I figured they were already tapping and recording everything, so it had to be something colloquial, you know, that their language computers would have trouble interpreting.'

She stopped suddenly, bringing her hand to her mouth. 'Oh no!'

'What?' Fiben edged forward.

She blinked for a moment, then motioned in the air. 'I told that fool operator at the Center how their emissary should dress, and where to meet me, then I said I'd pass myself off as a hooker – '

'As a what? I don't get it.' Fiben shook his head.

'It's an archaic term. Pre-Contact human slang for one who offers cheap, illicit sex for cash.'

Fiben snapped. 'Of all the damn fool, Ifni-cursed, loony ideas!'

Gailet Jones answered back hotly. 'All right, smartie, what *should* I have done? The militia was falling to pieces. Nobody had even considered what to do if every human on the planet was suddenly removed from the chain of command! I had this wild notion of helping to start a resistance movement from scratch. So I tried to arrange a meeting – '

'Uh huh, posing as someone advertising illicit favors, right outside a place where the Gubru were inciting a sexual *frenzy*.'

'How was *I* to know what they were going to do, or that they'd choose that sleepy little club as the place to do it in? I conjectured that social restraints would relax enough to let me pull the pose and so be able to approach strangers. It never occurred to me they'd relax *that* much! My guess was that anyone I came up to by mistake would be so surprised he'd act as you did and I could pull a fade.'

'But it didn't work out that way.'

'No it did not! Before you appeared, several solitary chens showed up dressed likely enough to make me put on my act. Poor Max had to stun half a dozen of them, and the alley was starting to get full! But it was already too late to change the rendezvous, or the password – '

Which nobody understood! *Hooker?* You should have realized something like that would get garbled!'

'I knew Dr Taka would understand. We used to watch and discuss old movies together. We'd study the archaic words they used. I can't understand why she ...' Her voice trailed off when she saw the expression on Fiben's face. 'What? Why are you looking at me like that?'

'I'm sorry. I just realized that you couldn't know.' He shook his head. 'You see, Dr Taka died just about the time they got your message, of an allergic reaction to the coercion gas.'

Her breath caught. Gailet seemed to sink into herself. 'I ... I feared as much when she didn't show up in town for internment. It's ... a great loss.' She closed her eyes and turned away, obviously feeling more than her words told.

At least she had been spared witnessing the flaming end of the Howletts Center as the soot-covered ambulances came and went, and the glazed, dying face of her mentor as the ecdemic gas took its cruel, statistical toll. Fiben had seen recordings of that fear-palled evening. The images lay in dark layers still, at the back of his mind.

Gailet gathered herself, visibly putting off her mourning for later. She dabbed her eyes and faced Fiben, jaw outthrust defiantly. 'I had to come up with something a chim would understand but the Eatees' language computers wouldn't. It won't be the last time we have to improvise. Anyway, what matters is that you are here. Our two groups are in contact now.'

'I was almost killed,' he pointed out, though this time he felt a bit churlish for mentioning it.

'But you weren't killed. In fact, there may be ways to turn your little misadventure into an advantage. Out on the streets they're still talking about what you did that night, you know.'

Was that a faint, tentative note of *respect* in her voice? A peace offering, perhaps?

Suddenly, it was all too much. Much too much for him. Fiben knew it was exactly the wrong thing to do, at exactly the wrong time, but he just couldn't help himself. He broke up.

'A hook ... ?' He giggled, though every shake seemed to rattle his brain in his skull. 'A *hooker*?' He threw back his head and hooted, pounding on the arms of the chair. Fiben slumped. He guffawed, kicking his feet in the air. 'Oh, Goodall. That was *all* I needed to be looking for!'

Gailet Jones glared at him as he gasped for breath. He didn't even care, right now, if she called in that big chim, Max, to use the stunner on him again.

It was all just too much.

If the look in her eyes right then counted for anything, Fiben knew this alliance was already off to a rocky start.

31

GALACTICS

The Suzerain of Beam and Talon stepped aboard its personal barge and accepted the salutes of its Talon Soldier escort. They were carefully chosen troops, feathers perfectly preened, crests neatly dyed with colors noting rank and unit. The admiral's Kwackoo aide hurried forth and took its ceremonial robe. When all had settled onto their perches the pilot took off on gravities, heading toward the defense works under construction in the low hills east of Port Helenia. The Suzerain of Beam and Talon watched in silence as the new city fence fell behind them and the farms of this small Earthling settlement rushed by underneath.

The seniormost stoop-colonel, military second in command, saluted with a sharp beak-clap. 'The conclave went well? Suitably? Satisfactorily?' the stoop-colonel asked.

The Suzerain of Beam and Talon chose to overlook the impudence of the question. It was more useful to have a second who could think than one whose plumage was always perfectly preened. Surrounding itself with a few such creatures was one of the things that had won the Suzerain its candidacy. The admiral gave its inferior a haughty eyeblink of assent. 'Our consensus is presently adequate, sufficient, it will do.'

The stoop-colonel bowed and returned to its station. Of course it would know that consensus was never perfect at this early stage in a Molt. Anyone could tell that from the Suzerain's ruffled down and haggard eyes.

This most recent Command Conclave had been particularly indecisive, and several aspects had irritated the admiral deeply.

For one thing, the Suzerain of Cost and Caution was pressing to release much of their support fleet to go assist other Gubru operations, far from here. And as if that weren't enough, the third leader, the Suzerain of Propriety, still insisted on being carried everywhere on its perch, refusing to set foot on the soil of Garth until all punctilio had been satisfied. The priest was all fluffed and agitated over a number of issues – excessive human deaths from coercion gas, the threatened breakdown of the Garth Reclamation Project, the pitiful size of the Planetary Branch Library, the Uplift status of the benighted, pre-sentient neo-chimpanzees.

On every issue, it seemed, there must be still another realignment, another tense negotiation. Another struggle for consensus.

And yet, there were deeper issues than these ephemera. The Three had also begun to argue over fundamentals, and *there* the process was actually starting to become enjoyable, somehow. The pleasurable aspects of Triumviracy were emerging, especially when they danced and crooned and argued over deeper matters.

Until now it had seemed that the flight to queenhood would be straight and easy for the admiral, for it had been in command from the start. Now it had begun to dawn on the Suzerain of Beam and Talon that all would not be easy. This was not going to be any trivial Molt after all.

Of course the best ones never were. Very diverse factions had been involved in choosing the three leaders of the Expeditionary Force, for the Roost Masters of home had hopes for a new unified policy to emerge from this particular Threesome. In order for that to happen, all of them had to be very good minds, and very different from each other.

Just how good and how different was beginning to become clear. A few of the ideas the others had presented recently were clever, and quite unnerving.

They are right about one thing, the admiral had to admit. *We must not simply conquer, defeat, overrun the wolflings. We must discredit them!*

The Suzerain of Beam and Talon had been concentrating so hard on military matters that it had got in the habit of seeing its mates as impediments, little more.

That was wrong, impertinent, disloyal of me, the admiral thought.

In fact, it was devoutly to be *hoped* that the bureaucrat and the priest were as bright in their own areas as the admiral was in soldiery. If Propriety and Accountancy handled their ends as brilliantly as the invasion had been, then they would be a trio to be remembered!

Some things were foreordained, the Suzerain of Beam and Talon knew. They had been set since the days of the Progenitors, long, long ago. Long before there were heretics and unworthy clans polluting the starlances – horrible, wretched wolflings, and Tymbrimi, and Thennanin, and Soro ... It was vital that the clan of Gooksyu-Gubru prevail in this era's troubles! The clan must achieve greatness!

The admiral contemplated the way the eggs of the Earthlings' defeat had been laid so many years before. How the Gubru force had been able to detect and counteract their every move. And how the coercion gas had left all their plans in complete disarray. These had been the Suzerain's own ideas – along with members of its personal staff, of course. They had been years coming to fruition.

The Suzerain of Beam and Talon stretched its arms, feeling tension in the flexors that had, ages before its species' own uplifting, carried his ancestors aloft in warm, dry currents on the Gubru homeworld.

Yes! Let my peers' ideas also be bold, imaginative, brilliant . . .

Let them be almost, nearly, close to – but not quite – as brilliant as my own.

The Suzerain began preening its feathers as the cruiser leveled off and headed east under a cloud-decked sky.

32

ATHACLENA

'I am going *crazy* down here. I feel like I'm being kept prisoner!'

Robert paced, accompanied by twin shadows cast by the cave's only two glow bulbs. Their stark light glistened in the sheets of moisture that seeped slowly down the walls of the underground chamber.

Robert's left arm clenched, tendons standing out from fist to elbow to well-muscled shoulder. He punched a nearby cabinet, sending banging echoes down the subterranean passageways. 'I warn you, Clennie, I'm not going to be able to wait much longer. When are you going to let me *out* of here?'

Athaclena winced as Robert slammed the cabinet again, giving vent to his frustration. At least twice he had seemed about to use his still-splinted right arm instead of the undamaged left. 'Robert,' she urged. 'You have been making wonderful progress. Soon your cast can come off. Please do not jeopardize that by injuring yourself—'

'You're evading the issue!' he interrupted. 'Even wearing a cast I could be out there, helping train the troops and scouting Gubru positions. But you have me trapped down here in these caves, programming minicomps and sticking pins in maps! It's driving me nuts!'

Robert positively radiated his frustration. Athaclena had asked him before to try to damp it down. *To keep a lid on it*, as the metaphor went. For some reason she seemed particularly susceptible to his emotional tides – as stormy and wild as any Tymbrimi adolescent's.

'Robert, you know why we cannot risk sending you out to the surface. The Gubru gasbots have already swept over our surface encampments several times, unleashing their deadly vapors. Had you been above on any of those occasions you would even now be on your way to Cilmar Island, lost to us. And that is at best! I shudder to think of the worst.'

Athaclena's ruff bristled at the thought; the silvery tendrils of her corona waved in agitation.

It was mere luck that Robert had been rescued from the Mendoza Freehold just before the persistent Gubru searcher robots swooped down upon the tiny mountain homestead. Camouflage and removal of all electronic items had apparently not been enough to hide the cabin.

Meline Mendoza and the children immediately left for Port Helenia and presumably arrived in time for treatment. Juan Mendoza had been less fortunate. Remaining behind to close down several ecological survey traps, he had been stricken with a delayed allergic reaction to the coercion gas and died within five convulsive minutes, foaming and jerking under the horrified gaze of his helpless chim partners.

'You were not there to see Juan die, Robert, but surely you must have heard reports. Do you want to risk such a death? Are you aware of how close we already came to losing you?'

Their eyes met, brown encountering gold-flecked gray. She could sense Robert's determination, and also his effort to control his stubborn anger. Slowly, Robert's left arm unclenched. He breathed a deep sigh and sank into a canvas-backed chair.

'I'm aware, Clennie. I know how you feel. But you've got to understand, I'm *part* of all this.' He leaned forward, his expression no longer wrathful, but still intense. 'I agreed to my mother's request, to guide you into the bush instead of joining my militia unit, because Megan said it was important. But now you're no longer my guest in the forest. You're organizing an army! And I feel like a fifth wheel.'

Athaclena sighed. 'We both know that it will not be much of an army ... a gesture at best. Something to give the chims hope. Anyway, as a Terragens officer you have the right to take over from me any time you wish.'

Robert shook his head. 'That's not what I mean. I'm not conceited enough to think I could have done any better. I'm no leader type, and I know it. Most of the chims worship you, and believe in your Tymbrimi mystique.

'Still, I probably *am* the only human with any military training left in these mountains ... an asset you have to use if we're to have any chance to—'

Robert stopped abruptly, lifting his eyes to look over Athaclena's shoulder. Athaclena turned as a small chimmie in shorts and bandoleer entered the underground room and saluted.

'Excuse me, general, Captain Oneagle, but Lieutenant Benjamin has just gotten in. Um, he reports that things aren't any better over in Spring Valley. There aren't any humans there anymore. But outposts all up and down every canyon are still being buzzed by the damn gasbots at least once a day. There doesn't seem to be any sign of it lettin' up anywhere where our runners have been able to get to.'

'How about the chims in Spring Valley?' Athaclena asked. 'Is the gas making them sick?' She recalled Dr Schultz and the effect the coercion gas had had on some of the chims back at the Center.

The courier shook her head. 'No, ma'am. Not anymore. It seems to be the same story all over. All the sus-susceptible chims have already been flushed out and gone to Port Helenia. Every person left in the mountains must be immune by now.'

Athaclena glanced at Robert and they must have shared the same thought.

Every person but one.

'Damn them!' he cursed. 'Won't they ever let up? They have ninety-nine point nine percent of the humans captive. Do they need to keep gassing every hut and hovel, just in order to get every last one?'

'Apparently they are afraid of *Homo sapiens,* Robert.' Athaclena smiled. 'After all, you are allies of the Tymbrimi. And we do not choose harmless species as partners.'

Robert shook his head, glowering. But Athaclena reached out with her aura to touch him, nudging his personality, forcing him to look up and see the humor in her eyes. Against his will, a slow smile spread. At last Robert laughed. 'Oh, I guess the damned birds aren't so dumb after all. Better safe than sorry, hmm?'

Athaclena shook her head, her corona forming a glyph of appreciation, a simple one which he might *kenn.* 'No, Robert. They aren't so dumb. But they have missed at least one human, so their worries aren't over yet.'

The little neo-chimp messenger glanced from Tymbrimi to human and sighed. It all sounded scary to her, not funny. She didn't understand why they smiled.

Probably, it was something subtle and convoluted. Patron-class humor ... dry and intellectual. Some chims batted in that league, strange ones who differed from other neo-chimpanzees not so much in intelligence as in something else, something much less definable.

She did not envy those chims. Responsibility was an awesome thing, more daunting than the prospect of fighting a powerful enemy, or even dying.

It was the possibility of being *left alone* that terrified her. She might not understand it, when these two laughed. But it felt good just to hear it.

The messenger stood a little straighter as Athaclena turned back to speak to her.

'I will want to hear Lieutenant Benjamin's report personally. Would you please also give my compliments to Dr Soo and ask her to join us in the operations chamber?'

'Yesser!' The chimmie saluted and took off at a run.

'Robert?' Athaclena asked. 'Your opinion will be welcome.'

He looked up, a distant expression on his face. 'In a minute, Clennie. I'll check in at operations. There's just something I want to think through first.'

'All right.' Athaclena nodded. 'I'll see you soon.' She turned away and followed the messenger down a water-carved corridor lit at long intervals by dim glow bulbs and wet reflections on the dripping stalactites.

Robert watched her until she was out of sight. He thought in the near-total quiet.

Why are the Gubru persisting in gassing the mountains, after nearly every human has already been driven out? It must be a terrific expense, even if their gasbots only swoop down on places where they detect an Earthling presence.

And how are they able to detect buildings, vehicles, even isolated chims, no matter how well hidden?

Right now it doesn't matter that they've been dosing our surface encampments. The gasbots are simple machines and don't know we're training an army in this valley. They just sense 'Earthlings!' – then dive in to do their work and leave again.

But what happens when we start operations and attract attention from the Gubru themselves? We can't afford to be detectable then.

There was another very basic reason to find an answer to these questions.

As long as this is going on, I'm trapped down here!

Robert listened to the faint plink of water droplets seeping from the nearest wall. He thought about the enemy.

The trouble on Garth was clearly little more than a skirmish among the greater battles tearing up the Five Galaxies. The Gubru couldn't just gas the entire planet. That would cost far too much for this backwater theater of operations.

So a swarm of cheap, stupid, but efficient seeker robots had been unleashed to home in on anything not natural to Garth ... anything that had the scent of Earth about it. By now nearly every attack dosed only irritated, resentful chims – immune to the coercion gas – and empty buildings all over the planet.

It was a nuisance, and it was effective. A way had to be found to stop it.

Robert pulled a sheet of paper from a folder at the end of the table. He wrote down the principal ways the gasbots might be using to detect Earthlings on an alien planet.

> OPTICAL IMAGING
> BODY HEAT INFRARED
> SCAN RESONANCE
> PSI
> REALITY TWIST

Robert regretted having taken so many courses in public administration, and so few on Galactic technologies. He was certain the Great Library's gigayear-old archives contained many methods of detection beyond just these five. For instance, what if the gasbots actually did 'sniff out' a Terran odor, tracing anything Earthly by sense of smell?

No. He shook his head. There came a point where one had to cut a list short, putting aside things that were obviously ridiculous. Leaving them as a last resort, at least.

The rebels did have a Library pico-branch he could try, salvaged from the wreckage of the Howletts Center. The chances of it having any entries of military use were quite slim. It was a tiny branch, holding no more information than all the books written by pre-Contact Mankind, and it was specialized in the areas of Uplift and genetic engineering.

Maybe we can apply to the District Central Library on Tanith for a literature search. Robert smiled at the ironic thought. Even a people imprisoned by an invader supposedly had the right to query the Galactic Library whenever they wished. That was part of the Code of the Progenitors.

Right! He chuckled at the image. *We'll Just walk up to Gubru occupation headquarters and demand that they transmit our appeal to Tanith ... a request for information on the invader's own military technology!*

They might even do it. After all, with the galaxies in turmoil the Library must be inundated with queries. They would get around to our request eventually, maybe sometime m the next century.

He looked over his list. At least these were means he had heard of or knew something about.

Possibility one: There might be a satellite overhead with

sophisticated optical scanning capabilities, inspecting Garth acre by acre, seeking out regular shapes that would indicate buildings or vehicles. Such a device could be dispatching the gasbots to their targets.

Feasible, but why were the same sites raided over and over again? Wouldn't such a satellite remember? And how could a satellite know to send robot bombers plunging down on even isolated groups of chims, traveling under the heavy forest canopy?

The reverse logic held for infrared direction. The machines couldn't be homing in on the target's body heat. The Gubru drones still swooped down on empty buildings, for instance, cold and abandoned for weeks now.

Robert did not have the expertise to eliminate all the possibilities on his list. Certainly he knew next to nothing about psi and its weird cousin, reality physics. The weeks with Athaclena had begun to open doors to him, but he was far from being more than a rank novice in an area that still caused many humans and chims to shudder in superstitious dread.

Well, as long as I'm stuck here underground I might as well expand my education.

He started to get up, intending to join Athaclena and Benjamin. Then he stopped suddenly. Looking at his list of possibilities he realized that there was one more that he had left out.

... A way for the Gubru to penetrate our defenses so easily when they invaded ... A way for them to find us again and again, wherever we hide. A way for them to foil our every move.

He did not want to, but honesty forced him to pick up the stylus one more time. He wrote a single word.

TREASON

33

FIBEN

That afternoon Gailet took Fiben on a tour of Port Helenia – or as much of it as the invader had not placed off limits to the neo-chimp population.

Fishing trawlers still came and went from the docks at the southern end of town. But now they were crewed solely by chim sailors. And less than half the usual number set forth, taking wide detours past the Gubru fortress ship that filled half the outlet of Aspinal Bay.

In the markets they saw some items in plentiful supply. Elsewhere there were sparse shelves, stripped nearly bare by scarcity and hoarding. Colonial money was still good for some things, like beer and fish. But only Galactic pellet-scrip would buy meat or fresh fruit. Irritated shoppers had already begun to learn what that archaic term, 'inflation,' meant.

Half the population, it seemed, worked for the invader. There were battlements being built, off to the south of the bay, near the spaceport. Excavations told of more massive structures yet to be.

Placards everywhere in town depicted grinning neo-chimpanzees and promised plenty once again, as soon as enough 'proper' money entered circulation. Good work would bring that day closer, they were promised.

'Well? Have you seen enough?' his guide asked.

Fiben smiled. 'Not at all. In fact, we've barely scratched the surface.'

Gailet shrugged and let him lead the way.

Well, he thought as he looked at the scant market shelves, *the nutritionists keep telling us neo-chimps we eat more meat than is good for us ... much more than we could get in the wild old days. Maybe this'll do us some good.*

At last their wanderings brought them to the bell tower overlooking Port Helenia College. It was a smaller campus than the University, on Cilmar Island, but Fiben had attended ecological conferences here not so very long ago, so he knew his way around.

As he looked over the school, something struck him as very strange.

It wasn't just the Gubru hover-tank, dug in at the top of the hill, nor the ugly new wall that grazed the northern fringe of the college grounds on its way around town. Rather, it was something about the students and faculty themselves.

Frankly, he was surprised to see them here at all!

They were all chims, of course. Fiben had come to Port Helenia expecting to find ghettos or concentration camps, crowded with the human population of the mainland. But the last mels and fems had been moved out to the islands some days ago. Taking their place had been thousands of chims pouring in from outlying areas, including those susceptible to the coercion gas in spite of the invaders' assurances that it was impossible.

All of these had been given the antidote, paid a small, token reparation, and put to work in town.

But here at the college all seemed peaceful and amazingly close to normal. Fiben and Gailet looked down from the top of the bell tower. Below them, chens and chimmies moved about between classes. They carried books, spoke to one another in low voices, and only occasionally cast furtive glances at the alien cruisers that growled overhead every hour or so.

Fiben shook his head in wonder that they persevered at all.

Sure, humans were notoriously liberal in their Uplift policy, treating their clients as near equals in the face of a Galactic tradition that was far less generous. Elder Galactic clans might glower in disapproval, but chim and dolphin members deliberated next to their patrons on Terragens Councils. The client races had even been entrusted with a few starships of their own.

But a *college* without *men*?

Fiben had wondered why the invader held such a loose rein over the chim population, meddling only in a few crass ways like at the Ape's Grape.

Now he thought he knew why.

'Mimicry! They must think we're playing pretend!' he muttered half aloud.

'What did you say?' Gailet looked at him. They had made a truce in order to get the job done, but clearly she did not savor spending all day as his tour guide.

Fiben pointed at the students. 'Tell me what you see down there.'

She glowered, then sighed and bent forward to look. 'I see Professor Jimmie Sung leaving lecture hall, explaining something to some students.' She smiled faintly. 'It's probably intermediate Galactic history ... I used to TA for him, and I well recall that expression of confusion on the students' faces.'

'Good. That's what *you* see. Now look at it through a Gubru's eyes.'

Gailet frowned. 'What do you mean?'

Fiben gestured again. 'Remember, according to Galactic tradition we neo-chimps aren't much over three hundred years old as a sapient client race, barely older than dolphins – only just beginning our hundred-thousand-year period of probation and indenture to Man.

'Remember, also, that many of the Eatee fanatics resent humans terribly. Yet humans had to be granted patron status and all the privileges that go along with it. Why? Because they already had uplifted chims and dolphins before Contact! That's how you get status in the Five Galaxies, by having clients and heading up a clan.'

Gailet shook her head. 'I don't get what you're driving at. Why are you explaining the obvious?' Clearly, she did not like being lectured by a backwoods chim, one without even a postgraduate degree.

'Think! How did humans win their status? Remember how it happened, back in the twenty-second century? The fanatics were outvoted when it came to accepting neo-chimps and neo-dolphins as sapient.' Fiben waved his arm. 'It was a diplomatic coup pulled off by the Kanten and Tymbrimi and other moderates before humans even knew what the issues were!'

Gailet's expression was sardonic, and he recalled that her area of expertise was Galactic sociology. 'Of course, but—'

'It became *a fait accompli*. But the Gubru and the Soro and the other fanatics didn't have to like it. They still think we're little better than animals. They *have* to believe that, otherwise humans have *earned* a place in Galactic society equal to most, and better than many!'

'I still don't see what you're—'

'*Look* down there.' Fiben pointed. 'Look with Gubru eyes, and tell me what you see!'

Gailet Jones glared at Fiben narrowly. At last, she sighed. 'Oh, if you insist,' and she swiveled to gaze down into the courtyard again.

She was silent for a long time.

'I don't like it,' she said at last. Fiben could barely hear her. He moved to stand closer.

'Tell me what you see.'

She looked away, so he put it into words for her. 'What you see are bright, well-trained animals, creatures *mimicking* the behavior of their masters. Isn't that it? Through the eyes of a Galactic, you see clever *imitations* of human professors and human students ... replicas of better times, reenacted superstitiously by loyal—'

'Stop it!' Gailet shouted, covering her ears. She whirled on Fiben, eyes ablaze. 'I hate you!'

Fiben wondered. This was hard on her. Was he simply getting even for the hurt and humiliation he had suffered over the last three days, partly at her hands?

But no. She had to be shown how her people were looked on by the enemy! How else would she ever learn how to fight them?

Oh, he was justified, all right. *Still*, Fiben thought. *It's never pleasant being loathed by a pretty girl.*

Gailet Jones sagged against one of the pillars supporting the roof of the bell tower. 'Oh Ifni and Goodall,' she cried into her hands. 'What if they are right! What if it's true?'

34

ATHACLENA

The glyph *paraphrenll* hovered above the sleeping girl, a floating cloud of uncertainty that quivered in the darkened chamber.

It was one of the Glyphs of Doom. Better than any living creature could predict its own fate, *paraphrenll* knew what the future held for it – what was unavoidable.

And yet it tried to escape. It could do nothing else. Such was the simple, pure, ineluctable nature of *paraphrenll*.

The glyph wafted upward in the dream smoke of Athaclena's fitful slumber, rising until its nervous fringe barely touched the rocky ceiling. That instant the glyph quailed from the burning reality of the damp stone, dropping quickly back toward where it had been born.

Athaclena's head shook slightly on the pillow, and her breathing quickened. *Paraphrenll* flickered in suppressed panic just above.

The shapeless dream glyph began to resolve itself, its amorphous shimmering starting to assume the symmetrical outlines of a face.

Paraphrenll was an essence – a distillation. Resistance to inevitability was its theme. It writhed and shuddered to hold off the change, and the face vanished for a time.

Here, above the Source, its danger was greatest. *Paraphrenll* darted away toward the curtained exit, only to be drawn short suddenly, as if held in leash by taut threads.

The glyph stretched thin, straining for release. Above the sleeping girl, slender tendrils waved after the desperate capsule of psychic energy, drawing it back, back.

Athaclena sighed tremulously. Her pale, almost translucent skin throbbed as her body perceived an emergency of some sort and prepared to make adjustments. But no orders came. There was no plan. The hormones and enzymes had no theme to build around.

Tendrils reached out, pulling *paraphrenll*, hauling it in. They gathered around the struggling symbol, like fingers caressing clay, fashioning decisiveness out of uncertainty, form out of raw terror.

At last they dropped away, revealing what *paraphrenll* had become ... A *face*, grinning with mirth. Its cat's eyes glittered. Its smile was not sympathetic.

Athaclena moaned.

A crack appeared. The face divided down the middle, and the halves separated. Then there were two of them!

Her breath came in rapid strokes.

The two figures split longitudinally, and there were four. It happened again, eight ... and again ... sixteen. Faces multiplied, laughing soundlessly but uproariously.

'Ah-ah!' Athaclena's eyes opened. They shone with an opalescent, chemical fear-light. Panting, clutching the blankets, she sat up and stared in the small subterranean chamber, desperate for the sight of real things – her desk, the faint light of the hall bulb filtering through the entrance curtain. She could still feel the thing that *paraphrenll* had hatched. It was dissipating, now that she was awake, but slowly, too slowly! Its laughter seemed to rock with the beating of her heart, and Athaclena knew there would be no good in covering her ears.

What was it humans called their sleep-terror? *Nightmare*. But Athaclena had heard that they were pale things, dreamed events and warped scenes taken from daily life, generally forgotten simply by awakening.

The sights and sensations of the room slowly took on solidity. But the laughter did not merely vanish, defeated. It faded into the walls, embedding there, she knew. Waiting to return.

'*Tutsunacann*,' she sighed aloud. Tymbrim-dialect sounded queer and nasal after weeks speaking solely Anglic.

The laughing man glyph, *tutsunacann*, would not go away. Not until something altered, or some hidden idea became a resolve which, in turn, must become a jest.

And to a Tymbrimi, jokes were not always funny.

Athaclena sat still while rippling motions under her skin settled down – the unasked-for *gheer* activity dissipating gradually. *You are not needed*, she told the enzymes. *There is no emergency. Go and leave me alone.*

Ever since she had been little, the tiny change-nodes had been a part of her life – occasionally inconveniences, often indispensable. Only since coming to Garth had she begun to picture the little fluid organs as tiny, mouselike *creatures*, or busy little gnomes, which hurried about making sudden alterations within her body whenever the need arose.

What a bizarre way of looking at a natural, organic function! Many of the animals of Tymbrim shared the ability. It had evolved in the forests of homeworld long before the starfaring Caltmour had arrived to give her ancestors speech and law.

That was it, of course ... the reason why she had never likened the nodes to busy little creatures before coming to Garth. Prior to Uplift, her pre-sentient ancestors would have been incapable of making baroque comparisons. And *after* Uplift, they knew the scientific truth.

Ah, but humans ... the Terran wolflings ... had come into intelligence without guidance. They were not handed answers, as a child is given knowledge by its parents and teachers. They had emerged ignorant into awareness and spent long millennia groping in darkness.

Needing explanations and having none available, they got into the habit of inventing their own! Athaclena remembered when she had been amused ... *amused* reading about some of them.

Disease was caused by 'vapors,' or excess bile, or an enemy's curse ... The Sun rode across the sky in a great chariot ... The course of history was determined by economics ...

And inside the body, there resided *animus* ...

Athaclena touched a throbbing knot behind her jaw and started as the small bulge seemed to skitter away, like some small, shy creature. It was a terrifying image, that *metaphor*, more frightening than *tutsunacann*, for it invaded her body – her very sense of self!

Athaclena moaned and buried her face in her hands. *Crazy Earthlings! What have they done to me?*

She recalled how her father had bid her to learn more about human ways, to overcome her odd misgivings about the denizens of Sol III. But what had happened? She had found her destiny entwined with theirs, and it was no longer within her power to control it.

'Father,' she spoke aloud in Galactic Seven. 'I fear.'

All she had of him was memory. Even the *nahakieri* glimmer she had felt back at the burning Howletts Center was unavailable, perhaps gone. She could not go down to seek his roots with hers, for *tutsunacann* lurked there, like some subterranean beast, waiting to get her.

More metaphors, she realized. *My thoughts are filling with them, while my own glyphs terrify me!*

Movement in the hall outside made her look up. A narrow trapezoid of light spilled into the room as the curtain was drawn aside. The slightly bowlegged outline of a chim stood silhouetted against the dim glow.

'Excuse me, Mizz Athaclena, ser. I'm sorry to bother you during your rest period, but we thought you'd want to know.'

'Ye ...' Athaclena swallowed, chasing more mice from her throat. She shivered and concentrated on Anglic. 'Yes? What is it?'

The chim stepped forward, partly cutting off the light. 'It's Captain Oneagle, ser. I'm ... I'm afraid we can't locate him anywhere.'

Athaclena blinked. 'Robert?'

The chim nodded. 'He's gone, ser. He's just plain disappeared!'

35

ROBERT

The forest animals stopped and listened, all senses aquiver. A growing rustle and rumble of footfalls made them nervous. Without exception they scuttled for cover and watched from hiding as a tall beast ran past them, leaping from boulder to log to soft forest loam.

They had begun to get used to the smaller two-legged variety, and to the much larger kind that chuffed and shambled along on three limbs as often as two. Those, at least, were hairy and smelled like animals. This one, though, was different. It ran but did not hunt. It was chased, yet it did not try to lose its pursuers. It was warm-blooded, yet when it rested it lay in the open noon sunshine, where only animals stricken with madness normally ventured.

The little native creatures did not connect the running thing with the kind that flew about in tangy-smelling metal and plastic, for that type had always made such noise, and reeked of those things.

This one, though ... this one ran unclothed.

'Captain, stop!'

Robert hopped one rock farther up the tumbled boulder scree. He leaned against another to catch his breath and looked back down at his pursuer.

'Getting tired, Benjamin?'

The chim officer panted, stooping over with both hands on his knees. Farther down slope the rest of the search party lay strung out, some flat on their backs, barely able to move.

Robert smiled. They must have thought it would be easy to catch him. After all, chims were at home in a forest. And just one of them, even a female, would be strong enough to grab him and keep him immobile for the rest to bundle home.

But Robert had planned this. He had kept to open ground and played the chase to take advantage of his long stride.

'Captain Oneagle ...' Benjamin tried again, catching his breath. He looked up and took a step forward. 'Captain, please, you're not well.'

'I feel fine,' Robert announced, lying just a little. Actually, his legs shivered with the beginnings of a cramp, his lungs burned, and his right arm itched all over from where he had chipped and peeled his cast away.

And then there were his bare feet ...

'Parse it logically, Benjamin,' he said. '*Demonstrate* to me that I am ill, and just maybe I'll accompany you back to those smelly caves.'

Benjamin blinked up at him. Then he shrugged, obviously willing to clutch at any straw. Robert had proven they could not run him down. Perhaps logic might work.

'Well, ser.' Benjamin licked his lips. 'First off, there's the fact that you aren't wearing any clothes.'

Robert nodded. 'Good, go for the direct. I'll even posit, for now, that the simplest, most parsimonious explanation for my nudity is that I've gone bonkers. I reserve the right to offer an alternative theory, though.'

The chim shivered as he saw Robert's smile. Robert could not help sympathizing with Benjamin. From the chim's point of view this was a tragedy in progress, and there was nothing he could do to prevent it.

'Continue, please,' Robert urged.

'Very well.' Benjamin sighed. 'Second, you are running away from chims under your own command. A patron afraid of his own loyal clients cannot be in complete control of himself.'

Robert nodded. 'Clients who would throw this patron into a straitjacket and dope him full of happy juice first chance they got? No good, Ben. If you accept *my* premise, that I have reasons for what I'm doing, then it only follows that I'd try to keep you guys from dragging me back.'

'Um . . .' Benjamin took a step closer. Robert casually retreated one boulder higher. 'Your reason could be a false one,' Benjamin ventured. 'A neurosis defends itself by coming up with rationalizations to explain away bizarre behavior. The sick person actually believes—'

'Good point,' Robert agreed, cheerfully. 'I'll accept, for later discussion, the possibility that my "reasons" are actually rationalizations by an unbalanced mind. Will you, in exchange, entertain the possibility that they might be valid?'

Benjamin's lip curled back. 'You're violating orders being out here!'

Robert sighed. 'Orders from an E.T. civilian to a Terragens officer? Chim Benjamin, you surprise me. I agree that Athaclena should organize the ad hoc resistance. She seems to have a flair for it, and most of the chims idolize her. But I choose to operate independently. You know I have the right.'

Benjamin's frustration was evident. The chim seemed on the verge of tears. 'But you're in danger out here!'

At last. Robert had wondered how long Ben could maintain this game of logic while every fiber must be quivering over the safety of the last free human. Under similar circumstances, Robert doubted many men would have done better.

He was about to say something to that effect when Benjamin's head jerked up suddenly. The chim put a hand to his ear, listening to a small receiver. A look of alarm spread across his face.

The other chims must have heard the same report, for they stumbled to their feet, staring up at Robert in growing panic.

'Captain Oneagle, Central reports acoustic signatures to the northeast. Gasbots!'

'Estimated time of arrival?'

'Four minutes! *Please*, captain, will you come now?'

'Come where?' Robert shrugged. 'We can't possibly make the caves in time.'

'We can hide you.' But from the tone of dread in his voice, Benjamin clearly knew it was useless.

Robert shook his head. 'I've got a better idea. But it means we have to cut our little debate short. You must accept that I'm out here for a valid reason, Chim Benjamin. At once!'

The chim stared at him, then nodded tentatively. 'I – I don't have any choice.'

'Good,' Robert said. 'Now take off your clothes.'

'S-ser?'

'Your clothes! And that sonic receiver of yours! Have everybody in your party strip. Remove everything! As you love your patrons, leave on nothing but skin and hair, then come join me up in those trees at the top of the scree!'

Robert did not wait for the blinking chim to acknowledge the strange command. He turned and took off upslope, favoring the foot most cut up by pebbles and twigs since his early morning foray had begun.

How much time remained? he wondered. Even if he was correct – and Robert knew he was taking a terrible gamble – he would still need to get as much altitude as possible.

He could not help scanning the sky for the expected robot bombers. The preoccupation caused him to stumble and fall to his knees as he reached the crest. He skinned them further crawling the last two meters to the shade under the nearest of the dwarf trees. According to his theory it wouldn't matter much whether or not he concealed himself. Still, Robert sought heavy cover. The Gubru machines might have simple optical scanners to supplement their primary homing mechanism.

He heard shouting below, sounds of chims in fierce argument. Then, from somewhere to the north, there came a faint, whining sound.

Robert backed further into the bushes, though sharp twigs scratched his tender skin. His heart beat faster and his mouth was dry. If he was wrong, or if the chims decided to ignore his command ...

If he had missed a single bet he would soon be on his way to internment at Port Helenia, or dead. In any event, he would have left Athaclena all alone, the sole patron remaining in the mountains, and spent the remaining minutes or years of his life cursing himself for a bloody fool.

Maybe Mother was right about me. Maybe I am nothing but a useless playboy. We'll soon see.

There was a rattling sound! – rocks sliding down the boulder scree. Five brown shapes tumbled into the foliage just as the approaching whine reached its crescendo. Dust rose from the dry soil as the chims turned quickly and stared, wide-eyed. An alien machine had come to the little valley.

From his hiding place Robert cleared his throat. The chims, obviously uncomfortable without their clothes, started in tense surprise. 'You guys had better have thrown everything away, including your mikes, or I'm getting out of here now and leaving you behind.'

Benjamin snorted. 'We're stripped.' He nodded down into the valley. 'Harry an' Frank wouldn't do it. I told 'em to climb the other slope and stay away from us.'

Robert nodded. With his companions he watched the gasbot begin its run. The others had witnessed this phenomenon, but he had not been in much shape to observe during the one opportunity he'd had before. Robert looked on with more than a passing interest.

It measured about fifty meters in length, teardrop-shaped, with scanners spinning slowly at the pointed, trailing end. The gasbot cruised the valley from their right to their left, disturbed foliage rustling beneath its throbbing gravities.

It seemed to be *sniffing* as it zigzagged up the canyon – and vanished momentarily behind a curve in the bordering hills.

The whine faded, but not for long. Soon the sound returned, and the machine reappeared shortly after. This time a dark, noxious cloud trailed behind, turbulent in its wake. The gasbot passed back down the narrow vale and laid its thickest layer of oily vapor where the chims had left their clothes and equipment.

'Coulda *sworn* those mini-coms couldn't have been detected,' one of the naked chims muttered.

'We'll have to go completely without electronics on the outside,' another added unhappily, watching as the device passed out of sight again. The valley bottom was already obscured.

Benjamin looked at Robert. They both knew it wasn't over yet.

The high-pitched moan returned as the Gubru mechanism cruised back their way, this time at a higher altitude. Its scanners worked the hills on both sides.

The machine stopped opposite them. The chims froze, as if staring into the eyes of a rather large tiger. The tableau held for a moment. Then the bomber began moving at right angles to its former path.

Away from them.

In moments the opposite hill was swathed in a cloud of black fog. From the other side they could hear coughing and loud imprecations as the chims who had climbed that way cursed this Gubru notion of better living through chemistry.

The robot began to spiral out and higher. Clearly the search pattern would soon bring it above the Earthlings on this side.

'Anybody got anything they didn't declare at customs?' Robert asked, dryly.

Benjamin turned to one of the other neo-chimps. Snapping his fingers, he held out his hand. The younger chim glowered and opened his hand. Metal glittered.

Benjamin seized the little chain and medallion and stood up briefly to throw it. The links sparkled for just a moment, then disappeared into the murky haze downslope.

'That may not have been necessary,' Robert said. 'We'll have to experiment, lay out different objects at various sites and see which get bombed ...' He was talking as much for morale as for content. As much for *his* morale as for theirs. 'I suspect it's something simple, quite common, but imported to Garth, so its resonance will be a sure sign of Earthly presence.'

Benjamin and Robert shared a long look. No words were needed. *Reason or rationalization.* The next ten seconds would tell whether Robert was right or disastrously wrong.

It might be us it detects, Robert knew. *Ifni. What if they can tune in on human DNA?*

The robot cruised overhead. They covered their ears and blinked as the repulsor fields tickled their nerve endings. Robert felt a wave of déjà vu, as if this were something he and the others had done many times, through countless prior lives. Three of the chims buried their heads in their arms and whimpered.

Did the machine pause? Robert felt suddenly that it *had*, that it was about to ...

Then it was past them, shaking the tops of trees ten meters away ... twenty ... forty. The search spiral widened and the gasbot's whining engine sounds faded slowly with distance. The machine moved on, seeking other targets.

Robert met Benjamin's eyes again and winked.

The chim snorted. Obviously he felt that Robert should not be smug over being right. That was, after all, only a patron's job.

Style counted, too. And Benjamin clearly thought Robert might have chosen a more dignified way to make his point.

Robert would go home by a different route, avoiding any contact with the still-fresh coercion chemicals. The chims tarried long enough to gather their things and shake out the sooty black powder. They bundled up their gear but did not put the clothes back on.

It wasn't only dislike of the alien stink. For the first time the items themselves were suspect. Tools and clothing, the very symbols of sentience, had become betrayers, things not to be trusted.

They walked home naked.

It took a while, afterward, for life to return to the little valley. The nervous creatures of Garth had never been harmed by the new, noxious fog that had lately come at intervals from a growling sky. But they did not like it any more than they liked the noisy two-legged beings.

Nervously, timorously, the native animals crept back to their feeding or hunting grounds.

Such caution was especially strong in the survivors of the Bururalli terror. Near the northern end of the valley the creatures stopped their return migration and listened, sniffing the air suspiciously.

Many backed out then. Something else had entered the area. Until it left, there would be no going home.

A dark form moved down the rocky slope, picking its way among the boulders where the sooty residue lay thickest. As twilight gathered it clambered boldly about the rocks, making no move to conceal itself, for nothing here could harm it. It paused briefly, casting about as if looking for something.

A small glint shone in the late afternoon sunshine. The creature shuffled over to the glittering thing, a small chain and pendant half hidden in the dusty rocks, and picked it up.

It sat looking at the lost keepsake for a time, sighing softly in contemplation. Then it dropped the shiny bauble where it had lain and moved on.

Only after it had shambled away at last did the creatures of the forest finish their homeward odyssey, scurrying for secret niches and hiding places. In minutes the disturbances were forgotten, dross from a used-up day.

Memory was a useless encumbrance, anyway. The animals had more important things to do than contemplate what had gone on an hour ago. Night was coming, and *that* was serious business. Hunting and being hunted, eating and being eaten, living and dying.

36

FIBEN

'We've got to hurt them in ways that they can't trace to us.'

Gailet Jones sat cross-legged on the carpet, her back to the embers in the fireplace. She faced the ad hoc resistance committee and held up a single finger.

'The humans on Cilmar and the other islands are completely helpless to reprisals. So, for that matter, are all the urban chims here in town. So we have to begin carefully and concentrate on intelligence gathering before trying to really harm the enemy. If the Gubru come to realize they're facing an organized resistance, there's no telling what they'll do.'

Fiben watched from the shadowed end of the room as one of the new cell leaders, a professor from the college, raised his hand. 'But how could they threaten the hostages under the Galactic Codes of War? I think I remember reading somewhere that – '

One of the older chimmies interrupted. 'Dr Wald, we can't count on the Galactic Codes. We just don't know the subtleties involved and don't have time to learn them!'

'We could look them up,' the elderly chen suggested weakly. 'The city Library is open for business.'

'Yeah,' Gailet sniffed. 'With a Gubru Librarian in charge now, I can just imagine asking one of them for a scan-dump on resistance warfare!'

'Well, supposedly . . .'

The discussion had been going on this way for quite a while. Fiben coughed behind his fist. Everyone looked up. It was the first time he had spoken since the long meeting began.

'The point is moot,' he said quietly. 'Even if we knew the hostages would be safe. Gailet's right for yet another reason.'

She darted a look at him, half suspicious and perhaps a little resentful of his support. *She's bright*, he thought. *Bur we're going to have trouble, she and I.*

He continued. 'We have to make our first strikes seem less than they are because right now the invader is relaxed, unsuspecting, and completely contemptuous of us. It's a condition we'll find him in only once. We mustn't squander that until the resistance is coordinated and ready.

'That means we keep things low key until we hear from the general.'

He smiled at Gailet and leaned against the wall. She frowned back, but said nothing. They had had their differences over placing the Port Helenia resistance under the command of a young alien. That had not changed.

She needed him though, for now. Fiben's stunt at the Ape's Grape had brought dozens of new recruits out of the woodwork, galvanizing a part of the community that had had its fill of heavy-handed Gubru propaganda.

'All right, then,' Gailet said. 'Let's start with something simple. Something you can tell your general about.' Their eyes met briefly. Fiben just smiled, and held her gaze while other voices rose.

'What if we were to . . .'

'How about if we blow up . . .'

'Maybe a general strike . . .'

Fiben listened to the surge of ideas – ways to sting and fool an ancient, experienced, arrogant, and vastly powerful Galactic race – and felt he knew exactly what Gailet was thinking, what she *had* to be thinking after that unnerving, revealing trip to Port Helenia College.

Are we really sapient beings, without our patrons? Do we dare try even our brightest schemes against powers we can barely perceive?

Fiben nodded in agreement with Gailet Jones. *Yes, indeed. We had better keep it simple.*

37

GALACTICS

It was all getting pretty expensive, but that was not the only thing bothering the Suzerain of Cost and Caution. All the new antispace fortifications, the perpetual assaults by coercion gas on any and every suspected or detected Earthling site – these were things insisted upon by the Suzerain of Beam and Talon, and this early in the occupation it was hard to refuse the military commander anything it thought needed.

But accounting was not the only job of the Suzerain of Cost and Caution. Its other task was protection of the Gubru race from the repercussions of error.

So many starfaring species had come into existence since the great chain of Uplift was begun by the Progenitors, three billion years ago. Many had flowered, risen to great heights, only to be brought crashing down by some stupid, avoidable mistake.

That was yet another reason for the way authority was divided among the Gubru. There was the aggressive spirit of the Talon Soldier, to dare and seek out opportunities for the Roost. There was the exacting taskmaster of Propriety, to make certain they adhered to the True Path. In addition, though, there must be Caution, the squawk of warning, forever warning, that daring can step too far, and propriety too rigid can also make roosts fall.

The Suzerain of Cost and Caution paced its office. Beyond the surrounding gardens lay the small city the humans called Port Helenia. Throughout the building, Gubru and Kwackoo bureaucrats went over details, calculated odds, made plans.

Soon there would be another Command Conclave with its peers, the other Suzerains. The Suzerain of Cost and Caution knew there would be more demands made.

Talon would ask why most of the battle fleet was being called away. And it would have to be shown that the Gubru Nest Masters had need of the great battleships elsewhere, now that Garth appeared secure.

Propriety would complain again that this world's Planetary Library was woefully inadequate and appeared to have been damaged, somehow, by the fleeing Earthling government. Or perhaps it had been sabotaged by the Tymbrimi trickster Uthacalthing? In any event, there would be urgent insistence that a larger branch be brought in, at horrible expense.

The Suzerain of Cost and Caution fluffed its down. This time it felt filled with confidence. It had let the other two have their way for a time, but things were peaceful now, well in hand.

The other two were younger, less experienced – brilliant, but far too rash. It was time to begin showing them how things were going to be, how they *must* be, if a sane, sound policy was to emerge. This colloquy, the Suzerain of Cost and Caution assured itself, it would prevail!

The Suzerain brushed its beak and looked out onto the peaceful afternoon. These were lovely gardens, with pleasant open lawns and trees imported from dozens of worlds. The former owner of these structures was no longer here, but his taste could be sensed in the surroundings.

How sad it was that there were so few Gubru who understood or even cared about the esthetics of other races! There was a word for this appreciation of otherness. In Anglic it was called *empathy*. Some sophonts carried the business too far, of course. The Thennanin and the Tymbrimi, each in their own way, had made absurdities of themselves, ruining all clarity of their uniqueness. Still, there were factions among the Roost Masters who believed that a small dose of this other-appreciation might prove very useful in the years ahead.

More than useful, caution seemed now to demand it.

The Suzerain had made its plans. The clever schemes of its peers would unite under its leadership. The outlines of a new policy were already becoming clear.

Life was such a serious business, the Suzerain of Cost and

Caution contemplated. And yet, every now and then, it actually seemed quite pleasant!

For a time it crooned to itself contentedly.

38

FIBEN

'Everything's all set.'

The tall chim wiped his hands on his coveralls. Max wore long sleeves to keep the grease out of his fur, but the measure hadn't been entirely successful. He put aside his tool kit, squatted next to Fiben, and used a stick to draw a rude sketch in the sand.

'Here's where th' town-gas hydrogen pipes enter the embassy grounds, an' here's where they pass under the chancery. My partner an' I have put in a splice over beyond those cottonwoods. When Dr Jones gives the word, we'll pour in fifty kilos of D-17. That ought to do the trick.'

Fiben nodded as the other chim brushed away the drawing. 'Sounds excellent, Max.'

It *was* a good plan, simple and, more important, extremely difficult to trace, whether it succeeded or not. At least that's what they all were counting on.

He wondered what Athaclena would think of this scheme. Like most chims, Fiben's idea of Tymbrimi personality had come mostly out of vid dramas and speeches by the ambassador. From those impressions it seemed Earth's chief allies certainly loved irony.

I hope so, he mused. *She'll need a sense of humor to appreciate what we're about to do to the Tymbrimi Embassy.*

He felt weird sitting out here in the open, not more than a hundred meters from the Embassy grounds, where the rolling hills of Sea Bluff Park overlooked the Sea of Cilmar. In oldtime war movies, men always seemed to set off on missions like this at night, with blackened faces.

But that was in the dark ages, before the days of high tech and infrared spotters. Activity after dark would only draw attention from the invaders. So the saboteurs moved about in daylight, disguising their activities amid the normal routine of park maintenance.

Max pulled a sandwich out of his capacious coveralls and took out large bites while they waited. The big chim was no less impressive here, seated cross-legged, than when they had met, that night at the Ape's Grape. With his broad shoulders and pronounced canines, one might have thought he'd be a revert, a genetic reject. In truth, the Uplift Board cared less about such cosmetic features than the fellow's calm, totally unflappable nature. He had already been granted one fatherhood, and another of his group wives was expecting his second child.

Max had been an employee of Gailet's family ever since she was a little girl and had taken care of her after her return from schooling on Earth. His devotion to her was obvious.

Too few yellow-card chims like Max were members of the urban underground. Gailet's insistence on recruiting almost solely blue and green cards had made Fiben uncomfortable. And yet he had seen her point. With it known that some chims were collaborating with the enemy, it would be best to start creating their network of cells out of those who had the most to lose under the Gubru.

That still didn't make the discrimination smell good to Fiben.

'Feelin' any better?'

'Hmm?' Fiben looked up.

'Your muscles.' Max gestured. 'Feelin' less sore now?'

Fiben had to grin. Max had apologized all too often, first for doing nothing when the Probationers began harassing him back at the Ape's Grape, and later shooting him with the stunner on Gailet's orders. Of course both actions were understandable in retrospect. Neither he nor Gailet had known what to make of Fiben, at first, and had decided to err on the side of caution.

'Yeah, lots better. Just a twinge now and then. Thanks.'

'Mmm, good. Glad.' Max nodded, satisfied. Privately, Fiben noted that he had never heard *Gailet* express any regret over what he'd gone through.

Fiben tightened another bolt on the sand-lawn groomer he had been repairing. It was a real breakdown, of course, just in case a Gubru patrol stopped by. But luck had been with them so far. Anyway, most of the invaders seemed to be down at the south side of Aspinal Bay, supervising another of their mysterious construction projects.

He slipped a monocular out of his belt and focused on the Embassy. A low plastic fence topped with glittering wire surrounded the compound, punctuated at intervals by tiny whirling watch buoys. The little spinning disks looked decorative, but Fiben knew better. The protection devices made any direct assault by irregular forces impossible.

Inside the compound there were five buildings. The largest, the chancery, had come equipped with a fall suite of modern radio, psi, and quantum wave antennae – an obvious reason why the Gubru moved in after the former tenants cleared out.

Before the invasion, the Embassy staff had been mostly hired humans and chims. The only Tymbrimi actually assigned to this tiny outpost were the ambassador, his assistant/ pilot, and his daughter.

The invaders weren't following that example. The place swarmed with avian forms. Only one small building – at the top of the far hill across from Fiben, overlooking the ocean – did not show a full complement of Gubru and Kwackoo constantly coming and going. That pyramidal, windowless structure looked more like a cairn than a house, and none of the aliens approached within two hundred meters of it.

Fiben remembered something the general had told him before he left the mountains.

'If you get an opportunity, Fiben, please inspect the Diplomatic Cache at the Embassy. If, by some chance, the Gubru have left the grounds intact, there might be a message from my father there.'

Athaclena's ruff had flared momentarily.

'And if the Gubru have violated the Cache, I must know of that, too. It is information we can use.'

It looked unlikely he'd have had a chance to do as she asked, whether the aliens respected the Codes or not. The general would have to settle for a visual report from far away.

'What d'you see?' Max asked. He calmly munched his sandwich as if one started a guerrilla uprising every day.

'Just a minute.' Fiben increased magnification and wished he had a better glass. As far as he could tell, the cairn at the top of the hill looked unmolested. A tiny blue light winked from the top of the little structure. Had the Gubru put it there? he wondered.

'I'm not sure,' he said. 'But I think – '

His belt phone beeped – another bit of normal life that might end once fighting began. The commercial network was still in operation, though certainly monitored by Gubru language computers.

He picked up the phone. 'That you, honey? I've been getting hungry. I hope you brought my lunch.'

There was a pause. When Gailet Jones spoke there was an edge in her voice. 'Yes, *dear.*' She stuck to their agreed-upon code, but obviously did not relish it. 'Pele's marriage group is on holiday today, so I invited them to join us for a picnic.'

Fiben couldn't help digging a little – just for verisimilitude, of course. 'That's fine, darling. Maybe you an' I can find time to slip into the woods for some, y'know, ook ook.'

Before she could do more than gasp, he signed off. 'See you in a little while, sweetie.' Putting down the phone, he saw Max looking at him, a wad of food in one cheek. Fiben raised an eyebrow and Max shrugged, as if to say, 'None of *my* business.'

'I better go see that Dwayne ain't screwed up,' Max said. He stood and dusted sand from his coveralls. 'Scopes up, Fiben.'

'*Filters* up, Max.'

The big chim nodded and moved off down the hill, sauntering as if life were completely normal.

Fiben slapped the cover back on the engine and started the groomer. Its motor whistled with the soft whine of hydrogen catalysis. He hopped aboard and took off slowly down the hill.

The park was fairly crowded for a weekday afternoon. That was part of the plan, to get the birds used to chims behaving in unusual ways. Chims had been frequenting the area more and more during the last week.

That had been Athaclena's idea. Fiben wasn't sure he liked it, but oddly enough, it was one Tymbrimi suggestion Gailet had taken up wholeheartedly. An anthropologist's gambit. Fiben sniffed.

He rode over to a copse of willows by a stream not far from the Embassy grounds, near the fence and the small, whirling watchers. He stopped the engine and got off. Walking to the edge of the stream, he took several long strides and leapt up onto the trunk of a tree. Fiben clambered to a convenient branch, where he could look out onto the compound. He took out a bag of peanuts and began to crack them one at a time.

The nearest watcher disk seemed to pause briefly. No doubt it had already scanned him with everything from X-rays to radar. Of course it found him unarmed and harmless. Every day for the last week a different chim had taken his lunch break here at about this time of day.

Fiben recalled the evening at the Ape's Grape. Perhaps Athaclena and Gailet had a point, he thought. If the birds try to condition us, why can't we turn the tables and do it to the birds?

His phone rang again.

'Yeah?'

'Uh, I'm afraid Donal's suffering from a little flatulence. He may not be able to make it to the picnic.'

'Aw, too bad,' he muttered, and put the phone away. So far, so good. He cracked another peanut. The D-17 had been put into the pipes delivering hydrogen to the Embassy. It would still be several minutes before anything could be expected to happen.

It was a simple idea, even if he had his doubts. The sabotage was supposed to look like an accident, and it had to be timed so that Gailet's unarmed contingent was in position. This raid was meant not so much to do harm as to create a *disturbance*. Both Gailet and Athaclena wanted information on Gubru emergency procedures.

Fiben was to be the general's eyes and ears. Over on the grounds he saw avians come and go from the chancery and other buildings. The little blue light atop the Diplomatic Cache winked against the bright sea clouds. A Gubru floater hummed overhead and began to settle toward the broad Embassy lawn. Fiben watched with interest, waiting for the excitement to begin.

D-17 was a powerful corrosive when left in contact with town-gas hydrogen for long. It would soon eat through the pipes. Then, when exposed to air, it would have yet another effect.

It would stink to high heaven.

He didn't have long to wait.

Fiben smiled as the first squawks of consternation began to emanate from the chancery. Within moments the doors and windows burst forth with feathered explosions as aliens boiled out of the building, chirping in panic or disgust. Fiben wasn't sure which and he didn't really care. He was too busy laughing.

This part had been his idea. He broke a peanut and tossed it up to catch in his mouth. This was better than baseball!

Gubru scattered in all directions, leaping from upper balconies even without antigravity gear. Several writhed on broken limbs.

So much the better. Of course this wasn't going to be much of an inconvenience to the enemy, and it could only be done once. The real purpose was to watch how the Gubru dealt with an emergency.

Sirens began to wail. Fiben glanced at his watch. A full two minutes had passed since the first signs of commotion. That meant the alarm was given manually. The vaunted Galactic defense computers weren't omniscient then. They weren't equipped to respond to a bad smell.

The watch buoys rose from the fence together, giving off a threatening whine, whirling faster than before. Fiben brushed peanut shells from his lap and sat up slowly, watching the deadly things warily. If they were programmed to extend the defense perimeter automatically, whatever the emergency, he could be in trouble.

But they merely spun, shining with increased vigilance. It took three more minutes, by Fiben's watch, for a triple sonic boom to announce the arrival of fighter craft, sleek arrows resembling sparrow hawks, which streaked in to pass low over the now empty chancery building. The Gubru on the lawn seemed too nervous to take much cheer in their arrival. They leapt and squawked as sonic booms shook trees and feathers alike.

A Gubru official strutted about the grounds, chirping soothingly, calming its subordinates. Fiben didn't dare lift his monocular with the protector-drones at such high alert, but he peered to try to get a better view of the avian in charge. Several features seemed odd about this Gubru. Its white plumage, for instance, looked more luminous, more lustrous than the others'. It also wore a band of black fabric around its throat.

A few minutes later a utility craft arrived and hovered until enough chattering avians had stepped aside to give it room to land. From the grounded floater a pair of invaders emerged wearing ornate, crested breathing masks. They bowed to the official, then strode up the steps and into the building.

Obviously the Gubru in charge realized that the stench from the corroded gas pipes posed no threat. All the noise and commotion was doing much more harm to his command of clerks and planners than the bad smell. No doubt he was upset because the work day was ruined.

More minutes passed. Fiben watched a convoy of ground vehicles arrive, sirens wailing, sending the agitated civil servants into a tizzy again. The senior Gubru flapped its arms until the racket finally cut off. Then the aristocrat waved a curt gesture at the supersonic fighters hovering overhead.

The warcraft swiveled about at once and departed as swiftly as they had come. Shock waves again rattled windows and sent the chancery staff shrieking.

'Excitable lot, aren't they?' Fiben observed. No doubt Gubru soldiery were better conditioned for this sort of thing.

Fiben stood up on his branch and looked over toward other areas of the park. Elsewhere the fence was lined with chims, and more streamed in from the city. They kept a respectful distance back from the barrier guardians, but still they came, babbling to each other in excitement.

Here and there among them were Gailet Jones's observers, timing and jotting down every alien response.

'Almost the first thing the Gubru will read about, when they study Library tapes on your species,' Athaclena had told him, *'will be the so-called "monkey reflex" ... the tendency of you anthropoids to scurry toward commotion, out of curiosity.*

'Conservative species find it strange, and this tendency of humans and chims will seem particularly bizarre to avian beings, which tend to lack even a semblance of a sense of humor.'

She had smiled.

'We will get them used to this type of behavior, until they grow to expect those strange Earthling clients always running toward trouble ... just to watch.

'They will learn not to fear you, but they should ... speaking as one monkey to another.'

865

Fiben had known what she meant, that Tymbrimi were like humans and chims in this way. Her confidence had filled him, as well – until he saw her frown suddenly and speak to herself, quickly and softly, apparently forgetting that he understood Galactic Seven.

'Monkeys … one monkey to another … Sumbaturalli! *Must I constantly think in metaphors?'*

It had perplexed Fiben. Fortunately, he did not have to understand Athaclena, only know that she could ask anything she wanted of him and he would jump.

After a while more maintenance workers arrived in ground vehicles, this time including a number of chims wearing uniforms of the City Gas Department. By the time they entered the chancery, the Gubru bureaucrats on the lawn had settled into the shade just outside, chirping irritably at the still potent stench.

Fiben didn't blame them. The wind had shifted his way. His nose wrinkled in disgust.

Well, that's that. We cost them an afternoon's work, and maybe we learned something. Time to go home and assess the results.

He didn't look forward to the meeting with Gailet Jones. For a pretty and bright chimmie, she had a tendency to get awfully officious. And she obviously bore some grudge against him – as if *he* had gunned *her* down with a stunner and carried *her* off in a sack!

Ah well. Tonight he would be off, back into the mountains with Tycho, carrying a report for the general. Fiben had been born a city boy, but he had come to prefer the kind of birds they had out in the country to the sort infesting town of late.

He turned around, grabbed the tree trunk with both arms, and started lowering himself. That was when, suddenly, something that felt like a big flat hand *slammed* hard against his back, knocking all the breath out of him.

Fiben clawed at the trunk. His head rang and tears filled his eyes. He managed just barely to keep his grip on the rough bark as branches whipped and leaves blew away in a sudden wave of palpable sound. He held on while the entire tree rocked, as if it were trying to buck him off!

His ears popped as the overpressure wave passed. The rip of rushing air dropped to a mere roar. The tree swayed in slowly diminishing arcs. Finally – still gripping the bark tightly – he gathered the nerve to turn around and look.

A towering column of smoke filled the center of the Embassy lawn where the chancery used to be. Flames licked at shattered walls, and streaks of soot showed where superheated gas had blasted in all directions.

Fiben blinked.

'Hot chicken in a biscuit!' he muttered, not ashamed at all of the first thing to come to mind. There was enough fried bird out there to feed half of Port Helenia. Some of the meat was pretty rare, of course. Some of it still moved.

His mouth was bone dry, but he smacked his lips nonetheless.

'Barbecue sauce,' he sighed. 'All this, an' not a truck-load of barbecue sauce to be seen.'

He clambered back onto the branch amid the torn leaves. Fiben checked his watch. It took almost a minute for sirens to begin wailing again. Another for the floater to take off, wavering as it fought the surging convection of superheated air from the fire.

He looked to see what the chims at the perimeter fence had done. Through the spreading cloud of smoke, Fiben saw that the crowd had not fled. If anything, it had grown. Chims boiled out of nearby buildings to watch. There were hoots and shrieks, a sea of excited brown eyes.

He grunted in satisfaction. That was fine, so long as nobody made any threatening moves.

Then he noticed something else. With an electric thrill he saw that the watch disks were down! All along the barrier fence, the guardian buoys had fallen to the ground.

'Bugger all!' he murmured. 'The dumb clucks are saving money on smart robotics. The defense mechs were all remotes!'

When the chancery blew up – for whatever ungodly reason it had chosen to do so – it must have taken out the central controller with it! If somebody just had the presence of mind to grab up some of those buoys ...

He saw Max, a hundred meters to his left, scurry over to one of the toppled disks and prod it with a stick.

Good man, Fiben thought, and then dropped it from his mind. He stood up and leaned against the tree trunk while tossing off his sandals. He flexed his legs, testing the support. *Here goes nothin'*, he sighed.

Fiben took off at full tilt, running along the narrow branch. At the last moment he rode the bucking tip like a springboard and leaped off into the air.

The fence was set back a way from the stream. One of Fiben's toes brushed the wire at the top as he sailed over. He landed in an awkward rollout on the lawn beyond.

'Oof,' he complained. Fortunately, he hadn't banged his still-tender ankle. But his ribs hurt, and as he panted sucked in a lungful of smoke from the spreading fire. Coughing, he pulled a handkerchief from his coveralls and wrapped it over his nose as he ran toward the devastation.

Dead invaders lay strewn across the once pristine lawn. He leapt over a sprawled, Kwackoo corpse – four-legged and soot-covered – and ducked through a roiling finger of smoke. He barely evaded collision with a living Gubru. The creature fled squawking.

The invader bureaucrats were completely disorganized, flapping and running about in total chaos. Their noise was overwhelming.

Slamming sonic booms announced the return of soldiery, overhead. Fiben suppressed a fit of coughing and blessed the smoke. No one overhead would spot him, and the Gubru down here were in no condition to notice much. He hopped over singed avians. The stench from the fire kept even his most atavistic appetites at bay.

In fact, he was afraid he might be sick.

It was touch and go as he ran past the burning chancery. The building was completely in flames. The hair on his right arm curled from the heat.

He burst upon a knot of avians huddling in the shadow of a neighboring structure. They had been gathered in a moaning cluster around one particular corpse, a remnant whose once-bright plumage was now stained and ruined. When Fiben appeared so suddenly the Gubru scattered, chirping in dismay.

Am I lost? There was smoke everywhere. He swiveled about, casting for a sign of the right direction.

There! Fiben spied a tiny blue glow through the black haze. He set off at a run, though his lungs already felt afire. The worst of the noise and heat fell behind him as he dashed through the small copse of trees lining the top of the bluff.

Misjudging the distance, he almost stumbled, sliding to a sudden halt before the Tymbrimi Diplomatic Cache. Panting, he bent over to catch his breath.

In a moment he realized that it was just as well he'd stopped when he had. Suddenly the blue globe at the cairn's peak seemed less friendly. It pulsed at him, throbbing volubly.

So far Fiben had acted in a series of flash decisions. The explosion had been an unexpected opportunity. It had to be taken advantage of.

All right, here I am. Now what? The blue globe might be original Tymbrimi equipment, but it also might have been set there by the invader.

Behind him sirens wailed and floaters began arriving in a continuous, fluttering whine. Smoke swirled about him, whipped by the chaotic comings and goings of great machines. Fiben hoped Gailet's observers on the roofs of the buildings nearby were taking all this down. If he knew his own people, most of them would be staring slack-jawed or capering in excitement. Still, they might learn a lot from this afternoon's serendipity.

He took a step forward toward the cairn. The blue globe pulsed at him. He lifted his left foot.

A beam of bright blue light lanced out and struck the ground where he had been about to step.

Fiben leaped at least a meter into the air. He had hardly landed before the beam shot forth again, missing his right foot by millimeters. Smoke curled up from smoldering twigs, joining the heavier pall from the burning chancery.

Fiben tried to back away quickly, but the damned globe wouldn't let him! A blue bolt sizzled the ground behind him and he had to hop to one side. Then he found himself being herded the other way!

Leap, zap! Hop, curse, zap again!

The beam was too accurate for this to be an accident. The globe wasn't trying to loll him. Nor was it, apparently, interested in letting him go!

Between bolts Fiben frantically tried to think how to get out of this trap ... this infernal practical joke ...

He snapped his fingers, even as he jumped from another smoldering spot. Of course!

The Gubru *hadn't* messed with the Tymbrimi Cache. The blue globe wasn't acting like a tool of the avians. But it was exactly the sort of thing *Uthacalthing* would leave behind!

Fiben cursed as a particularly near miss left one toe slightly singed. Damn bloody Eatees! Even the good ones were almost more than anybody could bear! He gritted his teeth and forced himself to take a single step forward.

The blue beam sliced through a small stone near his instep, cutting it precisely in half. Every instinct in Fiben screamed for him to jump again, but he concentrated on leaving the foot in place and taking one more leisurely step.

Normally, one would think that a defensive device like this would be programmed to give warnings at long range and to start frying in earnest when something came nearer. By such logic what he was doing was stupid as hell.

The blue globe throbbed menacingly and cast forth its lightning. Smoke curled from a spot between the tingers and tumb of his left foot.

He lifted the right.

First a warning, then the real thing. That was the way an Earthling defense drone would work. But how would a *Tymbrimi* program his? Fiben wasn't sure he should wager so much on a wild guess. A client-class sophont wasn't supposed to analyze in the middle of fire and smoke, and especially not when he was being shot at!

Call it a hunch, he thought.

His right foot came down and its toes curled around an oak twig. The blue globe seemed to consider his persistence, then the blue bolt lanced out again, this time a meter in front of him. A trail of sizzling humus walked toward him in a slow zigzag, the crackle of burning grass popping louder as it came closer and closer.

Fiben tried to swallow.

It's not designed to kill! he told himself over and over. *Why should it be? The Gubru could have blasted that globe at long range long ago.*

No, its purpose had to be to serve as a gesture, a declaration of rights under the intricate rules of Galactic Protocol, more ancient and ornate than Japanese imperial court ritual.

And it was designed to tweak the beaks of Gubru.

Fiben held his ground. Another chain of sonic booms rattled the trees, and the heat from the conflagration behind him seemed to be intensifying. All the noise pressed hard against his self-control.

The Gubru are mighty warriors, he reminded himself. *But they are excitable . . .*

The blue beam edged closer. Fiben's nostrils flared. The only way he could take his gaze away from the deadly sight was by closing his eyes.

If I'm right then this is just another damned Tymbrimi . . .

He opened them. The beam was approaching his right foot from the side. His toes curled from a deep will to leap away. Fiben tasted bile as the searing knife of light tore through a pebble two inches away and proceeded on to . . .

To hit and cross his foot!

Fiben choked and suppressed an urge to howl. Something was wrong! His head spun as he watched the beam cross his foot and then commence leaving a narrow trail of smoky ruin directly under his spread-legged stance.

He stared in disbelief at his foot. He had bet the beam would stop short at the last instant. It hadn't.

Still . . . there his foot was, unharmed.

The beam ignited a dry twig then moved on to climb up his left foot.

There was a faint tickling he knew to be psychosomatic. While touching him, the beam was only a spot of light.

An inch beyond his foot, the burning resumed.

His heart still pounding, Fiben looked up at the blue globe and cursed with a mouth too dry to speak.

'Very funny,' he whispered.

There must have been a small psi-caster in the cairn, for Fiben actually felt something like a *smile* spread in the air before him ... a small, wry, alien smirk, as if the joke had really been a minor thing, after all, not even worth a chuckle.

'Real cute, Uthacalthing,' Fiben grimaced as he forced his shaking legs to obey him, carrying him on a wobbling path toward the cairn. 'Real cute. I'd hate to see what gives you a belly laugh.' It was hard to believe Athaclena came from the same stock as the author of this little bit of whoopee cushion humor.

At the same time, though, Fiben wished he could have been present when the first Gubru approached the Diplomacy Cache to check it out.

The blue globe still pulsed, but it stopped sending forth pencil beams of irritation. Fiben walked close to the cairn and looked it over. He paced the perimeter. Halfway around, where the cliff overlooked the sea only twenty meters away, there was a hatch. Fiben blinked when he saw the array of locks, hasps, bolts, combination slots, and keyholes.

Well, he told himself, *it is a cache for diplomatic secrets and such.*

But all those locks meant that he had no chance of getting in and finding a message from Uthacalthing. Athaclena had given him a few possible code words to try, if he got the chance, but this was another story altogether!

By now the fire brigade had arrived. Through the smoke Fiben could see chims from the city watch stumbling over stick-figure aliens and stretching out hoses. It wouldn't be long before someone imposed order on this chaos. If his mission here really was futile, he ought to be getting out while the getting was still easy. He could probably take the trail along the bluff, where it overlooked the Sea of Cilmar. That would skirt most of the enemy and bring him out near a bus route.

Fiben bent forward and looked at the hatchway again. Pfeh! There were easily two dozen locks on the armored door! A small ribbon of red silk would be as useful in keeping out an invader. Either the conventions were being respected or they weren't! What the hell good were all these padlocks and things?

Fiben grunted, realizing. It was another Tymbrimi joke, of course. One the Gubru would fail to get, no matter how intelligent they were. There were times when personality counted for more than intelligence.

Maybe that means ...

On a hunch, Fiben ran around to the other side of the cairn. His eyes were watering from the smoke, and he wiped his nose on his handkerchief as he searched the wall opposite the hatch.

'Stupid bloody guesswork,' he grumbled as he clambered among the smooth stones. 'It'd take a Tymbrimi to think up a stunt like this . . . or a stupid, lame-brained, half-evolved chim client like m—'

A loose stone slipped slightly under his right hand. Fiben pried at the facing, wishing he had a Tymbrimi's slender, supple fingers. He cursed as he tore a fingernail.

At last the stone came free. He blinked.

He had been right, there *was* a secret hiding place here in back. Only the damn hole was empty!

This time, Fiben couldn't help himself. He shrieked in frustration. It was too much. The covering stone went sailing into the brush, and he stood there on the steep, sloping face of the cairn, cursing in the fine, expressive, indignant tones his ancestors had used before Uplift when inveighing against the parentage and personal habits of baboons.

The red rage only lasted a few moments, but when it cleared Fiben felt better. He was hoarse and raw, and his palms hurt from slapping the hard stone, but at least some of his frustration had been vented.

Clearly it was time to get out of here. Just beyond a thick wisp of drifting smoke, Fiben saw a large floater set down. A ramp descended and a troop of armored Gubru soldiery hurried onto the singed lawn, each accompanied by a pair of tiny, floating globes. *Yep, time to scoot.*

Fiben was about to climb down when he glanced one more time into the little niche in the Tymbrimi cairn. At that moment the diffusing smoke dispersed briefly under the stiffening breeze. Sunlight burst onto the cliffside.

A tiny flash of silvery light caught his eye. He reached into the niche and pulled on a slender thread, thin and delicate as gossamer, that had lined a crack at the back of the little crevice.

At that moment there came an amplified squawk. Fiben swiveled and saw a squad of Gubru Talon Soldiers coming his way. An officer fumbled with the vodor at its throat, dialing among the auto-translation options.

'. . . *Cathtoo-psh'v'chim'ph* . . .

    '. . . *Kah-koo-kee, k'keee! EeeEeEE! k* . . .

        '. . . *Hisss-s-ss pop *crackle!** . . .

            '. . . *una blwt mannennering* . . .'

                '. . . what you are doing there! Good clients do not play with what they cannot understand!'

Then the officer caught sight of the opened niche – and Fiben's hand stuffing something into a coverall pocket.

'Stop! Show us what . . .'

Fiben did not wait for the soldier to finish the command. He scrambled up the cairn. The blue globe throbbed as he passed, and in his mind terror was briefly pushed aside by a powerful, dry laughter as he dove over the top and slid down the other side. Laser bolts sizzled over his head, chipping fragments from the stone structure as he landed on the ground with a thump.

Damn Tymbrimi sense of humor, was his only thought as he scrambled to his feet and dashed in the only possible direction, down the protective shadow of the cairn, straight toward the sheer cliff

39

GAILET

Max dumped a load of disabled Gubru guard disks onto the rooftop near Gailet Jones. 'We yanked out their receivers,' he reported. 'Still, we'll have to be damn careful with 'em.'

Nearby, Professor Oakes clicked his stopwatch. The elderly chen grunted in satisfaction. 'Their air cover has been withdrawn, again. Apparently they've decided it was an accident after all.'

Reports kept coming in. Gailet paced nervously, occasionally looking out over the roof parapet at the conflagration and confusion in Sea Bluff Park. *We didn't plan anything like this!* she thought. *It could be great luck. We've learned so much.*

Or it could be a disaster. Hard to tell yet.

If only the enemy doesn't trace it to us.

A young chen, no more than twelve years old, put down his binoculars and turned to Gailet. 'Semaphore reports all but one of our forward observers has come back in, ma'am. No word from that one, though.'

'Who is it?' Gailet asked.

'Uh, it's that militia officer from th' mountains. Fiben Bolger, ma'am.'

'I might have guessed!' Gailet sighed.

Max looked up from his pile of alien booty, his face a grimace of dismay. 'I saw him. When the fence failed, he jumped over it and went running toward the fire. Um, I suppose I should've gone along, to keep an eye on him.'

'You should have done no such thing, Max. You were exactly right. Of all the foolish stunts!' She sighed. 'I might have known he would do something like this. If he gets captured, and gives us away ...' She stopped. There was no point in worrying the others more than necessary.

Anyway, she thought a little guiltily, *the arrogant chen might only have been killed.*

She bit her lip, though, and went to the parapet to look out in the direction of the afternoon sun.

40

FIBEN

Behind Fiben came the familiar *zip zip* of the blue globe firing again. The Gubru squawked less than he might have expected; these were soldiers, after all. Still, they made quite a racket and their attention was diverted. Whether the cache defender was acting to cover his retreat or merely harassing the invaders on general principles, Fiben couldn't speculate. In moments he was too busy even to think about it.

One look over the edge was enough to make him gulp. The cliff wasn't a glassy face, but neither was it the sort of route a picnicker would choose to get down to the shining sands below.

The Gubru were shooting back at the blue globe now, but that couldn't last long. Fiben contemplated the steep dropoff. All told, he would much rather have lived a long, quiet life as country ecologist, donated his sperm samples when required, maybe joined a real fun group family, taken up scrabble.

'*Argh!*' he commented in man dialect, and stepped off over the grassy verge.

It was a four-handed job, for sure. Gripping a knob with the tingers and tumb of his left foot, he swung way out to grab a second handhold and managed to lower himself to another ledge. A short stretch came easily, then it seemed he needed the grasping power of every extremity. Thank Goodall Uplift had left his people with this ability. If he'd had feet like a human's, he surely would have fallen by now!

Fiben was sweating, feeling around for a foothold that *had* to be there, when suddenly the cliff face seemed to lash out, batting away at him. An explosion sent tremors through the rock. Fiben's face ground into the gritty surface as he clutched for dear life, his feet kicking and dangling in midair.

Of all the damn ... He coughed and spat as a plume of dust floated down from the cliff edge. In peripheral vision he glimpsed bright bits of incandescent stone flying out through the sky, spinning down to hissing graves in the sea below.

The root-grubbing cairn must've blown!

Then something whizzed by his head. He ducked but still caught a flash of blueness and heard, within his head, a chuckling of alien laughter. The hilarity reached a crescendo as something seemed to brush the back of his head, then faded as the blue light zipped off again, dropping to skip away southward, just above the waves.

Fiben wheezed and sought frantically for a foothold. At last he found purchase, and he was able to lower himself to the next fairly safe resting place. He wedged himself into a narrow cleft, out of sight from the clifftop. Only then did he spare the extra energy to curse.

Some day, Uthacalthing. Some day.

Fiben wiped dust from his eyes and looked down.

He had made it about halfway to the beach. If he ever reached the bottom safely it should be an easy walk to the closed amusement park at the northwestern corner of Aspinal Bay. From that point it ought to be simple to disappear into back alleys and side streets.

The next few minutes would tell. The survivors of the Gubru patrol might assume he had been killed in the explosion, blown out to sea along with debris from the cache. Or perhaps they'd figure he would have fled by some other route. After all, only an idiot would try to climb down a bluff like this one without equipment.

Fiben hoped he had it thought out right, because if they came down here looking for him his goose was as surely cooked as those birds in the chancery fire.

Just ahead the sun was settling toward the western horizon. Smoke from this afternoon's conflagration had spread far enough to contribute brilliant umber and crimson hues to the gathering sunset. Out on the water he saw a few boats, here and there. Two cargo barges steamed slowly toward the distant islands – low, brown shapes barely visible on the decks – no doubt carrying food for the hostage human population.

Too bad some of the salts in the seawater on Garth were toxic to dolphins. If the third race of Terragens had been able to establish itself here, it would have been a lot harder for the enemy to isolate the inhabitants of the archipelago so effectively. Besides, fins had their own way of thinking. Perhaps they d have come up with an idea or two Fiben's people had missed.

The southern headlands blocked Fiben's view of the port. But he could see traces of gleaming silver, Gubru warships or tenders involved in the construction of space defenses.

Well, Fiben thought, *nobody's come for me yet. No hurry, then. Catch your breath before trying the rest of the trip.*

This had been the easy part.

Fiben reached into his pocket and pulled out the shimmering thread he had found in the niche. It might easily *be* a spider web, or something similarly insignificant. But it was the only thing he had to show for his little adventure. He didn't know how he would tell Athaclena that his efforts had come only to this. *Well, not only this.* There was also the destruction of the Tymbrimi Diplomatic Cache. That'd be another thing to have to explain.

He took out his monocular and unscrewed the lens cover. Fiben carefully wrapped the thread into the cap and replaced it. He put the magnifier away.

Yeah, it was going to be a real nice sunset. Embers from the fire sparkled, swept into whirling plumes by Gubru ambulances screaming back and forth from the top of the bluffs. Fiben considered reaching into a pocket for the rest of the peanuts while he watched, but right now his thirst was worse than his hunger. Most modern chims ate too much protein, anyway.

Life's rough, he thought, trying to find a comfortable position in the narrow notch. *But then, it's never been easy for client-class beings, has it?*

There you are, minding your own business in some rain forest, perfectly adequate in your ecological niche, then *bam*! Some authoritarian guy with delusions of godhood is sitting on your chest, forcing the fruit of the Tree of Knowledge down your throat. From then on you're inadequate, because you're being measured against the 'higher' standard of your patron; no freedom; you can't even breed as you please, and you've got all those 'responsibilities' – Who ever heard of responsibilities back in the jungle? – responsibilities to your patrons, to your descendants . . .

Rough deal. But in the Five Galaxies there's only one alternative, extermination. Witness the former tenants of Garth.

Fiben licked the sweat salt from his lips and knew that it was nervous reaction that had brought on the momentary wave of bitterness. There was no point to recriminations anyway. If he were a race representative – one of those few chims deputized to speak for all neo-chimpanzees before the Terragens and the great Galactic Institutes – the issues might be worth contemplating. As it was, Fiben realized he was just procrastinating.

I guess they forgot about me, after all, he thought, wondering at his luck.

Sunset reached its peak in a glory of color and texture, casting rich red and orange streamers across Garth's shallow sea.

Hell, after a day like this, what was climbing down a steep cliff in the dark? Anticlimax, that was all.

'Where the devil have you been!' Gailet Jones faced Fiben when he slumped through the door. She approached glowering.

'Aw, teach.' He sighed. 'Don't scold me. I've had a rough day.' He pushed past her and shuffled through the house library, strewn with charts and papers. He stepped right across a large chart laid on the floor, oblivious as two of Gailet's observers shouted indignantly. They ducked aside as he passed straight over them.

'We finished debriefing *hours* ago!' Gailet said as she followed him. 'Max managed to steal quite a few of their watch disks . . .'

'I know. I saw,' he muttered as he stumbled into the tiny room he had been assigned. He began undressing right there. 'Do you have anything to eat?' he asked.

'Eat?' Gailet sounded incredulous. 'We have to get your input to fill in gaps on our Gubru operations chart. That explosion was a windfall, and we weren't prepared with enough observers. Half of the ones we had just stood and stared when the excitement started.'

With a 'clomp' Fiben's coveralls fell to the floor. He stepped out of them. 'Food can wait,' he mumbled. 'I need a drink.'

Gailet Jones blushed and half turned away. 'You might have the courtesy not to scratch,' she said.

Fiben turned from pouring himself a stiff shot of ping-orange brandy and looked at her curiously. Was this actually the same chimmie who had accosted him with *'pink'* a fortnight or so ago? He slapped his chest and waved away plumes of dust. Gailet looked disgusted.

'I was lookin' forward to a bath, but now I think I'll skip it,' he said. 'Too sleepy now. Gotta rest. Goin' home, tomorrow.'

Gailet blinked. 'To the mountains?'

Fiben nodded. 'Got to pick up Tycho and head back to report to th' gen'ral.' He smiled tiredly. 'Don't worry. I'll tell her you're doin' a good job here. Fine job.'

The chimmie sniffed disgustedly. 'You've spent the afternoon and evening rolling in dirt and getting soused! Some militia officer! And I thought you were supposed to be a scientist!'

'Well, next time your precious general wants to communicate with our movement here in town, you make sure she sends somebody *else*, do you hear me?'

She swiveled and slammed the door behind her.

What'd I say? Fiben stared after her. Dimly he knew he could have

877

done better somehow. But he was so tired. His body ached, from his singed toes to his burning lungs. He hardly felt the bed as he collapsed into it.

In his dreams a blueness spun and pulsed. From it there emanated a faint *something* that could be likened to a distant smile.

Amusing, it seemed to say. *Amusing, but not all that much of a laugh.*

More an appetizer for things to come.

In his sleep Fiben moaned softly. Then another image came to him, of a small neo-chimpanzee, an obvious throwback, with bony eyeridges and long arms which rested on a keyboard display strapped to its chest. The atavistic chim could not speak, but when it grinned, Fiben shivered.

Then a more restful phase of sleep set in, and at last he went on in relief to other dreams.

41

GALACTICS

The Suzerain of Propriety could not set foot on unsanctioned ground. Because of this it rode perched upon a gilded staff of reckoning, guided by a convoy of fluttering Kwackoo attendants. Their incessant cooing murmur was more soothing than the grave chirps of their Gubru patrons. Although the Uplift of the Kwackoo had brought them far toward the Gubru way of viewing the world, they nevertheless remained less solemn, less dignified by nature.

The Suzerain of Propriety tried to make allowances for such differences as the clucking swarm of fuzzy, rotund clients carried the antigravity perch from the site where the body had lain. It might be inelegant, but already they could be heard gossiping in low tones over who would be chosen as replacement. Who would become the new Suzerain of Cost and Caution?

It would have to be done soon. Messages had already been sent to the Roost Masters on the homeworld, but if need be a senior bureaucrat would be elevated on the spot. Continuity must be preserved.

Far from being offended, the Suzerain of Propriety found the Kwackoo calming. It needed their simple songs for the distraction they offered. The days and weeks to come would be stressful. Formal mourning was only one of the many tasks ahead. Somehow, momentum toward a new policy must be restored. And, of course, one had to consider the effects this tragedy would have on the Molt.

The investigators awaited the arrival of the perch amid a copse of toppled trees near the still smoldering chancery walls. When the Suzerain nodded for them to begin, they proceeded into a dance of presentment – part gesticulation and part audiovisual display – describing what they had determined about the cause of the explosion and fire. As the investigators chirped their findings in syncopated, a cappella song, the Suzerain made an effort to concentrate. This was a delicate matter, after all.

By the codes the Gubru might occupy an enemy embassy, yet they could still be held responsible for any damage done to it if the fault was theirs.

Yes, yes, it occurred, did occur, the investigators reported. *The building is – has been made – a gutted ruin.*

No, no, no purposeful activity has been traced, is believed to have caused these happenings. No sign that this event path was pre-chosen by our enemies and imposed without our will.

Even if the Tymbrimi Ambassador sabotaged his own buildings, what of it? If we are not the cause, we need not pay, need not reimburse!

The Suzerain chirped a brief chastisement. It was not up to the investigators to determine propriety, only evaluations of fact. And anyway, matters of expense were the domain of the officers of the new Suzerain of Cost and Caution, after they recovered from the catastrophe their bureaucracy had suffered here.

The investigators danced regretful apologies. The Suzerain's thoughts kept hovering in numb wonderment about what the consequences would be. This otherwise minor event had toppled the delicate balance of the Triumvirate just before another Command Conclave, and there would be repercussions even after a new third Suzerain was appointed. In the short term, this would help both survivors. Beam and Talon would be free to pursue what few humans remained at large, whatever the cost. And Propriety could engage in research without constant carpings about how expensive it all would be.

And then there was the competition for primacy to consider. In recent days it had begun to grow clear just how impressive the old Suzerain of Cost and Caution had been. More and more, against all expectation, it had been the one organizing their debates, drawing their best ideas forth, pushing compromises, leading them toward consensus.

The Suzerain of Propriety was ambitious. The priest had not liked the direction things were heading. Nor was it pleasant seeing its cleverest plans tinkered with, modified, altered to suit a bureaucrat. Especially one with bizarre ideas about empathy with aliens!

No, this was not the worst thing to have happened. Not at all. A new Threesome would be much more acceptable. More workable. And in the new balance the replacement would start at a disadvantage.

Then why, for what reason, for what cause am I afraid? the high priest wondered.

Shivering, the Suzerain of Propriety fluffed its plumage and concentrated, bring its thoughts back to the present, to the investigators' report. They seemed to be implying that the explosion and fire had fallen into that broad category of events that the Earthlings might call *accidents*.

At its erstwhile colleague's urging, the Suzerain had of late been trying to learn Anglic, the wolflings' strange, non-Galactic language. It was a difficult, frustrating effort, and of questionable utility when language computers were facile enough.

Yet the chief bureaucrat had insisted, and surprisingly the priest discovered there were things to be learned from even so beastly a collection of grunts and moans, things such as the hidden meanings underlying that term, *accident*.

The word obviously applied to what the investigators said had happened here, a number of unpredicated factors combined with considerable incompetence in the City Gas Department after the human supervisors had been removed. And yet the way Earthlings defined 'accident' was wrong by definition! In Anglic the term actually had no precise meaning!

Even the humans had a truism, 'There are no accidents.'

If so, why have a word for a nonexistent thing?

Accident ... it served to cover anything from unperceived causality, to true randomness, to a full level seven probability storm! In every case the 'results' were 'accidental.'

How could a species be spacefaring, be classified at the high level of a *patron* of a clan with such a murky, undefined, context-dependent way of looking at the universe? Compared with these Earthlings, even the devil trickster Tymbrimi were transparent and clear as the very ether!

This sort of uncomfortable line of thought was the sort of thing the priest had most hated about the bureaucrat! It was one of the dead Suzerain's most irritating attributes.

It was also one of the things most beloved and valuable. It would be missed.

Such were the confusions when a consensus was broken, when a mating was shattered, half begun.

Firmly, the Suzerain chirped a word-chain of definition.

Introspection was taxing, and a decision had to made about what had happened here.

Under some potential futures the Gubru might have to pay damages to the Tymbrimi – and even to the Earthlings – for the destruction that occurred on this plateau. It was unpalatable to consider, and might be prevented altogether when the Gubru grand design was fulfilled.

Events elsewhere in the Five Galaxies would determine that. This planet was a minor, if important, nut to shell with a quick, efficient bill thrust. Anyway, it was the job of the new Suzerain of Cost and Caution to see that expenses were kept down.

To see that the Gubru Alliance – the true inheritors of the Ancient Ones – were not found failing in propriety when the Progenitors returned, that was the priest's own task. *May the winds bring that day,* it prayed. 'Judgment deferred, delayed, put off for now,' the Suzerain declared aloud. And the investigators at once closed their folders.

The business of the chancery fire being finished, the next stop would be the top of the hill, where there was yet another matter to be evaluated.

The cooing crowd of Kwackoo huddled close and moved as a mass, carrying the Perch of Reckoning with them, a flat ball of puffy clients surging placidly through a feathery crowd of their hopping, excitable patrons.

The Diplomatic Cache still smoked on top from the events of the day before. The Suzerain listened carefully as the investigators reported, sometimes one at a time, occasionally joining together to chirp in unison and then counterpoint. Out of the cacophony the Suzerain gathered a picture of the events that had led to this scene.

A local neo-chimpanzee had been found poking around the cache without first seeking formal passage by the occupying power, a clear violation of wartime protocol. Nobody knew why the silly half-animal had been present. Perhaps it was driven by the 'monkey complex' – that irritating, incomprehensible need that drove Earthlings to *seek out* excitement instead of prudently avoiding it.

An armed detachment had come upon the curious neo-chimp while routinely moving to secure the disaster area. The commander had urgently spoken to the furry client-of-humans, insisting that the Earthling creature desist at once and show proper obeisance.

Typical of the upspring of humans, the neo-chimp had been obdurate. Instead of behaving in a civilized manner it had run away. In the process of trying to stop it, some defense device of the cairn was set off. The cairn was damaged in the subsequent shooting.

This time the Suzerain decided that the outcome was most satisfactory. Subclient or no, the chimpanzee was officially an ally of the cursed Tymbrimi. By acting so, it had destroyed the immunity of the cache! The soldiers were within their rights to open fire upon either the chimp or the defender globe without restraint. There had been no violation of propriety, the Suzerain ruled.

The investigators danced a dance of relief. Of course, the more closely ancient procedures were adhered to, the more brilliant would be the plumage of the Gubru when the Progenitors returned.

May the winds hurry the day.

'Open, enter, proceed into the cache,' the priest commanded. 'Enter and investigate the secrets within!'

Certainly the cache fail-safes would have destroyed most of the contents. Still, there might be some information of value left to be deciphered.

The simpler locks came off quickly, and special devices were brought to remove the massive door. This all took some time. The priest kept occupied holding a service for a company of Talon Soldiers, preaching to reinforce their faith in the ancient values. It was important not to let them lose their keen edge with things so peaceful, so the Suzerain reminded them that in the last two days several small parties of warriors had gone missing in the mountains southeast of this very town. Now would be a useful time for them to remember that their lives belonged to the Nest. The Nest and Honor – nothing else mattered.

At last the final puzzle bolt was solved. For famous tricksters the Tymbrimi did not seem so clever. Their wards were easy enough for Gubru lockpick robots to solve. The door lifted off in the arms of a carrier drone. Holding instruments before them, the investigators cautiously entered the cairn.

Moments later, with a chirp-chain of surprise, a feathered form burst forth holding a black crystalline object in its beak. This one was followed almost immediately by another. The investigators' feet were a blur of dancing excitement as they laid the objects on the ground before the Suzerain's floating perch.

Intact! they danced. Two data-stores were found *intact*, shielded from the self-destruct explosions by a premature rockfall!

Glee spread among the investigators and from there to the soldiers and the civilians waiting beyond. Even the Kwackoo crooned happily, for they, too, could see that this counted as a coup of at least the fourth order. An Earthling client had destroyed the immunity of the cache through obviously irreverent behavior – the mark of flawed Uplift. And the result had been fully sanctioned access to enemy secrets!

The Tymbrimi and humans would be shamed, and the clan of Gooksyu-Gubru would learn much!

The celebration was Gubru-frenetic. But the Suzerain itself danced only for a few seconds. In a race of worriers, it had a role of redoubled concern. There were too many things about the universe that were suspect. Too many things that would be much better dead, lest they by some chance someday threaten the Nest.

The Suzerain tilted its head first one way then another. It looked down at the data cubes, black and shiny on the scorched loam. A strange juxtaposition seemed to overlie the salvaged record crystals, a feeling that *almost*, but not quite, translated into a brooding sense of dread.

It was not a recognizable psi-sense, nor any other form of scientific premonition. If it had been, the Suzerain would have ordered the cubes converted to dust then and there.

And yet... It was very strange.

For only a brief moment, it shuddered under the illusion that the faceted crystals were eyes, the shining, space-black eyes of a large and very dangerous snake.

42

ROBERT

He ran holding in one hand a new wooden bow. A simple, home-spun quiver containing twenty new arrows bounced gently against his back as he puffed up the forest trail. His straw hat had been woven from river rushes. His loincloth and the moccasins on his feet were made of native suede.

The young man favored his left leg slightly as he ran. The bandage on that thigh covered only a superficial wound. Even the pain from the burn was a pleasure of sorts, reminding him how much preferable a near miss was over the alternative.

Image of a tall bird, staring unbelievingly at the arrow that had split its breastbone, its laser rifle tumbling to the forest loam, released by death-numbed talons.

The ridge was quiet. Almost the only sound was his steady breathing and the soft rasp of moccasins against the pebbles. Prickles of perspiration dried quickly as the breeze laid tracks of goose bumps up his arms and legs.

The touch of wind freshened as he climbed. The slope of the trail tapered, and Robert at last found himself above the trees, among the towering hill-spines of the ridge crest.

The sudden warmth of the sun was welcome now that he had darkened nearly to the shade of a foon-nut tree. His skin had also toughened, making thorns and nettles less bothersome.

I'm probably starting to look like an oldtime Indian, he thought with some amusement. He leapt over a fallen log and slipped down along a lefthand fork in the trail.

As a child he had made much of his family name. Little Robert Oneagle had never had to take turns as a bad guy when the kids played Confederation Uprising. He *always* got to be a Cherokee or Mohawk warrior, whooping it up in make-believe spacesuit and warpaint, zapping the dictator's soldiers during the Power Satellite War.

When this is all over I've got to find out more about the family gene-history, Robert thought. *I wonder how much of it really is Amerindian stock.*

White, fluffy stratus clouds slid along a pressure ridge to the north, appearing to keep pace with him as he jogged along the ridgetops, across the long hills leading toward home.

Toward home.

The phrase came easily now that he had a job to do out under the trees and open sky. *Now* he could think of those catachtonian caves as home. For they did represent sanctuary in uncertain times.

And Athaclena was there.

He had been away longer than expected. The trip had taken him high into the mountains as far away as Spring Valley, recruiting volunteers, establishing communications, and generally spreading the word.

And of course, he and his fellow partisans had also had a couple of skirmishes with the enemy. Robert knew they had been little things – a small Gubru patrol trapped here and there – and annihilated to the last alien. The Resistance only struck where total victory seemed likely. There could be no survivors to tell the Gubru high command that Earthlings had learned to become invisible.

However minor, the victories had done wonders for morale. Still, while they might make things a bit warm for the Gubru up in the mountains, but what was the use if the enemy stayed out of reach?

Most of his trip had been taken up doing things hardly related to the Resistance. Everywhere Robert had gone he found himself surrounded by chims who whooped and chattered at the sight of him – the sole remaining free human. To his frustration they seemed perfectly happy to make him unofficial judge, arbitrator, and godfather to newborn babies.

Never before had he felt so heavily the burdens that Uplift demanded of the patron race.

Not that he blamed the chims, of course. Robert doubted that in their species' brief history so many chims had ever been cut off from humans for so long.

Wherever he went, it became known that the last human in the mountains would not visit any pre-invasion building or, indeed, even see anyone wearing any clothing or artifact of non-Garth origin. As word spread how the alien gasbots found their targets, chims were soon moving whole communities. Cottage industries sprang up, resurrecting the lost arts of spinning and weaving, of tanning and cobbling.

Actually, the chims in the mountains were doing rather well. Food was plentiful and the young still attended school. Here and there a few responsible types had even begun to reorganize the Garth Ecological Reclamation Project, keeping the most urgent programs going, improvising to replace the lost human experts.

Perhaps they don't really need us, he remembered thinking.

His own kind had come within a hair's breadth of turning Earth-homeworld into an ecological Chelmno, in the years just before humanity awakened into sanity. A horrible calamity was averted by the narrowest of margins. Knowing that, it was humbling to see so many so-called clients behaving more rationally than men had only a century before Contact.

Do we really have any right to play god with these people? Maybe when this blows over we should just go away and let them work out their future for themselves.

A romantic idea. There was a rub, of course.

The Galactics would never let us.

So he let them crowd around him, ask his advice, name their babies after him. Then, when he had done all he could for the time being, he took off down the trail for home. Alone, since by now no chim could keep up with his pace.

The solitude of the last day or so had been welcome. It gave him time to think. He had begun learning a lot about himself these last few weeks and months, ever since that horrible afternoon when his mind had crumpled under pounding fists of agony and Athaclena had come into his mind to rescue him. Oddly, it had not turned out to be the beasts and monsters of his neuroses that mattered most. Those were easily dealt with once he faced them and knew them for what they were. Anyway, they were probably no worse than any other person's burdens of unresolved business from the past.

No, what had been more important was coming to grips with what he was as a man. That was an exploration he had only just begun, but Robert liked the direction the journey seemed to be heading.

He jogged around a bend in the mountain trail and came out of the hill's shadow with the sun on his back. Ahead, to the south, lay the craggy limestone formations concealing the Valley of Caves.

Robert stopped as a metallic glint caught his eye. Something sparkled over the prominences beyond the valley, perhaps ten miles away.

Gasbots, he thought. Over in that area Benjamin's techs had begun laying out samples of everything from electronics to metals to clothing, in an effort to discover what it was the Gubru robots homed in on. Robert hoped they had made some progress while he was away.

And yet, in another sense he hardly cared anymore. The new longbow felt good in his hand. The chims in the mountains preferred powerful homemade crossbows and arbalests, requiring less coordination but greater simian strength to crank. The effect had been the same with all three weapons ... dead birds. The use of ancient skills and archaic tools had turned into a galvanizing theme, resonating with the mythos of the Wolfling Clan.

There were disturbing consequences as well. Once, after a successful ambush, he had noticed some of the local mountain chens drifting away from camp. He slipped into the shadows and followed them to what appeared to be a secret cook fire, in a side canyon.

Earlier, while they had stripped the vanquished Gubru of their weapons and carried off the bodies, he had noticed some of the chims glancing back at him furtively, perhaps guiltily. That night he watched from a dark hillside as long-armed silhouettes danced in the firelight under the windblown stars. Something roasted on a spit over the flames, and the wind carried a sweet, smoky aroma.

Robert had had a feeling there were a few things the chims did not want seen by their patrons. He faded back into the shadows and returned to the main camp, leaving them to their ritual.

The images still flickered in his mind like feral, savage fantasies. Robert never asked what had been done with the bodies of the dead Galactics, but since then he could not think of the enemy without remembering that aroma.

If only there were a way to get more of them to come into the mountains, he pondered. Only under the trees did it seem possible to hurt the invaders.

The afternoon was aging. Time to finish the long jog home. Robert turned and was about to start down into the valley when he stopped suddenly. He blinked. There was a blur in the air. Something seemed to flutter at the edge of his vision, as if a tricky moth were dancing just within his blind spot. It didn't seem to be possible to look at the thing.

Oh, Robert thought.

He gave up trying to focus on it and looked away, letting the odd *non-thing* chase him instead. Its touch laid open the petals of his mind like a flower unfolding in the sun. The fluttering entity danced timidly and winked at him ... a simple glyph of affection and mild amusement ... easy enough for even a thick-thewed, hairy-armed, road-smelly, pinkish-brown *human* to understand.

'Very funny, Clennie.' Robert shook his head. But the flower opened still wider and he *kenned* warmth. Without having to be told, he knew which way to go. He turned off the main trail and leapt up a narrow game path.

Halfway to the ridgetop he came upon a brown figure lounging in the shade of a thornbush. The chen looked up from a paperpage book and waved lazily.

'Hi, Robert. You're lookin' a lot better'n when I saw you last.'

'Fiben!' Robert grinned. 'When did you get back?'

The chim suppressed a tired yawn. 'Oh, 'bout an hour ago. The boys down in th' caves sent me right up here to see her nibs. I picked up somethin' for her in town. Sorry. Didn't get anythin for you, though.'

'Did you get into any trouble in Port Helenia?'

'Hmmm, well, some. A little dancin', a little scratchin', a little hootin'.'

Robert smiled. Fiben's 'accent' was always thickest when he had big news to downplay, the better to draw out the story. If allowed to get away with it, he would surely keep them up all night.

'Uh, Fiben ...'

'Yeah, yeah. She's up there.' The chim gestured toward the top of the ridge. 'And in a right fey mood, if you ask me. But don't ask me, I'm just a chimpanzee. I'll see you later, Robert.' He picked up his book again, not exactly the model of a reverent client. Robert grinned.

'Thanks, Fiben. I'll see ya.' He hurried up the trail.

Athaclena did not bother to turn around as he approached, for they had already said hello. She stood at the hilltop looking westward, her face to the sun, holding her hands outstretched before her.

Robert at once sensed that another glyph floated over Athaclena now, supported by the waving tendrils of her corona. And it was an impressive thing. Comparing her little greeting, earlier, to this one would be like standing a dirty limerick next to 'Xanadu.' He could not see it, neither could he even begin to *kenn* its complexity, but it was there, nearly palpable to his heightened empathy sense.

Robert also realized that she held something between her

hands ... like a slender thread of invisible fire – intuited more than seen – that arched across the gap from one hand to the other.

'Athaclena, what is – '

He stopped then, as he came around and saw her face.

Her features had changed. Most of the humaniform contours she had shaped during the weeks of their exile were still in place; but something they had displaced had returned, if only momentarily. There was an alien glitter in her gold-flecked eyes, and it seemed to dance in counterpoint to the throbbing of the half-seen glyph.

Robert's senses had grown. He looked again at the thread in her hands and felt a thrill of recognition.

'Your father ... ?'

Athaclena's teeth flashed white. *'With-tanna Uthacalthing belli-narri-t'hoo, haoon'nda! ...'*

She breathed deeply through wide-open nostrils. Her eyes – set as wide apart as possible – seemed to flash.

'Robert, he lives!'

He blinked, his mind overflowing with questions. 'That's great! But ... but where! Do you know anything about my mother? The government? What does he say?'

She did not reply at once. Athaclena held up the thread. Sunlight seemed to run up and down its taut length. Robert might have sworn that he heard sound, *real* sound, emitting from the thrumming fiber.

'With-tanna Uthacalthing!' Athaclena seemed to look straight into the sun.

She laughed, no longer quite the sober girl he had known. She chortled, *Tymbrimi* fashion, and Robert was very glad that *he* was not the object of that hilarity. Tymbrimi humor quite often meant that someone else, sometime soon, would definitely not be amused.

He followed her gaze out over the Vale of Sind, where a flight of the ubiquitous Gubru transports moaned faintly as they cruised across the sky. Unable to trace more than the outlines of her glyph, Robert's mind searched for and found something akin to it in the human fashion. In his mind he pictured a metaphor.

Suddenly, Athaclena's smile was something feral, almost *catlike*. And those warships, reflected in her eyes, seemed to take on the aspect of complacent, rather unsuspecting *mice*.

PART THREE

THE GARTHLINGS

The evolution of the human race will not be accomplished in the ten thousand years of tame animals, but in the million years of wild animals, because man is and will always be a wild animal.

CHARLES GALTON DARWIN

Natural selection won't matter soon, not anywhere near as much as conscious selection. We will civilize and alter ourselves to suit our ideas of what we can be. Within one more human lifespan, we will have changed ourselves unrecognizably.

GREG BEAR

43

UTHACALTHING

Inky stains marred the fen near the place where the yacht had foundered. Dark fluids oozed slowly from cracked, sunken tanks into the waters of the broad, flat estuary. Wherever the slick trails touched, insects, small animals, and the tough salt grass all died.

The little spaceship had bounced and skidded when it crashed, scything a twisted trail of destruction before finally plunging nose first into the marshy river mouth. For days thereafter the wreck lay where it had come to rest, slowly leaking and settling into the mud.

Neither rain nor the tidal swell could wash away the battle scars etched into its scorched flanks. The yacht's skin, once allicient and pretty, was now seared and scored from near-miss after near-miss. Crashing had only been the final insult.

Incongruously large at the stern of a makeshift boat, the Thennanin looked across the intervening flat islets to survey the wreck. He stopped rowing to ponder the harsh reality of his situation.

Clearly, the ruined spaceship would never fly again. Worse, the crash had made a sorrowful mess of this patch of marshlands. His crest puffed up, a rooster's comb ridged with spiky gray fans.

Uthacalthing lifted his own paddle and politely waited for his fellow castaway to finish his stately contemplation. He hoped the Thennanin diplomat was not about to serve up yet another lecture on ecological responsibility and the burdens of patronhood. But, of course, Kault was Kault.

'The spirit of this place is offended,' the large being said, his breathing slits rasping heavily. 'We sapients have no business taking our petty wars down into nurseries such as these, polluting them with space poisons.'

'Death comes to all things, Kault. And evolution thrives on tragedies.' He was being ironic, but Kault, of course, took him seriously. The Thennanin's throat slits exhaled heavily.

'I know that, my Tymbrimi colleague. It is why most registered nursery worlds are allowed to go through their natural cycles unimpeded. Ice ages and planetoidal impacts are all part of the natural order. Species are tempered and rise to meet such challenges.

'However, this is a special case. A world damaged as badly as Garth can only take so many disasters before it goes into shock and becomes completely barren. It is only a short time since the Bururalli worked out their madness here, from which this planet has barely begun to recover. Now our battles add more stress ... such as that filth.'

Kault gestured, pointing at the fluids leaking from the broken yacht. His distaste was obvious.

Uthacalthing chose, this time, to keep his silence. Of course every patron-level Galactic race was officially environmentalist. That was the oldest and greatest law. Those spacefaring species who did not at least declare fealty to the Ecological Management Codes were wiped out by the majority, for the protection of future generations of sophonts.

But there were degrees. The Gubru, for instance, were less interested in nursery worlds than in their products, ripe pre-sentient species to be brought into the Gubru Clan's peculiar color of conservative fanaticism. Among the other lines, the Soro took great joy in the manipulation of newly fledged client races. And the Tandu were simply horrible.

Kault's race was sometimes irritating in their sanctimonious pursuit of ecological purity, but at least theirs was a fixation Uthacalthing could understand. It was one thing to burn a forest, or to build a city on a registered world. Those types of damage would heal in a short time. It was quite another thing to release long-lasting poisons into a biosphere, poisons which would be absorbed and accumulate. Uthacalthing's own distaste at the oily slicks was only a little less intense than Kault's. But nothing could be done about it now.

'The Earthlings had a good emergency cleanup team on this planet, Kault. Obviously the invasion has left it inoperative. Perhaps the Gubru will get around to taking care of this mess themselves.'

Kault's entire upper body twisted as the Thennanin performed a sneezelike expectoration. A gobbet struck one of the nearby leafy fronds. Uthacalthing had come to know that this was an expression of extreme incredulity.

'The Gubru are slackers and heretics! Uthacalthing, how can you be so naively optimistic?' Kault's crest trembled and his leathery lids blinked. Uthacalthing merely looked back at his fellow castaway, his lips a compressed line.

'Ah. Aha,' Kault rasped. 'I see! You test my sense of humor with a statement of *irony*.' The Thennanin made his ridge crest inflate briefly. 'Amusing. I get it. Indeed. Let us proceed,'

Uthacalthing turned and lifted his oar again. He sighed and crafted *tu'fluk*, the glyph of mourning for a joke not properly appreciated.

Probably, this dour creature was selected as ambassador to an

Earthling world because he has what passes for a great sense of humor among Thennanin. The choice might have been a mirror image of the reason Uthacalthing himself had been chosen by the Tymbrimi ... for his comparatively serious nature, for his restraint and tact.

No, Uthacalthing thought as they rowed, worming by patches of struggling salt grass. *Kault, my friend, you did not get the joke at all. But you will.*

It had been a long trek back to the river mouth. Garth had rotated more than twenty times since he and Kault had to abandon the crippled ship in midair, parachuting into the wilderness. The Thennanin's unfortunate Ynnin clients had panicked and gotten their parasails intertangled, causing them to fall to their deaths. Since then, the two diplomats had been solitary companions.

At least with spring weather they would not freeze. That was some comfort.

It was slow going in their makeshift boat, made from stripped tree branches and parasail cloth. The yacht was only a few hundred meters from where they had sighted it, but it took the better part of four hours to wend through the frequently tortuous channels. Although the terrain was very flat, high grass blocked their view most of the way.

Then, suddenly, there it was, the broken ruin of a once-sleek little ship of space.

'I still do not see why we had to come back to the wreck,' Kault rasped. 'We got away with sufficient dietary supplements to let us live off the land. When things calm down we can intern ourselves – '

'Wait here,' Uthacalthing said, not caring that he interrupted the other. Thennanin weren't fanatical about that sort of punctilio, thank Ifni. He slipped over the side of the boat and into the water. 'There is no need that both of us risk approaching any closer. I will continue alone.'

Uthacalthing knew his fellow castaway well enough to read Kault's discomfort. Thennanin culture put great store in personal courage – especially since space travel terrified them so.

'I will accompany you, Uthacalthing.' He moved to put the oar aside. 'There may be dangers.'

Uthacalthing stopped him with a raised hand. 'Unnecessary, colleague and friend. Your physical form isn't suited for this mire. And you may tip the boat. Just rest. I'll only be a few minutes.'

'Very well, then.' Kault looked visibly relieved. 'I shall await you here.'

Uthacalthing stepped through the shallows, feeling for his footing in the tricky mud. He skirted the swirls of leaked ship-fluid and made toward the bank where the broken back of the yacht arched over the bog.

It was hard work. He felt his body try to alter itself to better handle the effort of wading through the muck, but Uthacalthing suppressed the reaction. The glyph *nuturunow* helped him keep adaptations to a minimum. The distance just wasn't worth the price the changes would cost him.

His ruff expanded, partly to support *nuturunow* and partly as his corona felt among the weeds and grass for presences. It was doubtful anything here could harm him. The Bururalli had seen to that. Still, he probed the surrounding area as he waded, and caressed the empathy net of this marshy life-stew.

The little creatures were all around him, all the basic, standard forms: sleek and spindly birds, scaled and horn-mouthed reptiloids, hairy or furry types which scuttled among the reeds. It had long been known that there were three classic ways for oxygen-breathing animals to cover themselves. When skin cells buckled outward it led to feathers. When they buckled inward there was hair. When they thickened, flat and hard, the animal had scales.

All three had developed here, and in a typical pattern. Feathers were ideal for avians, who needed maximum insulation for minimum weight. Fur covered the warm-blooded creatures, who could not afford to lose heat.

Of course, that was the only surface. Within, there was a nearly infinite number of ways to approach the problem of living. Each creature was unique, each world a wonderful experiment in diversity. A planet was *supposed* to be a great nursery, and deserved protection in that role. It was a belief both Uthacalthing and his companion shared.

His people and Kault's were enemies – not as the Gubru were to the humans of Garth, of course, but of a certain style – registered with the Institute for Civilized Warfare. There were many types of conflict, most of them dangerous and quite serious. Still, Uthacalthing liked this Thennanin, in a way. That was preferable. It was usually easier to pull a jest on someone you liked.

His slick leggings shed the greasy water as he slogged up onto the mudbank. Uthacalthing checked for radiation, then stepped lightly toward the shattered yacht.

Kault watched the Tymbrimi disappear around the flank of the broken ship. He sat still, as he had been bid, using the paddle occasionally to stroke against the sluggish current and keep away from the oozing spills. Mucus bubbled from his breathing slits to drive out the stench.

Throughout the Five Galaxies the Thennanin were known as tough fighters and doughty starfarers. But it was only on a living, breathing planet that Kault and his kind could relax. That was why their ships so resembled worlds themselves, solid and durable. A scout craft made by his people would not have been swatted from the sky as this one had, by a mere terawatt laser! The Tymbrimi preferred speed and maneuverability over armor, but disasters such as this one seemed to bear out the Thennanin philosophy.

The crash had left them with few options. Running the Gubru blockade would have been chancy at best, and the other alternative had been hiding out with the surviving human officials. Hardly choices one lingered over.

Perhaps the crash had been the best possible branching for reality to take, after all. At least here there was the dirt and water, and they were amid life.

Kault looked up when Uthacalthing reappeared around the corner of the wreck, carrying a small satchel. As the Tymbrimi envoy slipped into the water, Uthacalthing's furry ruff was fully expanded. Kault had learned that it was not as efficient at dissipating excess heat as the Thennanin crest.

Some groups within his clan took facts like these as evidence of intrinsic Thennanin superiority, but Kault belonged to a faction that was more charitable in outlook. Each lifeform had its niche in the evolving Whole, they believed. Even the wild and unpredictable wolfling humans. Even heretics.

Uthacalthing's corona fluffed out as he worked his way back to the boat, but it was not because he was overheated. He was crafting a special glyph.

Lurrunanu hovered under the bright sunshine. It coalesced in the field of his corona, gathered, strained forward eagerly, then catapulted over toward Kault, dancing over the big Thennanin's crest as if in delighted curiosity.

The Galactic appeared oblivious. He noticed nothing, and he could not be blamed for that. After all, the glyph *was* nothing. Nothing real.

Kault helped Uthacalthing climb back aboard, grabbing his belt and pulling him into the rocky boat head first. 'I recovered some extra dietary supplements and a few tools we might need,' Uthacalthing said in Galactic Seven as he rolled over. Kault steadied him.

The satchel broke open and bottles rolled onto the fabric bottom. *Lurrunanu* still hovered above the Thennanin, awaiting the right moment. As Kault reached down to help collect the spilled items, the whirling glyph pounced!

It struck the famed Thennanin obstinacy and rebounded. Kault's bluff stolidity was too tough to penetrate. Under Uthacalthing's prodding, *lurrunanu* leapt again, furiously hurling itself against the leathery creature's crest at just the moment Kault picked up a bottle that was lighter than the others and handed it to Uthacalthing. But the alien's obdurate skepticism sent the glyph reeling back once more.

Uthacalthing tried a final time as he fumbled with the bottle and put it away, but this time *lurrunanu* simply shattered against the Thennanin's impenetrable barrier of assumptions.

'Are you all right?' Kault asked.

'Oh, fine.' Uthacalthing's ruff settled down and he exhaled in frustration. Somehow, he would have to find a way to excite Kault's curiosity!

Oh well, he thought. *I never expected it to be easy. There will be time.*

Out there ahead of them lay several hundred kilometers of wildlands, then the Mountains of Mulun, and finally the Valley of the Sind before they could reach Port Helenia. Somewhere in that expanse Uthacalthing's secret partner waited, ready to help execute a long, involved joke on Kault. *Be patient,* Uthacalthing told himself. *The best jests do take time.*

He put the satchel under his makeshift seat and secured it with a length of twine. 'Let us be off. I believe we'll find good fishing by the far bank, and those trees will make for good shelter from the midday sun.'

Kault rasped assent and picked up his oar. Together they worked their way through the marsh, leaving the derelict yacht behind them to settle slowly into the endurant mud.

44

GALACTICS

In orbit above the planet the invasion force entered a new phase of operation.

At the beginning, there had been the assault against a brief, surprisingly bitter, but almost pointless resistance. Then came the consolidation and plans for ritual and cleansing. All through this, the major preoccupation of the fleet had been defensive.

The Five Galaxies were in a turmoil. Any of a score of other alliances might have also seen an opportunity in seizing Garth. Or the Terran/Tymbrimi alliance – though hard beset elsewhere – might choose to counterattack here. The tactical computers calculated that the wolflings would be stupid to do so, but Earthlings were so unpredictable, one could never tell.

Too much had been invested in this theater already. The clan of the Gooksyu-Gubru could not afford a loss here.

So the battle fleet had arrayed itself. Ships kept watch over the five local layers of hyperspace, over nearby transfer points, over cometary time-drop nexi.

News came of Earth's travails, of the desperation of the Tymbrimi, and of the tricksters' difficulties in acquiring allies among the lethargic Moderate clans. As the interval stretched it became clear that no threat would come from those directions.

But some of the other great clans *were* busy. Those who were quick to see advantage. Some were engaged in futile searches for the missing dolphin ship. Others used the confusion as a convenient excuse to carry through on ancient grudges. Millennia-old agreements unraveled like gas clouds before sudden supernovae. Flame licked at the ancient social fabric of the Five Galaxies. From the Gubru Home Perch came new orders. As soon as ground-based defenses were completed, the greater part of the fleet must go on to other duties. The remaining force should be more than adequate to hold Garth against any reasonable threat.

The Roost Masters did accompany the order with compensations. To the Suzerain of Beam and Talon they awarded a citation. To the Suzerain of Propriety they promised an improved Planetary Library for the expedition on Garth.

The new Suzerain of Cost and Caution needed no compensation. The orders were victory in themselves for they manifested caution in their essence. The chief bureaucrat won molt points, badly needed in its competition with its more experienced peers.

The naval units set forth for the nearest transfer point, confident that matters on Garth were well in beak and hand. The ground forces, however, watched the great battleships depart with slightly less certitude. Down on the planet's surface there were portents of a minor resistance movement. The activity – as yet hardly more than a nuisance – had started among the chimpanzee population in the back country. As they were cousins and clients of men, their irritating and unbecoming behavior came as no surprise. The Gubru high command took precautions. Then they turned their attention to other matters.

Certain items of information had come to the attention of the Triumvirate – data taken from an enemy source – information having to do with Planet Garth itself. The hint might turn out to be nothing at all. But if it were true the possibilities were vast!

In any event, these things had to be looked into. Important advantages might be at stake. In this, all three Suzerains agreed completely. It was their first taste of true consensus together.

A platoon of Talon Soldiers kept watch over the expedition making its way into the mountains. Slender avians in battle dress swooped just over the trees, the faint whine of their flight harnesses carrying softly down the narrow canyons. One hover tank cruised ahead on point and another guarded the convoy's rear.

The scientist investigators in their floater barges rode amidst this ample protection. The vehicles headed upland on low cushions of air. Perforce they avoided the rough, spiny ridgetops. There was no hurry, though. The rumor they chased was probably nothing at all, but the Suzerains insisted that it be checked out, just in case.

Their goal came into sight late on the second day. It was a flat-tened area at the bottom of a narrow valley. A number of buildings had burned to the ground here, not too long ago.

The hover tanks took positions at opposite ends of the scorched area. Then Gubru scientists and their Kwackoo client-assistants emerged from the barges. Standing back from the still stinking ruins, the avians chirped commands to whirring specimen robots, directing the search for clues. Less fastidious than their patrons, the fluffy white Kwackoo dove right into the wreckage, squawking excit-edly as they sniffed and probed.

One conclusion was clear immediately. The destruction had been deliberate. The wreckers had wanted to hide something under the smoke and ruin.

Twilight came with subtropical suddenness. Soon the investiga-tors were working uncomfortably under the glare of spotlights. At last the team commander ordered a halt. Full-scale studies would have to wait for morning.

The specialists retired into their barges for the night, chattering about what they had already discovered. There were traces, hints of things exciting and not a little disturbing.

Still, there would be ample time to do the work by day. The tech-nicians closed their barges against the darkness. Six drone watchers rose to hover in silent, mechanical diligence, spinning patiently above the vehicles. Garth turned slowly under the starry night. Faint creakings and rustles told of the busy, serious work of the nocturnal forest creatures – hunting and being hunted. The watcher drones ignored them, rotating unperturbed. The night wore on.

Not long before dawn, new shapes moved through the starlit

lanes underneath the trees. The smaller local beasts sought cover and listened as the newcomers crept past, slowly, warily.

The watcher drones noticed these new animals, too, and measured them against their programmed criteria. *Harmless,* came the judgment. Once again, they did nothing.

45

ATHACLENA

'They're sitting ducks,' Benjamin said from his vantage point on the western hillside.

Athaclena glanced up at her chim aide-de-camp. For a moment she struggled with Benjamin's metaphor. Perhaps he was referring to the enemy's avian nature?

'They appear to be complacent, if that is what you mean,' she said. 'But they have reason. The Gubru rely upon battle robots more extensively than we Tymbrimi. We find them because they are expensive and overly predictable. Nevertheless, those drones can be formidable.'

Benjamin nodded seriously. 'I'll remember that, ser.'

Still, Athaclena sensed that he was unimpressed. He had helped plan this morning's foray, coordinating with representatives of the Port Helenia resistance. Benjamin was blithely certain of its success.

The town chims were to launch a predawn attack in the Vale of Sind just before action was scheduled to begin here. The official aim was to sow confusion among the enemy, and maybe do him some harm he would remember. Athaclena wasn't certain that was really possible. But she had agreed to the venture anyway. She did not want the Gubru finding out too much from the ruins of the Howletts Center.

Not yet.

'They've set up camp under the ruins of the old main building,' Benjamin said. 'Right where we expected them to plant themselves.'

Athaclena looked at the chim's solid-state night binoculars uncomfortably. 'You are certain those devices aren't detectable?'

Benjamin nodded without looking up. 'Yes'm. We laid instruments like these out on a hillside near a cruising gasbot, and its flightpath didn't even ripple. We've narrowed down the list of materials the enemy's able to sniff. Soon ...'

Benjamin stiffened. Athaclena felt his sudden tension.

'What is it?'

The chen crouched forward. 'I see shapes movin' through the trees. It must be our guys gettin' into position. Now we'll find out if those battle robots are programmed the way you expected.'

Distracted as he was, Benjamin did not offer to share the binoculars. *So much for patron-client protocol*, Athaclena thought. Not that it mattered. She preferred to reach out with her own senses.

Down below she detected three different species of biped arranging themselves around the Gubru expedition. If Benjamin had spotted them they certainly had to be well within range of the enemy's sensitive watch drones.

And yet the robots did nothing! Seconds beat past, and the whirling drones did not fire on the shapes approaching under the trees. Nor did they alert their sleeping masters.

She sighed in increased hope. The machines' restraint was a crucial piece of information. The fact that they spun on silently told her volumes about what was happening not only here on Garth but elsewhere, beyond the flecked star-field that glittered overhead. It told her something about the state of the Five Galaxies as a whole.

There is still law, Athaclena thought. *The Gubru are constrained.*

Like many other fanatic clans, the Gubru Alliance was not pristine in its adherence to the codes of planetary/ecological management. Knowing the avians' dour paranoia, she had figured that they would program their defense robots one way if the rules were still valid, and quite another if they had fallen.

If chaos had completely taken over the Five Galaxies, the Gubru would have programmed their machines to sterilize hundreds of acres rather than allow *any* risk to their feathery frames.

But if the Codes held, then the enemy did not yet dare break them. For those same rules might protect *them*, if the tide of war turned against their faction.

Rule Nine Hundred and Twelve: *Where possible, non-combatants must be spared.* That held for noncombatant *species*, even more than individuals, especially on a catastrophe world such as Garth. Native forms were protected by billion-year-old tradition.

'You are trapped by your own assumptions, you vile things,' she murmured in Galactic Seven. Obviously the Gubru had programmed their machines to watch for the trappings of sapiency – factory-produced weapons, clothing, machinery – never imagining that an enemy might assail their camp naked, indistinguishable from the animals of the forest!

She smiled, thinking of Robert. This part had been his idea.

Gray, antelucan translucence was spreading across the sky, gradually driving out the fainter stars. To Athaclena's left their medic, the elderly chimmie Elayne Soo, looked at her all-metal watch. She tapped its lens significantly. Athaclena nodded, giving permission for matters to proceed.

Dr Soo cupped her mouth and uttered a high trilling sound, the call of a fyuallu bird. Athaclena did not hear the snapping twang of bowstrings as thirty crossbows fired. She tensed though. If the Gubru had invested in really sophisticated drones ...

'Gotcha!' Benjamin exulted. 'Six little tops, all broken to bits! The robots are all down!'

Athaclena breathed again. Robert was down there. Now, perhaps, she could believe that he and the others had a chance. She touched Benjamin's shoulder, and the chim reluctantly handed over the binoculars.

Someone must have noticed when the monitor screens went blank. There was a faint hum, and the upper hatch of one of the hover tanks opened. A helmeted figure peered about the quiet meadow, its beak working in alarm as it saw the wreckage of a nearby watch robot. A sudden movement rustled the branches nearby. The soldier whirled about with its laser drawn as something or someone leaped forth from one of the neighboring trees. Blue lightning blazed at the dark figure.

It missed. The confused Gubru gunner couldn't track a dim shape that neither flew nor fell but swung across the narrow clearing at the end of a long vine! Bright bolts went wide two more times, and then the soldier's chance was gone. There was a 'crack' as the shadowy figure wrapped its legs around the slender avian and snapped its spine.

Athaclena's triple pulse beat fast as she saw Robert's silhouette stand on the turret of the tank, over the crumpled body of the Talon Soldier. He raised an arm to signal, and suddenly the clearing was filled with running forms.

Chims hurried among the tanks and floaters, carrying earthenware bottles. Behind them shambled larger figures bearing bulky packs. Athaclena heard Benjamin mutter to himself in suppressed resentment. It had been her choice to include gorillas in this operation, and the decision was not popular.

' ... thirty-five ... thirty-six ... ' Elayne Soo counted off the seconds. As the dawn light spread they could see chims clambering over the alien vehicles. This was gamble number three. Would surprise delay the inevitable reaction long enough?

Their luck ran out after thirty-eight seconds. Sirens shrieked, first from the lead tank and then from the one in the rear.

'Look out!' someone cried below.

The furry raiders scattered for the trees as Talon Soldiers tumbled out of their hover barges, firing searing blasts from their saber rifles. Chims fell screaming, batting at burning fur, or toppled silently into the undergrowth, holed from front to back. Athaclena clamped down on her corona in order not to faint under their agony.

This was her first taste of full-scale war. Right now there seemed to be no joke, only suffering and pointless, hideous death.

Then Talon Soldiers began falling. The avians hopped about seeking targets that had disappeared into the trees and were struck down by missiles as they stood. The fighters adjusted their weapons to seek out energy sources, but there were no lasers out there to home in on, no pulse-projectors, not even chemically powered pellet guns. Meanwhile crossbow bolts whizzed like stinging gnats. One by one, the Gubru warriors jerked and fell.

First one tank, then the other, began to rise on growling blasts of air. The lead vehicle turned. Its triple barrels then started blasting swaths through the forest.

The tops of towering trees seemed to hang in midair for brief moments as their centers exploded, before plummeting earthward in a haze of smoke and flying wood chips. Taut vines whipped back and forth like agonized snakes, spraying their hard-won liquors in all directions. Chims screamed as they spilled from shattered branches.

Is it worth it? Oh, can anything be worth this?

Athaclena's corona had expanded in the emotion of the moment, and she felt a glyph start to take shape. Angrily she rejected the unformed sense image, an answer to her question. She wanted no laughing Tymbrimi poignancies now. She felt like weeping, human style, but did not know how.

The forest was afroth with fear, and native animals fled the devastation. Some ran right over Athaclena and Benjamin, squeaking in their panicked desperation to get away. The radius of slaughter spread as the deadly vehicles opened up on everything in sight. Explosions and flame were everywhere.

Then, as abruptly as it had started firing, the lead tank stopped! First one, then another barrel glowed reddish white and shut down. Half of the noise abated.

The other fighting machine seemed to be suffering similar problems, but that one tried to continue firing, in spite of its crackling, drooping barrels.

'Duck!' Benjamin cried out as he pulled Athaclena down. The crew on the hillside took cover just in time as the rear tank exploded in a searing, actinic flash. Pieces of metal and shape-plast armor whistled by overhead.

Athaclena blinked away the sharp afterimage. In a momentary confusion brought on by sensory overload, she wondered why Benjamin was so obsessed with Earthly waterfowl.

'The other one's jammed!' Somebody shouted. Sure enough, by the time Athaclena was able to look again it was easy to see smoke rising from the lead tank's apron. The turret emitted grinding noises, and it seemed unable to move. Mixed with the pungent odor of burning vegetation came the sharp smell of corrosion.

'It worked!' Elayne Soo exulted. Then she was over the top and gone, running to tend the wounded.

Benjamin and Robert had proposed using chemicals to disable a Gubru patrol. Athaclena then modified the plan to suit her own purposes. She did not want dead Gubru, as had been their policy so far. This time she wanted live ones.

There they were now, bottled up inside their vehicles, unable to move or act. Their communications antennae were melted, and anyway, by now the attacks in the Sind had surely begun. The Gubru High Command had worries enough closer to home. Help would be some time coming.

Silence held for a moment as debris rained to the forest floor. Dust slowly settled.

Then there was heard a growing chorus of high shrieks – shouts of glee unaltered since before Mankind began meddling with chimpanzee genes. Athaclena heard another sound, as well ... a rolling, ululating cry of triumph – Robert's 'Tarzan' call.

Good, she thought. *It is good to know he lived through all that killing.*

Now if only he follows the plan and stays out of sight from now on!

Chims were emerging from the toppled trees, some hurrying to help Dr Soo with the injured. Others took up positions around the disabled machines.

Benjamin was looking to the northwest, where a few stars faded before the dawn. Faint, warlike rumblings could be heard coming from that direction. 'I wonder how Fiben and the city boys are doin' at their end,' he said.

For the first time Athaclena set her corona free. Released at last, it crafted *kuhunnagarra* ... the essence of indeterminacy postponed. 'It is beyond our grasp,' she told him. 'Here, in this place, is where we act.'

With a raised hand she signaled her hillside units forward.

46

FIBEN

Smoke rose from the Valley of the Sind. Scattered fires had broken out in wheat fields and among the orchards, injecting soot into a morning fast growing pale and dim.

A hundred meters high in the air, perched on the rough wooden frame of a handmade kite, Fiben used field glasses to scan the scattered conflagrations. The fighting had not gone at all well here in the Sind. The operation had been intended as a quick hit-and-run uprising – a way to hurt the invader. But it had turned into a rout.

And now the cloud deck was dropping, as if overladen with dark smoke and the sinking of their hopes. Soon he wouldn't be able to see beyond a kilometer or so.

'*Fiben!*'

Below and to the left, not far from the kite's blocky shadow, Gailet Jones waved up at him. 'Fiben, do you see anything of C group? Did they get the Gubru guard post?'

He shook his head, exaggeratedly.

'No sign of them!' he called. 'But there's dust from enemy armor!'

'Where? How much? We'll give you more slack so you can get a better – '

'No way!' he shouted. 'I'm comin' down now.'

'But we need data – '

He shook his head emphatically. 'There are patrols all over the place! We've got to get out of here!' Fiben motioned to the chims controlling his tether rope.

Gailet bit her lip and nodded. They started reeling him in.

As the attack collapsed and their communications unraveled, Gailet had only become more frantic for information. Frankly, he couldn't blame her. He, too, wanted to know what was happening. He had friends out there! But right now it might be better to think of their own skins.

And it all started so well, he thought as his craft slowly descended. The uprising had begun when chim workers employed at Gubru construction sites set off explosives carefully emplaced over the last week. At five of the eight target sites, satisfying fiery plumes had risen to meet the dawn sky.

But then the advantages of technology began to be seen. It had been mind-numbing, witnessing how quickly the automated defense systems of the enemy responded, scything through advancing teams of irregular fighters before their assaults could barely begin. To his knowledge not a single of the more important objectives had been taken, let alone held.

All told, things did not look good at all.

Fiben was forced to luff the kite, spilling air as the crude glider dropped. The ground rushed up, and he gathered his legs for the impact. It came with a jarring thud. He heard one of the wooden spars break as the wing took up most of the shock.

Well, better a spar than a bone. Fiben grunted as he undid his harness and wrestled free of the heavy homespun fabric. A real parasail, with composite struts and duracloth wings, would have been an awful lot better. But they still didn't know what it was about some manufactured goods that the invader was able to home in on. So he had insisted on homemade – and clumsy – substitutes.

The big, scarred chim named Max stood watch nearby, a captured Gubru laser rifle in one hand. He offered a hand. 'You okay, Fiben?'

'Yeah, Max, fine. Let's get this thing broken down.'

His crew hurried to disassemble the kite and get it under the cover of the nearby trees. Gubru floaters and fighters had been whistling overhead ever since the ill-fated foray had begun before dawn. The kite was almost insignificant, virtually invisible to radar or infrared. Still, they had surely been pushing their luck using it in daylight like this.

Gailet met them at the edge of the orchard. She had been reluctant to believe in the Gubru secret weapon – the enemy's ability to detect manufactured goods. But she had gone along partway at his insistence. The chimmie wore a half-length brown robe over shorts and a homespun tunic. She clutched a notebook and stylus to her breast.

Getting her to leave behind her portable data screen had taken a major effort of persuasion.

If Fiben had imagined for a moment that he saw relief on her face when he picked himself out of the wreckage, he stood corrected. She was all business now.

'What did you see? How heavy were the enemy reinforcements from Port Helenia? How close did Yossy's team get to the skynet battery?'

Good chens and chimmies have died this morning, but all she seems to care about is her damned data!

The space-defense strongpoint had been one of several targets of opportunity. Until now the few piddling ambushes in the mountains had hardly been enough to raise the enemy's notice. Fiben had insisted that the first raid would have to count big. They would never find the enemy *so* unprepared again.

And yet Gailet had planned the operation in the Vale of Sind around her observers, not the fighting units. To her, information was more important than any harm they might do to the enemy. And to Fiben's surprise the general had agreed.

He shook his head. 'There's a lot of smoke over in that direction, so I guess maybe Yossy accomplished something.' Fiben dusted himself off. There was a tear in his homespun overalls. 'I saw plenty of enemy reinforcements moving about. It's all up here.' He tapped his head.

Gailet grimaced, obviously wishing she could hear it all right now. But the plan had been to be away well before this. It was getting awfully late. 'Okay, we'll debrief you later. By now this rendezvous must be compromised.'

You gotta be kidding, Fiben thought, sarcastically. He turned. 'You guys got that thing buried yet?'

The three chims in the late team were kicking leaves over a low mound under the bulging roots of a fook sap tree. 'All done, Fiben.' They began collecting their hunting rifles stacked beneath another tree.

Fiben frowned. 'I think we'd better get rid of those. They're Terran-make.'

Gailet shook her head emphatically. 'And replace them with what? If we're stuck with just our six or ten captured Gubru lasers, what can we accomplish? I'm willing to attack the enemy stark naked if I have to, but not unarmed!' Her brown eyes were hot.

Fiben felt his own anger. 'You're willing to attack. Why not go after the damn birds with a sharpened pencil then! That s your favorite weapon.'

'That's not fair! I'm taking all these notes because – '

She never finished the remark. Max interrupted, shouting, 'Take cover!'

The sudden whistle of split air became a rocking boom as something white flashed past nearly at treetop level. Fallen leaves whirled and floated out upon the meadow in its wake. Fiben did not remember diving behind a knotted tree root, but he peered over it in time to see the alien craft rise and come about at the crest of the far hill, then begin its return run.

He felt Gailet nearby. Max was to the left, already high in the branches of another tree. The others had flattened themselves over to the right, closer to the verge of the orchard.

Fiben saw one of them raise his weapon as the scoutcraft approached again.

'*No!*' he shouted, realizing he was already too late.

The edge of the meadow erupted. Gobbets of earth were thrown skyward, as if by angry demons. In the blink of an eye the maelstrom ripped through the nearest trees, propelling fragments of leaves, branches, dirt, flesh, and bone through the air in all directions.

Gailet stared at the chaos, slack-jawed. Fiben threw himself onto her just before the rolling explosion swept past them. He felt the wake of the white fighting craft as it roared past. Surviving trees rattled and shook from the momentum of displaced air. A steady rain of debris fell onto Fiben's back.

'Hmm-mmmph!'

Gailet's face emerged from under his arm. She gasped. 'Get friggin' offa me before I *suffocate*, you smelly, flea-crackin', moth-eaten ...'

Fiben saw the enemy scout plane disappear over the hill. He got up quickly. 'Come on,' he said, hauling her to her feet. 'We've got to get out of here.'

Gailet's colorful curses ceased abruptly as she stood up. She gasped at the sight of what the Gubru weapon had done, staring as one does at what is too horrible to believe.

Bits of wood had been stirred vigorously with the grisly remains of three would-be warriors. The chims' rifles lay scattered among the wreckage.

'If you're plannin' on grabbing one of those weapons, you're on your own, sister.'

Gailet blinked, then she shook her head and mouthed one word. *No.* She was convinced.

Then she whirled. 'Max!'

She started toward where they had last seen her big, dour servant. But just then there came a rumbling sound.

Fiben stopped her. 'Troop transports. We haven't got time. If he's alive and can get away he will. Let's go!'

The drone of giant machines drew closer. She resisted, still. 'Oh, for Ifni's sake, think of saving your notes!' he urged.

That struck home. Gailet let him drag her along. She stumbled after him for a few paces, then caught her stride. Together they began to run.

Some girl, Fiben thought as they fled under the cover of the trees. *She might be a pain in the ass, but at least she's got spunk. First time she's ever seen anything like that, and she doesn't even throw up.*

Yeah? Another little voice seemed to say inside him. *And when did you ever see such a mess, either? Space battles are neat, clean, compared to this.*

Fiben admitted to himself that the biggest reason he had not puked was that he'd be damned if he'd ever let himself lose his breakfast in front of this particular chimmie. He'd never give her the satisfaction.

Together they splashed across a muddy stream and sought cover away from there.

47

ATHACLENA

It was all up to Benjamin now.

Athaclena and Robert watched from cover up on the slopes as their friend approached the grounded Gubru convoy. Two other chims accompanied Benjamin, one holding high a flag of truce. Its device was the same as the symbol for the *Library* – the rayed spiral of Galactic Civilization.

The chim emissaries had doffed homespun and were now decked out in silvery formal robes, cut in a style appropriate for bipeds of their form and status. It took courage to approach this way. Although the vehicles were disabled – there had not been a sign of activity for more than half an hour – the three chims had to be wondering what the enemy would do.

'Ten to one the birds try using a robot first,' Robert muttered, his eyes intent on the scene below.

Athaclena shook her head. 'No bet, Robert. Notice! The door to the center barge is opening.'

From their vantage point they could survey the entire clearing. The wreckage of the Howletts Center buildings loomed darkly over one still smoldering hover tank. Its sister, useless barrels drooping, lay canted on its shattered pressure-skirts.

In between the two wrecked fighting machines, from one of the disabled barges, a floating shape emerged.

'Right,' Robert sniffed in disgust. It was, indeed, a robot. It, too, carried a flapping banner, another depiction of the rayed spiral.

'Damn birds won't admit chims are above the level of ground-worms, not unless they're forced to,' Robert commented. 'They'll try to use a machine to handle the parlay. I only hope Benjamin remembers what he's supposed to do.'

Athaclena touched Robert's arm, partly to remind him to keep his voice down. 'He knows,' she said softly. 'And he has Elayne Soo to help him.' Nevertheless, they shared a formless feeling of helplessness as they watched. This was patron-level business. Clients should not be asked to face a situation such as this alone.

The floating drone – apparently one of the Gubru's sample collection 'bots, hastily adapted to diplomatic functions – came to a halt four meters from the advancing chims, who had already stopped and planted their banner. The robot emitted a squeal of indignant chatter that Athaclena and Robert could not quite make out. The tone, however, was peremptory.

Two of the chims backed up a step, grinning nervously.

'You can do it, Ben!' Robert growled. Athaclena saw knots stand out in his well-muscled arms. If those bulges had been Tymbrimi change glands, instead ... She shivered at the comparison and looked back to the scene below.

Down in the valley, Chim Benjamin stood rock still, apparently ignoring the machine. He waited. At last its tirade ran down. There was a moment of silence. Then Benjamin made a simple arm motion – exactly as Athaclena had taught him – contemptuously dismissing the nonliving from involvement in sapient affairs.

The robot squawked again, this time louder, and with a trace of desperation.

The chims simply stood and waited, not even deigning to answer the machine. 'What hauteur,' Robert sighed. 'Good going, Ben. Show 'em you got class.'

Minutes passed. The tableau held.

'This convoy of Gubru came into the mountains without psi shields!' Athaclena announced suddenly. She touched her right temple as her corona waved. 'That or the shields were wrecked in the attack. Either way, I can tell they are growing nervous.'

The invaders still possessed some sensors. They would be detecting movement in the forest, runners drawing nearer. The second assault group would arrive soon, this time bearing modern weapons.

The Resistance had kept its greatest power in reserve for the sake of surprise. Antimatter tended to give off resonances that were detectable from a long way away. Now, though, it was time to show all of their cards. By now the enemy would know that they were not safe, even within their armored craft.

Abruptly, and without ceremony, the robot rose and fled to the center barge. Then, after a brief pause, the lock cycled open again and a new pair of emissaries emerged.

'Kwackoo,' Robert announced.

Athaclena suppressed the glyph *syrtunu*. Her human friend did have a propensity for proclaiming the obvious.

The fluffy white quadrupeds, loyal clients of the Gubru,

approached the parlay point gobbling to each other excitedly. They loomed large as they arrived in front of the chims. A vodor hung from one thick, feathery throat, but the translator machine remained silent.

The three chims folded their hands before themselves and bowed as one, inclining their heads to an angle of about twenty degrees. They straightened and waited.

The Kwackoo just stood there. It was apparent who was ignoring whom this time.

Through the binoculars Athaclena saw Benjamin speak. She cursed the need to watch all this without any way to listen in.

The chim's words were effective, however. The Kwackoo chirped and blatted in flustered outrage. Through the vodor came words too faint to pick out, but the results were nearly instantaneous. Benjamin did not wait for them to finish. He and his companions picked up their banner, turned about, and marched away.

'Good fellow,' Robert said in satisfaction. He knew chims. Right now their shoulder blades must be itching terribly, yet they sauntered coolly.

The lead Kwackoo stopped speaking. It stared, nonplussed. Then it began hopping and giving out sharp cries. Its partner, too, seemed quite agitated. Now those on the hill could hear the amplified voice of the vodor, commanding '... come back! ...' over and over again.

The chims continued walking toward the line of trees until, at last, Athaclena and Robert heard the *word*.

'... come back ... PLEASE! ...'

Human and Tymbrimi looked at each other and shared a smile. *That* was half of what this fight had been about.

Benjamin and his party halted abruptly. They turned around and sauntered back. With the spiral standard in place once more they stood silently, waiting. At last, quivering from what must have been terrible humiliation, the feathered emissaries bowed.

It was a shallow bow – hardly a bending of two out of four knees – but it served. Indentured clients of the Gubru had recognized as their equals the indentured clients of human beings. 'They might have chosen death over this,' Athaclena whispered in awe, though she had planned for this very thing. 'The Kwackoo are nearly sixty thousand Earth years old. Neo-chimpanzees have been sapient for only three *centuries*, and are the clients of wolflings.' She knew Robert would not be offended by her choice of words. 'The Kwackoo are far enough along in Uplift that they have the right to choose death over this. They and the Gubru must be stupefied, and have not thought out the implications. They probably can barely believe it is happening.

Robert grinned. 'Just wait till they hear the rest of it. They'll wish they'd chosen the easy way out.'

The chims answered the bow at the same angle. Then, with that distasteful formality out of the way, one of the giant avioids spoke quickly, its vodor mumbling an Anglic translation.

'The Kwackoo are probably demanding to speak with the leaders of the ambush,' Robert commented, and Athaclena agreed.

Benjamin betrayed his nervousness by using his hands as he replied. But that was no real problem. He gestured at the ruins, at the destroyed hover tanks, at the helpless barges and the forest on all sides, where vengeful forces were converging to finish the job.

'He's telling them he *is* the leader.'

That was the script, of course. Athaclena had written it, amazed all the while how easily she had adapted from the subtle Tymbrimi art of dissemblement to the more blatant, human technique of outright lying.

Benjamin's hand gestures helped her follow the conversation. Through empathy and her own imagination, she felt she could almost fill in the rest.

'*We have lost our patrons,*' Benjamin had rehearsed saying. '*You and your masters have taken them from us. We miss them, and long for their return. Still, we know that helpless mourning would not make them proud of us. Only by action may we show how well we have been uplifted.*

'*We are therefore doing as they have taught us – behaving as sapient creatures of thought and honor.*

'*In honor's name then, and by the Codes of War, I now demand that you and your masters offer their parole, or face the consequences of our legal and righteous wrath!*'

'He is doing it,' Athaclena whispered half in wonder.

Robert coughed as he tried not to laugh aloud. The Kwackoo seemed to grow more and more distressed as Benjamin spoke. When he finished, the feathery quadrupeds hopped and squawked. They puffed and preened and objected loudly.

Benjamin, though, would not be bluffed. He referred to his wrist chronometer then spoke three words.

The Kwackoo suddenly stopped protesting. Orders must have arrived, for all at once they bowed again, swiveled, and sped back to the center barge at a gallop.

The sun had risen above the line of hills to the east. Splashes of morning light blazed through the lanes of shattered trees. It grew warm out on the parlay ground, but the chims stood and waited. At intervals Benjamin glanced to his watch and called out the time remaining.

At the edge of the forest Athaclena saw their special weapons team begin setting up their only antimatter projector. Certainly the Gubru were aware of it, too.

She heard Robert softly counting out the minutes.

Finally – in fact nearly at the very last moment – the hatches of all three hover craft opened. From each emerged a procession. The entire complement of Gubru, dressed in the glistening robes of senior patrons, led the way. They crooned a high-pitched song, accompanied by the basso of their faithful Kwackoo.

The pageantry was steeped in ancient tradition. It had its roots in epochs long before life had crawled ashore on the Earth. It wasn't hard to imagine how nervous Benjamin and the others must feel as those to be paroled assembled before them. Robert's own mouth felt dry. 'Remember to *bow* again,' he urged in a whisper.

Athaclena smiled, having the advantage of her corona. 'Have no fear, Robert. He will remember.' And indeed, Benjamin folded his hands before him in the deeply respectful fashion of a junior client greeting a senior patron. The chims bowed low.

Only a flash of white betrayed the fact that Benjamin was grinning from ear to ear.

'Robert,' she said, nodding in satisfaction. 'Your people have done very well by theirs, in only four hundred years.'

'Don't give us the credit,' he answered. 'It was all there in the raw from the start'

The paroled avians departed toward the Valley of the Sind on foot. No doubt they would be picked up before long. Even if they were not, Athaclena had ordered that word go out. They were to reach home base unmolested. Any chim who touched one feather would be outlawed, his plasm dumped into sewers, his gene-line extinguished. The matter was that serious.

The procession disappeared down the mountain road. Then the hard work began.

Crews of chims hurried to strip the abandoned vehicles in the precious time remaining before retribution arrived. Gorillas chuffed impatiently, grooming and signing to one another as they awaited loads to carry off into the hills.

By then Athaclena had already moved her command post to a spine-covered ridge two miles farther into the mountains. She watched through binoculars as the last salvage was loaded and hauled away, leaving nearly empty hulks under the shadows of the ruined buildings.

Robert had left much earlier, at Athaclena's insistence. He was departing again on another mission tomorrow and needed to get his rest.

Her corona waved, and she *kenned* Benjamin before his softly slapping feet could be heard padding up the trail. When he spoke his voice was somber.

'General, we've had word by semaphore that the attacks in the Sind failed. A few Eatee construction sites were blown up, but the rest of the assault was nearly a total disaster.'

Athaclena closed her eyes. She had expected as much. They had too many security problems down below, for one thing. Fiben had suspected the town-side resistance was compromised by traitors.

And yet Athaclena had not disallowed the attacks. They had served a valuable purpose by distracting the Gubru defense forces, keeping their quick-reaction fighters busy far from here. She only hoped that not too many chims had lost their lives drawing the invader's ire.

'The day balances out,' she told her aide. Their victories would have to be symbolic, she knew. To try to expel the enemy with forces such as theirs would be futile. With her growing knack at metaphors she likened it to a caterpillar attempting to move a tree.

No, what we win, we will achieve through subtlety.

Benjamin cleared his throat. Athaclena looked down at him. 'You still do not believe we should have let them leave alive,' she told him.

He nodded. 'No, ser, I do not. I think I understand some of what you told me about symbolism and all that ... and I'm proud you seem to think we handled the parole ceremony all right. But I still believe we should've burned them all.'

'Out of revenge?'

Benjamin shrugged. They both knew that was how the majority of the chims felt. They couldn't care less about symbols. The races of Earth tended to look upon all the bowing and fine class distinctions of the Galactics as the mincing foolishness of a mired, decadent civilization.

'You know that's not what I think,' Benjamin said. 'I'd go along with your logic – about us scoring a real coup here today just by getting them to talk to us – if it weren't for one thing.'

'What thing is that?'

'The birds had a chance to snoop around the center. They saw traces of Uplift. And I can't rule out the possibility they caught a glimpse of the gorillas *themselves*, through the trees!' Benjamin shook his head. 'I just don't think we should've allowed them to walk out of here after that,' he said.

Athaclena put a hand on her aide's shoulder. She did not speak because there did not seem to be anything to say.

How could she explain it to Benjamin?

Syulff-kuonn took form over her head, whirling with satisfaction at the progress of things, things her father had planned.

No, she could not explain to Benjamin that she had insisted on bringing the gorillas along, on making them part of the raid, as a step in a long, involved, and very practical joke.

48

FIBEN AND GAILET

'Keep your head down!' Fiben growled.

'Will you stop snapping at me?' Gailet answered hotly. She lifted her eyes just to the tops of the surrounding grass stems. 'I just want to see if – '

The words cut off as Fiben swept her supporting arms out from under her. She landed with a grunt of expelled air and rolled over spitting dirt. 'You pit-scratching, flea-bitten – '

Her eyes remained eloquent even with Fiben's hand clamped firmly over her mouth. 'I told you,' he whispered. 'With their sensors, if you can see them it means they've *got* to see you. Our only chance is to crawl like worms until we can find a way to blend back into the civilian chim population!'

From not far away came the hum of agricultural machinery. The sound had drawn them here. If they could only get close enough to mingle with the farmers, they might yet escape the invaders' dragnet.

For all Fiben knew, he and Gailet might be the only survivors of the ill-fated uprising in the valley. It was hard to imagine how the mountain guerrillas under Athaclena's command could have done any better. The insurrection seemed all washed up from where he lay.

He drew back his hand from Gailet's mouth. *If looks could kill*, he thought, contemplating the expression in her eyes. With her hair matted and mud-splattered, she was hardly the picture of the serene chimmie intellectual.

'I ... thought ... you ... said ...' she whispered deliberately, emphasizing calmness, 'that the enemy couldn't detect us if we wear only native-made materials.'

'That's if they're being lazy and *only* counting on their secret weapon. But don't forget they've also got infrared, radar, seismic sonar, psi – ' He stopped suddenly. A low whine approached from his left. If it was the harvester they had heard before, there might be a chance to catch a ride.

'Wait here,' he whispered.

Gailet grabbed his wrist. 'No! I'm coming with you!' She looked quickly left and right, then lowered her eyes. 'Don't ... don't leave me alone.'

Fiben bit his lip. 'All right. But stay down low, right behind me.'

They moved single file, hugging the ground. Slowly the whine grew louder. Soon Fiben felt a faint tingling up the back of his neck. *Gravities*, he thought. *It's close.*

How close he didn't realize until the machine slipped over the grasstops, coming into view just two meters away.

He had been expecting a large vehicle. But this thing was about the size of a basketball and was covered with silvery and glassy knobs – sensors. It bobbed gently in the afternoon breeze, regarding them.

Aw hell. He sighed, sitting up on his haunches and letting his arms drop in resignation. Not far away he heard faint voices. No doubt this thing's owners.

'It's a battle drone, isn't it?' Gailet asked tiredly.

He nodded. 'A sniffer. Cheap model, I think. But good enough to find and hold us.'

'What do we do?'

He shrugged. 'What *can* we do? We'd better surrender.'

Behind his back, however, he sifted through the dark soil. His fingers closed around a smooth stone.

The distant voices were coming this way. *What th' heck*, he thought.

'Listen, Gailet. When I move, duck. Get outta here. Get your notes to Athaclena, if she's still alive.'

Then, before she could ask any questions, he let out a shout and hurled the stone with all his might.

Several things happened all at once. Pain erupted in Fiben's right wrist. There was a flash of light, so bright that it dazzled him. Then, during his leap forward, countless stinging pinpricks rained up and down his chest.

As he sailed toward the thing a sudden, strange feeling overcame Fiben, one that said that he had performed this act before – lived this particular moment of violence – not once or twice, but a hundred times, in a hundred prior lives. The wave of familiarity, hooked on the flickering edge of memory, washed over him as he dove through the drone's pulsing gravitic field to wrap himself over the alien machine.

The world bucked and spun as the thing tried to throw him off. Its laser blasted at his shadow and grass fires broke out. Fiben held on for his life as the fields and the sky blended in a sickening blur.

The induced sense of *déjà vu* actually seemed to help! Fiben felt as if he had done this countless times! A small, rational corner of his mind knew that he hadn't, but the memory misfunction said different and gave him a false confidence he badly needed right then as he dared to loosen the grip of his injured right hand and fumbled for the robot's control box.

Ground and sky merged. Fiben tore a fingernail prying at the lid, breaking the lock. He reached in, grabbed wires.

The machine spun and careened, as if sensing his intention. Fiben's legs lost their grip and whipped out. He was whirled around like a rag doff. When his left hand gave way he held on only by a weakening grip on the wires themselves – round and round and round . . .

At that moment only one thing in the world was not a blur: the lens of the robot's laser, directly in front of him.

Goodbye, he thought, and closed his eyes.

Then something tore loose. He flew away, still holding wires in his right hand. When crunching impact came, it was almost anticlimactic. He cried out and rolled up just short of one of the smoldering fires.

Oh, there was pain, all right. Fiben's ribs felt as if one of the big female gorillas at the Howletts Center had been affectionate with him all night. He had been shot at least twice. Still, he had expected to die. No matter what came after this, it was good just to be alive.

He blinked away dust and soot. Five meters away the wreckage of the alien probe hissed and sputtered inside a ring of blackened, smoking grass. So much for the vaunted quality of Galactic hardware.

What Eatee shyster sold the Gubru that piece of shit? Fiben wondered. *I don't care, even if it was a Jophur made of ten smelly sap rings, I'd kiss him right now, I really would.*

Excited voices. Running feet. Fiben felt a sudden hope.

He had expected Gubru to come after their downed probe. But these were chims! He winced and held his side as he managed to stand. He smiled.

The expression froze on his face when he saw who was approaching.

'Well, well, what do we have here? Mr Bluecard himself! Looks like you've been running more obstacle courses, college boy. You just don't seem to know when you're beat.'

It was a tall chen with carefully shaved facial hair and a mustache, elegantly waxed and curled. Fiben recognized the leader of the Probationer gang at the Ape's Grape. The one calling himself Irongrip.

Of all the chims in all the world, why did it have to be him?

Others arrived. The bright zipsuits bore an added feature, a sash and arm patch, each bearing the same sigil ... a claw outstretched, three sharp talons glistening in holographic threat.

They gathered around him carrying modified saber rifles, obviously members of the new collaborators' militia he and Gailet had heard rumors of.

'Remember me, college boy?' Irongrip asked, grinning. 'Yes, I thought you would. I sure do remember you.'

Fiben sighed as he saw Gailet Jones brought forward, held firmly by two other Probationers. 'Are you all right?' she asked softly. He could not read the expression in her eyes. Fiben nodded. There seemed to be little to say.

'Come on, my young genetic beauties.' Irongrip laughed as he took Fiben hard just above his wounded right wrist. 'We've got some people we want you to meet. And this time, there won't be any distractions.'

Fiben's gaze was torn away from Gailet's as a jerk on his arm sent him stumbling. He lacked the strength to put up a useless struggle.

As his captors dragged him ahead of Gailet, he had his first chance to look around and saw that they were only a few hundred meters from the edge of Port Helenia! A pair of wide-eyed chims in work dungarees watched from the running boards of a nearby cultivator.

Fiben and Gailet were being taken toward a small gate in the alien wall, the barrier that undulated complacently over the countryside like a net settled firmly over their lives.

49

GALACTICS

The Suzerain of Propriety displayed its agitation by huffing and dancing a brief series of hops on its Perch of Declamation. The half-formed squirms had actually delayed appearing before its judgment, withholding the news for more than a planetary rotation!

True, the survivors of the mountain ambush were still in shock. Their first thought had been to report to military command. And the military, busy cleaning up the last of the abortive insurrections in the nearby flatlands, had made them wait. What, after all, was a minor scuffle in the hills compared with a nearly effective assault on the deep-space defense battery?

The Suzerain could well understand how such mistakes were made. And yet it was frustrating. The affair in the mountains was actually far more significant than any of the other outbreaks of wild guerrilla warfare.

'You should have extinguished – caused an end – eliminated your-selves!'

The Suzerain chirped and danced out its chastisement before the Gubru scientists. The specialists still looked ruffled and unpreened from their long trek out of the hills. Now they slumped further in dejection.

'In accepting parole you have injured – caused harm – reduced our propriety and honor,' the Suzerain finished chiding.

If they had been military the high priest might have demanded reparations from these and their families. But most of their escorts had been killed, and scientists were often less concerned or knowl-edgeable in matters of propriety than soldiers.

The Suzerain decided to forgive them.

'Nevertheless, your decision is understood – is given sanction. We shall abide by your parole.'

The technicians danced in relief. They would not suffer humili-ation or worse upon returning to their homes. Their solemn word would not be repudiated.

The parole would be costly however. These scientists had to depart from the Garth system at once and not be replaced for at least a year. Furthermore, an equal number of human beings had to be released from detention!

The Suzerain suddenly had an idea. This brought on a rare flut-ter of that strange emotion, *amusement*. It would order sixteen humans freed, all right, but the mountain chimpanzees would not be reunited with their dangerous masters. The released humans would be sent to Earth!

That would certainly satisfy the propriety of the parole. The solu-tion would be expensive, true, but not nearly as much as letting such creatures loose again on the main continent of Garth!

It was stunning to contemplate that neo-chimpanzees might have achieved what these reported they had done in the mountains. How could it be? The proto-clients they had observed in town and in the valley hardly seemed capable of such finesse.

Might there, indeed, be humans out there still?

The thought was daunting, and the Suzerain did not see how it would be possible. According to census figures the number unac-counted for was too small to be significant anyway. Statistically, all of those should simply be dead.

Of course the gas bombings would have to be stepped up. The

new Suzerain of Cost and Caution would complain, for the program had proved very expensive. But now the Suzerain of Propriety would side with the military completely.

There was a faint stirring. The Suzerain of Propriety felt a twinge inside. Was it an early sign of a change of sexual state? It should not begin yet, when things were still so unsettled, and dominance not yet decided among the three peers. The molting must wait until propriety had been served, until consensus had been reached, so that it would be clear who was strongest!

The Suzerain chirped a prayer to the lost Progenitors, and the others immediately crooned in response.

If only there was some way to be sure which way the battles were going, out in the Galactic swirl! Had the dolphin ship been found yet? Were the fleets of some alliance even now approaching the returned Ancient Ones to call up the end of all things?

Had the time of Change already begun?

If the priest were certain that Galactic Law had indeed broken down irreparably, it would feel free to ignore this unpalatable parole and its implied recognition of neo-chimpanzee sapiency.

There were consolations, of course. Even with humans to guide them, the near-animals would never know the right ways to take advantage of that recognition. That was the way of wolfling-type species. Ignoring the subtleties of the ancient Galactic culture, they barged ahead using the direct approach, and nearly always died.

Consolation, it chirped. *Yes, consolation and victory.*

There was one more matter to take care of – potentially, the most important of all. The priest addressed the leader of the expedition again.

'Your final parole agreement was to avoid – to abjure – to forswear ever visiting that site again.'

The scientists danced agreement. One small place on the surface of Garth was forbidden the Gubru until the stars fell, or until the rules were changed.

'And yet, before the attack you found – did discover – did uncover traces of mysterious activity – of gene meddling – of secret Uplift?'

That too had been in their report. The Suzerain questioned them carefully about details. There had only been time for a cursory examination, but the hints were compelling. The implications staggering.

Up in those mountains the chimpanzees were hiding a pre-sentient race! Prior to the invasion, they and their human patrons had been engaging in Uplift of a new client species!

So! The Suzerain danced. The data recovered from the Tymbrimi cairn was no lie! Somehow, by some miracle, this catastrophe world has given birth to a treasure! And now, in spite of Gubru mastery of the surface and the sky, the Earthlings continued to hoard their discovery to themselves!

No wonder the planetary Branch Library had been ransacked of its Uplift files! They had tried to hide the evidence.

But now, the Suzerain rejoiced, *we know of this wonder.*

'You are dismissed – released – set upon your ships for home,' it told the bedraggled scientists. Then the Suzerain turned to its Kwackoo aides, gathered below its perch.

'Contact the Suzerain of Beam and Talon,' it said with unaccustomed brevity. 'Tell my peer that I wish a colloquy at once.' One of the fluffy quadrupeds bowed at once, then scurried off to call the commander of the armed forces.

The Suzerain of Propriety stood still upon its perch, disallowed by custom from setting foot upon the surface until the ceremonies of protection had been completed.

Its weight shifted from time to time, and it rested its beak on its chest while standing deep in thought.

PART FOUR

TRAITORS

Accuse not Nature, she hath done her part; Do thou but thine.

JOHN MILTON, *PARADISE LOST*

50

GOVERNMENT IN HIDING

The messenger sat on a couch in the corner of the Council Room, holding a blanket around his shoulders while he sipped from a steaming cup of soup. Now and then the young chen shivered, but mostly he looked exhausted. His damp hair still lay in tangled mats from the icy swim that had brought him on the last leg of his dangerous journey.

It's a wonder he made it here at all, Megan Oneagle thought, watching him. *All the spies and recon teams we sent ashore, carrying the finest equipment – none ever returned. But this little chim makes it to us, sailing a tiny raft made of cut trees, with homespun canvas sails.*

Carrying a message from my son.

Megan wiped her eyes again, remembering the courier's first words to her after swimming the last stretch of underground caves to their deep island redoubt.

'Captain Oneagle sends his felic— his felicitations, ma'am.'

He had drawn forth a packet – waterproofed in oli tree sap – and offered it to her, then collapsed into the arms of the medical techs.

A *message from Robert,* she thought in wonder. *He is alive. He is free. He helps lead an army.* She didn't know whether to exult or shudder at the thought.

It was a thing to be proud of, for sure. Robert might be the sole adult human loose on the surface of Garth, right now. And if his 'army' was little more than a ragged band of simian guerrillas, well, at least they had accomplished more than her own carefully hoarded remnants of the official planetary militia had.

If he had made her proud, Robert had also astonished her. Might there be more substance to the boy than she had thought before? Something brought out by adversity, perhaps?

There may be more of his father in him than I'd wanted to see.

Sam Tennace was a starship pilot who stopped at Garth every five years or so, one of Megan's three spacer husbands. Each was home for only a few months at a stretch – almost never at the same time – then off again. Other fems might not have been able to deal with such an arrangement, but what suited spacers also met her needs as a politician and career woman. Of the three, only Sam Tennace had given her a child.

And I never wanted my son to be a hero, she realized. *As critical as I have been of him, I guess I never really wanted him to be like Sam at all.*

For one thing, if Robert had not been so resourceful he might be safe now – interned on the islands with the rest of the human population, pursuing his playboy hobbies among his friends – instead of engaged in a desperate, useless struggle against an omnipotent enemy.

Well, she reassured herself. *His letter probably exaggerates.*

To her left, mutterings of amazement grew ever more pronounced as the government in exile pored over the message, printed on tree bark in homemade ink. 'Son of a bitch!' she heard Colonel Millchamp curse. 'So *that's* how they always knew where we were, what we were up to, before we even got started!'

Megan moved closer to the table. 'Please summarize, colonel.'

Millchamp looked up at her. The portly, red-faced militia officer shook several sheets until someone grabbed his arm and pried them out of his hand.

'Optical fibers!' he cried.

Megan shook her head. 'I beg your pardon?'

'They *doped* them. Every string, telephone cable, communications pipe ... almost every piece of electronics on the planet! They're all tuned to resonate back on a probability band the damn birds can broadcast ...' Colonel Millchamp's voice choked on his anger. He swiveled and walked away.

Megan's puzzlement must have shown.

'Perhaps I can explain, madam coordinator,' said John Kylie, a tall man with the sallow complexion of a lifetime spacer. Kylie's peacetime profession was captain of an in-system civilian freighter. His merchant vessel had taken part in the mockery of a space battle, one of the few survivors – if that was the right term. Overpowered, battered, finally reduced to peppering Gubru fighting planetoids with its comm laser, the wreck of the *Esperanza* only made it back to Port Helenia because the enemy was leisurely in consolidating the Gimelhai system. Its skipper now served as Megan's naval advisor.

Kylie's expression was stricken. 'Madam coordinator, do you remember that excellent deal we made, oh, twenty years ago, for a turnkey electronics and photonics factory? It was a state-of-the-art, midget-scale auto-fac – perfect for a small colony world such as ours.'

Megan nodded. 'Your uncle was coordinator then. I believe your first merchant command was to finalize negotiations and bring the factory home to Garth.'

Kylie nodded. He looked crestfallen. 'One of its main products is optical fibers. A few said the bargain we got from the Kwackoo was just too good to be true. But who could have imagined they might have something like this in mind? So far in the future? Just on the off chance that they might someday want to – '

Megan gasped. 'The Kwackoo! They're clients of – '

'Of the Gubru.' Kylie nodded. 'The damn birds must have thought, even then, that something like this might someday happen.'

Megan recalled what Uthacalthing had tried to teach her, that the ways of the Galactics are long ways, and patient as the planets in their orbits.

Someone else cleared his throat. It was Major Prathachulthorn, the short, powerfully built Terragens Marines officer. He and his small detachment were the only professional soldiers left after the space battle and the hopeless gesture of defiance at the Port Helenia space-field. Millchamp and Kylie held reserve commissions.

'This is most grave, madam coordinator,' Prathachulthorn said. 'Optical fibers made at that factory have been incorporated into almost every piece of military and civilian equipment manufactured on the planet. They are integrated into nearly every building. Can we have confidence in your son's findings?'

Megan nearly shrugged, but her politician's instincts stopped her in time. *How the hell would I know?* she thought. *The boy is a stranger to me.* She glanced at the small chen who had nearly died bringing Robert's message to her. She had never imagined Robert could inspire such dedication.

Megan wondered if she was jealous.

A woman Marine spoke next. 'The report is co-signed by the Tymbrimi Athaclena,' Lieutenant Lydia McCue pointed out. The young officer pursed her lips. 'That's a second source of verification,' she suggested.

'With all respect, Lydia,' Major Prathachulthorn replied. 'The tym is barely more than a child.'

'She's Ambassador Uthacalthing's daughter!' Kylie snapped. 'And chim technicians helped perform the experiments as well.'

Prathachulthorn shook his head. 'Then we have no truly qualified witnesses.'

Several councillors gasped. The sole neo-chimpanzee member, Dr Suzinn Benirshke, blushed and looked down at the table. But Prathachulthorn didn't even seem to realize he'd said anything insulting. The major wasn't known to be strong on tact. *Also, he's a Marine*, Megan reminded herself. The corps was the elite Terragens fighting service with the smallest number of dolphin and chim members. For that matter, the Marines recruited mostly males, a last bastion of oldtime sexism.

Commander Kylie sifted through the rough-cut pages of Robert

Oneagle's report. 'Still you must agree, major, the scenario is plausible. It would explain our setbacks, and total failure to establish contact, either with the islands or the mainland.'

Major Prathachulthorn nodded after a moment. 'Plausible, yes. Nevertheless, we should perform our own investigations before we commit ourselves to acting as if it is true.'

'What's the matter, major?' Kylie asked. 'You don't like the idea of putting down your phase-burner rifle and picking up bows and arrows?'

Prathachulthorn's reply was surprisingly mild. 'Not at all, ser, so long as the enemy is similarly equipped. The problem lies in the fact that he is not.'

Silence reigned for long moments. No one seemed to have anything to say. The pause ended when Colonel Millchamp returned to the table. He slammed the flat of his hand down. 'Either way, what's the point in waiting?'

Megan frowned. 'What do you mean, colonel?'

Millchamp growled. 'I mean what good do our forces do down here?' he demanded. 'We're all going slowly stir-crazy. Meanwhile, at this very moment, Earth herself may be fighting for her life!'

'There's no such thing as *this very moment* across interstellar space,' Commander Kylie commented. 'Simultaneity is a myth. The concept is imbedded in Anglic and other Earth tongues, but – '

'Oh, revert the metaphysics!' Millchamp snapped. 'What matters is that we can hurt Earth's enemies!' He picked up the tree-bark leaves. 'Thanks to the guerrillas, we know where the Gubru have placed many of their major planet-based yards. No matter *what* damned Library-spawned tricks the birds have got up their feathers, they can't prevent us from launching our flicker-swivvers at them!'

'But – '

'We have three hidden away – there weren't any used in the space battle, and the Gubru can't know we have any of 'em. If those missiles are supposed to be good against the Tandu, damn their seven-chambered hearts, they'll surely suffice for Gubru ground targets!'

'And what good will that do?' Lieutenant McCue asked mildly.

'We can bend a few Gubru beaks! Ambassador Uthacalthing told us that symbols are important in Galactic warfare. Right now they can pretend that we hardly put up a fight at all. But a symbolic strike, one that hurt them, would tell the whole Five Galaxies that we won't be pushed around!'

Megan Oneagle pinched the bridge of her nose. She spoke with eyes closed. 'I have always found it odd that my Amerindian ancestors' concept of "counting coup" should have a place in a hypertechnological galaxy.' She looked up. 'It may, indeed, come to that, if we can find no other way to be effective.

'But you'll recall that Uthacalthing also advised patience.' She shook her head. 'Please sit down, Colonel Millchamp. Everybody. I'm determined not to throw our strength away in a gesture, not until I know it's the only thing left to do against the enemy.

'Remember, nearly every human on the planet is hostage on the islands, their lives dependent on doses of Gubru antidote. And on the mainland there are the poor chims, for all intents abandoned, alone.'

Along the conference the officers sat downcast. *They're frustrated,* Megan thought. *And I can't blame them.*

When war had loomed, when they had begun planning ways to resist an invasion, nobody had ever suggested a contingency like this. Perhaps a people more experienced in the sophistications of the Great Library – in the arcane art of war that the aeons-old Galactics knew – might have been better prepared. But the Gubru's tactics had made a shambles of their modest defense plans.

She had not added her final reason for refusing to sanction a gesture. Humans were notoriously unsophisticated at the game of Galactic punctilio. A blow struck for honor might be bungled, instead giving the enemy excuse for even greater horrors.

Oh, the irony. If Uthacalthing was right, it was a little Earthship, halfway across the Five Galaxies from here, that had *precipitated* the crisis!

Earthlings certainly did have a knack for making trouble for themselves. They'd always had that talent.

Megan looked up as the small chen from the mainland, Robert's messenger, approached the table, still wearing his blanket. His dark brown eyes were troubled.

'Yes, Petri?' she asked.

The chim bowed.

'Ma'am, th' doctor wants me to go to bed now.'

She nodded. 'That's fine, Petri. I'm sure we'll want to debrief you some more, later ... ask you some more questions. But right now you should rest.'

Petri nodded. 'Yes'm. Thank you, ma'am. But there was somethin' else. Somethin' I'd better tell you while I remember.'

'Yes? What is it?'

The chen looked uncomfortable. He glanced at the watching humans and back at Megan. 'It's personal, ma'am. Somethin' Captain Oneagle asked me to memorize an' tell you.'

Megan smiled. 'Oh, very well. Will you all excuse me for a moment, please?'

She walked with Petri over to the far end of the room.

There she sat down to bring her eyes level with the little chim. 'Tell me what Robert said.'

Petri nodded. His eyes went unfocused. 'Captain Oneagle said to tell you that th' Tymbrimi Athaclena is actually doin' most of the organizing for th' army.'

Megan nodded. She had suspected as much. Robert might have found new resources, new depths, but he was not and never would be a born leader.

Petri went on. 'Cap'n Oneagle told me to tell you that it was important that th' Tymbrimi Athaclena have honorary patron status to our chims, legally.'

Again, Megan nodded. 'Smart. We can vote it and send word back.'

But the little chim shook his head. 'Uh, ma'am. We couldn't wait for that. So, uh, I'm supposed to tell you that Captain Oneagle an' th' Tymbrimi Athaclena have sealed a ... a *consort* bond ... I think that's what it's called. I ...'

His voice trailed off, for Megan had stood up.

Slowly, she turned to the wall and rested her forehead against the cool stone. *That damn fool of a boy!* part of her cursed.

It was the only thing they could do, another part answered.

So, now I'm a mother-in-law, the most ironic voice added.

There would certainly be no grandchildren from *this* union. That was not what interspecies consort marriages were for. But there were other implications.

Behind her, the council debated. Again and again they turned over the options, coming up dry as they had for months now.

Oh, if only Uthacalthing had made it here, Megan thought. *We need his experience, his wry wisdom and humor. We could talk, like we used to. And maybe, he could explain to me these things that make a mother feel so lost.*

She confessed to herself that she missed the Tymbrimi Ambassador. She missed him more than any of her three husbands and more even, God help her, than she missed her own strange son.

51

UTHACALTHING

It was fascinating to watch Kault play with a ne' squirrel, one of the native animals of these southern plains. He coaxed the small creature closer by holding out ripe nuts in his great Thennanin hands. He had been at it for over an hour while they waited out the hot noonday sun under the cover of a thick cluster of thorny bramble.

Uthacalthing wondered at the sight. His universe never seemed about to cease surprising him. Even bluff, oblivious, obvious Kault was a perpetual source of amazement.

Quivering nervously, the ne' squirrel gathered its courage. It took two more hops toward the huge Thennanin and stretched out its paws. It plucked up one of the nuts.

Astonishing. How did Kault do it?

Uthacalthing rested in the muggy shade. He did not recognize the vegetation here in the uplands overlooking the estuary where his pinnace had come down, but he felt he was growing familiar with the scents, the rhythms, the gently throbbing pain of daily life that surged and flowed through and all around the deceptively quiet glade.

His corona brought him touches from tiny predators, now waiting out the hot part of the day, but soon to resume stalking even smaller prey. There were no large animals, of course, but Uthacalthing *kenned* a swarm of ground-hugging insectoids grubbing through the detritus nearby, seeking tidbits for their queen.

The tense little ne' squirrel hovered between caution and gluttony as it approached once more to feed from Kault's outstretched hand.

He should not be able to do that. Uthacalthing wondered why the squirrel trusted the Thennanin, so huge, so intimidating and powerful. Life here on Garth was nervous, *paranoid* in the wake of the Bururalli catastrophe – whose deathly pall still hung over these steppes far east and south of the Mountains of Mulun.

Kault could not be soothing the creature as a Tymbrimi might – by glyph-singing to it in gentle tones of empathy. A Thennanin had all the psi sense of a stone.

But Kault spoke to the creature in his own highly inflected dialect of Galactic. Uthacalthing listened.

'Know you – sight-sound-image – an essence of destiny, yours? Little one? Carry you – genes-essence-destiny – the fate of star-treaders, your descendants?'

The ne' squirrel quivered, cheeks full. The native animal seemed mesmerized as Kault's crest puffed up and deflated, as his breathing slits sighed with every moist exhalation. The Thennanin could not commune with the creature, not as Uthacalthing might. And yet, the squirrel somehow appeared to sense Kault's love.

How ironic, Uthacalthing thought. Tymbrimi lived their lives awash in the everflowing music of life, and yet he did not personally identify with this small animal. It was one of hundreds of millions, after all. Why should he care about this particular individual?

Yet *Kault* loved the creature. Without empathy sense, without any direct being-to-being link, he cherished it *entirely in abstract*. He loved what the little thing represented, its potential.

Many humans still claim that one can have empathy without psi, Uthacalthing pondered. To 'put one's self into another's shoes,' went the ancient metaphor. He had always thought it to be one of their quaint pre-Contact ideas, but now he wasn't so certain. Perhaps Earthlings were sort of midway between Thennanin and Tymbrimi in this matter of how one empathized with others.

Kault's people passionately believed in Uplift, in the potential of diverse life forms eventually to achieve sapiency. The long-lost Progenitors of Galactic culture had commanded this, billions of years ago, and the Thennanin Clan took the injunction very seriously. Their uncompromising fanaticism on this issue went beyond being admirable. At times – as during the present Galactic turmoil – it made them terribly dangerous.

But now, ironically, Uthacalthing was counting on that fanaticism. He hoped to lure it into action of his own design. The ne' squirrel snatched one last nut from Kault's open hand and then decided it had enough. With a swish of its fan-shaped tail it scooted off into the undergrowth. Kault turned to look at Uthacalthing, his throat slits flapping as he breathed.

'I have studied genome reports gathered by the Earthling ecologists,' the Thennanin Consul said. 'This planet had impressive potential, only a few millennia ago. It should never have been ceded to the Bururalli. The loss of Garth's higher life forms was a terrible tragedy.'

'The Nahalli were punished for what their clients did, weren't they?' Uthacalthing asked, though he already knew the answer.

'Aye. They were reverted to client status and put under foster care to a responsible elder patron clan. My own, in fact. It is a most sad case.'

'Why is that?'

'Because the Nahalli are actually quite a mature and elegant people. They simply did not understand the nuances required in uplifting pure carnivores and so failed horribly with their Bururalli clients. But the error was not theirs alone. The Galactic Uplift Institute must take part in the blame.'

Uthacalthing suppressed a human-style smile. Instead his corona spiraled out a feint glyph, invisible to Kault. 'Would good news here on Garth help the Nahalli?' he asked.

'Certainly.' Kault expressed the equivalent of a shrug with his flapping crest. 'We Thennanin were not in any way associated with the Nahalli when the catastrophe occurred, of course, but that changed when they were demoted and given under our guidance. Now, by adoption, my clan shares responsibility for this wounded place. It is why a consul was sent here, to make certain the Earthlings do not do even more harm to this sorry world.'

'And have they?'

Kault's eyes closed and opened again. 'Have they what?'

'Have the Earthlings done a bad job, here?' Kault's crest flapped again.

'No. Our peoples may be at war, theirs and mine, but I have found no new grievances here to tally against them. Their ecological management program was exemplary.

'However, I do plan to file a report concerning the activities of the Gubru.'

Uthacalthing believed he could interpret bitterness in Kault's voice inflections. They had already seen signs of the collapse of the environmental recovery effort. Two days ago they had passed a reclamation station, now abandoned, its sampling traps and test cages rusting. The gene-storage bins had gone rancid after refrigeration failed.

An agonized note had been left behind, telling of the choice of a neo-chimpanzee ecology aide – who had decided to abandon his post in order to help a sick human colleague. It would be a long journey to the coast for an antidote to the coercion gas.

Uthacalthing wondered if they ever made it. Clearly the facility had been thoroughly dosed. The nearest outpost of civilization was very far from here, even by hover car.

Obviously, the Gubru were content to leave the station unmanned. 'If this pattern holds, it must be documented,' Kault said. 'I am glad you allowed me to persuade you to lead us back toward inhabited regions, so we can collect more data on these crimes.'

This time Uthacalthing did smile at Kault's choice of words. 'Perhaps we will find something of interest,' he agreed.

They resumed their journey when the sun, Gimelhai, had slipped down somewhat from its burning zenith.

The plains southeast of the Mulun range stretched like the undulating wavetops of a gently rolling sea, frozen in place by the solidity of earth. Unlike the Vale of Sind and the open lands on the other side of the mountains, here there were no signs of plant and animal life forms introduced by Earth's ecologists, only native Garth creatures.

And empty niches.

Uthacalthing felt the sparseness of species types as a gaping emptiness in the aura of this land. The metaphor that came to mind was that of a musical instrument missing half its strings.

Yes. Apt. Poetically appropriate. He hoped Athaclena was taking his advice and studying this Earthling way of viewing the world.

Deep, on the level of *nahakieri,* he had dreamt of his daughter last night. Dream-picted her with her corona reaching, *kenning* the threatening, frightening beauty of a visitation by *tutsunucann.* Trembling, Uthacalthing had awakened against his will, as if instinct had driven him to flee that glyph:

Through anything other than *tutsunucann* he might have learned more of Athaclena, of how she fared and what she did. But *tutsunucann* only shimmered – the essence of dreadful expectation. From that glimmer he knew only that she still lived. Nothing more.

That will have to do, for now.

Kault carried most of their supplies. The big Thennanin walked at an even pace, not too difficult to follow. Uthacalthing suppressed body changes that would have made the trek easier for a short while but cost him in the long run. He settled for a loosening in his gait, a wide flaring of his nostrils – making them flat but broad to let in more air yet keep out the ever-present dust.

Ahead, a series of small, tree-lined hummocks lay by a streambed, just off their path toward the distant ruddy mountains. Uthacalthing checked his compass and wondered if the hills should look familiar. He regretted the loss of his inertial guidance recorder in the crash. If only he could be sure . . .

There. He blinked. Had he imagined a faint blue flash?

'Kault.'

The Thennanin lumbered to a stop. 'Mmm?' He turned around to face Uthacalthing. 'Did you speak, colleague?'

'Kault, I think we should head that way. We can reach those hills in time to make camp and forage before dark.'

'Mmm. It is somewhat off our path.' Kault puffed for a moment. 'Very well. I will defer to you in this.' Without delay he bent and began striding toward the three green-topped mounds.

It was about an hour before sunset when they arrived by the watercourse and began setting camp. While Kault erected their camouflaged shelter, Uthacalthing tested pulpy, reddish, oblong fruits plucked from the branches of nearby trees. His portable meter declared them nutritious. They had a sweet, tangy taste.

The seeds inside, though, were hard, obdurate, obviously evolved to withstand stomach acids, to pass through an animal's digestive system and scatter on the ground with its feces. It was a common adaptation for fruit-bearing trees on many worlds.

Probably some large, omnivorous creature had once depended on the fruit as a food source and repaid the favor by spreading the seeds far and wide. If it climbed for its meals it probably had the rudiments of hands. Perhaps it even had Potential. The creatures might have someday become pre-sentient, entered into the cycle of Uplift, and eventually become a race of sophisticated people.

But all that ended with the Bururalli. And not only the large animals died. The tree's fruit now fell too close to the parent. Few embryos could break out of tough seeds that had evolved to be etched away in the stomachs of the missing symbionts. Those saplings that did germinate languished in their parents' shade.

There should have been a forest here instead of a tiny, scrabbling woody patch.

I wonder if this is the place, Uthacalthing thought. There were so few landmarks out on this rolling plain. He looked around, but there were no more tantalizing flashes of blue.

Kault sat in the entrance of their shelter and whistled low, atonal melodies through his breathing slits. Uthacalthing dropped an armload of fruit in front of the Thennanin and wandered down toward the gurgling water. The stream rolled over a bank of semi-clear stones, taking up the reddening hues of twilight.

That was where Uthacalthing found the artifact.

He bent and picked it up. Examined it.

Native chert, chipped and rubbed, flaked along sharp, glassy-edged lines, dull and round on one side where a hand could find a grip ...

Uthacalthing's corona waved. *Lurrunanu* took form again, wafting among his silvery tendrils. The glyph rotated slowly as Uthacalthing turned the little stone axe in his hand. He contemplated the primitive tool, and *lurrunanu* regarded Kault, still whistling to himself higher up the hillside.

The glyph tensed and launched itself toward the hulking Thennanin.

Stone tools – among the hallmarks of pre-sentience, Uthacalthing thought. He had asked Athaclena to watch out for signs, for there were rumors ... tales that told of sightings in the wild back country of Garth ...

'Uthacalthing!'

He swiveled, shifting to hide the artifact behind his back as he faced the big Thennanin. 'Yes, Kault?'

'I ...' Kault appeared uncertain. *'Metoh kanmi, b'twuil'ph ... I ...'* Kault shook his head. His eyes closed and opened again. 'I wonder if you have tested these fruits for my needs, as well as yours.'

Uthacalthing sighed. *What does it take? Do Thennanin have any curiosity at all?*

He let the crude artifact slip out of his hand, to drop into the river mud where he had found it. 'Aye, my colleague. They are nutritious, so long as you remember to take your supplements.'

He walked back to join his companion for a fireless supper by the growing sparkle of the galaxies' light.

52

ATHACLENA

Gorillas dropped over both sharp rims of the narrow canyon, lowering themselves on stripped forest vines. They slipped carefully past smoking crevices where recent explosions had torn the escarpment. Landslides were still a danger. Nevertheless, they hurried.

On their way down they passed through shimmering rainbows. The gorillas' fur glistened under coatings of tiny water droplets.

A terrible growling accompanied their descent, echoing from the cliff faces and covering their labored breathing. It had hidden the noise of battle, smothering the bellow of death that had raged here only minutes before. Briefly, the dinsome waterfall had had competition but not for long.

Where its fremescent torrent had formerly fallen to crash upon glistening smooth stones, it now splattered and spumed against torn metal and polymers. Boulders dislodged from the cliffsides had pounded the new debris at the foot of the falls. Now the water worked it flatter still.

Athaclena watched from atop the overlooking bluffs. 'We do not want them to know how we managed this,' she said to Benjamin.

'The filament we bunched up under the falls was pretreated to decay. It'll all wash away within a few hours, ser. When the enemy gets a relief party in here, they won't know what ruse we used to trap this bunch.'

They watched the gorillas join a party of chim warriors poking through the wreckage of three Gubru hover tanks. Finally satisfied that all was clear, the chims slung their crossbows and began pulling out bits of salvage, directing the gorillas to lift this boulder or that shattered piece of armor plate out of the way.

The enemy patrol had come in fast, following the scent of hidden prey. Their instruments told them that someone had taken refuge behind the waterfall. And it *was* a perfectly logical place for such a hideaway – a barrier hard for their normal detectors to penetrate.

Only their special resonance scanners had flared, betraying the Earthlings who had taken technology under there.

In order to take those hiding by surprise, the tanks had flown directly up the canyon, covered overhead by swarming battle drones of the highest quality, ready for combat.

Only they did not find much of a battle awaiting them. There were, in fact, no Earthlings at all behind the torrent. Only bundles of thin, spider-silk fiber. And a trip wire. And – planted all through the cliffsides – a few hundred kilos of homemade nitroglycerin.

Water spray had cleared away the dust, and swirling eddies had carried off myriad tiny pieces. Still the greater part of the Gubru strike force lay where it had been when explosions rocked the over-hanging walls, filling the sky with a rain of dark volcanic stone. Athaclena watched a chim emerge from the wreckage. He hooted and held up a small, deadly Gubru missile. Soon a stream of alien munitions found its way into the packs of the waiting gorillas. The large pre-sentients began climbing out again through the multi-hued spray.

Athaclena scanned the narrow streaks of blue sky that could be seen through the forest canopy. In minutes the invader would have its fighters here. The colonial irregulars must be gone by then, or their fate would be the same as the poor chims who rose last week in the Vale of Sind.

A few refugees had made it to the mountains after that debacle. Fiben Bolger was not one of them. No messenger had come with Gailet Jones's promised notes. For lack of information, Athaclena's staff could only guess how long it would take for the Gubru to respond to this latest ambush.

'Pace, Benjamin.' Athaclena glanced meaningfully at her time-piece.

Her aide nodded. 'Ill go hurry 'em up, ser.' He sidled over next to their signaler. The young chimmie began waving flapping flags.

More gorillas and chims appeared at the cliff edge, scrambling up onto the wet, glistening grass. As the chim scavengers climbed out of the water-carved chasm, they grinned at Athaclena and hurried off, guiding their larger cousins toward secret paths through the forest.

Now she no longer needed to coax and persuade. For Athaclena had become an honorary Earthling. Even those who had earlier resented taking orders 'from an Eatee' now obeyed her quickly, cheerfully.

It was ironic. In signing the articles that made them consorts, she and Robert had made it so that they now saw less of each other than ever. She no longer needed his authority as the sole free adult human, so he had set forth to raise havoc of his own elsewhere.

I wish I had studied such things better, she pondered. She was unsure just what was legally implied by signing such a document before witnesses. Interspecies 'marriages' tended to be more for official convenience than anything else. Partners in a business enterprise might 'marry,' even though they came from totally different genetic lines. A reptiloid Bi-Gle might enter into consort with a chitinous F'ruthian. One did not expect issue from such joinings. But it was generally expected that the partners appreciate each other's company.

She felt funny about the whole thing. In a special sense, she now had a 'husband.'

And he was not here.

So it was for Mathicluanna, all those long, lonely years, Athaclena thought, fingering the locket that hung from a chain around her throat. Uthacalthing's message thread had joined her mother's in there. Perhaps their *laylacllapt'n* spirits wound together in there, close as their bond had been in life.

Perhaps I begin to comprehend something I never understood about them, she wondered.

'Ser? . . . Uh, *ma'am?*'

Athaclena blinked and looked up. Benjamin was motioning to her from the trailhead, where one of the ubiquitous vine clusters came together around a small pool of pinkish water. A chimmie technician squatted by an opening in the crowded vines, adjusting a delicate instrument.

Athaclena approached. 'You have word from Robert?'

'Yesser,' the chimmie said. 'I definitely am detecting one of th' trace chemicals he took along with him.'

'Which is it?' she asked tensely.

The chimmie grinned. 'Th' one with th' left-handed adenine spiral. It's the one we'd agreed would mean victory.'

Athaclena breathed a little easier. So, Robert's party, too, had met with success. His group had gone to attack a small enemy observation post, north of Lome Pass, and must have engaged the enemy yesterday. Two minor successes in as many days. At this rate they might wear the Gubru down in, say, a million years or so.

'Reply that we, also, have met our goals.'

Benjamin smiled as he handed the signaler a vial of clear fluid, which was poured into the pool. Within hours the tagged molecules would be detectable many miles away. Tomorrow, probably, Robert's signaler would report her message.

The method was slow. But she imagined the Gubru would have absolutely no inkling of it – for a while, at least.

'They're finished with the salvage, general. We'd better scoot.'

She nodded. 'Yes. Scoot we shall, Benjamin.'

In a minute they were running together up the verdant trail toward the pass and home.

A little while later, the trees behind them rattled and thunder shook the sky. Clamorous booms pealed, and for a time the waterfall's roar fell away under a raptor's scream of frustrated vengeance.

Too late, she cast contemptuously at the enemy fighters.

This time.

53

ROBERT

The enemy had started using better drones. This time the added expense saved them from annihilation.

The battered Gubru patrol retreated through dense jungle, blasting a ruined path on all sides for two hundred meters. Trees blew apart, and sinuous vines whipped like tortured worms. The hover tanks kept this up until they arrived at an area open enough for heavy lifters to land. There the remaining vehicles circled, facing outward, and kept up nearly continuous fire in all directions.

Robert watched as one party of chims ventured too close with their hand catapults and chemical grenades. They were caught in the exploding trees, cut down in a hail of wooden splinters, torn to shreds in the indisciminate scything.

Robert used hand signals to send the withdraw-and-disperse order rippling from squad to squad. No more could be done to this convoy, not with the full force of the Gubru military no doubt already on its way here. His bodyguards cradled their captured saber rifles and darted into the shadows ahead of him and to the flanks.

Robert hated the way the chims kept this web of protection around him, forbidding him to approach a skirmish site until all was safe. There was just no helping it though. They were right, dammit.

Clients were expected to protect their patrons as individuals – and the patron race, in turn, protected the client race as a species.

Athaclena seemed better able to handle this sort of thing. She was from a culture that had come into existence from the start assuming that this was the way things were. *Also,* he admitted, *she doesn't worry about machismo.* One of his problems was that he seldom got to see or touch the enemy. And he so wanted to *touch* the Gubru.

The withdrawal was executed successfully before the sky filled with alien battlecraft. His company of Earthling irregulars split up into small groups, to make their separate ways to dispersed encampments until they received the call to arms again over the forest vine network. Only Robert's squad headed back toward the heights wherein their cave headquarters lay.

That required taking a wide detour, for they were far east in the Mulun range, and the enemy had set up outposts on several mountain peaks, easily supplied by air and defended with space-based weaponry. One of these stood along their most direct path home, so the chim scouts led Robert's group down a jungle crevice, just north of Lome Pass.

The ropelike transfer vines lay everywhere. They were wonders, certainly, but they made for slow going down here below the heights. Robert had had plenty of time to think. Mostly he wondered what the Gubru were doing coming up here into the mountains at all.

Oh, he was glad they came, for it gave the Resistance a chance to strike at them. Otherwise, the irregulars might as well spit at the enemy, with their vast, overpowering weaponry. But why were the Gubru bothering at all with the tiny guerrilla movement up in the Mulun when they had a firm grip on the rest of the planet? Was there some symbolic reason – something encrusted in Galactic tradition – that required they reduce every isolated pocket of resistance?

But even that would not explain the large civilian presence at those mountaintop outposts. The Gubru were pouring scientists into the Mulun. They were *looking* for something. Robert recognized this area. He signaled for a halt. 'Let's stop and look in on the gorillas,' he said. His lieutenant, a bespectacled, middle-aged chimmie named Elsie, frowned and looked at him dubiously. 'The enemy's gasbots sometimes dose an area without cause, sir. Just randomly. We chims will only be able to rest easy after you're safe underground again.'

Robert was definitely not looking forward to the caverns, especially since Athaclena wouldn't be back from her next mission for several days. He checked his compass and map.

'Come on, the refuge is only a few miles off our path. Anyway, if I know you chims from the Rowletts Center, you must be keeping your precious gorillas in a place that's even safer than the caves.'

He had her there, and Elsie clearly knew it. She put her fingers to her mouth and trilled a quick whistle, sending the scouts hurrying off in a new direction, to the southwest, darting through the upper parts of the trees.

In spite of the broken terrain, Robert made his way mostly along the ground. He couldn't dash pellmell along narrow branches, not

938

for mile after mile like the chims. Humans just weren't specialized for that sort of thing.

They climbed another side canyon that was hardly more than a split in the side of a mammoth bulwark of stone. Down the narrow defile floated soft wisps of fog, made opalescent by multiple refractions of daylight. There were rainbows, and once, when the sun came out behind, and above him, Robert looked down at a bank of drifting moisture and saw his own shadow surrounded by a triply colored halo, like those given saints in ancient iconography.

It was the *glory* . . . an unusually appropriate technical term for a perfect, one-hundred-and-eighty-degree reverse rainbow – much rarer than its more mundane cousins that would arch over any misty landscape, lifting the hearts of the blameless and the sinful alike.

If only I weren't so damn rational, he thought. *If I didn't know exactly what it was, I might have taken it as a sign.*

He sighed. The apparition faded even before he turned to move on.

There were times when Robert actually envied his ancestors, who had lived in dark ignorance before the twenty-first century and seemed to have spent most of their time making up weird, ornate explanations of the world to fill the yawning gap of their ignorance. Back then, one could believe in anything at all.

Simple, deliciously elegant explanations of human behavior – it apparently never mattered whether they were true or not, as long as they were incanted right. 'Party lines' and wonderful conspiracy theories abounded. You could even believe in your own sainthood if you wanted. Nobody was there to show you, with clear experimental proof, that there was no easy answer, no magic bullet, no philosopher's stone, only simple, boring sanity.

How narrow the Golden Age looked in retrospect. No more than a century had intervened between the end of the Darkness and contact with Galactic society. For not quite a hundred years, war was unknown to Earth.

And now look at us, Robert thought. *I wonder, does the Universe conspire against us? We finally grow up, make peace with ourselves . . . and emerge to find the stars already owned by crazies and monsters.*

No, he corrected himself. *Not all monsters.* In fact, the majority of Galactic clans were quite decent folk. But moderate majorities were seldom allowed to live in peace by fanatics, either in Earth's past or in the Five Galaxies today.

Perhaps golden ages simply aren't meant to last.

Sound traveled oddly in these closed, rocky confines, amid the crisscross lacing of native vines. One moment it seemed as if he were climbing in a world gone entirely silent, as if the rolling wisps of shining haze were folds of cotton batting that enveloped and smothered all sound. The next instant, he might suddenly pick up a snatch of conversation – just a few words – and know that some strange trick of acoustics had carried back to him a whispered remark between two of his scouts, possibly hundreds of meters away.

He watched them, the chims. They still looked nervous, these irregular soldiers who had until a few months ago been farmers, miners, and backwoods ecological workers. But they were growing more confident day by day. Tougher and more determined.

And more feral, Robert also realized, seeing them flit into and out of view among the untamed trees. There was something fierce and wild in the way they moved, in the way their eyes darted as they leaped from branch to branch. One seldom seemed to need words to know what the other was doing. A grunt, a quick gesture, a grimace, these were often more than enough.

Other than their bows and quivers and handspun weapons pouches, the chims mostly traveled naked. The softening trappings of civilization, the shoes and factory-made fabrics, were all gone. And with them had departed, some illusions.

Robert glanced down at himself – bare-shanked, clad in breechcloth, moccasins, and cloth knapsack, bitten, scratched and hardening every day. His nails were dirty. His hair had been getting in the way so he'd cut it off in front and tied it in back. His beard had long ago stopped itching.

Some of the Eatees think that humans need more uplifting – that we are ourselves little more than animals. Robert leaped for a vine and swung over a dark patch of evil-looking thorns, coming to land in an agile crouch upon a fallen log. *It's a fairly common belief among the Galactics, And who am I to say they're wrong?*

There was a scurry of movement up ahead. Rapid hand signals crossed the gaps between the trees. His nearby guards, those directly responsible for his safety, motioned for him to detour along the westward, upwind side of the canyon. After climbing a few score meters higher he learned why. Even in the dampness he caught the musty, oversweet smell of old coercion dust, of corroding metal, and of death.

Soon he reached a point where he could look across the little vale to a narrow scar – already healing under layers of new growth – which ended in a crumpled mass of once-sleek machinery, now seared and ruined.

There were soft chim whispers and hand signals among the scouts. They nervously approached and began picking through the debris while others fingered their weapons and watched the sky. Robert thought he saw jutting white bones amid the wreckage, already picked clean by the ever-hungry jungle. If he had tried to approach any closer, of course, the chims would have physically restrained him, so he waited until Elsie returned with a report.

'They were overloaded,' she said, fingering the small, black flight recorder. Emotion obviously made it hard for her to bring forth words. 'They were tryin' to carry too many humans to Port Helenia, the day just after th' hostage gas was first used. Some were already sick, and it was their only transport.'

'The flitter didn't clear th' peak, up there.' She gestured at the fog-shrouded heights to the south. 'Must've hit th' rocks a dozen times, to fall this far.'

'Shall . . . shall we leave a couple chims, sir? A . . . a burial detail?'

Robert scuffed the ground. 'No. Mark it. Map it. I'll ask Athaclena if we should photograph it later, for evidence.

'Meanwhile, let Garth take what she needs from them. I . . .'

He turned away. The chims weren't the only ones finding words hard right now. With a nod he set the party going again. As he clambered higher, Robert's thoughts burned. There *had* to be a way to hurt the enemy worse than they had so far!

Days ago, on a dark, moonless night, he had watched while twelve selected chims sailed down onto a Gubru encampment, riding the winds on homemade, virtually invisible paper gliders. They had swooped in, dropped their nitro and gas bombs, and slipped away by starlight before the enemy even knew anything was happening.

There had been noise and smoke, uproar and squawking confusion, and no way at all to tell how effective the raid was. Nevertheless, he remembered how he had hated watching from the sidelines. He was a trained pilot, more qualified than any of these mountain chims for a mission like that!

But Athaclena had given firm instructions to which the neo-chims all adhered. Robert's ass was sacred.

It's my own damn fault, he thought as he scrambled through a dense thicket. By making Athaclena his formal consort, he had given her that added status she had needed to run this small insurrection . . . and some degree of authority over him, as well. No longer could he do as he damn well pleased.

So, she was his *wife* now, in a fashion. *Some marriage,* he thought. While Athaclena kept adjusting her appearance to look more human, that only served to remind him of what she *couldn't* do, frustrating Robert. No doubt that was one reason why interspecies consortions were rare!

I wonder what Megan thinks of the news ... I wonder if our messenger ever got through.

'Hssst!'

He looked quickly to his right. Elsie stood balanced on a tree branch. She pointed upslope, to where an opening in the fog exposed a view of high clouds skimming like glass-bottomed boats on invisible pressure layers in the deep blue sky. Underneath the clouds could be seen the tree-fringed slope of a mountain. Narrow curls of smoke spiraled upward from shrouded places on its flanks.

'Mount Fossey,' Elsie said, concisely. And Robert knew, at once, why the chims felt this might be a safe place ... safe enough even for their precious gorillas.

Only a few semi-active volcanoes lay along the rim of the Sea of Cilmar. Still, all through the Mulun there were places where the ground occasionally trembled. And at rare intervals lava poured forth. The range was still growing.

Mount Fossey hissed. Vapor condensed in shaggy, serpentine shapes above geothermal vents, where pools of hot water steamed and intermittently burst forth in frothing geysers. The ubiquitous transfer vines came together here from all directions, twisting into great cables as they snaked up the flanks of the semi-dormant volcano. Here they held market in shady, smoky pools, where trace elements that had percolated through narrow trails of hot stone finally entered the forest economy.

'I should've guessed.' Robert laughed. Of course the Gubru would be unlikely to detect anything here. A few unclothed anthropoids on these slopes would be nothing amid all this heat, spume, and chemical potpourris. If the invaders ever did come to check, the gorillas and their guardians could just melt into the surrounding jungle and return after the interlopers left.

'Whose idea was this?' he asked as they approached under the shade of a high forest canopy. The smell of sulfur grew stronger.

'Th' gen'ral thought of it,' Elsie answered.

Figures. Robert didn't feel resentful. Athaclena was bright, even for a Tymbrimi, and he knew he himself wasn't much above human average, if that. 'Why wasn't I told about it?'

Elsie looked uncomfortable. 'Um, you never asked, ser. You were busy with your experiments, findin' out about the optical fibers and the enemy s detection trick. And ...'

Her voice trailed off.

'And?' he insisted.

She shrugged. 'And we weren't sure you wouldn't ever get dosed with th' gas, sooner or later. If that happened you'd have to report to town for antidote. You'd be asked questions – and maybe psi-scanned.'

Robert closed his eyes. Opened them. Nodded. 'Okay. For a moment there I wondered if you trusted me.'

'Ser!'

'Never mind.' He waved. Athaclena's decision had been proper, logical – once again. He wanted to think about it as little as possible.

'Let's go see the gorillas.'

They sat about in small family groups and were easily distinguished at a distance – much larger, darker, and hairier than their neo-chimpanzee cousins. Their big, peaked faces – as black as obsidian – bore expressions of peaceful concentration as they ate their meals, or groomed each other, or worked at the main task that had been assigned them, weaving cloth for the war.

Shuttles flew across broad wooden looms, carrying homespun weft over warped strands, snicking and clicking to a rhythm matched by the great apes' rumbling song. The ratcheting and the low, atonal grunting followed Robert as he and his party moved toward the center of the refuge.

Now and then a weaver would stop work, putting her shuttle aside to wave her hands in a flurry of motion, making conversation with a neighbor. Robert knew sign-talk well enough to follow some of the gossip, but the gorillas seemed to speak with a dialect that was quite different from that used by infant chims. It was simple speech, yes, but also elegant in its own way, with a gentle style that was all their own.

Clearly, these were not just big chims but a completely different race, another path taken. A separate route to sentience.

The gorilla groups each seemed to consist of a number of adult females, their young, a few juveniles, and one hulking silver-backed adult male. The patriarch's fur was always gray along his spine and ribs. The top of his head was peaked and imposing. Uplift engineering had altered the neo-gorilla's stance, but the bigger males still had to use at least one knuckle when they walked. Their huge chests and shoulders made them too top-heavy still to move bipedally.

In contrast, the lithe gorilla children moved easily on two legs. Their foreheads were rounded, smooth, without the severe sloping and bony brow ridges that would later give them such deceptively fierce countenances. Robert found it interesting how much alike infants of all three races looked – gorillas, chims, and humans. Only later in life did the dramatic differences of inheritance and destiny become fully apparent.

Neoteny, Robert thought. It was a classic, pre-Contact theory that had proven more valid than not – one proposing that part of the secret of sapiency was to remain as childlike as possible, for as long as possible. For instance, human beings retained the faces, the adaptability, and (when it was not snuffed out) the insatiable curiosity of young anthropoids, even well into adulthood.

Was this trait an accident? One which enabled pre-sentient *Homo habilis* to make the supposedly impossible leap – uplifting himself to starfaring intelligence by his own bootstraps? Or was it a gift from those mysterious beings some thought must have once meddled in human genes, the long-hypothesized missing patrons of humanity?

All that was conjecture, but one thing was clear. Other Earthly mammals largely lost all interest in learning and play after puberty. But humans, dolphins – and now, more and more with each generation, neo-chimpanzees – retained that fascination with the world with which they entered it.

Some day grown gorillas might also share this trait. Already these members of an altered tribe were brighter and remained curious longer than their fallow Earthly kin. Someday their descendants, too, might live out their life spans forever young.

If the Galactics ever allow it, that is.

Infant gorillas wandered about freely, poking their noses into everything. They were never slapped or chastised, only pushed gently aside when they got in the way, usually with a pat and a chuffed vocalization of affection. As he passed one group, Robert even caught a glimpse of a gray-flanked male mounting one of his females up in the bushes. Three youngsters crawled over the male's broad back, prying at his massive arms. He ignored them, simply closing his eyes and hunkering down – doing his duty by his species.

More infants scurried through breaking foliage to tumble in front of Robert. From their mouths hung strips of some plastic material that they chewed into frayed tatters. Two of the children stared up at him in something like awe. But the last one, less shy than the others, waved its hands in eager, if sloppy signs. Robert smiled and picked the little fellow up.

Higher on the hillside, above the chain of fog-shrouded hot springs, Robert saw other brown shapes moving through the trees. 'Younger males,' Elsie explained. 'And bulls too old to hold a patriarchy. Back before the invasion, the planners at th' Howletts Center were trying to decide whether to intervene in their family system. It's their way, yes, but it's so hard on the poor males – a couple years' pleasure and glory, but at the cost of loneliness most of the rest of their lives.' She shook her head. 'We hadn't made up our minds before the Gubru came. Now maybe we'll never get the chance.'

Robert refrained from commenting. He hated the restrictive treaties, but he still had trouble with what Elsie's colleagues had been doing at the Howletts Center. It had been arrogance to take the decision into their own hands. He could see no happy outcome to it.

As they approached the hot springs, he saw chims moving about seriously on various errands. Here one peered into the mouth of a huge gorilla easily six times her mass, probing with a dental tool. There another patiently taught sign language to a class of ten gorilla children.

'How many chims are here to take care of them?'

'Dr de Shriver from the Center, about a dozen of the chim techs that used to work with her, plus about twenty guards and volunteers from nearby settlements. It depends on when we sometimes take 'rillas off to help in the war.'

'How do they feed them all?' Robert asked as they descended to the banks of one of the springs. Some of the chims from his party had arrived ahead of them and were already lounging by the humid bank, sipping at soup cups. A small nearby cave held a makeshift storage chamber where resident workers in aprons were ladling out more steaming mugs.

'It's a problem.' Elsie nodded. 'The gorillas have finicky digestions, and it's hard to get them the right balance of foods. Even in th' restored ranges in Africa, a big silver-back needs up to sixty pounds of vegetation, fruit, an' insects a day. Natural gorillas have to move around a lot to get that kind of forage, an' we can't allow that.'

Robert lowered himself to the damp stones and released the gorilla infant, who scampered down to the poolside, still chewing his ragged strip of plastic. 'It sounds like quite a quandary,' he said to Elsie.

'Yeah. Fortunately, Dr Schultz solved the problem just last year. I'm glad he had that satisfaction before he died.'

Robert removed his moccasins. The water looked hot. He dipped a toe and pulled it back quickly. 'Ouch! How did he do it?'

'Um, beg your pardon?'

'What was Schultz's solution?'

'Microbiology, ser.' She looked up suddenly, her eyes bright. 'Ah, here they come with soup for us, too!'

Robert accepted a cup from a chimmie whose apron must have come from cloth woven on the gorillas' looms. She walked with a limp. Robert wondered if she had been wounded in some of the fighting.

'Thank you,' he said, appreciating the aroma. He hadn't realized how hungry he was. 'Elsie, what d'you mean, microbiology?'

She sipped delicately. 'Intestinal bacteria. Symbionts. We all have 'em. Tiny critters that live in our guts, an' in our mouths. They're harmless partners, mostly. Help us digest our food in exchange for a free ride.'

'Ah.' Of course Robert knew about bio-symbionts; any school kid did.

'Dr Schultz managed to come up with a suite of bugs that helps the 'rillas eat – and enjoy – a whole lot of native Garth vegetation. They –'

She was interrupted by a high-pitched little cry, unlike anything an ape might produce. 'Robert!' shrieked a piping voice.

He looked up. Robert grinned. 'April. Little April Wu. How are you, Sunshine?'

The little girl was dressed like Sheena, the jungle girl. She rode on the left shoulder of an adolescent male gorilla whose black eyes were patiently gentle. April tipped forward and waved her hands in a quick series of signs. The gorilla let go of her legs and she climbed up to stand on his shoulder, holding his head for balance. Her guardian chuffed uncomplainingly.

'Catch me, Robert!'

Robert hurried to his feet. Before he could say anything to stop her, she sprang off, a sun-browned windmill that streamed blond hair. He caught her in a tangle of legs. For a moment, until he had a sure grip, his heart beat faster than it had in battle or in climbing mountains.

He had known the little girl was being kept with the gorillas for safety. To his chagrin he realized how busy he had been since recovering from his injuries. Too busy to think of this child, the only other human free in the mountains. 'Hi, Pumpkin,' he said to her. 'How're you doing these days? Are you taking good care of the 'rillas?'

She nodded seriously. 'I've *gotta* take good care of th' 'rillas, Robert. We gotta be in charge, 'cause there's just us.'

Robert gave her a close hug. At that moment he suddenly felt terribly lonely. He had not realized how badly he missed human company. 'Yup. It's just you and me up here,' he said softly.

'You an' me an' Tymbimmie Athaclena,' she reminded him.

He met her eyes. 'Nevertheless, you're doing what Dr de Shriver asks, aren't you?'

She nodded. 'Dr de Shriver's nice. She says maybe I might get to go see Mommy and Daddy, sometime soon.'

Robert winced. He would have to talk to de Shriver about deceiving the youngster. The chim in charge probably could not bear to tell the human child the truth, that she would be in their care for a long time to come. To send her to Port Helenia now would be to give away the secret of the gorillas, something even Athaclena was now determined to prevent.

'Take me down there, Robert.' April demanded with a sweet smile. She pointed to a flat rock where the infant gorilla now capered before some of Robert's group. The chims laughed indulgently at the little male's antics. The satisfied, slightly smug tone in their voices was one Robert found understandable. A very young client race would naturally feel this way toward one even younger. The chims were very proprietary and parental toward the gorillas.

Robert, in turn, felt a little like a father with an unpleasant task ahead of him, one who must somehow break it to his children that the puppy would not remain theirs for long.

He carried April across to the other bank and set her down. The water temperature was much more bearable here. No, it was wonderful. He kicked off his moccasins and wriggled his toes in the tingling warmth.

April and the baby gorilla flanked Robert, resting their elbows on his knees. Elsie sat by his side. It was a brief, peaceful scene. If a neo-dolphin were magically to appear in the water, spy-hopping into view with a wide grin, the tableau would have made a good family portrait.

'Hey, what's that you've got in your mouth?' He moved his hand toward the little gorilla, who quickly shied back out of reach. It regarded him with wide, curious eyes.

'What's he chewing on?' Robert asked Elsie.

'It looks like a strip of plastic. But ... but what's it doing here? There isn't supposed to be anything here that was manufactured on Garth.

'It's *not* Garth-made,' someone said. They looked up. It was the chimmie who had served them their soup. She smiled and wiped her hands on her apron before bending over to pick up the gorilla infant. It gave up the material without fuss. 'All the little ones chew these strips. They tested safe, and we're absolutely positive nothing about it screams "Terran!" to Gubru detectors.'

Elsie and Robert exchanged a puzzled look. 'How can you be so sure? What is the stuff?'

She teased the little ape, waving the strip before its face until it chirped and grabbed it, popping the well-masticated piece back into its mouth.

'Some of their parents brought shredded bits of it back from our first successful ambush, back at the Howletts Center. They said it "smelled good." Now the brats chew it all the time.'

She grinned down at Elsie and Robert. 'It's that super-plastic fiber from the Gubru fighting vehicles. You know, that material that stops bullets flat?'

Robert and Elsie stared.

'Hey, Kongie. How about that?' The chimmie cooed at the little gorilla. 'You clever little thing, you. Say, if you like chewing armor plating, how about taking on something *really* tasty next? How about a *city?* Maybe something simple, like New York?'

The baby lowered the frayed, wet end long enough to yawn, a wide gaping of sharp, glistening teeth.

The chimmie smiled. 'Yum! Y'know, I think little Kongie likes the idea.'

54

FIBEN

'Hold still now,' Fiben told Gailet as he combed his fingers through her fur.

He needn't have said anything. For although Gailet was turned away, presenting her back to him, he knew her face bore a momentary expression of beatific joy as he groomed her. When she looked like that – calm, relaxed, happy with the delight of a simple, tactile pleasure – her normally stern countenance took on a glow, one that utterly transformed her somewhat ordinary features.

It was only for a minute, unfortunately. A tiny, scurrying movement caught Fiben's eye, and he pounced after it on instinct before it could vanish into her fine hair.

'Ow!' she cried when his fingernails bit a corner of skin, as well as a small squirming louse. Her chains rattled as she slapped his foot. 'What are you doing!'

'Eating,' he muttered as he cracked the wriggling thing between his teeth. Even then, it didn't quite stop struggling.

'You're lying,' she said, in an unconvincing tone of voice.

'Shall I show it to you?'

She shuddered. 'Never mind. Just go on with what you were doing.'

He spat out the dead louse, though for all their captors had been feeding them, he probably could use the protein. In all the thousands of times he had engaged in mutual grooming with other chims – friends, classmates, the Throop Family back on Cilmar

Island – he had never before been so clearly reminded of one of the ritual's original purposes, inherited from the jungle of long ago – that of ridding another chim of parasites. He hoped Gailet wouldn't be too squeamish about doing the same for him. After sleeping on straw ticks for more than two weeks, he was starting to itch something awful.

His arms hurt. He had to stretch to reach Gailet, since they were chained to different parts of the stone room and could barely get close enough to do this.

'Well,' he said. 'I'm almost finished, at least with those places you're willing to uncover. I can't believe the chimmie who said *pink* to me, a couple of months ago, is such a prude about nudity.'

Gailet only sniffed, not even deigning to answer. She had seemed glad enough to see him yesterday, when the renegade chims had brought him here from his former place of confinement. So many days of separate carceral isolation had made them as happy to see each other as long-lost siblings.

Now, though, it seemed she was back to finding fault with everything Fiben did. 'Just a little more,' she urged. 'Over to the left.'

'Gripe, gripe, gripe,' Fiben muttered under his breath. But he complied. Chims needed to touch and be touched, perhaps quite a bit more than their human patrons, who sometimes held hands in public but seldom more. Fiben found it nice to have someone to groom after all this time. Almost as pleasurable as having it done to you was doing it for somebody else.

Back in college he had read that humans once restricted most of their person-to-person touching to their sexual partners. Some dark-age parents had even refrained from hugging their kids! Those primitives hardly ever engaged in anything that could be likened to mutual grooming – completely nonsexual scratching, combing, massaging one another, just for the pleasure of contact, with no sex involved at all.

A brief Library search had verified this slanderous rumor, to his amazement. No historical anecdote had ever brought home to Fiben so well just how much agnosy and craziness poor human mels and fems had endured. It made forgiveness a little easier when he also saw pictures of old-time zoos and circuses and trophies of 'the hunt.'

Fiben was pulled out of his thoughts by the sound of keys rattling. The old-style wooden door slid open. Someone knocked and then walked in.

It was the chimmie who brought them their evening meals. Since being moved here, Fiben had not learned her name, but her heart-shaped face was striking, and somehow familiar.

Her bright zipsuit was of the style worn by the band of

Probationers that worked for the Gubru. The costume was bound by elastic bands at ankles and wrists, and a holo-projection armband picted outstretched birds' talons a few centimeters into space.

'Someone's comin' to see both of you,' the female Probie said lowly, softly. 'I thought you'd want to know. Have time to get ready.'

Gailet nodded coolly. 'Thank you.' She hardly glanced at the chimmie. But Fiben, in spite of his situation, watched their jailer's sway as she turned and walked away.

'Damn *traitors*!' Gailet muttered. She strained against her slender chain, rattling it. 'Oh, there are times when I wish I were a chen. I'd ... I'd ...'

Fiben looked up at the ceiling and sighed.

Gailet strained to turn and look at him. 'What! You've maybe got a comment?'

Fiben shrugged. 'Sure, if you were a chen, you just might be able to bust out of that skinny little chain. But then, they wouldn't have used something like that if you were a male chim, would they?'

He lifted his own arms as far as they would go, barely enough to bring them into her view. Heavy links rattled. The chafing hurt his bandaged right wrist, so he let his hands drop to the concrete floor.

'I'd guess there were other reasons she wishes she was male,' came a voice from the doorway. Fiben looked up and saw the Probationer called Irongrip, the leader of the renegades. The chim smiled theatrically as he rolled one end of his waxed mustache, an affectation Fiben was getting quite sick of.

'Sorry. I couldn't help but overhear that last part, folks.'

Gailet's upper lip curled in contempt. 'So you were listening. So what? All that means is you're an eavesdropper, as *well* as a traitor.'

The powerfully built chim grinned. 'Shall I go for *voyeur*, also? Why don't I have you two chained together, hm? Ought to make for lots of amusement, you like each other so much.'

Gailet snorted. She pointedly moved away from Fiben, shuffling over to the far wall.

Fiben refused to give the fellow the pleasure of a response. He returned Irongrip's gaze evenly.

'Actually,' the Probationer went on, in a musing tone, 'it's pretty understandable, a chimmie like you, wishing she was a chen. Especially with that white breeding card of yours. Why, a white card's damn near wasted on a girl!

'What I find hard to figure,' Irongrip said to Fiben, 'is why you two have been doin' what you were doin' – running around playing soldier for the man. It's hard to figure. You with a blue card, her with a white – jeez, you two could do it any time she's pink – with no pills, no asking her guardian, no by-your-leave from the Uplift Board. All th' kids you ever want, whenever you want 'em.'

Gailet offered the chim a chilled stare. 'You are disgusting.'

Irongrip colored. It was especially pronounced with his pale, shaved cheeks. 'Why? Because I m fascinated by what's been deprived me? With what I can't have?'

Fiben growled. 'More like with what you can't do.'

The blush deepened. Irongrip knew his feelings were betraying him. He bent over to bring his face almost even with Fiben's. 'Keep it up, college boy. Who knows what *you'll* be able to do, once we've decided your fate.' He grinned.

Fiben wrinkled his nose. 'Y'know, the color of a chen's card isn't everything. F'rinstance, even *you'd* probably get more girls if you just used a mouthwash once in a whi—'

He grunted and doubled over as a fist drove into his abdomen. *You pay for your pleasures,* Fiben reminded himself as his stomach convulsed and he fought for breath. Still, from the look on the traitor's face he must have struck paydirt. Irongrip's reaction spoke volumes.

Fiben looked up to see concern written in Gailet Jones's eyes. The expression instantly turned to anger.

'Will you two stop it! You're acting like children ... like pre-sentient – '

Irongrip whirled and pointed at her. 'What do *you* know about it? Hm? Are you some sort of expert? Are you a member of the goddam Uplift Board? Are you even a mother, yet?'

'I'm a student of Galactic Sociology,' Gailet said rather stiffly.

Irongrip laughed bitterly, 'A title given to reward a clever monkey! You must have really done some beautiful tricks on the jungle gym to get a real-as-life, scale-model, sheepskin doctorate!'

He crouched near her. 'Haven't you figured it out yet, little miss? Let me spell it for you. We're *all* goddam pre-sentients! Go ahead. Deny it. Tell me I'm wrong!'

It was Gailet's turn to change color. She glanced at Fiben, and he knew she was remembering that afternoon at the college in Port Helenia, when they had climbed to the top of the bell tower and looked out over a campus empty of humans, filled only with chim students and chim faculty trying to act as if nothing had changed. She had to be remembering how bitter it had been, seeing that scene as a Galactic would.

'I'm a sapient being,' she muttered, obviously trying to put conviction into her voice.

'Yeah,' Irongrip sneered. 'What you *mean* to say, though, is that you're just a little closer than the rest of us ... closer to what the

Uplift Board defines as a target for us neo-chims. Closer to what they think we *ought* to be.

'Tell me, though. What if you took a space trip to Earth, and the captain took a wrong turn onto D-level hyperspace, and you arrived a couple *hundred years* from now? What do you think would happen to your precious white card then?'

Gailet looked away. '*Sic transit gloria mundi.*' Irongrip snapped his fingers. 'You'd be a relic then, obsolete, a phase long bypassed in the relentless progress of Uplift.' He laughed, reaching out and taking her chin in his hand to make her meet his eyes. 'You'd be *Probationer*, honey.'

Fiben surged forward but was caught short by his chains. The jolting stop sent pain shooting up from his right wrist, but in his anger Fiben hardly noticed. He was too filled with wrath to be able to speak. Dimly, as he snarled at the other chen, he knew that the same held for Gailet. It was all the more infuriating because it was just one more proof that the bastard was right.

Irongrip met Fiben's gaze for a long moment before letting go of Gailet. 'A hundred years *ago*,' he went on, '*I* would've been somethin' special. They would've forgiven, ignored, my own little "quirks and drawbacks." They'd have given *me* a white card, for my cunning and my strength.

'*Time* is what decides it, my good little chen and chimmie. It's all what generation you're born in.'

He stood up straight. 'Or is it?' Irongrip smiled. 'Maybe it also depends on who your *patrons* are, hm? If the standards change, if the target image of the ideal future *Pans sapiens* changes, well ...' He spread his hands, letting the implication sink in.

Gailet was the first to find her voice.

'You ... actually ... expect ... th' Gubru ...'

Irongrip shrugged. 'Time's are a changin', my darlings. I may yet have more grandkids than either of you.'

Fiben found the key to drive out the incapacitating anger and unlock his own voice. He laughed. He guffawed. 'Yeah?' he asked, grinning. 'Well, first you'll haveta fix your *other* problem, boyo. How're you going to pass on your genes if you can't even get it up to—'

This time it was Irongrip's unshod foot that lashed out. Fiben was more prepared and rolled aside to take the kick at an angle. But more blows followed in a dull rain.

There were no more words, though, and a quick glance told Fiben that it was Irongrip's turn to be tongue-tied. Low sounds emerged as his mouth opened and closed, flecked with foam. Finally, in frustration, the tall chim gave up kicking at Fiben. He swiveled and stomped out.

The chimmie with the keys watched him go. She stood by the door, looking uncertain what to do.

Fiben grunted as he rolled over onto his back.

'Uh.' He winced as he felt his ribs. None seemed to be broken. 'At least Simon Legree wasn't able to perform a proper exit line. I half expected him to say: "I'll be back, just you wait!" or somethin' equally original.'

Gailet shook her head. 'What do you gain by baiting him?'

He shrugged. 'I got my reasons.'

Gingerly, he backed against the wall. The chimmie in the billowing zipsuit was watching him, but when their eyes met she quickly blinked and turned to leave, closing the door behind her.

Fiben lifted his head and inhaled deeply, through his nose, several times.

'*Now* what are you doing?' Gailet asked.

He shook his head. 'Nothin'. Just passin' the time.'

When he looked again, Gailet had turned her back to him again. She seemed to be crying.

Small surprise, Fiben thought. It probably wasn't as much fun for her, being a prisoner, as it had been leading a rebellion. For all the two of them knew, the Resistance was washed up, finished, kaput. And there wasn't any reason to believe things had gone any better in the mountains. Athaclena and Robert and Benjamin might be dead or captured by now. Port Helenia was still ruled by birds and quislings.

'Don't worry,' he said, trying to cheer her up. 'You know what they say about the truest test of sapiency? You mean you haven't heard of it? Why it's just comin' through when the chimps are down!'

Gailet wiped her eyes and turned her head to look at him. 'Oh, shut up,' she said.

Okay, so it's an old joke, Fiben admitted to himself. *But it was worth a try.*

Still, she motioned for him to turn around. 'Come on. It's your turn. Maybe ...' She smiled weakly, as if uncertain whether or not to try a joke of her own. 'Maybe I can find something to snack on, too.'

Fiben grinned. He shuffled about and stretched his chains until his back was as close to her as possible, not minding how it strained his various hurts. He felt her hands working to unknot his tangled, furry thatch and rolled his eyes upward.

'Ah, aahh,' he sighed.

A different jailer brought them their noon meal, a thin soup accompanied by two slices of bread. This male Probie possessed none of

Irongrip's fluency. In fact, he seemed to have trouble with even the simplest phrases and snarled when Fiben tried to draw him out. His left cheek twitched intermittently in a nervous tic, and Gailet whispered to Fiben that the feral glint in the chim's eyes made her nervous.

Fiben tried to distract her. 'Tell me about Earth,' he asked. 'What's it like?'

Gailet used a bread crust to sop up the last of her soup. 'What's to tell? Everybody knows about Earth.'

'Yeah. From video and from GoThere cube books, sure. But not from personal experience. You went as a child with your parents, didn't you? That's where you got your doctorate?'

She nodded. 'University of Djakarta.'

'And then what?'

Her gaze was distant. 'Then I applied for a position at the Terragens Center for Galactic Studies, in La Paz.'

Fiben knew of the place. Many of Earth's diplomats, emissaries, and agents took training there, learning how the ancient cultures of the Five Galaxies thought and acted. It was crucial if the leaders were to plan a way for the three races of Earth to make their way in a dangerous universe. Much of the fate of the wolfling clan depended on the graduates of the CGS.

'I'm impressed you even applied,' he said, meaning it. 'Did they ... I mean, did you pass?'

She nodded. 'I ... it was close. I qualified. Barely. If I'd scored just a little better, they said there'd have been no question.'

Obviously, the memory was painful. She seemed undecided, as if tempted to change the subject. Gailet shook her head. 'Then I was told that they'd prefer it if I returned to Garth instead. I should take up a teaching position, they said. They made it plain I'd be more useful here.'

'They? Who's this "they" you're talking about?'

Gailet nervously picked at the fur on the back of her arm. She noticed what she was doing and made both hands lay still on her lap. 'The Uplift Board,' she said quietly.

'But ... but what do they have to say about assigning teaching positions, or influencing career choices for that matter?'

She looked at him. 'They have a *lot* to say, Fiben, if they think neo-chimp or neo-dolphin genetic progress is at stake. They can keep you from becoming a spacer, for instance, out of fear your precious plasm might get irradiated. Or they can prevent you from entering chemistry as a profession, out of fear of unpredicted mutations.'

She picked up a piece of straw and twirled it slowly. 'Oh, we have

954

a lot more rights than other young client races. I know that, I keep reminding myself.'

'But they decided your genes were needed on Garth,' Fiben guessed in low voice.

She nodded. 'There's a point system, if I'd *really* scored well on the CGS exam it would've been okay. A few chims do get in.

'But I was at the margin. Instead they presented me with that damned white card – like it was some sort of consolation prize, or maybe a wafer for some sacrament – and they sent me back to my native planet, back to poor old Garth.

'It seems my raison d'être is the babies I'll have. Everything else is incidental.'

She laughed, somewhat bitterly. 'Hell, I've been breaking the law for months now, risking my life and womb in this rebellion. Even if we'd have won – fat chance – I could get a big fat medal from the TAASF, maybe even ticker tape parades, and it wouldn't matter. When all the hooplah died down I'd still be thrown into prison by the Uplift Board!'

'Oh, Goodall,' Fiben sighed, sagging back against the cool stones. 'But you haven't, I mean you haven't yet – '

'Haven't procreated yet? Good observation. One of the few advantages of being a female with a white card is that I can choose anyone blue or higher for the father, and pick my own timing, so long as I have three or more offspring before I'm thirty. I don't even have to raise them myself!' Again came the sharp, bitter laugh. 'Hell, half of the chim marriage groups on Garth would shave themselves bald for the right to adopt one of my kids.'

She makes her situation sound so awful, Fiben thought. *And yet there must be fewer than twenty other chims on the planet regarded as highly by the Board. To a member of a client race, it's the highest honor.*

Still, maybe he understood after all. She would have come home to Garth knowing one fact. That no matter how brilliant her career, how great her accomplishments, it would only make her ovaries all the more valuable ... only make more frequent the painful, invasive visits to the Plasm Bank, and only bring on more pressure to carry as many as possible to term in her own womb.

Invitations to join group marriages or pair bonds would be automatic, easy. Too easy. There would be no way to know if a group wanted her for herself. Lone male suitors would seek her for the status fathering her child would bring.

And then there would be the jealousy. He could empathize with that. Chims weren't often very subtle at hiding their feelings, especially envy. Quite a few would be downright mean about it.

'Irongrip was right,' Gailet said. 'It's got to be different for a chen. A white card would be fun for a male chim, I can see that. But for a chimmie? One with ambition to be something for herself?'

She looked away.

'I...' Fiben tried to think of something to say, but for a moment all he could do was sit there feeling thick-headed, stupid. Perhaps, some day, one of his great-to-the-nth grandchildren would be smart enough to know the right words, to know how to comfort someone too far gone into bitterness even to want comforting anymore.

That more fully uplifted neo-chim, a few score more generations down the chain of Uplift, might be bright enough. But Fiben knew he wasn't. He was only an ape.

'Um.' He coughed. 'I remember a time, back on Cilmar Island, it musta been before you returned to Garth. Let's see, was it ten years ago? Ifni! I think I was just a freshman...' He sighed. 'Anyway, the whole island got all excited, that year, when Igor Patterson came to lecture and perform at the University.'

Gailet's head lifted a little. 'Igor Patterson? The drummer?'

Fiben nodded. 'So you've heard of him?'

She smirked sarcastically. 'Who hasn't? He's –' Gailet spread her hands and let them drop, palms up. 'He's wonderful.'

That summed it up all right. For Igor Patterson was the best.

The thunder dance was only one aspect of the neo-chimpanzee's love affair with rhythm. Percussion was a favorite musical form, from the quaint farmlands of Hermes to the sophisticated towers of Earth. Even in the early days – back when chims had been forced to carry keyboard displays on their chests in order to speak at all – even then the new race had loved the beat.

And yet, all of the great drummers on Earth and in the colonies were humans. Everyone until Igor Patterson.

He was the first. The first chim with the fine finger coordination, the delicacy of timing, the sheer chutzpah, to make it alongside the best. Listening to Patterson play 'Clash Ceramic Lighting' wasn't only to experience pleasure; for a chim it was to burst with pride. To many, his mere existence meant that chims weren't just approaching what the Uplift Board wanted them to be, but what *they* wanted to be, as well.

'The Carter Foundation sent him on a tour of th' colonies,' Fiben went on. 'Partly it was as a goodwill trip for all the outlying chim communities. And of course it was also to spread the good luck around a bit.'

Gailet snorted at the obviousness of it. Of *course* Patterson had a white card. The chim members of the Uplift Board would have insisted, even if he weren't also as wonderfully charming, intelligent, and handsome a specimen of neo-chimpanzee as anyone could ask to meet.

And Fiben thought he knew what else Gailet was thinking. For a male having a white card wouldn't be much of a problem at all – just one long party. 'I'll bet,' she said. And Fiben imagined he detected a clear tone of envy.

'Yeah, well, you should've been there, when he showed up to give his concert. I was one of the lucky ones. My seat was way up in back, out of the way, and it happened that I had a real bad cold that night. That was damn fortunate.'

'What?' Gailet's eyebrows came together. 'What does that have to do with ... Oh.' She frowned at him and her jaw tightened. 'Oh. I see.'

'I'll bet you do. The air conditioning was set on high, but I'm told the aroma was still overpowering. I had to sit shivering under the blowers. Damn near caught my death—'

'*Will* you get to the point?' Gailet's lips were a thin line.

'Well, as no doubt you've guessed, nearly every green- or blue-card chimmie on the island who happened to be in estrus seemed to have a ticket to the concert. None of 'em used olfa-spray. They came, generally, with the complete okay of their group husbands, wearing flaming pink lipstick, just on the off chance—'

'I get the picture,' Gailet said. And for just an instant Fiben wondered if he saw her blink back a faint smile as she pictured the scene. If so, it was only a momentary flicker of her severe frown. 'So what happened?'

Fiben stretched, yawning. 'What would you expect to happen? A riot, of course.'

Her jaw dropped. 'Really? At the University?'

'Sure as I'm sitting here.'

'But – '

'Oh, the first few minutes went all right. Man, old Igor could play as good as his rep, I'll tell you. The crowd kept getting more and more excited. Even the backup band was feelin' it. Then things kinda got out of hand.'

'But – '

'Remember old Professor Olvfing, from the Terragens Traditions Department? You know, the elderly chim who sports a monocle? Used to spend his spare time lobbying to get a chim monogamy bill before the legislature?'

'Yes, I knew him.' She nodded, her eyes wide open.

Fiben made a gesture with two hands.

'No! In public? *Professor Olvfing?*'

'With th' dean of th' College of frigging Nutrition, no less.'

Gailet let out a sharp sound. She turned aside, hand to her breast. She seemed to suffer a sudden bout of hiccups.

'Of course, Olvfing's pair-bond wife forgave him later. It was that or lose him to a ten-group that said they liked his style.'

Gailet slapped her chest, coughing. She turned further away from Fiben, shaking her head vigorously.

'Poor Igor Patterson,' Fiben continued. 'He had problems of his own, of course. Some of th' guys from the football team had been drafted as bouncers. When it started getting out of hand, they tried using fire extinguishers. That made things slippery, but it didn't slow 'em down much.'

Gailet coughed louder. 'Fiben . . .'

'It was too bad, really,' he mused aloud. 'Igor was getting into a great blues riff, really pounding those skins, packin' in a backbeat you couldn't believe. I was groovin' on it . . . until this forty-year-old chimmie, naked and slick as a dolphin, dropped straight onto him from th' rafters.'

Gailet doubled over clutching her belly. She held up a hand, pleading for mercy. 'Stop, please . . .' she whimpered, weakly.

'Thank heavens it was the snare drum she fell through. Took her long enough gettin' untangled for poor Igor to escape out the back way, just barely ahead of the mob.'

She toppled over sideways. For a moment Fiben felt concern, her face was so flushed and red. She hooted, slapping the floor, and tears streamed from her eyes. Gailet rolled over onto her back, rocking with peals of laughter.

Fiben shrugged. 'And all that was just from playin' the first number – Patterson's special version of the bloody national anthem! What a pity. I never did get to hear his variation on "Inagadda Da Vita."

'Now that I think about it, though,' he sighed once more, 'maybe it's just as well.'

Power curfew came at 2000 hours, and no exception was made for prisons. A wind had risen before sunset and soon was rattling the shutters of their small window. It came in off the ocean, carrying a heavy salt smell. In the distance could be heard the faint rumblings of an early summer storm.

They slept curled in their blankets as close to each other as their chains allowed, head to head so they could hear each other breathing in the darkness. They slumbered inhaling the soft tang of stone and the mustiness of straw, and exhaled the soft mutterings of their dreams.

Gailet's hands moved in tiny jerks, as if trying to follow the rhythms of some illusory escape. Her chains tinkled faintly.

Fiben lay motionless, but now and then he blinked, his eyes occasionally opening and closing without the light of consciousness in them. Sometimes a breath caught and held for a long moment before releasing, at last.

They did not notice the low humming sound that penetrated from the hallway outside, nor the light which speared into their cell through cracks in the wooden door. Feet shuffled and claws clicked on flagstones.

When keys rattled in the lock, Fiben jerked, rolled to one side, and sat up. He knuckled his eyes as the hinges creaked. Gailet lifted her head. She used her hand to block the sharp glare of two lamps, held high on poles.

Fiben sneezed, smelling lavender and feathers. When he and Gailet were hauled to their feet by several of the zipsuited chims, he recognized the gruff voice of their head captor, Irongrip.

'You two better behave yourselves. You've got important visitors.'

Fiben blinked, trying to adjust to the light. At last he made out a small crowd of feathered quadrupeds, large balls of white fluff bedecked in ribbons and sashes. Two of them held staffs from which the bright lanterns hung. The rest twittered around what looked like a short pole ending in a narrow platform. On that perch stood a most singular-looking bird.

It, too, was arrayed in bright ribbons. The large, bipedal Gubru shifted its weight from one leg to another, nervously. It might have been the way the light struck the alien's plumage, but the coloration seemed richer, more luminous than the normal off-white shade. It reminded Fiben of something, as if he had seen this invader or one like it before, somewhere.

What the hell is the thing doing, moving around at night? Fiben wondered. *I thought they hated to do that.*

'Pay proper respect to honored elders, members of the high clan Gooksyu-Gubru!' Irongrip said, sharply, nudging Fiben.

'I'll show th' damn thing my respect.' Fiben made a rude sound in his throat and gathered phlegm.

'No!' Gailet cried. She grabbed his arm and whispered urgently. 'Fiben, don't! Please. Do this for me. Act *exactly* as I do!'

Her brown eyes were pleading. Fiben swallowed. 'Aw hell, Gailet.' She turned back toward the Gubru and folded her arms across her chest. Fiben imitated her, even as she bowed low.

The Galactic peered at them, first with one large, unblinking eye, then another. It shuffled to one end of the perch, forcing its holders to adjust their balance. Finally, it began chirping in a series of sharp, clipped squawks.

From the quadrupeds there emerged a strange, swooping accompaniment, rising and falling, sounding something like 'Zooooon.'

One of the Kwackoo servitors ambled forward. A bright, metallic disk hung from a chain around its neck. The vodor gave forth a low, jerky Anglic translation.

> 'It has been judged ...judged in honor
> > judged in propriety ...
> That you two have not transgressed ...
> > have not broken ...
> The rules of conduct ... the rules of war.
> > Zooooon.

> 'We judge that it is right ... proper ...
> > meet to allow for infant status ...
> To charitably credit ... believe ...
> > that your struggles were on your patrons' behalf.
> Zoooooon.

> 'It comes to our attention ... awareness ...
> > knowledge that your status is
> As leaders of your gene-flux ... race-flow ...
> > species in this place and time.
> > Zoooooooon.

> 'We therefore offer ... present ...
> > deign to honor you
> With an invitation ... a blessing ...
> > a chance to earn the boon of representation.
> > Zooooooon.

> 'It is an honor ... beneficence ...
> > glory to be chosen
> To seek out ... penetrate ...
> > create the future of your race.
> > Zoon!'

There it finished as abruptly as it had begun.

'Bow again!' Gailet urged in a whisper. She bent over with arms crossed, as she demonstrated. When Fiben looked up again, the small crowd of alien avians had swiveled and moved toward the doorway. The perch was lowered, but still the tall Gubru had to duck down, feathered arms splayed apart for balance, in order to pass through. Irongrip followed behind. The Probationer's parting glare at them was one of pure loathing.

Fiben's head rang. He had given up trying to follow the bird's queer, formal dialect of Galactic Three after the first phrase. Even the Anglic translation had been well nigh impossible to understand.

The sharp lighting faded as the procession moved away down the hallway in a babble of clucking gabble. In the remaining dimness, Fiben and Gailet turned and looked at each other.

'Now who th' hell was *that*?' he asked.

Gailet frowned. 'It was a Suzerain. One of their three leaders. If I'm not wrong – and I could easily be – it was the Suzerain of Propriety.'

'That tells me a whole lot. Just what on Ifni's roulette wheel is a Suzerain of Propriety?'

Gailet waved away his question. Her forehead was knotted in deep concentration. 'Why did it come to *us*, instead of having us brought to *it*?' she wondered aloud, though obviously she wasn't soliciting his opinion. 'And why meet us at night? Did you notice it didn't even stay to hear if we accepted its offer? It probably felt compelled, by propriety, to make it in person. But its aides can get our answer later.'

'Answer to what? *What* offer? Gailet, I couldn't even follow –'

But she made a nervous waving motion with both hands. 'Not now. I've got to think, Fiben. Give me a few minutes.' She walked back to the wall and sat down on the straw facing the blank stone. Fiben had a suspicion it would be considerably longer than she'd estimated before she was done.

You sure can choose 'em, he thought. *You deserve what you get when you fall in love with a genius . . .*

He blinked. Shook his head. *Say what?*

But movement in the hall distracted him from pursuing his own unexpected thought. A solitary chim entered, carrying an armload of straw and folded bolts of dark brown cloth. The load hid the short neochimp's face. Only when she lowered it to the ground did Fiben see that it was the chimmie who had stared at him earlier, the one who seemed so strangely familiar.

'I brought you some fresh straw, and some more blankets. These nights are still pretty cool.'

He nodded. 'Thank you.'

She did not meet his eyes. She turned and walked back toward the door, moving with a lithe grace that was obvious, even under the billowing zipsuit. 'Wait!' he said suddenly.

She stopped, still facing the door. Fiben walked toward her as far as the heavy chains would allow. 'What's your name?' he asked softly, not wanting to disturb Gailet in her corner.

Her shoulders were hunched. She still faced away from him. 'I'm . . .' Her voice was very low. 'S-some people call me Sylvie . . .'

Even in swirling quickly through the doorway she moved like a dancer. There was a rattle of keys, and hurried footsteps could be heard receding down the hall outside.

Fiben stared at the blank door. 'Well, I'll be a monkey's grandson.'

He turned around and walked back to the wall where Gailet sat, muttering to herself, and leaned over to drape a blanket upon her shoulders. Then he returned to his own corner to collapse into a heap of sweet-smelling straw.

55

UTHACALTHING

Scummy algae foamed in the shallows where a few small, stilt-legged native birds picked desultorily for insects. Bushy plants lay in clumps, outlining the surrounding steppes.

Footprints led from the banks of the small lake up into the nearby scrub-covered hillside. Just glancing at the muddy tracks, Uthacalthing could tell that the walker had stepped with a pigeon-toed gait. It seemed to use a three-legged stance.

He looked up quickly as a flash of blue caught the corner of his eye – the same glimmer that had led him to this place. He tried to focus on the faint twinkle, but it was gone before he could track it.

He knelt to examine the impressions in the mud. A smile spread as he measured them with his hands. Such beautiful outlines! The third foot was off center from the other two and its print was much smaller than the others, almost as if some bipedal creature had crossed from lake to brush leaning on a blunt-headed staff.

Uthacalthing picked up a fallen branch, but he hesitated before brushing away the outlines.

Shall I leave them? he wondered. *Is it really necessary to hide them?*

He shook his head.

No. As the humans say, do not change game plans in midstream.

The footprints disappeared as he swept the branch back and

forth. Just as he was finishing, he heard heavy footsteps and the sound of breaking shrubs behind him. He turned as Kault rounded a bend in the narrow game trail to the small prairie lake. The glyph, *lurrunanu*, hovered and darted over the Thennanin's big, crested head like some frustrated parasitic insect, buzzing about in search of a soft spot that never seemed to be there.

Uthacalthing's corona ached like an overused muscle. He let *lurrunanu* bounce against Kault's bluff stolidity for a minute longer before admitting defeat. He drew the defeated glyph back in and dropped the branch to the ground.

The Thennanin wasn't looking at the terrain anyway. His concentration was on a small instrument resting in his broad palm. 'I am growing suspicious, my friend,' Kault said as he drew even with the Tymbrimi.

Uthacalthing felt blood rush in the arteries at the back of his neck. *At last?* he wondered.

'Suspicious of what, my colleague?'

Kault folded an instrument and put it away in one of his many vest pouches. 'There are signs ...' His crest flapped. 'I have been listening to the uncoded transmissions of the Gubru, and something odd seems to be going on.'

Uthacalthing sighed. No, Kault's one-track mind was concentrating on a completely different subject. There was no use trying to draw him away from it with subtle clues.

'What are the invaders up to now?' he asked.

'Well, first of all, I am picking up much less excited military traffic. Suddenly they appear to be engaged in fewer of those small-scale fights up in the mountains than they were days and weeks ago. You'll recall we were both wondering why they were expending so much effort to suppress what had to be a rather tiny partisan resistance.'

Actually, Uthacalthing had been pretty certain he knew the reason for the frantic flurry of activity on the part of the Gubru. From what the two of them had been able to piece together, it seemed the invaders were very anxious to *find* something up in the Mountains of Mulun. They had thrown soldiers and scientists into the rough range with apparent reckless energy, and appeared to have paid a heavy cost for the effort.

'Can you think of a reason why the fighting has ebbed?' he asked Kault.

'I am uncertain from what I can decipher. One possibility is that the Gubru have found and captured the thing they were so desperately looking for – '

Doubtful, Uthacalthing thought with conviction. *It is hard to cage a ghost.*

'Or they may have given up searching for it – '

More likely, Uthacalthing agreed. It was inevitable that, sooner or later, the avians should realize they had been made fools of, and cease chasing wild gooses.

'Or, perhaps,' Kault concluded, 'the Gubru have simply finished suppressing all opposition and liquidated whoever was opposing them.'

Uthacalthing prayed the last answer was not the correct one. It was among the risks he had taken, of course, in arranging to tease the enemy into such a frenzy. He could only hope that his daughter and Megan Oneagle's son had not paid the ultimate price to further his own convoluted hoax on the malign birds.

'Hmm,' he commented. 'Did you say there was something else puzzling you?'

'This,' Kault went on. 'That after five twelves of planetary days, during which they have done nothing at all for the benefit of this world, suddenly the Gubru are making announcements, offering amnesty and employment to former members of the Ecological Recovery Service.'

'Yes? Well, maybe it just means they've completed their consolidation and can now spare a little attention to their responsibilities.'

Kault snorted. 'Perhaps. But the Gubru are accountants. Credit counters. Humorless, selfish worriers. They are fanatically prim about those aspects of Galactic tradition that interest them, yet they hardly seem to care at all about preserving planets as nursery worlds, only about the near-term status of their clan.'

Although Uthacalthing agreed with that assessment, he considered Kault less than an impartial observer. And the Thennanin was hardly the one to accuse others of being humorless.

Anyway, one thing was obvious. So long as Kault was distracted like this, thinking about the Gubru, it would be useless to try to draw his attention to subtle clues and footprints in the ground.

He could sense movement in the prairie all around him. The little carnivores and their prey were all seeking cover, settling into small niches and burrows to wait out midday, when the fierce heat of summer would beat down and it would cost too much energy either to give chase or to flee. In that respect, tall Galactics were no exception. 'Come,' Uthacalthing said. 'The sun is high. We must find a shady place to rest. I see some trees over on the other side of the water.'

Kault followed without comment. He appeared to be indifferent about minor deviations in their path, so long as the distant mountains grew perceptibly closer each day. The white-topped peaks were now more than just a faint line against the horizon. It might take weeks to reach them, and indeterminably longer to find a way through unknown passes to the Sind. But Thennanin were patient when it suited their purposes.

There were no blue glimmerings as Uthacalthing found them shelter under a too-tight cluster of stunted trees, though he kept his eye 'peeled' anyway. Still, with his corona he thought he *kenned* a touch of feral joy from some mind hiding out there on the steppe, something large, clever, and familiar.

'I am, indeed, considered to be something of an expert on Terrans,' Kault said a little later as they made conversation under the gnarled branches. Small insects buzzed near the Thennanin's breathing slits, only to be blown away every time they approached. 'That, plus my ecological expertise, won me my assignment to this planet.'

'Don't forget your sense of humor,' Uthacalthing added, with a smile.

'Yes,' Kault's crest puffed in the Thennanin equivalent of a nod. 'At home I was thought quite the devil. Just the sort to deal with wolflings and Tymbrimi pixies.' He finished with a rapid, low set of raspy breaths. It was obviously a conscious affectation, for Thennanin did not have a laughter reflex as such. *No matter,* Uthacalthing thought. *As Thennanin humor goes, it was pretty good.*

'Have you had much first-hand experience with Earthlings?'

'Oh, yes,' Kault said. 'I have been to Earth. I have had the delight of walking her rain forests and seeing the strange, diverse lifeforms there. I have met neo-dolphins and whales. While my people believe humans themselves should never have been declared fully uplifted – they would profit much from a few more millennia of polishing under proper guidance – I can admit that their world is beautiful and their clients promising.'

One reason the Thennanin were in this current war was in hopes of picking up all three Earthling species for their clan by forced adoption – 'for the Terrans' own good,' of course. Though, to be fair, it was also clear that there were disagreements over this among the Thennanin themselves. Kault's party, for instance, preferred a ten-thousand-year campaign of *persuasion,* to try to win the Earthlings over to adoption voluntarily, with 'love.'

Obviously, Kault's party did not dominate the present government.

'And of course, I met a few Earthlings in the course of a term working for the Galactic Institute of Migration, during an expedition to negotiate with the Fah'fah'n*fah.'

Uthacalthing's corona erupted in a whirl of silvery tendrils, an open show of surprise. He knew his stunned expression was readable even to Kault, and did not care. 'You ... you have been to meet the hydrogen breathers?' He did not even know the trick of pronouncing the hyper-alien name, not part of any sanctioned Galactic tongue.

Kault had surprised him once again!

'The Fah'fah'n*fah.' Again Kault's breathing slits pulsed in mimicry of laughter. This time, it sounded much more realistic. 'The negotiations were held in the Poul-Kren sub-quadrant, not far from what the Earthlings call the Orion sector.'

'That's very close to Terra's Canaan colonies.'

'Yes. That is one reason why they were invited to take part. Even though these infrequent meetings between the civilizations of oxygen breathers and hydrogen breathers are among the most critical and delicate in any era, it was thought appropriate to bring a few Terrans along, to show them some of the subtleties of high-level diplomacy.'

It must have been his state of confused surprise, but at that moment Uthacalthing thought he actually caught a *kenning* from Kault ... a trace of something deep and troubling to the Thennanin. *He is not telling me all of it*, Uthacalthing realized. *There were other reasons Earthlings were involved.*

For billions of years, uneasy peace had been maintained between two parallel, completely separate cultures. It was almost as if the Five Galaxies were actually Ten, for there were at least as many stable worlds with hydrogen atmospheres as planets like Garth and Earth and Tymbrim. The two strands of life, each supporting vast numbers of species and lifeforms, had almost nothing in common. The Fah'fah'n*fah wanted nothing of rock, and their worlds were too vast and cold and heavy for the Galactics ever to covet.

Also, they seemed even to operate on different levels or rates of *time*. The hydrogen breathers preferred the slow routes, through D-Level hyperspace and even normal space between the stars – the realm where relativity ruled – leaving the quicker lanes among the stars to the fast-living heirs of the fabled Progenitors.

Sometimes there were conflicts. Entire systems and clans died. There were no rules to such wars.

Sometimes there was trade, metals for gases, or machinery in exchange for strange things not found even in the records of the Great Library.

There were periods when whole spiral arms would be abandoned by one civilization or the other. The Galactic Institute of Migration organized these huge movements for the oxygen breathers, every hundred million years or so. The official reason was to allow great tracts of stars to 'go fallow' for an era, to give their planets time to develop new pre-sentient life. Still, the other purpose was widely known ... to put space between hydrogen and oxygen life where it seemed impossible to ignore each other any longer.

And now Kault was telling him that there had been a recent negotiation right in the Poul-Kren sector? And humans had been there?

Why have I never heard of this before? he wondered.

He wanted to follow this thread, but had no opportunity. Kault was obviously unwilling to pursue it, and returned to the earlier topic of conversation.

'I still believe there is something anomalous about the Gubru transmissions, Uthacalthing. From their broadcasts it is clear that they are combing both Port Helenia and the islands, seeking out the Earthlings' ecology and uplift experts.'

Uthacalthing decided that his curiosity could wait – a hard decision for a Tymbrimi. 'Well, as I suggested earlier, perhaps the Gubru have decided to do their duty by Garth, at last.'

Kault gurgled in a tone Uthacalthing knew denoted doubt. 'Even if that were so, they would require ecologists, but why Uplift specialists? I intuit that something curious is still going on,' Kault concluded. 'The Gubru have been extremely agitated for several megaseconds.'

Even without their small receiver, or any news over the airwaves at all, Uthacalthing would still have known that much. It was implicit in the intermittent blue light he had been following since weeks ago. The flickering glow meant that the Tymbrimi Diplomatic Cache had to have been breached. The bait he had left inside the cairn, along with numerous other hints and clues, could only lead a sapient being to one conclusion.

It was apparent his jest on the Gubru had proved very expensive for them.

Still, all good things come to an end. By now even the Gubru must have figured out that it was all just a Tymbrimi trick. The avians weren't exactly stupid. They had to discover sooner or later that there really weren't any such things as 'Garthlings.'

The sages say that it can be a mistake to push a joke too far. Am I making that error trying to pull the same jest on Kault?

Ah, but in this case the procedure was so totally different! Fooling Kault was turning into a much slower, more difficult, more *personal* task.

Anyway, what else have I to do, to pass the time?

'Do tell me more about your suspicions,' Uthacalthing said aloud to his companion. 'I am very, very interested.'

56

GALACTICS

Against all expectation, the new Suzerain of Cost and Caution was actually scoring points. Its plumage had barely even begun to show the royal hues of candidacy, and it had started out far, far behind its peers in the competition. Nevertheless, when it danced the other Suzerains were forced to watch closely and pay heed to its well-parsed arguments.

'This effort was misguided, costly, unwise,' it chirped and whirled in delicate rhythm. 'We have spent treasure, time, and honor
  seeking,
     chasing,
        hunting
  a chimera!'

The new chief bureaucrat did have a few advantages. It had been trained by its predecessor – the impressive deceased Suzerain of Cost and Caution. Also, to this conclave it had brought an equally impressive, indicting array of facts. Data cubes lay scattered across the floor. The presentation by the head civil servant had, in fact, been quite devastating.

'There is no way, no possibility, no *chance* that this world could have hidden upon it a pre-sentient survivor of the Bururalli! It was a hoax, a ruse, a fiendish wolfling-and-Tymbrimi plot to get us to
  waste,
     squander,
        throw away
  our wealth!'

To the Suzerain of Propriety this was most humiliating. In fact, it was not much short of catastrophic.

During the hiatus, while a new bureaucratic candidate was being chosen, the priest and the admiral had reigned supreme, with no one to hold them in check. They had well known that it was not wise to act so, without the voice of a third peer to restrain them, but what being always acted wisely when opportunity beckoned seductively?

The admiral had gone on personal search and destroy missions in pursuit of the mountain partisans, seeking gloss to add to its personal honor. For its part, the priest had ordered expensive new works built and had rushed the delivery of a new planetary Branch Library.

It had been a lovely interregnum of two-way consensus. The Suzerain of Beam and Talon approved every purchase, and the Suzerain of Propriety blessed every foray of the Talon Soldiers. Expedition after expedition was sent into the mountains as closely guarded scientists eagerly sought out a prize beyond price.

Mistakes were made. The wolflings proved diabolical in their ambushes and animal elusiveness. And yet, there would never have been any carping about cost had they actually found what they were looking for. It all would have been worth it, if only . . .

But we were tricked, fooled, made fools of, the priest thought bitterly. The treasure had been a lie. And now the new Suzerain of Cost and Caution was rubbing it in for all it was worth. The bureaucrat danced a brilliant dance of chastisement of excess. Already it had dominated several points of consensus – for instance, that there would be no more useless chases into the mountains, not until a cheaper way was found to eliminate the resistance fighters.

The plumage of the Suzerain of Beam and Talon drooped miserably. The priest knew how much this must gall the admiral. But they were both held hypnotized by the righteous correctness of the Dance of Chastisement. Two could not outvote one when that one was so clearly in the right.

Now the bureaucrat had launched into a new cadence, leading into a new dance. It proposed that the new construction projects be abandoned. They had nothing to do with defending the Gubru hold upon this world. They had been begun on the assumption that these 'Garthling' creatures would be found. Now it was simply pointless to continue building a hyperspace shunt and a ceremonial mound!

The dance was powerful, convincing, backed up with charts and statistics and tables of figures. The Suzerain of Propriety realized that something would have to be done and done soon, or this upstart would end the day in the foremost position. It was unthinkable that such a sudden reverse of order should happen just as their bodies were starting to give them twinges preliminary to Molt!

Even leaving out the question of molt order, there was also the message from the Roost Masters to consider. The queens and princes back home were desperate in their queries. Had the Three on Garth come up with a bold new policy yet? Calculations showed that it would be important to have something original and imaginative soon, or else the initiative would pass forever to some other clan.

It was intimidating to have the fate of the race riding in one's slipstream.

And for all of its obvious finesse and fine preening, one thing was readily apparent about the new chief bureaucrat. The new Suzerain of Cost and Caution lacked the depth, the clarity of vision of its dead predecessor. The Suzerain of Propriety knew that no grand policy was going to come out of picayune, short sighted credit-pinching.

Something had to be done, and done now! The priest took up a posture of presentiment, spreading its brightly feathered arms in display. Politely, perhaps even indulgently, the bureaucrat cut short its own dance and lowered its beak, yielding time.

The Suzerain of Propriety started slowly, shuffling in small steps upon its perch. Purposely, the priest adopted a cadence used earlier by its adversary.

'Although there may be no Garthlings, there remains a chance, opportunity, opening, for us to use the ceremonial site we have
  planned,
    built,
      dedicated
at such cost.

'There is a plan, scheme, concept, which may still yet win
  glory,
    honor,
      propriety
for our clan.

'At the center, focus, essence of this plan, we shall
  examine,
    inspect,
      investigate
the clients of wolflings.'

Across the chamber the Suzerain of Beam and Talon looked up. A hopeful light appeared in the dejected admiral's eye, and the priest knew that it could win a temporary victory, or at least a delay.

Much, much would depend in the days ahead upon finding out whether this bold new idea would work.

57

ATHACLENA

You see?' he called down to her. 'It moved during the night

Athaclena had to shade her eyes as she looked up at her human friend – perched on a tree branch more than thirty feet above the forest floor. He pulled on a leafy green cable that stretched down to him at a forty-five-degree angle from its even higher anchor.

'Are you certain that is the same vine you snipped last night?' she called.

'It sure is! I climbed up and poured a liter of chromium-rich water – the very stuff this particular vine specializes in – into the crotch of that branch, way up there above me. Now you can see this vine has reanchored itself to that exact spot!'

Athaclena nodded. She felt a fringe of truth around his words. 'I see it, Robert. And now I believe it.'

She had to smile. Sometimes Robert acted so much like a young Tymbrimi male – so quick, impulsive, puckish. It was a little disconcerting, in a way. Aliens were supposed to behave in strange and inscrutable ways, not just like ... well, *boys*.

But Robert is not an alien, she reminded herself. *He is my consort.* And anyway, she had been living among Terrans for so long, she wondered if she had started to think like one.

When – if – I ever get home, will I disconcert all around me, frightening and amazing them with metaphors? With bizarre wolfling attitudes? Does that prospect attract me?

A lull had settled over the war. The Gubru had stopped sending vulnerable expeditions into the mountains. Their outposts were quiescent. Even the ceaseless droning of gasbots had been absent from the high valleys for more than a week, to the great relief of the chim farmers and villagers.

With some time on their hands, she and Robert had decided to have themselves just one day off while they had a chance, to try to get to know each other better. After all, who knew when the fighting would resume? Would there ever be another opportunity?

They both needed distraction anyway. There had still been no reply from Robert's mother, and the fate of Ambassador Uthacalthing remained unclear, in spite of the glimpse she had been given of her father's design. All she could do was try to perform her part as well as possible, and hope he was still alive and able to do his.

'All right,' she called up to Robert. 'I accept it. The vines can be trained, after a fashion. Now come down! Your perch looks precarious.'

But Robert only smiled. 'I'll come down, in my own way. You know me, Clennie. I can't resist an opportunity like this.'

Athaclena tensed. There it was again, that whimsy at the edges of his emotional aura. It wasn't unlike *syulff-kuonn*, the coronal *kenning* surrounding a young Tymbrimi who was savoring an anticipated jest.

Robert gave the vine a hearty tug. He inhaled, expanding his ribcage to a degree no Tymbrimi could have equaled, then thumped his chest hollowly, rapidly, and gave out a long, ululating yodel. It echoed down the forest corridors.

Athaclena sighed. *Oh, yes. He must pay respects to their wolfling deity, Tarzan.*

With the vine clutched in both hands, Robert vaulted from the branch. He sailed, legs outstretched together, in a smooth arc down and across the forest meadow, barely clearing the low shrubs. He whooped aloud.

Of course it was just the sort of thing humans would have invented during those dark centuries between the advent of intelligence and their discovery of science. None of the Library-raised Galactic races, not even the Tymbrimi, would ever have thought up such a mode of transportation.

The pendulum swing carried Robert upward again, toward a thick mass of leaves and branchlets halfway up the side of a forest giant. Robert's warbling cry cut off suddenly as he crashed through the foliage with a splintering sound and disappeared.

The silence was punctuated only by a faint, steady rain of minor debris. Athaclena hesitated, then called out. 'Robert?'

There was neither reply nor movement up there in that high thicket. 'Robert! Are you all right? Answer me!' The Anglic words felt thick in her mouth.

She tried to locate him with her corona, the little strands above her ears strained forward. He was in there, all right . . . and in some degree of pain, she could tell.

She ran across the meadow, leaping over low obstacles as the *gheer* transformation set in – her nostrils automatically widening to accept more air as her heart rate tripled. By the time she reached the tree, her finger- and toenails had already begun to harden. She kicked off her soft shoes and began climbing at once, quickly finding holds in the rough bark as she shimmied up the giant bole to the first branch.

The ubiquitous vines clustered here, snaking at an angle toward the leafy morass that had swallowed Robert. She tested one of the ropy cables, then used it to shimmy up to the next level.

Athaclena knew she should pace herself. For all of her Tymbrimi speed and adaptability, her musculature wasn't as strong as a human's, and coronal-radiation didn't dissipate heat as well as Terran sweat glands. Still, she could not taper off from full, emergency speed.

It felt dim and close within the leafy blind where Robert had crashed. Athaclena blinked and sniffed as she entered the darkness. The odors reminded her that this was a wild world, and she was no wolfling to be at home in a ferine jungle. Athaclena had to retract her tendrils so they wouldn't get tangled in the thicket. That was why she was taken by surprise when something reached out from the shadows to grab her tightly.

Hormones rushed. She gasped and coiled around to strike out at her assailant. Just in time she recognized Robert's aura, his human male odor very near, and his strong arms holding her close. Athaclena experienced a momentary wave of dizziness as the *gheer* reaction braked hard.

It was in that stunned state, while still immobilized by change-rigor, that her surprise was redoubled. For that was when Robert began touching her *mouth* with his. At first his actions seemed meaningless, insane. But then, as her corona unwound, she started picking up feelings again . . . and all at once she remembered scenes from human video dramas-scenes involving mating and sexual play.

The storm of emotions that swept over Athaclena was so power-fully contradictory that she remained frozen for a while longer. Also, part of it might have been the relaxed power in his arms. Only when Robert finally let go of her did Athaclena back away from him quickly, wedging herself against the bole of the giant tree, gasping.

'*An . . . An-thwillathbielna! Naha* . . . You . . . you *blenchuq*! How dare you . . . *Cleth-tnub* . . . ' She ran out of breath and had to stop her polyglot cursing, panting slowly. It didn't seem to be penetrating Robert's mild expression of good cheer anyway.

'Uh, I didn't catch all that, Athaclena. My GalSeven is still pretty bad, though I've been working on it. Tell me, what's a . . . a *blenchuq*?'

Athaclena made a gesture, a twist of the head that was the Tymbrimi equivalent to an irritated shrug. 'Never mind that! Tell me at once. Are you badly hurt? And if not, why did you do what you just did?

'Third, tell me why I should not punish you for tricking and assaulting me like that!'

Robert's eyes widened. 'Oh, don't take it all so seriously, Clennie. I appreciate the way you came charging to my rescue. I was still a bit dazed, I guess, and got carried away being happy to see you.'

Athaclena's nostrils flared. Her tendrils waved, preparing she knew not what caustic glyph. Robert clearly sensed this. He held up a hand. 'All right, all right. In order – I'm not badly hurt, only a bit scraped. Actually, it was fun.'

He erased his smile on seeing her expression. 'Uh, as for question number two – I greeted you that way because it's a common human courtship ritual that I was strongly motivated to perform with you, even though I admit you might not have understood it.'

Now Athaclena frowned. Her tendrils curled in confusion.

'And finally,' Robert sighed. 'I can't think of a single reason why you shouldn't punish me for my presumption. It's your privilege, as it'd be the right of any human female to break my arm for handling her without permission. I don't doubt you could do it, too.

'All I can say in my defense is that a broken arm is sometimes an occupational hazard to a young human mel. Half the time a courtship can hardly get started unless a fellow pulls something impulsive. If he's read the signs right, the fem likes it and doesn't give him a black eye. If he's wrong, he pays.'

Athaclena watched Robert's expression turn thoughtful. 'You know,' he went on. 'I'd never quite parsed it out that way before. It's true, though. Maybe humans *are* crazy *cleth th-tnubs*, at that.'

Athaclena blinked. The tension had begun to leak away, dripping from the tips of her corona as her body returned to normal. The change nodes under her skin pulsed, reabsorbing the *gheer* flux.

Like little mice, she remembered, but she shuddered a little less this time.

In feet, she found herself smiling. Robert's strange confession had put matters – almost laughably – on a logical plane. 'Amazing,' she said. 'As usual, there are parallels in Tymbrimi methodology. Our own males must take chances as well.'

She paused then, frowning. 'But stylistically this technique of yours is so crude! The error rate must be tremendous, since you are without coronae to sense what the female is feeling. Beyond your crude empathy sense, you have only hints and coquetry and body cues to go on. I'm surprised you manage to reproduce at all without killing each other off well beforehand!'

Robert's face darkened slightly, and she knew he was blushing. 'Oh, I exaggerated a bit, I suppose.'

Athaclena couldn't help but smile once more, not only a subtlety of the mouth, but an actual, full widening of the separation between her eyes.

'That much, Robert, I had already guessed.'

The human's features reddened even more. He looked down at his hands and there was silence. Athaclena felt a stirring within her own deepself, and she *kenned* the simple sense-glyph *kiniwullun* ... the parable-boy caught doing what boys inevitably do. Sitting there, his open aura of abashed sincerity seemed to cover over his fix-eyed, big-nosed alien-ness and make him more familiar to her than most of her peers had been back in school.

At last Athaclena slipped down from the dusty corner where she had wedged herself in self-defense.

'All right, Robert,' she sighed. 'I will let you explain to me why you were "strongly motivated" to attempt this classical human mating ritual with a member of another species – me. I suppose it is because we have signed an agreement to be consorts? Did you feel honor bound to consummate it, in order to satisfy human tradition?'

He shrugged, looking away. 'No, I can't use that as an excuse. I know interspecies marriages are for business. It's just, well – I think it was just because you're pretty and bright, and I'm lonely, and ... and maybe I'm just a bit in love with you.'

Her heart beat faster. This time it was not the *gheer* chemicals responsible. Her tendrils lifted of their own accord, but no glyph emerged. Instead, she found they were *reaching* toward him along subtle, strong lines, like the fields of a dipole.

'I think, I think I understand, Robert. I want you to know that I ...'

It was hard to think of what to say. She wasn't sure herself just what she was thinking at that moment. Athaclena shook her head. 'Robert?' she said softly. 'Will you do me a favor?'

'Anything, Clennie. Anything in the world.' His eyes were wide open.

'Good. Then, taking care not to get carried away, perhaps you might go on to explain and demonstrate what you were doing, when you touched me just then ... the various physical aspects involved. Only this time, more slowly please?'

The next day they strolled slowly on their way back to the caves.

She and Robert dawdled, stopping to contemplate how the sunlight came down in little glades, or standing by small pools of colored liquid, wondering aloud which trace chemical was stockpiled here or there by the ubiquitous trade vines, and not really caring about the answer. Sometimes they just held hands while they listened to the quiet sounds of Garth Planet's forest life.

At intervals they sat and experimented, gently, with the sensations brought on by touching.

Athaclena was surprised to find that most of the needed nerve pathways were already in place. No deep auto-suggestion was required – just a subtle shifting of a few capillaries and pressure receptors – in order to make the experiment feasible. Apparently, the Tymbrimi might have once engaged in a courtship ritual such as kissing. At least they had the capability.

When she resumed her old form she just might keep some of these adaptations to her lips, throat, and ears. The breeze felt good on them as she and Robert walked. It was like a rather nice empathy glyph tingling at the tips of her corona. And kissing, that warm pressure, stirred intense, if primitive, feelings in her.

Of course none of it would have been possible if humans and Tymbrimi weren't already so very similar. Many charming, stupid theories had circulated among unsophisticated people of both races to explain the coincidence – for instance, proposing that they might once have had a common ancestor.

The idea was ridiculous, of course. Still, she knew that her case was not the first. Close association over several centuries had led to quite a few cases of cross-species dalliance, some even openly avowed. Her discoveries must have been made many times before.

She just hadn't been aware, having considered such tales rather seamy while growing up. Athaclena realized her friends back on Tymbrim must have thought her pretty much of a prude. And here she was, behaving in a way that would have shocked most of them!

She still wasn't sure she wanted anyone back home – assuming she ever made it there again – to think her consortium with Robert was anything but businesslike. Uthacalthing would probably laugh.

No matter, she told herself firmly. *I must live for today.* The experiment helped to pass the time. It did have its pleasant aspects. And Robert was an enthusiastic teacher.

Of course she was going to have to set limits. She was willing to adjust the distribution of forty tissues in her breasts, for instance, and it was fun to play with the sensations made possible by new nerve endings. But where it came to fundamentals she would have to be adamant. She wasn't about to go changing any really basic mechanisms ... not for any human being!

On the return trip they stopped to inspect a few rebel outposts and talk with small bands of chim fighters. Morale was high. The veterans of three months' hard battles asked when their leaders would find a way to lure more Gubru up into the mountains within reach. Athaclena and Robert laughed and promised to do what they could about the lack of target practice.

Still, they found themselves hard pressed for ideas. After all, how does one invite back a guest whose beak one has repeatedly bloodied? Perhaps it was time to try taking the war to the enemy, instead.

The problem was lack of good intelligence about matters down in the Sind and Port Helenia. A few survivors of the urban uprising had wandered in and reported that their organization was a shambles. Nobody had seen either Gailet Jones or Fiben Bolger since that ill-fated day. Contact with a few individuals in town was restored, but on a patchy, piecemeal basis.

They had considered sending in new spies. There seemed to be an opportunity offered by the Gubru public announcements, offering lucrative employment to ecological and uplift experts. But by now the avians must certainly have tuned their interrogation apparatus and developed a fair chim lie detector. In any event, Robert and Athaclena decided against taking the risk. For now, at least.

They were walking homeward up a narrow, seldom-visited valley, when they encountered a slope with a southern exposure, covered with a low-lying expanse of peculiar vegetation. They stood quietly for a time, looking over the green field of flat, inverted bowls.

'I never did cook you a meal of baked plate ivy root,' Robert commented at last, dryly.

Athaclena sniffed, appreciating his irony. The place where the accident had occurred was far from here. And yet, this bumpy hillside brought back vivid memories of that horrible afternoon when their 'adventures' all began.

'Are the plants sick? Is there something wrong with them?' She gestured at the field of plates, overlapping closely like the scales of some slumbering dragon. The upper layers did not look glassy smooth and fat, like those she recalled. The topmost caps in this colony seemed much less thick and sturdy.

'Hm.' Robert bent to examine the nearest. 'Summer's on its way out, soon. All this heat is already drying the uppermost plates. By mid-autumn, when the east winds come blowing down the Mulun range, the caps will be as thin and light as wafers. Did I ever tell you they were seed pod carriers? The wind will catch them, and they'll blow away into the sky like a cloud of butterflies.'

'Oh, yes. I remember you did mention it.' Athaclena nodded thoughtfully. 'But did not you also say that – '

She was interrupted by a sharp call.

'General! Captain Oneagle!'

A group of chims hurried into view, puffing along the narrow forest trail. Two were members of their escort squad, but the third was Benjamin! He looked exhausted. Obviously he had run all the way from the caves to meet them.

Athaclena felt Robert grow tense with sudden worry. But with the advantage of her corona, she already knew that Ben was not bringing dire news. There was no emergency, no enemy attack.

And yet, her chim aide clearly was confused and distraught. 'What is it, Benjamin?' she asked.

He mopped his brow with a homespun handkerchief. Then he reached into another pocket and drew out a small black cube. 'Sers, our courier, young Petri, has finally returned.'

Robert stepped forward. 'Did he reach the refuge?'

Benjamin nodded. 'He got there, all right, and he's brought a message from th' Council. This is it here.' He held out the cube.

'A message from Megan?' Robert sounded breathless as he looked down at the recording.

'Yesser. Petri says she's well, and sends her best.'

'But – but that's great!' Robert whooped. 'We're in contact again! We aren't alone anymore!'

'Yesser. That's true enough. In fact ...' Athaclena watched Benjamin struggle to find the right words. 'In fact, Petri brought more than a message. There are five people waiting for you, back at the caves.'

Both Robert and Athaclena blinked. 'Five humans?'

Benjamin nodded, but with a look that implied he wasn't exactly sure that term was the most applicable. 'Terragens Marines, ser.'

'Oh,' Robert said. Athaclena merely maintained her silence, *kenning* more closely than she was listening.

Benjamin nodded. 'Professionals, ser. Five humans. I swear, it's incredible how it feels after all this time without – I mean, with only th' two of you until now. It's made the chims pretty hyper right at the moment. I think it might be best if you both came on back as quick as possible.'

Robert and Athaclena spoke almost at once.

'Of course.'

'Yes, let's go at once.'

Almost imperceptibly, the closeness between Athaclena and Robert altered. They had been holding hands when Benjamin ran up. Now they did not renew that grasp. It seemed inappropriate as they marched along the narrow trail. A new unknown factor had slipped in between them. They did not have to look at each other to know what the other was thinking.

For better or for worse, things had changed.

58

ROBERT

Major Prathachulthorn pored over the readouts that lay like blown leaves spread across the plotting table. The chaos was only apparent, Robert realized as he watched the small, dark man work, for Prathachulthorn never needed to search for anything. Whatever it was he wanted, somehow he found it with barely a flick of his shadowed eyes and a quick grasp of his callused hands.

At intervals the Marine officer glanced over to a holo-tank and muttered subvocally into his throat microphone. Data whirled in the tank, shifting and turning in subtle rearrangements at his command.

Robert waited, standing at ease in front of the table of rough-cut logs. It was the fourth time Prathachulthorn had summoned him to answer tersely phrased questions. Each time Robert grew more awed by the man's obvious precision and skill.

Clearly, Major Prathachulthorn was a professional. In only a day he and his small staff had started to bring order to the partisans' makeshift tactical programs, rearranging data, sifting out patterns and insights the amateur insurgents had never even imagined.

Prathachulthorn was everything their movement had needed. He was exactly what they had been praying for.

No question about it. Robert hated the man's guts. Now he was trying to figure out exactly why.

I mean, besides the fact that he's making me stand here in silence until he's good and ready. Robert recognized that for a simple way of reinforcing the message of who was boss. Knowing that helped him take it with good grace, mostly.

The major looked every inch the compleat Terragens commando, even though his sole military adornment was an insignia of rank at his left shoulder. Not even in full dress uniform would Robert ever look as much a soldier as Prathachulthorn did right now, draped in ill-fitting cloth woven by gorillas under a sulfrous volcano.

The Earthman spent some time drumming his fingers on the table. The repetitious thumping reminded Robert of the headache he'd been trying to fight off with biofeedback for an hour or more. For some reason the technique wasn't working this time. He felt closed in, claustrophobic, short of breath. And seemed to be getting worse.

At last Prathachulthorn looked up. To Robert's surprise the man's first remark could be taken as something distantly akin to a compliment.

'Well, Captain Oneagle,' Prathachulthorn said. 'I confess to having feared things would be much, much worse than I find them here.'

'I'm relieved to hear it, sir.'

Prathachulthorn's eyes narrowed, as if he suspected an ever-so-thin veneer of sarcasm in Robert's voice. 'To be precise,' he went on, 'I feared I would discover that you had lied in your report to the Council in Exile, and that I would have to shoot you.'

Robert suppressed an impulse to swallow and managed to maintain an impassive expression. 'I'm glad that did not turn out to be necessary, sir.'

'So am I. I'm sure your mother would have been irritated, for one thing. As it is, and bearing in mind that yours was a strictly amateur enterprise, I'm willing to credit you with a good effort here.'

Major Prathachulthorn shook his head. 'No, that's unfairly restrained. Let me put it this way. There is much I'd have done otherwise, had I been here. But in light of how poorly the official forces have fared, you and your chims have performed very well indeed.'

Robert felt a hollowness in his chest begin to relax. 'I'm sure the chims will be glad to hear it, sir. I'd like to point out, though, that I was not sole leader here. The Tymbrimi Athaclena carried a good part of that burden.'

Major Prathachulthorn's expression turned sour. Robert wasn't sure if it was because Athaclena was a Galactic, or because Robert, as a militia officer, should have retained all authority himself.

'Ah, yes. The "General."' His indulgent smile was patronizing, at the very least. He nodded. 'I will mention her assistance in my report. Ambassador Uthacalthing's daughter is clearly a resourceful young alien. I hope she is willing to continue helping us, in some capacity.'

'The chims worship her, sir,' Robert pointed out.

Major Prathachulthorn nodded. As he looked over toward the wall, his voice took on a thoughtful tone. 'The Tymbrimi mystique, I know. Sometimes I wonder if the media knows what the hell it's doing, creating such ideas. Allies or no allies, our people have got to understand that Earthclan will always be fundamentally alone. We'll never be able to fully trust anything Galactic.'

Then, as if he felt he might have said too much, Prathachulthorn shook his head and changed the subject. 'Now about future operations against the enemy—'

'We've been thinking about that, sir. Their mysterious surge of activity in the mountains seems to have ended, though for how long we don't know. Still, there are some ideas we've been batting around. Things we might use against them when and if they come back.'

'Good.' Prathachulthorn nodded. 'But you must understand that in the future we'll have to coordinate all actions in the Mulun with other planetary forces. Irregulars are simply incapable of hurting the enemy where his real assets are. That was demonstrated when the city chim insurrectionists were wiped out trying to attack the space batteries near Port Helenia.'

Robert saw Prathachulthorn's point. 'Yessir. Although since then we have captured some munitions which could be useful.'

'A few missiles, yes. They might be handy, if we can figure out how to use them. And especially if we have the right information about where to point them.

'We have altogether too little data,' the major went on. 'I want to gather more and report back to the Council. After that, our task will be to prepare to support any action they choose to undertake.'

Robert finally asked the question that he had put off since returning to find Prathachulthorn and his small group of human officers here, turning the cave refuge upside down, poking into everything, taking over. 'What will be done with our organization, sir? Athaclena and I, we've given a number of chims working officer status. But except for me nobody here has a real colonial commission.'

Prathachulthorn pursed his lips. 'Well, you're the simplest case, captain. Clearly you deserve a rest. You can escort Ambassador Uthacalthing's daughter back to the Refuge with our next report, along with my recommendation for a promotion and a medal. I know the Coordinator would like that. You can fill them in on how you made your fine discovery about the Gubru resonance tracking technique.'

From his tone of voice, the major made it quite clear what he would think of Robert if he took up the offer. 'On the other hand, I'd be pleased to have you join my staff, with a brevet marine status of first lieutenant in addition to your colonial commission. We could use your experience.'

'Thank you, sir. I think I'll remain here, if it's all right with you.'

'Fine. Then well assign someone else to escort—'

'I'm sure Athaclena will want to stay as well,' Robert hurriedly added.

'Hmm. Well, yes. I am certain she could be helpful for a while. Tell you what, captain. I'll put the matter to the Council in my next letter. But we must be sure of one thing. Her status is no longer military. The chims are to cease referring to her as a command officer. Is that clear?'

'Yessir, quite clear.' Robert only wondered how one enforced that sort of order on civilian neo-chimpanzees, who tended to call anybody and anything whatever they pleased.

'Good. Now, as for those formerly under your command ... I do happen to have brought with me a few blank colonial commissions which we can assign to chims who have shown notable initiative. I have no doubt you'll recommend names.'

Robert nodded. 'I will, sir.'

He recalled that one other member of their 'army' besides himself had already been in the militia. The thought of Fiben – certainly dead for a long time, now – made him suddenly even more depressed. *These caves! They're driving me nuts. It's getting harder and harder to bear the time I must spend down here.*

Major Prathachulthorn was a disciplined soldier and had spent months in the Council's underground refuge. But Robert had no such firmness of character. *I've got to get out!*

'Sir,' he said quickly. 'I'd like to ask your permission to leave base camp for a few days, to run an errand down near Lome Pass ... at the ruins of the Howletts Center.'

Prathachulthorn frowned. 'The place where those gorillas were illegally gene-meddled?'

'The place where we won our first victory,' he reminded the commando, 'and where we made the Gubru accept parole.'

'Hmph,' the major grunted. 'What do you expect to find there?'

Robert suppressed an impulse to shrug. In his suddenly worsening claustrophobia, in his need for any excuse to get away, he pulled forth an idea that had until then only been a glimmer at the back of his mind.

'A possible weapon, sir. It's a concept for something that might help a lot, if it worked.'

That piqued Prathachulthorn's interest. 'What is this weapon?'

'I'd rather not be specific right now, sir. Not until I've had a chance to verify a few things. I'll only be gone three or four days at the most. I promise.'

'Hmm. Well.' Prathachulthorn's lips pursed. 'It will take that long just to put these data systems into shape. You'll only get underfoot till that's done. Afterwards, though, I'll be needing you. We've got to prepare a report to the Council.'

'Yessir, I'll hurry back.'

'Very well, then. Take Lieutenant McCue with you. I want one of my own men to see the countryside. Show McCue how you accomplished your little coup, introduce her to the leaders of the more important chim partisan bands in that area, then return without delay. Dismissed.'

Robert came to attention. *I think I know now why I hate him*, Robert realized as he saluted, performed an about-face, and walked out through the hanging blanket that served as a door to the subterranean office.

Ever since he had returned to the caves to find Prathachulthorn and his aides moving around like owners, patronizing the chims and judging everything they had all done together, Robert had been unable to stop feeling like a *child* who had, until that moment, been allowed to play a wonderful dramatic role, a really fun *game*. But now the child had to bear paternal pats on the head – strokes that burned, even if intended in praise.

It was an embarrassing analogy, and yet he knew that in a sense it was true after all.

Robert blew a silent sigh and hurried away from the office and dark armory he had shared with Athaclena, but which now had been completely taken over by grownups.

Only when he was finally back under the tall forest canopy did Robert feel he could breathe freely again. The trees' familiar scents seemed to cleanse his lungs of the dank cave odors. The scouts who flitted ahead of him and alongside were those he knew, quick, loyal, feral-looking with their crossbows and sooty faces. *My chims,* he thought, feeling a little guilty that it came to him in those words. But the feeling of proprietorship was there anyway. It was like the 'old days' – before yesterday – when he had felt important and needed.

The illusion broke apart, though, the next time Lieutenant McCue spoke.

'These mountain forests are very beautiful,' she said. 'I wish I'd taken the time to come up here before the war broke out.' The Earthling officer stopped by the side of the trail to touch a blue-veined flower, but it folded away from her fingers and retreated backward into the thicket. 'I've read about these things, but this is my first chance to see them for myself.'

Robert grunted noncommittally. He would be polite and answer any direct question, but he wasn't interested in conversation, especially with Major Prathachulthorn's second in command.

Lydia McCue was an athletic young woman, with dark, well-cut features. Her movements, lithe like a commando's – or an assassin's – were by that same nature also quite graceful. Dressed in homespun kilt and blouse, she might have been taken for a peasant dancer, if it weren't for the self-winding arbalest she cradled in the crook of one arm like a child. In hip pouches were enough darts to pincushion half the Gubru within a hundred kilometers. The knives sheathed at her wrists and ankles were for more than show.

She seemed to have very little trouble keeping up with his rapid pace through the criss-cross jungle mesh of vines. That was just as well, for he wasn't about to slow down. At the back of his mind Robert knew he was being unfair. She was probably a nice enough person in her own way, for a professional soldier. But for some reason everything likable about her seemed to irritate him all the more.

Robert wished Athaclena had consented to come along. But she had insisted on remaining in her glade near the caves, experimenting with tame vines and crafting strange, ornate glyphs that were far too subtle to be *kenned* by his own weak powers. Robert had felt hurt and stormed off, almost outracing his escorts for the first few kilometers.

'So much life.' The Earth woman kept pace beside him and inhaled the rich odors. 'This is a peaceful place.'

You're wrong on both counts, Robert thought, with a trace of contempt for her dull, human insensitivity to the truth about Garth, a truth he could feel all around him. Through Athaclena's tutoring he now could reach out – albeit tentatively, awkwardly – and trace the life-waves that fluxed through the quiet forest.

'This is an unhappy land,' he replied simply. He did not elaborate, even when she gave him a puzzled look. His primitive empathy sense withdrew from her confusion.

For a while they moved in silence. The morning aged. Once the scouts whistled, and they took cover under thick branches as great cruisers lumbered overhead. When the way was clear Robert took to the trail again without a word.

At last, Lydia McCue spoke again. 'This place we're heading for,' she asked, 'this Howletts Center. Would you please tell me about it?'

It was a simple request. He could not refuse, since Prathachulthorn had sent her along to be shown things. But Robert avoided her black eyes as he spoke. He tried to be matter-of-fact, but emotion kept creeping into his voice. Under her low prompting Robert told Lydia McCue about the sad, misguided, but brilliant work of the renegade scientists. His mother had known nothing of the Howletts Center, of course. It was only by accident that he himself had learned of it a year or so before the invasion, and he had decided to keep silent.

Of course the daring experiment was over now. It would take more than a miracle to save the neo-gorillas from sterilization, now that the secret was known to people like Major Prathachulthorn.

Prathachulthorn might hate Galactic Civilization with a passion that bordered on fanaticism, but he knew how essential it was that Terrans not break their solemn pacts with the great Institutes. Right now, Earth's only hope lay in the ancient codes of the Progenitors. To keep the protection of those codes, weak clans had to be like Caesar's wife, above reproach.

Lydia McCue listened attentively. She had high cheekbones and eyes that were sultry in their darkness. It pained Robert to look at them, though. Those eyes seemed somehow to be set too close together, too immobile. He kept his attention on the crooked path ahead of him.

And yet, with a soft voice the young Marine officer drew him out. Robert found himself talking about Fiben Bolger, about their narrow escape together from the gas-bombing of the Mendoza Freehold, and of his friend's first journey down into the Sind.

And the second, from which he never returned.

They crested a ridge topped with eerie spine-stones and came to an opening overlooking a narrow vale, just west of Lome Pass. He gestured to the tumbled outlines of several burned structures. 'The Howletts Center,' he said, flatly.

'This is where you forced the Gubru to acknowledge chim combatants, isn't it? And made them give parole?' Lydia McCue asked. Robert realized he was hearing *respect* in her voice, and turned briefly to stare at her. She returned his look with a smile. Robert felt his face grow warm.

He swung back quickly, pointing to the hillside nearest the center and rapidly describing how the trap had been laid and sprung, skipping only his own trapeze leap to take out the Gubru sentry. His part had been unimportant, anyway. The chims were the crucial ones that morning. He wanted the Earthling soldiers to know that.

He was finishing his story when Elsie approached. The chimmie saluted him, something that had never seemed necessary before the Marines arrived.

'I don't know about actually goin' down there, ser,' she said, earnestly. 'The enemy's already shown an interest in those ruins. They may have come back.'

Robert shook his head. 'When Benjamin paroled the enemy survivors, one condition they accepted was to stay out of this valley, and not even keep its approaches under surveillance, from then on. Has there been any sign of them breaking their word?'

Elsie shook her head. 'No, but – ' Her lips pressed together, as if she felt she ought to forbear comment on the wisdom of trusting the pledges of Eatees.

Robert smiled. 'Well, then. Come on. If we hurry we can be in and back out by nightfall.'

Elsie shrugged. She made a quick set of hand gestures. Several chims darted out of the spine-stones and down into the forest. After a moment there came an all-clear whistle. The rest of the party crossed the gap at a brisk run.

'They are very good,' Lydia McCue told him softly after they were back under the trees again.

Robert nodded, recognizing that she had not qualified her remark by adding, 'for amateurs,' as Prathachulthorn would have done. He was grateful for that, and wished she wasn't being so nice.

Soon they were picking their way toward tumbled ruins, carefully searching for signs that anyone else had been there since the battle, months ago. There did not seem to be any, but that did not diminish the intense vigilance of the chims. Robert tried to *kenn*, to use the Net to probe for intruders, but his own jumbled feelings kept getting in the way. He wished Athaclena were here.

The wreckage of the Howletts Center was even more complete than had been apparent from the hillside. The fire-blackened buildings had collapsed further under wild jungle vegetation now growing rampant over former lawns. The Gubru vehicles, long ago stripped of anything useful, lay in tangles of thick grass as tall as his waist.

No, clearly nobody's been here, he thought. Robert kicked through the wreckage. Nothing remained of interest. *Why did I insist on coming?* he wondered. He knew his hunch – whether it panned out or not – had actually been little more than an excuse to escape from the caves – to get away from Prathachulthorn.

To get away from uncomfortable glimpses of himself. Perhaps one reason he had chosen to come to this place was because it was here that he had had his own brief moment of hand-to-hand contact with the enemy.

Or maybe he had hoped to recreate the feelings of only a few days ago, traveling unfettered and unjudged. He had hoped to come here with different female company than the woman who now followed him, eyes darting left and right, putting everything under professional scrutiny.

Robert turned away from his brooding thoughts and walked toward the ruined alien hover tanks. He sank to one knee, brushing aside the tall, rank grass.

Gubru machinery, the exposed guts of the armored vehicles, gears, impellers, gravities . . .

A fine yellow patina overlay many of the parts. In some places the shining plastimesh had discolored, thinned, and even broken through. Robert pulled on a small chunk which came off, crumbling, in his hands.

Well I'll be a blue-nosed gopher. I was right. My hunch was right.

'What is it?' Lieutenant McCue asked over his shoulder. He shook his head. 'I'm not sure, yet. But something seems to be eating through a lot of these parts.'

'May I see?'

Robert handed her the piece of corroded ceramet. 'This is why you wanted to come here? You suspected this?'

He saw no point in telling her all the complex reasons, the personal ones. 'That was a large part of it. I thought, maybe, there might be a weapon in it. They burned all the records and facilities when they evacuated the center. But they couldn't eradicate all the microbes developed in Dr Schultz's lab.'

He didn't add that he had a vial of gorilla saliva in his pack. If he had not found the Gubru armor in this state, on arriving here, he had planned to perform his own experiments. 'Hm.' Lydia McCue crumbled the material in her hand. She got down and crawled under the machine to examine which parts had been affected. Finally she emerged and sat next to Robert.

'It could prove useful. But there would still be the problem of a delivery system. We don't dare venture out of the mountains to spray the little bugs over Gubru equipment in Port Helenia.

'Also, bio-sabotage weapons are very short term in their effectiveness. They have to be used all at once and by surprise, since
countermeasures are usually swift and effective. After a few weeks,
the bugs would be neutralized – chemically, with coatings, or by
cloning another beastie to eat ours.

'Still,' she turned another piece over and looked up to smile at
Robert. 'This is great. What you did here before, and now this ...
These are the right ways to fight guerrilla war! I like it. We'll find a
way to use it.'

Her smile was so open and friendly that Robert couldn't help
responding. And in that shared moment he felt a stirring that he had
been trying to suppress all day.

Damn, she's attractive, he realized, miserably. His body was sending him signals more powerful than it ever had in the company of
Athaclena. And he barely knew this woman! He didn't love her. He
wasn't bound up with her, as he was with his Tymbrimi consort.

And yet his mouth was dry and his heart beat faster as she looked
at him, this narrow-eyed, thin-nosed, tall-browed, female
human ...

'We'd better be heading home,' he said quickly. 'Go ahead and
take some samples, lieutenant. We'll test them back at base.'

He ignored her long look as he stood up and signaled to Elsie.
Soon, with specimens stowed away in their packs, they were climbing once more toward the spine-stones. The watchful guards showed
obvious relief as they shouldered their rifles and leaped back into the
trees.

Robert followed his escort with little attention to the path. He
was trying not to think of the other member of his own race walking beside him, so he frowned and kept himself banked in behind a
brumous cloud of his own thoughts.

59

FIBEN

Fiben and Gailet sat near each other under the unblinking regard of
masked Gubru technicians, who focused their instruments on the
two chims with dispassionate, clinical precision. Multi-lensed globes
and flat-plate phrased arrays floated on all sides, peering down at
them. The testing chamber was a jungle of glistening tubes and
shiny-faced machinery, all antiseptic and sterile.

Still, the place reeked of alien bird. Fiben's nose wrinkled, and once again he disciplined himself to avoid thinking unfriendly thoughts about the Gubru. Certainly several of the imposing machines must be psi detectors. And while it was doubtful they could actually 'read his mind,' the Galactics certainly would be able to trace his surface attitudes.

Fiben reached for something else to think about. He leaned to his left and spoke to Gailet.

'Um, I talked to Sylvie before they came for us this morning. She told me she hasn't been back to the Ape's Grape since that night I first came to Port Helenia.'

Gailet turned to look at Fiben. Her expression was tense, disapproving.

'So? Games like that striptease of hers may be obsolete now, but I'm sure the Gubru are finding other ways to use her unique talents.'

'She's refused to do anything like that since then, Gailet. Honestly. I can't see why you're so hostile toward her.'

'And *I* find it hard to understand how you can be so friendly with one of our jailers!' Gailet snapped. 'She's a probationer and a collaborator!'

Fiben shook his head. 'Actually, Sylvie's not really a probie at all, nor even a gray or yellow. She has a green repro-card. She joined them because – '

'I don't give a damn what her reasons were! Oh, I can imagine what sort of sob story she's told you, you big dope, while she batted her eyelashes and softened you up for – '

From one of the nearby machines came a low, atonal voice. '*Young neo-chimpanzee sophonts . . . be still. Be still, young clients . . .*' it soothed.

Gailet swiveled to face forward, her jaw set.

Fiben blinked. *I wish I understood her better,* he thought. Half the time he had no idea what would set Gailet off.

It was Gailet's moodiness that had started him talking with Sylvie in the first place, simply for company. He wanted to explain that to Gailet, but decided it would do no good. Better to wait. She would come out of this funk. She always did.

Only an hour ago they had been laughing, jostling each other while they fumbled with a complicated mechanical puzzle. For a few minutes they had been able to forget the staring mechanical and alien eyes while they worked as a team, sorting and resorting the pieces and arranging them together. When they stood back at last and looked on the completed tower they had made, they both knew that they had surprised the note-takers. In that moment of satisfaction, Gailet's hand had slipped, innocently and affectionately, into his.

Imprisonment was like that. Part of the time, Fiben actually felt as if he were profiting from the experience. It was the first time in his life, for instance, that he'd ever really had time to just sit and think. Their captors now let them have books, and he was catching up on quite a few volumes he'd always wanted to read. Conversations with Gailet had opened up the arcane world of alienology. He, in turn, had spoken to her of the great work being done here on Garth, delicately nudging a ruined ecosystem back toward health.

But then, all too common, had been the long, darker intervals, when the hours dragged on and on. A pall hung over them at such times. The walls seemed to close in, and conversation always came back to the War, to memories of their failed insurrection, to lost friends and gloomy speculations over the fate of Earth itself.

At such times, Fiben thought he might trade all hope of a long life for just an hour to run free under trees and clean sky.

So even this new routine of testing by the Gubru had come as a relief for both of them. At least it was a distraction.

Without warning, the machines suddenly pulled away, opening an avenue in front of their bench. *'We are finished, finished ... You have done well, done well, you have ... Now follow the globe, follow it, toward transportation.'*

As Fiben and Gailet stood up, a brown, octahedral projection took form in front of them. Without looking at each other they followed the hologram past the silent, brooding avian technicians, out of the testing chamber, and down a long hallway.

Service robots swept past them with the soft whisper of well-tuned machinery. Once a Kwackoo technician darted out of an office door, favored them with a startled look, then ducked back inside. At last Fiben and Gailet passed through a hissing portal and emerged into bright sunshine. Fiben had to shade his eyes. The day was fair, but with a bite that seemed to say that brief summer was now well on its way out. The chims he could see in the streets, beyond the Gubru compound, were wearing light sweaters and sneakers, another sure sign that autumn was near.

None of the chims looked their way. The distance was too great for Fiben to tell anything of their mood, or to hope that somebody might recognize him or Gailet.

'We won't be riding the same car back,' whispered Gailet. And she motioned down a long parapet toward the landing ramp below. Sure enough, the tan military van that had brought them had been replaced by a large, roofless hover barge. An ornate pedestal stood in the open deck behind the pilot's station. Kwackoo servitors adjusted a sunshade to keep the fierce light of Gimelhai off their master's beak and crest.

The large Gubru was recognizable. Its thick, faintly luminous plumage looked shaggier than the last time they had seen it, in the furtive darkness of their suburban prison. The effect was to make it seem even more different than the run-of-the-mill Gubru functionaries they had seen. In some places the allochroous feathers had begun to appear frayed, tattered. The avian aristocrat wore a striped collar. It paced impatiently atop its perch.

'Well, well,' Fiben muttered. 'If it ain't our old friend, the Somethin' of Good Housekeeping.'

Gailet snorted in something just short of a small laugh. 'It's called the Suzerain of Propriety,' she reminded him. 'The striped torc means it's the leader of the priestly caste. Now just you remember to behave yourself. Try not to scratch too much, and watch what I do.'

'I'll imitate yer very steps precisely, mistress.'

Gailet ignored his sarcasm and followed the brown guidance hologram down the long ramp toward the brightly colored barge. Fiben kept pace just a little behind her.

The guide projection vanished as they reached the landing. A Kwackoo, with its feathery ruff tinted a garish shade of pink, offered them both a very shallow bow. 'You are honored – honored . . . that our patron – noble patron does deign to show you – you half-formed ones . . . the favor of your destiny.'

The Kwackoo spoke without the assistance of a vodor. That in itself was no small miracle, given the creature's highly specialized speech organs. In fact, it spoke the Anglic words fairly clearly, if with a breathless quality which made the alien sound nervous, expectant.

It wasn't likely the Suzerain of Propriety was the easiest boss in the Universe to work for. Fiben imitated Gailet's bow and kept silent as she replied. 'We are honored by the attention that your master, the high patron of a great clan, condescends to offer us,' she said in slow, carefully enunciated Galactic Seven. 'Nevertheless, we retain, in our own patrons' names, the right to disapprove its actions.'

Even Fiben gasped. The assembled Kwackoo cooed in anger, fluffing up threateningly.

Three high, chirped notes cut their outrage off abruptly. The lead Kwackoo swiveled quickly and bowed to the Suzerain, who had scuttled to the end of its perch closest to the two chims. The Gubru's beak gaped as it bent to regard Gailet, first with one eye, then the other. Fiben found himself sweating rivulets.

Finally, the alien straightened and squawked a pronouncement in its own highly clipped, inflected version of Galactic Three. Only Fiben saw the tremor of relief that passed down Gailet's tense spine. He could not follow the Suzerain's stilted prose, but a vodor nearby commenced translating promptly.

'Well said – said well … spoken well for captured, client-class soldiers of foe-clan Terra … Come, then – come and see … come and see and hear a bargain you will certainly not disapprove – not even in your patrons' names.'

Gailet and Fiben glanced at each other. Then, as one, they bowed.

The late morning air was clear, and the faint ozone smell probably did not foretell rain. Such ancient cues were useless in the presence of high technology anyway.

The barge cruised south past the closed pleasure piers of Port Helenia and out across the bay. It was Fiben's first chance to see how the harbor had changed since the aliens had arrived.

The fishing fleet had been crippled for one thing. Only one in four trawlers did not lie beached or in dry dock. The main commercial port was almost dead as well. A clump of dispirited-looking seafaring vessels listed at their moorings, clearly untouched for months. Fiben watched one of the still working fishing trawlers heave into view around the point of the bay, probably returning early with a fortuitous catch – or with a mechanical failure the chim crew felt unable to deal with at sea. The tub-bottomed boat rose and fell as it rode the standing swell where sea met bay. The crew had to struggle since the passage was narrower than it had been in days of peace. Half of the strait was now blocked by a towering, curving cliff face – a great fortress of alien cerametal.

The Gubru battleship seemed to shimmer in a faint haze. Water droplets condensed at the fringes of its ward-screens, rainbows sparkled, and a mist fell over the struggling trawler as it forced its way past the northern tongue of land at last. Fiben could not make out the faces of the chim crew as the Suzerain's barge swept overhead, but he saw several long-armed forms slump in relief as the boat reached calm waters at last.

From Point Borealis the upper arm of the bayshore swept several kilometers north and east toward Port Helenia itself. Except for a small navigation beacon, those rough heights were unoccupied. The branches of ridgetop pines riffled gently in the sea breezes.

Southward, however, across the narrow strait, things were quite different. Beyond the grounded battleship, the terrain had been transformed. Forest growth had been removed, the contours of the bluffs altered. Dust rose from a site just out of view beyond the headland. A swarm of hovers and heavy lifters could be seen buzzing to and fro in that direction.

Much farther to the south, toward the spaceport, new domes had been erected as part of the Gubru defensive network – the facilities the urban guerrillas had only mildly inconvenienced in their abortive insurrection. But the barge did not seem to be heading that way. Rather they turned toward the new construction on the narrow, hilly slopes between Aspinal Bay and the Sea of Cilmar.

Fiben knew it was hopeless asking their hosts what was going on. The Kwackoo technicians and servitors were polite, but it was a severe sort of courtesy, probably on orders. And they were not forthcoming with much information.

Gailet joined him at the railing and took his elbow. 'Look,' she whispered in a hushed voice.

Together they stared as the barge rose over the bluffs.

A hilltop had been shorn flat near the ocean shoreline. Buildings Fiben recognized as proton power plants lay clustered around its base, feeding cables upward, along its flanks. At the top, a hemispherical structure lay face upward, glimmering and open like a marble bowl in the sunshine.

'What is it? A force field projector? Some kind of weapon?'

Fiben nodded, shook his head, and finally shrugged. 'Beats me. It doesn't look military. But whatever it does sure must take a lot of juice. Look at all those power plants. Goodall!'

A shadow slipped over them – not with the fluffy, ragged coolness of a cloud passing before the sun, but with the sudden, sharp chill of something solid and huge rumbling over their heads. Fiben shivered, only partly from the drop in temperature. He and Gailet couldn't help crouching as they looked up at the giant lifter-carrier that cruised only a hundred meters higher. Their avian hosts, on the other hand, appeared unruffled. The Suzerain stood on its perch, placidly ignoring the thrumming fields that made the chims tremble.

They don't like surprise, Fiben thought. *But they are pretty tough when they know what's happening.*

Their transport began a long, slow, lazy circuit around the perimeter of the construction site. Fiben was pondering the white, upturned bowl below when the Kwackoo with the pink ruff approached and inclined its head ever so slightly.

'The Great One deigns – does offer favor ... and will suggest commonality – complementarity ... of goals and aims.'

Across the barge, the Suzerain of Propriety could be seen perched regally on its pedestal. Fiben wished he could read expressions on a Gubru face. *What's the old bird got in mind?* he wondered. Fiben wasn't entirely sure he really wanted to know.

Gailet returned the shallow bow of the Kwackoo. 'Please tell your honored patron we will humbly attend his offer.'

The Suzerain's Galactic Three was stilted and formal, embellished with mincing, courtly dance steps. The vodor translation did not help Fiben much. He found himself watching Gailet, rather than the alien, as he tried to follow what the hell they were talking about.

'... *allowable revision to Ritual of Choice of Uplift Advisor ... modification made during time of stress, by foremost client representatives ... if performed truly in best interests of their patron race ...'*

Gailet seemed visibly shaken, looking up at the Gubru. Her lips pressed together in a tight line, and her intertwined fingers were white with tension. When the Suzerain stopped chirping, the vodor continued on for a moment, then silence closed in around them, leaving only the whistle of passing air and the faint droning of the hover's engines.

Gailet swallowed. She bowed and seemed to have difficulty finding her voice.

You can do it, Fiben urged silently. Speechlock could strike any chim, especially under pressure like this, but he knew he dared not do anything to help her.

Gailet coughed, swallowed again, and managed to bring forth words.

'Hon-honored elder, we ... we cannot speak for our patrons, or even for all the chims on Garth. What you ask is ... is ...'

The Suzerain spoke again, as if her reply had been complete. Or perhaps it simply was not considered impolite for a patron-class being to interrupt a client.

'You have no need – need not ... to answer now,' the vodor pronounced as the Gubru chirped and bobbed on its perch. 'Study – learn – consider ... the materials you will be given. This opportunity will be to your advantage.'

The chirping ceased again, followed by the buzzing vodor. The Suzerian seemed to dismiss them then, simply by closing its eyes.

As if at some signal invisible to Fiben, the pilot of the hover barge banked away from the frenzied activity atop the ravaged hilltop and sent the craft streaking back across the bay, northward, toward Port Helenia. Soon the battleship in the harbor – gigantic and imperturbable – fell behind them in its wreath of mist and rainbows.

Fiben and Gailet followed a Kwackoo to seats at the back of the barge. 'What was all that about?' Fiben whispered to her. 'What was the damn thing sayin' about some sort of ceremony? What does it want us to do?'

'Sh!' Gailet motioned for him to be silent. 'I'll explain later, Fiben. Right now, please, let me think.'

Gailet settled into a corner, wrapping her arms around her knees. Absently, she scratched the fur on her left leg. Her eyes were unfocused, and when Fiben made a gesture, as if to offer to groom her, she did not even respond. She only looked off toward the horizon, as if her mind were very far away.

Back in their cell they found that many changes had been made. 'I guess we passed all those tests,' Fiben said, staring at their transformed quarters.

The chains had been taken away soon after the Suzerain's first visit, that dark night weeks ago. After that occasion the straw on the floor had been replaced by mattresses, and they had been allowed books.

Now, though, that was made to seem Spartan, indeed. Plush carpeting had been laid down, and an expensive holo-tapestry covered most of one wall. There were such amenities as beds and chairs and a desk, and even a music deck.

'Bribes,' Fiben muttered as he sorted through some of the record cubes. 'Hot damn, we've got something they want. Maybe the Resistance *isn't* over. Maybe Athaclena and Robert are stinging them, and they want us to – '

'This hasn't got anything to do with your general, Fiben,' Gailet said in a very low voice, barely above a whisper. 'Or not much, at least. It's a whole lot bigger than that.' Her expression was tense. All the way back, she had been silent and nervous. At times Fiben imagined he could hear wheels turning in her head.

Gailet motioned for him to follow her to the new holo-wall. At the moment it was set to depict a three-dimensional scene of abstract shapes and patterns – a seemingly endless vista of glossy cubes, spheres, and pyramids stretching into the infinite distance. She sat cross-legged and twiddled with the controls. 'This is an expensive unit,' she said, a little louder than necessary. 'Lets have some fun and find out what it can do.'

As Fiben sat down beside her, the Euclidean shapes blurred and vanished. The controller clicked under Gailet's hand, and a new scene suddenly leaped into place. The wall now seemed to open onto a vast, sandy beach. Clouds filled the sky out to a lowering, gray horizon, pregnant with storms. Breakers rolled less than twenty meters away, so realistic that Fiben's nostrils flared as he tried to catch the salt scent.

Gailet concentrated on the controls. 'This may be the ticket,' he heard her mumble. The almost perfect beachscape flickered, and in its place there suddenly loomed a wall of leafy green – a jungle scene, so near and real that Fiben almost felt he could leap through and escape into its green mists, as if this were one of those mythical 'teleportation devices' one read of in romantic fiction, and not just a high-quality holo-tapestry.

He contemplated the scene Gailet had chosen. Fiben could tell at once that it wasn't a jungle of Garth. The creeper-entwined rain forest was a vibrant, lively, noisy scene, filled with color and variety. Birds cawed and howler monkeys shrieked.

Earth, then, he thought, and wondered if the Galaxy would ever let him fulfil his dream of someday seeing the homeworld. *Not bloody likely, the way things are.*

His attention drew back as Gailet spoke. 'Just let me adjust this here, to make it more realistic.' The sound level rose. Jungle noise burst forth to surround them. *What is she trying to do?* he wondered.

Suddenly he noticed something. As Gailet twiddled with the volume level, her left hand moved in a crude but eloquent gesture. Fiben blinked. It was a sign in baby talk, the hand language all infant chims used until the age of four, when speech finally became useful.

Grownups listening, she said.

Jungle sounds seemed to fill the room, reverberating from the other walls. 'There,' she said in a low voice. 'Now they can't listen in on us. We can talk frankly.'

'But – ' Fiben started to object, then he saw the gesture again. *Grownups listening . . .*

Once more his respect for Gailet's cleverness grew. *Of course* she knew this simple method would not stop snoopers from picking up their every word. But the Gubru and their agents might imagine the chims foolish enough to think it would! If the two of them acted as if they *believed* they were safe from eavesdropping . . .

Such a tangled, web we weave, Fiben thought. This was real spy stuff. Fun, in a way.

It was also, he knew, dangerous as hell.

'The Suzerain of Propriety has a problem,' Gailet told him aloud. Her hands lay still on her lap.

'It *told* you that? But if the Gubru are in trouble, why – '

'I didn't say the *Gubru* – although I think that's true, as well. I was talking about the Suzerain of Propriety itself. It's having troubles with its peers. The priest seriously overcommitted itself in a certain matter, some time back, and now it seems there's hell to pay over it.'

Fiben just sat there, amazed that the lofty alien lord had deigned to tell an earthworm of a Terran client such things. He wasn't comfortable with the idea. Such confidences were likely to be unhealthy. 'What were these overcommitments?' he asked.

'Well, for one thing,' Gailet went on, scratching her kneecap, 'some months ago it insisted that many parties of Talon Soldiers and scientists be sent up into the mountains.'

'What for?'

Gailet's face took on an expression of severe control. 'They were sent searching for . . . for Garthlings.'

'For *what*?' Fiben blinked. He started to laugh. Then he cut short when he saw the warning flicker in her eyes. The hand scratching her knee curled and turned in a motion that signified caution.

'For Garthlings,' she repeated.

Of all the superstitious nonsense, Fiben thought. *Ignorant, yellow-card chims use Garthling fables to frighten their children.* It was rich to think of the sophisticated Gubru falling for such tall tales.

Gailet did not seem to find the idea amusing, though.

'You can imagine why the Suzerain would be excited, Fiben, once it had reason to believe Garthlings might exist. Imagine what a fantastic coup it would be for any clan who claimed adoption rights on a pre-sentient race that had survived the Bururalli Holocaust. Immediate takeover of Earth's tenancy rights here would be the very least of the consequences.'

Fiben saw her point. 'But . . . but what in the world made it think in the first place, that – '

'It seems our Tymbrimi Ambassador, Uthacalthing, was largely responsible for the Suzerain's fixation, Fiben. You remember that day of the chancery explosion, when you tried to break into the Tymbrimi Diplomatic Cache?'

Fiben opened his mouth. He closed it again. He tried to think. What kind of game was Gailet playing now?

The Suzerain of Propriety obviously knew that he, Fiben, was the chim who had been sighted ducking through the smoke and stench of fried Gubru clerical workers on the day of the explosion at the one-time Tymbrimi Embassy. It knew Fiben was the one who had played a frustrated game of tag with the cache guardian, and who later escaped over a cliff face under the very beaks of a squad of Talon Soldiers.

Did it know because Gailet had told it? If so, had she also told the Suzerain about the secret message Fiben had found in the back of the cache and delivered to Athaclena?

He could not ask her these things. The warning look in her eyes kept him silent. *I hope she knows what she's doing,* he prayed fervently. Fiben felt clammy under his arms. He brushed a bead of sweat from his eyebrow. 'Go on,' he said in a dry voice.

'Your visit invalidated diplomatic immunity and gave the Gubru the excuse they were looking for, to break into the cache. Then the Gubru had what they thought was a real stroke of luck. The cache autodestruct partially failed. There was evidence inside, Fiben, evidence pertaining to private investigations into the Garthling question by the Tymbrimi Ambassador.'

'By *Uthacalthing?* But ...' And then it hit Fiben. He stared at Gailet, goggle-eyed. Then he doubled over, coughing as he fought not to laugh out loud. Hilarity was like a head of steam in his chest, a force in its own right, barely contained. A sudden, brief spell of speechlock was actually a blessing, as it kept Gailet from having to shush him. He coughed some more and slapped his chest. 'Excuse me,' he said in a small voice.

'The Gubru now believe that the evidence was contrived, a clever ruse,' she went on.

No kidding, Fiben thought silently.

'In addition to faked data, Uthacalthing also arranged to have the Planetary Library stripped of its Uplift files, making it seem to the Suzerain as if something was being hidden. It cost the Gubru a lot to find out that Uthacalthing had tricked them. A research-class Planetary Library was shipped in, for instance. And they lost quite a few scientists and soldiers up in the mountains before they figured it out.'

'*Lost* them?' Fiben sat forward. 'Lost how?'

'Chim irregulars,' Gailet answered tersely. And again there was that warning look. *Come on, Gailet,* he thought. *I'm not an idiot.* Fiben knew better than to refer in any way to Robert or Athaclena. He shied away from even thinking about them.

Still, he couldn't quite suppress a smile. So that was why the Kwackoo had been so polite! If chims were waging intelligent war, *and* by the official rules at that, then *all* chims had to be treated with some minimal degree of respect.

'The mountain chims survived that first day! They must've stung the invaders, and kept stingin' 'em!' He knew he was free to vent a bit of exultation. It would only be keeping in character.

Gailet's smile was thin. This news must have given rise to mixed feelings. After all, her own part of the insurrection had gone very much worse.

So, Fiben thought, *Uthacalthing's elaborate ruse persuaded the Gubru that there was something on the planet at least as important as the colony's value as hostage. Garthlings! Imagine that. They went up into the mountains chasing a myth. And somehow the general found a way to hurt them as soon as they came within reach.*

Oh, I'm sorry for all those things I thought about her old man. What a great jape, Uthacalthing!

But now the invaders are wise to it. I wonder if ...

Fiben glanced up and saw that Gailet was watching him intently, as if gauging his very thoughts. At last Fiben understood one of the reasons why she could not be completely open and frank with him.

We have to make a decision, he realized. *Should we try to lie to the Gubru?*

He and Gailet might make the attempt, try to prop up Uthacalthing's practical joke for just a while longer. They might succeed in convincing the Suzerain just one more time to go off hunting mythical Garthlings. It would be worth the effort if it drew even one more party of Gubru within reach of the mountain fighters.

But did either he or Gailet have anywhere near enough sophistication to pull off such a ruse? What would it take? He could just picture it. *Oh yes, massa, there is Garthlin's after all, yes boss. You can believe brer chim, yassa.*

Or, alternatively, they could try reverse psychology. *D-o-o-on't throw me in dot briar patch ... !*

Neither approach at all resembled the way Uthacalthing had done it, of course. The tricky Tymbrimi had played a game of subtle, colubrine misdirection. Fiben did not even toy with the idea of trying to operate on so sophisticated a plane.

And anyway, if he and Gailet were caught trying to lie to the Gubru, it could very well disqualify the two of them from whatever special status the Suzerain of Propriety seemed to be offering this afternoon. Fiben had no idea what the creature wanted of them, but it just might mean a chance to find out what the invaders were building out there by the Sea of Cilmar. That could be vital information.

No, it just wasn't worth the risk, Fiben decided.

Now he faced another problem, how to communicate these thoughts to Gailet.

'Even the most sophisticated sophont race can make mistakes,' he said slowly, enunciating carefully. 'Especially when they are on a strange world.' Pretending to look for a flea, he shaped the baby talk sign for *Game finished now?*

Obviously Gailet agreed. She nodded firmly. 'The mistake is over now. They're sure Garthlings are a myth. The Gubru are convinced it was just a Tymbrimi trap. Anyway, I get an impression the other Suzerains – the ones that share command with the high priest – won't allow any more pointless forays into the mountains, where they can be potshotted by guerrillas.'

Fiben's head jerked up. His heart pounded for a few, quick moments. Then it came to him what Gailet had meant ... how the last word she had spoken was intended to be spelled. Homonyms were one of many awkward drawbacks modern Anglic had inherited from old-style English, Chinese, and Japanese. While Galactic languages had been carefully designed to maximize information content and eliminate ambiguity, wolfling tongues had evolved rough and wild, with lots of idiosyncrasies, such as words with identical sounds but different meanings.

Fiben found his fists had clenched. He forced himself to relax. *Guerrillas, not gorillas. She doesn't know about the clandestine Uplift project in the mountains,* Fiben reassured himself. *She has no idea how ironic her remark sounded.*

One more reason, though, to end Uthacalthing's 'joke' once and for all. The Tymbrimi could not have been any more aware of the Howletts Center than his daughter. Had he known about the secret work there, Uthacalthing would certainly have chosen a different ruse, not one meant to send the Gubru into those very same mountains.

The Gubru must not go back into the Mulun, Fiben realized. *It's only luck they haven't already discovered the 'rillas.*

'Stupid birds,' he muttered, playing to Gailet's line. 'Imagine them falling for a dumb, wolfling folk tale. After Garthlings, what'll they go after next? Peter Pan?'

Superficially, Gailet's expression was reproving. 'You must try to be more respectful, Fiben.' Underneath, though, he felt a strong current of approval. They might not have the same reasons, but they were in agreement this far. Uthacalthing's joke was over.

'What they're going after next, Fiben, is us.'

He blinked. 'Us?'

She nodded. 'I'm guessing the war isn't going very well for the Gubru. Certainly they haven't found the dolphin ship that everyone's chasing, over on the other side of the Galaxy. And taking Garth hostage doesn't seem to have budged Earth or the Tymbrimi. I'd bet it only stiffened the resistance, and gained Terra some sympathy among former neutrals.'

Fiben frowned. It had been so long since he had thought about the larger scope – about the turmoil raging all across the Five Galaxies – about the *Streaker* – about the siege of Terra. Just how much did Gailet *know*, and how much was mere speculation?

In the nearby weather wall, a big black bird with a huge, gaily colored bill was depicted landing in a rustle very close to the carpet where Fiben and Gailet sat. It stepped forward and seemed to regard Fiben, first with one eye, then the other. The Toucan reminded him of the Suzerain of Propriety. Fiben shivered.

'Anyway,' Gailet went on, 'the enterprise here on Garth seems to be a drain on their resources that the Gubru can't afford too well, especially if peace does return to Galactic society, and the Institute for Civilized Warfare makes them give the planet back in only a few decades or so. I figure they're looking real hard for some way to make a profit out of all this.'

999

Fiben had an inspiration. 'All that construction by South Point is part of that, right? It's part of the Suzerain's plan to save his hash.'

Gailet's lips pursed. 'Colorfully put. Have you figured out what it is they're building?'

The multicolored bird on the branch cawed sharply and seemed to be laughing at Fiben. But when he glanced sharply that way it had already returned to the serious business of picking through the imaginary detritus on the forest floor. Fiben looked back at Gailet. 'You tell me,' he said.

'I'm not sure I can remember well enough to translate what the Suzerain said. I was pretty nervous, you'll remember.' Her eyes closed for a moment. 'Would – would a *hyperspace shunt* mean anything to you?'

The bird in the wall took off in an explosion of feathers and leaves as Fiben leaped to his feet, backing more than a meter away. He stared down at Gailet in disbelief.

'A *what*? But that's ... that's crazy! Build a shunt on the surface of a *planet*? It's just not – '

Then he stopped, remembering the great marble bowl, the mammoth power plants. Fiben's lips quivered and his hands came together, pulling on opposite thumbs. In this way, Fiben reminded himself that he was officially almost the equal of a man – that he should be able to think like one when facing such incredible improbability. 'What ...' He whispered, licked his lips, and concentrated on the words. 'What's it *for*?'

'I'm not so clear on that,' Gailet said. He could barely hear her over the squawking from the make-believe forest. Her finger traced a hand sign on the carpet, one which stood for confusion. 'I think it was originally intended for some ceremony, if they were ever able to find and claim Garthlings. Now, the Suzerain needs something to salvage out of their investment, probably another use for the shunt.

'If I understood the Gubru leader, Fiben, it wants to use the shunt for us.'

Fiben sat down again. For a long moment they did not look at each other. There were only the amplified jungle sounds, the colors of a luminescent fog flowing in between the leaves of a holographic rain forest, and the inaudible murmur of their own uncertain fear. The facsimile of a bright bird watched them for a little while longer from a replicant branch high overhead. When the ghostly fog turned to insubstantial rain, however, it finally spread fictitious wings and flew away.

60

UTHACALTHING

The Thennanin was obdurate. There did not seem to be any way to get through to him.

Kault seemed almost a stereotype, a caricature of his race – bluff, open, honorable to a fault, and so trusting that it threatened to drive Uthacalthing into fits of frustration. The glyph, *teev'nus*, was incapable of expressing Uthacalthing's bafflement. Over the last few days, something stronger had begun taking shape in the tendrils of his corona – something pungent and reminiscent of human metaphor.

Uthacalthing realized he was starting to get 'pissed off.'

Just what would it take to raise Kault's suspicions? Uthacalthing wondered if he should pretend to talk in his sleep, muttering dire hints and confessions. Would that raise an inkling under the Thennanin's thick skull? Or maybe he should abandon all subtlety and *write out* the entire scenario, leaving the unfolded pages in the open for Kault to find!

Individuals can vary widely within a species, Uthacalthing knew. And Kault was an anomaly, even for a Thennanin. It would probably never occur to the fellow to spy on his Tymbrimi companion. Uthacalthing found it hard to understand how Kault could have made it this far in the diplomatic corps of *any* race.

Fortunately, the darker aspects of the Thennanin nature were not also exaggerated in him. Members of Kault's faction, it seemed, weren't quite as smugly sanctimonious or utterly convinced of their own righteousness as those currently in charge of clan policy. More the pity, then, that one side effect of Uthacalthing's planned jest, if it ever succeeded, would be to weaken that moderate wing even more.

Regrettable. But it would take a miracle to ever bring Kault's group into power anyway, Uthacalthing reminded himself.

Anyway, the way things were heading, he was going to be spared the moral quandary of worrying about the consequences of his practical joke. At the moment it was getting exactly nowhere. So far this had been a most frustrating journey. The only compensation was that this was not, after all, a Gubru detention camp.

They were in the low, rolling countryside leading inexorably upward toward the southern slopes of the Mountains of Mulun. The variety-starved ecosystem of the plains was giving way gradually to somewhat less monotonous scenery – scrub trees and eroded terraces whose reddish and tan sedimentary layers glittered with the morning light, winking as if in secret knowledge of long departed days.

As the wanderers' trek brought them ever closer to the mountains, Uthacalthing kept adjusting their path, guided by a certain blue twinkle on the horizon – a glimmer so faint that his eyes could barely make it out at times. He knew for a fact that Kault's visual apparatus could not detect the spark at all. It had been planned that way.

Faithfully following the intermittent glow, Uthacalthing had led the way and kept a careful watch for the telltale clues. Every time he spotted one, Uthacalthing went through the motions, dutifully rubbing out traces in the dirt, surreptitiously throwing away stone tools, making furtive notes and hiding them quickly when his fellow refugee appeared around the bend.

By now anyone else would be positively *seething* with curiosity. But not Kault. No, not Kault.

Just this morning it had been the Thennanin's turn to lead. Their route took them along the edge of a mud flat, still damp from the recent onset of autumn rains. There, crossing their path in plain sight, had been a trail of footprints no more than a few hours old, obviously laid by something shuffling on two legs and a knuckle. But Kault just strode on past, sniffing the air with those great breathing slits of his, commenting in his booming voice on how fresh the day felt!

Uthacalthing consoled himself that this part of his scheme had always been a long shot anyway. Maybe his plan just wasn't meant to come about.

Perhaps I am simply not clever enough. Perhaps both Kault's race and my own assigned their dullest types to duty on this back-of-the-arm planet.

Even among humans, there were those who certainly would have been able to come up with something better. One of those legendary agents of the Terragens Council, for instance.

Of course there were no agents or other, more imaginative Tymbrimi here on Garth when the crisis hit. He had been forced to come up with the best plan he could.

Uthacalthing wondered about the other half of his jest. It was clear the Gubru had fallen for his ruse. But how deeply? How much trouble and expense had it cost them? More importantly from the point of view of a Galactic diplomat, how badly had they been embarrassed?

If the Gubru had proved as dense and slow as Kault . . .

But no, the Gubru are reliable, Uthacalthing reassured himself. *The Gubru, at least, are quite proficient at deceit and hypocrisy.* It made them easier enemies than the Thennanin.

He shaded his eyes, contemplating how the morning had aged. The air was getting warm. There was a swishing sound, the crackle of breaking foliage. Kault strode into view a few meters back, grumbling a low marching tune and using a long stick to brush shrubs out of his path. Uthacalthing wondered. *If our peoples are officially at war, why is it so hard for Kault to notice that I am obviously hiding something from him?*

'Hmmmph,' the big Thennanian grunted as he approached. 'Colleague, why have we stopped?'

The words were in Anglic. Recently they had made a game of using a different language every day, for practice. Uthacalthing gestured skyward. 'It is almost midday, Kault. Gimelhai is getting fierce. We had better find a place to get out of the sun.'

Kault's leathery ridge crest puffed. 'Get out of the sun? But we are not *in* . . . oh. Aha. Ha. Ha. A wolfling figure of speech. Very droll. Yes, Uthacalthing. When Gimelhai reaches zenith, it might indeed feel somewhat as if we were roasting in its outer shell. Let us find shelter.'

A small stand of brushy trees stood atop a hillock, not far away. This time Kault led, swinging his homemade staff to clear a path through the tall, grassy growth.

By now they were well practiced at the routine. Kault did the heavy work of delving a comfortable niche, down to where the soil was cool. Uthacalthing's nimble hands tied the Thennanin's cape into place as a sunshade. They rested against their packs and waited out the hot middle part of the day.

While Uthacalthing dozed, Kault spent the time entering data in his lap datawell. He picked up twigs, berries, bits of dirt, rubbed them between his large, powerful fingers, and held the dust up to his scent-slits before examining it with his small collection of instruments salvaged from the crashed yacht.

The Thennanin's diligence was all the more frustrating to Uthacalthing, since Kault's serious investigations of the local ecosystem had somehow missed every single clue Uthacalthing had thrown his way. *Perhaps it is* because *they were thrown at him.* Uthacalthing pondered. The Thennanin were a systematic folk. Possibly, Kault's worldview prevented him from seeing that which did not fit into the pattern that his careful studies revealed.

An interesting thought. Uthacalthing's corona fashioned a glyph of appreciated surprise as, all at once, he saw that the Thennanin approach might not be as cumbersome as he had thought. He had assumed that it was stupidity that made Kault impervious to his fabricated clues, but ...

But after all, the clues really are lies. My confederate out in the bush lays out hints for me to 'find' and 'hide.' When Kault ignores them, could it be because his obstinate worldview is actually superior? In reality, he has proven almost impossible to fool!

True or not, it was an interesting idea. *Syrtunu* riffled and tried to lift off, but Uthacalthing's corona lay limp, too lazy to abet the glyph.

Instead, his thoughts drifted to Athaclena.

He knew his daughter still lived. To try to learn more would invite detection by the enemy's psi devices. Still, there was something in those traces – trembling undertones down in the *nahakieri* levels of feeling – which told Uthacalthing that he would have much new to learn about Athaclena, should they ever meet again in this world.

'In the end, there is a limit to the guidance of parents,' a soft voice seemed to say to him as he drifted in half-slumber. *'Beyond that, a child's destiny is her own.'*

And what of the strangers who enter her life? Uthacalthing asked the glimmering figure of his long-dead wife, whose shape seemed to hover before him, beyond his closed eyelids.

'Husband, what of them? They, too, will shape her. And she them. But our own time ebbs.'

Her face was so clear ... This was a dream such as humans were known to have, but which was rarer among Tymbrimi. It was visual, and meaning was conveyed in words rather than glyphs. A flux of emotion made his fingertips tremble.

Mathicluanna's eyes separated, and her smile reminded him of that day in the capital when their coronae had first touched ... stopping him, stunned and still in the middle of a crowded street. Half-blinded by a glyph without any name, he had hunted the trace of her down alleyways, across bridges, and past dark cafes, seeking with growing desperation until, at last, he found her waiting for him on a bench not twelve sistaars from where he had first sensed her.

'You see?' she asked in the dream voice of that long ago girl. *'We are shaped. We change. But what we once were, that, too, remains always.'*

Uthacalthing stirred. His wife's image rippled, then vanished in wavelets of rolling light. *Syullf-tha* was the glyph that hovered in the space where she had been ... standing for the joy of a puzzle not yet solved.

He sighed and sat up, rubbing his eyes.

For some reason Uthacalthing thought that the bright daylight might disperse the glyph. But *syullf-tha* was more than a mere dream by now. Without any volition on his part, it rose and moved slowly away from Uthacalthing toward his companion, the big Thennanin.

Kault sat with his back to Uthacalthing, still absorbed in his studies, completely unaware as *syulff-tha* transformed ... changed subtly into *syulff-kuonn*. It settled slowly over Kault's ridge crest, descended, settled in, and disappeared. Uthacalthing stared, amazed, as Kault grunted and looked up. The Thennanin's breath-slits wheezed as he put down his instruments and turned to face Uthacalthing.

'There is something very strange here, colleague. Something I am at a loss to explain.'

Uthacalthing moistened his lips before answering. 'Do tell me what concerns you, esteemed ambassador.'

Kault's voice was a low rumble. 'There appears to be a creature ... one that has been foraging in these berry patches not long ago. I have seen traces of its eating for some days now, Uthacalthing. It is large ... very large for a creature of Garth.'

Uthacalthing was still getting used to the idea that *syulff-kuonn* had penetrated where so many subtler and more powerful glyphs had failed. 'Indeed? Is this of significance?'

Kault paused, as if uncertain whether to say more. The Thennanin finally sighed. 'My friend, it is most odd. But I must tell you that there should be no animal, since the Bururalli Holocaust, able to reach so high into these bushes. And its manner of foraging is quite extraordinary.'

'Extraordinary in what way?'

Kault's crest inflated in short puffs, indicating confusion. 'I ask that you do not laugh at me, colleague.'

'Laugh at you? Never!' Uthacalthing lied.

'Then I shall tell you. By now I am convinced that this creature has *hands*, Uthacalthing. I am sure of it.'

'Hm,' Uthacalthing commented noncommittally.

The Thennanin's voice dropped even lower. 'There is a mystery here, colleague. There is something very odd going on here on Garth.'

Uthacalthing suppressed his corona. He extinguished all facial expression. Now he understood why it had been *syulff-kuonn* – the glyph of anticipation of a practical joke fulfilled – that penetrated where none had succeeded before.

The joke was on me!

Uthacalthing looked beyond the fringe of their sunshade, where the bright afternoon had begun to color from an overcast spilling over the mountains.

Out there in the bush his confederate had been laying 'clues' for weeks, ever since the Tymbrimi yacht came down where Uthacalthing had intended it to, at the edge of the marshlands far southeast of the mountains. Little Jo-Jo – the throwback chim who could not even speak except with his hands – moved just ahead of Uthacalthing, naked as an animal, laying tantalizing footprints, chipping stone tools to leave in their path, maintaining tenuous contact with Uthacalthing through the blue Warder Globe.

It had all been part of a convoluted plan to lead the Thennanin inexorably to the conclusion that pre-sentient life existed on Garth, but Kault had seen none of the clues! None of the specially contrived hints!

No, what Kault had finally noticed was Jo-Jo *himself* ... the traces the little chim left as he foraged and lived off the land!

Uthacalthing realized that *syulff-kuonn* was exactly right. The joke on himself was rich, indeed.

He thought he could almost hear Mathicluanna's voice once again. 'You *never know* ... ' she seemed to say.

'Amazing,' he told the Thennanin. 'That is simply amazing.'

61

ATHACLENA

Every now and then she worried that she was getting too used to the changes. The rearranged nerve endings, the redistributed fatty tissues, the funny protrusion of her now-so-humanoid nose – these were things now so accustomed that she sometimes wondered if she would ever be able to return to standard Tymbrimi morphology.

The thought frightened Athaclena.

Until now there had been good reasons for maintaining these humaniform alterations. While she was leading an army of half-uplifted wolfling clients, looking more like a human female had been more than good politics. It had been a sort of bond between her and the chims and gorillas.

And with Robert, she remembered.

Athaclena wondered. Would the two of them ever again experiment, as they once had, with the half-forbidden sweetness of interspecies dalliance? Right now it seemed so very unlikely. Their consortship was reduced to a pair of signatures on a piece of tree bark, a useful bit of politics. Nothing else was the same as before.

She looked down. In the murky water before her, Athaclena saw her own reflection. 'Neither fish nor fowl,' she whispered in Anglic, not remembering where she had read or heard the phrase, but knowing its metaphorical meaning. Any young Tymbrimi male who saw her in her present form would surely break down laughing. And as for Robert, well, less than a month ago she had felt very close to him. His growing attraction toward her – the raw, wolfling hunger of it – had flattered and pleased her in a daring sort of way.

Now, though, he is among his own kind again. And I am alone.

Athaclena shook her head and resolved to drive out such thoughts. She picked up a flask and scattered her reflection by pouring a quarter liter of pale liquid into the pool. Plumes of mud stirred near the bank, obscuring the fine web of tendrils that laced through the pond from overhanging vines.

This was the last of a chain of small basins, a few kilometers from the caves. As Athaclena worked she concentrated and kept careful notes, for she knew she was no trained scientist and would have to make up for that with meticulousness. Still, her simple experiments had already begun to bear promising results. If her assistants returned from the next valley in time with the data she had sent for, she might have something of importance to show Major Prathachulthorn.

I may look like a freak, but I am still Tymbrimi! I shall prove my usefulness, even if the Earthmen do not think of me as a warrior.

So intense was her concentration, so quiet the still forest, that sudden words were like thunderclaps.

'So this is where you are, Clennie! I've been looking all over for you.'

Athaclena spun about, almost spilling a vial of umber-colored fluid. The vines all around her suddenly felt like a net woven just to catch her. Her pulse pounded for the fraction of a second it took to recognize *Robert*, looking down at her from the arching root of a giant near-oak.

He wore moccasins, a soft leather jerkin, and hose. The bow and quiver across his back made him look like the hero of one of those old-time wolfling romances Athaclena's mother used to read to her when she was a child. It took longer to regain her composure than she would have preferred.

'Robert. You startled me.'

He blushed. 'Sorry. Didn't mean to.'

That wasn't strictly true, she knew. Robert's psi shield was better than before, and he obviously was proud of being able to approach undetected. A simple but clear version of *kiniwullun* flickered like a pixie over Robert's head. If she squinted, she might almost imagine a young Tymbrimi male standing there ...

Athaclena shuddered. She had already decided she could not afford this. 'Come and sit down, Robert. Tell me what you have been doing.'

Holding onto a nearby vine, he swung lightly onto the leaf-strewn loam and stepped over to where her experiment case lay open beside the dark pool. Robert slipped off his bow and quiver and sat down, cross-legged.

'I've been looking around for some way to be useful.' He shrugged. 'Prathachulthorn's finished pumping me for information. Now he wants me to serve as sort of a glorified chim morale officer.' His voice rose a quarter octave as he mimicked the Terragens Marine's South Asian accent. 'We must keep the little fellows' chins up, Oneagle. Make them feel they're important to the Resistance!'

Athaclena nodded, understanding Robert's unspoken meaning. In spite of the partisans' past successes, Prathachulthorn obviously considered the chims superfluous – at best useful in diversions or as grunt soldiery. Liaison to childlike clients would seem an appropriate cubbyhole to assign the undertrained, presumably spoiled young son of the Planetary Coordinator.

'I thought Prathachulthorn liked your idea of using digestion bacteria against the Gubru,' Athaclena said.

Robert sniffed. He picked up a twig and twirled it deftly from finger to finger. 'Oh, he admitted it was intriguing that the gorillas' gut critters dissolved Gubru armor. He agreed to assign Benjamin and some of the chim techs to my project.'

Athaclena tried to trace the murky pattern of his feelings. 'Did not Lieutenant McCue help you persuade him?'

Robert looked away at the mention of the young Earthling woman. His shield went up at the same time, confirming some of Athaclena's suspicions.

'Lydia helped, yeah. But Prathachulthorn says it'd be next to impossible to deliver enough bacteria to important Gubru installations before they detect it and neutralize it. I still get the impression Prathachulthorn thinks it a side issue, maybe slightly useful to his main plan.'

'Do you have any idea what he has in mind?'

'He smiles and says he's going to bloody the birds' beaks. There's been intelligence of some major facility the Gubru are building, south of Port Helenia, and that may make a good target. But he won't go into any more detail than that. After all, strategy and tactics are for professionals, don't y'know.'

'Anyway, I didn't come here to talk about Prathachulthorn. I brought something to show you.' Robert shrugged out of his pack and reached inside to pull out an object wrapped in cloth. He unfolded the coverings. 'Look familiar at all?'

At first sight it appeared to be a pile of wrinkled rags with knotted strings hanging off the edges. On closer examination, the thing on Robert's lap reminded Athaclena of a shriveled fungus of some sort. Robert grabbed the largest knot, where most of the thin fibers came together in a clump, and extended the strings until the filmy fabric unfolded entirely in the gentle breeze.

'It ... it looks familiar, Robert. I would say it was a small parachute, but it is obviously natural ... as if it came from some sort of plant.' She shook her head.

'Pretty close. Try to think back a few months, Clennie, to a certain rather traumatic day ... one I don't think either of us will ever forget.'

His words were opaque, but flickerings of empathy drew her memories forth. 'This?' Athaclena fingered the soft, almost translucent material. 'This is from the *plate ivy?*'

'That's right.' Robert nodded. 'In springtime the upper layers are glossy, rubbery, and so stiff you can flip them and ride them as sleds – '

'If you are coordinated,' Athaclena teased.

'Um, yeah. But by the time autumn rolls around, the upper plates have withered back until they're like this.' He waved the floppy, parachute-like plate by its fibrous shrouds, catching the wind. 'In a few more weeks they'll be even lighter.'

Athaclena shook her head. 'I recall you explained the reason. It is for propagation, is it not?'

'Correct. This little spore pod here' – he opened his hand to show a small capsule where the lines met – 'gets carried aloft by the parachute into the late autumn winds. The sky fills with the things, making air travel hazardous for some time. They cause a real mess down in the city.

'Fortunately, I guess, the ancient creatures that used to pollinate the plate ivy went extinct during the Bururalli fiasco, and nearly all of the pods are sterile. If they weren't, I guess half the Sind would be covered with plate ivy by now. Whatever used to eat it is long dead as well.'

'Fascinating.' Athaclena followed a tremor in Robert's aura. 'You have plans for these things, do you not?'

He folded the spore carrier away again. 'Yeah. An idea at least. Though I don't imagine Prathachulthorn will listen to me. He's got me too well categorized, thanks to my mother.'

Of course Megan Oneagle was partly responsible for the Earthling officer's assessment and dismissal of her son. *How can a mother so misunderstand her own child?* Athaclena wondered. Humans might have come a long way since their dark centuries, but she still pitied the *k'chu-non,* the poor wolflings. They still had much to learn about themselves.

'Prathachulthorn might not listen to you directly, Robert. But Lieutenant McCue has his respect. She will certainly hear you out and convey your idea to the major.'

Robert shook his head. 'I don't know.'

'Why not?' Athaclena asked. 'This young Earthwoman likes you, I can tell. In fact, I was quite certain I detected in her aura – '

'You shouldn't *do* that, Clennie,' Robert snapped. 'You shouldn't nose around in people's feelings that way. 'It's . . . it's none of your business.'

She looked down. 'Perhaps you are right. But you are my friend and consort, Robert. When you are tense and frustrated, it is bad for both of us, no?'

'I guess so.' He did not meet her gaze.

'Are you sexually attracted to this Lydia McCue, then?' Athaclena asked. 'Do you feel affection for her?'

'I don't see why you have to ask – '

'Because I cannot *kenn* you, Robert!' Athaclena interrupted, partly out of irritation. 'You are no longer open to me. If you are having such feelings you should share them with me! Perhaps I can help you.'

Now he looked at her, his face flushed. '*Help* me?'

'Of course. You are my consort and friend. If you desire this woman of your own species, should I not be your collaborator? Should I not help you achieve happiness?'

Robert only blinked. But in his tight shield Athaclena now found cracks. She felt her tendrils wafting over her ears, tracing the edges of those loose places, forming a delicate new glyph. 'Were you feeling guilty over these feelings, Robert? Did you think they were somehow being *disloyal* to me?' Athaclena laughed. 'But interspecies consorts may have lovers and spouses of their own race. You knew that!

'So what would you have of me, Robert? I certainly cannot give you children! If I could, can you imagine what mongrels they would be?'

This time Robert smiled. He looked away. In the space between them her glyph took stronger form.

'And as for recreational sex, you know that I am not equipped to leave you anything but frustrated, you overendowed/underendowed, wrong-shaped ape-man! Why should I *not* take joy in it, if you find one with whom you might share such things?'

'It's . . . it's not as easy as that, Clennie. I . . .'

She held up a hand and smiled, at once beseeching him to be quiet and to let go. 'I am here, Robert,' she said, softly.

The young man's confusion was like an uncertain quantum potential, hesitating between two states. His eyes darted as he glanced upward and tried to focus on the *nonthing* she had made. Then he remembered what he had learned and looked away again, allowing *kenning* to open him to the glyph, her gift.

La'thsthoon hovered and danced, beckoning to him. Robert exhaled. His eyes opened in surprise as his own aura unlocked without his conscious will. Uncurling like a flower. Something – a twin to *la'thsthoon* – emerged, resonating, amplifying against Athaclena's corona.

Two wisps of nothing, one human, one Tymbrimi, touched, darted apart playfully, and came together again.

'Do not fear that you will lose what you have with me, Robert,' Athaclena whispered. 'After all, will any human lover be able to do *this* with you?'

At that, he smiled. They shared laughter. Overhead, mirrored *la'thsthoon* manifested intimacy performed in pairs.

Only later, after Robert had departed again, did Athaclena loosen the deep shield she had locked around her own innermost feelings. Only when he was gone did she let herself acknowledge her envy.

He goes to her now.

What Athaclena had done was right, by any standard she knew. She had done the proper thing.

And yet, it was so unfair!

I am a freak. I was one before I ever came to this planet. Now I am not even anything recognizable any longer.

Robert might have an Earthly lover, but in that area Athaclena was all alone. She could seek no such solace with one of her own kind.

To touch me, to hold me, to mingle his tendrils and his body with mine, to make me feel aflame . . .

With some surprise, Athaclena noticed that this was the first time she had ever felt this thing . . . this longing to be with a man of her own race – not a friend, or classmate, but a *lover* – perhaps a mate.

Mathicluanna and Uthacalthing had told her it would happen someday – that every girl has her own pace. Now, however, the feeling was only bitter. It enhanced her loneliness. A part of her blamed Robert for the limitations of his species. If only he could have changed *his* body, as well. If only he could have met her halfway!

But she was the Tymbrimi, one of the 'masters of adaptability.' How far that malleability had gone was made evident when Athaclena felt wetness on her cheeks. Miserably, she wiped away salty tears, the first in her life.

That was how her assistants found her hours later, when they returned from the errands she had sent them on – sitting by the edge of a small, muddy pool, while autumn winds blew through the tree-tops and sent gravid clouds hurrying eastward toward the gray mountains.

62

GALACTICS

The Suzerain of Cost and Caution was worried. All signs pointed to a molting, and the direction things appeared to be going was not to its liking.

Across the pavilion, the Suzerain of Beam and Talon paced in front of its aides, looking more erect and stately than ever. Beneath the shaggy outer feathers there was a faint reddish sheen to the military commander's underplumage. Not a single Gubru present could help but notice even a trace of that color. Soon, perhaps within only a twelve-day, the process would have progressed beyond the point of no return.

The occupation force would have a new queen.

The Suzerain of Cost and Caution contemplated the unfairness of it all as it preened its own feathers. They, too, were starting to dry out, but there were still no discernible signs of a final color.

First it had been elevated to the status of candidate and chief bureaucrat after the death of its predecessor. It had dreamed of such a destiny, but not to be plunged into the midst of an already mature Triumvirate! Its peers were already well on the way toward sexuality by that time. It had been forced to try to catch up.

At first that had seemed to matter little. To the surprise of all, it had won many points from the start. Discovering the foolishness the other two had been up to during the interregnum had enabled the Suzerain of Cost and Caution to make great leaps forward.

Then a new equilibrium was reached. The admiral and the priest had proven brilliant and imaginative in the defense of their political positions.

But the molting was supposed to be decided by correctness of policy! The prize was supposed to go to the leader whose wisdom had proven most sage. It was the way!

And yet, the bureaucrat knew that these matters were as often decided by happenstance, or by quirks of metabolism.

Or by alliance of two against the third, it reminded itself. The Suzerain of Cost and Caution wondered if it had been wise to support the military against Propriety, these last few weeks, giving the admiral by now an almost unassailable advantage.

But there had been no choice! The priest *had* to be opposed, for the Suzerain of Propriety appeared to have lost all control!

First had come that nonsense about 'Garthlings.' If the bureaucrat's predecessor had lived, perhaps the extravagance might have been kept down. As it was, however, vast amounts had been squandered ... bringing in a new Planetary Branch Library, sending expeditions into the dangerous mountains, building a hyperspace shunt for a Ceremony of Adoption – before there was any confirmation that anything existed to adopt!

Then there was the matter of ecological management. The Suzerain of Propriety insisted that it was essential to restore the Earthlings' program on Garth to at least a minimal level. But the Suzerain of Beam and Talon had adamantly refused to allow any humans to leave the islands. So, at great cost, help was sent for off-planet. A shipload of Linten gardeners, neutrals in the present crisis, were on the way. And the Great Egg only knew how they were to pay for them!

Now that the hyperspace shunt was nearing completion, both the Suzerain of Propriety and the Suzerain of Beam and Talon were ready to admit that the rumors of 'Garthlings' were just a Tymbrimi trick. But would they allow construction to be stopped?

No. Each, it seemed, had its reasons for wanting completion. If the bureaucrat had agreed it would have made a consensus, a step toward the policy so much desired by the Roost Masters. But how could it agree with such nonsense!

The Suzerain of Cost and Caution chirped in frustration. The Suzerain of Propriety was late for yet another colloquy. Its passion for rectitude did not extend, it seemed, to courtesy to its peers.

By this point, theoretically, the initial competitiveness among the candidates should have begun transforming into respect, and then affection, and finally true mating. But here they were, on the verge of a Molt, still dancing a dance of mutual loathing.

The Suzerain of Cost and Caution was not happy about how things were turning out, but at least there would be one satisfaction if things went on in the direction they seemed headed – when Propriety was brought down from its haughty perch at last.

One of the chief bureaucrats' aides approached, and the Suzerain took its proffered message slab. After picting its contents, it stood in thought.

Outside there was a commotion ... no doubt the third peer arriving at last. But for a moment the Suzerain of Cost and Caution still considered the message it had received from its spies.

Soon, yes soon. Very soon we will penetrate secret plans, plans which may not be good policy. Then perhaps we shall see a change, a change in sexuality ... soon.

63

FIBEN

His head ached.

Back when he had been a student at the University he had also been forced to study hour after hour, days at a stretch, cramming for tests. Fiben had never thought of himself as a scholar, and sometimes examinations used to make him sick in anticipation.

But at least back then there were also extracurricular activities, trips home, *breathing spells*, when a chen could cut loose and have some fun!

And back at the University Fiben had liked some of his professors. Right at this moment, though, he had had just about as much as he could take of Gailet Jones.

'So you think Galactic Sociology's stuffy and tedious?' Gailet accused him after he threw down the books in disgust and stalked off to pace in the farthest corner of the room. 'Well, I'm sorry Planetary Ecology isn't the subject, instead,' she said. 'Then, maybe, you'd be the teacher and I'd be the student.'

Fiben snorted. 'Thanks for allowing for the possibility. I was beginning to think you already knew everything.'

'That's not fair!' Gailet put aside the heavy book on her lap. 'You know the ceremony's only weeks away. At that point you and I may be called upon to act as spokesmen for our entire race! Shouldn't we try to be as prepared as possible beforehand?'

'And you're so certain you know what knowledge will be relevant? What's to say that Planetary Ecology *won't* be crucial then, hm?'

Gailet shrugged. 'It might very well be.'

'Or mechanics, or space piloting, or. . . or beer-swilling, or *sexual aptitude*, for Goodall's sake!'

'In that case, our race will be fortunate you were selected as one of its representatives, won't it?' Gailet snapped back. There was a long, tense silence as they glared at each other. Finally, Gailet lifted a hand. 'Fiben. I'm sorry. I know this is frustrating for you. But I didn't ask to be put in this position either, you know.'

No. But that doesn't matter, he thought. *You were designed for it.*

Neo-chimpdom couldn't hope for a chimmie better suited to be rational, collected, and oh, so cool when the time comes.

'As for Galactic Sociology, Fiben, you know there are several reasons why it's the essential topic.'

There it was again, that *look* in Gailet's eyes. Fiben knew it meant that there were levels and levels in her words.

Superficially, she meant that the two chim representatives would have to know the right protocols, and pass certain stringent tests, during the Rituals of Acceptance, or the officials of the Institute of Uplift would declare the ceremonies null and void.

The Suzerain of Propriety had made it abundantly clear that the outcome would be most unpleasant if that happened.

But there was another reason Gailet wanted him to know as much as possible. *Sometime soon we pass the point of no return ... when we can no longer change our minds about cooperating with the Suzerain. Gailet and I cannot discuss it openly, not with the Gubru probably listening in all the time. We'll have to act in consensus, and to her that means I've got to be educated.*

Or was it simply that Gailet did not want to bear the burden of their decision all by herself, when the time came?

Certainly Fiben knew a lot more about Galactic civilization than before his capture. Perhaps more than he had ever wanted to know. The intricacies of a three-billion-year-old culture made up of a thousand diverse, bickering patron-client clan lines, held together loosely by a network of ancient institutes and traditions, made Fiben's head swim. Half the time he would come away cynically disgusted – convinced that the Galactics were little more than powerful spoiled brats, combining the worst qualities of the old nation-states of Earth before Mankind's maturity.

But then something would crystallize, and Gailet would make clear to him some tradition or principle that displayed uncanny subtlety and hard-won *wisdom*, developed over hundreds of millions of years.

It was getting to the point where he didn't even know what to think anymore. 'I gotta get some air,' he told her. 'I'm going for a walk.' He stepped over to the coatrack and grabbed his parka. 'See you in an hour or so.'

He rapped on the door. It slid open. He stepped through and closed it behind him without looking back.

'Need an escort, Fiben?'

The chimmie, Sylvie, picked up a datawell and scribbled an entry. She wore a simple, ankle-length dress with long sleeves. To look at her now, it was hard to imagine her up on the dance mound at the Ape's Grape, driving crowds of chens to the verge of mob violence.

Her smile was hesitant, almost timid. And it occurred to Fiben that there was something unaccountably nervous about her tonight.

'What if I said no?' he asked. Before Sylvie could look alarmed he grinned. 'Just kidding. Sure, Sylvie. Give me Rover Twelve. He's a friendly old globe, and he doesn't spook the natives too much.'

'Watch robot RVG-12. Logged as escort to Fiben Bolger for release outside,' she said into the datawell. A door opened down the hallway behind her, and out floated a remote vigilance globe, a simple version of a battle robot, whose sole mission was to accompany a prisoner and see that he did not escape.

'Have a nice walk, Fiben.'

He winked at Sylvie and affected an airy burr. 'Now, lass, what other kind is there, for a prisoner?'

The last one, Fiben answered himself. *The one leading to the gallows.* But he waved gaily. 'C'mon, Rover.' The front door hissed as it slid back to let him emerge into a blustery autumn afternoon.

Much had changed since their capture. The conditions of their imprisonment grew gentler as he and Gailet seemed to become more important to the Suzerain of Propriety's inscrutable plan. *I still hate this place*, Fiben thought as he descended concrete steps and made his way through an unkempt garden toward the outer gate. Sophisticated surveillance robots rotated slowly at the corners of the high wall. Near the portal, Fiben came upon the chim guards.

Irongrip was not present, fortunately, but the other Probationers on duty were hardly friendlier. For although the Gubru still paid their wages, it seemed their masters had recently deserted their cause. There had been no overturning of the Uplift program on Garth, no sudden reversal of the eugenics pyramid. *The Suzerain tried to find fault in the way neo-chimps are being uplifted*, Fiben knew. *But it must've failed. Otherwise, why would it be grooming a blue card and a white card, like me and Gailet, for their ceremony?*

In fact, the use of Probationers as auxiliaries had sort of backfired on the invaders. The chim population resented it.

No words passed between Fiben and the zipsuited guards. The ritual was well understood. He ignored them, and they dawdled just as long as they dared without giving him an excuse to complain. Once, when the claviger delayed too long with the keys, Fiben had simply turned around and marched back inside. He did not even have to say a word to Sylvie. Next watch, those guards were gone. Fiben never saw them again.

This time, just on impulse, Fiben broke tradition and spoke. 'Nice weather, ain't it?'

The taller of the two Probationers looked up in surprise. Something about the zipsuited chen suddenly struck Fiben as eerily familiar, although he was certain he had never met him before. 'What, are you kidding?' The guard glanced up at rumbling cumulonimbus clouds. A cold front was moving in, and rain could not be far off.

'Yeah,' Fiben grinned. 'I'm kidding. Actually, it's too sunny for my tastes.'

The guard gave Fiben a sour look and stepped aside. The gate squeaked open, and Fiben slipped out onto a back street lined by ivy-decked walls. Neither he nor Gailet had ever seen any of their neighbors. Presumably local chims kept a low profile around Irongrip's crew and the watchful alien robots.

He whistled as he walked toward the bay, trying to ignore the hovering watch globe following just a meter above and behind him. The first time he had been allowed out this way, Fiben avoided the populated areas of Port Helenia, sticking to back alleys and the now almost abandoned industrial zone. Nowadays he still kept away from the main shopping and business areas, where crowds would gather and stare, but he no longer felt he had to avoid people completely.

Early on he had seen other chims accompanied by watch globes. At first he thought they were prisoners like himself. Chens and chimmies in work clothes stepped aside and gave the guarded chims wide berth, as they did him.

Then he noticed the differences. Those other escorted chims wore fine clothes and walked with a haughty bearing. Their watch globes' eye facets and weaponry faced *outward*, rather than upon the ones they guarded. *Quislings*, Fiben realized. He was pleased to see the faces many chim citizens cast at these high-level collaborators when their backs were turned – looks of sullen, ill-concealed disdain.

After that, in his quarters, he had stenciled the proud letters P-R-I-S-O-N-E-R on the back of his parka. From then on, the stares that followed him were less cold. They were curious, perhaps even respectful.

The globe was not programmed to let him speak to people. Once, when a chimmie dropped a folded piece of paper in his path, Fiben tested the machine's tolerance by bending over to pick it up ...

He awoke sometime later in the globe's grasp, on his way back to prison. It was several days before he was allowed out again.

No matter. It had been worth it. Word of the episode spread. Now, chens and chimmies nodded as he passed storefronts and long ration lines. Some even signed little messages of encouragement in hand talk.

They haven't twisted us, Fiben thought proudly. A few traitors hardly mattered. What counted was the behavior of a people, as a whole. Fiben remembered reading how, during the most horrible of Earth's old, pre-Contact world wars, the citizens of the little nation of Denmark resisted every effort of the Nazi conquerors to dehumanize them. Instead they behaved with startling unity and decency. It was a story well worth emulating.

We'll hold out, he replied in sign language. *Terra remembers, and will come for us.*

He clung to the hope, no matter how hard it became. As he learned the subtleties of Galactic law from Gailet, he came to realize that even if peace broke out all across the spiral arms, it might not be enough to eject the invaders. There were tricks a clan as ancient as the Gubru knew, ways to invalidate a weaker clan's lease on a planet like Garth. It was apparent one faction of the avian enemy wanted to end Earth's tenancy here and take it over for themselves.

Fiben knew that the Suzerain of Propriety had searched in vain for evidence the Earthlings were mishandling the ecological recovery on Garth. Now, after the way the occupation forces had bollixed decades of hard work, they dared not raise that issue.

The Suzerain had also spent months hunting for elusive 'Garthlings.' If the mysterious pre-sentients had proven real, a claim on them would have justified every dime spent here. Finally, they saw through Uthacalthing's practical joke, but that did not end their efforts.

All along, ever since the invasion, the Gubru had tried to find fault with the way neo-chimpanzees were being uplifted. And just because they seemed to have accepted the status of advanced chims like Gailet, that did not mean they had given up completely.

There was this business of the damned Ceremony of Acceptance – whose implications still escaped Fiben no matter how hard Gailet tried to make them clear to him.

He hardly noticed the chims on the streets as his feet kicked windblown leaves and snatches of Gailet's explanations came back to him.

' ... *client species pass through phases, each marked by ceremonies sanctioned by the Galactic Uplift Institute ... These ceremonies are expensive, and can be blocked by political maneuvering ... For the Gubru to offer to pay for and support a ceremony for the clients of wolfling humans is more than unprecedented ... And the Suzerain also offers to commit all its folk to a new policy ending hostilities with Earth ...*

' ... *Of course, there is a catch ...* '

Oh, Fiben could well imagine there would be a catch!

He shook his head, as if to drive all the words out of it. There was something unnatural about Gailet. Uplift was all very well and good, and she might be a peerless example of neo-chimpdom, but it just wasn't natural to think and talk so much without giving the brain some off-time to air out!

He came at last to a place by the docks where fishing boats lay tied up against the coming storm. Seabirds chirped and dove, trying to catch a last meal in the time remaining before the water became too choppy. One of them ventured too close to Fiben and was rewarded with a warning shock from 'Rover,' the watch robot. The bird – no more a biological cousin to the avian invaders than Fiben was – squawked in anger and took off toward the west.

Fiben took a seat on the end of the pier. From his pocket he removed half a sandwich he had put there earlier in the day. He munched quietly, watching the clouds and the water. For the moment, at least, he was able to stop thinking, stop worrying. And no words echoed in his head.

Right then all it would have taken to make him happy would have been a banana and a beer, and freedom.

An hour or so later, 'Rover' began buzzing insistently. The watch robot maneuvered to a position interposing itself between him and the water, bobbing insistently.

With a sign Fiben got up and dusted himself off. He walked back along the dock and soon was headed past drifts of leaves toward his urban prison. Very few chims were still about on the windy streets.

The guard with the oddly familiar face frowned at him when Fiben arrived at the gate, but there was no delay passing him through. *It's always been easier gettin' into jail than getting' out,* Fiben thought.

Sylvie was still on duty at her desk. 'Did you have a nice walk, Fiben?'

'Hm. You ought to come along sometime. We could stop at the Park and I'd show you my Cheetah imitation.' He gave her an amiable wink.

'I've already seen it, remember? Pretty unimpressive, as I recall.' But Sylvie's tone did not match her banter. She seemed tense. 'Go on in, Fiben. I'll put Rover away.'

'Yeah, well.' The door hissed open. 'Good night, Sylvie.'

Gailet was seated on a plush throw rug in front of the weather wall – now tuned to show a scene of steamy savannah heat. She looked up from the book on her lap and took off her reading glasses. 'Hello. Feeling better?'

'Yeah.' He nodded. 'Sorry about earlier. I guess I just had a bad case of cabin fever. I'll knuckle down and get back to work now.'

'No need. We're done for today.' She patted the rug. 'Why don't you come over and give me back a scratch? Then I'll reciprocate.'

Fiben did not have to be asked twice. One thing he had to grant Gailet, she was a truly fine grooming partner. He shrugged out of his parka and came over to sit behind her. She laid one hand idly on his knee while he began combing his fingers through her hair. Soon her eyes were closed. Her breath came in soft, low sighs.

It was frustrating trying to define the relationship he had with Gailet. They were not lovers. For most chimmies, that was only possible or practical during certain parts of their bodily cycles, anyway. And Gailet had made it clear that hers was a very private sense of sexuality, more like a human female's. Fiben understood this and had put no pressure on her.

Trouble was, he just could not get her out of his mind.

He reminded himself not to confuse his sex drive with other things. *I may be obsessed with her, but I'm not crazy.* Lovemaking with this chimmie would require a level of bonding he wasn't sure he was ready to think about.

As he worked his way through the fur at the back of Gailet's neck he encountered knots of tension. 'Say, you're really tight! What's the matter? Have th' damn Gu—'

The fingers on his knee dug in sharply, though Gailet did not move otherwise. Fiben thought quickly and changed what he had been about to say.

'... g-guards been making moves on you? Have those Probationers been getting fresh?'

'And what if they had? What would you do about it, march out there and defend my honor?' She laughed. But he felt her relief, expressed through her body. Something was going on. He had never seen Gailet so worked up.

As he scratched her back, his fingers encountered an object embedded in the fur ... something round, thin, disk-like. 'I think there's a knot of hair, back there,' Gailet said quickly as he started to pull it free. 'Be careful, Fiben.'

'Uh, okay.' He bent over. 'Um, you're right. It's a knot all right. I'm gonna have to work this out with my teeth.'

Her back trembled and her aroma was sweaty as he brought his face close. *Just as I thought. A message capsule!* As his eye came even with it, a tiny holographic projector came alight. The beam entered his iris and automatically adjusted to focus on his retina.

There were just a few, simple lines of text. What he read, however, made him blink in surprise. It was a document written in his own name!

STATEMENT OF WHY I AM DOING THIS: RECORDED BY
LUTENANT FIBEN BOLGER, NEOCHIMPANZEE.

ALTHOUGH IVE BEEN WELL TREATED SINCE BEING CAP-
TURED, AND I APPRECIATE THE KIND ATTENTION IVE
BEEN GIVEN, IM AFRAID I JUST HAVE GOT TO GET OUT OF
HERE. THERES STILL A WAR GOING ON, AND ITS MY DUTY
TO ESCAPE IF I CAN.

IN TRYING TO ESCAPE I DONT MEAN ANY INSULT TO THE
SUZERAIN OF PROPRIETY OR THE CLAN OF THE GUBRU.
ITS JUST THAT IM LOYAL TO THE HUMANS AND MY CLAN.
THAT MAKES THIS SOMETHING I JUST HAVE TO DO.

Below the text was an area that *pulsed* redly, as if expectantly.
Fiben blinked. He pulled back a little and the message disappeared.

Of course he knew about records such as this. All he had to do
was look at the red spot, and earnestly will it, and the disk would
record his assent, along with his retinal pattern.

The document would be at least as binding as a signature on
some piece of paper.

Escape! The very thought made Fiben's heart race faster: *But . . .
how?*

He had not failed to notice that the record mentioned only *his*
name. If Gailet had intended to go with him, she surely would have
included herself.

And even if it were possible, would it be the *right* thing to do? He
had apparently been chosen by the Suzerain of Propriety to be
Gailet's partner in an enterprise as complex and potentially hazardous as any in the history of their race. How could Fiben desert
her at a time like this?

He brought his eye close and read the message again, thinking
furiously.

When did Gailet ever have a chance to write this? Was she in contact with elements of the Resistance somehow?

Also, something about the text struck Fiben as *wrong*. It wasn't
just the misspellings and less than erudite grammar. Just at a glance,
Fiben could think of several improvements the statement badly
needed if it was to do any good at all.

Of course. Someone other than Gailet must have written it, and
she was just passing it on for him to read!

'Sylvie came in a while ago,' Gailet said. 'We groomed each other.
She had trouble with the same knot.'

Sylvie! So. No wonder the chimmie had been so nervous, earlier.

Fiben considered carefully, trying to reassemble a puzzle. Sylvie must have planted the disk on Gailet ... No, she must have worn it *herself*, let Gailet read it, and then transferred it to Gailet's fur with her permission.

'Maybe I was wrong about Sylvie,' Gailet continued. 'She strikes me as a rather nice chimmie after all. I'm not sure how dependable she is, but my guess is she's pretty solid, down deep.'

What was Gailet telling him now? That this wasn't her idea at all but Sylvie's? Gailet would have had to consider the other chimmie's proposition without being able to speak aloud at all. She would not even be able to give Fiben any advice. Not out in the open, at least.

'It's a tough knot,' Fiben said, leaving a patch of wet fur as he sat back. 'I'll try again in a minute.'

'That's all right. Take your time. I'm sure you'll work it out.'

He combed through another area, near her right shoulder, but Fiben's thoughts were far from there.

Come on, think, he chided himself.

But it was all so damn murky! The Suzerain's fancy test equipment must have been on the fritz when the technicians selected him as an 'advanced' neo-chimp. At that moment Fiben felt far from being anyone's sterling example of a sapient being.

Okay, he concentrated. *So I'm being offered a chance to escape. First off, is it valid?*

For one thing, Sylvie could be a plant. Her offer could be a trap.

But that didn't make any sense! For one thing, Fiben had never given his parole, never agreed not to run away, if he ever got the chance. In fact, as a Terragens officer it was his duty to do so, especially if he could do it *politely*, satisfying Galactic punctilio.

Actually, accepting the offer might be considered the *correct* answer. If this were yet another Gubru test, his proper response might be to say yes. It could *satisfy* the inscrutable ETs ... show them he understood a client's duties.

Then again, the offer might be for real. Fiben remembered Sylvie's agitation earlier. She had been very friendly toward him the last few weeks, in ways a chen would hate to think were just play-acting.

Okay. But if it's for real, how does she plan to pull it off?

There was only one way to find out, and that was by asking her. Certainly, any escape would have to involve fooling the surveillance system. Perhaps there was a way to do that, but Sylvie would only be able to use it one time. Once he and Gailet started asking open questions aloud, the decision would already have to be made.

So what I'm really deciding is whether to tell Sylvie, 'Okay, let's hear your plan.' If I say yes, I had better be ready to go.

Yeah, but go where?

There was only one answer, of course. Up to the mountains, to report to Athaclena and Robert all he had learned. That meant getting out of Port Helenia, as well as this jail.

'The Soro tell a story,' Gailet said in a low voice. Her eyes were closed, and she seemed almost relaxed as he rubbed her shoulder, 'they tell about a certain Paha warrior, back when the Paha were still being uplifted. Would you like to hear it?'

Puzzled Fiben nodded. 'Sure, tell me about it, Gailet.'

'Okay. Well, you've surely heard of the Paha. They're tough fighters, loyal to their Soro patrons. Back then they were coming along nicely in the tests given by the Uplift Institute. So one day the Soro decide to give 'em some responsibility. Sent a group of them to guard an emissary to the Seven Spin Clans.'

'Seven Spin ... Uh, they're a machine civilization, right?'

'Yes. But they aren't outlaws. They're one of the few machine cultures who've joined Galactic society as honorary members. They keep mostly out of the way by sticking to high-density spiral arm areas, useless to both oxygen and hydrogen breathers.'

What's she getting at? Fiben wondered.

'Anyway, the Soro Ambassador is dickering with the high muckity mucks of the Seven Spinners when this Paha scout detects something out at the edge of the local system and goes to investigate.

'Well, as luck would have it, he comes upon the scene to find one of the Seven Spinners' cargo vessels under attack by rogue machines.'

'Berserkers? Planet busters?'

Gailet shuddered. 'You read too much science fiction, Fiben. No, just outlaw robots looking for loot. Anyway, when our Paha scout gets no answer to his calls for instructions, he decides to take some initiative. He dives right in, guns blazing.'

'Let me guess, he saved the cargo snip.'

She nodded. 'Sent the rogues flying. The Seven Spinners were grateful, too. The reward turned a questionable business deal into a profit for the Soro.'

'So he was a hero.'

Gailet shook her head. 'No. He went home in disgrace, for acting on his own without guidance.'

'Crazy Eatees,' Fiben muttered.

'No, Fiben.' She touched his knee. 'It's an important point. Encouraging initiative in a new client race is fine, but during sensitive Galactic-level negotiations? Do you trust a bright child with a fusion power plant?'

Fiben understood what Gailet was driving at. The two of them were being offered a deal that sounded very sweet for Earth – on the surface, at least. The Suzerain of Propriety was offering to finance a major Ceremony of Acceptance for neo-chimps. The Gubru would end their policy of obstructing humanity's patron status and cease all hostilities against Terra. All the Suzerain seemed to want in exchange was for Fiben and Gailet to tell the Five Galaxies, by hyperspacial shunt, what great guys the Gubru were.

It sounded like a face-saving gesture for the Suzerain of Propriety, and a major coup for Earthkind.

But, Fiben wondered, did he and Gailet have the *right* to make such a decision? Might there be ramifications beyond what they could figure out for themselves? Potentially deadly ramifications?

The Suzerain of Propriety had told them that there were reasons why they weren't allowed to consult with human leaders, out on the island detention camps. Its rivalry with the other Suzerains was reaching a critical phase, and they might not approve of how much it was planning on giving away. The Suzerain of Propriety needed surprise in order to outmaneuver them and present a *fait accompli*.

Something struck Fiben as odd about that logic. But then, aliens were alien by definition. He couldn't imagine any Terran-based society operating in such a way.

So was Gailet telling him that they should pull out of the ceremony? Fine! As far as Fiben was concerned, she could decide. After all, they only had to say *no* . . . respectfully, of course.

Gailet said. 'The story doesn't end there.'

'There's more?'

'Oh, yes. A few years later the Seven Spin Clans came forward with evidence that the Paha warrior really had made every effort to call back for instructions before beginning his intervention, but subspace conditions had prevented any message from getting through.'

'So?'

'So that made all the difference to the Soro! In one case he was taking responsibility he didn't merit. In the other he was only doing the best he could!

'The scout was exonerated, posthumously, and his heirs were granted advanced Uplift rights.'

There was a long silence. Neither of them spoke as Fiben thought carefully. Suddenly it was all clear to him.

It's the effort that counts. That's what she means. It'd be unforgivable to cooperate with the Suzerain without at least trying to consult with our patrons. I might fail, probably will fail, but I must try.

'Let's take a look at that knot again.' He bent over, brought his eye close to the message capsule. Again the lines of text appeared, along with the pulsing red spot. Fiben looked right at the expectant blob and thought hard.

I agree to this.

The patch changed color at once, signifying his assent. *Now what?* Fiben wondered as he sat back.

His answer came a moment later, when the door opened quietly. Sylvie entered, wearing the same ankle-length dress as before. She sat down in front of them.

'Surveillance is off. I'm feeding the cameras a tape loop. It ought to work for at least an hour before their computer gets suspicious.'

Fiben plucked the disk out of Gailet's fur and she held out her hand for it. 'Give me a minute,' Gailet whispered, and hurried over to her personal datawell to drop the capsule inside. 'No offense, Sylvie, but the wording needs improvement. Fiben can initial my changes.'

'I'm not offended. I knew you'd have to fix it up. I just wanted it to be clear enough for you two to understand what I was offering.'

It was all happening so fast. And yet Fiben felt the adrenaline already starting to sing in his veins. 'So I'm going?'

'We're going,' Sylvie corrected. 'You and me. I've got supplies stashed, disguises, and a route out of town.'

'Are you with the underground, then?'

She shook her head. 'I'd like to join, of course, but this is strictly my own show. I . . . I'm doing this for a price.'

'What is it you want?'

Sylvie shook her head, indicating she would wait for Gailet to return. 'If you two agree to take the chance, I'll go back outside and call in the night guard. I picked him out carefully and worked hard to get Irongrip to assign him duty tonight.'

'What's so special about that guy?'

'Maybe you noticed, that Probationer looks a lot like you, Fiben, and he's got a similar build. Close enough to fool the spy-comps in the dark for a while, I'd guess.'

So that was why that chen at the gate had looked so familiar! Fiben speculated concisely. 'Drug him. Leave him with Gailet while I sneak out in his clothes, using his pass.'

'There's a lot more to it, believe me.' Sylvie looked nervous, exhausted. 'But you get the general idea. He and I both go off shift in twenty minutes. So it's got to be before then.'

Gailet returned. She handed the pellet to Fiben. He held it up to one eye and read the revised text carefully, not because he planned to criticize Gailet's work, but so he would be able to recite it word for word if he ever did make it back to Athaclena and Robert.

Gailet had entirely rewritten the message.

STATEMENT OF INTENT: RECORDED BY FIBEN BOLGER, A-CHIM-AB-HUMAN, CLIENT CITIZEN OF THE TERRAGENS FEDERATION AND RESERVE LIEUTENANT, GARTH COLO-NIAL DEFENSE FORCE.

I ACKNOWLEDGE THE COURTESY I HAVE BEEN SHOWN DURING MY IMPRISONMENT, AND AM COGNIZANT OF THE KIND ATTENTION GIVEN ME BY THE EXALTED AND RESPECTED SUZERAINS OF THE GREAT CLAN OF THE GUBRU. NEVERTHELESS, I FIND THAT MY DUTY AS A COM-BATANT IN THE PRESENT WAR BETWEEN MY LINE AND THAT OF THE GUBRU COMPELS ME TO RESPECTFULLY REFUSE FURTHER CONFINEMENT, HOWEVER COURTEOUS.

IN ATTEMPTING TO ESCAPE, I IN NO WAY SPURN THE HONOR GRANTED ME BY THE EXALTED SUZERAIN, IN CONSIDERING ME FOR THE STATUS OF RACE-REPRESEN-TATIVE. BY CONTINUING HONORABLE RESISTANCE TO THE GUBRU OCCUPATION OF GARTH, I HOPE THAT I AM BEHAVING AS SUCH A CLIENT-SOPHONT SHOULD, IN PROPER OBEDIENCE TO THE WILL OF MY PATRONS.

I ACT NOW IN THE TRADITIONS OF GALACTIC SOCIETY, AS BEST I HAVE BEEN GIVEN TO UNDERSTAND THEM.

Yeah. Fiben had learned enough under Gailet's tutelage to see how much better this version was. He registered his assent again, and once more the recording spot changed color. Fiben handed the disk back to Gailet.

What matters is that we try, he told himself, knowing how forlorn this venture certainly was.

'Now.' Gailet turned to Sylvie. 'What is this fee you spoke of? What is it you want?'

Sylvie bit her lip. She faced Gailet, but pointed at Fiben. 'Him,' she said quickly. 'I want you to share him with me.'

'*What?*' Fiben started to get up, but Gailet shushed him with a quick gesture. 'Explain,' she asked Sylvie.

Sylvie shrugged. 'I wasn't sure what kind of marriage arrange-ment the two of you had.'

'We don't have any!' Fiben said, hotly. 'And what business – '

'Shut up, Fiben,' Gailet told him evenly. 'That's right, Sylvie. We have no agreement, group or monogamous. So what's this all about? What is it you want from him?'

'Isn't it obvious?' Sylvie glanced over at Fiben. 'Whatever his Uplift rating was before, he's now effectively a white card. Look at his amazing war record, and the way he foiled the Eatees against all odds, not once but twice, in Port Helenia. Any of those'd be enough to advance him from blue status.

'And now the Suzerain's invited him to be a race-representative. That land of attention sticks. It'll hold *whoever* wins the war, you know that, Dr Jones.'

Sylvie summarized. 'He's a white card. I'm a green. I also happen to like his style. It's that simple.'

Me? A Goodall-damned whitie? Fiben burst out laughing at the absurdity of it. It was just dawning on him what Sylvie was driving at.

'Whoever wins,' Sylvie went on, quietly ignoring him. 'Whether it's Earth or the Gubru, I want my child to ride the crest of Uplift and be protected by the Board. My child is going to have a destiny. I'll have grandchildren, and a piece of tomorrow.'

Sylvie obviously felt passionately about this. But Fiben was in no mood to be sympathetic. *Of all the metaphysical claptrap!* he thought. And she wasn't even telling this to *him*. Sylvie was talking to *Gailet*, appealing to her! 'Hey, don't I have anything to say about this?' he protested.

'Of course not, silly,' Gailet replied, shaking her head. 'You're a chen. A male chim will screw a goat, or a leaf, if nothing better is available.'

An exaggeration, but a stereotype based on enough truth to make Fiben blush. 'But – '

'Sylvie's attractive and approaching pink. What do you *expect* you'll do once you get free, if all of us have agreed in advance that your duty *and* pleasure coincide?' Gailet shifted. 'No, this is not your decision. Now for the last time be quiet, Fiben.'

Gailet turned back to ask Sylvie a new question, but at that moment Fiben could not even hear the words. The roaring in his ears drowned out every other sound. All he could think of at that moment was the drummer, poor Igor Patterson. *No. Oh, Goodall, protect me!*

' . . . males work that way.'

'Yes, of course. But I figure you have a bond with him, whether it's formal or not. Theory is fine, but anyone can tell he's got an honor-streak a mile thick. He might prove obstinate unless he knew it was all right with you.'

Is this how females think of us chens, down deep? Fiben pondered. He remembered secondary school 'health' classes, when the young male chims would be taken off to attend lectures about procreative rights and see films about VD. Like the other boy-chims, he used to wonder what the chimmies were learning at those times. *Do the schools teach them this cold-blooded type of logic? Or do they learn it the hard way? From us?*

'I do not own him.' Gailet shrugged. 'If you are right, nobody will ever have that sort of claim on him . . . nobody but the Uplift Board, poor fellow.' She frowned. 'All I demand of you is that you get him to the mountains safely. He doesn't touch you till then, understood? You get your fee when he's safe with the guerrillas.'

A male human would not put up with this, Fiben pondered bitterly. But then, male humans weren't unfinished, client-level creatures who would 'screw a goat, or a leaf, if nothing better was available,' were they?

Sylvie nodded in agreement. She extended her hand. Gailet took it. They shared a long look, then separated.

Sylvie stood up. 'I'll knock before I come in. It'll be about ten minutes. When she looked at Fiben her expression was *satisfied*, as if she had done very well in a business arrangement. 'Be ready to leave by then,' she said, and turned to go.

When she had left, Fiben finally found his voice. 'You assume too much with all your glib theories, Gailet. What the hell makes you so sure – '

'I'm not sure of anything!' she snapped back. And the confused, hurt look on her face stunned Fiben more than anything else that had happened that evening.

Gailet passed a hand in front of her eyes. 'I'm sorry, Fiben. Just do as you think best. Only please don't get offended. None of us can really afford pride right now. Anyway, Sylvie's not asking all that much, on the scale of things, is she?'

Fiben read the suppressed tension in Gailet's eyes, and his outrage leaked away. It was replaced by concern for her. 'Are . . . are you sure you'll be okay?'

She shrugged. 'I guess so. The Suzerain'll probably find me another partner. I'll do my best to delay things as long as I can.'

Fiben bit his lip. 'We'll get word back to you from the humans, I promise.'

Her expression told him that she held out little hope. But she smiled. 'You do that, Fiben.' She reached up and touched the side of his face gently. 'You know,' she whispered. 'I really will miss you.'

The moment passed. She withdrew her hand and her expression

was serious once more. 'Now you'd better gather whatever you want to take with you. Meanwhile, there are a few things I suggest you ought to tell your general. You'll try to remember, Fiben?'

'Yeah, sure.' But for one instant he mourned, wondering if he would ever again see the gentleness that had shone so briefly in her eyes. All business once more, she followed him around the room as he gathered food and clothing. She was still talking a few minutes later when there came a knock on the door.

64

GAILET

In the darkness, after they had left, she sat on her mattress with a blanket over her head, hugging her knees and rocking slowly to the tempo of her loneliness.

Her darkness was not entirely solitary. Far better if it had been, in fact. Gailet sensed the sleeping chen near her, wrapped in Fiben's bedclothes, softly exhaling faint fumes from the drug that had rendered him unconscious. The Probie guard would not awaken for many hours yet. Gailet figured this quiet time probably would not last as long as his slumber.

No, she was not quite alone. But Gailet Jones had never felt quite so cut off, so isolated.

Poor Fiben, she thought. *Maybe Sylvie's right about him. Certainly he is one of the best chens I'll ever meet. And yet ...* She shook her head. *And yet, he only saw part of the way through this plot. And I could not even tell him the rest. Not without revealing what I knew to hidden listeners.*

She wasn't sure whether Sylvie was sincere or not. Gailet never had been much good at judging people. *But I'll bet gametes to zygotes Sylvie never fooled the Gubru surveillance.*

Gailet sniffed at the very idea – that one little chimmie could have bollixed the Eatees' monitors in such a way that they would not have instantly noticed it. *No, this was all far too easy. It was arranged.*

By whom? Why?

Did it really matter?

We never had any choice, of course. Fiben had to accept the offer.

Gailet wondered if she would ever see him again, if this were just another sapiency test ordered by the Suzerain of Propriety, then Fiben might very well be back tomorrow, credited with one more 'appropriate response' ... appropriate for an especially advanced neo-chimpanzee, at the vanguard of his client-level race.

She shuddered. Until tonight she had never considered the implications, but Sylvie had made it all too clear. Even if they were brought together again, it would never be the same for her and Fiben. If her white card had been a barrier between them before, his would almost certainly be a yawning chasm.

Anyway, Gailet had begun to suspect that this wasn't just another test, arranged by the Suzerain of Propriety. And if not, then some faction of the Gubru had to be responsible for tonight's escapade. Perhaps one of the *other* Suzerains, or ...

Gailet shook her head again. She did not know enough even to guess. There wasn't sufficient data. Or maybe she was just too blind/stupid to see the pattern.

A play was unfolding all around them, and at every stage it seemed there was no choice which way to turn. Fiben *had* to go tonight, whether the offer of escape was a trap or not. She *had* to stay and wrestle with vagaries beyond her grasp. That was her written fate.

This sensation of being manipulated, with no real power over her own destiny, was a familiar one to Gailet, even if Fiben was only beginning to get used to it. For Gailet it had been a lifelong companion.

Some of the old-time religions of Earth had included the concept of predetermination – a belief that all events were foreordained since the very first act of creation, and that so-called free will was nothing more than an illusion.

Soon after Contact, two centuries ago, human philosophers had asked the first Galactics they met what they thought of this and many other ideas. Quite often the alien sages had responded patronizingly. *'These are questions that can only be posed in an illogical wolfling language,'* had been a typical response. *'There are no paradoxes,'* they had assured.

And no mysteries left to be solved ... or at least none that could ever be approached by the likes of Earthlings.

Predestination was not all that hard for the Galactics to understand actually. Most thought the wolfling clan predestined for a sad, brief story.

And yet, Gailet found herself suddenly recalling a time, back when she was living on Earth, when she had met a certain neo-dolphin – an elderly, retired poet – who told her stories about occasions when he had swum in the slipstreams of great whales, listening for hours on end to their moaning songs of ancient cetacean gods. She had been flattered and fascinated when the aged fin composed a poem, especially for her.

> *Where does a ball alight,*
> *Falling through the bright midair?*
> *Hit it with your snout!*

Gailet figured the haiku had to be even more pungent in Trinary, the hybrid language neo-dolphins generally used for their poetry. She did not know Trinary, of course, but even in Anglic the little allegory had stuck with her.

Thinking about it, Gailet gradually came to realize that she was smiling.

Hit it with your snout, indeed!

The sleeping form next to her snored softly. Gailet tapped her tongue against her front teeth and pretended to be listening to the rhythm of drums.

She was still sitting there, thinking, some hours later when the door slid open with a loud bang and light spilled in from the hall. Several four-legged avian forms marched in. Kwackoo. At the head of the procession Gailet recognized the pastel-tinted down of the Servitor of the Suzerain of Propriety. She stood up, but her shallow bow received no answer.

The Kwackoo stared at her. Then it motioned down at the form under the blankets. 'Your companion does not rise. This is unseemly.'

Obviously, with no Gubru around, the Servitor did not feel obligated to be courteous. Gailet looked up at the ceiling. 'Perhaps he is indisposed.'

'Does he require medical assistance?'

'I imagine he'll recover without it.'

The Kwackoo's three-toed feet shuffled in irritation. 'I shall be frank. We wish to inspect your companion, to ascertain his identity.'

She raised an eyebrow, even though she knew the gesture was wasted on this creature. 'And who do you think he might be? Grandpa Bonzo? Don't you Kwackoo keep track of your prisoners?'

The avian's agitation increased. 'This confinement area was placed under the authority of neo-chimpanzee auxiliaries. If there was a failure, it is due to their animal incompetence. Their unsapient negligence.'

Gailet laughed. 'Bullshit.'

The Kwackoo stopped its dance of irritation and listened to its portable translator. When it only stared at her, Gailet shook her head. 'You can't palm this off on us, Kwackoo. You and I both know putting chim Probationers in charge here was just a sham. If there's been a security breach, it was inside your own camp.'

The Servitor's beak opened a few degrees. Its tongue flicked, a gesture Gailet by now knew signified pure hatred. The alien gestured, and two globuform robots whined forward. Gently but firmly they used gravitic fields to pick up the sleeping neo-chimp without even disturbing the blankets, and backed away with him toward the door. Since the Kwackoo had not bothered to look under the covers, obviously it already knew what it would find there.

'There will be an investigation,' it promised. Then it swiveled to depart. In minutes, Gailet knew, they would be reading Fiben's 'goodbye note,' which had been left attached to the snoring guard. Gailet tried to help Fiben with one more delay.

'Fine,' she said. 'In the meantime, I have a request ... No, make that a demand, that I wish to make.'

The Servitor had been stepping toward the door, ahead of its entourage of fluttering Kwackoo. At Gailet's words, however, it stopped, causing a mini traffic jam. There was a babble of angry cooing as its followers brushed against each other and flicked their tongues at Gailet. The pink-crested leader turned back and faced her.

'You are not able to make demands.'

'I make this one in the name of Galactic tradition,' Gailet insisted. 'Do not force me to send my petition directly to its eminence, the Suzerain of Propriety.'

There was a long pause, during which the Kwackoo seemed to contemplate the risks involved. At last it asked. 'What is your foolish demand?'

Now though, Gailet remained silent, waiting.

Finally, with obvious ill grace, the Servitor bowed, a bending so minuscule as to be barely detectable. Gailet returned the gesture, to the same degree.

'I want to go to the Library,' she said in perfect GalSeven. 'In fact, under my rights as a Galactic citizen, I insist on it.'

65

FIBEN

Exiting in the drugged guard's clothes had turned out to be almost absurdly simple, once Sylvie taught him a simple code phrase to speak to the robots hovering over the gate. The sole chim on duty had been mumbling around a sandwich and waved the two of them through with barely a glance.

'Where are you taking me?' Fiben asked once the dark, vine-covered wall of the prison was behind them.

'To the docks,' Sylvie answered over her shoulder. She maintained a quick pace down the damp, leaf-blown sidewalks, leading him past blocks of dark, empty, human-style dwellings. Then, further on, they passed through a chim neighborhood, consisting mostly of large, rambling, group-marriage houses, brightly painted, with doorlike windows and sturdy trellises for kids to climb. Now and then, as they hurried by, Fiben caught glimpses of silhouettes cast against tightly drawn curtains.

'Why the docks?'

'Because that's where the boats are!' Sylvie replied tersely. Her eyes darted to and fro. She twisted the chronometer ring on her left hand and kept looking back over her shoulder, as if worried they might be followed.

That she seemed nervous was natural. Still, Fiben had reached his limit. He grabbed her arm and made her stop. 'Listen, Sylvie. I appreciate everything you've done so far. But now don't you think it's time for you to let me in on the plan?'

She sighed. 'Yeah, I suppose so.' Her anxious grin reminded him of that night at the Ape's Grape. What he had imagined then to be animal lust that evening must have been something like this instead, fear suppressed under a well-laid veneer of bravado.

'Except for the gates in the fence, the only way out of the city is by boat. My plan is for us to sneak aboard one of the fishing vessels. The night fishers generally put to sea at' – she glanced at her finger watch – 'oh, in about an hour.'

Fiben nodded. 'Then what?'

'Then we slip overboard as the boat passes out of Aspinal Bay. We'll swim to North Point Park. From there it'll be a hard march north, along the beach, but we should be able to make hilly country by daybreak.'

Fiben nodded. It sounded like a good plan. He liked the fact that there were several points along the way where they could change their minds if problems or opportunities presented themselves. For instance, they might try for the *south* point of the bay, instead. Certainly the enemy would not expect two fugitives to head straight toward their new hypershunt installation! There would be a lot of construction equipment parked there. The idea of stealing one of the Gubru's own ships appealed to Fiben. If he ever pulled something like *that* off, maybe he'd actually merit a white card after all!

He shook aside that thought quickly, for it made him think of Gailet. Damn it, he missed her already.

'Sounds pretty well thought out, Sylvie.'

She smiled guardedly. 'Thanks, Fiben. Uh, can we go now?'

He gestured for her to lead on. Soon they were winding their way past shuttered shops and food stands. The clouds overhead were low and ominous, and the night smelled of the coming storm. A southwesterly wind blew in stiff but erratic gusts, pushing leaves and bits of paper around their ankles as they walked.

When it started to drizzle, Sylvie raised the hood of her parka, but Fiben left his own down. He did not mind wet hair half as much as having his sight and hearing obstructed now.

Off toward the sea he saw a flickering in the sky, accompanied by distant, gray growling. *Hell*, Fiben thought. *What am I thinking!* He grabbed his companion's arm again. 'Nobody's going to go to sea in this kind of weather, Sylvie.'

'The captain of this boat will, Fiben.' She shook her head. 'I really shouldn't tell you this, but he's ... he's a smuggler. Was even before the war. His craft has foul weather integrity and can partially submerge.'

Fiben blinked. 'What's he smuggling, nowadays?'

Sylvie looked left and right. 'Chims, some of the times. To and from Cilmar Island.'

'Cilmar! Would he take *us* there?'

Sylvie frowned. 'I promised Gailet I'd get you to the mountains, Fiben. And anyway, I'm not sure I'd trust this captain that far.'

But Fiben's head was awhirl. Half the humans on the *planet* were interned on Cilmar Island! Why settle for Robert and Athaclena, who were, after all, barely more than children, when he might be able to bring Gailet's questions before the experts at the University!

'Let's play it by ear,' he said noncommittally. But he was already determined to evaluate this smuggler captain for himself. Perhaps under the cover of this storm it might turn out to be possible! Fiben thought about it as they resumed their journey.

Soon they were near the docks – in fact, not far from the spot where Fiben had spent part of the afternoon watching the gulls. The rain now fell in sudden, unpredictable sheets. Each time it blew away again the air was left startlingly clear, enhancing every odor – from decaying fish to the beery stink of a fisherman's tavern across the way, where a few lights still shone and low, sad music leaked into the night.

Fiben's nostrils flared. He sniffed, trying to trace something that seemed to fade in and out with the fickle rain. Likewise, Fiben's senses fed his imagination, laying out possibilities for his consideration.

His companion led him around a corner and Fiben saw three piers. Several dark, bulky shadows lay moored next to each. One of those, no doubt, was the smugglers' boat. Fiben stopped Sylvie, again with a hand on her arm.

'We'd better hurry,' she urged.

'Wouldn't do to be too early,' he replied. 'It's going to be cramped and smelly in that boat. Come on back here.

There's something we may not have a chance to do for some time.'

She gave him a puzzled expression as he drew her back around the corner, into the shadows. When he put his arms around her, she stiffened, then relaxed and tilted her face up.

Fiben kissed her. Sylvie answered in kind.

When he started using his lips to nibble from her left ear across the line of her jaw and down her neck, Sylvie sighed. 'Oh, Fiben. If only we had time. If only you knew how much ...'

'Shh,' he told her as he let go. With a flourish he took off his parka and laid it on the ground. 'What ...?' she began. But he drew her down to sit on the jacket. He settled down behind her.

Her tension eased a bit when he began combing his fingers through her hair, grooming her.

'Whoosh,' Sylvie said. 'For a moment I thought – '

'Who me? You should know me better than that, darlin'. I'm the kind who likes to build up slowly. None of this rush-rush stuff. We can take our time.'

She turned her head to smile up at him. 'I'm glad. I won't be pink for a week, anyway. Though, I mean, we don't really have to wait *that* long. It's just – '

Her words cut short suddenly as Fiben's left arm tightened hard around her throat. In a flash he reached into her parka and clicked open her pocket knife. Sylvie's eyes bulged as he pressed the sharp blade close against her carotid artery.

'One word,' he whispered directly into her left ear. 'One sound and you feed the gulls tonight. Do you understand?'

She nodded, jerkily. He could feel her pulse pound, the vibration carrying up the knife blade. Fiben's own heart was not beating much slower. 'Mouth your words,' he told her hoarsely. 'I'll lip read. Now tell me, where are tracers planted?'

Sylvie blinked. Aloud, she said, 'What – ' That was all. Her voice stopped as he instantly increased pressure.

'Try again,' he whispered.

This time she formed the words silently.

'What ... are ... you talking about, Fiben?'

His own voice was a barely audible murmur in her ear. 'They're waiting for us out there, aren't they, darlin'? And I don't mean fairy tale chim smugglers. I'm talking *Gubru*, sweets. You're leading me right into their fine feathered clutches.'

Sylvie stiffened. 'Fiben ... I ... no! No, Fiben.'

'I smell bird!' he hissed. 'They're out there, all right. And as soon as I picked up that scent it all suddenly made perfect sense!'

Sylvie remained silent. Her eyes were eloquent enough by themselves.

'Oh, Gailet must think I'm a prize sap. Now that I think on it, of *course* the escape must've been arranged! In fact, the date must've been set for some time. You all probably didn't count on this storm tying up the fishing fleet. That tale about a smuggler captain was a resourceful ad lib to push back my suspicions. Did you think of it yourself, Sylvie?'

'Fiben'

'Shut up. Oh, it was appealing, all right, to imagine some chims were smart enough to be pulling runs to Cilmar and back, right under the enemy's beak! Vanity almost won, Sylvie. But I was once a scout pilot, remember? I started thinking about how hard that'd be to pull off, even in weather like this!'

He sniffed the air, and there it was again, that distinct musty odor.

Now that he thought about it, he realized that none of the tests he and Gailet had been put through, during the last several weeks, had dealt with the sense of smell. *Of course not. Galactics think it's mostly a relic for animals.*

Moisture fell onto his hand, even though it was not raining just then. Sylvie's tears dripped. She shook her head.

'You ... won't ... be harmed, Fiben. The Suz – Suzerain just wants to ask you some questions. Then you'll be let go! It ... It promised!'

So this was just another test, after all. Fiben felt like laughing at himself for ever believing escape was possible. *I guess I'll see Gailet again sooner than I thought.*

He was beginning to feel ashamed of the way he had terrorized Sylvie. After all, this had all been just a 'game' anyway. Simply one more examination. It wouldn't do to take anything too seriously under such conditions. She was only doing her job.

He started to relax, easing his grip on her throat, when suddenly part of what Sylvie had said struck Fiben.

'The Suzerain said it'd let me go?' he whispered. 'You mean it'll send me back to jail, don't you?'

She shook her head vigorously. 'N-no!' she mouthed.

'It'll drop us off in the mountains. I meant that part of my deal with you and Gailet! The Suzerain promised, if you answer its questions – '

'Wait a minute,' Fiben snapped. 'You aren't talking about the Suzerain of Propriety, are you?'

She shook her head.

Fiben felt suddenly lightheaded. 'Which ... *Which* Suzerain is waiting for us out there?'

Sylvie sniffed. 'The Suzerain of Cost and ... of Cost and Caution,' she whispered.

He closed his eyes in the dreadful realization of what this meant. This was no 'game' or test, after all. *Oh, Goodall*, he thought. Now he had to think to save his own neck!

If it had been the Suzerain of Beam and Talon, Fiben would have been ready to throw in the towel right then and there. For then all of the resources of the Gubru military machine would have been arrayed against him. As it was, the chances were slim enough. But Fiben was starting to get ideas.

Accountants. Insurance agents. Bureaucrats. Those made up the army of the Suzerain of Cost and Caution. *Maybe*, Fiben thought. *Just maybe.*

Before doing anything, though, he had to deal with Sylvie. He couldn't just tie her up and leave her. And be simply wasn't a bloody-minded killer. That led to only one option. He had to win her cooperation, and quickly.

He might tell her of his certainty that the Suzerain of Cost and Caution wasn't quite the stickler for truth the Suzerain of Propriety was. When it was its word against hers, why should the bird keep any promise to release them?

In fact, tonight's raid on its peer might even be illegal, by the invaders' standards, in which case it would be stupid to let two chims who knew about it run around free. Knowing the Gubru, Fiben figured the Suzerain of Cost and Caution would probably let them go, all right – straight out an airlock into deep space.

Would she believe me, though, if I told her?

He couldn't chance that. Fiben thought he knew another way to get Sylvie's undivided attention. 'I want you to listen to me carefully,' he told her. 'I am not going out to meet your Suzerain. I am not going out there for one simple reason. If I walk out there, *knowing what I now know*, you and I can kiss my white card goodbye.'

Her eyes locked onto his. A tremor ran down her spine.

'You see, darlin'. I have to behave like a superlative example to chimpdom in order to qualify for that encomium. And what kind of superchimp goes and walks right into somethin' he *already knows* is a trap? Hmm?

'No, Sylvie. We'll probably still get caught anyway. But we've gotta be caught tryin' our very best to escape or it just won't count! Do you see what I mean?'

She blinked a few times, and finally nodded.

'Hey,' he whispered amiably. 'Cheer up! You should be *glad* I saw through this stunt. It just means our kid'll be all the more clever a little bastard. He'll probably find a way to blow up his kindergarten.'

Sylvie blinked. Hesitantly, she smiled. 'Yeah,' she said quietly. 'I guess that's right.'

Fiben let his knife hand drop away and released Sylvie's throat. He stood up. This was the moment of truth. All she probably had to do was let out a shout and the followers of the Suzerain of Cost and Caution would be on them in moments.

Instead, though, she pulled off her ring watch and handed it to Fiben. *The tracer.*

He nodded and offered her his hand to help her rise. She stumbled at first, still trembling from reaction. But he kept his arm around her as he led her back one block and a little south.

Now, if only this idea works, he thought.

The dovecote was where he remembered it, behind an ill-kempt group house in the neighborhood bordering the harbor. Everyone was asleep apparently. But Fiben nevertheless kept quiet as possible as he cut a few wires and crept into the coop.

It was dank and smelled uncomfortably of bird. The pigeons' soft cooing reminded Fiben of Kwackoo.

'Come on, kids,' he whispered to them. 'You're gonna help me fool your cousins, tonight.'

He had recalled this place from one of his walks. The proximity was more than convenient, it was probably essential. He and Sylvie dared not leave the harbor area until they had disposed of the tracer.

The pigeons edged away from him. While Sylvie kept watch, Fiben cornered and seized a fat, strong-looking bird.

With a piece of string he bound the ring watch to its foot. 'Nice night for a long flight, don't ya think?' he whispered, and threw the pigeon into the air. He repeated the process with his own watch, for good measure.

He left the door open. If the birds returned early, the Gubru might follow the tracer signal here. But their typically noisy arrival would send the whole flock flapping off again, starting another wild goose chase.

Fiben congratulated himself on his cleverness as he and Sylvie ran eastward, away from the harbor. Soon they were in a dilapidated industrial area. Fiben knew where he was. He had been here before, leading the placid horse, Tycho, on his first foray into town after the invasion. Sometime before they reached the wall he signaled for a stop. He had to catch his breath, though Sylvie seemed hardly winded at all.

Well, she's a dancer, of course, he thought.

'Okay, now we strip,' he told her.

To her credit, Sylvie did not even bat an eye. The logic was inescapable. Her watch might not have been the only tracer planted on their person. She hurried through the disrobing and was finished before him. When everything lay in a pile, Fiben spared her a brief, appreciative whistle. Sylvie blushed. 'Now what?' she asked.

'Now we go for the fence,' he answered.

'The fence? But Fiben – '

'C'mon. I've wanted to look at the thing close up for some time anyway.'

It was only a few hundred yards farther before they reached the broad strip of ground the aliens had leveled all the way around Port Helenia. Sylvie shivered as they approached the tall barrier, which glistened damply under the light of bright watch globes placed at wide intervals along its length.

'Fiben,' Sylvie said as he stepped out onto the strip. 'We can't go out there.'

'Why not?' he asked. Still, he stopped and turned to look back at her. 'Do you know anyone who has?'

She shook her head. 'Why *would* anybody? It's obviously crazy! Those *watch globes* . . . '

'Yeah,' Fiben said contemplatively. 'I was just wondering how many of 'em it took to line a fence around the whole city. Ten thousand? Twenty? Thirty?'

He was remembering the guardian drones that had lined the much smaller and much more sensitive perimeter around the former Tymbrimi Embassy, that day when the chancery building exploded and Fiben had had his lesson in ET humor. Those devices had turned out to be pretty unimpressive compared with 'Rover,' or the typical battle robot the Gubru Talon Soldiers took into battle.

I wonder about these, he thought, and took another step forward.

'Fiben!' Sylvie sounded close to panic. 'Let's try the gate. We can tell the guards . . .we can tell them we were robbed. We were hicks from the farms, visiting town, and somebody stole our clothes and ID cards. If we act dumb enough, maybe they'll just let us through!'

Yeah, sure. Fiben stepped closer still. Now he stood no more than half a dozen meters from the barrier. He saw that it comprised a series of narrow slats connected by wire at the top and bottom. He had chosen a point between two of the glowing globes, as far from each as possible. Still, as he approached he felt a powerful sensation that they were *watching* him.

The certainty filled Fiben with resignation. By now, of course, Gubru soldiery were on their way here. They would arrive any minute now. His best course was to turn around. To run. Now!

He glanced back at Sylvie. She stood where he had left her. It was easy to tell that she would rather be almost anywhere else in the world than here. He wasn't at all sure why she had remained.

Fiben grabbed his left wrist with his right hand. His pulse was fast and thready and his mouth felt dry as sand. Trembling, he made an effort of will and took another step toward the fence.

An almost palpable dread seemed to close in all around him, as he had felt when he heard poor Simon Levin's death wail, during that useless, futile battle out in space. He felt a dark foreboding of imminent doom. Mortality pressed in – a sense of the futility of life.

Fiben turned around, slowly, to look at Sylvie.

He grinned.

'Cheap chickenshit birds!' he grunted. 'They aren't watch globes at all! They're stupid *psi radiators*!'

Sylvie blinked. Her mouth opened. Closed. 'Are you *sure*?' she asked unbelievingly.

'Come on out and see,' he urged. 'Right there you'll suddenly be sure you're being watched. Then you'll think every Talon Soldier in space is coming after you!'

Sylvie swallowed. She clenched her fists and moved out onto the empty strip. Step by step, Fiben watched her. He had to give Sylvie credit. A lesser chimmie would have cut and run, screaming, long before she reached his position.

Beads of perspiration popped out on her brow, joining the intermittent raindrops.

Part of him, distant from the adrenaline roar, appreciated her naked form. It helped to distract his mind. *So, she really has nursed.* The faint stretch marks of childbearing and lactation were often faked by some chimmies, in order to make themselves look more attractive, but in this case it was clear that Sylvie had borne a child. *I wonder what her story is.*

When she stood next to him, eyes closed tightly, she whispered. 'What ... what's happening to me right now?'

Fiben listened to his own feelings. He thought of Gailet and her long mourning for her friend and protector, the giant chim Max. He thought of the chims he had seen blown apart by the enemy's overpowering weaponry.

He remembered Simon.

'You feel like your best friend in all the world just died,' he told her gently, and took her hand. Her answering grip was hard, but across her face there swept a look of relief.

'Psi emitters. That's ... that's all?' She opened her eyes. 'Why ... why those cheap, chickenshit birds!'

Fiben guffawed. Sylvie slowly smiled. With her free hand she covered her mouth.

They laughed, standing there in the rain in the midst of a riverbed of sorrow. They laughed, and when their tears finally slowed they walked together the rest of the way to the fence, still holding hands.

'Now when I say push, push!'

'I'm ready, Fiben.' Sylvie crouched beneath him, feet set, shoulder braced against one of the tall slats, arms gripping the part of the wall next to it.

Standing over her, Fiben took a similar stance and planted his feet in the mud. He took several deep breaths.

'Okay, *push!*'

Together they heaved. The slats were already a few centimeters apart. As he and Sylvie strained, he could feel the space begin to widen. *Evolution is never wasted,* Fiben thought as he heaved with all his might.

A million years ago humans were going through all the pangs of self-uplift, evolving what the Galactics said could only be given – sapiency – the ability to think and to covet the stars.

Meanwhile, though, Fiben's ancestors had not been idle. *We were getting strong!* Fiben concentrated on that thought while sweat popped out on his brow and the plastisheath slats groaned. He grunted and could feel Sylvie's own desperate struggle as her back quivered against his leg.

'Ah!' Sylvie lost her footing in the mud and her legs flew out, throwing her backward hard. Recoil spun Fiben about, and the springy slats bounced back, tossing him on top of her.

For a minute or two they just lay there, breathing in shuddering gasps. Finally though, Sylvie spoke.

'Please, honey ... not tonight. I gotta headache.'

Fiben laughed. He rolled off of her and onto his back, coughing. They needed humor. It was their best defense against the constant hammering of the psi globes. Panic was incipient, ever creeping on the verge of their minds. Laughter kept it at bay.

They helped each other up and inspected what they had accomplished. The gap was noticeably larger, perhaps ten centimeters, now. But it was still far from wide enough. And Fiben knew they were running out of time. They would need at least three hours to have any hope of reaching the foothills before daybreak.

At least if they made it through they would have the storm on their side. Another sheet of rain swept across them as he and Sylvie settled in again, bracing themselves. The lightning had drawn closer over the last half hour. Thunder rolled, shaking trees and rattling shutters.

It's a mixed blessing, Fiben thought. For while it no doubt hampered Gubru scanners, the rain also made it hard to get a good grip on the slippery fence material. The mud was a curse.

'You ready?' he asked.

'Sure, if you can manage to keep that thing of yours out of my face,' Sylvie said, looking up at him. 'Its distracting, you know.'

'It's what you told Gailet you wanted to share, honey. Besides, you've seen it all before, back at the Thunder Mound.'

'Yes.' She smiled. 'But it didn't look quite the same.'

'Oh, shut up and push,' Fiben growled. Together they heaved again, putting all their strength into the effort.

Give! Give way! He heard Sylvie gasp, and his own muscles threatened to cramp as the fence material creaked, budged ever so slightly, and creaked again.

This time it was Fiben who slipped, letting the springy material bounce back. Once more they collapsed together in the mud, panting.

The rain was steady now, Fiben wiped a rivulet out of his eyes and looked at the gap again. *Maybe twelve centimeters. Ifni! That's not anywhere near enough.*

He could feel the captivating power of the psi globes broadcasting their gloom into his skull. The message was sapping his strength, he knew, pushing him and Sylvie toward resignation. He felt terribly heavy as he slowly stood up and leaned against the obdurate fence.

Hell, we tried. We'll get credit for that much. Almost made it, too. If only . . .

'No!' he shouted suddenly. '*No!* I won't let you!' He hurled himself at the gap, tried to pry his body through, wriggled and writhed against the recalcitrant opening. Lightning struck, somewhere in the dark realm just beyond, illuminating an open countryside of fields and forests and, beyond them, the beckoning foothills of the Mulun range.

Thunder pealed, setting the fence rocking. The slats squeezed Fiben between them, and he howled in agony. When they let go he fell, half-numbed with pain, to the ground near Sylvie. But he was on his feet again in an instant. Another electric ladder lit the glowering clouds. He screamed back at the sky. He beat the ground. Mud and pebbles flew up as he threw handfuls into the air. More thunder drove the stones back, pelting them into his face.

There was no longer any such thing as speech. No words. The part of him that knew such things reeled in shock, and in reaction other older, sturdier portions took control.

Now there was only the storm. The wind and rain. The lightning and thunder. He beat his breast, lips curled back, baring his teeth to the stinging rain. The storm *sang* to Fiben, reverberating in the ground and the throbbing air. He answered with a howl.

This music was no prissy, human thing. It was not poetical, like the whale dream phantoms of the dolphins. No, *this* was music he could feel clear down to his bones. It rocked him. It rolled him. It lifted Fiben like a rag doll and tossed him down into the mud. He came back up, spitting and hooting.

He could feel Sylvie's gaze upon him. She was slapping the ground, watching him, wide-eyed, excited. That only made him beat his breast harder and shriek louder. He knew he was not drooping now! Throwing pebbles into the air he cried defiance to the storm, calling out for the lightning to come and *get* him!

Obligingly, it came. Brilliance filled space, charging it, sending his hair bristling outward, sparking. The soundless bellow blew him backward, like a giant's hand come down to slap him straight against the wall.

Fiben screamed as he struck the slats. Before he blacked out, he distinctly smelled the aroma of burning fur.

66

GAILET

In the darkness, with the sound of rain pelting against the roof tiles, she suddenly opened her eyes. Alone, she stood up with the blanket wrapped around her and went to the window.

Outside, a storm blew across Port Helenia, announcing the full arrival of autumn. The caliginous clouds rumbled angrily, threateningly.

There was no view to the east, but Gailet let her cheek rest against the cool glass and faced that way anyway.

The room was comfortably warm. Nevertheless, she closed her eyes and shivered against a sudden chill.

67

FIBEN

Eyes ... eyes ... eyes were everywhere. They whirled and danced, glowing in the darkness, taunting him.

An elephant appeared – crashing through the jungle, trumpeting with red irises aflame. He tried to flee but it caught him, picked him up in its trunk, and carried him off bouncing, jouncing him, cracking his ribs.

He wanted to tell the beast to go ahead and eat him already, or trample him ... only to get it over with! After a while, though, he grew used to it. The pain dulled to a throbbing ache, and the journey settled into a steady rhythm ...

The first thing he realized, on awakening, was that the rain was somehow missing his face.

He lay on his back, on what felt like grass. All around him the sounds of the storm rolled on, scarcely diminished. He could feel the wet showers on his legs and torso. And yet, none of the raindrops fell onto his nose or mouth.

Fiben opened his eyes to look and see why ... and, incidentally, to find out how he happened to be alive.

A silhouette blocked out the dun underglow of the clouds. A lightning stroke, not far away, briefly illuminated a face above his own. Sylvie looked down in concern, holding his head in her lap.

Fiben tried to speak. 'Where ...' but the word came out as a croak. Most of his voice seemed to be gone. Fiben dimly recalled an episode of screaming, howling at the sky ... That had to be why his throat hurt so.

'We're outside,' Sylvie said, just loud enough to be heard over the rain. Fiben blinked. *Outside?*

Wincing, he lifted his head just enough to look around.

Against the stormy backdrop it was hard to see anything at all. But he was able to make out the dim shapes of trees and low, rolling hills. He turned to his left. The outline of Port Helenia was unmistakable, especially the curving trail of tiny lights that followed the course of the Gubru fence.

'But ... but how did we get here?'

'I carried you,' she said matter-of-factly. 'You weren't in much shape for walking after you tore down that wall.'

'Tore down ...'

She nodded. There appeared to be a shining light in Sylvie's eyes. 'I thought I'd seen thunder dances before, Fiben Bolger. But that was one to beat all others on record. I swear it. If I live to ninety, and have a hundred respectful grandchildren, I don't imagine I'll ever be able to tell it so I'll be believed.'

Dimly, it sort of came back to him now. He recalled the anger, the outrage over having come so close, and yet so far from freedom. It shamed him to remember giving in that way to frustration, to the animal within him.

Some white card. Fiben snorted, knowing how stupid the Suzerain of Propriety had to be to have chosen a chim like him for such a role.

'I must've lost my grip for a while.'

Sylvie touched his left shoulder. He winced and looked down to see a nasty burn there. Oddly, it did not seem to hurt as badly as a score of lesser aches and bruises.

'You taunted the storm, Fiben,' she said in a hushed voice. 'You *dared* it to come down after you. And when it came ... you made it do your bidding.'

Fiben closed his eyes. *Oh, Goodall. Of all the silly, superstitious nonsense.*

And yet, there was a part of him, deep down, that felt warmly satisfied. It was as if that portion actually believed that there had been cause and effect, that he had done exactly what Sylvie described!

Fiben shuddered. 'Help me sit up, okay?'

There was a disorienting moment or two as the horizon tilted and vision swam. At last, though, when she had him seated so the world no longer wavered all around him, he gestured for her to help him stand.

'You should rest, Fiben.'

'When we reach the Mulun,' he told her. 'Dawn can't be far off. And the storm won't last forever. Come on, I'll lean on you.

She took his good arm over her shoulder, bracing him. Somehow, they managed to get him onto his feet.

'Y'know,' he said. 'You're a strong lil' chimmie. Hmph. Carried me all the way up here, did you?'

She nodded, looking up at him with that same light. Fiben smiled. 'Okay,' he said. 'Pretty damn okay.'

Together they started out, limping toward the glowering dark hummocks to the east.

PART FIVE

AVENGERS

In ancient days, when Poseidon still reigned and the ships of man were as weak as tinder, bad luck struck a certain Thracian freighter, who foundered and broke apart under an early winter storm. All hands were lost under those savage waves, save one – the boat's mascot – a monkey.

As the fates would have it, a dolphin appeared just as the monkey was gasping its last breath. Knowing of the great love between man and dolphin, the monkey cried out, 'Save me! For the sake of my poor children in Athens!'

Quick as a streak, the dolphin offered its broad back. 'Thou art very strange, small, and ugly for a man,' the dolphin said as the monkey took a desperate grip.

'As men go, I might be quite handsome,' replied the monkey, who coughed, holding on tightly as the dolphin turned towards land, 'You say you are a man of Athens?' the wary sea creature asked.

'Indeed, who would claim it were he not?' the monkey proclaimed.

'Then you know Piraeus?' the suspicious dolphin inquired further.

The monkey thought quickly. 'Oh, yes!' he cried. 'Piraeus is my dear friend. I only spoke with him last week!'

With that the dolphin bucked angrily and flung the monkey into the sea to drown. The moral of the story, one might suppose, is that one should always get one's story straight, when pretending to be what one is not.

M. N. PLANO

68

GALACTICS

The image in the holographic display flickered. That was not surprising, since it came from many parsecs away, refracted through the folded space of the Pourmin transfer point. The muddy picture wavered and occasionally lost definition.

Still, to the Suzerain of Propriety the message was coming in all too clearly.

A diverse collection of beings stood depicted before the Suzerain's pedestal. It recognized most of the races by sight. There was a Pila, for instance – short, furry, and stubby-armed. And there was a tall, gangling Z'Tang who stood beside a spiderlike Serentin. A Bi-Gle glowered lazily, coiled next to a being the Suzerain did not immediately recognize, and which might have been a client or a decorative pet.

Also, to the Suzerain's dismay, the delegation included a Synthian and a human.

A human!

And there was no way to complain. It was only appropriate to include a Terran among the official observers – if a qualified human were available – since this world was registered to the wolflings. But the Suzerain had felt certain that there *were* none employed by the Uplift Institute in this sector!

Perhaps this was one more sign that the political situation in the Five Galaxies had worsened. Word had come from the homeworld Roost Masters telling of serious setbacks out between the spiral arms. Battles had gone badly. Allies had proven unreliable. Tandu and Soro fleets dominated once profitable trade routes and now monopolized the siege of Earth.

These were trying times for the great and powerful clan of the Gooksyu-Gubru. All now depended on certain important neutralist patron-lines. Should something happen to draw one or two of them into an alliance, triumph might yet be attained for the righteous.

On the other side of the wing, it would be disastrous to see any of the neutrals turn against the Great Clan!

To influence such matters had been a major reason, back when the Suzerain of Propriety originated the idea of invading Garth in the first place. Superficially this expedition had been intended to seize hostages for use in prying secrets out of the High Command of Earth. But psychological profiles had always made success in that seem unlikely. Wolflings were obstinate creatures.

No, what had won the Roost Masters over to the priest's proposal was the possibility that this would bring honor to the cause of the clan – to score a coup and win new alliances from wavering parties. And at first all seemed to go so well! The first Suzerain of Cost and Caution –

The priest chirped a deep note of mourning. It had not before realized what wisdom they had lost, how the old bureaucrat had tempered the rash brilliance of the younger two with deep and reliable sense.

What a consensus, unity, policy we might have had. Now, though, in addition to the constant struggles among the still disunited Triumvirate, there was this latest bad news. A *Terran* would be among the official observers from the Uplift Institute. The implications were unpleasant to consider. And that was not to be the worst of it! As the Suzerain watched in dismay, the Earthling stepped forward as spokesman! Its statement was in clear Galactic Seven.

'Greetings to the Triumvirate of the Forces of Gooksyu-Gubru, now in contested occupation of the limited-leasehold world known as Garth. I greet you in the name of Cough'Quinn*3, Grand High Examiner of the Uplift Institute. This message is being sent ahead of our vessel by the quickest available means, so that you may prepare for our arrival. Conditions in hyperspace and at transfer points indicate that causality will almost certainly allow us to attend the proposed ceremonies, and administer appropriate sapiency tests at the time and place requested by you.

'You are further informed that Galactic Uplift Institute has gone to great lengths to accommodate your unusual request – first in exercising such haste and second in acting on the basis of so little information.

'Ceremonies of Uplift are joyous occasions, especially in times of turmoil such as these. They celebrate the continuity and perpetual renewal of Galactic culture, in the name of the most revered Progenitors. Client species are the hope, the future of our civilization, and on such occasions as this we demonstrate our responsibility, our honor, and our love.

'We approach this event, then, filled with curiosity as to what wonder the clan of Gooksyu-Gubru plans to unveil before the Five Galaxies.'

The scene vanished, leaving the Suzerain to contemplate this news.

It was too late, of course, to recall the invitations and cancel the ceremony. Even the other Suzerains recognized this. The shunt must be completed, and they must prepare to receive honored guests. To do otherwise might damage the Gubru cause irrevocably.

The Suzerain danced a dance of anger and frustration. It muttered short, sharp imprecations.

Curse the devil-trickster Tymbrimi! In retrospect, the very idea of 'Garthlings' – native pre-sentients that survived the Holocaust of the Bururalli – was absurd. And yet the trail of false evidence had been so startlingly plausible, so striking in its implied opportunity!

The Suzerain of Propriety had begun this expedition in a lead position. Its place in the eventual Molt had seemed assured after the untimely demise of the first Suzerain of Cost and Caution.

But all that changed when no Garthlings were found – when it became clear just how thoroughly Propriety had been tricked. Failure to find evidence of human misuse of Garth or their clients meant that the Suzerain still had not yet set foot upon the soil of this planet. That, in turn, had retarded the development of completion hormones. All of these factors were setbacks, throwing the Molt into serious doubt.

Then, insurrection among the neo-chimpanzees helped bring the military to the fore. Now the Suzerain of Beam and Talon was rapidly growing preeminent, unstoppable.

The coming Molt filled the Suzerain of Propriety with foreboding. Such events were supposed to be triumphant, transcendent, even for the losers. Moltings were times of renewal and sexual fulfillment for the race. They were also supposed to represent *crystallization of policy* – consensus on correct action.

This time, however, there was little or no consensus. Something was very wrong, indeed, about this molting.

The only thing all three Suzerains were in agreement about was that the hyperspace shunt must be used for some sort of Uplift ceremony. To do otherwise would be suicidal at this point. But beyond that they parted company. Their incessant arguing had begun affecting the entire expedition. The more religious Talon Soldiers had taken to bickering with their comrades. Bureaucrats who were retired soldiers sided with their former comrades over logistical expenditures, or turned sullen when their chief overruled them. Even among the priesthood there were frequent arguments where there should already be unanimity.

The priest had just recently discovered what factionalism could do. The divisiveness had gone all the way to the point of betrayal! Why else had one of its two race-leader chimpanzees been stolen?

Now the Suzerain of Cost and Caution was insisting on a role in choosing the new male. No doubt the bureaucrat was responsible for the 'escape' of the Fiben Bolger chimp in the first place! Such a promising creature it had been! By now it no doubt had been converted to vapor and ashes;

There would be no way to pin this on either of the rival Suzerains, of course.

A Kwackoo servitor approached and knelt, proffering a data cube in its beak. Given assent, it popped the record into a player unit.

The room dimmed and the Suzerain of Propriety watched a camera's-eye view of driving rain and darkness. It shivered involuntarily, disliking the ugly, dank dinginess of a wolfling town.

The view panned over a muddy patch in a dark alley ... a broken shack made of wire and wood, where Terran birds had been kept as pets ... a pile of soggy clothing beside a padlocked factory ... footprints leading to a churned up field of mud beside a bent and battered fence ... more footprints leading off into the dim wilderness ...

The implications were apparent to the Suzerain before the investigators' report reached its conclusion.

The male neo-chimpanzee had perceived the trap set for it! It appeared to have made good its escape!

The Suzerain danced upon its perch, a series of mincing steps of ancient lineage.

> *'The harm, damage, setback*
> *to our program is severe.*
> *But it is not, may not be*
> *irreparable!'*

At a gesture its Kwackoo followers hurried forward. The Suzerain's first command was straightforward.

> *'We must increase, improve, enhance*
> *our commitment, our incentives.*
> *Inform the female that we agree,*
> *accept, acquiesce to her request.*

> *'She may go to the Library.'*

The servitor bowed, and the other Kwackoo crooned.
'Zoooon!'

69

GOVERNMENT IN EXILE

The holo-tank cleared as the interstellar message ran to its end. When the lights came on, the Council members looked at each other in puzzlement. 'What ... what does it mean?' Colonel Maiven asked.

'I'm not sure,' said Commander Kylie. 'But it's clear the Gubru are up to something.'

Refuge Administrator Mu Chen drummed her fingers on the table. 'They appeared to be officials from the Uplift Institute. It seems to mean the invaders are planning some sort of Uplift ceremony, and have invited witnesses.'

That much is obvious, Megan thought. 'Do you think this has anything to do with that mysterious construction south of Port Helenia?' she asked. The site had been a topic of much discussion lately.

Colonel Maiven nodded. 'I had been reluctant to admit the possibility before, but now I'd have to say so.'

The chim member spoke. 'Why would they want to hold an Uplift ceremony for the Kwackoo here on Garth? It doesn't make sense. Would that improve their claim on our leasehold?'

'I doubt it,' Megan said. 'Maybe ... maybe it isn't for the Kwackoo at all.'

'But then for who?'

Megan shrugged. Kylie commented. 'The Uplift Institute officials appear to be in the dark as well.'

There was a long silence. Then Kylie broke it again.

'How significant do you think it is that the spokesman was human?'

Megan smiled. 'Obviously it was meant as a dig at the Gubru. That man might have been no more than a junior clerk trainee at the local Uplift Institute branch. Putting him out in front of Pila and Z'Tang and Serentini means Earth isn't finished yet. And certain powers want to point that out to the Gubru.'

'Hm. Pila. They're tough customers, and members of the Soro clan. Having a human spokesman might be an insult to the Gubru, but it's no guarantee Earth is okay.'

Megan understood what Kylie meant. If the Soro now dominated Earthspace, there were rough times ahead.

Again, another long silence. Then Colonel Maiven spoke.

'They mentioned a hyperspace shunt. Those are expensive. The Gubru must set great store by this ceremony thing.'

Indeed, Megan thought, knowing that a motion had been put before the Council. And this time she realized that it would be hard to justify holding to Uthacalthing's advice.

'You are suggesting a target, colonel?'

'I sure am, madam coordinator.' Maiven sat up and met her eyes. 'I think this is the opportunity we've been waiting for.'

There were nods of agreement up and down the table.

They are voting out of boredom, and frustration, and sheer cabin fever, Megan knew. *And yet, is this not a golden chance, to be seized or lost forever?*

'We cannot attack once the emissaries from the Uplift Institute have arrived,' she emphasized, and saw that everybody understood how important that was. 'However, I agree that there may be a window of opportunity during which a strike could be made.'

Consensus was obvious. In a corner of her mind, Megan felt there really ought to be more discussion. But she, too, was near filled to bursting with impatience.

'We shall cut new orders to Major Prathachulthorn then. He shall receive carte blanche, subject only to the condition that any attack be completed by November first. Is it agreed?'

A simple raising of hands. Commander Kylie hesitated, then joined in to make it unanimous.

We are committed, Megan thought. And she wondered if Hell reserved a special place for mothers who send their own sons into battle.

70

ROBERT

She didn't have to go away, did she? I mean she herself said it was all right.

Robert rubbed his stubbled chin. He thought about taking a shower and shaving. Major Prathachulthorn would be calling a meeting sometime after it reached full light, and the commander liked to see his officers well groomed.

What I really should be doing is sleeping, Robert knew. They had just finished a whole series of night exercises. It would be wise to catch up on his rest.

And yet, after a couple of hours of fitful slumber he had found himself too nervous, too full of restless energy to stay in bed any longer. He had risen and gone to his small desk, setting up the datawell so its light would not disturb the chamber's other occupant. For some time he read through Major Prathachulthorn's detailed order of battle.

It was ingenious, professional. The various options appeared to offer a number of efficient ways to use limited forces to strike the enemy, and strike him hard. All that remained was choosing the right target. There were several choices available, any of which ought to do.

Still, something about the entire edifice struck Robert as *wrong*. The document did not increase his confidence, as he had hoped it would. In the space over his head Robert almost imagined something taking form – something faintly akin to the dark clouds that had shrouded the mountains in storms so recently – a symbolic manifestation of his unease.

Across the little chamber a form moved under the blankets. One slender arm lay exposed, and a smooth length of calf and thigh.

Robert concentrated and erased the nonthing that he had been forming with his simple aura-power. It had begun affecting Lydia's dreams, and it wouldn't be fair to inflict his own turmoil upon her. For all of their recent physical intimacy, they were still in many ways strangers.

Robert reminded himself that there were some positive aspects to the last few days. The battle plan, for instance, showed that Prathachulthorn was at last taking some of his ideas seriously. And spending time with Lydia had brought more than physical pleasure. Robert had not realized how much he missed the simple touch of his own kind. Humans might be able to withstand isolation better than chims – who could fall into deep depression if they lacked a grooming partner for very long. But mel and fem humans, too, had their apelike needs.

Still, Robert's thoughts kept drifting. Even during his most passionate moments with Lydia, he kept thinking of somebody else.

Did she really have to leave? Logically there was no reason to have to go to Mount Fossey. The gorillas were already well cared for.

Of course, the gorillas might have been just an excuse. An excuse to escape the disapproving aura of Major Prathachulthorn. An excuse to avoid the sparking discharges from human passion.

Athaclena might be correct that there was nothing wrong with Robert seeking his own kind. But logic was not everything. She had feelings, too. Young and alone, she could be hurt even by what she knew to be right.

'Damn!' Robert muttered. Prathachulthorn's words and graphs were a blur. 'Damn, I miss her.'

There was a commotion outside, beyond the flap of cloth that sectioned off this chamber from the rest of the caves. Robert looked at his watch. It was still only four a.m. He stood up and gathered his trousers. Any unplanned excitement at this hour was likely to be bad news. Just because the enemy had been quiet for a month did not mean it had to stay that way. Perhaps the Gubru had gotten wind of their plans and were striking preemptively!

There was the slap of unshod feet upon stone. 'Capt'n Oneagle?' a voice said from just beyond the cloth. Robert strode over and pulled it aside. A winded chim messenger breathed heavily. 'What's happening?' Robert asked.

'Um, sir, you'd better come quick.'

'All right. Let me get my weapons.'

The chim shook her head. 'It's not fighting, sir. It's ... it's some chims just arrivin' from Port Helenia.'

Robert frowned. New recruits from town had been arriving in small groups all along. What was all the excitement about this time? He heard Lydia stir as the talking disturbed her sleep. 'Fine,' he told the chimmie. 'We'll interview them a little later – '

She interrupted. 'Sir! It's Fiben! Fiben Bolger, sir. He's come back.'

Robert blinked. 'What?'

There was movement behind him. 'Rob?' a feminine voice spoke. 'What is – '

Robert whooped. His shout reverberated in the closed spaces. He hugged and kissed the surprised chimmie, then caught up Lydia and tossed her lightly into the air.

'What ... ?' she started to ask, then stopped, for she found herself addressing only the empty space where he had been.

Actually, there was little need to hurry. Fiben and his escorts were still some distance away. By the time their horses could be seen, puffing up the trail from the north, Lydia had dressed and joined Robert up on the escarpment. There dawn's gray light was just driving out the last wan stars.

'Everybody's up,' Lydia commented. 'They even roused the major. Chims are dashing all over the place, jabbering in excitement. This must be some chen we're waiting for.'

'Fiben?' Robert laughed. He blew into his hands. 'Yeah, you might say old Fiben's unusual.'

'I gathered as much.' She shaded her eyes against the glow to the east and watched the mounted party pass a switchback climbing the narrow trail. 'Is he the one in the bandages?'

'Hm?' Robert squinted. Lydia's eyesight had been bio-organically enhanced during her Marine training. He was envious. 'It wouldn't surprise me. Fiben's always getting banged up, one way or another. Claims he hates it. Says it's all due to innate clumsiness and a universe that has it in for him, but I've always suspected it was an affinity for trouble. Never known a chim who went to such lengths just to get a story to tell.'

In a minute he could make out the features of his friend. He shouted and raised his hand. Fiben grinned and waved back, although his left arm was immobilized in a sling. Next to him, on a pale mare, rode a chimmie Robert did not recognize.

A messenger arrived from the cave entrance and saluted. 'Sers, the major requests that you an' Lieutenant Bolger come down just as soon's he's here.'

Robert nodded. 'Please tell Major Prathachulthorn we'll be right there.'

As the horses climbed the last switchback, Lydia slipped her hand into his, and Robert felt a sudden wave of both gladness and guilt. He squeezed back and tried not to let his ambivalence show.

Fiben's alive! he thought. *I must get word to Athaclena. I'm sure she'll be thrilled.*

Major Prathachulthorn had a nervous habit of tugging at one ear or the other. While listening to reports from his subordinates, he would shift in his chair, occasionally leaning over to mumble into his datawell, retrieving some quick dollop of information. At such times he might seem distracted, but if the speaker stopped talking, or even slowed down, the major would snap his fingers, impatiently. Apparently, Prathachulthorn had a quick mind and was able to juggle several tasks at once. However, these behaviors were very hard on some of the chims, often making them nervous and tongue-tied. That, in turn, did not improve the major's opinion of the irregulars that had only recently been under Robert's and Athaclena's command.

In Fiben's case, though, this was no problem. As long as he was kept supplied with orange juice, he kept on with his story. Even Prathachulthorn, who usually interrupted reports with frequent questions, probing mercilessly for details, sat silently through the tale of the disastrous valley insurrection, Fiben's subsequent capture, the interviews and tests by the followers of the Suzerain of Propriety, and the theories of Dr Gailet Jones.

Now and then Robert glanced at the chimmie Fiben had brought with him from Port Helenia. Sylvie sat to one side, between the chims Benjamin and Elsie, her posture erect and her expression composed. Occasionally, when asked to verify or elaborate on something, she answered in a quiet voice. Otherwise, her gaze remained on Fiben constantly.

Fiben carefully described the political situation among the Gubru, as he understood it. When he came to the evening of the escape, he told of the trap that had been laid by the 'Suzerain of Cost and Caution,' and concluded simply by saying, 'So we decided, Sylvie and I, that we'd better exit Port Helenia by a different route than by sea.' He shrugged. 'We got out through a gap in the fence and finally made it to a rebel outpost. So here we are.'

Right! Robert thought sardonically. Of course Fiben had left out any mention of his injuries and exactly *how* he escaped. He would no doubt fill in the details in his written report to the major, but anyone else would have to bribe them out of him.

Robert saw Fiben glance his way and wink. *I'd bet this is at least a five-beer tale,* Robert thought.

Prathachulthorn leaned forward. 'You say that you actually saw this hyperspace shunt? You know exactly where it is located?'

'I was trained as a scout, major. I know where it is. I'll include a map, and a sketch of the facility, in my written report.'

Prathachulthorn nodded. 'If I had not already had other reports of this thing I'd never have credited this story. As it is though, I am forced to believe you. You say this faculty is expensive, even by Gubru standards?'

'Yessir. That's what Gailet and I came to believe. Think about it. Humans have only been able to throw one Uplift ceremony for each of their clients in all the years since Contact, and both had to be held on Tymbrim. That's why other clients like the Kwackoo can get away with snubbing us.

'Part of the reason has been political obstruction by antagonistic clans like the Gubru and the Soro, who've been able to drag out Terran applications for status. But another reason is because we're so frightfully poor, by Galactic standards.'

Fiben had been learning things, obviously. Robert realized part of it must have been picked up from this Gailet Jones person. With his heightened empathy sense, he picked up faint tremors from his friend whenever her name came up.

Robert glanced at Sylvie. *Hmm. Life seems to have grown complicated for Fiben.*

That reminded Robert of his own situation, of course. *Fiben isn't the only one,* he thought. All his life he had wanted to learn to be more sensitive, to better understand others and his own feelings. Now he had his wish, and he hated it.

'By Darwin, Goodall, and Greenpeace!' Prathachulthorn pounded the table. 'Mr Bolger, you bring your news at a most opportune time!'

He turned to address Lydia and Robert. 'Do you know what this means, gentlemen?'

'Um,' Robert began.

'A target, sir,' Lydia answered succinctly.

'A target is right! This fits perfectly with that message we just received from the Council. If we can smash this shunt – preferably before the dignitaries from the Uplift Institute arrive – then we could rap the Gubru right where it pains them most, in their wallets!'

'But – ' Robert started to object.

'You heard what our spy just told us.' Prathachulthorn said. 'The Gubru are *hurting* out there in space! They're overextended, their leaders here on Garth are at each other's throats, and this could be the last straw! Why, we might even be able to time it so their entire Triumvirate is at the same place at the same time!'

Robert shook his head. 'Don't you think we ought to give it some thought, sir? I mean, what about the offer that the Suzerain of Probity – '

'Propriety,' Fiben corrected.

'Propriety. Yes. What about the offer it made to Fiben and Dr Jones?'

Prathachulthorn shook his head. 'An obvious trap, Oneagle. Be serious now.'

'I *am* being serious, sir. I'm no more an expert on these matters than Fiben, and certainly less of one than Dr Jones. And certainly I concede it *may* be a trap. But on the surface, at least, it sounds like a terrific deal for Earth! A deal I don't think we can pass up without at least reporting this back to the Council.'

'There isn't time.' Prathachulthorn said, shaking his head. 'My orders are to operate at my own discretion and, if appropriate, to act before the Galactic dignitaries arrive.'

Robert felt a growing desperation. 'Then at least let's consult with Athaclena. She's the daughter of a diplomat. She might be able to see some ramifications we don't.'

Prathachulthorn's frown spoke volumes. 'If there's time, of course I'll be happy to solicit the young Tymbrimi's opinion.' But it was clear that even mentioning the idea had brought Robert down a peg in the man's eyes.

Prathachulthorn slapped the table. 'Right now I think we had better have a staff meeting of commissioned officers and discuss potential tactics against this hypershunt installation.' He turned and nodded to the chims. 'That will be all for now, Fiben. Thank you very much for your courageous and timely action. That goes the same to you too, miss.' He nodded at Sylvie. 'I look forward to seeing your written reports.'

Elsie and Benjamin stood up and held the door. As mere brevet officers they were excluded from Prathachulthorn's inner staff. Fiben rose and moved more slowly, aided by Sylvie.

Robert hurriedly spoke in a low voice to Prathachulthorn. 'Sir, I'm sure it only slipped your mind, but Fiben holds a foil commission in the colonial defense forces, If he's excluded it might not go down well, um, politically.'

Prathachulthorn blinked. His expression barely flickered, though Robert knew he had once again failed to score points. 'Yes, of course,' the major said evenly. 'Please tell Lieutenant Bolger he is welcome to stay, if he's not too tired.'

With that he turned back to his datawell and started calling up files. Robert could feel Lydia's eyes on him. *She may despair of my ever learning tact,* he thought as he hurried to the door and caught Fiben's arm just as he was leaving.

His friend grinned at him. 'I guess it's grownup time again, here,' Fiben said, sotto voce, glancing in Prathachulthorn's direction.

'It's worse even than that, old chim. I just got you tapped as an honorary adult.'

If looks could maim, Robert mused on seeing Fiben's sour expression. *And you thought it was Miller time, didn't you?* They had argued before about the possible historical origins of that expression.

Fiben squeezed Sylvie's shoulder and hobbled back into the room. She watched him for a moment, then turned and followed Elsie down the hall.

Benjamin, however, lingered for a moment. He had caught Robert's gesture bidding him to stay. Robert slipped a small disk into the chim's palm. He dared not say anything aloud, but with his left hand he made a simple sign.

'*Auntie,*' he said in hand talk.

Benjamin nodded quickly and walked away.

Prathachulthorn and Lydia were already deep into the arcana of battle planning as Robert returned to the table. The major turned to Robert, 'I'm afraid there just won't be time to use enhanced bacteriological effects, as ingenious as your idea was on its own merits ...'

The words washed past unnoted. Robert sat down, thinking only that he had just committed his first felony. By secretly recording the meeting – including Fiben's lengthy report – he had violated procedure. By giving the pellet to Benjamin he had broken protocol.

And by ordering the chim to deliver the recording to an alien he had, by some lights, just committed treason.

71

MAX

A large neo-chimpanzee shambled into the vast underground chamber, hands cuffed together, drawn along at the end of a stout chain. He remained aloof from his guards, chims wearing the invader's livery, who pulled at the other end of his leash, but occasionally he did glare defiantly at the alien technicians watching from catwalks overhead.

His face had not been unblemished to start with, but now fresh patterns of pink scar tissue lay livid and open, exposed by patches of missing fur. The wounds were healing, but they would never be pretty.

'C'mon, Reb,' one of the chim guards said as he pushed the prisoner forward. 'Bird wants to ask you some questions.'

Max ignored the Probie as best he could as he was led over to a raised area near the center of the huge chamber. There, several Kwackoo waited, standing upon an elevated instrument platform.

Max kept his eyes level on the apparent leader, and his bow was shallow – just low enough to force the avian to give one in return.

Next to the Kwackoo stood three more of the quislings. Two were well-dressed chims who had made tidy profits providing construction equipment and workers to the Gubru – it was rumored that some of the deals had been at the expense of their missing human business partners. Other stories implied approval and direct connivance by men interned on Cilmar and the other islands. Max didn't know which version he wanted to believe. The third chim on the platform was the commander of the Probie auxiliary force, the tall, haughty chen called Irongrip.

Max also knew the proper protocol for greeting traitors. He grinned, exposing his large canines to view, and spat at their feet. With a shout the Probies yanked at his chain, sending him stumbling. They lifted their truncheons. But a quick chirp from the lead Kwackoo stopped them in mid-blow. They stepped back, bowing.

'You are sure – certain that this one – this individual is the one we have been looking for?' the feathered officer asked Irongrip. The chim nodded.

'This one was found wounded near the site where Gailet Jones and Fiben Bolger were captured. He was seen in their company before the uprising, and was known to be one of her family's retainers for many years before that. I have prepared an analysis showing how his contact with these individuals makes him appropriate for close attention.'

The Kwackoo nodded. 'You have been most resourceful,' he told Irongrip. 'You shall be rewarded – compensated with high status. Although one of the candidates of the Suzerain of Propriety has escaped our net somehow. *We* are now in a good position to choose – select his replacement. You will be informed.'

Max had lived under Gubru rule long enough to recognize that these were *bureaucrats*, followers of the Suzerain of Cost and Caution. Though what they wanted from him, what use he could be to them in their internal struggles, he had no idea.

Why had he been brought here? Deep in the bowels of the handmade mountain, across the bay from Port Helenia, there sat an intimidating honeycomb of machinery and humming power supplies. During the long ride down the autolift, Max had felt his hair stand out with static electricity as the Gubru and their clients tested titanic devices.

The Kwackoo functionary turned to regard him with one eye. 'You will serve two functions,' it told Max. 'Two purposes now. You will give us information – data about your former employer, information of use to us. And you will help – assist us in an experiment.'

Again, Max grinned. 'I won't do neither, an' I don't even care if it is disrespectful. You can go put on a clown suit an' ride a tricycle, for all I'll tell you.'

The Kwackoo blinked once, twice, as it listened to a computer translation for verification. It chirped an exchange with its associates, then turned back to face him.

'You misunderstand – mistake our meaning. There will be no questions. You need not speak. Your cooperation is not necessary.'

The complacent assuredness of the statement sounded dire. Max shivered under a sudden premonition.

Back when he had first been captured, the enemy had tried to get information out of him. He had steeled himself to resist with all his might, but it really rocked him when all they seemed to be interested in were 'Garthlings.' That's what they asked him about again and again. '*Where are the pre-sentients?*' they had inquired.

Garthlings?

It had been easy to mislead them, to lie in spite of all the drugs and psi machines, because the enemy's basic *assumptions* had been so cockeyed dumb. Imagine Galactics falling for a bunch of children's tales! He had had a field day, and learned many tricks to fool the questioners.

For instance, he struggled hard *not* to 'admit' that Garthlings existed. For a while that seemed to convince them all the more that the trail was hot.

At last, they gave up and left him alone. Perhaps they finally figured out how they'd been duped. Anyway, after that he was assigned to a work detail at one of the construction sites, and Max thought they'd forgotten about him.

Apparently not, he now knew. Anyway, the Kwackoo's words disturbed him.

'What do you mean, you won't be asking questions?'

This time it was the Probationer leader who replied. Irongrip stroked his mustache with relish. 'It means you're going to have everything you know *squeezed* out of you. All this machinery' – he waved around him – 'will be focused on just little ol' you. Your answers will come out. But you won't.'

Max inhaled sharply and felt his heart beat faster. What kept him steady was one firm resolve; he wasn't going to give these traitors the satisfaction of finding him tongue-tied! He concentrated to form words.

'That ... that's against th' ... the Rules of War.'

Irongrip shrugged. He left it to the Kwackoo bureaucrat to explain.

'The Rules protect – provide for species and worlds far more than individuals. And anyway, none of those you see here are followers of priests!'

So, Max realized. *I'm in the hold of fanatics.* Mentally he said farewell to the chens and chimmies and kids of his group family, especially his senior group wife, whom he now knew he would never see again. Also mentally, he bent over and kissed his own posterior goodbye.

'Y'made two mistakes,' he told his captors. 'Th' first was lettin' it slip that Gailet is alive, an' that Fiben's made a fool of you again. Knowin' that makes up for anythin' you can do to me.'

Irongrip growled. 'Enjoy your brief pleasure. You're still going to be a big help in bringing your ex-employer down a few pegs.'

'Maybe.' Max nodded. 'But your second mistake was leaving me attached to this – '

He had been letting his arms go slack. Now he brought them back with a savage jerk and pulled the chain with all his might. It yanked two of the Probie guards off their feet before the links flew out of their hands.

Max planted his feet and snapped the heavy chain like a whip. His escorts dove for cover, but not all of them made it in time. One of the chim contractors had his skull laid open by a glancing blow. Another stumbled in his desperation to get away and knocked down all three Kwackoo like bowling pins.

Max shouted with joy. He whirled his makeshift weapon until everyone was either toppled or out of reach, then he worked the arc sideways, changing the axis of rotation. When he let go, the chain flew upwards at an angle and wrapped itself around the guardrail of the catwalk overhead.

Shimmying up the heavy links was the easy part. They were too stunned to react in time to stop him. But at the top he had to waste precious seconds unwrapping the chain. Since it was attached to his handcuffs, he'd have to take it along.

Along where? he wondered as he got the links gathered. Max spun about when he glimpsed white feathers over to his right. So he ran the other way and scurried up a flight of stairs to reach the next level.

Of course escape was an absurd notion. He had only two short-term objectives: doing as much harm as possible, and then ending his own life before he could be forced against his will to betray Gailet.

The former goal he accomplished as he ran, flailing the tip of the chain against every knob, tube, or delicate-looking instrument within reach. Some bits of equipment were tougher than they looked, but others smashed and tinkled nicely. Trays of tools went over the edge, toppling onto those below.

He kept a watch out, though, for other options. If no ready implement or weapon presented itself before the time came, he ought to try to get high enough for a good leap over the railing to do the trick.

A Gubru technician and two Kwackoo aides appeared around a corner, immersed in technical discussions in their own chirping dialect. When they looked up Max hollered and swung his chain. One Kwackoo gained a new apterium as feathers flew. During the backstroke Max yelled, 'Boo!' at the staring Gubru, who erupted in a squawk of dismay, leaving a cloud of down in its wake.

'With respect,' Max added, addressing the departing avian's backside. One never knew if cameras were recording an event. Gailet had told him it was okay to kill birds, just so long as he was polite about it.

Alarms and sirens were going off on all sides. Max pushed a Kwackoo over, vaulted another, and swept up a new flight of steps. One level up he found a target just too tempting to pass by. A large cart carrying about a ton of delicate photonics parts lay abandoned very near the edge of a loading platform. There was no guardrail to the lifter shaft. Max ignored all the shouts and noise that approached from every side and put his shoulder to the back end. *Move!* he grunted, and the wheeled wagon started forward.

'Hey! He's over this way!' he heard some chim cry out. Max

strained harder, wishing his wounds had not weakened him so. The cart started rolling.

'You! Reb! Stop that!'

There were footsteps, too late, he knew, to prevent inertia from doing its work. The wagon and its load toppled over the edge. *Now to follow it,* Max thought.

But as the command went to his legs they spasmed suddenly. He recognized the agonizing effects of a neural stunning. Recoil spun him about in time to see the gun held by the chim called Irongrip.

Max's hands clenched spastically, as if the Probie's throat were within reach. Desperately, he willed himself to fall backward, into the shaft.

Success! Max felt victory as he plummeted past the landing. The tingling numbness would not last long. *Now! we're even, Fiben,* he thought.

But it wasn't the end after all. Max distantly felt his nerve-numbed arms half yanked out of their sockets as he came up suddenly short. The cuffs around his wrists had torn bleeding rents, and the taut chain led upward past the end of the landing. Through the metal mesh of the platform, Max could see Irongrip straining, holding on with all his might. Slowly, the Probie looked down at him, and smiled.

Max sighed in resignation and closed his eyes.

When he came to his senses Max snorted and pulled away involuntarily from an odious smell. He blinked and blearily made out a mustachioed neo-chimp holding a broken snap-capsule in his hand. From it still emitted noxious fumes.

'Ah, awake again, I see.'

Max felt miserable. Of course he ached all over from the stunning and could barely move. But also his arms and wrists seemed to be burning. They were tied behind him, but he could guess they were probably broken.

'Wh . . . where am I?' he asked.

'You're at the focus of a hyperspace shunt,' Irongrip told him matter-of-factly.

Max spat. 'You're a Goodall-damned liar.'

'Have it your way.' Irongrip shrugged. 'I just figured you deserved an explanation. You see, this machine is a special kind of shunt, what's called an *amplifier*. It's s'pozed to take images out of a brain and make 'em clear for all to see. During the ceremony it'll be under Institute control, but their representatives haven't arrived yet. So today we're going to overload it just a bit as a test.

'Normally the subject's supposed to be cooperative, and the

process is benign. Today though, well, it just isn't going to matter that much.'

A sharp, chirping complaint came from behind Irongrip. Through a narrow hatch could be seen the technicians of the Suzerain of Cost and Caution. 'Time!' the lead Kwackoo snapped. 'Quickly! Make haste!'

'What's your hurry?' Max asked. 'Afraid some of the other Gubru factions may have heard the commotion and be on their way?'

Irongrip looked up from closing the hatch. He shrugged.

'All that means is we've got time to ask just one question. But it'll serve. Just tell us all about Gailet.'

'Never!'

'You won't be able to help it.' Irongrip laughed. 'Ever tried *not* to think about something? You won't be able to avoid thoughts about her. And once it's got somethin' to get a grip on, the machine will rip the rest out of you.'

'You ... you ...' Max struggled for words, but this time they were gone. He writhed, trying to move out of the focus of the massive coiled tubes aimed at him from all sides. But his strength was gone. There was nothing he could do.

Except not think of Gailet Jones. But by trying *not* to, of course, he *was* thinking about her! Max moaned, even as the machines began giving out a low hum in superficial accompaniment. All at once he felt as if the gravitic fields of a hundred starships were playing up and down his skin.

And in his mind a thousand images whirled. More and more of them pictured his former employer and friend.

'No!' Max struggled for an idea. He mustn't try *not* to think of something. What he had to do was find something *else* to contemplate. He had to find something *new* to focus his attention on during the remaining seconds before he was torn apart.

Of course! He let the enemy be his guide. For weeks they had questioned him, asking only about Garthlings, Garthlings, nothing but Garthlings. It had become something of a chant. For him it now became a mantra.

'Where are the pre-sentients?' they had insisted. Max concentrated, and in spite of the pain it just had to make him laugh. 'Of... all th' stupid ... dumb ... idiotic ...'

Contempt for the Galactics filled him. They wanted a projection out of him? Well let them amplify *this*!

Outside, in the mountains and forests, he knew it would be about dawn. He pictured those forests, and the closest thing he could imagine to 'Garthlings,' and laughed at the image he had made.

His last moments were spent guffawing over the idiocy of life.

72

ATHACLENA

The autumn storms had returned again, only this time as a great cyclonic front, rolling down the Valley of the Sind. In the mountains the accelerated winds surged to savage gusts that sloughed the outer leaves from trees and sent them flying in tight eddies. The debris gave shape and substance to whirling devil outlines in the gray sky.

As if in counterpoint, the volcano had begun to grumble as well. Its rumbling complaint was lower, slower in building than the wind, but its tremors made the forest creatures even more nervous as they huddled in their dens or tightly grasped the swaying tree trunks.

Sentience was no certain protection against the gloom. Within their tents, under the mountain's shrouded flanks, the chims clung to each other and listened to the moaning zephyrs. Now and then one would give in to the tension and disappear screaming into the forest, only to return an hour or so later, disheveled and embarrassed, dragging a trail of torn foliage behind him.

The gorillas also were susceptible, but they showed it in other ways. At night they stared up at the billowing clouds with a quiet, focused concentration, sniffling, as if searching for something expectantly. Athaclena could not quite decide what it reminded her of, that evening, but later, in her own tent under the dense forest canopy, she could easily hear their low, atonal singing as they answered the storm.

It was a lullaby that eased her into sleep, but not without a price.

Expectancy ... such a song *would*, of course, beckon back that which had never completely gone away.

Athaclena's head tossed back and forth on her pillow. Her tendrils waved – seeking, repelled, probing, compelled. Gradually, as if in no particular hurry, the familiar essence gathered.

'*Tutsunucann* ...' she breathed, unable to awaken or avoid the inevitable. It formed overhead, fashioned out of that which was not.

'*Tutsunucann, s'ah brannitsun. A'twillith't* ...' A Tymbrimi knew better than to ask for mercy, especially from Ifni's universe. But Athaclena had changed into something that was both more and less than mere Tymbrimi. *Tutsunucann* had allies now. It was joined by visual images, *metaphors*. Its aura of threat was amplified, made

1067

almost palpable, filled out by the added substance of human-style nightmare. ' ... *s'ah brannitsun,* ... ' she sighed, pleading antephialticly in her sleep.

Night winds blew the flaps of her tent, and her dreaming mind fashioned the wings of huge birds. Malevolent, they flew just over the tree tops, their gleaming eyes searching, searching ...

A faint volcanic trembling shook the ground beneath her bedroll, and Athaclena shivered in syncopation, imagining burrowing creatures – the *dead* – the unavenged, wasted Potential of this world – ruined and destroyed by the Bururalli so long ago. They squirmed just underneath the disturbed ground, seeking.

'S'ah brannitsun, tutsunucann!'

The brush of her own waving tendrils felt like the webs and feet of tiny spiders. *Gheer* flux sent tiny gnomes wriggling under her skin, busy fashioning unwilled changes.

Athaclena moaned as the glyph of terrible expectant laughter hovered nearer and regarded her, bent over her, reached down –

'General? Mizz Athaclena. Excuse me, ma'am, are you awake? I'm sorry to disturb you, ser, but – '

The chim stopped. He had pulled aside the tent flap to enter, but now he rocked back in dismay as Athaclena sat up suddenly, eyes wide apart, catlike irises dilated, her lips curled back in a rictus of somnolent fear.

She did not appear to be aware of him. He blinked, staring at the pulsations that coursed slowly, like soliton waves, down her throat and shoulders. Above her agitated tendrils he briefly glimpsed something terrible.

He almost fled right then. It took a powerful effort of courage to swallow instead, to bear down, and to choke forth words.

'M-Ma'am, p-please. It's me ... S-Sammy ... '

Slowly, as if drawn back by the sheerest force of will, the light of awareness returned to those gold-flecked eyes. They closed, reopened. With a tremulous sigh, Athaclena shuddered. Then she collapsed forward.

Sammy stood there, holding her while she sobbed. At that moment, stunned and frightened and astonished, all he could think of was how light and frail she felt in his arms.

'*... That was when Gailet became convinced that any trick, if th' Ceremony was a trick at all, had to be a subtle one.*

'*You see, the Suzerain of Propriety seems to have done a complete about-face regarding chim Uplift. It had started out convinced it would find evidence of mismanagement, and perhaps even cause to take neo-chimps away from humans. But now the Suzerain seemed to be earnest in searchin' out ... in searchin' out appropriate race repre-sentatives ...'*

The voice of Fiben Bolger came from a small playback unit resting on the rough-hewn logs of Athaclena's table. She listened to the recording Robert had sent. The chim's report back at the caves had had its amusing moments. Fiben's irrepressible good nature and dry wit had helped lift Athaclena's limp spirits. Now, though, while relating Dr Gailet Jones's ideas about Gubru intentions, his voice had dropped, and he sounded reticent, almost embarrassed.

Athaclena could feel Fiben's discomfort through the vibrations in the air. Sometimes one did not need another's presence in order to sense their essence.

She smiled at the irony. *He is starting to know who and what he is, and it frightens him.* Athaclena sympathized. A sane being wished for peace and serenity, not to be the mortar in which the ingredients of destiny are finely ground. In her hand she held the locket containing her mother's legacy thread, and her father's. For the moment, at least, *tutsunucann* was held at bay. But Athaclena knew somehow that the glyph had returned for good. There would be no sleep now, no rest until *tutsunucann* changed into something else. Such a glyph was one of the largest known manifestations of quantum mechanics – a probability amplitude that hummed and throbbed in a cloud of uncertainty, pregnant with a thousand million possibilities. Once the wave function collapsed, all that remained would be fate.

'... delicate political maneuverings on so many levels – among the local leaders of th' invasion force, among factions back on the Gubru homeworld, between the Gubru and their enemies and possible allies, between the Gubru and Earth, and among th' various Galactic Institutes ...'

She stroked the locket. Sometimes one does not need another's presence in order to sense their essence.

There was too much complexity here. What did Robert think he would accomplish by sending her this taping? Was she supposed to delve into some vast storehouse of sage Galactic wisdom – or perform some incantation – and somehow come up with a policy to guide them through this? Through *this*?

She sighed. *Oh father, how I must be a disappointment to you.*

The locket seemed to vibrate under her trembling fingers. For some time it seemed that another trance was settling in, drawing her downward into despair.

'...By Darwin, Goodall, and Greenpeace!'

It was the voice of Major Prathachulthorn that jarred her out of it. She listened for a while longer.

'...a target!...'

Athaclena shuddered. So. Things were, indeed, quite dire. All was explained now. Particularly the sudden, gravid insistence of an impatient glyph. When the pellet ran out she turned to her aides, Elayne Soo, Sammy, and Dr de Shriver. The chims watched her patiently.

'I will seek altitude now,' she told them.

'But – but the storm, ma'am. We aren't sure it's passed. And then there's the volcano. We've been talking about an evacuation.'

Athaclena stood up. 'I do not expect to be long. Please send nobody along to guard or look out for me, they will only disturb me and make more difficult what I must do.'

She stopped at the flap of the tent then, feeling the wind push at the fabric as if searching for some gap at which to pry. *Be patient. I am coming.* When she spoke to the chims again, it was in a low voice. 'Please have horses ready for when I return.'

The flap dropped after her. The chims looked at each other, then silently went about preparing for the day.

Mount Fossey steamed in places where the vapor could not be entirely attributed to rising dew. Moist droplets still fell from leaves that shivered in the wind – now waning but still returning now and then in sudden, violent gusts.

Athaclena climbed doggedly up a narrow game trail. She could tell that her wishes were being respected. The chims remained behind, leaving her undisturbed.

The day was beginning with low clouds cutting through the peaks like the vanguards of some aerial invasion. Between them she could see patches of dark blue sky. A human's eyesight might even have picked out a few stubborn stars.

Athaclena climbed for height, but even more for solitude. In the upper reaches the animal life of the forest was even sparser. She sought emptiness.

At one point the trail was clogged with debris from the storm, sheets of some clothlike material that she soon recognized. *Plate ivy parachutes.*

They reminded her. Down in the camp the chim techs had been striving to meet a strict timetable, developing variations on gorilla gut bacteria in time to meet nature's deadline. Now, though, it looked as if Major Prathachulthorn's schedule would not allow Robert's plan to be used.

Such foolishness, Athaclena thought. *How did humans last even this long, I wonder?*

Perhaps they had to be lucky. She had read of their twentieth century, when it seemed more than Ifni's chance that helped them squeeze past near certain doom ... doom not only for themselves but for all future sapient races that might be born of their rich, fecund world. The tale of that narrow escape was perhaps one reason why so many races feared or hated the *k'chu'non*, the wolflings. It was uncanny, and unexplained to this day.

The Earthlings had a saying, 'There, but for the love of God, go I.' The sick, raped paucity of Garth was mild compared to what they might easily have done to Terra.

How many of us would have done better under such circumstances? That was the question that underlay all the smug, superior posturings, and all of the contempt pouring from the great clans. For they had never been tested by the ages of ignorance Mankind suffered. What might it have felt like, to have no patrons, no Library, no ancient wisdom, only the bright flame of mind, unchanneled and undirected, free to challenge the Universe or to consume the world? The question was one few clans dared ask themselves.

She brushed aside the little parachutes. Athaclena edged past the snagged cluster of early spore carriers and continued her ascent, pondering the vagaries of destiny.

At last she came to a stony slope where the southern outlook gave a view of more mountains and, in the far distance, just the faintest possible colored trace of a sloping steppe. She breathed deeply and took out the locket her father had given her.

Growing daylight did not keep away the thing that had begun to form amid her waving tendrils. This time Athaclena did not even try to stop it. She ignored it – always the best thing to do when an observer does not yet want to collapse probability into reality.

Her fingers worked the clasp, the locket opened, and she flipped back the lid.

Your marriage was true, she thought of her parents. For where two threads had formerly lain, now there was only one larger one, shimmering upon the velvety lining.

An end curled around one of her fingers. The locket tumbled to the rocky ground and lay there forgotten as she plucked the other end out of the air. Stretched out, the tendril *hummed*, at first quietly. But she held it tautly in front of her, allowing the wind to stroke it, and she began to hear harmonics. Perhaps she should have eaten, should have built her strength for this thing she was about to attempt. It was something few of her race did even once in their lifetimes. On occasions Tymbrimi had *died* ...

'*A t'ith'tuanoo, Uthacalthing,*' she breathed. And she added her mother's name. '*A t'ith'tuanine, Mathicluanna!*'

The throbbing increased. It seemed to carry up her arms, to resonate against her heartbeat. Her own tendrils responded to the notes and Athaclena began to sway. '*A t'ith'tuanoo, Uthacalthing . . .* '

'It's a beauty, all right. Maybe a few more weeks' work would make it more potent, but this batch will do, an' it'll be ready in time for when the ivy sheds.'

Dr de Shriver put the culture back into its incubator. Their makeshift laboratory on the flanks of the mountain had been sheltered from the winds. The storm had not interfered with the experiments. Now, the fruit of their labors seemed nearly ripe.

Her assistant grumbled, though. 'What's th' use? The Gubru'd just come up with countermeasures. And anyway, the major says the attack is gonna take place before the stuff's ready to be used.'

De Shriver took off her glasses. 'The point is that we keep working until Miss Athaclena tells us otherwise. I'm a civilian. So're you. Fiben and Robert may have to obey the chain of command when they don't like it, but you and I can choose . . .'

Her voice trailed off when she saw that Sammy wasn't listening any longer. He stared over her shoulder. She whirled to see what he was looking at.

If Athaclena had appeared strange, eerie this morning, after her terrifying nightmare, now her features made Dr de Shriver gasp. The disheveled alien girl blinked with eyes narrow and close together in fatigue. She clutched the tent pole as they hurried forward, but when the chims tried to move her to a cot she shook her head.

'No,' she said simply. 'Take me to Robert. Take me to Robert now.'

The gorillas were singing again, their low music without melody. Sammy ran out to fetch Benjamin while de Shriver settled Athaclena into a chair. Not knowing what to do, she spent a few moments brushing leaves and dirt from the young Tymbrimi's ruff. The tendrils of her corona seemed to give off a heavy, fragrant heat that she could feel with her fingers.

And above them, the thing that *tutsunucann* had become made the air seem to ripple even before the eyes of the befuddled chim.

Athaclena sat there, listening to the gorillas' song, and feeling for the first time as if she understood it.

All, all would play their role, she now knew. The chims would not be very happy about what was to come. But that was their problem. Everybody had problems.

'Take me to Robert,' she breathed again.

73

UTHACALTHING

He trembled, standing there with his back to the rising sun, feeling as if he had been sucked as dry as a husk.

Never before had a metaphor felt more appropriate. Uthacalthing blinked, slowly returning to the world ... to the dry steppe facing the looming Mountains of Mulun. All at once it seemed that he was old, and the years lay heavier than ever before.

Deep down, on the *nahakieri* level, he felt a numbness. After all of this, there was no way to tell if Athaclena had even survived the experience of drawing so much into herself.

She must have felt great need, he thought. For the first time his daughter had attempted something neither of her parents could ever have prepared her for. Nor was this something one picked up in school.

'You have returned,' Kault said, matter-of-factly. The Thennanin, Uthacalthing's companion for so many months, leaned on a stout staff and watched him from a few meters away. They stood in the midst of a sea of brown savannah grass, their long shadows gradually shortening with the rising sun.

'Did you receive a message of some sort?' Kault asked. He had the curiosity shared by many total nonpsychics about matters that must seem, to him, quite unnatural.

'I – ' Uthacalthing moistened his lips. But how could he explain that he had not really *received* anything at all? No, what happened was that his daughter had taken him up on an offer he had made, in leaving both his own thread and his dead wife's in her hands. She had called in the debt that parents owe a child for bringing her, unasked, into a strange world.

One should never make an offer without knowing full well what will happen if it is accepted.

Indeed, she drained me dry. He felt as if there was nothing left. And after all that, there was still no guarantee she had even survived the experience. Or that it had left her still sane.

Shall I lie down and die, then? Uthacalthing shivered. *No, I think. Not quite yet.*

'*I* did experience a communion, of sorts,' he told Kault.

'Will the Gubru be able to detect this thing you have done?'

Uthacalthing could not even craft a *palanq* shrug. 'I do not think so. Maybe.' His tendrils lay flat, like human hair. 'I don't know.'

The Thennanin sighed, his breathing slits flapping. 'I wish you would be honest with me, colleague. It pains me to be forced to believe that you are hiding things from me.'

How Uthacalthing had tried and tried to get Kault to utter those words! And now he could not really bring himself to care. 'What do you mean?' he asked.

The Thennanin blew in exasperation. 'I mean that I have begun to suspect that you know more than you are telling me about this fascinating creature I have seen traces of. I warn you, Uthacalthing, I am building a device that will solve this riddle for me. You would be well served to be direct with me before I discover the truth all by myself!'

Uthacalthing nodded. 'I understand your warning. Now, though, perhaps we had better be walking again. If the Gubru did detect what just happened, and come to investigate, we should try to be far from here before they arrive.'

He owed Athaclena that much, still. Not to be captured before she could make use of what she had taken.

'Very well, then,' Kault said. 'We shall speak of this later.'

Without any great interest, more out of habit than for any other reason, Uthacalthing led his companion toward the mountains – in a direction selected – again by habit – by a faint blue twinkling only his eyes could see.

74

GAILET

The new Planetary Branch Library was a beauty. Its beige highlights glistened on a site recently cleared atop Sea Bluff Park, a kilometer south of the Tymbrimi Embassy.

The architecture did not blend as well as the old branch had, into the neo-Fullerite motif of Port Helenia. But it was quite stunning nevertheless – a windowless cube whose pastel shades contrasted well with the nearby chalky, cretaceous outcrops.

Gailet stepped out into a cloud of dry dust as the aircar settled onto the landing apron. She followed her Kwackoo escort up a paved walkway toward the entrance of the towering edifice.

Most of Port Helenia had turned out to watch, a few weeks ago, as a huge freighter the size of a Gubru battleship cruised lazily out of a chalybeous sky and lowered the structure into place. For a large part of the afternoon the sun had been eclipsed while technicians from the Library Institute set the sanctuary of knowledge firmly into place in its new home.

Gailet wondered if the new Library would ever really benefit the citizens of Port Helenia. There were landing pads on all sides, but no provision had been made for groundcar or bicycle or foot access to these bluffs from the town nearby. As she passed through the ornate columned portal, Gailet realized that she was probably the first chim ever to enter the building.

Inside, the vaulted ceiling cast a soft light that seemed to come from everywhere at once. A great ruddy cube dominated the center of the hall, and Gailet knew at once that this was, indeed, an expensive setup. The main data store was many times larger than the old one, a few miles from here. It might even be bigger than Earth's Main Library, where she had done research at La Paz.

But the vastness was mostly empty compared to the constant, round-the-clock bustle she was used to. There were Gubru, of course, and Kwackoo. They stood at study stations scattered about the broad hall. Here and there avians clustered in small groups. Gailet could see their beaks move in sharp jerks, and their feet were constantly in motion as they argued. But no sound at all escaped the muffled privacy zones.

In ribbons and hoods and feather dyes she saw the colors of Propriety, of Accountancy, and of Soldiery. For the most part, each faction kept apart in its own area. There was bristling and some ruffling of down when the follower of one Suzerain passed too close to another.

In one place, however, a multi-hued gaggle of fluttering Gubru displayed that some communication remained among the factions. There was much head ducking and preening and gesturing toward floating holographic displays, all apparently as much ritualistic as based on fact and reason.

As Gailet hurried by, several of the hopping, chattering birds turned to stare at her. Pointing talons and beak gestures made Gailet guess that they knew exactly who she was, and what she was supposed to represent.

She did not hesitate or linger. Gailet's cheeks felt warm.

'Is there any way I can be of service to you, miss?'

At first Gailet thought that what stood at the dais, directly beneath the rayed spiral of the Five Galaxies, was a decorative plant of some sort. When it addressed her, she jumped slightly.

The 'plant' spoke perfect Anglic! Gailet took in the rounded, bulbous foliage, lined with silvery bits which tinkled gently as it moved. The brown trunk led down to knobby rootlets that were mobile, allowing the creature to move in a slow, awkward shuffle.

A Kanten, she realized. *Of course, the Institutes provided a Librarian.*

The vege-sentient Kanten were old friends of Earth. Individual Kanten had advised the Terragens Council since the early days after Contact, helping the wolfling humans weave their way through the complex, tricky jungle of Galactic politics and win their original status as patrons of an independent clan. Nevertheless, Gailet restrained her initial surge of hope. She reminded herself that those who entered the service of the great Galactic Institutes were supposed to forsake all prior loyalties, even to their own lines, in favor of a holier mission. Impartiality was the best she could hope for, here.

'Um, yes,' she said, remembering to bow. 'I want to look up information on Uplift Ceremonies.'

The little bell-like things – probably the being's sensory apparatus – made a chiming that almost sounded *amused*.

'That is a very broad topic, miss.'

She had expected that response and was ready with an answer. Still, it was unnerving talking with an intelligent being without anything even faintly resembling a face. 'I'll start with a simple overview then, if you please.'

'Very well, miss. Station twenty-two is formatted for use by humans and neo-chimpanzees. Please go there and make yourself comfortable. Just follow the blue line.'

She turned and saw a shimmering hologram take form next to her. The blue trail seemed to hang in space, leading around the dais and on toward a far corner of the chamber. 'Thank you,' she said quietly.

As she followed the guide trail she imagined she heard sleigh bells behind her.

Station twenty-two was like a friendly, familiar song. A chair and desk and beanbag sat next to a standard holo-console. There were even well-known versions of datawells and styluses, all neatly arranged on a rack. She sat at the desk gratefully. Gailet had been afraid she would have to stand stiltwise, craning her neck to use a Gubru study station.

As it was, she felt nervous. Gailet hopped slightly as the display came alight with a slight 'pop.' Anglic text filled the central space. PLEASE ASK FOR ADJUSTMENTS ORALLY. REQUESTED REMEDIAL SURVEY WILL BEGIN AT YOUR SIGNAL.

'Remedial survey ...' Gailet muttered. But yet, it would be best to begin at the simplest level. Not only would it guarantee that she had not forgotten some vital fundamental, but it would tell her what the Galactics themselves considered most basic.

'Proceed,' she said.

The side displays came alight with pictures, displaying images of faces, the faces of other beings on worlds far away in both space and time.

'When nature brings forth a new pre-sentient race, all Galactic society rejoices. For it is then that the adventure of Uplift is about to begin ...'

Soon the old patterns reasserted themselves. Gailet swam easily into the flow of information, drinking from the font of knowledge. Her datawell filled with notes and cross-references. Soon she lost all sense of the passage of time.

Food appeared on the desktop without Gailet ever becoming aware of how it arrived. A nearby enclosure took care of her other needs, when nature's call grew too insistent to ignore.

During some periods of Galactic history, Uplift Ceremonies have been almost purely ceremonial. Patron species have been responsible for declaring their clients suitable, and their word was simply accepted that their charges were ready. There have been other epochs, however, in which the role of the Uplift Institute has been much stronger, such as during the Sumubulum Meritocracy, when the entire process was under direct Institution supervision in all cases.

The present era falls somewhere in between these extremes, featuring patron responsibility but with medium to extensive Institute involvement. The latter participation has increased since a rash of Uplift failures forty to sixty thousand GYUs ago* resulted in several severe and embarrassing ecological holocausts (Ref: Gl'kahesh, Bururalli, Sstienn, Muhurn8.) Today the patron of a client cannot vouch alone for its client's development. It must allow close observation by the client's Stage Consort, and by the Uplift Institute.

Uplift Ceremonies are now more than perfunctory celebrations. They serve two other major purposes. First, they allow representatives from the client race to be tested – under rigorous and stressful circumstances – to satisfy the Institute that the race is ready to assume the rights and duties appropriate to the next Stage. Also, the ceremony allows the client race an opportunity to choose a new consort for the subsequent Stage, to watch over it and, if necessary, to intercede on its behalf.

*GYU = Galactic year unit (approximately fourteen Earth months)

The criteria used in testing depend upon the level of development the client race has reached. Among other important factors are phagocity type (e.g., carnivore, herbivore, autophagic, or ergogenic), modality of movement (e.g., bipedal or quadrupedal walker, amphibious, roller, or sessile), mental technique (e.g., associative, extrapolative, intuitive, holographic, or nulutative) . . .

Slowly she worked her way through the 'remedial' stuff. It was fairly heavy plodding. This Library branch would need some new translation routines if the chim-on-the-street in Port Helenia was going to be able to use the vast storehouse of knowledge. Assuming Joe and Jane Chim ever got the opportunity.

Nevertheless, it was a wonderful edifice – far, far greater than the miserable little branch they'd had before. And unlike back at La Paz, there was not the perpetual hustle and bustle of hundreds, thousands of frantic users, waving priority slips and arguing over access timeslots. Gailet felt as if she could just sink into this place for months, years, drinking and drinking knowledge until it leaked out through her very pores.

For instance, here was a reference to how special arrangements were made to allow Uplift among machine cultures. And there was one brief, tantalizing paragraph about a race of *hydrogen breathers* which had seceded from that mysterious parallel civilization and actually applied for membership in Galactic society. She ached to follow that and many other fascinating leads, but Gailet knew she simply did not have the time. She had to concentrate on the rules regarding bipedal, warm-blooded, omnivorous Stage Two clients with mixed mental faculties, and even that made for a daunting reading list.

Narrow it down, she thought. So she tried to focus on ceremonies which take place under contention or in time of war. Even under those constraints she found it hard slogging. Everything was all so complicated! It made her despair over the shared ignorance of her people and clan.

. . . whether an agreement of co-participation is or is not made in advance, it can and shall be verified by the Institutes in a manner taking into account methods of adjudication considered traditional by the two or more parties involved . . .

Gailet did not recall felling asleep on the beanbag. But for some time it was a raft, floating upon a dim sea which rocked to the rhythm of her breathing. After a while, mists seemed to close in, coalescing into a black and white dreamscape of vaguely threatening shapes. She saw contorted images of the dead, her parents, and poor Max.

'Mm-mm, no,' she muttered. At one point she jerked sharply. 'No!'

She started to rise, began to emerge from slumber. Her eyes fluttered, fragments of dreams clinging in shreds to the lids. A *Gubru* seemed to hover overhead, holding a mysterious device, like those which had probed and peered at her and Fiben. But the image wavered and fell apart as the avian pressed a button on the machine. She slumped back, the Gubru image rejoining the many others in her disturbed sleep.

The dream state passed and her breathing settled into the slow cycle of deep somnolence.

She only awoke sometime later, when she dimly sensed a hand stroke her leg. Then it seized her ankle and pulled hard.

Gailet's breath caught as she sat up quickly, before she could even bring her eyes to focus. Her heart raced. Then vision cleared and she saw that a rather large chim squatted beside her. His hand still rested on her leg, and his grin was instantly recognizable. The waxed handlebar mustache was only the most superficial of many attributes she had come to detest.

So suddenly drawn out of sleep, she had to take a moment to find speech again. 'Wh ... what are *you* doing here?' she asked acerbically, yanking her leg away from his grasp.

Irongrip looked amused. 'Now, is that the way to say hello to someone as important as I am to you?'

'You do serve your purpose well,' she admitted. 'As a bad example!' Gailet rubbed her eyes and sat up. 'You didn't answer my question. Why are you bothering me? Your incompetent Probies aren't in charge of guarding anybody anymore.'

The chen's expression soured only slightly. Obviously he was relishing something. 'Oh, I just figured I ought to come on down to th' Library and do some studying, just like you.'

'*You*, studying? Here?' She laughed. 'I had to get special permission from the Suzerain. *You're* not even supposed – '

'Now those were the exact words I was about to use,' he interrupted.

Gailet blinked. 'What?'

'I mean, I was gonna tell you that the Suzerain told me to come down here and study with you. After all, partners ought to get to know each other well, especially before they step forward together as race-representatives.'

Gailet's breath drew in audibly. 'You ... ?' Her head whirled. 'I don't believe you!'

Irongrip shrugged. 'You needn't sound so surprised. My genetic scores are in the high nineties almost across the board ... except in two or three little categories that shouldn't ever have counted in the first place.'

That Gailet could believe easily enough. Irongrip was obviously clever and resourceful, and his aberrant strength could only be considered an asset by the Uplift Board. But sometimes the price was just too great to pay. 'All that means is that your loathsome qualities must be even worse than I had imagined.'

The chen rocked back and laughed. 'Oh, by human standards, I suppose you're right,' he agreed. 'By those criteria, most Probationers *shouldn't* be allowed anywhere near chimmies and children! Still standards change. And now I have the opportunity to set a new style.'

Gailet felt a chill. It was just sinking in what Irongrip was driving at.

'You're a liar!'

'Admitted, *mea culpa*.' He pretended to beat his breast. 'But I'm not lying about being in the testing party, along with a few of my fellow donner boys. There've been some changes, you see, since your little mama's boy and teacher's pet ran off into the jungle with our Sylvie.'

Gailet wanted to spit. 'Fiben's ten times the chen you are, you, you atavistic mistake! The Suzerain of Propriety would never choose *you* as his replacement!'

Irongrip grinned and raised a finger. 'Aha. *There's* where we misunderstand each other. You see we've been talking about different birds, you and I.'

'Different ...' Gailet gasped. Her hand covered the open collar of her shirt. 'Oh Goodall!'

'You get it,' he said, nodding. 'Smart, aristophrenic little monkey you are.'

Gailet slumped. What surprised her most was the depth of her mourning. At that moment she felt as if her heart had been torn out.

We were pawns all along, she thought. *Oh, poor Fiben!*

This explained why Fiben had not been brought back the evening he took off with Sylvie. Or the next day, or the next. Gailet had been so *sure* that the 'escape' would turn out to have been just another propriety and intelligence test.

But clearly it wasn't. It had to have been arranged by one or both of the other Gubru commanders, perhaps as a way to weaken the Suzerain of Propriety. And what better way to do that than by robbing it of one of its most carefully chosen chim 'race-representatives.' The theft couldn't even be pinned on anybody, for no body would ever be found.

Of course the Gubru would have to go ahead with the ceremony. It was too late to recall the invitations. But each of the three Suzerains might prefer to see different outcomes.

Fiben . . .

'So, professor? Where do we start? You can start teaching me how to act like a proper white card now.'

She closed her eyes and shook her head. 'Go away,' she said. 'Just please go away.'

There were more words, more sarcastic comments. But she blocked them out behind a numbing curtain of pain. Tears, at least, she managed to withhold until she sensed that he was gone. Then she burrowed into the soft bag as if it was her mother's arms, and wept.

75

GALACTICS

The two danced around the pedestal, puffing and cooing. Together they chanted in perfect harmony.

> *'Come down, come down,*
> *down, come down!*
> *Come down off your perch.*
>
> *'Join us, join us,*
> *– us, join us,*
> *Join us in consensus!'*

The Suzerain of Propriety shivered, fighting the changes. They were completely united in opposition now. The Suzerain of Cost and Caution had given up hope of achieving the prized position – and was supporting the Suzerain of Beam and Talon in its bid for dominance. Caution's objective was now second place – the male Molt-status.

Two out of three had agreed then. But in order to achieve their objectives, both sexual and in policy, they had to bring the Suzerain of Propriety down off its perch. They had to force it to step onto the soil of Garth.

The Suzerain of Propriety fought them, squawking well-timed counterpoint to disrupt their rhythm and inserting pronouncements of logic to foil their arguments.

A proper Molt was not supposed to go this way. This was coercion, not true consensus. This was rape.

For this the Roost Masters had not invested so much hope in the

Triumvirate. They needed policy. Wisdom. The other two seemed to have forgotten this. They wanted to take the easy way out with the Uplift Ceremony. They wanted to make a terrible gamble in defiance of the Codes.

If only the first Suzerain of Cost and Caution had lived! The priest mourned. Sometimes one only knew the value of another after that one was gone, gone.

> *'Come, down come down,*
> *Down off your perch.'*

Against their united voice it was only a matter of time, of course. Their unison pierced through the wall of honor and resolve the priest had built around itself and penetrated down to the realm of hormone and instinct. The Molt hung suspended, held back by the recalcitrance of one member, but it would not be forestalled forever.

> *'Come down and join us.*
> *Join us in consensus!'*

The Suzerain of Propriety shuddered and held on. How much longer it could do so, it did not know.

76

THE CAVES

'Clennie!' Robert shouted joyfully. When he saw the mounted figures come around a bend in the trail he nearly dropped his end of the missile he and a chim were carrying out of the caves.

'Hey! Watchit with that thing, you ... captain.' One of Prathachulthorn's Marine corporals corrected himself at the last second. In recent weeks they had begun treating Robert with more respect – he'd been earning it – but on occasion the noncoms still showed their fundamental contempt for anyone non-Corps.

Another chim worker hurried up and easily lifted the nose cone out of Robert's grasp, looking disgusted that a human should even *try* lifting things.

Robert ignored both insults. He ran to the trailhead just as the band of travelers arrived and caught the halter of Athaclena's horse. His other hand reached out for her.

'Clennie, I'm glad you ...' His voice faltered for an instant. Even as she squeezed his hand he blinked and tried to cover up his discomfiture. '... um, I'm glad you could come.'

Athaclena's smile was unlike any he remembered her ever wearing before, and there was sadness in her aura that he had never *kenned*.

'Of course I came, Robert.' She smiled. 'Could you ever doubt I would?'

He helped her dismount. Underneath her superficial air of control he could feel her tremble. *Love, you have gone through changes.* As if she sensed his thought, she reached up and touched the side of his face. 'There are a few ideas shared by both Galactic society and yours, Robert. In both, sages have spoken of life as being something like a wheel.'

'A wheel?'

'Yes.' Her eyes glittered. 'It turns. It moves forward. And yet it remains the same.'

With a sense of relief he felt *her* again. Underneath the changes she was still Athaclena. 'I missed you,' he said.

'And I, you.' She smiled. 'Now tell me about this major and his plans.'

Robert paced the floor of the tiny storage chamber, stacked to the overhead stalactites with supplies. 'I can argue with him. I can try persuasion. Hell, he doesn't even mind if I yell at him, so long as it's in private, and so long as after all the debate is over I still leap two meters when he says "Jump."' Robert shook his head. 'But I can't actively obstruct him, Clennie. Don't ask me to break my oath.'

Robert obviously felt caught between conflicting loyalties. Athaclena could sense his tension.

His arm still in a sling, Fiben Bolger watched them argue, but he kept his silence for the time being.

Athaclena shook her head. 'Robert, I explained to you that what Major Prathachulthorn has planned is likely to prove disastrous.'

'Then tell *him*!'

Of course she had tried, over dinner that very evening. Prathachulthorn had listened courteously to her careful explanation of the possible consequences of attacking the Gubru ceremonial site. His expression had been indulgent. But when she had finished, he only asked one question. Would the assault be considered one against the Earthlings' legitimate enemy, or against the Uplift Institute itself.

'After the delegation from the Institute arrives, the site becomes their property,' she had said. 'An attack then would be catastrophic for humanity.'

'But *before* then?' he had asked archly.

Athaclena had shaken her head irritably. 'Until then the Gubru still own the site. But it's not a military site! It was built for what might be called holy purposes. The propriety of the act, without handling it just right...'

It had gone on for some time, until it became clear that all argument would be useless. Prathachulthorn promised to take her opinions into account, ending the matter. They all knew what the Marine officer thought of taking advice from 'E.T. children.'

'We'll send a message to Megan,' Robert suggested.

'I believe you have already done that,' Athaclena answered.

He scowled, confirming her guess. Of course it violated all protocol to go over Prathachulthorn's head. At minimum it would seem like a spoiled boy crying to mama. It might even be a court-martial offense.

That he had done so proved that it wasn't out of fear for himself that Robert was reticent about directly opposing his commander, but out of loyalty to his sworn oath.

Indeed, he was right. Athaclena respected his honor.

But I am not ruled by the same duty, she thought. Fiben, who had been silent so for, met her gaze. He rolled his eyes expressively. About Robert they were in complete agreement.

'I already suggested to th' major that knocking out the ceremonial site might actually be doin' the enemy a favor. After all, they built it to use it on Garthlings. Whatever their scheme with us chims, it's probably a last ditch effort to make up some of their losses. Rut what if th' site is insured? We blow it up, they blame us and collect?'

'Major Prathachulthorn mentioned your idea about that.' Athaclena said to Fiben. 'I find it acute, but I'm afraid he did not credit it as very likely.'

'Y'mean he thought it was a cuckoo pile of apeshi—'

He stopped as they heard footsteps on the cool stone outside. 'Knock knock!' A feminine voice said from beyond the curtain. 'May I come in?'

'Please do, Lieutenant McCue,' Athaclena said. 'We were nearly finished anyway.' The dusky-skinned human woman entered and sat on one of the crates next to Robert. He gave her a faint smile but soon was staring down at his hands again. The muscles in his arms rippled and tensed as his fists clenched and unclenched.

Athaclena felt a twinge when McCue placed her hand on Robert's knee and spoke to him. 'His nibs wants another battle-planning conference before we all turn in.' She turned to look at Athaclena and smiled. Her head inclined. 'You're welcome to attend should you wish. You're our respected guest, Athaclena.'

Athaclena recalled when she had been the mistress of these caverns and had commanded an army. *I must not let that influence me,* she reminded herself. All that mattered now was to see that these creatures harmed themselves as little as possible in the coming days.

And, if at all possible, she was dedicated to furthering a certain jest. One that she, herself, still barely understood, but had recently come to appreciate.

'No, thank you, lieutenant. I think that I shall go say hello to a few of my chim friends and then retire. It was a long several days' ride.'

Robert glanced back at her as he left with his human lover. Over his head a metaphorical cloud seemed to hover, flickering with lightning strokes. *I did not know you could do that with glyphs,* Athaclena wondered. Every day, it seemed, one learned something new.

Fiben's loose, unhinged grin was a boost as he followed the humans. Did she catch a sense of something from him? A conspiratorial wink?

When they were gone, Athaclena started rummaging through her kit. *I am not bound by their duty,* she reminded herself. *Or by their laws.*

The caves could get quite dark, especially when one extinguished the solitary glow bulb that illuminated an entire stretch of the hallway. Down here eyesight was not an advantage, but a Tymbrimi corona gave quite an edge.

Athaclena crafted a small squadron of simple but special glyphs. The first one had the sole purpose of darting ahead of her and to the sides, scouting out a path through the blackness. Since cold, hard matter was searing to that which was not, it was easy to tell where the walls and obstacles lay. The little wisp of nothing avoided them adroitly.

Another glyph spun overhead, reaching forth to make certain that no one was aware of an intruder in these lower levels. There were no chims sleeping in this stretch of hallway, which had been set aside for human officers.

Lydia and Robert were out on patrol. That left only one aura beside hers in this part of the cave. Athaclena stepped toward it carefully.

The third glyph silently gathered strength, awaiting its turn.

Slowly, silently, she padded over the packed dung of a thousand generations of flying insectivore creatures who had dwelt here until being ousted by Earthlings and their noise. She breathed evenly, counting in the silent human fashion to help maintain the discipline of her thoughts.

Keeping three watchful glyphs up at once was something she'd not have attempted only a few days ago. Now it seemed easy, natural, as if she had done it hundreds of times.

She had ripped this and so many other skills away from Uthacalthing, using a technique seldom spoken of among the Tymbrimi, and even less often tried.

Turning jungle fighter, trysting with a human, and now this. Oh, my classmates would be amazed.

She wondered if her father retained any of the craft she had so rudely taken from him.

Father, you and mother arranged this long ago. You prepared me without my even knowing it. Did you already know, even then, that it would be necessary some day?

Sadly, she suspected she had taken away more than Uthacalthing could afford to spare. *And yet, it is not enough.* There were huge gaps. In her heart she felt certain that this thing encompassing worlds and species could not reach its conclusion without her father himself.

The scout glyph hovered before a hanging strip of cloth. Athaclena approached, unable to see the covering, even after she touched it with her fingertips. The scout unraveled and melted back into the waving tendrils of her corona.

She brushed the cloth aside with deliberate slowness and crept into the small side chamber. The watch glyph sensed no sign that anyone was aware within. She only *kenned* the steady rhythms of human slumber.

Major Prathachulthorn did not snore, of course. And his sleep was light, vigilant. She stroked the edges of his ever-present psi-shield, which guarded his thoughts, dreams, and military knowledge.

Their soldiers are good, and getting better, she thought. Over the years Tymbrimi advisors had worked hard to teach their wolfling allies to be fierce Galactic warriors. And the Tymbrimi, in truth, often came away having learned some fascinating bits of trickery themselves, ideas that could never have been imagined by a race brought up under Galactic culture.

But of all Earth's services, the Terragens Marines used no alien advisors. They were anachronisms, the *true* wolflings.

The glyph *z'schutan* cautiously approached the slumbering human. It settled down, and Athaclena saw it metaphorically as a globe of liquid metal. It *touched* Prathachulthorn's psi-shield and slid in golden rivulets over it, swiftly coating it under a fine sheen.

Athaclena breathed a little easier. Her hand slipped into her pocket and withdrew a glassy ampule. She stepped closer and carefully knelt next to the cot. As she brought the vial of anesthetic gas near the sleeping man's face, her fingers tensed.

'I wouldn't,' he said, casually.

Athaclena gasped. Before she could move his hands darted out, catching her wrists! In the dim light all she could see were the whites of his eyes. Although he was awake his psi-shield remained undisturbed, still radiating waves of slumber. She realized that it had been a phantasm all along, a carefully fabricated trap!

'You Eatees just have to *keep* on underrating us, don't you? Even you smarty-pants Tymbrimi never seem to get it.'

Gheer hormones surged. Athaclena heaved and pulled to get free, but it was like trying to escape a metal vice. Her clawed nails scratched, but he nimbly kept her fingers out of reach of his callused hands. When she tried to roll aside and kick he deftly applied slight pressure to her arms, using them as levers to keep her on her knees. The force made her groan aloud. The gas pellet tumbled from her limp hand.

'You see,' Prathachulthorn said in an amiable voice, 'there are some of us who think it's a mistake to compromise at all. What can we accomplish by trying to turn ourselves into good Galactic citizens?' he sneered. 'Even if it worked, we'd only become horrors, awful things totally divorced from what it means to be human. Anyway, that option isn't even open. They won't let us become citizens. The deck is stacked. The dice are loaded. We both know that, don't we?'

Athaclena's breath came in ragged gasps. Long after it was clearly useless, the *gheer* flux kept her jerking and fighting against the human's incredible strength. Agility and quickness were to no avail against his reflexes and training.

'We have our secrets, you know,' Prathachulthorn confided. 'Things we do not tell our Tymbrimi friends, or even most of our own people. Would you like to know what they are? Would you?'

Athaclena could not find the breath to answer. Prathachulthorn's eyes held something feral, almost animally fierce.

'Well, if I told you some of them it would be your death sentence,' he said. 'And I'm not ready to decide that quite yet. So I'll tell you one fact some of your people already know.'

In an instant he had transferred both of her wrists to one hand. The other sought and found her throat.

'You see, we Marines are also taught how to disable, and even kill, members of an allied Eatee race. Would you like to know how long it will take me to render you unconscious, miss? Tell you what. Why don't you start counting?'

Athaclena heaved and bucked, but it was useless. A painful

pressure closed in around her throat. Air started getting thick. Distantly, she heard Prathachulthorn mutter to himself.

'This universe is a goddam awful place.'

She would never have imagined it could get blacker, but an even deeper darkness started closing in. Athaclena wondered if she would ever awaken again. *I'm sorry, father.* She expected those to be her last thoughts.

Continued consciousness came as something of a surprise then. The pressure on her throat, still painful, eased ever so slightly. She sucked a narrow stream of air and tried to figure out what was happening. Prathachulthorn's arms were quivering. She could tell he was bearing down hard, but somehow the force wasn't arriving!

Her overheated corona was no help. It was in total ignorance and amazement – when Prathachulthorn's grip loosened – that she dropped limply to the floor.

The *human* was breathing hard, now. There were grunts of exertion, and then a crash as the cot toppled over. A water pitcher shattered and there was a sound like that a datawell would make, getting smashed.

Athaclena felt something under her hand. *The ampule,* she realized. But what had happened to Prathachulthorn?

Fighting enzyme exhaustion, she crawled in a random direction until her hand came down upon the broken datawell. By accident her fingers brushed the power switch, and the rugged machine's screen spilled forth a dim luminescence.

In that glow, Athaclena saw a stark tableau ... the human mel straining – his powerful muscles bulged and sinewy – against two long brown arms that held him from behind.

Prathachulthorn bucked and hissed. He threw his weight left and right. But every effort to get free was to no avail. Athaclena saw a pair of brown eyes over the man's shoulder. She hesitated for only a moment, then hurried forward with the ampule.

Now Prathachulthorn had no psi-shield. His hatred was open for all to *kenn* if they had the power. He heaved desperately as she brought forward the little cylinder and broke it under his nose.

'He's holdin' his breath,' the neo-chimpanzee muttered as the cloud of blue vapor hovered around the man's nostrils, then slowly fell groundward.

'That is all right,' Athaclena answered. From her pocket she drew forth ten more.

When he saw them, Prathachulthorn let out a faint sigh. He redoubled his efforts to get away, but all it served to was to bring closer the moment when he would. finally have to breathe. The man was stubborn. It took five minutes, and even then Athaclena suspected he had fainted of anoxia before he ever felt the drug.

'Some guy,' Fiben said when he finally let go. 'Goodall, they make them Marines strong.' He shuddered and collapsed next to the unconscious man.

Athaclena sat limply across from him.

'Thank you, Fiben,' she said quietly.

He shrugged. 'Hell, what's treason an' assault on a patron? All in a day's work.'

She indicated his sling, where his left arm had rested ever since the evening of his escape from Port Helenia. 'Oh, this?' Fiben grinned. 'Well, I guess I have been milking the sympathy a bit. Please don't tell anybody, okay?'

Then, in a more serious mood, he looked down at Prathachulthorn. 'I may not be any expert. But I'll bet I didn't win any points with th' old Uplift Board, tonight.'

He glanced up at Athaclena, then smiled faintly. In spite of everything she had been through, she found she could not help but find everything suddenly *hilarious*.

She found herself laughing – quietly, but with her father's rich tones. Somehow, that did not surprise her at all.

The job wasn't over. Wearily, Athaclena had to follow as Fiben carried the unconscious human through the dim tunnels. As they tiptoed past Prathachulthorn's dozing corporal, Athaclena reached out with her tender, almost limp tendrils and soothed the Marine's slumber. He mumbled and rolled over on his cot. Especially wary now, Athaclena made doubly sure the man's psi-shield was no ruse, that he actually slept soundly.

Fiben puffed, his lips curled back in a grimace as she led him over a tumbled slope of debris from an ancient landslide and into a side passage that was almost certainly unknown to the Marines. At least it wasn't on the cave map she had accessed earlier today from the rebel database.

Fiben's aura was pungent each time he stubbed his toes in the dim, twisting climb. No doubt he wanted to mutter imprecations over Prathachulthorn's dense weight. But he kept his comments within until they emerged at last into the humid, silent night.

'Sports an' mutations!' he sighed as he laid his burden down. 'At least Prathachulthorn isn't one of th' tall ones. I couldn't've managed with his hands and feet dragging in the dust all the way.'

He sniffed the air. There was no moon, but a fog spilled over the nearby cliffs like a vaporous flood, and it gave off a faint lambience. Fiben glanced back at Athaclena. 'So? Now what, chief? There's gonna be a hornet's nest here in a few hours, especially after Robert and that Lieutenant McCue get back. Do you want I should go get Tycho and haul away this bad example to Earthling clients for you? It'll mean deserting, but what the hell, I guess I was never a very good soldier.'

Athaclena shook her head. She sought with her corona and found the traces she was looking for. 'No, Fiben. I could not ask that of you. Besides, you have another task. You escaped from Port Helenia in order to warn us of the Gubru offer. Now you must return there and face your destiny.'

Fiben frowned. 'Are you sure? You don't need me?'

Athaclena brought her hands over her mouth. She trilled the soft call of a night bird. From the darkness downslope there came a faint reply. She turned back to Fiben. 'Of course I do. We all need you. But where you can do the most good is down there, near the sea. I also sense that you want to go back.'

Fiben pulled at his thumbs. 'Gotta be crazy, I guess.

She smiled. 'No. It is only one more indicator that the Suzerain of Propriety knew its business in choosing you ... even though it might prefer that you showed a little more respect to your patrons.'

Fiben tensed. Then he seemed to sense some of her irony. He smiled. There was the soft clattering of horses' hooves on the trail below. 'All right,' he said as he bent over to pick up the limp form of Major Prathachulthorn. 'Come on, papa. This time I'll be as gentle as I would with my own maiden aunt.' He smacked his lips against the Marine's shadowed cheek and looked up at Athaclena.

'Better, ma'am?'

Something she had borrowed from her father made her tired tendrils fizz. 'Yes, Fiben.' She laughed. 'That's much better.'

Lydia and Robert had their suspicions when they returned by the dawn's light to find their legal commander missing. The remaining Terragens Marines glared at Athaclena in open distrust. A small band of chims had gone through Prathachulthorn's room, cleaning away all signs of struggle before any humans got there, but they couldn't hide the fact that Prathachulthorn had gone without a note or any trace.

Robert even ordered Athaclena restricted to her chamber, with a Marine at the door, while they investigated. His relief over a likely delay in the planned attack was momentarily suppressed under an outraged sense of duty. In comparison, Lieutenant McCue was an eddy of calm. Outwardly, she seemed unconcerned, as if the major had merely stepped out. Only Athaclena could sense the Earth woman's underlying confusion and conflict.

In any event, there was nothing they could do about it. Search parties were sent out. They caught up with a party of Athaclena's chims returning on horseback to the gorilla refuge. But by that time Prathachulthorn was no longer with them. He was high in the trees, being passed from one forest giant to another, by now conscious and fuming, but helpless and trussed up like a mummy.

It was a case of humans paying the penalty for their 'liberalism.' They had brought up their clients to be individualists and citizens, so it was possible for chims to rationalize imprisoning one man for the good of all. In his own way Prathachulthorn had helped to bring this about, with his patronizing, deprecating attitudes. Nevertheless, Athaclena was certain the Marine would be delicately, carefully treated.

That evening, Robert chaired a new council of war. Athaclena's vague status of house arrest was modified so could attend. Fiben and the chim brevet lieutenants were present, as well as the Marine noncommissioned officers.

Neither Lydia nor Robert brought up going ahead with Prathachulthorn's plan. It was tacitly assumed that the major wouldn't want it put under way without him.

'Maybe he went off on a personal scouting trip, or snap inspection of some outpost. He might return tonight or tomorrow,' Elayne Soo suggested in complete innocence.

'Maybe. We'd best assume the worst, though,' Robert said, He avoided looking at Athaclena. 'Just in case, we'd better send word to the refuge. I suppose it'll take ten days or so to get new orders from the Council, and for them to send a replacement.'

He obviously assumed that Megan Oneagle would never leave him in charge.

'Well, I want to go back to Port Helenia,' Fiben said simply. 'I'm in a position to get close to the center of things. And anyway, Gailet needs me.'

'What makes you think the Gubru will take you back, after running away?' Lydia McCue asked. 'Why won't they simply shoot your'

Fiben shrugged. 'If I meet up with the wrong Gubru, that's what they'll probably do.'

There was a long silence. When Robert asked for other suggestions, the humans and remaining chims remained silent. At least when Prathachulthorn had been here, dominating the discourse and the mood, there had been his overbearing confidence to override their doubts. Now their situation came home to them again. They were a tiny army with only limited options. And the enemy was about to set into motion things and events they could not even understand, let alone prevent.

Athaclena waited until the atmosphere was thick with gloom. Then she said four words. 'We need my father.'

To her surprise, both Robert and Lydia nodded. Even when orders finally arrived from the Council-in-Exile, those instructions would likely be as confused and contradictory as ever. It was obvious that they could use good advice, especially with matters of Galactic diplomacy at stake.

At least the McCue woman does not share Prathachulthorn's xenophobia, Athaclena thought. She found herself forced to admit that she approved of what she *kenned* of the Earthling female's aura.

'Robert told me you were sure your father was alive.' Lydia said. 'That's fine. But where is he? How can we find him?'

Athaclena leaned forward. She kept her corona still. 'I know where he is.'

'You do?' Robert blinked. 'But ...' His voice trailed off as he reached out to touch her with his inner sense, for the first time since yesterday. Athaclena recalled how she felt then, seeing him holding Lydia's hand. She momentarily resisted his efforts. Then, feeling foolish, she let go.

Robert sat back heavily and exhaled. He blinked several times. 'Oh.' That was all he said.

Now Lydia looked back and forth, from Robert to Athaclena and back again. Briefly, she shone with something faintly like envy.

I, too, have him in a way that you cannot, Athaclena mused. But mostly, she shared the moment with Robert.

' ... N'tah'hoo, Uthacalthing,' he said in GalSeven. 'We had better do something, and fast.'

77

FIBEN AND SYLVIE

She awaited him as he led Tycho up the trail emerging out of the Valley of Caves. She sat patiently next to an overhanging fip pine, just beyond a switchback, and only spoke when he drew even. 'Thought you'd just sneak out without saying goodbye, did you?' Sylvie asked. She wore a long skirt and kept her arms wrapped around her knees.

He tied the horse's tether to a tree limb and sat down next to her. 'Nah,' Fiben said. 'I knew I wouldn't be so lucky.'

She glanced at him sidelong and saw that he was grinning. Sylvie sniffed and looked back into the canyon, where the early mists were slowly evaporating into a morning that promised to be clear and cloudless. 'I figured you'd be heading back.'

'I have to, Sylvie. It's – '

She cut him off. 'I know. Responsibility. You have to get back to Gailet. She needs you, Fiben.'

He nodded. Fiben didn't have to be reminded that he still had a duty to Sylvie as well. 'Um. Dr Soo came by, while I was packing. I ...'

'You filled the bottle she gave you. I know.' Sylvie bowed her head. 'Thank you. I consider myself well paid.'

Fiben looked down. He felt awkward, talking around the edges of the topic like this. 'When will you – '

'Tonight, I guess. I'm ready. Can't you tell?'

Sylvie's parka and long skirt certainly hid any outward signs. Still, she was right. Her scent was undisguised. 'I sincerely hope you get what you want, Sylvie.'

She nodded again. They sat there awkwardly. Fiben tried to think of something to say. But he felt thick headed, stupid. Whatever he tried, he knew, would surely turn out all wrong.

Suddenly there was a small rustle of motion down below, where the switchbacks diverged into paths leading in several directions. A tall human form emerged around a rocky bend, jogging tirelessly. Robert Oneagle ran toward a junction in the narrow trails, carrying only his bow and a light backpack.

He glanced upward, and on spotting the two chims he slowed. Robert grinned in response as Fiben waved, but on reaching the fork he turned southward, along a little-used track. Soon he had disappeared into the wild forest.

'What's he doing?' Sylvie asked.

'Looked like he was running.'

She slapped his shoulder. 'I could see that. Where is he *going*?'

'He's gonna try to make it through the passes before it snows.'

'Through the *passes*? But – '

'Since Major Prathachulthorn disappeared, and since time is so short, Lieutenant McCue and th' other Marines agreed they'd go along with the alternative plan Robert and Athaclena have cooked up.'

'But he's running south,' Sylvie said. Robert had taken the little-used trail that led deeper into the Mulun range.

Fiben nodded. 'He's going looking for somebody. He's the only one who can do the job.' It was obvious to Sylvie from his tone that that was all he would say about the matter.

They sat there for a little while longer in silence. At least Robert's brief passage had brought a welcome break in the tension. *This is silly,* Fiben thought. He liked Sylvie, a lot. They had never had much chance to talk, and this might be their last opportunity.

'You never ... you never did tell me about your first baby,' he said in a rush, wondering, as the words came out, if it was any of his business to ask.

Of course it was obvious that Sylvie had given birth before, and nursed. Stretch marks were signs of attractiveness in a race a quarter of whose females never bred at all. *But there is pain there as well,* he knew.

'It was five years ago. I was very young.' Her voice was level, controlled. 'His name was – we called him Sichi. He was tested by the Board, as usual, but he was found ... "anomalous."'

'Anomalous?'

'Yes, that was the word they used. They classified him superior in some respects ... "odd" in others. There were no obvious defects, but some "strange" qualities, they said. A couple of the officials were concerned. The Uplift Board decided they'd have to send him to Earth for further evaluation.

'They were very nice about it.' She sniffed. 'They offered me the choice of coming along.'

Fiben blinked. 'You didn't go, though.'

She glanced at him. 'I know what you're thinking. I'm terrible. That's why I never told you before. You'd have refused our deal. You think I'm an unfit mother.'

'No, I – '

'At the time it seemed different, though. My mother was ill. We didn't have a clan-family, and I didn't feel I could just leave her in the care of strangers, an' probably never see her again.

'I was only a yellow card at the time. I knew my child would get a good home on Earth or ... Either he'd find favored treatment and be raised in a high-caste neo-chimp home or he'd meet a fate I didn't want to know. I was so worried we would go all that way and they would only take him away anyway. I guess I also dreaded the shame if he was declared a Probationer.'

She stared down at her hands. 'I couldn't decide, so I tried to get advice. There was this counselor in Port Helenia, a human with the local Uplift Board. He told me what he thought th' odds were. He said he was sure I'd given birth to a Probie.

'I stayed behind when they took Sichi away. Six ... six months later my mother died.'

She looked up at Fiben. 'And then, three years after that, word came back from Earth. The news was that my baby was now a happy, well-adjusted little blue card, growing up in a loving blue-card family. And oh, yeah, I was to be promoted to green.'

Her hands clenched. 'Oh, how I hated that damned card! They took me off compulsory yearly contracept injections, so I didn't have to ask permission anymore if I wanted to conceive again. Trusted me to control my own fertility, like an adult.' She snorted. 'Like an adult? A chimmie who abandons her own child? They ignore *that*, and promote me because he passes some damn tests!'

So, Fiben thought. This was the reason for her bitterness, and for her early collaboration with the Gubru. Much was explained.

'You joined Irongrip's band out of resentment against the system? Because you hoped things might be different under the Galactics?'

'Something like that, maybe. Or maybe I was just angry.' Sylvie shrugged. 'Anyway, after a while I realized something.'

'What was it?'

'I realized that, however bad the system was under humans, it could only be far worse under the Galactics. The humans are arrogant all right. But at least a lot of them feel guilty over their arrogance. They try to temper it. Their horrible history taught them to be wary of hub ... hub ...'

'Hubris.'

'Yeah. They know what a trap it can be, acting like gods and coming to believe it's true.

'But the Galactics are *used* to this meddlesome business! It never occurs to them to have any doubts. They're so damned smug ... I hate them.'

Fiben thought about it. He had learned much during the last few months, and he figured Sylvie might be stating her case a little too strongly. Right now she sounded a lot like Major Prathachulthorn. But Fiben knew there were quite a few Galactic patron races who had reputations for kindness and decency.

Still, it was not his place to judge her bitterness.

Now he understood her nearly single-minded determination to have a child who would be at least a green card from the very start. There had to be no question. She wanted to keep her next baby, and to be sure of grandchildren.

Sitting there next to her, Fiben was uncomfortably certain of Sylvie's present condition. Unlike human females, chimmies had set cycles of receptivity, and it took some effort to hide them. It was one reason for some of the social and family differences between the two cousin species.

He felt guilty to be aroused by her condition. A soft, poignant feeling lay over the moment, and he was determined not to spoil it by being insensitive. Fiben wished he could console her somehow. And yet, he did not know what to offer her.

He moistened his lips. 'Uh. Look, Sylvie.'

She turned. 'Yes, Fiben?'

'Um, I really do hope you get ... I mean I hope I left enough ...' His face felt warm.

She smiled. 'Dr Soo says there probably was. If not, there's more where that came from.'

He shook his head. 'Your confidence is appreciated. But I wouldn't bet I'll ever be back again.' He looked away, toward the west.

She took his hand. 'Well, I'm not too proud to take extra insurance if it's offered. Another donation will be accepted, if you feel up to it.'

He blinked, feeling the tempo of his pulse rise. 'Uh, you mean right now?'

She nodded. 'When else?'

'I was hoping you'd say that.' He grinned and reached for her. But she held up a hand to stop him.

'Just a minute,' she said. 'What kind of girl do you think I am? Candlelight and champagne may be in short supply up here, but a fem generally appreciates at least a little foreplay.'

'Fine by me,' Fiben said. He turned around to present his back for grooming. 'Do me, then I'll do you.'

But she shook her head. 'Not that kind of foreplay, Fiben. I had in mind something much more stimulating.'

She reached behind the tree and brought forth a cylindrical object made of carved wood, one end covered by a tautly stretched skin. Fiben's eyes widened. 'A *drum*?'

She sat with the little handmade instrument between her knees. 'It's your own damn fault, Fiben Bolger. You showed me something special, and from now on I'll never be satisfied with anything less.'

Her deft fingers rattled off a quick rhythm.

'Dance,' she said. 'Please.'

Fiben sighed. Obviously she wasn't kidding. This choreo-maniac chimmie was crazy, of course, whatever the Uplift Board said. It seemed to be the type he fell for.

There are some ways we'll never be like humans, he thought as he picked up a branch and shook it tentatively. He dropped it and tried another. Already he felt flushed and full of energy.

Sylvie tapped the drum, starting with a rapid, exhilarating tempo that made his breath sharpen. The shine in her eyes seemed to warm his blood.

That is as it should be. We are our own selves, he knew.

Fiben took the branch in a two-handed grip and brought it down on a nearby log, sending leaves and brush exploding in all directions. 'Ook ...' he said.

His second blow was harder though, and as the beat picked up his next cry came with more enthusiasm.

The morning fog had evaporated. No thunder rolled. The uncooperative universe had not even provided a single cloud in the sky. Still, Fiben figured he could probably manage this time without the lightning.

78

GALACTICS

In Gubru Military Encampment Sixteen, the chaos at the top had begun affecting those lower down in the ranks. There were squabbles over allotments and supplies, and over the behavior of common soldiers, whose contempt for the support staff reached new and dangerous levels.

At afternoon prayer time, many of the Talon Soldiers put on the traditional ribbons of mourning for the Lost Progenitors and joined the priestly chaplain to croon in low unison. The less devout majority, who generally kept a respectful silence during such services, now seemed to make it a special occasion for gambling and loud commotion. Sentries preened and purposely sent loose feathers drifting in strong breezes so they would pass distractingly among the faithful.

Discordant noises could be heard during work, during maintenance, during training exercises.

The stoop-colonel in charge of the eastern encampments happened to be on an inspection tour and witnessed this disharmony in person. It wasted no time on indecision. At once the stoop-colonel ordered all personnel of Encampment Sixteen assembled. Then the officer gathered the camp's chief administrator and the chaplain by its side upon a platform and addressed those gathered below.

> 'Let it not be said, bandied, rumored,
> That Gubru soldiers have lost their vision!
> Are we orphans? Lost? Abandoned?
> Or members of a great clan!
> What were we, are we, shall we be?
> Warriors, builders, but most of all –
> Proper carriers of tradition!'

For some time the stoop-colonel spoke to them so – joined in persuasive song by the camp's administrator and its spiritual advisor – until, at last, the shamed soldiers and staff began to coo together in a rising chorus of harmony.

They made the effort, invested the time, one small united regiment of military, bureaucrats, and priests, and struggled as one to overcome their doubts.

For a brief while then, there did indeed take shape a consensus.

79

GAILET

... Even among those rare and tragic cases, wolfling species, there have existed crude versions of these techniques. While primitive, their methods also involved rituals of 'combat-of-honor,' and by such means kept aggressiveness and warfare under some degree of restraint.

Take, for example, the most recent clan of wolflings – the 'humans' of Sol III. Before their discovery by Galactic culture, their primitive 'tribes' often used ritual to hold in check the cycles of ever-increasing violence normally to be expected from such an unguided species. (No doubt these traditions derived from warped memories of their long lost patron race.)

Among the simple but effective methods used by pre-Contact humans (see citations) were the method of counting coup for honor *among the 'american indians,'* trial by champion among the *'medieval europeans,' and* deterrence by mutual assured destruction, *among the 'continental tribal states.'*

Of course, these techniques lacked the subtlety, the delicate balance and homeostasis, of the modern rules of behavior laid out by the Institute for Civilized Warfare ...

'That's it. Break time. I'm puttin' a T on it. Enough.'

Gailet blinked, her eyes unfocusing as the rude voice drew her back out of her reading trance. The library unit sensed this and froze the text in front of her.

She looked to her left. Sprawled in the beanbag, her new 'partner' threw his datawell aside and yawned, stretching his lanky, powerful frame. 'Time for a drink,' he said lazily.

'You haven't even made it through the first edited summary,' Gailet said.

He grinned. 'Aw, I don't know why we've got to study this shit. The

Eatees'll be surprised if we remember to bow and recite our own species-name. They don't expect neo-chimps to be geniuses, y'know.'

'Apparently not. And your comprehension scores will certainly reinforce the impression.'

That made him frown momentarily. He forced a grin again. 'You, on the other hand, are tryin' so hard – I'm sure the Eatees will find it terribly cute.'

Touché, Gailet thought. It hadn't taken the two of them very long to learn how to cut each other where it hurt.

Maybe this is yet another test. They are seeing how far my patience can be stretched before it snaps.

Maybe ... but not very likely. She had not seen the Suzerain of Propriety for more than a week. Instead, she had been dealing with a committee of three pastel-tinged Gubru, one from each faction. And it was the blue-tinted Talon Soldier who strutted foremost at these meetings.

Yesterday they had all gone down to the ceremonial site for a 'rehearsal.' Although she was still undecided whether to cooperate in the final event, Gailet had come to realize that it might already be too late to change her mind.

The seaside hill had been sculpted and landscaped so that the giant power plants were no longer visible. The terraced slopes led elegantly upward, one after another, marred only by bits of debris brought in by the steady autumnal winds. Already, bright banners flapped in the easterlies, marking the stations where the neo-chimp representatives would be asked to recite, or answer questions, or submit to intense scrutiny.

There at the site, with the Gubru standing close by, Irongrip had been to all outward appearances a model student. And perhaps it had been more than a wish to curry favor that had made him so uncharacteristically studious. After all, these were facts that had direct bearing upon his ambitions. That afternoon, his quick intelligence had shone.

Now though, with them alone together under the vast vault of the New Library, other aspects of his nature came to the fore. 'So how 'bout it?' Irongrip said, as he leaned over her chair and gave her a cyprian leer. 'Want to step outside for some air? We could slip into the eucalyptus grove and – '

'There are two chances of that,' she snapped. 'Fat and slim.'

He laughed. 'Put it off until the ceremony, then, if you like it public. Then it'll be you an' me, babe, with the whole Five Galaxies watchin'.' He grinned and flexed his powerful hands. His knuckles cracked.

Gailet turned away and closed her eyes. She had to concentrate to keep her lower lip from trembling. *Rescue me,* she wished against all hope or reason.

Logic chided her for even thinking it. After all, her white knight was only an ape, and almost certainly dead.

Still, she couldn't help crying inside. *Fiben, I need you. Fiben, come back.*

80

ROBERT

His blood sang.

After months in the mountains – living as his ancestors had, on wits and his own sweat, his toughened skin growing used to the sun and the scratchy rub of native fibers – Robert still had not yet realized the changes in himself, not until he puffed up the last few meters of the narrow, rocky trail and crossed in ten long strides from one watershed to another.

The top of Rwanda Pass ... I've climbed a thousand meters in two hours, and my heart is scarcely beating fast.

He did not really feel any need to rest, however Robert made himself slow down to a walk. Anyway, the view was worth lingering over.

He stood atop the very spine of the Mulun range. Behind him, to the north, the mountains stretched eastward in a thickening band, and westward toward the sea, where they continued in an archipelago of fat, towering islands.

It had taken him a day and a half of running to get here from the caves, and now he saw ahead of him the panorama he would have yet to cross to reach his destination.

I'm not even sure how to find what I'm looking for! Athaclena's instructions had been as vague as her own impressions of where to send him.

More mountains stretched ahead of him, dropping away sharply toward a dun-colored steppe partially obscured by haze. Before he reached those plains there would be still more rise and fall over narrow trails that had only felt a few score feet even during peacetime. Robert was probably the first to come this way since the outbreak of war.

The hardest part was over, though. He didn't enjoy downhill running, but Robert knew how to take the jolting, fall-stepping so as to avoid damaging his knees. And there would be water lower down.

He shook his leather canteen and took a sparing swallow. Only a few deciliters remained, but he was sure they'd do.

He shaded his eyes and looked beyond the nearest purple peaks to the high slopes where he would have to make his camp tonight. There would be streams all right, but no lush rain forests like on the wet northern side of the Mulun. And he would have to think about hunting for food soon, before he sallied forth onto the dry savannah.

Apache braves could run from Taos to the Pacific in a few days and not eat anything but a handful of parched corn along the way.

He wasn't an Apache brave, of course. He did have a few grams of vitamin concentrate with him, but for the sake of speed he had chosen to travel light. For now, quickness counted more than his grumbling stomach.

He skirted aside where a recent landslide had broken the path. Then he set a slightly faster pace as the trail dropped into a set of tight switchbacks.

That night Robert slept in a moss-filled notch just above a trickling spring, wrapped in a thin silk blanket. His dreams were slow and as quiet as he imagined space might be, if one ever got away from the constant humming of machines.

Mostly, it was the stillness in the empathy net, after months living in the riot of the rain forest, that lent a soft loneliness to his slumber. One might *kenn* far in an empty land such as this – even with senses as crude as his.

And for the first time there was not the harsh – metaphorically almost *metallic* – hint of alien minds to be felt off in the northwest. He was shielded from the Gubru, and from the humans and chims for that matter. Solitude was a strange sensation.

The strangeness did not evaporate by the dawn's light. He filled his canteen from the spring and drank deeply to take the edge off his hunger. Then the run began anew.

On this steeper slope the descent was wearing, but the miles did go by quickly. Before the sun was more than halfway toward the zenith the high steppe had opened up around him. He ran across rolling foothills now – kilometers falling behind him like thoughts barely contemplated and then forgotten. And as he ran, Robert probed the countryside. Soon he felt certain that the expanse held odd entities, somewhere out there beyond or among the tall grasses.

If only *kenning* were more of a localizing sense! Perhaps it was this very imprecision that had kept humans from ever developing their own crude abilities.

Instead, we concentrated on other things.

There was a game that was often played both on Earth and

among interested Galactics. It consisted of trying to reconstruct the fabled 'lost patrons of humanity,' the half-mythical starfarers who supposedly began the Uplift of human beings perhaps fifty thousand years ago and then departed in mystery, leaving the job 'only half done.'

Of course there were a few bold heretics – even among the Galactics – who held that the old Earthling theories were actually true, that it was somehow possible for a race to Uplift itself ... to *evolve* starfaring intelligence and pull itself up by its bootstraps out of darkness and into knowledge and maturity.

But even on Earth most now thought the idea quaint. Patrons uplifted clients, who later took their own turn uplifting newer pre-sentients. It was the way and had been ever since the days of the Progenitors, so long ago.

There was a real dearth of clues. Whoever the patrons of Man might have been, they had hidden their traces well, and for good reason. A patron race who abandoned a client was generally branded as an outlaw.

Still, the guessing game went on.

Certain patron clans were ruled out because they would never have chosen an omnivorous species to raise. Others were unsuited to living on Earth even for short visits – because of gravity or atmosphere or a host of other reasons.

Most agreed that it couldn't have been a clan which believed in specialization either. Some uplifted their clients with very specific goals in mind. The Uplift Institute demanded that any new sapient race be able to pilot starships, exercise judgment and logic and be capable of patron status itself someday. But beyond that the Institute put few constraints on the types of niches into which client species might be made to fit. Some were destined to become skilled craftsmen, some philosophers, and some mighty warrior castes.

But humanity's mysterious patrons had to have been generalists. For Man, the animal, was very much a flexible beast.

Yes, and for all of the vaunted flexibility of the Tymbrimi, there were some things not even those masters of adaptation could even think of doing.

Such as this, Robert thought.

A covey of native birds exploded into the air in a flurry of beating wings as Robert ran across their feeding grounds. Small, skittering things felt the rumble of his approach and took cover.

A herd of animals, long-legged and fleet like small deer, darted away, easily outdistancing him. They happened to flee southward, the direction he was going anyway, so he followed them. Soon Robert was approaching where they had stopped to feed again.

Once more they bolted, opened a wide berth behind them, then settled down again to browse.

The sun was getting high. It was a time of the day when all the plains animals, both the hunters and the hunted, tended to seek shelter from the heat. Where there were no trees, they scraped the soil in narrow runnels to find cooler layers and lay down in what shade there was to wait out the blazing sun.

But on this day one creature did not stop. It kept coming. The pseudo-deer blinked in consternation as Robert approached again. Once more, they arose and took flight, leaving him behind. This time they put a little more distance in back of them. They stood atop a small hill, panting and staring unbelievingly.

The thing on two legs just kept coming!

An uneasy stir riffled through the herd. A premonition that this just might be serious.

Still panting, they fled once more.

Perspiration shone like oil on Robert's olive skin. It glistened in the sunlight, quivering in droplets that sometimes shook loose with the constant drumming of his footsteps.

Mostly, though, the sweat spread out and coated his skin and evaporated in the rushing wind of his own passage. A dry, south-easterly breeze helped it change state into vapor, sucking up latent heat in the process. He maintained a steady, even pace, not even trying to match the sprints of the deerlike creatures. At intervals he walked and took sparing swigs from his water bag, then he resumed the chase.

His bow lay strapped across his back. But for some reason Robert did not even think of using it. Under the noonday sun he ran on and on. *Mad dogs and Englishmen*, he thought.

And Apache . . . and Bantu . . . and so many others . . .

Humans were accustomed to thinking that it was their brains which distinguished them so from the other members of Earth's animal kingdom. And it was true that weapons and fire and speech had made them the lords of their homeworld long before they ever learned about ecology, or the duty of senior species to care for those less able to understand. During those dark millennia, intelligent but ignorant men and women had used fires to drive entire herds of mammoths and sloths and so many other species over cliffs, killing hundreds for the meat contained in one or two. They shot down millions of birds so the feathers might adorn their ladies. They chopped down forests to grow opium.

Yes, intelligence in the hands of ignorant children was a dangerous weapon. But Robert knew a secret.

We did not really need all these brains in order to rule our world.

He approached the herd again, and while hunger drove him, he also contemplated the beauty of the native creatures. No doubt they were growing rapidly in stature with each passing generation. Already they were far larger than their ancestors had been back when the Bururalli slew all the great ungulates which used to roam these plains. Someday they might fill some of those empty niches. Even now they were already far swifter than a man.

Speed was one thing. But *endurance* was quite another matter. As they turned to flee him again, Robert saw that the herd members had begun to look a little panicky. The pseudo-deer now wore flecks of foam around their mouths. Their tongues hung out, and their rib cages heaved in rapid tempo.

The sun beat down. Perspiration beaded and covered him in a thin sheen. This evaporated, leaving him cool. Robert paced himself.

Tools and fire and speech gave us the surplus. They gave us what we needed to begin culture. But were they all we had?

A song had begun to play in the network of fine sinuses behind his eyes, in the gentle squish of fluid that damped his brain against the hard, driving accelerations of every footstep. The throbbing of his heartbeat carried him along like a faithful bass rhythm. The tendons of his legs were like taut, humming bows ... like violin strings.

He could smell them now, his hunger accentuating the atavistic thrill. He identified with his intended prey. In an odd way Robert knew a fulfillment he had never experienced before. He was *alive*.

He barely noticed as he began overtaking deer who had collapsed to the ground. Mothers and their fawns blinked in dull surprise as he ran past them without a glance. Robert had spotted his target, and he projected a simple glyph to tell the others to relax, to slip aside, while he chased a big male buck at the head of the herd.

You are the one, he thought. *You have lived well, passed on your genes. Your species does not need you anymore, not as much as I do.*

Perhaps his ancestors actually used empathy-sense quite a bit more than modern man. For now he saw a real function for it. He could *kenn* the growing dread of the buck as, one by one, its overheated companions dropped aside. The buck put in a desperate burst of speed and leaped far ahead. But then it had to rest, panting miserably to try to cool off, its sides heaving as it watched Robert come on. Foaming, it turned to flee again. Now it was just the two of them. Gimelhai blazed. Robert bore on. A little while later he brought his left hand to his belt as he ran, and loosened the sheath of his knife. Even that tool he chose with some reluctance. What decided him to use it, instead of his bare hands, was empathy with his prey, and a sense of mercy.

*

It was some hours later, his stomach no longer growling urgently, that Robert felt his first glimmerings of a clue. He had begun making his way southwestward, in the direction Athaclena had hoped would lead him to his goal. As the day aged, Robert shaded his eyes against the late afternoon glare. Then he closed them and reached forth with other senses.

Yes, something was close enough to *kenn*. If he thought of it metaphorically, it came as a very familiar flavor.

He headed forth at a jog, following traces that came and went, sometimes cool and sentient and sometimes as wild as the buck who had shared its life with Robert so recently.

When the traces grew quite strong, Robert found himself near a vast thicket of ugly thorn bush. Soon it would be sunset, and there was no way he would be able to chase down the thing emanating those vibrations, not in this dense, hurtful undergrowth. Anyway, he did not want to 'hunt' this creature. He wanted to talk to it.

He was sure the being was aware of him now. Robert halted. He closed his eyes again and cast forth a simple glyph. It darted left, right, then plunged into the vegetation. There came a rustle.

He opened his eyes. Two dark, glittering pools blinked back at him. 'All right,' he said, softly. 'Please come on out now. We had better talk.'

There was another moment's hesitation. Then there shambled forth a long-armed chim, hairier than most, with thick brows and a heavy jaw. He was dirty, and totally naked.

There were a few stains that Robert was sure came from caked blood, and it had not come from the chim's own minor scratches. *Well, we are cousins, after all. And vegetarians don't live long on a steppe.*

When he sensed that the comate chim was reluctant to make eye contact, Robert did not insist. 'Hello, Jo-Jo,' he said softly, and with sincere gentleness. 'I've come a long way to bring a message to your employer.'

81

ATHACLENA

The cage consisted of thick wooden slats bound by wire. It hung from a tree branch in a sheltered vale, under the leeward shoulder of a simmering volcano. Still the guy cables holding it in place trembled under occasional gusts of wind, and the cage itself swayed.

Its occupant – naked, unshaven, and looking very much the wolfling – stared down at Athaclena with an expression that would have burned even without the loathing he radiated. To Athaclena it felt as if the little glade were saturated with the prisoner's hatred. She planned to keep her visit as short as possible.

'I thought you would want to know. The Gubru Triumvirate has declared a protocol truce under the Rules of War,' she told Major Prathachulthorn. 'The ceremonial site is now sacrosanct, and no armed force on Garth can act except in self-defense for the duration.'

Prathachulthorn spat through the bars. 'So? If we'd attacked when I planned, we'd have made it before this.'

'I find it doubtful. Even the best plans are seldom executed perfectly. And if we were forced to abort the mission at the last minute, every secret we had would have been revealed for nothing.'

'That's your opinion,' Prathachulthorn snorted.

Athaclena shook her head. 'But that is not the only or even the most important reason.' She had grown tired of fruitlessly explaining the nuances of Galactic punctilio to the Marine officer, but somehow she found the will to try one more time. 'I told you before, major. Wars are known to feature cycles of what you humans sometimes call "tit-for-tat" where one side punishes the other side for its last insult, and then that other side retaliates in turn. Left unconstrained, this can escalate forever! Since the days of the Progenitors, there have been developed rules which help keep such exchanges from growing out of all proportion.'

Prathachulthorn cursed. 'Damn it, you admitted that our raid would've been legal if done in time!'

She nodded. 'Legal, perhaps. But it also would have served the enemy well. Because it would have been the *last* action before the truce!'

'What difference does that make?'

Patiently, she tried to explain. 'The Gubru have declared a truce while still in an overpowering position of strength, major. That is considered honorable. You might say they "win points" for that.

'But their gain is multiplied if they do so immediately after taking *damage*. If they show restraint by not retaliating, the Gubru are then performing an act of forbearance. They gather credit – '

'Ha!' Prathachulthorn laughed. 'Fat lot of good it'd do them, with their ceremonial site in ruins!'

Athaclena inclined her head. She really did not have time for this. If she spent too long here, Lieutenant McCue might suspect that this was where her missing commander was being hidden. The Marines had already swooped down on several possible hiding places.

'The upshot might have been to force *Earth* to finance a new site as a replacement,' she said.

Prathachulthorn stared at her. 'But – but we're at *war*!'

She nodded, misunderstanding him. 'Exactly. One cannot allow war without rules, and powerful neutral forces to enforce them. The alternative would be barbarism.'

The man's sour look was her only answer.

'Besides, to destroy the site would have implied that humans do not want to see their clients tested and judged for promotion! But now it is the *Gubru* who must pay honor-gild for this truce. Your clan has gained a segment of status by being the aggrieved party, unavenged. This sliver of propriety could turn out to be crucial in the days ahead.'

Prathachulthorn frowned. For a moment he seemed to concentrate, as if a thread of her logic hung almost within reach. She felt his attention shimmer as he tried ... but then it faded. He grimaced and spat again. 'What a load of crap. Show me dead birds. That's currency I can count. Pile them up to the level of this cage, little Miss Ambassador's Daughter, and maybe, just *maybe* I'll let you live when I finally break out of here.'

Athaclena shivered. She knew how futile it was to try to hold a man such as this prisoner. He should have been kept drugged. He should have been killed. But she could not bring herself to do either, or to further prejudice the fate of the chims in her cabal by involving them in such crimes.

'Good day, major,' she said. And turned to go.

He did not shout as she left. In a way, the parsimonious use he made of his threats made those few seem all the more menacing and believable.

She took a hidden trail from the secret glade over a shoulder of the mountain, past warm springs that hissed and steamed uncertainly. At the ridge crest Athaclena had to draw in her tendrils to keep them from being battered in the autumn wind. Few clouds could be seen in the sky, but the air was hazy with dust blowing in from faraway deserts.

Hanging from a nearby branch she encountered one of the parachutelike kite and spore pod combinations blown up here from some field of plate ivy. The autumn dispersal was fully under way now. Fortunately, it had begun in earnest more than two days ago, before the Gubru announced their truce. That fact might turn out to be very important indeed.

The day felt odd, more so than any time since that night of terrible dreams, shortly before she climbed this mountain to wrestle with her parents' fierce legacy.

Perhaps the Gubru are warming up their hyperwave shunt, again.

She had since learned that her fit of dreams on that fateful night had coincided with the invaders' first test of their huge new facility. Their experiments had let surges of unallocated probability loose in all directions, and those who were psychically sensitive reported bizarre mixtures of deathly dread and hilarity.

That sort of mistake did not sound like the normally meticulous Gubru, and it seemed to be validation of Fiben Bolger's report, that the enemy had serious leadership problems.

Was that why *tutsunucann* collapsed so suddenly and violently that evening? Was all that loose energy responsible for the terrific power of her *s'ustru'thoon* rapport with Uthacalthing?

Could that and the subsequent tests of those great engines explain why the gorillas had begun behaving so very strangely?

All Athaclena knew for certain was that she felt nervous and afraid. *Soon,* she thought. *It will all approach climax very soon.*

She had descended halfway down the trail leading back to her tent when a pair of breathless chims emerged from the forest, hurrying uphill toward her. 'Miss ... miss ...' one of them breathed. The other held his side, panting audibly.

Her initial reading of their panic triggered a brief hormone rush, which only subsided slightly when she traced their fear and *kenned* that it did not come from an enemy attack. Something *else* had them terrified half out of their wits.

'Miss Ath-Athaclena,' the first chim gasped. 'You gotta come quick!'

'What is it, Petri? What's happening?'

He swallowed. 'It's the 'rillas. We can't control 'em anymore!'

So, she thought. For more than a week the gorillas' low, atonal music had been driving their chim guardians to nervous fits. 'What are they doing now?'

'They're leaving!' the second messenger wailed plaintively.

She blinked. 'What did'you say?'

Petri's brown eyes were filled with bewilderment. 'They're leaving. They just got up and left! They're headin' for the *Sind,* an' there doesn't seem t'be anythin' we can do to stop 'em!'

82

UTHACALTHING

Their progress toward the mountains had slackened considerably recently. More and more of Kault's time seemed to be spent laboring over his makeshift instruments ... and in arguing with his Tymbrimi companion.

How quickly things change, Uthacalthing thought. He had labored long and hard to bring Kault to this fever pitch of suspicion and excitement. And now he found himself recalling with fondness their earlier peaceful comradeship – the long, lazy days of gossip and reminiscences and common exile – however frustrating they had seemed at the time.

Of course that had been when Uthacalthing was whole, when he had been able to look upon the world through Tymbrimi eyes, and the softening veil of whimsy.

Now? Uthacalthing knew that he had been considered dour and serious by others of his race. Now, though, they would surely think him crippled. Perhaps better off dead.

Too much was taken from me, he thought, while Kault muttered to himself in the corner of their shelter. Outside, heavy gusts blew through the veldt grasses. Moonlight brushed long hillcrests that resembled sluggish ocean waves, locked amid a rolling storm.

Did she actually have to tear away so much? he wondered, without really being able to feel or care very much.

Of course Athaclena had hardly known what she was doing, that night when she decided in her need to call in the pledge her parents had made. *S'ustru'thoon* was not something one trained for. A recourse so drastic and used so seldom could not be well described by science. And by its very nature, *s'ustru'thoon* was something one could do but once in one's lifetime.

Anyway, now that he looked back upon it, Uthacalthing remembered something he hadn't noticed at the time.

That evening had been one of great tension. Hours beforehand he had felt disturbing waves of energy, as if ghostly half-glyphs of immense power were throbbing against the mountains. Perhaps that explained why his daughter's call had carried such strength. She had been tapping some outside source!

And he remembered something else. In the *s'ustru'thoon* storm Athaclena triggered, not *everything* torn from him had gone to her!

Strange that he had not thought of it until now. But Uthacalthing now seemed vaguely to recall some of his essences flying *past* her. But where they had actually been bound he could not even imagine. Perhaps to the source of those energies he had felt earlier. Perhaps ...

Uthacalthing was too tired to come up with rational theories. *Who knows? Maybe they were drawn in by Garthlings.* It was a poor joke. Not even worth a tiny smile. And yet, the irony was encouraging. It showed that he had not lost absolutely everything.

'I am certain of it now, Uthacalthing.' Kault's voice was low and confident as the Thennanin turned to face him. He put aside the instrument he had constructed out of odd items salvaged from the wrecked pinnace.

'Certain of what, colleague?'

'Certain that our separate suspicions are focusing in on a probable fact! See here. The data you showed me – your private spools regarding these "Garthling" creatures – allowed me to tune my detector until I am now sure that I have found the resonance I was seeking.'

'You are?' Uthacalthing didn't know what to make of this. He had never expected Kault to find actual *confirmation* of mythical beasts.

'I know what concerns you, my friend,' Kault said, raising one massive, leather-plated hand. 'You fear that my experiments will draw down upon us the attention of the Gubru. But rest assured. I am using a very narrow band and am reflecting my beam off the nearer moon. It is very unlikely they would ever be able to localize the source of my puny little probe.'

'But ...' Uthacalthing shook his head. 'What are you looking for?'

Kault's breathing slits puffed. 'A certain type of cerebral resonance. It is quite technical,' he said. 'It has to do with something I read in your tapes about these Garthling creatures. What little data you had seemed to indicate that these pre-sentient beings might have brains not too dissimilar to those of Earthlings, or Tymbrimi.'

Uthacalthing was amazed by the way Kault used his faked data with such celerity and enthusiasm. His former self would have been delighted. 'So?' he asked.

'So ... let me see if I can explain with an example. Take humans – '

Please, Uthacalthing inserted, without much enthusiasm, more out of habit.

' – Earthlings represent one of many paths which can be taken to arrive eventually at intelligence. Theirs involved the use of *two* brains that later became one.'

Uthacalthing blinked. His own mind was working so slowly.

'You ... you are speaking of the fact that their brains have two partially independent hemispheres?'

'Aye. And while these halves are similar and redundant in some ways, in others they divide the labor. The split is even more pronounced among their neo-dolphin clients.

'Before the Gubru arrived, I was studying data on neo-chimpanzees, which are similar to their patrons in many respects. One of the things the humans had to do, early in their Uplift program, was find ways to unite the functions of the two halves of pre-sentient chimpanzee brains comfortably into one consciousness. Until that was done neo-chimpanzees would suffer from a condition called "bicamerality" ...'

Kault droned on, gradually letting his jargon grow more and more technical, eventually leaving Uthacalthing far behind. The arcana of cerebral function seemed to fill their shelter, as if in thick smoke. Uthacalthing felt almost tempted to craft a glyph to commemorate his own boredom, but he lacked the energy even to stir his tendrils.

'... so the resonance appears to indicate that there are, indeed, bicameral minds within the range of my instrument!'

Ah, yes, Uthacalthing thought. Back in Port Helenia, at a time when he had still been a clever crafter of complex schemes, he had suspected that Kault might turn out to be resourceful. That was one reason why Uthacalthing chose for a confederate an atavistic chim. Kault was probably picking up traces from poor Jo-Jo, whose throwback brain was in many ways similar to fallow, non-uplifted chimpanzees of centuries ago. Jo-Jo no doubt retained some of this 'bicamerality' characteristic Kault spoke of.

Finally Kault concluded. 'I am therefore quite convinced, from your evidence and my own, that we cannot delay any longer. We must somehow get to and use a facility for sending interstellar messages!'

'How do you expect to do that?' Uthacalthing asked in mild curiosity.

Kault's breathing slits pulsed in obvious, rare excitement. 'Perhaps we can sneak or bluff or fight our way to the Planetary Branch Library, claim sanctuary, and then invoke every priority under the fifty suns of Thennan. Perhaps there is another way. I do not care if it means stealing a Gubru starship. Somehow we must get word to my clan!'

Was this the same creature who had been so anxious to flee Port Helenia before the invaders arrived? Kault seemed as changed outwardly as Uthacalthing felt inwardly. The Thennanin's enthusiasm was a hot flame, while Uthacalthing had to stoke his own carefully.

'You wish to establish a claim on the pre-sentients before the Gubru manage it?' he asked.

'Aye, and why not? To save them from such horrible patrons I would lay down my life! But there may be need for much haste. If what we have overheard on our receiver is true, emissaries from the Institutes may already be on their way to Garth. I believe the Gubru are planning something big. Perhaps they have made the same discovery. We must act quickly if we are not to be too late!'

Uthacalthing nodded. 'One more question then, distinguished colleague.' He paused. 'Why should I help you?'

Kault's breath sighed like a punctured balloon, and his ridge crest collapsed rapidly. He looked at Uthacalthing with an expression as emotion-laden as any the Tymbrimi had ever seen upon the face of a dour Thennanin.

'It would greatly benefit the pre-sentients,' he hissed. 'Their destiny would be far happier.'

'Perhaps. Arguable. Is that it, though? Are you relying on my altruism alone?'

'Errr. Hm.' Outwardly Kault seemed offended that anything more should be asked. Still, could he really be surprised? He was, after all, a diplomat, and understood that the best and firmest deals are based on open self-interest. 'It would ... It would greatly help my own political party if I delivered such a treasure. We would probably win government,' he suggested.

'A slight improvement over the intolerable is not enough to get excited about.' Uthacalthing shook his head. 'You still haven't explained to me why I should not stake a claim for my own clan. I was investigating these rumors before you. We Tymbrimi would make excellent patrons for these creatures.'

'*You!* You ... *K'ph mimpher'rrengi?*' The phrase stood for something vaguely equivalent to 'juvenile delinquents.' It was almost enough to make Uthacalthing smile again. Kault shifted uncomfortably. He made a visible effort to retain diplomatic composure.

'You Tymbrimi have not the strength, the power to back up such a claim,' he muttered.

At last, Uthacalthing thought. *Truth.*

In times like this, under circumstances as muddy as these, it would take more than mere priority of application to settle an adoption claim on a pre-sentient race. Many other factors would officially be considered by the Uplift Institute. And the humans had a saying that was especially appropriate. 'Possession is nine points of the law.' It certainly applied here.

'So we are back to question number one.' Uthacalthing nodded.

'If neither we Tymbrimi nor the Terrans can have the Garthlings, why should we help *you* get them?'

Kault rocked from one side to the other, as if he were trying to work his way off a hot seat. His misery was blatantly obvious, as was his desperation. Finally, he blurted forth, 'I can almost certainly guarantee a cessation of all hostilities by my clan against yours.'

'Not enough,' Uthacalthing came back quickly.

'What more could you ask of me!' Kault exploded.

'An actual alliance. A promise of Thennanin aid against those now laying siege upon Tymbrim.'

'But – '

'And the guarantee must be firm. In advance. To take effect *whether or not* these pre-sentients of yours actually turn out to exist.'

Kault stammered. 'You cannot expect – '

'Oh, but I can. Why should *I* believe in these "Garthling" creatures? To me they have only been intriguing rumors. I *never* told you I believed in them. And yet you want me to risk my life to get you to message facilities! Why should I do that without a guarantee of benefit for my people?'

'This ... this is unheard of!'

'Nevertheless, it is my price. Take it or leave it.'

For a moment Uthacalthing felt a thrilled suspicion he was about to witness the unexpected. It seemed as if Kault might lose control ... might actually burst forth into violence. At the sight of those massive fists, clenching and unclenching rapidly, Uthacalthing actually felt his blood stir with change enzymes. A surge of nervous fear made him feel more alive than he had in days.

'It ... it shall be as you demand,' Kault growled at last.

'Good.' Uthacalthing sighed as he relaxed. He drew forth his datawell. 'Let us work out together how to parse this for a contract.'

It took more than an hour to get the wording right. After it was finished, and when they had both signified their affirmation on each copy, Uthacalthing gave Kault one record pellet and kept the second for himself.

Amazing, he thought at that point. He had planned and schemed to bring about this day. This was the second half of his grand jest, fulfilled at last. To have fooled the Gubru was wonderful. This was simply unbelievable.

And yet, right now Uthacalthing found himself feeling numb rather than triumphant. He did not look forward to the climb ahead, a furious race into the steep towers of the Mulun range, followed by a desperate attempt that would, no doubt, result only in the two of them dying side by side.

'You know of course, Uthacalthing, that my people will not carry out this bargain if I turn out to be mistaken. If there are no Garthlings after all, the Thennanin will repudiate me. They will pay diplomatic gild to buy out this contract, and I will be ruined.'

Uthacalthing did not look at Kault. This was another reason for his sense of depressed, detachment, certainly. *A great jokester is not supposed to feel guilt,* he told himself. *Perhaps I have spent too much time around humans.*

The silence stretched on for a while longer, each of them brooding in his own thoughts.

Of course Kault would be repudiated. Of course the Thennanin were not about to be drawn into an alliance, or even peace with the Earth-Tymbrimi entente. All Uthacalthing had ever hoped to accomplish was to sow confusion among his enemies. If Kault should by some miracle manage to get his message off and truly draw Thennanin armadas to this backwater system, then two great foes of his people would be drawn into a battle that would drain them ... a battle over nothing. Over a nonexistent species. Over the ghosts of creatures murdered fifty thousand years ago.

Such a great jest! I should be happy. Thrilled.

Sadly, he knew that he could not even blame *s'ustru'thoon* for his inability to take pleasure out of this. It was not Athaclena's fault that the feeling clung to him ... the feeling that he had just betrayed a friend.

Ah, well, Uthacalthing consoled himself. *It is all probably moot, anyway. To get Kault the kind of message facilities he needs now will take seven more miracles, each greater than the last.*

It seemed fitting that they would probably die together in the attempt, uselessly.

In his sadness, Uthacalthing found the energy to lift his tendrils slightly. They fashioned a simple glyph of regret as he raised his head to face Kault.

He was about to speak when something very surprising suddenly happened. Uthacalthing felt a *presence* wing past in the night. He started. But no sooner had it been there than it was gone.

Did I imagine it? Am I falling apart?

Then it was back! He gasped in surprise, *kenning* as it circled the tent in an ever-tightening spiral, brushing at last against the fringes of his indrawn aura. He looked up, trying to spot something that whirled just beyond the fringe of their shelter.

What am I doing? Trying to see *a glyph?*

He closed his eyes and let the un-thing approach. Uthacalthing opened a *kenning.*

'Puyr'iturumbul!' he cried.

Kault swiveled. 'What is it, my friend? What ... ?'

But Uthacalthing had risen. As if drawn up by a string he stepped out into the cool night.

The breeze brought odors to his nostrils as he sniffed, using all his senses to seek in the acherontic darkness. 'Where are you?' Uthacalthing called. 'Who is there?'

Two figures stepped forward into a dim pool of moonlight. *So it is true!* Uthacalthing thought. *A human* had sought him out with an empathy sending, one so skillful it might have come from a young Tymbrimi.

And that was not the end to surprises. He blinked at the tall, bronzed, bearded warrior – who looked like nothing but one of the heroes of those pre-Contact Earthling barbarian epics – and let out another cry of amazement as he suddenly recognized Robert Oneagle, the playboy son of the Planetary Coordinator!

'Good evening, sir,' Robert said as he stopped a few meters away and bowed.

Standing a little behind Robert, the neo-chimpanzee, Jo-Jo, wrung his hands nervously. This, certainly, was not according to the original plan. He did not meet Uthacalthing's eyes.

'V'hooman'ph? Idatess!' Kault exclaimed in Galactic Six. 'Uthacalthing, what is a human doing here?'

Robert bowed again. Enunciating carefully, he made formal greetings to both of them, including their full species-names. Then he went on in Galactic Seven.

'I have come a long way, honored gentlebeings, in order to invite you all to a party.'

83

FIBEN

'Easy, Tycho. Easy!'

The normally placid animal bucked and pulled at its reins. Fiben, who had never been much of a horseman, was forced to dismount hurriedly and grab the animal's halter.

'There now. Relax,' he soothed. 'It's just another transport going by. We've heard 'em all day. It'll be gone soon.'

As he promised, the shrieking whine faded as the flying machine passed quickly overhead and disappeared beyond the nearby trees, traveling in the direction of Port Helenia.

A lot had changed since Fiben had first come this way, mere

weeks after the invasion. Then he had walked in sunshine down a busy highway, surrounded by spring's verdant colors. Now he felt blustery winds at his back as he passed through a valley showing all the early signs of a bitter winter. Half the trees had already dropped their leaves, leaving them in drifts across meadows and lanes. Orchards were bare of fruit, and the back roads devoid of traffic.

Surface traffic, that is. Overhead the swarm of transports seemed incessant. Gravities teased his peripheral nerves as Gubru machines zoomed past. The first few times, his hackles had risen from more than just the pulsing fields. He had expected to be challenged, to be stopped, perhaps to be shot on sight.

But in fact the Galactics had ignored him altogether, apparently not deigning to distinguish one lonely chim from others who had been sent out to help with the harvest, or the specialists who had begun staffing a few of the ecological management stations once again.

Fiben had spoken with a few of the latter, many of them old acquaintances. They told of how they had given their parole in exchange for freedom and low-level support to resume their work. There wasn't much to be done, of course, with winter coming on. But at least there was a program again, and the Gubru seemed quite satisfied to leave them alone to do their work.

The invaders were, indeed, preoccupied elsewhere. The real focus of Galactic activity seemed to be over to the southwest, toward the spaceport.

And the ceremonial site, Fiben reminded himself. He didn't really know what he was going to do in the unlikely event he actually made it through town. What would happen if he just marched right up to the shabby house that had been his former prison? Would the Suzerain of Propriety take him back?

Would Gailet?

Would she even be there?

He passed a few chims dressed in muffled cloaks, who desultorily picked through the stubble in a recently harvested field. They did not greet him, nor did he expect them to. Gleaning was a job generally given the poorest sort of Probationer. Still, he felt their gaze as he walked Tycho toward Port Helenia. After the animal had calmed a bit, Fiben clambered back onto the saddle and rode.

He had considered trying to reenter Port Helenia the way he left it, over the wall, at night. After all, if it had worked once, why not a second time? Anyway, he had no wish to meet up with the followers of the Suzerain of Cost and Caution.

It was tempting. Somehow, though, he figured that once was lucky. Twice would be simple stupidity.

Anyway, the choice was made for him when he rounded a bend and found himself staring at a Gubru guard post. Two battle robots of sophisticated design whirled and focused upon him.

'Easy does it, guys.' Fiben said it more for his own benefit than theirs. If they were programmed to shoot on sight, he never would have seen them in the first place.

In front of the blockhouse there sat a squat armored hover craft, propped up on blocks. Two pairs of three-toed feet stuck out from underneath, and it did not take much knowledge of Galactic Three to tell that the chirped mutterings were expressing frustration. When the robots' warning whistled forth there came a sharp bang under the hover, followed by an indignant squawk.

Soon a pair of hooked beaks poked out of the shadows. Yellow eyes watched him unblinkingly. One of the disheveled Gubru rubbed its dented head frill.

Fiben pressed his lips together to fight back a smile. He dismounted and approached until he was even with the bunker, puzzled when neither the aliens nor the machines spoke to him.

He stopped before the two Gubru and bowed low.

They looked at each other and twittered irritably to each other. From one there came something that sounded like a resigned moan. The two Talon Soldiers emerged from under the disabled machine and stood up. Each of them returned a very slight but noticeable nod.

Silence stretched.

One of the Gubru whistled another faint sigh and brushed dust from its feathers. The other simply glared at Fiben.

Now what? He tried to think, but what was he supposed to *do*? Fiben's toes itched.

He bowed again. Then, with a dry mouth, he backed away and took the horse's tether. With affected nonchalance he started walking toward the dark fence surrounding Port Helenia, now visible just a kilometer ahead.

Tycho nickered, swished his tail, and cut loose an aromatic crepidation.

Tycho, pu-lease! Fiben thought. When a bend in the road at last cut off all view of the Gubru, Fiben sank to the ground. He just sat and shook for a few moments.

'Well,' he said at last. 'I guess there really is a truce after all.'

After that, the guard post at the town gate was almost anticlimactic. Fiben actually enjoyed making the Talon Soldiers acknowledge his bow. He remembered some of what Gailet had taught him about Galactic protocol. Grudging acknowledgment from the client-class

Kwackoo had been vital to achieve. To get it from the Gubru was delicious.

It also clearly meant that the Suzerain of Propriety was holding out. It had not yet given in.

Fiben left a trail of startled chims behind him as he rode Tycho at a gallop through the back streets of Port Helenia. One or two of them shouted at him, but at that moment he had no thought except to hurry toward the site of his former imprisonment.

When he arrived, however, he found the iron gate open and untended. The watch globes had vanished from the stone wall. He left Tycho to graze in the unkempt garden and beat aside a couple of limp plate ivy parachutes that festooned the open doorway.

'Gailet!' he shouted.

The Probationer guards were gone too. Dustballs and scraps of paper blew in through the open door and rolled down the hall. When he came to the room he had shared with Gailet, Fiben stopped and stared.

It was a mess.

Most of the furnishings were still there, but the expensive sound system and holo-wall had been torn out, no doubt taken by the departing Probies. On the other hand, Fiben saw his personal datawell sitting right where he had left it that night.

Gailet's was gone.

He checked the closet. Most of their clothes still hung there. Clearly she hadn't packed. He took down the shiny ceremonial robe he had been given by the Suzerain's staff. The silky material was almost glass-smooth under his fingers.

Gailet's robe was missing.

'Oh, Goodall,' Fiben moaned. He spun about and dashed down the hall. It took only a second to leap into the saddle, but Tycho barely looked up from his feeding. Fiben had to kick and yell until the beast began to comprehend some of the urgency of the situation. With a yellow sunflower still hanging from his mouth, the horse turned and clomped through the gate and back onto the street. Once there, Tycho brought his head down and gamely gathered momentum.

They made quite a sight, galloping down the silent, almost empty streets, the robe and the flower flapping like banners in the wind. But few witnessed the wild ride until they finally approached the crowded wharves.

It seemed as if nearly every chim in town was there. They swarmed along the waterfront, a churning mass of brown, callipose bodies dressed in autumn parkas, their heads bobbing like the waters of the bay just beyond. More chims leaned precariously over the rooftops, and some even hung from drainage spouts.

It was a good thing Fiben wasn't on foot. Tycho was really quite helpful as he snorted and nudged startled chims aside with his nose. From his perch on the horse's back, Fiben soon was able to spy what some of the commotion was about.

About half a kilometer out into the bay, a dozen fishing vessels could be seen operating under neo-chimpanzee crews. A cluster of them jostled and bumped near a sleek white craft that glistened in cliquant contrast to the battered trawlers.

The Gubru vessel was dead in the water. Two of the avian crew members stood atop its cockpit, twittering and waving their arms, offering instructions which the chim seamen politely ignored as they tied hausers to the crippled craft and began gradually towing it toward the shore.

So what? Big deal, Fiben thought. So a Gubru patrol boat suffered a breakdown. For this all the chims in town had spilled out into the streets? The citizens of Port Helenia really must be hard up for entertainment.

Then he realized that only a few of the townfolk were actually watching the minor rescue in the harbor. The vast majority stared southward, out across the bay.

Oh. Fiben's breath escaped in a sigh, and he, too, was momentarily struck speechless.

New, shining towers stood atop the far mesa where the colonial spaceport lay. The lambent monoliths looked nothing like Gubru transports, or their hulking, globular battleships. Instead, these resembled glimmering steeples – spires which towered high and confident, manifesting a faith and tradition more ancient than life on Earth.

Tiny winklings of light lifted from the tall starships – *carrying Galactic dignitaries*, Fiben guessed – and cruised westward, drawing nearer along the arc of the bay. At last the aircraft joined a spiral of traffic descending over South Point. That was where everyone in Port Helenia seemed to sense that something special was going on.

Unconsciously, Fiben guided Tycho through the crowd until he arrived at the edge of the main wharf. There a chain of chims wearing oval badges held back the crowd. *So there are proctors again*, Fiben realized. *The Probationers proved unreliable, so the Gubru had to reinstate civil authority.*

A chen wearing the brassard of a proctor corporal grabbed Tycho's halter and started to speak. 'Hey, bub! You can't . . . ' Then he blinked. 'Ifni! Is that you, Fiben?'

Fiben recognized Barnaby Fulton, one of the chims who had

been involved in Gailet's early urban underground. He smiled, though his thoughts were far across the choppy waters. 'Hello, Barnaby. Haven't seen you since the valley uprising. Glad to see you still scratchin'.'

Now that attention had been drawn his way, chens and dummies started nudging each other and whispering in hushed voices. He heard his own name repeated. The susurration of the crowd ebbed as a circle of silence spread around him. Two or three of the staring chims reached out to touch Tycho's heavy flanks, or Fiben's leg, as if to verify that they were real.

Barnaby made a visible effort to match Fiben's insouciance. 'Whenever it itches, Fiben. Uh, one rumor had it you were s'pozed to be over there.' He gestured toward the monumental activity taking place across the harbor. 'Another said you'd busted out an' taken to the hills. A third . . .'

'What did the third say?'

Barnaby swallowed. 'Some said your number'd come up.'

'Hmph,' Fiben commented softly. 'I guess all of them were right.'

He saw that the trawlers had dragged the crippled Gubru patrol boat nearly to the dock. A number of other chim-crewed vessels cruised farther out, but none of them crossed a line of buoys that could be seen stretching, all the way across the bay.

Barnaby looked left and right, then spoke in a low voice. 'Uh, Fiben, there are quite a few chims in town who . . . well, who've been reorganizing. I had to give parole when I got my brassard back, but I can get word to Professor Oakes that you're in town. I'm sure he'd want to get together a meetin' tonight . . .'

Fiben shook his head. 'No time. I've got to get over there.' He motioned to where the bright aircraft were alighting on the far headlands.

Barnaby's lips drew back. 'I dunno, Fiben. Those watch buoys. They've kept everybody back.'

'Have they actually burned anybody?'

'Well, no. Not that I've seen. But – '

Barnaby stopped as Fiben shook the reins and nudged with his heels. 'Thanks, Barnaby. That's all I needed to know,' he said.

The proctors stood aside as Tycho stepped along the wharf. Farther out the little rescue flotilla had just come to dock and were even now tying up the prim white Gubru warcraft. The chim sailors did a lot of bowing and moved in uncomfortable crouched postures under the glare of the irritated Talon Soldiers and their fearsome battle drones.

In contrast, Fiben steered his steed just outside of the range that would have required him to acknowledge the aliens. His posture was erect, and he ignored them completely as he rode past the patrol boat to the far end of the pier, where the smallest of the fishing boats had just come to rest.

He swung his feet over the saddle and hopped down. 'Are you good to animals?' he asked the startled sailor, who looked up from securing his craft. When he nodded, Fiben handed the dumb-founded chim Tycho's reins. 'Then we'll swap.'

He leaped aboard the little craft and stepped behind the cockpit. 'Send a bill for the difference to the Suzerain for Propriety. You got that? The Gubru Suzerain of Propriety.'

The wide-eyed chen seemed to notice that his jaw was hanging open. He closed it with an audible clack.

Fiben switched the ignition on and felt satisfied with the engine's throaty roar. 'Cast off,' he said. Then he smiled. 'And thanks. Take good care of Tycho!'

The sailor blinked. He seemed about to decide to get angry when some of the chims who had followed Fiben caught up. One whis-pered in the boatman's ear. The fisherman then grinned. He hurried to untie the boat's tether and threw the rope back onto the foredeck. When Fiben awkwardly hit the pier backing up, the chim only winced slightly. 'G-good luck,' he managed to say.

'Yeah. Luck, Fiben,' Barnaby shouted.

Fiben waved and shifted the impellers into forward. He swung about in a wide arc, passing almost under the duraplast sides of the Gubru patrol craft. Up close it did not look quite so glistening white. In fact, the armored hull looked pitted and corroded. High, indig-nant chirps from the other side of the vessel indicated the frustration of the Talon Soldier crew.

Fiben spared them not a thought as he turned about and got his borrowed boat headed southward, toward the line of buoys that split the bay and kept the chims of Port Helenia away from the high, patron-level doings on the opposite shore.

Foamed and choppy from the wind, the water was cinerescent with the usual garbage the easterlies always brought in, this time of year – everything from leaves to almost transparent plate ivy para-chutes to the feathers of molting birds. Fiben had to slow to avoid clots of debris as well as battered boats of all description crowded with chim sightseers.

He approached the barrier line at low speed and felt thousands of eyes watching him as he passed the last shipload, containing the most daring and curious of the Port Helenians.

Goodall, do I really know what I'm doing? he wondered. He had been acting almost on automatic so far. But now it came to him that he really was out of his depth here. What did he hope to accomplish by charging off this way? What was he going to do? Crash the ceremony? He looked at the towering starships across the bay, glistening in power and splendor.

As if he had any business sticking his half-uplifted nose into the affairs of beings from great and ancient clans! All he'd accomplish would be to embarrass himself, and probably his whole race for that matter.

'Gotta think about this,' he muttered. Fiben brought the boat's engine down to idle as the line of buoys neared. He thought about how many people were watching him right now.

My people, he recalled. *I . . . I was supposed to represent them.*

Yes, but I ducked out, obviously the Suzerain realized its mistake and made other arrangements. Or the other Suzerain's won, and I'd simply be dead meat if I showed up!

He wondered what they would think if they knew that, only days ago, he had manhandled and helped kidnap one of his own patrons, and his legal commander at that. Some race-representative!

Gailet doesn't need the likes of me. She's better off without me.

Fiben twisted the wheel, causing the boat to come about just short of one of the white buoys. He watched it go by as he turned.

It, too, looked less than new on close examination – somewhat corroded, in fact. But then, from his own lowly state, who was *he* to judge?

Fiben blinked at that thought. Now that was laying it on *too* thick!

He stared at the buoy, and slowly his lips curled back. *Why . . . why you devious sons of bitches . . .*

Fiben cut the impellers and let the engine drop back to idle. He closed his eyes and pressed his hands against his temples, trying to concentrate.

I was girding myself against another fear *barrier . . . like the one at the city fence, that night. But this one is more subtle! It plays on my sense of my own unworthiness. It trades on my humility.*

He opened his eyes and looked back at the buoy. Finally, he grinned.

'*What* humility?' Fiben asked aloud. He laughed and turned the wheel as he set the craft in motion again. This time when he headed for the barrier he did not hesitate, or listen to the doubts that the machines tried to cram into his head.

'After all,' he muttered, 'what can they do to shake the confidence of a fellow who's got delusions of adequacy?' The enemy had made a serious mistake here, Fiben knew as he left the buoys behind him and, with them, their artificially induced doubts. The resolution that flowed back into him now was fortified by its very *contrast* to the earlier depths. He approached the opposite headland wearing a fierce scowl of determination.

Something flapped against his knee. Fiben glanced down and saw the silvery ceremonial robe – the one he had found in the closet back at the old prison. He had crammed it under his belt, apparently, just before leaping atop Tycho and riding, pell-mell, for the harbor. No wonder people had been staring at him, back at the docks!

Fiben laughed. Holding onto the wheel with one hand, he wriggled into the silky garment as he headed toward a silent stretch of beach. The bluffs cut off any view of what was going on over on the sea side of the narrow peninsula. But the drone of still-descending aircraft was – he hoped – a sign that he might not be too late.

He ran the boat aground on a shelf of sparkling white sand, now made unattractive under a tidal wash of flotsam. Fiben was about to leap into the knee-high surf when he glanced back and noticed that something seemed to be going on back in Port Helenia. Faint cries of excitement carried over the water. The churning mass of brown forms at the dockside was now surging to the right.

He plucked up the pair of binoculars that hung by the capstan and focused them on the wharf area.

Chims ran about, many of them pointing excitedly eastward, toward the main entrance to town. Some were still running in that direction. But now more and more seemed to be heading the other way ... apparently not so much in fear as in *confusion*. Some of the more excitable chims capered about. A few even fell into the water and had to be rescued by the more level-headed.

Whatever was happening did not seem to be causing panic so much as acute, near total bewilderment.

Fiben did not have time to hang around and piece together this added puzzle. By now he thought he understood his own modest powers of concentration.

Focus on just one problem at a time, he told himself. *Get to Gailet. Tell her you're sorry you ever left her. Tell her you'll never ever do it again.*

That was easy enough even for him to understand.

Fiben found a narrow trail leading up from the beach. It was crumbling and dangerous, especially in the gusting winds. Still, he hurried. And his pace was held down only by the amount of oxygen his limited lungs and heart could pump.

84

UTHACALTHING

The four of them made a strange-looking group, hurrying northward under overcast skies. Perhaps some little native animals looked up and stared at them, blinking in momentary astonishment before they ducked back into their burrows and swore off the eating of overripe seeds ever again.

To Uthacalthing, though, the forced march was something of a humiliation. Each of the others, it seemed, had advantages over him.

Kault puffed and huffed and obviously did not like the rugged ground. But once the hulking Thennanin got moving he kept up a momentum that seemed unstoppable.

As for Jo-Jo, well, the little chim seemed by now to be a creature *of* this environment. He was under strict orders from Uthacalthing never to knuckle-walk within sight of Kault – no sense in taking a chance with arousing the Thennanin's suspicions – but when the terrain got too rugged he sometimes just scrambled over an obstacle rather than going around it. And over the long flat stretches, Jo-Jo simply rode Robert's back.

Robert had insisted on carrying the chim, whatever the official gulf in status between them. The human lad was impatient enough as it was. Clearly, he would rather have run all the way.

The change in Robert Oneagle was astonishing, and far more than physical. Last night, when Kault asked him to explain part of his story for the third time, Robert clearly and unself-consciously manifested a simple version of *teev'nus* over his head. Uthacalthing could *kenn* how the human deftly used the glyph to contain his frustration, so that none of it would spill over into outward discourtesy to the Thennanin.

Uthacalthing could see that there was much Robert was not telling. But what he said was enough.

I knew that Megan underestimated her son. But of this I had no expectation.

Clearly, he had underrated his own daughter as well.

Clearly. Uthacalthing tried not to resent his flesh and blood for her power, the power to rob him of more than he had thought he could ever lose.

He struggled to keep up with the others, but Uthacalthing's change nodes already throbbed tiredly. It wasn't just that Tymbrimi were more talented at adaptability than endurance. It was also a fault in his *will*. The others had purpose, even enthusiasm.

He had only duty to keep him going.

Kault stopped at the top of a rise, where the looming mountains towered near and imposing. Already they were entering a forest of scrub trees that gained stature as they ascended. Uthacalthing looked up at the steep slopes ahead, already misted in what might be snow clouds, and hoped they would not have to climb much farther.

Kault's massive hand closed around his as the Thennanin helped him up the final few meters. He waited patiently as Uthacalthing rested, breathing heavily through wide-open nostrils.

'I still can scarcely believe what I have been told,' Kault said. 'Something about the Earthling's story does not ring true, my colleague.'

'*T'funatu* ... ' Uthacalthing switched to Anglic, which seemed to take less air. 'What – what do you find hard to believe, Kault? Do you think Robert is lying?'

Kault waved his hands in front of himself. His ridgecrest inflated indignantly. 'Certainly not! I only believe that the young fellow is naive.'

'Naive? In what way?' Uthacalthing could look up now without his vision splitting into two separate images in his cortex. Robert and Jo-Jo weren't in sight. They must have gone on ahead.

'I mean that the Gubru are obviously up to much more than they claim. The deal they are offering – peace with Earth in exchange for tenancy on some Garthian islands and minor genetic purchase rights from neo-chimpanzee stock – such a deal seems barely worth the cost of an interstellar ceremony. It is my suspicion that they are after something else on the sly, my friend.'

'What do you think they want?'

Kault swung his almost neckless head left and right, as if looking to make sure no one else was within listening range. His voice dropped in both volume and timbre.

'I suspect that they intend to perform a snap-adoption.'

'Adoption? Oh ... you mean – '

'Garthlings,' Kault finished for him. 'This is why it is so fortunate your Earthling allies brought us this news. We can only hope that they will be able to provide transport, as they promised, or we will never be in time to prevent a terrible tragedy!'

Uthacalthing mourned all that he had lost. For Kault had raised a perplexing question, one well worth a well-crafted glyph of delicate wryness.

He had been successful, of course, beyond his wildest expectations. According to Robert, the Gubru had swallowed the 'Garthling' myth 'hook, line, and sinker.' At least for long enough to cause them harm and embarrassment.

Kault, too, had come to believe in the ghostly fable. But what was one to make of Kault's claim that his own instruments *verified* the story?

Incredible.

And now, the Gubru seemed to be behaving as if they, too, had more to go on than the fabricated clues he had left. They, too, acted as if there were confirmation!

The old Uthacalthing would have crafted *syulff-kuonn* to commemorate such amazing turns. At this moment, though, all he felt was confused, and very tired.

A shout caused them both to turn. Uthacalthing squinted, wishing right then that he could trade some of his unwanted empathy sense for better eyesight.

Atop the next ridge he made out the form of Robert Oneagle. Seated atop the young human's shoulders, Jo-Jo waved at them. And something else was there, too. A blue glimmering that seemed to spin next to the two Earth creatures and radiate all of the good will of a perfect prankster.

It was the beacon, the light that had led Uthacalthing ever onward, since the crash months before.

'What are they saying?' Kault asked. 'I cannot quite make out the words.'

Neither could Uthacalthing. But he knew what the Terrans were saying. 'I believe they are telling us that we don't have very much farther to go,' he said with some relief. 'They are saying that they have found our transport.'

The Thennanin's breathing slits puffed in satisfaction. 'Good. Now if only we can trust the Gubru to follow custom and proper truce behavior when we appear and offer correct diplomatic treatment to accredited envoys.'

Uthacalthing nodded. But as they began marching uphill together again, he knew that that was only one of their worries.

85

ATHACLENA

She tried to suppress her feelings. To the others, this was serious, even tragic.

But there was just no way to keep it in; her delight would not be contained. Subtle, ornate glyphs spun off from her waving tendrils and diffracted away through the trees, filling the glades with her hilarity. Athaclena's eyes were at their widest divergence, and she covered her mouth with her hand so the dour chims would not see her human-style smile as well.

The portable holo unit had been set up on a ridgetop overlooking the Sind to the northwest in order to improve reception. It showed the scene being broadcast just then from Port Helenia. Under the truce, censorship had been lifted. And even without humans the capital had plenty of chim 'newshounds' on the spot with mobile cameras to show all the debris in stunning detail.

'I can't stand it,' Benjamin moaned. Elayne Soo muttered helplessly as she watched. 'That tears it.'

The chimmie spoke volumes, indeed. For the holo-tank displayed what was left of the fancy wall the invaders had thrown around Port Helenia ... now literally ripped down and torn to shreds. Stunned chim citizens milled about a scene that looked as if a cyclone had hit it. They stared around in amazement, picking through the shattered remnants. A few of those who were more exuberant than thoughtful threw pieces of fence material into the air jubilantly. Some even made chest-thumping motions in honor of the unstoppable wave that had crested there only minutes before, then surged onward into the town itself.

On most of the stations the voice-over was computer generated, but on Channel Two a chim announcer was able to speak over his excitement.

'At – at first we all thought it was a nightmare come true. You know ... like an archetype out of an old TwenCen flatmovie. Nothing would stop them! They crashed through the Gubru barrier as if it was made of tish-tissue paper. I don't know about anybody else, but at any moment I expected the biggest of them to go around grabbing our prettiest chimmies and drag them screaming all the way to the top of the Terragens Tower ...'

Athaclena clapped her hand tighter over her mouth in order to keep from laughing out loud. She fought for self-control, and she was not alone, for one of the chims – Fiben's friend, Sylvie – let out a high chirp of laughter. Most of the others frowned at her in disapproval. After all, this was serious! But Athaclena met the chimmie's eyes and recognized the light in them.

'But it – it appears that these creatures aren't complete kongs, after all. They – after their demolishment of the fence, they don't seem to have done much more damage in their s-sudden invasion of Port Helenia. Mostly, right now, they're Just milling around, opening doors, *eating fruit, going wherever they want to. After all, where does a four-hundred-pound gor ... oh, never mind.'*

This time, another chim joined Sylvie. Athaclena's vision blurred and she shook her head. The announcer went on.

'They seem completely unaffected by the Gubru's psi-drones, which apparently aren't tuned to their brain patterns ...'

Actually, Athaclena and the mountain fighters had known for more than two days where the gorillas were headed. After their first frantic attempts to divert the powerful pre-sentients, they gave up the effort as useless. The gorillas politely pushed aside or stepped over anybody who got in their way. There had simply been no stopping them.

Not even April Wu. The little blond girl had apparently made up her mind to go and find her parents, and short of risking injury to her, there was no way anybody would be able to pry her off the shoulders of one of the giant, silver-backed males.

Anyway, April had told the chims quite matter-of-factly, *somebody* had to go along and supervise the 'rillas, or they might get into trouble!

Athaclena remembered little April's words as she looked at the mess the pre-sentients had made of the Gubru wall. *I'd hate to see the trouble they could cause if they* weren't *supervised!*

Anyway, with the secret out, there was no reason the human child should not be reunited with her family. Nothing she said could hurt anybody now.

So much for the last secrecy of the Howletts Center Project. Now Athaclena might as well just toss away all the evidence she had so dutifully gathered, that first, fateful evening so many months ago. Soon the entire Five Galaxies would know about these creatures. And by some measures that was, indeed, a tragedy. And yet .....

Athaclena remembered that day in early spring, when she had been so shocked and indignant to come upon the illegal Uplift experiment hidden in the forest. Now she could scarcely believe she had actually been like that. *Was I really such a serious, officious little prig?*

Now, *syulff-kuonn* was only the simplest, most *serious* of the glyphs she sparked off, casually, tirelessly, in joy over a simply marvelous joke. Even the chims could not help being affected by her profligate aura. Two more laughed when one of the channels showed an alien staff car, manned by squawking irate Kwackoo, in the process of being peeled back by gorillas who seemed passionately interested in how it would taste. Then another chim chuckled. The laughter spread.

Yes, she thought. *It is a wonderful jest.* To a Tymbrimi, the best jokes were those that caught the joker, as well as everybody else. And this fit the bill beautifully. It was, in truth, a religious experience. For her people believed in a Universe that was more than mere clock-work physics, more than even Ifni's capricious flux of chance and luck.

It was when something like this happened – the Tymbrimi sages said – that one really knew that God, Himself, was still in charge.

Was I, then, also an agnostic before? How silly of me. Thank you then, Lord, and thank you too, father, for this miracle.

The scene shifted to the dock area, where milling chims danced in the streets and stroked the fur of their giant, patient cousins. In spite of the likely tragic consequences of all this, Athaclena and her warriors could not help but smile at the delight the brown-furred relations obviously took in each other. For now, at least, their pride was shared by all the chims of Port Helenia.

Even Lieutenant Lydia McCue and her wary corporal could not help but laugh when a gorilla baby danced past the cameras, wear-ing a necklace made of broken Gubru psi-globes. They caught a glimpse of little April, riding in triumph through the streets, and the sight of a human child seemed to galvanize the crowds.

By now the glade was saturated with her glyphs. Athaclena turned and walked away, leaving the others to resonate in the wry joy. She moved up a forest trail until she came to a place with a clear view of the mountains to the west. There she stood, reaching and *kenning* with her tendrils.

It was there that a chim messenger found her. He hurried up and saluted before handing her a slip of paper. Athaclena thanked him and opened it, though she thought she already knew what it would say.

'W'ith'tanna, Uthacalthing,' she said, softly. Her father was back in touch with the world again. For all of the events of the past few months, there was a solid, practical part of her, still, who was relieved to have this confirmation by radio.

She had had faith that Robert would succeed, of course. That was why she had not gone to Port Helenia with Fiben, or after that with the gorillas. What could she accomplish there, with her poor expert-ise, that her father could not do a thousand times better? If anyone could help turn their slim hopes into more and still greater miracles, it would be Uthacalthing.

No, her job was to remain here. For even in the event of miracles, the Infinite expected mortals to provide their own insurance.

She shaded her eyes. Although she had no hope of personally sighting a little aircraft against the bright clouds, she kept looking for a tiny dot that would be carrying all her love and all her prayers.

86

GALACTICS

Gay pavilions dotted the manicured hillside, occasionally billowing and flapping in the gusting breeze. Quick robots hurried to pluck up any debris brought in by the wind. Others fetched and carried refreshments to the gathered dignitaries.

Galactics of many shapes and colors milled in small groups that merged and separated in an elegant pavane of diplomacy. Courteous bows and flattenings and tentacle wavings conveyed complex nuances of status and protocol. A knowledgeable observer might tell a great deal from such subtleties – and there were many knowledgeable observers present on this day.

Informal exchanges abounded as well. Here a squat, bearlike Pila conversed in clipped, ultrasonic tones with a gangling Linten gardener. A little upslope, three Jophur ring-priests keened in harmonious complaint to an official from the War Institute over some alleged violation out among the starlanes.

It was often said that much more practical diplomacy was accomplished at these Uplift Ceremonies than at formal negotiation conferences. More than one new alliance might be made today, and more than one broken.

Only a few of the Galactic visitors spared more than passing attention to those being honored here today – a caravan of small, brown forms which had taken the entire morning to labor halfway up the mound, circling it four times along the way.

By now nearly a third of the neo-chimpanzee candidates had failed one test or another. Those rejected were already trooping back down the sloping path, in downcast ones and twos.

The remaining forty or so continued their ascent, symbolically reiterating the process of Uplift that had brought their race to this stage in its history, but ignored, for the most part, by the bright crowds on the slopes.

Not all of the observers were inattentive, of course. Near the pinnacle, the Commissioners from the Galactic Uplift Institute paid close attention to the results relayed up by each test station. And nearby, from beneath their own pavilion, a party of the neo-chimpanzees' human patrons watched, glumly.

Looking somewhat lost and helpless, they had been brought out from Cilmar Island only this morning – a few mayors, professors, and a member of the local Uplift Board. The delegation had put forward a procedural protest over the irregular way the ceremony had come about. But when pressed, none of the humans actually claimed a right to cancel it altogether. The possible consequences were potentially just too drastic.

Besides, what if this were the real thing? Earth had been agitating to be allowed to hold just such a ceremony for neo-chimpanzees for two hundred years.

The human observers definitely looked unhappy. For they had no idea what to do, and few of the grand Galactic envoys present even deigned to acknowledge them amid the flurry of informal diplomacy.

On the opposite side of the Evaluators' pavilion sat the elegant Sponsors' Tent. Many Gubru and Kwackoo stood just outside, nervously hopping from time to time, watching every detail with unblinking, critical eyes.

Until moments ago, the Gubru Triumvirate had been visible also, two of them strutting about with their Molt colorings already starting to show and the third still obstinately perched upon its pedestal.

Then one of them received a message, and all three disappeared into the tent for an urgent parlay. That had been some time ago. They still had not emerged.

The Suzerain of Cost and Caution fluttered and spat as it let the message drop to the floor.

'I protest! I protest this interference! This interference and intolerable betrayal!'

The Suzerain of Propriety stared down from its perch, totally at a loss. The Suzerain of Cost and Caution had proved to be a crafty opponent, but never had it been purposely obtuse. Obviously something had happened to upset it terribly.

Crouching Kwackoo servitors hurriedly plucked up the message pellet it had dropped, duplicated the capsule, and brought copies to the other two Gubru lords. When the Suzerain of Propriety viewed the data, it could scarcely believe what it saw.

It was a *solitary neo-chimpanzee*, climbing the lower slopes of the towering Ceremonial Mound, passing rapidly through the automatic first-stage screens and gradually beginning to close the wide gap separating it from the official party, higher on the hillside.

The neo-chimp moved with an erect determination, a clearness of purpose that could be read in its very posture. Those of its conspecifics who had already failed – and who were spiraling slowly down the long trail again – first stared, then grinned and reached out to touch the newcomer's robe as he passed. They offered words of encouragement.

'This was not, cannot have been rehearsed!' the Suzerain of Beam and Talon hissed. The military commander cried out, 'It is an interloper, and I shall have it burned down!'

'You should not, must not, *shall* not!' the Suzerain of Propriety squawked back in anger. 'There has not yet been a coalescence! No complete molting! You do not yet have a queen's wisdom!

'Ceremonies are run, governed, ruled by traditions of honor! *All* members of a client race may approach and be tried, tested, evaluated!'

The third Gubru lord snapped its beak open and shut in agitation. Finally, the Suzerain of Cost and Caution fluffed its ragged feathers and agreed. 'We would be charged reparations. The Institute officials might leave, depart, lay sanctions ... The cost ... ' It turned away in a downy huff. 'Let it proceed, then. For now. Alone, solitary, in isolation it can do no harm.

But the Suzerain of Propriety was not so sure. Once, it had set great store in this particular client. When it seemed to have been stolen, the Suzerain of Propriety suffered a serious setback.

Now, however, it realized the truth. The neo-chimp male had *not* been stolen and eliminated by its rivals, the other Suzerains. Instead, the chimp had *actually* escaped!

And now it was back, alone. How? And what did it hope to accomplish? Without guidance, without the aid of a group, how far did it think it could go?

At first, on seeing the creature, the Suzerain of Propriety had felt joyful amazement – an unusual sensation for a Gubru. Now its emotion was something even more uncomfortable ... a worry that this was only the *beginning* of surprise.

87

FIBEN

So far it had been a piece of cake. Fiben wondered what all the fuss was about.

He had feared they would ask him to solve calculus problems in his head – or recite like Demosthenes, with marbles in his mouth. But at first there had only been a series of force-screen barriers that peeled back for him automatically. And after that there were only more of those funny-looking instruments he had seen the Gubru techs use weeks, months ago – now wielded by even funnier-looking aliens.

So far so good. He made it around the first circuit in what had to be record speed.

Oh, a few times they asked him some questions. What was his earliest memory? Did he enjoy his profession? Was he satisfied with the physical form of this generation of neo-chimpanzee, or might it be improved somehow? Would a prehensile tail be a convenient aid in tool use, for instance?

Gailet would have been proud of the way he remained polite, even then. Or at least he hoped she'd be proud of him.

Of course the Galactic officials had his entire record – genetic, scholastic, military – and were able to access it the moment he passed a group of startled Talon Soldiers on the bayside bluffs and strode through the outer barriers to meet his first test.

When a tall, treelike Kanten asked him about the note he had left, that night when he 'escaped' from imprisonment, it was clear that the Institute was capable of subpoenaing the invaders' records as well. He answered truthfully that Gailet had worded the document but that he had understood its purpose and concurred.

The Kanten's foliage tinkled in the chiming of tiny, silvery bells. The semi-vegetable Galactic sounded pleased and amused as it shuffled aside to let him pass.

The intermittent wind helped keep Fiben cool as long as he was on the eastward slopes, but the westward side faced the afternoon sun and was sheltered from the breeze. The effort of maintaining his rapid pace made him feel as if he were wearing a thick coat, even though a chim's sparse covering of body hair was technically not fur at all.

The parklike hill was neatly landscaped, and the trail paved with a soft, resilient surface. Nevertheless, through his toes he sensed a faint trembling, as if the entire artificial mountain were throbbing in harmonies far, far below the level of hearing. Fiben, who had seen the massive power plants before they were buried, knew that it was not his imagination.

At the next station a Pring technician with huge, glowing eyes and bulging lips looked him up and down and noted something in a datawell before allowing him to proceed. Now some of the dignitaries dotting the slopes seemed to have begun to notice him. A few drifted nearer and accessed his test results in curiosity. Fiben bowed courteously to those nearby and tried not to think about all the different kinds of eyes that were watching him like some sort of specimen.

Once their ancestors had to go through something like this, he consoled himself.

Twice Fiben passed a few spirals below the party of official candidates, a gradually dwindling band of brownish creatures in short, silvery robes. The first time he hurried by, none of the chims noticed him. On the second occasion, though, he had to stand under the scrutiny of instruments held by a being whose species he could not even identify. That time he was able to make out a few figures among those up above. And some of the chims noticed him as well. One nudged a companion and pointed. But then they all disappeared around the comer again.

He had not seen Gailet, but then, she would likely be at the head of the party, wouldn't she? 'Come on,' Fiben muttered impatiently, concerned over the time this creature was taking. Then he considered that the machines focused on him might read either his words or his mood, and he concentrated on preserving discipline. He smiled sweetly and bowed as the alien technician indicated a passing score with a few terse, computer-mediated words.

Fiben hurried on. He grew more and more irritated with the long distances between the stations and wondered if there wasn't any dignified way he could run, in order to cut down on the gap even faster.

Instead though, things only started going slower as the tests grew more serious, calling for deeper learning and more complex thought. Soon he met more chims on their way back down. Apparently these were now forbidden to talk to him, but a few rolled their eyes meaningfully, and their bodies were damp with perspiration.

He recognized several of these dropouts. Two were professors at the college in Port Helenia. Others were scientists with the Garth Ecological Recovery Program. Fiben began to grow worried. All of these chims were blue-card types – among the brightest! If they were failing, something had to be very wrong here. Certainly this ceremony wasn't perfunctory, as that celebration for the Tytlal, which Athaclena had told him about.

Perhaps the rules *were* stacked against Earthlings.

That was when he approached a station manned by a tall Gubru. It did not help that the avian wore the colors of the Uplift Institute and was supposedly sworn to impartiality. Fiben had seen too many of that clan wearing Institute livery today to satisfy him.

The birdlike creature used a vodor and asked him a simple question of protocol, then let him proceed.

A thought suddenly occurred to Fiben as be quickly left that test site. What if the Suzerain of Propriety had been completely defeated by its peers? Whatever its real agenda, that Suzerain had, at least, been sincere about wanting to run a real ceremony. A promise made had to be kept. But what of the others? The admiral and the bureaucrat? Certainly they would have different priorities.

Could the whole thing be rigged so that neo-chimps could not win, no matter how ready they were for advancement? Was that possible?

Could such a result be of real benefit to the Gubru in some way?

Filled with such troubling thoughts, Fiben barely passed a test that involved juggling several complex motor functions while having to solve an intricate three-dimensional puzzle. As he left that station, with the waters of Aspinal Bay falling under late afternoon shadows to his left, he almost failed to notice a new commotion far below. At the last moment he turned to see where a growing sound was coming from.

'What in Ifni's incontinence?' He blinked and stared.

He was not alone in that. By now half of the Galactic dignitaries seemed to be drifting down that way, attracted by a brown tide that was just then spilling up to the foot of the Ceremonial Mound.

Fiben tried to see what was happening, but patches of sunlight, reflected by still-bright water, made it hard to make out anything in the shadows just below. What he could tell was that the bay appeared to be covered with *boats,* and many were now emptying their passengers onto the isolated beach where he had landed, hours before.

So, more of the city chims had come out to get a better look after all. He hoped none of them misbehaved, but he doubted any harm would be done. The Galactics surely knew that monkey curiosity was a basic chimp trait, and this was only acting true to form. Probably the chims'd be given a lower portion of the slope from which to watch, as was their right by Galactic Law.

He couldn't afford to waste any more time dawdling, though. Fiben turned to hurry onward. And although he passed the next test on Galactic History, he also knew that his score had not helped his cumulative total much.

Now he was glad when he arrived on the westward slope. As the sun sank lower, this was the side on which the wind did not bite quite as fiercely. Fiben shivered as he plodded on, slowly gaining on the diminishing crowd above him.

'Slow *down,* Gailet,' he muttered. 'Can't you drag your feet or somethin'? You don't haveta answer every damn question the very second it's asked. Can't you tell I'm comin'?'

A dismal part of him wondered if she already knew, and maybe didn't care.

88

GAILET

She found it increasingly hard to feel that it mattered. And the cause of her depression was more than just the fatigue of a long, hard day, or the burden of all these bewildered chims relying upon her to lead them ever onward and upward through a maze of ever more demanding trials.

Nor was it the constant presence of the tall chen named Irongrip; It certainly was frustrating to see him breeze through tests that other, better chims failed. And as the other Sponsors' Choice, he was usually right behind her, wearing an infuriating, smug grin. Still, Gailet could grit her teeth and ignore him most of the time.

Nor, even, did the examinations themselves bother her much. Hell, they were the best part of the day! Who was the ancient human sage who had said that the purest pleasure, and the greatest force in the ascent of Mankind, had been the skilled worker's joy in her craft? While Gailet was concentrating she could block out nearly everything, the world, the Five Galaxies, all but the challenge to show her skill. Underneath all the crises and murky questions of honor and duty, there was always a clean sense of satisfaction whenever she finished a task and *knew* she had done well even before the Institute examiners told her so.

No, the tests weren't what disturbed her. What bothered Gailet most was the growing suspicion that she had made the wrong choice after all.

I should have refused to participate, she thought. *I should have simply said no.*

Oh, the logic was the same as before. By protocol and all of the rules, the Gubru had put her in a position where she simply had no choice, for her own good and the good of her race and clan.

And yet, she also knew she was being *used*. It made her feel defiled.

During that last week of study at the Library she had found herself repeatedly dozing off under the screens, bright with arcane data. Her dreams were always disturbed, featuring birds holding threatening instruments. Images of Max and Fiben and so many others lingered, thickening her thoughts every time she jerked awake again.

Then the Day arrived. She had donned her robe almost with a sense of relief that now, at least, it was all finally approaching an end. But *what* end?

A slight chimmie emerged from the most recent test booth, mopped her forehead with the sleeve of her silvery tunic, and walked tiredly over to join Gailet. Michaela Noddings was only an elementary school teacher, and a green card, but she had proven more adaptable and enduring than quite a few blues, who were now walking the lonely spiral back down again. Gailet felt deep relief on seeing her new friend still among the candidates. She reached out to take the other chimmie's hand.

'I almost flunked that one, Gailet,' Michaela said. Her fingers trembled in Gailet's grasp.

'Now, don't you dare flake out on me, Michaela,' Gailet said soothingly. She brushed her companion's sweaty locks. 'You're my strength. I couldn't go on if you weren't here.'

In Michaela's brown eyes was a soft gratitude, mixed with irony. 'You're a liar, Gailet. That's sweet of you to say, but you don't need any of us, let alone little me. Whatever I can pass, you take at a breeze.'

Of course that wasn't strictly true. Gailet had figured out that the examinations offered by the Uplift Institute were *scaled* somehow, in order to measure not only how intelligent the subject was but also how hard he or she was trying. Sure, Gailet had advantages over most of the other chims, in training and perhaps in IQ, but at each stage her own trials got harder, too.

Another chim – a Probationer known as Weasel – emerged from the booth and sauntered over to where Irongrip waited with a third member of their band. Weasel did not seem to be much put out. In fact, all three of the surviving Probationers looked relaxed, confident. Irongrip noticed Gailet's glance and winked at her. She turned away quickly.

One last chim came out then and shook his head. 'That's it,' he said.

'Then Professor Simmins … ?'

When he shrugged, Gailet sighed. This just did not make sense. Something was wrong when fine, erudite chims were failing, and yet the tests did not cull out Irongrip's bunch from the very start.

Of course, the Uplift Institute might judge 'advancement' differently than the human-led Earthclan did. Irongrip and Weasel and Steelbar were *intelligent*, after all. The Galactics might not view the Probationers' various character flaws as all that terrible, loathsome as they were to Terrans.

But no, that wasn't the reason at all, Gailet realized, as she and Michaela stepped past the remaining twenty or so to lead the way upward again. Gailet knew that something else had to be behind this. The Probies were just too cocky. Somehow they knew that a fix was in.

It was shocking. The Galactic Institutes were supposed to be above reproach. But there it was. She wondered what, if anything, could be done about it.

As they approached the next station – this one manned by a plump, leathery Soro inspector and six robots – Gailet looked around and noticed something for the first time, that nearly all of the brightly dressed Galactic observers – the aliens unaffiliated with the Institute who had come to watch and engage in informal diplomacy – nearly all of them had drifted away. A few could still be seen, moving swiftly downslope and to the east, as if drawn by something interesting happening off that way.

Of course they won't bother telling us what's going on, she thought bitterly.

'Okay, Gailet,' Michaela sighed. 'You first again. Show 'em we can talk real good.'

So, even a prim schoolteacher will use grunt dialect as an affectation, a bond. Gailet sighed. 'Yeah. Me go do that thing.'

Irongrip grinned at her, but Gailet ignored him as she stepped up to bow to the Soro and submit to the attentions of the robots.

89

GALACTICS

The Suzerain of Beam and Talon strutted back and forth under the flapping fabric of the Uplift Institute pavilion. The Gubru admiral's voice throbbed with a vibrato of outrage.

'Intolerable! Unbelievable! Impermissible! This invasion must be stopped, held back, put into abeyance!'

The smooth routine of a normal Uplift Ceremony had been shattered. Officials and examiners of the Institute – Galactics of many shapes and sizes – now rushed about under the great canopy, hurriedly consulting portable Libraries, seeking precedents for an event none of them had ever witnessed or imagined before. An unexpected disturbance had triggered chaos everywhere, and especially in the corner where the Suzerain danced its outrage before a spiderlike being.

The Grand Examiner, an arachnoid Serentini, stood relaxed in a circle of datatanks, listening attentively to the Gubru officer's complaint.

'Let it be ruled a violation, an infraction, a capital offense! My soldiers shall enforce propriety severely!' The Suzerain fluffed its down to display the pinkish tint already visible under the outer feathers – as if the Serentini would be impressed to see that the admiral was nearly female, almost a queen.

But the sight failed to impress the Grand Examiner. Serentini were *all* female, after all. So what was the big deal?

The Grand Examiner kept her amusement hidden, however. 'The new arrivals fit all of the criteria for being allowed to participate in this ceremony,' she replied patiently in Galactic Three. 'They have caused consternation, of course, and will be much discussed long after this day is done. Still, they are only one of many features of this ceremony which are, well, unconventional.'

The Gubru's beak opened, then shut. 'What do you mean by that?'

'I mean that this is the most irregular Uplift Ceremony in megayears. I have several times considered canceling it altogether.'

'You dare not! We should appeal, seek redress, seek compensation . . .'

'Oh, you would love that, wouldn't you?' The Grand Examiner sighed. 'Everyone knows the Gubru are overextended now. But a judgment against one of the Institutes could cover some of your costs, no?'

This time, the Gubru was silent. The Grand Examiner used two feelers to scratch a crease in her carapace. 'Several of my associates believe that that was your plan all along. There are so many irregularities in this ceremony you've arranged. But on close examination each one seems to stop *just* short of illegality. You have been clever at finding precedents and loopholes.

'For instance, there is the matter of human approval of a ceremony for their own clients. It is unclear these hostage officials of yours understood what they were agreeing to when they signed the documents you showed me.'

'They were – had been – offered Library access.'

'A skill for which wolflings are not renowned. There is suspicion of coercion.'

'We have a message of acceptance from Earth! From their homeworld! From their nest-mothers!'

'Aye,' the Serentini agreed. 'They accepted your offer of peace and a free ceremony. What poor wolfling race in their dire circumstances could turn down such a proposal? But semantic analysis shows that they thought they were only agreeing to *discuss* the matter further! They obviously did not understand that you had purchased liberation of their *old* applications, some made more than fifty paktaars ago! This allowed the waiting period to be waived.'

'Their misunderstandings are not our concern,' clipped the Suzerain of Beam and Talon.

'Indeed. And does the Suzerain of Propriety hold with this view?'

This time there was only silence. Finally, the Grand Examiner lifted both forelegs and crossed them in a formal bow. 'Your protest is acknowledged. The ceremony shall continue, under the ancient rules set down by the Progenitors.'

The Gubru commander had no choice. It bowed in return. Then it swiveled and flounced outside, angrily pushing aside a crowd of its guards and aides, leaving them cackling, disturbed, in its wake.

The Examiner turned to a robot assistant. 'What were we discussing before the Suzerain arrived?'

'An approaching craft whose occupants claim diplomatic protection and observer status,' the thing replied in Galactic One.

'Ah, yes. Those.'

'They are growing quite perturbed, as Gubru interceptors now seem about to cut them off, and may do them harm.'

The Examiner hesitated only a moment. 'Please inform the approaching envoys that we will be only too happy to grant their request. They should come directly to the Mount, under the protection of the Uplift Institute.'

The robot hurried off to pass on the order. Other aides then approached, waving readouts and picting preliminary reports on still more anomalies. One after another of the holo-screens lit up to show the crowd that had arrived at the base of the hill, tumbling out of rusty boats and surging up the unguarded slopes.

'This event grows ever more interesting,' the Grand Examiner sighed reflectively. 'I wonder, what will happen next?'

90

GAILET

It was after sunset and Gimelhai had already sunk below a western horizon turbid with dark clouds by the time the worn-down survivors finally passed through the last examination screen to collapse in exhaustion upon a grassy knoll. Six chens and six chimmies lay quietly close to each other for warmth. They were too tired to engage in the grooming all felt they needed.

'Momma, why didn't they choose dogs to uplift, instead? Or pigs?' One of them moaned.

'Baboons,' another voice suggested, and there was a murmur of agreement. Such creatures deserved this kind of treatment.

'Anybody but us,' a third voice summarized, succinctly.

Ex exaltavit humilis, Gailet thought silently. *They have lifted up the humble of origins.* The motto of the Terragens Uplift Board had its origins in the Christian Bible. To Gailet it had always carried the unfortunate implication that someone, somewhere, was going to get crucified.

Her eyes closed and she felt a light sleep close in immediately. *Just a catnap,* she thought. But it did not last long. Gailet felt a sudden return of that dream – the one in which a Gubru stood over her, peering down the barrel of a malevolent machine. She shivered and opened her eyes again.

The last shreds of twilight were fading. Bitterly clear, the stars twinkled as if through something more refracting than mere atmosphere.

She and the others stood up quickly as a brightly lit floater car approached and settled down in front of them. Out stepped three figures, a tall, downy-white Gubru, a spiderlike Galactic, and a pudgy human mel whose official gown hung on him like a potato sack. As she and the other chims bowed, Gailet recognized Cordwainer Appelbe, the head of Garth's local Uplift Board.

The man looked bewildered. Certainly he must be overawed to be taking part in all this. Still, Gailet also wondered whether Appelbe was drugged.

'Um, I want to congratulate you all,' he said, stepping just ahead of the other two. 'You should know how proud we are of all of you. I've been told that, while there are certain test scores that are still in dispute, the overall judgment of the Uplift Institute is that *Pan argonostes* – the neo-chimpanzees of Earthclan – are, or, well, actually have been ready for stage three for quite some time.'

The arachnoid official stepped forward then. 'That is true. In fact, I can promise that the Institute will favorably consider any future applications by Earthclan for further examinations.'

Thank you, Gailet thought as she and the others bowed again. *But please, don't bother picking me for the next one.*

Now the Grand Examiner launched into a lengthy speech about the rights and duties of client races. She spoke of the long-departed Progenitors, who began Galactic civilization so long ago, and the procedures they set down for all succeeding generations of intelligent life to follow.

The Examiner used Galactic Seven, which most of the chims could at least follow. Gailet tried to pay attention, but within her troubled thoughts kept turning to what was certainly to come after this.

She was sure she felt underfoot an increase in the faint trembling which had accompanied them all the way up the mountain. It filled the air with a low, barely audible rumbling. Gailet swayed as a wave of *unreality* seemed to pass through her. She looked up and saw that several of the evening stars appeared to flare suddenly brighter. Others fled laterally as an oval distortion inserted itself directly overhead. A *blackness* began to gather there.

The Examiner's aeolian speech droned on. Cordwainer Appelbe listened raptly, a bemused expression on his face. But the white-plumed Gubru grew visibly impatient with each passing moment. Gailet could well understand why. Now that the hyperspace shunt was warmed up and ready, every passing minute was costing the invaders. When she realized this, Gailet felt warmer toward the droning Serentini official. She nudged Michaela when her friend seemed about to doze off, and put on an attentive expression.

Several times the Gubru opened its beak as if about to commit the ungraceful act of interrupting the Examiner. Finally, when the spiderlike being stopped briefly for a breath, the avian cut in sharply. Gailet, who had been studying hard for months, easily understood the clipped words in Galactic Three.

'—*delaying, dawdling, stalling! Your motives are in doubt, incredible, suspect! I insist that you proceed, move along, get on with it!*'

But the Examiner scarcely missed a beat, continuing in Galactic Seven.

'In passing the formidable gauntlet you faced today, more rigorous than any testing I have heretofore witnessed, you have demonstrated your worthiness as junior citizens of our civilization, and bring credit to your clan.

'What you receive today, you have earned – the right to reaffirm your love of your patrons, and to choose a stage consort. The latter decision is an important one. As consort you must select a known, oxygen-breathing, starfaring race, one that is not a member of your own clan. This race will defend your interests and impartially intercede in disputes between you and your patrons. If you wish, you may select the Tymbrimi, of the Clan of the Krallnith, who have been your consort-advisors up until now. Or you may make a change.

'Or, you may choose yet another option – to end your participation in Galactic civilization, and ask that the meddling of Uplift be reversed. Even this drastic step was prescribed by the Progenitors, as insurance of the fundamental rights of living things.'

Could we? Could we really do that? Gailet felt numb at the very idea. Even though she knew that it was almost never allowed in practice, the option was there!

She shuddered and refocused her attention as the Grand Examiner lifted two arms in a benediction. 'In the name of the Institute of Uplift, and before all of Galactic civilization, I therefore pronounce you, the representatives of your race, qualified and capable of choosing and bearing witness. Go forth, and do all living things proud.'

The Serentini stepped back. And at last it was the turn of the ceremony sponsor. Normally, this would have been a human, or perhaps a Tymbrimi, but not this time. The Gubru emissary did a little dance of impatience. Quickly, it barked into a vodor, and words in Galactic Seven boomed forth.

'Ten of you shall accompany the final representatives to the shunt and offer witness. The selected pair shall carry the burden of choice and honor. These two I shall name now.

'Doctor Gailet Jones, female, citizen of Garth, Terragens Federation, Clan of Earth.'

Gailet did not want to move, but Michaela, her friend, betrayed her by planting a hand in the small of her back and gently urging her forward. She stepped a few paces toward the dignitaries and bowed. The vodor boomed again.

'Irongrip Hansen, male, citizen of Garth, Terragens Federation, Clan of Earth.'

Most of the chims behind her gasped in shock and dismay. But Gailet only closed her eyes as her worst fears were confirmed. Up until now she had clung to a hope that the Suzerain of Propriety might still be a force among the Gubru. That it might yet compel the Triumvirate to play fair. But now . . .

She felt *him* step up next to her and knew the chen she hated most was wearing that grin.

Enough! I've stood for this long enough! Surely the Grand Examiner suspects something. If I tell her . . .

But she did not move. Her mouth did not open to speak.

Suddenly, and with brutal clarity, Gailet realized the real reason why she had gone along with this farce for so long!

They've fooled with my mind!

It all made sense. She recalled the dreams . . . nightmares of helplessness under the subtle, adamant coercion of machines held in ruthless talons.

The Uplift Institute wouldn't be equipped to test for that.

Of course they wouldn't! Uplift Ceremonies were invariably joyous occasions, celebrated by patron and client alike. Who ever heard of a race-representative having to be conditioned or forced to participate?

It must've been done after Fiben was taken away. The Suzerain of

Propriety couldn't have agreed to such a thing. If the Grand Examiner only knew, we could squeeze a planet's worth of reparation gild from the Gubru!

Gailet opened her mouth. 'I ...' She tried to make words come. The Grand Examiner looked at her.

Perspiration condensed on Gailet's brow. All she had to do was make the accusation. Even *hint* at it!

But her brain was frozen. It felt as if she had forgotten *how* to make words!

Speechlock. Of course. The Gubru had learned how easy it was to impose on a neo-chimpanzee. A human, perhaps, might have been able to break the hold, but Gailet recognized how futile it was in her case.

She could not read arthropoid expressions, but it seemed somehow as if the Serentini looked disappointed. The Examiner stepped back. 'Proceed to the hyperspace shunt,' she said.

No! Gailet wanted to cry. But all that escaped was a faint sigh as she felt her right hand lift of its own accord and meet Irongrip's left. He held on and she could not let go.

That was when she felt an image begin to form in her mind – an avian face with a yellow beak and cold, unblinking eyes. No effort could rid her of the picture. Gailet knew with terrible certainty that she was about to carry that image with her to the top of the ceremonial mound, and once there she and Irongrip would send it upward, into the oval of warped space overhead, for all to see, here and on a thousand other worlds.

The part of her mind that still belonged to her – the logical entity, now cut off and isolated – saw the cold covinous logic of the plan.

Oh, humans were sure to claim that the choice made today had been rigged. And probably more than half of the clans in the Five Galaxies would believe it. But that wouldn't change anything. The choice would still stand! The alternative would be to discredit the entire system. Stellar civilization was under such pressure, right now, that it could not stand much further strain.

In fact, quite a few clans might decide that there had already been quite enough trouble over one little tribe of wolflings. Whatever the rights and wrongs, there would be substantial sentiment for ending the problem, once and for all.

It came to Gailet all in a rush. The Gubru did not merely want to become chims' new stage consort 'protectors.' They meant to bring about the extinction of *humanity.* Once that was accomplished, her own people would be up for adoption, and she had little doubt how *that* would go!

Gailet's heart pounded. She struggled not to turn in the direction

Irongrip was guiding her, But to no avail. She prayed that she would have a stroke.

Let me die!

Her life hardly mattered. They certainly planned to have her 'disappear' immediately after the ceremony anyway, to dispose of the evidence. *Oh, Goodall and Ifni, strike me down now!* She wanted to scream.

At that moment, words came. *The* words ... but it was not her voice that spoke them.

'Stop! An injustice is being done, and I demand a hearing!'

Gailet had not thought her heart could beat any quicker, but now tachycardia made her feel faint. *Oh God, let it be* ...

She heard Irongrip curse and let go of her hand. That alone brought her joy. There was the sound of squawking Gubru anger, and high 'eeps' of chim surprise. Someone – Michaela, she realized – took her arm and turned her around.

It was full night now. Scattered clouds were underlit by the bright beacons of the mound, and by the turbulent, lambent tunnel of energy now taking form above the artificial mountain. Into the stark light of the floater car's headlamps a solitary neo-chimpanzee in a dust-coated formal robe approached from the last test station. He wiped sweat from his brow and strode purposefully toward the three surprised officials.

Fiben, Gailet thought. Dazed, she found that old habits were the first to reassert themselves. *Oh, Fiben, don't swagger! Try to remember your protocol* ...

When she realized what she was doing, Gailet suddenly giggled in a brief wave of hysteria. It shook her partially free of her immobility, and she managed to lift her hand to cover her mouth. 'Oh, Fiben,' she sighed.

Irongrip growled, but the new arrival only ignored the Probationer. Fiben caught her eye and winked. It struck Gailet how the gesture that had once so infuriated her now made her knees feel weak with joy.

He stepped before the three officials and bowed low. Then, with hands clasped respectfully, Fiben awaited permission to speak.

' – dishonorable, incorrigible, impermissible interruptions – ' the Gubru's vodor boomed. 'We demand immediate removal and sanction, punishment – '

The noise suddenly cut off as the Grand Examiner used one of her forward arms to reach up and switch the vodor off. She stepped daintily forward and addressed Fiben.

'Young one, I congratulate you on making your way up to this place all alone. Your ascent provided much of the excitement and unconventionality that is making this one of the most memorable of all ceremonies on record. By virtue of your test scores and other accomplishments, you have earned a place on this pinnacle.' The Serentini crossed two arms and lowered her forebody. 'Now,' she said as she rose again, 'can we assume that you have a complaint to voice? One important enough to explain such abruptness of tone?'

Gailet tensed. The Grand Examiner might be sympathetic, but there was a veiled threat implied in those words. Fiben had better make this good. One mistake and he could make matters even worse than before.

Fiben bowed again. 'I – I respectfully request an explanation of ... of how the race-representatives were chosen.'

Not too bad. Still, Gailet struggled against her conditioning. If only she could step forward and help!

For some time the dim slopes beyond the circle of lights had begun to fill with the Galactic dignitaries – those who had departed earlier to watch unknown events downslope. Now they were all hushed, watching a humble client from one of the newest of all species demand answers from a lord of the Institute.

The Grand Examiner's voice was patient when she answered. 'It is traditional for the ceremony sponsors to select a pair from among those who pass all trials. While it is true that the sponsors are, on this occasion, declared enemies of your clan, their enmity will officially end upon completion of the rites. Peace will exist between the clan of Terrans and that of Gooksyu-Gubru. Do you object to this, young one?'

'No.' Fiben shook his head. 'Not to that. I just want to know this: Do we absolutely *have to accept* the sponsors' choice as our representatives?'

The Gubru emissary immediately squawked indignantly. The chims looked at one another in surprise. Irongrip muttered, 'When this is over, I'm gonna take that little frat boy an' ...'

The Examiner waved for silence. Its many-faceted eyes focused upon Fiben. 'Young one, what would you do, were it up to you? Would you have us put it to a vote of your peers?'

Fiben bowed. 'I would, your honor.'

This time the Gubru's shriek was positively painful to the ear. Gailet tried once again to step forward, but Irongrip held her arm tightly. She was forced to stand there, listening to the Probationer's muttered curses.

The Serentini official spoke at last. 'Although I am sympathetic, I cannot see how I can allow your request. Without precedent – '

'But there *is* precedent!'

It was a new, deep voice, coming from the dim slope behind the officials. From the crowd of Galactic visitors four figures now emerged into the light, and if Gailet had felt surprise before, now she could only stare in disbelief.

Uthacalthing!

The slender Tymbrimi was accompanied by a bearded human mel whose ill-fitting formal robe had probably been borrowed from some bipedal but not quite humanoid Galactic and was thrown over what seemed to be *animal skins*. Beside the young man walked a neo-chimp who had obvious trouble standing completely erect and who bore many of the stigmata of atavism. The chim hung back when they approached the clearing, as if he knew he did not belong on this ground.

It was the fourth being – a towering figure whose bright, inflated crest ballooned upward in dignity – who bowed casually and addressed the Grand Examiner.

'I see you, Cough*Quinn'3 of the Uplift Institute.'

The Serentini bowed back. 'I see you, honored Ambassador Kault of the Thennanin, and you, Uthacalthing of the Tymbrimi, and your companions. It is pleasant to witness your safe arrival.'

The big Thennanin spread his arms apart. 'I thank your honor for allowing me to use your transmitting facilities to contact my clan, after so long an enforced isolation.'

'This is neutral ground,' the Uplift official said. 'I also know that there are serious matters regarding this planet which you wish to press with the Institute, once this ceremony is at an end.

'But for now, I must insist we maintain pertinence. Will you please explain the remark you made on your arrival?'

Kault gestured toward Uthacalthing. 'This respected envoy represents the race which has served as stage consort and protector to the neo-chimpanzees ever since their wolfling patrons encountered Galactic society. I shall let him tell you.'

All at once Gailet noticed how *tired* Uthacalthing looked. The tym's usually expressive tendrils lay flat, and his eyes were set close together. It was with obvious effort that he stepped forward and offered a small, black cube. 'Here are the references,' he began.

A robot came forward and plucked the data out of his hand. From that instant the Institute's staff would be inspecting the citations. The Examiner herself listened attentively to Uthacalthing.

'The references will show that, very early in Galactic history, Uplift Ceremonies evolved out of the Progenitors' desire to protect themselves from *moral fault*. They who began the process we now know as Uplift frequently consulted with their client races, as humans do with theirs, today. And the clients' representatives were never imposed upon them.'

Uthacalthing gestured toward the assembled chims.

'Strictly speaking, the ceremonial sponsors are making a *suggestion*, when they make their selection. The clients, having passed all the tests appropriate to their stage, are legally permitted to ignore the choice. In the purest sense, this plateau is their territory. We are here as their guests.'

Gailet saw that the Galactic observers were agitated. Many consulted their own datawells, accessing the precedents Uthacalthing had provided. Polylingual chatter spread around the periphery. A new floater arrived, carrying several Gubru and a portable communications unit. Obviously, the invaders were doing furious research of their own.

All this time the power of the hyperspace shunt could be felt building just upslope. The low rumbling was now omnipresent, making Gailet's tendons quiver in imposed rhythm.

The Grand Examiner turned to the nominal human official, Cordwainer Appelbe. 'In the name of your clan, do you support this request for a departure from normal procedure?'

Appelbe bit his lower lip. He looked at Uthacalthing, then at Fiben, then back at the Tymbrimi Ambassador. Then, for the first time, the man actually smiled. 'Hell, yes! I sure do!' he said in Anglic. Then he blushed and switched to carefully phrased Galactic Seven. 'In the name of my clan, I support Ambassador Uthacalthing's request.'

The Examiner turned away to hear a report from her staff. When she came back the entire hillside was hushed. Suspense held them all riveted until she bowed to Fiben.

'Precedent is, indeed, interpretable in favor of your request. Shall I ask your comrades to indicate their choice by hand? Or by secret ballot?'

'Right!' came an Anglic whisper. The young human who had accompanied Uthacalthing grinned and gave Fiben a thumbs-up sign. Fortunately, none of the Galactics were looking that way to witness the impertinence.

Fiben forced a serious expression and bowed again. 'Oh, a hand vote will do nicely, your honor. Thank you.'

Gailet was more bemused than anything as the election was held. She tried hard to decline her own nomination, but the same captation, the same implacable force that had kept her from speaking earlier made her unable to withdraw her name. She was chosen unanimously.

The contest for male representative was straightforward as well. Fiben faced Irongrip, looking calmly up into the tall Probationer's fierce eyes. Gailet found that the best she could make herself do was abstain, causing several of the others to look at her in surprise.

Nevertheless, she almost sobbed with relief when the poll came in nine to three … in favor of Fiben Bolger. When he finally approached, Gailet sagged into his arms and sobbed.

'There. There,' he said. And it wasn't so much the cliché as the sound of his voice that comforted her. 'I told you I'd come back, didn't I?'

She sniffed and rubbed away tears as she nodded. One cliché deserved another. She touched his cheek, and her voice was only slightly sardonic as she said, 'My hero.'

The other chims – all except the outnumbered Probies – gathered around, pressing close in a jubilant mass. For the first time it began to look as if the ceremony just might turn into a celebration after all.

They formed ranks, two by two, behind Fiben and Gailet, and started forth along the final path toward the pinnacle where, quite soon, there would be a physical link from this world to spaces far, far away.

That was when a shrill whistle echoed over the small plateau. A new hover car landed in front of the chims, blocking their path. 'Oh, no,' Fiben groaned. For he instantly recognized the barge carrying the three Suzerains of the Gubru invasion force.

The Suzerain of Propriety looked dejected. It drooped on its perch, unable to lift its head even to look down at them. The other two rulers, however, hopped nimbly onto the ground and tersely addressed the Examiner.

'We, as well, wish to present, offer, bring forward … a precedent!'

91

FIBEN

How easily is defeat snatched from the jaws of victory?

Fiben wondered about that as he stripped out of his formal robe and allowed two of the chims to rub oil into his shoulders. He stretched and tried to hope that he would remember enough from his old wrestling days to make a difference.

I'm too old for this, he thought. *And it's been a long, hard day.*

The Gubru hadn't been kidding when they gleefully announced that they had found an out. Gailet tried to explain it to him while he got ready. As usual, it all seemed to have to do with an *abstraction.*

'As I see it, Fiben, the Galactics don't reject the idea of evolution itself, just evolution of *intelligence*. They believe in something like what we used to call "Darwinism" for creatures all the way up to pre-sentients. What's more, it's assumed that nature is wise in the way she forces every species to demonstrate its fitness in the wild.'

Fiben sighed. 'Please get to the point, Gailet. Just tell me why I have to go face to face against that momzer. Isn't trial-by-combat pretty silly, even by Eatee standards?'

She shook her head. For a little while she had seemed to suffer from speechlock. But that had disappeared as her mind slipped into the familiar pedantic mode.

'No, it isn't. Not if you look at it carefully. You see, one of the risks a patron race runs in uplifting a new client species all the way to starfaring intelligence is that by meddling too much it may deprive the client of its essence, of the very *fitness* that made it a candidate for Uplift in the first place.'

'You mean – '

'I mean that the Gubru can accuse humans of doing this to chims, and the only way to disprove it is by showing that we can still be passionate, and tough, and physically strong.'

'But I thought all those tests – '

Gailet shook her head. 'They showed that everyone on this plateau meets the criteria for Stage Three. Even' – Gailet grimaced as she seemed to have to fight for the words – 'even those Probies are superior, at least in most of the ways Institute regulations test for. They're only deficient by our own, quaint, Earth standards.'

'Such as decency and body odor. Yeah. But I still don't get – '

'Fiben, the Institute really doesn't *care* who actually steps into the shunt, not once we've passed all its tests. If the Gubru want our male race-representative to prove he's better by one more criterion – that of "fitness" – well it's precedented all right. In fact, it's been done more often than voting.'

Across the small clearing, Irongrip flexed and grinned back at Fiben, backed up by his two confederates. Weasel and Steelbar joked with the powerful Probationer chief, laughing confidently over this sudden swerve in their favor.

Now it was Fiben's turn to shake his head and mutter lowly. 'Goodall, what a way to run a galaxy. Maybe Prathachulthorn was right after all.'

'What was that, Fiben?'

'Nothin',' he said as he saw the referee, a Pila Institute official, approach the center of the ring. Fiben turned to meet Gailet's eyes. 'Just tell me you'll marry me if I win.'

'But – ' She blinked, then nodded. Gailet seemed about to say something else, but that *look* came over her again, as if she simply could not find the phrases. She shivered, and in a strange, distant voice she managed to choke out five words.

'Kill – him – for – me, Fiben.'

It was not feral bloodlust, that look in her eyes, but something much deeper. Desperation.

Fiber nodded. He suffered no illusions over what Irongrip intended for him.

The referee called them forward. There would be no weapons. There would be no rules. Underground the rumbling had turned into a hard, angry growl, and the zone of nonspace overhead flickered at the edges, as if with deadly lightning.

It began with a slow circling as Fiben and his opponent faced each other warily, sidestepping a complete circuit of the arena. Nine of the other chims stood on the upslope side, alongside Uthacalthing and Kault and Robert Oneagle. Opposite them, the Gubru and Irongrip's two compatriots watched. The various Galactic observers and officials of the Uplift Institute took up the intervening arcs.

Weasel and Steelbar made fist signs to their leader and bared their teeth. 'Go get 'im, Fiben,' one of the other chims urged. All of the ornate ritual, all of the arcane and ancient tradition and science had come to this, then. This was the way Mother Nature finally got to cast the tie-breaking vote.

'Be-gin!' The Pila referee's sudden shout struck Fiben's ears as an ultrasonic squeal an instant before the vodor boomed.

Irongrip was quick. He charged straight ahead, and Fiben almost decided too late that the maneuver was a feint. He started to dodge to the left, and at barely the last moment changed directions, striking out with his trailing foot.

The blow did not finish in the satisfying crunch he'd hoped for, but Irongrip did cry out and reel away, holding his ribs. Unfortunately, Fiben was thrown off balance and could not follow up his brief opportunity. In seconds it was gone as Irongrip moved forward again, more warily this time, with murder written in his eyes.

Some days it just doesn't pay to get out of bed, Fiben thought as they resumed circling.

Actually, today had begun when he awoke in the notch of a tree, a few miles outside the walls of Port Helenia, where plate ivy parachutes festooned the stripped branches of a winter-barren orchard ...

Irongrip jabbed, then punched out with a hard right. Fiben

ducked under his opponent's arm and riposted with a backhand blow. It was blocked, and the bones of their forearms made a loud *crack* as they met.

... The Talon Soldiers had shown grudging courtesy, so he rode Tycho hard until he arrived at the old prison ...

A fist whistled past Fiben's ear like a cannonball. Fiben stepped inside the outstretched arm and swiveled to plant his elbow into his enemy's exposed stomach.

... Staring at the abandoned room, he had known that there was very little time left. Tycho had galloped through the deserted streets, a flower dangling from his mouth ... The jab wasn't hard enough. Worse, he was too slow to duck aside as Irongrip's arm folded fast to come around to cross his throat.

... and the docks had been filled with chims – they lined the wharves, the buildings, the streets, staring ...

A crushing constriction threatened to cut off his breath. Fiben crouched, dropping his right foot backward between his opponent's legs. He tensed in one direction until Irongrip counterbalanced, then Fiben whirled and threw his weight the other way while he kicked out. Irongrip's right leg slipped out from under him, and his own straining overbalance threw Fiben up and over. The Probationer's incredible grasp held for an astonishing instant, tearing loose only along with shreds of Fiben's flesh.

... He traded his horse for a boat, and headed across the bay, toward the barrier buoys ...

Blood streamed from Fiben's torn throat. The gash had missed his jugular vein by half an inch. He backed away when he saw how quickly Irongrip found his feet again. It was downright intimidating how fast the chen could move.

... He fought a mental battle with the buoys, earning – through reason – the right to pass through ...

Irongrip bared his teeth, spread his long arms, and let out a blood-curdling shriek. The sight and sound seemed to pierce Fiben like a memory of battles fought long, long before chims ever flew starships, when *intimidation* had been half of any victory.

'You can do it, Fiben!' Robert Oneagle cried, countering Irongrip's threat magic. 'Come on, guy! Do it for Simon.'

Shit, Fiben thought. *Typical human trick, guilt-tripping me!*

Still, he managed to wipe away the momentary wave of doubt and grinned back at his enemy. 'Sure, you can scream, but can you do this?'

Fiben thumbed his nose. Then he had to dive aside quickly as Irongrip charged. This time both of them landed clear blows that sounded like beaten drums. Both chims staggered to opposite ends of the arena before managing to turn around again, panting hard and baring their teeth.

... The beach had been littered, and the trail up the bluffs was long and hard. But that turned out to be only the beginning. The surprised Institute officials had already started disassembling their machines when he suddenly appeared, forcing them to remain and test just one more. They assumed it would not take long to send him home again ...

The next time they came together, Fiben endured several hard blows to the side of his face in order to step inside and throw his opponent to the ground. It wasn't the most elegant example of jiu-jitsu. Forcing it, he felt a sudden tearing sensation in his leg.

For an instant, Irongrip was rolling, helpless. But when Fiben tried to pounce his leg nearly collapsed.

The Probationer was on his feet again in an instant. Fiben tried not to show a limp, but something must have betrayed him, for this time Irongrip charged his right side, and when Fiben tried to backpedal, the left leg gave way.

... grueling tests, hostile stares, the tension of wondering if he would ever make it in time ...

As he fell backward, he kicked out, but all that earned him was a grip that seized his ankle like a roller-press. Fiben scrambled for leverage, but his fingers clawed in the loose soil. He tried to slip aside as his opponent hauled him back and then fell upon him.

... And he had gone through all of that just to arrive here? Yeah. All in all, it had been one hell of a day ...

There are certain tricks a wrestler can try against a stronger opponent in a much heavier weight class. Some of these came back to Fiben as he struggled to get free. Had he been a little less close to utter exhaustion, one or two of them might even have worked.

As it was, he managed to reach a point of quasi-equilibrium. He attained a small advantage of leverage which just counterbalanced Irongrip's horrendous strength. Their bodies strained and tugged as hands clutched, probing for the smallest opening. Their faces were pressed near the ground and close enough together to smell each other's hot breath.

The crowd had been silent for some time. No more shouts of encouragement came, from one side or the other. As he and his enemy rocked gradually back and forth in a deadly serious battle of deceptive slowness, Fiben found himself with a clear view of the downward slope of the Ceremonial Mound. With a small corner of his awareness, he realized that the crowd was gone now. Where there had been a dense gathering of multiformed Galactics, now there was only an empty stretch of trampled grass.

The remnants could be seen hurrying downhill and eastward,

shouting and gesticulating excitedly in a variety of tongues. Fiben caught a glimpse of the arachnoid Serentini, the Grand Examiner, standing amid a cluster of her aides, paying no attention any longer to the two chims' fight. Even the Pila referee had turned away to face some growing tumult downslope.

This, after talking as if the fate of everything in the Universe depended upon a battle to the death between two chims? That same detached part of Fiben felt insulted.

Curiosity betrayed him, even here and now. He wondered. *What in th' world are they up to?*

Lifting his eyes even an inch in an attempt to see was enough to do it. He missed by milliseconds an opening Irongrip created as the Probationer shifted his weight slightly. Then, as Fiben followed through too late, Irongrip took advantage in a sudden slip and hold. He began applying pressure.

'Fiben!' It was Gailet's voice, thick with emotion. So he knew that at least *somebody* was still paying attention, if only to watch his final humiliation and end.

Fiben fought hard. He used tricks dragged up out of the well of memory. But the best of them required strength he no longer had. Slowly he was forced back.

Irongrip grinned as he managed to lay his forearm against Fiben's windpipe. Suddenly breath came in hard, high whistles. Air was very dear, and his struggles took on new desperation.

Irongrip held on just as urgently. His bared canines reflected bitter highlights as he panted in an open-mouthed grin over Fiben.

Then the glints faded as something occulted the lights, casting a dark shadow over both of them. Irongrip blinked, and all at once seemed to notice that something bulky had appeared next to Fiben's head. A hairy black *foot*. The attached brown leg was short, as stout as a tree trunk, and led upwards to a mountain of fur ...

For Fiben the world, which had started to spin and go dim, came slowly back into focus as the pressure on his airpipe eased somewhat. He sucked air through the constricted passage and tried to look to see why he was still alive. The first thing he saw was a pair of mild brown eyes, which stared back in friendly openness from a jet black face set at the top of a hill of muscle.

The mountain also had a smile. With an arm the length of a small chimpanzee, the creature reached out and touched Fiben, curiously. Irongrip shuddered and rocked back in amazement, or maybe fear. When the creature's hand closed on Irongrip's arm, it only squeezed hard enough to test the chim's strength.

Obviously, there was no comparison. The big male gorilla chuffed, satisfied. It actually seemed to laugh.

Then, using one knuckle to help it walk, it turned and rejoined the dark band that was even then trooping past the amazed rank of chims. Gailet stared in disbelief, and Uthacalthing's wide eyes blinked rapidly at the sight.

Robert Oneagle seemed to be talking to himself, and the Gubru gabbled and squawked.

But it was Kault who was the focus of the gorillas' attention for a long moment. Four females and three males clustered around the big Thennanin, reaching up to touch him. He responded by speaking to them, slowly, joyfully.

Fiben refused to make the same mistake twice. What *gorillas* were doing here, here atop the Ceremonial Mound the Gubru invaders had built, was beyond his ability to guess, and he wasn't even about to try. His concentration returned just a split instant sooner than his opponent's. When Irongrip looked back down, the Probie's eyes betrayed instantaneous dismay as he recognized the looming shape of Fiben's fist.

The small plateau was a cacophony, a mad scene devoid of any vestige of order. The boundaries of the combat arena did not seem to matter anymore as Fiben and his enemy rolled about under the legs of chims and gorillas and Gubru and whatever else could walk or bounce or slither about. Hardly anybody seemed to be paying them any attention, and Fiben did not really care. All that mattered to him was that he had a promise that he had to keep.

He pummeled Irongrip, not allowing him to regain balance until the chen roared and in desperation threw Fiben off like an old cloak. As he landed in a painful jolt, Fiben caught a glimpse of motion behind him and turned his head to see the Probationer called Weasel lifting his leg, preparing to strike down with his foot. But the blow missed as the Probie was grabbed up by an affectionate gorilla, who lifted him into a crushing embrace.

Irongrip's other comrade was held back by Robert Oneagle – or, rather, held *up*. The male chim might have vastly greater strength than most humans, but it did him no good suspended in midair. Robert raised Steelbar high overhead, like Hercules subduing Anteus. The young man nodded to Fiben.

'Watch out, old son.'

Fiben rolled aside as Irongrip hit the ground where he had lain, sending dust plumes flying. Without delay Fiben leaped onto his opponent's back and slipped into a half-Nelson hold.

The world spun as he seemed to ride a bucking bronco. Fiben tasted blood, and the dust seemed to fill his lungs with clogging, searing pain. His tired arms throbbed and threatened to cramp. But when he heard his enemy's labored breathing he knew he could stand it for a little while longer.

Down, down Irongrip's head went. Fiben got his feet around the chim and kicked the other's legs out from under him.

The Probationer's solar plexus landed on Fiben's heel. And while a flash of pain probably meant several of Fiben's toes were broken, there was also no mistaking the whistling squeak as Irongrip's diaphragm momentarily spasmed, stopping all flow of air.

Somewhere he found the energy. In a whirl he had his foe turned over. Gripping in a tight scissors lock, he brought his forearm around and applied the same illegal-but-who-cares strangulation hold that had earlier been used on him.

Bone ground against gristle. The ground beneath them seemed to throb and the sky rumbled and growled. Alien feet shuffled on all sides, and there was the incessant squawking and chatter of a dozen jabbering tongues. Still, Fiben listened only for the breath that did not flow through his enemy's throat . . . and felt only for the throbbing pulse he so desperately had to silence . . .

That was when something seemed to explode inside his skull.

It was as if something had broken open within him, spilling what seemed a brilliant light *outward* from his cortex. Dazzled, Fiben first thought a Probationer or a Gubru must have struck him a blow to the head from behind. But the luminance was not the sort coming from a concussion. It hurt, but not in that way.

Fiben concentrated on first priorities – holding tightly to his steadily weakening opponent. But he could not ignore this strange occurrence. His mind sought something to compare it to, but there was no correct metaphor. The soundless outburst felt somehow simultaneously alien and eerily familiar.

All at once Fiben remembered a blue light which danced in hilarity as it fired infuriating bolts at his feet. He remembered a 'stink bomb' that had sent a pompous, furry little diplomat scurrying off in abandoned dignity. He remembered stories told at night by the general. The connections made him suspect . . .

All around the plateau, Galactics had ceased their multi-tongued babble and stared upslope. Fiben would have to lift his head a bit to see what so captivated them. Before he did so, however, he made certain of his foe. When Irongrip managed to drag in a few thin, desperate breaths, Fiben restored just enough pressure to keep the big chen balanced on the edge of consciousness. That accomplished, he raised his eyes.

'Uthacalthing,' Fiben whispered, realizing the source of his mental confusion.

The Tymbrimi stood a little uphill from the others. His arms opened wide and the capelike folds of his formal robe flapped in the cyclone winds circling the gaping hyperspace shunt. His eyes were set far apart.

Uthacalthing's corona tendrils waved, and over his head *something* whirled.

A chim moaned and pressed her palms against her temples. Somewhere a Pring's tooth-mashies clattered. To many of those present, the glyph was barely detectable. But for the first time in his life, Fiben actually *kenned*. And what he *kenned* named itself *tutsunucann*.

The glyph was a monster – titanic with long-pent energy. The essence of delayed indeterminacy, it danced and whirled. And then, without warning, it blew apart. Fiben felt it sweep around and through him – nothing more or less than distilled, unadulterated *joy*.

Uthacalthing poured the emotion forth as if a dam had burst. '*N'ha s'urustuannu, k'hammin't Athaclena w'thtanna!*' he cried. 'Daughter, do you send these to me, and so return what I had lent you? Oh, what interest compounded and multiplied! What a fine jest to pull upon your proud parent!'

His intensity affected those standing nearby. Chims blinked and stared. Robert Oneagle wiped away tears.

Uthacalthing turned and pointed up the trail leading toward the Site of Choosing. There, at the pinnacle of the Ceremony Mound, everyone could see that the shunt was connected at last. The deeply buried engines had done their job, and now a *tunnel* gaped overhead, one whose edges glistened but whose interior contained a color emptier than blackness.

It seemed to *suck away* light, making it difficult even to recognize that the opening was there. And yet Fiben knew that this was a link in real time, from this place to countless others where witnesses had gathered to observe and commemorate the evening's events.

I hope the Five Galaxies are enjoying the show. When Irongrip showed signs of reviving, Fiben gave the Probie a whack to the side of the head and looked up again.

Halfway up the narrow trail leading to the pinnacle there stood three ill-matched figures. The first was a small neo-chimpanzee whose arms seemed too long and whose ill-formed legs were bowed and short. Jo-Jo held onto one hand of Kault, the huge Thennanin, ambassador. Kault's other massive paw was grasped by a tiny human girl, whose blond hair flapped like a bright banner in the whirling breeze.

Together, the unlikely trio watched the pinnacle itself, where an unusual band had gathered.

A dozen gorillas, males and females, stood in a circle directly under the half-invisible hole in space. They rocked back and forth, staring up into the yawning emptiness overhead, and crooned a low, atonal melody.

'I believe ...' said the awed Serentini Grand Examiner of the Uplift Institute. '... I believe this has happened before ... once or twice ... but not in more than a thousand aeons.'

Another voice muttered, this time in gruff, emotion-drenched Anglic. 'It's no fair. This was s'pozed t'be *our* time!' Fiben saw tears streaming down the cheeks of several of the chims. Some held each other and sobbed.

Gailet's eyes welled also, but Fiben could tell that she saw what the others did not. Hers were tears of relief, of joy.

From all sides there were heard other expressions of amazement.

'But what sort of creatures, entities, beings can they *be*?' One of the Gubru Suzerains asked.

'... pre-sentients,' another voice answered in Galactic Three.

'... They passed through all the test stations, so they *had* to be ready for a stage ceremony of some sort,' mumbled Cordwainer Appelbe. 'But how in the world did goril—'

Robert Oneagle interrupted his fellow human with an upraised hand. 'Don't use the old name anymore. Those, my friend, are *Garthlings.*'

Ionization filled the air with the smell of lightning. Uthacalthing chanted his pleasure at the symmetry of this magnificent surprise, this great jest, and in his Tymbrimi voice it was a rich, unearthly sound. Caught up in the moment, Fiben did not even notice climbing to his feet, standing to get a better view.

Along with everyone else he saw the coalescence that took place above the giant apes, humming and swaying on the hilltop. Over the gorillas' heads a milkiness swirled and began to thicken with the promise *of shapes*.

'In the memory of no living race has this happened,' the Grand Examiner said in awe. 'Client races have had countless Uplift Ceremonies, over the last billion years. They have graduated levels and chosen Uplift consorts to assist them. A few have even used the occasion to request an end of Uplift ... to return to what they had been before ...'

The filminess assumed an oval outline. And within, dark forms grew more distinct, as if emerging slowly from a deep fog.

'... But only in the ancient sagas has it been told of a new species coming forth *of its own will*, surprising all Galactic society, and demanding the right to select its own patrons.'

Fiben heard a moan and looked down to see Irongrip beginning to rise, trembling, to his elbows. A cruor of blood-tinted dust covered the battered chen from face to foot.

Got to hand it to him. He's got stamina. But then, Fiben did not imagine he himself looked a whole lot better.

He raised his foot. It would be so easy ... He glanced aside and saw Gailet watching him.

Irongrip rolled over onto his back. He looked up at Fiben in blank resignation.

Aw, hell. Instead he reached down and offered his hand to his former foe. *I don't know what we were fighting over. Somebody else got the brass ring, anyway.*

A moan of surprise rippled through the crowd. From the Gubru came grating wails of dismay. Fiben finished hauling Irongrip to his feet, got him stable, then looked up to see what the gorillas had wrought to cause such consternation.

It was the face of a *Thennanin*. Giant, clear as anything, the image hovering in the focus of the hyperspace shunt looked enough like Kault to be his brother.

Such a sober, serious, earnest expression, Fiben thought. *So typically Thennanin.*

A few of the assembled Galactics chattered in amazement, but most acted as if they had been frozen in place. All except Uthacalthing, whose delighted astonishment still sparked in all directions like a Roman candle.

'Z'wurtin's'tatta ... I worked for this, and never knew!'

The titanic image of the Thennanin drifted backward in the milky oval. All could see the thick, slitted neck, and then the creature's powerful torso. But when its arms came into view, it became clear that two figures stood on either side of it, holding its hands.

'Duly noted,' the Grand Examiner said to her aides. 'The unnamed Stage One client species tentatively called Garthlings have selected, as their patrons, the Thennanin. And as their consorts and protectors, they have jointly chosen the neo-chimpanzees and humans of Earth.'

Robert Oneagle shouted. Cordwainer Appelbe fell to his knees in shock. The sound of renewed Gubru screeching was quite deafening.

Fiben felt a hand slip into his. Gailet looked up at him, the poignancy in her eyes now mixed with pride.

'Oh, well,' he sighed. 'They wouldn't have let us keep 'em, anyway. At least, this way, we get visitation rights. And I hear the Thennanin aren't too bad as Eatees go.'

She shook her head. 'You knew something about these creatures and didn't tell me?'

He shrugged. 'It was supposed to be a secret. You were busy. I didn't want to bother you with unimportant details. I forgot. *Mea culpa*. Don't hit, please.'

Briefly, her eyes seemed to flash. Then she, too, sighed and looked back up the hill. 'It won't take them long to realize these aren't really Garthlings, but creatures of Earth.'

'What'll happen then?'

It was her turn to shrug. 'Nothing, I guess. Wherever they come from, they're obviously ready for Uplift. Humans signed a treaty – unfair as it was – forbidding Earthclan to raise 'em, so I guess this'll stand. *Fait accompli*. At least we can play a role. Help see the job's done right.'

Already, the rumbling beneath their feet had begun to diminish. Nearby, the cacophony of Gubru squawking rose in strident tones to replace it. But the Grand Examiner appeared unmoved. Already she was busy with her assistants, ordering records gathered, detailing followup tests to be made, and dictating urgent messages to Institute headquarters.

'And we must help Kault inform his clan,' she added. 'They will no doubt be surprised at this news.'

Fiben saw the Suzerain of Beam and Talon stalk off to a nearby Gubru flyer and depart at top speed. The boom of displaced air ruffled the feathers of the avians who remained behind.

It happened then that Fiben's gaze met that of the Suzerain of Propriety, staring down from its lonely perch. The alien stood more erect now. It ignored the babbling of its fellows and watched Fiben with a steady, unblinking yellow eye.

Fiben bowed. After a moment, the alien politely inclined its head in return.

Above the pinnacle and the crooning gorillas – now officially the youngest citizens of the Civilization of the Five Galaxies – the opalescent oval shrank back into the narrowing funnel. It diminished, but not before those present were treated to yet one more sight none had ever seen before … one they were not likely ever to see again.

Up there in the sky, the image of the Thennanin and those of the chim and human all looked at each other. Then the Thennanin's head rocked back and he actually *laughed*.

Richly, deeply, sharing hilarity with its diminutive partners, the leathery figure chortled. It roared.

Among the stunned onlookers, only Uthacalthing and Robert Oneagle felt like joining in as the ghostly creature above did what Thennanin were never known to do. The image kept right on laughing even as it faded back, back, to be swallowed up at last by the closing hole in space and covered by the returning stats.

PART SIX

CITIZENS

I am a kind of farthing dip,
Unfriendly to the nose and eyes;
A blue-behinded ape, I skip
Upon the trees of Paradise.

ROBERT LOUIS STEVENSON, 'A PORTRAIT'

92

GALACTICS

'They exist. They have substance! They are!'

The assembled Gubru officials and officers bobbed their downy heads and cried out in unison.

'Zooon!'

'This prize was denied us, honor was set aside, opportunity abandoned, all in the name of penny-pinching, miserly bean-counting! Now the cost will be greater, multiplied, exponentiated!'

The Suzerain of Cost and Caution stood miserably in the corner, listening amid a small crowd of loyal assistants while it was berated from all sides. It shivered each time the conclave turned and shouted its refrain.

The Suzerain of Propriety stood tall upon its perch. It stepped back and forth, fluffing up to best display the new color that had begun to show under its molting plumage. The assembled Gubru and Kwackoo reacted to that shade with chirps of passionate devotion.

'And now a derelict, recalcitrant, stubborn one forestalls our Molt and consensus, out of which we might at least regain something. Gain honor and allies. Gain peace!'

The Suzerain spoke of their missing colleague, the military commander, who dared not, it seemed, come and face Propriety's new color, its new supremacy.

A four-legged Kwackoo hurriedly approached, bowed, and delivered a message to its leader's perch. Almost as an afterthought, a copy made its way to the Suzerain of Cost and Caution as well.

The news from the Pourmin transfer point was not surprising – echoes had been heard of great starships bearing down upon Garth in mighty numbers. After that debacle of an Uplift Ceremony, the new arrivals were only to be expected.

'Well?' The Suzerain of Propriety queried the several military officers who were present. 'Does Beam and Talon plan a defense of this world, against all advice, all wisdom, and all honor?'

The officers, of course, did not know. They had deserted their warrior leader as the confusing, unhappy Molt-coalescence suddenly reversed direction.

The Suzerain of Propriety danced a dance of impatience. 'You do me no good, do the clan no good, standing about in righteousness.

Go back, seek out, return to your posts. Do your duties as he commands, but keep me informed of what he plans and does!'

Use of the male pronoun was deliberate. Though Molt was not yet complete, anyone could tell without dropping feathers which way the wind was blowing.

The officers bowed and rushed as one out of the pavilion.

93

ROBERT

Debris littered the now quiescent Ceremonial Mound. Stiff easterly winds riffled the lawnlike slopes, tugging at stringy rubbish blown in earlier from the distant mountains. Here and there, city chims poked through trash on the lower terraces, looking for souvenirs.

Higher up only a few pavilions still stood. Around these several dozen large black forms lazily groomed each other's fur and gossiped with their hands, as if they had never had anything more momentous on their minds than who would mate with whom and what they would be fed next meal.

To Robert it seemed as if the gorillas were quite well satisfied with life. *I envy them*, he thought. In his case even a great victory did not bring an end to worry. Things were still quite dangerous on Garth. Perhaps even more so than two nights ago, when fate and coincidence intervened to surprise them all.

Life was troubling sometimes. All the time.

Robert returned his attention to his datawell and the letter the Uplift Institute officials had relayed to him only an hour before.

... Of course it's very hard for an old women – especially one who, like me, has grown so used to having her own way – but I know I must acknowledge how mistaken I was about my own son. I have wronged you, and for that I am sorry.

In my own defense I can only say that outward appearances *can* be misleading, and you were outwardly such an aggravating boy. I suppose I should have had the sense to see underneath, to the strength you have shown during these months of crisis. But that just never occurred to me. Perhaps I was afraid of examining my own feelings too closely.

In any event, we'll have much time to talk about this after

peace comes. Let's let it go now by saying that I am very proud of you. Your country and your clan owe you much, as does your grateful mother.

With affection,
    Megan

How odd, Robert thought, that after so many years despairing of ever winning her approval, now he had it, and didn't know how to deal with it. Ironically, he felt sympathy for his mother; it was obviously so very difficult for her to say these things at all. He made allowances for the cool tone of the words themselves.

All Garth saw Megan Oneagle as a gracious lady and fair administrator. Only her wandering husbands and Robert himself knew the other side, the one so utterly terrified by permanent obligation and issues of private loyalty. This was the first time in all his life that Robert recalled her apologizing for something really important, something involving family and intense emotions.

Blurring of vision made him close his eyes. Robert blamed the symptoms on the fringing fields of a lifting starship, whose keening engines could be heard all the way from the spaceport. He wiped his cheeks and watched the great liner – silvery and almost angelic in its serene beauty – rise and pass overhead on its leisurely way out to space and beyond.

'One more batch of fleeing rats,' he murmured.

Uthacalthing did not bother turning to look. He lay back on his elbows watching the gray waters. 'The Galactic visitors have already had more entertainment than they bargained for, Robert. That Uplift Ceremony was plenty. To most of them, the prospect of a space battle and siege are much less enticing.'

'One of each has been quite enough for me,' Fiben Bolger added without opening his eyes. He lay a little downslope, his head on Gailet Jones's lap. For the moment, she also had little to say, but concentrated on removing a few tangles from his fur, careful of his still livid black and blue bruises. Meanwhile, Jo-Jo groomed one of Fiben's legs.

Well, he's earned it, Robert thought. Although the Uplift Ceremony had been preempted by the gorillas, the test scores handed down by the Institute still held. If humanity managed to get out of its present troubles and could afford the expense of a new ceremony, two rustic colonials from Garth would lead the next procession ahead of all the sophisticated chims of Terra. Though Fiben himself seemed uninterested in the honor, Robert was proud of his friend.

A female chim wearing a simple frock approached up the trail.

She bowed languidly in a brief nod to Uthacalthing and Robert. 'Who wants the latest news?' Michaela Noddings asked.

'Not me!' Fiben grumped. 'Tell th' Universe t'go f—'

'Fiben,' Gailet chided gently. She looked up at Michaela. 'I want to hear it.'

The chimmie sat and began working on Fiben's other shoulder. Mollified, he closed his eyes again.

'Kault has heard from his people,' Michaela said. 'The Thennanin are on their way here.'

'Already.' Robert whistled. 'They aren't wasting any time, are they?'

Michaela shook her head. 'Kault's folk have already contacted the Terragens Council to negotiate purchase of the fallow gorilla genetic base and to hire Earth experts as consultants.'

'I hope the Council holds out for a good price.'

'Beggars can't be choosers,' Gailet suggested. 'According to some of the departing Galactic observers, Earth is in pretty desperate straits, as are the Tymbrimi. If this deal means we lose the Thennanin as enemies, and maybe win them as allies instead, it could be vital.'

At the price of losing gorillas – our cousins – as clients of our own. Robert mulled. On the night of the ceremony he had only seen the hilarious irony of it all, sharing that Tymbrimi way of viewing things with Uthacalthing. Now, though, it was harder not to count the cost in serious terms.

They were never really ours in the first place, he reminded himself. *At least we'll have a say in how they're raised. And Uthacalthing says some Thennanin aren't as bad as many.*

'What about the Gubru?' he asked. 'They agreed to make peace with Earth in exchange for acceptance of the ceremony.'

'Well, it wasn't exactly the sort of ceremony they had in mind, was it?' Gailet answered. 'What do you think, Ambassador Uthacalthing?'

The Tymbrimi's tendrils waved lazily. All of yesterday and this morning he had been crafting little glyphs of puzzlelike intricacy, far beyond Robert's limited ability to *kenn,* as if he were delighting in the rediscovery of something he had lost.

'They will act in what they see to be their own self-interest, of course,' Uthacalthing said. 'The question is whether they will have the sense to *know* what is good for them.'

'What do you mean?'

'I mean that the Gubru apparently began this expedition with confused goals. Their Triumvirate reflected conflicting factions back home. The initial intent of their expedition here was to use the hostage population of Garth to pry secrets out of the Terragens Council. But then they learned that Earth is as ignorant as everybody else about what that infamous dolphin-ship of yours discovered.'

'Has there been any new word about the *Streaker*?' Robert interrupted.

Spiraling off a *palanq* glyph, Uthacalthing sighed. 'The dolphins seem to have miraculously escaped a trap set for them by a dozen of the most fanatic patron lines – an astonishing feat by itself – and now the *Streaker* seems to be loose on the starlanes. The humiliated fanatics lost tremendous face, and so tensions have reached an even higher level than before. It is one more reason why the Gubru Roost Masters grow increasingly frightened.'

'So when the invaders found they couldn't use hostages to coerce secrets out of Earth, the Suzerains searched for other ways to make some profit out of this expensive expedition,' Gailet surmised.

'Correct. But when the first Suzerain of Cost and Caution was killed it threw their leadership process out of balance. Instead of negotiating toward a consensus of policy, the three Suzerains engaged in unbridled competition for the top position in their Molt. I'm not sure that even now I understand all of the schemes that might have been involved. But the final one – the one they settled on at last – will cost them very dearly. Blatantly interfering with the proper outcome of an Uplift Ceremony is a grave matter.'

Robert saw Gailet wince in revulsion as she obviously recollected how she had been used. Without opening his eyes, Fiben reached out and took her hand. 'Where does that leave us now?' Robert asked Uthacalthing.

'Both common sense and honor would demand the Gubru keep their bargain with Earth. It's the only way out of a terrible bind.'

'But you don't expect them to see it that way.'

'Would I remain confined here, on neutral ground, if I did? You and I, Robert, would be with Athaclena right now, dining on *khoogra* and other delicacies I'd cached away, and we would speak for hours of, oh, so many things. But that will not happen until the Gubru decide between logic and self-immolation.'

Robert felt a chill. 'How bad could it get?' he asked in a low voice. The chims, too, listened quietly.

Uthacalthing looked around. He inhaled the sweet, chill air as if it were of fine vintage. 'This is a lovely world,' he sighed. 'And yet it has suffered horror. Sometimes, so-called civilization seems bent on destroying those very things which it is sworn to protect.'

94

GALACTICS

'After them!' cried the Suzerain of Beam and Talon. 'Chase them! Pursue them!'

Talon Soldiers and their battle drones swooped down upon a small column of neo-chimpanzees, taking them by surprise. The hairy Earthlings turned to fight, firing their ill-sorted weapons upward at the stooping Gubru. Two small fireballs did erupt, emitting sprays of singed feathers, but for the most part resistance was useless. Soon, the Suzerain was stepping delicately among the blasted remains of trees and mammals. It cursed as its officers reported only chim bodies.

There had been stories of others, humans and Tymbrimi and, yes, thrice-cursed Thennanin. Had not one of them suddenly appeared out of the wilderness? They had to all be in league together! It had to be a plot!

Now there were constant messages, entreaties, demands that the admiral return to Port Helenia. That it join with the other commanders for a conclave, a meeting, a new struggle for consensus.

Consensus! The Suzerain of Beam and Talon spat on the trunk of a shattered tree. Already it could feel the ebbing of hormones, the leaching away of color that had *almost* been its own!

Consensus? The admiral would show them consensus! It was determined to win back its position of leadership. And the only way to do that, after that catastrophe of an Uplift Ceremony, was to demonstrate the efficacy of the military option. When the Thennanin came to claim their 'Garthling' prizes, they would be met with force! Let them engage in Uplift of their new clients from deep-space!

Of course, to keep them at bay – in order to return this world for the Roost Masters – there must be complete surety that there would be no attacks from behind, from the surface. The ground opposition had to be eliminated!

The Suzerain of Beam and Talon refused even to consider the possibility that anger and revenge might also have colored its decisions. To have admitted that would be to begin to fall under the sway of Propriety. Already, several good officers had deserted down that path, only to be ordered back to their posts by the sanctimonious high priest. That was particularly galling.

The admiral was determined to win their loyalty back in its own right, with victory!

'The new detectors work, are effective, are efficient!' It danced in satisfaction. 'They let us hunt the Earthlings without needing to scent special materials. We trace them by their very blood!'

The Suzerain's assistants shared its satisfaction. At this rate, the irregulars should soon all be dead.

A pall fell over the celebration when it was reported that one of the troop carriers that had brought them here had broken down. Another casualty of the plague of corrosion that had struck Gubru equipment all over the mountains and the Vale of Sind. The Suzerain had ordered an urgent investigation.

'No matter! We shall all ride the remaining carriers. Nothing, nobody, no event shall stop our hunt!'

The soldiers chanted.

'*Zooon!*'

95

ATHACLENA

She watched as the hirsute human read the message for the fourth time, and could not help wondering whether she was doing the right thing. Rank-haired, bearded, and naked, Major Prathachulthorn looked the very essence of a wild, carnivorous wolfling ... a creature far too dangerous to trust.

He looked down at the. message, and for a moment all she could read were the waves of tension that coursed up his shoulders and down his arms to those powerful, tightly flexed hands.

'It appears that I am under orders to forgive you, and to follow your policies, miss.' The last word ended in a hiss. 'Does this mean that I'll be set free if I promise to be good? How can I be sure this order is for real?'

Athaclena knew she had little choice. In the days ahead she would not be able to spare the chimpower to continue guarding Prathachulthorn. Those she could rely upon to ignore the human's command-voice were very few, and he had already nearly escaped on four separate occasions. The alternative was to finish him off here and now. And for that she simply had not the will.

'I have no doubt you would kill me the instant you discovered the message wasn't genuine,' Athaclena replied.

His teeth seemed to flash. 'You have my word on that,' he assured her.

'And on what else?'

He closed and then reopened his eyes. 'According to these orders from the Government in Exile, I have no choice but to act as if I was never kidnapped, to pretend there was no mutiny, and to conform my strategy to your advice. All right. I agree to this, as long as you remember that I'm going to appeal to my commanders on Earth, first chance I get. And they will take this to the TAASF. And once Coordinator Oneagle is overruled, I will find you, my young Tymbrimi. I will come to you.'

The bald, open hatred in his mind simultaneously made her shiver and also reassured her. The man held nothing back. *Truth* burned beneath his words. She nodded to Benjamin.

'Let him go.'

Looking unhappy, and avoiding eye contact with the dark-haired human, the chims lowered the cage and cut open the door. Prathachulthorn emerged rubbing his arms. Then, quite suddenly, he whirled and leaped in a high kick landing in a stance one blow away from her. He laughed as Athaclena and the chims backed away.

'Where is my command?' he asked tersely.

'I do not know, precisely,' Athaclena answered, as she tried to abort a *gheer* flux. 'We've scattered into small parties and even had to abandon the caves when it was clear they were compromised.'

'What about this place?' Prathachulthorn motioned to the steaming slopes of Mount Fossey.

'We expect the enemy to stage an assault here at any moment,' she replied honestly.

'Well,' he said. 'I didn't believe half of what you told me, yesterday, about that "Uplift Ceremony" and its consequences. But I'll give you this; you and your dad do seem to have stirred up the Gubru good.'

He sniffed the air, as if already he were trying to pick up a spoor. 'I assume you have a tactical situation map and a datawell for me?'

Benjamin brought one of the portable computer units forward, but Prathachulthorn held up a hand. 'Not now. First, let's get out of here. I want to get away from this place.'

Athaclena nodded. She could well understand how the man felt.

He laughed when she declined his mock-chivalrous bow and insisted that he go first. 'As you wish,' he chuckled.

Soon they were swinging through the trees and running under the thick forest canopy. Not much later, they heard what sounded like thunder back where the refuge had been, even though there were no clouds in the sky.

96

SYLVIE

The night was lit by fiery beacons which burst forth actinically and cast stark shadows as they drifted slowly groundward. Their impact on the senses was sudden, dazzling, overwhelming even the noise of battle and the screams of the dying.

It was the defenders who sent the blazing torches into the sky, for their assailants needed no light to guide them. Streaking in by radar and infrared, they attacked with deadly accuracy until momentarily blinded by the brilliance of the flares.

Chims fled the evening's fireless camp in all directions, naked, carrying only food and a few weapons on their backs. Mostly, they were refugees from mountain hamlets burned down in the recent surge of fighting. A few trained irregulars remained behind in a desperate rearguard action to cover the civilians' retreat.

They used what means they had to confuse the airborne enemy's deadly, precise detectors. The flares were sophisticated, automatically adjusting their fulminations to best interfere with active and passive sensors. They slowed the avians down, but only for a little while. And they were in short supply.

Besides, the enemy had something new, some secret system that was letting them track chims even under the heaviest growth, even naked, without the simplest trappings of civilization.

All the pursued could do was split up into smaller and smaller groups. The prospect facing those who made it away from here was to live completely as animals, alone or at most in pairs, wild-eyed and cowering under skies that had once been theirs to roam at will.

Sylvie was helping an older chimmie and two children climb over a vine-covered tree trunk when suddenly upraised hackles told her of gravities drawing near. She quickly signed for the others to take cover, but something – perhaps it was the unsteady rhythm of those motors – made her stay behind, peering over the rim of a fallen log. In the blackness she barely caught the flash of a dim, whitish shape, plummeting through the starlit forest to crash noisily among the branches and then disappear into the jungle gloom.

Sylvie stared down the dark channel the plunging vessel had cut. She listened, chewing on her fingernails, as debris rained down in its wake.

'Donna!' she whispered. The elderly chimmie lifted her head from under a pile of leaves. 'Can you make it with the children the rest of the way to the rendezvous?' Sylvie asked. 'All you have to do is head downhill to a stream, then follow that stream to a small waterfall and cave. Can you do that?'

Donna paused for a long moment, concentrating, and at last nodded. 'Good,' Sylvie, said. 'When you see Petri, tell him I saw an enemy scout come down, and I'm goin' to go and look it over.'

Fear had widened the older chimmie's eyes so that the whites shone around her irises. She blinked a couple of times, then held out her arms for the children. By the time they were gathered under her protection, Sylvie had already cautiously entered the tunnel of broken trees.

Why am I doing this? Sylvie wondered as she stepped over broken branches still oozing pungent sap. Tiny skittering motions told of native creatures seeking cover after the ruination of their homes. The smell of ozone put Sylvie's hair on end. And then, as she drew nearer, there came another familiar odor, one of overripe bird.

Everything looked eerie in the dimness. There were absolutely no colors, only shades of stygian gray. When the off-white bulk of the crashed aircraft loomed in front of her, Sylvie saw that it lay canted at a forty degree slope, its front end quite crumpled from the impact.

She heard a faint crackling as some piece of electronics shorted again and again. Other than that, there came no sound from within. The main hatch had been torn half off its hinges.

Touching the still warm hull for guidance, she approached cautiously. Her fingers traced the outlines of one of the gravitic impellers, and flakes of corrosion came off. *Lousy maintenance,* she thought, partly in order to keep her mind busy. *I wonder if that's why it crashed.* Her mouth was dry and her heart felt in her throat as she reached the opening and bent to peer around the corner.

Two Gubru still lay strapped at their stations, their sharp-beaked heads lolling from slender, broken necks.

Sylvie tried to swallow. She made herself lift one foot and step gingerly onto the sloping deck. Her pulse threatened to stop when the plates groaned and one of the Talon Soldiers moved.

But it was only the broken vessel, creaking and settling slightly. 'Goodall,' Sylvie moaned as she brought her hand down from her breast. It was hard to concentrate with all of her instincts screaming just to get the hell out of here.

As she had for many days, Sylvie tried to imagine what Gailet Jones would do under circumstances like this. She knew she would never be the chimmie Gailet was. That just wasn't in the cards. But if she tried *hard* ...

'Weapons,' she whispered to herself, and forced her trembling hands to pull the soldiers' sidearms from their holsters. Seconds seemed like hours, but soon two racked saber rifles joined the pistols in a pile outside the hatch. Sylvie was about to lower herself to the ground when she hissed and slapped her forehead. 'Idiot! Athaclena needs intelligence more than popguns!'

She returned to the cockpit and peered about, wondering if she would recognize something significant even if it lay right in front of her.

Come on. You're a Terragens citizen with most of a college education. And you spent months working for the Gubru.

Concentrating, she recognized the flight controls, and – from symbols obviously pertaining to missiles – the weapons console. Another display, still lit by the craft's draining batteries, showed a relief territory map, with multiple sigils and designations written in Galactic Three.

Could this be what they're using to find us? she wondered.

A dial, just below the display, used words she knew in the enemy's language. 'Band Selector,' the label said. Experimentally, she touched it.

A window opened in the lower left corner of the display. More arcane writing spilled forth, much too complex for her. But above the text there now whirled a complex design that an adult of any civilized society would recognize as a chemical diagram.

Sylvie was no chemist, but she had had a basic education, and something about the molecule depicted there looked oddly familiar to her. She concentrated and tried to sound out the indentifier, the word just below the diagram. The CalThree syllabary came back to her.

'Hee … Heem … Hee Moog …'

Sylvie felt her skin suddenly course with goose bumps. She traced the line of her lips with her tongue and then whispered a single word.

'Hemoglobin.'

97

GALACTICS

'Biological warfare!' The Suzerain of Beam and Talon hopped about the bridge of the cruising battleship on which it held court and pointed at the Kwackoo technician who had brought the news. 'This corrosion, this decay, this blight on armor and machinery, it was created by *design*?'

The technician bowed. 'Yes. There are several agents – bacteria, prions, molds. When we saw the pattern counter-measures were instituted at once. It will take time to treat all affected surfaces with organisms engineered against theirs, but success will eventually reduce this to a mere nuisance.'

Eventually, the admiral thought bitterly. 'How were these agents delivered?'

The Kwackoo pulled from its pouch a filmy clump of clothlike material, bound by slender strands. 'When these things began blowing in from the mountains, we consulted Library records and questioned the locals. Irritating infestations occur regularly on this continental coast with the onset of winter, so we ignored them.

'However, it now appears the mountain insurgents have found a way to infect these airborne spore carriers with biological entities destructive to our equipment. By the time we were aware, the dispersal was nearly universal. The plot was most ingenious.'

The military commander paced. 'How bad, how severe, how catastrophic is the damage?'

Again, a deep bow. 'One third of our planet-side transport is affected. Two of the spaceport defense batteries will be out of commission for ten planetary days.'

'Ten days!'

'As you know, we are no longer receiving spares from the homeworld.'

The admiral did not need to be reminded. Already most routes to Gimelhai had been interdicted by the approaching alien armadas, now patiently clearing mines away from the fringes of Garth system.

And if that weren't enough, the two other Suzerains were now united in opposing the military. There was nothing they could do to prevent the coming battles if the admiral's party chose to fight, but they could withhold both religious and bureaucratic support. The effects of that were already showing.

The pressures had built until a steady, throbbing pain seemed to pulse within the admiral's head. 'They will pay!' the Suzerain shrieked. *Curse* the limitations of priests and egg counters!

The Suzerain of Beam and Talon recalled with fond longing the grand fleets it had led into this system. But long ago most of those ships had been pulled away by the Roost Masters to meet other desperate needs, and probably quite a few of them were already smoking ruins or vapor, out on the contentious Galactic marches.

In order to avoid such thoughts the admiral contemplated instead the noose now tightening around the shrinking mountain strong-holds of the insurgents. Soon that worry, at least, would be over forever.

And then, well, let the Uplift Institute enforce the neutrality of its sacred Ceremonial Mound in the midst of a pitched planet-space battle! Under such circumstances, missiles were known to fall astray – such as into civilian towns, or even neutral ground.

Too bad! There would be commiseration, of course. Such a pity. But those were the fortunes of war!

98

UTHACALTHING

No longer did he have to hold secret the yearnings in his heart, or keep contained his deep-stored reservoir of feelings. It did not matter if alien detectors pinpointed his psychic emanations, for they surely would know where to find him, when the time came.

At dawn, while the east grew gray with the cloud-shrouded sun, Uthacalthing walked along the dew-covered slopes and reached out with everything he had.

The miracle of some days back had burst the chrysalis of his soul. Where he thought only winter would forever reign, now bright shoots burst forth. To both humans and Tymbrimi, *love* was considered the greatest power. But there was, indeed, something to be said for *irony*, as well.

I live, and kenn the world as beautiful.

He poured all of his craft into a glyph which floated, delicate and light, above his wafting tendrils. To be brought to this place, so near where his schemes began ... and to witness how all his jests had been turned around upon himself, giving him all he had wanted, but in such amazing ways ...

Dawn brought color to the world. It was a winter land- and sea-scape of barren orchards and tarp-covered ships, The waters of the bay wore lines of wind-flecked foam. And yet, the sun gave warmth.

He thought of the Universe, so strange, often bizarre, and so filled with danger and tragedy.

But also surprise.

Surprise ...the blessing that tells one that this is real – he spread his arms to encompass it all – *that even the most imaginative of us could not have made all of this up within his own mind.*

He did not set the glyph free. It cast loose as if of its own accord and rose unaffected by the morning winds, to drift wherever chance might take it.

Later came long consultations with the Grand Examiner, with Kault and Cordwainer Appelbe. They all sought his advice. He tried not to disappoint them.

Around noon Robert Oneagle drew him aside and brought up again the idea of escape. The young human wanted to break out of their confinement on the Ceremonial Mound and head off with Fiben to cause the Gubru grief. They all knew of the fighting in the mountains, and Robert wanted to help Athaclena in any way possible.

Uthacalthing sympathized. 'But you underestimate yourself in thinking you could ever do this, my son,' he told the young man.

Robert blinked. 'What do you mean?'

'I mean that the Gubru military are now well aware of how dangerous you and Fiben are. And perhaps through some small efforts of my own they include me on their list. Why do you think they maintain such patrols, when they must have other pressing needs?'

He motioned at the craft which cruised just beyond the perimeter of Institute territory. No doubt even the coolant lines leading to the power stations were watched by expensive drones of deadly sophistication. Robert had suggested using handmade gliders, but the enemy was surely wise even to that wolfling trick by now. They had had expensive lessons.

'In this way we help Athaclena,' Uthacalthing said. 'By thumbing our noses at the enemy, by smiling as if we have thought of something special which they have not. By frightening creatures who deserve what they get for having no sense of humor.'

Robert made no outward gesture to show that he understood. But to Uthacalthing's delight he recognized the glyph the young man formed, a simple version of *kiniwullun*. He laughed. Obviously, it was one Robert had learned – and earned – from Athaclena.

'Yes, my strange adopted son. We must keep the Gubru painfully aware that boys will do what boys do.'

It was later, though, toward sunset, that Uthacalthing stood up suddenly in his dark tent and walked outside. He stared again to the east, tendrils waving, seeking.

Somewhere, out there, he knew his daughter was thinking furiously. Something, some news perhaps, had come to her. And now she was concentrating as if her life depended on it.

Then the brief, fey moment of linkage passed. Uthacalthing turned, but he did not go back to his own shelter. Instead, he wandered a little north and pulled aside the flap of Robert's tent. The human looked up from his reading, the light of the datawell casting a wild expression onto his face.

'I believe there actually is one way by which we could get off of this mountain,' he told the human. 'At least for a little while.'

'Go on,' Robert said.

Uthacalthing smiled. 'Did I not once say to you – or was it your mother – that all things begin and end at the Library?'

99

GALACTICS

Matters were dire. Consensus was falling apart irreparably, and the Suzerain of Propriety did not know how to heal the breach.

The Suzerain of Cost and Caution had nearly withdrawn into itself. The bureaucracy operated on inertia, without guidance.

And their vital third, their strength and virility, the Suzerain of Beam and Talon, would not answer their entreaties for a conclave. It seemed, in fact, bound and determined upon a course that might bring on not only their own destruction but possibly vast devastation to this frail world as well. If that occurred, the blow to the already tottering honor of this expedition, this branch of the clan of Gooksyu-Gubru, would be more than one could stand.

And yet, what could the Suzerain of Propriety do? The Roost Masters, distracted with problems closer to home, offered no useful advice. They had counted on the expedition Triumvirate to meld, to molt, and to reach a consensus of wisdom. But the Molt had gone wrong, desperately wrong. And there was no wisdom to offer them.

The Suzerain of Propriety felt a sadness, a hopelessness, that went beyond that of a leader riding a ship headed for shoals – it was more that of a priest doomed to oversee sacrilege.

The loss was intense and personal, and quite ancient at the heart of the race. True, the feathers sprouting under its white down were now red. But there were names for Gubru queens who achieved their femaleness without the joyous consent and aid of two others, two who share with her the pleasure, the honor, the glory.

Her greatest ambition had come true, and it was a barren prospect, a lonely and bitter one.

'The Suzerain of Propriety tucked her beak under her arm, and in the way of her own people, softly wept.

100

ATHACLENA

'Vampire plants,' was how Lydia McCue summed it up. She stood watch with two of her Terragens Marines, their skins glistening under painted layers of monolayer camouflage. The stuff supposedly protected them from infrared detection and, one could hope, the enemy's new resonance detector as well.

Vampire plants? Athaclena thought. *Indeed. It is a good metaphor.*

She poured about a liter of a bright red fluid into the dark waters of a forest pool, where hundreds of small vines came together in one of the ubiquitous nutrient trading stations.

Elsewhere, far away, other groups were performing similar rituals in little glades. It reminded Athaclena of wolfling fairy tales, of magical rites in enchanted forests and mystical incantations. She would have to remember to tell her father of the analogy, if she ever got the chance.

'Indeed,' she said to Lieutenant McCue. 'My chims drained themselves nearly white to donate enough blood for our purposes. There are certainly more subtle ways to do this, but none possible in the time available.'

Lydia answered with a grunt and a nod. The Earth woman was still in conflict with herself. Logically, she probably agreed that the results would have been catastrophic had Major Prathachulthorn been left in charge, weeks ago. Subsequent events had proven Athaclena and Robert right.

But Lieutenant McCue could not disassociate herself so easily from her oath. Until recently the two women had begun to become friends, talking for hours and sharing their different longings for Robert Oneagle. But now that the truth about the mutiny and kidnapping of Major Prathachulthorn was out, a gulf lay between them.

The red liquid swirled among the tiny rootlets. Clearly, the semimobile vines were already reacting, drawing in the new substances.

There had been no time for subtlety, only a brute force approach to the idea that had struck her suddenly, soon after hearing Sylvie's report. *Hemoglobin. The Gubru had detectors that can trace resonance against the primary constituent of Earthling blood. At such sensitivity, the devices must be frightfully expensive!*

A way had to be found to counteract the new weapon or she might be left the only sapient being in the mountains. The one possible approach had been drastic, and symbolic of the demands a nation made of its people. Her own unit of guerrillas now tottered around, so depleted by her demands for raw blood that some of the chims had changed her nickname. Instead of 'the general' they had taken to referring to Athaclena as 'the countess,' and then grimacing with outthrust canines.

Fortunately, there were still a few chim technicians – mostly those who had helped Robert devise little microbes to plague enemy machinery – who could help her with this slapdash experiment.

Bind hemoglobin molecules to trace substances sought by certain vines. Hope the new combination still meets their approval. And pray the vines transfer it along fast enough.

A chim messenger arrived and whispered to Lieutenant McCue. She, in turn, approached Athaclena.

'The major is nearly ready,' the dark human woman told her. Casually, she added, 'And our scouts say they detect aircraft heading this way.' Athaclena nodded.

'We are finished here. Let us depart. The next few hours will tell.'

101

GALACTICS

'There! We note a concentration, gathering, accumulation of the impudent enemy. The wolflings flee in a predictable direction. And now we may strike, pounce, swoop to conquer!'

Their special detectors made plain the quarry's converging trails through the forest. The Suzerain of Beam and Talon spoke a command, and an elite brigade of Gubru soldiery stooped upon the little valley where their fleeing prey was trapped, at bay.

'Captives, hostages, new prisoners to question . . . these I want!'

102

MAJOR PRATHACHULTHORN

The bait was invisible. Their lure consisted of little more than a barely traceable flow of complex molecules, coursing through the

intricate, lacy network of jungle vegetation. In fact, Major Prathachulthorn had no way of knowing for certain that it was there at all.
He felt awkward laying enfilade and ambush on the slopes overlooking a series of small ponds in an otherwise unoccupied forest
vale.

And yet, there was something symmetrical, almost poetic about
the situation. If this trick by some chance actually worked, there
would be the joy of battle on this morn.

And if it did not, then he intended to have the satisfaction of
throttling a certain slender alien neck, whatever the effects on his
career and his life.

'Feng!' he snapped at one of his Marines. 'Don't scratch.' The
Marine corporal quickly checked to make sure he had not rubbed
off any of the monolayer coating that gave his skin a sickly greenish
cast. The new material had been mixed quickly, in hopes of blocking the hemoglobin resonance the enemy were using to track
Terrans under the forest canopy. Of course, their intelligence on that
matter might be completely wrong. Prathachulthorn had only the
word of *chims*, and that damned Tym –

'Major!' someone whispered. It was a neo-chimpanzee trooper,
looking even more uncomfortable in green-tinted fur. He motioned
quickly from midway up a tall tree. Prathachulthorn acknowledged
and sent a hand gesture rippling in both directions.'

Well, he thought, *some of these local chims are turning into pretty
fair irregulars, I'll admit.*

A series of sonic booms rocked the foliage on all sides, followed
by the shriek of approaching aircraft. They swept up the narrow
valley at treetop level, following the hilly terrain with computer-
piloted precision. At just the right moment, Talon Soldiers and their
accompanying drones spilled out of long troop carriers to fall
serenely toward a certain jungle grove.

The trees there were unique in only one way, in their hunger for
a certain trace chemical brought to them by far-reaching, far-trad-
ing vines. Only now those vines had delivered something else as
well. Something drawn from Earthly veins.

'Wait,' Prathachulthorn whispered. 'Wait for the big boys.'

Sure enough, soon they all felt the effects of approaching gravities, and on a major scale. Over the horizon appeared a Gubru
battleship, cruising serenely several hundred meters above.

Here was a target well worth anything they had to sacrifice. Up
until now, though, the problem had been how to know in advance
where one would come. Flicker-swivvers were wonderful weapons,
but not very portable. One had to set them up well in advance. And
surprise was essential.

'Wait,' he murmured as the great vessel drew nearer. 'Don't spook 'em.'

Down below, the Talon Soldiers were already chirping in dismay, for no enemy awaited them, not even any chim civilians to capture and send above for questioning. At any moment, one of the troopers would surely guess the truth. Still, Major Prathachulthorn urged, 'Wait just a minute more, until – '

One of the chim gunners must have lost patience. Suddenly, lightning lanced upward from the heights on the opposite side of the valley. In an instant, three more streaks converged. Prathachulthorn ducked and covered his head.

Brilliance seemed to penetrate from *behind*, through his skull. Waves of *déjà vu* alternated with surges of nausea, and for a moment it felt as if a tide of anomalous gravity were trying to lift him from the forest loam. Then the concussion wave hit.

It was some time before anyone was able to look up again. When they did, they had to blink through clouds of drifting dust and grit, past toppled trees and scattered vines. A seared, flattened area told where the Gubru battle cruiser had hovered, only moments ago. A rain of red-hot debris still fell, setting off fires wherever the incandescent pieces landed.

Prathachulthorn grinned. He fired off a flare into the air – the signal to advance.

Several of the enemy's grounded aircraft had been broken by the overpressure wave. Three, however, lifted off and made for the sites where the missiles had been fired, screaming for vengeance. But their pilots did not realize they were facing Terragens Marines now. It was amazing what a captured saber rifle could do in the right hands. Soon three more burning patches smoldered on the valley floor.

Down below grim-faced chims moved forward, and combat soon became much more personal, a bloody struggle fought with lasers and pellet guns, with crossbows and arbalests.

When it came down to hand-to-hand, Prathachulthorn knew that they had won.

I cannot leave all of the close-in stuff to these locals, he thought. That was how he came to join the chase through the forest, while the Gubru rear guard furiously tried to cover the survivors' escape. And for as long as they lived thereafter, the chims who saw it talked about what they saw: a pale green figure in loin cloth and beard, swinging through the trees, meeting fully armed Talon Soldiers with knife and garrote. There seemed to be no stopping him, and indeed, nothing living withstood him.

It was a damaged battle drone, brought back into partial

operation by self-repair circuitry – perhaps making a logical connection between the final collapse of the Gubru forces and this fearsome creature who seemed to take such joy in battle. Or maybe it was nothing more than a final burst of mechanical and electrical reflex.

He went as he would have wanted to, wearing a bitter grin, with his hands around a feathered throat, throttling one more hateful thing that did not belong in the world he thought ought to be.

103

ATHACLENA

So, she thought as the excited chim messenger gasped forth the joyous news of total victory. On any scale, this was the insurgents' greatest coup.

In a sense. Garth *herself became our greatest ally. Her injured but still subtly powerful web of life.*

The Gubru had been lured by fragments of chim and human hemoglobin, carried to one site by the ubiquitous transfer vines. Frankly, Athaclena was surprised their makeshift plan had worked. Its success proved just how foolish had been the enemy's over-dependence on sophisticated hardware.

Now we must decide what to do next.

Lieutenant McCue looked up from the battle report the winded chim messenger had brought and met Athaclena's eyes. The two women shared a moment's silent communion. 'I'd better get going,' Lydia said at last. 'There'll be reconsolidation to organize, captured equipment to disburse ... and I am now in command.'

Athaclena nodded. She could not bring herself to mourn Major Prathachulthorn. But she acknowledged the man for what he had been. A warrior.

'Where do you think they will strike next?' she asked.

'I couldn't begin to guess, now that their main method of tracking us has been blown. They act as if they haven't much time.' Lydia frowned pensively. 'Is it certain the Thennanin fleet is on its way here?' Lydia asked.

'The Uplift Institute officials speak about it openly on the airwaves. The Thennanin come to claim their new clients. And as part of their arrangement with my father and with Earth, they are bound to help expel the Gubru from this system.'

Athaclena was still quite in awe over the extent to which her father's scheme had worked. When the crisis began, nearly one Garth year ago, it had been clear that neither Earth nor Tymbrim would be able to help this faraway colony. And most of the 'moderate' Galactics were so slow and judicious that there was little hope of persuading one of those clans to intervene. Uthacalthing had hoped to fool the Thennanin into doing the job instead – pitting Earth's enemies against each other.

The plan had worked beyond Uthacalthing's expectations because of one factor her father had not known of. *The gorillas.* Had their mass migration to the Ceremonial Mound been triggered by the *s'ustru'thoon* exchange, as she had earlier thought? Or was the Institute's Grand Examiner correct to declare that fate itself arranged for this new client race to be at the right time and place to choose? Somehow, Athaclena felt sure there was more to it than anyone knew, or perhaps ever would know.

'So the Thennanin are coming to chase out the Gubru.' Lydia seemed uncertain what to make of the situation. 'Then we've won, haven't we? I mean, the Gubru can't hold them off indefinitely. Even if it were possible militarily, they'd lose so much face across the Five Galaxies that even the moderates would finally get upset and mobilize.'

The Earth woman's perceptiveness was impressive. Athaclena nodded. 'Their situation would seem to call for negotiation. But that assumes logic. The Gubru military, I'm afraid, is behaving irrationally.'

Lydia shivered. 'Such an enemy is often far more dangerous than a rational opponent. He doesn't act out of intelligent self-interest.'

'My father's last call indicated that the Gubru are badly divided,' Athaclena said. The broadcasts from Institute Territory were now the guerrillas' best source of information. Robert and Fiben and Uthacalthing had all taken turns, contributing powerfully to the mountain fighters' morale and surely adding to the invader's severe irritation.

'We'll have to act under the assumption the gloves are off then.' The woman Marine sighed. 'If Galactic opinion doesn't matter to them, they may even turn to using space weaponry down here on the planet. We'd better disperse as widely as possible.'

'Hmm, yes.' Athaclena nodded. 'But if they use burners or hell bombs, all is lost anyway. From such weapons we cannot hide.

'I cannot command your troops, lieutenant, but I would rather die in a bold gesture – one which might help stop this madness once and for all – than end my life burying my head in the sand, like one of your Earthly oysters.'

Despite the seriousness of the proposition, Lydia McCue smiled. And a touch of appreciative irony danced along the edges of her simple aura. 'Ostriches,' the Earth woman corrected gently. 'It's big birds called ostriches that bury their heads.

'Now why don't you tell me what you have in mind.'

104

GALACTICS

Buoult of the Thennanin inflated his ridgecrest to its maximum height and preened his shining elbow spikes before stepping out upon the bridge of the great warship, *Athanasfire*. There, beside the grand display, where the disposition of the fleet lay spread out in sparkling colors, the human delegation awaited him. Their leader, an elderly female whose pale hair tendrils still gleamed in places with the color of a yellow sun, bowed at a prim, correct angle. Buoult replied with a precise waistband of his own. He gestured toward the display.

'Admiral Alvarez, I assume you can perceive for yourself that the last of the enemy's mines have been cleared. I am ready to transmit to the Galactic Institute for Civilized Warfare our declaration that the Gubru interdiction of this system has been lifted by *force majeur*.'

'That is good to hear,' the woman said. Her human-style smile – a suggestive baring of teeth – was one of their easier gestures to interpret. One as experienced with Galactic affairs as the legendary Helene Alvarez surely knew the effect the wolfling expression often had on others. She must have made a conscious decision to use it.

Well, such subtle intimidations played an acceptable role in the complex game of bluff and negotiation. Buoult was honest enough to admit that he did it too. It was why he had inflated his towering crest before entering.

'It will be good to see Garth again,' Alvarez added. 'I only hope we aren't the proximate cause of yet another holocaust on that unfortunate world.'

'Indeed, we shall endeavor to avoid that at all costs. And if the worst happens – if this band of Gubru are completely out of control – then their entire nasty clan shall pay for it.'

'I care little about penalties and compensation. There are people and an entire frail ecosphere at risk here.'

Buoult withheld comment. *I must be more careful,* he thought. *It is not meet for others to remind Thennanin – defenders of all Potential – of the duty to protect such places as Garth.*

It was especially galling to be chided righteously by wolflings.

And from now on they will be at our elbows, carping and criticizing, and we will have to listen, for they will be stage consorts to one of our clients. It is only one price we must pay for this treasure Kault found for us.

The humans were pressing negotiations hard, as was to be expected from a clan as desperate for allies as they. Already Thennanin forces had withdrawn from all areas of conflict with Earth and Tymbrim. But the Terragens were demanding much more than that in exchange for help managing and uplifting the new client race called 'Gorilla.'

In effect, they were demanding that the great clan of the Thennanin ally itself with forlorn and despised wolflings and bad-boy prankster Tymbrimi! This at a time when the horrible Soro–Tandu alliance appeared to be unstoppable out on the star-lanes. Why, to do so might conceivably risk annihilation for the Thennanin themselves!

If it were up to Buoult, who had had enough of Earthlings to last him a lifetime, the choice would be to tell them to go to Ifni's Hell and seek their allies there.

But it was not up to Buoult. There had long been a strong minority streak of sympathy for Earthclan, back home. Kault's coup, allowing the Great Clan to achieve another treasured laurel of patronhood, could win that faction government soon. Under such circumstances, Buoult figured it wise to keep his own opinions to himself.

One of his undercommanders approached and saluted. 'We have determined the positions taken up by the Gubru defense flotilla,' he reported. 'They are clustered quite close to the planet. Their dispersement is unusual. Our battle computers are finding it very hard to crack.'

Hmm, yes, Buoult thought on examining the close-in display. *A brilliant arrangement of limited forces. Even original, perhaps. How unlike the Gubru.*

'No matter,' he huffed. 'Even if there is no subtle way, they will nonetheless see that we came with more than adequate firepower to do the job by brute force if necessary. They will concede. They must concede.'

'Of course they must,' the human admiral agreed. But she did not sound convinced. In fact, she seemed worried.

'We are ready to approach to fail-safe envelopment,' the officer of the deck reported.

Buoult nodded quickly. 'Good. Proceed. From there we can contact the enemy and announce our intentions.'

Tension built as the armada advanced closer to the system's modest yellow sun. Although the Thennanin claimed proudly to possess no psychic powers, Buoult seemed to *feel* the gaze of the Earthling woman upon him, and he wondered how it was possible that he found her so intimidating.

She is only a wolfling, he reminded himself.

'Shall we resume our discussions, commander?' Admiral Alvarez asked at last.

He had no choice but to comply, of course. It would be best if much was decided before they arrived and the siege manifesto was read aloud.

Still, Buoult planned to sign no agreements until he had a chance to confer with Kault. That Thenananin had a reputation for vulgarity and, well, *frivolity*, that had won him exile to this backwater world. But now he appeared to have achieved unprecedented miracles. His political power back home would be great.

Buoult wanted to tap Kault's expertise, his apparent knack at dealing with these infuriating creatures.

His aides and the human delegation filed out of the bridge toward the meeting room. But before Buoult left he glanced one more time back at the situation tank and the deadly-looking Gubru battle array. Air noisily escaped his breathing slits.

What are the avians planning? he wondered. *What shall I do if these Gubru prove to be insane?*

105

ROBERT

In some parts of Port Helenia, there were more guard drones than ever, protecting their masters' domains rigorously, lashing out at anyone who passed too near.

Elsewhere, however, it was almost as if a revolution had already taken place. The invader's posters lay tattered in the gutters. Above one busy street corner Robert glimpsed a new mural that had recently been erected in place of Gubru propaganda. Painted in the style called Focalist Realism, it depicted a family of gorillas staring with dawning but hopeful sentience out upon a glowing horizon.

Protectively standing beside them, showing the way to that wonderful future, was a pair of idealized, high-browed neo-chimpanzees.

Oh, yes, there had also been a human and a Thennanin in the picture, vague and in the background. Robert thought it really nice of the artist to have remembered to include them.

The heavily guarded shuttle he was in passed through the intersection too quickly to see much detail, but he thought the rendering of the female chim hadn't quite done Gailet justice. *Fiben*, on the other hand, ought to be flattered.

Soon the 'free' parts of town were behind them, and they passed westward into areas patrolled with strict military discipline. When they landed their Talon Soldier guards hurried outside and stood watch as Robert and Uthacalthing left the shuttle to climb the ramp leading to the shining new Branch Library.

'This is an expensive setup, isn't it?' he asked the Tymbrimi Ambassador. 'Do we get to keep it if the Thennanin manage to kick the birds out?'

Uthacalthing shrugged. 'Probably. And maybe the Ceremonial Mound as well. Your clan is due reparations, certainly.'

'But you have your doubts.'

Uthacalthing stood in the vast entranceway surveying the vaulted chamber and the towering cubic data store within. 'It is just that I think it would be unwise to count your chickens before they have met the rooster.'

Robert understood Uthacalthing's point. Even defeat for the Gubru might come at unthinkable cost.

'It's counting one's *eggs* before they're *laid,*' he told the Tymbrimi, who was always anxious to improve his grasp of Anglic metaphors. This time, however, Uthacalthing didn't thank Robert. His widespread eyes seemed to flash as he looked back, sidelong. 'Think about it,' he said.

Soon Uthacalthing was deep in conversation with the Kanten Chief Librarian. At a loss to follow their rapid, inflected Galactic, Robert started a circuit of the new Library, taking its measure and looking at its current users.

Except for a few members of the Grand Examiner's team, all of the occupants were avians. The Gubru present were divided by a gulf he could *kenn*, as well as see. Nearly two thirds of them clustered over to the left. They cooed and cast disapproving glances at the smaller group, which consisted almost entirely of soldiers. The military did not give off happy vibrations, but they hid it well, strutting about their tasks with crisp efficiency, returning their peers' disapproval with arrogant disdain.

Robert made no effort to avoid being seen. The wave of stares he attracted was pleasing. They obviously knew who he was. If just passing near caused an interruption in their work, so much the better.

Approaching one cluster of Gubru – by their ribbons obviously members of the priestly Caste of Propriety – he bowed to an angle he hoped was correct and grinned as the entire offended gaggle was forced to form up and reply in kind.

Finally Robert came upon a data station formatted in a way he understood. Uthacalthing was still immersed in conversation with the Librarian, so Robert decided to see what he could find out on his own.

He made very little progress. The enemy had obviously set up safeguards to prevent the unauthorized from accessing information about near-space, or the presumably converging battle fleets of the Thennanin. Still, Robert kept on trying. Time passed as he explored the current data net, finding out where the invaders had set up their blocks.

So intense was his concentration that it took a while before he grew aware that something had changed in the Library. Automatic sound dampers had kept the growing hubbub from intruding on his concentration, but when he looked up at last Robert saw that the Gubru were in an uproar. They waved their downy arms and formed tight clusters around holo-tanks. Most of the soldiers had simply vanished from sight.

What on Garth has gotten into them? he wondered.

Robert didn't imagine the Gubru would welcome him peering over their shoulders. He felt frustrated. Whatever was happening, it sure had them perturbed!

Hey! Robert thought. *Maybe it's on the local news.*

Quickly he used his own screen to access a public video station. Until recently censorship had been severe, but during the last few days, as soldiers were called away to combat duty, the networks had fallen under the control of the Caste of Cost and Caution. Those glum, apathetic bureaucrats now hardly enforced even modest discipline.

The tank flickered, then cleared to show an excited chim reporter.

'... and so, at latest reports, it seems the surprise offensive from the Mulun hasn't yet engaged the occupation forces. The Gubru seem unable to agree on how to answer the manifesto of the approaching forces ...'

Robert wondered, had the Thennanin made their pronouncement of intent already? That had not been expected for a couple of days at least. Then one word caught in his mind.

From the *Mulun*?

'... We'll now rebroadcast the statement read just five minutes ago by the joint commanders of the army right now marching on Port Helenia.'

The view in the holo-tank shifted. The chim announcer was replaced by a recently recorded image showing three figures standing against a forest background. Robert blinked. He knew these faces, two of them intimately. One was a chen named Benjamin. The other two were women he loved.

'... and so we challenge our oppressors. In combat we have behaved well, under the dicta of the Galactic Institute for Civilized Warfare. This cannot be said of our enemies. They have used criminal means and have allowed harm to noncombatant fallow species native to a fragile world.

'Worst of all, they have *cheated*.'

Robert gaped. The image panned back to show platoons of chims – bearing a motley assortment of weapons – trooping forth from the forest out into the open, accompanied by a few fierce-eyed humans. The one speaking into the camera was Lydia McCue, Robert's human lover. But Athaclena stood next to her, and in his alien consort's eyes he saw and knew who had written the words.

And he knew, without any doubt, whose idea this was.

'We demand, therefore, that they send forth their best soldiers, armed as we are armed, to meet our champions out in the open, in the Valley of the Sind ...'

'Uthacalthing,' he said, hoarsely. Then again, louder. '*Uthacalthing!*'

The noise suppressors had been developed by a hundred million generations of librarians. But in all that time there had been only a few wolfling races. For just an instant the vast chamber echoed before dampers shut down the impolite vibrations and imposed hushed quiet once again.

There was nothing, however, to be done about running in the halls.

106

GAILET

'Recombinant Rats!' Fiben cried upon hearing the beginnings of the declaration. They watched a portable holo set up on the slopes of the Ceremonial Mound.

Gailet gestured for silence. 'Be quiet, Fiben. Let me hear the rest of it.'

But the meaning of the message had been obvious from the first few sentences. Columns of irregulars, wearing makeshift uniforms of homespun cloth, marched steadily across open, winter-barren fields. Two squads of *horse cavalry* skirted the ragged army's perimeter, like escapees from some pre-Contact flatmovie. The marching chims grinned nervously and watched the skies, fondling their captured or mountain-made weapons. But there was no mistaking their attitude of grim resolve.

As the cameras panned back, Fiben did a quick count. 'That's everybody,' he said in awe. 'I mean, allowing for recent casualties, it's everybody who's had any training or would be any good at all in a fight. It's all or nothing.' He shook his head. 'Clip my blue card if I can figure what she hopes to accomplish.'

Gailet glanced up at him. 'Some blue card,' she sniffed. 'And I'd have to say she knows *exactly* what she's doing, Fiben.'

'But the city rebels were *slaughtered* out on the Sind.'

She shook her head. 'That was then. We didn't know the score. We hadn't achieved any respect or status. Anyway, there weren't any witnesses.

'But the mountain forces have won victories. They've been acknowledged. And now the Five Galaxies are watching.'

Gailet frowned. 'Oh, Athaclena knows what she's doing. I just didn't know things were this desperate.'

They sat quietly for a moment longer, watching the insurgents advance slowly across orchards and winter-barren fields. Then Fiben let out another exclamation. 'What?' Gailet asked. She looked where he pointed in the tank, and it was her turn to hiss in surprise.

There, carrying a saber rifle along with the other chim soldiers, strode someone they both knew. Sylvie did not seem uncomfortable with her weapon. In fact, she appeared an island of almost zenlike calm in the sea of nervous neo-chimpanzees.

Who would've figured it? Gailet thought. *Who would've thought that about her?*

They watched together. There was little else they could do.

107

GALACTICS

'This must be handled with delicacy, care, rectitude!' the Suzerain of Propriety proclaimed. 'If necessary, we must meet them one on one.'

'But the expense!' wailed the Suzerain of Cost and Caution. 'The losses to be expected!'

Gently, the high priest bent over from her perch and crooned to her junior.

'Consensus, consensus ... Share with me a vision of harmony and wisdom. Our clan has lost much here, and stands in dire jeopardy of losing far more. But we have not yet forfeited the one thing that will maintain us even at night, even in darkness – our nobility. Our honor.'

Together, they began to sway. A melody rose, one with a single lyric.

'*Zoooon ...*'

Now if only their strong third were here! Coalescence seemed so near. A message had been sent to the Suzerain of Beam and Talon urging that he return to them, join them, become one with them at last.

How, she wondered. *How could he resist knowing, concluding, realizing at last that it is his fate to be my male? Can an individual be so obstinate?*

The three of us can yet be happy!

But a messenger arrived with news that brought despair. The battle cruiser in the bay had lifted off and was heading inland with its escorts. The Suzerain of Beam and Talon had decided to act. No consensus would restrain him.

The high priest mourned.

We could have been happy.

108

ATHACLENA

'Well, this may be our answer,' Lydia commented resignedly.

Athaclena looked up from the awkward, unfamiliar task of controlling a horse. Mostly, she let her beast simply follow the others. Fortunately, it was a gentle creature who responded well to her coronal singing.

She peered in the direction pointed out by Lydia McCue, where scattered clouds and haze partially obscured the western horizon. Already many of the chims were gesturing that way. Then Athaclena also saw the glint of flying craft. And she *kenned* the approaching forces. Confusion ... determination ... fanaticism ... regret ... loathing ... a turmoil of alien-tinged feelings bombarded her from the ships. But one thing was clear above all.

The Gubru were coming with vast and overwhelming strength.

The distant dots took shape. 'I believe you are right, Lydia,' Athaclena told her friend. 'It seems we have our answer.'

The woman Marine swallowed. 'Shall I order a dispersal? Maybe a few of us can get away.' She sounded doubtful.

Athaclena shook her head. A sad glyph formed. 'No. We must play this out. Call all units together. Have the cavalry bring everyone to yonder hilltop.'

'Any particular reason we should make things easy for them?'

Above Athaclena's waving tendrils the glyph refused to become one of despair. 'Yes,' she answered. 'There is a reason. The best reason in all the world.'

109

GALACTICS

The stoop-colonel of Talon Soldiers watched the ragged army of insurgents on a holo-screen and listened as its high commander screamed in delight.

'They shall burn, shall smoke, shall curl into cinders under our fire!'

The stoop-colonel felt miserable. This was intemperate language, bereft of proper consideration of consequences. The stoop-colonel knew, deep within, that even the most brilliant military plans would eventually come to nothing if they did not take into account such matters as cost, caution, and propriety. Balance was the essence of consensus, the foundation of survival.

And yet the Earthlings' challenge had been honorable! It might be ignored. Or even met with a decent excess of force. But what the leader of the military now planned was unpleasant, his methods extreme.

The stoop-colonel noted that it had already come to think of the Suzerain of Beam and Talon as 'he.' The Suzerain of Beam and Talon was a brilliant leader who had inspired his followers, but now, as a prince, he seemed blind to the truth.

To even think of the commander in this critical way caused the stoop-colonel physical pain. The conflict was deep and visceral.

The doors to the main lift opened and out onto the command dais stepped a trio of white-plumed messengers – a priest, a bureaucrat, and one of the officers who had deserted to the other Suzerains. They strode toward the admiral and proffered a box crafted of richly inlaid wood. Shivering, the Suzerain of Beam and Talon ordered it opened.

Within lay a single, luxuriant feather, colored iridescent red along its entire length except at the very tip.

'Lies! Deceptions! An obvious hoax!' the admiral cried, and knocked the box and its contents out of the startled messengers' arms.

The stoop-colonel stared as the feather drifted in eddies from the air circulators before fluttering down to the deck. It felt like sacrilege to leave it lying there, and yet the stoop-colonel dared not move to pick it up.

How could the commander ignore *this*? How could he refuse to accept the rich, blue shades spreading now at the roots of his own down? 'The Molt can reverse again,' the Suzerain of Beam and Talon cried out. 'It can happen if we win victory at arms!'

Only now what he proposed would not be victory, it would be slaughter.

'The Earthlings are gathering, clustering, coming together upon a single hillmount,' one of the aides reported. 'They offer, display, present us with a single, simple target!' The stoop-colonel sighed. It did not take a priest to tell what this meant. The Earthlings, realizing that there would be no fair fight, had come together to make their demise simple. Since their lives were already forfeit, there was only one possible reason.

They do it in order to protect the frail ecosystem of this world. The purpose of their lease-grant was, after all, to save Garth. In their very helplessness the stoop-colonel saw and tasted bitter defeat. They had forced the Gubru to choose flatly between power and honor.

The crimson feather had the stoop-colonel captivated, its colors doing things to its very blood. 'I shall prepare my Talon Soldiers to go down and meet the Terrans,' the stoop-colonel suggested, hopefully. 'We shall drop down, advance, attack in equal numbers, lightly armed, without robots.'

'No! You must not, will not, shall not! I have carefully assigned roles for all my forces. I need, require them all when we deal with the Thennanin! There shall be no wasteful squandering.

'Now, heed me! At this moment, this instant, the Earthlings below shall feel, bear, sustain my righteous vengeance!' the Suzerain of Beam and Talon cried out. 'I command that the locks be removed from the weapons of mass destruction. We shall sear this valley, and the next, and the next, until all life in these mountains –'

The order was never finished. The stoop-colonel of Talon Soldiers blinked once, then dropped its saber pistol to the deck. The clatter was followed by a double thump as first the head and then the body of the former military commander tumbled as well.

The stoop-colonel shuddered. Lying there, the body clearly showed those iridescent shades of royalty. The admiral's blood mixed with the blue princely plumage and spread across the deck to join, at last, with the single crimson feather of his queen.

The stoop-colonel told its stunned subordinates, 'Inform, tell, transmit to the Suzerain of Propriety that I have placed myself under arrest, pending the outcome, result, determination of my fate.

'Refer to Their Majesties what it is that must be done.'

For a long, uncertain time – completely on inertia – the task force continued toward the hilltop where the Earthlings had gathered, waiting. Nobody spoke. On the command dais there was hardly any movement at all.

When the report arrived it was like confirmation of what they had known for some time. A pall of mourning had already settled over the Gubru administration compound. Now the former Suzerain of Propriety and the former Suzerain of Cost and Caution crooned together a sad dirge of loss.

Such great hopes, such fine prospects they had had on setting out for this place, this planet, this forlorn speck in empty space. The Roost Masters had so carefully planned the right oven, the correct crucible, and just the right ingredients – three of the best, three fine products of genetic manipulation, their very finest.

We were sent to bring home a consensus, the new queen thought. *And that consensus has come.*

It is ashes. We were wrong to think this was the time to strive for greatness.

Oh, many factors had brought this about. If only the first candidate of Cost and Caution had not died ... If only they had not been fooled *twice* by the trickster Tymbrimi and his 'Garthlings.' ... If only the Earthlings had not proven so wolfishly clever at capitalizing on every weakness – this last maneuver for instance, forcing Gubru soldiery to choose between dishonor and regicide ...

But there are no accidents, she knew. *They could not have taken advantage if we had not shown flaws.*

That was the consensus they would report to the Roost Masters. That there were weaknesses, failures, mistakes which this doomed expedition had tested and brought to light.

It would be valuable information.

Let that console me for my sterile, infertile eggs, she thought, as she comforted her sole remaining partner and lover.

To the messengers she gave one brief command.

'Convey to the stoop-colonel our pardon, our amnesty, our forgiveness. And have the task force recalled to base.'

Soon the deadly cruisers had turned about and were headed homeward, leaving the mountains and the valley to those who seemed to want them so badly.

110

ATHACLENA

The chims stared in amazement as Death seemed to change its mind. Lydia McCue blinked up at the retreating cruisers and shook her head. 'You knew,' she said as she turned to look at Athaclena. Again she accused. 'You knew!'

Athaclena smiled. Her tendrils traced faint, sad imprints in the air.

'Let us just say that I thought there was a possibility,' she said at last. 'Had I been wrong, this would still have been the honorable thing to do.

'I am very glad, however, to find out that I was right.'

PART SEVEN

WOLFLINGS

Not a whit, we defy augury; there's a special providence
in the fall of a sparrow. If it be now, 'tis not to come;
if it be not to come, it will be now;
if it be not now, yet it will come;
the readiness is all.

HAMLET, ACT V, SCENE II

III

FIBEN

'Goodall, how I hate ceremonies!'

The remark brought a jab in his ribs. 'Quit fidgeting, Fiben. The whole world is watching!'

He sighed and made an effort to sit up straight. Fiben could not help remembering Simon Levin and the last time they had stood parade together, just a short distance from here. *Some things never change,* he thought. Now it was Gailet nagging him to try to look dignified.

Why did everyone who loved him also incessantly try to correct his posture? He muttered. 'If they wanted clients who looked elegant, they'd have uplif—'

The words cut short in an 'oof! of exhaled breath. Gailet's elbows were sure a lot sharper than Simon's had been. Fiben's nostrils flared and he chuffed irritably, but he kept quiet. So prim in her well-cut new uniform, *she* might be glad to be here, but had anyone asked *him* if he wanted a damn medal? No, of course not. Nobody ever asked him.

At last the triple-cursed Thennanin admiral finished his droning, boring homily on virtue and tradition, garnering scattered applause. Even Gailet seemed relieved as the hulking Galactic returned to his seat. Alas, so many others also seemed to want to make speeches.

The mayor of Port Helenia, back from internment on the islands, praised the doughty urban insurrectionists and proposed that his chim deputy ought to take over City Hall more often. That got him hearty applause ... and probably a few more chim votes, come next election, Fiben thought cynically.

Cough*Quinn'3, the Uplift Institute Examiner, summarized the agreement recently signed by Kault on behalf of the Thennanin, and for Earthclan by the legendary Admiral Alvarez, under which the fallow species formerly called gorillas would henceforth enter upon the long adventure of sapiency. The new Galactic citizens – already widely known as 'The Client Race That Chose' – would be given leasehold on the Mountains of Mulun for fifty thousand years. Now they were, in truth, 'Garthlings.'

In return for technical assistance from Earth, and fallow gorilla genetic stock, the mighty clan of the Thennanin would also undertake to defend the Terran leasehold of Garth, plus five other human and Tymbrimi colony worlds. They would not interfere directly in conflicts now raging with the Soro and Tandu and other fanatic clans, but easing pressure on those fronts would allow desperately needed help to go to the homeworlds.

And the Thennanin themselves were no longer enemies of the trickster-wolfling alliance. That fact alone was worth the power of great armadas.

We've done what we can, and more, Fiben thought. Until this point, it had seemed that the great majority of Galactic 'moderates' would simply sit aside and let the fanatics have their way. Now there was some hope that the apparent 'inevitable tide of history' that was said to doom all wolfling clans would not be seen as quite so unstoppable. Sympathy for the underdogs had grown as a result of events here on Garth.

Whether there actually were more allies to be won, more magic tricks to be pulled, Fiben couldn't predict. But he was pretty sure the final outcome would be decided thousands of parsecs away from here. Perhaps on old mother Earth herself.

When Megan Oneagle began speaking Fiben realized it was finally time to get through the morning's worst unpleasantness.

' ... will turn out to be a total loss if we do not learn from months such as those we have just passed through. After all, what is the use of hard times if they do not make us wiser? For what did our honored dead give up their lives?'

The Planetary Coordinator coughed for a brief moment and rustled her old-fashioned paper notes.

'We shall propose modification of the probation system, which causes resentments the enemy were able to exploit.

We'll endeavor to use the new Library facilities for the benefit of all. And we certainly shall service and maintain the equipment on the Ceremonial Mound, against the day when peace returns and it can be used for its proper purpose, the celebration of status the race of *Pan argonostes* so richly deserves.

'And most important of all, we shall use Gubru reparations to finance resumption of our major job here on Garth, reversing the decline of this planet's frail ecosphere, using hard-won knowledge to halt the downward spiral and return this, our adopted home, to its proper task – the task of breeding wonderful species diversity, the wellspring of all sentience.

'More of these plans will be presented for public discussion over the coming weeks.' Megan looked up from her notes and smiled. 'But today we also have an added chore, the pleasurable chore of honoring those who have made us proud. Those who made it possible for us to stand here in freedom today. It is our chance to show them how grateful we are, and how very much they are loved.'

You love me? Fiben asked silently. *Then let me outta here!*

'Indeed,' the Coordinator went on. 'For some of our chim citizens, recognition of their achievements will not finish with their lives or even with their places in history books, but shall continue in the veneration with which we hold their descendants, the future of their race.'

From his left, Sylvie leaned forward far enough to look across Fiben to Gailet on his right. The two shared a glance and a grin.

Fiben sighed. At least he had persuaded Cordwainer Appelbe to keep that damned upgrade to white card secret! Fat lot of good it would do, of course: Green- and blue-status chimmies from all over Port Helenia were after him already. And Gailet and Sylvie were hardly any help at all. Why the hell had he married them, anyway, if not for protection! Fiben sniffed at the thought. Protection, indeed! He suspected the two of them were interviewing and evaluating *candidates*.

Whether or not two species came from the same clan, or even the same planet, there would always be some basics that were different between them. Look at how much pre-Contact humans had varied for simply cultural reasons. Of course matters of love and reproduction among chims had to be based on their own sexual heritage, from long before Uplift.

Still, there was enough human conditioning in Fiben to make him blush when he thought of what these two were going to put him through, now that they were close friends. *How did I let myself get into such a situation?*

Sylvie caught his eye and smiled sweetly. He felt Gailet's hand slip into his.

Well, he admitted with a sigh. *I guess it wasn't all that hard.*

They were reading names now, calling people up to accept their medals. But for a while Fiben felt just the three of them, sitting there together, as if the rest of the world were only an illusion. Actually, under his outward cynicism, he felt pretty good.

Robert Oneagle rose and stepped to the dais to accept his medal, looking much more comfortable in his uniform than Fiben felt. Fiben watched his human pal. *I've got to ask him who his tailor is.*

Robert had kept his beard, and the hard body won in rugged mountain living. He was no stripling any longer. In fact, he looked every inch a storybook hero.

Such nonsense. Fiben sniffed in disgust. *Gotta get that boy pissed drunk real soon. Beat him arm-wrestling. Save him from believing ever'-thing the press writes.*

Robert's mother, on the other hand, seemed to have aged appreciably during the war. Over the last week Fiben had seen her repeatedly blink up at her tall, bronzed son, walking by with the grace of a jungle cat. She seemed proud but bewildered at the same time, as if the fairies had taken away her own child and left a changeling in its place.

It's called growing up, Megan.

Robert saluted and turned to head back toward his seat. As he passed in front of Fiben, his left hand made a quick motion, sign talk spelling out a single word.

Beer!

Fiben started laughing but choked it back as both Sylvie and Gailet turned to look at him sharply. No matter. It was good to know Robert felt as he did. Talon Soldiers were almost preferable to this ceremonial nonsense.

Robert returned to his seat next to Lieutenant Lydia McCue, whose own new decoration shone on the breast of her glistening dress tunic. The woman Marine sat erect and attentive to the proceedings, but Fiben could see what was invisible to the dignitaries and the crowd, that the toe of her boot had already lifted the cuff of Robert's trouser leg.

Poor Robert fought for composure. Peace, it seemed, offered its own travails. In its way, war was simpler.

Out in the crowd Fiben caught sight of a small cluster of humanoids, slender bipedal beings whose foxlike appearance was belied by fringes of gently waving tendrils just above their ears. Among the gathered Tymbrimi he easily picked out Uthacalthing and Athaclena. Both had declined every honor, every award. The people of Garth would have to wait until the two departed before erecting any memorials. That restraint, in a sense, would be their reward.

The ambassador's daughter had erased many of the facial and bodily modifications which had made her look so nearly human. She chatted in a low voice with a young male Tym who Fiben supposed could be called handsome, in an Eatee sort of way.

One would think the two young people – Robert and his alien consort – had readjusted completely to returning to their own folk. In fact, Fiben suspected each was now far more at ease with the opposite sex than they had been before the war.

And yet . . .

He had seen them come together once, briefly, during one of the endless series of diplomatic receptions and conferences. Their heads had drawn quite near, and although no words were exchanged, Fiben was certain he saw or sensed *something* whirl lightly in the narrow space between them.

Whatever mates or lovers they would have in the future, it was clear that there was something Athaclena and Robert would always share, however much distance the Universe put between them.

Sylvie returned to her seat upon receiving her own commendation. Her dress could not quite hide the rounding of her figure. Another change Fiben would have to get used to pretty soon. He figured the Port Helenia Fire Department would probably have to hire more staff when that little kid started taking chemistry in school.

Gailet embraced Sylvie and then approached the podium herself. This time the cheers and applause were so sustained that Megan Oneagle had to motion for order.

But when Gailet spoke, it was not the rousing victory paean the crowd obviously expected. Her message, it seemed, was much more serious.

'Life is not fair,' she said. The murmuring audience went silent as Gailet looked out across the assembly and seemed to meet their eyes as individuals. 'Anyone who says it is, or even that it *ought* to be, is a fool or worse. Life can be *cruel*. Ifni's tricks can be capricious games of chance and probability. Or cold equations will cut you down if you make one mistake in space, or even step off the sidewalk at the wrong moment and try too quickly to match momentum with a bus.

'This is not the best of all possible worlds. For if it were, would there be illogic? Tyranny? Injustice? Even evolution, the wellspring of diversity and the heart of nature, is so very often a callous process, depending on death to bring about new life.

'No, life is not just. The Universe is not fair.

'And yet' – Gailet shook her head – 'and yet, if it is not fair, at least it can be *beautiful*. Look around you now. There is a sermon greater than anything *I* can tell you. Look at this lovely, sad world that is our home. *Behold* Garth!'

The gathering took place upon the heights just south of the new Branch Library, in a meadow with an open view in all directions. To the west, all could see the Sea of Cilmar, its gray-blue surface colored with streaks of floating plant life and dotted with the spumelike trails of underwater creatures. Above lay the blue sky, scrubbed clean by the last storm of winter. Islands gleamed in the morning sunlight, like distant magical kingdoms.

On the north side of the meadow lay the beige tower of the Branch Library, its rayed spiral sigil embossed in sparkling stone. Freshly planted trees from two score worlds swayed gently in the breezes stroking over and around the great monolith, as timeless as its store of ancient knowledge.

To the east and south, beyond the busy waters of Aspinal Bay, lay the Valley of the Sind, already beginning to sprout with early green shoots, filling the air with the aromas of spring. And in the distance the mountains brooded, like sleeping titans ready to shrug off their brumal coats of snow.

'Our own petty lives, our species, even our clan, feel terribly important to us, but what are they next to this? This nursery of creation? *This* was what was worth fighting for. Protecting this' – she waved at the sea, the sky, the valley, and the mountains – 'was our success.

'We Earthlings know better than most how unfair life can be. Perhaps not since the Progenitors themselves has a clan understood so well. Our beloved human patrons nearly destroyed our more beloved Earth before they learned wisdom. Chims and dolphins and gorillas are only the beginnings of what would have been lost had they not grown up in time.'

Her voice dropped, went hushed. 'As the true Garthlings were lost, fifty thousand years ago, before they ever got the chance to blink in amazement at a night sky and wonder, for the first time, what that light was that glimmered in their minds.'

Gailet shook her head. 'No. The war to protect Potential has gone on for many aeons. It did not finish here. It may, indeed, never end.'

When Gailet turned away there was at first only a long, stunned silence. The applause that followed was scattered and uncomfortable. But when she returned to Sylvie's and Fiben's embrace, Gailet smiled faintly.

'That's tellin' 'em,' he said to her.

Then, inevitably, it was Fiben's turn. Megan Oneagle read a list of accomplishments that had obviously been gone over by some publicity department hack in order to hide how dirty and smelly and founded on simple dumb *luck* it all had been. Read aloud this way, it all sounded unfamiliar. Fiben hardly remembered doing half the stuff attributed to him.

It hadn't occurred to him to wonder why he'd been selected to go last. Probably, he assumed, it had been out of pure spite. *Following an act like Gailet will be pure murder,* he realized.

Megan called him forward. The hated shoes almost made him trip as he made his way to the dais. He saluted the Planetary Coordinator and tried to stand straight as she pinned on some garish medal and an insignia making him a reserve colonel in the Garth Defense Forces. The cheers of the crowd, especially the chims, made his ears feel hot, and it only got worse when, per Gailet's instructions, he grinned and waved for the cameras.

Okay, so maybe I can stand this, in small doses. When Megan offered him the podium Fiben stepped forward. He had a speech of sorts, scrawled out on sheets in his pocket. But after listening to Gailet he decided he had better merely tell them all thank you and then sit down again.

Struggling to adjust the podium downward, he began. 'There's just one thing I want to say, and that's – YOWP!'

He jerked as sudden electricity coursed through his left foot. Fiben hopped, grabbing the offended member, but then another shock hit his right foot! He let out a shriek. Fiben glanced down just in time to see a small blue brightness emerge slightly from beneath the podium and reach out now for *both* ankles. He leaped, hooting loudly, two meters into the air – alighting atop the wooden lectern.

Panting, it took him a moment to separate the panicked roaring in his ears from the hysterical cheering of the crowd. He blinked, rubbed his eyes, and stared.

Chims were standing on their folding chairs and waving their arms. They were jumping up and down, howling. Confusion reigned in the ranks of the polished militia honor guard. Even the humans were laughing and clapping uproariously.

Fiben glanced, dumbfounded, back at Gailet and Sylvie, and the pride in their eyes explained what it all meant.

They thought that was my prepared speech! he realized. In retrospect he saw how perfect it was, indeed. It broke the tension and seemed an ideal commentary on how it felt to be at peace again.

Only I didn't write it, damnit!

He saw a worried look on the face of his lordship the mayor of Port Helenia. *No! Next they'll have me running for office!*

Who did this to me?

Fiben searched the crowd and noticed immediately that one person was reacting differently, completely unsurprised. He stood out from the rest of the crowd partly due to his widely separated eyes and waving tendrils, but also because of his all too human expression of barely contained mirth.

And there was something else, some nonthing that Fiben somehow *sensed* was there, floating above the laughing Tymbrimi's wafting coronae.

Fiben sighed. And if looks alone could maim, Earth's greatest friends and allies would have to send a replacement ambassador to the posting on Garth right away.

When Athaclena winked at Fiben, it just confirmed his suspicions.

'Very funny,' Fiben muttered caustically under his breath, even as he forced out another grin and waved again to the cheering crowds.

'T'rifically funny, Uthacalthing.'

POSTSCRIPT AND ACKNOWLEDGMENTS

First we feared the other creatures who shared the Earth with us. Then, as our power grew, we thought of them as our property, to dispose of however we wished. The most recent fallacy (a rather nice one, in comparison) has been to play up the idea that the animals are virtuous in their naturalness, and it is only humanity who is a foul, evil, murderous, rapacious canker on the lip of creation. This view says that the Earth and all her creatures would be much better off without us.

Only lately have we begun embarking upon a fourth way of looking at the world and our place in it. A new view of life.

If we evolved, one must ask, are we then not like other mammals in many ways? Ways we can learn from? And where we differ, should that not also teach us?

Murder, rape, the most tragic forms of mental illnesses – all of these we are now finding among the animals as well as ourselves. Brainpower only exaggerates the horror of these dysfunctions in us. It is not the root cause. The cause is the darkness in which we have lived. It is ignorance.

We do not have to see ourselves as monsters in order to teach an ethic of environmentalism. It is now well known that our very survival depends upon maintaining complex ecological networks and genetic diversity. If we wipe out Nature, we ourselves will die.

But there is one more reason to protect other species. One seldom if ever mentioned. Perhaps we *are* the first to talk and think and build and aspire, but we may not be the last. Others may follow us in this adventure.

Some day we may be judged by just how well we served, when alone we were Earth's caretakers.

The author gratefully acknowledges his debt to those who looked over this work in manuscript form, helping with everything from aspects of natural simian behavior to correcting bad grammar outside quotation marks.

I want to thank Anita Everson, Nancy Grace, Kristie McCue, Louise Root, Nora Brackenbury, and Mark Grygier for their valued insights. Professor John Lewis and Ruth Lewis also offered observations, as did Frank Catalano, Richard Spahl, Gregory

Benford, and Daniel Brin. Thanks also to Steve Hardesty, Sharon Sosna, Kim Bard, Rick Sturm, Don Coleman, Sarah Bartter, and Bob Goold.

To Lou Aronica, Alex Berman, and Richard Curtis, my gratitude for their patience.

And to our hairy cousins, I offer my apologies. Here, have a banana and a beer.

David Brin
November 1986

GLOSSARY AND CAST OF CHARACTERS

Acceptor – A member of a Tandu client race. A psychic adept.

Akki (Ah-kee) – A dolphin midshipman from Calafia.

Anglic – The language most commonly used by the Terragens – people descended from Earth humans, chimpanzees, and dolphins.

Athaclena – Daughter of the Tymbrimi ambassador, Uthacalthing. Leader of the Irregular Army of Garth.

Gillian Baskin – A physician and agent for the Terragens Council. A product of human genetic engineering.

Beie Chohooan (Bay Choe-hoo-wan) – A Synthian spy.

Fiben Bolger – A neo-chimpanzee ecologist and lieutenant in the colonial militia.

Brookida (Broo-kee-dah) – A dolphin metallurgist.

Brothers of the Night – A Galactic patron race.

Bururalli – The last prior race to be allowed to lease Garth; a newly uplifted race which reverted and nearly ruined the planet.

Calafia – A human/neo-dolphin colony world.

'Chen' – Anglic term for a male neo-chimpanzee.

'Chim' – Anglic term for a member of the neo-chimpanzee client race (male or female).

'Chimmie' – Anglic term for a female neo-chimpanzee.

Client – A species that owes its full intelligence to genetic uplift by its patron race. And *indentured* client species is one which is still working off this debt.

Creideiki (Cry-dye-kee) – Captain of the exploration vessel *Streaker*.

Emerson D'Anite – A human engineer assigned to the *Streaker*.

Charles Dart – A neo-chimpanzee planetologist.

Derelict fleet – A drifting collection of giant starships, ancient and long undiscovered until found by the Streaker.

Episiarch – A member of a client race indentured to the Tandu. A psychic adept.

'Fem' – Anglic term for a female human being.

'Fin' – Vernacular for a neo-dolphin. ('Fen' – plural.)

Galactic – One of the senior starfaring species which comprise the community of the Five Galaxies. Many have become patron races, participating in the ancient tradition of uplift.

Garthling – A rumored native creature of Garth – a large animal survivor of the Bururalli Holocaust.

Gubru (Goo-broo) – A pseudo-avian Galactic race hostile to Earth.

Haoke (Ha-oh-kay) – A *Tursiops* neo-dolphin.

Herbie – The mummy of an ancient starfarer, of unknown origin.

Heurkea (Hee-urk-eeah) – A *Stenos* neo-dolphin.

Hikahi (Hee-kah-hee) – A female neo-dolphin, third in command of the *Streaker*.

Ifni – 'Infinity' or Lady Luck.

Iki – An ancient island of death and destruction.

Toshio Iwashika – A midshipman from the colony world Calafia.

Gailet Jones – Chimmie expert on Galactic Sociology. Holder of an unlimited birthright ('white card'). Leader of the urban uprising.

Kanten – One of a few Galactic species openly friendly to Earthmen.

Karrank% (Impossible for humans to pronounce properly) – A Galactic species so thoroughly modified during its indenture as a client race that it was driven insane.

Kault – Thennanin ambassador to Garth.

Keneenk – A hybrid school of discipline, combining logical, human-style thought with the heritage of the *Whale Dream*.

Keepiru (Kee-peer-ooh) – First pilot of the *Streaker*. A native of Atlast.

Kiqui (Kee-kwee) – Amphibious pre-sentient creatures native to the planet Kithrup.

Krat – Commander of the Soro forces. '

K'tha-jon (K'thah-jon) – A special variant *Stenos* neo-dolphin. One of the *Streaker*'s petty officers.

Library – The information storehouse that holds Galactic society together; an archive of cross-referenced knowledge accumulated since the age of the Progenitors.

Makanee (Ma-kah-nay) – Ship's surgeon aboard the *Streaker*; a female neo-fin.

'Man' – Anglic term referring to both male and female human beings.

Mathicluanna – Athaclena's deceased mother.

Lydia McCue – An officer in the Terragens Marines.

'Mel' – Anglic term referring specifically to a male human.

Ignacio Metz – An expert on uplift, assigned to the *Streaker*.

Moki (Moe-kee) – A *Stenos* neo-fin.

Nahalli – A race that was patron to the Bururalli and paid a great penalty for the crimes of their clients.

The Niss Machine – A pseudo-intelligent computer, lent to Thomas Orley by Tymbrimi agents.

Megan Oneagle – Planetary Coordinator for the Terran leasehold colony world on Garth.

Robert Oneagle – Captain in the Garth Colonial Militia Forces and son of the Planetary Coordinator.

Thomas Orley – An agent of the Terragens Council and a product of mild genetic engineering.

Pan argonostes – Species name of the Uplifted client race of neo-chimpanzees.

Pila – A Galactic patron race, part of the Soro clan and hostile to Earth.

Major Prathachulthorn – A Terragens Marine officer.

Primal Delphin – The semi-language used by natural, unmodified dolphins on Earth.

Progenitors – The mythical first species, who established Galactic culture and the Library several billion years ago.

Sah'ot (Sah-ote) – A *Stenos* neo-dolphin. A civilian linguist onboard the *Streaker*.

'Ser' – A term of respect used toward a senior Terran of either gender.

Shallow Cluster – A seldom-visited, unpopulated globular cluster, where the derelict fleet was discovered.

Soro – A senior Galactic patron race hostile to Earth.

Stenos – A vernacular term for neo-fins whose genes include grafts from natural *Stenos bredanensis* dolphins.

Stenos bredanensis – A species of natural dolphins on Earth.

Streaker – A dolphin-crewed starship that has made a critical discovery far across the galaxy from Garth. The repercussions of this discovery have led to the present crisis.

Dennie Sudman – A human exobiologist.

Hannes Suessi – A human engineer.

Suzerain – One of three commanders of the Gubru invasion force, each in charge of a different area: Propriety, Bureaucracy, and the Military. Overall policy is decided by consensus of the three. A Suzerain is also a candidate for Gubru royalty and full sexuality.

Sylvie – A 'green-card' female neo-chimpanzee.

Synthian(s) – A member of one of three Galactic races friendly to Earth.

Takkata-Jim (Tah-kah-tah-jim) – A *Stenos* neo-fin, Vice-Captain of the *Streaker*.

Tandu – A militant Galactic species hostile to Earth.

Thennanin (Thenn-an-in) – A militant Galactic species.

'Tingers and tumb' – The small and large toes of a neo-chimpanzee, which retain some grasping ability.

Tsh't (Tish-oot) – A female neo-fin, the *Streaker*'s fourth officer.

Tursiops – A vernacular word for neo-dolphins without *Stenos* gene grafts.

Tursiops amicus – A modern neo-dolphin. 'Friendly bottle-nose.'

Tursiops truncatus – Natural bottlenose dolphins on Earth.

Tymbrimi (Tim-brye-me) – A Galactic race friendly to Earthmen, renowned for its cleverness.

Uplift – The process by which older spacefaring races bring new species into Galactic culture, through breeding and genetic engineering. The resulting client species serves its patron for a period of indenture to pay for this favor.

Uthacalthing – Tymbrimi ambassador to the colony world of Garth.

Wattaceti – A neo-fin non-commissioned officer.

Wolflings – Members of a race which achieved starfaring status without the help of a patron.